MW00784000

Valkyrie

By: Stephan Grundy

TLS

ISBN13: 978-1-989033-59-3

Set in: Athelas 11pt/Cheddar Gothic Sans 27pt/Mjolnir 11pt

The Three Little Sisters LLC
www.the3littlesisters.com
USA/CANADA

©The Three Little Sisters

CHAPTER I. HOILOGAE

He sits on top of the mound, watching the sunset-lit clouds sweep in from the North Sea over the darkening sky. Though Austarjon's feast has just called summer in, the wind bites keener and colder as the heavens begin to deepen into night. It is time for him to shout the sheep together and drive them down to their pen. Still, the hoar-gray stone against which he leans is warm with the last sunlight, his sheep mill about him, their bodies shielding him from the sharpest edges of the wind, and so he has no will to move. Beneath the mound rests the body of his great-grandfather, Herwamundaz, who won these lands for his own three generations ago. The oaken coffin in which the hero lies has tanned his skin to a brown leather bag holding his long bones, weighted down by the bronze sword lying over him and the torc of twisted gold sunken into the folds of his neck. Herwamundaz's grandson Herwawardhaz tried to give his first-born son the mound-dweller's name, but to no avail. Herwamundaz keeps his lands still, warding and keeping the fields fruitful from within the howe, and Herwawardhaz's son stays nameless, good only for herding sheep. He speaks little, and no name will fasten to him.

Now the wind is blowing harder. He can hear the beating of the waves against the shore, their white rims glimmering through the blue twilight. The sound rises into the air, the hollow note of the storm wind over the hills rising to a singing shriek from above him. His sheep, startled as if a wolf's scent ran on the wind, wheel and bleat down the howe, leaving only the patchy wool of his cloak to keep the cold off. He lifts his gaze to the deepening purple of the sky, where the clouds now seem to glow bluish-white against the darkness. They curl and twist, shaping hooves and manes, spears and shields and the long streaming hair of nine mighty women who ride before the storm that rips the sea into fountains of gleaming spray. It is their voices that he hears howling together, their wind high and piercing as arrows of ice through his skull.

These are the walkurjons, the daughters of Wodhanaz, Choosers of the Slain. Their glance is awe and death, but he sits with his back to the warm stone and watches. One rides a little before the others, it seems to him that she is the tallest and most shining of the nine, her spear-point glinting starlight against the storm clouds behind her. It seems to turn slowly in her hand, pointing straight at him as her voice thrills through his head.

"Late, Hoilogae, thou apple-tree of battle, shalt thou rule over rings, nor over Rodulsvales. Early cried the eagle, if you still remain silent, though, warrior, you show a hard soul!"

With her words, the first gust of rain stings into his face and fills his open mouth, the echo of sweet mead icy in the back of his throat and whirling dizziness into his head. It seems to him that the sound of her voice has loosed all the fetters on him, as though the unseen collar of heavy bronze that had always bound him from speaking fell away at the moment she named him, Hoilogae, the Holy One. He cannot turn his gaze from her, nor will he, as she rides closer and he sees her swan-white face clearly through the darkness.

He leaps to his feet, raising his arms towards her and crying out joyously. "What will you let follow the name of Hoilogae, bright-lightening bride, and all you speak to offer? Think wisely of all, well must you speak. I will have none of it, unless I have thee!"

"I know swords lying in Sigisharjaz's Holm. Four are lacking from five tens. One of them is better than all. The harm of spears, wrought with gold. A ring is in the hilt, in the heart is soul, awe is in the edge, for owning winner, a blood-dyed wyrm on the blade turns, upon the guard an adder winds tail. Can you claim it? No hero living will be your like. It is Wejlunduz who has made it, from northern iron, the bane of all bronze. When you have won the sword, you shall win your mother's udal lands that she should hold from her father. There lie the bones of your mother's kin that shaped you, there lies the soul-might that you should bear, and there the foes from the south threaten the life of the northern folk. Only when those kin-mounds are ruled by your clan again will your shame be fully slain, only when you have taken up all that belonged to your forebears shall you see me again, for only thus can you bring the walkurjon the bride-gift she wishes, yourself, holy and whole."

As she speaks, Hoilogae feels the might whirling up into him from the howe, down into him from the storm. His body seems to flare bright as a new-kindled torch, even as he feels the blood of his kin crying out within his own blood and bones for the deeds that will make them all whole. Yet her fair glimmering calls him even more strongly, he opens his arms to the wind, wanting it to sweep him up to her cold embrace. "A name you have given me, now tell me yours, for I will wed you."

"Seek you Swaebhon, the daughter of Aiwilimae. Fare well, Hoilogae."

The glittering point of Swaebhon's spear catches Hoilogae's gaze even as the rain blows into his eyes, starring its brightness out into burning white rays that draw nearer and nearer. He feels the sign she traces with it as if a keen bronze blade cut it into his flesh. Three triangles woven into each other, a sharp-edged knot tightening about his heart. Swaebhon turns her spear again, lifting it upwards. She and the eight maids who follow her ride away on the wind as the clouds curl up from their horses' hooves, galloping into the dark forest of the storm. Hoilogae's cloak is soaked through with the salt-edged sea-rain, his long hair woven wet across his eyes. He laughs as he runs down from the howe, bare feet skidding through the muddy grass as he hastens towards his father's hall.

HAILGI

The screaming of the eagles sounds clearly through the waterfall-beating of the storm on the roof of the hall, drowning out any moans that Bergohildar may be making in her labor. The midwife looks up a moment. The firelight shows her teeth to Bergohildar, though the young woman cannot tell whether the old one is smiling or grimacing. Then she does not think about it. Her womb grips tighter again, her hands tightening on the square edges of the house-pillar as she strains to push her child out. She can feel the frantic struggling within her, trying to beat its way out or fighting to stay in, she cannot tell.

Sigismundar Halfdane sees the eagles on the beach in the first flash of lightning. Great black shapes against the white sand, beating wings the size of shields and screaming over something that lies long on the beach. He does not stop to look, hastening ahead of the rowers who pull the boat up onto the shore behind him. The message that his wife was birthing came to him, it seemed, only a few breaths after the battle was ended, hardly before he had finished swearing the oaths of a blood-bought truce with Hunding. Now, his shoulders aching from rowing, he scrambles up along the well-known path to the hall, cursing the storm which has shattered the warmth of summer with unseasonable iciness.

He does not mean for anything to stop him, but the flash of red-gold lightning above blinds him for a moment, so that he has to blink the sudden brightness from his eyes. In the shining shadow against his lids, he sees three darker shadows, as if of cloaked women raising their hands. Another line of gold lightning stitches across the sky, then another and another, threads of might coming together from east, west, and north, to meet in the middle of the moon's shadowed hall.

Sigismundar sets his shoulders and clutches his sodden cloak more tightly in front of him, forcing his way through the torrent-laden wind towards his hall. He is almost to the gate in the fence which surrounds the hamlet when his boot slips in the mud. He grabs out for a branch to break his fall, but misses, going down hard on the wet earth, his clutching hand tears a wild leek from the ground, its green scent sharp through the wind. He lies there for a moment, panting, before he pushes himself up and goes on.

The wind tears the door from Sigismundar's hand, blowing the echoes of the eagles' screams in with him like a tattered rag of sound. At first he thinks the cry he hears is part of that calling. Then it comes again, more piercing, and he sees the small fists and feet striking out from the little shadow in the midwife's cloaked lap. This is his firstborn, now that he is here, he does not quite yet dare to ask—son or daughter?

"Did you see that lightning?" A man's hushed voice whispers behind him. "Did you see?" The familiar tones of his men break Sigismundar's iced-in nerves, but before he can speak, the midwife answers.

"It's a son for you," she says. "A son, and your frowe's well. What's that in your hand?"

Sigismundar holds up the leek. Its white root gleams in the firelight, the fountain of green leaves above it is only a shadow. Swiftest-growing, most shining of grasses. He knows the leek is a hero's herb. He is stepping forward almost before he knows it, his cold hand seeking the warmth of his son's little fingers and pressing the leek into them. Even through the battle and arguing the truce afterwards with Hunding, he has thought of this moment, readying all his hopes. Now he cannot keep from lifting his son up, though this should not be done till nine nights after the birth. The soul given with the name should not be breathed in until the child is proven strong.

"I name you Hailgi," he says swiftly, the words tumbling irretrievably out of his mouth like gold rings from an overturned bag. "Hailgi, the Holy One, after the hero Hailgi the son of Herwowardar, beloved of the walkurja Swafa. May your deeds be as mighty as his. With the name I give you Ring-stead, Sun-Fell, Snow-Fell, and Sigisharjar's Vale, Hatun and Heaven-Meadows, and my father's sword wrought with a blood-colored wyrm."

With his left hand, Sigismundar wrings some of the water from his cloak and sprinkles it on Hailgi's head. Hailgi opens his eyes, squalling in fury.

"He'll be a true drighten," murmurs Bernu's deep voice approvingly.

"Good harvest will come for him," Thonarwaldar says softly. Each of the men speaks a blessing in turn as the midwife gives the child over to Bergo-hildar and she folds a corner of her blanket down from one swollen breast. The rain is already softening as Hailgi begins to suck.

Sigimundar awakens a little before dawn, when the first blue-gray light is just glimmering through the smoke hole. His wife is sleeping soundly, with Hailgi enfolded warmly in the sheepskins and woolen blankets beside her, but he feels suddenly that he must get out of the stink of old smoke and stale birthing-blood. He wraps a dry cloak around himself, but does not stop to pull on his boots, stepping barefoot out into the wet grass like a boy. The rain is over, the paling crescent of the moon and the morning star shining clear through the fresh air of early dawn. Dizzy with the rain washed green scent of the summer wood, he moves lightly along the path, not thinking of where he goes till he is almost to the top of the hill where a tall ash stands with a rotting rope dangling from one of its sturdy branches.

The harsh call of a raven brings him up short, he stands still for a moment before he turns to go back. But something in the sound catches his ear. The deep resonant croak breaks into words he can understand if he does not listen too closely but simply lets them sound in his skull.

"I know something," the raven on the gallows tree says, and a second coughs in answer. "Sigismundar's bairn stands in his byrnie, though only one day old. Now day is come, he has the keen eyes of a warrior. He shall be a friend to wargs. We two shall be glad!"

Sigismundar turns again to look up into the tree, hardly believing that he has heard the raven speak. At his movement, the two great black birds rise heavily into the air, circling the tree for a moment before they fly off to the north. Sigismundar touches the lump of amber that hangs on a leather thong around his neck. A sure warding against ill, if any should threaten. He wonders for a moment if it was wise for him to name his son after a hero who had dread such a weird one as Hailgi Herwowardar's son.

The name, he knows, bears the life's shape and length together with the soul, all reborn together, and though the Holy One was mighty, he was not long-lived. Nor was it often done, to name a child before nine nights had passed. If he should be weak, there would be no helping the choice, and to speak such sureness in the babe's health might bring down some bad luck, or the gaze of ill wights upon him. It is done, in the echoes of the raven's speech, Sigismundar hears the strength of his son's orlog, which he himself cannot shift.

HELGI

The heavy hammer-blow of thunder rattles the window-panes. Kirsten's smile is strained as she glances up at Roger, her hands go protectively to her belly, swollen to full ripeness under the white folds of her maternity dress.

"We haven't had a blackout here in three years," Roger Hadding says reassuringly to his wife as he folds her robe and puts it into her hospital bag. "Anyway, we should be glad about this storm. It makes it that much less likely that disappointed trick- or-treaters will soap our windows or whatever it is kids do here."

Kirsten's laugh chokes on a soft gasp. Roger imagines that he can see the ripples of the contraction moving across her body like a line of swells on the ocean.

"What if it's a boy?" She says. "We haven't even decided on a name for a boy yet."

"Doe," answers Roger, doing his best Sean Connery imitation. "James Doe."

This time her laughter is real, though quiet. "No, but....."

Helga for her dead mother, if it's a girl, they had decided that easily, long ago.

"It's almost a fifty-percent chance. Anyway, we'll think of something when the moment comes. If the moment comes. There, that's all the clothes.

Which books do you want?"

Kirsten leans her head to the right, scanning the titles on the shelves. She is about to speak when the doorbell rings.

"Son of a bitch! I'll take care of them and then we'll go, okay?"

Roger runs through the living room, barely swinging his long legs around the sharp edges of the coffee table in time to avoid barking his shins. The Frankenstein mask he had bought "to scare the kids with" lies forgotten on the mantel, a slumped heap of warty green rubber and glistening black hair with one eye showing empty.

Hurried as he is, Roger turns on the porch light and looks through the keyhole first. Kids, after all. One dripping, chest-high werewolf, one waist-high, sodden witch.

"Trick-or-treat!"The little witch cries in a piercing voice, holding out a plastic bag as Roger opens the door. The bigger kid says nothing, though he does deign to extend his own booty bag.

Although the witch is wearing a full-face mask, Roger recognizes her at once by the long blond braid which hangs halfway to her waist. This is Karin Jensen from two blocks down the road, the werewolf, he thinks, must be her big brother Olaf.

"What are you two doing out in this weather?" He asks as he pours candy into their bags. He smiles wryly, hearing the tones of parent-to-be in his own voice.

"I didn't want to come. I thought it was stupid," Olaf mutters. "She made me."

"We're Vikings," Karin asserts clearly. "Vikings never turn away from storms."

"And there I thought you were a witch and a werewolf," Roger says before he could stop himself.

"I'm a troll-woman, not a witch," answers Karin. "He's a wolf. Troll-women ride wolves."

"Oh." A white track of lightning slices the sky, the thunder crying out a moment after it. "Well, we've got to go. Ah, can we give you two a ride home? It's getting worse out there."

"Yes," says Olaf, just as Karin says, "No." The two of them stare at each other a moment before Olaf drops his eyes. Finally he looks up at Roger. "I can get my sister home okay. Thank you for offering," he adds quickly.

"Will you go straight home?"

The lightning and the thunder seem to come almost at once as Karin nods reluctantly.

"We promise," Olaf says, more cheerfully. "Come on, Karin. Moder gør sorg om os."

They turn back, their dark shapes almost vanishing in the rain-thick blackness between the white halos of the Haddings' porch light and the streetlight at the corner. Then a sudden flash of alarm spears through Roger Hadding. He tightens his hand on the door handle, ready to run out. A tall shadow stands just at the edge of the streetlight's brightness—body hidden in the folds of a huge coat, face hidden by a low-brimmed hat. A thousand horrors throng through Roger's mind, kidnapping, rape, slaughter.

He is ready to run out, to scream warning, when the wind shifts a little, casting back the branches of the old alder tree like an arm full of thick hair. Now the light gleams faintly from the wet bark of the tree's trunk, and Roger laughs in nervous relief, but he waits until the Jensen children are down to the streetlight, and safe out of the alder-tree's grip before turning the porch light off and locking the door again. There is something about what Karin said, her words calling up the trace of a memory, like a scent brushing past him on the wind.

"Are you all through?" Kirsten calls. "I've finished packing."

"How often are the contractions coming now?"

"Twenty minutes between the last two."

"Do you think we can wait until the storm slacks off a bit? I'd rather not drive in this if I can help it."

Kirsten bites her lower lip. "The weather report said the storm is only going to get worse, there will be a tornado watch from eight-thirty as well as heavy storming. I think we should go as soon as we can."

"All right." Roger picks up his wife's bag and the two of them go through the house to the garage. As he puts the bag in the trunk, he asks, "Dear, do you know anything about troll-women riding wolves?"

"What?"

"Karin Jensen says they do."

"It sounds a little familiar. Maybe out of a folktale? Or the Norse sagas?"

"Hmm." He walks around the car to help Kirsten in. As she closes the door, his memory suddenly snaps into focus, as if a dial in his head had clicked into place. "Just a second."

Roger runs upstairs to the room where he keeps all the books from his high school and undergraduate days, the books with the gaudy paper covers designed by people like Boris Vallejo and Frank Frazetta. Among these, (he still knows just where,) is a gold trilogy-case, decorated with spiky runes and a fiery ring, which holds three books with sober, delicately drawn maps and trees upon their covers. And beside that is a larger paperback, whose black lettering on a red-gold spine reads, THE POETIC EDDA. He snatches it from its place and runs back down again.

"What was all that about?" Kirsten asks as Roger presses the button to raise the garage door and starts the car. The rush of rain beating against the roof as he drives out drowns his muttered non-answer.

It is not until they are in the hospital, with Kirsten flattened in her bed and waiting for the anesthesiologist to come and give her a spinal block, that Roger has a chance to check the index and flip through the book to find the passage he remembers, in a poem called "The Lay of Helgi Hjörvarðsson."

"Helgi's brother Heðinn 'fared home by himself through the wood on Yule evening, and found a troll woman, who rode a warg and had wyrms for reins, and bade Heðinn to follow her.' And then later it says that Helgi thought 'that Heðinn had seen his fetch, when he saw the woman riding the warg.'"

"I don't see why you were making such a fuss about it," Kirsten says, rather crossly.

"It was an odd thing to have come up. It startled me, that's all."

"I didn't know you were interested in the old Norse stories."

"When I was an undergraduate I used to read Tolkien a lot. I rescued an English grade once by writing a paper on his mythological sources. That passage was...let me see...it corresponded to the goblins riding wargs in The Hobbit."

Kirsten clutches Roger's hand in one of hers and the bed frame in the other, her fingers whitening to bone with the pain of the contraction. When she is done, Roger gently disengages his hand and massages the blood back into it.

"Not long now," he says.

"No. The anesthesiologist should get here soon." She is still a moment. "If it's a boy, that's not a bad name."

"What?"

"Helgi."

"The other kids will tease him something awful, you know."

"He's ours. He'll be tough."

"The 'Boy Named Sue' theory of child-raising."

Kirsten wrinkles her nose at him. "It's a good Danish name. It means something like a saint, I think, I remember my grandmother talking about den hellige Olav. Anyway, it's very Danish."

"Hey, we're not the Jensens, remember? We don't have an ethnos to keep up."

"Speak for yourself. My mother was first generation."

"Anyway, it'll probably be a girl."

"Helga for a girl, Helgi for a boy. You promise?"

"Okay."

Something is still itching in Roger's memory, he turns back towards the beginning of the poem, seeking, yes, there is the footnote he remembered. "The name 'Helgi', meaning 'The Holy One', may originally have been a cult-title of the Norse religion, perhaps signifying a priest, though the tales of Helgi Hjörvarðsson and Helgi Hunding's-Bane suggest that the 'Holy One' was actually a sacrifice to Óðinn, chosen by the Valkyrie. The repetition of the name makes the connection between the Helgi/Valkyrie poems clear. In Norse belief, the act of naming a newborn after a dead person signified that the deceased was reborn in the child, and perhaps even determined the process of rebirth, as the name and the soul were so closely linked." There is no more about the name, Roger's gaze flicks back to the text again.

"Hjörvarðr and Sigrlinn got a large and handsome son. He was silent, no name would fasten on him. He sat on a howe, he saw nine Valkyries riding, and one was stateliest of them. She said, 'Late shall you rule over rings, Helgi, thou apple-tree of battle'"

CHAPTER II

The three men sitting in the hut rose to their feet at once as Hoilogae flung the door open and burst inside. His younger brother Hedhinaz reached for the bronze sword at his side, the other two, Herwawardhaz and Attalae, glanced towards the spears that leaned in the corner by the door. Wary as the startled hounds by her feet, Sigislinthon looked up from the pot she was stirring, the long wooden spoon stilling in her hand.

"Have you seen raiders, boy?" Herwawardhaz asked.

Hoilogae shook his head. "No one."

"What's wrong with you, then?" Hedhinaz snapped, his breaking voice high and sharp.

Hoilogae found that he could not speak, he could not tell them about what he had seen. He only shook his head. Hedhinaz stared at him for another moment, then it seemed to Hoilogae that he could feel the walkurjon's gaze still burning in his own eyes, and, suddenly fearful of harming his brother, turned his face away. Hedhinaz's thin nostrils tightened with familiar scorn as he shifted a fold of his dark cloak away from his throat and turned back to his father and Attalae.

Hoilogae made his way around the three of them as they began to talk again, sitting down beside the fire-pit as he was used to doing, close enough that the hem of his cloak was always stained with ashes and the coarse strands of wool pitted by the little scorch-scars of sparks. His mother worked around him with the ease of long custom, as though he were no more than another heap of firewood. Sitting there, one night had always been the same as another, the red-glowing snakes of fire through the gray-furred coals drawing his mind into a dreamy stillness where he neither needed to hear nor speak. But now his ears felt keen as if the wind had stripped them raw, he could not help but listen to what the other men were saying, their voices echoing deep below the song of need that still wailed in his head, driving him on like a ship before a strong gale.

"There is not too much risk in faring against Wulfahardhaz and his folk," Attalae said, tugging thoughtfully at his short gray beard. "I think there is also a good deal to be gotten by it, their lands are rich enough, and Wulfahardhaz has been the chief dealer with traders from the south for some time. Too, it would be better if our trade were less hampered. It is only to be expected that we gain less from the amber we gather because it must pass through several neighbors. The iron-folk are rich, and those closer to them gain by it. I would not choose to live too close to the southerners, since they are also greedy for land, but two marches yet would stand between us and them."

Hoilogae marked the way Herwawardhaz looked at his second son. Their father's pockmarked cheeks seemed less drawn, his brooding eyebrows easing from the bewildered half-frown that Hoilogae knew better.

"Well, Hedhinaz," the drighten said. "What do you think?"

Hedhinaz coughed, as if to knock his voice down to a man's deepness before he spoke. Hoilogae could hear his brother straining to keep his words low and even, it seemed that he could almost feel the tightness in Hedhinaz's sinews and in the back of his skull as the youth tried to give a wise answer.

"Attalae is older than I and knows more about battle, so I would believe him when he says there is not much risk. I would guess that if we go swiftly, Wulfahardhaz will have little time to gather his friends from the lands around, and once the fighting is over, there are no drightens with blood-ties who should feel bound to avenge him.

Then there is little reason not to make war, and much in favor of it." He glanced from his father to Attalae, who nodded his head. "Perhaps it would be best to go before planting, rather than after, the way is not far or very muddy, and most men ween summer to be the time for readying their weapons."

"This will not give us long to summon our folk to us either," Herwawardhaz pointed out mildly.

"Nor will it give word time to spread."

Herwawardhaz smiled, then clapped his younger son on the shoulder. "You have a good wit."

Hoilogae saw—the blink of a lash would have hidden it from him—the flicker of his father's eyes in the firelight, a whip-flick whose sting had never touched his bare skin before. Still, something else stung deeper. Not a lash on his hide, but an ache rising from within his memory, of words which had sunk into the well of his mind without a ripple as he sat staring at the fire. Now it seemed to him as though the weight of years of shame was falling on him again like many man-weights of wool, ready to crush him down into the coal-biter's sullen witlessness, it seemed that Swaebhon's song was fading in his ears, and with it that sudden rush of keen joy that had dawned with his awakening on the mound.

Hoilogae clenched his fists to kindle his own need-fire against his years of silence, struggling to force himself up. He had no sword to clasp his hand to, no keen weapon to show he had proved himself a man. The space at his belt seemed like a hollow in the marrow of his bones, weakening all his strength where it should have stiffened him with hard metal and letting the old bonds tighten about his throat again. Swaebhon's brightness glimmered against the smoky roof for a moment, wavering and vanishing like a swan's reflection in a wind-tossed lake.

I will have my sword, I will! Hoilogae cried to himself. With the strength of his silent shout, he surged to his feet. The unseen thrall-collar binding his neck snapped, and he spoke with the same sureness with which he had answered Swaebhon. "You are not given a hale rede, Herwawardhaz Kin-Leader, edge-wise and famed though you are, if you let the fire eat the dwelling of a battle-boar who has never done ill towards you. Now Hrothamaraz has rule over rings which he got from our kinsmen. Though kin are living, he thinks to rule the inheritance of all the dead ones."

"Who are you to speak to our father like that?" Hedhinaz cried out at once. "What do you know about the counsels of men, coal-biter? You don't even have a name, how can you say our rede is wrong?"

The shame of his long silence burned in Hoilogae's face like coals when the gray ash is blown from them, so kindled, he answered, "I am Hoilogae. I have gotten my name this day, and what I see is what is true. Our mother's father Swafnijaz lies dead by Hrothamaraz's hand, and he holds the land and wealth that should have come to Sigislinthon and through her to us."

"That slaying was a long time ago." Herwawardhaz' voice trailed off as he stared at his eldest son, his dark eyes shocked wide. The firelight gleamed from the darkness of his pupils, tiny reflections of the flames that Hrothamaraz set to burning throughout Swafnijaz's lands on the night that Herwawardhaz and Attalae took the women Sigislinthon and Anulaibho from their hiding place in the house of Anulaibho's father Frahanamariz and rode for their own lands, and their lives.

"It still is, the years have not changed it."

Herwawardhaz's face was already settling into a look familiar through Hoilogae's veiled memories, as though he had dreamed it in another life—soft contempt for the words of a witling, underscored with the arrow-jab on arrow-jab of the shame his son's weak mind had brought on him. "You were wiser not to speak of things you cannot understand. Men know where their strength comes to end, only luck brought me Sigislinthon when Hrothamaraz would have wedded her, and it was as well that he was content to take the land without the woman."

"More than luck," Attalae murmured softly enough that his words did not turn the heads of either Herwawardhaz or Hedhinaz. Only Hoilogae looked into his eyes as he whispered, startled to see the clear spark answering his gaze from the blue depths—a light that showed more than might be seen by the flickering light of the fire within the hall. The older warrior raised his voice. "Hoilogae is well named."

Herwawardhaz twisted a strand of his beard, staring at his rede-giver. "What do you mean by that?"

"Let us think about fighting Hrothamaraz. It would bring more wealth, and more fame, than making war on Wulfahardhaz."

The drighten's heavy brows creased, he shook his head. "Has some ill spell come over you, that a fool's rede has struck a man who was always wise? We would be outnumbered by a great many, and many of his men are armed with iron from the south. His war band has always been made strong by southerners who fought for pay."

"We have won battles before when everything seemed to turn against us."

"Not by going into them with the knowledge that we were weaker. Indeed—as you know better than any—it was the rede of wise and battle-skilled men that brought us sig in place of loss, and not the words of an alf-struck witling."

"Perhaps you should ask Sigislinthon whether she wishes to see the hall where she was born, or to have the gold that she was brought up to play with."

"I have done well enough for her!" Herwawardhaz's voice was alive with hurt now, but though he straightened his back as if in pride, Hoilogae could hear the soft scuffling of his shoes on the earthen floor. "Sigislinthon, have you ever lacked for anything since I brought you here?"

"I have always been glad of it," Sigislinthon replied, beginning to ladle stew into the clay bowls beside the fire pit. "If you have given me less gold than my father did, you have given me more amber, and I have not lacked rule over those things I wished for myself." She paused, wiping the sweat from her creased forehead with the back of her hand. "Still," she went on slowly, the faint wistfulness in her soft voice like a mist over far-off hills, "I have often missed the land of my birth, and often mourned over my father, though he would not willingly give me to you. Sometimes I have thought that his lack of vengeance. I have heard that such things appear in one's children, I had thought that perhaps Hoilogae"

"Though Hoilogae is not, after all, witless," Attalae said, his voice crackling dry as fallen leaves. "Well, Hoilogae? Since you have offered rede, will you go on to tell us how this deed ought to be accomplished? Do you remember what you have heard of Hrothamaraz's strength of arm and folk, or of the paths that lead to his lands? When shall we go?"

Hoilogae was not sure whether it was mockery, or merely the cracking of age, that dusted the old man's voice, but he was sure of what he saw in the twisting of Hedhinaz's thin lips and in the lines scored about his father's brows. "There is something I must do first," Hoilogae declared. "Then you shall see whether I am witless or mad, for the giver of my battle-rede also told me this." For a moment, Swaebhon's voice was clearer in his head than the crackling of the flames in the fire pit, the bubbling of his mother's stew or Hedhinaz's harsh, angry breath, the fire lit darkness of the hall faded into the softly glowing blue of twilight before his eyes, and in the blurred light it seemed to him that he could see her bright shadow again. "A sword has been wrought of northern iron, lying south in Sigisharjaz's Holm. I must go to find it before I lead the folk against Hrothamaraz, or else I shall have no luck in the battle. But when I come back with it, then you shall see the proof of my worth."

"You've sat on the mound too long, and the alfs have stolen whatever wits you had." Hedhinaz's voice broke as he spoke, cracking up to a raw note. "What madness tells you that an iron sword should be made for you? I think you're no better now than you were before, even though you've found your tongue."

"Hush, Hedhinaz," Attalae said. "You shouldn't need a spae-wife to tell you that there is more in this than you can see."

The youth closed his mouth, but the muscles of his jaw still rippled as though he were speaking his anger aloud.

"Attalae, what rede can you give me?" Herwawardhaz asked softly. "Let me believe that you, at least, have not gone mad."

Attalae shook his hoary head "I will go with Hoilogae to find his sword. Then you will see the truth of this matter clearly enough when we come back, and know whose sight is most to be trusted."

Herwawardhaz only stood looking at his rede-giver. "Who will trust my rule, if I do such a thing? Our folk will say that I, too, have grown foolish in my age, if I have at last made myself believe the untruth of what all need to be true. If I have told myself that a nameless and useless youth is holy, or one who can barely herd sheep fit to give rede to men."

"Say that I have gone faring to Sigisharjaz's Holm on quiet matters, and I took him to row and bear my burdens, because he could not speak unwisely, or betray secrets even by chance."

"What weapon shall he bear on the journey, then? Sigislinthon's eldest son," he spoke the words slowly, tasting them like fresh bread after a long journey, "ought to set out fittingly from the beginning. If one of us had a sword that will not be needed" He looked about the hall, his eyes moving as slowly as if he had been struck hard on the skull. At last it was the movement of Hedhinaz's hand covering the pommel of his sword which drew his gaze. "Hedhinaz," Herwawardhaz said wonderingly, "you are young for battle still, and there is not likely to be fighting until Hoilogae comes back, so you have little need for that."

"That is not fair," Sigislinthon protested before Hedhinaz's answer could slice through the knot of anger in his throat. "Herwawardhaz, you cannot take away what one son has for the other's sake, no matter what you had thought. If Hedhinaz got his sword earlier than he should have otherwise, that is your fault, not his. And you are not yourself this night, or you would not have thought otherwise."

"I don't need you to fight for me," Hedhinaz said to his mother. "I won't give up my sword."

"No," Herwawardhaz said. "You're right, of course. Let me think." His silence grew heavier as the moments passed, his shaggy brown head swaying a little.

"I shall give him my spear," Attalae said at last, when it seemed that Herwawardhaz would not speak again. "Let that do till he has proved himself."

Without waiting for Herwawardhaz to answer, Attalae went over to the corner where the shafts were propped together, taking his own spear in his hand and bringing it back to Hoilogae. "Let this be my naming-gift to you within the Middle-Garth's ring, Hoilogae. It shall serve you well until you have found your sword."

Hoilogae opened his hand, wrapping his fingers around the smooth wood. The spear-shaft fit into his palm as if long use had worn its groove into his flesh. He hefted it, turning the weapon as if to throw it and feeling it light with the memory of a thousand flights—most into practice straw, a few singing into the bodies of men on the battlefield.

"The time we spent trying to teach you to fight wasn't wasted after all, was it?" Herwawardhaz murmured in amazement. "What, in Tiwaz's name, has happened here? I don't understand"

"We'll leave tomorrow morning," Attalae told him flatly.

"Do you know where you're going?"

"We shall," Hoilogae answered.

Hedhinaz turned away, taking the bowl of stew that Sigislinthon held out to him and squatting down on his haunches by the fireplace like a warrior keeping watch in his foe man's lands. The frowe of the hall bore a second bowl to her husband, she offered the third to Attalae, but he waved her away.

"Hoilogae and I have more to do tonight before we go. We'll be back tomorrow at first light. Have you got a couple of torches we can use?"

Sigislinthon went to the stack that lay against the far wall, coming back with a pitch-tipped stick in each hand. Attalae took them, thanking her, and thrust them into the fire, where they flared bright yellow beneath swift-rising streams of black smoke. He handed one to Hoilogae, keeping the other for himself.

"Tomorrow," he said, striding briskly towards the door. Hoilogae followed him out into the rain. The storm had lightened, though the torches hissed and spit, they did not go out.

"Where are we going?"

"To get an ox."

Hoilogae followed the old warrior to the low fence where the kine were kept, then around and past. Attalae had not meant the pens for the cows and bulls of the hamlet, he realized, but the one farther along where three golden-horned beasts grazed. One of these was given in offering at Yule every year and another set in its place, but now Attalae guided Hoilogae in through the gate and told him to take the ox's bridle. The rain on the beast's horns shone in wet golden ripples when Hoilogae held the hissing torch up before it.

"Why are we doing this?" Hoilogae asked as they walked slowly through the mud towards the hamlet's hof, the little hall where the gods and goddesses were worshiped and sacrifices made.

Attalae said nothing until they had gotten indoors and he had laid fire to the dry wood which always stood ready in the low pit before the harrow of heaped stones. Then, with the brightness crackling up from the sticks and the fire's warmth reaching out to steam the rain from their cloaks, he said, "I have never told anyone of this before."

"Of what?"

The old warrior stroked the ox between its golden horns to quiet its rest-less shifting, Hoilogae wondered if it smelt the old blood that had soaked into the wooden walls and earthen floor through years of sacrifice.

"When your father was young and I was younger than I am now, he had other wives, Alfahildjoz and Saiwahraifaz and Sindrfethro, and sons by them who are dead now. But he had sworn an oath to marry the woman whom he knew to be most beautiful. He had heard that the drighten Swaf-nijaz had the daughter who was fairest of all, who was named Sigislinthon. I went to ask for Sigislinthon's hand for the kin-leader, and dwelt there the whole winter. But Sigislinthon's foster-father Frahanamariz, the father of Anulaibho, gave Swafnijaz rede against it, and so I fared home again. Then, it was at summer's beginning, only a little after Austarjon's feast, I stood in a certain grove. A bird sat above me in the branches, it spoke, and I listened to what it said. I think that you will not be amazed by this, nor doubt it. It spoke in verse to me, saying,

'Saw thou Sigislinthon Swafnijaz's daughter,
fairest of maidsin Munar-Home?
though handsome are Herwawardhaz's women,
and goodly seemin Glasislund.'

Then I asked it if it would speak further with me, for I knew that it was wise. It said, 'I shall, if to me the mighty makes offering, and choose I, what I will from kin-leader's garth.'

But I said that it should not choose Herwawardhaz, nor his sons, nor any of his women, but it should deal fairly with me as between friends. For such wights often ask a geld that is higher than anyone wishes to pay, and Victo-ry-Father is gladdened most of all by the lives of men.

And the bird said, 'I choose a hof and harrow great,
gold-horned cows from garth of the warrior,
if Sigislinthon shall sleep in his arms,
and free-willing follows the drighten.'

And so Herwawardhaz and I rode together through the hills like raiders going after a cow, and then we came to the hall of Frahanamariz. An eagle was sitting on the roof. There was something in its eye that I disliked, and when it cried out I could feel my heart slowing and my breath stopping, and so I cast a spear at it and killed it. And then we went inside and found Sigis-linthon and Anulaibho. Frahanamariz was there too, lying beneath a blanket as if he slept and still quite warm, but he was dead as a stone, he must have died the moment before we came in."

Attalae looked up at Hoilogae, his age-lined face set grimly, as if daring the youth to laugh at his words. "So, I gave your father rede to have this hof built as it is now. Now, as I am recked wise, I think that you would be a fool to set forth without making a gift to the one who brought about your birth—to the Ansuz, whose name men do not often speak." With his last words, he pulled the ox's halter tight, as though he meant to strangle it.

Hoilogae stepped back a few paces, then let the spear fly from his hand. Attalae leapt back as it struck, cracking in a rib and sinking through the great muscles of the ox's chest till no more than half an arms length of the shaft showed. The beast bellowed in pain, falling to its knees and then crashing to the earth like a toppling oak.

"To Wodhanaz," Hoilogae said slowly. He felt no fear as he spoke the name, much as other men feared to call the gaze of the Drighten of Death to them. Instead he thought of Swaebhon, and the spear-keen joy he had felt when her eyes met his.

Hoilogae braced his foot on the quivering body of the ox and pulled his spear out in a single swift movement. The ox's blood spurted out behind the blade, spraying over Hoilogae in a warm waterfall, blood enameled the spear's length in gleaming deep-red, running in warm rivulets down the haft to his hands.

"Well-done," Attalae murmured. "That was not the throw of a weak-armed man. Now you'll have to wash and we'll get some rest. Dawn comes earlier than I've ever liked at the beginning of a faring."

Neither Attalae nor Hoilogae marked that the door they had shut behind them when they went in was ajar when they went out. Hedhinaz stepped back around the corner of the hof, staring at the gleam of their torches through the misty rain as they walked towards Attalae's home. In the clouded night, cloaked in black with a fold of his cloak drawn down over his face, he knew that they could not see him unless they tripped over him.

When the darkness of Attalae's doorway swallowed the torches' light, Hedhinaz pushed the hof's door open again and felt his way in, following the hot coppery scent of blood and scuffling his feet a little ahead of him till one searching shoe met the yielding flesh of the dead ox. Hedhinaz crouched down, feeling the cold metal of its gilded horns, stroking down its rough-haired face and neck till his hand sank into the viscous warmth his brother's spear had left behind.

"Why not me?" He asked aloud, feeling his voice crack like a shard of pottery in his throat. He touched the pommel of his sword with his clean hand, calling his mood into bravery. "Wodhanaz, why not me?"

Hedhinaz did not know what he awaited—the harsh croak of a bird, the howling of a wolf, a whisper in the darkness? But none of it came. The air in the hof was still, heavy with no more than the smell of blood and pierced bowels. After a while Hedhinaz's legs began to ache and his feet to fade into numbness. He stood unsteadily, stretching his hand out before him till his fingers found the rough wood of the doorpost. He had to guess at his path, scuffling his feet from side to side of the bare earth till he found the edges of grass, and moving slowly along between the borders till he found himself at the top of his great-grandfather's mound.

His legs were trembling so hard that he had to sit down, then it seemed to him that he could hear a rustling within, as if of a hand reaching through the grave-linen. It was well enough for Hoilogae—his brother, to whom their father could give no name—to sit here by day with his sheep, but Austarjon's feast was not long past, and the nights were still long enough for the dead to walk again.

"Herwamundaz," Hedhinaz whispered. The sound of his own voice, like wind through the dry grass of summer's end, startled him, he gulped, clutching at his sword's smooth pommel again, before he could go on. "Why him? Why not me?" He could not go on, but his thoughts flowed clearly enough. The aches of muscles strained in sword-practice were still with him, the marks he knew well enough were left by trying to do more than his body would let him, he could feel the lines grooving themselves into his forehead above brows that were always drawn with trying to think, trying to be the man that his father's other son, four years older, could not be. Now it was bitter as the spoor of gall in an ill-cut deer's liver, knowing that his father had not given him a sword early because of his own worth, but only because of his brother's shame, and seeing Hoilogae, who had not done more than sit on a stone by day and sit by the fire at night for as long as Hedhinaz could remember, suddenly stand up to take a man's place. And more. He had named himself 'the holy one', stepping easily past all Hedhinaz's wit and effort into a realm that only Attalae could share with him.

"It's not fair." Hedhinaz felt that he did not care whether the dead man seized him now, he leaned forward till he toppled face-down, stretching himself full-length on the wet grass with his arms and legs spread out and his hands clutching at the earth.

"What happened here?" He asked, his voice muffled by the ground. "Why?"

Hedhinaz felt a tingle of cold through his limbs, his body tightened, waiting, but nothing more happened, except that the mist-soft rain fell more heavily upon him. At last, bewildered and unhappy, he got to his feet again and looked up at the black sky. "At least let me have my share of my brother's part," he said quietly. "I've earned that much."

Hedhinaz turned again and went down, not waiting for an answer. If the gods meant to answer him, they would have to show him with more than they had given him yet.Though she rode aloft over the waves, skimming swift as a spear's flight through the coiling storm clouds, it was not a short faring from the shores of Jutland to the hall that was Swaebhon's home within the Middle-Garth. The earth was black beneath her, woods and lakes and high troll-ridden crags, but the maiden could see the pale lights of those who dwelt in the bergs and ancient barrows, and the shifting glow of the wyrms far beneath the earth.

Behind Swaebhon rode her troop of eight mist-women, true walkurjons from the hall of Wodhanaz. She did not know whether they were the ghosts of women like herself who had once walked the Middle-Garth, or came of other kin, but their might swept always behind her when she fared forth from her own hide. Still, she turned her wolf-gray steed higher as they passed above Hati's Firth. The old etin who dwelt there would be a fell foe to battle with, but it was his daughter Rime-Gerdhaz who bore the greatest hate for the fair women who rode through the sky. But Hati's Firth was the last marking before Swaebhon came to her home, the high hall bright with the fires of fellowship where her father was drighten and held rule over the folk of their land, and so it was never wholly unwelcome for her to look down and see the twisted shapes of the etin-clan moving far below her.

After the clear rushing of the air above, the first breaths Swaebhon took in her own body always felt like breathing in the steam from the stones of the bathhouse, chokingly hot and thick. She lay on her back for a moment, staring up into the shifting fire-shadows of the thatch. Someone had come into her house and built up the fire while she slept, otherwise it would have burnt down to embers. As she slowly gathered her strength and soul together, Swaebhon stared unblinkingly at the black blot on one straw—a spot or a spider, she could not tell, but it was there, steady enough for her to fix on as if it were the pole-star of the Wain. Still, she could not fix her gaze, her eyes slewed away, head roaring and body whirling as if she had drunken herself witless. She grasped at the edge of the furs over her, but could not hold them, her fingers weak as fire-softened butter, and a rush of sparkling mist swept over her sight.

The storm wind howling through her ears rose and broke like a great wave, and in its wake she heard a raven croaking, its rasping depth slowly clearing into words. Now Swaebhon could see the ring of shadows around her, the trunks of great trees dark through gray mist. She did not know where she stood, but her spear was in her hand, holding her shaking soul upright.

"Swaebhon, chooser of the slain." The raven called, its voice deepening in her ears until it rang all about her. "Whom have you chosen to die?"

"I do not mean him to die!" Swaebhon answered, even as she thought of Hoilogae, her breath tightened in her lungs and her heart quickened. He had sat so still that she had thought him an alf or stone-wight at first, still as a stock of wood set to mark the barrow's dweller. But then he had raised his head, flint-gray eyes glinting up from a fair face beneath a tangle of amber hair, and she had seen what she had never seen before—a living man who could gaze up at the riding of Wodhanaz's daughters with his heart rock-steady beneath his ribs and no more than wonder in his eyes. "I love him, I mean for him to live and dwell ever beside me. Others I shall choose for his sword, his bright blade shall not go hungry, and he shall slay where Wodhanaz wishes."

The low laughter sounded through the mist. "That he shall. Now bronze and iron are weighed on the scales, and iron must win, the harder ever has sig. But iron bites at the will of the ones who shape it, the rich folk, the southern folk—their swords are sharper, their hammers heavier. I would not see my children cut down before their flower, I would not have their greatest songs stilled unsung, nor their weapon arms broken long before the worst of all foes treads the field. Now Hoilogae, and you stand at the doorway. The battle you win on the Middle-Garth's green meadows shall shape much, but more shall be shaped when Hoilogae's blood is spilled on the earth, for it shall feed the songs that shall be the breath of folk in days to come. You have become a walkurjon, a Chooser of the Slain, and this few living maids may bear, for you go but to wreak the deaths of men and, above all, the death of him you love." The croaking raven-voice softened now, lowering until its sound was hardly a whisper thrumming through the cracked stones beneath Swaebhon's feet. "This I will give you for comfort, Swaebhon. Once you are wedded to your Hoilogae, death shall never part you from life for too long, nor shall one be born into the Middle-Garth without the other following close behind."

Then the words were drowned in the wind blowing hard through the mist, blowing Swaebhon's eyes to blackness and her ears to deafened stillness. She tightened her fists. The polished wood of the spear melted beneath them, and she could feel only the softness of fur and the smoothness of hide crumpling beneath her grasp. She lay in her bed, breathing deeply until she could feel the weight of her body about her again, broad shoulders and solid breasts and long legs all comfortable and well known as her old winter cloak. Knowing how hungry she always was after a long faring, Swaebhon had left half her mid-day share of milk and cheese on a little stool by her sleeping-furs before she had lain down. As soon as she could sit up, she reached for them and began to eat. Only then, steadied in her body, did she let herself think again of the man she had seen at her faring's end. Many men had tried to win Swaebhon from her father's hall, but all their boasts of claiming and taming her had been no more than noise made to drown the ringing bronze shiver of fear in their bodies.

One alone had felt more, and paid for it, but men had been nothing to her until she saw Hoilogae sitting on the howe in his rough shepherd's rags, and felt the hidden fire within him spring forth at her call. Without his deep well-spring of life, eighteen years untapped, to draw on, Swaebhon would not have been able to show herself and speak to him within the Middle-Garth's ring. Now that he lived fully, she would be weaker—till he had done the deeds which would bring them together again, the deeds whose might would be her strength. Swaebhon's eyes stung as though a gust of smoke had blown into her face, it was a long faring from Jutland to her father's hall. Chaidhamariz the Traveler had set out on the southward path last summer, with a broken-hearted thrall by his side, but no one knew what had become of them. No other had ever made that faring, news of the south lands, of drightens such as Sigisharjaz of Jutland and Nidhadhuz of the Swihonez folk, came to the north only along a lengthy chain of telling. And if he comes? She asked herself. Why must I lure him to his death, why has Wodhanaz made such an ill doom of me?

Swaebhon heard the whisper from within herself, and did not know whether it was some part of her soul, her fetch or a ghostly sister-wight that spoke, or whether the god answered her through her heart. You chose to be a walkurjon before you knew love, you chose Wodhanaz before you chose a living man, and you are kin to raven and eagle and the ravening wolf. If Hoilogae knows the price he must pay, who are you to say he may not pay it if he can win the right to it, and does not die in the winning. Swaebhon blinked her sight clear and stood, breathing deeply until she had her balance again. When she opened the door, she saw two amber eyes glowing in the reflected firelight outside, a wolf's shape dark against the snow. She stepped forward boldly, lifting the bronze-tipped staff that she used to test the depths of the thicker drifts and steady herself on the ice.

A wild wolf would have fled, unless it were sick with the howling wod, but this beast's ears pricked up and it nuzzled towards her, wagging its tail, it was one of the half-wolfish hunting dogs that she and her father bred for bringing down elk and deer. Swaebhon scratched it behind the ears.

"Good dog, sa, good hound." She had hunted in the moonlight before, when her prey was more easily found, but this would not be the night for it. The brothers Wiwastanaz and Ehwastanaz had speared a walrus at dawn, since Austarjon's feast had been thin the night before, they had known the rare kill to be a gift of the gods, and brought it for all the folk to share instead of smoking and salting the meat for themselves.

She could smell the meat already, and so could the hound, frisking about her in a spray of snow. Her father Aiwilimae sat at the table farthest from the stabled cattle and horses, with the fire burning to warm his back and cast his shadow high over the hall. The seat beside him was empty. Since her mother had died three years before, only Swaebhon had sat there. The hall-folk had not waited in carving the walrus and serving it out, the men and women were eating greedily, bare chins and beards glistening with fat.

There had been no great hunger that year, but the meal had run out early and the storms been harsh, so that few had eaten as well as they might have wished since Yule. A piece of the liver and a good-sized slice of meat lay on a wooden trencher before Swaebhon's chair, and she was quick to take her place and claim them. The meat was dark and rich with a fishy tang to it, somewhat stronger-tasting and less tender than seal, but good for all that.

"So, my daughter," Aiwilimae said when she had cut her second helping from the broad roast at their table, "what did you see on your faring? Was it anything I have need to know?" His voice was steady, though the drighten was one of the many who would not speak the name of Wodhanaz, placing his own trust in Tiwaz and the Thunderer, he held his daughter's redes dear.

Swaebhon looked up at her father, considering. The firelight gleamed from the palm-wide bald spot in the middle of his thick fair hair, but his craggy face was shadowed, only his pale blue eyes lighting from beneath his heavy brows. She had seen Aiwilimae's face grow dark and rough as a troll's with anger when others said that she might be married away from his hall, there was no need to sorrow him too soon with news that they should part.

"I saw wind, and wave, and a man sitting upon a howe far from here. No one moves to do battle against us, nor are the land-wights wroth. Though the snow-clouds still rise thickly from the north, nothing should hinder our planting when the time is come."

"Then it is good." Aiwilimae reached out to squeeze his daughter's shoulders in a brief, bear-strong hug. "The Ansuz blessed our folk when he chose you for one of his walkurjons."

Swaebhon smiled at her father, but his words pricked a shiver of unease down her spine. When Wodhanaz chose me? She wondered. It was I who chose to follow his ways, and ride the wind-paths over air and water. The god had thralls as well as thanes, and if he was cruel to the strong, he was worse to the weak, if he could get use from them. She, thirteen winters old, had chosen to go out alone and sit on the howe raised so long since that no one remembered what mighty ruler lay buried there.

With only the light of the stars to guide her hand, she had made the spear-nick above her own heart, between her little unflowered breasts, and as her blood began to well dark, the wind had risen. She had spoken the god's own name, as few folk dared, it was she who had called his gaze to her. And to Hoilogae. Now, Swaebhon remembered tracing the threefold triangle, the walknot, knot of the slain, with the point of her spear. This I will give you for comfort, once you are wedded to your Hoilogae.

It shall be worth it! Swaebhon thought fiercely, biting into the slice of walrus-liver so that the rich blood ran heavy down her chin. If I must lose him, at least our wedding shall be a worthy geld for his death. Still, the tears stung her eyes like the sharp whipping of birch-trees in the wind, and the blood in her mouth seemed like a fore-taste of a chilling kiss. Her bones shook within her like aspen-leaves, and she did not know whether it was from dread or hope.

CHAPTER III

Helgi sat at the piano with Lays of Beleriand open before him, a pencil propped beside the sheets of blank music paper. It seemed to him that he could already hear the song, the rippling arpeggios in the upper keys that were Luthien's elven voice rising winged above the deep and steady notes of Beren, and it was not long before he began to pick them out and write them down, one by one, singing each measure twice and three times through.

"'A night there was when winter died, then all alone she sang and cried...'"

The wind was rising outside, blowing snowflakes to star and melt against the glass of the windowpanes. After a while, Helgi stopped, getting up and hurrying to look outside. The snow was falling hard enough that he could hardly see across the street. He pressed his palms against the icy glass, staring out as if he could draw the snowstorm in through his gaze. The snow was not yet lying on the street, but he thought that if it could fall till night, it might stay for a day or two.

Although it was only a little past three-thirty in the afternoon, Helgi plugged in the lights that ringed the ornament-hung pine in a thousand points of colored fire, then took the matches down from over the fireplace and lit the candles of the iron wreath on the mantel. He stood looking at their warm glow against the white light from the window. In two hours, his mother would be home and then she would take him over to the Jensens' for their Yule party, and he would see Karin if the roads hadn't iced over and the weather wasn't too bad to walk in. His parents had both called already, forbidding him to drive.

Helgi hurried back to the window, torn between his wish to see the snow fall harder and his hope that the weather would not keep him locked inside. Karin's leave was only for a week, since he did not dare to write to her, this was his only chance for her to notice him. One hour, fifty minutes, he thought, looking at the clock, then back outside. When he glanced upward, the sky seemed blacker against the torrent of white flakes, a strange birthing of light from darkness that caught his gaze for a moment, as though he stared up from the bottom of a great abyss.

Helgi turned back to the piano, already feeling his rising fear turn to a minor key, twisting down to the uncomfortable notes of the diminished fifth and up to the unfulfilled demands of the augmented.

"'He lay upon the leafy mold,
his face upon earth's bosom cold'"

The golden beeswax candles had burned half down, their warm scent filling the room, by the time the door which led from the garage into the kitchen opened and Helgi's mother called, "Helgi? Are you there?"

Helgi leapt up from the piano, dropping his pencil as he hurried to meet her. His mother was muffled in a thick camel's-hair coat, the dark blue woven hat pulled down over her ears sharpening the delicate points of her nose and chin so that she looked like a pretty troll-woman.

"Better get dressed for the cold, Helgi. It's a long walk."

Helgi ran to his room and pulled on a bulky sweater, then zipped his ski jacket over it. "Mom, I can't find my gloves or my hat," he wailed.

"They're in our closet," she shouted back.

The hat fit, but Helgi had outgrown his gloves. "Wear your father's," his mother told him. "It doesn't matter if they're a little bit too large. Now go put out the candles."

Helgi blew out each of the six flames on the wreath in turn, making a silent wish with each. Let Karin notice me. He picked up the little silver-wrapped box he had gotten for her himself and the larger package with the Christmas-tree wrapping—a box of chocolates which his mother had chosen for the Jensen family.

By the time Helgi and his mother started out the door, it was almost dark, the streetlights haloed in rings of light glimmering off the streaming snow. Helgi moved in front of his mother as they stepped out into the wind, trying to shield her slim form with his own. She laughed.

"This reminds me of when I was a girl in Minnesota," she said. "This isn't anything, we used to have to hold onto a rope tied to the house door when we went out to the outhouse, because otherwise you could get lost and freeze to death ten feet from the door."

Helgi looked at his mother in disbelief. She seldom talked about her childhood, but now she was laughing, the snowflakes melting to tiny drops in her fair eyebrows and the wisps of hair sticking out from beneath her woolly hat. "Is that really true?" he asked. "An outhouse?"

"We didn't get indoor plumbing until I was twelve. It's too bad we live in Dallas now, you've never seen a real winter."

"Why don't we go up to Minnesota for Christmas, then?"

"Because it's real winter up there, and Emma and Jetta want to come down here where it's warm."

Helgi held out his gloved palm to the wind, catching a fine scurf of white crystals on the dark leather. Although he had three layers of socks underneath his hiking boots, his toes had already gone numb. "Warm?"

"Compared to Minnesota," his mother answered.

The Jensens' lawn was lightly covered in snow by the time Helgi and his mother got there, though the walkway was still wetly bare. Their curtains were pulled back, light shining through to mark the night-paleness of their lawn with a barred rectangle of gold like the map of a fortress' foundations against the snow.

The horrible scream behind them almost made Helgi drop his packages. He jerked back, turning so fast he nearly fell as a huge white furry thing hurtled, howling, out of the dark bushes along the walkway. With the self-conscious ease of three months' lessons, Helgi dropped into a karate crouch to face it.

His mother recovered faster, beginning to laugh. "Karin," she said, "you'll give someone a heart attack doing that. Don't you think you're a little old for leaping out of bushes?"

The white furry thing straightened up, throwing back her hood. Helgi could see the gleam of Karin's teeth and eyes as her high bright laugh joined his mother's. "Let me be a little silly," she said. Helgi knew she had grown up in Dallas, but the Danish language still showed through in her slight accent and the way she carefully set her words, as though expecting them to slip from their places at any moment.

"I've just gotten leave from the federal penitentiary which we jokingly call our Armed Forces, I've earned the right to be crazy. Come in and have some eggnog to settle your nerves. Come in quickly, the ghosts come out at Yule and the Wild Hunt rides."

"Not to mention people leaping out from behind bushes?" Helgi added.

Karin glanced quickly down at him, her eyes were such a pale blue that, in the darkness, they seemed to reflect the shadowed whiteness of the snow. "That's right. Werewolves and berserks run around at Yule, you've started martial arts training, haven't you?"

"Shotokan karate," Helgi answered.

"Right." Karin eased into a fighting crouch.

"I'll leave you warriors out here," Helgi's mother said, taking the presents and going on up the walkway.

Karin and Helgi sparred for a few moments. He could tell she was going easy on him, she was as big as he and much better trained, but she carefully held back from thumping him until he tried to show off with a high kick to her shoulder. She grabbed his leg and dumped him into the snow.

"Kicks above the waist are for katas and chop-sockey movies," Karin admonished him lightly. "Don't try it when you're fighting. You're doing well, though, keep it up."

Helgi scrambled to his feet, brushing the snow off.

"You really think so?"

"Sure. You've got good form and you're fast. How long have you been doing it?"

"Three months. I just got my red belt—I double-graded," he added proudly.

"Very good. If you stay with it, you'll make a fine fighter."

The warmth inside the Jensens' house stung Helgi's cheeks with fresh blood as he shucked his coat and sweater. He turned to Karin, but she was gone already, leaving her white fell empty behind her. The snow-crystals in the fur had melted already, water-droplets pearling the tiny hairs.

The Jensens' living room was full of people already, talking and laughing through the pure keen notes of a soprano singing "O Holy Night" through the speakers on either side of the room. Karin's brother Olaf stood behind the white-draped table that had been set up as a makeshift bar, handing out drinks by candlelight and talking to the dark-haired woman who leaned against the cabinet beside him. A saint and a witch, Helgi thought as he got into line, looking at the glitter of the candle's flames off Olaf's white-blond hair and eyebrows, and the shadow of the slender woman's long pointed nose across the sharp plane of her cheek.

"Hi, Helgi," he said. "Coke, Sprite, or Dr. Pepper?"

"Eggnog, please."

The woman beside Olaf laughed. "Oh, let him have it. He's not driving, is he?" Olaf poured a cupful of frothy whiteness out of the blender.

Even in a candlelit room full of party, Helgi had no trouble seeing Karin, with her height and the fair hair that shimmered like a pale helmet above her white blouse, she stood out in his sight like lightning against the clouds. It was not until he had edged his way closer to her that he saw she was actually talking to his mother. He strained to hear what they were saying. Was Karin talking about him?

"Instead of Christmas?"

Karin's laugh tinkled like light off crystal. "Mother's not just being idiosyncratic. It's practical too. Everyone is at home with their families on Christmas Eve and Christmas Day, but not so many are busy on the solstice—the old Yule. Therefore, a 'Yule party'. You ask this every year, don't you?"

"I suppose I do."

"Can I get you another cup of eggnog?"

"That's very kind of you."

By the time Helgi had made it to his mother's side, Karin was already over at the bar.

"Did she say anything about me?" He whispered.

"No. Should she have?"

"I just thought" Helgi trailed off, glancing away to avoid his mother's eyes. His heart was beating so swiftly that it seemed to thrum in his breast. He was sure he must be sweating terribly, but when he passed his hand across his forehead, both were dry. He could hear his own music in his skull, drowning out the beginning notes of "Silent Night ."

"As she went, he swiftly came
and called her with the tender name,
of nightingales in elvish tongue,
that all the woods now sudden rung,
'Tinuviel! Tinuviel!'"

Karin moved through the party like a swan breasting the swell of a wave, gliding slowly so as not to spill a drop of the brimming cups in her hand. Helgi could not turn his gaze away from her. The curve of hip and length of leg filling out her faded blue jeans, the rounded muscles of her white arms beneath the thin rim of lace ringing her short sleeves, high cheekbones strengthened by the shadowy candlelight, blue-gray eyes light-filled as an Arctic wolf's. He realized that she was staring back at him, one corner of her mouth tilting upward.

"Uh," Helgi said desperately. "Uh, I brought you something." He took the little box from his mother's hand and pushed it towards Karin. He caught his breath as her cool fingers brushed his, it felt as though her touch had sent a stream of icy champagne-bubbles up his veins. At the same moment, he felt warmth throbbing in his groin with his heartbeat. Oh, God, he thought desperately, not now! But the heat was already draining away again, betrayed, thankfully, by his nervousness.

"Shall I open it now, or save it for Christmas?" Karin asked.

"Open it now."

Karin tore into the wrapping, shreds of silver dangling down from her fingers as she freed the box and flipped its top up. She drew in her breath. Real surprise, Helgi thought, hoping that the open-eyed look of delight that followed was as real.

"That is beautiful. Look, Mrs. Hadding, what your son has gotten me!" She held out the box so that Helgi's mother could see the pendant that lay gleaming against its pale cotton nest. Although he had turned it over and over in his hands by sunlight and electrical light, Helgi could not help looking at it again, to see it in the glow of the candle-flames as Karin saw it now. The piece was made of silver, unevenly cast but burnished smooth so that it had the look of ice that had dripped and frozen to gleaming clearness again. It showed a single strand angling sharply and weaving into itself again and again, weaving into the shape of three interlocked triangles. "It looks as though it must be handmade. Where-ever did you find it?"

"I got it at the Texas Renaissance Festival this October. I, uh, remembered you like Viking things, and the silversmith said this was a Viking symbol.

There's a card in the box that tells about it."

Karin lifted the pendant and the cotton beneath it, taking out the little square of folded parchment-paper to read the inscription that Helgi had long since learned by heart. "'Kveldúlfr Gundarsson wrought this valknútr in silver. The valknútr is an ancient Viking symbol from the Gotlandic picture stones, holy to the god Ódhinn (Wotan).' Then he's got something in runes, let me see."

"I tried to translate them, but they didn't make any sense," Helgi said. "I was able to find all but a couple of the runes, but when I put them together I couldn't spell anything with them." The silversmith had said something about the three strands of fate—past, present, and future—weaving together in a single knot, and something else about Norse time all being one within Wyrd, past lives and present bound by the sign, but Helgi could not remember it very well, and the runes had not helped him.

"Uh huh. I bet you were using Tolkien, weren't you?"

"Guilty as charged," Helgi admitted.

"These are real runes, from the older runic alphabet. I used to know it well enough to write graffiti in it, let me see, now, sowilo, isa, gebo, sig, sigfödr sael sigruna merki." Karin shrugged. "The first word is a name for Ódhinn, Sigfader, you would say, 'Victory-Father'. And sigruna has to be 'victory-runes'. I'm not sure about the rest of it, but I'm pretty sure it's in Old Norse."

Karin took a deep drink of her eggnog, dashing the froth from her upper lip afterwards with the tips of her fingers, then lifted the pendant from its cotton and hung it about her neck. "Thank you so much, Helgi. I wish I had thought to get something for you."

"That's all right."

"I shall remember, at your birthday—for Halloween. I was there the night you were born, you know. Yours was the last house we visited, because of the storm." Karin looked over to the fireplace, where a squat dark shadow had moved before the flames, the shadow of a sitting woman on the hearth. "Mother's about to start the Yule ghost stories. Come on, let's listen."

Helgi followed her over, settling down in one of the thick fluffy sheepskins on the floor as Karin turned off the tape player and called out, "Ghost stories! Anyone for Yule ghosts?"

Mrs. Jensen sat quietly, not saying anything until Karin had shepherded the guests into a half-circle around the fireplace, some on folding chairs and some, like Helgi, on the floor. At last, when Karin had blown out all the candles in the room and seated herself next to her mother, the older woman began to speak.

"This is a story about something that happened on a farm in Vintens, near Horsens in Jutland, not so far from where I grew up," Mrs. Jensen said quietly. Although Helgi knew she had lived in America since Karin was three, the sounds of the Danish coast still echoed in her voice like waves in a seashell, her accent much stronger than the slight flavoring in Karin's words. "I know it is true because the farm where it happened is still standing, and if you are brave enough to go into the barn in daylight and look very carefully, you can still see the traces of blood on the roof beams, and those who sleep in the house at night often hear things in the barn as well—most especially at Yule, when the darkness is strongest.

"'There was once a serving-maid on that farm, and she was a strong and brave maiden. Folk said she was not even afraid of the Devil himself. One winter the lads had carved a Yule-buck, and set it up as we did in the old days. Now the Yule-buck," Mrs. Jensen added, "is a thing that we make with a goat's head on a pole, it has a long red tongue and jaws that clack, so that a young man, who is sometimes dressed in a furry cape, can carry it about to frighten people with on Yule Eve. Sometimes it is called the Devil, but there are many who think that it goes back to the old gods of Denmark, Oden and Tor.'"

When Mrs. Jensen had finished her story, she paused to let her listeners shudder in the darkness a moment before she moved aside from the hearth. "Halfdan, it's your turn now." Mr. Jensen rose from his seat and settled himself again in his wife's stead before the fire. The shadow of his broad shoulders hid the flames, but their light wavered behind him, his skull gleamed ruddy through his thinning blond hair, and the fire's bright reflection shone from the glossy paper cover of the book in his hand.

"Thorodd Thorbrandsson was still farming at Altafjord, and owned the lands at Ulfarsfell and Orlygsstad as well," Mr. Jensen began, his slow deep voice taking on a measured tone and pace as he read, as though he were long used to telling stories by the fireplace. "'Thorolf Twist-Foot's ghost haunted these farms so viciously that no one would live there. Bolstad was abandoned now, for as soon as Arnkel was dead, Thorolf had begun to haunt there too, killing men and beasts alike, so that no one has been brave enough to farm there since.'" He read of how Thorodd and his neighbors broke open the knoll where Thorolf Twist-Foot was buried, to find the long-dead man uncorrupted, but black as death and swollen to the size of an ox, how, after Thorolf Twist-Foot had been burnt, one of his cows would lick the stones where the ashes had blown about, and men often saw the cow up on the mountainside with a dapple-gray bull, but no one knew of any such bull there. In time the cow gave birth to a bull-calf, when Thorodd's old foster-mother heard it bellowing, she prophesied that it would bring unhappiness if it were let to live.

But the calf grew and grew, they named him Glæsir, and he became a fine-looking beast, but Thorodd's foster-mother still wished to have him destroyed, saying that he would be Thorodd's death. And towards the end of the summer, Glæsir went mad, and when Thorodd heard what Glæsir was doing, he rushed out of the house and grabbed a large birch log from the stack of firewood, striking the bull between the horns. Thorodd's farm-hands got their weapons and tried to help, but when Glæsir saw them coming, it tossed Thorodd and gored him, then fled down to the river until it sank in a quagmire.

"To our ancestors, the dead were never quite dead—even burning was not enough to finish Thorolf Twist-Foot," Halfdan went on. "Our ghosts are stronger in the North, when the winters are dark all day and the snow howls outside the doors, but even here, they may come back from their graves at Yule." The fire glinted from his teeth as he moved aside to let Karin take his place by the hearth.

Karin read the last story, "The Mezzo-Tint", about a picture of a house which changed to show a thing creeping across the lawn, getting into the house, and carrying off a child. Helgi hardly listened to it. It was enough for him to be able to stare freely at Karin as she sat with her head bent over the book, peering at the words in the firelight.

When her tale was done, Karin lit a candle from the fireplace and carried the flame about the room, kindling all the sooty wicks into life again as Olaf turned on the CD player. The voice of Luciano Pavarotti singing "Adeste Fideles" swelled strong and warm through the room, bringing a wash of talk in its wake as the guests began to stand up and move about once more.

"Are you enjoying being in the Air Force?" Helgi asked Karin when she had set her candle back into its place between two straw goats on the mantel's wreath of pine.

Karin paused, cocking her head as if to catch the sound of a wind that brushed by Helgi without touching him. "All the rules and regulations. I don't like those so much," she said slowly. "A woman takes a lot of special crap, but so does everyone who stands out. I knew it would be like that, it's the price I expected to pay. To fly, they'll let women be fighter pilots within the next five to ten years, there's no doubt about it. And flying like that. There's nothing better. I'm not allowed to fly by myself yet, but I've been up in the air in some of the real planes. It's power and speed. It's splitting the sky with my flight—that is worth everything."

"Couldn't you have been a commercial pilot? Why the Air Force?"

"Flying a bus! If I wanted to do that, I'd drive one on the ground. I'm not up there for safety, I'm up there to push it to the limit." She was staring over Helgi's head now, gazing at the candles whose flames were mirrored for Helgi in her ice-gleaming valknútr.

"Ten o'clock," Helgi's mother said. "Time to go."

"Already?"

"Your father will call out the Mounties if we don't. Come on."

"Take care, Helgi." Karin touched her pendant lightly. "Thank you, again."

"You're welcome. Um, I hope I can see you again before you have to go back."

"Maybe so. If not, well, Merry Christmas."

"You too."

The snow had stopped falling, the air was so still that Helgi did not notice how cold it was until they had been walking for several minutes. Suddenly his mother lost her footing, windmilling her arms as she tried to catch herself. Helgi reached out for her, but she was already half-stepping, half-falling backward onto better footing.

"Ice," she said when she'd recovered her balance. Carefully she stuck out a boot, scraping the thin layer of snow away from the gleaming patch of smooth darkness with the side of her sole. "Watch out for it. The roads must have frozen over before the snow started sticking. It's a good thing we didn't drive."

They went more cautiously after that, each ready to catch the other. It seemed like a very long time before the two of them, shivering through all their winter clothes, were at their own door. Helgi's mother had to try three times before her stiff fingers could fit the key into the keyhole.

"My God, I'm glad the two of you are back!" Helgi's father said as they came through the door. "The radio said there was a bad accident right over there by the Jensens'. I called and they said you'd left nearly forty-five minutes ago. I was almost ready to get in the car and go looking for you." He rubbed at his grizzled temples as if to loosen the deep threads of worry graven across his long forehead.

"The sidewalks were icy and we had to go carefully," Helgi's mother answered. "I don't suppose you thought to soothe your nerves with hot chocolate, did you?"

"We can make some if you'd like. Did you enjoy the party, Helgi?"

"Yes, very much," Helgi answered.

He waited until his parents had gone into the kitchen, then sat down at the piano, playing the music that was already piercing clear through his head and writing it down, bar by bar. If only I could bring in the instruments to play this with me, he thought. If only I had a synthesizer or something like that. He could hear the high notes of the flames on silver against the dark shivering of the wintry cold and the murmur of the snow, he sang softly, bar by bar, catching the sounds and making them fast before him.

"Thus in anguish Beren paid
for that great doom upon him laid,
the deathless love of Luthien,
too fair for love of mortal Men,
and in his doom was Luthien snared,
the deathless in his dying shared,
and Fate them forged a binding chain
of living love and mortal pain."

The cup of chocolate on top of the piano was quite cold when he looked up and saw it, a trail of droplets already clotted to stickiness around the rim of its wooden coaster. The ghostly green digits glowing from the VCR's time-keeper read 1.23. Helgi drank his chocolate down quickly, then coughed to clear his throat and sat down again, beginning his song from the beginning. He had to go slowly, he had written the piano part for a better player. But even so, he could hear it singing through his throat and the piano together, dizzying him with what he had wrought.

Helgi sat still for a few moments after the last note had died away. He wondered if he could make a recording of it and send it to Karin. Not yet, he thought. Maybe if I can get some of the guys from the orchestra to play with me. He could see himself standing up in front of the musicians, feel the thrumming of strings through polished wood and the breath bringing voice to gleaming brass as his own breath filled his throat with words, and Karin sitting in the audience, the pale-gilded helm of her hair glowing in the shadowed auditorium.

Not satisfied yet, but happy enough with what he had done, Helgi turned off the light and went to get ready for bed. He did not see Karin again before her leave was over, but the Christmas holidays were full enough to keep him from brooding on it. Aunt Emma and Uncle Karl with their children Tony and Christian and Lisa, Aunt Jetta and Uncle Mike with Margrete and Barney, flew down from Minnesota on December twenty-second and stayed until the fourth of January.

Helgi was set to playing Christmas carols on the piano for everyone to sing, he himself sang as powerfully as he could, and was gratified when Aunt Jetta finally said, "My, your voice has certainly improved, Helgi. I think changing has done it some good." He wasn't ready yet to perform his song for his relatives' approval, though he thought he could sing it well enough, he couldn't play it up to speed yet, and it seemed to him that the one was of little good without the other.

But on Christmas Eve he played *Silent Night* on his trombone, between Christian's display of magical tricks and the moment when little Lisa was encouraged to hold up a crayon-scratched piece of paper and say shyly, "It's a cat. I drew it this morning because I saw a cat outside the window."

Then, after Tony had told a horde of jokes (and been suppressed by his mother when he started on dead-baby jokes) and Margrete had stood on her head and Barney had recited "The Burial of Sam McGee" with only two glances at the book, Helgi sang "It Came Upon a Midnight Clear ." He got through with only a couple of bad moments on the high notes, and thought he had done rather well.

"Tell me, Helgi," Uncle Karl said quietly to him after the family recital was over and the children under twelve, Lisa, Margrete, and Barney had been sent to bed, "have you ever thought about taking singing lessons?"

"No. Do you think I should? Is something wrong with my voice?"

His uncle blinked behind his black-rimmed glasses. "Why should there be? You take lessons on the trombone, don't you?"

"Well, yes."

"It's the same thing. If you want to sing, you ought to learn to do it as well as you can, and a good teacher can help a lot. Even the best operatic singers still have vocal coaches, just like football players do." Uncle Karl tapped the arm of the sofa twice with a single twitch of his wrist, Helgi remembered how last year, when his uncle had still smoked, he had tapped the ash off his cigarette with just the same gesture. "Your voice is still changing, so you have to be careful with it. I thought I heard you straining a bit on the high notes there."

"Well, yes," Helgi admitted, relieved that there was no more to it than that.

"So there you are. Are you in the school choir?"

"Yes."

His uncle nodded. "I don't know where you get all your music from. No one else in the family can carry a tune in a bucket, well, I guess you can hear that for yourself. But the important thing is how much we enjoy it, not how it sounds."

Helgi nodded respectfully. Still, the thought echoed as if through a hollow dark place in his chest. If the singer doesn't sound good, no one will listen to the song.

The first day of school was a mess as usual, with everyone running madly through the halls in search of classrooms believed not to exist in any real sense. Helgi wandered aimlessly about the band room, staring darkly at his schedule card and muttering, for no real reason, about the death of Western civilization, until someone punched him on the arm. He looked up along the gangley length of his friend Mark Tippet.

"Marcus, Marcum, Marci, Marco, Marco, O Marce," he intoned. "Mark Heil!"

Mark thumped his fist against his chest, giving Helgi a Roman salute. "Hail, Hell-Guy, O barbarian from the frozen north. What lunch period do you have?"

"Third."

Mark checked his own card. "Crap. I've got first. Match cards."

They compared their schedules. Mark sighed. "Well, four together ain't too bad, especially for the last semester of senior year. How'd you get a study hall?"

"By not doing chemistry. Sleep seemed infinitely better than explosions."

Mark blew a raspberry and Helgi took the mouthpiece out of his trombone case and replied with an amplified one which slid into a rude rendition of "Taps" before they sat down and began to warm up.

Helgi shook his sneakers as he walked out of the room where Major Works Geometry was taught.

"What're you doing?" Mark asked.

"Shaking the dust of mathematics from my feet before I aspire to the peak of human endeavor."

"You've switched into chemistry already."

"Music. Vocal production. That which separates man from beast."

"That which doesn't separate you from a donkey with a throat condition."

Helgi punched Mark beneath the ribs, not quite hard enough to double him over. "Die, infidel swine."

"Oink," Mark answered, shoving him back. "Go on, go howl, I'll vouch that you've had your rabies shots when they come to take you away."

"May you blow your dick into a thousand pieces—if you can find it."

The two of them parted, laughing, and Helgi hurried back to the music room, taking his place between John Gowdy and Craig Hermann in the middle row of the bass section. It was a minute or two past the bell when the music director, Mr. Stravich, came panting in, clutching a stack of folders. "Sorry I'm late, folk," he said. "I had some trouble with the Xerox machine." He handed the folders to Laura Raphael at the short end of the first sopranos. "Pass 'em along, please. We're going to choose six out of eight for our spring concert. Why so few? Because our program will also include four soloists, two boys and two girls. I'd like to have more, but there's not time in the program. I do want to encourage all of you to work on an audition piece. Even if you don't feel like singing in front of people, it's good practice, and it's always nice to have something performance-ready."

Helgi's heart leapt like a salmon over the rocks, he could hardly keep from grinning maniacally. His song. He could sing it after all! He was sure that a piece he had composed himself would be more interesting, worth more, than anything anyone else was likely to do. Again, he felt himself standing at the front of the stage and Karin shining in the darkness of the auditorium, her face pale against her shadowy uniform as she stared up at him, drawn in by the sound of his voice

"Wake up, asshole," John hissed out of the corner of his mouth, poking Helgi with the corner of the folders. He took one and passed the rest to Craig. In despite of the notes and words black before him, he could still hear his own song, "A night there was when winter died."

Helgi practiced his song for an hour every day, until the arpeggios rippled easily from his fingers and his hands stretched without a thought to form the chords he had written for himself. After a little thought, remembering what Uncle Karl had said, he moved the highest notes down by a third, but kept the piano part where it was to compensate for his loss of the vocal tones. Finally he played and sang it for Mark.

"What do you think?" He asked when he was done.

"Pretty music, I guess. Sounds too opera like for me. Why don't you take to writing metal?"

"This is Tolkien, fool. Elves do not sing metal."

"I guess so. Can I see the words?"

"Couldn't you understand them?"

"Not all that well. You know it's always harder to understand something that's sung. Remember how long it took us to figure out the lyrics to 'Another Brick in the Wall'?"

Until they'd gotten the album and read them off the cover, yeah.

"Okay. You want me to do it again?"

"Just play the music, well, yeah, you might as well sing too."

Helgi played his song again, enunciating the words as carefully as he could. Mark nodded when he was done.

"That's better. I understood you a lot more clearly that time."

"You think I'll make it?"

"I don't know. Shit, I'm a clarinet player, I'm no judge of singing. Sounded okay to me."

The tryouts for the soloists were held in February. Mr. Stravich had a panel of three boys, Helgi, Mike Albercht, and Chuck Gosforth, judging the girls and three girls, Michelle Snyder, Farrell Ashcroft, and Marcia Albani, judging the boys. He explained to Helgi's panel that he had chosen them because they were both section leaders in the band and orchestra and also members of the choir, and so he expected them to be able to judge musical capability from both a vocal and a general standpoint. The girls sang first.

Most of them had enlisted either vocal teachers or piano students from the university as accompanists. The outstanding soloist was clearly Farrell, whose rich mezzo-soprano rendition of "Memories" brought a prickle to the backs of Helgi's eyes and an ache of sympathetic desire to the back of his throat. You're a wimp, he told himself severely, blinking hard several times, but that evening he practiced for an hour and a half, till he was too hoarse to hit even the B-flat below middle C that he had chosen as the comfortable limit of his top range.

He shook all through the next day, staring out into the rain and trying to calm himself by breathing deeply. Third up, he thought, over and over again. Not last, not first. It's a good place to be. He stared at the sheets of music hidden beneath his homework in Geometry, he moved his fingers and shaped his mouth softly around the silent sounds of Tolkien's words while his English teacher droned on about Dickens. Third up. I can do it, I know my song is good.

Still, Helgi's nerve nearly failed him when he got into the large practice room after school and saw Michelle, Farrell, and Marcia staring at him like three cats on a fence, while Mr. Stravich blinked softly. He remembered what the music director had told the class about auditioning and stepped forward, smiling as if his hands were not shaking at all.

"I'm Helgi Hadding. The lyrics of my song are excerpted from Tolkien's Lay of Leithian, Canto III, the music is my own composition." He sat down at the piano, placing his fingers carefully on the keys. I know this song, I cannot screw it up, he murmured silently to himself.

The music beneath his fingers calmed him, he had played it so many times that he could no longer get it wrong. Now it seemed as though his blood ran through the keys, as his breath gave life to the words. The dark wood of the piano seemed to glimmer with a red tracery of strange runes before his eyes, and the notes he hammered out drowned the judges' breath in his hearing. It was easy, then, for Helgi to open his mouth and let the words flow freely through him, holding them in the spell of his song till he was done.

The names of the soloists were to be posted the next day. Helgi raced over to the band room during the five minutes between each class, staring at the door as if his gaze could bring his name forth from the wood. It was not until after the last bell had rung that the piece of paper appeared there.

Female Soloists.

Ashcroft, Farrell ("Memories")

Tolliver, Rhonda ("La Violetta")

Male Soloists.

Hirsch, Max ("Death and the Maiden")

Infano, David ("If Ever I Would Leave You")

Helgi stared at it, the hot choking in his throat rising in a flood towards his eyes. He bit it back viciously. He would ask, he would find out what had gone wrong.

Mr. Stravich was in his office, shuffling through his file cabinet. He turned around quickly when Helgi cleared his throat, almost losing his balance.

"What can I do for you, Helgi?" He asked.

Helgi felt himself at a loss. He did not know where to start or what to say. Finally he choked out, "Um, the solos, UmWhat was wrong with mine?"

The music director winced, his plump face crumpling into lines of sudden age. "Helgi," he said gently, "there were only two places, and Max and David are both really quite exceptional singers. You mustn't feel bad because you didn't make it. You're only seventeen, and your voice may still be changing."

"Is there anything I could have done better? Is there anything I could change about the song?"

Mr. Stravich looked down at his desk for a few moments. Helgi could see the tightening of sinews beneath the soft flesh of his hands as he gripped the file he held. "Ah." Then he looked up, looking Helgi straight in the eye. "Helgi, I think you're mature enough for me to tell you the truth."

Helgi nodded, the chill of sickness was upon him, but its cold grip held his feet to the ground as he met the music director's gaze.

"You're a fairly good pianist and your composition is excellent. It shows a great deal of musical talent. But, well, there's no way I can say this kindly, and I hope you won't take it too personally. Your singing voice is very bad."

"What's wrong with it?"

"Um. It's harsh, grating, and off-key. I don't really think there's much you can do about it, except wait until your voice has finished changing all the way, until you're nineteen or twenty, at the earliest, low voices always take the longest to come on-stream, but even so, well."

Helgi barely noticed as Mr. Stravich came around the desk to pat him on the shoulder.

"You're a very good trombonist, and quite a remarkable composer for your age. For your own sake, Helgi, stick to the gifts you have and don't put your heart into something you can't do well. It was sensible of you to apply to Jefferson as a trombone major, if you'd like to perform one of your own pieces as a trombone solo, or even piano at the band's spring concert, I think you should. It would be well worthwhile. It wouldn't be fair of me. For your sake as much as anyone else's, to let you perform as a solo vocalist."

"Would it help if I took voice lessons?" Helgi asked, doing his best to keep his voice steady.

"Ah, Helgi, lessons can't do that much if the voice isn't there. Stick to what you're good at, that's the best you can do."

"Should I quit the choir, then?"

"Not if you enjoy singing. Choir is for fun, no one really stands out in it. But don't put your heart into doing solo vocal work. All right?"

"All right. Thank you."

"Think about writing a piece for instrumental performance," Mr. Stravich urged as Helgi turned to go out. "You really ought to keep developing your compositional work, I think you have a very good future there."

"Thank you," Helgi said again, and got out while he could still see to turn the doorknob.

He cried silently in a stall in the boys' room for quite a long time, rocking back and forth as his sobs racked his body with the despair he could not let sound. Grasping at his neck, he could feel the sharp edges of his Adam's apple lodged like a half-swallowed rock in his throat, and thought how easy it would be to tear his broken voice-box loose with his hand. But finally, exhausted, he dropped his arm again and picked up his book-bag. Helgi did not look about him as he plodded home, only lowered his head against the cold edge of wind. When he got home, he sat down at the piano and stared at the betraying notes that leapt winged on the pages before him. He took the sheets in his hand, meaning to tear them across again and again till no one could transform their silence into sound again, but he could not.

Instead he crumpled them, standing and lifting the lid of the piano stool and forcing the rustling cream-white ball into the corner beneath the hinge, then sitting down hard upon it again and staring at the row upon row of blank lines in the music notebook before him. Why? He thought. If I can compose, if I can play the trombone, why should I have to sing? The names of composers whirled through his heads—Beethoven, Mozart, Wagner, all empty and common as plaster busts on a piano. No words without breath, no song without words, no might without song. Only his own croaking, harsh and grating, could bring what he heard forth from the hidden world around him, flesh the bare bones and green the dry sticks of the notes before him. There was something more. Helgi's eyes blurred until he could see the earthen walls rising dark around him, skulls and rot sealing him in, and it seemed to him that his voice alone was the wind that could open the way and bear him forth from that place. There was some strength in his song, something he could not name, but he had felt it when singing, bearing him up on eagle-wings, spilling golden and glittering from his mouth, but he could not sing, the door of the flood was broken, wings walled within the stone of his throat. Helgi could not cry out his hurt, he could not speak it alone without the tones sounding around and through it, and before long he beat a vicious discord on the piano with one hand, lifting the other to write.

"I know my own damnation," he wrote, half-spoken to a cruel chord within whose bounds no note would quite be off-key and no note quite on. Then the words came easily, rushing up on the music that bore them like life rushing freely on the blood-spurt from an artery, their flow swiftly numbing his shock.

"Howls the wolf and hates the sound,
Harsh the throat in hemp-noose bound,
Choking chains of flesh and bone."
His chord modulated, down a half-step.
"Scars on soul are cruelest scarred,
Bitterest hate from love is barred,
Coldest cries, who cries alone."
Up a fifth now, with the perfect fifth still ringing underneath—the eerie sound that all his books on composition said to avoid.
"If the horn blows, who will hear?
'Neath its roughness, need and fear,
Wordless cries weens none to know."
Then Helgi's left hand began to beat the deep notes, pounding out triplets with his painful cry sounding above in a double rhythm. The words hurt, ripping out of his throat as he scribbled them down, but he could not still them nor stanch the flow of their music.
"Day shall hide in dark wolf's fell,
Fair moon fade 'neath bat-wing swell.
Iron now shall eat the gold,
Day-spring dark to winter's cold.
Wolves run wild as goblins' steeds,
Wyrm-sword spring up, wound now bleeds.
Now I care not. Night or day,
Rent my heart from ribs away,
Stand I stung in snake-pit deep,
Nor was pain here paid for cheap.
All I've wrought, my words and will,
Cast away as carrion still,
How can I tell, what took so long
To build, and burnt before its dawn?"
He went back to his first chord, holding it till his nerves ached in sympathy with the discord.

"The light unlit I to dark,
Troll wild be woman most fair,
A wolf-song I wield alone."

Down a half-step again, the sound scraping across his skin until he must cry out in answer.

"Ill, stands my voice yet not stilled,
To ring the holy steads round,
My heart more hides than you know."

Up a fifth for the last piercing cry, now truly howling, unbound from the bonds of tones and harmony from which Helgi had called hurt in stead of help,

"I curse all who won't hear,
I howl my hopes beyond Hell,
My sight shines through my sounds
So stand I as I am!"

The song fully wrought, Helgi began again. This time he could feel his song cutting keen through him, rope-rough scratching in his throat as he battered against the black wall of earth and stone. He sang it twice, then a third time. His tone was dropping, his lungs beating like great black wings against the wind to keep his voice strong as the oxygen rush buzzed in his head. It seemed to him that his voice was deeper than it had been—no, that another voice, rough and deep as a raven's croak, echoed him from far away.

Helgi closed his eyes, crying out the last words with all his strength. Something burst bright within his head, a shadow loomed before the fireworks glittering on the back of his eyelids. A man in a blue-black cloak, one eye gleaming bright beneath his eagle-beaked helm. The burning spark of a spear-tip, pointing as if to show him the way, and then Helgi sat dazed and panting on the hard edge of the piano bench, looking at the swift scribblings before him. It was no longer weeping that ached in his throat. The muscles hurt as though he had lifted something far too heavy for his strength. He tore the new song out of his music notebook, then lifted the piano bench and pulled out the crumpled ball of the old, smoothing it and folding the two carefully together before putting them away again.

CHAPTER IV

Hailgi moved carefully, keeping his head down as he passed through the hall. A greasy hood of grayish-white wool covered his warrior's knot of amber-fair hair, his dirty cloak hid the sword on his belt, and he dragged one foot a little behind him. When he came to the ring of tall posts around the garth, he shifted the pebble in his mouth with his tongue.

Aiwarikijar, who warded the gate in the afternoon, did not bother to stand up, merely tossing thick brown hair back from his eyes as Hailgi came closer. "Where did you come from, boy, and where are you going?" He asked. Hailgi bit back a snort at the skinny warrior's use of the word "boy", though Aiwarikijar stood most of a handspan taller than Hailgi, he was only two years older.

"Home," Hailgi grunted. "Came up to sell cheese this morning."

"Go on, then."

Hailgi limped through the gate, walking along the path to the woods as slowly as he could bear to until a horde of smooth gray trunks misted by green wood-dimness hid the hall from his sight. Then he spat out the pebble and began to run, lighter in his legs than usual with the fresh ease of losing his feigned limp, but hampered in his breath by biting his lip to keep back the laughter. He'd made it! If he could pass unknown through Hagalar's garth, where he'd grown up in foster care for the past three years, then surely no one in Hunding's hall would be able to recognize him. It was easy, he thought, to make oneself seem less, to hide wit and strength till they were needed and to turn a twitch of rage into a flinch of fear.

Now, though he had reached fifteen and not yet blooded his sword, though years of frith had kept battle-fame from his grasp, when other men in the hall boasted of having slain their first foes at twelve or thirteen. He would be able to do a deed worth remembering, any man could swing a blade, but he would be known first for wit and skill. It was finer yet that he should dare it from his place as Hagalar's fosterling.

Hagalar had held the lands between Hunding and Sigismundar since Hailgi's birth, and held the frail frith between the two drighten alive as well. By buying land from each, he had ended their first quarrel over their march-lands, if not the lasting hate that had sprung from the fight. Hagalar had held his place carefully. His eldest daughter was wed to Hunding's second son Aiwulfar, but he had fostered Hailgi, weighting each side of the scale hanging between northern Jutland's great drightens with a kin-bond.

Now Hailgi would use that to his own clan's gain—if only in the smallest way, he would tip the scales of honor, of soul-strength, by winning his will here, and begin to turn Wyrd so that the Wolfings' might could rise over that of Hunding and his sons. Hailgi kept walking steadily, making a bag of his cloak and picking up dry wood when he passed it until sundown began to darken the shadows of the trees. When he could no longer see sunlight through the branches, he stopped beneath the roots of a wide-spreading oak, scraping twigs into a loose pile and weaving a few pieces of his firewood together over it.

Even with dusk creeping swiftly over him, it did not take Hailgi long to find a piece of flint, and the curved fire-iron at the bottom of his belt pouch rested in a nest of fluffy tinder. Two sharp strikes at the stone's shiny gray edge, and the tiny flame was already flaring up in his hand. Hailgi blew on it carefully, cupping his hand as he moved it to set fire to the tattered edge of a fallen leaf, then another. Before long, Hailgi had a good fire going and was resting against the trunk of the tree almost as comfortably as he would have within Hagalar's hall. Although he could hear the noises of something moving not too far away, he was not very afraid, he had his sword, and if he had to, he could easily get up the oak.

As for outlaws, though he was not as large as a full-grown man and had not begun to grow a beard yet, he was fast and strong enough to make most of Hagalar's warriors wary even in practice fights, where a wooden sword could easily leave a bright bruise or crack a bone. His only real worry was that Hunding's men would come upon him before he was ready to meet them, for the best he could hope for then was that Sigismundar would be able to pay whatever geld Hunding asked for giving him back alive and unhurt. A warrior must be willing to risk his hide, he told himself, otherwise there's no worth in his deeds.

For all his brave thoughts, Hailgi slept uneasily that night. When the sun was up, it was easy not to fear wood-ghosts and the cold hands of those who walked in darkness, but it was also easy for Hailgi to see and hear things that others walked on past, and easier yet for him to call up sights in his mind which could not be banished so lightly. Now he remembered tales of bodies buried shallowly in the woods that cast off their thin cloaks of earth to rise and walk again, and of those who rested half-living in the mounds among the trees, and sleep did not come swiftly to him. He twitched awake each time a stick cracked beneath the greedy jaws of the flames, several times, he got up to throw more wood onto the fire. The sky was just beginning to gray by the time he fell into a deep sleep.

When Hailgi awoke, his fire had burned down to a thick layer of ash over the coals and the Sun was halfway up the clear cold morning sky. He sprang up, drawing his cloak around him and pulling the hood down over his head again, and began to walk briskly. He had not thought that he would sleep so late, but now that he was awake, his tautened nerves thrummed like the wind off the North Sea singing through bare winter branches. Although Hunding's battle-banner was not flying over his garth, Hailgi knew it at once by its size.

Only his father's holdings were as great. Tugging his hood low as if against the sharp wind of summer's end, he limped towards the gate. The hefty guard only grunted and waved him through with his spear, lifting the clay pot in his hand to his lips again as Hailgi passed.

It did not take much thinking to know that the great hall which stood among the flock of lesser huts like an eagle in a hen house would have to be Hunding's own. Hailgi thought that it would be wiser of him not to walk straight up to it in daylight. Instead he drifted towards a pen where a red-haired youth about his own age—fourteen or fifteen winters, Hailgi guessed—sat on top of the low wooden wall ringing the cattle-garth and prodded at the cows with a long stick every now and then.

"What're you doing?" Hailgi asked, after watching the other for a little while.

"Not much," the boy answered. "It's what I'm not doing that means more."

"All right. What aren't you doing?"

"I'm not herding sheep. I'm not looking after swine."

"Ah. Yes. I see you're not," Hailgi said, feeling very much at a loss. "So why is this better?"

The other youth's pale eyes narrowed as he looked at Hailgi. "Are you simple-minded? You look as though you ought to know what it's like."

"Never thought it was so bad," Hailgi muttered. He was glad of the hood that hid his burning ears. He hoped it shadowed his blush as well, quiet as he might learn to keep his mouth and eyes, his feelings still showed through his fair skin at the least chance.

"Well, you may not care, but I can tell you, I was meant for better things. Anything's better, really," he added with a grimace. "But I've been practicing with a spear, and when I'm a little better, I'll try to get into the drighten's band. Catch me looking after a sheep then!" He grinned at Hailgi, showing the snaggle-gap between his brown-stained front teeth.

"What's your name?" Hailgi asked.

"I'm called Swain Redhair. Everyone knows me here. Where did you come from, anyway? Did you run away from somewhere?"

"M'father died half a moon ago," Hailgi mumbled, thrusting his thumb through his fist under his cloak to turn away the ill weird that his words might wreak. "I've been looking for a place to work where I could get food and a warm bed."

"You've come to the right place," Swain told him. "There's always lots of work at the great hall. More work than anyone really wants to do. What's your name? I'll take you along when I go up to help with the food tonight, and you'll get plenty to eat when the thanes are done. Whatever folk may say about Hunding, I'd fight any man who says he's not free with his food. He's not here now, but Heming and the rest of his sons are, and Heming's almost as good as his father, though he's still getting over the fever he had after Midsummer's, that's why he's not out with Hunding now."

"My name's Hamal," Hailgi answered. He pulled himself up to sit on the fence beside Swain. "Why isn't Hunding here?"

"He went off to the west with a small troop yesterday. They were bearing white shields, I think he meant only to remind Anulaibhar who his oaths were sworn to. I shouldn't think he'll be gone more than a few days, since it's almost time to begin harvesting. How are you with a sickle?"

Hailgi smiled to himself, now he knew what he had come to learn. Still, he thought there would be no harm in staying the night here and leaving at the first light of dawn instead of starting back now and sleeping in the wood again, and the rede his stomach was giving him seemed well worth listening to.

"I've been taught to gather grain," he said, thinking of how he had heard a skop in Hagalar's Hall call gold the grain-harvest of southern lands. "This seems like a garth worth staying in." For tonight, at least, he whispered inside his head.

Swain had not said how many men made up "a small troop", but Hailgi guessed that if only twenty had gone with Hunding, the drighten's band was at least the match of his father's. Carrying full platters of meat from the roasts dripping into the long fire at one end of the hall to the men who shouted for more at the other end gave him plenty of time to reckon up the war band's strength. Hunding's son Heming was too thin to fill his father's high seat. Even in the fire lit dimness, Hailgi could see the unhealthy sallowness of his skin, and he often shifted on the smooth wood as if his bones were chafing through his flesh. Heming's mouth was narrow beneath his thick beard, his brown hair already beginning to thin at the back.

"The fair one to Heming's left, the young one, him who's trying to make a beard out of three hairs on his chin, is his brother Lingwe," Swain hissed out of the corner of his mouth as he and Hailgi passed one another. "Watch out for him, he's got a nasty temper, and the rings on his hands make his blows sting.

He's angry now because Hunding said he was too young to go out with the war band this season, though he's only fourteen winters old. Don't let him see you pinching meat off the plate, or he'll give you something to remember. The big graybeard beside him is Blindi. Blindi Bale-Wise, some folk call him, because he knows more about working ill than anyone else, but he's Hunding's best rede-giver. The best thing to do is keep out of his way."

"Thanks."

"There on the other side, those are Alfarath, Aiwulfar, Herwowardhar and Hawarthar....oh shit," he added at Lingwe suddenly turned to look at them.

Hunding's youngest son banged his fist on the table and pointed at Hailgi. "You! Over here, boy!"

Hailgi's lips tightened over his teeth, but he hurried towards the head of the hall anyway. After he had set the plate down, he waited a moment to see if Lingwe meant to do anything more, but the young man had already turned back to talk with his brother.

By the time he and Swain were pressed into helping some of the thralls pull the tables back so that the real ale-drinking could begin, it felt very late to Hailgi, but when he went out to piss, he saw by the lay of the Moon's thin white crescent in the sky that it had not been dark more than a couple of hours. He went back in to join Swain and the thralls in slicing remnants of roasted meat from their bones and gnawing until their stomachs were full and mouths and hands slick with grease. Every so often Hailgi had to elbow away one of the hounds which nosed in towards his food or tried to lick the taste of meat from his face.

Tired as he was, he finally gave in and let it have the gnawed bone so that it would go away and leave him alone. Another, a gray bitch about to whelp, took its place at once, whining in a low and mournful key and rubbing her head against Hailgi's leg. As he would have in Hagalar's hall, Hailgi wrenched two meaty ribs from the lamb's side and gave them to her.

"Hey!" Swain said, jabbing a sharp elbow into Hailgi's ribs. "If you don't want any more, get away and let me eat it. D'you think you're an atheling who can give good meat to a hound?"

His side aching, Hailgi was ready to strike the other youth back, but he minded that he was far from safe in the hall of his father's foe. Instead of giving the blow back in kind, he chose an answer to satisfy himself.

"My father did not let gray hounds go hungry often, they often had the bones of boars he had slain. And you have not the wit to know what I mean by it."

"You must have come from a good way off, then. I know all the foresters in these parts. Had enough?"

Hailgi did not have to feign his yawn. "Where can I sleep?"

"Oh, anywhere, long as you're out of the way of the men. Some of them don't stop to look before they piss."

"See you in the morning." Hailgi got up and kicked a pile of dirty straw together close to the wall, then lay down on it with his sword beneath his leg and pulled a fold of his cloak up to shield his ears from the talking and laughter at the other end of the hall.

He woke to a nudge from Swain's foot, opening bleary eyes to let the gray light coming through the door and the smoke hole into his skull.

"You hurry, you might get some porridge," the redheaded youth said as Hailgi carefully shifted his hidden sword from the hollow it had worn in his leg and twisted about so that he could stand without it jutting out beneath his cloak.

His limp was real enough as he followed Swain to the low fire where a fat little thrall-maiden whose dark hair curled low over the iron ring around her neck ladled out the gruel.

"Where's your bowl, then?" She asked Hailgi. "You don't want me to pour it into your face."

"You can use mine for now," Swain offered, handing Hailgi a wooden bowl. Only a thin trail of white clots in the shallow crack that ran halfway down its side showed that Swain had already eaten his breakfast out of it. "I swear, you should thank all the gods that I'm looking after you. You don't have a spoon either, I guess."

Hailgi had a spoon in his waist-pouch, it was beaten from good silver, its handle adorned with finely twisted wire and set with a little piece of amber at the end. "May I borrow yours?"

Swain was already giving him a clean-licked little spoon of horn. "Mind you don't give it to the hounds or break it or anything. It's the only one I've got."

"Thanks."

When Hailgi had finished his breakfast, he and Swain went out to the pens. "No getting out of it today," Swain said gloomily. "It's sheep, and more sheep shit."

The two of them opened the gate and herded the sheep out. As they did, one of the hounds began to bark and the sheep began to run. Swain took off after them at once, Hailgi followed him.

"No, over there, dimwit!" The shepherd boy shouted. "Herd them this way. Don't let them break up!" As if they had heard his words, three of the sheep dashed away from the main herd. Hailgi hurried after them, but instead of coming back they ran straight away from him. It took him a little while to realize that he had to get around them and frighten them back to the main herd.

"Anyone would think you'd never seen sheep before," Swain panted disgustedly. "I thought you said you knew how to herd them."

Hailgi only shrugged, letting the other youth complain until they had driven the sheep through the gate of the garth and almost to the edge of the wood where a lone pig grunted and snuffled among the beech-trees' roots. Then he pulled out the long thorn that held his cloak, swirling the wide square of dirty wool from his shoulders to drape over one arm and waiting for Swain to turn and look at him.

The redhead did not seem to mark the change in his fellow at first, though he looked straight at the sword. Then his mouth shut in the middle of a word, shut, and opened again, though no sound came out. Hailgi could not hold back his smirk. "You like telling things, I've got a message for you. Say to Heming that Hailgi minds who, in byrnie, felled the heroes, and that Hunding had the gray wolf within his hall, though men thought it was Hamal. But I thank you for your kindness to the guest whom you did not know." Hailgi drew the silver spoon from his pouch and held it out to the other, stunned as Swain seemed to be, he did not lose a moment in getting it into the little bag hanging from his own belt. Hailgi turned and walked away, as slowly and proudly as he could, hoping his newly straight and bold gait showed his atheling-blood as clearly as his sword and the gift he had given.

It was just past sundown by the time Hailgi came to Hagalar's garth again. The gate was closed, he knocked once on the heavy wooden cross-beam.

"Who's there?" The answer cracked with startled suddenness, Hailgi recognized Eburhelmar's voice.

"It's me, Hailgi Sigimundar's son. Are you going to let me in?"

"Are you living?"

"Of course I am, you old fool." Hailgi banged twice more on the gate. "Does that make you happy? Stick a torch out here, you'll see I'm no draug."

"All right, all right. Can't be too careful," Eburhelmar mumbled. "I ought to make you wait out there till daylight, just to be sure."

"Let me in, curse your beard. I've been walking all day with nothing to eat, and I'm hungry."

Hailgi heard the creak as the old warrior heaved his bulk from his wooden stool, then the gate swung slowly open. "Where in Thonarar's name have you been, anyway?" Eburhelmar asked, peering down at Hailgi from beneath the snouted crest of the boar-helm that held his luck together with his name. "Hagalar's been having nine sorts of fits looking for you."

"I've been out, finding things."

"Hah. Go on, then."

Hailgi's step slowed as he came nearer to the hall. He moved as slowly and carefully as if he were trying to muffle the clinking of a byrnie, making his way unwillingly through the smoky firelight to stand beside one of the two pillars that flanked Hagalar's high seat. The light of the long fires was kind to the drighten's age, hiding the gray in his fair hair and beard and softening the wrinkles about his eyes and mouth, but Hailgi knew how old Hagalar was in sunlight, and the cold worm of guilt began to twist in the youth's entrails.

"Foster-father," Hailgi said. Softly as he spoke, Hagalar started as though Hailgi had prodded him with a spear point.

"Hailgi! Where have you been?" Hagalar broke off and breathed deeply, his open look of startled relief falling suddenly down into a grimness that Hailgi knew better. "There had better," he added more slowly, "be good grounds for whatever you've done. I suppose you climbed over the wall?"

"I went out through the gate," Hailgi answered. "I was well- masked."

"And where did you go?"

Hailgi braced himself. There was no sense in putting things off, and he had tidings worth telling, he hoped. "I went to Hunding's garth. He's off in the west frightening Anulaibhar before harvest begins, we're not likely to see him here this year. He left his sons behind, but Heming's been ill and he still looks too sickly to go to battle."

"And how did you find all this out?"

"I talked to one of the shepherd boys there, and helped with the food at the night meal."

"Hah. You do know the sort of risk you took?"

"I thought it was worth it."

Hagalar sighed, shaking his head. "What am I going to do with you, Hailgi? You can't lock yourself in a chest and stay there for just a year, till I send you home to your father again, can you?"

"I don't think so."

"Where did you get the idea of doing this?"

Hailgi looked down at a dark little heap of shadowed straw near his boots. "Uh, from some of the tales of Wodhanar. Masking himself, creeping into a foe man's hold getting what he wanted and going away again, with no one the wiser."

Hagalar raised a shaggy eyebrow. "'The day after, the rime-thurses went to ask of the High One's knowledge in the High One's hall, they asked about Bale-Worker, if he had come among the gods, or if he were slain by Suth-thungar.'"

"What do you mean?"

"I mean that you had better lie low for a while. My soul tells me that you did not pass wholly unknown out of Hunding's garth, did you?"

Unwillingly, Hailgi shook his head, kicking at the pile of straw with the toe of one boot. His foot found it solid, the small heap gave out a soft, high-pitched growl and raised its head to show the dark gleam of eyes and the white gleam of sharp little teeth.

"Let me consider this. You go and have something to eat, and be up early tomorrow." Then Hagalar's mouth opened in a slow, wicked grin, a grin that Hailgi had seen only a few times in the course of his six years' fostering. "I may well have a way to keep you safe, and be sure you don't do anything like this again."

"What?"

"Go eat. You'll find out what it is if I decide it will work."

Hailgi grabbed a hunk of bread and a thick slice of cheese from the table, then went out to the little house that lay behind Hagalar's hall. Because of his father's might, Hailgi did not have to share his place with any of the other warriors. Most of the time he was glad of it, but the ashes in the round fireplace at his house's middle were cold now, and the night was getting chilly. He could kindle a fire well enough, but he had forgotten to bring in more wood before he left, and there was no more in the house to burn. For a moment he thought of Swain, wondering if he could somehow bring the shepherd boy back with him—he had no doubt that Swain would like tending his things better than herding swine and sheep.

"A man who wants to live well sees to his own affairs, and a warrior who wants to live long sees to his own weapons," Hailgi reminded himself, though it was he who spoke, his tongue only echoed Hagalar's voice in his head. He sighed and burrowed under his blankets, lying on his belly and propping his head on his hand. Though his stomach churned with acrid sourness, he forced himself to eat his bread and cheese. If Hagalar meant to lay something unhappy on him in the morning, he wanted to have his strength about him so that he could meet what came to pass as well as he might.

Sigrun awoke early that morning, a little before dawn. A strange tingling was running through her long limbs, she felt that she must rise and do something, though she did not know what. She sat up among her blankets, breathing deeply to gather her might into the single point beneath her navel, as her mother had taught her to do. She could hear the thralls clattering about in the hall, like the hammering of woodpeckers at the edge of her awareness, and smell the porridge. Something else laced the grain's scent, at once sharp and a little stale, like the first spoor of fermentation bubbling in malt. Sigrun breathed in more slowly, and the coppery smell became stronger.

It is blood that I smell, she thought, and felt an answering twinge deep within her body. Sigrun reached down carefully between her legs. She could feel the gritty stain on the skin of her inner thighs, and streaks showed black on her fingers in the dim gray light when she looked at her hand. Not much had flowed from her body yet, only a few spots stained her pale shift. Sigrun was not frightened. She knew that women bled at the dark of the Moon and were likeliest to get children when he shone full on the Earth, and at fifteen winters, she was older than many women who had already given birth.

A washcloth and bowl of water stood by the table at her bedside, for Sigrun liked to greet the morning with her face well-scrubbed. She washed her face quickly now, then sat down on the side of her bed, wetting the cloth again and sponging the blood from her thighs. It seemed to her that she could feel something welling within her, like water frothing up from a great depth, and for a moment she was so dizzy that she had to drop the wash cloth and hold tightly to the edge of the table to keep from toppling from the bed. Sigrun made herself close her eyes and breathe in slowly and strongly, and in a few breaths the dizziness had eased, though the strange tingling in her body seemed to grow stronger.

Carefully Sigrun unfolded herself and straightened her shift, then belted on her keys and walked out through the hall to the storehouse where the cloth was kept. Women had their own breech clouts, she would have to sew one for herself today, but for now, a few strips of linen could be made to serve. When she had finished her work and changed her clothes, Sigrun went back into the hall for breakfast. She was not hungry, but she thought that if she was losing blood, it would be best for her to eat something to strengthen herself. Her father Haganon and her two brothers were already seated there. Bragi, fourteen winters old, was gobbling his food between breathless words of how he would try his new bow at hunting that day, the younger boy, Dagar, ate more slowly, his pale eyes staring over his father's shoulder.

Sigrun filled her bowl and joined them, Thonargardhar came over at once to put a horn of warm milk in her mistress' hand.

"You seem pale, Sigrun, and your hands are shaking" Haganon rumbled as his daughter lowered the horn and wiped the milk-froth from her upper lip. "Are you well?"

Sigrun glanced up at her father. The old bear was aging, his long hair and beard gone to the grayish-yellow of dead grass and massive shoulders slumping in a little as he hunched over his porridge, but the blue brightness of Haganon's eyes had not softened with the years. It seemed to her that a strand of calculation wove through his concern. Sigrun had heard mutterings that it would be hard to find a man for her, and knew it would be twice as hard if she got a name for being sickly, but there was no less love in him, for all that.

"I am," she answered. "It is only...a woman's matter."

Haganon's face eased into a smile, showing his cracked yellow teeth. "Ah. I see."

"What does she mean by that?" Dagar asked.

His father laid a large hand on his shoulder, shaking him lightly. "You are too young to be worried about it yet."

Bragi leaned over, whispered something to Dagar. Together they burst into high giggles, Bragi's suddenly cracking down into a rusty croak.

Sigrun glared at both of them, putting down her spoon. "Why don't the two of you get your training gear out now? Let's see how many bruises I can leave on your worthless little hides."

"Women are bad-tempered at this time of month," Bragi told Dagar with authority, deepening his voice as much as he could.

Dagar glanced swiftly up at his sister through the fringe of blond hair falling over his eyes. "How can you tell? Isn't she always bad-tempered?"

Sigrun drained the last milk from her horn and banged it down on the table, then stood up and stalked from the hall. One of the thralls could eat her porridge, or the dogs would get it, she really didn't care which. She went to the storeroom that housed the weapons, tucking three throwing-spears under one arm and a straw-man target under the other. The Sun had hardly risen over the world's rim, though the herders were out with the beasts already, she would have the empty meadow where the thanes practiced fighting and shooting all to herself.

Sigrun set up her target, then counted her paces back to the farthest edge of her range, the hem of her dress swishing heavily through the damp grass. The cold dew had already soaked through the slats of her shoes, so that she might as well have been barefoot. The spear was light in her hand as she raised her arm, her sight shooting ahead of the weapon's keen singing path. Draw back, cast, the spear flew straight and smoothly, half the length of the spear passing through the target's lower belly. Not a clean kill, but a sure one. He would not fight again. Still, her next cast was higher—a fine throw, taking him through the heart. The third went a little too high. It killed the straw man, right through the left side of his head, but it might have glanced from a good helmet or even a strong skull. Though women did not ride out with the war bands, there was no atheling's hall so mighty that a foe might not come to it with sword and flame someday.

Then the women must know how to cast spears and shoot arrows, or even take up swords when there was no other way out save becoming an enemy's bonds maids or burning like cows in a barn, and if that day ever came for the Skjolding hall, it would be Sigrun who would lead the fight when her father and brothers were dead. A sudden yawn cracked the mask of grimness that had settled on Sigrun's face. Out of habit, she put her hand to her mouth, then yawned again. Perhaps it is too early to be casting spears, after all, she thought. As Sigrun walked towards the straw man to pull her weapons free, she yawned once more, stumbling to her knees. Her legs would not bear her, she realized in a moment of sudden fright, her eyes were closing. She would get up! She told herself fiercely. Pushing hard against the ground and gritting her teeth, Sigrun heaved herself from the wet grass.

As she stood again, it seemed to her that she could see the meadow shining around her, waves of green and silver glimmering over the grass like the invisible veils of heat wavering up from a fire. Amazed, she looked down at her feet, and saw her own body lying as she had fallen, head pillowed on the smooth curve of one arm and long fair hair flung out over her face. A strand hung over her open mouth, wavering with her deep breaths. Sigrun stretched herself, flinging back her head and raising her arms to the Sun's bright light which flowed over her like a warm waterfall. She knew that she was still within the Middle-Garth's ring, it was a long faring from here to the other realms within the World-Tree's grasp. But now she could see the other thin stream flowing around her feet, seething with eggshell-white froth that rose and fell in a pattern of shifting runes, it stretched west towards Jutland like a long white strand of linen. This was the might she had felt on waking.

A stream flowing from the well of Wyrd, a thread spun by the Norns' distaff. Something cold and soft nudged the back of Sigrun's arm. The nose of a bright-eyed gray horse which stood beside her. The steed's hooves were misted, now there seemed to be four, now eight, as it shifted its weight in the grass. Gladly Sigrun mounted, tucking her skirts up so that she could get a good grip with her knees. With a sudden rush that took her breath away, the gray horse leapt up into the air, galloping higher and higher. Sigrun could see the bright rim of sand around Sealand's edge, like a golden bezel rimming a smooth jewel, and the threads of streams and rivers glittered bright below her. A wisp of cloud blurred past, stroking damp along her hair, it seemed to her that the wind itself was bearing her up. She was not surprised to find a spear resting lightly in her hand, nor the cool smoothness of a helm weighting her head and a gleaming byrnie upon her body. Some battle is doomed this day, she thought, and laughed. The stream fell downward towards Jutland, a thin white waterfall, and Sigrun turned her horse to follow it. She saw no sign that men were ready to fight, a few bright shapes came together on a green field, but the weapons in their hands were wood-dull.

The hall below was much smaller than her father's, a rather poor thing, if she had to liken the two. Sigrun did not know why she should suddenly be clenching her fist on her spear, urging her gray steed onward as the horse's muscles surged and bunched beneath her, but then it seemed to her that she could feel the unseen currents about her, the ripples of Wyrd, crossing and weaving in towards a single point, down there, inside the little hall. Though Sigrun knew it was darker inside, she could see as easily there as in the sunlight. The drighten who sat in the high seat was tall and spare, his hair graying much of an age with her father, she guessed. The frowe beside him was both tall and heavy, wearing adornments that seemed too rich for such a small holding, unless her husband had the favor of mightier men, Sigrun began to understand. There were two girls, fair-haired and dark, and one thrall-maid, but it seemed to her that she felt no special strength in any of them, nor did the thickening ripples of might seem to swirl about anyone. Then the door opened.

The women began to giggle, but Sigrun was deaf to all but the roaring in her ears, a deep blue mist, glimmering with rainbow sparks, rose up about the sides of her sight, blinding her to everything but the shining shape in the doorway. For a moment it seemed to her that she stared at her own image in a pool, but no, this other was a young man, slim-hipped with only the flat curves of muscle at his chest. His hair was redder than hers, the color of pale amber, and his gray eyes dark enough to seem almost black in the hall's shadows. He was smaller than Sigrun as well, but about her age, she guessed, he would soon begin to shoot upward like a leek. White brightness flared from him, a glowing might that left Sigrun breathless, even as the tip of her spear tilted downward to point at him, tracing the three woven triangles of Wodhanar's sign, the walknot, the Knot of the Slain.

"Hailgi", she whispered. The Holy One. Now Sigrun was sure where she was. All knew of the long warring of Sigismundar Half-Dane and Hunding, and it was also known that Sigismundar's son Hailgi was fostered by the drighten Hagalar, who kept the marches between the two great leaders of Jutland. And we have been long together, never parted, though I have not Wodhanar's sight into the Well of Memory, that I might see when we were bound.

A tide of red washed over Hailgi's high cheekbones as he walked towards the little group at the end of the hall. Sigrun could feel the waves of heat flowing off him beneath the giggling of the women. Feeling with him, she closed her eyes for a moment, and it seemed to her then that she was looking out from behind Hailgi's gaze, hearing his thoughts within her own head. Although Hagalar's voice was calm when he spoke, amusement crackled behind it like footsteps behind a thicket.

"Since I can't lock you away or send you to get lost in the woods, we'll have to put you in a disguise that Hunding or his men will never guess at. Everyone knows how proud you are, you might dress as a shepherd boy for a jest, but never a bonds maid."

Hailgi stepped forward in anger, his fist raised as the women broke out in gales of laughter. Hagalar also stepped forward a pace. Though the drighten's body was spare, he seemed to loom before his foster-son like an ancient pine-tree. "You do have a choice, Hailgi. You can let us hide you like this, and if you do it well enough, no one will ever know. And if you don't blush yourself to death before it's over, this will teach you more about thinking before you act than any thrashing I could give you. Or you can go running back to your father in shame with a witling's prank hanging about your neck. Now, which would you rather?"

For a moment Hailgi did not answer. The odd clash of anger on laughter in Hagalar's voice, like a smith's hammer beating folded layers of iron and gold together into a single rippling wyrm-pattern, caught his mind up wholly.

"Well?" Hailgi was ready to shout out his fury, to rage that he would live as a wolf in the woods first. But now he saw what he had done. If his foster-father had been more on his mind two nights ago, he would not have gone. Now Hagalar's stead between Sigismundar and Hunding seemed not like a wall that Hailgi must leap, but like a wicker fence between two roaring bulls, that either, or both, could destroy with a single rush. Now, Hailgi realized, he had tilted the scale as he had meant to, but whoever won in the end, it was from Hagalar's holdings that the geld for his game would be wrung. Hagalar needed say nothing. Hailgi knew well enough that if Hunding did not slay the march-drighten for harboring a spy, as he would if Hailgi fled home, he would surely do some harm to Hailgi himself, and then it would be Sigismundar who would burn Hagalar's hall for his ill care. Whatever happened, Hagalar's blood would redden the clean straw that Wulfaruna had spread on the floor, if she lived, an iron collar would ring Ingwibjorg's neck instead of amber strands, and rough blades would hack Gunthahildar's long chestnut hair to a thrall-crop.

Hailgi lowered his fist. It was fair enough. He had earned some shame, he would not add cowardice to it.

"All right."

Sigrun started at Hailgi's voice, deep with the rough dark resonance of a raven's croak, like no one else's and as familiar as her own. She could not have called the sound pretty, but its raw might tingled through her, and even as she longed to embrace him, it seemed as though his thoughts rose to drown her own.

Hagalar patted Hailgi on the shoulder. "I'll leave you to the women, then. If anyone asks, I'll say you've gone out hunting."

He walked out of the hall. Hailgi looked around at the women, staring angrily into their faces. "What are you waiting for?"

"Don't snarl so, dear," Wulfrun said, patting his hot cheek as the girls sniggered. "Smile and be charming, you're not a shield-maiden. Now come with us and we'll dress you properly."

She started towards the chambers behind the main feasting hall, graceful as a ship on the wave despite her bulk. Hailgi stalked stiff-legged after her.

"No, no," Gunthahildar chided. "That's not how you ought to walk. Like this, see?" She moved in front of Hailgi, swaying her hips so that the hem of her skirt swung from side to side. Though she was only thirteen winters old two younger than Hailgi her buttocks were already well-formed and plump, swelling out beneath a long torrent of red-brown hair.

"You're watching closely enough," Audhar said. "But I don't think you're walking any differently."

"Skirts will make a difference," Wulfrun answered. "Don't tease him any more, now."

When Audhar had closed the door behind them, Gunthahildar and Ingwibjorg closed on Hailgi from each sides, grasping at the hem of his tunic and pulling it up over his head. He let them take it, standing bare to the waist before them, but when Ingwibjorg reached for the string of his breeches he caught her wrist.

"Let go of me," she said breathlessly, looking into his eyes and tugging lightly against his grasp. She was close enough for him to see the tiny flecks of brown in her green eyes, her lashes, he marked, were the same dark ash-blond as her low-curved eyebrows and thick wavy hair. Her breath smelled of fresh milk, and her skin felt smooth as a rose's white petal in his rough grasp. Flustered, Hailgi opened his hand, but she did not move away.

"Be kind to Ingwibjorg," Wulfrun told him. "She'll be lending you her clothes, after all, the two of you are close enough to a size. But perhaps we'll let you put your skirt on before you have to drop your breeches."

Ingwibjorg went to a chest by the wall and pulled out a skirt of a tabby green-and-blue weave and a white upper garment. "This on first," she said, slipping the short tunic over his head. Hailgi remembered that the same garment had fallen loosely about Ingwibjorg's shoulders and molded itself closely over her breasts, but, though he had thought himself slimmer than she, it was uncomfortably tight across Hailgi's shoulders and back, he was sure he would break it if he moved too swiftly.

"That won't do," Wulfrun said. "No, Hailgi, don't you try to take it off, you'll split the seams. Audhar, go get one of my tunics. He'll be lost in it, of course, but that's all to the good. The more we can hide, the better."

When Wulfrun had carefully stripped the garment from him, Hailgi straightened his shoulders, marking out of the corner of his eye how Ingwibjorg's gaze flickered from the smooth swell of his chest muscles to the wide curves of her mother's bosom, then to her younger sister's jutting breasts.

Wulfrun's tunic was loose enough across Hailgi's shoulders, belling out like a wind-filled sail beneath his armpits. Hailgi stepped into Ingwibjorg's skirt by himself, loosening the waist-ties to fit more comfortably. Full-bosomed and wide-hipped as Ingwibjorg was, her middle was surprisingly small. He raised his gaze to her face, only to find her smiling knowingly at him.

"Let me tuck that in for you," she said, pushing several folds of his upper garment beneath the skirt's waistline. Hailgi held still as a troll caught by sunlight, the pounding in his ears beat time to the throbbing in his groin.

He was glad to be able to turn away from her when he reached beneath the skirt to untie his breeches. For a moment he stood, unwilling to drop the thin wall of wool that stood between him and all that went with a woman's clothes.

"Find something that shouldn't be there?" Audhar screeched at him. "You don't have to make the disguise that complete if you don't want to."

Wulfrun's laughter was muffled behind her hand, her daughters giggled without restraint. Hailgi dropped his breeches and kicked them away defiantly, though he could not help thrusting his thumb through his fist to ward off whatever ill the woman's garb might work upon him and whispering the name of Thonar, who had also dressed so to gain his hammer back. He lost no manhood through that, Hailgi told himself, nor shall I!

"Now there's only your hair," Wulfrun told him. "Sit down and let us comb it out properly."

Hailgi walked carefully over to the sheepskin in front of Ingwibjorg's chest and settled down in front of it. Ingwibjorg sat on one side of him, Gunthahildar on the other. They disentangled the warrior's knot over his right ear and unbraided the thick braid, then set to combing.

"I'd give an armload of gold rings for hair like his," Gunthahildar declared. She leaned forward, her left breast just grazing Hailgi's right ear, and held a strand of his hair up to her necklace of light amber. "See, it's just the same color, and so fine. It's not fair to waste that hair on a man."

"And such long dark eyelashes, too," Ingwibjorg sighed.

"Yes, she's a remarkably pretty girl," Wulfrun answered. "We'll have to give her a proper name, we certainly can't call her Hailgi. I'm not sure where he went"

Gunthahildar smiled sweetly. "Father says he's out hunting."

Ingwibjorg traced the line of Hailgi's cheekbone with her finger. "Look, she blushes at his name...perhaps she's in love?"

Even as Hailgi choked on his anger, he would not move away from her touch, he wanted to fling himself on her there and then, to still her mockery beneath his body. He shifted position, suddenly glad of the skirt's concealment.

"What shall we call you then, dear?" Wulfrun asked Hailgi. "Answer softly and sweetly, now, remember that you're a lark and not an eagle."

"Perhaps she needs to see herself first in order to remember," Ingwibjorg suggested. She stood up, shooing her younger sister off the chest, and pulled out a wide piece of polished bronze, holding it out to Hailgi. "Stand up so you can see how your new clothes look on you."

Hailgi clenched his jaw as he stood up and took the mirror from her hand and raised it. He was about to sling it into the corner, but its bright gleam drew his gaze inward.

He stared at the image in the mirror, pierced by his own reflection. Hair reddened by the burnished bronze tumbled around a fair, high-boned face, the eyes that gleamed back at him from beneath winged eyebrows were gray as flint or polished iron. Her sharp features were finely chiseled, but the slight bulge of muscles at the hinge of her narrow jaw showed a terrifying strength of will. Do I look like that to other folk? Hailgi wondered. He had seen his own reflection in ponds and the shining metal of swords and shield-bosses before. His face, though sharp, had never seemed finely wrought to him, though fair enough, he had never thought his looks beautiful. As Hailgi stared into the mirror, Sigrun could feel her own soul slowly swimming free of his again. It seemed to her that she was looking out of the polished bronze into Hailgi's gray eyes, the keenness of his gaze rending her heart. She could still hear his thoughts, clear as her own in her head. He does not know who I am, she realized with a pang of fear, how will he ever know how to find me?

The faint hammer-marks on the mirror's bronze rippled behind the maiden's face like the wings of a ghostly swan arching up behind her. Then it came to Hailgi that, though the ebbing and flowing heat in his cheeks was at full tide, no warm pink tinted the reflection's fairness, nor, hard as his hand was shaking, did her image waver before him.

It seemed to him that her mouth moved, shaping a name. "Sigrun," he heard his own voice say, it cracked down on the second syllable, and his hand dropped to his side.

"Sigrun," Ingwibjorg echoed. "That's a lovely name for you. I think you sound as though you've caught a nasty cold, though. Give my mirror back and Audhar will fix you some hot ale with honey to soothe your throat."

"It wouldn't hurt," Wulfrun murmured, then, "Hail, ah, Sigrun, are you all right? You've gone awfully pale."

Hailgi sat down again very suddenly, catching at the edge of the chest to keep from falling. He felt dizzy and ill, his hands and feet numb, as though he had risen a little way from his body and then been slammed suddenly back in. He barely felt Ingwibjorg's hand stroking his hair.

As Hailgi's legs gave way under him, Sigrun stepped free. She did not know what to do. It seemed to her that she must find a way to speak to him, but Hailgi seemed as deaf to her as if a helm blocked his ears, and only shivered a little beneath her ghostly touch.

Wulfrun took off her own shawl and draped it over Hailgi's shoulders. "Go on, Audhar. Some hot ale will do her good. There, Gunthahildar, let me borrow your amber a moment." She took the necklace from her daughter and draped it over Hailgi's head. "That should chase out what's troubling you, ill can't stay in the same hall as amber."

Slowly Hailgi's shaking died down under the warmth of the woolen cloak. When Audhar came back with the honeyed ale, he took a deep gulp of it.

"Slowly, Sigrun," Wulfrun counseled, in the same tone that Hailgi had heard her using to her daughters. "Sip, don't gulp. A woman is a pourer of ale, not a guzzler, and if you spill anything on our clothes, you'll be the one to wash them." She waited until Hailgi had finished the cup, then went on. "You three, you go out. I need to talk to Sigrun alone."

When the two of them were alone, Wulfrun sank carefully down onto the chest. The wood creaked under her as she bent down to look more closely at Hailgi. He knew she was a little short-sighted, though she seldom showed it, now her forehead wrinkled as she strove to gaze into his eyes. "You think this is rather cruel for a joke, don't you?"

Hailgi nodded.

"But if you think about it, we could do no better than hiding you here, not only for our sake, but for your father's. Now that you've seen Hunding's strength, you can guess what a meeting between the two war bands would bring."

"Yes. I can." Whoever won the day would likely be too weakened to hold what he had won. A hundred small leaders would circle in, like dogs pulling down a half-dead stag, and then no stead would be safe in Jutland for a man's lifetime, if one of the great rulers did not lead a host from Gautland or Sealand to make all the Jutlanders his thralls. And if Hailgi fled from Hunding to his father, it was not sure whose pride would start the fighting.

"So you will have to be a maiden very well indeed now. Firstly to save yourself when Hunding's men come looking for you, and secondly, because you don't want anyone here to recognize you in Ingwibjorg's clothes." Wulfrun stared at him sharply for a long moment.

"It will not be so hard as you think to hide you even from men who know you. You truly look as though you have become another person altogether. Turn your hands to spinning and weaving, baking and grinding at the quern, and no one will ever know you. I will not ask you to serve ale in the hall, some of the men can't keep their hands to themselves, and your temper is too rough to bear what women must learn to deal with. Will you do your best, since you must?"

"I will."

"For Frija's sake, don't say anything unless you have to, and if you must, then whisper. I'm afraid there's nothing to be done about your voice. We might as well try to make a raven into a thrush. It would be hard enough for anyone to mistake you for another man, no matter how sweetly you speak, you'll never sound at all like a woman."

Haili nodded.

"Good girl, Sigrun. I'll call the others in now, and they can start by teaching you to spin. Cheer up, harvest will be starting in just a few days, and if Hunding's men haven't come by then, they won't come."

Sigrun settled herself to watch Hailgi try to spin. If he could feel the spindle's turning, the shaping of the thread, then the sword-clashing thoughts in his skull would fall still, then he could hear her voice. But spinning did not come easily to Hailgi. When he tried to measure the wool between his clenching fingers, it slithered into great loose lumps along the thread, when he let the spindle's whirling weight tug it out, it dwindled too thin and broke. By the eighth or ninth time this happened, he was angry enough to pick up the spindle and hurl it end-over-end against the chamber's far wall, shattering the clay whorl into bits.

"You are a fierce walkurja, aren't you, Sigrun?" Ingwibjorg said. "Perhaps you'll do better at weaving."

For a little while Hailgi worked quietly standing before the loom, slinging the shuttle to hiss through from one side to the other. "So, like that," Sigrun murmured to him, stepping closer, "through, and through, weave the web, shape the threads."

She laid her hand gently on the back of Hailgi's. He started, slinging the shuttle through with both their strengths behind it. The woolen threads snapped with a deep twang, the stone weights of the warp clattering to the floor.

"I see that a shield-maiden makes a poor bonds maid," Hagalar's low voice said behind Hailgi. "Go on out to the grain storerooms, Sigrun, my wife has a task that she thinks you can do rather better than the other maidens."

"You want me to go outside?" Hailgi whispered.

"Unless you want to ask a couple of men to carry the grinding stones in for you, you'll have to."

"I can't."

"It won't do you any harm. If Wulfrun hadn't told me what to expect, I'd never have known you myself. Go on, then."

Unhappily Hailgi walked out of the hall. The brushing of his skirt against his ankles and the odd nakedness of going without breeches reminded him to move carefully, he did not feel inclined to step as widely as he was wont to.

Wulfrun was waiting by the quern, two large leather sacks by her feet. One had the lumpy look of a bag filled with grain, the other lay in a shapeless pile on the earth. "Did your spinning go well?"

Hailgi shook his head.

"It's harder than it looks, isn't it?"

He nodded.

"You'll find this easier. Lift the top stone up a moment for me, will you?"

Hailgi raised it a little and Wulfrun poured a stream of golden-brown grain in between the two round rocks. "There you go. Now you've only to turn it till the meal is ground fine."

He sat down on the smoothed rock that served as a seat for whichever of the garth's women was set to grind the grain and grasped the wooden handle that rose from a hole in the top most stone, turning it slowly around the creaky wooden axle that pegged the two grindstones together. Although he found it hard to be outside where he could hear the crack of wooden sword on wooden sword and shield, the thudding of wood on flesh and the curses of soft grunts as some of the thanes, those who weren't off hunting or inside the hall drinking, sparred with one another, at least he could keep his head down and face in shadow as he worked, so that no one would see him too easily.

Before long, Hailgi knew why Wulfrun had called him out to do the grinding. Though he wore a woman's skirts, he would not need to worry about his sword-arm losing its strength. Still, there was something oddly soothing in the round of stone on stone.

Sigrun settled in beside Hailgi again, she did not try to touch him this time, but whispered into his ear instead. The quern-stone crushing the grain seemed to circle as slowly and steadily as the ring of summer and winter that had grown it, sprouts of green seemed to shimmer before Hailgi's half-closed eyes, ripening to gold.

"Bread and beer and barley," he whispered to himself, the refrain of a song that he had heard women singing over the grindstones, and Sigrun murmured with him, "barley and bread and beer ." One-third of the seeds went back into the ground, one-third were ground as Hailgi ground them now, to bake a year's worth of bread.

The last third were roasted and beaten, heated with hot stones in the malting tub, then the frothy spittle of the women brought froth fermenting to the top as their magic worked in the depths, working the wort into the ale that held luck and madness, the holy draught that made men wise or cast mind from the high seat of the skull, as Wodhanar should deem it. It seemed to Hailgi as he worked that he could feel all that seedling might thrumming through the stones beneath his hands, that neither the grain within the wheeling stone ring nor what would grow from it had changed since his first fore-fathers came to gather amber and flint by Jutland's coast, nor would it change in a thousand generations more, woven like a triple golden braid through the whirling stones of birth and death.

It was strange to him, to see like that. He wondered if such sight was why women were named wise, but he would not have put it away from him. Soon, Sigrun whispered into Hailgi's ear, you shall reap Wodhanar's fair barley, cutting down men on the field of battle for the Dread One's harvest. Watching the turning of the quern-stone, she could see the shadow of fighting now—the broad shape of Hunding falling before Hailgi's blade, before the Moon had waxed to full again. That should come to pass. Soon you shall see me more clearly, for your deeds shall give me the might to show myself more strongly, and bring us ever closer.

Her own words did not echo back from Hailgi's skull, but she hoped that some shadow of them had gotten through, he seemed to be cheered a little. At mealtime, Hailgi crept into the women's chamber through the back of the hall so that he would not have to see any of the war band. Ingwibjorg and Gunthahildar brought him his food, spreading his bread thick with butter and pressing a second cup of strong ale on him when he had finished his first.

"You'll have to eat more than that, Sigrun," Ingwibjorg chided him when Gunthahildar had gone out to refill her own plate. "If you mean to find a husband, you'll have to be a bit plumper than you are now." She pressed her palm flat against Hailgi's chest, breathing deeply at the same time so that her large breasts swelled upward. "You're much too thin there—I can almost feel your ribs." Ingwibjorg ran her hand down Hailgi's left side, along his flank and down the outside of his thigh. "Such slender hips. I'm afraid you won't give birth very easily."

It seemed to Sigrun now that Hailgi's strength was pushing her back and away as his thoughts turned towards the woman stroking him, but at the same time, she could feel a slight flare of strength through her as his blood surged. She reached out, tugged against one of the thin veils of might fluttering through the hall.

Ingwibjorg jerked back guiltily as the door opened. "What are you doing?" Gunthahildar asked. "Don't answer that, I saw where your hand was."

"You did not," Ingwibjorg hissed at her. "Close that door and be quiet."

Gunthahildar closed the door, smirking at her sister and Hailgi. "What will you give me if I don't tell, huh?"

"I won't cut your nose off your face," Ingwibjorg answered. "That's worth a lot, you'd look very funny without a nose. Talk funny, too. Besides, all I was doing was putting Sigrun's skirts to rights. She still doesn't wear them as easily as she ought."

"Hah," Gunthahildar muttered, though the glint of glee in her leaf-shaped brown eyes had dimmed. "I'll be watching the two of you. Just wait."

After the evening meal, Wulfrun told Hailgi that he would be sleeping in the same chamber as her daughters and Audhar. He took the news meekly, worse, he thought, could easily have befallen him.

He was almost asleep on the heap of straw and furs which the maidens shared when he felt a hand pushing his skirts up. "What are you doing?" He whispered.

"Hush."

Hailgi reached out until his hand met the springy mass of Ingwibjorg's curls. Entwining his fingers in them, he drew her head in for a kiss.

Unseen and unheard, Sigrun stalked over to her horse and mounted up again, staring at the two beneath the blankets. The darkness did not hide them from the walkurja's gaze, but Hailgi's mind was already set. He would not listen to her now, although her strength was rising with the desire that brightened his body. *If only my flesh were here, if only he could turn that desire to me!* Sigrun thought. She watched angrily, listening to the echo of Hailgi's thoughts and the soft whispering in the dark.

"Hush," Ingwibjorg murmured again. "We have to be quiet. Let me. I've never felt" Her hand moved upward between Hailgi's thighs, seeking and finding. Carefully he reached for her again, pulling her upper garment loose from her skirt and sliding his hand up to stroke her breasts. Her breath came a little faster as her nipples hardened beneath his fingers.

"Careful," Ingwibjorg whispered to him, then, as he tried to tug her skirts upward with his other hand, "No, don't. Lie still, just let me touch you."

"I want you," Hailgi hissed urgently.

The rustle of Gunthahildar turning over froze them both, Hailgi felt his might draining out from between Ingwibjorg's fingers. The moment of fear stretched into a vast lake of still black ice, going on until they heard the sound of her breathing deepen into a soft snore. Then Ingwibjorg began to caress Hailgi again. He lay where he was, his hand over her swift-beating heart, caught between the stroking that urged him to pull her closer and seek passage between her thighs and his keen sense of the two who lay sleeping lightly beyond her, set—whether witting or not—as warders against the cuckoo in the women's nest. Hailgi could hear his own breath hissing harshly through his teeth as he bit back the sounds of pleasure, he knew he must spill soon.

"Harder," he murmured to Ingwibjorg. She pressed tighter, moving her fingers faster on him. He pulled the furs beneath him away till he lay on bare straw, then gave himself over entirely to her caresses and the warmth of her breasts beneath his hand.

Ingwibjorg drew in a deep gasp as he spurted into the straw, stroking away the last of the drops with the tip of one finger and holding him fast as his manhood shrank. Hailgi caressed the soft curve of her cheek with his free hand, feeling the curve of her smile.

"What are you smiling at?"

"Nothing. Go to sleep, Hailgi." She patted him one more time and let go as he unwillingly took his hand from her breast. Hailgi tugged the furs back over the stain he'd left in the straw and pulled his skirt back down. He felt achingly empty, not only in his ballocks, but all thorough his body, as though his ribs were the staves of a cask drained of ale.

Sigrun felt herself burning atop her steed, half-angry at Hailgi, but filled with the raging might that had roared through her from the moment he had spurted. As Hailgi's heart and breathing slowed, it seemed to Sigrun that her horse's hide was growing thicker and softer, its shape shifting between her thighs. Now a wolf's long-muzzled face looked back at her, eyes glowing red in the darkness, now she knew that she must ride away from the garth of men, for the darkest shape of Wodhanar's wish-daughters was coming upon her, the shadow of Hailgi's fetch, her own shadow, answering the roaring in her blood. Sigrun's adder-reins writhed in her hands as she turned her wolf's head away from where the women lay sleeping, digging in her heels as they ran out and through the black trees.

Ingwibjorg's soft snoring soon blended with her sister's, but Hailgi, though he turned from side to side, could not sleep. At the feast of Yule, when his father had last come to see Hagalar, Sigismundar had spoken about wedding Hailgi to a girl called Borghild, the daughter of a drighten in southern Jutland. Now Ingwibjorg, but he did not know if he could have her, or if he wanted her. It seemed to him that, while he wore women's skirts, he was not really Hailgi, that what Ingwibjorg said or did to him now would be gone like mist in the sunlight when he pulled on his breeches and girded on his sword again, and that she must know it too, or she would not have touched him as she did.

Still, dream that it might be, he felt emptied and lonely. Aching within, Hailgi thought of the maiden he had seen in Ingwibjorg's mirror, and knew that he himself was not so fair. Sometimes women saw things in still pools of water, things that had been or might yet become, caught unchanged in the clear depths, it was told that Wodhanar had given his eye for such sight, that it was kept deep in the well of Mimir which held all that had come to be. Hailgi did not know why he should have seen such a thing, but he could not turn it from his thoughts.

At last Hailgi pushed his shaggy-wool blanket aside and stood up, creeping carefully past the sleeping women and out through the hall. The night was very clear, the Moon's thread-thin sickle gleaming like fine and frost-edged steel through the biting air. The stars seemed brighter than Hailgi had ever seen them, dazzling a shower of silver into his eyes. He blinked the light away like a tear, gliding over to the gate. Although the man who stood watch seemed to be awake, he did not speak a word, not even when Hailgi cast aside the thick beam of oak that barred the gate and pushed it open.

He did not know where he was going, only that his feet had found the path that led between the tall beech trees, their gray trunks shimmering white as birch bark in the keen moonlight. He did not stop until he came to the edge of a clearing where white mist glowed pale against the dark, seething over the ground. Then he heard a high wild howl rising from the middle of the clearing. Though wolves were not often seen in the north of Jutland, and hardly ever came so close to humans' garths, Hailgi knew the wolf's cry at once. He reached for the sword that was not by his side as he saw the dark shadow against the moonlit mist.

The moonlit mist curled around Sigiruna as though she had sunken into the frothing waters of Wyrd's Well. Helgi's shape glowed fair against it, Sigiruna raised her hand to reach towards him, but he did not step any closer, and she could see the little rivulets of shivering running over his skin like washes of clear rain.

"Are you afraid?" Sigiruna asked, hoping that the mocking in her voice would drown out her own trembling. "Does your heart match your clothes?"

"I'm not afraid," he answered boldly. "Who are you?"

"Who are you?"

"Hailgi the son of Sigismundar Half-Dane."

"That's not the name you spoke for yourself today."

"Who are you?" Hailgi challenged. Then, though he seemed to be looking straight at her, "Show yourself to me, if you're not afraid, you wanderer in night and mist."

Sigiruna breathed deeply, drawing the might of the stream that frothed about her wolf's feet up into herself. She could feel the tears of joy glittering in her eyes, as Hailgi's face grew better-known to her in every passing moment. She did not know how they could ever have been parted, for it seemed to her that his shape had always been before her sight, though she had not known it.

"I fare where ravens fare," she replied. "I choose the meat for my steed, but mead I bear to his drighten. Ever I follow the eagle, for I love those birds who fly above the others and whose talons tear their foes, and the fields of the slain are my joy, for the might of my wolf must be fed."

"Why have you come to me?"

"I have never left you, Hailgi, but you were not able to see me since your birth. You shall hear me again when you need me, then you must fare forth, to spatter the earth with the blood of the slain and joy the ravens. Only thus shall you see Sigiruna again. Your deeds are her might, and only with her warding can you do the deeds that shall bring you to her side. Only one bride-gift can win you the walkurja, but soon you must avenge your shame, or she will be lost to you."

"What do you mean?" Hailgi cried. He ran forward, trying to clutch at Sigiruna, but his touch seemed to pass like mist over her skin. His eyes opened wider, as though he were straining to pierce the night fog with his gaze, and Sigiruna knew she had faded once more from his sight, leaving him to stand bewildered in his skirts like a maid without a lover beneath the moon. After a while he turned, making his way slowly along the path between the trees.

It seemed to Sigrun as though the next day passed in the flickering of an eyelid, it was mid-afternoon before the sheath-muted songs of swords rang in her ears, shivering over her skin like a fine whetstone running along her nerves. Hailgi raised his head, sniffing at the air as though her sudden wakefulness had stirred him, though it would still be a little while before he could hear the sound of hoof beats above the crunching of grain between his grindstones. Sigrun could feel that was a large troop. More than half a hundred men, she could tell that even without seeing. Now she could hear the faint thoughts from the head of the leader, Heming.

Hunding's sons had left a good many of their warriors home to guard their hall, but the force they had brought was near-equal to that of Hagalar's whole war band. They would have what they wanted, or Hagalar would answer for it. The smooth wood of the grindstone's handle was slick with sweat beneath Hailgi's palms, warm as the sun was on his back, he shuddered as though a cold hand had been laid upon his head. He kept his face low as he ground the corn without a pause, listening to the men at the gate.

"Hail, Heming," Hagalar said, his quiet words cool and even. "What brings you to my gate?"

"Your foster-son Hailgi paid us a visit, and we've come to return it," Heming answered. His voice sounded sharp as the taste of cheese about to go moldy.

"Hailgi is not here now. He went out several days ago, and has not come back. He said that he was going hunting, I believe, though he may merely have sought to get away from the work of harvesting."

"Then you won't mind if we come in and have a look for him?"

"Come as you will. You must tie your horses outside, though. We have no pen large enough for all of them."

Hailgi heard the rustling and the mutters among Heming's men, he thought that they must not have awaited that answer. He kept his head down, grinding quietly as Heming's men scattered out through the garth.

"Hai, girl, do you know where Hailgi is?" a voice asked by his ear. Only just remembering his garb in time, Hailgi looked up and shook his head.

A stocky, fair-haired young man squatted down beside him, close enough for Hailgi to see the light dusting of freckles over his crooked nose and wide cheeks.

"You don't need to be afraid of me," the young warrior coaxed. "If you know, tell me, and I'll give you this gold ring from my finger." He turned his hand so that the beaten metal glinted sparks of sunlight into Hailgi's eyes.

"I haven't seen him for days," Hailgi whispered, mindful of the depth lurking in his throat.

Hunding's man patted him on the cheek, his touch bringing the blood of fury as if he had struck Hailgi in the face. "You are shy, aren't you? Are you one of Hagalar's daughters?"

Hailgi shook his head again, turning the quern-stone harder. "Hai, Hrabanar," called one of the other warriors, by his looks a brother of the man he addressed, though somewhat taller and slimmer. "Have you found him yet? You won't get anywhere there. She looks too skinny to cover him beneath her skirts, and we didn't come to play hide-the-sausage with bond maids."

Hrabanar rose wrathfully to his feet. "You can go play hide-the-sausage with the sheep, Hrodhiwulfar," he answered, but to Hailgi's relief, he walked away to join the other men. Hailgi lowered his head again, grinding harder and harder, but Sigrun could feel the great might drawing nearer to them, like the storm clouds running dark on a screaming wind from the north. Now Hailgi would need the strength of both of them, she stepped within him, binding herself to him as closely as she could. The one who was coming closer might wish them well, but only if they could withstand his gaze, for he had no use for those who failed beneath his testing. Hailgi felt a cold shadow falling across him, and glanced upward, tightening his hand on the quern's handle to keep from reaching for the sword that was no longer at his side. The voice that spoke from above him was deep and harsh, like a raven's croak through the clashing of iron blades in the frost.

"Keen are the eyes of Hagalar's bonds maid. The one who sits at the quern comes of no Carl's kin, the stones shake, the bin is about to burst. Now a hard deeming has fettered the warrior, when the leader must mill barley, it would rather be seemly for those hands to hold a sword-grip than a milling handle."

The man who had spoken was taller than Hagalar by half a head, his long gray beard fell almost to his waist, mingling with the gray hair that streamed out from beneath the wide brim of his deep blue hat. The eye that Hailgi could see was dimmed, as though a shield of white mist lay over it, the hat's brim hung over the other. By his size and beard, Hailgi knew the man he had seen beside Lingwe in Hunding's hall. Blindi Bale-Wise, as Swain had named him.

"It is little wonder if the stones thrum," Hagalar answered. "A kin-leader's maid turns the mill. She rushed forward through the clouds above, and dared to do battle like a warrior. Before Hailgi put fetters upon her, she was a sister of Sigiharjar, thus the eyes of the Wulfing maid are awesome."

"Will she serve ale in your hall tonight? I would see how used those hands are to meting out mead."

"If you wish it, she will."

"Speak to me, maiden," Blindi commanded. "What is your name?"

"Sigrun," Hailgi whispered. He could not keep from raising his eyes to the old rede-giver's, though he knew that his anger must glint in his face like the hilt of a sword jutting through a clumsily draped cloak. The quern-stones thrummed harder beneath his hands, groaning under the strength that turned them.

"Sigrun the daughter of Haganon I know, you have her look, but I had not heard that a walkurja could be made a thrall-maiden so easily."

"Frodhi might have said the same to Fenja and Menja when they ground for him," Hailgi answered, keeping his voice as soft and high as he could. "Before you taunt me, think on what weird I may turn for you from these stones."

Blindi's laugh was oddly high, ringing for a very long time. "Those are surely the words of Haganon's daughter, but not her voice, it sounds as though the noose that fettered you crushed your throat. Can you speak more clearly, Sigrun?"

"No."

The rede-giver laughed again. "Don't you fear the gray wolf you keep, Hagalar? Surely you know that a walkurja brings nothing but death to the men around her, with her love and her wrath alike. You'd be better off without this one in your hall."

"I'll keep what I have," Hagalar answered. "May I bid you and the men with you to eat with us tonight? It is not my way to turn wanderers out unfed, even those who come to my gates unasked."

"I'm sure Hunding's sons will gladly accept your kind offer."

Hagalar beckoned to Hailgi. "Sigrun, go tell my wife to ready dinner for our guests. Then wash yourself and put on your finest clothes, you'll serve at table tonight."

Well done! Sigrun said to Hailgi as she stepped away from him again. He started, turning his head sharply, but he could not see her, not now in clear daylight with no mist or cloud to give her shape. Though Hailgi's hands had been steady as he spoke to Blindi, they were shaking as if he had just done battle. Sigrun would have given him a horn of mead then if she could, and hailed him proudly, but now she could do no more than stroke his shoulders and his long amber hair, hoping that he could feel at least the shadow of her touch. As he walked about pouring the ale into the horns and cups of the men that night, Hailgi marked how carefully Hagalar had mingled his own men between those of Hunding's sons.

A sudden attack would come to confusion, with each man flanked by his foes. One or two of Hagalar's warriors looked sharply at Hailgi as he filled their horns, but none said anything. Firelight often betrays the eyes, he thought hopefully, no one can see anything too clearly within a fire lit hall. He had almost finished his second round, he was near the head of the long table again when he felt the calloused hand sliding up beneath his skirt to his buttocks. Hailgi turned and struck as hard as he could. His blow flung the groper to the floor, the sound of his clay pitcher shattering on the wall was almost drowned by the angry shout of rage as the young man got to his feet again. He was blond and almost beardless, no older than Hailgi himself and little taller. Hailgi knew the glittering rings on his fingers first, though he had not looked too closely in Hunding's hall, he remembered Lingwe with little difficulty.

"You're going to be sorry for this," the youth hissed, stalking towards Hailgi as a roar of laughter rose from the benches.

"Hai, Lingwe!" Someone shouted. "Are you sure you want to fight her? I think you're over matched!"

Lingwe whirled towards the speaker, his hand clenching into a fist, but someone else was already shouting.

"Give her your breeches, the skirts are more fitting to you!"

Even beneath the flickering red-gold of the firelight, Hailgi saw the youth's face go deathly pale. The soft rasp of his sword coming from the sheath was almost lost beneath the laughter around, but the flame-gleam off its edges slashed through the noise, leaving the hall very still.

"Who said that?" Lingwe asked. "Does he have the bravery to stand?"

Hailgi, forgotten, backed into the shadow of one of the pillars to watch as the men glanced at one another.

Finally Hagalar leaned forward from the high seat. "Put your sword away, Lingwe. I do not wish to see the frith of my hall broken."

"Then let the man who spoke come outside with me. I will have his blood, I am no nithling, to thole such words."

"It was a poor jest, leave it be," Hagalar answered, but Blindi spoke above him.

"Lingwe has the right to do battle, few greater insults can be given a man. Lingwe, if you let this pass, you will be a laughing-stock all your days. Think of your line and do what you ought."

"Who spoke?" Lingwi asked again, scanning the benches.

At last one of Hagalar's men, Thonarstainar, got to his feet. "I did," he said easily. "I'll apologize if you like, I meant no stain on your manhood."

"Only your blood will make it good," Lingwe answered. "Draw your sword now, or come out with me if your drighten's too weak- stomached to bear the sight of fighting with his meal."

Thonarstainar drew his blade at once, stepping forward. "I'd offer to teach you better manners, but you're not going to live to learn them, boy," he rumbled. Hailgi thought he would agree. Thonarstainar had a hand span of reach and considerable weight over Lingwe, and Hailgi knew from his own experiences that the man was a fine fighter.

Hailgi had expected Lingwe to rush forward, but the youth hung back a little and let the other come to him, judging his strength, Hailgi thought. Lingwe was fast, too, he must have learned early to use his young speed and agility against the size and strength of older men, just as Hailgi had. Twice his blade hissed before Thonarstainar's belly, the second time, it tore away a rag of tunic, but left the other's skin white and unscratched. Wary, the older warrior stepped carefully towards the younger again. Lingwe moved a little too soon, and Thonarstainar caught his sword on his own, using his strength and weight to press the youth back towards one of the hall-pillars. For a moment it seemed that Lingwe would be pinned against the great upright beam, but then his glance flickered towards Blindi. The wood at his back, he dropped suddenly to his knees. Thonarstainar's own strength, unexpectedly loosed, lodged his blade in the pillar. Before he could wrench it free, Lingwe stood again, thrusting his sword up as he did. The tip came out at Thonarstainar's throat.

Thonarstainar gulped bloodily, letting go of his sword hilt and clutching at the air a moment before he dropped.

"Now I have avenged the insult." Lingwe's voice shook only a little as he spoke. "Now I have avenged the insult." He bent down to pull the bloody sword out.

"Your man began it, and the match was fair," Blindi said before Hagalar could speak again. "Will you say that what was done was not within right?"

Though his tongue moved slowly, as though weighted with something heavy, Hagalar answered, "I cannot say that."

Lingwe took his place at the table again, draining his silver cup dry. Before he could look about for Hailgi, Wulfrun was there to fill it again for him. Hailgi went back into the women's chambers, deeply shaken. He had not liked Lingwe much from the first, but he could not deny that the other youth was brave, and had acted like a man, while Hailgi wore a woman's garb. Sigrun saw the shadows that stretched out before, more clearly than she ever had, and she knew that Hailgi could hear her wolfish whisper.

Lingwe's overweening mood shall doom him someday, he shall not always have Blindi's help in battle, someday the blood-eagle shall be scored on his back, to pay the geld of an old slaying, and his flesh shall gladden the ravens. Hailgi did not know that this thought was any fairer to him than the first, but he could be rid of neither. Tomorrow, he thought, they will go away and I can put on my breeches and gird on my own sword again. Though it was still early, he lay down upon the furs and straw of the bedding, wishing that the day were there already.

CHAPTER V

Hoilogae was awake before dawn, creeping out into the cold star-bitten air. The clouds had fled, now the sickle Moon stood as bright drighten of the sky. Hoilogae turned his face up to meet the gray-soaked god's keen light, eyes dazed by his brilliance. If the Moon is so bright, how shall I ever bear the Sun? He thought. After a moment he had to turn his head away, looking among the dark humps of the huts to see if Attalae had come out yet. It was still too early, though, Hoilogae knew it, though he did not know how. Instead he made his way softly down the path that led to the strand. The sea often cast amber up here, thus Herwawardhaz's lands were often called Glazaleunduz the Amber Grove. The sea was still now, all Agjiwaz's wild mood calmed and his leaping daughters sleeping again. The Moon's light glimmered down the way across the waters. Wodanaz's walkurjons, so Hoilogae remembered, could ride over water and air, his own path must be trodden by the wave-steed, if he was to find the sword which Swaebhon had spoken of. He walked down from the grasses onto the pale sand which sifted through the slits in his hide shoes. Only the thinnest rim of foam rolled up the beach before him, hissing over the fine pebbles and shifting the fronds of the seaweed lying dark against the beach. Bending down to touch the swift-moving edge as it began to roll back from him, Hoilogae still felt the strength beneath the light tug. The etin-maid's finger pulling at his own. He raised his spear, holding it over the water as it fell back. The moonlight glittered pale gold off the stone-sharpened bronze.

"Wodhanaz hallow my way," he murmured. "Sink, you greedy ones, I am not for you."

Footfalls whispered through the sand behind him. Spear ready, Hoilogae turned, only to see Attalae's gray hair pale as a young man's fairness beneath the moonlight. The old warrior brought out a clay jar from beneath his cloak.

"What are you doing?" Hoilogae asked.

"Pouring a gift to Agjiwaz and his clan."

Hoilogae looked out over the still sea again. Its mirrored moonlight seemed to him betraying as green grass over the black water of a bog.

"They are no friends to me."

"Still, it is not wise to wish their hate."

Attalae raised the clay jar high. He did not trace the hallowing sun-wheel over it, nor the hammer of Thonaraz. Such things were ill to the etin-kin. Instead he murmured swiftly. "Agjiwaz, have this alu, Ran, rend us not! This gift we give you, grant us a smooth and free way."

He stood still until the thin edge of foam had risen almost to his feet, then poured out the ale into it. The drink's froth sank back with the sea-foam, Attalae let his breath out again. "So it is done."

Hoilogae would not have noticed what lay beneath his feet if he had not kicked it. He drew in his breath, awaiting the sharp pain from his toe, but there was no pain, the big stone skittered ahead of his foot, weightless as wood. He bent down to pick it up. Its rough near-warmth thrilled through his fingers with its lightness.

"What have you got there?"

Hoilogae held out his hand. The piece of amber covered his palm, it was a little bigger than his clenched fist, and when he raised it to the Moon, his light glowed clear and gold through it, as though the amber had transformed it to sunlight.

"There is little doubt that we shall need it, since you have found it now. Keep it well, such gifts are not found twice. Still, you should not love it too much, for my soul tells me that you shall not have it by the end of our faring."

Hoilogae nodded soberly. Though the amber was rough as a rock in his hand, its lightness made it seem less there, nor did it have the cold truth of stone to the touch. He well believed that it would not stay in his grasp for long.

"Do you know where we're going?"

"I know." Although the Moon had lowered since they had spoken, his path on the waters changing, Hoilogae could still see the ghost of his first light glimmering against the darkness. He pointed. "That way, then southward to Sigisharjaz's Holm."

"Sigisharjaz is a great drighten, who may well hold many iron swords," Attalae said softly. "If your soul leads you there, I would say it has led you truly."

Attalae and Hoilogae went back from the beach, back to the storehouses where Attalae chose smoked meat and fish and twice-baked bread for their journey, stacking them carefully inside waxed skins. Hoilogae watched without speaking. It seemed to him now that there were many things he must know, which his soul would not tell him of.

"Why waxed?" He asked at last.

"It keeps the water from getting in and rotting them," Attalae answered as he worked. "I hope that last night's storm was the last of the year's turning, but he who trusts hope alone while faring on the sea is not very likely to make land again."

"How far do we have to go?"

"Two days and a night to Sigisharjaz's Holm, if we are not driven off-course. If we are a week or more. Though Herwawardaz and he have never been foes, we do not know if he will meet us with friendship either."

"Oh." Hoilogae watched carefully as Attalae finished packing the food and drink for their faring, then helped him carry it to the boat that was moored to a pine-tree above high-tide mark. The first pale streaks of dawn were rising through the eastern darkness when they were done, pinkish-gold against the deep blue of night.

"So you're ready?" Attalae asked Hoilogae when they had finished loading the boat.

"As far as I know."

"There's no reason to wait, then."

"Shouldn't I say farewells to my family?"

Attalae did not answer, and Hoilogae thought about it for a few moments. What will I be bidding farewell to, then? He wondered. It seemed to him that he could feel all the sideways glances at once, all the words cast towards the one who did not understand, and a lifetime of shame heated his cheeks. He was less than unknown at home. He was known to be worthless, witless and without might, and he knew he could not stay to bear what his years of sleep within himself had won.

"Get in," he said roughly. "I'll push off."

Attalae stepped high over the boat's side without another word, sitting in the stem and turning his head to watch. His stiff beard jutted gray against the pale glow of dawn as Hoilogae dug his feet into the soft sand of the beach and pushed. The boat moved swiftly beneath his hands, hissing through the sand like seawater as he pushed it towards the reaching edge of the waves. The water of the North Sea was icy around his ankles, numbing his feet as he felt the boat take flight above it, leaping over the first swell like a fine horse leaping the wooden ring around the garth.

"Get in, Hoilogae," Attalae cried, digging his oars into the water. Hoilogae leapt up into the middle of the boat, it hardly tilted as he steadied himself. Another wave met them, and then another, the foam sprayed white around them like cold sea-blood as their boat cut through the swells. Hoilogae held his spear ready to cast as Attalae rowed, till they were through the surf and out onto the great quiet swells of the open ocean.

"We shall not speak the name of the Awesome One, nor that of his bride, nor shall we name his daughters till we are safe at land again," Attalae said quietly. "Do you understand, you who have named yourself Hoilogae?"

Hoilogae looked over the side of the boat. Close to the water's surface, he could see the purple-wrought clearness of jellyfish as they wove through the waves, beneath, he thought he saw the flash of fish, but below that there was only darkness and more darkness.

"I understand."

That night on the sea was an easy faring. Attalae kept watch, and Hoilogae slept as if his mother rocked him again, fierce as Ran might be, she knew the cradle-rhythm as well as any earthly frowe. When the first light-fingers of dawn pressed between his eyes, Hoilogae rose to take the oars from Attalae, chewing on dried meat and hard bread as he steered south of the sunrise.

As Attalae had promised, Sunna was sinking towards the sea when they first saw the lowering bank of cloud to their south.

"There stands Sigisharjaz's Holm," said the old warrior. "Pull towards the cloud."

"I can't see land," Hoilogae complained.

"The cloud always stands above it, the land-wights will hide it from the sea, who wishes the earth no good. Pull towards the cloud, I swear to you, we will find land there, and if no ill wights have deceived us, it will be Sigisharjaz's Holm."

"What lands does this drighten rule?" Hoilogae asked as he bent towards the oar-pull again.

"He rules the holm here, and more. Here is his hold, from which he harries all the lands along the coast. Nearby is Sigisharjaz's Field, where the mightiest heroes bid one another to battle, one man to another beneath the drighten's eyes. Here all hate is paid with a red geld, where his name shall not soon be forgotten."

After a while, Hoilogae could see the dark rim of land against the fading circle of sunlight around the sea. He pulled more strongly as the waves near the land rose higher, but in a short time, when his might had overcome them, they turned to bear his boat inward, dragging it forth more powerfully than his own strength could bear it.

Attalae took the oars from his hands. "Now let me row, though it is still day, the rocks here are baleful to ships."

Hoilogae let the older man steer between the ripples on the water, marking the hidden shadows of the rocks beneath as Attalae guided their boat through the sharp black edges that rent the sea's clear depths like great claws.

"We have been lucky," Attalae said when they dragged the boat up onto land at last. "Often the land-warders are not so kind to those who come by sea, and Sigisharjaz's ghosts are mighty, or he would not have won as much as he has."

Hoilogae touched the lump of amber that lay thick in his belt-pouch, his other hand tightening on his spear-shaft. It seemed to him that he was murmuring again, the furrowed cliff-face before him blurring in the twilight, but his own voice sank in the sea's hissing through the rocks, what he was saying seemed less to him than the cold wind echoing through his ears.

"The walkurjon will bring you no weal, Hoiloge," Attalae answered, his face crumpled with care like a brown leaf at winter's beginning. "Be wary of her gifts, though she bring you mead, she sates herself on men's flesh at the last. Troll-women are as trusty, and do not daze you with beauty to hide greed."

Hoilogae whirled on the older man. For the first time, he felt his own size and strength. Attalae seemed like a wizened child before him, the frost on his hair and ice-gray beard no more than snow on the face of a boy playing in winter.

"What do you know of it?" He demanded fiercely. "Were you there when I saw her riding? Don't speak to me of this again, judge by the worth of her rede, if you must judge at all."

Attalae's face was pale in the twilight, his wrinkles shadowing into deep crevasses. "What gift is it, to be awakened only for your slaying? Perhaps you were better, had you been left to sleep. Only the Ansuz and his black-feathered kin are the winners of every battle."

"You know that is not true. Wodhanaz is also the lord of the clan-howe, and it is for kin both living and dead that the walkurjon awakened me. If I am to be slain, it is by her love, and as a gift to the god, if we can win through what must be done."

"As you will," Attalae murmured at last, casting the boat's rope around a great rock that jutted forth from the sand at the cliff's edge. "I await my end, it shall come before yours."

"What do you mean by that?"

"Only that I am old."

The lights were bright in Sigisharjaz's hall, torches standing outside the door to mark how the drighten welcomed wayfarers. The shadows they cast hid the warders by the door, but they could not hide the dark-silver gleam of their iron spearheads, nor the light echoing off the beaten edges which no bronze sword could mar.

"Who are you?" A voice demanded from the darkness. Hoilogae turned his eyes from the light to the shadow, staring till the corner of his gaze caught the glint of the spearhead moving back.

"Hoilogae the son of Herwawardhaz and his man Arnulita, whom most know as Attalae. We have fared in friendship, will you stand against us, or bid us welcome?"

"Be welcome, guests, to Sigisharjaz's hall," the voice from the shadows said hastily. The bright spear-head turned, pointing down towards the earth, the man stepped forward into his shadow against the torchlight. "Come, the feasting begins. Sigisharjaz welcomes all wayfarers, and Attalae has fair fame."

Hoilogae looked down at the back of the man's fair head as he led them into the hall, staring at the pinkish spot where the blond hairs grew more sparsely. As if he felt the cold touch of his guest's gaze, the hall-warder brushed his hand uneasily over his head. Sigisharjaz's hall was much bigger than his father's, filled with enough men for three villages, and every one of them, as well as Hoiloge could tell in the torchlight, finely dressed and adorned with spiral rings of bronze and gold. The maids who carried the meat around were simply clad, but the frost-haired woman pouring out the ale wore several lengths of large amber beads around her cream-white neck, glowing dark off her short yellow tunic.

As if it were a high feast, her navel was covered by a wide round plate with a spike jutting from its center, the fine carvings upon it shattered the firelight into a hundred spiral swirls of glittering light-beads. The skirt of woven strings she wore swished about her knees as she moved, glimpses of white thighs gleaming through like pale driftwood through the waves. She turned without hurry as she saw the two guests, gesturing for one of the maids to bring cups as she made her way over to them.

"Greeting and welcome, guests," she said, taking the glazed clay mugs from the maiden's hands and giving them to Attalae and Hoilogae before pouring them full of ale. The heady scent of fruit mixed with barley and honey and bog-myrtle rose from the thin rim of froth on the cup, filling Hoilogae's mouth with longing. His mother brewed a like brew, but it had never been offered to him before. "What names shall I know you by?"

"Arnulita the son of Athalwulfaz and Hoilogae, the son of Herwaward-haz," Attalae replied. Hoilogae watched her carefully. It seemed to him that he could see her thoughts grinding swiftly through, giving the name to Herwawardhaz's nameless son. He did not miss how her gaze slid from him, as if he had become a stock of wood beside the living man. "Has it been so long since my last faring here?"

She peered at him more closely, one of her eyes refocusing as the other cleared. "My sight is growing no better, and it is very dark in here," she apologized. "My husband will be glad to see you again."

Sigisharjaz's wife and Attalae walked through the benches and long tables to the high seat at the end of the hall, Hoilogae trailing behind and looking about him in wonder. One man was showing another a sword that was all of iron, short and keen-edged, Hoilogae caught the name "Wejlunduz" as he passed them. It seemed to him that he could feel the warriors' deep voices and the strength of their moods like heavy surf around him, as if, walking towards Sigisharjaz, he breasted the tingling waves to move deeper out to sea.

These were chosen men, strong and trained, he realized. The pick of many villages. Still, he could feel their souls giving way like the waters as he passed unshaken among them. Sigisharjaz was a smaller man than Hoilogae had expected, though broad-shouldered and heavy of arm. The war leader's hair and stiff short beard were iron-gray, his keen eyes dark beneath shaggy gray brows. A pale banner stitched with the shape of an eagle hung behind his seat, though it had often been washed clean, Hoilogae could see the shadows of bloodstains on it, and when he looked at it out of the corner of his eye, the brightness of Sigisharjaz's battle-luck shimmered around it like the clear waves of heat over a flame. Sigisharjaz raised his cup to his guests, Hoilogae followed Attalae in raising his own and drinking from it. The malty brew was sweet and strong, easing his throat and bearing his mood upward.

"Welcome, Attalae," the drighten said. His voice was very deep, scarred rough by years of shouting on the battlefield. "What brings you to my hall?" Sigisharjaz looked carefully at Hoilogae. "Have you brought this man to seek a sword in my war band? He has the look of a keen warrior, who might well bear shield with my own. What is your name, then?"

"I am Hoilogae, the eldest son of Herwawardhaz."

Sigisharjaz's brows drew together a little, but his dark gaze did not falter. "Now that you are named, you seem a better man than you were weened to be. Are you seeking a stead away from your kin?"

"I am seeking a sword of iron. I was told that it lies here, among fifty less four."

Sigisharjaz rose to his feet in a single swift movement. The sounds of talking stilled as the men turned to watch their drighten and his guests, a few reaching for their swords.

"How do you know this?" He asked softly. The tingle of nervousness trickling down Hoilogae's back froze to chill-gleaming ice at once. He could feel the keen tip of Wodhanaz's spear touching the blood-beat in his throat, and knew that Sigisharjaz was half a breath from spilling his life onto the earthen floor.

"Through no means that will bring ill to you," Attalae broke in swiftly. "Nor has he spoken to any other of it. Have Herwawardhaz or his kin ever raised hand against you and yours?"

The war leader stood staring hard at the two of them for a few moments. It seemed to Hoilogae that he could see the ghost-shape of a grizzled wolf beneath the bones of Sigisharjaz's face. An old wolf, testing the scent on the wind. Slowly Hoilogae began to breathe again. The god's spear had pulled back, but every tight sinew corded along Sigisharjaz's shoulders showed that it was still poised.

"Come with me," the drighten said, turning towards the door beside the eagle-banner. He led Hoilogae and Attalae out of the hall and into a smaller, richly furnished house where the bed was heaped high with gleaming furs and the floor strewn with sweet-scented herbs. Sigisharjaz seated himself in one of the two heavy wooden chairs, resting his mug upon one of the carven raven-heads that jutted from the end of each arm and gesturing for his guests to seat themselves where they would. "Now you may speak freely. Hoilogae, tell me how this news came to you."

Hoilogae opened his mouth, but could not speak, it was as though his throat had been bound in a threefold knot. Sigisharjaz reached behind himself, taking a short throwing-spear from the corner and raising it. His shape seemed to shimmer in the cloaking shadows of the firelight, although Hoilogae could not tell what lay behind him now.

Slowly Sigisharjaz stretched the spear-tip towards Hoilogae, stopping it just before his breastbone. "Now let the Ansuz choose what shall come to you if you tell me a mis-truth."

Hoilogae's breath suddenly loosed, and with it his words. Swiftly he told Sigisharjaz of all that had come to pass, and the words of the walkurjon.

The drighten lowered his spear when Hoilogae had finished, putting it back in its place by the wall. He raised his mug, taking a deep drink before he stood and walked to two large chests which stood side by side at the foot of the bed. Drawing his iron dagger, he cut straight through the complex weave of knotted leather thongs which held them safely unopened.

The chests were both full of swords, iron swords, keen and deadly, lying over one another like a nest of dark-shining adders. Hoilogae could not think of how much wealth had bought them, but he knew that they were the loom-beaters of a new web stretching out from Sigisharjaz's eagle banner.

"Tell no one of these," the war-leader said softly. "You may choose from among them, for the favor of our god, for you war as he wills, that our ways not be swept off in the iron tide rising from the south or our lore forgotten in the times that shall come."

Hoilogae knelt down, reaching carefully into the chest to take the swords out one by one. He had never seen such weapons, each forged and polished as cleanly as if it had come whole and perfect from the rock. Some were adorned about the hilt with twisted wire, a few with inlay of silver and gold. Touching the iron was not like touching bronze. He could feel it scathing through all the hidden realms, cutting through all the woven layers at once. One chest emptied and refilled, he started on the other, his hands beginning to shake as he moved faster and faster, searching for the ring-hilted sword that was not there, the serpent-adorned blade and haft that were not among the iron hoard.

"Where is it?" He asked, looking wildly up at Sigisharjaz, staring at the drighten's own sword as if his gaze could fasten the troth-ring to its hilt.

"These are all that Wejlunduz had when I went to him, there were three more to be made, but he had not finished them yet. It must be that the sword you seek is among them."

"Will he give it to me?"

Sigisharjaz looked thoughtfully down at the two chests of swords. "He has already been paid for the full number." The drighten drew a small piece of amber, carved in the likeness of an eagle's head, from his belt-pouch and pressed it into Hoilogae's hand. "Show this to him and tell him that I have sent you to bring the blades back to me."

A knock sounded against the door. "Everything's fine," Sigisharjaz shouted. "We'll be back in just a moment. Now go away!"

He closed the chests, squatting beside Hoilogae and muttering something as he tied the cut thongs again, his fingers skillfully weaving the leather together until the ties looked as they had before.

"We might as well go back now, before all the food's been eaten. There's no point to doing anything more before the morning."

Sigisharjaz and Attalae stayed up talking late into the night, while Hoilogae ate and drank and listened carefully to them. They said nothing more of Wejlunduz, nor were their words openly of battle, instead they talked of harvests and the trade from the South, of the weight of amber and furs needed to buy bronze and fine work. Still, it seemed to Hoilogae that he could hear the clashing beneath their speech, as though cattle and swords, trade and spears, could not be cut one from the other. At last Sigisharjaz's wife Gunthahildjoz showed Attalae and Hoilogae to another outbuilding.

When she set her torch to the ready-laid fire, Hoilogae saw that, though not as finely furnished as Sigisharjaz's own, the guest-house was better than most homes he had seen. He wondered, as he lay down and tugged the shaggy woolen blanket over himself, if his mother had grown up in such a hall, and how it had been for her to lose it at her father's death.

"Does Hrothamaraz rule as much as Sigisharjaz?" He asked Attalae quietly.

For a moment there was no answer from the darkness. When he finally spoke, Attalae's voice sounded very tired and old. "He has more lands, though fewer men. His fame is not so wide-spread as Sigisharjaz's, and he does not ever look to rule more than he has, warriors do not come from other steads to seek a place in his hall. Still, his might is closer to that of Sigisharjaz than to that of your father. It was not cowardice that made us content with what we had when we won our brides."

I have brought us to fight against him, Hoilogae thought. He knew that it would not be well to ask Sigisharjaz for help in this. His father's lands lay between those of the two great drightens, and if Sigisharjaz's band once marched into them, Herwawardhaz would not long hold his steads alone. He tried to bring Swaebhon's shining image into his mind again, but she melted again and again into the wild-haired shape of a troll, her horse's gray face narrowing to a wolf's grim and blood-stained muzzle. Halfway between waking and sleep, he turned restlessly, pushing at the heavy blanket, but its weight grew greater and greater, the sights that stirred his anxiety fading beneath the cloud of dark warmth until at last he slept. Hoilogae and Attalae set off again the next day. Sigisharjaz had given them a larger boat to use, for it was a week's sailing in fair weather to the shore where they would have to land, then another three days up a river to the lake by which Wejlunduz dwelt, so that they had to be well-supplied.

"He is a strange man," Sigisharjaz warned them as they were about to cast off. "If he is wholly a man, he has the craft of the dwarves, and there are some who say that he once dwelt among them. Anyway, he and his brothers have dealt in Wolf Dales for a very long time, and it is an uncanny place." The drighten paused, the deep lines on his brow wrinkling. "It is said that they are sons of a king in Finland. Be careful that you deal well with him, and do not ask for more than he offers. Though he has never been known to do harm, I have met him, and there is no one I would less wish to have as my foe. Fare well, and the gods be with you."

The snow melted quickly from the rocks and crags around Aiwilimae's hall in the half-moon after Austarjon's feast. The first silver-furred buds of Austarjon's willows, which hailed the coming of summer, had burst free of their brown hulls a few days before, now, with the goddess called forth, it was not too long before Swaebhon saw the little green birch leaves starting to unfurl and smelled their clean scent sharp through the dripping icicles. Those were the best of days, she thought, when the birch twigs were leafy enough to use in the bath-house and yet the ice was still crusted over the lake so that she could plunge in through a hole in its white rim after the long sweating of the bath.

But those times also brought burden to her, for now that the Moon was dark and the women's blood flowing, she must go up the mountainside with the other women to tap the birch trees' springing sap in the grove around the holy white stone. The sweet syrup they boiled was not as good as honey, but there was more of it, and the birch sap could also be brewed into a fine drink. When they had malt, they blended the birch-ale with that, but there was no grain left this year save that which they had kept for the sowing, unless they found honey for mead, there would only be the brews of birch sap and berry-juices until after harvest. In other years Swaebhon had less to bear than most of the other women. The others had carried her clay pot and buckets and divided her sleeping gear among them, for the drighten's daughter also had to carry her hunting weapons, bow and arrows, and a spear with a crosspiece fixed on it. She did not mean to go hunting boar by herself, much less to come to close quarters with a bear, lynx, or wolverine, but there was always the chance that the troop would start up a winter-hungry beast, women had been killed on the way to the mountainside before, though not since Swaebhon had been old enough to join the other maids.

Swaebhon was not the only one of the women who hunted, nor the only one who went weaponed up the mountain. Most of them walked with the help of spear-staves, and several also had bows, but she was the strongest and most skilled of them, and so she was always allowed to have her hands and shoulders free. This morning, however, her bedroll of Lappish reindeer-fur and the bundle of oiled wool wrapped around carven tent-stakes still lay in the straw by her feet beside the fire-blackened cauldron, though the other women were beginning to pick up their own gear and cast cold glances towards Swaebhon where she stood in her white wolf-cloak with her bow slung over her shoulder and her spear in her hand. It is because of Wulfaz, she thought, sighing silently.

She had thought that the ill mood that many had shown towards her in the hall since last summer might have faded by now, but it had lingered through the winter as stubbornly as the last stink of sickness in the straw. If she were not Aiwilimae's daughter, and he so loathed to see her wedded, things would have gone far worse for her. If the sea were above the clouds, we would shoot fish down with arrows! Swaebhon said to herself, crouching down to sling the yoke of the buckets across her neck. She could brace the pot on her right shoulder with one hand and tuck her sleeping gear beneath her arms as the other women did. Her spear would be useful only for a walking staff, and there would be no hope of slinging her bow in time to shoot anything with it, but she would ask for no help from those who liked her so ill.

As Swaebhon straightened up under her burden again, she saw that the knot of women by the doorway had broken up, and Thonaradis was walking over to her. The other maiden carried a like load with grace, despite her small slightness, but her unstrung bow stave was strapped across her back beneath her long tail of leather-wrapped brown hair. Though Thonaradis was a fine shooter, her bow was too light for any beast bigger than a small deer, she would be bringing down rabbits and birds for their meals when they were up on the mountain.

"I will take your sleeping furs," the smaller maiden said to Swaebhon. "They are not so heavy, but you must have your hands free on the way."

Swaebhon looked down into Thonaradis' upturned face, meeting the other girl's hazel gaze. Thonaradis had spoken to her little all winter, though they had often gone hunting together in other years. "I would not burden you with what I can carry myself."

Thonaradis' fine nostrils tightened, and Swaebhon saw her little jaw setting firmly. "I know you are stronger than I, no one asked to spare you the weight. But if no woman is free to guard us on the way, we must ask a man to come to the grove's edge with us, and that would be a shame to us. Far better to have you do it."

Not friendship nor frith then, but pride. That, Swaebhon understood well enough. Still, she was glad enough to set down all but her hunting gear, feeling her bow and spear ready again. Hlothawina stumped over to take up her pot and tent, the set of her broad shoulders under her thin fall of white-blond hair showed that she thought she could have borne much more, though she said nothing. The morning was fair, though clouds passed over the Sun now and again. A clean cool breeze rustled through the springing leaves, birds called and answered back and forth through the wood.

Swaebhon strode a little ahead of the others, her eyes flickering over the muddy pathway to see who had passed there. Several times she saw the curving tracks of cold-sluggish adders, for the wyrms were just wakening now, but she did not call out to the others. They knew when the snakes wriggled from their burrows just as well as she did, and walked warily at this season. A burst of bright laughter rang out from behind her, and Swaebhon could feel her ears burning with blood beneath her wolf-head hood. She did not know that they were speaking of her, she had been listening to the woodland noises, not the muttering of the other women's voices. Still, they did not mean for her to share in their talk. Though she warded the other women on the way to the birch grove, or sat spinning with them in the hall, it might be that she would never be one of their number again. Swaebhon had often been alone, and seldom made friends, but she could feel the difference between that and being counted an outcast by the women of the settlement.

But there is one, Swaebhon thought, walking a little more quickly and holding her head high against the arrowing giggles. There is one within the Middle-Garth's ring who both knows and loves me, though he be yet far from here. She would have traded the whole troop of women for Hoilogae's friendship, even as she had given Wulfaz's life for it, though she had not known what she bought with that geld. The day was a little too warm for her wolf skin cloak, Swaebhon could feel the sweat trickling down her temples and between her breasts, soaking into the back of her linen dress. She cast back her hood, lifting her heavy pale hair free and letting the wind stroke cool over the back of her neck. So Hoilogae might stroke her, his strong hands moving gently over her body.

Her nipples ached, and she could feel an answering throbbing between her thighs as she thought of him. Suddenly she longed to be far away from the other women, in a safe stead where she might leave her lich to sleep as she mounted her horse and rode over air and water to see how her hallowed one fared. No ill threatened him now, or she would feel it in every breath, but she wished she could know where Hoilogae was now, and guess from that when he might begin the long faring northward. Swaebhon tightened her grip on her spear, her feet leaving deeper tracks in the leaf-thick mud as she walked faster. She had let the other women take her burden from her, if her dreams of Hoilogae drew her mind too far and her spear was not there to meet the winter-thin bear or crouching raider that might burst from the bushes at any time, only her life would pay for the shame. The grove's edge was marked by two high pillars of pink-gray granite, like the door-pillars of an unseen hall. Swaebhon stopped, stepping aside as the other women came up. Though she often led the rites for the folk at the great feast, only a woman who had borne children could lead the troop into the birch-grove. Swaebhon waited with the other unwedded maidens, who would enter the grove last.

Thonaradis, Badhwa-child-hioz, and the rest . She was the oldest of them by a good three winters, she marked, and the next eldest, Badhwa-child-hioz and Ingwadis were both promised to wed at harvest-time. It was Child-hagardhaz who came forward between the other women, tossing her gray braid back over her bucket-yoked shoulders as she struck the butt of her spear into the ground before the tall stones. "Berkanon, birch-goddess holy, we hail you!" She cried straightaway. "Frijjo, wife of the Ansuz, our daughters greet you, as our blood flows to your might, give you your blood for ours. We who have given birth, those whose wombs wait for your blessing, we all wish to tread within the hallowed grove, around the shining stone."

For a moment, only the soft wind rustled through the new leaves. No woman spoke, no birdsong sounded, and the Sun was shadowed. Then the cloud that had hidden the sky's bright frowe passed on, the Sun's bright light pierced free through the leaves, shining on the gateway before Child-hagardhaz.

"Holy frowe, mother of light and life, bless us! Let our children be strong, our lives be glad. Bless us in coming, bless us in staying, bless us in going. Dark Frowe Berkanon, bright Frowe Sun, we tread between the hall-posts of your realm. Give us greeting!"

Child-Hagardhaz stepped forward between the stones. Although the snow was not long melted, and white patches shone yet around the edges of the grove where the trees' shadows hid the ice from the Sun's light, the grass within already brushed high over the edges of her skirt's hem. She stalked up to the white stone in the middle of the grove, laying both palms upon it, and tilted her head back to gaze at the sky for a long moment. Then she whirled, thick arms spread out as if to embrace the troop of women that waited beyond the grove's edge. "My daughters bright and dark, fare within! The birch-queen gives you blessing!"

After the women had stepped inside and touched the holy stone, Child-hagardhaz gestured the maidens in. Swaebhon was the first one past the pillars, it seemed to her that Child-hagardhaz's smile tightened as she saw her, but that might have been her own thoughts casting an ill shadow upon the older woman's deep-lined face. I have full right here, Swaebhon thought. My blood flows in answer to the birch-tree's sap, my breasts have flowered fully.

She stepped forward to lay her own palms upon the holy stone, whispering; "Frijjo, blessing between us." She could feel the stone thrumming beneath her hands, though it was sometimes said that Frijjo and Wodhanaz strove against each other for their own purposes, she knew that the goddess looked kindly upon her now, and that was comfort against the side-glances the other women gave her as they stepped up to touch the hallowed rock.

The first task was to drive the taps into the birch-trees, to bleed the sap from the white maidens. By this, Swaebhon thought, might a woman be known for there were many among them who flinched with the pain of their own bleeding. Thonaragardhaz, the sister of Thonaradis, would not come up to them until they were almost done, for she lay on her own sleeping furs with only the tea of willow-bark Swaebhon had left her to ease her hurt. Though Ingwachildhaz had borne her own weight, carried her gear, and walked without complaint, her round face was whitish-green beneath its light dusting of freckles and the sweat that glimmered on her forehead, and now and again she bent lower as though she were ready to spew. That is a strong woman, Swaebhon thought. She herself had been blessed with ease in her bleeding, but now and again she felt a twinge that hinted to her of the pangs her sisters might feel as their wombs wound, readying for births that might come, or angered at their barrenness. She did not know which, and she doubted that any other might. Before she raised the mallet to drive the tap into the slim white trunk of the birch before her, Swaebhon had to breathe deeply to steady her hand, thinking of the blood that trickled from between her own legs.

"What I bear, you can bear," she whispered to the tree, "I ask you for nothing that I do not give."

Swaebhon clenched her thighs tight as she knocked the tap in and set the bucket beneath it. Slowly an amber droplet welled up, dripping into the waiting willow-wood, then another. She stroked the birch tree's soft white bark as if to soothe her, easing the sap up again as her empty womb twinged in answer. Someday this blood will strengthen my own child, she thought. Though I am Wodhanaz's wish-maiden, he will not gainsay Frijjo's blessing if she gives it to me.

When all the buckets were set beneath the waiting taps, the women gathered in the middle of the grove to talk, and once again, no one looked at Swaebhon or offered her greeting. And she would not make the first move, she leaned on her spear near the gate-stones for a moment, then unslung her bow and stretched it to its fullest, aiming it at points around the clearing. Most of the thanes in Aiwilimae's hall could not draw Swaebhon's bow fully, and among the women of the settlement, only Hlothawina and Swaebhon herself could pull it back all the way. Swaebhon had made it herself, it could drive an arrow fully through the body of an elk and halfway into an oak tree, as she had shown many times.

She did not know if matters would be different for a man whether strength and skill were enough to win friendship there, or whether they, too, would peck and peck at a cuckoo in the nest, but as she stood testing her weapons away from the murmuring women, she felt like a bear being stung to death by wasps. Still, as the hallowed garth's warder, she could not walk away from the ones she had silently sworn to guard. Though Swaebhon usually fell asleep quickly, the sharp scent of the birch-sap and the slow dripping from the taps kept her awake that night. She tossed from one side of her tent to the other, rucking her reindeer hides up above and beneath her. Her own heat in the fur seemed to stifle her. Though she had left her tent-flap open, she could not see the stars, only the ghostly gleam of the pillar-stones at the grove's gateway. Still, she could hear the voices of the other women well enough.

"If she is a woman."

"Well, her breasts are big enough, and I've seen her in the bath-house, if she's hiding cock and balls between her thighs, she's got them well tucked up. She surely doesn't care much for men, best you not bare your tender little teats in the stream near her when we wash, Thonaradis, you're too small to fight her off."

Swaebhon's face flushed white-hot with anger, she clenched her hands tight to keep them from shaking as Thonaradis' higher voice answered, "Best you not bare your own teats, if you think those floppy udders would charm man or woman!" Swaebhon heard a scuffle and a brief ripple of giggles, then the rustling of sleeping furs settling back down.

"Ah, but if Wulfaz wasn't good enough for her, there's no man in the world who can have her, and no woman with a heart would do what she did to him."

"With a heart, aye Softer! She might hear, and I do not wish that walkurjon-gaze turned on me. It was fear enough to see her face when she spoke the poor man's doom."

Even as Swaebhon heard the other women whispering their soft agreement, she ground her teeth together. I did not tell him to vow our wedding, I never hinted that he was welcome in my arms! She thought. Why should his need have made him any worthier, when I did not want him?

"If only he had turned to me!" Arnibergo's sharp-edged soprano murmured. "What did he see in her, that great lumpy huntress with her thick arms? He was a fine man, he could have had any of us"

"You want to know how a man thinks?" Child-hagardhaz's rough voice answered. Swaebhon heard the furs rustling, she could guess at the older woman's gesture. "No brains in that little head! They're blinder than pigs, they do not see what we do. He saw teats and hips, and if he thought at all, he saw the drighten's daughter."

Swaebhon could feel her fury swelling through her body, she was ready to stamp out, to tear the tents down around the other women's heads, but that would mean admitting that she had listened to their bed-talk, that she cared what they said about her. She clenched her left hand tight on the shaft of the spear that lay beside her bed, until she heard the cracking sound of her nails and felt the broken pain splintering down her forefinger. In the morning she would see to it, but now its ache drowned out whatever the other women were muttering in the darkness. Hoilogae, she whispered to herself. The broad set of his shoulders, the milky white skin of his chest where his rough brown herder's tunic had fallen open. Perhaps she could calm herself enough to gather her might so that she could fare forth from her body, but Swaebhon still had to answer for the women who whispered and gossiped behind her in the night. Even the holy grove must be warded, or its frith would surely be broken someday. If she went forth now, it would be for that end and no other.

Swaebhon drew her feet under her, tucking the topmost reindeer skin around her shoulders like a cloak. The muttering behind her faded to the low murmuring of a stream as she breathed deeply, thinking of the glowing white stone that shone like a beacon-fire in the middle of the clearing, that would guide her back from her faring. Yet she feared to go, not for her own sake, but for Hoilogae's. It seemed to her that she could see the grim shadows of the walkurjons in the darkness about her, see their bony hands reaching white as ice-crusted willow-branches. She had seen the Choosers of the Slain as dark battle-ghosts, their mouths black with the blood of men. Those who rode with her wished to feed on Hoilogae's slain flesh.

"Oh, but he is dear to me," she murmured. "If any tastes his blood, it shall only be myself" but the tears were already in her eyes, in spite of her words. Her own wrists glimmered pale against the darkness, and it seemed to her that it would be easier to draw her spear-edge over them than over Hoilogae's throat, and let Wodhanaz have her as sacrifice in Hoilogae's stead. "Why should I have been chosen, and why he? Why could I not have contented myself with the man who came before him, who would better have been chosen for death than for the woeful wyrd I gave him?"

The sound that whispered to her was soft as the rustling of an eagle's feathers, Swaebhon's own mind shaped the words. It was from the blood of slain Kwasajaz that the mead Wod-Stirrer was brewed, that honey-draught which Wodhanaz gives to singers, from the blood of the slain their songs are often brewed, as you shall brew life from your own. The dwarves blended honey with Kwasajaz's spilled life, deep in the dead-halls, the wise one and the shrieking one brewed it.

And deep in the etin's cave the maid Guntholathjo guarded it, and Wodhanaz crept in the grave-fish's shape, the crawling wyrm in the mound, to fill himself on that blood, and afterwards rose, on atheling-bird's wings. Swaebhon's high voice rasped softly in her own ears as she chanted the words that flowed through her, she did not know whether it was she herself who wreaked the spell, or whether the breath that flowed through her was Wodhanaz's wind. Out of the etins' clutches, out of the grasp of ice, the eagle flew to the gods' fair garth. Bright was the burden of mead he bore, and sweet he spilled it for gods and men, the eagle's flood streaming gold to green earth.

Who drinks that draught is a singer blessed, with all the god's galdor might, shining there, Wodhanaz's seeds spring forth, and the walkurjons feed the spear-shoots with blood, and ready for battle again, sowing the barley of the slain that the worlds may sprout green and live once more. The better the seed, the better the harvest. The best of all is sown in joy. The faring of Hoilogae and Attalae from Sigisharjaz's Holm to Wolf Dales did not go so easily as their first. Though the heavy clouds veiling the horizon with rain passed them by, a strong wind whipped up the waves and forced the traveler to seek land and wait for two days until the sea was calm enough for them to row out again. Attalae said it was the best of luck that they had been near the shore when the wind blew up.

After that, it was easy for them to make their way along the coastline to the mouth of the river Sigisharjaz had told them about, though rowing upstream asked more of their strength. Often Attalae would lean back from his oar with a little sigh, and Hoilogae marked a bluish tinge to his lips, like the faint shadow of a dead man's darkness. But he always recovered swiftly, and was ready to row on after a few breaths. It was almost noon of the third day when the river opened out into a wide, still lake. A few ducks and a pair of white geese floated, quiet as sleepers, on the water's surface, but only the ripples of rowing stirred the deep-towering reflections of the heavy cloud-cliffs moving slowly across the blue sky, only the splashing of their oars broke the quiet.

Then another sound rang out across the lake, clear and sharp. Within one of the four small huts on the shore, metal beat against metal, again and again. Hoilogae and Attalae rowed over to the huts. When they were close enough to the lake's sandy beach, Hoilogae took off his shoes, tucked his tunic's hem up under his belt, and stepped into the water to pull the boat up onto the shore. When he looked up again, Hoilogae saw the white figure gleaming before the doorway of the hut. His breath caught in his throat. For a moment, he thought that Swaebhon was before him again. But this was not she. The hair that fell straight over her slim shoulders was black as midnight, her eyes dark against her fair face as a swan's eyes against snowy feathers. Her cheekbones were very wide, her eyes a little slanted, her mouth was pale as the petals of a wild rose. Her arms and fingers were all bedecked with silver and gold more finely wrought than anything Hoilogae had ever seen, so that each movement cast a shower of reflected glitters on the shadowed door behind her.

"Are you Sigisharjaz's men?" She asked.

"We have come from Sigisharjaz," Attalae answered. "Is Wejlunduz here?"

"Wejlunduz is forging," she said. "If you have come to see him, you must wait here until the evening. It is more pleasant out here. I shall bring you drink, if you like, and then you shall tell me about what is happening in the world beyond this wood."

"Thank you," Attalae said. "We shall be very glad to."

The woman went back into the hut, vanishing into the shadows past the door just as the door of another opened. Hoilogae blinked, staring hard, it seemed to him that the woman coming out was the same as the one who had just gone in. But though her face was the same, she was not woven about with so many ornaments, and the hem and sleeves of her dress were trimmed with shimmering silver fur.

"Greetings, wayfarers," she said. "I am Swanahwit, wife of Slegifedera, my sisters are Alurunon, wife of Agilaz," she gestured to the third hut, where another dark-haired woman, clad all in furs, stood silently watching, "and Aljawihtiz the wife of Wejlunduz."

Aljawihtiz came out of her hut again, bearing two long-stemmed silver flowers. The blooms were not fully open, wide petals still cupped upward, it was only when Hoilogae, a little bewildered, took the blossom from her hand and felt the cold of metal beneath his fingers as the heady scent of fine ale rose up to him that he realized that this was Wejlunduz's work. He heard Attalae's soft gasp of amazement beside him. Aljawihtiz's lips curled into a smile as her two sisters giggled softly.

Hoilogae and Attalae raised their cups, first to Aljawihtiz, then to Swanahwit and Alurunon. "Hail to our hosts!" Attalae said. Hoilogae echoed him, and they drank. Although he had thought Gunthahildjoz's ale good, this washed the memory of it from Hoilogae's mind as if it had been water. The cup was empty, almost as light in his hand as if it were a flower in truth, before he realized that he had taken more than a sip.

Fur-clad Alurunon went into her house again and came out swiftly with a pitcher and more cups, then the three women sat down on the grass by the shore and beckoned Hoilogae and Attalae to join them.

"Now you shall talk to us," Swanahwit said. She did not look at them, but out over the water. Aljawihtiz and Alurunon stared up at the clouds as they echoed her softly. Something in their voices cut keen and cold at Hoilogae, so that he wanted to reach up to the wind and cry out Swaebhon's name, it seemed to him that the longing ringing beneath their voices was somehow akin to his own, though he did not know how it might be. But Alurunon refilled his cup. He drank again, and words were already pouring from his mouth, tales of things he had heard as he sat by the fire in his long sleep.

Attalae spoke as readily as Hoilogae did, all his wariness forgotten, so that everything the old rede-giver had heard of battles planned and words whispered between drightens lay spread before the maidens like a peddler's wares. Now and again, Hoilogae saw one or another of the white hands tighten like a warrior's closing on a sword hilt of air, once Aljawihtiz seemed to draw her arm back as if she were about to cast a spear, but her gesture turned to a smoothing of silver-adorned hair.

The Sun was growing lower, casting the dark peaks of the pines long across the reddening reflection of the lake. Suddenly a long arrow ripped through the air between Hoilogae and Attalae, thunking into the wood of their boat, and a gruff male voice called out, "Stay where you are!"

Hoilogae and Attalae sat quite still, only turning their eyes towards the edge of the wood. Two large and furry figures bears on their hind legs, it seemed stood with drawn bows in their hands. A slain deer drooped bloodily down the back of one, a string of rabbits and birds hung from the shoulders of the other. Only by looking very closely could Hoilogae see where the bear-pelts stopped and the hair and beards of men began.

"We have come peacefully, to get the last swords which Sigisharjaz bought from Wejlunduz," Hoilogae said to them. "By what right do you threaten us?"

"What are you doing with our wives?"

Swanahwit and Alurunon rose gracefully to their feet, each of them walking to one of the hunters and laying a hand upon the point of his arrow. As if enchanted, the men slowly eased their bows away from the draw. "We welcomed them as guests, and asked them to give us news of Jutland," Swanahwit told her man. "They have done no more than that. Will you look me in the eye if you mean to accuse me of not being true?"

The man looked down and shook his shaggy head. "I meant little by it," he muttered. Hoilogae had never heard speech like his before. Though he spoke clearly enough, his words had an odd singsong lilt to them, and he drew out the sounds as if he were used to singing rather than talking. "Could we not have shot a single hair off the head of either of them, if we had wished? My arrow did not come near enough to fright them."

"I am Agilaz," the other man, the one with the string of small game hanging down his back, said unexpectedly. "My brother is Slegifedera. He doesn't mean to be rude, but we don't see other folk often here. We are the brothers of Wejlunduz the Smith. Be welcome here, guests, since our wives have greeted you already." He cocked his head towards the smithing hut, as if he were listening to a sound that Hoilogae could not hear. "Wejlunduz should be done with his day's work now. He shall be out soon, and then you can speak with him. Do you want to eat with us? There's no bale in the food or drink, I swear it, you don't have any reason to be afraid, whatever folk may have told you."

"We will eat with you gladly," Attalae answered.

Hoilogae rose to his feet, only now feeling the stiffness of long sitting in his legs. His head was spinning more than he liked, and his bladder pressed painfully against the walls of his belly.

"I'll be back in a moment," he said, going towards the trees. Attalae followed him more clumsily, the hours of sitting had taken a harder toll on his old bones and joints than on Hoilogae's.

"Did those women enchant us?" Hoilogae whispered to Attalae when they had made their way out of sight among the pines.

Attalae sighed in relief as a long stream of piss hissed out of him. He did not answer until they had both finished and straightened their tunics again. Then he murmured very softly, so that Hoilogae had to lean in towards him, half-reading his lips. "I think no harm will come to us from them. After all, we shall not be here very long." He stared off into the gloomy depths of the darkening forest. "I cannot blame Slegifedra for his ill thoughts. Even old as I am, I could not have turned away from one of them if I thought that I might win her, and I have not wished for a woman since Anulaibhon's death."

"I did not feel so," was all Hoilogae could answer.

When they came back to the shore, the doors of the huts were wide open and the smell of roasting meat wafted out of one over the bright shadows of firelight on the shadow-darkened sand. A black shape filled one doorway a moment before the man stepped out. Wejlunduz was smaller than his brothers, much shorter than Hoilogae and, aside from the heavy muscles of the smith's arms and shoulders, much more finely built. He was clean-shaven, he looked more than a little like his wife, with the same broad cheekbones and tilted eyes. His cheeks were stippled with black, but whether it was fresh beard-growth or the ingrained coal of his forging was something Hoilogae could not tell in the bad light.

The smith's dark eyes were keener than those of his brothers, shining with a light that Hoilogae thought he knew well. Little would be hidden from Wejlunduz's sight. His black hair was twisted into a long braid down his back, woven tightly with silver wires. It seemed at first glance that a serpent twined about his waist, but it was only a skillfully worked leather belt, with a sword hanging from it from the right side, Hoilogae knew from this that the smith was left-handed. His hands were unadorned, very long and narrow. The sinews on their backs stood out like bands of tightened wire. Wejlunduz looked at Hoilogae and Attalae without speaking.

Hoilogae could not break the hold of his gaze. Evenly matched, they stared into one another's eyes until Hoilogae, without looking, reached into his pouch and drew out the amber eagle's-head Sigisharjaz had given him as a token. Then the smith's glance dropped, his gaze running over the sign as carefully as skilled fingers.

"I told him that Agilaz would bring him the swords," Wejlunduz said brusquely. "Still, they're done. Will you look at them now, or wait till morning?"

"Now."

"Come, then." He walked back to his forging hut, coming out a few moments later with a long leather-wrapped bundle which he bore into his house. Hoilogae followed him, treading carefully down several wooden steps onto the sunken floor.

Wejlunduz unwrapped the swords beside the fire, laying them out so that Hoilogae could see them. It needed only a glance for him to see that his was not among them.

"Where is it?" He cried.

Wejlunduz's hand was already on his own sword-hilt. "Sigisharjaz paid me for one less than five tens of swords. These are the three that were lacking when he came last time. Do you claim that I have cheated him?"

Four are lacking from five tens, rang Swaebhon's voice again in Hoilogae's mind, and suddenly he knew what she had meant. "No. But there is one more that you must make, which is not like these."

Wejlunduz looked at Hoilogae with a sudden keen interest, as if he were measuring a beam of wood for the shaping. "Is it for you?"

"Yes."

"You have something better than the finest swords I have made for Sigisharjaz in your thought, and it will call for a high price. What have you brought with you?"

Hoilogae, lost, looked at Attalae for help.

"We have brought amber for trading, and some gold," the older man said.

"It is my way to give wrought iron only when a share and a half of the rough bog-iron is added to the price. I cannot be gathering ore all my days. Still, let me see what you have, Aljawihtiz is fond of amber, and we see little of it here. It may do for a first payment. Have you cloth with you, or meal or grain? Those are of as much use to us as gold."

"None of that, though it may be that we could get some at need."

Attalae went out to the boat, leaving Wejlunduz and Hoilogae silent until he came back with a small sack in his hand. Wejlunduz opened the bag, running his hands through it. He lifted out two thin gold arm rings, then the largest pieces of amber one the size of a plum, several as big as hazelnuts. Finally he shook his head. "This would do for a sword of bronze, though I do not often make bronze weapons any more. It will not buy iron."

Hoilogae stared in despair at him a moment. "What do I need, then?"

"Tell me of the sword you want."

Hoilogae repeated Swaebhon's words to him. The smith's wide brow furrowed, he pinched the nape of his nose and squeezed his eyes shut. "I do not yet know how to make such a blade. It would need ores I do not have, and other things I would have to find out it will take time, and I will not begin it until I have the full price."

"What do you want?"

Wejlunduz was about to speak when Attalae broke in. "Hoilogae, you have something else to show him." He handed Hoilogae a smaller bag, its weight light in the younger man's hand. When Hoilogae reached in, his fingers met the warm roughness of the great lump of amber. He had forgotten it, though, touching it again, he did not know how he could have.

"What will this buy?" He asked, pulling it out.

Wejlunduz drew in his breath as he looked at the flickering firelight through the unmarred golden depths. Carefully he took it from Hoilogae's palm. It nearly covered both of the smith's own fine-fingered hands. As he caressed it lightly, it seemed to Hoilogae that he could see the shape of a swan caught in its curves, that only the lightest touch of the knife would bring the proud bird forth in honey-rich amber, a fair gift for Wejlunduz's wife.

"This will buy your sword," he said.

Hoilogae and Attalae ate with the others that night, feasting on the wild fowl and rabbits the two hunters had brought back. Slegifedra had not boasted too broadly of the skill he and his brothers shared. Each of the little beasts, Hoilogae saw when he looked at the pelts that were now spread out for tanning, had been shot neatly through the eye. Free of their suspicion and mellowed by Alurunon's drink, the brothers were cheerful companions, laughing and breaking into song now and again. Only Wejlunduz was silent, sitting a little to one side, his keen eyes misted as if he gazed on the others from far away. Finely herbed and cooked as the food was, white and fine as the bread was, he ate as if he did not taste any of the care that had gone into readying it for him. This look Hoilogae knew from within, but he guessed that the smith was learning more from the shifting pattern of air-stirred fire through wood and embers than he ever had.

When Hoilogae came out of Slegifedra's house the next morning, Attalae and the boat were both gone. Suddenly unsettled, he looked about swiftly as if they might have been hiding from him.

"You don't need to worry," said Alurunon from where she leaned against the wall of Agilaz's home. "We didn't send him off alone. Agilaz went with him."

"Oh. Why did he leave me here?"

"You'll have to talk to Wejlunduz about that when he comes out for his midday meal. He was the one who said you should stay." She glanced up at the Sun, standing more than halfway up the morning sky. "I think there are some things he wants you to get for him."

"Wood for charcoal," the smith told Hoilogae as they sat on the shore eating bread and cold meat from the night before. "Certain kinds of stone. Herbs. The work will go faster if I have someone to do some of the rough jobs for me."

"Why haven't you taken a boy on to learn from you? There must be a hundred who would be glad to."

Wejlunduz looked aside almost as if embarrassed, Hoilogae thought. For the first time, he realized how young the smith was. No more than a few years older than himself, he thought. Finally Wejlunduz raised his head to gaze straight into Hoilogae's eyes again. "I don't know enough to teach someone else," he admitted. "When I'm ready, I will."

"But there can't be a finer smith than you in the world," protested Hoilogae. "How can you not know enough to teach?"

The corner of Wejlunduz's mouth quirked into an odd half-smile. "Oh, yes," he said. "There are still many finer. Though in time" His quiet laugh was like the brush of a soft cloth, as if he were dusting the thought and setting it carefully aside again. "Anyway, we are used to living alone here."

"How long have you been wedded?"

"Seven years."

"Where did you find your wives? Are they Finnish?"

Wejlunduz cracked his last bone and licked the marrow clean, then tossed it back towards the woods. "Come with me. I'll show you what you need to do."

The Moon had been just past full when Hoilogae had reached Wejlunduz's steading, as he waned and waxed once more, Hoilogae searched for stones with a certain color or sheen, sometimes lending his strength to aid the smith in crushing them. Often he brought clay, wood, and coals, helping to build up the man-high raised cones outside the smithy where Wejlunduz melted the true iron out of ore, often he broke the crust of slag and hard-cooked clay to pieces again. Three times he bore a bucket of glittering filings out of the smithy to mix in with the chickens' feed, three times, without asking why, he swept up their droppings and brought them to Wejlunduz again. He did not follow the smith out to the woods any more, though sometimes he lay awake in the night and listened for the sound of footsteps outside, the hairs prickling up on the back of his spine.

The other women, spoke little to Swaebhon while they were on the mountain, but she did not hear them speaking ill of her or doubting her womanhood again, and now and again one of the maids would smile at her. Still, their gazes sheered away from meeting hers, and no one lingered by her at mealtimes not even when the food had been felled by her own bow. On the last day of their stay in the holy grove, when the taps had been drawn from the slim bodies of the birches and their wounds smeared with pitch, Swaebhon's anger threaded wondering overcame her pride. When Thonaragardhaz went to the stream, Swaebhon followed her, laying aside her spear to kneel beside the smaller maid and beginning to scrub the pitch from her fingers with a handful of coarse gravel as the other was doing.

"You are silent today, Thonaragardhaz," Swaebhon said.

The point of Thonaragardhaz's nose tilted suddenly downward. She kept cleaning her hands without so much as glancing sideways, but she muttered something under her breath.

"Yes?"

The little maiden's cheeks colored brightly. She still did not look up, even as she spoke.

"I said, I do not know what I should have to say."

"There are a great many women in the grove who know no more," Swaebhon answered, her anger flaring like dry leaves on the fire. "If you wish to cast me out, you ought to hold a Thing over it, and see who among you would rather give herself to an unwanted man than say him nay."

The water splashed beneath Thonaragardhaz's trembling hands, splattering both their skirts as she dumped the little rocks back into the stream.

"Why have you chosen me for this?" She asked, her high voice breaking beneath the words. "What have I done?"

"I have not chosen you from anything. I will get my answers from who-ever has the bravery to tell me why none of you dares to meet my eyes."

Swaebhon could hardly hear Thonaragardhaz's next mumble, but when Aiwilimae's daughter rose to her full height, the other maid spoke clearly enough.

"Because we fear your gaze! You have surely been hallowed since the Thing. The light of the Ansuzis in your eyes, even when you stand in your own hide in the Middle-Garth, in the full light of the sun. I am afraid to look too long on you, for I fear to see my death awaiting me." Then Thonaragardhaz scrambled to her feet, fleeing as though Swaebhon ran, spear raised, on her trail.

Swaebhon turned her weapon in her hand, running her forefinger thoughtfully along the glittering bronze edge until a thin red line showed bright against the golden metal. Now she must walk with care among the women, now that she knew how their minds shaped her. It had been easier to rage against their mocking, if their hate had turned wholly to thoughts of hallowing, she did not know how she should bear it every day. But Swaebhon had led the rites from her mother's death onward, and she knew how the gods' might could drown all fear and unsureness she knew it, as well, from the rare moments of true sight that came upon her when she was among folk in her own hide, when she spoke from the soul without a single catch of thought. Icy clouds blew in from the far north overnight, rattling a scatter of sleet over the women's tents a little before dawn. Swaebhon stood leaning on her spear at the gate-stones, watching the others take turns at scraping the heavy birch-syrup from the pots and the rocks that had been cast in to heat them.

She did not let her gaze linger too long on any one of them, lest they become too afraid, but when their work was done, she came mildly as any to lay her hands on the holy white stone for the last time. In spite of the cold wind, its rough surface was warm from the fires that had burned by it, and the life of summer leaping up within it, springing new from the earth with the rising year. Like the other women, Swaebhon touched her lips to the stone in farewell, and it seemed to her that she could feel her new-cleansed womb tingling in answer to its might, like one lur-horn's bronze ringing softly to the other's deep sound. By the time the women had borne their heavy burdens back to the garth, late in the afternoon, the snow was falling hard and straight from the sea-gray sky.

Swaebhon did not linger in the hall as the others set down their burdens and unwrapped their leggings by the fire, calling laughingly that the men had lazed indoors all day and should bring them something hot to drink, the door had hardly closed behind the last of the women's troop before she was out it again, walking along the path that sloped down to the end of the firth. The wide slab of stone where the folk held their rites was dark gray against the snow, no more than dampened by the icy showers that had whitened the earth around it, the green grass sprouted unscathed about its edges. So it was always, even in the deepest winters when the drifts rose to thrice the height of a man and the firth's ice was thick enough for the folk to build their Yule bone-fires and dance on the frozen sea. Swaebhon sat herself down in the middle of the rock, staring out through the veils of white sweeping over the water.

The wind was whipping up the waves, the last plates of ice at the water's edge groaned as they rose and fell over the rocks, breaking with sharp crystal cracks through a low steady crunching. Now she might fare to find Hoilogae, now the storm would aid her flight, giving strength to her gray steed. Swaebhon rode swift as a spear keening through the wind, the snow flying like dust beneath her horse's hooves. She could hear the laughter of the wild ones from Hati's Firth. The etins often drew up such storms for their joy, when the seething winds between summer and winter made them able, and they had sunk many ships in the sea or broken them against their rocks, feasting on the sailors' bones. Swaebhon sped forward before the mocking taunts of the troll-maiden Rime-Gerdhaz could reach her, following the white-frothing stream that would lead her to Hoilogae.

Her path did not lead her so far up to the south as it had before, she would not cross the North Sea to Jutland, but instead turned eastward, over the lands of the Gauts and the Swihonez-folk, and farther, across the waters to the lands of the Finns. Now she saw the spark of red-gold within Wejlunduz's forge, the glowing might of the lore the smith had learned from the swart alfs who dwelt within the stones. Swaebhon cried out in joy as she rode above his roof, for she could see the sword he was sharpening, and knew that it was the one she had spoken for Hoilogae. And Hoilogae himself was there, in one of the little houses where the fettered swan-brides sat spinning and weaving, dreaming of the feather-cloaks they had worn before Wejlunduz and his brothers stole those hides away and took the women to wife.

Hoilogae sat indoors, listening to the rain rattling against the thatch. The storm had blown up suddenly, and Slegifedera had chosen to stay in the house past daybreak, as he did not often do, his flint-dark eyes sparking suspicion every time they struck against Hoilogae. It seemed to Hoilogae that other men must have some way of easing a husband's worry about a strange man and his wife, but he, for whom women had been no more than patches of wool-pale or -dark mist through his life, had learned none of them, nor did his sleeping memory bring any chance words up to help him. Should he be careful not to touch Alurunon's hand on the goblet she bore him, or step an extra pace away from Swanahwit's leg when he passed the stool where she sat spinning, Slegifedera glared closer, when he smiled at Aljawihtiz to thank her for the honeyed porridge she brought him for breakfast, the wood-man showed his snaggly teeth in a snarl.

At last Hoilogae grew tired of Slegifedera's angry stare and turned to face him squarely. The other rose, huge and shaggy as a bear in the little hut, gazing down into his eyes, Hoilogae stayed seated. He could hear the women's breaths hissing like arrows through the air hissing with eagerness, he thought. It seemed to him that Swanahwit was standing between himself and Slegifedera, but she was not, there was no one else there, no, there were two shapes of glimmering white, women's slim arms wrestling between the men. One was pressing the other back.

The near-stillness was broken by Swanahwit's cry as her distaff dropped to the floor. "Cursed thing!" She bent down to pick it up, pulling crossly at the thread. "The thread isn't falling as it should this morning. It's the damp that's gotten into it from this weather, I think."

As if Thonaraz had heard her words, the thunder of the god's ax striking down boomed across the lake. Slegifedera pulled his furs around himself, glaring about. "I won't stay in with spinning women all day," he muttered. "See if I can catch anything in this rain. It'll last a good while, you'll see."

He hurried out the door while his wife was still trying to tug her thread out evenly. Hoilogae shook his head to clear it of its dizziness.

"Will Wejlunduz be angry if I go into his smithy before mid-day?" He asked.

Swanahwit and Alurunon glanced at one another, then at Aljawihtiz. At last the smith's wife said, "I think you may go safely now. Perhaps it would be better for you to spend the day there."

Hoilogae did not knock at the door, Wejlunduz had told him earlier that he must come and go quietly, lest he should break the smith's thoughts at the wrong moment. Instead he slipped carefully inside the smithy, biting back his breath as he watched.

An adder of flame ran coiling up and down the dark iron blade as Wejlunduz turned it before his fire. The edges flared with a biting glitter, but the golden glow of the ring on the hilt was steady and true above the curling of the serpent's tail. Suddenly the smith slashed it through the keening air, to Hoilogae's bewitched eyes, it left a trail of unseen blue light, the scar of lightning on storm clouds.

"So it is done," Wejlunduz murmured to himself. He regarded the sword for a moment, hefting it in his hand. Then Hoilogae saw his smile break through the dark veil of soot on his face, bright as a shaft of sunlight cutting through the storm. He felt almost ashamed to be watching the craftsman as he stood in the first moment with his full-wrought work, but he knew that Wejlunduz could not begrudge him his share in that joy.

"So it is done," Hoilogae echoed softly.

The brightness faded from Wejlunduz's face, though not from his eyes, as he turned to face Hoilogae. Flicking the sword about as lightly as a wand in his hand, he set the hilt into its owner's palm. "There you are, then. What shall you name it?"

The thunder above them drowned out anything Hoilogae might have said for a moment. When the echoes had died away over the lake, he said, "I think it can have no name other than the one I bear."

"Give it, then." Wejlunduz stood watching him, with no further hints. Hoilogae stood staring at the blade in his hand, at the wyrm-ripples of light and dark steel along it and the wyrm that rose from them to coil its tail about the hilt below the ring. It seemed to him that he could taste the fresh-forged iron in his mouth with the keen after-path of the lightning, and that both tasted sharp with blood.

"Iron is like blood," the smith murmured softly. "And blood calls for blood."

Hoilogae raised his left hand, piercing the palm on the sword's tip. The red rivulet sprang out at once, following the wyrm's wavy line down the edge to dye the serpent-shape upon the blade. "Hoilogae," he said, the name as strange and wonderful from his mouth as it had been from Swaebhon's. He whipped the sword suddenly through the air, swiftly enough to dash the blood from it. The dark drops hissed into the fire and were gone.

"Good enough," Wejlunduz said. "Iron is not like bronze, though. I'll need to teach you how to care for it. The best is most easily ruined. Water will eat the iron, and so will sweat, and blood even more. Each time you use it, you must clean it, and oil it before you put it back in the sheath."

"Does it have a sheath?"

Wejlunduz pointed to the thin length of leather-covered wood that lay across one of the smith's stools. "I do all things to the full," he said, and this time his smile was narrow-lipped as a snake's. He handed Hoilogae a small clay pot and a soft cloth. "Now, this is how you must clean the blade"

When Hoilogae had cleaned his sword to Wejlunduz's content and sheathed it, the two of them left the forge together, walking swiftly through the rain to the smith's own hut. Wejlunduz stopped Hoilogae with the palm of his hand on the larger man's chest just before they opened the door.

"I do have one favor to ask of you," Wejlunduz said in a low voice. "Might I borrow the blade tonight, just for a short time? I shall not use it, but" he looked down at his muddy bare feet a moment, then up at Hoilogae again. "It is the best sword I have made, and I wish to show it to someone."

Hoilogae touched the ring on the hilt. He was not willing to let the sword leave his side, nor go from him for a moment, but he knew the Finn's pride, though the sword bore Hoilogae's own name, it was still Wejlunduz's work. Calling all his strength of will to him, he nodded his head. "You may."

Hoilogae lay awake long after the fire had burned down to a soft glow of coals through the darkness, listening to Slegifedra's heavy snores and the soft breathing of Swanahwit. If the night had not been so still by the lake, he would never have heard the rustling outside. At first it might have been a hare, but a hare did not move steadily towards a goal. Then Hoilogae heard the leather-muffled clink of metal on metal, and his thoughts told him that it must be Wejlunduz going somewhere in the night. He waited until he could hear the noise no longer, then stealthily pushed his way out from beneath the bearskin he had been given as a blanket and picked his way between the sleepers and the fire pit. The moon was near full outside, bleaching the sands white as old bones. It was easy for Hoilogae to see the narrow foot-prints that led in a close-set line from Wejlunduz's hut to a thick hedge of blackberries at the edge of the forest.

Treading in the smith's own tracks, he found himself slipping between the thorny walls without scathe, though he had to duck and turn where Wejlunduz could pass easily. Then he had no choice but to follow the trail or turn back. Hoilogae moved very slowly and carefully, trying to make no sound. He did not know how far away from him Wejlunduz was, and he was sure that the smith would be angry with him if he caught him following. As the path broke suddenly out into a moonlit clearing, Hoilogae's foot slipped and came down on a branch with a loud crack. He could not bite back the gasp as his heart struck hard against his ribs, but he froze without moving. His breath came back to him only slowly as he looked about to see if he had been found out.

A huge gray boulder stood in the middle of the clearing, the moon silvering the pale lichens growing on it into patches of hoarfrost. Wejlunduz sat cross-legged in front of the stone, his palms against it. He did not stir or give any sign that he had heard Hoilogae. After a while, when the smith did not move, Hoilogae crept closer. Wejlundaz's eyes were dark and empty in the shadow of his brow.

He sat so still that Hoilogae was not sure he was breathing, his chest did not seem to rise or fall. As Hoilogae neared the rock, the hairs on the back of his neck prickled up. He could feel the might thrumming around the stone, and felt, too, that if whatever dwelt within was not his foe, it was no friend to him either. He was about to back away from it when he heard the echoes of the voices from within the rock. They rang oddly, as if the speakers were within a house built all of stone slabs, but he could still recognize the sing-song speech of Wejlunduz, and hear that the rumbling answer was deeper than any human voice could be. Fascinated, Hoilogae listened as closely as he dared. He could make out few words, but those that he heard spoke of temper and the color of iron's glow, ore and charcoal and hammer-weights.

This was a lore he did not know enough to share, what he stole by eaves-dropping would do the thief no good. So he backed away carefully, stepping backwards in the crushed grass of his own tracks and Wejlunduz's until he was at the edge of the forest again and had to turn to see his way. As he turned, Hoilogae bumped into something dark, rough with linen and soft with fur. He stepped back, steadying himself and readying an apology. The shape before him was taller and broader than he, one of Wejlunduz's broth-ers, he thought, until he heard the soft deep laugh.

"You are wise to seek knowledge of the making of your sword," the cloaked man rumbled, "For there is such wyrd wrought in its shaping that it will turn the path of many folk for many lifetimes to come." The thin curved blade of the Moon glimmered silver onto his face as he turned his head, one eye shone icy gray, but shadows pooled dark as spilt ale in the other.

Hoilogae's windpipe seemed to snap like a dry twig. He could neither draw nor let breath, and his words lay still in his mouth.

"Now the southern folk push upward, Hrothamaraz has bought more warriors and swords than his land can feed, and if you do not strike now, you and he will be eaten alike by his host. But if your strength and your sword are worthy of each other, and you move when the way is clear, there will come a day when your kin ride onward when Wodhanaz's spear flies over hosts by the Rhine, and gifts to Frijjo are cast into the Danu, when Thonaraz's Hammer and Tiwaz's true star are hailed on the highest moun-tains from south to north. Then the pattern-forged swords shall be the strength of those who call on myself and my kin, all the Ases and Wans. I lay the stones, I shape the posts, and your bones shall shore up the foundation of the holy stead of the gods, if you will give them."

"I asked for the walkurjon's love, and she showed me the way to a sword," Hoilogae croaked, his mouth dry as the ashes of a burnt corpse. "I think the bargain more than good."

The one-eyed man laughed again, and this time the keen hissing of whetstone on steel edged the sound. "Be sure, all you give will come back to you again. You shall build on the mounds of the dead, you shall claim your forebears' might, not once, but thrice and the last deed you do for me shall be the most needed."

Then he was gone. Hoilogae blinked the darkness from his sight. His limbs were still shaking, carefully he walked to the hut and lay down.

CHAPTER VI

The snow whirled against the briefing room's windows, flakes starring the glass and slowly freezing to one another. Karin leaned her chin in her palm and her elbow against the table. Straight from Arizona to this, she thought fire to ice. Still, the harsh cold of the Colorado mountains in December was a relief to her after the months of sweating from the first step outside in the morning to her shower at the end of the day, she would be just as glad never to see Luke AFB again in her life.

"Hel og hæglbyge, but I hate being too hot," Karin murmured to herself. Even after four years away from her family, she still thought in Danish most of the time. Words had never come easily to her.

She glanced up at the clock on the bare white wall. Ten to seven. The other pilot-trainees would be crowding in soon. Even as she thought, the door swung open and Lt. Galloway wandered in. His mouth hardly twitched, but the freckled skin at the corners of his eyes twitched as he settled his long body a couple of chairs away from her.

"Hey, Jensen."

He turned his right hand towards her, middle finger extended. Karin leapt up, ready to grab his arm and crank it till he screamed, but he sprang backwards out of the chair, dodging neatly.

"What did you mean by that, you asshole?"

Galloway grinned. "The early worm deserves the bird." He bent over, laughing like a hyæna, but softly, their C.O. might be right outside the door.

Karin shook her head in disgust and sat back down. "Aahh," she muttered. "Shithead." Galloway was better than good in the air, or he would have been somewhere else, but on the ground he was still about twelve years old. "Gods help you if you ever get assigned as GIB in any plane I'm flying. I'll have you puking your guts within half an hour."

"Not gonna happen," Galloway said confidently.

The others in their small group of trainees were starting to file in now. Peters, Rodriguez, Schroeder, and Bergmann. The four men nodded to Galloway and Karin, taking their places at the table. All of them were new on base, FNGs, Fucking New Guys, as the others called them. Still undergoing local training and familiarization before they could be worked into their squadron.

"Whatcha bet we get a little Survival & Resistance review today, on account of this nice weather?" Bergmann asked. He glanced over at his reflection in the frosted window, straightening his cap and brushing down a few short spikes of brown hair. Even in uniform, Karin thought, he still had that sharp East Coast look to him, he could have been a young lawyer in an Air Force uniform.

"It could happen," Schroeder agreed dolefully.

"You got no reason to bitch, you grew up in Minnesota," Bergmann told him. "Should be used to it."

As the door opened again, the six trainees stood up and turned to face it, standing at attention as Lieutenant Colonel Yorke, their squadron commander, strode in, crumbs of snow still sprinkling from the shoulders of his overcoat. He saluted, they saluted back.

"At ease," Yorke said. "Sit down." He walked around the table and slapped his plastic folder down, then stood facing them with hands on hips, his short squat figure a dark rock against the white wall. "Nice day, isn't it, Lieutenant Jensen?"

"Yessir."

"Glad you think so. Now, we are told that conditions will become rapidly more inclement during the day, culminating in a full-scale blizzard early this afternoon. Lieutenant Rodriguez, what do you think such a day is ideal for?"

Rodriguez's dark eyes flickered towards the icy window. Karin remembered that he had treated his first snowfall on base like an act of the gods well, he had lived in San Diego until the Air Force sent him to Arizona. "Uh, inclement weather flight training, sir," he said hopefully. Karin saw his fingers twitching as if telling a rosary bead. None of the pilot-trainees was happy to be on the ground when they might have been in the air, but she was willing to bet that Rodriguez had given Mary a few extra Hails that morning against the chance of a day at Survival & Resistance in the snow.

"Very good, Lieutenant. After all, the action may be over the sand now, but what happens next, no one knows. You may see flying in the Urals yet. Our job is to be ready for anything." Yorke was about forty-eight, Karin remembered, though his shortness and his swift crisp movements made him look ten years younger. He had flown missions over the Red River Valley in Viet Nam, and trained most of his life thinking of the enemy as a MiG pilot with a red star on his badge.

"Therefore," the major went on, "the six of you will get a lovely day playing in the snowy clouds and the mountains zero-zero weather, IFR all the way, I promise you won't be able to see a thing out of your canopies, and after a day with the rocks reaching up to grab you. You will probably want to take your TFR out of the plane and buy it a drink after you RTB. Remember that the winds are going to get a hell of a lot worse as the day rolls on, and that the rocks out there are treacherous sons-a-bitches. When in doubt, head for the heights. I don't want to be scraping any of you off the side of a mountain this afternoon."

Schroeder raised his hand, his broad fair forehead creasing. "Permission to ask a question, sir?"

"Ask away."

"Any dogfighting today?"

"No way. I'm not gonna let you practice combat against live opposites till you've racked up a few more hours in heavy snow and rough terrain, getting used to your all-weather capabilities and sudden mountains in your face. You'll do enough piccolo playing to keep in the air and follow the plan on your mission cards without live bandits to worry about. For the moment." Yorke snapped his folder open, his little square hands shuffling out the cards to the trainees. "Here you go, gentlemen. Prick up your ears."

The maneuverers were basic enough. Air to air. Air to ground, nothing she had not flown many times before, but Karin could hear the wind rising above Lieutenant Colonel Yorke's words and the scratching of the pilots' pencils, and the windows were thickly crusted with ice now. This would be real flying, she thought, her breath quickening. Riding the storm or being cast down by it. She had logged a few hours in simulated conditions like this, but to feel the wind and rocks around her. Her own body flung about as her plane swooped and rolled in the twisting currents of air, that was something else!

"Finally, I shouldn't need to tell you this by now, but I'll tell you anyway. Conditions are deteriorating rapidly out there, this is supposed to be the storm of the century. Your birds are capable of putting a bomb right through a shit house window in the middle of a blizzard, you should be able to handle everything out there. Nevertheless, there is always the minute possibility that you may hear a still small voice in your headset saying 'RTB', and you will RTB that moment, as straight and fast as you can while maintaining optimal safety precautions. No hanging out there for just one last loop or one final dump Return To Base." Yorke's green eyes glared straight at Karin. "This means you, Brünnhilde. No matter how good you can fly in clear weather."

"Yessir. RTB ASAP, sir."

"Survival suits and Combat Edge gear. Get moving. Pre-flight check at the hangar in minus twenty."

The grainy snow rasped harshly against Karin's face as she walked towards her plane her F-16D! In spite of the cold, she could feel the sweat starting under her rubberized survival suit. She breathed in carefully, sucking the freezing air in slowly through her nose. The Combat Edge vest pressed the sharp edges of her valknútr pendant into her skin, it also squeezed her breasts uncomfortably tight against her body. Like a lot of fighter gear, it had not been designed with women in mind. She was lucky to be tall and wide-shouldered, but having large breasts was sometimes downright painful. Still, she had never suffered G-LOC with the Combat Edge system on, and staying conscious through a 9g turn was worth discomfort.

The ladder was slick with ice under Karin's gloves and boots as she climbed up and hit the switch to open the F-16's bubble canopy. Ground crew had cleaned the clear plastic off, but the snow was already frosting onto it again. Popeye, for sure. She would be almost totally dependent on her instruments to show her where she was flying and what was around her, like night-flying in a storm.

A bulky shape was clambering up the ladder behind her not a designated GIB, Karin was flying alone today with the rear seat empty. It was one of the ground crew coming up to strap her in. She recognized Sgt. Petrowsky's broad cheekbones and china-blue eyes beneath the cap pulled low over his face.

Petrowsky grunted, tugging her straps tight. "Whuffo' a pretty gal like you flying on a day like this?"

Karin's eyes narrowed, but she already knew him well enough to know he was just running his mouth to hear himself talk. If you didn't want to take crap for being a woman, you shouldn't have gone into fighter training, Karin reminded herself, and forced a smile. "Same thing a cute boy like you is doing on that ladder with the wind whistling up your butt, sergeant. Practice for freezing to death in Siberia." She waited to see if he was going to try to cop a feel as he strapped her, no joy through all the flight gear anyway, but there were some assholes who just couldn't keep their hands to themselves when they thought they might have a chance to brush a tit. But Petrowsky wasn't one of them, he straightened up after his final check.

"There y'go. Fly careful, the shit's coming thick and fast. Ma'am."

"I can see that, sergeant. Thanks."

Petrowsky slowly made his way back down the icy ladder. His foot skidded on a patch of ice as he stepped onto the ground, and he flailed a moment before catching his balance again.

Karin flicked the battery switch and closed the canopy. The low hum of her engine rose through her bones, the wind-up of her gyros grinding in her ears as her instrument panel glowed to life. Now the tight binding of her g-suit and Combat Edge system did not seem to constrict her breathing, nor did the straps that held her tight to the F-16's reclining seat, they were armor bracing her flesh, but the boundaries of her body were her plane's metal and plastic, thrumming with the blood that ran more swiftly through her veins as she began her pre start up check. This was the hardest thing of all. Not to let the joyous rushing of wind in her skull dull the keen edge of her observations, or sweep her away from the discipline of her training. Karin's systems checks were always careful, but this time her gloved fingers lingered a little longer than usual on each button and switch, her gaze sharpening to look for the least hairsbreadth variation on the dials or nervous flicker of the glowing digital displays.

Horizontal Situation Indiator, Inertial Navigational System, radar, and her TIDS, the Tactical Information Display System that gave her all the mission info she could call for. All of that, and if Karin failed to glance over the right indicator at the right moment, or her fingers were a little too slow at the wrong time, her F-16 would live up to the nickname "Lawn Dart ." It would be shrapnel scattered over the Rockies, and there might not be enough of her body left to scrape up. She checked the TFR (Terrain-Following Radar) three times to be sure. Any glitches there, and her next base transfer would be to Valhöll.

"Operation Jötunheimr about to commence," Karin muttered to herself, her voice muffled and dull through the helmet's clasp on her ears. Engine running, brakes still locked. She could not see the ground crew completing the final checks beneath the F-16's wings and body, but she knew that they were there. It seemed to her that she could feel when they were done, her INS display settled into full alignment, and she saw the dark shadows stepping away in the snow. One lifted an arm, waving her off the pan. She taxied slowly forward to the 'last chance' stop, where the armory would take the pins from her weapons load.

Karin's headset crackled a moment, Yorke's voice was hissy with static. "Condition, Jensen?"

"FMC, sir." Fully Mission Capable, Karin whispered to herself again, smiling. She could just see the lights of two other aircraft from her canopy, she flicked her TIDS display to show the full formation. Schroeder's F-16C, single-seater bastard, they'd have him in combat the moment hostilities started. Even though she was the better pilot, she would be damned lucky if she ever flew anything but an instructor's two-seater model, or got to shoot at anyone who was firing live armaments back. Around them were ranged Rodriguez's Tomcat, Peters and Bergmann in the Phantom, and Galloway in his A-10 Warthog. Within a month, the six of them would be slotted into squadron places, but for now they flew together.

Her headset sizzled again, this time it was the voice of Berkeley Tower. "Valkyrie, cleared for takeoff."

"Roger, Tower ." Karin let the throttles ease forward, felt her wheels begin to roll. The runway ahead of her was a blurry dark strip, hardly visible through her iced canopy and the blowing snow, two streams of white ghost-lights shone along its edges. The F-16 bumped along, picking up speed as the thunder of the turbofans beat through Karin's ears, as the ground-speed needle turned swiftly upward. When it hit 120 knots, Karin stroked the control stick at her side. She felt the nose gear leaving the wet tarmac and yanked the stick back hard, screaming up into the whirling snow. Her altimeter swung around as the rush dragged the blood from her head, she could see the radar blips of the other planes shifting on the green screen of her TIDS as they rose and leveled out. Behind her, the white glow of the landing field's powerful searchlights faded out in her screaming wake.

As per their mission plan, Karin and Schroeder were a little ahead of the others, she slowed a little to pace him more closely, even as his F-16 pressed forward to match hers. If only he were like that on the ground, Karin thought for a moment but her Terrain-Following Radar was already warning her to swing upwards again.

Static crackled in her ears for several breaths before she heard Yorke's voice. "Planned."

"Come again, sir? Bad static."

Karin heard indistinct muttering through the frying-bacon noise of interference, then the squadron commander's words came through clearly. "Do you read me now, Jensen?"

"Loud and clear, Major."

"Minus thirty seconds, begin maneuverers as scheduled."

"Roger, sir."

As Karin swung into the first loop, a bad cross-wind caught her. The F-16's design was nearly buffet-proof, but this gust actually swung her a few degrees off track. All her hairs were prickling now, tingling like fine living nerve-ends as her touch on the control stick shifted with the shifting storm. Her speed had raked the crust of ice from her canopy, but the whirling of gray clouds and snow hid everything around her, it was the glowing shapes moving on her TFR as the radar traced the jagged mountains and deep crevasses beneath her that she answered to, swooping down and pulling straight up before the crags that lurked behind the seething waves of the storm. The other pilots had dropped a little behind her, their reflexes not quite as fast as hers, or nerves not quite as good, the winds were blowing more strongly all the time, and the terrain here was rougher than anything they had trained on in Arizona. Got you, Karin thought, grinning as she pulled up into the vertical again.

The move killed some of her forward velocity, she hung a moment, waiting for them to catch up. Yorke would be watching them closely on his own TIDS, and he had made it clear that teamwork counted as highly as talent in his eyes. He had already ranked Karin out once for hot dogging to leave the other trainees behind. Then there was no time to think as she wove the F-16 through its high-G curves. Here the swift fighter earned its other name, the Viper. No bandits glowed on her TIDS screen, and the audio warning of her headset was not beeping, but as the storm raged towards its full fury and the mountain-peaks surged and leapt below her, Karin knew that her death was no more than the brushing of a cloak-edge away. Her lips pulled back taut against her teeth, she could feel her Combat Edge system forcing air into her crushed lungs.

If only I had a target! She thought her flight was so close to perfect. The clouds writhed away from the F-16 like deep blue smoke, a flash of lightning blinded Karin's eyes for a heartbeat. She blinked hard, letting her trained instinct move her hand on the side-stick controller as the thunder boomed muffled through her headset. The lightning burst around her like enemy fire, her Viper spearing straight and clean through the writhing snakes of brightness. This is Valhöll! She thought, skimming down into a low fast series of rolls only seconds above a mountain peak, as the warnings flared before her. It seemed that she could feel the cold wind as the snow-hidden rocks blurred past beneath. The trainees' ground targets were set out for them individually, the simulated bunkers would need no camouflage today, but they glowed bright and clear on Karin's cockpit screen. In this weather, infra-red was a waste of time, but her radar would give her enough targeting to do her job. Between the mountains and figuring the winds in, though, the low bombing passes were going to be a real bitch, even with all the help of the F-16's computer systems. Here and there, Karin could see the dark edges of raw rock blurring through the snow as she swept down along the mountain's steep slope.

Even as her eyes constantly flickered over her HUD and the dials around it, watching the ADI's indications shift, part of her mind was visualizing the bunker with the enemy in it, shadows hunkered over their anti-aircraft guns, staring at the bright spark of her Viper in their radar. Perhaps her Radar Lock warning light would be glowing now, a low whine moaning in her ears to let her know she was targeted. Cross-winds gusting constantly, to actually hit the fucking target she would have to get in as low as possible jink fast and hard to avoid fire. Karin twisted, and an overhanging crag swept before her canopy like a huge fist hooking an inch too short, her TFR was jittering about madly as she closed in on her target. There! Dear gods, she could actually see its black shape, the wind must have swept the snow from the roof or something just get her cross-hairs on it, dive on in there and pull out sharp, the computer would pickle it for her. Karin hit the bottom of her pass as hard as if she were landing on rock, it felt as though the sheer momentum of her fall had flung her violently backward. She glanced down, and bit her lip hard. Something big and dark was moving down there in her target area. Then it burst in orange brightness, and Karin was not sure what she had seen. She was climbing rapidly, out of firing range by now and safe, but she could hear her own harsh panting through her helmet.

"Jeg tænker, at jeg dræbte en troll," she whispered.

The head seat crackled. "Say again, Jensen?"

"Got him!"

"Sure did. Nice comp, I bet that wind's a bitch. Carry on."

"Roger."

Karin climbed for a few more seconds, dragging the next scheduled maneuverers back into her brain. Her next run was a strafe pass another mountainside target, she would have to skim around rather than going straight down. Up to the farthest edge, and no further, that's what makes a fighter pilot, Colonel Roberts had said when he first spoke to her training group, and she had held tight to those words since. As she slid between the peaks, Karin kept her gaze on her control panel, but she could not keep from watching the snow-blurred crags with her peripheral vision. Now it seemed to her that she could see more of the rocks moving, that the snow twisted around them into half-human shapes. The warmth of her flight gear did not keep a shiver of cold from thrilling up her spine, but her touch on the stick was light and sure as she moved into position for her pass. Men or trolls, she thought, you get in my path and you're gone! Karin's targets were marked out clearly on her screen, she moved her pipper fast as she swept in, marking each of them for her bullets.

Dø! She thought Die! Swept up again, rising swiftly through the flickering lightning to the heights where the purple-black anvil-heads towered into the deep blue sky. The last target was a long way away, ten minutes for the F-16 at max velocity, but Karin already had it marked. One bomb left, then she would have to turn homeward, RTB, and spend the rest of the day filling out paperwork and watching analyses of her flight. No way to stay up here any longer than scheduled for her, Yorke would notice all delays and unplanned fuel use, especially if it went for aerobatics. One more bomb drop. The terrain was so irregular here, it would have to be on manual. Get you on one pass, Karin thought, gritting her teeth. But not only would she have to come in low here, she would have to sweep slower than she liked to deal with the vicious cross-winds. The storm was raging around her at her fullest, lightning playing over her F-16's body and wings, even though she was squinting against the flashing brightness, the searing afterimages still stitched through her sight every time she blinked.

Karin turned the Viper's nose down, swooping over the snow-softened rocks. The shapes that twisted past her in the whirling storm were clearer in her sight, dancing wildly to the screaming of the wind as her F-16 swept past them. It seemed to her that she could hear the music from Peer Gynt inside her head. Trond i Valfjeldet! Bård og Kåre!Slagt Ham! Kristenmands Sön har dåret Dovregubbens veneste Mö! Trond, Dovregubben the Mountain King, the king of the trolls. Now she dove about the gables of his hall, the crags that reached and struck for her plane now her battle was with him, the old berg-dweller. No visual yet, the snow was blowing straight across in a thick blanket between Karin and her target, but her radar showed her where to aim, clear and clean, and her cross-hairs were centered right on. Lightning burst brightness over the front of Karin's canopy as she pressed the pickle button, clawed blackness flashed before her eyes like a giant hand slapping at the F-16. She tore back, rolling upward through the swirling snow. The green blip on her screen had winked out.

Target annihilated. Slowly Karin forced her breathing to steady as she dove up through the clouds. Then her heart clenched within her ribs, as though her legs had suddenly dropped from under her. Her radar was dead, her TIDS blank and instrument landing system gone, and the warning lights were glowing at the bottom of the panel. *You're supposed to be insulated against lightning, damn you!* Karin swore at the Lawn Dart, but she was not sure the plane deserved it.

Well, it was time to RTB anyway, Tower could talk her down, and anyway, if Karin couldn't fly without instruments, she should give up planes and stick to computers. "Tower, this is Valkyrie. Radar and TIDS failure, ILS fucked. Position on INS still clear, no problem finding you, but you'll have to give me more than a little help getting down. Standard GCA won't do it without radar."

"Roger, Valkyrie. What happened?"

"Lightning strike. Looks like something shorted out."

"That's not s'posed to happen, is it?"

"I fucking know that! But it fucking well did."

"Sorry, Valkyrie. We'll get you down."

Karin flew low above the seething mass of clouds. The Sun had just gone beneath their edge, though her mission had seemed to take no more than a few moments, the afternoon was wearing on. The flight gear braced her tired muscles, holding her ready for the half-blind descent into the blizzard. *The mission's not over until the paperwork is done,* Karin reminded herself. She checked her INS reading again.

"ETA minus five minutes, Tower."

"Rog. Ground standing by."

Onward. "Preparing for descent."

Karin sloped her nose downward, slow and steady, as Tower began feeding her a string of numbers. Blinded again by the dark clouds and the snow streaming over her bubble, she had to trust in her abilities and the man talking her in. If her nerve failed, she would circle till she fell, if her skill failed, she would crash. She slid in carefully through the winds that tried to catch and tear at her plane, constantly shifting with the voice hissing in her headset. Now she could see the brighter whiteness through the snow, the beams of light spearing up into the storm, she corrected her course again.

"On target, Valkyrie. Two thousand feet, fifteen hundred" The F-16 was slowing, the landing gear chunking out. Karin had the runway on infra-red now, landing would be no problem. In and then she was down, the Lawn Dart bumping along the salted tarmac as it gradually rolled to a halt. Ground crew was already waiting, it would be a long time before that plane flew again.

"Nice landing, Jensen," Lt. Colonel Yorke said as Karin walked into his office. "Now, what happened?"

"Sir, I was struck by lightning as I made the last drop. Next thing I saw was the warning lights."

Yorke tapped his pencil thoughtfully on the sheaf of forms in front of him, heavy dark brows creasing over his green eyes. "The Lawn Dart's pretty heavily insulated, Lieutenant. No signs of trouble earlier?"

"Nothing whatsoever, sir. Not a flicker." Sweat dry in her uniform, adrenalin-laced blood no longer thrilling through her hands, Karin was already finding it hard to recall what she had seen on the mountainside if she had seen it, and not simply been dazzled by snow and lightning and the speed of her own flight.

The squadron commander picked up the low stack of papers and handed it to her. "I want these done and back at seventeen-thirty. Maintenance should have their report to me by then. We'll go over it then."

"Yes, sir."

"I'd tell you what excellent flying that was out there, but I suspect you already know it. Good bombing is magic, Jensen."

"Yes, sir. Thank you, sir."

Karin was driving off-base by eighteen-hundred, her jeep crawling along the streets with brights on full. The windshield wipers and defroster were fighting a losing battle against the snow freezing onto the glass, although the snowploughs must have been along less than an hour ago, the road was already crusted white again. It had been an unexplained power surge within the plane that had knocked out her instrumentation. Maintenance swore up and down that the lightning could not have done it. Karin was going to be grounded while they tore the F-16's machinery apart and rebuilt it. Cause not immediately apparent. One of the great joys of being a lieutenant was the private housing, Karin thought as she unlocked the door of her efficiency apartment. Her BAQ wasn't enough for a very large home off-base, but what she had suited her well enough. She shucked her coat and uniform jacket, hanging them up neatly on the hook beside the door, then bent down to pick up the envelopes scattered on the floor under the mail slot.

"Sierra Hotel!" She muttered. Air Force for shit hot. Not one, but both of the Asatro magazines she subscribed to, Mountain Thunder and Idunna, had come in. Karin glanced swiftly at the other letters. Publishers Sweepstakes wanted to let her know that she could win a million dollars, and TV Guide wanted to sell itself.

She tossed those two in the trash unopened, then spun the magazines gently onto her bed. She deserved a beer or few. She wouldn't get drunk, but since there was no chance of flying tomorrow, a little pollution in her bloodstream wouldn't hurt her. When Karin had settled down in her chair with a bottle of Elephant and the new issue of Mountain Thunder on the table beside her, she reached down to her little portable CD player, punching it on. As she took her first sip, the dark growl of Bathory's lead singer sounded through the apartment, the opening words of "Hammerheart."

"Now that the wind called my name.."

Karin raised her eyes to the poster taped to the door. Except for her gun-metal gray bookshelf, it was the one decoration breaking up her apartment's whiteness. Twisted knot work serpents and ravens writhed around its edges, deep black and shining white against the gray background, but it was the pale face in the middle of the dark center square that drew the gaze. The light shining from the high cheekbones and gray-white beard of the old man whose dark hat drooped over one eye, picking out the rune-carved shaft of the spear he held. Although she knew her voice was off-key, she sang softly with the music. "With my blood brothers at side, all sons of father with one eye, we all were born in the land of the blood on ice." She lifted her beer bottle in her left hand, tracing the valknútr's triple triangle over it with the right.

"Óðinn," Karin murmured. "Grim One, you might have had me today, if it was not you who helped me against the berg-dwellers." Karin had never doubted her god, not since she, six years old, had seen his single eye staring at her from the illustrated Norse Gods and Giants her mother had given her for her birthday, but she knew the price he always asked in the end. She could not tell whether the mouth beneath Óðinn's white-stranded mustache was smiling or frowning, but his eye was gazing straight at her as she downed her beer in a single draught. Someday she would make herself a proper drinking horn, if she ever had the time, there were directions in Our Troth and a couple of her other Asatro books. Else buy one at a Renaissance Faire.

For now, she drank beer from the bottle, milk from the carton, and tap water from her cupped hands, and liked it well enough. Karin got up to fetch herself another beer, the glass bottle smooth and cool in her left palm. There might be another in my other hand, she thought. I might be bringing ale to a hero. She laughed, thinking of Galloway's dimwitted jokes, Schroeder's sulks, the clicking of Rodriguez's rosary beads. If there was no one among her fellow fighter pilots who seemed worth bringing a beer to, she was probably S.O.L. Maybe I'm looking in the wrong place, she thought, as she had many times before. Karin knew damned well there was always a sharp edge of competition between herself and the other pilots, no matter how well and closely they could work together. If she could find an Army man, now, maybe a tanker. Karin settled back into her chair, taking a long pull of her beer and letting the familiar fantasy roll up in her mind. Friendly and enemy ground forces blipping on her screen from below, the bandits screaming in above as the American tanks rolled through the sand towards the anti-aircraft guns.

Her man was down there, broad shoulders hunched above the tank's controls. He knew she was above him, swooping and diving close on the tail of the foe who would assail him from the air, and his tank's guns were hammering, beating against the bastards who would shoot her from the sky like a duck in October. One unit, ground and air, and there was no one who could stand against them, her lightning and his steel. En helt som Helge, she thought wistfully, a hero like Helgi. Karin did not know whether it was Helgi Hjörvardhsson or Helgi Hunding's-Bane she meant, but thinking of the first of them reminded her of the strange thing she had seen in the mountains. She reached over to her bookshelf for her battered copy of the Poetic Edda. It fell open to the page she had chosen.

"Helgi slew Hati the etin, who sat on a certain mountain" Karin glanced over the words between Helgi's man Atli and the troll-woman Rime-Gerd, Hati's daughter, seeking the passage in which Helgi and the etin-maid spoke together

"'You would rather have her, Helgi, who watched over harbor last night with the men, here she rode over land and water and so made fast your fleet. She alone ruled there, so that I might not be bane to the prince's men.'"

Well, I have battled with trolls now, Karin thought. Surely it will not be too much longer before I find my Helgi. She touched the silver valknútr around her neck and smiled. Now that she thought about it, Helgi was also the name of the Haddings' kid, though he hardly looked like a hero, even for a seventeen year-old, he was a scrawny little creature. Helgi must have been a family name on Fru Hadding's side, although the other Völsungs, Sigurd the Dragon-Slayer and Sigmund, were well-known, no one who didn't read the Eddic poems closely had ever heard of either of the Helgis. Chances were that Helgi Hadding would never know that he had been given the name of an ancestral hero, Karin had sent him a copy of Crossley-Holland's The Norse Myths for his sixteenth birthday, a little over a year ago, but the Helgi stories had not been included in that book, and she doubted he would ever find out about them elsewhere. Perhaps I should write to him, Karin thought, then shook her head.

The Hadding kid might have had a crush on her then, but he had probably forgotten her altogether by now. She put down the book and picked up her Mountain Thunder, pausing a moment to admire the high-resolution photograph on the front cover. A raven swooping over the snow between two tall pines, every black feather and needle as sharp as if they had been outlined with the corner of a razor blade.

"Evige Asatro," Karin murmured as she opened the magazine, everlasting Ásatrú, the troth of the gods of the North. Her troth, whether there would ever be someone in her life to share it with or not.

CHAPTER VII

Soon he will come to me, Swaebhon thought, riding up through the glittering clouds again as the lightning sparked from her silvery helm and byrnie. The web was fully set now, beaten into its shape by the sword in Hoilogae's hand, he would linger no longer than he must, drawn to her by their need, his way lighted over the sea as hers was lighted through the air by the beacon of the hallowed stone at the firth's edge. Swaebhon was stiff and sore when she arose from her seat on the rock, stretching her arms above her head and stamping on the stone to drive the blood back into her feet. The grainy snowflakes beat harshly against her face, stinging her eyes. As she drew deep life-breaths of the icy air, it seemed to her that she could see shadowed shapes between the alf-cups that pitted the water-darkened stone. The long spear of Wodhanaz in a man's hand, and two wolves running beneath it, Thonaraz's ax lifted high over the hallowed couple below him, the curling prow and stern of a ship. She blinked again, and the shadows on the rock glowed red as the after-image of lightning against the dark backs of her lids, burning within her skull so that she was sure of them. Then she saw only the rough-grained surface of the stone and the melted water that had run to pool in the alf-cups like the blood and ale poured over the gods' rock at the high feasts.

Still, its might thrummed up through Swaebhon's feet, live and strong as the back of a sun-warmed snake. She did not know whether the signs to be carved were meant to bring Hoilogae to her, or to help spread the rock's blessings to the folk, or whether all would be wrought together in one work when the two of them wed upon its face, but she was sure that the holy ones had given her true sight, and it would be the worst of ill luck to gainsay them. She strode back to the hall, flinging the door open and standing between the threshold-posts. The women were chattering with their men, spinning and carving wood. Aiwilimae sat in his high seat, running a whetstone briskly along a bronze arrow-tip, a pile of arrows lay on the table before him.

"Hear me!" Swaebhon cried. Heads turned all about the hall, eyes wide in its dim light as they stared up at her. "I sat at the edge of the firth, on the holy stone, and the gods showed me what they will. Come, you who have skill at stone-chipping. Bring your mallets and chisels, for there is work for you to do, and much must be done to ready the rock before the next folks' blessing."

There was a shuffling as a few of the men slowly rose to their feet, Child-iowulfaz and Ehwastanaz and Arnubernu reaching for their cloaks. No one spoke, but Swaebhon could see the smile beneath her father's beard as he, too, set aside his work and lifted himself from his seat. Such a sign of the holy ones' care gave Aiwilimae's folk clear hope for a good harvest and a light winter, and though men seldom set the knowledge out in words, if the gods turned their faces away too long, it was the fro and his nearest kin who must pay the geld for whatever had been ill-done, just as it was they who led the rites and called the gods' might into the Middle-Garth's ring.

The sound of Wejlunduz's hammer rang through the thunder early the next morning, sparks flew from his smithy door into the rain. Hoilogae drew his sword and wondered at the light twisting through the dark iron along the fair. Had the craftsman in the rock not found it good enough? Or was Wejlunduz seeking, of his own will, to shape something even better than his last work? Whichever, what he had was his, as Swaebhon had promised him. Attalae and Agilaz were back a little after the full moon, their boat riding low under a heavy cargo of full sacks. As they rowed across the lake, Hoilogae marked that Agilaz was doing nearly all of the work, though the shaggy man showed no sign of minding, he was as merry as if he were in the middle of a feast.

"Hai! Alurunon!" Agilaz shouted across the water. "Pry the ale away from that lazy lout so he can help us unload."

Hoilogae set his goblet down carefully on a nearby stone and went to the edge of the water, catching the rope that Attalae flung out and towing the boat in to shore. Although both the wayfarers were looking at the hilt and scabbard at his side, neither of them said anything about it until all of the sacks of grain, flax, and wool were carefully stacked away in the common storehouse behind the huts. Only then did Agilaz say, "Well, let us see if what you've got there was worth all the fuss Wejlunduz was making."

Hoilogae drew his sword, tilting it so that they could see the way the sun's light coiled and uncoiled along the blade. Agilaz drew in his breath in a long, low whistle, Attalae only stared.

"I would not have thought it," the old warrior murmured softly at last. He half-reached out with his hand, as if about to ask if he might heft it, then drew his arm back suddenly to his side. "When do you want to turn homeward and gather the host, then? It is yours to say from now on."

Hoilogae glanced upward at the Sun. She had only begun to ride past the noonday mark, they would have many hours of daylight until the short darkness. "We may as well go as soon as we can. We'll go straight home, when we bring Sigisharjaz's boat back to him, I mean to have own a fine gift to bring with it, to thank him for all his help. Now if Wejlunduz will come out to bid us farewell, I think he would like to look on his work one last time."

"So I would," the smith's singsong voice said from behind him. "I hope to make better in time, but I have not yet." Then he grinned at Hoilogae. "Nor has any other! Swing it, I would see the blade living."

Hoilogae stepped back as he turned to face the smith. He whirled the blade about himself as he had seen men do to awe children. A showy under-and-over stroke past each shoulder, with what he knew somehow was of no use in battle, but one which showed the light on the blade and let its hissing stroke keen through the air. Wejlunduz gazed at it for a long moment, the pride that lit his dark eyes casting shadows of sorrow underneath.

He bent down, plucking the white puff-head of a dandelion and holding it up. "Do that again."

As Hoilogae swung the sword once more, Wejlunduz blew the seeds free. A few of the white threads floated onto its edge, parting before it. The seed-ends tumbled downward, the down-ends floated on, as if touched by no more than the wind.

Suddenly Wejlunduz chopped the knife-edge of his hand through the air between them, as if bringing a chisel down to snap taut-drawn wire. "There it is, then. Fare well, and don't forget to clean it properly and sharpen it only as I showed you how."

"I won't forget."

The women had come out of their huts by this time. Attalae turned away from their gazes, getting into the boat and shifting the food and drink that were left about.

"Fare well, Hoilogae," they said together, and he bade them farewell in turn.

"Wait," Alurunon said as he was about to turn away. "We have something for you. Agilaz, go and get the cask by the door in our house."

Wejlunduz's brother fetched it at once, setting it carefully in the middle of the boat. "That ought to ballast you well enough, and I think it shouldn't be any hard task for you to lighten it when you need to."

"I think not," agreed Hoilogae, he had heard the gurgle as Agilaz moved it, and thought he knew what the cask held. "Thank you."

He pushed off until the water was up to his knees and the boat floated loose, then jumped in and took up his oars, helping Attalae to steer it about. Before they had crossed the lake, they heard the ring of Wejlanduz's hammer again. Agilaz had disappeared, whether into one of the houses or the wood Hoilogae did not know, but three white shapes still stood on the fading shore, heads turned as if staring after the two who rode over the water again.

With the summer well begun, the weather was clear and the faring home smooth. Nine days after they left the steading of Wejlunduz and his brothers, Hoilogae and Attalae were pulling their boat up on the strand Glaszaleunduz. Hoilogae hoisted the cask of ale to his shoulder as Attalae made the boat fast, at the older man's bidding, they had not drunk from it along the way.

"Stay behind me and keep quiet for now," Attalae told him. "There are a few things which must be made ready before we summon the host." He pulled a fold of Hoilogae's tunic out from his belt, arranging it to cover the hilt of the sword.

"Why should I go this way, as if I were no more than..?" Than I was, he thought, but would not say it.

"Because what you have to say will have more might if it is shown all at once, rather than letting men whisper about your weapon before you have a chance to draw it, and because some folk's glances of doubt can steal the strength from a thing. Do you trust me?"

"Attalae," Hoilogae answered. The Little Father hardly anyone called Herwawardhaz's rede-giver by any other name. "I trust you."

He stood still until Attalae was finished with him, then meekly followed the other man up the shore to Herwardaz's hall. Blankets dangled from the branches of the slender ash-tree beside the hall like cloaks draped over a young man's outstretched arms, their shadows wavering softly over the sunlit grass below.

The hall's doors stood open to the mild summer breeze, airing out whatever spoor of winter's sourness might still lie sunk into the wood within. A shift of the wind brought the fresh scent of Sigislinthon's baking wafting over the fire's pale smoke to the two wayfarers a trace of honey sweetening the warm odor of the bread, and they quickened their steps.

The sunlight from the door brightened the back of Sigislinthon's ash-blond head and the braids down her back to true gold. Though she wore only a short cream-colored shift, sweat darkened the hollow between her shoulder blades, beneath the hem, her white legs were slim and firm as a young girl's. She did not stand up or turn around as they came in, only said softly, "Not yet, Hedhinaz, they'll be ready soon."

"Mother, it's me," Hoilogae said, easing his cask of ale to the floor.

Sigislinthon's quickness saved the long-handled baking shovel in her hands from falling into the fire, only the two honey-cakes at the end slid off, one to sizzle into blackness in the flames and one to roll onto the floor. Carefully she put the baking shovel aside and picked up the lost cake, scraping the dust off and putting it back with the others. Only then did she run to her eldest child, embracing him hard enough for him to feel her shaking.

The bronze disk-brooch on her right shoulder dug painfully into Hoilogae's chest just below the nipple, but he did not break the embrace until she pulled away to look at him.

"Did you not think I would come back, then?"

"I didn't know what to think. Only, that I'm glad you are back and safe."

"You knew I wouldn't let him come to any harm, I hope," Attalae said, dry amusement scratching at his voice. Hoilogae did not miss the glance his mother cast at the warrior before answering him, her mouth twisting between fear and relief like a strand of clay between two strong hands, it seemed to him that they had not yet passed out of the night when Attalae had cast his spear at the eagle so that Herwawardhaz might claim his bride.

"You have always been a good warder to those in your keeping," Sigislinthon agreed. "And you've come almost in time for some honey-cakes, if you'll let me finish them." She blinked hard, several times, looking about until Hoilogae quietly pointed to where the baking shovel lay beside the fire. "I must be getting old," she muttered.

Attalae laughed. "You're a long way from it still. Wait until your hair is as white as mine. Have you more baking to do after this?"

"This was the last of it, I thought."

"Do you have meal for a large lot of bread? Hoilogae means to raise the host as soon as he may."

"Meal? Yes." Sigislinthon stood with the baking shovel raised in her hand, looking at her son again. "To march against Hrothamaraz?"

"Yes."

"Do you really think, yes, of course." Her pale eyes flickered aside, "After all of this, how could I ask?" She coughed out a soft laugh. "It will be a fair thing for my father to be avenged."

Attalae said nothing, but Hoilogae thought he could feel the other man's faint stiffening beside him. And how would it be if he and my father had done the slaying, as they meant to? He wondered, but he did not wonder long, for his mother was still speaking. "I'll start the bread baking as soon as I'm done with this, then."

"How long will it take?" Hoilogae asked.

"How much help may I have? When I bake for your father, several women often bake with me, and everyone in our lands knows that the host will be called up before long."

"This is not to be known before it is time for me to speak."

"Then you shall have to wait until close to nightfall."

Hoilogae moved without thinking, going over to put a careful arm around his mother where she stood over the fire. Only when he saw the shock bright on her sweaty face did he think that he had never touched her before, and that she might not care for it. But Sigislinthon let go of her pan's wooden handle with one hand, hugging him in turn for a moment before she went back to moving the tool about, careful that the flames not heat the bronze too long in one spot and sear the cakes above.

It was not long before Hedhinaz's thin shadow dulled the sunlight through the door. "Hai, Mother, are the honey-cakes done?" He called. "It smells as though they might" A gasp cut off his words, as though the butt of a spear had caught him in the throat. He stood staring at his brother, his mouth writhing in silent astonishment, or anger, Hoilogae thought, seeing the way Hedhinaz's eyes gleamed through his own shadow.

He marked that the flesh around his brother's right eye was puffy with dark bruises, and more bruises, some purple and some fading to paler stains of green and yellow against the youth's tanned skin, marred his arms and legs. Hedhinaz had not rested in frith while Hoilogae was away.

"So you're back," Hedhinaz said at last. If his sharp voice was not angry, Hoilogae heard no softness in it either. "Was your alf-dream real?"

Hoilogae twitched back the flap of tunic that Attalae had laid over it, half-drawing the sword from its sheath so that his brother could see the fine patterning Wejlunduz had wrought into it. Hedhinaz leaned closer, his teeth biting his lower lip thin and white.

"Your turn will come," Hoilogae assured him. The words laughed hollowly at him as he spoke them, dull as the slag cast off from Wejlunduz's clay smelting ovens. Nor did Hedhinaz seem to take them any more fairly, though he said nothing except, "It is a very fine blade."

"The honey-cakes are ready now," Sigislinthon told them, straightening up and wiping the sweat from her flushed brow with the back of one hand. "Be careful, they're hot."

Attalae took his cake from the baking shovel and set to eating it at once, with the stolid ease of a man whose fingers were calloused too thickly to feel the heat. Hoilogae and Hedhinaz both had to juggle theirs carefully from hand to hand for a few moments before the sweet buns were cool enough for them to hold. When they were done, Sigislinthon took one for herself and said, "Hedhinaz, I think your father would like a honey-cake as well. Would you mind taking it out to him?"

"Such work is his" Hedhinaz began, gesturing at Hoilogae. His arm dropped like an arrow-felled goose halfway through its arc. Hoilogae's jaw tightened. Even the brightness of his sword had not burned through the memories that veiled him in the sight of his kin.

"No more," Sigislinthon answered. "Go and tell your father all the tidings, but tell him quietly. No one else is to know. Can I trust you?"

"Herwawardhaz gave me my own sword," Hedhinaz answered. Hoilogae could tell that he was doing his best to sound manly, but his voice broke beneath the weight of his words like a thin bough.

"Of course he did. Well. Tell Herwawardhaz that Hoilogae is back, that he has found his iron sword as he said he would, and that he means to call the host up this evening."

"I'll tell him," Hedhinaz said, picking up the honey-cake for his father. He jerked his hand back from the hot bronze paddle quickly, as if it had seared his fingertips, but he made no sound and gave no other sign that he might have been burnt.

Sigislinthon sighed as her younger son left the house. "Be kind to him," she said softly to Hoilogae. "He is not. It is hard for him to find out that he is no longer the chosen one. You must remember this, and be careful of him."

He was not often careful of me, Hoilogae thought, though with little bitterness. Still, he said, "I shall."

"Now tell me about your faring, if you may." Sigislinthon turned to the large clay jars that stood near the fire, heaving one up and pouring a stream of pale meal into the bronze cauldron where she mixed the dough for her baking as well as cooking stews and porridge. Hoilogae and Attalae sat down on the bench beside her, Hoilogae let the older man do most of the talking, only adding a few words of his own now and then.

Although his mother's pale eyes widened now and again, her hands never slowed their work as she mixed and stirred and kneaded the dough, setting each batch aside to rise in its turn and beginning the next. Three long hundreds of loaves, though they might be small ones, were a good number for a single woman to bake between midday and sunset. It was not long before Herwawardhaz came in. Drops of sweat rolled down his forehead, damp circles blackened his gray tunic beneath the armholes, and a dark stain like a long plait of hair spread between his shoulder blades and dribbled down to a point at the small of his back. His bare legs were already brown from the sun, had it not been for the bronze sword at his side, he might have been any farmer resting from the afternoon's work. He walked slowly, staring at Hoilogae as if he were trying to see whether a wyrm's patterned scales warned of an adder or a grass-snake. Hoilogae half-drew his sword again, seeing how the woven light and darkness of its iron drew his father's gaze. Herwawardhaz reached out as if to touch the blade, Hoilogae put his own hand out, palm forward. Herwawardhaz stopped as if his fingers had met a stone wall, drawing his arm back slowly.

"Your rede was more than words of madness." Herwawardhaz's voice rang hollow, but Hoilogae could hear something sparking within it, sharp and bright as a pine-twig beginning to crackle from a banked coal.

"I have proved it, as I said I would," Hoilogae answered, binding the fierce shout that wanted to burst from him into his few soft words. "And more. If we do not move against Hrothamaraz now, he shall surely move against us soon, for he has bought more warriors and iron swords than his land can feed, and they must soon turn on someone."

"From where do you know of this, Hoilogae?" His father whispered through tight-reined lips, his blue eyes wide and pale in the shaft of sunlight that bleached his face to bone and glittered from the droplets of sweat starring his forehead. "Thonaraz and Tiwaz ward us, are you truly my witling son, or some alf-kin out of the mound?"

"Neither witling nor alf," Hoilogae answered, the words bitter as ill-rinsed acorn meal in his mouth. "You need not beat me longer with the silence of my youth. Had I not been still so long, I would never have heard the holy words we need."

Herwawardhaz moved his hand, as if to turn the question away, and stepped out of the door's light. "No, forget that I spoke. If one strange rede is good, so is another like to be, and if the gods have turned against me or the Norns mean ill, there is naught that can be done in any case. Keep baking, Sigislinthon, Hoilogae must call the host when you are done."

Herwawardhaz went quickly out again, his broad shoulders blackening the door-brightness for a moment. Hoilogae stared after him. He had hoped for kinder words, or some sign of pride.

"He sees his own doom in you," Attalae said, his voice so low that Hoilogae thought he alone could hear it. "And he did not await it, he had not thought to be old before Dagar was full-grown."

Hoilogae did not know how to answer, or if he should. But Sigislinthon began to pat together a new batch of bread, and asked whether they had seen Wejlunduz or his brothers bind and loose winds with knots in a rope, as she had heard that the Finns often did, and there was no time to ask the old rede-giver what he had meant.

A pink blush was beginning to stain the clear light, like a few drops of red gold alloyed into the white silver, by the time Sigislinthon lifted the last loaves from the fire and traced the sign of Thonaraz's ax over them to ward off and drive out any ill magic.

Her breaths were coming more quickly, a new brightness shone beneath the dusting of meal on her hair and her face. "Blessed be these loaves for your giving, blessed be the might they give your men for battle. Fro Ingwaz and the Frowe ward the battle-boars and weave your following together behind you, Nerthuz fill you warriors with strength. Thonaraz hallow you, Tiwaz grant you victory." She paused, tilting her head as if she heard something far away. "And may the Ansuz, Father of the Slain, not look ill upon you, but he and his daughters choose death for your foe-men," she whispered at last, her shift rippling in a chill shudder. Sigislinthon traced the four crooked arms of the sun-wheel over the baskets of loaves, then straightened her back and dusted the meal from her hands. She went to the wall where Herwawardhaz's pair of gold-bound aurochs-horns hung, taking them down and giving them to her son.

"Now it is yours to do."

Attalae lifted the baskets in his arms, Hoilogae lifted the cask of ale to his shoulder. Together they went out to Herwamundaz's howe. A few sheep still grazed on top of the howe, but the boy who looked after them now did not sit on the mound, nor rest within its shadow.

"Blow the horn," Attalae said when they had put their burdens down. Hoilogae set the drinking horn on top of the ale-cask and raised the blowing horn to his lips.

Its first tone startled him, moaning deep through the air and shaking through the mound beneath him as though it would rouse Herwamundaz from his long slumber. He cut it off sharply, but the tone still sang in his skull like a draught of rich dark ale, drawing him to crave it again and again. The horn's second note lasted as long as there was breath in Hoilogae's lungs, and by that time the men were running from the fields and from their houses, hurrying to the mound.

By the time the third note had died away, Herwawardhaz stood fully weaponed at the mound's foot, with the swiftest of his thanes around him, their bronze spears shining red as true gold in the slowly lowering light. When the drighten turned his gaze up to his son, his eyes were dark as skull-sockets against his pale face. It seemed to Hoilogae that he could feel Herwawardhaz's trembling in his own limbs, his own body echoing his father's like that of the gilded image in a mirror of polished bronze. He breathed in deeply, looking up at the streaks of pink and gold spreading across the still pale sky. Swaebhon was not to be seen in this peace.

If he was to be the folk-leader, he must do it with what she had given him already. He waited until all the men of his village were gathered before him and the low green rolling of the hills around glinted bronze sparks with the hurrying of the warriors from west and south-west. Then he was about to speak, but Herwawardhaz spoke before him.

"Why have you called us here, Arnulita? Why do you stand on my grandfather's mound and break his stillness? What foe threatens us, or what is to be won?"

"I have not called you here," Attalae answered. "It is Hoilogae, your son, who blew the horn, it is he who has called the host together."

Hoilogae had known too little to await anything, thus the spurt of high laughter from amid the throng, bursting into a wave of mirth, did not surprise him. But even as his face heated, his entrails knotted iron-cold with anger, stilling his throat for a moment.

"It's half a moon too early for the Midsummer's jesting to start, Attalae," Ingwagairaz shouted. "Have you been into the ale?"

"Hoilogae!" Someone else called, laughing. "You look like a hof-ox, where are your gilded horns?"

The laughter swelled as more men came panting to the edges of the throng and the words "Hoilogae summoned the host" Rippled outward to them.

Hoilogae stepped forward and drew his sword. "Silence!" He shouted, his voice cutting keenly through all the laughter. "You dare to laugh at me, do any of you dare to fight me?"

The icy shock of silence fell over the host, they stared at him, and Hoilogae marked more than one man clutching at the amber ax-sign of Thonaraz or bronze spear-sign of Tiwaz around his neck.

"Now hear my words! Hrothamaraz holds lands that are rightfully my mother's, your frowe Sigislinthon waits for her father's vengeance. The time for sitting by the fire is over. I say that we must rise and march against him, to win those lands and riches back. Will you follow me?"

The men looked at one another, tugging at cloaks or shifting their grips on their weapons. Hrothamaraz stared straight ahead at the mound-grass before him, his grasp frozen to his spear and feet to the ground. No one met Hoilogae's eyes.

"Will you follow me?" Hoilogae asked again. "Are you afraid?"

"Afraid of troll-craft, yes!" Thonarabernu answered, still not raising his gaze to the top of the mound. The burly man spat on the earth between himself and Hoilogae. "You have the shape of a witling, but you are not he, and you have our wisest man in your thrall."

"If we go against Hrothamaraz, we'll be slaughtered," Hrothirikaz added. "There are many wights that love the blood of battle-slain men walkurjons and wolves, trolls and more. How do we know this isn't a trap to bring us to our deaths?"

Hoilogae did not know how to answer, and as he stood silent more whispers sprang up, rippling through the men like frosty breezes through fresh grain-shoots. "Don't look at his eyes, no human, troll-crafted blade. Thonaraz ward us."

"Will you believe it if the gods themselves show you the truth?" Attalae demanded at last. He had to shout his words three times before the rising swell of muttering sank back into stillness again.

"How?" Thonarabernu asked. Holding to the amber ax at his throat, he glanced about as if he thought to see some sign before him.

"Let us put the question of the battle to the test by slaying one of the holy horses, and let Hoilogae be the one to hold the reins. Then the gods may show you how to trust him, for the horses will bear nothing unholy near them, and the signs of its slaying shall show us what to await from Hroth-amaraz's host."

"It has been many years since this was done last," Herwawardhaz said slowly. "If the matter is not worthy, we shall bring the wrath of the gods by scathing their stallion."

"There has not been a greater matter among us while we have lived," Attalae answered. "If we win through, only Sigisharjaz shall be like to us, if we do not, none of our men shall see another harvest. What more is there? Who can speak against this?"

Although Hoilogae heard the rustling of boots shuffling through grass as men shifted their weight and moved about uneasily, no one spoke.

"Come, Hoilogae," Attalae said softly. He straightened his back and strode down the mound. Hoilogae followed him, but did not sheath his sword, he could feel the fear of the men behind him, cold as a spear-point sped by winter's winds.

Most of the time, only Attalae, Herwawardhaz, and Sigislinthon were allowed to tread between the stones that marked the borders of the grove where the holy horses grazed. Only in times of strife, when the neighing of the horses, the shaking of their heads and stamping of their feet, gave signs for the whole folk, might anyone else pass within the grove. Thus it was now, the men moved very slowly, as if bound by hidden fetters, each treading without a single mis-step on the narrow way between the trees. Oak, ash, and elm cast dark twilight shadows through the grove, misting the white shapes of the horses moving between the trees and across the grass of the clearing in the middle of the hallowed wood.

They were not tamed or broken, these horses were set aside for the gods and goddesses alone, and given worship for their wisdom. Hoilogae hefted the reins and bridle that Attalae had taken out of the hof for him. He could feel the might of the gods thrumming through the silent grove. At first it seemed to him that a few steps along the right way would take him wholly from the Middle-Garth and into the garth where the holy ones dwelt. Then he knew that they dwelt in this place, though his eyes were not yet keen enough to see more than the faint shape of shadow standing tall and dark on the gray slab of stone that slanted down between two ash-trees. Across the clearing, the great white stallion raised his head and neighed, his voice running down the back of Hoilogae's spine with the clean cold pain of ice.

Hoilogae lifted his face to meet the dark gaze of the horse. When their eyes met, he felt as though a taut rope had been flung between them, binding and drawing them closer together. The stallion stood quite still, letting Hoilogae walk up to him. His dark eye seemed to deepen into a well of whirling black water as the man drew nearer. Hoilogae's breath came more slowly, as though water filled his chest instead of air, he was growing dizzy, gleams of unseen light sparkling through the twilight shadows around him. He felt himself beginning to stagger, as though a mighty wind blew against him and clenched his teeth, summoning all his will to hold himself upright. The hilt of his sword bit cold into the palm of his hand, steadying him. Then it seemed that he saw the glimmering shape on the stallion's back the long-haired maid, her ice-gray eyes gazing into his. "Stay with me," he breathed.

Swaebhon stroked the horse's white mane, and it seemed to Hoilogae that he could feel her touch on his own hair. "Hoilogae," she murmured, "Let the gods see your strength in the hallowed gift. Win through blood and death to me." Then she was gone. Only a shimmer of bright tears lightened Hoilogae's eyes as he looked up to where she had been. Hoilogae and the stallion stood staring at each other for another moment before the horse lowered his head for Hoilogae to bridle. Side by side they walked from the grove, the host following them out in silence. No blood could be shed in there, for the place would no longer be holy afterward. Living gifts to the gods were given elsewhere.

The gold-horned cattle and Yule boar were slain at the hof, in another place among the trees, those who had done ill were lifted from the earth and pierced with spears to still the Ansuz's wrath, but other sacrifices were made farther from the village, by the shore of a shallow, boggy lake, and it was to this place that Hoilogae led the host. Although the light lasted for a long time in the summer, blood stained the pale gold sky-banners and their mirrored lake-glow now, and the eastern blue was deepening. Still, there was enough light to see the stunned numbness on Herwawardhaz's face as he stepped before Hoilogae and the hallowed stallion.

"Tiwaz, Fro Ingwaz, mighty horse-gods!" He called. His voice was not loud, but there was no other sound to deafen the ear to it. "You have ridden this stallion, well you know him. Now he rides to dwell wholly within your lands. Let his death show us your favor for a battle with Hrothamaraz show victory or death for its slayers. Ansuz, look not ill upon us, for we give your steed wholly to you, we scathe it not lightly, and with no ill-will. Thonaraz, hallow this work!"

Herwawardhaz stepped back, and Hoilogae tightened his grip upon the reins, bracing himself against the strength of the earth beneath his feet. "Now!" Attalae cried, and the host drew their weapons and began to circle.

The stallion also shifted, but Hoilogae held him fast, unshaken even when Thonarabernu stepped forward and the horse reared to strike at him. Hoilogae yanked down hard on the reins, drawing his head into the path of Thonarabernu's ax. The blade glanced off the stallion's skull, a trail of dark blood scattered from his white forehead behind its glittering path. The stallion's lunge almost wrenched the reins from Hoilogae's hands, he did not know how he held to the fighting steed as the host closed in. He saw one man fall beneath a hoof's blow as the stallion reared again, heard the thudding grunt behind him as the horse's back-kick dropped another. The holy stallion's white coat was swiftly streaked with black, one rib jutted through the blood like a pale spear of broken bone. His head was more dark than bright with wounds, but he still rose and kicked, straining against the reins that bound him to Hoilogae.

He would not fall, but, blackened with his blood, fought like a fierce shadow of the fair steed that had grazed in the grove. He could not hold for ever, as his life flowed onto the soft earth, the men closed in again and again, beating him down till he could not rear on broken legs, till at last Hoilogae could no longer pull him upright by the reins, but had to let his corpse drop to the ground. Without speaking, Attalae, Herwawardhaz, and Thonarabernu came forward. Hoilogae bent with them to lift the stallion's weight. They walked out into the boggy lake until their feet began to sink dangerously into the soft mud beneath them, then eased the body of the gods' gift into the water where the holy ones would take it in their time.

"Will you follow me now?" Hoilogae said when they had come back to shore.

"We will!" Thonarabernu answered, half a word before the rest of the host roared, "We will!"

They surged forward, Hoilogae felt himself lifted from his feet, onto the hard seat of a shield, as his father's men bore him back to the mound, shouting and cheering. They set him down at the foot, letting him walk up to the crown himself.

"Will you drink my ale and take my loaves, and hold me for your drighten till the battle is done?"

"We will!" They shouted. Hoilogae filled the drinking horn from his keg and took up one of the loaf-baskets.

Attalae was first up the mound, first to take a sip from the horn and to get a loaf from Hoilogae's hand. After him came Herwawardhaz, then Thonarabernu, Ingwiawaldaz, Laithingaz, Dagastiz, all the men of the three villages. Hoilogae did not know all their names. Hedhinaz, too, came up at the last, though the twist of his mouth said that the ale and loaf did not taste as sweet to him as to the others.

"Tomorrow we fare," said Hoilogae, and was answered by a cry of "Tomorrow!"

CHAPTER VIII

The pale light of dawn through the smoke hole was the first thing Hailgi saw when he opened his eyes. Ingwibjorg lay sprawled out with her arms flung to either side over the blanket, her mouth open in soft snoring, Gunthahildar was curled on her side with her thumb in her mouth. Audhar also slept on her side, her face turned towards the wall. Hailgi reached over to caress Ingwibjorg's breast. He could feel her nipple hardening beneath the thin linen of her sleeping shift, and moved closer to her. Ingwibjorg stirred a little in her sleep, shifting away from him and mumbling something that he couldn't quite make out. He stroked her hair softly until she moved her head away, then crept out from beneath the blankets. The cool morning air was heavy with old smoke and stale sleep, Hailgi coughed softly once, smothering the low sound with his hand. Now that day had come, he knew he ought to lie low until Hunding's men were gone, but his throat was aching for the taste of fresh air as badly as his bladder ached for easing. They will still be sleeping, he told himself, I heard them shouting until late into the night.

Despite his words to himself, a few men were starting to awaken in the hall. Hailgi hurried past them as swiftly as he dared, turning his face away. He hoped that Lingwe still slept, he hoped that he had forgotten their quarrel, for it would have been too bitter to him to be unmasked by the son of Hunding. The village outside seemed almost empty, gloomy and still in the gray light as if a sickness had stricken it overnight. Only one of Hagalar's thanes, Gleaugir, stood outside pissing against the wall. Seeing the keen-eyed gaze the warrior turned on him as he passed, Hailgi walked faster, almost running towards the shelter of the woods where he could loose his own bladder unseen.

As he sped up, Hailgi's skirts twined between his legs, tangling in his step before he could stop himself. He fell heavily to the ground with a sharp grunt of "Shit!"

Gleaugir's lanky legs brought him to Hailgi's side before the youth could get to his feet again. The thane stood staring down at him for a few moments. Then a raucous burst of laughter snorted out through his beak-like nose. "Hailgi! Are you going to meet a lover? Who is he, then?"

Hailgi grasped two fistfuls of earth, gripping hard enough to rip the grass free by its roots. When he thought he could speak again, he said "If you tell anyone, I'll kill you," trying hard to keep his voice low and even. Carefully he pulled his skirts out of the way and got to his feet.

Gleaugir only laughed harder. "You look more fit to take a sword than to stab with one," he answered, making a gesture that Hailgi could not mistake. Hailgi reached without thinking for the weapon that was not at his belt, angry at himself for forgetting, angrier with Gleaugir, he leapt at the other man.

Taken by surprise, Gleaugir stumbled back a few paces, barely getting his hands up in time to fend off Hailgi's lunge for his throat and catch the youth's wrists. The two of them wrestled back and forth for a few moments, Gleaugir's reach and weight against Hailgi's agility and anger. Neither had much advantage, and at last Hailgi's temper began to cool.

"Look," he said softly, still bracing his grip against Gleaugir's long arms, "I'll take this up with you when Hunding's sons are gone. The drighten told me to hide from them in this manner, I don't think he'd like it if you spoiled his plan for the sake of laughing at me."

Slowly Gleaugir lowered his arms. "All right," he murmured back. "But you'll have a lot to answer for when they're gone. It's hardly a man's deed to put on skirts for fear of a foe I name it ergi, as much as if you'd let Lingwe bed you."

"Later," Hailgi said.

He began to walk, Gleaugir stretched his long legs, hurrying around to block the way. The thane leaned down, closely enough for Hailgi to see the red pimples on his forehead through the strands of his loose black hair. "You'd better be glad Thonarastainar had no kinsmen in this hall," he muttered. Soft as his voice was, Hailgi could hear the edges of his teeth in it. "If it weren't for you, he'd be alive now."

"If you want were-gild, take it up with Lingwe," Hailgi answered. Even as he spoke, he could feel the cold mouth of guilt sucking strength from his limbs, he was shaking as though he had vomited himself past emptiness. Still, he walked away to the woods as proudly as he could between the aching of his strained bladder and his care not to trip over his clothing again.

He had no right to say that to me, Hailgi told himself as he walked, and the glowing coal of anger began to bring his might back to him. What does he know? It was Thonarastainar's own words that killed him, and Gleaugir dares to use worse ones to me! As Hailgi walked and thought, his blood seethed within him, so that even when he had gotten far away to feel safe in lifting his skirts, it was some time before he could loose the hot tide of piss bound up in his body, and the stream's pattern wavered on the beech's smooth gray bark. Once eased, he felt better, his hands no longer trembled so badly as he arranged his clothing again, and the knotted muscles of his belly began to loosen. Still, he waited on the edge of the wood longer than he might have, glancing about to see that he was not watched before he darted back to the hall. The thick fog of smells within. Old food and smoke, dogs and unwashed men, stuffed Hailgi's nose numb within a few breaths, by the time he had scuttled halfway down the hall, he marked them no longer.

He flung himself into the women's chamber like a wolf fleeing to his den from a pack of hounds, turning as he passed the doorway to be sure that no eyes had followed him.

Audhar yawned, rolling over and sitting up with her knees to her chest. "What's wrong with you?" She muttered sleepily. "Be quiet and let the girls sleep a little longer. Anyone would think you were still playing games. I suppose you want me to bring your breakfast to you, too. They stirring in there yet?"

Audhar stumped out of the room, mumbling about her knees all the way. Hailgi waited until the door had closed behind her, then crawled under the covers next to Ingwibjorg, fitting his body into the hollow his weight had crushed into the straw during the night, where a little warmth still lingered. Although he closed his eyes, their lids did not shut the light from his thoughts. He still saw the blood-dark steel sticking out beneath Thonarastainar's beard. It had been a good stroke, the man had died quickly, but it was not hard for Hailgi to feel the cold iron slicing through his own bowels, slitting his lungs and choking through his throat. And it was for me, he thought. If I had not, if I were not so, but Wyrd weaves as she will, he answered, and if I were not as I am, I should be someone else, with a different doom. If I did not have a warrior's mood, I should be no warrior. If I were not and suddenly he remembered the face he had seen in the mirror, the face that went with the name of Sigiruna. Sigiruna the daughter of Haganon is known to me, you have her look, but I had not heard that a walkurja could be made a thrall-maiden so easily. Hailgi did not open his eyes, but a shudder of excitement ran through his body. I was not dreaming, I am not mad, he told himself.

I did see. The face that was almost his own was clear in the mirror of his mind, keen blue-gray eyes and pale hair glowing in his skull-darkness, but unbidden, the memory of the wolf-riding woman with the dark stains about her mouth shadowed there as well. He could feel himself trembling again, though not with fear, his manhood was stiffening against his skirt. It seemed to him that if he did not act soon, he would be torn apart by the cross-winds of feeling that had blown harder and harder through him since he had put on the woman's garb, but he did not know what he might do. It seemed to him that it would be no help to ask for Ingwibjorg's touch again, that spilling his seed would only madden him further. Sigiruna, Sigiruna, Hailgi thought, who are you? What have you done to me? He lay without moving, staring into the darkness behind his eyelids for what seemed like a very long time, till the pounding of his blood through his body quieted, till he could hear the sounds of Gunthahildar getting up and Ingwibjorg's grumble of..."*Lemme sleep, Frija curse it!*"

Hailgi raised his head, but Gunthahildar shook her finger at him. "You, stay where you are. I'll go see if breakfast is ready yet. You, Ingwibjorg, you ought to get up. The sooner we can get those pigs from Hunding's hall fed, the sooner we can get them out of here."

Ingwibjorg sat up, clutching the blankets around her with one hand and rubbing her eyes with the other. "I'm all for that. I'll wager you a gold ring my arse is black and blue from last night. You'd think we were thrall-maidens, the way they acted."

"None of our men would ever behave that way to a drighten's daughter," Gunthahildar agreed. "Then, Hunding's only got sons, and his wife's been dead a while, so there's no one to teach them any better. What can you expect when a bunch of men are used to feasting together? There's not a man alive who's anything but a bear with an ale-horn, no matter what they may say."

Ingwibjorg snorted, nodding. Hailgi still said nothing, but he thought that Sigiruna, whoever she might be, would thole the handling Hunding's men had dealt out no better than he himself had. Ingwibjorg and Gunthahildar went out, Hailgi stayed in the women's chamber, waiting until Ingwibjorg came back with a bowl of porridge and a warm mug of fresh milk for him.

"They ought to be leaving soon," she told him. "I heard Blindi saying that he thought they had a few days, but that they should be home before Hunding got back to find his hall empty and his men chasing a ghost."

"Good," Hailgi said with his mouth full. He swallowed, coughed to clear his sticky throat. "Does that mean they've given up on me?"

"I think so."

Hailgi waited in the women's chambers until a little after midmorning, listening to the rumble of talk and the sound of Hunding's men gathering themselves to leave. Even when they had left the hall, he did not leave his place nor make a move towards changing his clothes, he thought that Blindi might well have readied a ruse to draw him out.

He stayed in the women's chamber until Gunthahildar came scampering back to tell him that the sons of Hunding had ridden past Hagalar's marches again. Then he gratefully pulled his breeches up beneath his skirt again, casting off shift and skirt and Wulfrun's tunic and pulling on his own. Though finely woven, the wool felt scratchy against his thighs and buttocks, oddly binding between his legs. But the weight of his sword at his side helped to steady him, its ring-hilt comfortably smooth beneath his palm. Swiftly he bound his hair into the warrior's knot at the side of his head again, pulling the amber strands tight against his skull.

"Can I help you?" Ingwibjorg asked. Hailgi turned to look at her. The memory of her touch was still uncomfortably warm on his body, but her eyes were open and guileless as clear pools. Suddenly he wanted to speak to her of what had taken place between them, but he could not. Her hand reaching for the manhood beneath his skirts was something that could not be spoken of in plain words, and so had not been. The crevasse of the last two days was narrow enough, but it dropped down too far for any of their eyes to see what lay in its depths.

"I'm all right."

Hailgi shook himself like a dog shaking off water, then straightened his tunic and shifted his belt so that his sword lay more easily against his thigh. It felt strange, stepping out into the hall in his man's garb, he felt as much an impostor as he had in the women's clothing. Only the women were there. Audhar was sweeping up the filthy straw, the rest of them strewing fresh straw and sweet herbs. The clean scents as Wulfrun crushed the leaves in her hands and scattered them around were already driving out the stale smells like wind clearing away the morning fog.

"Hai, so you're back, Hailgi," Wulfrun said, smiling at him warmly. "You missed all the excitement."

"Did I? I was out hunting."

"Did you catch anything?"

"I didn't get caught, at least, although I heard the baying of hounds close to me once or twice."

"Good enough," Wulfrun said. She patted him on the shoulder with a balm- and rosemary-scented hand. "Go on with you, then. This is women's work in here."

The sky had cleared to a hard blue, the sharp wind herding a few gray-fleeced clouds across it. Sunna's light was harsh against Hailgi's eyes, the wind rough on his face, he felt as though he had been flayed, so that the rustling of the leaves rasped against his ears and the sight of the gilded fields and orange-touched rowan berries struck through his skull. Though harvest had not yet started, the cold came through Hailgi's cloak as if it were an ill-chinked wall.

He raised his chin, turning towards the sound of men's voices down by the practice fields. He could feel the muscles tightening through his shoulders and down his back, as if his flesh were forging itself into a byrnie against whatever they might say to him, his face tightened into the iron mask of a helm. I shall not flinch, he whispered fiercely to himself. I shall face them as a man ought. The hollow sounds of wooden sword beating on wooden shields stilled as he strode down towards the grassy sward where the thanes practiced their fighting. Although he had clenched his heart to firmness, the first gust of laughter beat against him like a high wave striking a boat. Still, he did not falter until he was down among them, nor did he stop walking until he saw all the thanes ringed around him. Gleaugir and Aiwimundar, Thurir and Leugar, Thonaraharjar and Fastawulfar, the curly-haired brothers Angantiwar and Athawulfar, who had most often been on Hailgi's side in ball-games and mock battles alike, all the men who were there had laid down their weapons and come to watch. Hailgi had thought some of them his friends and none his foes, but now they had him at bay. Aiwimundar's scar-split mouth was drawn into a smile, his broken teeth gleaming like brown-glazed pottery, grim as Gleaugir's face was, his dark eyes glittered with unkind glee. Hagalar was not there, and Hailgi did not know where he might be, whether he had chosen to leave his foster-son to the war band or whether he simply did not know what was about to happen. This is not fair, this is too much! He cried out silently to the drighten who was not there. I did not earn this!

But he was here, and Leugar, who thought himself a skop, was already speaking, chanting his shameful verse in a sharp voice that ill-fitted his burly body,

"Methinks a manrode mare by night,
swiftly she trotsand swishes her tail.
Why are you here? Wish you another?
could Hunding's sonnot help your lust?"

Leugar stepped back out of reach as Hailgi whirled on him, his grin pulling his ruddy-cheeked face into a mockery of goodwill. "You'll find fights easier to start when you put your skirts back on, little walkurja. Those breeches don't become you at all, a woman's heart should be clad in woman's weeds."

As Hailgi flung himself at Leugar, hard hands seized him from behind and held him back. His arms pinned, he kicked backward, stamping down along a shin, and wrenched himself free as his attacker grunted with pain. At once he turned and struck, flesh giving way beneath his sharp knuckles, he struck again, but Hlauthwigar had already limped swiftly out of reach, holding his side and muttering to himself. Hailgi felt his lips pulling back from his teeth. They would not be so swift to make free with his body, whatever they said. No one had ever called him a poor fighter, and his rage had risen to drown out any fear or pain.

"Why so angry?" Thonaraharjar called from the other side of the circle. His blue eyes were open as wide as if he sought to make a maiden believe the truth of his words, they looked very pale against his tanned face. "Is Leugar too old a swain for you? Or is his word-craft too clumsy? I have a better verse, here.

Necklace-Freyjafriend to all men
in woods of your homeween I to find
for my thrust-steelforge most hot,
to soften by strikingman's strong, hard blade."

Some of the men laughed at once, it took others a moment to work the verse out. It took Hailgi no time at all, he was already running for Thonaraharjar, who dodged nimbly behind one man and then another as they shifted around to keep Hailgi ringed in.

"Are you afraid of me, then?" He called out harshly. "You mock easily, don't you have the heart to back up your words?"

"'The bravest man may fear woman's wrath,'" answered Thonaraharjar. "Come, walkurja, what hero have you chosen, for me to please you so ill?"

"You know little about wooing women," Aiwimundar told him. "Though I am old and my head is balding, I know what pleases them better than you. From atheling-frowes to thrall-maidens, they are all kin to the goddess who bought Brisingamen." The thane pushed his stained yellow sleeve back to show the gold ring spiraling around his hairy forearm, a glittering serpent winding its fairness four times around the ugly gnarling of his muscles.

He stepped forward till he was only two arms lengths from Hailgi, then pulled the ring from his arm. "Come, my sweet, I have a ring to soothe your mood, and a ring can easily bring frith between men and women, as you may have found already."

Hailgi drew his sword and sliced down. Aiwimundar leapt back in time to save his hand, but the sword's tip cut through the first ring of the spiral and stuck fast halfway through the second. Hailgi swung it back past his shoulder, then down again, flinging the gold ring off the blade and straight into Aiwimundar's face. It struck the thane across nose and mouth with a crunch, splitting his lips so that blood started forth, running down into his grizzled beard.

As Aiwimundar cursed and wiped his mouth with his sleeve, Thonaraharjar hooted with laughter. "Will you give me more rede on wooing?" He asked. "I think my word-craft was more pleasing to her, or else an old man needs more gold than that to bring a young maid joy."

His blade still out, Hailgi rounded upon Thonaraharjar. The sword's tip wavered a little, casting out the Sun's mirrored brightness like light on rippling water. Though a few men still laughed, the sound was thin as ale watered with snow melt at winter's end.

"Now take back your verse," Hailgi said. The draught of strong rage seething through his veins unsteadied his words, his lips and tongue felt numb, but his head was clear with the sharp sight of the sword-thrusts to come. "Take it back, or you will never speak another unless your flesh speaks in the bale fire's sizzling."

"What are you doing?" Hagalar's voice boomed suddenly from behind Hailgi. "All of you! What has come upon you? Hailgi, as you owe me a fosters honor, put down your sword!"

Hailgi lowered his blade, slowly turning to face his foster-father. Hagalar's pale blue cloak was askew across his shoulders, the Sun's brightness made fine steel from the silvering through his hair, and a few droplets of sweat gleamed crystalline from the crevasses in his forehead. The drighten was breathing hard, he must have run down from the hall, Hailgi thought.

"What honor can he give?" Gleaugir shouted, his voice brittle as iron ground too thin. "He has worn a woman's clothes to hide from his foe, and that is ergi, he has no place with us."

Hagalar stood for a moment before he answered, gathering his breath. Slowly he straightened his cloak, as if he had all the time he could wish. "It was my rede that he hide himself from Hunding's sons, that I not be forced to send him away in shame. I do not wish to know which of you saw through his guise, but it were better for all of us if you had not, or, if seeing, you had been wise enough to keep silence."

Gleaugir did not turn his eyes away until Hagalar's gaze left him, but then he stared angrily down at the ground, and Hailgi saw the flush darkening his pockmarked cheeks. "What's done is done," he muttered angrily. "I think you did him no kindness, he will have to leave this hall in shame now, or else go back to spinning with the women."

"I say, that he shall not. He is my foster-son, and has a year to bide here before I send him home to Sigismundar. Do you wish to soil our honor by breaking my oaths for me?"

"Hagalar," Thurir said softly. "Listen to me."

Thurir spoke seldom, though his hollow-cheeked face was seldom missing when difficult matters were spoken of. His quiet voice was not often heard when men spoke loudly, but when it was, men often thought his redes fairer than those of others. So now Hagalar asked him only, "What do you have to say, then?"

"Some blame is yours, for giving Hailgi such an ill counsel, but more is his for following it willingly. Nothing would shame us more than claiming as a shield-fellow one who dressed as a woman out of fear, his ergi can bring us no luck, but the shame he has won by it would fall upon all of us. I shall bring the tidings to Sigismundar myself, if no one else will. Greatly as it may grieve him, he can get more sons, but if we lose our luck by this, it shall not be so easy to get again."

"What is your rede, then?"

Thurir said only, "He cannot live among us. Cowardice is not fit to be shown in the light of day," and Hailgi heard the mutterings behind him, rising like a slow tide of peat-black water. "In older times" "Not so long ago" "Our fathers knew how to."

"He is my foster-son. Neither I nor you may raise hand against him," Hagalar said firmly, and as he spoke, Hailgi heard a howling in his head over the drighten's voice, a woman's high call fading in and out of the wolf's song. *Only one bride-gift can win you the walkurja but soon you must avenge your shame, or she will be lost to you.*

He did not listen to the words spoken after that, Sigiruna's mirrored shadow was before his mind, and his heart battered at his ribs in desperation, for he knew that the mirror was about to slip from his grasp and he did not know how to hold it fast. *Avenge my shame on whom?* His glance fell first on Hagalar, whose mouth was still moving, though Hailgi could no longer hear him, his foster-father's blood would only add the nith of oath-breaking to that of ergi. Nor was Thurir at fault, though no distress seemed to stir his quiet ease at the thought of giving Hailgi to the bog. There stood Thonar-aharjar, quiet now, his sun streaked brown hair falling over his shoulders, he had not thought beyond a moment's mirth, nor had he been the one to bring Hailgi's shame on him. Nor Gleaugir, though his keen eyes had seen through Hailgi's guise, he was far from its root, Hailgi's own folly was closer, but he could hardly cry revenge self on self. It seemed to Hailgi that he could see the depths stretching further back, to the first clash between his father's men and Hunding's, when Hunding had first slain his father's brother's son Guthmundar.

What but that had brought him to Hagalar's hall? What but the fear of being grist ground between two stones had given the drighten's shameful rede to Hailgi? At last, he knew his foe, and the knowledge unfettered the strength of his arm till the sword no longer weighted it, but was light in his hand as a shaft of sun through the mist. Hailgi whirled, swinging his sword, and began to run down to the shore. Hagalar's thanes sheared away from him before he came near. He heard the shouting now, though it was only a far-off echo roaring through his ear-caves.

Now over grass, now over stones, the sand slowed him, but only a little. None of the men had come near him by the time he was splashing through the knee-high surf, no one was close enough to catch hold of him before he stumbled into the deeper water, nor to stop him before he swung himself up and over the side of the warship that floated by the shore, rope-moored to a great boulder, and heaved the anchor up with a sudden surge of strength. He stood with one foot on the headless prow, his sword held ready to swing down and cut the bond that held ship to land.

Hagalar was in the lead of the pack that stopped on the shore, staring at Hailgi.

"Hagalar!" Hailgi shouted. "What is your oath to my father worth?"

"How can you ask that?" Hagalar's care-creased face was white as if with pain, his eyes squinting shut against the Sun's light as he looked up at Hailgi. "Sheath your sword. None of my men will harm you, I give you my oath on that they must slay me before they slay you."

"Only one deed will clean my name, only when Hunding is dead can I be free of this nith! Now let all the men who stand on the shore sail with me, and we shall meet Hunding and his warriors as they come back from Anu-laibhar's hall, and then I shall win free of what my folly and your rede have bound upon me."

"We can pull him down from there!" Aiwimundar broke in hotly. "Hagalar, only give us leave, and we shall take him, even if he breaks the mooring, he cannot row out to deep water by himself."

"Yes, shame your drighten and break his oath for him!" Hailgi answered him. "How will you take me without harming me? I will kill Hunding and whoever seeks to keep me from him, or I will die. True, I will find it difficult to row this ship by myself, but if you do not come with me, I shall do as best I can, and if I fail, my death shall be upon your heads."

"You think we'll follow you?" Gleaugir cried.

"Hagalar! You granted that Lingwe was right to slay Thonarastainar for saying that he would be fit for wearing a woman's clothes. What claim do I have against you, who put them on me?"

"Gleaugir, be still," Hagalar said heavily as the angry thane drew breath to speak again. For the first time since Hailgi had known him, the drighten looked down from his foster-son's gaze, casting his glance over the pebbles on the beach as though seeking for amber's gold among the smooth gray sea-stones.

"A very great claim," Hagalar admitted at last. "I can not deny you whatever you should ask of me. Your shame must also be mine, for it was my fear of two mighty men that led me to twist those ropes upon you."

Hagalar turned his back to Hailgi, facing the thanes. Though he did not speak loudly, the water carried his voice so clearly that Hailgi might have been standing at his right hand.

"If you are still my men, who have taken my rings and drunk my ale. If all of this has not turned you from me then gather your weapons and byrnies and food for the voyage, and be back here as soon as you can. Nor shall you say anything to anyone who is not here now, we must go swiftly and without warning. The fight I gathered you to wait has come sooner than I weened, but Wyrd cannot be gainsaid." His next words were less clear, for he mumbled them through his teeth, but he seemed to say, "Least of all when she turns about one such as Hailgi."

Only Thurir did not hurry away, but stood looking gravely at his drighten. Before he could speak, Hailgi called out, "Thurir! You will not come with us, but you offered to go to my father. Now ride to him as swiftly as you may, and let him know all the tidings, and bid him to Hagalar's hall, for Hunding's sons may be expected to raise their host when they hear their father is dead, and without his help there is little hope."

"All the tidings, Hailgi?"

"All that you think fit for him to hear. You were swift enough to say what you thought not long ago."

"I shall tell him what he needs to hear," Thurir answered. "Though Wodhanar is called the Swift-Changer, it seems to me that you have a right to the name as well."

By the time he had stridden up the beach, Hailgi still did not know whether he had been insulted or given an honor, but then only Hagalar stood before him.

The drighten walked to the edge of the water, his boots leaving prints of damp sand through the salty ale-froth the waves had left on the shore. "Shall I come with you as well?"

"Stay here. No one must guess what is to happen, you must hold your hall as you have always done."

"You have left me more than I might have looked for," Hagalar murmured. For a moment it seemed as though he might say something more, he stood with his gaze turned up past Hailgi towards the sky, his eyes mirroring the blue like still puddles. But then he, too, went away, leaving Hailgi to stand alone at the boat's prow, his own breathing sounding harsh above the beating of the waves in his ears.

The carven dragon-head lay on its side across the two fore-benches, taken from its socketed stand while the ship was still at sea, lest it anger or frighten the land-wights and so end the luck of Hagalar's rule. One red-ochre eye stared flatly at the sky, its ruddy rings of eye and iris and pupil set apart by thin circles of black. Its gaze was dull as a dead thing's, though it was said that the wyrm could see the way through the waters and guide the ship to its prey. As a swell rocked the ship, Hailgi's knees bent suddenly, so that he sat down on the bench beside the dragon's head. Hardly thinking about it, but drawn by the soft sheen of the carving, he began to run his fingers over the smooth wood of its diamond-shaped scales, tracing the red-painted grooves that ran between them. The turning of the even lines, slanting across each other in two neat rows of parallels, slowly began to steady his hands.

They hardly shook at all by the time Angantiwar and Athalwulfar, burdened with byrnies and sacks of food, were splashing through the waves towards him. The other thanes were strung out across the beach and the greensward above, bearing their gear steadily towards the ship, if they did not hurry as eagerly as Hailgi had seen them do in some times before, at least few of them were dragging their feet. Hailgi took the sword from the bench beside him. He sheathed it, but his hand did not leave the hilt until Athalwulfar called, "Hai, you could help us up here, Hailgi! This stuff's heavy, and we've got your things as well." Then he bent over the side, reaching down to grasp the other youth's sinewy hand and helping him to heave himself up. Though Athawulfar smiled brightly at him, as if to say that nothing had happened, the strain of it trembled in his lips beneath the scanty hairs of his beard and mustache. Hailgi showed his teeth in return, Athawulfar did not quite sigh in relief, but a long breath came out of him as he eased his sack to one of the benches. The two of them helped his heavier brother up together. Angantiwar's smile at Hailgi only lasted a moment, and he did not look into Hailgi's eyes.

But he had not refused the help offered, nor shunned Hailgi's touch, and that, Hailgi thought, must be counted as a beginning. By ones and twos, the other thanes made their way through the water and into the boat. Gleaugir and Aiwimundar were last, they did not let Hailgi help them, but grimly pulled themselves up over the side. Hailgi saw that Aiwimundar had not scorned to pick up the arm ring he had sheared through. Three coils twisted about the old thane's right wrist, a single ring was bent about his left. He fore bore to say anything about it, but it seemed to him that he had not done so ill there. Hailgi waited until each of the men had taken his place by an oar. Then he stepped up to the prow again, drew his sword, and cut through the rope. The next swell lifted the boat from its place. Hagalar's men knew their work well, for this too was a part of war, the oars dug into the water, and the ship began to turn as the waves bore it out to sea. When they were facing away from the land, Hailgi lifted the wyrm-prow from where it lay. Wrought from solid oak, it was heavier than he had thought, but he managed to raise it without showing the strain.

"Show us the way well, to where Hunding rides for home," he whispered as he wrestled it up and dropped its long neck down into the deep wooden well that had been made for it. "Guide us through the waters and bring us to the foe-land where we need to be."

"Which way, Hailgi?" Hagalar's steersman Berikan asked.

Hailgi pointed towards the northwest. "We must be out of sight when we pass Hunding's lands. Around that way, then we'll turn in to land again and follow the coast until we find them. They shouldn't be too far from Anulai-bhar's hall yet."

"A wise enough rede," the steersman said, nodding his heavy head slowly. "Wise enough."

There was little talking that day. The thanes rowed grimly, as though the pulling of the oars against their arms could draw the thoughts from their minds. Berikan leaned on the rudder, his face half-turned away so that Hailgi could see only his shaggy brown hair and beard. After a while, the wind grew stronger, lashing the waves up into little whitecaps so that the boat rolled swiftly from side to side. Hailgi marked that the ruddy hue had drained from Leugar's face, his skin was a sickly greenish-white against his straw-colored mane, nor did Athalwulfar and Angantiwar look as well as they had when the faring began.

It was only a few moments more before Leugar leaned over the side to spew his breakfast into the leaping spray. Hailgi remembered the verse he had made, and it was not in his mind to offer any easing, but a missing oars-man was like a flight-feather plucked from a hawk's wing, and the sea-eagle would fly, limping without him.

Hailgi made his way over the benches to the seasick thane. "Hai, let me take your place," he said softly. "Lie down and close your eyes, if you can."

Leugar looked at him mistrustfully for a moment, then moved over so that Hailgi could take his oar. "Thank you," he muttered. It sounded to Hailgi as though the words choked in his throat. A flare of anger leaped from Hailgi's heart is it so hard for them to give me thanks? Then Leugar leaned over the side again, and he felt a little ashamed. He turned his mind to the rowing. His oar threshed about a little before he could get it to turn in the same round as the others, but soon he was bending his back in the same steady rhythm, helping to speed his ship forward.

Some of the men tired more quickly than the others, as would always be true, and as the afternoon wore on, the rowing began to grow ragged. Then Aiwimundar growled out, "Berikan, give us a song to row by."

The steersman was still for a moment, thinking, before he began to chant. His strong tenor voice rose easily above the slapping of waves against the boat and the mewing of the gulls that followed.

"Agjiwar brewsale for gods,
but gods drink deepgoodly must be
the sea-lord's kettle seething with foam -
forth Thonarar went a fit one to get."

All the men who had breath for it sang with him on the refrain,

"Thonarar, hail! Thurses' foe!
Fisherman, Wyrm's baneWarder of Men!"

Berikan went on to sing of how Thonarar and Tiwar came to the house of the etin Hymir and shielded themselves behind a stone pillar, which shattered at the giant's awful glance. By the third refrain, Hailgi was gasping out the song with the rest, though he was little used to rowing, and his right shoulder and arm were beginning to ache, the rhythm of the song seemed to row through him.

"Thonarar, hail! Thurses' foe!
Fisherman, Wyrm's baneWarder of Men!"

Hailgi knew the tale well. How Thonarar and Hymir had gone fishing the next morning, baiting their hooks with the heads of bulls. Hymir caught whales, but Thonarar drew up the Middle-Garth's Wyrm and did battle with it, striking its head with his Hammer.

"Shook the seas then,shook the earth,
the hills all howled, the high cliffs fell.
but Hymir, heart-weak, hewed through line,
sank the Wyrmto wend to depths."

"Thonarar, hail! Thurses' foe!
Fisherman, Wyrm's baneWarder of Men!"

The last cry was louder than before, Hailgi thought, and then it seemed to him that he could feel all the fathoms of dark water sinking below him, down to the stone and mud of the sea's floor where the Middle-Garth's Wyrm coiled, and he knew that the wooden planking of the boat was very thin. Well indeed, he thought, to call on Thonarar at sea! But the song went on, telling of Hymir's rime-crystal cup, which Thonarar threw twice through the stone hall-pillars and shattered at last on the etin's skull, winning the cauldron in which Agjiwar might brew ale enough for all the gods.

"Agjiwar brewsale for gods,
now gods drink deepand goodly is
the sea-lord's kettleseething with foam
Thonarar has drinkhis thirst to quench!"

"Thonarar, hail! Thurses' foe!
Fisherman, Wyrm's baneWarder of Men!"

Leugar sat up again when the song was done. Although he was still pale, his color seemed a little better. "I'll take my oar again now, if you're willing," he offered. Gladly, Hailgi moved aside to let him have it. Sunna was lowering before them, her brightness blushing redder as streaks of yellow and pink stretched out across the pale sky. Behind them, the wind was freshening, but it had swept all the clouds away, there would be no ill weather that night. Hailgi made his way back over the lurching benches to the prow where Berikan held tightly to the rudder.

"What do you think?" Hailgi asked. "How far have we gotten?"

Berikan put his hand over his eyes, peering at the Sun's stead in the sky through his fingers. "I can tell you better when the stars are out," he said slowly. "Still, we've made good time, with the wind behind us and strong rowing. If we slant in towards land now, it might be that we could make landfall past Hunding's marches by the time night is fully on us."

"We'll do that, then."

Berikan merely nodded, pulling at the rudder.

As the steersman had told Hailgi, they were rowing into a sheltered bay by the time darkness set. Though the men raised their tents, they were still too close to Hunding's lands to risk kindling fires, instead, they ate hard bread and salted fish by the light of the half-full Moon, talking in whispers and tossing dice as they drank small beer.

His cloak wrapped tightly around him against the cold wind, Hailgi sat a little apart from the rest, looking out at the long wyrm-headed shadow of his ship rising and falling with the swells. The white-capped waves shattered the moon's silver-gilt light into a tossing trail of gold coins over the black water, the soft crashing as they broke on the shore and the hissing of the water drawing back over the stony strand blended into the river-rushing of the wind through the beeches behind him. Hailgi held the first watch himself, sitting up while the men slept. Though his cloak was warm, Hailgi could feel his bones beginning to tremble. Now the roaring of the waves sounded far away in his ears, as though he already floated out of sight of land. He felt rootless as a spear caught by a gale, and did not know whether the wind would blow him straighter to his goal, or cast him aside. So Wyrd is shaped, he thought.

My guising was mightier than I knew, for now I shall win my father's battle, or lose my life with it. Now the frith of my birthing-night is truly sundered, and I shall find if my days were measured by its length, or if I was born to fulfill the Wolfings' might. All through his watch, such thoughts twined through Hailgi's mind like eels in seaweed. Now glimmering silver and fair, now black as the dead. Every so often he rose to wander between the tents, listening to the snoring that grated through wind and wave. Once a wolf howled, but it was a very long way away, and if others answered, they were too far off for Hailgi to hear them. He woke Fastawulfar for the second watch, taking the thane's place in the warm nest of blankets he had made for himself, he was tired enough to fall asleep at once. Sigiruna leaned eagerly over the edge of the ship, staring at the helm that rose low and green from the sea before her. This was the island Fyn, where the greatest hof in the North, save perhaps the Inglings' hof at Uppsala, stood.

Since anyone could remember, the wagon of Nerthus had been brought forth from that island every year at the beginning of planting-season, making the rounds of Sea land, Jutland, and sometimes part of the coast lands of Saxony and Frisia before coming back to the hidden sacrifice by the hof's lake. The other gods and goddesses were worshiped there too. Nerthus' children, Ingwi-Freyjar and his twin sister Freyja, the Thing-rulers Tiwar and Fosite, Thonarar and his bride Sibja, the hunters from the far north, Wuldhur and Skadhi, Frija and all her handmaidens, the goddesses of healing and oaths, marriage and wisdom and fruitfulness, and Wodhanaz, though many of his rites were still held on Jutland, where the ravens flew about the hanging-tree in Fetter-Grove.

"Do you see the hof?" Bragi asked, leaning over beside her. His brownish-gold hair had come loose from the thong that held it back, wisps whipping about his face. Impatiently he pushed it back with one hand as the other touched the gold ring in the hilt of his new sword. At fourteen winters, this was the first time he had been allowed to go weaponed from home, he might even, Sigiruna thought, think that he was leading the little band of warriors that had come with them. She straightened herself, tilting the spear in her hand to look at the head. A few spots of spray had already reddened its silver-wrought iron, she sighed, reaching in her bag for a little wand of whetstone to scour it clean.

"Not yet. You know, Bragi, they're going to make you take your sword off before you come into the holy garth. The only weapons they allow there are the ones that belong to the gods."

Her brother's light-fuzzed jaw jutted out, brows lowering over his gray eyes. "I'm not stupid. I know what a frith-garth is, and I wouldn't break the holy peace. But why'd you bring a spear, since you're not going to need it?" He knew better than to add that women seldom went armed, in any case, it was no very strange thing for a woman to weapon herself with spear or bow on a faring.

"In case we get attacked on the way, or maybe outside the frith-garth."

Bragi grinned. "Think we will?"

Sigiruna looked down at him. He was big for a fourteen year-old, and strong as well, more heavily-built than she or Dagar, or Hailgi, she thought, almost unwillingly remembering the taut-muscled, wiry body of the Wolfing. The thickness of Bragi's arms was mostly bone, he was a long way from a man's full growth yet, and she little liked the thought of him going into battle, even as she looked at him, she could see his head thrown back, pale in death, the broken shaft of a spear standing out from his body. Sigiruna reached out to touch her little brother's shoulder, as if to reassure herself that he still lived and was hale.

"Don't hope for it too loudly. It is often said that the gods hear men's words, and that the Father of Battles delights in fulfilling such wishes. Hold my spear a moment while I see to your hair again, I think we will be landing soon, and Haganon's son should not look unkempt as a thrall when he meets new folk."

Bragi took the spear and stood still as Sigiruna took her comb out of her belt-pouch and began to tidy his hair back. Her own was tied into a thick knot at the nape of her neck, from which her long braid dangled down her back, but she would be happy if her brother would stay in one place long enough for her to get all his stray wisps caught and neatly bound up with the thong. Not all the butter in the world could keep his hair in its place, though their mother had slicked it down with great care that morning. The thanes had taken the sail down and lifted their oars, rowing over to the wooden pier that jutted out from the sand. There were several other ships tied up there as well, their banners showing the clans that owned them. Though Sigiruna was sure Hailgi would not be there, she could not help looking for the sign of the Wolfing line, but she did not see it. The Skjolding emblem was not a battle-flag, but a red shield raised high on a pole, its rim and boss glittering with gold and gilded ornaments riveted to the painted linden, on any other island, the sign would be a call to battle.

Steadying herself with her spear, Sigiruna stepped up onto the pier and walked to the end, waiting for the thanes to make the boat fast. Bragi leapt up behind her, scampering along the wooden planking as he glanced back and forth at the men who sat guarding the other ships. A couple stared stolidly back at him, but most of them ignored him, their gazes resting either on Sigiruna or on the warriors who followed the two young Skjoldings.

Sigiruna straightened her skirts, settling her belt of gilded plates more comfortably across her hips and brushing a few flecks of dust from the cuffs of her sleeves. The white horsehair patterning the red tablet-woven bands of trim with interwoven triangles gleamed very nicely in the Sun's light, she marked, brightening the deep rich blue of her linen dress. Though it was too warm for a cloak and the long sleeves of her dress hid the rings on Sigiruna's arms, the gold snake-rings on her fingers and the matching pair of great brooches on her shoulders, as well as the garnets and gold of her southern-worked girdle clasp, showed that she was a woman of atheling-kin and not to be treated lightly, if the spear in her hand, with the circles of silver inlay on its blade and the narrow bands of silver about its shaft were not enough to impress by itself.

Her belt-knife had a golden hilt, and the small drinking horn that dangled by a looped thong against her other thigh was bound with well-wrought silver. Bragi looked very fine as well, she thought. The gold buttons glittered on the cuffs of his narrow sleeves and along the sides of his red tunic, and the gilded hilt of his sword and the ornaments of its sheath shone as though he had been polishing them all day. Which was near enough to the truth. Not one of the eleven thanes who had come with them lacked either byrnie or sword of his own, and four of them had fine helms as well. Hrabanawulfar bore up the bag of gifts which the Skjoldings were sending to the hof. For a moment he looked back and forth between Bragi and Sigiruna, as though unsure which of them should bear it. Then Sigiruna gestured at her brother. It mattered little which of them actually set the gifts in the hands of the hof-folk, but she wished to walk unburdened.

The hof God-Home lay only a little way inland, set on the top of a small hill which was fenced about with heaps of stone and carven posts. The wood of its roof-shingles was gilded, and wooden horse-heads with staring eyes rose high over the gables. Sigiruna shivered with awe as she looked up at it, even though she was a long way from the boundaries of the frith-garth, it seemed to her that she could feel the stead's holiness thrumming through the land about her. Beyond the hof was the grove where no one save the gud-hes and gudhijas might tread, Nerthus' lake lay in the middle of the woods, and to see it was to die, unless one were already hallowed to the mighty life-giver. But before it was a lively settlement, bright with the canopies of merchant-booths and the tunics of folk in their feast-day finery.

This was a merry time, these last days before the harvest started and everyone, atheling and thrall alike, worked from dawn to dusk in the race to bring the grain in before the first storms of winter ravaged the fields. Later, Sigiruna thought, she would go among the stalls and see if there was anything there she wished to buy. There might, perhaps, be Roman glass for sale, she had long wanted a rime-clear cup or even a pitcher, and she ought to celebrate becoming a woman. The man who stood at the foot of the hill before the two great posts that marked the way up to the hof was old, his thick hair and curly beard the white-streaked gray of a storm-swept sea, but Sigiruna had no doubt that he could have warded the path against a host.

He over topped the tallest of the thanes, Thonarastainar Broad-Nose, by a full hand span, his shoulders were near massive enough to block the gateway between the pillars, and Sigiruna could not have gotten both hands around the rippling forearm-muscles that bulged beneath the sleeves of his loose gray tunic. He must have looked like Thonarar walking the Middle-Garth in truth when he was young, she thought, staring up at him. Though he bore neither shield nor spear, the oaken staff that leaned on the pillar beside him was thicker than Sigiruna's thigh, and she was sure he could swing it with crushing speed. She had heard that the great berg-etins of the North sometimes mated with the children of Ash and Elm, perhaps he came of that kin?

"Hail and welcome, Skjoldings," the hof-warder said softly. His voice rumbled as though it might set the earth to shaking should he raise it. "The holy ones wait within. Will you come in frith, into the garth of the gods?"

"We will," Sigiruna answered firmly, handing her spear to him and look-ing meaningfully at Bragi, who was gazing at the huge warrior with a look of wonder on his broad-boned face. It seemed to her that she could almost hear her brother's thoughts. If I could only grow to be that big, that strong. Then the Skjolding youth handed the bag to his sister, fumbling quickly to unhook the sword from his belt and give it over. Behind them, Hrabanawul-far started to do likewise, but the warder stilled him with a gesture of his massive hand.

"These two shall go up alone for now. Tomorrow the hof shall be open to all who wish to make gifts or ask for blessing, and then you may come freely and be welcome. A place in the town is being readied for your stay even now, God-Home is ever glad to guest the Skjoldings and their folk, the more so since we still hold blithe memories of the days when the frowe Sigigafja dwelt among us." The hof-warder's lips curved into a smile for a moment beneath his thick beard before he stepped aside, waving Sigiruna and Bragi through the pillars.

Passing between the door-posts of the frith-garth's fence was like walking through a waterfall that tingled ice-cold over Sigiruna's body. She breathed deeply, standing with her feet rooted in the black earth and drawing as much air into her lungs as she could as she tried to settle the sudden rush of might flowing through her. Bragi seemed to feel nothing, he had already walked ahead, not marking that his sister had paused. Sigiruna hurried to catch up with him, so that the two of them went up the hill side by side. The hof's door was made of heavy oak, carved with writhing wyrms and the twisting shapes of strange beasts. Sigiruna did not know whether she should open it and step in, or wait for it to open before her. They seemed to know we were here quickly enough, she thought.

Bragi was watching her, the bag in his hands jingling as he shifted restlessly from foot to foot, he seemed to have forgotten that he was supposed to be a man grown, who little needed an elder sister to tell him what to do. At last she lifted her fist, knocking thrice. The hof door swung open. Squinting into the shadows within, Sigiruna could see no one, only the huge dark shapes of the gods and goddesses looming between the tall pillars, the long fires along the floor lighting their rough hewn wooden faces and gleaming from the two shield-shaped rounds of bronze that hung by the stone harrow. Her spine prickled, until a slight movement drew her gaze downward. She had been looking too high, the hof-gudhija who had opened the door was a very small woman, the top of her gray head no higher than Sigiruna's breasts. The soft wrinkles of her face gave her a kind look, her eyes gleamed bright in the gloom as she lifted the two horns she held, placing one in the hand of each Skjolding.

"Hail to you!" The gudhija said. "Come within, Sigiruna and Bragi, be welcome as guests in the hall of the gods. I am Hredhild, one of the keepers of this holy stead." Her voice was slightly breathy, warm as a cat's back, though she spoke with a strong Saxon accent, shortening many of her words and chewing others in the way the coast-folk had.

The two Skjoldings stepped between the door-posts and raised their horns. "Hail the gods and goddesses, and all the folk of this hallowed stead," Sigiruna replied, Bragi murmuring the words half a breath behind her. They drank together, then followed the gudhija to the long bench placed before the great stone harrow in the middle of the hof. Sigiruna knew from her mother's stories of life at God-Home that tables were brought in for the feasting that the folk shared with the gods, but now the holy hall was furnished only with the single bench.

She looked around herself, trying to guess which of the hallowed images was who. She knew that the veiled shape at the end of the hall must be Nerthus. Freyjar sat to the right, the tree-bark had been left on the great phallus that jutted from his lap, polished only from the knob at its end. On Nerthus' other side was Freyja, a huge collar of four filigree-wrought gold rings resting upon her wooden shoulders. No clothing hid the curves of her breasts, nor the cleft cut between the forked branches of her legs. Wodhanar stood byrnie-clad and helmed, his spear in his hand, Thonarar's beard was carefully marked and painted red, his broad staring eyes gilded and the haft of his Hammer wrapped with gold wire.

Frija was fully clad as a house-frowe, with a great ring of golden keys at her side, the other goddesses were harder to tell apart, but Sigiruna guessed that the one with the cluster of dried herbs thrust into the wooden ring of her hand was Airi the Healer, the one who held the oath-ring must be Wara, and she with the golden cup was surely Saga.

Hredhild gestured for them to sit, settling herself beside them. "It is good to see that Sigigafja's children are growing so well. You both have much of her look about you."

Sigiruna nodded, not knowing what to say, but Bragi answered, "I am told that is so, but that I am more like my father Haganon."

The hof-gudhija smiled, Sigiruna marked that she still had all her teeth. "That may well be."

Something cold pressed against Sigiruna's back. She froze in shock, breath clenched between her teeth, then turned her head slowly to see what it might be. When she did, she let her breath free in a slow sigh. It was only the wet nose of a big hound that had touched her, a beautiful hound, like a golden wolf with a little gray stranded through her fur. The dog leaned its head on the bench beside Sigiruna's thigh, rolling big brown eyes up at her.

Hredhild snapped her fingers. "Selha, here!" The hound came slowly around the bench, head down and tail wagging in supplication. Sigiruna reached down to pet her, smiling in spite of herself. Selha was a well-fed hound, Sigiruna could not feel her ribs beneath her soft coat. The hall of the gods was not so different from her own home, after all. She could see Bragi's muscles easing as well, the color coming back to his freckled face as he, too, stroked the dog.

"Tell me, is there any news from Sealand?" The gudhija asked as Selha lay down by their feet.

"All is well, last year's harvest was fair, and few folk tried to raid our shores this summer."

"Only twice, and neither was worth the name of raid," Bragi broke in. "I have not yet had any foes to swing my blade against."

Hredhild looked at him, and for a moment it seemed to Sigiruna as though she could see the bones tightening to steel beneath the old gudhija's sweet face. "Well, I have heard men say that the first battle is the hardest, if you live through your first, you are likely to see many more. What of you, Sigiruna? Surely it will not be long before there is talk of having you wed?"

"Nothing has been spoken yet," Sigiruna said slowly. Then a rush of dizziness swept over her, as though the hof-bench were rolling beneath her like a ship on the wave, it seemed to her that she could see Hailgi before her again, and that he was no longer clad in skirts, but wore tunic and breeches, with a sword girded to his side. He was staring out over the waves, the Sun's setting light glimmering gold from his gray eyes"Holy frowe, I would speak to you by myself, if I may. There is a matter."

Hredhild's blue gaze met Sigiruna's for a moment, it seemed to the younger woman as though the hof-gudhija were searching through her very skull. Then Hredhild patted the Skjolding's shoulder, nodding. "We shall speak of it. Bragi, you have had a long faring, and there is no need for you to sit through talk that will be tiresome to you. Perhaps you would like to share the company of Wihastainar, who wards our hof? He has many tales of battle to tell, and might be willing to show you some of his skills as well."

Bragi looked at the gudhija, then at his sister. For a moment he frowned fiercely, as though he meant to complain about being sent away, then a smile struggled through, and he stood. "I would be glad to," he answered. "Thank you, holy frowe. I'll see you tonight, Sigiruna!" He drained his horn, laying it down carefully on the bench, and hurried out of the hof as quickly as he could, if he had not still felt some awe of the holy stead, Sigiruna knew, he would have run full-tilt.

"Now you shall tell me," Hredhild said, and Sigiruna did told her all she had seen and done, all she knew of Hailgi. The gudhija nodded, sitting quietly as she listened.

"There is no doubt that you are one of Wodan's wish-daughters, though I do not yet know how deeply your doom is set. Much hangs on the Wolfing's deeds now, for a man cannot do as he has done and come unchanged from it. It seems to me that it would be well for you to speak with the hof-gudhe who best knows the ways of Wodan. Karl son of Habukar, whom we call Wodan's-Karl, for he can best give you rede in this, then, if we deem it fitting, I shall find out what lies in the well of Wyrd for you."

"II thank you," Sigiruna began, but Hredhild shook her head.

"There is no need to thank me. This is part of our duty, both to the holy folk and to our kin in the Middle-Garth, and you have the look of one who will give much to the god in times to come. But I am afraid you will have to wait until tomorrow to speak with Wodan's-Karl. He is old, and has been struck three times by elf-shot, so that he tires easily and goes to bed early, often before sunset. And he cannot come here, you will have to go to his dwelling on Hawk's Height, though it is not so far away."

"That will be little hardship to me," Sigiruna replied.

Hredhild rose, brushing her hands together. "Well, then. Will you and your brother come back to the hof to eat with us when the Sun has set below the hilltop? Feast is the fitting time for gift-giving, and then the Skjolding clan shall get the blessings for which you were sent."

"That will be well."

"You may leave your bag here if you would rather not carry it, you may be sure that it will be safe."

The Sun's light dazzled Sigiruna's eyes as she stepped outside, she had to stand blinking for several moments before she could see her way down the path. At the foot of the hill, just outside the frith-garth's gate-posts, Wihastainar and Bragi were laying about one another Bragi wielding his sheathed sword, Wihastainar prodding at him with the butt-end of Sigiruna's spear and calling helpful hints. Though she could see how the hof-warder was holding back, the mock-fight still did not look too bad, her brother was living up to the promise everyone had seemed to see in him since he was young. Well, it is no surprise that Sigigafja and Haganon should have gotten good warriors, Sigiruna thought, smiling to herself.

Even Dagar seems no weakling when matched against the other boys his age, though he may be the runt of our litter. She slipped out between the pillars and waited for a break in the fighting. When Wihastainar finally let Bragi step back to get his breath, Sigiruna cleared her throat. The hof-warder looked down at her, it was hard to tell the look on his face through his gray-white thicket of beard and the hair that had fallen over his face, but she thought there might be a little guilt there.

He handed back her spear, massive hand uncurling from the shaft that had looked like a child's stick in his grasp. "I have handled your weapon carefully, frowe, I hope you do not feel that my touch has done it harm. I would not have taken it, but your brother gave me leave and asked me to."

Sigiruna glared swiftly at Bragi, who flinched beneath her gaze and glanced away as he hooked his sword back to his belt. She had the right to be truly angered with both of them, but in front of the hof, even outside the frith-garth, was no place to let her temper burn free, and she had no wish for the hof-folk to think her ungracious, so she eased her snarl into a smile as she looked back at Wihastainar.

"Well, he should not have done that, but there is no harm taken. Truly, I am honored that such a mighty warrior has used my spear, even in teaching. May some of your strength and skill linger in the weapon, should I ever need it in battle."

Wihastainar grinned down at her. "What strength or skill of mine is in it may stay there, freely given. Your brother is becoming a worthy warrior, and I am sure your arms are no weaker, you are much like your mother."

Sigiruna's smile warmed with the compliment, and she could feel the blush rising in her cheeks. She murmured her thanks and turned to Bragi. "Will you come into the town with me? Or would you like to stay here a while longer? We have been bidden to feast with the hof-folk at sunset, but there is still some time between now and then."

Bragi looked from Wihastainar to the tents raised at the town's edge, gray eyes wide, like a hound raising his head from the trail to sniff a strange scent, unsure whether to follow his track or go haring off after new prey. "What are we going to do tomorrow?"

"I am going to see one of the hof-gudhes, you may do as you please, but I remember that the hof is to be open to all tomorrow, so this good warrior may have little time for you."

"Alas, that is so," Wihastainar agreed.

Bragi nodded, his head jerking with the sharp firm movement of a fist banging on a table one of Haganon's gestures, Sigiruna thought, truly folk are born again in their children. "I will stay with you, then."

When Sigigafja had brought her daughter to God-Home for blessing before, Sigiruna had still been a child, and, now that she thought of it, that had actually been during planting-time, so that there were few guests on the holm. Surely the town had not been so full of folk, nor had there been merchants' tents set up everywhere and folk crying their wares in the dusty streets.

In spite of Wihastainar's assurances, the Skjolding maid kept one hand over her belt-pouch as she made her way along. She could smell roast lamb somewhere, the rich sweet scent reminded her that she had not eaten more that day than a piece of bread and a cup of milk at dawn, and so she followed it to the open-air booth where a broad-bellied man stood by the spitted carcase with a grease-shiny knife in his hand. A little silver bead from the handful of small trade-things in the bottom of her pouch got Sigiruna both a thick slice of lamb and a horn full of yeasty ale. It was a little awkward to eat with the spear in one hand and both food and drink in the other, but she was in no hurry. She licked the dripping fat and meat-juice off her fingers as she walked slowly past the merchant-stalls, careful not to get any grease on her fine dress.

There was one man with a table of hawking-gear before his tent and two fair Northern falcons perched on a wooden mount within, their golden eyes gleaming from the shadows. Sigiruna stopped a moment to admire the birds, but she had seldom enough time for hawking, and such fine creatures were worthy of more time and care than she could give them. There were plenty of merchants selling trinkets, beads of glass and amber, boars' tusks and the teeth and claws of bears, there were tents with strings of furry hides dangling from their roof-posts and bales of fur heaped up within, cups and pitchers, woven lengths of bright-dyed cloth and embroidered cloaks.

Many of the goods were no different from those sold at the Midsummer Thing in the Skjoldings' lands, when the folk gathered to deem laws and lawsuits, were gilds for injury and bridal portions, but Sigiruna also marked that there were more things from far-off lands for sale here, from a strip of southern silk to the white fox-furs of the farthest North. As she came closer to the middle of the town, walking among the thatched houses and more sturdily built wooden stalls, she saw that the goods were growing finer and rarer. One booth held carefully stoppered jars of herbs and tools for cutting everything from hair to bone, after a moment of thought, Sigiruna paused there to trade two heavy coils of twisted gold wire from her fingers for a lump of poppy-gum.

That would be her gift to Dagar, she thought. Getting something rare for his herb-craft and knowing that she had thought of him should go a long way towards soothing the quiet disappointment that had clouded her younger brother's face when he heard that both his older siblings were going to God-Home, but he would be left behind. Finally Sigiruna found what she was looking for. A stall where a few pieces of Roman glass were displayed among the smooth earth-red cups and pitchers the southern folk made. The slim dark-haired woman who sat on a stool inside looked up and nodded as Sigiruna stepped beneath the canopy's shadow.

"Greetings, atheling-frowe," she said. Her voice was pleasantly low, though a fraction loud, her smile showed that two of her bottom teeth were missing. "Are you looking for anything special?"

Sigiruna shook her head, considering the glasswares ranked on the stall's shelves for a moment. A pale blue glass cone with clear trails wriggling up its side like adder-tracks, a clear green horn wound about with spirals of solid white and yellow, two cups so black and shiny they might have been carved from stone, and a tall, rime-clear pitcher with an elegant curving handle. Sigiruna could already see the mead glowing like fire lit amber within it. Sigiruna lifted the pitcher, and the merchant-woman raised her narrow brows, cool green eyes taking Sigiruna's measure. It would not be cheap, this was not the Thing-fair on Sealand, where traders often thought to keep the good favor of the Skjolding clan by easy bargaining.

When the haggling was done, Sigiruna was left with only a few small coils of silver in the bottom of her pouch. She feared that she might find herself borrowing from Bragi before they went home. The bargain had included a large basket all padded with wool to keep the pitcher from breaking, and the merchant-woman had told her tales of how the Romans made their glass-ware, by heating the raw sand until it melted clear and glowed and could be spun into whatever shapes the workers wished. Sigiruna knew that if she did not listen in wonder to such things, she would be a better bargain-er, but it was hardly fitting for an atheling to argue over goods better to be open-handed to those who brought fine wares from far-off places. Sigiruna bumped into a man as she walked out of the stall, she was about to excuse herself, but it seemed to her that he moved to keep his thigh against hers a little longer.

"Who are you?" She asked tightly, stepping back and looking coldly at him. He was a few finger widths shorter than she, widely-built and heavy-boned, clean-shaven, with thick wavy brown hair falling around a square, broad-cheeked face. He smiled easily at her, as though his mouth-hinges were greased.

"I know who you are, Sigiruna daughter of Haganon the Skjolding."

"Good. Who are you?"

"I am Hadubroddar the son of Granamarar, best known as Isung's Bane for I slew the Gautish drighten in a great battle, as you may have heard. I am a sea-king, and the men of my band are the best to be found. I take only those war-eagles who dare the greatest heights."

Sigiruna knew that she had heard a song or two about Hadubroddar, Isung's Bane. She considered him more carefully. Hadubroddar's white tunic glittered with broad buttons and brooches, his sword-hilt was so orna-mented that she wondered how he could wield it. Still, there seemed to her something not quite true about the color of the gold he wore, she was sure that much of it was brass with the gilding wearing off, and the crafting of many of his big tunic-clasps seemed over-wrought and cheap. He would do better, she thought, to wear fewer things of finer make, if he boasts himself a sea-king, he is not able to take land and hold it. She did not like the look shining in his eyes, it seemed to her that he was gloating already. Still, her father's words sounded in her mind.

There are few allies who are not worth having. It was that wisdom which had helped him to keep the might of the Skjolding line as great as that which their forebears from Skjold Sheaf onward had known, so she had little place to doubt him, Isung's Bane and his men might yet prove a help to the Skjolding host in battle.

"It is good to meet you," she said carefully. "What brings you here to God-Home?"

"To pay my troth to the gods and goddesses, as is always my way. Wodhanar gives me victory, for I have always dared to be true to him!" Hadubroddar's smooth voice grew louder as he spoke, he almost shouted out the words dared and true! Sigiruna thought that he meant to stir her heart, but she remembered the raven-depth of Hailgi's voice as he called her forth from the misted darkness, and it seemed to her that this loud raider, who spoke of himself like a peddler boasting his wares, was like to think more of himself than of the holy ones. When Hadubroddar saw that folk were starting to turn their heads, he spoke more softly. "I know that you are no stranger to that troth, for you are here as well, and I know also that your mother is a walkurja, who rides over land and water to bring victory to her husband in his battles."

"It was Sigigafja's sword that brought Haganon victory the last time raiders from the sea came against the Skjoldings' hall," Sigiruna answered, also softly. Even though Hadubroddar spoke words of truth, there was something she disliked in the way he mouthed them. Perhaps it was only that he was not Hailgi, and she found it ill to share with a stranger words that so much as touched on her thoughts of the Wolfing, or perhaps it was the way he seemed to be closing on her even when he stood still.

Hadubroddar shrugged, the movement hardly more than a wriggling of the heavy muscles that bulked over his shoulders. Sigiruna marked that the sea-king's neck was thicker than his head, his jawline seeming to slope smoothly out to his body. The long sword at his side was very heavy, tugging his belt down beneath his bulging sides, she guessed that he would trust more to its weight than its edge. She spoke before Hadubroddar could say anything else about Wodhanar or walkurjas.

"In your farings, have you heard news of the Wolfing clan, or of their foe Hunding?"

"There is little news, Hagalar keeps the march between them. I believe that the Wolfing boy is still fostered in his hall. He is of your age, fifteen winters, but not," Hadubroddar added, his words slicking a little faster, "a promising young man. I have heard that he is not well-skilled at sword-play and seldom shows much soul or thought when men are gathered to speak. But he is the only child that Sigismundar and Borghildar could get, perhaps there is some weakness in their lines."

Sigiruna thought of the taut-muscled body of the youth she had seen the warrior's lines of his lithe body impossible to hide, even when blurred by a woman's skirts, and forebore to speak. Sweat from her palm slicked the smooth shaft of her spear as she watched the slight shifting of Hadu-broddar's face. This man may be dangerous, she thought. What if I had not known Hailgi? Why does he tell me these things?

Hadubroddar's gaze slid downward, to the basket in her hand. "What do you have in there?"

"Some glass I bought earlier. I am sure it would break in a moment on shipboard," she added sharply.

The sea-king laughed. "So you like glass! Were there any other pieces in there that you wished to own?"

Sigiruna's grip on her spear tightened, she could hear the soft crackling of the woven straw handle in her other hand. "That would be more than a gift of friendship to the Skjoldings. It would be a courting-gift, and my father has said that I am yet too young to think on wedding." Friendship for friendship, she thought to herself, and eke lies for lies, that was Wodhanar's rede.

Hadubroddar smiled slowly. "I see that you are thought-wise. A fair thing in a young maiden though fifteen winters is hardly less than a grown woman's count of years."

The Sun's edge was nearly hidden behind the hill, the high-arching horse-heads of the gables black against her ruddy light. "I must go. My brother and I were bidden to the hof for feasting this night."

"Then you must go. Fare well, Sigiruna. It will gladden me greatly when we see each other again."

Sigiruna turned and walked off as swiftly as she could, trying to still the anger that swirled up in her like river-mud beneath the splashing hooves of a horse. Whether Isung's Bane was a mighty warrior or not, she was sure there was little to trust in him, and yet it seemed to her that he would not be sure to displease her father and Bragi, should he bring his band to the Skjolding hall in frith.

Then it would be well for Sigiruna that Haganon listened to his wife's redes and often knew them for wiser than his own thoughts. Bragi was waiting for her at the foot of the hill, trying hastily to straighten his own hair and clothes. Sigiruna set her basket and spear down and grasped him by the shoulders. "No use trusting you to care for yourself, is there?" She said, her voice harsher than she meant it to be. This is no foe, she reminded herself, he is my dear little brother, who may have his own sword, but still cannot quite straighten his own tunic. "Never mind, I'll have you fit to come to feasting in a moment. Have you been here fighting all this time?"

"Yes!" Bragi answered. Then, glancing sideways at Wihastainar, who stood leaning against a gatepost with his arms folded, "Well, he talked about fighting to me too, and told me about battles he's been in."

Sigiruna smiled. "And now you're hungry as a bear at winter's end."

"Hungry enough to eat a hungry bear!"

"I'm sure the hof has better food than that." She pulled the last knot of Bragi's hair-thong tight, looked at him a moment. The sweat-stains on his tunic had dried, they would not show in the firelight. "That's good enough. Let's not make the holy folk wait for us."

CHAPTER IX

Like a yew-berry stuck within my throat,
Red the stilled flesh, still the seed within,
Hidden, and its life hidden in the hull
Fire hidden in wood and wood hid in seed.
And I, for four autumns' berry-turnings,
Silent, not as stone, but as a seed.
There is no sureness of spring-tide growth,
Nor of fresh birth from the fleshy cairn.
Still, it has come before, for seeds do sprout.
Time may have brewed a stronger ale,
To free the yew-seed, loose the choking knot,
To spew the seed forth to new birth,
To open the way to eagle's flood.

The bell shuddered its grating note through the university classroom as
Helgi wrote the last few words. He closed his notebook and got up, stuffing
his history book into his bag. The heat wrapped around him like a damp
warm blanket as soon as he stepped outside from the air-conditioned hall,
slowing his steps. "It's fall," he muttered. "Today really is September 28."
Somewhere, he knew, people were putting on sweaters and looking up at
gray skies. Somewhere, the wind was cold as the flat of a steel blade against
the back of the neck, ready to turn towards the cutting edge of winter. Here,
a slight yellowish haze sickened the sky's unbroken blueness, and tanned
legs reached down everywhere beneath the edges of shorts.

Jefferson University was a great sprawling complex of a place, graced by
a number of neo-Classical columns and Latin motto over the doors where
Helgi had hoped to find helpful building-names. Wide expanses of grass
stretched like green seas between each clump of buildings, the leaves of
the live-oaks that lined them were just beginning to turn brown in hopes of
the autumn ahead. After three years, he had gotten to know the path to the
music department well enough. Over the steps of the university library, past
another great green sea, past the World War I memorial fountain, and five
buildings to the right after that. It was too hot to jog, but Helgi walked as
swiftly as he could bring himself to, hurrying from the scattered shade of the
live oaks into the shade of building after building.

Helgi had three minutes left by the time he got to the door marked 12. He raised his hand to the doorknob, then let it drop back, he could hear a woman talking inside, though he couldn't make out her words. Helgi could feel the strings of his throat tightening already as his stomach knotted coldly. *What am I doing here, anyway?* He asked himself. *What will I do if she tells me I'm not good enough for her to teach?* For a moment he was tempted just to turn around, walk away, and drive home, and leave everything to do with singing where it had lain since high school. But when the door opened, he stepped forward at once, though the soles of his feet prickled at each step as though each nerve ending were sticking needle-pointed through the skin.

The young man who came out was an inch or two taller than Helgi and more heavily built, with a crew-cut. He was big enough for the football team, but not in training, his belly slopped over the embossed belt running through the loops of his faded jeans. "G'bye, Miz Devereaux," he muttered. "See you next week."

"Goodbye, Johnny," the woman answered. Her neatly outlined black eyes swiveled past Helgi as she looked out into the hall. Helgi coughed, and she glanced back at him. "Are you waiting for something? I have a new student who ought to be here." Ms. Devereaux's voice was sharper than he had expected, as though the black bun twisted at the nape of her neck had screwed her vocal cords tight. Although no age-creases outlined her mouth or starred from the corners of her eyes, Helgi guessed her to be in her mid-thirties.

"Ms. Devereaux?"

"Yes?"

"I'm Helgi Hadding. I think you're waiting for me."

Ms. Devereaux looked down at the yellow square of gummed note-paper fluttering from her piano. A faint blush tinted the smooth olive skin of her cheeks. "I'm sorry. I thoughtI wrote the name down as Helga."

"It happens all the time." Then, before she could ask, "It's a Danish name, from my mother's family."

"Right. Well, come on in and let's get started."

The practice room was very small, barely large enough for the scarred old piano and two people.

"Have you ever sung before?" She asked. "What sort of musical training do you have?"

"I was in choir in high school," Helgi admitted. "I'm a music major, in the first trombone section in the band and orchestra here. I've never had singing lessons."

"What made you decide to do it now?"

His sneakers were very dirty, Helgi noticed as he looked at them. The spatter of blue ink where his fountain pen had leaked on the right one was still there, though it had faded a little in the month since school had started. *Don't be a wimp*, he told himself severely. *All she can do is tell you to fuck off.* He raised his gaze to meet her eyes. "I thought I ought to learn properly," he answered. "I'm planning to stay for graduate study in composition, and I'd like to add voice." There, the words were scored on the air now, and he could not scratch them out.

"That's quite ambitious, especially if you haven't had much vocal training. Unless you turn out to be quite naturally gifted, I can't promise to teach you enough for you to pass the spring auditions for graduate work. I don't want to discourage you, but, as you know, this department does have quite high standards. On the other hand, if you're accepted for graduate study in composition, you might be able to add voice later."

"All right."

"Do you have any other languages?"

"I've done three years of Latin and three of German."

"No French or Italian?" Helgi shook his head.

Ms. Devereaux pointed to the corner farthest from the piano. "Stand there and don't look at the keyboard. Just sing after me and follow the notes. This is an exercise to give me some idea of what your range is and how much you know about singing."

Dutifully, Helgi looked at the cracked plaster in the corner in front of him as she played three notes slowly, singing, "Aaa-eee-aaa." Even on the nonsense syllables, he could hear the richness and power of her contralto voice. He took a deep breath and repeated "Aaa-eee-aaa" after her, even in his own ears, his own voice sounded thin and flat.

"Your breathing's all wrong. Breathe from the stomach, so, and don't let your shoulders move." Ms. Devereaux stood, placing a thin hand beneath her solar plexus, and inhaled to show him. "Again."

Helgi breathed in deeply, as he had been taught for the trombone letting the wind breathe through him without strain, himself the instrument first, and his teacher nodded. "Better. Let's keep going up, though, and see how high you can get."

Helgi gave it his best try, but as soon as his voice cracked the first time, it seemed as though his throat completely shut down, he could not hit the note again, although Ms. Devereaux urged him towards it twice.

"Well, let's see what kind of low range you have."

Going down, Helgi felt easier, his throat loosed, rather than knotting, and he sang a little more loudly.

"Well, you have a workable range, anyway," she said at last. "From low G, down here, she plunked the note, "to high D." She struck the note just above middle C. "With a little work, you can train up at the very least to the E or the F above that, which means that you'll be able to sing most things written for baritone and some moderate bass pieces. A bit more warm-up work, now."

By the end of the lesson, Helgi was exhausted. He could not sing more than a few notes without her stopping to correct him, if his breathing was not wrong, then his stance was, or he was producing sound from too far down in the throat, or else he had wandered off pitch.

"Fairly simple songs to begin with," she said at last. "You must get really thoroughly grounded in the basics before you push on to more serious singing. Then, your voice is still in the process of fully settling and it's very important not to strain it at this point."

Helgi nodded. "Can I, Um, do you think?"

"If you work on the exercises and songs I give you and you will certainly get better. I can't say at this point whether you might have a solo-quality voice or not." Ms. Deveraux's dark eyes looked smooth and polished as shards of flint against the pale earth of her face, if Helgi saw no yielding there, he saw no eiderdown-softness of lies either. He grasped the keen edges of her truthfulness as a sign of hope, but now he knew it was a cutting hope, whose wounds had kept him bitterly silent for four years. But he could not stand mute while others sang his songs, and he could not keep from shaping them. That, too, he had learned as his need grew with his skill and his skill grew with every new piece he heard. *If only I can be good enough,* he thought *just good enough that people will be willing to listen to my music?* He did not yet dare shape his dearest dream. That his voice itself could strengthen the songs.

Two of the pieces she chose for him looked disappointingly simple. A silly English folk song that began, "Oliver Cromwell is buried and dead. Hey, ho, buried and dead. There grew an old apple tree over his head," and another, translated from the Italian. The third, Schubert's setting of a song by Goethe called "Wandrer's Nachtlied", seemed more promising to Helgi, though it was very slow and very short.

"Work on these for now. Later in the year we shall do Christmas carols, if you like."

When Helgi got back to his student apartment, Mark Tippet's blue Volkswagen bug was sitting in front of the driveway where he usually parked. "Ah, shit," he muttered to himself as he remembered. He glanced at his watch, it was almost seven-thirty, and he'd invited Mark over for six-thirty. He maneuvered the Impala into place behind the bug.

Mark stood in the lobby, leaning against the door with HADDING on the mail slot. "Hey, where were you?" Mark said as Helgi walked in. "Mike let me in half an hour ago, and I thought I was late. Is *Grapes of Wrath* that bad, you have to go nearly an hour out of your way to try and avoid talking about it?"

"I forgot you were coming over. I had a singing lesson."

"I thought you'd given up on singing." Then Mark raised his hands, palm forward and stepped back hastily. "Hey, I'm sorry, Helgi, really. I didn't mean."

"Yah." Helgi was breathing hard, his body tightened as if against the stinging shock of a snakebite. *Him too,* he couldn't help thinking. *I know what he meant.* "It's okay. You want something to drink?"

"Wouldn't mind a beer, if you've got one."

"Sorry. No beer." Helgi led Mark up the stairs and opened the door, bending down to fend off the rush of his elk hound puppy, Elric, before the dog could make it outside. He was just locking it when the phone outside his apartment door rang. "Shit! Wait a minute."

The voice crackling on the other end of the line was his mother's. "Helgi?"

"Yes?"

"Home at last. I've been trying to catch you all day. How do you feel about Minnesota for Christmas?"

"Won't the Jensens be disappointed if we miss their Yule party?"

"Karin won't have her leave till February."

Helgi's teeth ground tightly together, he would not voice any sign of the iron-clad hooves beating at his guts. *I am not a child, I do not have a crush on her anymore!* He thought angrily, and straightened his back, though he could not drive away the image of Karin as he had seen her last, with his gleaming silver valknútr hanging from her throat. She must wear it sometimes, the sharp points against her white skin. If her uniform let her have no jewelery except the marks of bravery, still she was free sometime, if she did not love him, then she loved the heritage from which the valknútr stemmed. Sigfödhr saelsigruna merki. And she had sent him a birthday present that year, a copy of Kevin Crossley-Holland's The Norse Myths with a runic inscription inside the front cover. *May you love these tales of our ancestors as much as I do.*

"Yeah. I'd like to see real snow."

Simple as the songs seemed, Helgi found that singing them was harder than he had thought. He sat in the practice room for an hour every day, wrestling with the notes, with his breath, his own body, until he was too tired to sing any more, and still the sounds hovered just a little beyond his reach. *I am better, I must be better,* he told himself. *I can hear it myself,* but even when he taped his own voice and listened as Ms. Devereaux had told him to, he felt as though he were treading among trembling bog-grasses, his voice had always sounded strong and pure in his own ears, and he could not judge it now. All he could do through that autumn, until Jefferson let out for Christmas vacation, was wrestle with the ghost-foe of himself as long as he was able.

As Helgi's mother had promised, the drifts of snow in Minnesota were higher than Helgi's head. He stared unbelievingly at the high white heaps standing against the ice-starred night sky as he and his parents walked from the airport to the taxi stand.

"I told you so," Helgi's mother said smugly from the depths of her blue scarves and woolly hat. "See what we've been missing out on all these years, Roger?"

"Aren't you glad you came to live in the south with me?" Helgi's father replied, pulling his glossy black fur hat down to cover more of his ears. "A week of winter is all I really need. What do you think, Helgi?"

"I think it's pretty awesome," Helgi answered. The cold tingled in his face like a slap wakening him out of the indoors warmth, sharpening the edges of everything around him. Anything might be lurking in snow like that, he thought as the smaller drifts melted to the low sleek shapes of wolves in the corners of his sight. There, just over there, something was moving in the snow, a sudden white whirling. No, disappointed, he saw that it was just the wind lifting a swirl of flakes from the ground.

"Helgi?"

"What? Sorry. Can't hear a thing through these scarves."

"I was just saying," his father repeated more loudly, "that it's fine for a little while, but round about February you'd be pretty sick of it."

Helgi looked around at the white snow-fields in the darkness. It seemed to him that he could feel the night stretching to months, mewed up in a small and smoky house thick with the smell of humans and animals.

"Yeah. Maybe so. Are there wolves in Minnesota?"

His mother laughed. "You're thinking of Siberia, Helgi. We're not going to be attacked by wolves on the way to the taxi stand."

"But there are wolves here?"

"There are wolves in parts of Minnesota, but there are no wolves here. If you want to see wolves, you are just going to have to go to the zoo."

Helgi's knuckles whitened and his jaw clenched at each turn as the taxi-cab skidded skillfully over the snowy road. From the way his father's thick eyebrows crawled closer and closer together, he saw that he was not the only nervous person in his cab, but his mother seemed perfectly at her ease, chatting on about past winters.

"Yep, this'll be a hard one," the cab driver said. "Got our first snow at the end of September, and there's been something mean in the wind since. Straight down out of the north without a change, all winter long, would you believe it? Light-show's been nice, though." He switched hands on the wheel, puffing on his cigarette as he casually spun the cab out of a sideways skid.

"You mean the northern lights?" Helgi asked.

"Sure do. Where are you from, anyway?"

"Dallas."

"Dallas, huh? You know J.R.?"

Helgi and his father looked at each other, rolling their eyes up together.

When they got to Karl and Emma's house, Helgi went ahead of his parents to kick the way clear through the knee-deep snow over the path that led to the door, the soles of his boots rasping over damp cement. Snow mounded high on either side of the pathway, someone must have shoveled it clear again and again. The house's roof slanted at a sharp angle, its dark shingles were bare near the top, where the snow had slipped away. Long twisted ice-fangs stretched down from the eaves.

"Is that you, Kirsten?" Aunt Emma called, opening the door as they came up the walk. She was wearing an apron and her cheeks were flushed, trails of gray-blond hair floating loosely from the pile on top of her head. She had gotten plumper since last Christmas, when she had been constantly insisting that she was On A Diet.

"No, it's a family of trolls come to move in for the winter," Helgi's mother answered. "Got any young children for us to eat?"

"There's Lisa, but she's a little too thin to make much of a meal out of. Tony's too old, and I don't think troll-folk want a child named Christian. Sorry, you'll have to content yourself with ham and beer soup."

"Beer soup?" Helgi said as they came into the living room and began to shed their layers of garments.

"It's an old Danish recipe," Aunt Emma answered cheerfully. "Not nearly as horrid as it sounds, I promise. And it's just the thing to feed trolls who turn up on your doorstep."

The Christmas tree was up already, packages heaped about the bottom and a spiral of colored lights blinking up around it like the coiling of a bright snake through its branches. The wrought-iron wreath above the huge fireplace was a twin to the one at home, though this one was woven through with glossy green twigs of pine and red-berried holly. As the eldest sister, Emma had inherited the house which the Anderssens had built when they first moved from Denmark. The ceiling in the living room was very high, held up by heavy planks with a cross-beam running a couple of feet below its peak, the walls were lined with pale pine.

"Why is there a bowl on the roof-beam?" Helgi asked as he sat down on the couch beside Lisa. She was eight now, he thought. She wore a red velvet dress with a little amber brooch at her throat, and she was petting her soft skirt as if it were a cat.

"It's for the nisse," she answered, looking shyly up at him. "He gets porridge every night at Christmas-time. I make it for him and Daddy holds me up so I can put it up there."

Helgi tugged gently on the red bow at the end of one of her golden-brown braids. "What's a nisse, then?"

"He's a little man who lives here and looks after things. He wears a little red cap and sometimes you can see him peeking over the beam. Mother told me about him. She said he came over with our grandparents, and he might be one of our relatives from way back."

"Ah," Helgi said, nodding. "I see. Very good."

"Mother said that the nisse lived in one of the little mounds on the old farm in North Jutland," Helgi's mother said unexpectedly. "She brought some of the earth from the mound to put in the foundations of this house. She said he was the luck of the family."

Helgi glanced up again, looking into the shadows clustered at the beam's ends. The luck of the family

"Did he have a name?"

His mother blinked, shaking back her silver-gilt curls. "You know, I think he did, but I can't remember what. It was like something out of Wagner Sieg-fried? No, not Siegfried.Emma, do you remember what the nisse's name is?"

Emma brushed a strand of hair from her sweaty forehead, squinting her eyes until she looked like a plump gnome-woman. "Ah. Mother used to call him. Old somebody, what was that Danish word she used for 'old', some-thing like 'camel' Gammel Sigmund, that was it! Old Sigmund."

"Old Sigmund," Helgi echoed. "Did she really believe in him?"

"Oh, she was most particular about him," Emma smiled. "Gammel Sig-mund had to have his beer and porridge, and we shouldn't make noise on Thursdays, because that was his day off and he might be angry."

"It was a good way to keep us quiet," Helgi's mother agreed. "Mother had all sorts of horrible stories about the things nissen did when they were an-gry, throwing plow boys over the barn was the least of it."

Uncle Karl tapped his fingers against the arm of his chair. "My, we are ver-itable mines of Danish folklore today. I've told you before, Emma, you ought to talk to an ethnologist, they live for this sort of thing."

Emma laughed a small embarrassed laugh, Helgi's mother only shrugged. "I hadn't thought about our nisse in years. I don't think he comes down to Dallas."

"Why should he, when he gets his porridge here?" Uncle Karl asked lightly. "Speaking of living quarters, Helgi, do you mind sharing a room with Tony and Christian, do you? It'll be a bit of a squeeze, I'm afraid."

"I don't mind at all," Helgi answered. "Do they?"

"They'd better not. It's upstairs, the second door on the right."

"Okay." Helgi got up again and took his suitcase up. A third bed had already been set up in the middle of the room, straddling the scuffed line of duct tape that divided it in two. Its neatly tucked corners and smooth quilt looked strange between the blanket-heaped messes to either side of it. Helgi dumped his suitcase on top of it and started to drag out the presents he had brought for his relatives.

The planked walls in this room were marred by a number of scars and gashes. Above one bed, a skeleton scowled from the back of a motorcycle, next to a giant Gray's Anatomy poster showing a flayed man with neatly labeled internal organs, the brooding leather shadow of Jim Morrison stared from the opposite side. There was only one window, set into the wall that slanted sharply upward over the foot of Helgi's bed, the glass was blanked out by snow. Curious, Helgi went to it and opened the panes outward.

Through the rush of icy air, Helgi saw that he was actually looking out from halfway up the house's roof. Then he stopped stock-still, his breath freezing in his throat as he stared at the glowing banners of ghost-light in the sky. Red and pale blue against the deep blue-black of the sky, they shift-ed and flared and wove about each other in the eerie stillness of the snowy night. Here a spear of white streaked through the air, there a flickering violet aura flared up to outline what might have been a dark-cloaked head and hunched shoulders.

Helgi clung numb-fingered to the icy window-frame, the shifting lights playing through his skull.

"Hey! Close the window, it's getting cold in here!"

Unwillingly Helgi glanced behind him. Tony's black hair flopped to one side of his face as he cocked his head to look up at his cousin. "What're you staring at out there?"

"The lights."

"Oh, yeah. Haven't you ever seen them before? We see them all the time."

"I haven't. I'm going out to look at them."

Anchored by one hand on the banister, Helgi took the stairs in great flying leaps of four at a time. Everyone looked up as he ran into the living room and started to scrabble for his coat. "The lights," he panted. "Mom, Dad, come out and look at them."

Helgi's father grabbed his coat and hat almost as quickly as Helgi had. His mother smiled, following along more slowly with her sister and Karl as Roger and Helgi hurried out onto the lawn. The light-veils drifting over the sky were more awesome now that Helgi had to stand on the snow and tilt his head back to see them burning coldly above him.

"That's something. That's really something," Helgi's father said, his voice soft and blurred with amazement. Helgi's mother said something in answer, but Helgi did not hear it. If Karin were here, he thought. She could fly them up through the shifting lights, through the icy night-rainbows of fire.

So swift, and he could see their radiance flaring about her, white streaks of aurora feathering out behind her like long hair, pale blue light glimmering out from her eyes and shining in a corona around her head, the dawn-red streaks trailing from her plane as it clove the frozen sky.

Helgi stood and watched the lights until long after everyone had gone in, until his mother came out to say, "Don't you want to come in for dinner, Helgi?" She took one last glance up at the brightened sky as Helgi urged his snow-numb feet towards the house. "I thought I'd remembered what they were like, but it's always a shock, every winter you think you'd imagined some of it, but it's all real."

"Will it do this every night?"

"I don't know. If it stays clear it might, but the weather report said another storm was coming in around the middle of the day tomorrow. I hope Jetta and Mike get here early."

"It's going to snow more?"

"You think this is snow? Oh, wait until you see what's left when the storm has passed. I've seen it get past the eaves of the house."

"How did anyone ever live here?"

"We're tough Vikings," his mother answered, patting him on the shoulder. "You'd be surprised what people can learn to live with. Go on, go wash up, dinner's about to be served. I think the bathroom's the first door on the right upstairs, right next to your room."

The clouds had rolled in by morning, the first flakes of snow had just started to fall when Uncle Mike and Aunt Jetta came bustling up the walkway with Margrete and Barney in tow. They had brought an immense array of pickled and smoked foodstuffs for a lunchtime cold table.

"My, my, we are being ethnic this Christmas, aren't we?" Helgi's father said teasingly as Aunt Emma brought in a tray of drinks. Next to each beer bottle stood a tiny frosted glass of ice-cold akavit, all neatly arranged in a double ring.

"We thought as long as you'd come all the way up here, we ought to entertain you with our quaint native customs," Emma answered. "Skoal?"

"Just beer for me, I think. Helgi," he added as Helgi reached towards the tray, "you watch out for that stuff. It will take your head off. Believe me, I know."

"The beer goes with the akavit," Tony said, helping himself to both. "You shoot down the akavit and then you have a drink of beer to wash the taste out of your mouth. Every time someone raises their glass and says 'Skoal' to you, and you have to empty your glass."

"You may be starting pre-med, but if I catch you doing it more than once, you'll be washing dishes from now till next Christmas," Emma told him. "Don't you give any of it to the little kids, either."

"I'm not a little kid this year," Christian said, smiling up at his mother with what looked to Helgi like a practiced expression of blond angelicas. "I'm seventeen. Can I have a beer?"

"One. Just one."

"Well," Uncle Karl said when everyone had a plateful of food, "here's to us. Skoal!" He raised his akavit.

"Skoal!" The rest of the family echoed, raising their glasses and drinking. Helgi tipped his akavit back in one swift motion. The icy cold burned his throat, shocking it numb, it was a moment before he got enough breath back to cough. Tony laughed.

"A little strong for you, huh?"

"Tony," Emma said warningly.

Helgi nodded ruefully. "Nice once it's down, though." He took a sip of beer to wash down the caraway-taste the akavit had left in his mouth, then started to eat. Suddenly a flare of light shocked through the window, followed by a thunderclap that rattled the glass in its frame. A moment later, everything outside was entirely blotted out by whiteness as a gust of wind filled the window with snow.

"Going to be a bad one," Uncle Mike said. "We were listening to the weather reports on the way over, and they said it looked like to be the worst storm in ten years."

"Well, there's plenty of food and drink in the house, and the woodshed's full," Emma answered. "I think we'll probably survive."

It was snowing too hard for them to see the lightning, but the thunder crashed now and again. To Helgi's surprise and delight, the wind was actually beginning to moan over the rooftop and in the chimney something he had never heard in his life. The sound was eerily monotonous and a little disappointing at first. No one could possibly mistake that for voices, he thought.

But after he had listened to it for a few minutes, Helgi began to see how it could work on the mind, until the howl gave birth to something calling in words. The thunder boomed against the wind, its deep note steady and oddly reassuring through the wailing that rushed over the house. Karin would say, Helgi thought, that Thor was fighting the Frost Giants now. He wondered if she liked this kind of weather, and what it was like where she was stationed in Southern California or Arizona, she might be swimming in an outdoors pool, or sweating in full uniform under a winter-softened sun.

"Does this mean we don't get to stay up and go to the midnight Christmas Eve service?" Margrete asked. Her big horn-rimmed glasses hid most of the expression on her thin face, but Helgi could hear the disappointment in her voice. "Last Christmas, you promised me I could carry a candle this year."

"You can carry a candle here," Jetta promised her quickly. "If the storm's died down a little by midnight, we can carry candles around the house and sing carols in the snow. And if it hasn't, we'll do it inside."

"Can Santa Claus come through the snow?" Lise asked. Ignoring everything on the table, she had gotten her mother to make her a peanut butter sandwich, and the peanut butter was smeared around her mouth. "They said on the TV that the weather was going to be too bad for flying."

"Santa Claus is stopped by no storms," Margrete told her. "His reindeer can fly through anything." She glanced up at Helgi, as if for confirmation.

"That's why two of them are named Donner and Blitzen," he agreed solemnly. "Which is German for 'Thunder' and 'Lightning'."

Uncle Karl smiled, leaning forward. "But in Germany, he drives a wagon which is pulled by two goats, because reindeer come from the very far North. They are herded by Lapps up above the Arctic circle, and do not appear in Germany."

"Huh," said Barney. "What do Germans know about Christmas?"

"Oh, they know quite a lot about it. They gave us Christmas trees, for one thing. As far as I know, setting up trees and decorating them was originally a German custom. In fact, most Danes didn't have Christmas trees until sixty or seventy years ago. Instead we had wreaths like the wreath on the mantle piece, which has been in your mother's family for generations without end, as far as I know. Speaking of the wreath, Christian, why don't you go get the fire going and light the candles?"

"I read somewhere that decorating the Christmas tree came from pagan sacrificial customs," said Tony, grinning, as his brother crouched down in front of the fireplace. "The old Germanic tribesmen used to hang people and animals on trees, see, and stick spears through them and...."

"Enough, Tony."

"They did. This is very educational. Freedom of information, Dad."

"Does not extend to you discussing the gruesome details of early Germanic human sacrifice over lunch. Before you get started, we don't want to hear about bog people either, or mummification in ancient Egypt, or anything else concerned with similar topics. I am declaring a unilateral moratorium on morbidity for the time being."

"Okay. Anyway, I was just going to say that when the Christians wouldn't let them do that anymore, they hung up little dolls and bread things instead, and that's why we decorate trees the way we do."

Helgi looked over at the Christmas tree, hung about with glittering balls and winking lights, candy canes and strings of popcorn and cranberries dangling over the gifts heaped below. Many of the decorations were wooden, snowflakes and dolls and stars carved out by his grandfather, some were stuffed cloth, embroidered by his grandmother, and some were bits of wood brightened by markers or dabs of glitter, which the children must have made when they were younger. He could see its roots stretching back across the ocean into a well of darkness, its branches reaching outward as green shadows through the room. A higher tree, with holy gifts hanging from it, dangling dark through the windswept branches that gleamed green and living beneath the winter's weight of snow, an ancient, ever-green tree, roots reaching deep between the earth-shrouded stones of a burial mound, twined about bones and gold. The tree he looked at was rootless, but if it could sprout again. Dizzied by his sight, Helgi raised his bottle and took a deep drink of the malty beer.

After lunch, Helgi, Margrete, and Barney hung their stockings from the mantel, across from the other three children's. Emma and Helgi's mother disappeared into the kitchen, Uncle Karl turned on the TV. "Anyone want to watch a video?" He asked. "We've got The Court Jester, healthy and relatively innocent amusement for the whole family." Everyone did, except Tony, who had already sat down in front of the living-room computer.

"Want to play World Conquest?" He said to Helgi as Karl slotted the video into place. "Great game. The goal is total violent domination of everything and everybody. Much more fun than healthy and relatively innocent amusement."

Since Helgi had already seen the movie, he pulled one of the folding chairs over beside his cousin. "How does it work?"

"This is the test scenario, see."

Tony and Helgi played World Conquest through the afternoon, until their mothers drafted them to help set the table and carry in plates of food.

"Where's the main dish?" Tony asked his mother, after they had carried in mashed potatoes, cranberry jelly, fruit salad, rye and white bread, butter, and a host of lesser foods, arranging the dishes carefully between the china and the three large silver candelabras on the table.

"In the top oven. Shoo," Aunt Emma added, moving her ample body between her son and his goal. "You'll see it soon enough. It's a surprise."

"So surprise me now."

"No way. Out of here, out." Emma flapped her sauce-spotted apron at her son. "You too, Helgi. Don't even think of poking your nose in there."

"I know what it is," Margrete said from behind them. "I was coming through to see a man about a chimera when you were putting it in. You can bribe me."

"See a man about a chimera?" Helgi echoed.

Margrete turned a scathing glance on him. "Dogs are so ordinary." Helgi looked at her blankly. "What I meant was, I had to pee. I was using a ladylike expression. Now, Auntie Em, what about that bribe? Is there an extra portion of dessert?"

"Margrete, sweetie, come here," Emma told her. "You see this oven? There's just enough room left just enough for you."

Helgi's mother looked at the digital clock flashing above the oven. "I think it ought to be done by now, anyway. What do you say we let these two stalwart Danish heroes bear it in triumphantly?"

A gleam of light traveled up and down Margrete's huge glasses as she considered her cousins. "Tony doesn't look very stalwart. He's too scrawny."

"Oh, thank you so much, Runt," Tony answered. "Let's talk about the bird, huh?"

"What bird?"

"The bird you traded legs with."

Margrete looked down demurely at the thin calves beneath the lace-edged hem of her dress. "I have the elegant and slender legs of a future fashion model," she replied, turning and stalking out on them before Tony could say anything else. Helgi snickered, Emma sighed.

"Ah, the trials of having genius children in the house. Well, you wanted to see it, boys, here it is. Specially ordered in October, slaughtered and prepared by trained specialists, roasted by people who had absolutely no clue." She flung the oven door open, a warm gust of rich scent blowing out into the kitchen.

"Oh my god what is it?" Tony gasped in one breath. Helgi blinked, staring at the browned thing inside. It stared back at him out of glazed and horrible eyes.

"I think it's a pig's head," he answered in a low voice. "Is it dead yet? It must be, it hasn't eaten its apple."

"We're actually going to eat this?"

Helgi's mother and Aunt Emma each took one side of the roasting pan, easing the pig's head out of the oven. Now over his first shock, Helgi began to grin. "That's excellent."

Aunt Emma beamed back at him. "I'm glad you like it. It took us forever to figure out how to do it. We're still not sure we did it right, but there's some alternate meat."

Helgi's mother bent down to open the bottom oven, taking a large joint of pork out. "We would have gotten a whole pig to roast, but it wouldn't fit in any of the fireplaces."

The two women transferred the head and the joint to a huge silver platter. Helgi recognized the pattern of interlaced roses around the edge, it was the same as the pattern on his mother's best silverware, which she had inherited from her mother. Aunt Emma added a big silver fork and the matching silver-handled carving knife, crossing them carefully in front to the head.

"Now, you two wait in here until you hear the music," Emma instructed them. "Then I want you to bring it in and carry it around the table before you put it down. And if you spill so much as one drop of grease on my carpet." She slashed her finger across her throat.

"Yassuh, boss massa," Tony answered, going into a swift funky shuffle.

The two women left the kitchen. Helgi heard the ding of a bell, then his mother's voice announcing, "Dinner is served!"

He and Tony stood and waited through the muffled comments on the beauty of the table, how good the food smelled, and all the other things the family said every year. Then the plinking notes of a harp came clearly through the voices. The two of them hefted the heavy platter between them and began to walk slowly.

The dining room was lit only by flickering candles, their light gleaming off the china and crystal and casting wavering shadows over the pale wooden walls. As Helgi and Tony started to carry the pig's head around the table, a trio of men's voices began to sing from the stereo,

"'The boar's head in hand bear I,
 All bedecked with bay and rosemary,
 And I pray you, masters, be merry,
 quod estis in convivio.'"

When Helgi and Tony had finished their round of the dining room, they stood at the foot of the table holding the pig's head up between them.

"'Caput apri defero
Reddens laudes domino,
Caput apri defero
Reddens laudes domino.'"

Everyone applauded at the song's end, as the two boar-bearers lifted their burden up and placed it carefully in the center of the table.

"There's a traditional Yule dish for you, Roger!" Aunt Emma said. "You're the guest from far away, do you want the honor of carving it?"

Helgi's father looked dubiously at the pig's head. "I thought the boar's head was English."

"Well, it's somebody's traditional Yule dish one side of the North Sea or the other. Go on, have a go at it."

He picked up the carving knife and fork, poising them above the pig's head as he looked for a likely place to start.

Tony snickered. "Looks as though you're about to sacrifice it."

"Shut up, Tony," Christian said.

Uncle Karl looked over the rim of his glasses at his elder son. "I'm beginning to reconsider my opposition to human sacrifice. Someone was giving me full instructions on the traditional method earlier, do I see a volunteer over there?"

"Not me."

Helgi's father raised the carving knife. "Okay, watch this, everyone. I dedicate this pig to whoever the Vikings dedicated pigs to. Freyr and Freyja, if I remember rightly." He plunged the knife dramatically into the pig's head. It grated on the skull before the blade got half an inch in. "Um, yeah. Maybe the sacrifice got away that time."

"Try slicing the meat off bit by bit," Helgi's mother suggested. "I don't think you'll get very far if you try to cut off big hunks of it like that."

Everyone moved into the living room after dinner, except for Lise and Aunt Emma who went into the kitchen to cook the nisse's porridge.

"Any chance we could turn on the news?" Uncle Mike asked. "I'd kind of like to hear what the weather's planning to do tomorrow."

Christian flicked on the television. The screen-light burst into a patter of static as he punched the remote-control buttons, searching for a station.

"What channel are you on there?" Uncle Karl asked.

"I'm on 7. You think the storm's knocked our aerial down again?"

"Well, I'm not going up on the roof to see. Keep trying."

Finally the flickering hiss of light-snow cleared into grainy shapes. "Got it!" Christian said gleefully. "I guess the weather's just interfering with the signal. This is thirty-nine, it should be the news."

"Really bad snow," the voice of the static-shadowed announcer said. "We warned you yesterday, and all our predictions are coming true. It's dumped over two feet since this morning, and there's no sign of a letup anytime tonight or tomorrow. Stay indoors and enjoy your holiday. Do not attempt to drive anywhere. In case of medical emergency, call..." He started to give a list of phone numbers for various areas. Helgi noticed that Aunt Jetta had gotten a pen out of her purse and was jotting them down. "Finally, we're getting a lot of thunder and lightning with this one. Be aware of the possibility of a power failure and be sure you've got plenty of fuel for those old wood stoves. Ah, just a moment." A second shadow came onto the screen, something passed between them. "Special bulletin from Santa Watch. We've had a sleigh sighting over one of the suburbs north of Toronto, and it looks like he's heading in our direction. If he keeps due on course, he ought to get here just after midnight, so get those cakes and milk out for the jolly old elf. Bruce Keynes reporting for 39 Weather, Merry Christmas and goodnight."

"Well, that's that," Jetta said, dropping her list back into her purse and snapping it shut. "Don't worry, Mike, no one's going to work until the roads are cleared, and tomorrow's Christmas anyway."

Uncle Mike's heavy brow eased smooth as he looked at his wife. "I guess you're right."

Aunt Emma and Lise came into the living room, Emma carrying a steaming bowl of porridge. Lise hurried over to stand under the roof beam, looking expectantly at her father.

"Daddy? Will you lift me up?"

"Why don't you let someone else do it for a change? Helgi seems to have grown into a tall and sturdy sort of chap, maybe you should ask him."

Lise turned her gaze up to Helgi. "Will you pick me up so I can give the nisse his porridge?"

"Sure."

Helgi came over to her and crouched down so that she could seat herself on his shoulders. Her little body seemed almost weightless as he rose slowly up to his full height. Emma carefully handed the porridge up to her daughter.

"Careful, dear, it's hot, and Helgi won't like it if you spill it on him. Hold still, Helgi, and help her keep her balance. She's got to reach up quite high now. There, Lise, straighten up."

Helgi held quite still, keeping a fast grip on Lise's legs as her weight shifted.

"Nisse, nisse, here is your porridge with honey and milk, for a happy Yule and a good year ahead," his cousin chanted as she set the bowl on the roof beam. "Now I'm up here, will you give me a horsey back ride, Helgi?"

Helgi trotted about the room a few times as Lise clung to his hair and drummed lightly against his chest with her heels, calling out "Giddyup." Finally Aunt Emma rescued him by declaring it to be Lise's bedtime.

The blizzard was still raging outside at midnight, but at Margrete's insistence, they turned off all the lights and lit candles.

"We ought to sing carols, too," she said. "We always sing 'Silent Night' when we walk out with the candles at church."

"The night's not very silent," Barney objected, waving a chubby hand at the window. "How can we sing 'Silent Night' with the storm making all that noise?"

Margrete looked down her nose at her brother. "The night is silent in spirit," she said loftily. "And we always do it. Everyone has to sing."

"I'll put the CD on, and those who want to can sing along," Aunt Emma suggested. She slid the disk into place, checking the song-list on the jacket by the light of her candle and forwarding till a digital 5 gleamed green from the darkness. "Everyone ready? All right, then!"

Helgi took a deep breath as the first slow strains of the music sounded, getting into his place in the line of light-bearers. Margrete walked before them, holding her candle high as if to light the way around the living room for the others.

"'Silent night, holy night,'" he sang, shifting to match his voice's own key to the choir singing from the stereo. "'All is calm, all is bright'" My god, he thought as the others joined in one by one, we really do sound terrible. I wonder why I never noticed before? Helgi sang more loudly, trying to keep his pitch true for the rest of the family to follow. "'Round yon Virgin Mother and Child, holy infant so tender and mild. Sleep in heavenly peace, sleep in heavenly peace.'"

Helgi hoped that someone would say something about his singing, but at the same time he remembered how Aunt Jetta had commented on its improvement two years ago, and he knew he could not bear to hear that again. However, when the song was over and Emma had turned the lights back on, Jetta only said, "Now it really is time for us all to go to bed. Merry Christmas, everyone."

The family parted with a ragged chorus of mutual Merry Christmases, some going up the stairs and some going into the guest bedrooms past the kitchen. Although Helgi had felt a little drowsy earlier in the evening, he was wide awake now. Up here, under the roof, the wind was louder, its cry scraping the snow from the shingles above him. He showered quickly, sliding into the thick flannel pajamas Uncle Karl had lent him.

"You play any sports at college?" Christian asked him.

"I'm in the marching band. Does that count as a sport?"

"Nope. You look like you ought to play something."

"I do. It's called a trombone."

"Sport, sport."

"Well. If it makes you any happier, I do karate."

"What belt are you?"

"First dan, that's a black belt to you."

"How many bricks can you break now?"

Helgi took a deep breath, ready to repeat his sensei's lecture on the futility of brick- and board-breaking.

"Ignore him," Tony advised as he walked in, rubbing his wet hair up into spiky dampness with a towel. "He doesn't believe in anything that can't be kicked, hit, or rewired so that it only works when the moon is full and the wind is blowing from the south."

"He's jealous because I got onto the varsity soccer team this year and they wouldn't even take him as a bench-warmer when he was a senior. That's all it is, jealousy."

Christian and Tony glared at each other across Helgi's bed. So this is what having a brother is like, Helgi thought. And sometimes I wish I did, and sometimes. He held out one hand, palm forward, to either of them. "Hey, guys. Merry Christmas. Peace and goodwill, and all that nice shit, remember?"

"Yeah, right," Tony muttered. "Okay, peace and goodwill, more or less. Merry Christmas."

"Merry Christmas," Christian echoed, walking over to turn off the light.

Helgi lay still in his bed, staring at the window as he listened to the wind snarling over the roof and keening through the icicle-hung eaves. The thunder was very far away now, its crashing drowned in the wind, but every so often the snow lit blue, and he could feel the electricity tingling through him, sparking between the blankets and his pajamas every time he moved. Tony shifted in his bed, turning his back to Helgi and curling up like a shrimp, Christian lay flat on his stomach with his head turned to the side, his open mouth dark against his pale face. Helgi turned to one side, then to the other, but he could not find ease. He felt as though his bones were willfully setting their edges against the soft mattress, as though his body were raising its own wolfish night-wakening against the stillness of sleep.

Helgi did not know how long he lay twisting about like that, nor could he mark the moments when his two cousins slid into their own dreams. But after a while he simply lay still on his back again, letting the sounds of the wind rush through his head until they twisted into words. "Out of the way! Let the way be clear!"

He blinked several times against the white afterimage of the frosted window, then suddenly rolled out of the bed. When he stepped off the braided rug, the wooden floor shocked cold through his feet. I am awake, I am awake, Helgi thought. Each of his hairs seemed to prickle with unseen sparks as a little ice-shiver rippled along his back. He could still hear the calling, and behind it the wind rising into a host of other sounds.Quickly, softly, he tiptoed over to open the window. The wind was cold enough to numb his face and hands at once as he looked out, hooding his hair and cloaking half his face in snow. It was blowing harder, though he could see darkness through the swirling white, and now the words that had sounded in the wind rose to men's voices shouting above the howling of wolves, though Helgi could not make out what they were saying. The wind swirled a blast of snowflakes harsh as sand-grains across his eyes, he blinked again and again as the snow-shadowed darkness melted into shapes, riding before him over the high snow-field.

He was crying out as he leaned out the window, his mouth was open, and he could feel the cry in his throat, but he could not hear it through the sound of the horns and the howling. The wolves that ran before the wind were dark, but their ember-eyes glowed red, their white fangs dripped down into icicles. The horse galloping behind them shone grayish-white as old bones in the storm, its many hooves churning the blowing snow into a swirling mist around its eight legs. A broad-brimmed hat hid one of its rider's eyes, the other was red as a wolf's, glowing from the shadowed hollow above his snow filled beard. He held a spear above his head, poised for throwing, his dark blue cloak flapped behind him like the wings of the ravens that wheeled through the snow above him. One of the black birds croaked loudly as it flew, the other was silent, a pale eyeball clenched in its beak.

Behind the host's dreadful leader, some rode on limping three-legged steeds, some, their blue-black faces swollen, swung on the ropes knotted around their necks. Helgi saw the glint of byrnies in the blue lightning, and the ghastly black streaks of blood flowing from the wounded warriors as they fought, old wounds bleeding still and new ones springing fresh as sword and spear scathed them again. Maimed, some headless, some holding limbs or clutching at the ice-glistening entrails that twisted out behind them in the wind, they rode wildly, their battle-cries rising into trailing screams. Helgi thought he glimpsed gleams of bronze beside iron, flint striking on steel.

Here sparks leapt from the spike of a World War I helmet, there tatters of a jungle-blotched camouflage uniform blew back from a soldier's rent and rotting flesh, there a knight rode in full armor, the side of his helm caved in and blood spurting through his visor. Beside the dead warriors rode gray women on gray wolves, snow-whitened hair streaming behind and mouths black with blood. Now and again woman and wolf turned to tear at those who hastened beside them, muffling their own ice-keen howling in mouthfuls of flesh as fury masked the rending pain. Some of the shapes shifted as the host rushed onward, beast-jaws jutting from men's faces and fierce muzzles melting back to open mouths, fur thickening like coats of snow or stripping away again beneath the rasping wind, others seemed masked, their warped heads swollen and fierce grimaces carved deep and unchanging.

Their riding pounded an awful music through Helgi's head, horn and drum and screaming flute thundering through his bones and rising high within his skull. Breathless, he would be, if the wind had not ripped his breath from him already, and the music was calling him on to ride with them behind the eight-legged horse. Now he could hear his own voice singing wordlessly above them not wordlessly, there were words, though he could not understand them. He wanted it, he wanted the sound of his own singing to the maddened music, and he reached outward towards the riders, about to run towards them, except that something was tugging at his legs to hold him back. He turned, striking out blindly, and at the same moment a sharp pain scored down his back and flashed brilliantly through his eyes. Helgi cried out, covering his eyes with his hands. He could hear a deep growling, only after a moment did he realize that it was coming from his own throat.

Slowly he took his hands from his eyes, letting the brightness seep into them again. Tony half-sat, half-lay against the far wall, his eyes very wide and his mouth open as he stared at his cousin. Helgi shook his head hard, as if he could shake off whatever had come over him.

"What happened?" He whispered.

"I was going to ask you that," Tony hissed back. "What the fuck were you doing?"

"What happened?"

"I woke up, it was cold. I turned on the light to see what was going on and you were almost all the way out the window. I tried to drag you back and you lost your balance you were lucky, you fell in instead of out, and you hit me. What the fuck were you doing out there?"

"I don't know. I think maybe I was sleepwalking."

"Climbing out the window in a blizzard?"

"I guess so."

Tony used the wall to heave himself up, limped over to the window and looked out. He shut it, shaking his head. "Nothing out there but snow and wind. Fuck, it's cold in here. That must have been why I woke up. I wonder why no one's come to see what happened."

"Why should they?"

"You knocked me across the room, I landed hard. You were making noises."

"Christian's still asleep."

Tony looked down at his slumbering brother. He shook his head. "That's not possible. He's got to be faking." He reached down for Christian's shoulder, shook him hard. Christian muttered something indistinct and rolled over. "Pretty good fake." He leaned down, hissing in Christian's ear, "Christian don't you smile, don't you dare laugh," but got no response. "Damn, that always gets him. Maybe he really is asleep. Helgi, tell me, dammit, I know something's going on. Do you have drugs here? I guess you could've tranquilized him while I was in the shower or something."

"No drugs. Nothing. I swear." Helgi reached around to rub his aching back, then gulped back a hiss of pain. The pajamas were torn, a wet flap of flannel hanging loose behind him, and his fresh blood was warm on his hands. "Shit! I hurt myself coming in there, I think. How bad does it look?"

"It's real bloody. I can't tell unless we get it cleaned up."

The two of them crept into the bathroom. Helgi pulled the pajama top off carefully and let Tony sponge his back clean with a wad of damp tissues.

"Ah it's not that bad. You just managed to skin yourself a little, and the bleeding's stopping now. The great future Dr. Antonio Schumacher will take care of you for only a moderate fee. Hold still."

Helgi waited while Tony got a pad of gauze and some white surgical tape out of the cabinet below the sink. "Good thing for you my brother thinks he's a jock. He's always bunging himself up, so we've got loads and loads of medical supplies up here. There you go, now. Wash the blood out of your pajamas and go back to the room. I'll be back up in a moment with my final prescription. No good doctor leaves a patient in pain."

Helgi sat on his bed until Tony crept back in, a frosted shot glass in each hand and two bottles of beer clutched under his arm. "Here you go. Purely medicinal, of course." He handed one to Helgi, the sharp scent of akavit rose up as a cold mist. "Skoal!"

"Skoal!" Helgi echoed. They tapped glasses and downed the drinks. Knowing what to expect this time, Helgi braced himself for the burning burst of cold in his throat, and let it ebb away a little before he quenched it with a draught of beer. "Thanks."

"One thing, though. Mom keeps count. If she asks about the missing beers, you drank both of them."

"Okay."

"What were you dreaming, then?"

"I don't remember. Hey, thanks for pulling me back. I'm sorry I hit you. I hope I didn't hurt you."

"Nah. Knocked the breath out of me, and I'll probably have a few bruises. Good thing you didn't hit me in the face, though, or my nose would be on the other side of my head."

"I really am sorry."

"So, tell me what was going on, and I'll forgive you."

"I thought, I guess I was dreaming. I dreamed I saw a bunch of dead people riding outside in front of the window, and I was going to go join them."

Tony shook his head in disgust. "You were going to go join them, all right. You'd have wound up at the bottom of a snowdrift on our lawn, and we wouldn't have found you till the spring thaw. Dead people riding, hmm, sounds like that dumb cowboy song 'Ghost Riders in the Sky', or something. You sleepwalk often?"

"Not as far as I know. No one's ever told me I did, anyway." Helgi yawned. The akavit had eased the aching in his back, and he was bone-weary. He did not want to think about what had happened, or what he had seen. Though he could still hear the echoes whispering through his skull, it was no more than a faint tugging, he was out of the undertow's grasp.

Helgi finished off his beer, then crawled beneath his cold quilt. "Good night. Merry Christmas."

"Merry Christmas to you too. Don't do it again, okay?" Tony said, turning off the light. Helgi heard the sound of glugging in the darkness, then the rustling of blankets, and nothing more until Lise's shrill voice shouted "Merry Christmas! Wake up, guys, it's Christmas!" He opened his eyes to snowy morning light.

Helgi's back was very stiff and sore. He was careful to keep it turned away from Christian as he dressed.

"You didn't hear anything strange last night, did you?" Tony asked his brother.

"Nah. Slept like the dead. Something wrong, Helgi?"

"No. Why?" Helgi asked, pulling his T-shirt down hastily and tucking it into his jeans.

"You just got a funny look on your face there."

"Nothing's wrong." The window was a solid square of frost this morning, dimming the light to a pure translucent whiteness. The wind was still blowing hard, now and again the roof would creak beneath its force. "I wonder if it's still snowing."

"Sure to be."

Helgi followed his cousins down the stairs, walking very quietly. He felt very strange, as though he were only half-there, bones delicate as crystal within ghost-clear flesh. He could not shake the feeling that he had actually gone out the window, that this was the dream now, or else a ghost's dreaming half-life. He squeezed his left arm tightly with his right hand. The bones and muscles were solid as wood under his grasp, his fingers dug in hard enough to ache.

Margrete, Lise, and Barney were already gathered in front of the fireplace, staring at the full stockings which now lay neatly before the hearth, odd corners and curves bulging against the red wool. The electric lights were on, the snow outside was higher than the windows.

"Where's everyone else?" Christian asked as he put more wood on the banked fire.

"They're waking up. They told me they'd come in at nine-thirty," answered Lise, as Christian set to poking at the embers and working the fireplace bellows until the new wood caught. It was always like this on Christmas morning. The stockings had to wait untouched until the first adult appeared.

Tony checked his watch. "Any minute now. There! Merry Christmas, Dad, Aunt Kirsten, Uncle Roger."

"Merry Christmas, everyone," Uncle Karl and Helgi's parents answered. Uncle Karl bent to start the Christmas music, and the children all pounced on their stockings. As he unearthed each new treasure, a box of Anton Berg chocolates, a Led Zeppelin CD, the sheet music for a trombone solo. Helgi did his best to show as much enthusiasm as the others. Now and again, though an image from his dream would twist before him in the shadows and flames of the fireplace. A wolf-rider, the broad-hatted spear-bearer, a masked or beast-faced shape, drawing his mind away from the gifts under his hands again and again. Yet terrible as some of the shapes were, it was not gruesomeness that shadowed Helgi's vision, but awe, for with each memory came an echo of the music which he had heard last night, which still longed through him, its driving rhythm pounding through the sound of 'Adeste Fideles'. Am I going nuts? He wondered. Visual and audible hallucinations, sleep walking. For a brief moment it occurred to Helgi that Tony could have slipped some acid into something he drank last night, but then he remembered reading that acid trips lasted something like eight hours.

Not possible, he decided.

"Everything all right, Helgi?" His father asked.

"Oh. Yes, everything's fine. I was just thinking how this is almost everything I wanted."

"Well, go on. That stocking doesn't look empty to me yet."

The last thing in the toe of Helgi's stocking was a small gift-wrapped box. It rattled heavily as he tore into it, he did not have to fake his yelp of delight when he saw the gold-plated Mirafone trombone mouthpiece inside. Better shape, better tone-quality, he had been nagging for it for months, and the delight of its gleaming weight in his hand brought him back into the ring of celebration.

"Too bad I didn't bring my trombone with me," Helgi said, grinning. Then he sobered, thinking, I could have played this music, I can hear it, but there was no instrument in the old Anderssen house, no one in the family except Helgi played anything.

"Sorry about that. We didn't want to warn you, besides, who can say what Santa might be bringing?" Helgi's father winked at him.

"Who can say, indeed?"

Helgi lay awake for a very long time that night, but heard nothing except the wind over the roof and through the eaves. The next day, the storm had passed, and the boys joined their fathers in moving the snow that lay higher than their heads, while the snowploughs rumbled and scraped their way through the streets. The moments of memory pressed less and less frequently on Helgi's mind as the week went by, the howling wind had stilled, and he tried to think of it only when no one could see his face.

CHAPTER X

The Sun was up by the time Hailgi woke, shining brightly through the open tent-flap. He wanted to pull his cloak over his head and go back to sleep again, but his bleary eyes fell on the empty ground around him, and he realized that he was alone in the tent. The shock woke him fully, he was on his feet and out of the tent in a moment, blinking fiercely against the warm morning light.

The other tents had already been loaded, and most of the thanes were in the ship already. Only Berikan, Athalwulfar, Angantiwar, and Leugar stood on the shore, Hailgi realized that they had been waiting for him.

"Why didn't you wake me?" He asked fiercely.

The men glanced at each other, avoiding his gaze. Leugar scuffled the toe of his shoe through a fall of little pebbles and broken shells. "We weren't going to leave you," he muttered, looking down. "We only thought you wouldn't care for being woken too suddenly."

"We'll get your tent," Athawulfar said. He and his brother hurried towards it without waiting for another word from Hailgi. They pulled out the wooden pegs swiftly, easing the stakes down and folding the heavy wool. Hailgi watched them for a moment, then shrugged and waded out to the ship with Leugar and Berikan splashing behind him.

"Have your gear ready, all of you," he said when Athawulfar and Angantiwar had climbed aboard and stowed the tent with the others. "We should see them on the road sometime today, but I don't know when, so be ready." He bent to put his arms through the sleeves of his own byrnie, straightening his back and heaving his hands upward so that the chain-shirt slithered down over his body. Reaching under it, he unbuckled his sword-belt and put it back on, a hole looser, on top of his byrnie, then settled his iron cap upon his head.

Berikan steered the ship along the shore. As before, Hailgi sat beside him, but now, instead of staring into the waves, he strained his eyes towards land, looking for the shapes of men on horseback. Sigiruna awoke early, gasping in deep breaths of cold dawn air. She did not know whether she was glad or sorry to see the faint gray light through the guest-house's smoke hole, her eyes were still dazzled with the beating of raven-wings and the brightness of blood, Hailgi's face pale as a lightning-bolt through a shower of arrows and spears.

The linen that had been smooth and clean last night was rucked up around her, wet as a warrior's tunic after battle, and Sigiruna could smell her own sweat above the sweet freshness of the new straw tick she had slept on. Her heartbeat slowed as she lay there, trying to call her dream back to her mind.

It seemed to her that she had led wolves to the battlefield, and that one of the gray heath-walkers had shifted like mist, rising into Hailgi's shape, but the young warrior's mouth had still frothed like that of a wolf long ill with the howling wod, his face twisted with its madness as the rising wind swept her on before him, her sword beating aside the sharp-edged hail of arrows dropping down towards him.

Even as Sigiruna strove to remember the rest of the dream, she could feel it slipping from her mind, like a little grass snake slithering between her fingers and away. Hawk's Height was a good walk from the hof. Sigiruna had to skirt the boggy ground around the edge of Nerthus' grove, then make her way over the low rising and falling of the land for some way before she saw the tall mound with the house on top of it. Its shadow was short, for the Sun was nearing her mid-day's height, and Sigiruna could see that the hill's edges were too regular and its shape too smooth for it to have grown from the earth. Some great one of elder days must lie buried under it, Wodhanar's-Karl was a brave man, and mighty, to live so closely with the dead. Sigiruna hurried up the hill, pausing before the door.

The gables were carved with small shapes, men in horned helms and birds of prey with curling beaks. Their swirling lines drew her gaze in, winding her thoughts about their haunting patterns. It was a struggle for Sigiruna to pull herself away from the designs graven in the dark wood, to raise her hand and knock on the door. For a moment she heard nothing within, then a slow, heavy shuffle moved closer to her. The door opened. Although Wodhanar's-Karl was stooped within the thick muffling of his deep blue cloak, Sigiruna could see that he was a tall man, and very thin.

His hair shone pure white in the light from the doorway, and his pale blue eyes caught the Sun's brightness so keenly that they seemed to glow like clear gems. Without thinking, Sigiruna reached out to clasp his arm as if they were two warriors meeting. The gudhe returned her grip. Though he must once have been very strong, she could feel his muscles trembling beneath her own with the shaking of the alf-shot's bale Hredhild had told her of. That is ever the risk of one who does battle in the worlds beyond the Middle-Garth, she thought. Who has made danger his calling, may ever go into the earth through it. Already she felt herself awed by Wodhanar's-Karl, and swallowed hard, trying to think of fitting words to speak to him.

"I am very glad that you are here, maiden of the Skjoldings," the old gudhe said to her. His voice was very high, but strong and pure, like the keen sound of a metal horn. "Come in and sit down, I think we have much to speak of."

Wodhanar's-Karl left the door open, the clean wind blowing through his house. Everything within was very neat, the byrnie and helm of his younger days draped over a wooden mount in the corner and the wolf-hide that lay over his bed straightened with paws and tail outstretched so that the beast might have been sleeping with its chin on the lower pillow. There was a row of small iron tools and three mallets of different sizes on one of the shelves that hung from the ceiling, perhaps he had once worked the thin temple-to-kens of gold with the shapes of gods and heroes beaten or stamped into the metal.

Two long harps, one greater and one lesser, hung from hooks on the wall. Although the day was warm, the fire burned brightly in the middle of his hearth. The gudhe reached down to the keg that rested on his table, clearly meaning to offer Sigiruna a drink, but as she slid her horn from its loop, she saw that his hands shook so badly that he could not grasp the tap.

Sigiruna picked up the wide-mouthed cup beside the keg. "Holy fro, please let me pour the draught for us, it is little fitting that you should have to bear it to me," she said swiftly.

"I thank you," Wodhanar's-Karl replied, stepping back so that she could fill his cup and her horn. Slowly he lowered himself onto the bench, and Sigiruna sat down beside him. She had been careful not to pour the cup too full, and now she saw that she had done rightly, though he clasped it in both hands, it would surely have split if it were fuller. She raised her horn to him and they drank together.

The draught was the finest mead, sweet and strong, with a warm taste of berries beneath its honey.

"How did you know who I am?" Sigiruna asked Wodhanar's-Karl curious-ly. The old gudhe smiled, his eyes glowing warmly at her.

"I knew your mother well. And news fares fast on such a small holm, it is seldom that a maid so tall and fair comes here with a spear in her hand, as though Wodhanar had sent her straight from Walhall."

As he spoke, a wisp of memory floated through Sigiruna's head. She thought that there had been dead men fighting in her dream, warriors bat-tling beyond the field of the fallen, as in Walhall, where the walkurjas ever waked the slain to do battle again. She watched Wodhanar's-Karl closely, trying to guess what the grave look on his long face might mean. But instead he turned to asking her how matters went with the Skjolding clan, questions that anyone might ask, and Sigiruna knew better than to press him into deeper speech before he was ready.

"But you are not yet betrothed?" The gudhe said.

"There is only one man I would have for my own, and I do not know how matters are with him," Sigiruna answered. Even as she spoke, it seemed to her that she could feel her body beginning to thrum, like a bronze harp string twisted tightly and plucked. Her breath was coming more swiftly, her heart beating faster, as though she had been running full-tilt up a hill, and she could feel the blood burning in her face. Her own hands were beginning to shake now. She leaned her horn against the wall behind her before she could spill it.

"Lie down," Wodhanar's-Karl said. The two harps on the wall rang with the echoes of his strong high voice, the sound through the small house dazing Sigiruna so that she could not think of doubting him, or doing other than he told her. She leaned her back down on the bench, swirls of brightness and darkness rising over her sight. "Your hero has need of you now. You must gird yourself with sword and spear, a bright helm on your head and byrnie on your body. Now you must mount the wind-gray steed, ride over air and water to his side."

The white glow in the gudhe's blue eyes brightened as he spoke, it seemed to Sigiruna that she could see that light shining through the house, the red network of runes that warded the walls and the lightning-hot eyes of the hawk that sat unseen on the highest gables. The horse that stood beside her, waiting for her to mount, was gray and shaggy as a wolf, her own shape on the bench was hardly more than a pale wisp of mist in her sight, but sparks flew from the tip of the spear in her hand as she rode forth into the Sun's light.

When Hailgi finally saw Hunding's band, a little before midday, he could not help glancing upward to silently thank Wodhanar for his help. His foe man's warriors had dismounted, and sat around a fire by the side of the road with their horses tethered to the trees behind them, eating and drinking. Hunding's dog's-head banner stood with the butt of its pole planted deeply in the ground, the warm breeze lifting it enough for Hailgi to recognize it, there was no doubt that he had found what he was seeking. A rise in the land would hide the ship from them when it had come in closer to the beach, so that Hailgi and his men could easily come to land without being marked. Hunding's band was bigger than Hailgi had thought, thirty or thirty-five men to his own twenty, but Hailgi knew that if he moved swiftly, he could keep the advantage.

Berikan was already steering inward without being told, until the little hill cut Hunding's band from their view and the ship's bottom bumped gently against the slope of the shore. Hailgi was first over the side. He did not look back to see if the others were following him, but rushed through the water and up the beach, his sword drawn and shield in his hand. Flashes of sight blurred sharp across his mind. The spray splashing from beneath his boots, a gray sea-hollowed boulder in his path, then below him as he leapt up over it, the pale sand falling away beneath the dandelion-starred grass and the rounded sea-pebbles studding the sandy path upward.

Hunding's men were just rising to their feet as he leapt howling among them, Hailgi saw bearded faces frozen open in shock, hands clenched tight on the hilts of undrawn swords, as though his cry had fettered them. His blade was already moving, its tip cutting through the sparse blond hairs of another youth's throat to open the hollows and slice the blood-strings within. The young man cried out soundlessly in a gout of bubbling blood, tears started from his blue eyes as he fell forward, hands scrabbling uselessly at his neck. Hunding's warriors rushed forward at once, but by that time Hailgi's thanes had caught up with him. The two bands met with the resounding crash of stag's antlers breaking on stag's antlers.

Shield shattered against shield as sword clashed on sword, spears bit into byrnie and flesh, but the battle-cries drowned out any lower grunts of pain. A glancing blow rang off the side of Hailgi's helm, staggering him for a moment, he thrust out blindly, feeling his blade cut deep into flesh, and jerked the edge sideways through the falling man's guts as he wrenched it free. Men's voices roared in his ears, but he could not hear the shapes of the words.

He was dimly aware of the froth running down his chin as he cut his way through the battle, maddened by the blood like a wolf among a herd of deer. The high brightness of one high-standing helm drew his eye to a massive graybeard, who howled like a deep-voiced hound as he fought. Hailgi strove nearer to him, saw his sword break through the side of Athawulfar's byrnie and the dark-glistening entrails slithering tangled over the bloody rings as the youth twisted away from him. Then Hailgi was before his foe at last, hewing at the big man with all the fury that his days in a woman's garb had stoked up in him. Although the other's great strength forced Hailgi back now and again, his own wrath and swiftness gained more ground for him, till he had his foe's back to a beech tree. The graybeard was bleeding from a dozen small wounds, Hailgi had laid his sword-wrist open, so that he moved more and more slowly. With a last roar, he flung himself up from the tree behind his shield.

Almost too late, Hailgi saw that he meant to strike with the linden-wood, not stab, he leapt aside, in time to turn the blow that would have brought him down into a glancing slam that cracked his own shield's edge. He staggered from the weight of it, but his swift move had thrown his foe off balance too. Hailgi recovered a moment more quickly, stabbing beneath the edge of the other's shield before he could turn, and his blade went in deep. The stroke was almost Hailgi's death as well, for the big man did not fall as Hailgi had thought he would, but turned and brought his sword down. The blade rang from the edge of Hailgi's helmet, whispering cold past the edge of his jaw and sinking deep into his shield. Hailgi wrenched the linden away, it cracked in two, but the swift movement tore the sword from his foe man's hand. The point of Hailgi's blade ripped its way up the arm, driving up under the helmet's edge and through till it stuck in the other warrior's skull.

He did fall then, taking Hailgi's sword with him. Hailgi did not bend to pull it out, but turned and leapt backward over him, covering himself as well as he could with his half-shield as he looked about to see which way the next foe was attacking. It took his battle-glazed eyes a moment to see that all the men standing were the thanes he knew, as the roaring in his ears slowly shaped itself to a cry of "Hailgi, Hailgi!" Suddenly he felt very weak, he staggered backward till he could lean against the tree that had braced his foe's back a few moments ago, its solid wood anchoring him against the sudden wave of dizziness sweeping over him. He shook his head, wiping the froth from his face, then grunted in pain as his hand caught in the torn flesh along his jaw, where a flap of skin the width and half the length of his finger dangled.

He pressed the skin back and held his palm tightly against it as Hagalar had taught him, trying to stop the bleeding and still the throbbing ache with one gesture.

"Hailgi, are you all right?" Thonaraharjar asked, leaning over him. "How badly are you hurt?" The other men had crowded around as well, their shadows blocking the light through the beech's leaves.

"Not badly," Hailgi answered, straightening himself up and stepping away from the tree. "I think this scratch on my face is my only wound, and my beard will hide it well enough in a year or two. How many of ours are down?"

"Hlauthwigar and Katilar are dead, Gjardhjarjar, Athalwulfar, and Hadhu-wardhar are badly wounded and will soon die."

Hailgi walked back to the bloodied grass where the fighting had been. The ground was so badly torn up that he could no longer see where the sandy path had been, the bodies of men lay here and there, cast about the wal-stead like rock-torn seals flung up on the beach by a winter storm. Athalwulfar lay face down, moaning and clinging to the slippery things falling from his side. Hailgi crouched down beside him, his need to help prickling against the back of his eyes and aching in his throat even as it closed against the stink of shit. Then he froze motionless, he could see that there would be no healing for Athawulfar's wound.

"Athawulfar," he said softly. "Can you hear me?"

The other youth moaned something Hailgi could not quite make out, then, more strongly, "Hailgi?"

"It's me," Hailgi said. He saw the clear drop fall from his face onto Athawulfar's side, he could not help it.

"Don't let me die," Athawulfar pleaded. He turned his head, looking up towards his friend. His blue-green eyes were open wide, swollen pupils staring blindly. Suddenly his teeth clenched as his hands tightened on his side. "It hurts, Hailgi, it hurts! Help me, please."

Hailgi glanced up at the older men, as if they might know something more than he did, but Aiwimundar only shook his head and Leugar turned away.

Hailgi wanted to close his eyes as he drew his dagger, but he knew the only kindness he could give his friend was to cut hard and sure. He laid one hand on Athawulfar's shoulder to hold him steady, he thought that the youth never saw his other hand move.

Athawulfar gave a single bubbling sigh, rolling over onto his face again as the life left him. Shakily, Hailgi wiped his knife on the torn grass, wiping again and again till grass and sandy earth had scoured away every trace of blood.

"That was bravely done," Aiwimundar said, bending to help Hailgi up. "Don't feel ill about it, did he know what would have lain before him, he'd have thanked you for it, and you may yet thank someone else for the same. If you doubt me, ask his brother, he'd have done it if you didn't."

Hailgi glanced at Angantiwar before he could help himself. The older youth nodded, then turned quickly away, his shoulders shaking. "His first battle, too," Aiwimundar murmured. "Leave him be."

"What about the other two?"

Aiwimundar's dark eyes flickered to one spot, then the other. "They've been cared for. Now, Hailgi, we've three living battle-captives and a mess of dead bodies to see to. What shall we do with them?"

There would be no bale-fire, they were too close to Hunding's marches to send up such a cloud of smoke.

"Can we take our dead with us?"

"Think again. It's summer, and not such a cold one either. There's little extra room in the boat, and most of us won't be rowing so hard as we were going out, nor is the weather as fine as it was. Now we could take them with us if you really thought we ought to, but you wouldn't like them nearly as much by the time we got home, and there's more than a little risk in it."

Hailgi looked up at the sky. Although it was blue above their heads, a bank of dark clouds was rising in the east, and a sudden gust of cool wind blew an early leaf past his face.

"No," he said unwillingly. A few dark shapes were circling high above, like black leaves in the wind, he could not tell whether they were ravens or sea-eagles. "Wodhanar has given us the victory, then let his birds have the slain, and the fowl of Gunthar and her walkurja-sisters may feed well upon the wal-stead. As for the men we have taken, we shall take them to Fetter-Grove." A sudden thought struck him, he glanced anxiously about. "What of Hunding? He didn't get away, did he?"

"Don't you know?" Aiwimundar asked. It was hard to see surprise on the thane's battered face, but Hailgi heard its note uplifting his voice. "It was he whom you killed, there at the last the big man with your sword still in his head." He pulled the thrice-coiled ring from his right wrist. "I hope you won't throw this in my face again, but a name needs a gift to go with it. Hailgi Hunding's-Bane. That's how you'll be known from here on, and I daresay that no one will be likely to mock you for this summer's deeds again."

"I thank you," Hailgi said, taking the ring from him and bending it to fit around his more slender forearm. "Shall we go now?"

"I think we've a few things still to pick up. If you take my meaning."

Hailgi looked around at the field again. Hunding's men had fared finely, with many gold rings and well-wrought silver brooches as well as their armor and weapons, and these belonged to those who had won the day, as much as they might belong to anyone. There were the horses, too, pawing wildly at the ground and straining against their tethers, they would not fit in the warship, and if they were loosed they were likely to run straight back to Hunding's hall, so there was only one thing that might be done with them.

"So we do."

Hailgi pulled his sword from Hunding's head, cleaned it on the grass, and sheathed it at his side again. That done, he picked up one of the spears that lay on the ground. "You all belong to Wodhanar!" He cast it over the horses, it shot through the leafy branches and was lost to sight. He and Hildigairar went among the steeds then, stepping carefully as cats between the tossing manes and sharp-edged hooves as they slit the great neck-veins one by one. Dark sprays of blood stained the beeches' smooth gray trunks, the two slayers were bathed in blood when they were done, hair clotted and byrnies blackened.

Two of the flying ravens had already come to earth, croaking over the slain. The flies were gathering as well, drawn to the wounds of the living and the dead. Hailgi could not hope to beat them all from him, but he brushed a black cluster from the scrape on his face and kept his hand over it as he walked down to the beach to wash himself. He took his byrnie off and left it in the sand, then squatted down in the cold waves and ducked his head under. His gasp of startled pain filled his mouth with salt water as the sea bit into his bloodied jaw, but he clenched his teeth against the pain and scrubbed his hair and body as hard as he could. At last he got out, and scuffled his byrnie through the sand until all the blood was scoured from it.

When Sigiruna opened her eyes again, she thought it must be dawn, but the light outside was too bright, she must have slept a long time. Then she saw the pale, lined face of Wodhanar's-Karl above her, and stared up at him in wonder. "I did the walkurja's work, as if I were never born a living woman," she murmured. "I strove against Hunding's idises, the ancient kinswomen who warded him on the battle-field, and my might overcame them, I turned aside the blow that would have split Hailgi's skull." She stopped. It seemed too much to believe, the memory already blurring into the past night's dream.

"That is the walkurja's work," the old gudhe agreed. "Tell me. What else did you see?"

"I saw hook-nibbed birds above the warriors' heads, and wyrms with wings and beaks, all of them dark and baleful, and I saw men fall where they lighted. And it seemed to me that they flew most thickly in that part of the fray where Hailgi did battle, and it was no easy thing for me to ward him from them."

"Wights of ill-luck and baleful idises often follow the hero, for his doom hovers ever near to him, as near as you yourself. What else did you see?"

"I saw the shapes of ghosts behind the living men. Though often they were naked, they wore helms horned with the heads of birds, and their hands guided the aim of the spears."

"Those were Walfather's wish-sons, Wodhanar's harriers, who have their share in the choosing of the slain. Did you see more?"

"When Hailgi slew Hunding at the battle's end, it seemed to me that the shadow of a great eagle's wings fell across the wal-stead, and the storm-wind of their beating swept me up, so that I might not linger by my beloved when the fighting was done, but must ride back here, back to my own hide again."

As Sigiruna pushed herself up to sit straight-backed on the bench again, she saw that something gold glittered in Wodhanar's-Karl's long-fingered hand, gleams of light sparkling out as his grip shook. It was a thin round nearly as large as his palm, stamped with sharp lines and swirling lines. Sigiruna had to blink several times before she could see the shapes clearly. A man stood, or danced, one leg was lifted to cross over the other in a half-hedged enclosure, he held a ring in one hand, but she could not be sure of what was in the other. From his middle jutted a broken twig. Before him was a winged figure, behind him, a man who held a spear, but above the dancer's head was a shape like those Sigiruna had seen flying greedily over the field of battle, a snakelike bird with huge beak and cruel talons.

"There is Baldhrar, the brightest hero among the gods, wounded by the mist-twig that was grown to be his bane." Each time Wodhanar's-Karl stopped for breath, Sigiruna could hear the wood and strings of the harps on the wall ringing beneath his keen voice, until it seemed that her own skull rang in answer. "Before him is Loki, winged in Frija's falcon-hide. But above him is Hella's messenger, for the Death-Frowe long wished for Baldhrar to lie in her embrace, in the world of the grave, and behind him stands Wodhanar with his spear." It seemed to Sigiruna that the glittering of Loki's winged shape mirrored the leaping flames of the gudhe's hearth, but Wodhanar's shape was shadowed, only his spear gleaming from the gold. "There Baldhrar stands in the hallowed stead. You can see that he is hedged about by the wall of the garth, and the ring he holds is Wodhanar's ring Draupnir, his own death-gift that shall be laid on the bale-fire with him, Wodhanar's spear-point is down, for his deeming is already done."

"Are you saying that Hailgi is doomed to death?"

"You and he have both made your choices. If he were not death-doomed, you should never have ridden to him. Wodhanar's eye watches over you, and I have seen his madness whirling about you. It is seldom indeed that a walkurja-ghost is born into the Middle-Garth, and Wodhanar's maids do not love men not unless the god orders one to wed, to bring a hero to his doom and death-joy to his battle-women. But without your warding, Hailgi Hunding's-Bane should not have lived out this battle, nor should his deeds have given new might to the hero's name he bears."

Sigiruna saw Hailgi's gray eyes wide beneath his helmet again, and it seemed to her that the sound of his wild howling still echoed in her ears. How his sword had shone, cleaving keenly through the weaves of flesh and soul to slice death from life, how fair it had been to fight above him, where the battle was mirrored in the hidden world of the blood-thirsting war-wights and the dark-winged ones strove for their prey!

"I would not have it otherwise," she said slowly, "not though it meant his death, and mine, and many more. I am not yet betrothed, and there is no cause why he and I should not wed."

The gudhe pressed the thin round of gold into Sigiruna's fingers. It was very warm from his hand, as though he had held it near the fire while she slept. She could not look away from the white pools of light in his eyes as he spoke. "Hold to this," Wodhanar's-Karl told her. "It will show you much as you think on it, and in time be a fair gift to leave for Wodhanar when you come to his blessings in Fetter-Grove."

Sigiruna curled her fingers around the bracteate. She was about to speak when Wodhanar's-Karl said, "There is one who can teach you more than I, if she will."

"Hredhild?"

"No, the woman I speak of does not dwell in God-home, but in your own island, by the holy stone half a day's ride north of your father's hall. She is a Frisian woman, called Ansuwunja, and she is seldom seen among men, for she was wedded to the Last Sheaf in her youth, and given with the hallowed grain, to be Wodhanar's bride. Even when I knew her, she was more skilled in the runes and galdor-craft than any, now she must be mighty indeed."

"I had heard that a madwoman lived there," Sigiruna said slowly, "for my mother fares at times with food and clothing for her. I did not know that she was Wodhanar's bride."

"Even here, it has been long since a maid was truly bound to the Sheaf. But Ansuwunja went willingly." Wodhanar-Karl turned his gaze away from the light, and the white glow faded from his pale eyes. "She is as close to a true walkurja as will ever tread this earth, she has never loved a living man, but has slain several with her own hands, as gifts to Wodhanar. She may not speak to you, but you should at least lay eyes on her, if you would know how strongly our god walks the world."

It was growing late in the day when at last Hailgi and his men were ready to set off. The wind had begun to blow hard drops of rain in their faces, and the sky was darkening before sunset.

"We won't be able to get too far tonight," Berikan told Hailgi. "Nor will it be wise to get out of sight of land. Push there for me, my right arm's stiff." Hailgi saw the stain of dried blood around the rent in the shoulder of the steersman's tunic, and took the rudder without any questions. The ship turned easily under his hand. "Good, you'll do well. We'd best make for Bruni Bay, though it's on Hunding's land, it's well sheltered, and if we don't light fires, there's small risk of us being seen."

"All right."

Hailgi followed Berikan's guidance, steering the ship around the coast. Between the wind that blew against them and the nine men that were too badly wounded to help with the rowing, they moved slowly, wallowing through the rising seas until they got to the deep crescent-bay Berikan had chosen for their night's rest. There, the waves no longer lifted their heads angrily against the wind, and the ship glided to an easy stop. Those who were whole carried the leg-wounded and the three captives ashore, and set at once to raising their tents beside the little stream that flowed from the wood into the ocean.

Gleaugir paused at his work, raising his head and staring intently among the trees. "Look! Hailgi, do you see the cow over there?"

Hailgi looked through the shadows, he thought he could just see the lighter brown shadows among them. "Someone had best go see if there's a cowherd with her, then. I think some good fresh meat would make a fine supper."

"Funny, that was just my thought." Gleaugir's thin mouth cracked open in a grin.

Tired as he was, Hailgi thought that if Gleaugir was ready to show him friendship again, he ought not to waste the moment. "Let's go, then."

The cows was alone. As Gleaugir and Hailgi came close, she looked up and mooed plaintively.

"Looks lost to me," Gleaugir said.

"Well, she's found now." Hailgi and Gleaugir grabbed her by the halter, and together they led the cow back to the camp.

"Fresh meat!" Fastawulfar rejoiced softly, pulling his swollen lips into a smile. He flipped his sun-whitened hair from his eyes with a toss of his head, bending to stroke the cow's neck. "Let me get to know you better, darling."

"It'll be very fresh," Eburhelmar's son Eburgairar said sardonically from where he sat propped against one of the tents, his wounded leg stretched straight in front of him. "Since we can't start a fire to roast it, there'll be none fresher."

"I think that wound's curdled your blood," Fastawulfar answered. "Who's too weak to eat raw meat? At home they always said it was the making of warriors."

"Very likely, where you come from. I don't think your kin have learned to make fire yet."

"Say that again when your leg's whole, and see what happens to you!" The other thane replied. With half a front tooth missing, his grin was more jagged than it had been before the battle.

Hungry as they were from the fight and the long day's rowing, it did not take Hailgi and his men long to carve the cow into bloody hunks of meat, nor was anyone too squeamish to tear into the warm flesh. The rain had driven the flies away, now it washed the cow's blood swiftly from the grass and ran in pink rivulets down the arms of the men. Ingwiawaldar cut the finest pieces of liver and shoulder for Hailgi, giving them to him without a word. Hailgi thanked him, the thane hunched his huge shoulders and glanced away as if embarrassed, muttering something into his bushy black beard.

Salted with its thickening blood, the meat tasted strong and fine. Hailgi had not realized how hungry he was until he bit into it. He hardly chewed the pieces of liver, but the stringier meat of the cow's shoulder took more work to get down, he had to grind the rich taste nearly out of each mouthful before he could swallow it.

"Look at us!" Leugar guffawed, glancing about at the bloody mouths and hands of his comrades who crouched inside the tent-mouths. "We look like a bunch of bear-sarks or wolf-coats."

"Well, why not?" Thonaraharjar replied. "We've fought as if we were, haven't we?"

A few of the men shouted approval, others laughed. Angantiwar sat silently, staring out at the ship as if he still hoped to see his brother's curly head shadowed against the rain. The three men they'd taken were glum, sitting with bound hands and legs as they watched the others eat.

"We might as well feed our captives too," Hailgi said.

Aiwimundar stuck a finger into his mouth, scraping a strand of meat out of an empty tooth-socket and swallowing it before he answered. "Why bother? You're not planning to keep them."

"There's plenty of meat, and they might as well be strong when we give them to Wodhanar."

"Well enough." He looked about. "Hai, Angantiwar, and you, Fastawulfar. Cut some of that cow for our captives, why don't you?"

Angantiwar stood up slowly and went out into the rain. Fastawulfar looked up from the piece of meat he was gnawing to say, "Cut it yourself if you care so much about it. I'm still eating."

Hailgi, who had finished his own meat, stood. He meant to go and help Angantiwar, but Fastawulfar's blunt face sharpened into a sudden nervous wariness as he took the first step.

"It's all right," the thane said hastily, putting his meat down on his blanket. "I'll be glad to do it, Hailgi."

Hailgi suddenly noticed that the other men had all found corners of the tent or interesting bits of their meat to look at. Slowly he sat down as Fastawulfar went out. Blessed gods, he thought, I think they're frightened of me. Did he think I meant to attack him? Then Hailgi looked about at the other men, hunching in the darkening tent with their faces masked by shadows and blood, and their wariness seemed a little less strange to him.

Angantiwar and Fastawulfar came back in, faces washed rain-clean and hands full of meat. Hailgi quickly went across to the captives and untied the ropes around their wrists. One was a short, heavily muscled youth a few years older than Hailgi, with a scraggly dark mustache and clean-shaven jaw, the other two looked to be in their middle years. The long welt swelling purplish-blue on the big redhead's temple showed how he had been captured. He had the hard and oak-ugly face of a man who had been knocked down and gotten back up many times, Hailgi thought he would not have been easy to take if he had been on his feet, but the spear-shaft or shield-rim had done its job neatly enough.

The third man's long legs were bound up in cloths. Though the work had been done with little care for neatness, it must have been done well enough, for the blood on the bandages was all dry. His face was keen and narrow, with an eagle's curve to the nose, his black hair was bound into a warrior's knot like that Hailgi wore. The youth and the lamed man set to stretching the blood back into their hands and rubbing the white marks of the rope from their wrists at once. Hailgi was expecting trouble from the other, and so was ready to rise and turn a little, taking the blow on the muscle of his thigh instead of in his groin.

"Through now?" He asked calmly. His leg felt as though a hammer had struck it, but he would not rub it.

"Yah. Till you come closer."

Hailgi took a piece of meat from Angantiwar's hands and held it out to him. The captive grabbed at it, he meant to grab Hailgi's hands as well, but Hailgi was a little swifter.

"I'm Frodhamarar, the son of Frodhabernu," the young man said suddenly as Fastawulfar gave him his share. "My father will pay a fair geld to get me back alive and well, if that was your thought."

"Didn't you listen, boy?" The redhead growled. "They're taking us to Fetter-Grove. I hope you count Wodhanar your friend, 'cause it won't be long before you're seeing him as closely as you ever might have wanted to."

Frodhamarar said nothing, but Hailgi could see his skin paling beneath the shadows as he sat with his untouched meat in his hands. The lamed man closed his hand slowly and painfully into a fist, as if his fingers were still numb, and thumped his younger companion softly on the shoulder. "Wyrd writes as she will," he murmured. "We're not hanged yet, so be as cheerful as you can while you may."

The youth nodded and set grimly to eating. After a moment the red-haired man raised his head again. "This meat's tough as an old boot, and I don't think much of your cooking either. If you're going to send us to Walhall, you might give us something worth eating first, or at least something to wash it down with."

"That's not a bad idea," Aiwimundar agreed. "Not for us, anyway. I know there's a barrel of strong ale out in the ship, I loaded it myself. Hailgi? Should we open the ale yet?"

"Go on, but leave some for tomorrow. Give them some, I don't want them complaining to Wodhanar about the way we treated his hallowed ones before we sent them off." Fastawulfar, Thonaraharjar, and Leugar began to laugh, laughing until Hailgi looked at them. "Go on, go get it." He rubbed at his temples. Suddenly he felt very tired, and he wanted to be alone. Over the land, the rain had not eased, but he could see an reddish shaft of sunlight shooting through the swift-moving clouds just above the far-off rim of the sea. "I'll be back in a little while. Save some ale for me, too."

Hailgi pulled a fold of his cloak over his head and walked out into the rain, going past the arching white bones of the half-cleaned cows and down to the shore till he felt the wave-wet sand firm beneath his feet. Then he turned towards the left, following the curve of the coast around until the ship and the tents were lost to his sight. After a little while, he threw the wet cloak back from his hair, letting the rain wash his face and hands clean. The cold of the water running from his scalp down his spine tingled through him, the air tasted very clear. Tatters of cloud hung dark and thick from the sky, chasing the wind-swept veils of rain over the darkened sea. The light in the west shone bloodier against them, as if the flames leaping from a burning ship glowed through a chink in the cloud-wall.

He had come to a rocky part of the beach now, where Agjiwar's mighty arms had cast great loose boulders up on top of the cracked slabs of living bedrock. Slimy with green and black moss, they loomed treacherous in the shadows, so that Hailgi picked his way up the heap with care, not raising one foot until he was sure that the other was firm enough to hold him if he should slip forward or teeter back. One boulder was higher than the rest, and when he had reached that one he sat down to breathe for a moment, watching the low-moving cloud shards run swiftly along beneath the storm-clouded sky. Towards the west, the clouds were breaking before the sunset, Hailgi could not stare through the parting veil for long.

A sudden gust of changing wind struck his face with a stinging slap of rain, the water blinding his eyes into a blurry dazzle of ruddy light. When he had wiped them clear, he saw the wind-blown mists turning towards him, curling into a half-seen shape before his dazed eyes. He caught his breath, staring, his body felt as numb as if he stood drunken in the snow, but his sight was sharpening painfully, resolving the drifting cloud into the shape of a rider on horseback. A helm darkened the rider's face to a grim mask, but long pale hair twisted out beneath its edge to stream behind, her byrnie gleamed in gray rain-droplets, and her steed's legs melted in and out of one another, from four to eight and back again as it galloped towards him.

Her high voice howled pure through his head, wind wrought to steel-silver words. "Who lets the fleet float in the harbor? Where do you warriors have your home? For what do you wait in Bruni Bay? Where do you look to know your road?"

Hailgi did not know who she was, only that she was an awesome wight. So he answered with wary words, "Hamall lets float the fleet in the harbor! We have our home in Hles Isle. We wait for good winds in Bruni Bay, we look eastward to know our road."

"Where have you, warrior, wakened battle and fed the goslings of Gunthr's sister? Why is your byrnie spattered with blood? Why, helmed, do you eat raw meat?"

Hailgi had taken off his byrnie, and wore no helm, but as the woman spoke, it seemed that he could feel them weighing on him, bloody from the battle. A trickle of warmth ran down his neck among the cold rivulets of rain, and he knew that the cut on his jaw had begun to bleed again.

"That most newly won the child of the Wolfings in the west, if you list to know, when I took bears in Bragi Lund, and sated the kin of eagles with edges. Now it is said, maiden, for what reason these things are done and why by the sea's edge we eat little-streaked meat."

"Tell thou of battle! Hunding the kin-leader sank to the field before Hailgi. He bore battle, who revenged a kinsman, and blood streamed over the blade's edge. I was not far, folk's edge-leader, from the ruler's death that morning, though I ween Sigismundar's bairn is wise, to tell of battle-play with wal-runes."

Hailgi's breath was coming fast as he stared at her, and her gray shape was ever sharper and clearer against the deepening red of the Sun. It seemed to him that he must know her now, but her name had fled him. If she would only take off her helm!

"How do you know, wise-understanding one, who it was that revenged a kinsman? Many are the keen sons of warriors, and all like to our kindred."

"I watched you in the fore of the long ship, there where you stood in the bloody stem and the spray-cold waves played. Now the day-bright seeks to hide himself from me, but Haganon's daughter kens Hailgi!"

"Sigiruna!" He cried, leaping from the rock and flinging himself forward. The wind caught him at the moment his foot slipped on a patch of seaweed. He went down hard, both knees banging on the stone with a sharp shock that brought tears to his eyes. For a moment he could do nothing but rock back and forth, clutching his legs and breathing silent pain between his clenched teeth, until the pain eased a little and he could make sure that his kneecaps were unbroken.

When Hailgi looked up again, the storm had broken in a long path upward from the west. The sunset's red light faded to blue-gold a little way along the bridge, beyond that, the road through the clouds was the deep pure blue of night. It was no longer raining. Leaning on a boulder, Hailgi levered himself slowly to his feet. He was very careful making his way back over the rocks, especially since the shadows kept moving, black water-weed shifting into stone and rough stone melting into slimy leaves, he went in a crouching half-crawl like a troll, with one hand always clinging to the rock.

He loosed his breath in a deep sigh when at last he stood on the sand again, straightening his back and looking out over the waves. Sigiruna's steed had left no track, neither in water nor aloft, he did not know how he might follow her, and so he went back along the strand where the sea and wind had washed his own tracks away, back to the men.

Someone thrust a horn of ale into Hailgi's hand as soon as he ducked beneath the tent-flap, it was too dark to see who, but he heard Thonaraharjar's voice, "It was hard work keeping these thirsty hounds off your drink, Hailgi, but I did it anyway, and made a verse about you while I was at it."

Hailgi stiffened, the froth slopping over onto his wrist. Thonaraharjar was already speaking.

"Troll-woman's horse harries less fierce
than Wolfings' brightest warrior, Hailgi!
Hunding's-Bane bested the strongest,
Wodhanar's oak awesome, brought down.
The friend to war gsis free with their meat,
No gloom to ravens glad be they now!
The eagle mead-drunk eke shall be joyful
When kin-leader gives the geld for his aid."

Hailgi pulled the gold ring Aiwimundar had given him from his wrist, twisting at one of the coils until it broke off. Thus was a drighten called ring-breaker. "A well-made verse, Thonaraharjar. May you make many more." He pressed the ring into Thonaraharjar's hand.

"May your victories give me cause to," the thane answered, a gleam of delight brightening his mellow voice.

"The best verses are always made after a hero is dead," an unfamiliar voice murmured from the darkness. Halgi heard the sound of a foot, or perhaps a fist, meeting flesh, then a biting hiss of pain, he realized that it was the wounded captive who had spoken.

"Leave him alone," Hailgi said sharply to the darkness. No one answered straight out, though Hailgi thought he heard a couple of muttering whispers.

Hailgi only stepped on a couple of legs as he made his way to his own heap of blankets by touch, casting off his wet cloak and pulling the covers up around his neck to warm himself before taking a deep gulp of the ale. The horn was empty before he would have liked, but he knew he had to save some for Fetter-Grove.

Aiwimundar had gone to sleep in a moment, as most of the older thanes seemed able to do, he was already snoring like a boar with a snout of roughened iron. It was not long before Hailgi heard a thump and a sleepy mutter of "Roll over and shut up," answered by a more garbled, but less friendly, mutter that ended in "yourself."

Although his tiredness weighed upon him like a night-mare, sleep came slowly to Hailgi. He lay with his eyes closed, trying to compass the day, but his thoughts wandered off the path again and again. He had woken late, Angantiwar was already asleep, or was it Frodhamarar? That soft breathing was surely a young man's. Angantiwar must sleep, else his eyes would stare into the darkness just as his brother's did now, watching for the dark-winged ones who had their choice of the slain. Then they had found Hunding and fought. Blindi Balewise, no, Blindi was with Lingwe.

He had known Sigiruna, or at least known of her, but surely Hailgi couldn't ask him. No one would laugh at him now, though. No one was allowed to laugh in Fetter-Grove, they had to go bound, and silent, to the clearing in the middle of the grove, where the horse grazed freely. The troll-woman's horse, the gray wolf, grazed on the field of battle, now that night had come and the eagle flown to his stead in the ash-tree, the raven's song would greet the bright day. As before, it was Sunna's light that woke him. Hailgi sat up, looking around himself.

The other men were already up, seeing to the tents or sitting on the ground chewing twice-baked bread and drinking water. Hailgi was about to ask why they had let him sleep, but no one would meet his gaze. Silently he rose and rolled his blankets up, then stood gnawing on his breakfast bread as he watched the others take down and load the tents again. Angantiwar stood near him, staring at the ground as he ate and drank. Suddenly moved by his thoughts, Hailgi walked over to the other young warrior. Angantiwar looked up as he came nearer, turning and bracing himself as though he expected a blow.

"Are you getting on all right?" Hailgi asked gently.

"Well enough. We always knew it could happen to either of us, any time, and there's nothing to be done when Wodhanar has made his choice. You avenged him, right enough, though I wish it had been me to do it."

"It's done, anyway. He didn't go to Walhall alone."

"Yes." Angantiwar turned his gaze down to the half-eaten round of brown bread in his right hand and the mug of water in his left. After a little thought, he slowly raised the bread to his mouth.

"Why didn't you wake me up?" Hailgi finally asked. "When we fared south to hold the Winter nights feast with Wulfrun's kin, no one ever let Hagalar sleep past the dawn. Is there a reason why no one bothers to awaken me?"

Muscles moved in Angantiwar's jaws as he slowly chewed the hard bread, finally washing it down with a swallow of spring-water. "Um." He coughed softly, then swallowed again. "Well, the truth is, you swear not to be angry with me for saying it?"

"How can I, when I don't know what it is?"

"Um. You've never woken up very friendly, and now. Well, no one wants to cross you. That's all. You talk in your sleep. Some of the men who were in the tent with you last night had to get up and crowd their way into the other tents because of it."

"I see," Hailgi mused. "What did I say?"

"I don't remember," Angantiwar muttered hastily. He was pale, quite pale in the shadow of the long-feathered cloud drifting across the Sun. "Um, Hailgi, we're taking the captives to Fetter-Grove today?"

"Yes?"

"May I stay to ward the boat? I don't want to go in there, and Wodhanar's taken more than I wanted to give him anyway."

"You'd better stay outside the grove, then."

Angantiwar nodded gratefully and went back to eating, as though he hoped that Hailgi was quite done with him. Feeling oddly lost, Hailgi wandered away again, watching his men until the ship was loaded and it was time for everyone to wade out and climb on board. The wind had changed, it no longer blew against them, but from behind, casting high banners of long thin cloud out before Hailgi and his warriors. Hailgi gazed up at the scattered sky-mists, hoping to see the shadow of the woman and her steed in them, but his eyes could not shape the clouds into more than the streaming tails of white mares.

The three captives sat bound beside him. The big redhead's hands and feet had been tied down to the bench as well, to make sure that he stayed where he had been put, Aiwimundur and Thonaraharjar had not had an easy time tying his hands again the night before. Frodhamarar sat slumped with his knees drawn up, leaning against the side of the boat, while the other man rested calmly on the bench, only clenching his jaw a little when the ship's rocking jarred his wounded leg against the wood.

It was not hard at all for Hailgi to think of himself in their place. He had risked capture three times now, and he was sure that Hunding would not have dealt any more kindly with Sigismundar's son than he himself was dealing with, Frodhabernu's son Frodhamarar, who were the others?

"What are your names?" He asked.

"Why should I tell you?" The redhead replied at once. "What can you do to me that you're not already planning to do? If I don't want to tell you my name, there's nothing you can do about it." He knotted his thick brows, staring straight up into Hailgi's eyes as he locked the muscles that bulged along his jaw.

"I can let you die with your name forgotten, and no one will ever know whether you went bravely to the tree or whimpered and begged to be set loose."

The captive hacked and spat, very near to Hailgi's boots. Hailgi waited patiently, thinking. If I were in his place, I would do the same.

At last the big warrior looked down at the puddle of bilge water by his feet. "All right," he muttered unhappily. "I've got a wife and three sons to home. Will you swear to let them know how things went?"

"I swear."

"My name's Ansumundar, the son of Ansuwaldur. My frowe's Sigiridha everyone calls her Sigga."

Hailgi nodded. "And you?" He said to the man with the wounded legs.

"Will knowing my name make it easier for you to kill me?" The eagle-nosed man replied smoothly. Hailgi winced. Frodhamarar closed his eyes for a moment, as though he could not bear the sight and the words of his doom together.

"Will not telling me make your death easier?" Hailgi replied harshly. The words hurt his throat as he spoke them, as though he were coughing out chunks of flint. At once he wished he had not said it, but it was too late.

The man smiled at him, the thin white rim of teeth-edges showing just beneath his curled lips. "Maybe not. And after all, it is you, Hailgi, who ought to be afraid of us knowing your name. You, of all folk, should know the might of a slain man's word, I heard the things you said in your sleep last night. It's little wonder no one cares to share your tent or touch you, the wonder is that you can fare among living folk when the Sun's light is on you."

A man who could wound while he was bound hand and foot was rare indeed, Hailgi thought, his admiration for the captive's brave mood was already swelling over the hurt he felt at the man's words. "You already know my name, so you may as well tell me yours."

"I am Gunthabrandar, the son of Gunthadis. Does this make you any more joyful?"

"No," Hailgi answered truthfully. He stood looking at them a little longer. Gunthabrandar, Ansumundar, Frodhamarar. Suddenly a great wish rose up in him to turn the rudder back towards Hagalar's lands, to leave Fetter-Grove as it was and take the geld that Frodhabernu would pay for his son and Sigga for her husband and whoever loved Gunthabrandar for him. Gunthadis for her son, perhaps?, And let them go, free from the knots of orlog. It could be me there, he thought again.

Then, The ravens have pecked out Athalwulfar's eyes by now. The three captives looked back at Hailgi. Frodhamarar's eyes were blue with green flecks, widened as if the Sun's light would drive out the shadow of fear behind them. Ansumundar's eyes were the bright blue-gray of a well-polished blade, Gunthabrandar's were deep brownish-black, set deeply beneath the rims of his narrow black brows like gems in the curve of two matched cups. Hailgi's own mirror-shape shone back at him six times over from their pupils, as tiny as if he stood very far away, so that he could only see the glints of his byrnie and his bright hair clearly. As he gazed with all his mind caught up by the image, the eyes around it seemed gray as his own, mirroring himself back again in his own pupils. Shaken, Hailgi turned away.

The boat lurched, so that the bench hit him just behind the knees, he went with it, sagging down to sit. He could not deny Wodhanar his geld, for the god had given him victory, and he had pledged it, only a nithling would go back on his pledge. Hailgi could no more keep these chosen men from him than he could keep himself from Sigiruna, and it was at Wodhanar's will that the walkurja rode. No one spoke very much during the day. They rowed with all their strength, for the faring towards Fetter-Grove was long enough and, Hailgi guessed, there was no one there who did not want to be well-gone from the stead of awe by nightfall. But wind and wave were with them now, not against them, and they made landfall not far from the grassy mound beneath the gray stone which Berikan said marked the beginning of the pathway from the sea to the grove.

"I won't need more than eight of you with me," Hailgi said as Raginaharjar lowered the anchor. "Who is willing?"

After a few moments, Raginaharjar nodded, then Aiwimundar.

"I'll go, I guess," Fastawulfar mumbled.

"Me too," whispered Sigibernu. His brothers Sigihadhur and Sigifrodhar jerked their fair heads in agreement without speaking, though the stubbly lump of Sigihadur's voice-box rose and fell in a sudden gulp.

Hailgi looked around at the others. His eyes met Gleaugir's, he stared until the thane lowered his head in a nod.

"I'll come as well, then," Thonaraharjar finally said, when no one else spoke.

The chosen men heaved the three captives over, lugging them to the beach. They went in byrnies, but bore no weapons, the only weapon in Fetter-Grove was Wodhanar's own. Hailgi waded back to the boat with Aiwimundar behind him. Leugar was already leaning over the side with two thick coils of rope when he got there. As Hailgi took them, he felt a slight tremor in the thane's big hands, but the breath he heard as he relieved Leugar's arms of the weight was deep with relief. He made his way back through the low-rippling waves, Aiwimundar followed him with the lightened ale-cask and a horn.

No one might enter Fetter-Grove unbound, bindings must be laid upon each man, and he who fell could not raise himself to his feet again, but had to crawl or roll from the grove as best he might. Thus had Wodhanar wrought it in earlier times, for it was his might to lay and loose fetters over all that lived and died. Hailgi first bent to loosen the bonds on the legs of the captives so that they might walk to the grove. He was wary as he untied and retied the ropes around Ansumundar's ankles, waiting on another attack, but the warrior stood without struggle, straightening his back as though his sons could see that he would not fight against his wyrd out of fear. Frodhamarar's face was set firmly, jaw clenched over any sound he might make. The dark stubble on his face, Hailgi marked suddenly, was still patchy, the little clusters of hairs would not have made a good beard for two or three years yet.

Gunthabrandar still sat on the sand. He looked coldly at Hailgi as the youth loosened his leg-fetters. "How shall I walk into the grove?" He whispered. "If I were so steady on my feet, you should not have taken me."

"We shall go together," Hailgi murmured back. "You'll lean on my shoulder."

Aiwimundar, Thonaraharjar, and Sigifrodhar took the captives away in turn to let them empty their bladders and bowels, so that they might not shame themselves or stain the hallowed grove. One by one, Hailgi's warriors came before him and let him tie their legs with the same loose bonds that fettered their captives, so that they might not step more than half a pace at a time. Their arms he tied more freely, so that, though he made a rope-end fast around each man's wrist, the loop dangling between was long enough that they could still move their arms freely enough to cast a spear. Sigibernu and Sigihadhur, Fastawulfar, Raginaharjar, and Gleaugir, finally, when their work was done, Aiwimundar, Thonaraharjar, and Sigifrodhar. Hailgi bound them, then, with Gleaugir's help, fastened the same bonds upon himself.

He tucked the other coil of rope under his arm and bent to help Gunthabrandar up. Thin as he was, the wounded man was heavier than Hailgi had thought. His weight was solid as a corpse's, pressing the rings of Hailgi's byrnie hard into the bones and muscles of his shoulder. It took a moment for the two of them to find their balance together, they walked clumsily, like two horses yoked to one wain for the first time. Ansumundar and Frodhamarar followed Hailgi and Gunthabrandar down the path, with the rest of the men in single file behind them. The cool wind stirred the leaves above their heads, scattering golden sunlight over the shadowy pathway, the stones that marked it and the sharp-nailed wolf-prints sunk deep into the leaf-mold. Hailgi's head was down, his back bent a little so that Gunthabrandar could lean on him, and they moved very slowly.

Of a sudden, Hailgi felt all his hairs prickling as though he were walking through a thorn bush. He raised his head, looking around to see if the others felt anything. The two captives behind him showed nothing but the set mood with which they would meet what lay before them. Aiwimundar's eyebrows were drawn down in thought, his swarthy forehead wrinkled, Fastawulfar was staring fixedly at the path beneath his feet.Hailgi did not know if the sound he heard then sounded within his skull or outside it.

It might have been a low growl, it might have been a man's deep voice muttering a few words, though he could not make out what they might be. He kept on walking. He set his feet carefully to keep from giving Gunthabrandar more pain than he had to, but after they had gone a little way, he could see the brightness of fresh blood beginning to break through the brown-crusted bandages on the thane's legs. The low voice muttered through the wood again. This time, it sounded more like a growl, it was clear enough that Hailgi knew he was hearing it through his ears.

"Wait," Fastawulfar whispered. Hailgi stopped, turning his head to glance back at him. The young thane was looking at the ground, his lips pressed whitely together. He bent his knees, crouching down.

"They're only a single wolf's tracks," Hailgi murmured in answer.

"See how the toes are spread? I've seen this before. And look, there." Fast-awulfar pointed to the side of the path with a broken-nailed finger, Hailgi marked the spatters of foam for the first time. "It's well gone in the howling madness, and it's not far away. It's a big one too, the biggest I've seen. We'd do best to cut our fetters now, before we cross the grove's markers, and go back for weapons or something."

"No." Hailgi did not whisper, though he spoke softly, his voice rang raven-harsh in his own ears. "Wodhanar chooses what he shall have from each garth for his help. It is not for us to flee from his holy stead, when we have said that we shall come within. The wod-greedy wolf may never come near us, but walk warily, all, and listen carefully."

Though no one spoke against him, Hailgi could hear them shuffling more and more swiftly behind him, and had to mend his own pace. He was almost carrying Gunthabrandar by the time Aiwimundar whispered, "There it is."

The way into Fetter-Grove was marked by a huge, slanted slab of gray stone lying flat against the ground, they would have to walk over it to enter the grove. A row of deep cup-marks ran down it like a line of hoof prints in the rock. As he got closer, Hailgi could see that what had looked at first like splotchy irregularities on the stone's flat face were images that had been ground into the rock. The shadow-shape of a huge figure, his manhood upright, cast a spear over the long curves of skeleton ships, the stick-figures of two dogs ran beneath his feet. Aiwilimo came past the two hale captives and nudged Hailgi on the shoulder with the corner of the ale-barrel.

"I'll take care of this one," he whispered. "You fill the horn and pour the first draught into the highest alf-cup." He set the barrel down and stood up beneath Hailgi's burdened arm, shifting Gunthabrandar's weight easily to his own shoulder.

As Hailgi walked closer to the rock, the soles of his feet began to tingle. The prickling in them was almost painful by the time he stepped onto the stone itself. But he carried the horn to the alf-cups and raised it, looking into the grove. Although the holy stead stood within a beech-wood, only ash and oak grew there. Hailgi's spread arms could not have half-spanned many of the tree-trunks, neither the gnarled oak nor the smoother ash, some might have stood since the folk of early years had shaped the shadows on the stone.

A straight path led from the rock to the middle of the clearing, where a harrow of heaped stones stood beneath the most awesome ash-tree of all, an old giant towering above all the others. Its branches shadowed a great wooden shape. The image of Wodhanar, his face masked by the shape of a helm with a crudely-cut eagle's head jutting from between the eyes and his body hidden by the deep hack-marks that showed the folds of his cloak, sat throned behind the harrow. A spear stood loose in the ring of his closed fist, its butt resting on the ground and its other end lashed to a branch of the tree. No rust marred the iron point that gleamed above the god's head.

Beside his seat stood a rootless tree-stump, smoothed by the same crafts-man's hand and worn by use.

"Wodhanar, grant us leave to come here," Hailgi said softly. "Fettered, we come to Fetter-Grove, we bring you gifts won in fight."

He poured the ale out, its stream frothing up from the first alf-cup to spill down into the next and the next and the next, until the horn was empty and each of the little hollows gleamed full. Then, careful not to let his clum-sy-bound feet slip on the sloping rock, he stepped down into the grove. It was silent with awe, ringing soundlessly through his skull and thrumming up through his feet. Sparkles of unseen light burst before his eyes, as though he had held his breath too long, each draught of air he drank filled him until he, too, felt that he must shimmer with the might of the hallowed stead. He walked straight to the harrow and laid the horn and his coil of rope down on it. He did not turn his head, but only listened as the other men made their way over the marker-stone and into the grove to him.

Wodhanar's spear was not easy to lift from his hand. A chain looped about the shaft just below the iron head made the weapon fast to a branch of the tree, above a man's reach, so that one who came bound and alone would have little chance of loosing it. Hailgi pointed to Fastawulfar and Gleaugir. They came forward, bending their backs before the harrow. Hailgi used the heap of stones to help him pull himself up, then crouched with one foot on each man and slowly straightened himself until his outstretched hand touched the spear's fetter. He had heard that it did not always come free, it was Wodhanar's runes of unbinding that loosened it at his will. The chain fell away easily in his hand.

Hailgi had just begun to lift the spear up through the god's loose fist when the howl wavered through the clearing. Only his firm grasp on the weapon saved him from falling as Fastawulfar jerked beneath his feet, but he could not keep from twisting to look. The snarling wolf leapt stiff-legged over the stone at the path's end. Hailgi's first sight was of its lightning-white fangs melting into unreal length, stretching and twisting down past the edges of its gaping jaw, then he realized that what he saw was the froth of the howling madness running from its mouth. Its eyes were black against the pale mask of its face, ears laid out to the sides, ash-black fur bristled up along its back. The wod-wolf stopped for a moment, swinging its head from side to side as it saw the fettered men before it. Then it leapt forward towards the two who were bent beneath Hailgi's feet.

Hailgi did not know how he had been able to take the spear from Wodhanar's hand, then turn and cast it in the half-heartbeat while the wolf was in the air. His throw was true. The god's weapon took the maddened beast through the chest, knocking it back to the earth. Then Hailgi realized that he was standing on the ground as well, as though he had leapt towards the wolf while casting the spear. Carefully he walked towards where it lay. The wolf raised its head and looked at him. The strands of slobber twisting from its mouth were red now, its growl bubbled in its throat. The wolf's wide paws scrabbled at the ground for a moment as it tried to rise against the spear, thick black nails cutting brown scars of earth through the grass. Then it slumped back and lay still. Hailgi grasped the spear's shaft with both hands and braced one foot against the wolf's body, pulling the weapon out. He leaned the shaft against the harrow and took the coil of rope, looping one end roughly around the corpse's neck and making it fast. It was not easy to drag the huge wolf over to the ash-tree. It weighed as much as Hailgi himself, and seemed heavier in death, and Hailgi's shaking legs kept trying to fall from under him. Still, he got it there and cast the rope over a low branch of the ash, then pulled.

The wolf's head rose, then its body, until it swung freely with a span of air above its head and beneath its dangling hind feet. Quickly Hailgi tied off the rope and sliced the rest of the coil free with the sharp spear-edge. When he turned to look at his men again, he saw that Sigihadur was sitting on the ground, his pale blue eyes very wide as he stared at Hailgi and the wolf. Fastawulfar leaned against the harrow, panting with his mouth open as though he were about to be sick. The others had borne it better, but to be fettered before the howling madness was no easy thing, and none of them looked unshaken. Only the three battle-captives seemed unscathed in mood, as though a sure death were hardly worse one way or the other. There would be three gifts, yes, but a wolf's life was worth the life of a man. One, Hailgi knew now, must go free, for Wodhanar had made a choice. Ansumundar, Frodhamarar, Gunthabrandar the god would choose among them. Having no knife, Hailgi could not score the lots on wood. Instead, he picked up three flat pebbles from the ground.

He cast about for a moment in search of something to mark them with, then dipped his forefinger into the little pool of ale-dregs that had collected near the mouth of the horn. On one he traced the Ansur-rune, that would be Ansumundar's. Fehu for Frodhamarar, Gebo for Gunthabrandar, then he cupped his hands like a dice-cup and shook the rattling stones, breathing deeply. Face-up or face-down, the odd one out would live. Hailgi looked up at the helm-masked face of the god, then past him into the ash-tree's reaching branches. It seemed to him that he could feel the flowing pathways of the water from below that fed and shaped the tree, that the same might flowed up through his feet and out through his cupped hands, bearing the pebbles with it. The stave that showed ale-dark against the gray stone was straight with two down-slanted branches. Ansur.

The other two were faceless. Moving slowly, as if in a dream, Hailgi beckoned to Frodhamarar. The great ash-tree's shadow lay gray over the young man's face as he stumbled over to Hailgi. Hailgi put his hand on Frodhamarar's muscular shoulder for a moment to steady him before he looped the rope about his neck and tied the knot. A gust of wind rushed through the ash's leaves, turning the dangling body of the wolf. Frodhamarar's green-flecked eyes flickered over to the swaying corpse for a moment. Hailgi led the other youth to the tree. Aiwimundar followed quietly behind them, it took three to make the gift to Wodhanar. The old thane moved the rootless stump beneath a branch a little higher than the one Hailgi had hung the wolf from, Frodhamarar stepped up, and Aiwimundar took the rope from Hailgi's hand, looping it over the branch. Hailgi went back to the harrow and took the spear in his hand again. Its shaft was very smooth. Long as it was, it seemed oddly light, as though the wind were already bearing it up in flight. He did not look at Frodhamarar, but at the god who sat between warrior and wolf.

I wot that I hungon the windy tree
nights all nine.
Wounded by spear

Hailgi raised the weapon, turning his gaze back to the other youth. "To Wodhanar given," he murmured.

Myself to me myself.

Aiwimundar kicked the stool from beneath Frodhamarar's feet and leapt back, pulling the rope. The spear flew eagle-swift from Hailgi's hand, Hailgi's own breath rushed out of him as it thunked home beneath Frodhamarar's breastbone. His body swung wildly under the blow, as though a storm wind beat about it. Frodhamarar's neck had broken cleanly, his head rolling onto his shoulder as he swung. His face was already beginning to darken. After a moment, Hailgi steadied Frodhamarar with his hand again and wrenched the spear from his chest. It came free in a gout of blood that splattered over Hailgi's byrnie, as though he stood in the wal-stead again.

Aiwimundar pointed silently, Hailgi cut the rope where the thane showed him, leaving the other to tie it fast to the branch. Fastawulfar and Sigibernu had to carry Gunthabrandar forward. They held him as Hailgi knotted the rope around his neck. Hailgi did not want to look into the wounded man's eyes, but he would not turn away. He met Gunthabrandar's brown-black gaze, holding his stare. His own shadow, with the warrior's knot dark against the side of his head. The ravens, the choosers of the slain, would come soon enough for those baleful eyes, Wodhanar's winged ones flew unfettered through Fetter-Grove. Hailgi took up the god's spear again, waiting until Fastawulfar and Sigibernu had heaved Gunthabrandar into place beside Frodhamarar. He nodded. Fastawulfar kicked the tree-stump free as Sigibernu pulled on the rope.

Hailgi's throw was hard enough that the spear ran more than halfway through Gunthabrandar's body, its tip sticking in the ash-tree's blood-sprinkled bark. Hailgi heard the warrior's choking sound as he tried to double around it, his movement pulling the strangling rope tighter around his neck. His wounded legs kicked, scattering drops of fresh blood to the ground.

Then a pale stain soaked through the front of his breeches, his seed spilling with the last of his life. Sigibernu held Gunthabrandar's corpse still as Hailgi freed the spear from him. Hailgi leaned it against the harrow and filled the horn with the last cloudy ale from the barrel's depths, raising it to the god's grim image and the three who wavered in the wind. He drank and passed it to Aiwimundar. The horn went about the ring of men, each drinking a small mouthful, until it came to Ansumundar, whose hands were still bound. Sigifrodhar, who held it, looked uncertainly at Hailgi. Hailgi came forward and took the horn from his hands, raising it to Ansumundar's lips himself.

When the captive had drunk, Hailgi took another sip, then poured what was left of the ale out over the spear's tip to wash the blood from it. Fastawulfar and Gleaugir bent down again, Hailgi climbed up on their backs to drop the spear-shaft down into Wodhanar's hand and chain it fast to the rope-bound bough again. They left as silently as they had come, though more slowly, for they had to wait for Sigihadhur to drag himself along the ground and up over the rock. He was able to stand when they had passed beyond the grove's markers, but the men still went fettered until they had come out into the warm sunlight that shone without shadows on the strand.

Then Hailgi untied all of his warriors, though he left Ansumundar bound.

"What are you going to do with me?" Ansumundar asked. Although his husky voice was still fierce, Hailgi could hear the genuine curiosity in it as well.

"I don't know. Keep you as a hostage until we find out what Hunding's sons are going to do, I guess. What do you want me to do with you?"

Ansumundar cleared his throat and spat to the side, flushing beneath his red beard. "I don't know. I don't favor any of his sons, and it's my thought that they won't find it easy to rule together. He was my drighten, so I guess I ought to think about coming after you, but Thonarar, this isn't what I thought would happen. I just don't know. Can you leave me a while to think about it?"

"I suppose so. If I can have your oath that you won't try to escape or attack me or my men without warning us first, I'll even untie you."

"Hah!" Ansumundar barked, an odd sound halfway between a cough and a laugh. "I guess you can. I swear by, well, by the wolf that took my place on Wodhanar's tree," he added in a lower voice.

Hailgi untied his bonds. The big warrior stood up, stretching his arms towards the sky. Hailgi's head did not quite reach to his chin. He'd be a good man to have in my own war band someday, Hailgi thought.

The Sun was almost halfway down the western sky. They would be sailing with her light in their eyes, but there was no mistaking the eagerness of the men who crowded through the waves towards the boat. Though the wind would be in their faces now, Hailgi thought it was likely that they could make it back to Hagalar's shore before the Sun had set. After Sigiruna had given her parents the greetings of the gudhes and gudhijas and gotten her treasures safely stored away, she mounted her dun mare Folwa and turned the horse's head northward, urging her along the track that led to Ansuwunja's house.

The mid-day sunlight was hot on Sigiruna's fair hair, as though she wore a steel cap. Eager as her rider was, Folwa trotted along only lazily in the warmth, wending from side to side and lowering her head to chomp up big mouthfuls of grass whenever Sigiruna's hands slackened on the reins.

"Hurry, worthless nag, or I'll see you seething in the stew pot at Winter nights," Sigiruna threatened, tapping the mare's sides lightly with her heels. Folwa mended her pace for a moment, then slowed again. Sigiruna could not bring herself to kick the horse any harder. Folwa was old, older than Sigiruna herself, and had been her steed since she had been large enough to climb onto the mare's back, but she told herself that she would ask her father for a livelier mount soon.

The holy stone stood near the road, in the middle of a grove of oak-trees. It was a rock strange to this land, a rough, broad cube of granite pink as flesh, flecked with little glitters of white ice-stone and speckles of black. No men could have lifted the great head-high boulder, no ship borne it from Gautland to Sealand without foundering. It was said that in elder days, Thonarar had stood among the Gautish cliffs and the etin-maid Laikino had stood in the grove, shouting taunts at him and saying that it was little worthy of his manhood to threaten a woman with his Hammer, though she was of the worst troll-kin.

Thonarar had replied, "If you are not worthy of my Hammer, then let stone be the death of the stone-wife!" Cast the boulder across the sea to break her skull. It was sure that the rock thrummed with an awesome holiness that only the touch of Thonarar the Hallower could have given it. Men went there to ask Might-Father's strength for their arms, women asked the Hallower to bless their wombs with fruitfulness, all folk came there to call for rain in dry years, and brought their sick children and beasts so that the Troll-Slayer could drive out whatever ill had beset them. Garlands of flowers, some dry and some with fresh petals just starting to droop, lay upon the wide face of the ruddy rock.

Its base was heaped with shards of clay and broken drinking horns where folk had given a draught, vessel and all, to the god, and about it were ringed the horns of the goats that were slain for Thonarar every year at the high feasts, or whenever there was need. The madwoman's, Ansuwunja's, house was hidden back in the beech wood behind the holy grove. The path was small and winding, Folwa had to pick her way carefully over stumps and stones, lifting and placing her hooves as delicately as a feast-clad frowe walking through an unmucked byre. Though Sigiruna had never seen Ansuwunja's house, it was plain to know.

It had been built beneath a great ash, and was half-hedged about by the gray-green fronds of sharp-scented junipers, a raven's head was carved at either side of the roof beam, and the oaken half-beams of the door were scarred with the deep-hacked triple triangle of the walknot. A wave of eagerness sparkled through Sigiruna as she saw the holy sign of Wodhanar. She leapt from Folwa's back, tying her horse to a low-hanging beech branch. Raising her spear, she knocked at the heart of the walknot with its butt.

"Who is it?" A loud, cracked voice screeched from inside. The Frisian accent was so thick that Sigiruna had trouble understanding the words at first.

"Sigiruna, daughter of Haganon and Sigigafja!"

"Who sent you here? What are you doing here?"

"I was sent here by one of the gudhes in God-Home, Wodhanar's-Karl, who knew you once. He says that you are to teach me about being a walkurja."

Sigiruna heard crashing inside, the sound of something heavy banging over, followed by a shriek of "Wodaaaan!" The door flew open, Sigiruna had to leap back quickly to keep from being hit by it. The woman who stood inside was almost as tall as Sigiruna, but no wider than a maid of eleven winters, her breasts seemed barely blossomed, her hips flared only by her long blue skirts.

Only the white tufts in her arched eyebrows and the lines scoring the edges of her eyes and cutting deeply about either side of her mouth showed her age. Her hair was hidden beneath a deep blue veil bound about with a silver circlet, as might be expected for the most modest of wedded women. Her eyes were dual colored, the right greener and the left bluer, and the left eye seemed to skew off to the side, its pupil misted. Her dress was plain deep blue, her red apron was embroidered with shiny dark horse-hair in a running pattern of holy signs, walknot, hook-cross, trefot, and sun-wheel, set among rows of rune-staves. Ansuwunja wore a large necklace with the rune-row all graven into bone beads strung between beads of swirling blue and black glass. Several stamped gold rounds like the one Wodhanar's-Karl had given Sigiruna hung upon it, Sigiruna could see one with a man walking between nine little whorls, two with a long-haired rider followed by a bird of prey, one with a bird-crowned man sitting upon a high seat. A large droplet of polished golden amber hung in the middle, its spangles glimmering in the sunlight.

"So Wodan's-Karl sent you, did he? He's a good old man. Tell me, how does he fare?"

"He shakes badly from alf-shot, but seems hale otherwise," Sigiruna answered. "The hof-folk make sure that all is well with him, I think."

"Well, they'd better!" The Frisian woman shrieked. "If they left the old man to rot, the god would curse them with sickness, eat the flesh from their bones and let their guts rot within them!" She smacked her fist hard into her palm. "I'd curse them to foul death myself, for Wodan's walked in Karl's hide more than once, he's dear as a brother to me." Sigiruna tried to rein back her startle at the other woman's fierceness, but Ansuwunja shook her head, the grim line of her narrow jaw tightening. "You may not have seen it, living among good kin as you do, but I can tell you, there's plenty of scum out there who would say an old man like Wodan's-Karl was worthless and have him out in the cold quick as that." She snapped her fingers.

"The other gudhes and gudhijas hold him to be of the highest worth, frowe," Sigiruna answered.

Ansuwunja laughed, a cackle loud enough to make Sigiruna wince. The Skjolding guessed that the older woman must have dwelt alone a long time, or else that she had never cared about the thoughts of other folk. "Don't call me frowe, girl. My father was a Frisian carle with three cows and twelve children, and my mother sold me off to be a thrall as soon as ever she could. I'm no one's frowe, well." Her hard glare softened suddenly, her face easing to a young girl's smoothness as she glanced up at the rustling leaves of the big ash-tree whose branches reached over her cottage like a husband's arms. Now she might have been a maiden bride, fine sharp features framed by her blue wedding-veil, pointed chin tipped upward and eyes half-closed in the joy of her love. "I'm Wodan's frowe, the wife of the best of the gods," she said quietly. "After all these years, I can still hardly believe it, that he chose me, of all folk!" She crossed bone-thin arms over her chest, hugging herself tightly. "I'm mad, am I?"

Sigiruna was not sure what to answer, as she was already half-sure of it, but a sudden gust of cold wind whirled through the ash-tree's leaves, brightening Ansuwunja's light eyes as if it blew coals to flame, and Sigiruna felt the same burst of joy sparking in herself, as if she were a dry pine-sap torch catching fire from Ansuwunja's flare. "As mad as Wodhanar," she answered truthfully. She could not keep herself from laughing, but the Frisian threw her straw-brittle arms about her, squeezing hard enough to knock the Skjolding's breath out for a moment. Letting go, she waved Sigiruna in, rings of silver and red gold flashing from the thin brown sticks of her fingers. Sigiruna blinked against the darkness as she lowered her spear and ducked in under the low wooden lintel. Ansuwunja's house was thick with smoke, that soaked into the wooden walls from many years of burning holy herbs.

Sigiruna could pick out the heavy odors of scorched juniper and hedge-thorn berries, mug wort and hemp and mist-twig, pine and birch and the sweet, penetrating scent of burning hwanna roots. The walls had once been painted blue with woad, now they were a deep blue-black. As if the little house were a hall, a great high-seat stood at one end. A raven's skull had been mounted on the wing-carven posts that would rise to either side of a sitter's head, and a gray wolf's hide lay furry over the back of the seat. A spear leaned behind it, its head hidden by the wide hat that hung lopsided over it. In the chair itself stood a large figure of straw, half the size of a man and dressed in a deep blue cloak and a broad-brimmed hat that had been pulled low over one eye.

Sigiruna had seen god-shapes made of sheaves before. The Skjoldings were born of Skjold Sheafing, and after her father had carried the Last Sheaf in from the field, the women of the family made it into a gold-cloaked and berry-crowned straw man and set him high in the hall, that Ingwe-Freyjar might watch over his kin all winter, and bring them a good planting when he was plowed into the field at winter's end. But this figure had been wrought on bones of wood with tighter wrapping and plaiting. He had clearly been meant to stand for a lifetime. His hair and beard were too fine to be straw, as Sigiruna's eyes cleared, she saw that they were plaited from deep gold human hair. A small spear was bound into one of his hands, a little drink-ing-horn into the other, and his straw chest was stained dark as if ale or blood had often been poured upon him. A hempen noose dangled from his neck. Sigiruna stood staring at the sheaf-Wodhanar as the hairs rose in little prickles along her spine. She could feel the god-might beating out from him, as clearly as she had felt it in the great hof, no, more clearly, more keenly, for there was no might but Wodhanar's in that house. It was a stead wholly given to him, hallowed by the life of his bride and gudhija through the many years she had dwelt and worshiped there.

"Wodhanar's-Karl said I should see you, if I would know how strongly our god walks the world," Sigiruna murmured, and did not know quite whether she spoke to Ansuwunja or to the sheaf-god in his high seat.

"This whole house is Wodan's home, his own stead rooted in the Mid-dle-Garth," the Frisian said proudly. "Every breath I take, every word I speak, all of it gives might to him." She threw back her head, crying "WOOOODAAAN" so loudly that Sigiruna's ears rang with pain. Instead of wincing back from the shriek that speared through her eardrums, Sigiruna screamed the god's name in answer, her high, harsh-edged voice cutting through the other woman's lower shout.

Ansuwunja smiled at her in the ringing stillness afterwards, a pleased, tight-lipped smile. "I am called Hlakka and Skogla, for I shriek and strike forward, as is the way of the walkurja. Now sit down and I shall get you some ale while you tell me more of why you have come here and what you know already."

The Frisian's stools and little table were plain, but clean and well-polished, Sigiruna marked when she sat down, the hard earthen floor was well-swept, and the stones lining the fire-pit in the middle were freshly scrubbed. For all she might seem mad to some, Wodhanar's bride took better care of her home than many another housewife. Sigiruna knew the barrel from which Ansuwunja drew the ale.

She had helped her mother to load it onto the back of the horse that had brought it here, and wondered why she had never come here with Sigigafja. A white house-cat leapt into Sigiruna's lap, purring and butting a furry head against her hand to be scratched, a larger one slept curled up on the other bench. Sigiruna had seldom seen such beasts, they were not often found here in the North, though she had heard that they were common in Britain. She leaned her own spear against the wall behind her and petted the cat with both hands.

"That's my little Frowe, and her brother the Fro over there," Ansuwunja told her. "They were gifts to me from God-Home, they'll make a fine pair of white gloves for me someday." Sigiruna was a little taken aback by her words, but she also marked that the cat she petted was sleek, with no ribs to be felt beneath her soft fur, and the sides of the sleeping one bulged with fat. The cats were better fed than the woman who kept them.

When each of the women had a cup of ale in her hand, Sigiruna told Ansuwunja of all that had happened to her. The Frisian squinted one eye as she listened, her other eye stayed fixed piercingly on Sigiruna.

"So what do you want me to teach you?" She asked when Sigiruna had finished her tale. "You can ride out and help this man of yours in battle without me." Then Ansuwunja leaned over and slapped Sigiruna backhanded across the face. The blow was not hard, but one of her rings cut the corner of the Skjolding's mouth. Sigiruna blinked, licking the blood away and wondering if she should hit the other woman back. She would not have paused a moment if a man had struck her, but she surely outweighed Ansuwunja by half again, and she remembered how fragile the Frisian's bones had felt. "You lucky whore, having one of Wodan's heroes all to yourself! He never gave me one."

"He surely wanted you all for himself," Sigiruna answered, her liking for Ansuwunja rising again to overcome the sting of the other woman's friendly blow.

Ansuwunja smiled. "You truly think so? Yesss, that must be it. Oh, he has given me so much, I have nothing to complain about. I've given him my whole life. He can take me whenever he wants, see?" She unbuckled her belt, pulling up her dress and apron. Between the little cups of her breasts, Ansuwunja was marked with the walknot, its lines scarred into her flesh and darkened with something, ash, perhaps to make them show against her pale skin.

"I marked Hailgi with that same sign," Sigiruna said slowly. "I touched him with my spear and traced it on his heart."

"Yes, that's right, it must be scarred on his soul, whether it marks his body or not, for you are both gifts to Wooodaaan!"

Sigiruna thought to herself as Ansuwunja dropped her skirts and fastened her belt again that it was a wonder they had never heard the woman shrieking in Haganon's hall, her voice was surely loud enough to carry across half a day's ride. As the ringing of the Frisian's call to the god faded from her ears, the lingering echo of Ansuwunja's scream reminded Sigiruna of something else Wodhanar's-Karl had said.

"I was told that you are skilled at galdor and runes. Will you teach me those crafts? I know the staves and their sounds, but little of their secrets, or how to use them for more than scratching a message on a stick."

"Wodan has blessed you, for him, I'll teach you anything you want to know." Ansuwunja rose and filled their cups again. She sat down, squinting with her bad eye, then suddenly got up and took the wide-brimmed hat from her spearhead, tugging it low to hide that eye. Now her fine features seemed sharp and grim in the dimming twilight, hard as a man's. Her voice came deep and scratchy from her throat, and Sigiruna saw that her neck was braided about with little age-lines like the faint scars of a noose. "Galdor and runes are one and the same. The staves shape the rune-sounds for all the worlds to see, setting them forever in tree and stone, but it is the galdor, the song that reddens them with blood, the song that breathes them full of life. Thus men may carve staves and say little, if they do not sing forth the holy runes in blood and breath. Do you know how the galdor-mead was won by Wodan in elder times?"

"I know that the dwarves slew Kwasijar, and brewed it from his blood, wisdom and sweet honey blended together. The etin Suththungar took it from them, and set his daughter Guntholathja to ward it in a cave's depth, but Wodhanar crept to her in a wyrm's shape, and slept with her three nights, and drank all the mead in three great draughts. He flew away afterwards in the shape of an eagle, leaving Guntholathja to weep."

"Yes it was that mead Wodan longed for when he won the holy staves, the horn for which he thirsted when he hung nine nights on the World-Tree. There he won the staves for shaping, but the soul flows from the song-mead, and the wisdom to use it springs from Mimir's Well, the Well of Memory, where Wodan sank his eye. The true rune is the galdor of might, the words of strength, though the staves are runes as well, and 'runes' men call them betimes. Would you know more, or what?"

"I would," Sigiruna whispered.

Ansuwunja opened her mouth to speak again, then suddenly shook her body, darting her head forward like a great raven pecking at Sigiruna's face. "Hai, I've just heard something. Hsh. Your Hailgi! You said that he had slain Hunding and some of his men the other day."

"Yes. He did."

"Well, Hunding has sons, did you think of that? Strong sons, I've heard of them even here. What do you think will happen, when they learn that their father is dead?"

Sigiruna's heart knocked hard once against her ribs, hard as a metal-bound spear-butt rapping on the door of a hall.

"Not many folk speak to me, but I'm no half-wit. I know what's going on, you can be sure of that. Wodan told you to ask me about galdor-craft, you'll learn it now, for you and I must do a mighty galdor against Hunding's sons now. Take up your spear and stand there, in the middle of the house by the hearthstone."

Sigiruna did as she was told, staring up at the bearded sheaf-face of the god. Ansuwunja went to the little chest by the high seat, lifting out a small wooden wand with a horse's head carved on the end. There were rune-staves graven into it, black with old blood, but the Frisian's hand covered some so that Sigiruna could not read them. Ansuwunja took her own spear in her left hand and, holding the wand in her right, began to trace the stave-shapes and chant the names of the runes, turning in a slow sun wise circle as her voice rose to a high rough shriek that filled the whole room, running up and down Sigiruna's spine like a wyrm streaked with fire and ice.

"Fehu. Uruz. Thurisaz. Ansuz!" The angular shapes of the runes seemed to burn red as after flashes of lightning in Sigiruna's sight, glowing ghostly against the deep blue evening-light that filled the house. Ansuwunja's rune-song never ceased, her cry echoing between the dark walls even as she drew slow breaths between each stave. By the time she had made the full round, might pounded through the smoky air like the rain and sparks of a thunderstorm, Sigiruna had to hold tight to her spear for balance. Ansuwunja traced the hallowing shape of Thonarar's whirling Hammer, the hook-cross, above and below, and it seemed to Sigiruna that the spinning sign drew a great river of shining white might down from the heavens to whirl at the crown of her head, shining black might up from the earth to tingle in the soles of her feet.

"Wodan!" Ansuwunja cried. "Galdor-father, Rune-Father, Sig-Father, Beloved, your bride calls you! Fly on raven-wings, run on wolf-feet, soar in an eagle's hide here! Walker between the worlds, winner of the holy mead, wal-stead's mighty drighten, your walkurjas call you here! Wooodaaan." Sigiruna's own mouth opened, and she was singing the god's name together with Ansuwunja, her voice rising high above the Frisian's until the walls of the house seemed to tremble with their awe-full chord.

Then it seemed to Sigiruna that the sound was lifting her up, forth from her body, that she could see the high-timbered hall where Hunding's corpse lay raven-torn and rotting upon the table, where the brothers pulled their byrnies on and called for their swords with wild cries of rage and grief, sending their men out to summon the host that would drown the small band around Hailgi, tear him to pieces and tread his bones into the ground before ever the wolves could feed on his flesh, but one man watched silent, a tall graybeard with misted eyes. He glanced up, the dull gleam of his gaze brightening as he peered towards Sigiruna.

Then the might Sigiruna and Ansuwunja had called seemed to grind against the Skjolding's fear for her beloved like wood on dry wood, kindling a coal that sprang to a flame hotter than the strongest mead in her throat. Ansuwunja was chanting more rune-names, weaving their sharp-edged shapes in burning staves with the flaring tip of her wand, over the Frisian's low drone, Sigiruna cried out...

"Walkurjas' song-might, wailing,
 winds the warriors, binding,
 Wodhanar's steeds, wild-lathered,
 wield your blades on shield-kin!"

Another voice was singing with her a deep man's voice, sounding far below Ansuwunja's runes. It seemed to Sigiruna that the sound poured from the mist-eyed man in the dark blue cloak, though he sat silent in the hall with only a little smile curling like an adder's tail through his beard. It was as though he were singing through her throat a two-noted horn brought to life by the wind of his breath, and for a moment Sigiruna saw a glimmering of a pattern that stretched far beyond her sight, the threads of crimson and death-gray that flowed from her mouth already woven into Wodhanar's plan.

"Brother-bane be athelings,
 black-winged host and pack gray
 harvest have of reaving,
 hate alone be sated!"

With the last line of her song, Sigiruna threw her spear with all her might. She saw it skimming over the hall, bright and cruel as a falling star, its burning tail setting fire to the thatch, she heard a harsh laugh rising from within, followed by deeper cries, and then a solid thunk shook through her, dropping her dazed onto Ansuwunja's floor. Her spear still shivered in the wall, sunk head-deep where she had thrown it.

Ansuwunja drew a deep breath, leaning on her own spear to straighten herself. "Wodan Beloved," she said quietly. "Hail and thanks, stay with us ever, here in this hallowed stead." She lifted her spear, tracing a widdershins ring around the room. "Rune-staves' might, rise to highest worlds, sink down to murky depths. Be awe-strength to Ases, to the alfs all good, and wisdom aye to Wodan."

The Frisian hung her hat on her spear-point and stood it behind the god's high-seat again, then came back to help Sigiruna up. "Are you well?" Ansuwunja asked, though her own hands were shaking harder than the Skjolding's.

"I am," Sigiruna said, pushing herself to her feet.

Ansuwunja clasped her in another wire-bruising embrace. "That was wonderful, girl! You're a galdor-crafter born, well, it's Wodan's blessing, nothing strange in that. Here, you look like you could use some more ale. It's too late for you to ride home tonight, stay here, and in a while I'll tell you more of the runes."

Sigiruna made her way to the stool, gratefully taking the newly filled cup from Ansuwunja's hand and draining it. Her hide still felt hollow, but it seemed to her that she was starting to come back to herself, and she knew, with no chance to question or fear, that the sons of Hunding would soon ride out against Hailgi. As the Sun lowered and they grew closer to Hagalar's lands, Hailgi found that he was straining his eyes towards the shore, looking for the plume of rising black smoke. It was not hard for him to see Ingwibjorg's reddened thighs wrenched apart, or Lingwe's ringed hand over her mouth as he forced himself into her.

A knife cutting into Gunthahildar's breast, as Hagalar's head watched through glazed blue eyes, drops from the tattered flesh of his neck still dripping into the dark pool of clotting blood at the foot of the spear that held it up. They might see no smoke. Hunding's sons might have come and gone. Even now, Hagalar's hall could be standing roofless, the dead within black with flies or charred and twisted from the flames.

I must not think these things, Hailgi told himself as sternly as he could. Fear will make things no better, and speaking of ill often brings it on. He stood up, climbing up to the prow and lifting the wyrm's head down before its gaze could fall upon Hagalar's lands. "You've done well," he whispered to it beneath his breath. "Rest now, you'll have no more work till the spring."

As they rowed closer, Hailgi could see that the fields had not been burned or ridden down, they rippled beneath the softly purpling evening sky, golden-ripe for harvest. See, all is well, he thought, though he could not bring himself to speak it aloud and risk the ill-luck that might follow if some trollish wight heard it. The wooden palisade still stood, sturdy as when they had left it, the roof of Hagalar's hall rose above it, its thatches unscorched.

They beached the boat and hurried eagerly up to the hall, the whole men helping the wounded. As they came closer to the gate, however, Hailgi's steps slowed. The muddy road had been churned by a troop of horsemen, a greater troop than Hagalar's. Though the tracks were muddled, he could see that none of them led away from the garth, only inward.

Hailgi straightened his back and strode up to the gate. If this was a trap, then so it would be. He would not hide from his foe again.

"Hai!" He called. "Hailgi is here! Will you let me in?"

The gate swung open. It was Eburhelmar who guarded it, his glance went past Hailgi at once to the troop behind him, flickering among the men until at last the sight of his son eased his anxious gaze. Hailgi could see the horses tethered to stakes within the garth. He recognized the tall bay with the white splotch over his nose at once. These were the horses of his father's war band here. No one cheered, but Hailgi saw the grins of relief. Now that Sigismundar was here, Hagalar had no need to fear the slaughter that Hunding's sons would have wreaked on him. The battle would be even at worst.

"What tidings?" Eburhelmar asked. "We've heard all sorts of stories, and the drighten sent his daughters south to dwell with Wulfaruna's kin for a while. Is Hunding coming?"

"I slew Hunding," Hailgi answered. "Is everyone in the hall?"

"Yes."

Hailgi went on, walking proudly at the head of his men. Between the rushing of the past days and his own tiredness, he had not had time to think about his own deeds, but now the realization burst before his eyes like the lights flashing from a heavy blow to the skull. He had slain his father's foe, one of the two great drightens of North Jutland fifteen winters old and still beardless, he had led a troop into battle and won the victory, and he knew of no one else who could say the same, and now he felt drunken with it. He could not have thought of a fairer wyrd for himself if he had been asked. At that moment, the throbbing cut no longer ached in his jaw, it seemed to him that his high mood must last forever, and that all he had given was a small price to pay for becoming Hailgi Hunding's-Bane.

The hall was brightly lit with torches. Wulfaruna and Audhar were moving about serving ale to the men within. Hailgi did not know all of his father's men, though he recognized some of them. In his time away, he had forgotten how large Sigismundar's war band was, Hagalar's hall had never been built to hold so many, so that some of the men were leaning against the walls or the hall-pillars as they ate and drank.

"Here they are!" Someone shouted. A pathway cleared through the men so that Sigismundar could hurry down the hall to his son. Although Hailgi's father had only a few winters less than Hagalar, none of their frost had settled on his ruddy hair, and he ran like a young man.

"What have you done? Hailgi, tell me!"

"I have killed Hunding myself, with my grandfather's sword which you gave me at my birth," Hailgi answered proudly. "We found him as he came along the shore, and slew him and all with him."

Their byrnies grated together as Sigismundar clasped his son around the shoulders. "A mighty deed, truly! The old blood of the Wolfing line still lives in you. Is that slice on your face your only wound?"

"It is."

"Was that from Hunding? It was not his way to deal such light blows when he was younger," said Sigismundar, and laughed.

Hailgi grinned back at his father. "He had my sword in his guts, I think that took his mind from his work."

"I suppose it might have," Sigismundar replied. "Now come and talk with Hagalar and me. It is not unlikely that we will be fighting by each other's side as soon as the sons of Hunding find out what has happened. We have only to decide whether we shall go to him or let him come to us."

Hailgi and his father went up to the head of the table where Hagalar sat. Wulfaruna was there with a horn of ale before Hailgi sat down. "It's easy to see what sort of tasks you are best fitted for, isn't it?" She said softly to him.

"It is," he answered. He smiled at her, there was no more anger left in him.

Hailgi told the whole tale of their faring to Hagalar and his father. The two men listened carefully, only now and again murmuring in approval or surprise. At the end of the story, Sigismundar said, "Very well done indeed. But what made you decide to do it?"

He did not think about the words until they were out of his mouth. "Sigiruna the daughter of Haganon."

Sigismundar cocked his head sideways, staring at his son. Hailgi thought of how the shadows on the ward-stone had suddenly resolved into shapes, and wondered if his own face had borne the same look of wary realization then.

"What about her? I think that you have not gone to her father's dwellings in Sealand, and I should have known if she had come here."

"I have heard of her," Hailgi muttered lamely. "I was told that she would be lost to me unless I acted quickly to avenge our clan on Hunding." He tilted his horn, but only a few dark drops dribbled into his mouth. He was drunk already, he realized numbly, and no surprise, he had gulped a full horn of Wulfaruna's strong ale on an empty stomach, when he was already tired enough to drop.

Wulfaruna set a platter of bread and cheese in front of him before she took the horn out of his hands to refill it. Not waiting for his father to ask him any more questions, Hailgi began to gobble his food.

"Don't ask him any more questions about it, Sigismundar," Hagalar told the other drighten in a low voice. "A great deal has happened here. But if I had not believed that there was no other choice, I would not have sent my men with him."

"No, you wouldn't have. Well, what then? Do we attack now or wait for them?"

"It would be best to strike as soon as we can, I think. Hunding's sons will find the bodies before long, if they haven't already, and they will be gathering their host. If we can go now, before they have readied themselves, we will have the stronger hand. Then, the harvest must be brought in soon."

"Yes," Sigismundar said musingly. "It must. Still, Hunding has not been dead long, and you said they did not know the day he would come back. And then, my men are tired from the long ride we hastened as swiftly as we could, since Thurir said he thought there was need, and Hailgi and his men look ready to fall asleep in their food."

"I'm not," Hailgi said with his mouth full, but he was.

"If we can ready ourselves to leave a little before dawn, that should do well enough."

"Yes. All right, then."

Since Hagalar's daughters had been sent away, Hailgi and Sigismundar were put in their chamber for the night. Hailgi's last thoughts on falling asleep were the hope that his father, if no one else, would wake him up before the host left.

"Hailgi, Hailgi!" Someone was shouting through the darkness. "Hailgi, wake up! Wake up!"

"Huh? Whassat?" Hailgi muttered, sitting up. He tried to focus his eyes on the torch wavering before him. "Are we leaving?"

"Come on," his father's voice said. Sigismundar's big hand wrapped around his arm, helping him to his feet. "It's still night. There's someone outside who says he'll only talk to you."

Hailgi flung his cloak over his shoulders and followed his father out to the gate. Hagalar and Eburhelmar stood there, looking at something that glittered in the torchlight. He could hear the sound of someone sucking in deep sobbing gulps of air outside the gate.

"Is this your spoon, Hailgi?" Hagalar asked, holding it out. Hailgi recognized the amber-set handle at once. It was the spoon he had given to Swain.

"Let me in!" The herder-boy's strained voice called. "I've got to talk to Hailgi. Hailgi, are you there?"

"Are you alone?"

"Yes. Hailgi, do you remember how I helped you when you came to me? Will you take me as your man and give me shelter?"

"I will," Hailgi answered. "Eburhelmar, let him in."

Sigismundar and Hagalar drew their swords, Eburhelmar picked up his spear, holding it halfway along the shaft so that he could stab with it. Slowly he opened the door a little way, standing ready to close it.

Swain's thin body squeezed in through the gap, the warder closed the gate and banged the bar down at once. The youth was shuddering, tunic dark with stains of sweat and night-grayed hair standing up in spikes.

"Hailgi," he gasped. "They're killing each other, they're all killing each other."

"Who are? Calm down and tell me what's happened from the beginning." Hailgi took off his cloak and wrapped it around the herder.

Slowly Swain's breaths eased and the tremors that shivered through his body began to die down.

"They got word that Hunding had been slain a little before sunset. Then they were going to gather the host and ride here, but then Blindi Bale-Wise asked who would lead it. And that was all he had to say. None of Hunding's sons got a word in after that. Some of the men favored one, and some another, and then one of the thanes hit another one, and he drew his knife, and then they all had weapons out. That was when I got out of the hall," he added, "and when I saw them riding and fighting through the wheat I started running because I knew they had all gone mad for the slaughter."

"What about Blindi?" Hagalar asked quietly. "Who does he favor?"

"I think he's always been fondest of Lingwe. And he was standing beside him when the fight started, and I think the two of them left together."

"So." Hagalar looked at Sigismundar.

"It seems that our work has been done for us," Sigismundar replied. "If they're riding down their own harvest, Hunding's sons will not be ready to trouble us for some time after this. We may well win a more thorough victory by simply waiting to see what happens, and if a madness has come upon them, it is better for us not to go among them."

"True enough."

"My men and I will stay here for the next few days, or until we hear more. Then we will have to go back to help get in our own harvest. Hailgi will come with us," he added.

"Are you sure?"

"Now that he has led a troop of his own, I think he needs no more fostering."

"I suppose not. It will be quieter here without him."

"It's sure to be," Sigismundar admitted. "Well, it's too cold to be standing out here without a good reason, and I expect our messenger here could do with something to drink."

It was not more than three days later when more news of Hunding's sons came to them. This time it was brought by one of the older warriors from Hunding's hall, a burly man whose short black hair and stiff beard were shot through with gray. He told them that Swain's tale was true. Hunding's sons and their thanes had fallen to fighting, and many of the thanes had been slain. Blindi Bale-Wise and Lingwe had gone off with a small band, and no one knew yet what had become of them, though most thought they were likely to be faring towards the kin of Lingwe's mother.

Between them, the sons of Hunding now had no more than half the men their father had ruled over, and they now wished to offer Hagalar frith, and to let him know that they would want to buy whatever grain he could spare, for the fighting had spoiled more than half their harvest. If Hagalar mistrusted them, Heming, Alfarath, and Aiwulfar were each willing to send a son to him as hostage in proof of their friendship.

"It seems a fair offer," Hagalar said after some thought, "and my harvest looks as though it will be good this year, if no ill comes to it before it is brought in. Tell them I am willing to do that, then."

"So we have no need to stay longer," Sigismundar said when Hagalar told him of what had happened.

"It would seem not."

"Good enough, then. Will you and your family come to keep Yule with us?"

"We'll be glad to."

Hailgi did not wait by the two older men any longer, but went off and set Swain to packing his things, then wandered down to the shore. The sea was very still in the warm day, its water clear enough for him to see every blade of the reddish-brown seaweed that swayed gently in the tide. He stood looking over the waters till they curved and dropped away from his sight. I have avenged my shame, I have won good words and might, and shown that I am truly a son of my clan, Hailgi thought. And yet his heart beat a hollow drumbeat of longing against his ribs, and not even a wisp of cloud misted the sky over the wave-path to Sealand, so that his dearest hopes could not dream the shape of the gray wind-rider before him. I am Hailgi Hunding's-Bane.

I have led my men in battle, and given the holiest of gifts to Wodhanar, but still I am only fifteen, and a thane in my father's house. I cannot yet seek a bride, for winning a battle is a long way from winning a hall, and I have little wealth of my own to show an atheling-maid and her kin, though there is no doubt that my fame will be well-met when I go to wed. Still, the road glittered on the sea before him. Hailgi knew that he would fare to Sigiruna on that bright bridge, as soon as his own strength was full-waxed, and the clan of the Wolfings rooted deeply enough to grow again. After Hunding's sons had sworn a lasting frith, or been given to the more lasting frith of the old earth-house, for Hailgi knew, as well, that the Hound's clan would ever seek to tear down the Wolf's while both lived. After a while, Hailgi turned around and went back to the garth to say farewell to Hagalar's men and see if he could talk Ansumundar into coming back to his father's hall with him.

CHAPTER XI

"So," Ms. Devereaux said when Helgi came back for his first lesson after the holidays. "Do you still want to try out for graduate studies in voice?"

"Do you think I'm good enough?"

"It's hard to say. You've come an amazingly long way in a relatively short time, and I can tell you've been working hard, but you still have some problems with pitch and tone, and you're not nearly as steady in the top of your range as you ought to be. You can think about it."

After she had taken him through his warm-up, Ms. Devereaux handed him a music book titled Solo Songs for Low Voice, and Helgi flipped through the book until one page caught his gaze. The words were in German, their sense came to him more slowly than their sound, like a light shimmering through marsh-mists. "Wer reitet so spät, durch Nacht und Wind? Es ist ein Vater mit seinem Kind. 'Mein Sohn, was birgst du so bang dein Gesicht?' 'Siehst, Vater, du, den Erl-König nicht?'" Who rides so late, through night and wind? It is a father with his child'. My son, why do you hide your face, so frightened?' 'Father, don't you see the Erl-King?' A shiver of recognition sliced through him like cold steel through the strings of his guts.

"This one," he said.

Ms. Devereaux looked at it, shaking her head. A strand of hair had come loose from her bun, drifting across the nape of her neck like a tendril of seaweed. "You're still too ambitious, Helgi. I wouldn't recommend that for performance for a couple of years yet."

"Why not? If I can hit all the notes in it"

"There's far more to it than that. This is a complicated piece and it really requires a much more mature singer to interpret it properly. If you really want to do well, choose something more within your reach."

"Would it be all right for me to work on this, anyway?"

"Hmm." She tapped an apricot nail on the piano bench several times. "I wouldn't advise you to waste too much time on it. Look, let's try it now so you can see for yourself how difficult it is."

Ms. Devereaux turned back to the piano and began to play. The rushing rhythms caught Helgi by surprise, the bass runs pounding beneath his feet like a horse's hooves sweeping him away. He tried to keep abreast of his place in the music, but the sound overwhelmed him, stealing his breath and dizzying his sight, so that Ms. Devereaux had to stop the ceaseless beating of her right hand on the keys in order to plunk out Helgi's own notes for him to follow. He limped through the song, he knew he was limping, and that the music limped beneath his clumsiness, but in spite of that, he could hear the might hidden within it, like a fine blade wrapped in a filthy piece of cloth. Though his voice was tired well before the end, well before the high death-cry of "Erl-König hat mir ein Leid getan!", He knew that he had to sing this piece.

"You see?" Ms. Devereaux said.

"Let me work on it, anyway, and see how it goes."

Ms. Devereaux speared him with a sideways glance, tightening her mouth. Helgi stared into her eyes, as though the night-wind's rushing could blow through his gaze, blow what he had heard in the music, and what he thought he could sing into it, into her skull.

At last she nodded. "I suppose it won't hurt you to study it, anyway. Don't try to do it all through too often, and don't strain your voice. When you start getting tired, stop and rest. I suggest you get a professional recording, Dietrich Fischer-Dieskau has a nice version in his '21 Schubert-Lieder'."

The wind bit bitterly into Helgi's ears and face when he came out from his lesson, the streetlamps lining the pavement shone bright through the cold air, brighter than the city-dimmed stars above. Hands thrust deeply in his pockets, music held tightly between his left arm and his side as if to protect it from the cold, he hurried to his car. The radio had gone out on him in November, but the heater still worked. Helgi turned it up full blast and drove out of the parking lot, making his way slowly through the maze of one-way streets that twisted unpredictably through the campus. The old Impala coughed and jerked a couple of times as he stepped on the gas and steered out onto Mockingbird. Now that all the Christmas lights had been taken down, the street looked strangely stark, white lights against black sky and black asphalt misting everything between into shades of gray. The words to his new song ran through Helgi's head as he drove towards Sound Warehouse, their rhythm riding through the rolling of the car.

Shivering, he sang softly to himself, hardly knowing that he sang, "*Den Erlen-König, mit Kron und Schweif!' 'Mein Sohn, es ist ein Nebelstreif.'"* 'The Erl-King, with crown and (something, have to look that up).' 'My son, it is a streak of mist.'

Once home, he hurried up to his room where Elric was curled up on the foot of his bed. The elk hound opened one eye and regarded his master mournfully. Helgi slipped the '21 Lieder' into his CD player, fast-forwarding until he got to 'Erlkönig', and thumbed it on, sitting down beside his puppy to listen. He was disappointed by the way the song sounded on CD. It was too fast, too light, the piano tinkling rather than thundering.

"This is not the way I would do it," Helgi murmured to his dog. Fischer-Dieskau's changes in tone were something else, though. Helgi could hear the different voices speaking, the frightened child, his father calming him, the Erl-King calling sweetly, then fearsomely, and all woven together by the same music, by the same pounding bass run. He ran the CD back when the song was over, the second time, he tried to sing along. Not there, his voice was still too weak, too shaky, to bear the music, but he was starting to hear it now, the voices and horns rising behind his own in the wind, the wind blowing through his bookshelves, stirring through the sheets of music and the dirty socks scattered around his room and soundlessly rattling the posters on his walls. Elric stood and stretched, shaking the bed, then suddenly jumped off and ran to the door where he stood staring back at Helgi. He lowered his muzzle, letting out a low whine.

"You're no appreciator of music, Elric, you dog," Helgi muttered to him, breaking off in mid-line. "Come on back, I'll take you for a walk when the song's over." At the word walk, the elk hound began to frisk about, then ran up to Helgi and laid his head on his knee, looking up soulfully. Helgi did not know whether his hand was shaking from anger or relief as he punched the CD player off.

"You're not going to let me go nuts, are you, fur ball?" Helgi said to the dog. "Come on, walk. Woof woof." Elric aimed his nose towards the door and barked sharply. "Good boy."

Helgi hesitated with his hand on the doorknob a moment before going out. His memory had not dimmed at all since Christmas Eve, it took little imagination for him to see the host of the dead sweeping between the pale streetlights, their wounds lit starkly by the ghostly electricity. I imagined it, anyway, he told himself sternly, and besides, no wind was blowing now, only the city-lights hazed the winter sky. When Helgi and his dog came back in from their walk, Helgi went to the phone, dialing Mark Tippet's number. Two rings, three, four...

"Hello?" He said.

"Al's Mortuary," a deep voice answered. "You stab 'em, we slab 'em."

"Y'know, Mark, that was old when your ancestors were painting graffiti in caves and gnawing raw meat from mammoth bones."

"Very probably. What can I do to you?"

"Nothing to do around here. I wondered if I could come over for a while."

"Sure. How do you feel about some beer? Bring money, I'll take you out to my newest discovery."

"You found a blind doorman who believes your fake ID?"

"Why, you know an upright and upstanding university student such as myself would not carry a fake ID, any more than you would. Shame on you, Hell-Guy."

"My ID is real now, remember. It's not my fault you were born six months too late."

"Probably was. See you in ten."

Mark was already in his bug trying to get the motor started when Helgi pulled up in front of his house. Helgi rolled his window down and called, in a high lisping voice, "Hello, sailor! Your car or mine?"

"Looks like yours. Plague Bug doesn't like the cold."

"I thought Volkswagens were designed for the autobahns of Russia after the Nazi conquest."

"You sure about that? I thought it was Mercedese." Tippet got out of his car, muttering to it, "You're doomed. You useless bucket of bolts, the moment I get a real job, you're doomed."

"So, where are we going?" Helgi asked when Mark had settled in.

"It's down on Greenville. Well, more sort of off Greenville. Take Central to Mockingbird, hang a left."

The traffic on Central was running swift and thick, lights skimming along the road in a steady stream. "Prepare for kamikaze maneuver, honorable Marcus-san. Ich, ni, san, shiBanzai!" Helgi stomped on the accelerator, zooming in just in front of a pickup truck. He saw the driver's raised middle finger in the rear view mirror, but ignored it, concentrating on getting up to speed and sliding over into the left lane.

"No fake ID required, actually," Mark said as they sped along. "Aaron's bar tending there part-time, and he told me how to get in through the back. It's not the kind of place where they check real close, anyway."

"How come Aaron's working? I thought he had a graduate scholarship."

"He does, but he's getting Real Serious about this girl Lisa. He said UTD cafeteria is not the ideal place for a romantic evening out, and Bud Lite is not the wine to convince her that he is a smoothly sophisticated man of high class. An overproduction of semen has backed up in his system and poisoned his brain."

It took them a while to crawl through the traffic on Greenville. The street wasn't crowded with tables and pedestrians the way it was in the summer, no one eating outside or just hanging out at this time of year, but the cars were still bumper-to-bumper on the street, and the parking lots jammed full.

"Now, I realize this place is not going to win any prizes for decor, so don't say anything about it," Mark warned Helgi. "Think of it like this. It's off the beaten path, and there are parking places nearby."

"How sleazy is it? Do we have to show a razor and puke blood to get in?"

"Nah, it's just, um, kinda run-down, and the music's real inferior. But, they'll serve us beer. Think of donative equines."

"I am suddenly reminded more of equine hindquarters."

They drove around a row of shoddy-looking buildings, to a parking lot with a few battered cars in it. Behind one of the buildings was a garbage dumpster and a stack of cardboard boxes. "Over here," Mark hissed, leading Helgi around the dumpster. He fumbled with the door a moment, then pulled it open. They slipped through a grimy bathroom, carefully avoiding the wet patches on the tiles, and into the darkened bar.

The first thing Helgi noticed was that the piano was a bit out of tune, and the player was just barely competent. The men who sat at tables or hunched on their barstools like great birds in the rain were mostly middle-aged or older, as far as Helgi could tell in the bad light, they slouched like men who had been beaten a few times. There were a few more blacks than whites in the room, though not many. The haze of cigarette smoke in the air gave Aaron a grey and tired look as well. Although he was dressed in a white shirt and bow tie, his longish hair slicked back under his collar, he looked more rumpled than he did wearing T-shirt and jeans in full daylight. He rolled his eyes back when he saw his brother and Helgi.

"Heineken," Mark told him.

Aaron leaned over the bar towards him. "You shit, Mark," he hissed, "I told you not to bring any of your buddies in with you. What happens if one of these guys complains to the owner about the Children's Crusade taking over the place during my shift?"

"We'll stay in the corner and be real quiet, I promise. Anyway, Helgi's of age."

Aaron straightened up, glaring at Helgi. "What can I get you sir?"

"I'll have a Heineken too."

Aaron gave them their beers, relieved them of $2.50 each, and gestured towards an empty table in the dark corner nearest the bathroom.

"Convenient for escape?" Helgi asked quietly as he sat down.

"Yeah. If the owner comes in, I'm gone."

"How glad I am that I'm no longer a second-class citizen. Back of the bus, back of the line."

"Separate but equal, yeah. Is this place a dump, or what?"

"It is, but beer is beer, where-ever you go." Helgi took a deep drink of his. The Heineken was lighter than the British ales his father drank, but he could still taste the grain's gold beneath the bitter edge of hops. Beer and bread, he thought, and remembered that he hadn't had dinner. "Do they serve food here?"

"Have to get a different license. You know, Helgi, you could probably get a job playing the piano somewhere like this."

"I think I plan to set my sights a little higher, thank you."

"You know what I meant."

"I'm afraid I do." Helgi stared up at the cigarette smoke curling through the glow of the dim yellow lights set into the barroom ceiling, reflected in the mirror behind the bar. Shapes in smoke, in cloud, in snow but it was the mind that did all of it, the mind and the gullible eyes. Lights and mirrors and smoke, and a sucker. If it could be real? He thought. If it could be, then he was not gazing into an abyss that yawned before his feet, if it could not, then Schubert and Goethe had stood here before him, and stared into the same grinning gap. And if you look into an abyss long enough

"What's wrong?"

"Nothing. Why?"

"You went real pale and sick-looking there for a moment."

Helgi's story beat against the back of his throat, raven-words trying to wing free. He was used to telling Mark things, he was used to hearing what his friend had to say. But he knew trying to describe this thing would cripple it, whatever it was. He would be still, he told himself, he would say nothing until he knew how to say it so that no one would mishear.

"No. I guess I'm hungrier than I thought."

Helgi finished his beer and Mark followed suit. They went up to the bar to grab two more, when no one was watching them, they left the bar.

"Burger King?" Helgi asked as he started the car, his beer cold between his thighs.

"Good enough. Or at least mediocre enough."

When Helgi realized that they had been driving silently for a very long time, he glanced over to Mark. Mark was no longer in his seat, only a shadow rode beside Helgi, without shape or face. Did I drop him off? Am I losing my mind? Helgi wondered. He stepped on the accelerator as if to flee the thought, speeding up and weaving between the bobbing headlights that zoomed towards him in a thunderstorm of raucous honking. His hands locked on the wheel, a sudden storm of panic sleeted cold through his body as he realized that he had taken the wrong turn. He was driving the wrong way on the freeway as the speedometer needle wavered upward against the pale glow of the instrument panel and the headlights exploded up towards him and sheared away in squealing brakes in front of him. I've got to pull over, I've got to get off! Helgi thought, but as he tried to raise his foot from the accelerator, a cold boot stamped down over it and a pair of icy hands closed over his own, holding the wheel straight as the road twisted off and upward into the wide arc of an overhead ramp. The speedometer needle crossed the red 90 mark as the car started to make the curve. Helgi was too scared to cry out, he clung tightly to the wheel, trying to wrest it away, but the old Impala was going too fast for him to control it now. He could feel the car's own speed catching it like a mighty wind, flinging its wheels free of the road and over the low concrete barrier at the ramp's edge.

He was tumbling now, slowly, slow-motion, enough time to think, "This is it, this is really it, I'm going to die now", and the car was falling faster and faster, the city lights swirling into a giant pinwheel around him as his momentum flung him downwards, Crash.

Helgi lay shaking in the darkness, staring at the patterns of lightless color his eyes made on the blackness and breathing hard, as if he were trying to suck breath back into crushed lungs. The sweat was already chilling on his face and in the twisted sheets winding around him.

"Just a dream," he whispered to himself. "It was only a dream. Calm down, guy."

Helgi sat up, reaching blindly towards the light switch at the foot of the bed. As he groped about in the dark, something cold and wet pressed against the pulse inside his wrist.

He cried out, a fright-strangled gulp of "Aaagh", and jerked his hand away, slapping the light on. Elric's deep brown eyes looked inquisitively up at him as the elk hound thumped his tail twice against the bed.

"My God, dog, you scared me. Don't do that when I've just had a nightmare, okay?"

Elric licked his hand, the warmth of the dog's tongue making Helgi realize just how cold he was. He scooted closer, burying both hands in Elric's deep fur and hugging the dog's body to him. Eventually Helgi's shivering eased. He turned the light off and crawled back under the covers. "No more of those dreams," he muttered, pressing his feet up against Elric's back and waiting for the warmth to soak through to him. He closed his eyes, breathing deeply and trying to clear his mind.

Helgi did not sleep, though he rolled from side to side, he could not sleep. He wasn't even drowsy now, it seemed as if the pounding speed of the dream still ran through him, muted down from its screaming pitch of fear into a rush of energy throbbing through his body. Elric shifted restlessly at his feet, then raised his muzzle and whined.

Helgi patted his dog with one hand while turning the light back on with the other. "Must be catching, huh? Well, as long as I'm awake, I might as well do something useful."

He plugged his headphones into his CD player, cranking up the bass as high as he could, and put "Erlkönig" on again. After a moment he stopped the CD, then went for the music he had borrowed from Ms. Devereaux and his German dictionary so that he could look up the vocabulary he didn't know before he went any further. He worked slowly, penciling the English in above the German every so often as he came across strange words.

"Wer reitet so spät, durch Nacht und Wind?
Who rides so late, through night and wind?
Es ist ein Vater mit seinem Kind.
It is a father with his child.
Er hat den Knabe wohl in dem Arm, he has the boy close in his arm,
Er fasst ihn sicher, er hält ihn warm.
He holds him tight, he keeps him warm.
'Mein Sohn, was birgst du so bang dein Gesicht?'
'My son, why hide you, so frightened, your face?
'Siehst, Vater, du, den Erl-König nicht?
'Father, don't you see the Erl-King?
Den Erlen-König, mit Kron und Schweif?
'The Erl-King, with crown and trail?'
'Mein Sohn, es ist ein Nebelstreif.'
'My son, it is a streak of mist.'
'Du liebes Kind, komm, geh mit mir,
'You darling child, come, go with me,
Gar schöne Spielen spiel ich mit dir,
I will play lovely games with you.

Manch' bünte Blumen sind an den Strand,
Many bright flowers are on the shore,
 Meine Mutter hat manch' gülden Gewand.'
My mother has many golden clothes.'
'Mein Vater, mein Vater, und hörest du nicht,
'My father, my father, and don't you hear
Was Erlen-König mir leise verspricht?
'What the Erl-King softly promises me?'
'Sei ruhig bleibe ruhig, mein Kind,
'Be still stay still, my child,
 In dürren Blättern rauschelt der Wind.
'The wind rustles through dry leaves.'
'Willst, feiner Knabe, du mit mir gehen?
'Will you go with me, fine youth?
 Meine Töchter sollen dir warten schon,
My daughters shall wait upon you,
 Meine Töchter führen den nächtlichen Reihn,
My daughters lead the nightly row,
 Und wiegen und tanzen und singen dich ein,
And sway and dance and sing to you,
 Sie wiegen und tanzen und singen dich ein.
'They sway and dance and sing to you.'
'Mein Vater, mein Vater, und siehst du nicht dort,
'My father, my father, and don't you see there
Erl-König's Töchter in düsterem Ort?
'Erl-King's daughters in the shadowy place?'
'Mein Sohn, mein Sohn, ich seh es genau,
'My son, my son, I see it well,
 Es scheinen die alten Weiden so grau.
'The old willows shine gray.'
'Ich liebe dich, mich reizt deine schöne Gestalt,
'I love you, your beautiful shape tears at me,
 Und bist du nicht willig, so brauch ich Gewalt!
'And if you're not willing, I shall se force!'
'Mein Vater, mein Vater, jetzt fasst er mich an,
'My father, my father, now he grasps me,
 Erl-König hat mir ein Leid getan!
'Erl-King has done me a harm!'
 Den Vater grauset's, er reitet geschwind,
It frightens the father, he rides swiftly,
 Er hält in Armen den ächzehnten Kind.
He holds the moaning child in arms.
 Erreicht den Hof mit Müh und
Not -Reaches the hall with toil and need -
 In seinen Armen das Kindwar tot.
In his arms the child was dead."

Helgi started the CD again and lay back to listen to it, closing his eyes and letting the words bring their shapes to his mind. Rushing, the horse galloping along, frighteningly fast, and suddenly the shadow beside him, the cloaked shadow of the Erl-King, followed by the glimmering shapes of his daughters with their long hair twisting in the wind behind him, some mounted on gray horses and some on gray wolves. I have seen this, I know this, part of his mind whispered through the sudden coldness that grasped him. The Erl-King, leading his host of the dead, calling me to him.

You were going to go join them, all right, Tony had said.

"'Erl-König hat mir ein Leid getan!'"

It didn't frighten me. I wanted it, I wanted power and speed, splitting the sky with my flight, Karin's voice said silently to him. Would falling have been like his dream, spinning slowly down with the snow whirling around him? Or would he have been swept up in the wind, howling up through the clouds till he broke through among the banners of light that flared across the glittering sky above?

"These are crazy thoughts," Helgi whispered to himself as the last two chords pounded down. "Maybe I am really going crazy."

He sat up, reaching out for Elric he wanted to lean against the solidness of the elk hound's body, to prove to himself the firmness of real and not-real. But Elric had jumped down sometime during the song, leaving only a depression in the blankets and a brindled spoor of shed hair. Resolutely Helgi punched the CD back again, started the song again. It wasn't the child who spoke first. All of them. I have to sing all of them. He could see the father and the Erl-King facing each other, one bright, one dark, seen and unseen, the same shape and the same face.

They both lose the boy, and they both claim him, Helgi thought dizzily. Death is the blind one, but it's the father who doesn't see the Erl-King's daughters riding through the wind. Helgi woke up slowly the next morning, sleep lying heavy through his limbs like leaden marrow in his bones as he showered and shaved and gathered his books. By the time Helgi got to Jefferson, his head had begun to ache, a vague pain, as though his skull were just a little too tight. It could be a brain tumor, the still small Voice of Doom muttered in the back of his mind. It could be an aneurysm about to blow. It could be what I get for not getting enough sleep last night, Helgi answered himself, picking up his trombone and starting to warm up. The slide was moving slowly today, he pulled it all the way out and spritzed it with a few shots of lubricant.

"Yo," said Mark from behind him. "Hung over after two beers? You have that coveted gray and dead look about you."

"Wait till I tell you what you look like," Helgi said automatically, though he couldn't think of anything to follow the threat up with.

"Has anyone told you that the dead are not required to attend classes? It's as good as having mono, you get an automatic vacation for the duration of the condition."

"Lay off, Tippet. I didn't sleep real well last night, okay?"

"Sorry. Well, you've got a German class next period, don't you? An hour of guaranteed sleep."

"Yeah."

As Helgi watched the music in front of him, playing mostly by habit, the black notes would begin to swirl and vanish into a whirlpool of colored sparks. He kept blinking the lights away, but if he looked at the page for more than a few seconds, they would rise out of it again, throwing off his timing and obscuring his entrances. No one else seemed to notice that he wasn't playing as well as usual. The pieces were still fairly new, and other sections' mistakes were far more audible, but he knew, and he could feel his frustration beginning to cramp in his guts. Most of the time his glances at the round white clock-face staring from the wall were looks of hope meant to slow the turning of its time, today, streaks of sweat slicked the slim tubes of gleaming metal beneath his hands, and his trombone's last note as the bell rang trailed off into a deep moan of relief.

Helgi sat in the back of the class in "Goethe and His Contemporaries", twice Fräulein Doktor Friedmann called on him, and twice he made simple mistakes of case and gender, die for der, der for dem, that he would not have made two years ago. As always when confronted with great stupidity, Fräulein Friedmann finally threw up her thin hands and rolled her dark eyes in a way that Helgi had always thought was more suited to a French teacher than a German professor.

She moaned "Ach, was tu' ich mit dir?" Then moved on to Brad Eliot, who sat in front of him, even as Helgi's head began to droop towards the desk. When the bell rang to wake him up and his eyelids grated back across his eyes, he felt worse, not better. Helgi stumbled to his car, letting his habit of driving that path through the network of roads carry him home. Elric met him with a rush of joy that nearly knocked Helgi down, if elk hounds were not particularly tall dogs, they were very strong, bred to wrestle moose to the ground. Helgi pushed him off feebly, making his way into the bathroom and taking the thermometer out of its place in the medicine rack.

It was very cool in his mouth. Tighten his teeth a little more, the mercury would run free and silvery down his throat, coating it. Don't even think that, he told himself. He knew mercury poisoning would be a nasty way to die, even if it killed at once. Which it might not, he had heard that people used to say "mad as a hatter" because hatters breathed mercury fumes which ate their brains. Helgi could almost feel the mercury spearing from his mouth, flung outward by his own heat. When he took the thermometer out, it read 103.0.

"I am sick," Helgi muttered to himself. "Oh, I am sick." He got two Tylenol, moved very carefully towards his bed, and collapsed.

Helgi's own thrashings against the twisted blankets woke him up. The only sound in his room was his own harsh breath panting through his aching throat. Shivering with the cold, he untangled his blankets and pulled them back up over himself. He looked at his clock. The digits glowing against the dark read 2.30.

Helgi reached out to flick the light on, then dragged himself over to his bookshelf, pulling down his boxed Lord of the Ring trilogy. Holding the case in his hands, he stared at the runes running around its edges. When he was thirteen, he had been able to read and write Tolkien's runes. Now they were strange to him, a garble of stick-shapes almost like letters, but with their sounds scrambled beyond recognition. The runes writhed beneath his gaze, the flames that burned from the ring's gold beginning to twist in his sight. Helgi hastily turned the case around and carefully dislodged the first book from its place. He had read only a few pages when the letters began to dissolve again. The blood was pounding hotly in his temples, pressing against the inside of his head as though a noose were tightening around his jugular vein, cutting off the down-flow of blood and breath.

The words, the music of "Erlkönig" beat through his mind with his quickened heartbeat, dizzyingly fast, Helgi clamped his jaw shut, afraid that he was going to throw up again. He lay back, breathing hard through his mouth and trying to cast off the feeling of strangulation as the lightless sparkles pinwheeled before his eyes. When the noose loosened and his breathing eased again, he closed his eyes, but he could not get back to sleep. After a little while, he felt a heavy thump at the end of the bed. The weight shifted, moving up towards the head, then Helgi smelled the effluvia of liver-flavored horse meat on Elric's warm breath.

"Dog, you've got a bad case of dog breath," he muttered, turning his face away. "Uck, ptoo. Back, boy." Helgi levered himself up to a sitting position, holding onto the dog's muscular body for support. Elric settled down on his haunches, his tongue lolling out between long white fangs, and Helgi patted him weakly. "My faithful friend. Who'd ever guess that you're only a couple of genes away from chasing sledges through the snow in Siberia?" And would his dark eyes gleam red in the night when the wind brought him the scent of blood? Helgi felt Elric's fur stir beneath his hand as the thick muscles of the elk hound's shoulders bunched. Elric drew back his upper lip, a soft rumble starting in his chest. He was not looking at Helgi now, but staring at the shadowed crack of the door.

"What's wrong?" Helgi whispered. He could feel the chill sweat dewing on his forehead and limbs, as if he were walking through a patch of thick fog. He felt the shaking in his hand, but he could not tell if it was he who trembled, or Elric.

The dog's body convulsed in two sharp, deep barks. "Hush now," Helgi muttered. "Easy, boy, what is it?" A burglar? He thought. Shit why now?

Helgi held his breath, listening, but heard nothing no footsteps on the stairs, no breathing but Elric's. Suddenly the dog lowered his muzzle, letting out a low whine that shivered chill through Helgi's body to set his teeth on edge. There is something bad out there, Helgi thought. He put his arm around the trembling elk hound, who still stared at the doorway, at the darkness lurking in the edges of the door. Glancing around his room, he saw nothing he could use as a weapon, nothing more dangerous than his old Boy Scout knife and a couple of empty Coke bottles.

Carefully he swung his legs over the side of the bed and stood up, steadying himself with a hand against the wall. He felt very light, dizzyingly light, like the shell of a blown egg, and the edges of his peripheral vision were foggy, but he could walk.

He picked up a Coke bottle by the neck and crept to the door, his bare feet whispering soundlessly over the carpet. Helgi flattened himself against the wall, opening the door very slowly and peering around it to the spot fixed by Elric's frozen stare. His sight dulled by the clear electric light flooding his room, at first Helgi saw nothing but darkness outside. As his eyes adjusted, some of the darkness slowly grayed, and amid the darkness, he saw the shadow standing on the stair. His heart clenched tightly, knocking a rush of blood through his head, he could feel the ice slicked his entrails. 'Du liebes Kind, komm, geh mit mir.' Though he could see no face, Helgi suddenly knew that it was watching him from beneath its shadow-hood. He half-wanted to flee yammering back into the full light, slamming the door behind him and leaping to his bed where he could hold tight to his watchful dog, but he could already hear Karin's laughter above the wing beats of blood in his ears. As if she were watching him, he clenched the Coke bottle more tightly, holding it up before his face, his other fist raised to guard his body as he eased into fighting stance. Just let it move, he thought fiercely let it come nearer me! He could feel his own weight shifting forward, it was he who was moving closer to the edge of the light, to the top of the stair where the dark shape waited for him.

The shadow showed no movement, but Helgi felt the wind brushing his face a cold wind, tainted by a hint of rot. He swayed beneath a sudden wave of dizziness, the fever-heat burning back into his cheeks. The gleaming glass of the bottle in his hand shook reflections back into his eyes, in the lightning-blue afterimage, he saw, or he thought he saw the figure raise a hand towards him, a fold of shadow falling down from its arm like a huge raven's drooping wing. It moved a step closer, and Helgi felt his windpipe beginning to tighten again, choking the breath that scratched like hemp through his sore throat. Suddenly his nerve broke. He leapt forward, knocking the outstretched arm away with his empty fist and swinging the bottle at the shadow's head. It slipped from his hand at the same moment as his foot slipped on the stair, shattering on the banister as he went down.

Helgi blinked hard against the sudden brightness in his eyes. He was sitting on the stair where he had fallen, yes, he could see the shards of the Coke bottle sprayed out over the carpet on the last two steps and the wooden floor beneath, but the hall light above him and the staircase light were both on. His legs were shaking as he got up, badly enough that he had to cling to the banister for support, standing hunched over like an old man. Carefully he dragged himself back up to his room. Elric was curled up on the end of his bed, he looked asleep, until one dark eye opened to regard Helgi. Helgi's knees melted beneath him, dropping him to the floor. After a little while, Helgi was able to get up and crawl back into bed. I must have been sleepwalking again, he thought as Elric settled in beside him. Maybe I should tell someone. I could have broken my neck on the stairs. I could have done anything.

"I wish you could tell me what you saw," he said to the elk hound. "Was it just me getting up and running around like an idiot? Or were you really barking at something?" He knew how sounds from the waking world could creep into dreams, a song on the radio finding its own place in the realm of sleep or a voice calling through the wide drowsy place between sleep and awakening, but Elric would not answer.

Helgi looked at the clock. It was four-eighteen. "The hour of the wolf," he whispered to Elric. "Woof woof." At the command, Elric barked, Helgi started violently enough to bring the darkness up before his eyes again. Its tide swirled slowly back as he got control of his breathing again. The dog nosed enquiringly at him. "It's okay, Elric. Everything's just fine. I hope." He picked up Fellowship of the Ring again and started to read, more or less where he thought he had left off.

The next day was worse, a daze of sleep broken by feverish tossing. Fortunately, Helgi had a few cans of frozen orange juice concentrate and a couple of croissants in the apartment, as well as a full bottle of Tylenol. Each dose of medicine took about half an hour to ease his aching joints and lower his fever, then he slept for another two or three hours before his own tossing about woke him up again. He would drink a few sips of the juice and nibble a few flakes of croissants, watching the clock until he could take more Tylenol.

It was past eleven when the phone rang. Helgi dragged himself out to answer it, groaning with the strain.

"Hello, Helgi."

"Karin!" The delighting shock drove the shaking of sickness from Helgi's limbs. "You're back."

"It's just for a little while. I'll be back in Colorado tomorrow. Can I see you tonight?"

"Sure, sure, I'd love to," Helgi stammered. "Where..? But, but I'm sick. I might not be very good company for you. I don't want you to catch what I've got."

Karin's laugh's crystal had a cutting edge to it, the mockery so keen Helgi was hardly sure it was more than his imagination. "Are you too sick to come out with me? If you are, you can't expect many more chances to see me."

"I'm not," he answered hastily. "Where can I meet you?"

"I'll pick you up in a few minutes." The line went dead.

Helgi dressed hastily in the darkness, hurried down the stairs and out the door. Feverish as he was, he hardly felt the icy spattering of the sleet, it was as though his own heat melted it warm before it could touch him. A car was already driving up a hulking old beast of a vehicle, gray under the street-lights, its exhaust pipe breathing a roiling cloud of pale steam out behind it. The car's windows were rolled all the way down, Karin's pale face glimmered from the darkness inside, and Helgi saw the glitter of the valknut at her throat.

"Get in, min helt," Karin called to him. Helgi hurried around the car, pulling the door open and climbing in. He reached around for the shoulder belts. "None in this car. You'll just have to trust my driving. Do you?"

"Yes," Helgi answered, although he could see the ice glittering bright above the black asphalt on the road ahead of them. It won't be easy for me to get to the doctor's tomorrow, he thought. But Karin guided the car over the slippery road with ease, driving so gracefully she might have been ice-skating. They spun out onto the icy stretch of Central Expressway, laughing, Karin stepped on the accelerator, flying them more and more swiftly down the road, weaving between the other cars without ever braking or taking her foot from the gas. Helgi's face was so numb from the wind that he could not tell whether he was smiling or not, but he tasted the keen cold rushing in the back of his throat, its breath rising to ring through his head as if he were singing a perfect high note.

"Where are we going?" He asked.

Karin turned her head to smile at him. "You'll find out."

The spatters of sleet on the windshield shattered the lights of downtown Dallas into a myriad of colored stars, the neon-edged towers fire working before Helgi's eyes as the windshield wipers scraped and smeared the freezing droplets. Karin pulled off onto a ramp that spiraled down to the right and across into a full circle before it came to ground.

Instead of slowing down as she turned, Karin went faster, Helgi caught his breath, but the car floated smoothly over the ice, skimming down and straight onto the I-30, leading through to the Dallas Zoo, and Fort Worth after that.

"Isn't it kind of late for the zoo?"

"You'd be amazed." But it was the Fair Park exit she took, slowing at last as she drove behind a block of buildings and into a dark parking lot, where she stopped and got out. Helgi was about to protest, this was a dangerous area, no place to be at night, but Karin was in uniform, and he was damned if he'd show himself to be less brave than she was.

His fever-heat rose again as she took him by the arm, throbbing through his body and tingling in his groin. He could feel the strength in her grasp as she guided him towards the alleyway between two of the building-blocks. He remembered how easily she had dumped him in the snow before, and he realized how much he'd grown since. He was almost two inches taller than Karin now.

Karin turned him towards the left, towards the squiggles of neon that glowed through the windows of one place. The bar was decorated with crazed paintings, streaks of bright color gleaming here and there against the wall, the people inside were alive with scruffiness, every scuff on leather or denim a note of defiance, proclaiming a fight or a night on the street lived through. Helgi liked the place at once, his blood throbbing with the bass beat pulsing through the room from the group set up beside the bar.

"Two Bass Ales," Karin hollered through the din as the bartender turned his dark curly head towards her. She raised her bottle towards Helgi, downing the beer in a single swift gulp. "Skoal." Helgi followed suit as well as he could, opening his throat to let it flow down. Karin was already beckoning for two more.

"Are you trying to get me drunk?" Helgi asked dizzily. He felt as though the alcohol were feeding his fever, blowing up the fire in his head.

Karin laughed. "I know what you can take. Do you trust me?" Her hand rested on his thigh a moment.

"I think so."

"Good. Keep that in mind." She sipped at her second beer, Helgi followed her example. Dew beading on the outside of the bottle, the taste of grain beneath the icy glass, he felt that he was on the edge of a memory, but she stopped him before he plunged. "Do you love me?"

"I think so."

"Will you come with me?"

"I've come this far."

"Last time you fought me."

"You jumped out at me from the bushes. What did you expect?"

Karin said nothing, but finished her beer and got to her feet. After a heartbeat, Helgi followed her. "Where are we going now?"

She turned around and put her forefinger across his lips, the calloused pad harsh against his soft flesh. The silencing press of her finger felt close as a kiss, a shiver trembled through Helgi's body at her touch. He followed her out past the two doors marked with simple Male and Female symbols and the roped-off room set apart for an absent band, past the laundromat that took up the back half of the building, its few machines endlessly whirling a frothing cycle of clothes. Karin pushed aside the FIRE ALARM bar shutting off the back door and led Helgi outside again. A sleet-swirl of wind dimmed his eyes with cold tears as he pressed after her in the darkness, guided only by the glimmer of her pale hair ahead of him. She was walking faster now, so that he had to hurry, trying to catch up with her, but no matter how he lengthened his stride, Karin stayed just a little bit ahead of him.

Once he reached out for her. His fingertips just brushed the back of her uniform. She looked back at him, laughing through the blowing sleet. "Come on," she said. "Hurry!"

Karin began to run, and Helgi still followed her. The icy needles of sleet prickled against his hot face like a tingle of excitement as they ran beneath the white-haloed streetlights and out across the road. Helgi heard the screech of brakes behind them, the huge shape of a truck rumbled past in front of them, its rushing wake of air nearly knocking Helgi down. "Faster, faster!" Karin cried to him. "Run faster, or I'll lose you!"

I'm sick, I have a fever, I can't run any faster, Helgi was about to call back to her, but then he felt her strong cold hand gripping his, pulling him along, and the roaring of the wind drowned out the noise of the cars as the pounding of his feet rose to match the pounding of his blood in his ears. They ran along the edge of the overpass, buffeted by the waves of wind from the road and the whirling of the storm from the other side. Karin leapt up to the concrete buffer, balancing easily as she ran along. "Up here!"

Helgi tried to match her leap onto the ice-slicked concrete. His feet skidded, but Karin was still pulling him forward on the slippery pathway, forward into the darkness. He could hear the howling around him now, though he saw nothing until he looked down to the streetlights far below, their light showing him the shadows swirling out of the sleet around him. Now he knew the cloaked shadow, the Erl-King riding ahead of him with his great spear raised high as he stormed through the air. Helgi reached out, clasping Karin about the waist and pulling himself closer to her. They were riding, not running, he could feel the hooves pounding on the wind beneath them, tearing faster and faster through the sky. Karin turned, smiling sharptoothed at Helgi. One breast pressed against his chest as she drew his head down into a kiss.

Her mouth tasted of honey mingled with blood, her buttocks were wedged against his groin, her body cool to his fever-heat as the two of them rode among the wild throng of ice-pale ghosts. Helgi clasped her tightly to him as he threw back his head and cried out, his voice rising through the hoof beats on the wind to a pure sound that speared through his chest, its pain growing to a sudden burst of pleasure so strong that he could feel his body tearing apart beneath it. Panting, Helgi lay on his back, staring up at the light. His pyjamas were wet, his sheets tangled about him in sweat-damp coils. Although he still felt weak and tired, he was able to sit up, then to stand and put on clean pyjamas. The thermometer lay on the tray beside the pitcher of orange juice. When he took it out of his mouth again, it read 98.60.

His fever had broken. Suddenly Helgi began to scrabble around for pencil and music paper, then plugged in his earphones and flicked his little synthesizer on. What he had seen pressed against the inside of his skull, its music rising around it again, and now he could make it fast and hold it for his own. It began with the upward bass-run from "Erl-König", shifted up into the treble for the wind's voice and then sweeping down again and rising to a high shriek before the heavy chords began to beat in the bass, the same driving beat he had heard in the storm, hard and fast enough to bear him over the edge and up without letting him fall. He did not dare to sing aloud, and his throat would not have borne it anyway, but he whispered the words as they ran into his mind and out through his pencil.

"Wind is howling through black pines,
  Winter wolf-night's driving snow,
  Who will ride the road this night?
  Who dares to follow the wood-mad wind?"

Now a treble interlude, he could hear a piccolo alone, keening through the long twists of icicles before the depth swept back to overwhelm it.

"Who can hear the horn's deep call,
  When the dark shadows skim swift through trees?
  Harrying dead from howe ride forth,
  White bone, rot-flesh, red-eyed steeds!
  Holy maid and howling wolf,
  Lightning fair through lashing storm,
  Rend the sky, you riders swift,
  Speed behind the spear wind-borne."

A longer interlude this time, the high and low lines swirling in and out of each other, twisting just at the edge of discord with the horn-call's pure fifth ringing through to hold them fast. Now the beat changed, moving to a flowing six-eight, the bass line running in shifting upward arpeggios.

"One-eyed the awful one storming before,
  Gallops on ghost-gray, eight-legged horse.
  Death as the Erl-King rides on the wind,
  Seeking the one who sees him too clear.
  The hunt hares above as I sink to the ground,
  The willow-gray maiden wheels in the sky,
  Blood raining black from the host of the slain,
  The hemp of the hang-noose harsh-brushing my face.
  I give this death as a gift to myself,
  As Erl-King's daughter cuts my chains loose.
  Gray-shining, grips me, pulling me up,
  My bride and my bane, bright the death-maid.
  Sharp is the spear I raise in my hand,
  I too shall ride and I too shall run,
  And have my share in the hunt's downed prey,
  The one who waits on the earth below."

Now back to the original music, the wing-beating chords dark beneath the wind.

"Sweet in my mouth, the mead of her kiss,
The spear of her song cuts keen as ice,
Battle-bright, she shines through storm,
Rune-wise maid who rides with me.
Haro, halloo, sound the horn
For raven, wolf, and rushing ghost,
Ride with the hunt or flee before,
For Erl-King, awesome, rules the night!"

Helgi finished with a final crashing of chords, then sat back to look at what he had written, the swift pencil-slashes of notes and his shorthand chord-markings leaping over the page above the hasty scribbling of his words. His sinuses were full, his head clogged and beginning to ache, he did not have the strength to play the song again, but worn and sick as he was, he felt eased at last. He was too weak to think about his dream, or what the song might mean.

It was enough that it had sprung from the same wellspring as his dream, a spell he could sing to bring back the moment of riding with Karin through the sky to draw her back to him, if she could ever hear his voice. Helgi touched the paper as though to fasten it tightly into being, to keep it from misting away with the rest of his fever-dream, then turned off the light and crept upstairs again.

CHAPTER XII

Hoilogae woke to the sound of men's low mutterings in the dark hut. The first red of sunrise gleamed dully through the open door like the faint ruddy glow of banked embers, shadows moved against the pale morning light. He rolled up to his feet in a single smooth motion, stretching and spitting the sour taste of sleep from his mouth to hiss in the hot ashes. His mother was there beside him in a moment, handing him a clean tunic and cloak. She glanced over at Hedhinaz, who sat by the fire pit with his back to them, honing the bronze leaf of his spear-blade. Siglinthon beckoned Hoilogae to lower his head. "These are the clothes you must wear when you come to the battle," she whispered. "I wove them with my best wishes to ward you."

"Thank you, Mother," Hoilogae answered, just as softly.

The shadows were gathering against the dawn outside, the men would soon be ready to march. Hoilogae took the bread and milk his mother gave him and went to join the low talking of his father and Attalae.

"There's no hope of catching him by surprise, is there?" Herwawardhaz was saying.

"Not unless the gods give better luck than I guess. At best, he won't have time to call his host together."

Herwawardhaz kneaded at his temples as if the touch would soothe his thoughts. He turned to look at his wife where she stood by Hedhinaz with a clay pot and the foaming pitcher of fresh milk in her hands, looking at her, Hoilogae thought for a moment, as if to weigh the worth of her gilded hair and the strand of amber looped twice around her neck. His gaze softened a moment, then he glanced quickly out the door.

"Well, we can't wait too much longer. Are you ready, Hoilogae?"

"I'm ready."

"Hedhinaz?"

Hedhinaz took the bread and milk from his mother, gulping the food down and draining the clay mug dry in a single long swallow. He rasped the ball of his thumb over the edge of the spearhead. "I'm ready."

Sigislinthon came forward to embrace her husband. She held Herwawardhaz tight, kissing him for what seemed to Hoilogae to be a very long time before letting him go. When she turned to hug her elder son, Hoilogae could feel the shivering that fluttered through her light bones and held her as gently as if he cupped a moth in the palm of his hand.

Hedhinaz suffered his mother's embrace less easily, but even in the dimness of dawn, Hoilogae could see his brother's mouth trembling, as if Hedhinaz fought against some fetter that bound the words down in his throat.

"Fare well and safely, my brave ones, and come home to me again soon."

"If the gods and our luck are with us, we shall bring you to the hall which was your home first, and the years of waiting shall be over for you at last," Herwawardhaz answered gravely, his deep voice very soft and sure. He and Sigislinthon looked at one another for a moment longer. Hoilogae felt as though he ought to turn away from what their gaze shared, but he could not help remembering the searing keenness of Swaebhon's eyes first meeting his own, and an envious aftershock of longing rumbled through his body as he watched his parents' parting glance.

Wheels creaked outside, Hoilogae heard the whinnying of a horse above a man's murmur, "Sa, sa, easy, now. Attalae raised his head at the noise. "Wains loaded at last, sounds like. We might as well be off."

"So you must," Sigislinthon agreed, and smiled at him. Though the light through door and smoke hole was brightening, it was still too dim to show the wrinkles about her eyes, and Attalae looked twenty years younger as he grinned back at her. "Take good care of my men, and make sure they come back safely."

"Always."

The lightening sky was blue-gray as polished iron in the dawn. The host was already gathered around the wains that held their tents and food for the days of travel to the hall of Hrothamaraz, the horses lowered their heads and fretted against their bindings as if eager to set their strength against the weights behind them. Hoilogae himself would ride in the foremost wain, as if he were making the first fruitfulness-faring around the fields at winter's end. It was done so when men went to war, to call the blessing of Ingwaz and the strength of Nerthuz to aid in the fight.

Hoilogae waited beside the wain, standing silently while Attalae went down to the hof and came back with a heavy bronze helm. Two long horns of bronze arched up from its temples like matched lurs, huge round bronze eyes stared out from beneath them. Hoilogae felt doubly awkward when Attalae lifted the helm up and lowered it onto his bent head. He knew that now he must look like one of the hof-oxen. That, too, was as things were done. It would not ward his skull well in the fighting, but hamper him and make him a target for shots and spears. Slowly he climbed up, standing above the heads of his father's men. The two lur-players, Hoilogae could not think of their names, though they had played the horns at every rite since he could remember, raised the great coils of bronze to their shoulders and blew the call to battle, the metal tags that dangled from the instruments jingling beneath the long notes.

Attalae handed Hoilogae the reins and goad, Hoilogae prodded his two oxen until they began to plod forward, and the march had begun. They followed the wide road that ran from north to south along the spine of Jutland, a track beaten down by the yearly oxen-drives, which men called the Host-Way.

This time, they were too many to scatter through the forests, or ride here and there among the low hills. The day warmed as the sun rose, but it was not long before the host had passed beneath the green shadows of the beech trees that rose gray above their heads on either side of the path. The helmet was starting to chafe on Hoilogae's head, so he rolled up his hair in long twists and stuffed it up underneath the bronze rim to cushion it. Hedhinaz was walking beside the wain, face set and fist clutched tight on his spear. Every now and again he glanced sideways up at his brother, snapping his gaze away whenever Hoilogae looked down at him. Around them, the men walked in small clumps, talking softly as they went.

Now and again, a deer would dash away from its grazing at the side of the road, once a red streak of fox flickered across the path. One of the men started to sing, a few others picked up the melody, and they swung along a little more briskly. A little past midday, they came to a small river. Hoilogae's oxen stopped at the shore, their hooves sinking in the mud, and turned their heavy heads from side to side as if refusing to cross.

"The ford's a little way upriver," Herwawardhaz said, and so they followed the river up to the two heaps of piled stones that marked safe crossing. Hoilogae was about to get out to lead the beasts through, but his father stopped him with a gesture. "No, stay where you are. Hedhinaz, you lead them."

Hoilogae's younger brother rolled up his breeches and went to his task without a word, stepping between the two oxen with his left hand on the yoke and tugging until they pulled their hooves from the sticky mud at the river's edge and stepped into the fall of stones that lay over its bed. The oxen snorted as the water frothed from their splashing hooves on the rocks, but Hedhinaz led them smoothly until they were about halfway across. Hoilogae did not quite see what happened then, but he thought a stone must have turned under his brother's foot. Hedhinaz lurched, flailing for balance with his spear, then went down, his head going beneath the water for a moment. He kept hold of the yoke, but his right hand was empty when he came up again. A little way downriver, the pale shaft of his spear flashed through the leaf-shadowed water like a long fish's back, then was gone again in the frothing eddies.

The oxen waited, their sullen stillness unstirred, until Hedhinaz pulled on the yoke and Hoilogae prodded them from behind, then they plodded forward as before until they had come out on the other side and onto firm land. When the other wains had forded, the host halted by the edge of the road to eat. Hedhinaz sat alone on a rock, looking off into the woods as he chewed. He had taken off his soaked tunic, wrung it out, and hung it over one of the wains, it would dry quickly enough in the summer warmth. The ridges of ribs and sinew pushed against the white skin of his back, droplets ran from his long water-darkened tail of hair down the knoted cord of his spine. His amber luck-necklace draped over the narrow cords of muscle along his shoulders, butter-white and honey-gold and blood-dark amber strung in careful threes along it.

Hoilogae knew that he must have looked something like his brother years ago, but that memory, too, was drowned in his skull. He walked over and squatted down beside Hedhinaz.

"Are you all right?"

"Yes."

"It looked as though you went down hard there. Did you hurt yourself?"

"Twisted my ankle a little," Hedhinaz grunted. "I've done worse to myself before. I'll be all right. You don't need to worry about me."

Hoilogae cast about for something else to say. "This is your first battle, isn't it?"

"Yes. I've only got thirteen winters. It's your first, too." Hedhinaz looked hard at his brother out of one bruised eye, the fading bruises on his ribs were a darker pattern beneath the shifting shadows of the leaves.

"So it is. You're upset, aren't you?"

"I lost my spear."

"Attalae will lend you another one. I'll ask him for you, if you like."

"I'll ask him myself. I don't need you to do things for me," Hedhinaz added. His thin lips pulled back, showing white teeth with only a couple of careless crockery-chips at their edges.

"All right," Hoilogae answered. He glanced down at his brother's ankle, already beginning to swell into adder-bitten redness. "Do you want to ride for a while? There's room in the wain for two, and you won't be able to fight if you strain your foot any worse now."

Hedhinaz dusted the crumbs of bread off his lap and stood up, testing his ankle. Hoilogae saw his brother's narrow brows draw together as he rested his weight on the leg. "Guess maybe I'd better," Hedhinaz muttered. It seemed to Hoilogae that the bruises under his eye darkened into a pool like ale spilt in the shadows, a pool with a strong undercurrent, drawing downward. He grasped his brother's hand to help him to the wain, and in Hedhinaz's warm grip he could feel the life stretching on and on from beneath the cold spattering of the youth's fear.

"That stumble was no ill sign for you," Hoilogae said softly, so that only Hedhinaz could hear his words above the slow noises of the ox-cart as the host began to move on again. "You are not fey, I think that you'll live longer than I do. You have nothing to fear in this battle."

Hedhinaz seemed about to say something, but the words broke in his throat as he looked up at his brother. He fell silent again, staring at the reddened ankle propped up on a bag of hard bread before him, then over the side of the wain. Now it was Hoilogae's turn to feel the current of cold beneath the warm light through the leaves, as the sureness of his feeling drained slowly away like water from a cracked pot. He had no surety that he would come whole through this battle, no more than any of the men who followed the Host-Way beside him.

If he fell, he reminded himself, he would see Swaebhon before him again, and he had chosen her when he took her rede. Herwawardhaz and Attalae called the host to a halt a little before sunset. They were still in the woods, but here there were many ax-bitten stumps, and many of the beeches around were fresh-sprung saplings, or young trees with trunks thin as a woman's waist.

"We'll eat here, and sleep for a while," Herwawardhaz said to his sons, "then go on past the village after it's gotten full dark, when maybe the folk will be sleeping." He laid down a bundle of dried sticks, weaving one over another until they were ready to light.

"Have we reached Hrothamaraz's lands yet?" Hedhinaz asked, a spark of eagerness kindling his voice.

"Not yet. We should be there by sundown," Herwawardhaz looked up through the leaves, as if counting on their rustling shapes, "two days from now, and at the door of his hall by midday after that."

"We never thought it a long way between ourselves and Hrothamaraz before," Attalae said dryly. The old man crouched down, stirring among Herwawardhaz's twigs until he had them arranged to his liking, then drew a small bow-drill from his belt-pouch and settled down to bring the fire forth from the wood. His hands moved swiftly in the well-known rhythm, until the smoke began to curl up from the little glowing coal where the drill-stick met the wood beneath it. Blowing softly, he sprinkled fluffy tinder onto it, then little twigs to catch the flames, then larger ones, until the fire was going strongly.

Attalae looked up to see Hedhinaz and Hoilogae both staring at him. "Start fires as often as I have, and it'll go as quickly for you." He smiled easily at both of them. "When you're my age"

"Won't it look suspicious if we go through the village in the middle of the night?" Hedhinaz asked.

"It's our best hope to avoid being noticed. The wains have to stay on the road, the rest of us can skirt the edges. As long as we keep well clear of the houses, we won't be seen in the dark, and nothing will tell them that the whole host is coming through."

"What will we do if we come to a garth by full day?"

"Go straight on through and hope whoever lives there doesn't raise the alarm for miles around. We're almost certain to be seen before we get to Hrothamaraz's hall, but if we can get by for another day, our chances will be better. Even if, " Attalae shut his mouth.

It's summer, and there are plenty of folk on the road, Hoilogae thought. We're sure to be seen soon. "'No wings fly swifter than those bearing news,'" he murmured to himself, words brushing dark across his mind.

Across the fire from him, Hedhinaz twitched, his eyes wide. "What? What did you say?"

"Nothing."

Hedhinaz stared accusingly at him for a moment, but dropped his gaze when Hoilogae met his eyes.

Hoilogae sprang awake at once when his father touched him on the shoulder. He stood, picking up the helmet. "Should I leave this off?" He whispered. "If anyone sees us...."

"You must wear it for the whole faring," Attalae answered softly.

Herwawardhaz handed Hoilogae a wide strip of soft cloth. "Wrap this around your head," he murmured. "I had forgotten how badly the war-helm chafes."

Hoilogae wrapped his head as his father had told him, then eased the helmet's weight back onto his skull. The fires were all out or hidden beneath a weight of earth, only stars and the waning crescent of the Moon lit their pathway. Hoilogae boosted his brother up into the foremost wain and climbed up after him. Hedhinaz hesitated a moment, then stretched out a hand to steady Hoilogae as he came over the wagon's rim.

"Thanks," Hoilogae whispered, leaning forward to prod the oxen into a walk again. Behind them, he could hear the other wains' wheels beginning to turn. The men around were melting into the woods, shadowing between the trees like saplings swaying in the wind. Every so often, he heard a muffled grunt or a whispered curse as a root caught someone by the foot or a branch lashed across a face, but as those who went by foot made their way farther from the road, the sounds of the wood. The cool wind through the leaves, the high chirping of the crickets by the roadside, drowned out the noises of the men.

Hoilogae felt his skin prickling against the fresh wool of his tunic, the wind stirring through his fine beard-hairs as his eyes opened to the faint brightness of the night. They were almost to the edge of the wood when they saw the woman standing in the middle of the road before them, her white gown pale against the night. Her face was shadowed, but her long hair streamed moonlit down like a river of shining iron around her shoulders. Hoilogae heard his brother bite back a gasp, jerking upright as if caught by lightning, he himself was on his feet with his sword in his hand. She turned her hidden gaze up to him, and he saw the glint of white teeth in her face as he lowered his weapon and stretched his other hand out as if to grasp the arm she raised towards him.

The oxen plodded on as if there was no one there. At the last moment, Hoilogae realized that the woman would not move out of their way and grasped for their yoke to pull them back, but they were already walking through the patch of mist where she had been. He felt a slight chill as they passed the place, no more. Hoilogae and Hedhinaz turned to meet each other's gaze as Hoilogae sheathed his sword.

"What did you see?" Hedhinaz murmured.

"I saw a woman."

"She wore a war-helm, but it was silver in the moonlight, it looked like iron? And there were black streaks on the silver, like blood, and she rode on a gray horse."

"That's not what I saw."

"Could you see her face?"

"No."

"Nor could I." Hedhinaz shivered, but Hoilogae could see his brother smiling at the same time, although the youth had turned his face half-away as if to hide his expression. "She was reaching out to me."

"Not to you," Hoilogae said, more sharply than he meant to. "To me."

"Shhh!" Hedhinaz hissed, his voice suddenly so soft Hoilogae could hardly hear him. "You'll wake someone. Don't you have the sense to be quiet? We're in the village now."

Hoilogae was about to answer in kind, but he could hear the wound beneath his brother's sharpness. He replied in a like whisper, "It may be that we each saw what we were meant to see."

Then they said no more as they passed between the houses, each creak of the wain loud as the breaking of a bow in the quiet night. A dog's sudden bark startled Hoilogae's hand to his sword again, his head jerking towards the sound. He could see the hound sitting by the door of one of the little huts with its nose to the wind.

It barked again, thrice, and Hedhinaz began to scrabble about in the bottom of the wain for a bow.

"No," Hoilogae whispered. "If we shoot it they'll know." He crouched down so that he wouldn't be seen if anyone came out of the hut.

"The dog's running away now," Hedhinaz murmured to him. "No one's come out yet."

Hoilogae stayed down until they were through the hamlet, well along the road through the fields. Then he sat up and dusted himself off. "You didn't see anyone?"

"No."

They went on into the woods, then stopped, waiting for the rest of the host. Men on foot might move more swiftly than the ox-wains on the open road, but the others had a longer way around the hamlet with the night and the forest in their way. So it was a while yet before the shadows of men started to come out of the trees and Hoilogae heard Attalae's soft voice in his ear.

"There's a good-size clearing up and off the road just a little way. We'll make camp there."

It was just before midday the next day when they saw their first northern traveler on the Host-Way, a tall man in a dusty cloak, walking beside a freshly-painted horse-cart. He looked up to Hoilogae, then guided his cart to the side of the road and stood still. Hoilogae thought at first that the man merely meant to let them pass, but then the cart-man began to unload his top bag, and Hoilogae realized he was a merchant. He tugged his wain to a halt and got down.

"Where have you come from?" Hoilogae asked.

The merchant waved a hand southward. "Back there. Are you folk going home?" His accent was thick, not familiar to Hoilogae. Although crows-feet marked the corners of his eyes, his heavy features were smooth otherwise, and only a few threads of silver gleamed in his brown-black hair and beard.

The sword at his hip had a bronze hilt, but it was longer and thinner than most bronze blades could be cast and still be useful in a fight.

"We could be," Hoilogae answered cautiously.

"Ha, I thought so. No other reason for three settlements in a row to have no one in 'em but gaffers, gamers, and little children. Might you be looking to buy any weapons?"

"Do you have any iron?"

"Ah well, everyone wants iron now, it goes fast. Still, I had a mind that I might want to carry some amber south with me on the next trip, and I've heard that up here is the best place for it."

"You heard rightly," Herwawardhaz said. With an unheard breath of relief, Hoilogae stepped back to the side of the wain, leaving his father and the other men to dicker with the peddler.

"Hoilogae!" Hedhinaz called softly. "Over here." He had lifted his luck-necklace from around his neck, now he sat with the strand of amber dangling from his hand, looking at it sadly. "Amber is easy enough to find," he murmured, "but this is our mother's finest work." Hoilogae touched the soft wool of his tunic and said nothing. "Still, I would very much like an iron weapon. I know I can't get a sword for this, but a knife, or an iron spearhead in the stead of the one I lost? Help me down, Hoilogae."

Hoilogae lifted his brother down from the wain. Hedhinaz was walking more easily now, but he still favored his tightly bandaged ankle.

The peddler grinned at him. "Ah, wounded, but still walking. And what might you want, young warrior?"

It took some long dickering, but few of the men had brought amber with them, and fewer of those could bring themselves to part with their luck-pieces, so Hedhinaz was well-placed for bargaining. When Hoilogae boosted his brother back into the wain, the youth had a new head for a thrusting-spear and a small belt-knife.

"I'd hoped for better," the peddler said with a grimace as he finally put his wares away. "You've come from the north? Is there anyone left there for me to sell to?"

"If you go far enough, all the way up to the coast and east of the Host-Way a bit, you'll get to the strand called Glazaleunduz," Herwawardhaz told him. "The best amber in Jutland comes from that shore, and you'll be given a good welcome when you get there."

As they rode on, Hedhinaz sat stroking his iron spearhead lightly, with the tips of his fingers, as if he feared the edge would turn to slice him. "It feels so different," he murmured. "As if."

As if it would cut the web of being like cloth, Hoilogae thought, his own hand going to the hilt of the sword at his side. He looked through the green depths of the wood around them, thinking of the shadow-shapes that moved there at twilight and dawn, the dancing alf-shapes that could lure a man deeper and deeper among the trees, whose spell no bronze could break, but only the flint thunder-stones shaped like axes or arrowheads.

The iron he and his brother bore would scathe them to the bone, and many other wights.

"Be careful with it," Hoilogae answered. "It will be easy to cut where you do not wish to, or slay a wight who would be better alive." Could a high sword-swing in battle harm the women who fought unseen above the warriors, or an iron spear-cast strike one of them from the air like a pierced swan? The thought knotted cold in Hoilogae's guts as he thought of Swaebhon hovering over his head with her shield before him. Thoughts of the keen blade slicing through byrnie-shimmering breasts or white swan-feathers.

Hedhinaz glanced sideways at him, eyes dark beneath his tangle of bronze-bright hair. "That's easy enough with any weapon," he answered. "I notice you aren't afraid to bear iron yourself."

There were a few extra spear-shafts in the bottom of the wain, some were always broken in battle, but though the heads were dear, spare shafts were cheap. Hedhinaz got down and began to try his new spear-head to see which one would need the least whittling for a good fit. His brother's prize would be light for a thrusting weapon, but heavy for throwing, Hoilogae thought. Still, he kept his thoughts to himself, he knew Hedhinaz would not thank him for unsought rede.

As Herwawardhaz had promised, they were at the edge of Hrothamaraz's lands by sundown the next day. Hoilogae and Hedhinaz did not recognize the stead, but their father came forward and caught their oxen by the yoke before they could pass between the two high mounds that rose shadowy on either side of the road, a yew-tree spreading dark branches over the eastern howe and a birch's white trunk shining bright above the western.

"Your mother's elder kin dwell there," he said in a low voice. "You two must pour drink to them and tell them that you have come to claim Swafnijaz's land for his daughter and her kin again."

A prickling shiver of warning ran through Hoilogae's body as Hedhinaz began to climb from the wain, he could feel the painful tingle swirling out from his brother. Hoilogae reached down to catch his brother by the shoulder before he got more than halfway out of the wain.

Hedhinaz looked up angrily. "What now?" Although his voice was fierce, he whispered as though he feared to disturb a sleeper. "Are you going to deny me my right?"

"Your knife," Hoilogae murmured back. "Unhallowed iron will frighten the mound-dwellers."

"You took your sword up on Herwamundaz's mound, and drew it there," Hedhinaz answered sulkily. "What difference is there between the two?"

"Will you trust me? Take off your knife and leave it here, you'll be safer on the mound without it."

Hedhinaz's gaze flickered into the darkening depths of the wood, then up to the dark burgs of brush-covered earth looming above them. "What have we to fear from our kin?"

"Nothing, so long as we deal well with them. See, I'll leave my sword here, though it is hallowed." Hoilogae unfastened his sword-belt and laid it down in the bottom of the wain. Hedhinaz slipped the knife from his own belt and retied it. Without speaking again, the two of them took the horns from Attalae's hands. Hoilogae went to the left the eastern mound and Hedhinaz to the right, where Sunna's tree-broken light twisted his shadow long over the road.

The mound was overgrown with knee-high blueberry bushes, though the berries were not yet ripe. Hoilogae climbed up to the top in a long spiral, feeling the might rising up beneath his feet as his winding path stirred the one who dwelt within to slow wakefulness. When he had come to the end of his way, he was looking eastward, face towards the dark yew and without ward back to the road.

"Hear me, you who dwell here," he murmured. "I have come, I, Sigislinthon's son to win Swafnijaz's land for his daughter and her children, that your blood may rule here again. Do not hinder our way, but let us fare swiftly through, and help us along our paths to revenge our mother's father and lift up the soul of our clan. Now I share with you, from whom my sib has stemmed, a drink of friendship and frith." Hoilogae raised the horn, drinking of the thick ale himself and then pouring it out in a foaming stream to the ground. Without thought he crouched down, holding the horn between his knees as he pushed the low bushes aside and pressed both his palms to the drink-wet earth between the yew's rough roots. "Be well, my kin," he said softly before he stood and retraced his ring-spiraling track down around the mound.

Hedhinaz was already in the ox-cart by the time Hoilogae got back, staring fixedly at the other mound. His knife hung at his belt again. Hoilogae climbed up and put his sword on, then clicked his tongue to move the oxen on again. As the wain rolled between the two mounds, it seemed to Hoilogae for a moment as though they passed between two huge doorposts, stretching up higher than he could see. A shudder of awe ran through his body, but then they were past and he could not look back until the slow way and the darkening twilight had hidden the mounds from his sight.

It was not long after that they came to the shadow of a giant tree-stump, its jagged black edges reaching up three times the height of a man. They had just passed it when Attalae came to the fore and took Hoilogae's left ox by the harness, leading it around.

"When I was here before, that stump was a great oak," he said. "It marks where a short road leads off to a clearing in which we can all rest easily." He paused as the oxen's hooves began to beat their way along the overgrown path. "There was a time when whoever fared through here left a gift to Thonaraz among its roots. It looks as though he has taken his last gift from it."

Hoilogae glanced back at the lightning-blasted stump, black against the sky's deepening blue. "Hallowed with his Hammer."

Attalae shrugged. "As may be."

As the old warrior crouched down to start kindling his fire, Hedhinaz began to feel about on the ground, coming up with a lump of dark rock in his hand. "May I have a bit of your kindling?" He asked Attalae. The old man nodded, never ceasing to turn the stick in his hand, and Hedhinaz took a pinch of the fluffy stuff and drew his knife.

"What are you going to do with that?" Hoilogae asked.

"Watch."

Hedhinaz turned the blunt side of the blade to his stone and struck it sharply downwards against the flint's rim. A shower of sparks burst up into the air, one falling upon the kindling. It went out before he could blow it to life, it took several more strikes before Hedhinaz got a small flame going, just as the wood was beginning to smoke under Attalae's hands. Quickly the youth laid his fire into the small sticks Attalae had gotten ready, feeding the flame upward.

"Neatly done," Herwawardhaz said as Attalae leaned forward to put his rubbing-sticks into the blaze. Hedhinaz's fire reflected brightly off the youth's teeth as he smiled upward at his father.

There was no singing that night, they were too close to Hrothamaraz's folk to make much noise. Instead they spoke softly. "If you get killed, can I marry your wife?" "They say Hrothamaraz has plenty of gold, and more than a few of us are like to come home with iron blades. I'm planning to get at least a sword out of it, myself." "If I don't make it, will you make sure my brother doesn't try to do my wife out of my stud bull? He's the best beast in the herd, and,"

Hoilogae leaned back against a tree-trunk, staring into the flames as he chewed slowly on his hard bread and smoked fish. Their bright weaving drew his eye along, teasing it with patterns that melted even as they shaped themselves, each blending into the next so smoothly that he could not tell where the life of one flame began and the next ended. He might have sat like that the whole night, except that Hedhinaz's knuckles jabbed in hard under his ribs.

"Hey! Are you listening?"

Hoilogae painfully blinked the brightness from his eyes and turned to where his kinsmen and Attalae sat.

"What are you thinking, Hoilogae?" Attalae asked softly. "What do you see?"

"Nothing. Only....only...the fire."

Hoilogae's eyes were too blinded by the brightness to see if the old warrior's face showed any signs of disappointment at his words, Attalae's voice did not change as he went on.

"Our best chance is to march straight on to his garth tomorrow. At worst, they'll be drawn up in full array when we get there, but if we try to spread out through the woods, we're likely to do no more than confuse ourselves, and give Hrothamaraz that much more time to call more men together. And who knows, maybe we'll surprise him out in the fields or in bed with his wife."

"It can always happen." Herwawardhaz's voice rustled dry with doubt, and it seemed to Hoilogae that he could hear a dark echo behind it. His father hardly seemed eager for the fight. "At least I have no better plan. Do you my sons?" He added, turning his gaze suddenly from Hedhinaz to Hoilogae, as though his long habit of ignoring his eldest son had only broken that moment.

"I have no better," Hoilogae answered. Hedhinaz shook his head silently.

"So it ought to be, then," Attalae answered, his voice at once brisker and more youthful. "Go to sleep, we'll want to march out at dawn if we're to be there by midday, and you'll need to be as rested as you can." He slid down into his own cloak, twisting so that more of his body lay near the fire's warmth, he had complained of the chill in his bones at every dawn since they had started out. Hoilogae finished the last of his food and lay down himself, resting his chin on his fists and staring into the flames again.

Swaebhon had prowled restless all day, pacing the dry path between houses and fields until the track of her bare feet walking back and forth blurred into a single brown stream like a wagon's trail and her calves were caked with dust beneath the swishing of her string-skirt. She had cast off her tunic when the day grew bright, now, in the afternoon warmth, the Sun's light stroked her bare back and trailed between her breasts in little hot rivulets of sweat, and the spiked round of bronze that fastened her belt seared her skin when she brushed her fingertips over it. So close to Midsummer, the fields needed no work but a little weeding, and that was already done.

Most of the folk of the settlement had gone down to the sea, to fish or swim, a few lay on the green meadows where the cattle grazed, spinning or carving wood in the Sun's brightness. She, too, should be swimming in the cold water or lazing in the grass like a snake with the lump of a fresh-swallowed mouse weighting its body, but there was no one she wished to see there, and she could not still the rushing movement of her body for more than a few heartbeats. Perhaps it would be a good day for me to look for herbs, Swaebhon thought. The dried bunches that dangled from the rafters of her house had grown thin and tattered, and worts seldom held much strength after a year or two. Even as she thought it, she was turning, grinding the dust beneath the thick callous of her heel. With spear, wort-bags, and a skin of ale in her hands and her hound trotting behind her, Swaebhon started off into the cool green shadow of the wood.

The dark needles above dappled spiky patterns across her hound's brindled fur and her own white shoulders and breasts, the brown needles below pricked softly against her hard soles. She trotted along in the smooth gait she had learned when her breasts began to blossom, covering the ground quickly as her gaze flickered from side to side. Most of the worts she sought today grew along stream sides, farther along the edge of the mountain, she knew their steads well, for she had learned them while her mother lived and come back every year. But there were other herbs on Swaebhon's path. She turned aside where speckled spires of adder's blue weed rose high from a spill of loose stones, their long spikes of bee-hung flowers glowing fresh pink and older blue. Kneeling among the sharp rocks, she leaned close to hear the plants' buzzing voices. Adder's blue weed was one of the most needful worts in her store. It drove out the bale of wyrms and alf-shot alike, and was good in cooling fevers.

Carefully Swaebhon dripped a little ale around the roots of the plants, whispering among the bees, "I ask your gifts, you holy herbs, and give to you again. Let me have your healing might, the blessings honey-handed Aizio gives to folk through her fosterling shoots, made strong by the fro Ingwaz, made fair by his sister, the holy Frowe, by Nerthuz and Earth, who give to all." She reached slowly towards the spotted stem, until its little hairs prickled at her fingertips with a faint welcoming warmth. Heartened, Swaebhon took firm hold and snapped it off, shaking the spear of flowers until the bees buzzed up and settled on the blooms around. No fewer than one shot in three could be left, one standing for one taken was better, for she would need to pluck again next year, and if she were dead by then, other women would come to gather herbs in this stead.

Thus she picked only her share and went on, leaving the golden bees to feed behind her. As often happened in the summer, when Sunna only dipped behind the mountains for a little time, Swaebhon lost all thought of how late in the day it might be, only when her wort-bags were bulging with leaves and the cool breeze began to stroke goosebumps along her bare skin did she look up to mark the reddish light staining the sky like streaks of blood streaming into clear water. So close to Midsummer, it would not grow darker than twilight, but Swaebhon knew that she should not stay away too long, lest her father fear that some ill had befallen her. She whistled sharply, her hound came bounding out of the trees, crashing through the low blueberry bushes to roll over at her feet with his tongue lolling between sharp teeth.

Swaebhon could still hear the snapping of green twigs and the rustling of leaves, growing louder as if a bear were nearing. She grasped her spear, glancing at the trees around her to see which she could climb most swiftly. As well for her that she wore only the little skirt of woven cords. But the sound that came from the shadows between the trees was not the growling of the Brown One. It was a man's laugh, stroking up the little hairs along her spine like a breath of winter wind. Swaebhon turned her spear to point towards him. Outlaw or troll, she did not fear him.

"It is not me at whom you should point your spear, walkurjon," the deep voice murmured, humming strong as a draught of mead through Swaebhon's blood. "Your hero battles tomorrow, if his foes meet him as one, he shall surely fall."

Swaebhon drove her spear-butt deep into the soft stream side earth, the breath choked dumb in her throat.

"No words without breath, no song without words," the shadow-cloaked stranger told her softly. "The walkurjon's song is the keening of edge on edge, her rune is the song of battle. That rune must you sing tonight, to set strife between the rich iron-folk and the drighten they serve, that the eagle stoop not on a single bear, but on a pair of battling wyrms."

He raised his hand, and Swaebhon saw that he held an aurochs horn, bound with silver at the rim, tipped with a silver eagle's head, and carved with a winding row of strange sharp twig-shapes. "Drink of my galdor-craft, and sing them strife, drink the raven's call, the eagle's harsh scream and the howl of the wolf."

Swaebhon moved forward, taking the horn. Its graven rind was smooth beneath her fingers, cold as rime where he had held it. She lifted it and drank, opening her throat so that the strong mead could flow freely into her. Only a few drops spattered from the rim when she shook the horn empty and gave it back, but her head was whirling with drunkenness. She tried to fix her gaze upon him again, but he was already gone, lost in the shadows, and her legs were giving way, so that she must sink to the damp grasses by the stream side. The sound that came out of Swaebhon's mouth when she opened it raised her hackles again. a low moan, tinged with the shrillness of bronze scraping against bronze.

It seemed to her that she could see the hall looming before her, a bigger hall than her father's. Her gaze pierced through the woven wands and clay, she saw the gray-tipped spears leaning against the walls. Though the only iron Swaebhon had ever seen was the little knife Chaidhamaraz the Traveler had bought in the south lands, she knew the southern metal at once. She could feel its keenness already, as though it might slice ghost as well as flesh. Many of the words swirling around her sounded in a different tongue, their rhythm lilting and chanting. She could tell which warriors were southerners easily. Their hair stood out in ruddy mane-spikes, as though brightened and stiffened by lime water, and most of them were clean-shaven except for long mustaches shaped, like their hair, into sharp points. The gold of their brooches was finer than the work she knew. Fine feathered birds with inlay of strange red stones, helmed men battling little beasts, swine and stags, all wrought down to the least hair.

More than a few of their belts were plated with gold and silver. Well were the southerners called the rich folk, for their gear made the simple rings of twisted gold about the necks and arms of the Northern drighten and his son look plain and poor. The clean-boiled skulls of men stood spiked between the spear points, and Swaebhon could see the red brightness flaming around them those skulls had been taken in war, and stood now as both the boast and the soul-strength of their slayers. That hall was a stead of might, and there was little ill in it, yet she knew Hoilogae would die before the doors and the iron-folk flood down to the North with his dear skull among their banners if she did nothing. Then her bowels coiled cold within her, and she tightened her hand on her spear.

For Wyrd was turning her spindle here, and Hoilogae's life would hold by a thinly spun strand. I must be his strength in the battle, Swaebhon whispered to herself. I must ward him against the war-idises of the iron clans, Wodhanaz, let my fear for him only give me might! A raven sat on the hall's roof, a great she-raven, who opened her beak and laughed at Swaebhon. "Did you think the holy ones work each other ill?" She croaked. "Slaughter is good, blood waters the earth, and my little sisters who are yours as well shall be full-fed. Often the Wod-Filled and I have joyed in the same wars, often shall we in times to come." She rose from the roof and winged slowly thrice about the hall, her feathers waving a cold wind down over Swaebhon.

Swaebhon looked at the folk within. The broad-shouldered graybeard who sat in the high seat, the stocky, fair-haired youth beside him, and the iron folk, red and dark, woven thickly through the paler heads. The blood-spoor rose from them already. The hall-lord's scent sharp with the edge of worry, his son rough with anger at the strangers who laughed and boasted in their own tongue without thought to the folk who held the land, and the rich greed of the southerners, who thought they would soon have all they had come to claim, and more, when they stormed down to the amber-strewn edge of the North Sea. The seeds of flame were set, the little coals kindled. It would take only the wind to blow them up to a raging fire.

Now Swaebhon knew that she understood the rune Wodhanaz had given her, and now the words rushed winging from her, to sing unheard through the hall and wrap the warriors in her winding coil of soul-sound.

Who is the leader in land and in war,
whose sword is strongest, who swings the rule?
Who is the heroin hall and on field,
whose right to sit in seat of the lord?

They were twitching now, she could see the fear sparking in the hall-lord's dark eyes, the green glints of rage in his son's, and feel the warm thoughts kindling in the strangers' breasts.

Only the fearful fails to take
what might has won for him man does not halt!
Who would hold land here? Who would be ruler?
Iron-men awesome? Or old man in chair?

Swaebhon could hear the muttering now, but it was already fading, even as the brightness of the hall dimmed into shining mist before her vision. She breathed deeply. Though she had sung only a short chant, her throat ached with its weight. Now she must start back, for Hoilogae would battle tomorrow and he would surely need her help then. The dawn cold eased swiftly into warmth as the Sun rose, well before midday, Hoilogae could feel his helmet's warmth through the wrappings that cushioned his head, and the drops of sweat were trickling over his temples and down the slanted planes of his face into his beard.

The oxen pulled more slowly in the heat, the sun warming their blood to sluggishness as the frost might chill a snake's cold veins. Hoilogae reached forward now and again to prick them on with his goad, a new eagerness warming in his entrails as he drew nearer and nearer to his midday goal. The Sun was nearly at her height when the road broke out of the wood, sloping gently downward through a cow-studded meadow to a wide village built around a single high-timbered dwelling.

A ring of wooden posts circled three sides of the settlement, the fourth bordered on the shore of a small lake, whose waters gleamed sky-blue in the midday's brightness. The ragged youth who stood among the cows shoved a mass of pale hair out of his face as he turned to stare at them, light blue eyes wide. Hedhinaz' spear took him in the side as he turned to run, his shout died to a gurgle in his throat.

Hoilogae met his brother's eyes as the other lowered himself down. "Go on," Hedhinaz said. "I'll run down with the others. I need my weapon."

Hoilogae nodded. He was already breathing hard from the shock of the sudden killing, the blue sky and green field burning in his eyes. For a moment, he could feel the iron fetters tightening on his limbs, but now Wyrd was full-reded. He could win through or die, but he would never live in shame again. As soon as Hedhinaz was clear, Hoilogae pricked both oxen hard with the goad, then brought it down on the wain's side with a lightning-sharp crack.

The pieces flew free, the oxen lumbered into a run, pulling the wagon downward towards the settlement. Hoilogae heard his men shouting, their feet pounding behind him. He stayed on his feet, hanging onto the edge of the wain with one hand and drawing his sword with the other, dizzy with the rolling might of the charge. He did not know whether it was fear or joy whirling in his head. He only knew that it was driving him forward as the wheels thrummed under him like Wyrd's swift-turning spindles, like a hundred singing bowstrings. Even as Hoilogae rode, he could hear the shouting and clashing of metal not behind him, but before him, and the ravens screamed and wheeled above, swooping down and up again. His first dazed thought was that his men had somehow managed to break through before him, but the gate was still shut. Something was happening within, but it was too late to stop for it now. The blurring wind ripped the shout from his mouth, the oxen were heading straight for the gate.

This is my death, this is our end, Hoilogae thought in a sheer naked flash of fear as the oaken beams rose up before him, but the gate flew open just before the oxen struck it, as though the wind of his riding had riven it apart. Then he was driving through breakers of glittering iron and bronze, his sword shearing through blades and flesh together. The roaring in his ears sharpened as the wind of a spear brushed past his cheek, something else rang from his helmet. The ox-cart stopped in its tracks, the beasts slumping down before it. Hoilogae swung his sword in a hissing arc around himself as he leapt down.

It wedged in a shield, he wrenched it free of the shattered linden and swung again. Then there was no one within arm's reach, the fighting was pushing out the gate, where the garth's warders struggled to push Hoilogae's men back, and those who were still within were running around him to get to the main throng. There were more defenders than attackers, many more, Hoilogae thought. But as the first flush cleared from his eyes he saw that more than a few of the garth-folk had ragged bandages tied around arms or legs, brown-stained with blood, and they moved their swords like weary men, and the battle within was still going on, his foes were cutting each other down, the metal-belted warriors with long mustaches and hair spiky beneath their iron helms fighting against those who could hardly be told from Hoilogae's men on sight. Hoilogae's foot caught on a dead man's arm, he stumbled and caught himself, leaping back to see that the foreigner's corpse had already been plundered of helmet and belt and sword. A rush of joy burst through him. By the workings of the gods, a witling's rede could win the day!

"To me!" Hoilogae shouted. He caught himself before he could thrust his iron blade up into the shimmering air above him, Sunna's light on his towering helm was enough to show where he was. He ran towards the defenders, forcing them to turn towards him, away from the foe pressing towards their gate. More than once a bronze blade slipped along the side of his tunic, but Hoilogae felt no sting until a spear point of black iron tore through his left sleeve and scored its track down the outside of his arm.

It pricked him to fight more fiercely, battling his way through to where a stocky graybeard stood with his back against a gatepost, the coils of gold on his arm burning out sharp flashes of sunlight as he held Herwawardhaz and Attalae at bay. The sword in the foe man's hand was a finely polished blade of gray iron, as Hoilogae watched, it cut half-through Attalae's bronze weapon. The graybeard wrenched his sword free with a practiced twist that swept it around to meet Herwawardhaz's stroke and beat his blade aside. Hoilogae stepped in swiftly enough to block the return thrust that would have pierced his father's body. His own sword notched the other, though not deeply enough to ruin it. Now it was only the two of them, beating and stabbing. Hoilogae knew if he stopped moving for a moment he would be dead, he could only trust in his body's memory of the warrior's training which his mind had never noticed.

Still, he could not keep his eyes from flickering upwards, and in that moment his muscles locked, for the swan-bright shape of the woman above him blinded him as if he had foolishly glanced into the Sun, but the bloody gray shadows riding behind her rimmed Hoilogae's awestruck gaze with ice, and their gore-black mouths seemed to suck the marrow from his bones, so that he could not move. The empty air where his blade no longer warded called to the keen gray snake in the other man's hand, its glittering point striking swift and true towards his vitals. Hoilogae's limbs and gaze were frozen, and yet it seemed to him then that Swaebhon spurred her steed closer, that her glistening shield swept down before him. The clean death-stroke slid sideways, slipping from its straight aim to hiss through the air beside Hoilogae's limbs.

Then Swaebhon's spear-point glittered down to touch the gray-bearded man. His weathered face froze in a cold grimace of fear. He seemed fettered tightly as Hoilogae had been a heartbeat ago.

Hoilogae stepped forward and ran him through.Hedhinaz's voice cracked up to a high screech, "Hoilogae! Behind you", and Hoilogae whirled just in time to block another blow.

As he swung, he saw a second man stepping in behind his sword's arch with blade swinging forward. His weight thrown into his own blow, he could not turn, but Hedhinaz's spear-shaft crashed against the outstretched arm as Hoilogae's blade cut through his foe man's stomach in a stinking torrent of blood and guts. Hedhinaz's spear-tip came out the second man's side, Hoilogae stood to ward his brother as Hedhinaz wrenched his weapon loose. Now Hoilogae saw the gray women clearly, their mouths bloody as ravens' beaks. Their spears stabbed down into the host, whirling spindles weighted with men's corpses and wound with men's guts, and the white one rode before them, her spinning shield flashing the battle-sparks of clashing iron to glint gem-red from blood. At last the women rose higher, wheeling above the field, and Hoilogae knew the battle was won. "Swaebhon!" He called out joyfully, dropping his sword and lifting his hands to the sky.

A fierce gladness washed through him. Now he had won through, now she must come to him, and be clasped solid in his arms!

"Swaebhon, come down to me!"

The fair rider's steed circled downwards, Hoilogae's heart sang like a bow-string at the sight of Swaebhon's face against the bright sky. But her look did not answer his joy. Her pale eyes were half-closed, as though to hide tears.

"I cannot come to you. You must come to me, if you would wed me within the Middle-Garth's ring. Hoilogae, my love, you have won the battle, but there is a long faring yet before you see me stand before you as a living woman."

"Then stay with me a little longer and let me have you beside me for the feast."

"I cannot. My hide tires already, and if I stay much longer, I shall be lost outside the Middle-Garth."

"Then go," Hoilogae cried, the words rending their way from his chest. "Go swiftly and safely, my beloved, I shall come to you." Heedless of the others on the field, he stood and watched till no pale clouds blurred the brightened sky. A few scattered fights were still going on around the edges of the throng, but they were quickly over. Hrothamaraz's men fell, or threw down their weapons and bowed their heads.

The weight of his helm was bearing down more and more heavily on Hoilogae's neck now, its bronze bowl had become a heated oven. He raised his hand to take it off, then jerked his burnt fingers from the metal.

"Hoilogae, Hoilogae!" Someone was shouting. More men took up the cry, the way between the warriors parted for him, so that he could lead the host in victory to Herwawardhaz's garth. A red-haired youth, whose freckled fore-head was already swelling blue around the cut that scored its length, ran up to him with the notched iron sword in his hands. "Don't you want this? You killed Hrothamaraz, it's yours by right."

"Give it to my brother. He's earned it as fully as anyone, and I owe him my life for this day's work."

Hedhinaz stretched out his hand slowly. The sword trembled in his grasp as he took it, and though he showed his teeth, Hoilogae could not tell what he was thinking from the look on his pale face.

"I thank you. This is a noble gift," Hedhinaz said, his voice breaking down-ward. He breathed deeply, as though he had just come up from deep water, and Hoilogae thought, Our first battle is over, and we're both still alive! The thought stunned him, he knew that his brother must be feeling much the same shock.

Instead of marching straight up to the drighten's dwelling, Hoilogae led his host around the settlement. Some of the men looked into the houses, seeing if any other fighting men were hidden, or else looking for women and treasures, but most followed him around to the shore of the lake. Then, no longer caring what they did or thought, Hoilogae waded out a little way and crouched down.

The war-helm sizzled angrily as he dunked his head into the cool water. When Hoilogae came up for a deep, grateful breath, he was bare-headed, the horned helmet in his hand. He shook the water from his lightened head in a long torrent of drops and stood again, unwillingly easing the cooled helm back onto his wet hair before going on to finish his ringing of the garth and leading the host to the hall where Herwawardhaz had dwelt.

Polished skulls stood on poles about the long hall, dark eyes looking emptily down at the wounded men who lay below them, some on benches and some in heaps of blankets and straw on the floor. Hoilogae blinked, unsure that the darkness was not deceiving him. Surely his men could not have brought all the wounded in and tended to them already? But he knew none of the pale faces that stared up at him, neither from the three days of marching nor from the dream-memories that sometimes glimmered in his mind. Beside him, Attalae drew in his breath in a long murmur of "Ahhhh," then stepped forward.

"We have slain your drighten Hrothamaraz and all of his men who were still hale," the old warrior said gruffly. "You are too wounded to fight. If you yield to us and swear us your troth, we shall treat you like our own men, if not, we shall cut your throats where you lie."

Some of the wounded rustled in their straw, painfully turning over to look at him. A stocky, fair-haired man pushed himself up against the high seat. "Who are you?" he asked. "What right do you have here?"

"I am Hoilogae, the son of Sigislinthon, the daughter of Swafnijaz, who once ruled here by the right of his elder kin who dwell in the mounds at the northern marches of these lands," Hoilogae replied. "Now I have avenged my mother's father with my own hands. Which of you can question my right to take this stead?"

"I am Hrothagaisaz, the son of Hrothamaraz. My father won these lands in battle, by the gods' blessing, and while I live I shall not give them up, whoever lies buried beneath them. I was wounded fighting the folk from the south when they turned on us this morn, but I fought as long as I could stand, I do not wish to give myself up to you, who have done no better than chewing the last of the battle's carrion, striking unfairly when we had nearly overcome our foes. I shall not lie to you, nor lurk in wait. Slay me, and you slay a helpless man, let me live, and I shall destroy you."

Hoilogae turned towards Attalae. The older man shrugged. "This is your choice, Hoilogae. I cannot aid."

"There are few fairer causes for revenge, and it is true that we surprised you in the middle of your own battle," Hoilogae answered. "Still, your father slew my mother's father, and no were-gild was ever offered for that, so I have done no more than is fair in winning back my lands. Now I shall offer you a mighty were-gild, as your father's worth shall be deemed."

"Who should deem it? You? Your kinsmen? The vanquished can look for little at the victor's hands. Or would you leave me to choose my own? I have heard that Sigislinthon's eldest son is witless, but even a fool should hardly let his victim set all terms."

"You seem an honorable man, but you are bent on revenge. Let Sigisharjaz choose the were-gild, little binds him to either of us, and few would question his wisdom."

"Sigisharjaz," Hrothagaisaz said musingly. "However he deems, he will favor himself most of all, and he has long cast a watchful eye towards these lands."

"Can you think of one more suited to choose between us?" Hoilogae countered.

The fair-haired looked down at the dry brown crust rimming the edge of the bandage around his right leg. Hoilogae waited for him, another breath and another. He has just lost his father, Hoilogae thought. How would I feel if? It was Attalae who lay pale on the bier in his mind, short gray beard jutting stiffly up above the twisted wires of his gold torc and a hound slain at his feet. Hoilogae could feel the first coils of smoke stinging tears into his eyes, and had to glance swiftly to the side, to where the living man stood by him, to press them back.

"Swear now that none of our women shall be dishonored, nor our folk shamed or slain, nor the goods of the living taken from them, and I will agree to let Sigisharjaz set the terms of my father's were-gild."

"For the battle's loser, you ask a goodly price already," Attalae countered, his voice dry. "Will you challenge our right to the spoils we have won?"

"You did not win this battle, it was the iron-folk who swore troth to my father's war band and then turned against us. Had they not weakened us, you would have been slaughtered like cows at summer's end. Take the weapons and gear of the slain, and even their gold, for all the riches the southerners had, the cold leavings are the fit part of wolf and raven. But before you harm our women or chain our sons, you must kill each of us who sits here." Hrothagaisaz looked back at Hoilogae. His brown eyes were flecked with glints of green, like glimmers of light in a forest pool. "If you had meant to do that, we'd be dead already."

"You would," Hoilogae admitted. He looked about at the wounded, his own men had started to carry more in already. Outside a woman screamed, her cry choked off abruptly. Hrothagaisaz half-rose with his sword drawn, then his leg-wound brought him back down.

"Attalae, stop that," Hoilogae ordered. "Sigisharjaz may add these terms to the weight of his deeming." The old warrior hurried out. He limped a little, but moved swiftly enough, and no blood stained his breeches.

The pyre was raised for the dead before sundown. The heap of bodies was woven through with branches and bundles of dry straw, pitch had been poured over the dead to hasten their burning, and the pole-mounted skulls that the iron-folk had raised had been ranged carefully on top of the black mound of the slain. Hrothagaisaz had been brought out of the drighten's hall to call the news of their safety to his own people. The women of the village, freed to grieve by the loosing of their fears, were coming out of their houses one by one. Each bore something, a blanket, a comb, a loaf of bread or pot of beer, to put on the pyre beside her dead man.

Except for Hrothamaraz, who had been given a bronze spear in place of the sword Hedhinaz held, none of the garth's warders bore weapons for their faring, but many of Hoilogae's slain had kept their own bronze blades, for the fallen iron-folk, or Hrothamaraz's men who had taken short-lived plunder from them had left many swords to be claimed by the winners. Hoilogae touched his own sword-hilt as he watched the others arrange the bodies. It would be ill for his own blade to be taken from him at his last faring, he thought, but he had little hope that a sword of iron would be put on pyre or laid in mound.

Two small children, dusty-brown hair long around their tear muddied faces, came up to where Hoilogae stood by the heaped mound for the burning. The bigger of the two wore a pair of ragged breeches, the other was quite naked. Both were tanned as deeply as if they had spent the summer in the bog's brown waters, rather than soaking in the Sun's light. A dead dove's body lay limply in the larger one's hands, head rolling over the edge of his palm on a broken neck.

"Please, fro, can we put this on the fire with our father?" The bird-carrier said. Hoilogae could see him trembling perhaps with fear of the enemy warrior, perhaps frightened by the war-helm which made Hoilogae look tall as a shadow at sunrise, but the child did not turn his face away from Hoilogae's gaze.

"Why?" Hoilogae asked, mildly curious.

"The wings will help him f-fly to Walhall," the smaller one said. He bit back a sob, added very fast, "And once he's there, he can eat it."

Hoilogae knew that he could not laugh at the children's grief. He nodded his head soberly. "A worthy gift."

"We'll avenge him someday," the elder boy promised fiercely. "Just you wait"

His sibling kicked him sharply on the ankle. "Hush, Siggi, can't you tell that's their leader?"

"I'll speak as I like, and Hrothagaisaz told us he swore not to hurt us. So what can he do?"

"Who was your father?" Hoilolgae asked.

"Gunthabrandaz son of Gunthahelmaz," the older child replied, drawing his back up. "He fought all day against the iron-folk, and was the first one to stand against you when you rode in."

"His bravery lives in his son," Hoilogae said, laying his hand onto the boy's head and turning him about towards the pyre. "Go and make your gift."

The two of them stood looking up at him for another breath's time. Hoilogae looked over their head to the pyre, where hacked branches wove about hacked limbs, sap and blood and adder-shiny rivulets of black pitch running together. "Would you rather I took it to him for you?" Hoilogae asked gently.

"We'll do it," the younger child said. He turned, walking before his brother to the heaped dead. The flies buzzed up here and there, like black dust stirred by sudden puffs of wind, as the women and children of the village brought gifts to their fallen and Hoilogae's men to their slain friends. Will those two live to turn against me someday? Hoilogae wondered. A wolf often lives in a young son. His other choice was to slay and slay till nothing but himself was left alive in the earth, not those children nor Hrothagaisaz nor his brother Hedhinaz who stood behind him with a naked sword in the sinking light.

"This is a very fine blade you have given me," Hedhinaz said.

Hoilogae faced towards his brother, glad to have a reason to turn away from the dead and their mourners. Hedhinaz had the iron sword out, running his fingertips caressingly down the blade. His iron bladed spear stood within the crook of his arm, leaning against his right shoulder. Behind him, the ravens called back and forth from the top of a high beech tree, their rusty voices sawing through the warm evening air. "Not everyone has a reason to thank me," he replied. He gestured towards the black bird-shadows outlined against the reddened sky. "I've cheated them of their food."

"There's usually plenty left for the ravens when the fire's died down. Even with pitch, dead men take a lot of burning." Hedhinaz's voice was careless, his eyes drawn only to the sheen of his new sword. "Shall we build a mound for them afterwards?"

"No. If there are bones left in the morning, we'll pour more pitch onto them and light the fire again." He would not grant Hrothamaraz a home in his mother's lands, that would not be fitting, and a land could not do well if its wights warred within it. "Careful how you touch that blade. The iron must be perfectly clean before you sheathe it, or the rust will eat it. Here, let me show you."

Hedhinaz opened his hand so that Hoilogae could take the sword, looking stiff-necked on while his brother cleaned the weapon as Wejlunduz had taught him how.

"Thank you," Hedhinaz said. His words sounded as if a sudden sour taste had twisted his tongue in his mouth, but he smiled pleasantly enough as he sheathed the blade at his side.

"Time for the burning," Attalae said. "Come, Hoilogae."

The old warrior led Hoilogae and Hedhinaz to the head of the pyre, where Hrothamaraz was laid out amid a weaving of branches. The pitch made him black and shiny as a bog-troll, and Hoilogae's men had stripped his treasures from him. Herwawardhaz stood before him, with a burning torch in his fist and all the men of the band gathered about him, the women and children, and those wounded who could still walk, were ringed around the rest of the death-heap. Someone had carried Hrothagaisaz out as well. He sat on a little stool near his father's head, his wounded leg stretched stiffly before him. His eyes were black as skull-sockets in his pale face, only the sunset's gleam reflecting their life.

The wailing of the women and the low talking of the men stilled as Hoilogae stepped forward to take the torch from his father's hand.

"Now the Ansuz has taken his own," Hoilogae said, his voice deepening in his throat till he hardly knew it. "Wodhanaz, here are your gifts, given to you for the victory I've won." He turned to take Hedhinaz's spear from him, raised it in his left hand and cast it over the heap of bodies. The weapon whirred in a long low arc through the air, thunking deep into the heart of an old ash tree. Hoilogae heard a gasp from one of the women, but hardly heeded it, he knew he had cast rightly. He raised the torch till its black smoke coiled into the long shadow of his arm over the heap of the slain, then turned it suddenly, plunging it into Hrothamaraz's hair. The hair flared up in a bright burst of stink, the pitch was only a little slower to catch, scorching the flesh beneath it as the flame ran along its black rivers, climbing more slowly onto the dry branches that wove the pyre together. Although twilight had hardly dimmed the air, Hoilogae held the torch before him as he led the way back to the hall, finally thrusting it into the earthen floor before the high seat.

"Will you take your place there?" Hoilogae asked Hrothamaraz.

The drighten shook his head. "You won the day. It is your place to take."

Hoilogae was about to sit down when a wave of dizziness overtook him. His sight twisted so that he seemed to look out from between the high-pillars, at a bloodied giant in the inhuman horned mask of the war-helm, with the reek of carrion rising from him and his bloodied blade in his hand, and his guts twisted in anger and loathing. What have I done wrong? Hoilogae thought as he looked out of his own eyes again.

Have I done ill to the wights here? No, it was only that he was still wearing the war-helm, and could not sit as fro in the high-seat till he had taken it from his head. However the lands were won, the one who sat there must come as friend, or the wights would never look well upon him.

Hoilogae lifted the war-helm from his head and handed it to Hedhinaz. "Bring Hrothamaraz's son here."

Hrothagaisaz came limping, with his arms around the necks of two men who had arm-wounds, but he stood to face Hoilogae. "What do you want of me now?"

"I have this seat by right of my ancestors' blood in the earth and the blood of battle spilt today. Can you challenge my right to take it?"

Hrothagaisaz's strength seemed to flow from him like blood from a vein-wound, one of the men holding him up half-stumbled beneath the sinking of his weight. "I cannot challenge," he said, his voice low. "I yield it to you while you live." In his words, Hoilogae heard the hollow splash of a stone falling into a deep well, its cold waters rippling up his spine.

"So it is," Hoilogae said, and sat down in the high seat. He bent to take a pinch of the earthen floor, passed it three times through the torch's flame. "When you are well enough, Hrothagaisaz, we shall fare to Sigisharjaz's Holm for his deeming. Till then, you are my honored guest in this hall."

The fair man's thick brows beetled close as he looked through the torch-smoke curling up between him and Hoilogae. "Either you are wiser than I am, or more a fool than men say you are. I will take your offer of guest-right, for myself and my men, for you slew our foes as well as our folk. The ale-casks are in the storehouses down by the stream, and in the one on the far right you will find two casks of a strong mead. As your guest, I would ask for drink, this standing has wearied my leg."

Fresh blood was already soaking through the bandages around Hro-thagaisaz's thigh. Hoilogae called for a bench to be brought up, so that Hrothamaraz's son and his own kinsmen could sit beside him. Someone had already put the women to work, and they were bringing in bread and cheese for the warriors. Hoilogae could smell roasting meat, but he did not know whether the sweet scent came from a fire pit nearby or from the corpses burning on the bier. In the short summer darkness, Hoilogae lay awake while the others slept, staring out at the stars that glimmered through the smoke hole and trying to shut his ears to the snores grating against each other. Swaebhon, he thought, fixing his gaze on a single high white point of light.

Swaebhon, have I not done well? Come to me, holy maid, tell me what you will of me. I have my sword, and I have proved myself, but my naming-gift is not whole until you come to me. Swaebhon has your strength come back to you, will you show yourself again now? Only a tattered stream of smoke across the starlight answered him, the pyre still burned outside, its fire keeping the wolves from their night-food. Hoilogae pushed his blanket aside and rose as quietly as he could, though the straw beneath him crack-led soft warning. The wounded shifted and moaned in their beds, but none hailed him as he walked to the door. It creaked open beneath his hand and he slipped out into the night, past the glowing coals and the sputtering of charring flesh on the fire. His walk became swifter as he got farther from the settlement, until he was running lightly along the road where his war-wain had rumbled that morning. Hoilogae's feet were far swifter than the sluggish oxen, his legs were dropping beneath him and he gasped harsh flame with each breath by the time he had come to the mounds, but the first dew of dawn-light was only starting to bleach the sky.

He dragged himself slowly along the overgrown spiral track up the eastern howe. Now he could feel the warmth burning up through his body from the earth, the howe-fire blown to life by the heaving bellows of his chest. When he had reached the top, he pushed his way in between the yew's dark-nee-dled branches, standing with his back to the old tree's trunk. It seemed to him that he could feel its limbs stretching up above him as if they sprang from his body, fresh strength flowing into him from its roots where they twined about the bones and gold of his elder kinsman. He stared at the white birch-tree rising from the other mound, the pale bark shimmering against the blue light of first dawn. The air seemed to sparkle between the two mounds, opening like a doorway. A shadow stood between them.

"Swaebhon," Hoilogae murmured, but it was not she. Sigisharjaz's grizzled wolf-face tilted up above the dark sweep of cloak-wings, one eye gleaming gray and one hidden by the dim shadow of Hoilogae's mound, the old drighten lifted his spear, pointing northwards at a flicker of white glinting against the sky.

His voice thrummed through Hoilogae's body, low and harsh-edged as the call of a lurhorn. "Her work is wrought, the day won. She fares over water and aloft and you must fare over sea after her, north past holm and high cliffs. Now you have won your soul, now your forebears' full might flows through you. Now you may seek your bride, if you dare to wed your doom."

Hoilogae stared into the drighten's eye. Its brightness seemed to swell to the edges of his vision, until it seemed that he stood in the middle of a great mountain of clear blue-gray ice, staring into a black pool where two blue-gray eyes glimmered back at him above high arches of bone, swept about with long ripples of pale hair. He reached out for her, and the sight was gone. The steel-blue light of dawn shone about him, and the road between the mounds was empty. Hoilogae had no doubt of the message. He would fare to Sigisharjaz's Holm, and hail the drighten again in Wodhanaz's name.

CHAPTER XIII

When Helgi was well enough to sing again, he spent every moment that he could working on one or the other of his two songs through the springtime thunders, when the radio warned ominously of tornadoes and flooding, through the heat that began to choke its coils tight around the city in April. Halfway through the month, Ms. Devereaux found an accompanist for him, a short, swarthy Hispanic named Federico who was a graduate studying piano. Helgi dreaded singing in front of him at first, but Federico never said anything except, "Okay, man," or, sometimes, "Late entrance. Count the beats."

Karin had been at Preddy Base in Colorado for nearly six months when she got her next transfer orders. She stood before Lt. Colonel Yorke's desk with the slip of paper in her hand, staring at it. She was scheduled to be at Sijan Base near Dallas in two days, to take up duties described as "squadron and instructional."

"Questions, Lieutenant?" Yorke asked her.

"Military or civilian transport, sir?"

"No military flights scheduled. You'll be flying into DFW. A pickup at the airport will be arranged when you have ETA."

"Yes, sir."

"Got much to pack?"

"No, sir. Books and clothes, maybe two suitcases worth."

"Okay. Well, consider yourself relieved of duty anyway. Go take a last look at the mountains or something." Yorke smiled, the corners of his eyes and his mouth creasing so that he suddenly looked his full forty-eight years. "We're going to miss you here, Brünnhilde. You're a helluva pilot. I wish you'd been with us over the Red River."

Karin stood speechless for a moment. She had often heard her flying praised, but she had never been given such a compliment. Her throat closed for a moment, and she could feel the hot blood brightening her cheeks. She coughed. "Uh. Thank you, sir!"

"Something else. Don't get discouraged. Not that I think you would, but I know you're always wondering whether you'll really be allowed to fly combat missions when the next war breaks out. The US military moves slowly, Jensen, but nevertheless it does move. Keep that in mind."

"Yes, sir."

"Dismissed, Lieutenant. Go buy a plane ticket."

It felt strange to Karin to be driving her jeep off-base at ten-thirty in the morning, the clear sunlight slanting through her windshield. She felt like a teenager ditching class, she started when the gate guard saluted and waved her through. After a moment, she turned on the radio, twisting the dial until she heard Bruce Dickinson's voice chanting his eerie, wailing version of "*Rime of the Ancient Mariner,*" fragments about Death and Life-in-Death. Karin cranked the volume up until the bass shook the pedals beneath her feet, swinging the jeep easily around the twisting mountain road. Back to Dallas, she thought, that will gladden my parents. She glanced up at the dark pine trees and overhanging crags looming above her, the signs posted at every curve to warn of skidding cars and falling rocks.

No more Survival & Resistance in blizzards, Karin thought, shivering at the memory of a snow-hidden outcropping of rotten rock breaking away beneath her foot as she crawled slowly down a cliff face. No more of the guys bitching about the motherfucking cold. No more following the clean graceful moves of Captain Perry, wingman protecting her leader, sweeping through the sky together like skaters dancing on clear ice, no more leading combat exercises with the sure knowledge that Rodriguez had her area scoped, her ass guarded, and her exit clear.

Instead, she'd have a whole new set of guys to convince that a woman flying a fighter plane was more than a dancing bear, and she'd probably get tagged with a nickname a whole lot less flattering than, "*Brünnhilde.*" Back at Luke, a few of the guys had referred to her as Clinton's Case, not that Karin cared if they thought she was a dyke, it scared off some of the particular bastards by whom she least wanted to be hit on. But maybe they would give her an F-16C in Texas, with the matching assurance that she would be going into combat? No, the word "instructional" had been quite clear on her orders, she'd be in a two-seater again, and probably spending more time in back than in front. Damn it. Maybe someday.

There was more for Karin to do than ordering a plane ticket, she had to arrange for transfer of her bank account, explain to her apartment manager that she had been moved, thank gods, it had been just about rent time anyway, so she wasn't going to be stuck paying for space she wouldn't be using, and call around a few agencies to find someone who would drive her jeep down to Dallas, insured, without charging her more arms and legs than she had to spare. Finally, she phoned her parents' house.

"Moder? Er du hjemme?" Often her mother turned the machine on to screen calls when she was at home, but Karin waited a few heartbeats and heard nothing except the faint hiss of the tape turning. She left her message, promising to come home for a visit as soon as she was able, and hung up.

Karin looked at her watch. Its flat black-on-gray digital screen showed 13.32. Most of a day to myself, she thought, and nothing to do in it. There was a bar in town where she sometimes went on her off-duty evenings, but it was likely too early for them to be open. Perhaps she would go up to the mountains, after all. She drove until the winding little road up the mountain turned to dirt and the thunder of planes cleaving the sky was no more than a vague rumble, only an echo of memory, that another might not have heard in her place. When she came to a thin waterfall that fell like a frothing thread down the cliff, tumbling hundreds of feet into a small deep pool, Karin pulled her jeep over and got out.

She had packed herself a picnic lunch, bread and hard sausage from the German deli and beer. As she settled herself on a mossy rock by the side of the pool, at the edge of the waterfall's rainbow-bright ring of spray, Karin could feel her shoulders easing and her lungs unlocking to draw in deeper and deeper breaths of the clear cool air. She was almost up past the tree line here, only a few scraggly pines thrusting their branches against the rocks. Only a few yards from the edge of the pond, the land dropped away as suddenly as the plummeting stoop of a falcon, far beneath, she could see the brighter green of oak, ash, and birch mottling the dark carpet of conifers.

The only sounds she could hear were the rushing of the water over the rocks and the clear call of a bird. Karin twisted a little to dig her utility knife out of the tight front pocket of her jeans. It seemed to her that there was something very familiar about this stead so high in the mountains. Yes, the summer she was twelve, the whole Jensen family, Danish and American branches together, had gone to Norway to rent vacation cottages in the Jotunheimen mountains for a month. Her cousin Nils, seventeen then, had told the younger children stories about trolls and ghosts every night, then lurked with a fright mask on to leap out at them from the darkness. She popped the top off her Elephant, watching the beer froth up into the neck and slowly settle down.

Karin had never told anyone what she had seen on her first heavy-weather flight at Preddy, nor had Maintenance ever found out what had killed her TIDS and radar. Several times she had thought she heard mocking laughter in the wind while fighting her way through the mountains on Survival & Resistance, and always it had been just before the ice gave way under her feet, before a rock dropped from above or a sudden gust of snow-laden wind blinded her eyes as she scrabbled on stone for a hand- or foothold, but that giggle of cracking rock had been her best help on the last bad winter exercise in February, warning her on the same blizzard-swept path where Schroeder had broken his leg and Galloway dislocated his shoulder.

"So, Dovregubber," Karin murmured, lifting her beer bottle. "Du gammel troll måske, at jeg savner dig." I might miss you. You old troll. "You and all the wights here in your kingdom can rest a little easier when the planes come over now. You don't have too much cause to be angry with me, you came close enough to getting me a good share of times." She poured a few amber drops out to froth from the rocks, another splash of beer to be lost in the foam floating out from the waterfall's frothing foot, then drank a deep swallow herself.

Her ears humming from the long draught, it seemed to Karin that she could hear a deep voice murmuring something through the rushing water. She could not make out the words, but the tone did not seem angry or harsh. When she had finished eating, Karin carefully picked up everything she had brought with her, but she left her last slice of bread and sausage on the rock where she had been sitting. Squadron 106 was not likely to hold much of a going-away party for her, and her move was too sudden, and her wing had ACM, air combat maneuvers, scheduled for tomorrow, but the land-wights would have their share of her feast, and the Mountain King would not forget her. Karin spent most of the flight to DFW reading Red Storm Rising, carefully ignoring the stares and drawling mutters of the men in the row of seats across from her. Middle-aged, two a little paunchy and one health-club trim, dark suits, short-cropped hair. They were probably coming back from a convention or something. Likely more so now, since the state's anti-gay Amendment 2 was finally repealed and Colorado was no longer under boycott. She knew she was hardly inconspicuous, since it was a commercial flight, she could have dressed in civvies, but she had chosen to wear her service dress uniform so that she wouldn't have to change clothes before reporting on base.

She did not start staring out the window until the plane's nose began to slope downward, getting ready to begin the descent into DFW. The first thing Karin thought as she looked down at the green and brown squares of field beneath her was that she had forgotten how flat Texas was. She could have been looking at an irregularly checkered chessboard, or the top of a mosaic table with a model of a space-age city of spired steel and glass set in its center. The next thing she noticed was the faint grungy yellowness of the air, she could almost feel its thickness after the clear bright sky of color, perhaps it was the way the plane wallowed in the light crosswinds, heavy and coarse as her grandmother's sow in farrow. Karin's hand closed on the thick edge of the Tom Clancy book as if it were the control stick of her Lawn Dart, wishing that the silver flash in the corner of her eye gleamed from her sleek narrow wing, that the seatbelt pulled taut across her hips was attached to the straps of her harness. The takeoff from Colorado had been clumsy enough that she put little trust in the pilot, but even a bus driver should be able to land in such still weather, at least she hoped. Karin walked slowly to the exit after collecting her bags, looking over the crowd. She had also forgotten how many Texans actually did wear cowboy boots and hats, how thick that drawl of "Wa-yell" and "y'all" really sounded. She knew it must be hot outside.

The sweat gleamed on shoulders and arms, the heavy biceps of the men and the tank-top cleavage of the women, as they made their way through the airport's glass doors, and they sucked up the air-conditioning like cold beer. The heavy Dallas air was already pressing on her, stifling her. Like Skaði, the hunt-goddess, Karin thought, she had come down from the mountains to sea-level, and like Skaði, she longed to go back to the cold winds of the heights. Skaði had married the sea-god Njörðr, and not been able to dwell in his home, and he could not bear the howling wind and wolves of her crags, so they had parted. And later she had gone with Óðinn, and borne a son, from whom were descended the Jarls of Hladhir, that defended the gods and goddesses of Norway against the kings who would convert. A flash of Air Force storm-blue caught the corner of Karin's eye, and she turned her head, raising her own hand automatically as she saw the descending salute. The sergeant who stood there was a huge man, seven or eight inches taller than Karin's own five-eleven and muscled like a romantic nineteenth-century painting of Thórr. His skin was deep purple-black, his features were broad, definitely African, but clearly cut. Karin turned on her heel, striding over to him. "Sergeant."

"Ma'am. Sergeant Thorne here." His speech was so thick that Karin could not understand his next words.

"Come again, sergeant?"

Thorne coughed. "Uh. Instructions to convey you and your gear to Sijan Base ASAP, ma'am." Not only did he speak more slowly, but his speech was so perfect that Karin wondered for a moment if he had been a television or radio announcer before joining the military.

"Thank you, sergeant. Carry on."

Thorne glanced at her bags, not actually reaching for them the way most men did, but opening his huge pink-palmed hands as if to let her know that he was ready and willing to take them if she said so. No threat to my womanhood, Karin thought, no need to stand on feminist principle. She handed one up to him, leaning slightly to one side to compensate for the sudden imbalance, and started briskly out to the parking lot.

"Ah, ma'am," Thorne said when he had threaded his way through the maze of cement and cars.

"Yes, sergeant?"

"I'm crew chief for your bird."

Karin smiled. "What condition is she in now?"

"FMC, ma'am. Fully Mission Capable," he told her, rolling the words lovingly off his tongue. "You won't be disappointed, ma'am." Sergeant Thorne dropped into a rhythm that was almost a chant, she could hear the natural sounds of his voice straining against the precision with which he spoke. "Gleaming like a queen, eagle-sight focused for the tiniest sparrow's fall, the lightning is in her talons, an' the thunder is in her grip." Though he never shifted his gaze from the road ahead of them, Karin could see the brightness glowing suddenly from his deep brown eyes as he spoke.

"I suspect I won't be disappointed at all, Sergeant Thorne."

Karin had been assigned a temporary room of her own in one of the barracks, where she would stay for the next few nights, until she had a chance to check out the available housing and decide whether she wanted to live on-base or off. The room was a four-bunker, all of the beds except the one on the lower right stripped. A sheaf of information about Sijan Base lay on the flat pillow. Karin dumped her bags on the floor, locked up, and went looking for the toilet so she could neaten herself and wash her face before reporting to the base commander, checking that her badges and insignia were perfectly aligned on her blue uniform jacket and parallel to the floor.

The door to General Voorhies' office was open when Karin got there. She slowed, wiping the sweat from her forehead with the back of her hand and straightening her cap before she strode ahead to stop at the threshold. As the man sitting at the desk looked up, she saluted without thinking, staring at his bandaged right eye and the spidery network of scars, some white against his ruddy skin, some pink, around the fresh scabbed gash through his gray eyebrow. He looked like a big man, heavily built with the beginnings of a solid paunch, Karin could see his scalp gleaming through the little gray bristles of his crew-cut.

"Sir, Lieutenant Jensen reporting, sir!"

"Come in, Jensen." The general's voice was very deep, with an echoing tone like rocks rattling in an empty fuel drum. "At ease. Sit down. Welcome to Sijan Base." He tapped a blunt finger on the papers in front of him, his clear blue eye staring keenly up at her. "Your reputation has preceded you, Lieutenant. I expect to be impressed."

"You won't be disappointed, sir."

Voorhies' heavy head moved down, then up in a slow nod. "Confidence is a good thing, Lieutenant. So long as it doesn't become overconfidence. Is that clear?"

"Yes, sir. An overconfident pilot is a danger to himself and his wing, sir."

"Good, Lieutenant. Keep it in mind, or get your butt kicked from here to Hanoi. Do you play bridge?"

"Yes, sir," Karin answered, bewildered by the sudden change of subject.

"My wife is the president of the Ladies' Bridge Club here on base. You are invited for tomorrow night, nineteen-thirty. When you have received your roster of duties from your squadron commander, Colonel Douglas, you are to let me know whether you will be able to make it."

"Yes, sir. Thank you, sir."

"You can thank my wife. It was her idea. Dismissed, Lieutenant."

Wonderful, Karin thought, sitting on her hard bed and looking at her orders for the upcoming week. More Survival & Resistance, in other words, heatstroke training and the chance to practice hiding on flat fields. On the other hand, should she ever have to do S&R in wartime, it would be a hell of a lot more likely to be on terrain like Texas than like Colorado.

Rejoice that you are in the Air Force, she said to herself, and will always be able to fly back to air conditioning, showers, and all your favorite amenities of life, whilst the poor grunts are stuck out there in the field. And do not bitch about running around in the heat and diving face-first into the dirt. She unpacked her uniforms, hanging them up and brushing the wrinkles out, she would have to take an iron to them that night. There was no point in setting up her books, since she wasn't going to be there more than three or four days. Karin was getting hungry, and for a few moments she wavered between the choices of going to the officers' mess or calling a cab to take her into the nearest small town. Finally she decided that when she met the guys she'd be flying with, she would rather that they could see her in action before getting too much time to discuss her and work up their doubts or whatever they were going to work up.

Anyway, going out would show her whether it was worthwhile to try and get an apartment off-base, or whether she should stick with base housing. Karin stripped off her uniform and stood beneath the air conditioning vent in bra and panties a moment, letting its breeze cool her damp skin. She had sweated nearly through the uniform jacket already, just from walking between the buildings in the full late afternoon sunlight. Water was going to be her first priority tomorrow, no question. She shuddered, remembering the time she had passed out from the heat in Basic, her sight darkening as her knees gave way and she crashed to the ground beneath her pack, then waking up in the infirmary with teeth chattering and limbs shaking, terrified that she was going to be handed her medical discharge as soon as she was on her feet. Water, more water, and force 24 sunblock, she thought, those had been her mainstays during training in Arizona, and she was sure it would be no different here. Thinking of the heat outside, Karin was about to pull on minimal civvies, shorts and a tank top, when she remembered that different bases had different policies on uniform wear. Here it would have been decided by General Voorhies. I am under the gaze of the Dread Eye, Karin said solemnly to herself, and suddenly laughed. A woman who followed the Asatro should not be disheartened by a one-eyed commander.

She looked at the packet of information, flipping through until she found the section she wanted. Uniforms were to be worn at all times on-base with the standard prohibitions against bearing uniforms in connection with "any meeting, demonstration, movement, group, or combination of persons that the Attorney General of the United States has designated as totalitarian, fascist, communist, or subversive activities such as public speeches, interviews, picket lines, marches, rallies, or any public demonstration, including those pertaining to civil rights, not approved by the Air Force." Well, that settled that. The uniform she had worn that day was still clammy to the touch, so she put on a fresh one, thinking that the pathway to the base laundry service would soon become very familiar.

The cab driver took Karin to a small diner called Bobbi's Bar & Grill, about fifteen minutes' drive away. "Yeah, lots of the guys from base come out here to eat. Bobbi makes the best steaks in Tarrant County, and there's just 'bout always a pool game goin' on in the back room. Y'all play pool, ma'am?"

To hear a civilian saying "ma'am" to her seemed strangely disorienting to Karin, so that she paused before replying, she had forgotten how Texans always called strangers "ma'am" and "sir ."

"Uh, no, I don't."

"I could teach y'all sometime, if y'wanted," the cabby offered. As they pulled into the parking lot, he glanced in the rear view mirror, as if to check the reaction of Karin's reflection.

"That's nice of you," she said coolly. "But I was just assigned, and I don't think I'll be able to get off-base very often for a while."

"Oh. Well, when y'all do need to come into town, just call Yellow Cab and ask for Mike Fielding, okay? I usually work late afternoons and evenings on weekdays, daytime shift on Sunday."

Bobbi's Bar & Grill was dimly lit, the pink and red neon of the jukebox and the lurid glow of the video games and pinball machine by the door lending it a cheap atmosphere. There was no music going, Karin could hear the clicking of pool balls and a tired "Shee-it" from the back room. She looked at the jukebox, flipping through the racks of song titles, and decided to leave it be. Instead she ordered a medium rare steak and a Corona from the big red-haired woman behind the counter, and settled herself in a corner where she could eat and read Red Storm Rising without drawing too much attention.

Karin was almost through with her meal when a movement caught her eye and she looked up from her book. For a moment she was a child again, staring up from her bed at the huge troll-shape bulking dark against her wall. Then her sight settled, shaping the faint gleams of neon off blackness and the shadows between them into the features of the big sergeant who had driven her from the airport.

"Good evening, Lieutenant," Sgt. Thorne rumbled. "I see you're finding your way around. Spent all afternoon polishing up your bird, but I hear you're scheduled for S&R this week."

"News travels fast, doesn't it?" Officers and enlisted men had separate messes for a reason, but the better terms she was on with her maintenance crew, the happier her life would be, Karin thought. "Sit down and I'll buy you a drink. Beer?"

"Suits me just fine, Lieutenant. Thank you."

Karin turned her book face-down. Thorne looked at it, nodding. "One of his best, isn't it?"

"I think so."

"Those Icelanders in there, they are some interesting people." For a moment, the sergeant's eyes met hers, gleaming reddish-black in the gloom. "You aren't Icelandic, are you? Must be something Scandinavian."

STEPHAN GRUNDY

"Danish."

"Not a native English-speaker, either. Shows in the way you talk an' you be havin' a little trouble understandin' me when I talk my way, I think." Thorne grinned, showing a row of square white teeth, and Karin had to smile with him.

"You caught me by surprise the first time," Karin admitted. "And my first language is Danish. But we moved here when I was three, and I grew up in Dallas, so I think I can follow you."

The sergeant laughed. "You bein' a Scandinavian, maybe you can tell me somethin'. I've heard that black folks can't be posted to Keflavík Base in Iceland, 'counta the natives still bein' real superstitious, thinkin' we be trolls or somethin'. There any truth to that, Lieutenant?"

"I don't know," Karin answered slowly. She could not see through the dark mask of Sgt. Thorne's face, his teeth still grinned at her, but it seemed to her that she could feel his steady gaze hard against her own. "I know that many of them still believe in elves and land-wights, and that a few trust in the gods of their ancestors, but I had not heard that. Certainly it is not so in Denmark, anyway."

"Mmm." Thorne looked down at the cover of the book again, the gold and red lettering gleaming against the background of black smoke rising from hot yellow-white flames. He seemed about to say something more, but Bobbi had come out from behind the counter, tossing her huge mass of curly auburn hair over one thick shoulder as she walked over to them.

"What're you havin' tonight, Rof?"

"Got paid las' week believe I'll have me one of them fourteen-ounce steaks you cook so good."

"Drink?"

"Beer for both of us," Karin said swiftly. "It's on me."

The deep laugh-lines around Bobbi's eyes crinkled as she grinned. "Ain't you ashamed, Rof? You got no manners, makin' the lady buy the drinks. You better buy the next round, or I'll kick your big studly ass right out the door, you believe me." She balled her big freckled fist and shook it jokingly under his nose.

"Oh, I do, I do," Thorne laughed. "Wouldn' want to make you mad at me, not at all. You don' want to see her beat me up, do you, Lieutenant?"

Karin shook her head. "I guess I could handle one more beer to save my crew chief's ass." It is not going to be so bad for me here at all, she realized suddenly. Not with Sergeant Thorne on my side.

Helgi's first audition, performing one of his own compositions for trombone and piano, went easily. No fear gripped his guts as he came to stand before the two men and one woman who sat behind a long white-topped table in the big audition room Dr. Richie, the head of the Music department, Ms. Clairmont, the director of the university orchestra, and Dr. Alexander, the composition specialist.

Helgi's trombone teacher, Mr. Guest, didn't work for the university and so was able to accompany him for the audition, they had practiced this piece together until Helgi no longer needed the battered and pencil-marked pages taped together on the music stand in front of him. Helgi slid up and down octaves of scales on command, then told them the title of his solo and was away, letting the hollow clear voice of his trombone build the sounds above and through the piano. The piece was harder than it sounded, the long notes made to let any flaws of intonation show sharply through, and the slow rhythms built to disintegrate at the least hairsbreadth of a slip in Helgi's counting.

It was a melancholy piece, full of twilight longing, but the longing Helgi played into it was his own longing after words that would make more sense than the twining patterns of the music, that would bring the half-vision of the sounds out into something known and named. He thought of his own voice speaking through the golden length of his horn, singing with all the clarity and truth that the instrument lent his sound. Once or twice he saw a pencil scratch, no more. At the end of the piece, the three judges clapped with, Helgi thought, more warmth than politeness. Dr. Richie's smile crinkled a few wrinkles into the corner of his mouth, and he nodded.

"Very good. Thank you."

"You done good, kid," Mr. Guest said as they walked along the hall together, the heels of their shoes clicking loudly against the hard white floor. "That's as nice as I've heard you play that yet, and I've heard worse compositions in concert halls. I don't think there's any doubt about you getting in."

"I hope not."

"Going to go out to celebrate?"

"I've got another audition here this afternoon. I'm going for graduate study in voice as well as composition."

"Huh! I didn't know you sang. Well, good luck then. I hope you do as well on that as you did just now."

"Thanks."

A wave of heat swept in when Mr. Guest opened the exit door. "See you later," the old trombonist said, squaring his stocky shoulders beneath the unaccustomed hang of his grey suit and stepping out into the sweltering sunlight like a swimmer plunging into the water. Helgi turned back into the cool of the air conditioning as the door swung shut, making his way down in search of an empty practice room. Although the auditions had been running late, Helgi's watch told him that he still had two hours before he was scheduled to sing, but the first flies of nervousness were already starting to buzz in his bowels.

He found a free room and wedged himself in before the piano. The deep breath he needed to sing with calmed him. He began his warm-up, taking it slow and easy, testing his voice like a skater moving bit by bit out onto fresh ice. No cracks here, go on a little roughness, a little mucus caught in his throat, making him want to cough it clear, but Ms. Devereaux had warned him against that, so that he stopped himself before the cough was more than a breath and went out to clear his throat at the drinking fountain in the hall. Half an hour of warm-up, another half-hour of singing, then he quit before he could tire his voice too badly. I'd better go get some lunch, he told himself, I'll drive myself crazy if I sit around here too much longer. But he did not push the piano bench back and get to his feet. The runes of black notes woven with words drew his eyes again, swirling before him like flies above pale sand. Helgi yawned suddenly, his jaws cracking as they stretched. His skull was swimming, dizzy, he felt as though he were about to faint. Something rustled behind him, soft as the shuffling of papers, and he turned slowly on the bench. The pasteboard walls of the practice room stretched out before his dazzled eyes, the wall that had been at his back was lost in pale fog.

Helgi clenched his fists tight, breathing deeply in through the nose, out through the mouth, as his sensei had taught him to, feeling the warmth of his chi, his life-force, strengthening him. Now something was moving, and it seemed to Helgi that he could see the shape forming before him. A man riding on a horse, the bay steed's hooves churning through the mist as though he galloped hard. The man wore helm and byrnie, a spear was in his right hand, and a cone of green glass in the left he leaned forward along the horse's neck, and the wind was blowing his ruddy braids back. Helgi did not dare to blink, lest his sight be lost, stinging tears welled in his fixed eyes, dripping hot down his cheeks. The wind was rising around him, a low moan through his ears shifting into the far-off calling of a man's breathy voice.

"Helgi do you hear me?"

"I hear you," Helgi whispered. "Who are you?"

Though the rider galloped yet, he seemed to come no nearer, Helgi did not know how far away he was, but his words blew faint on the wind.

"Sigismundar, sword-glad,
swung his blade in young days,
Spear of Wodhanar spared not,
saved who came from blade-play.
Hero, my son, hare I
high from mound depth, riding -
bring for brave youth's song-war,
bright mead, eagle's flight-gold,
bright mead, High One's flight-gold."

Sigismundar stretched out a mist-blurred hand, holding the green cone of glass out towards Helgi. Slowly Helgi stood, raising his own arm towards the rider. A freezing shock leapt through his fingertips. The rime-covered glass was cold as ice from the green heart of a glacier. Helgi's hand was already moving, his head tilting before he could stop to think.

The drink froze his throat, its cold burning down into his stomach, but its ice was sweet across his tongue, its blood-scent rich in his mouth and nose. Three swallows, and he had downed it. The strength of the draught rose suddenly to his head, his legs lowered beneath him, dropping him onto the piano bench again. Helgi closed his eyes as a long, thrilling shudder ran through him. When he looked up again, the rider was gone. Before him, Helgi saw only the pockmarked yellow pasteboard of the practice room's flimsy wall, scratched with the faint little words "john sucks cock" in half-erased pencil. He raised his hand to his throat.

It seemed to him that the sudden burst of cold had faded into a gentle warmth, thrumming just behind his vocal cords. A shrill beep shot through Helgi's ears, he started, almost falling off the bench, then slapped his alarm clock down before hastily gathering his music together and shoving it into his backpack. He had five minutes to get upstairs to the audition room five minutes before he had to sing. The sudden shaking rush of adrenalin drove other thoughts from Helgi's mind. There would be time to sit and think about what had happened later, but now...

"They're running late," a short girl who wore her red hair in a long ponytail said softly as Helgi paced up to glance back and forth between his watch and the list. "I was supposed to be up fifteen minutes ago, and there's one more before me."

Federico had been leaning against the wall, reading a newspaper, now he glanced up at Helgi. "They're always late," he grunted, lowering his gaze to his paper again. Helgi looked back at the little redhead.

"What's your name?"

"Luann O'Roarke."

Her name was third from the top, his was about halfway down the list. This is all going to be over eventually, Helgi reminded himself.

"Graduate or undergraduate?" He said, hoping that the conversation would distract him.

"Graduate. What about you?"

"Graduate, likewise. Composition and voice. I hope."

"Good luck." Luann slid down the wall, folding herself boneless into lotus position when her bottom reached the floor. She patted her mouth with her hand, half-covering a wide yawn, then picked up the music book that lay face-down beside her Favorite Opera Arias, for mezzo-soprano, and began to hum very quietly as her eyes tracked over the notes.

Helgi tried not to listen to the sounds coming from behind the door. He couldn't hear clearly enough to tell what the song was, or how well the singer was doing, but each snatch of sound plucked at his tightened nerves. He walked down the hall, then back the other way, looking for Federico.

When they finally went in, Dr. Richie was still there. Ms. Devereaux sat on his right, a slim blond woman one of the choir directors, to his left. At first Helgi saw no recognition in the man's dark eyes, and even his slight formal smile of that morning had worn off beneath the horde of auditions. Then Dr. Richie looked down at the list before him, and Helgi could see his face easing. "You're applying for graduate studies in voice as well as composition, Mr. Hadding?"

"I am."

"Carry on."

Federico seated himself at the piano and Helgi moved to stand in his place before it, facing the three judges. For a fainting moment he saw the pitiless eyes of Michelle, Farrell, and Marcia staring from their skulls, as if he were living his first audition through again, then the music of "Erlkönig" began to run, bearing his fear up on its back. His hands shaking with the night's deep cold, palms damp with the cool sweat of fog-dew, and the sweet ghost-drink blowing through his throat like the first breath of a storm wind.

"'Wer reitet so spät, durch Nacht und Wind?'" And in his voice, the youth's longing to go together with his terror, the wonder of the sights he sees in the night and mist, the Erl-King's fatherly claim on the son who is surely his own, his hope for life as well as his slain booty, and the father's blind calmness which must finally break, when the Erl-King's gift cannot be kept from him and he too shudders at the youth's voice calling on the wind.

And he knew they could hear it too now, those flesh-masked skulls misted by the sparkling darkness that rose before his sight, the Erl-King's fury finally reaching through his mead-wet throat to still the blond woman's scribbling pencil and grasp Dr. Richie's gaze by force. "'Und bist du nicht willig, so brauch ich Gewalt!'" And so the last line blended brightness with the dark chords, winning woven with the loss. "In seinen Armen das Kindwar tot."

Helgi was breathless when he was done, breathless and drenched with sweat like a horse lathered from running. He saw Ms. Devereaux's faint nod, and his tight-thudding heart loosened a little in his chest. Dismissed, he and Federico went out together.

"What do you think?" Helgi asked his accompanist.

Federico shrugged. "Who can say, man? Sounded way better than you did in practice. Don't worry."

"Thanks for working with me on it."

"Yah. No problem."

Helgi went home to change out of his suit and into shorts and a T-shirt, then drove over to Mark's house. Tippet was out mowing the lawn, wearing only a ragged pair of cut-off denims and flip-flop sandals, his shirt was flung over the low hedge that separated their lawn from the one next door. Rivulets of sweat rolled down from the knobby arch of his backbone, and his tan was already deep enough for Helgi to feel a trifle inferior when he glanced down at his own white legs.

"Kind of hot to work now, isn't it?" Helgi asked, scooting into the shade of the porch. "I thought all you peons were supposed to take siesta in the afternoon."

"Come the revolution, Yuppie slime, you're up against the wall," Tippet answered, kicking the lawnmower off. "Fuck it, I'm almost done, I'll finish it tomorrow. How'd it go?"

"Pretty good."

"Great. I got some really excellent news today."

"Do tell."

"MIT finally decided to accept me for grad work. No scholarship, but at least I'm in." Mark grinned, shaking his clasped hands victoriously over his head. Helgi grinned back.

"Excellent! This calls for celebration."

"Bet your ass. Hey, stay over tonight and we can get drunk in Aaron's place after my mom goes to bed."

"Sounds good to me."

At seven, Helgi came down out of Mark's room to the kitchen, where a phone clung brown against the wall beside the stove, and took Ms. Devereaux's home number out of his wallet. The knotting in his guts did not pull his fingers' sinews too tight to press the phone buttons, nor did the buzzing in his ears drown out the three rings and her sharp, "Hello?"

"Ms. Devereaux?"

"Hello, Helgi. What do you want?"

"I wanted to know if, I mean, did I..?"

"Helgi, you know I'm not supposed to tell you anything about that. The auditions are supposed to be confidential. You'll find out when you get the notice in the mail." Helgi waited. After a moment, he heard her gusty sigh. "All right. I won't torture you, then. You made it."

Helgi was about to whoop with delight, but she went on, cutting him off. "You should know that I was rather surprised. Even given the great improvement you've made in the last semester, as I told you. You really should not have expected to get in. Your pitch was shaky in places, and you still have some basic problems with tone and sound production, which will not be easy to correct. However, the judges were very impressed with your general musical skills and your interpretation of that particular piece, unreasonably ambitious as it was in terms of range and skill. And in performance, you have a certain vocal presence which had not appeared in practice, enough to overwhelm many of your voice's current flaws to a degree that I would not have suspected possible. So the final consensus was that you showed enough potential to be encouraged to continue with serious vocal study."

"Oh. Thank you."

"You're welcome. Now remember, I didn't tell you any of this. Call me in a week or so that we can schedule lessons over the summer."

"All right."

Helgi went back to Mark's room, kicking his way through the heaps of shed clothes and empty Coke cans to the bed.

"What news?" Mark said, looking up from his White Dwarf magazine.

"I made it."

"All right! Congratulations."

Getting into Plague Bug, they rolled the windows down all the way to let the warm night air flow through, though Mark waited till they were heading towards the freeway ramp to crank up the radio and let the sound of Jethro Tull boom out on the wind behind them. Helgi could not hear his own laughter beneath the music and the rushing air, but he could feel the lightness of his limbs, suddenly strong as if a long sickness had fallen from him in a single breath. Late as it was, Greenville Avenue was still loud with music throbbing through the hot night, the street clogged with cars and pedestrians weaving among them. The sidewalks in front of the cafés and bars bloomed with night-grayed parasols, now shading the frozen margaritas and beers on the tables beneath from the glare of the streetlights and the colored heat of neon signs. Mark skillfully steered Plague Bug through the gaps in traffic, shouting at drunken walkers now and then. One or two shouted back, most ignored him. He swerved viciously close to a big Chevy, forcing it to brake hard.

"You're going to get killed doing this someday!" Helgi shouted to him.

"Relax, I know what I'm doing. I'll live to dance on your grave, wait and see."

Busy as the main street was, the parking lot behind the bar where Aaron worked was no fuller than it had been the other times Mark and Helgi had come here, and when they got in, they saw that there were only four men drinking inside. The piano stood silent, its player gone home.

Even through the dim light, Helgi could see how bloodshot Aaron's eyes were, the irises melted into black pupils. He stared at them for a moment, then nodded. "Hi, guys. What do you want?"

"Bass Ale?" Helgi asked.

"None of that limey piss here. Try again."

"Two Heinekens. I'm buying, Mark. Are you going to tell your brother the good news?"

"I'm glad somebody's got good news," Aaron muttered. "Yeah, tell me."

Mark told him about MIT. Aaron handed the two of them beers. "Congrats, kid. Good job. These are on the house."

Mark leaned over the bar, looking closer at his elder brother. "You're stoned, aren't you?"

"Yeah. You think anyone here is going to care?"

Helgi glanced back at the men, three black and one white, who sat with their beer bottles, still as if they were listening to the silent piano.

"You might as well sit at the bar," Aaron went on. "No one's going to notice."

"So, what's wrong with you?" Mark asked.

"Lisa dumped me for a goddamn undergraduate football player. I wined and dined her with all the class I had, and she gave it up in favor of two hundred fifty pounds of Big Macs. You got a girlfriend, Helgi?"

"No."

"Good move. Don't trust them." He looked around vaguely. "Y'know, I sure wish this place had a jukebox. The quiet is getting to me."

"Where's the piano player?"

"He claims he's got the flu. It's probably AIDS."

"Helgi just got accepted as a music graduate at Jefferson," Mark said. "Why don't you play the piano for a while, Helgi? It'll be your first chance for a real live public performance. You'll have groupies clinging to your ankles by the time you're done."

Helgi took a deep drink of his beer and belched loudly at his friend. But if I do? He thought suddenly. There was hardly anyone to hear him nothing to lose.

"Yeah, go on," Aaron urged him. "I'll give you free beer the rest of the night if you'll play for a while, okay?"

"Why not?" Helgi said. He picked up his beer and went over to the piano. The microphone was dead, but the bar was small and quiet enough for that not to matter, and the piano was still a little out of tune, but not badly enough to make him stop playing. He started with the accompaniment to *"Wandrer's Nachtlied,"* then chugged the rest of his beer down and plunged into his own version of *"Stairway to Heaven"* as Mark carried another drink over to him. Now he could imagine the bar full, the silence not empty but full of people listening to his music, and after two more songs, he thought, Well, why not? He couldn't remember the accompaniment to *"Erl-König"* quite well enough to play it, but the memory of its melody was already waking his own song from the bone-yellow ivory beneath his hands. My kingdom for a synthesizer, he thought.

The piccolo's scream, the horn and deep-thrumming strings only sounded in his skull, but the words to summon them lay hoarded in his throat, and so Helgi breathed deeply and began to sing into the waiting music.

"Wind is howling through black pines." His voice sounded clearer and stronger in his own ears than he had heard it before, he half-closed his eyes to see the shapes through the thin haze of smoke as he sang, the walls of the bar stretching further and further back until he crouched on stage at the bottom of a great arena, huge speakers casting his song out through the waiting crowd.

Helgi could not lie to himself long, he knew the room was small and empty, and that the ears that heard were too dulled by drink and their own thoughts to care what he sang. Still, he was doing it, and that bore him up and forward till he was done. Mark and Aaron both began to clap when he was done. A shock of anger jerked Helgi's head up in the thought that they were mocking him, but no laughter lightened the shadows across their faces as they watched him stand and come back to the bar.

"Did you write that?" Mark asked as Aaron got Helgi another beer.

"Yes."

"You've gotten a lot better. You really have. That was..," Mark's shoulders twitched, as though to shake the memory of the song off like cold water, and Helgi felt the warmth of triumph flushing in his cheeks as his friend went on, "really good. I remember when your singing used to sound like shit."

"Thanks, asshole." Though he tried to keep his tone light, the edge of bitterness sliced Helgi's tongue as he spoke. Better and better, and never yet good, he thought. He wanted to fling his bottle across the room, but drank it empty instead, keeping a tight hold on its neck so that it would not slip from his hand. The pain was still keen through the numbness the draught left in the pit of his stomach. I made it in, he told himself.

Enough potential to be encouraged to continue."Another beer?"

"Sure," Aaron said. "You've earned it. I just hope you're not driving."

"I'm driving," Mark told him. "You think I'd let this drunken maniac get me killed?"

"You're not much better off," Aaron answered. He got Helgi his beer, but gave his brother a Coke. "Don't bitch, Mark, you're not paying for it anyway."

Helgi hardly heard the brothers arguing, he looked at the little bubbles rising behind the cold-dewed green glass, slow as the amber fermentation of the layers of peat and mold beneath dark bog-water, and wondered what he would do.

"I will get better!" He whispered angrily to himself, and drank on it.

Aaron looked at his watch. "Well, guys," he said to the air in general, "it's quarter till two last call for drinks." Two of the men got up and headed towards the bar, one moved for the door, and one stayed where he was. "You two might as well drink up and move on. You sure I can't call you a taxi? I seem to remember getting a lot of beers."

"I've only had three," Mark protested. "He's the drunk one."

"Not that drunk," Helgi replied, getting to his feet. "Thanks, Aaron. It was a great evening."

"I'm glad someone enjoyed it. I'm going to get fired when Prune-Bowels gets back, but what the hell, I only took the job for one reason anyway. See you later."

Mark and Helgi managed to get in without waking Mark's mother. Helgi felt fine until he lay down and closed his eyes, then the room began to spin around him. He clenched his eyelids tighter, feeling himself sucked through the eye of the whirlwind. But I did it, he thought. I made it, and as he thought that, the spinning sped up to the rock-steady whirling of the earth beneath him, braced against the winds that still rushed through his head.

CHAPTER XIV

Hair hooded against the light rain, Hailgi stood beside the deep scar through the green turf, where the earth for the mound had been ripped away. The mound stood high in the middle of the dark wet soil, a drighten's new hall among the grass-grown heaps that rose low beside it. Time might weather his father's howe down, Hailgi knew, but now it stood as a fresh wound among the faded scars. It had not been sealed yet, on the other side, his mother still guided the bondsmen and women to arrange the drighten's grave-goods within his howe. Two days ago, Sigismundar had been strong and hale, laughing as he sparred with Hailgi, who had almost grown to match his father's height in the three years since he came back from Hagalar's fosterage. The Sun was warm for Ostara-month, as though the three moons until Midsummer's had turned already. Dripping with sweat beneath her noonday light, Sigismundar leapt back to push a wave of ruddy hair back from his eyes, then raised his wooden sword again.

Hailgi leapt forward, straight in, the wind of his own rush brushing past him like a spear's swift breeze or a raven's wingtip. He did not notice his father's sudden gasp as the blunt weapon drooped in his hand, nor the stricken look on his graying face, until his own blade was already thumping against the drighten's ribcage. Then Sigismundar was falling. Hailgi was barely able to catch him, to lower him easily to the clover-starred grass. His father's mouth was blue as if with frost, his skin the gray of death already, though he still breathed in great rattling gasps. Hailgi crouched down beside him, grasping Sigismundar's cold hands in his own, trying to pour his own warmth into his father's body, as if the furious racing of his heart could quicken Sigismundar's again. Wodhanar, did I do it? Hailgi thought, his heart clutching inwards in sudden terror. He glanced at his practice sword. He had heard of a reed cast in jest becoming a spear, of a weak loop of withies that became a hangman's noose, but his sword was only wood, and no rent or stain of blood marred Sigismundar's onion-gold tunic. It was not I who dropped him, surely not I witch shot or elf-shot, that leaves no mark.

The cool shadows of men were falling over both of them, the thanes hurrying around.

"What's happened, Hailgi?" Arnugrimar's raspy voice asked. "What's wrong with the drighten?"

Hailgi looked wildly up at the thane's ugly face. When he was very small, he had tugged at Arnugrimar's swollen lump of a nose and poked at the wen above his eye over and over again while the warrior held him up and laughed at his spirit. The memory of his childhood reminded him that he was a man now, and so he answered as evenly as he could, "I don't know. We were sparring. He was fine and then he dropped his sword and fell down. Someone fetch old Amma, fetch her right now! He's still breathing, she may know some healing for it. Stand back, let Sunna's light shine full on him, she'll help him more than any of us can. Ansumundar, give me your Hammer."

The red haired thane took Thonarar's amulet from around his neck. Hailgi swung it over his father's body three times, deosil, murmuring, "Drive out hag-shot, drive out elf-shot, drive out the shot of ill wights."

The thanes moved back a pace, but Hailgi did not rise from his place nor let go of his father's hand. Sigismundar drew in a deep breath, coughed. "Hailgi," he whispered. "My heart struck into my heart, just before you hit me. The god's spear, no healing. Don't let Bergohildar"

The sky's blue still glimmered from his eyes, and his hands grew no colder, but Hailgi knew that his father was dead. Still he did not move until the fat old healer whom everyone in the settlement called Amma came puffing down the hill with her little bags and boxes of herbs and medicines.

"Away now, let me see," she panted.

Hailgi got to his feet, but shook his head. "There's no more you can do." He was surprised at how steady his voice was, how his hands, still cool from his father's dead grasp, did not shake as he took the herb-wife by the shoulders and turned her gently towards the hall. "Go to my mother. He spoke of her at the last. I think he feared that she would try to join his death." He looked at Ansumundar, who stood staring at the earth. "Get together as many of the men as you can and set to building up a mound in the middle of the grave-field by the shore. Arnugrimar, help me here."

Hailgi squatted down, taking his father by the shoulders and heaving the corpse up. Arnugrimar took Sigismundar's legs and they began to make their way back up the hill to their settlement, following a good way behind the herb-wife. They stopped by the gate, standing with their burden. It seemed to Hailgi as though his father's corpse was growing heavier and colder with each breath, he could taste the strong earth in his own mouth.

His mother came out of the gate. Her high-boned face was quite still, the silver pins holding her dark hair in place as neatly and tightly placed as the pegs of a fresh-launched ship.

"Bear him into our house," Bergohildar said. "I have readied our bed for him, you need only to lay him down and I shall see to the rest."

They followed her to the chamber the drighten and his wife had shared, where the fine furs were heaped on the bed and fresh straw strewn on the floor. Sigismundar's best feast tunic was laid out over one of his chests, and the gold and silver threads which adorned it glittered very finely in the noon sunlight flooding through the smoke hole.

"Now leave us be," she ordered. Arnugrimar twisted his hands together, looking down at the floor. He scuffled one foot backward, then forward again.

"I shall stay with you," Hailgi insisted. "You cannot tell me to go away."

"Some things are between man and wife," Bergohildar answered, and his mother's voice, clear and still as snow melt in a hollow of stone, chilled Hailgi to the bone.

"Mother, you shall not follow him. He told me at the last not to let you."

"Go," she said to Arnugrimar and Amma, waving at the door, and both of them went. "This is your hall now, Hailgi. You know as much as your father and I could teach you. You must rule here, with a wife beside you, and no old woman sitting by the fire to give her trouble. I have been frowe in my time. I need no more."

Hailgi wanted to take her by the shoulders and shake her until the brittle ice over her eyes cracked into hot tears. He could not quite bring the wish to his hands, instead he embraced her around the shoulders, pulling the slight bones of her frame into the warm ring of his arms. "I need you, Mother," he murmured. "Life in the mound is long enough, and Father will surely wait for you there, but while you live, I need your rede and help. If you fear he will be lonely within the howe, there are enough maidservants around the hall that the loss of one will not keep us from holding a fitting funeral feast for him in three days' time."

"See, you are ruling the hall already," Bergohildar answered. "What do you need me for? I shall only get in your way. You must be from here, and that is as it should be."

"I cannot rule well without a woman by my side, and none will speak to me about the one I have chosen."

Hailgi's mother pulled away, looking sharply up at him. "You have been told often enough that Sigiruna the daughter of Haganon is not a fitting match for you."

"Why not? No one has ever given me a reason."

Hailgi sat down in his father's large carven chair, his mother sat in her own. She leaned forward, her gray eyes holding his gaze. "Sigiruna comes of strange kin on her mother's side. Some say that she was a walkurja, it is certain that she joyed in strife and the deaths of men, and that she was full of herb-craft and trolldom beyond the knowledge of others. Some have said that while Sigiruna lies at home asleep, her soul fares out to the battlefield to choose the slain, and that she weaves blood and death into her webs. She is surely uncanny. Some young warrior may ask for her hand because her father is the greatest drighten in Sealand, but you have land and might enough that Sigiruna's kin has nothing to buy you with."

"We are kin to the Walsings, and they are uncanny enough," Hailgi argued. "Wasn't Sigimund's own mother a walkurja, and didn't he and Sinfjotli become wolves in the wood up in Gautland?"

"And that is sung to their shame," Bergohildar replied. "No man has ever had joy of a walkurja-bride. Think of Ingwibjorg, Hagalar's daughter, she is of a good age to be married, and I have heard that you might have found her fair."

The warmth rose in Hailgi's face, but did not betray his thoughts. As if she took the echo of red shame for a lover's blush, his mother smiled, and now the tears began to well up in her eyes remembering her own wedding, Hailgi guessed. There was no kindness in speaking further to her of Sigiruna. Now that he was drighten here, he could send his bidding to the Skjoldings soon enough.

"I shall help you here, Mother," he said firmly. "It is my right."

Bergohildar did not protest as Hailgi helped her to strip Sigismundar's body and force his finest feasting clothes over his stiffening limbs. Hailgi saw how his mother's hands trembled, touching his father's cool skin as she had once touched him when he was warm with life. She turned away quickly to get the gold-worked cloak Sigismundar had worn to the high feasts. Hailgi reached beneath his father's body, lifting Sigismundar up so that Bergohildar could spread the cloak beneath him.

"We shall put the rest of his treasures on the bed, and have it borne to the mound. It was our marriage bed, my brother's gift to me, and I shall not sleep in it again until Sigismundar's mound is opened for me."

"Shall he fare alone?"

Bergohildar looked down at the body of her husband, and the tears broke into her voice. "No other woman shall lie beside him in the grave, if you will not let me go now, he must wait for me. Perhaps we should send a thrall to serve him in the mound. it is not fitting that he should kindle his own fires and tend horse and hound within his own hall."

Together Bergohildar and Hailgi chose what Sigismundar should take with him to the mound. They laid the cone-shaped goblet of green Roman glass by his head, but Hailgi kept the silver-bound aurochs horn that his father had drunk from at the holy feasts. Hailgi put the spear into his father's hand and closed Sigismundar's cold fingers around it, as Sigismundar had once curled his son's little hand about a shaft nearly too large for the boy to grip. Bergohildar girded her husband's sword to his side and fastened his cloak with a crystal-set silver fibula as long as a man's hand. They twisted gold rings around his arms and fingers, so that he seemed all twined about with red-glittering wyrms.

At last Bergohildar closed her husband's mouth, then his eyes, and laid two Roman coins on the lids to weight them shut. Only then did she sink down beside his body, her tears flowing. She turned her face away so that the salt droplets would not fall onto the body and torment Sigismund- ar's ghost, the tears were lost in the fresh straw beneath her knees. Hailgi stood staring at his father's face, remembering how pride had lit it for his son's deeds. Sigismundar had never known what had driven Hailgi to slay Hunding never known of the need the woman's skirts had kindled in his son. Hailgi's chest ached as though he had taken the blunt blow of the practice sword full across his own ribs. He felt the hot prickling of tears behind his own eyes, blurring his father's body before him.

A fly buzzed in through the smoke hole, circling Sigismundar's body before lighting at the corner of his mouth. Hailgi reached for it, but it had flown up and away before his hand could touch it. There will be time for me to weep later, he thought. He went to the door, opened it to see Arnugrimar and Amma standing outside in the warm sunlight. "Amma, see to my moth- er," Hailgi ordered, then, to Arnugrimar, "We'll bear his bier to the great hall and drink his arvel tonight, when I take the high seat."

Hailgi and Arnugrimar went to either end of the bed and lifted it up, bear- ing it out. It was only a short way from the drighten's house to his feasting hall, but Hailgi's breath was coming hard and fast by the time they had laid Sigismundar down before the high seat. The smoke-darkened oak of the benches and tables seemed almost unbearably bright to Hailgi, the motes of dust that glimmered in the shafts of light from door and smoke hole glit- tering like sunlight from a gilded byrnie. Hailgi's mouth was too dry for him to speak, his belly taut as a harp's tight-drawn wires. He could not feel the straw and hard earth beneath his shoes, it was as though he were an uproot- ed tree lifted into the air by a strong wind.

He could feel the wind blowing against him, hastening him on faster and faster, its rushing like the sound of an army marching through dry leaves. Hailgi reached for the house pillar beside him, pressing his palms against its sharp corners. The touch of the smooth wood, anchored deep in the earthen floor and rising above him to the roof, slowly brought him down to himself again.

"Are you all right, Hailgi?" Arnugrimar asked.

Hailgi coughed, swallowed hard, licked his lips. "I'm fine." He looked about the hall. Only one of his mother's bonds maidens stood within, leaning on her broom as she watched wide-eyed. "You, Oddny, stop staring and fetch us some ale. Then get the other women to work, we have a funeral feast to hold tonight."

Oddny scurried off at once, Arnugrimar nodded. "You're not wasting any time, are you?"

"There's no time to waste," Hailgi answered. "I think we will not have long to wait in frith, once it is known that Sigismundar is dead. For this reason, I want you to send riders out through all my father's lands, calling all the men who can fight to come here with their weapons ready, for Sigismundar's honor."

Then Hailgi was alone in the hall with his father. He went to kneel down beside the bed. He wanted to speak, but was not sure what to say. Though his sorrow at the sight of his father's gray face ran deep, it bore something better. Sigismundar's son had won the Wolfings' battle, but now he would win the war, and each man slain was another plank in the bridge between Hailgi and Sigiruna, for once the sons of Hunding were dead, Hailgi would hold the north of Jutland without fear of foes at his back, and even the Skjoldings must own him the worthiest man for their maid.

Hailgi knew that Sigismundar must know the thoughts that were in his mind, now, the fallen drighten could see the weave of Hailgi's wyrd more clearly than Hailgi himself could. "I trust in you and your rede, Father," Hailgi murmured. "I know you haven't forsaken me."

Sudden as Sigismundar's death was, the richness of the funeral feast they held that night showed the reach of his might and the fruitfulness his rule had brought to his lands. There was ale enough for all the men who had come at Hailgi's bidding, though more and more byrnie-clad warriors crowded into the hall as the long summer day slowly darkened, and no one could complain that the food was scanty. The high seat was empty till sunset. Hailgi wandered about the hall, greeting the men who had sworn troth to his father. They were watching him carefully to see how he would bear himself, he knew. It would be some time before his place was truly fast among them, for he was young and his father's death had been very sudden. At sunset, Hailgi lifted Sigismundar's war-horn from his father's chest and blew three long blasts of it. The deep notes shook the buzz of talk to silence within the hall, as all the men turned to stare at him. Hailgi set the war-horn down and raised up his father's drinking-horn.

"Now Sigismundar fares to dwell with his kin in the howe, and I alone, I, Hailgi Hunding's-Bane, am left to rule these lands. I have proven myself in battle, and my father placed his trust in me. Would any here question my right to sit in Sigismundar's high seat, or to call the host to the field?" Hailgi looked over the gathered thanes, their faces shadowed by the shifting of sunset light and torch-fires. "Is there any man here who holds that his troth to Sigismundar is not also troth sworn to Sigismundar's son? Speak now, while he lies here to hear it, if you do!"

Hailgi heard the whispers, saw the light gleaming sideways from a few eyes. It was a brave man who would dare the dead, and most of them would be sleeping in the hall that night. He counted nine heartbeats. No one spoke aloud.

"Let the holy ones hear! Wodhanar, first father of the Wolfing line, Ingwe-Freyjar, Tiwar, Thonarar, all you gods, and you kinsmen who have fared before me, I hail you! Bless my rule in my father's steads, bring me sig in battle, and fruitfulness to my folk. Thus I take my udal lands, the earth Sigismundar has left me."

Hailgi took a burning brand from the fire that blazed before the bier. Slowly he walked around the hall, ringing it three time as the folk within his circle watched him in silence. The fire was scorching his knuckles when he cast the stick back into the blaze. He mounted to the high-seat and sat down in it. Bergohildar rose from her own chair and filled his horn with ale. Hailgi raised the drink high.

"Now drink Sigismundar's arvel! He was a mighty drighten, a beloved from to the folk of these lands. We feast to his memory and our love for him, that he shall look well upon us from his howe's high hall."

"Hail Sigismundar!" The warriors shouted, their deep voices like waves crashing upon polished rock. Hailgi drank a mighty draught from the horn, the rich ale spreading its warmth through his body. He had not eaten since early that morning, nor known his hunger until now. The fat cattle roasted for this feast and the plentiful bread and ale had been his father's gift to his folk, Hailgi ate eagerly, looking down to Sigismundar's gold-covered eyes. Now it was Hailgi to whom the gods and goddesses would deem their favor or disfavor. The fruit of sacrifices on Wodhanar's tree would grow into the land's fruitfulness, the flesh of the Yule boar slain for Ingwe-Freyjar would strengthen Hailgi's warriors with the boar's fierce mood in battle. It seemed to Hailgi that he could see the braid winding forward through the twilight, glimmering white and blood-red twining over and under earthy darkness. It was his will that would have to wind it now. That inheritance, too, he had won.

"Hail, Hailgi," a low voice said beside him. He looked up, along the lanky body of the drighten Freyjawulfar Long-Ears, who had held the lands southward of his father's, but always followed Sigismundar in wartime and come to his halls at the high feasts. Freyjawulfar's long nose poked out from a tangle of gray-streaked red hair above and beard below, he looked unkempt as a thistle in late summer, but Hailgi knew he was one of the most powerful men who had followed Sigismundar. Freyjawulfar was not called Long-Ears because of his looks, but because it was said that no word could be whispered in Jutland or Sealand without it coming swiftly to him, and Hailgi knew his father had placed great worth on his friendship.

"Hail, Freyjawulfar," Hailgi answered. "My father would be pleased to see his friend come to his feast."

Freyjawulfar's dark eyes shifted, glancing at the corpse glittering in the firelight, then at the gleams of byrnies and swords around the hall. "It seems as though you expect more than your father's friends here."

"Hunding also had friends, and sons. If we are not ready for them, I think it will not be long before they are here in this hall and drinking the funeral ale of others."

"There are some who might think you are rather over-eager for battle, and that a youth who seeks needless fighting is not the best leader for as many folk as gathered under your father."

"Some might think that," Hailgi said calmly. "But I shall not be surprised if news of their host's marching has reached us before the last spadeful of dirt is flung onto my father's mound. If they do not seek to seize this moment and avenge their father, then I may be called a fool, and they, perhaps, may be called nithlings. You, I trust, mean to keep the troth you swore to my father." Hailgi drank from his horn, then stretched it out to Freyjawulfar. "It gladdens me to share my ale and my father's friendship with you."

Freyjawulfar looked down at the horn. It seemed to Hailgi that he could see the lanky drighten wavering as though he hung in the wind. Hailgi watched steadily, sure that he had left the other no way out. At last Freyjawulfar took the horn from his hand, though he did not yet drink.

"If you prove wrong in this, you shall, no doubt, find that you wish to seek the rede of your father's older friends in matters afterwards?"

"I shall," Hailgi agreed.

Freyjawulfar drank. When he lowered the horn again, beads of froth gleamed white from his tangled beard.

So Hailgi stood by the open mound, while the thralls and bonds maids bore food and ale within for Sigismundar and the thrall Brandar whom they had sent to be the drighten's servant in the howe, when the horseman came from the west, from Hagalar's lands. Hailgi recognized Thurir at once. Dark hollows ringed the quiet thane's eyes, and sweat mingled with rain to drip from the tips of his hair and droopy mustache.

"Hailgi!" He called. "Hagalar calls you to his aid. The sons of Hunding are gathering their host."

"We are ready to ride," Hailgi answered. "Go in and rest now, my mother will give you food and drink. We have only to close my father's mound, and by that time the men will all be gathered here."

The sound of his horn surprised no one, before long, the men of Hailgi's war band and of those drightens who had fought under his father, Freyjawulfar, Hrothormar Bear-Sark, Raganar, and Theudowinar, were mounted and drawn up in lines. Swain had saddled Hailgi's horse and stood holding it together with his own, waiting for his drighten. When everyone was looking at him, Hailgi turned and walked alone into the mound. Sigismundar's bed had been laid inside a low boat. The ship's oars and mast were broken, and a hole had been staved into the bottom to slay it into the worlds beyond. A full keg of ale stood beside it, a wooden plate with cheese and bread and a bowl filled with dried apples and fresh strawberries.

The body of the thrall Brandar lay inside the boat, at the foot of the bed, he had been beheaded and his limbs tied up to keep him from walking back to the lands of the living. Sigismundar's treasures had been moved to one side of the bed, the other was empty, waiting for the day when the mound should be opened again and Bergohildar laid in beside her husband. It was too dark inside the mound for Hailgi to see his father's body very clearly, nor did he wish to look more closely. A hint of rot tainted the howe's air already, and Sigismundar's clothes were tight on him, as if he were swelling in death.

"Father," Hailgi murmured, "give your blessing to this faring. My victory here shall hold your lands safe for my lifetime, if I win. Let me bear your luck into battle."

Hailgi did not know what he awaited, but when his father's right arm dropped, flopping limply from his chest across the empty half of the bed, his awe choked the cry of shock in his throat. Hailgi waited a moment, but Sigismundar did not move again. He knew that the death-stiffening of bodies did not last forever, but the loosening of his father's limbs struck him speechless.

The movement had dislodged one of the gold rings around Sigismundar's wrist, so that it had come half-off. This, Hailgi knew, must be his father's gift to him and the sign of his blessing. He pulled it free and slipped it onto his own arm. "Thank you, Father," he murmured. "I'll bear it well." Swiftly, before his own thoughts could betray him into cowardice, he bent to hug the dead man about the shoulders, then recrossed Sigismundar's arms and folded his hands around his spear again. The clear gray light outside the mound hurt Hailgi's eyes when he straightened up into the daylight. He blinked back tears, walking before his men and raising his arm.

"Sigismundar has given us his blessing and his battle-luck!" He called. "Now we shall surely have victory!"

A cheer went up as Swain brought Hailgi's horse Wigablajar over and handed him the reins. The youth's eyes were very wide, his hand shaking, and he pulled back from Hailgi as quickly as he could, as though the awe of the dead still hung about him. Hailgi's fallow steed danced about him uneasily, nostrils flaring, until Hailgi put a firm hand on his neck to still his shivering. He mounted up and took a spear from Swain's hand, waiting until the other young man had also mounted. Then Hailgi raised his spear, pointing it westward, towards Hunding's lands. "Forward!" He cried, spurring his horse to a trot. A host of hooves churned the wet earth behind him.

After a little while, Freyjawulfar rode up beside Hailgi, though he kept as much space between them as the road allowed. "You were right about the sons of Hunding," the older drighten admitted. "I hadn't thought they'd be ready to move against you so fast not since the hard times they had after you killed old Hunding."

Hailgi did not answer. He remembered his father's dying words, and that Sigismundar had thought himself struck down by a spear, one cast from an unseen hand.

"Can you speak of what happened in the mound?" Freyjawulfar asked. "Your face is pale."

"Sigismundar lowered his arm, and gave me a ring for his blessing. This faring will be lucky, as I said before. I am not fey, nor are many of those who ride with us."

Freyjawulfar passed a hand over the bronze boar that crested his helmet, as if to call Ingwe-Freyjar to ward him. "Good seldom comes from coming too close to the dead. Going of your own will into the mound is hardly safer than pledging your troth to one of War Father's wish-maidens who choose the slain."

"What do you know about Wodhanar's wish-maidens?" Hailgi answered. "Do you know anything of Sigiruna the daughter of Haganon, who dwells in Sealand?"

"I know that it will be a long time, if ever, before a man comes to wed her, and that for your father's sake, I would give you rede against thinking too much on her. He was no friend who spoke of her to you. There are many maidens fairer, and few so uncanny or perverse of will. I do not know whether she is truly one of the Grim One's own maids or not, but I am sure that her favor would be no kindlier than his." Freyjawulfar stroked his helm-crest again, dashing a few droplets of rain from the boar's gleaming back. "Some gifts are not worth their price, and victory is little comfort to a corpse."

Hailgi said nothing. He could not set into words what Sigiruna's gaze had been to him, only remember fierce joy bleeding from a wound and his strength bearing up the weight of byrnie and helm as he looked upward to where she rode. Speechless as a sword in the scabbard, he could only shake his head.

"There will be time later for you to think on marriage, if you live out this battle," Freyjawulfar said when they had ridden a little way. "Tell me now, how do you mean to fight the sons of Hunding?"

Hailgi remembered the night of strife that had followed Hunding's death. Though his sons had made peace among themselves, he thought it could hardly be an easy one. "They will find it hard to fight together, and none will be like to take orders from another. We must do our best to scatter them on the field, and stay together ourselves, perhaps in a tight wedge or shield-wall. Past that, I can only tell when I have seen the field where we'll fight. There will be no hope of taking them by surprise, and little chance to send our men about." He paused. "Has anyone heard tidings of Blindi Bale-Wise coming back to Hunding's hall?"

"Lingwe still dwells with his mother's kin, or so he did when I last heard of him, and the two of his brothers who are nearest to him in age have joined him there. No one has spoken of Blindi for near to three years now, perhaps he is dead, and good riddance if it's so."

"I would find it fair to meet Lingwe on the field," Hailgi murmured. He could feel the treacherous blush in his cheeks as he remembered the shameful touch of Hunding's youngest son, the heat flared the more at Freyjawulfar's chuckle.

"You've all the warrior-mood that men say you have," the older man marked. "Maybe the fight after next, if Hunding's other sons are slain, I've little doubt that Lingwe will be swift to try claiming his inheritance." He spat into the wet grass. "The little shit's Blindi's fosterling through and through. Can't quite call him a coward. I've heard he's showed himself brave enough in sword-play, in battle and single fighting both, but there's something nasty about him."

"There is," Hailgi agreed, feeling oddly reprieved.

Ansumundar and Swain set up Hailgi's tent that night, they said they would be sharing it with him, and Hailgi could not argue. Of all the men there, they had been his thanes first.

"No ill feelings about fighting men you used to know?" Hailgi asked the big warrior when they settled down by the fire.

Ansumundar grunted. "I'm your thane now, and my family's settled on your lands. What's to feel ill about?"

"There's some I'll be glad to see at the other end of my spear," Swain chimed in. Like Hailgi, he had grown a great deal in the last three years. A lot of training had made the shepherd boy a passable warrior, though he would never be Hailgi's match. "I remember how they used to cuff me when I wasn't fast enough, or when they had nothing else to do. I used to think then how I'd like to pay them back in iron, and now you're giving me my chance."

"So long as you remember to hold tight with us, and don't break the shield-line," Hailgi warned. "An over-eager attack is little help."

His deep yawn caught him off-guard, he had no chance to muffle it or turn it into a cough.

"Sounds like you need to go to sleep," Ansumundar commented. The big man's gaze suddenly slid downward, and he cleared his throat. "Uh, Hailgi, we'll be in the tent with you. If you should start shouting, or saying um, strange things in your sleep, should we better wake you, or leave you be? You weren't an easy sleeping companion on the way to Fetter Grove."

"Wake me," Hailgi said. "And be sure to wake me at dawn this time, no matter what I'm doing or saying in my sleep."

Hailgi slept soundly that night, with no dreams that he remembered, and woke stiff and cold to the gray-green light of dawn, it was he who wakened Ansumundar and Swain. The rain had stopped for the moment, but the beeches were still dripping beneath the clouded sky, and the fires were all out. The men breakfasted on dried fish and hard bread, muttering about the cold and damp as they mounted. Wigablajar's warm hide felt good under Hailgi, the fallow horse's heat working into his body as he rode and loosening his muscles. A shroud of gray-beaded spiderwebs draped the green bushes along the side of the road, veiling the white dog-roses like rain hiding clouds.

Behind him, Hailgi could hear Bow-Athalwulfar's nasal voice complaining about the weather and what it would do to his strings if it kept up. If the weather held damp, there would be little use for archery on either side, Hailgi thought. They would be fighting toe to toe along the field. He thought he would have the advantage there. He was likely to have more men, and more experienced warriors as well. Still, his father had told him that such battles were best avoided when he could. When closely matched forces met head-on, even the winner was likely to find he had lost more than he could spare at the end of the day. He glanced back along the road, where the horsemen rode by twos and threes.

They trust me, he thought. Or at least they trusted my father enough to risk their lives on his son's leadership. Hailgi's place alone at the head of the host hardly seemed real to him. Sigismundar's laugh was more real, the sense that his father had just dropped back behind him for a moment to speak to one of the other men, and the feeling of Sigismundar's warm hand patting his shoulder to steady him. In time Sigismundar would have sent Hailgi out from his hall to lead a band, not the full host, but that was only a matter of numbers, and waited in his hall, as he waited now. The thought strengthened Hailgi's heart, and more when he thought that it was truly his own battle he would be fighting, against foes he had won for himself.

Cheered, Hailgi began to sing very softly to himself. His raven hoarse voice croaked worse than usual in the dampness, but no one was close enough to hear.

"Light goes the dance through land and grove
The helm-proud drighten rode high through the wood,
to his bridal ale bade he the folk come,
light goes the dance through land and grove"

By the time they stopped for their mid-day meal, the sky had lightened and a sharp wind from the west was beginning to break through the clouds. Hailgi was the first to hear the sound of hooves on the muddy road. A single rider, moving briskly. He set his half-eaten bread down on a flat stone and stood with his spear in his hand, straining his eyes through the trees to see who was coming. Hailgi did not recognize the tall blond man who rode up on a long-legged gray horse. His bright red cloak and the gold clasp pinning it showed him to be an atheling, but he was not one of Hagalar's men. The rider turned his spear so that the butt of it pointed at Hailgi.

"Hai, boy! I have come under the seal of frith, with a message for Hailgi Sigismundar's son. Can you tell me where to find him?"

Hailgi held tight to his temper. It seemed to him that the first skirmish of the battle had begun.

"I am Hailgi Hunding's-Bane, whom you seek," he replied calmly. "What message do you bring?"

The rider looked down his long nose at him, pursing thin lips as his gaze moved up and down Hailgi's body. "You are fair-faced enough, and your beard scant enough, that the stories may be true, though I will grant that you are too well-thewed now to easily be taken for a maiden."

Hailgi's rage shuddered through his body like wind shaking an aspen leaf, but he gripped his spear-shaft and brought a smile to his face. "I think Hunding could have told you the difference three years ago if the ravens had not eaten out his tongue where I left him lying on the wal-stead."

"You may have bought free of your shame there, but the geld will be very high now. The sons of Hunding have sent me to claim the payment for their father. Two dozen marks of gold is the price they ask for Hunding's death, and Hagalar, who helped you in the killing, must yield up his land and folk to them. If you do not have the gold, your land from its eastern march to the place where your hall stands will serve as payment in its place. This will buy your life, if you cannot pay for it, then meet the sons of Hunding at the field below Loga Fells and give up your life there beside the Eagle's Stone."

"For beggars, the sons of Hunding are oddly arrogant," Hailgi answered. "Most who cannot work or fight for their livelihoods ask no more of their betters than an egg or a piece of bread. If they are so hungry, I am free with my food, and I have pigs and cattle enough to find work for all of them on my land. If they have learned bravery after three years, and think they can threaten me with their strength, I have another payment for them." Hailgi raised his spear to the sky, high into the rising wind, as a heavy cloud's shadow passed over his face. "I offer them a great storm of gray spears, of Wodhanar's wrath. Frodhi's frith shall shatter between us, and the Storm-Bringer's gray hounds shall feed well on the field when I have walked from it with my winnings. Bear this message to the sons of Hunding, boy, and take yourself and your nag from our road before we ride you down!"

The spear turned in Hailgi's hand, hissing through the air to pass within a hairsbreadth of the messenger's narrow skull, and thunked deep into the trunk of an ash-tree behind him. Pale eyes wide, the man backed his horse up a few steps, then whirled and galloped off with the laughter of Hailgi's men rising behind him as the first heavy spatters of rain beat against his back.

"Hail Hailgi!" Helmbernu shouted. "We'll send the Hound's sons back to their kennels with a whipping!" Other warriors were laughing and cheering agreement. Freyjawulfar watched from the side, a slow smile spreading across his face as Hailgi wrenched his spear from the tree and turned back towards his host.

Hailgi saw the lightning flickering against the black clouds sweeping in from the west as the rain fell harder, he raised his weapon to it, staring along the spear's length as though the lightning's flash from its tip might point the way to the maiden who rode white through the storm. He did not see her, but he felt as though the lightning's might tingled down the spear into his own body.

"See! Wodhanar and Thonarar ride with us," he called, his voice ringing harsh through the cheers of his men and the rising hiss of the heavy rain through the leaves. "Onward now, the sooner we're there, the sooner we can fight them!"

Hailgi mounted up, and the others scrambled to follow him. Wigablajar stood trembling with eagerness as Hailgi climbed to his back, and Hailgi had to rein him in to keep him from dashing down the road ahead of the others as they began to ride again. The storm was waxing, new green leaves, torn early from their limbs, whipped past Hailgi on the wind, tangling in the amber strands of wet hair that beat about his face, and the back of his cloak was quickly soaked through. When Hailgi could bear it no longer, he loosed Wigablajar's reins, shouting, and let his steed bear him as swiftly as he could, hooves scattering the mud in a spray behind him. It seemed to Hailgi that his galloping was its own wild drumbeat, that he could hear high voices crying on the wind, cutting through his cold-numbed ears.

He brandished his spear as he rode, crying out, "Sigiruna, Sigiruna" for he was sure she could not be far. The lightning's great flash blinded Hailgi, the crash of Thonarar's Hammer shaking the earth under him. Wigablajar stopped dead, shivering, as Hailgi tried to blink the brightness from his eyes. The lightning's afterimage was burning through the rain, a tree whose trunk had been twice as wide as Hailgi's outstretched arms flaring into flames before him with a greedy wyrm-hiss of steam billowing out as the rain poured down into the fire. Shaken, Hailgi looked around. He had not left the road, but he had ridden far ahead, out of sight of the others. He stroked Wigablajar's rain-darkened neck until the horse's shivering died down, then turned his head about to ride back to the host. By sunset they had crossed the marches of Hagalar's lands, though they were still some way from his hall.

Hrothormar Bear-Sark rode up beside Hailgi. His furred hood up over his head, he looked like a troll or beast on horseback in the rain and gathering dark, and the low muttering in his throat sounded much like a growl. He had come down from the north with his band of twelve berserks a few years before Hailgi was born, and taken a fair piece of land before Sigismundar led the other drightens of the area against him. No one knew whether it was good sense or some whisper from Wodhanar, giver of the berserk-wod, that had caused Hrothormar to take the frith Sigismundar had offered and pledge his troth to the Wolfing drighten, but he had kept that troth, and a score of years had long eased his allies' wariness of the berserk-band.

"Going on, or stopping here?" Bear-Sark asked. "Be too dark to ride soon, unless you know the way well."

"I know it well enough to find Hagalar's hall in the dark. It's straight along the road, anyway, and if each man follows the one in front of him, no one will get lost."

"Too wet for torches," Bear-Sark grumbled in agreement. "It won't be bad sleeping indoors tonight, especially with a battle laid for tomorrow. My bones've been moaning at me since this morning, maybe I'm just getting old, but I don't think the weather's like to be any better by morning." He rode back to spread the word to his own men.

Luckily, the road was straight and smooth, so that even in the rain-thick darkness the host could follow it through until they saw the torchlight gleaming between the logs ringing Hagalar's garth. Hailgi rode ahead of the rest, beating on the gate with the butt of his spear.

"Hai!" He shouted. "Hailgi Hunding's-Bane has come with his host. Will you let us in?"

The gate swung aside and Hailgi rode in. The fires burning in the little shelter where the guard sat showed him Hagalar's deep creased face, the drighten's look of strain not easing as he hurried up to Hailgi's side.

"You came more swiftly than we had feared you might," Hagalar rumbled. "Let my men take care of your horses, and come in. There is little time to talk. Have you brought all those who rode behind your father?"

"I have," said Hailgi. He swung out of the saddle, handing his horse's reins to Swain.

Wulfrun met him with a horn of hot ale as he walked in. "Greetings, Hailgi, and our thanks for the help you have brought us." The frowe's dark dress hung heavily on her frame, she had grown thinner, and white coils wound through her dark braids like pale serpents creeping through the earth. Something in her manner made Hailgi uneasy, and he glanced swiftly about the hall.

"Where are Ingwibjorg and Gunthahildar?" He asked.

Wulfrun's wince tightened the lines of pain about her eyes and mouth. "Hunding's sons have taken them as pledges, so that we will be able to give you no help in the battle tomorrow." She did not say it aloud, but it seemed to Hailgi that he could hear the words in the frowe's mind. *Whether you win or lose, we fear for what may befall them when they are no longer useful to Hunding's sons.*

Hailgi thought again of how Lingwe had handled him, at another man's feast, when there had been no blood-strife between Hagalar and Hunding's sons, and this time, the hot blood rose from his anger at the thought of how Hunding's men had found it right to deal thus with maids.

"We shall win them back safe for you tomorrow," Hailgi answered her. "Be sure of that, and if any has harmed them, I shall cut the guilty man's living guts from his body myself." He raised the horn to drink upon his pledge, letting the hot ale flow down his throat to soak the cold from his bones. It was very strong, as ale often became by winter's end, and Wulfrun had sweetened the draught with honey and herbs.

Hagalar called his thralls to build up the fires and bring food as Hailgi's dripping troops began to make their way in. The warmth of the hall was welcome, Hailgi found himself standing close enough to the flames for steam to rise from his sodden cloak. The other drightens gathered close by him to talk about their battle-plans for the next day. The Loga Fells were well within Hagalar's land, but Hailgi had little doubt that the sons of Hunding would be drawn up on the field already by the time his own host got there. It was Hailgi's thought that a swine-wedge would be the strongest formation for the full host, but Raginar reminded him that many of their men were farmers just come from the spring planting, and little-used to fighting closely together. At best, they could hold to a straight shield-wall.

"Sometimes," said Fastawulfar, taking a slow draught from his own horn, "your father would gather the best-trained thanes into a swine-wedge to break the foe's line, with the shield-wall following to bear them down afterwards. It is in my mind that this would serve you well against the sons of Hunding."

Hailgi had to agree with him, and their talk turned to the questions of who should stand where, and how Hunding's sons were likeliest to deal with them. It had been a hard ride, however, and soon the mixture of the hall's warmth and Wulfrun's strong ale brought Hailgi to yawning. He was not the only one, either, more than a few warriors had already draped their cloaks on benches by the fires to dry and made themselves beds in the dry straw.

"You can sleep back in the girls' chamber if you like, Hailgi," Hagalar offered. "Audhar will go somewhere else, and you'll be more comfortable there than you will out here."

"I thank you for the offer, but I ought to stay out here with my men," Hailgi answered. Still, it would be well to sleep early. They would be rising at dawn, with a half day's march and then a battle ahead of them. The spot he chose was no further from the fire than was needed to keep the sparks from flying into the straw, and the low sea-roar of men's voices in his ears faded swiftly into the darkness of sleep.

Hailgi woke struggling against the hands that held him, twisting and kicking in the darkness until he broke free, his shoulders thumping down into the straw. The grasp on his feet let go quickly, and he rolled over into a fighting crouch, drawing his sword. His hair was wet, sweat stinging in his eyes and dripping salty as blood into his mouth. He could just barely see the shapes around him in the dim glow of the embers, but he could tell that he had been carried out of the great hall into one of the rear chambers.

"Hailgi, it's us," Ansumundar's voice said softly. Now Hailgi could make out his thane's hulking shadow. "You told us to wake you, but you lay with your eyes open, and wouldn't move."

"You were crying out in your sleep, and saying things," Swain added. "Some of the men, those who don't know you so well, were becoming a feared, not me, but one of Hagalar's thanes said you'd done the same when you went to fight with Hunding."

"And on the way to Fetter-Grove" Ansumundar cut off sharply. "It means no ill for us, I'd guess."

"Lie down, Hailgi," Freyjawulfar's calm voice broke in. "You ought to be in here, anyway, not out there in the straw. Rest, we'll need you at your best in the morning."

Hailgi lay down, letting the others cover him with blankets. He thought a scent of roses and sea-salt still hung about the bedding. They had brought him into the room where Ingwibjorg and Gunthahildar had slept, after all. His body ached as though he had been wrestling all night.

Ansumundar and Swain went out, but Freyjawulfar stayed back a moment. "What did you see?" He whispered. "Were you speaking to our foes, or to us?"

"I don't know," Hailgi answered. He tried to remember, to dredge something of his dream up from the dark well of the night. Closing his eyes and letting the drowsiness rise around him, he could feel the words dripping into his throat, coming faster and faster like ale from a new-breached cask. "The dead were all around me, and she was there, bright in the howe. The gray heath-dwellers wait for the sons of Hunding, the Wolfing is the troll-woman's brother, but the bloody eagle shall tear Lingwe in a land far from here for my kinsman's vengeance, and the raven's song shall rule the swan, the wolf's howl fair-worded for those who know his blood. A great slaying, but no end, the dead rise weaponed and their wounds still run with walkurjas' wine to lure their kisses, but you shall live through this day and I shall live through that and through the day's spear and come again from the mound of my kin, we shall all."

Freyjawulfar's hand cracked against Hailgi's face, shocking him into still wakefulness. "No more!" The older drighten whispered. "Hailgi, no more!"

Hailgi blinked, shaking his head. "Did you understand any of what I said?"

"Very little, I think. You must sleep alone after this. I had heard before that you said strange things in your sleep and that Hagalar's men had become wary of what the Grim One or his daughters might say to you in the night, but nothing had been spoken of it in the past three years, and men often cry out in their sleep after their first battles. And so it is often, but you must sleep alone." Freyjawulfar paused. "It may be Hrothormar Bear Sark can give you better rede in this than I. The kin-soul of the Wolfings is not ill-suited to his teachings, though they might make you less suited to your place if you follow his ways too closely."

Hailgi settled back and closed his eyes, but his face still stung from Frey-jawulfar's slap, and his entrails felt deeply unsettled. If I win tomorrow, he thought, no one will look ill upon me for what I say in my sleep, and if I lose, then I will have no reason to worry within the howe. Still, he could hear the sounds of soft talking in the hall beneath the grating rumble of snores, and he felt as far from the fellowship of men as he had been when he had slept in this chamber before.

Sigiruna would understand. Folk looked upon her with the same wari-ness, for she, too, fared beyond their home-ring into the worlds beyond the Middle-Garth. There beneath the same blankets that had covered Ingwib-jorg and himself, Hailgi curled around his loneliness, calling Sigiruna's mir-rored image to his mind again. If she were here beside me, I would not be alone, nor would my limbs feel so cold, Hailgi thought. The ache he felt was much like the longing for home he had felt in his first months with Haga-lar, honed keener by his knowledge that he might die without ever holding Sigiruna in his arms. Lying awake would bring her no nearer, and loss of sleep tonight would do him little good in the battle tomorrow, so Hailgi let himself dream of holding her warmth against his body, strength beneath slim softness, the rose-scent of her amber-bright hair, and so to ease into a fairer dream of Sigiruna than the one which had wakened his fellows.

CHAPTER XV

As the summer heat of Dallas rose through June and into a scorching, steamy July, Karin found that she was meeting Rof at Bobbi's steakhouse more and more often when the two of them were off duty. It was only a few days after the Fourth when she noticed that they were both automatically glancing about themselves for other base personnel, then sliding into the darkest booth at the far back of the eatery where they would be least likely to draw notice, like pilots lurking in a cover of heavy cloud lest they draw fire.

"We have to stop meeting like this," Karin said. She meant it as a joke, but Rof did not laugh. He shrugged his heavy shoulders, straightening the straps of his dun coveralls.

"Yeah, yo' right. I've heard a few words already 'bout it, won' be too long befo' you do, too. Fraternization down here it's not jus' court-martial, it's lynchin', if you know what I mean. Only protection you got so far, most of the guys still think yo' a dyke. No offense."

"None taken. So, if we don't meet here, where can we meet?"

Rof lowered his voice, a soft rumbling whisper through the neon-lit gloom. "You really talkin' about fraternization?"

Karin blinked. Rof sat still, his big hands resting on the table, she stared at them, remembering how gently and skillfully they caressed the wires of her plane, Rof's rich chocolate skin glistening with oil against the shining metal as he checked and repaired and polished. "I don't know yet," she murmured back. "At least not being separated from the only friend I've got down here and the man to whom I trust my life."

"Yes," Rof murmured, his deep, soft voice shaking through Karin like the first bone-trembling growl of her engines. "That be a mighty trust. Well."

The sergeant glanced upwards, his heavy brows drawn as though he were staring into the dark air for an answer. He shook his head slightly, as if to twitch off a gnat, then settled his huge body more comfortably in the cramped space between table and bench.

"Well. Seems to me, if we want to get to know each other better, we ought to be learnin' a little of where we come from. I tell you what. You give me a couple o' them Vikin' books you always readin', let me find out more about yo' folk, and when we both have a night off again, you come to my momma's house fo' dinner. She, I better tell you this now, befo' we get too much farther. She an orisha-priestess, given to Oya. That mean anything to you? No? Well, some folks might call it voodoo, and some might call it Santeria. Got you there! Ain't nobody got cause to fear her, so long as they don' do harm to her or hers, but she be a mighty powerful woman."

Rof's face was set like a wide carved mask of ebony, but his dark eyes held Karin's, warm and alive, and she could feel her breath quickening. At last, she had found a man who cared about his own roots and traditions as she did. "Do you also do this?" She asked.

"Not me. No, I got a little sight, can read people pretty good, but I ain't no orisha priest. Never had the time to learn or be initiated, and never wanted to get too far into the mojo, my momma cast the cowries when I was born, warn me all my life that I better not get too close, lest it be my death. Someone got to do it, everywhere, but I be happy enough to leave it to them that does. An' you?"

"I worship the gods of my forebears, I follow the Asatro," Karin answered slowly. "I don't know anyone else who does, except maybe."

"Except who?" Rof asked. Though he sat still, Karin could see the great muscles tightening beneath his dark skin, like a huge black panther scenting the prey.

"A boy I used to know, the son of my parent's friends, five years younger than me, the one who gave me my valknútr." She touched the silver pendant at her throat. "He was interested in the runes and I sent him a book of myths, but I think it was all Dungeons and Dragons to him, I'm sure he never believed in the old ways. He was just a kid, anyway. He's probably long since forgotten it."

Rof's eyes narrowed slightly, but he said nothing. Karin could not help remembering Helgi's skinny, pale figure against the snow, his rough teenage awkwardness, so weak and frail in her memory against Rof's solid sureness. "There were never any little neighborhood girls with crushes on you when you were the high school football hero, Rof?" She asked lightly. "Come on, I don't believe that."

Rof laughed, and Karin could feel his body easing. She could almost feel his warmth across the booth, like a thick arm around her shoulder. "Guess there mighta been a few. Mostly my teammates' little sisters, at that. Well, you wanta come meet my momma next Friday?"

"Sure."

As Rof and Karin drove towards Oakcliff, Karin noticed that the houses were getting dingier, that the folk living in them were sitting out on screened porches in the heat of the early dusk, and more and more car windows and house doors were open to catch the slight breeze, rather than closed to seal in air conditioning. Karin also noticed that the children playing on the spotty yellow lawns among the pieces of bright plastic and rusty lawnmower guts were nearly all black or Hispanic, with only a few poor whites mixed in here and there. She knew that her military training would make her more, not less, careful if she had to walk there alone, she watched the news often enough to know how many shootings took place in the area and, even behind the wheel of her jeep, the back of her neck prickled when a cluster of youths in wide trousers with the baggy rears hanging to their knees and backward-turned caps stared in through the window at her as she waited for the light to change.

Now Karin knew in her heart that she was an invader here, a foreigner who would have to watch her step and speak softly, waiting for Rof to guide her into his culture. A guide such as he would not be needed when she brought him to meet her parents. She had already heard him speak as clearly as any television broadcaster, and seen his manner switch to military precision in the flicker of an eyelid, she suspected that he would be able to carry himself perfectly where ever he went. Rof's family home was a big shingled house, though the white paint on the wooden pillars around the edge of the porch showed dingy stains of weathering, and the cracked slabs of cement that led through the lawn to the steps in tilted at different angles, the lawn was clean and neatly mowed, and the sprinklers were just sputtering down. Karin let her jeep coast into the driveway, gliding over the shuddering potholes as if they were patches of rough air, and parked neatly behind an ancient brown Mustang.

"Now, remember about that crowned pot," Rof murmured to Karin. "Don' touch it, don' ask about it, don' get near it without Momma invite you to. Think of, well, Oya, she a little like your Freyja, a fierce, fiery woman, but she also got wind and lightnin' in her hands, like a Valkyrie. She dangerous as hell when roused, that sure."

"I will remember."

The first thing that struck Karin was the heavy sweet smell of perfume, like a rain-forest riot of flowers just passing ripeness. The inside of the house was darker than Karin expected. She had to blink a few times, letting her eyes shift downward to the rich amber gloom. The walls of the living room where they had come in were painted deep brown, only a single lamp glowed, its light struggling through a thick orange shade. The lamp burned next to a chest covered with a cloth in a multi-colored floral pattern, on top of the cloth rested several rattles and big cheap paper fans. In the middle of the chest squatted the wide shape of a pot draped in the same cloth, on top of it was a copper crown adorned with cut-outs of stars, crescent moon, and lightning bolt.

It seemed to Karin that she could feel the power beating out of it like a hot wind, she nodded towards it, a respectful tilt of her head. Everything in the room was kept tidier than Karin could keep her own apartment on base. The gleaming brown linoleum, the immaculately dusted shelves of fans, knickknacks, and tall orange candle-glasses with pictures and short prayers frosted onto the glass, the maroon couch where only the end of a mended rip showed beneath the clean golden slipcover. The woman who ghosted out of one of the open doorways was much taller than Karin, but very thin, her skin shone eggplant-dark in the dim amber light, and the turban she wore a rich winding of maroon and burnt pumpkin, brown and gold and orange towered high even above Rof's head. A thick tangle of colored bead-strands hung about her neck like an Egyptian collar, her loose tunic and floor-length skirt were the same fabric as that which covered her shrine, all the burning shades of autumn blossoming in great flowers. Karin could see the fire deep within her dark brown eyes, like the heat deep within coals. She braced her own back straight, as if she were a private on review, and met the priestess' gaze squarely.

"So," the woman whispered, her deep, heavily accented voice a bare breath hissing out of her mouth. "Mah son brings you here, we see how wise he choose?"

Karin did not know what Rof's mother meant, but she nodded nevertheless. If it were a challenge, she would not be found wanting.

"Ovah heah, wheah Lady of the Winds can see you cleah." Rof's mother took a small orange-striped bag and a square of patterned maroon cloth from the top of the shrine, squatting down before it and gesturing Karin towards her. Karin crouched down on the other side, carefully poised to spring up. She could feel the power prickling more strongly over her skin, and did not know yet whether it meant her well or ill.

"Now we cast the cowries we see whet hah you bring good or evil to mah son."

The orisha-priestess began to murmur beneath her breath, rubbing the bag between her hands. It seemed to Karin that her movements stirred something deep in memory, cupped hands pale in the darkness, shaking something that clattered not with the porcelain clinking of the shells, but with the duller rattling of blood-stained wood, the rattling of Óðinn's runes, lots cast before the holy harrow to gain the will of the gods.

The cowries fell out of the bag, sixteen little shells, pale toothed ovals with gold-ringed backs. Karin could not read their falling, some close and some scattered, but she could see the sharp facial muscles tightening under the other woman's purple-black skin, and hear the soft snake-hiss through her teeth.

"Touch nothin'," she said to Karin, standing up and shaking a brief shudder of breeze from her full skirt. "Best you stand outside. Rof, you stay heah."

Bewildered, Karin walked carefully out. She stood with her back braced against the jeep as if she were practicing S&R in a war zone, ready to dodge behind or beneath it, or leap in and roar off, if she could.

It was only a few minutes before Rof stormed out, his teeth showing yellow in a snarl of anger and the screen door banging shut behind him. But his voice was mild by the time Karin had started the jeep up. "You know anywheres good to drink? Guess I wouldn' mind havin' a few shots o' whiskey and sayin' a few words, if it don' offend you an' you don' mind drivin' me back to base. Nothin' bad about you, I don' think," he added hastily.

Karin shrugged. "I left here before I was legal. Anywhere you want to go?"

They ended up at a bar down across from Fair Park, where the walls were all painted black and most of the customers were neo-Goths staring moodily into huge martini glasses. "Mostly I drink at Bar o' Soap across the alleyway," Rof apologized, "but they don' got no hard liquor license, and tonight I jus' feel the need." He downed his shot, waved for another. Karin sipped on her beer, watching him.

"My momma, she tell me the cowries, they talk 'bout yo' early death, mine too, if I stay with you. She tell me, get away, transfer off base or get you to go."

"What do you think?"

"I think. I read them books. You follow the Grim One, the One-Eyed, that so?"

"Yes."

"I think yo' in danger. And yeah, I think if I don' watch close, I could be too. They ain't nothin' set so hard it can' be changed. Job I got, I watch over you better than anyone could, and I aim to keep doin' that 'cause I want to see you alive an' well till the end of your days. And that fo' sure won' happen if I turn an' run like a dog with his tail between his legs. My momma say stay away, but a grown man's got to make his choices, you understan'? An' I'll choose to stay with you, if you'll have me."

Karin reached out and took Rof by the hand. His grasp was warm and rough, strong enough to hold her hand safe without seeming to trap her.

"I wouldn't mind breaking a few regulations with you, Sergeant Rof."

Rof's kiss was rich and musky with the whiskey he had drunk, his lips tenderly easing into Karin's, the first kiss she had given anyone since high school, she suddenly realized. The neo-Goths stared white-faced from under their dyed black bangs as Karin and Rof stood, making their way out of the bar and towards the parking lot.

"Weird women winging, the white swan's singing,

The sky is a bell and the lightning's ringing,

Eagle rides bright above black raven's flight,

Wolf is waiting for gray-grim wight."

Helgi shifted a few of the levers on his new synthesizer and punched a setting button with one hand, changing his instrumentation as he moved out of the song's chorus into the next verse. The instrument that took up his entire desk was half a graduation present, half-bought with money from two months of working at the gas station, and he had spent every free moment at it for the last month.

He had moved out of student housing and lived in his own apartment now, in Oakcliff, near I-30. It was only two cramped rooms, a bathroom, and a kitchen he could hardly turn around in. Rap music boomed out all night from the windows across the street, and he had needed to install extra chains on the doors and bars on the windows, but it was Helgi's own, the rent paid with his first check as a teacher's assistant in the music department at Jefferson, and no one complained if he cranked his synthesizer up full blast, even after midnight. It also had a little fenced backyard where Helgi could practice his katas for the amusement of the Claymore children who lived downstairs or, if he was so inclined during the daytime, gaze out his window at the sun-burnt sweep of Mr. Claymore's broad belly as the man lay dozing on his recliner. Helgi changed his left-hand drums from their running triads to a sharp hard double beat, right hand ripping out a high lead guitar with enough distortion to give it a cutting edge.

"Rain beats hard in the streets,
our battle's harsh between sheets.
Driving fast with lightning's lash,
trusting in thunder's crash."

If Helgi were careful of his range, he could get four instruments at a time on the same keyboard, from a bass like mountains walking to a trumpet setting which he'd modified for his solo interludes on this song until it sounded like a human voice wailing through the brass. It was wailing finely now, calling through the rain that hissed in Helgi's saxophone and the soft tympani running on auto-accompany.

"Word-spears fly swift through the years,
the warrior's wounded by tears.
I bear my shield, dead on the field,
and still I will not yield."

As Helgi reached up to change settings again, the high beep of his watch needled through the music.

"Shit," he muttered, shutting down the synthesizer in mid-note and picking up the pile of music that lay beside it. As always when he had finished playing well, the space around him seemed eerily still and drab, as though he had stepped through a hidden curtain into a haze of gray fog. Helgi had given himself five minutes to gather his stuff and get his car started. The heat made it balkier than usual. He sat with the door open in hopes of stirring the baking air inside, nudging the gas pedal over and over again with his foot.

At last the engine coughed into life, and he backed out of the driveway, checking his directions and wondering again why Ms. Devereaux had referred him away to this Dr. Sachs for vocal coaching. Dr. Sachs lived out past White Rock Lake, in a well-kept residential neighborhood with a lot of trees and winding streets. Helgi took the wrong turn twice, and spent fifteen minutes driving slowly trying to see house numbers and locate missing street signs before he found Cherry Stone Lane. By the time he had found a parking place, he was a few minutes past the hour.

Sweaty and disheveled, Helgi breathed in relief when he saw the brass letters of the name "Dr. J. Sachs" bright against the gleaming white mailbox in front of 1503 Cherry Stone. He hurried up the walkway and knocked on the door. The man who opened the door was much older than Helgi had expected. His mane of hair and neat goatee were grayish-white, his face deeply scored with a web of lines. He was short, but still powerful despite his age, heavy muscles bulging beneath his neat gray coat. He looked up into Helgi's face, adjusting wire-rimmed glasses to peer more closely at the young man.

"You are Helgi Hadding?" His voice was deep and soft, with a strong German accent.

"Ich bin Helgi Hadding," Helgi answered. "Möchten Sie Deutsch mit mir sprechen?"

Dr. Sachs chuckled, gesturing Helgi in. "Please, I am an old man and, also, very proud of my English. Your accent is very good, but there is no need to trouble yourself for me. You will get enough of German when you are singing for me."

The cool air of Dr. Sachs' house settled over Helgi like a soothing shower of rain as he stepped inside. The house was simply furnished, with heavy wooden chairs, small oaken tables, and full bookshelves everywhere Helgi looked. A grizzled Siamese tom looked up from a chair as Helgi passed, snarling low in warning.

"Tiberius! Raus!" Dr. Sachs said, striking his hands sharply together. The cat jumped off the chair, weaving smoothly among the table legs and running from the room. "He is a very bad cat. He knows he is not allowed to come in here, but he waits until I look somewhere else or leave the door open a moment, and then, pffft! I have raised him from a kitten and he has trained me to live with his bad behavior. Do you keep animals, Helgi?"

"I have a Norwegian elk hound."

The old man nodded. "Helgi is a good Scandinavian name. Is your family Norwegian?"

"Danish, on my mother's side."

Dr. Sachs' keen blue gaze slid past Helgi, softening as if he were looking far away. Helgi thought that he might be about to say something more, but instead Sachs stepped past him, opening another door. "This is my studio. Come in, please." Helgi was about to ask if Dr. Sachs had ever been to Denmark, but it occurred to him then that the old teacher had been a young man in 1940, and might have come into Scandinavia with the German army. The thought made him uncomfortable, as if he were trying to turn his gaze unobtrusively away from a maimed man's empty sleeve.

The room was bare except for a bookcase full of scores and the dark-polished grand piano which took up a quarter of one wall. A single large window showed a carefully landscaped garden with young oak trees leading down to a small creek. High brick walls running from the sides of the house down to the water closed Dr. Sachs' garden off from his neighbors on either side.

The German took off his coat and hung it neatly on a hook by the door, then sat down on the piano bench. "Now we shall see," he said comfortably. "Ms. Devereaux only sends two sorts of students to me. Problems and geniuses. Which are you, Helgi?"

"Uh. I guess I'm a problem," he admitted as truthfully as he could. To his humiliation, Helgi could feel himself blushing. He wanted to crawl out of the house right then and there.

Dr. Sachs' laugh was soft and kindly. "The two go most together. Ms. Devereaux would not have sent you to me if she did not think I could do something with your voice. She told me that you were very ambitious, and that you were always surprising her. So, we shall see. Put your books down and stand here, your back to the piano. For now you must trust your ears to find the notes, not your eyes. Sing with your full strength, I want to hear you filling this room with sound."

As Helgi had expected, Dr. Sachs brought him slowly up the scale to test his range. When they had reached its high end, the old teacher stopped him. "You are tightening your throat, you will choke your notes to death. Do not worry about your neck. Let the sound come out from between your eyes, so." He stood, tapping the middle of Helgi's forehead lightly with a thick-knuckled index finger. The touch of his fingertip against Helgi's skull felt like an electrical shock, almost painfully intense. Helgi blinked, still feeling the tingle in his head as Dr. Sachs sat down and struck the note again.

This time, the sound rang easily, as though his voice were spearing out from the spot where the teacher had touched him. They went up several notes higher before starting down again.

"A bit better than two octaves," Dr. Sachs said when he had taken Helgi's voice as low as it would go without growling. "Low F to high A flat, a full bass-baritone range. Much better than you thought, yes? Proper training will widen it also and make it easier for you to use highest and lowest without strain. A bit more warming up, and then we will come to some real music."

After Dr. Sachs had put Helgi through a long and complex series of vocal exercises, he picked up the book of Schubert songs Helgi had brought. "Ms. Devereaux tells me you sang 'Erlkönig' as your audition piece? Also, we shall hear it." Its spine often folded back, the music book opened easily to the song. Dr. Sachs' gnarled hands moved lightly on the piano, he hardly glanced at the keys galloping beneath his fingers, but watched Helgi very closely through the song.

"We shall work on your pitches," he stated. "Your interpretation is very understanding, and you feel the music. Your voice itself," Dr. Sachs tugged at his beard, regarding Helgi thoughtfully, and Helgi felt his guts cramp inward.

"There is something to it, something 'eigenartig?'" Helgi shook his head, he did not know the word. "There is some music for which it will never do. You will not become a great singer of Mozart, I think. But in five years, you will do well for der fliegende Holländer, in ten or fifteen, with the most careful training and work and if you do not fall by the wayside, you might perhaps have the possibility of becoming a fine Wotan. Your tone is unusual to you, but if you learn to use it as I teach you, those who hear you will have to listen to you. There is much strength in your voice. It needs only to be disciplined and brought into your control. Do you understand me?"

"I think so," Helgi answered breathlessly.

Dr. Sachs smiled, showing strong brown-streaked teeth, and sang softly, "Und wie er musst, so konnt er's, das merkt ich ganz besonders." As he had to, so he was able, that I marked most particularly. He laughed at Helgi's blank look. "From Meistersinger. Do you like Wagner well now?"

"I don't know much Wagner. Only 'Ride of the Valkyries' oh, and we played 'Siegfried's Funeral March' in the orchestra last year."

"You shall not sing Wagner at all for several years yet. Your voice is too young for you to even think about it. However, you shall listen to his operas and study the music and his meanings against the day when your voice is ready. 'A man's reach should exceed his grasp, or what's a heaven for?' Jefferson's Music library has very fine recordings together with the scores, and you shall go there and listen to them. Now you shall work on Lieder, Schubert and Schumann, and we shall perhaps find you some Handel in a month or two. Will you like that?"

"Yes.....Only," The words spilled out of Helgi's mouth, he could not keep them back. "I write songs also, both the music and the words. Could I, would it be possible, for me to bring them in to you so that I could learn to sing them properly? What I really want is to be able to perform my own works. Uh, they might be more rock than. I wrote them for synthesizer."

He stopped, afraid of the old German's reaction this is no classical music, this is a boy's silliness, you must learn from the masters, not from yourself, but Dr. Sachs was nodding slowly. "I will be pleased to see them. Who better than yourself to write songs that fit to your voice? Have you any with you?"

"Not today."

"You shall bring them next week, then. Now, enough of talking. You are here to sing." He stood up, lifted a tape recorder out of the piano bench. "You shall sing 'Erl-König' again for my machine, and then you should not sing it even in the shower for the next six months. In half a year we will go back to it and you should see how far you have come."

First-year music classes started at eight in the morning on Monday, and Helgi had a long drive over to Jefferson for his first teaching assignment. Only the battered old piano facing the row of desks from beneath the window made it different from any of the chalk dusted rooms in which Helgi had sat for nine months a year since he was six, but now he was on the other side of the desk.

He glanced down at his lesson plans, the words he had heard on his first day in Jefferson's music department coming to him. One out of three of you will not be here by the time you graduate. Talent is not enough, there are hundreds of thousands of talented musicians out there. Helgi had two morning introductory classes, from eight to ten, then three hours free before the next one. His work over, he made his way to the teachers' lounge, pouring himself a cup of coffee. The red-haired woman from the auditions was there too, he reached for her name, missed it, but sat beside her anyway.

"I see you made it," he said.

The creases over her rounded brows smoothed as she looked up. "Yeah. Hairy, isn't it? Did you give the 'One in Three Of You Is a Weed, So You Might As Well Quit Now' lecture?"

"I was going to, but," Helgi could see himself mirrored in her brown eyes, a pale shape against the darkness. "I remembered getting it, I would have picked up singing again a lot sooner if I hadn't.

"I didn't give it either. I remembered thinking I'd probably be a weed and my brother went through here a few years ago. He says it changed a lot after Dr. Sachs retired. When he was head of the department, they used to try to get at least a couple of basic music classes for everyone. Now they can't stand wasting their precious time on minors or people who just want lessons as electives, the non-professionals."

Head of the department, huh? Helgi thought. It probably explained something about why Ms. Devereaux had referred him, but he wasn't sure what. "Is your brother a professional musician now?" He asked, choosing to deal with the easier question.

"He actually works as a free-lance programmer, but he's in this band Fluorescent, they're playing tonight, in fact, out at Bar of Soap. Which," she amplified at Helgi's bewildered look, "is a bar slash-laundromat across from the main gates of Fair Park. You want to come?" Her brown eyes dropped when he tried to meet her gaze, mouth shutting firmly.

Helgi smiled, trying to put her a little more at ease. "Sure. Meet you there?" No commitment, not so much as he would have made to Tippet for an evening out, depending on whose car was working best.

"Okay. They start around eight. If you get there an hour early, you can have the incredible privilege of helping Mike and his merry men set up."

The man working the door at the Bar of Soap was very short and muscular, blue tattoos writhing and twining over his bare arms. Neon squiggles gleamed on the bar's walls, twisting green and pink and blue between paintings of things that wiggled from shapes to shapelessness in shades of purple and black. All the paintings had price tags on them, except for the large one on the wall behind the bar which was marked SOLD. The bartender, a tall, lean man with a mass of golden-brown curls spilling down the back of his black leather jacket, sat hunched up on a stool near the end of the bar, flicking cigarette ash into a Budweiser ash tray and talking to a couple of customers. He stuck the cigarette in his mouth when he saw Helgi.

"Bass Ale, please," Helgi said.

"One of them large-mouth beers, huh? Two-fifty." The bartender beheaded the bottle neatly and Helgi handed his money over.

"Is Mike here yet?"

"Back there, setting up." He waved Helgi back to the passage leading from the main room. Past the bathrooms, the little hallway opened up to a makeshift stage on the left side, on the right, another empty doorway led to a row of washers and dryers.

A shiver crawled down Helgi's spine as he looked down to the open fire exit at the end of the hall. It was as though something tingled like static-charged fur just at the ends of his nerves, just out of his reach. Hot air seeped in through the open door, blowing back the coolness of the bar behind Helgi. A thin red-haired man wedged himself and the giant speaker in his arms sideways through the door. Helgi recognized him at once. His hair was in a ponytail just like his sister's, and despite his droopy mustache, their rounded faces were remarkably similar. He frowned at Helgi as he made his way back.

"Hey, help me with this shit or get out of the way, but stop staring."

"Sorry," Helgi said. He followed the guy, Mike, in then set his beer down on the stage and helping the other lower the heavy speaker on the opposite side of the room.

Mike straightened up, rubbing at his back. "Solid motherfucker. Everyone's late again, they're just waiting until I've hauled all our shit in by my lonesome. Hey, are you the one Luann called me about?"

"Probably. My name's Helgi Hadding."

Mike shook his hand. His grip was firm, lean hands heavily calloused. "You mind doing a little work, then?"

"Nah."

Together they toted the rest of the sound equipment in from Mike's truck, then Helgi carried Mike's electronic keyboard while the other man brought his guitar. When they had everything hooked up, Mike got himself a beer and came back, sitting on the edge of the stage beside Helgi and lighting up a cigarette. "Smoke?" He offered, waving the pack of Marlboros at Helgi.

"No, thanks."

Mike checked his watch. "Shit, they oughta be here by now. I have a drummer, a rhythm guitarist, and a bass player, and sometimes I think not one of them has the brains God gave a turd squished on the road."

"You play keyboard?"

"Yeah, and lead guitar, and sing. I started out with a vocal major at Jefferson, back when Dr. Sachs was still there. You missed the best time there, kid. He quit my sophomore year, and I didn't like the way things were going, so I changed to computers."

"I'm studying with Dr. Sachs now, I'm a grad student, but I was referred for lessons."

Mike tugged at his mustache, deep brown eyes narrowing as he regarded Helgi thoughtfully. "You must be some good, huh? He didn't teach much even when he was chairman of the department, said he was too old to deal with anything but problems and geniuses. We all thought he was the nearest thing to God."

Helgi grunted noncommittally, but within he felt the warmth of excitement clashing with the cold of fear, like winter and summer winds swirling together into a spring tornado. His mind whirled up by the storm, he heard himself saying, "I play keyboard, too. You need someone else in your band? I might even be able to give your average squished turd some intellectual competition."

Caught with the bottle at his mouth, Mike's laugh sprayed beer froth onto the stage. "Might could," he said. He waved his bottle at the keyboard. "Go on, play something hell, sing something. I want to hear what Dr. Sachs is teaching these days."

"I just started with him last week," Helgi confessed.

"That's okay, sing something for me anyway."

Helgi felt himself settling in the moment he sat down behind the keyboard and flicked it on, he felt as though the current were flowing through him, bearing him through. He flicked through some of the settings until he found one that suited him and began.

"Wind is howling through black pines."

As he started over the bridge, the icy wind suddenly swept down his back, a spattering of sleet needling goosebumps along his arms. He could hear his voice flung out along the howling wind, calling to the silver-winged shape that wheeled above, and he remembered. I dreamed this place, Helgi realized. I dreamed Karin here, the Erl-King's daughter. The hot summer air blowing through the open door could not warm him now, the sweat lay cold as grave-dew on his forehead by the time he had reached the last words, "Ride with the hunt or flee before, For Erl-King, awesome, rules the night!"

"I detect the heavy hand of Schubert resting upon the composer's shoulder," Mike said dryly when Helgi was done. The eagerness open in his eyes gave him away. Helgi just smiled at him, and he grinned back. Mike turned to three young men who had come in while Helgi had been singing. "Hey, what do you-all think? Aside from that you're late enough to get out of setting up, again."

"Hey, I've still gotta bring m'set in," the plumpish youth with crew-cut blond hair complained. His high drawl sounded as though he had just come out from the cow pastures of West Texas. "Don't gimme shit about it."

The other two, a light-skinned black man with heavy features under a huge fluff of Afro and a big burly fellow whose greased back hair tapered into a pencil-thin braid that fell halfway down his back, looked back and forth from each other to Helgi and Mike. The guy with the Afro spoke first.

"He got a real spooky voice, man. Real spooky. Don't take it personal or nothing," he added to Helgi, "but I wouldn' like hearin' too much of that voice. Keyboard's all right, but I don' nohow like that music."

"Weird fucking song," the other one grunted. "I didn't understand a word of it. What's an Erl-King?" Helgi couldn't answer him, so he said nothing. "Music sounded fine to me, though. Betcha a band could do something with it."

Mike looked back at the blond. "You got an opinion, Rack? How would you feel about having him in the band?"

"I've heard better keyboard players, but ain't none of those asking to be in our band, and you sure as shit ain't one of them. Let him sing the psycho songs, man, you do the rest. Yup, I think we should give him a chance."

"Josh?" Mike asked, looking at the guy with the braid.

"We might as well try him out. We can always tell him to fuck off if he doesn't work out."

"Widget?"

"Do we gotta play his music?"

"We'll see what the rest of it's like. Personally I think it won't hurt to have some new songs, kinda break up the monotony, but we'll see how it goes. You have any objection to giving him a try?"

Widget scratched the bristles on his chin, looking thoughtfully at Helgi. The combination of light-caramel skin and heavy features made him look more Turkish or Middle Eastern than Negro to Helgi. He straightened his back and looked down into the band member's dark eyes, fixing him with a keen stare. Widget dropped his gaze quickly and looked away, one foot scraping against the concrete floor as if he were trying to step backwards as his hand lifted halfway to the little gold cross at his neck, then dropped. "I guess we can," he muttered. "Guess it won' hurt."

"How about it, Helgi? Dollar a gig and all the empty Styrofoam beer cups you can eat."

"Sounds good."

"Meet the band, then. This is Rack, our drummer," the blond raised a hand, "Josh, rhythm guitar."

"Meetcha," the burly man grunted, trying to crush Helgi's hand. Helgi crushed back, and Josh eased up.

"Widget, bass, more or less sometimes."

"Yo' mamma," the Afro'd musician answered. He let out a surprising high cackle.

"Eat me, Widget," Mike replied. "Guys, this is Helgi Hadding."

"Helga?" Josh muttered. "That's a girl's name. You don't look good enough to be no girl."

"Not Helga," Helgi said patiently. "Helgi. My mother's family is Danish." I will get a T-shirt, he thought, and I will wear it all the time, and it will say, MY MOTHER'S FAMILY IS DANISH. DO NOT MAKE FUN OF MY NAME.

"Whatever you say, Helga."

"I will beat the living shit out of you if you keep calling me that," Helgi answered, trying to keep his voice calm. He was already running attack combinations through his mind. He guessed Josh had been in a lot more fights than he had, but he doubted that the other man was going to pull a knife or a gun on him right there. Helgi could feel the excitement rising in him, and knew that he was hoping for a fight.

"You and what army?" Josh shot back, stepping closer. Mike moved between them, hands outstretched.

"Cool it, guys. Josh, clean the fucking wax out of your ears, okay? We've got a gig to play in just about fifteen minutes, and this shit isn't going to cut it. Now make nice, okay?"

Josh glowered, but stuck out his hand again. "Sorry, Helgi. Just razzing you. Don't take it so personal."

This time the crushing contest went on longer. Haven't done this since I was a sophomore in high school, Helgi thought. He could feel his hand getting numb, but the sweat slicking their palms let their grips slide a little and he was able to start grinding Josh's knuckles. Josh let up quickly, sliding his hand loose. "Good grip there," he grunted.

"You too," Helgi said, willing to be gracious in victory.

Rack had moved closer and was rising up and down on the toes of his black cowboy boots, reminding Helgi of a puppy in need of a walk. "Come on, guys, let's get my set in before one'a those gah damn S.O.B's out there rips it off. No drums, no music, man."

Luann showed up just as the music began, making her way through the thickening crowd to where Helgi was leaning against the wall by the stage. "Can I get you anything to drink?" Helgi asked.

Luann glanced at the near empty beer in his hand. Helgi emptied it. "Well, as long as you're going up there anyway, I wouldn't mind a wine cooler." When Helgi carried the drinks back and gave Luann hers, he thought the light had changed, gleaming from her brown eyes and bringing out the look of bright alertness from the curves of her features.

"What do you think of them?" She asked after they had been listening a little while.

Helgi sipped at his cold beer before answering. The neon squiggles glinted in curves off the slick patches his grasp left on the dew-beaded bottle, twisting like colored flames as he moved. "They'll be better when I'm playing keyboard with them." It was true. Flourescent's members were all fine musicians, but it seemed to Helgi that he could feel a lack in their music, no seed of fire, steel and tinder without a flint.

"You're going to join?"

"They're trying me out?"

"All right!"

Luann stuck around till the end of the set. "I still have a lot of things to do," she explained as the sound of U-2 rose from the jukebox to fill the brief silence following Flourescent's last song. "Mason dumped me with a load of first-year 'who are you, what do you play, why are you here' essays to process, among other crap."

"I'd probably better be moving pretty soon too," Helgi said. "Thanks for inviting me here."

"Hey, you're welcome. You'll probably see quite a bit more of me, since Flourescent mostly rehearses in my parents' garage and I still live with them."

She went off, and Helgi made his way over to Mike to trade phone numbers and get rehearsal times.

"Bring your songs with you, too. I liked that one you did this evening, Schubert ripoff and all."

Helgi's car surged under him like an eager steed as he turned onto the freeway, speeding up to weave into the long spinal cord of lights that ran through the city's asphalt backbone. He felt dazed by Mike's praise, dazed but not surprised, he had felt a sureness in his song that he could not have hidden from himself. "A spooky voice," Helgi thought, and it seemed to him that he could not argue with Josh's words.

When Dr. Sachs had played his "Erlkönig" back to him, Helgi had been most conscious of the places where he had strained at the top of his range, listening for pitch rather than tone, but now he could remember, a deep, large tone, with an eerie harshness to it, like the echo of a raven's resonant croaking or a hempen noose scratching lightly against his throat, and sometimes he had seemed to hear the chilling overtones of a howl in his singing.

"A spooky voice," he murmured to himself, and now his speech sounded ghastly to him, as if a dead man had spoken. He shivered, looking at his pale face in the rear view mirror and then glancing back over his shoulder at the back seat, but there was nothing there. Someone, Helgi told himself severely, has a hyperactive imagination. He turned on the radio. *"Immigrant Song"* was just starting, he cranked it up high to drive away the demons, letting the heavy drumbeat crash over him and singing beneath Robert Plant's voice, wailing about new lands, battle, and Valhalla.

Helgi's only assistant work on Thursdays was the 9.30-11.00 seminar "Nietzsche and Wagner", and he only had to attend and help grade papers, not teach. When that class was over, he made his way to the music library, intending to follow Dr. Sachs' advice on Wagner. He knew that he should probably start with one of the earlier works, but threads from the Ring Cycle were running through his head. An orchestral setting of "Siegfried's Funeral March" that he had played in as an undergraduate, the high ringing "Glorification of Brünnhilde" theme that Dr. Mason had used as an example of Wagnerian motifs.

"All right," Helgi said to himself. "I'll try it."

He made his way through the maze of paperwork that attended using the audio facilities, and at last got permission to sit down and listen. Only when the first torrent of music began to rush through his headphones did Helgi realize that he had forgotten to check out the score first. He shrugged, he would have more chances to study it. Instead he read the booklet that had come with the set of records. Siegmund collapsing, exhausted, in the house of his clan's foe Hunding, naming himself Wehwalt, the Wolfing, reunited with his twin sister Sieglinde and falling in love with her. Pulling the sword Nothung from the trunk of the tree and running away with Sieglinde. Helgi read more swiftly than the music sang. He stopped reading when he had reached the end of the first act, before Hunding's bass had yet sounded over his headphones, and reached into the bag that held his texts for *"Nietzsche and Wagner"*, pulling out the heavy two-volume set of Nietzsche's collected works.

Helgi did not try to read any part of it straight through. Rather, he flipped pages, letting his gaze fall upon phrases as the music seared through his skull. Now and again the pure voices of the singers would ravish him to stunned senselessness. Though he could only make out a few words here and there, it seemed to him that the music called to something in his soul past his understanding, awakening a part of himself to which he was still blind.

"'Among the Persians, a true priest could only be born through incest. The rainbow is the bridge to the Übermensch, the lightning is the Übermensch." He had heard of the idea of the "Superman" before, but that was not what Helgi understood now by Übermensch, though he was not sure what he did understand. "Blessed is he who goes to ground and goes under in his calling the will to live is the will to power."

It was the beginning of the third act that tore him away from the book again, the dialogue between Siegmund and Brunnhilde, where most of the words came slow and clear.

"Siegmund! Look at me!"

"Who are you, say, who appear so beautiful and grave to me?"

"Only the death-hallowed see my image. Who I appear to parts from life's light. On the stead of the slain alone I appear to athelings."

"Who follows you, where do you lead the hero?"

"To Valfather, who chose you, I lead, to Valhall you follow me."

Helgi could feel the tears coming to his eyes as the steely clear music of the Valkyrie's call to her hero rose, blurring the page before him. "Wotan's daughters shall truly offer you drink." If death were the price of a drink from Karin's hands, he thought. He blinked again, and the words shone clear. "Nur ein Gebot gilt dir. Sei rein!" There is only one commandment for you. Be pure! This purity, he thought, Wagner's hero must be Nietzsche's Übermensch. "What makes heroic? To face simultaneously one's greatest suffering and one's highest hope. The lightning is the Übermensch!" Then after Ride of the Valkyries, for the first time, he heard the Valkyrie singing Siegfried's motif to Sieglinde. "For the hero you bear in womb shall become the greatest hero of the world," and again, with Wotan's final words. "Who fears my spear's point shall never step through this fire!"

Helgi was cramped and aching when he finally rose from his seat, he would have to hurry to get home, change into his gi, and make it to the dojo on time. He felt as though a hammer had struck his head, he knew that his eyes must be pools of blackness, drugged with the sounds and words. The brightness outside hurt as though he were wrapped in a lightning flash that went on and on forever in the moment of striking. He slitted his eyes, trying to shut the light down to a bearable level, and after a few moments he was able to go on, though his head had begun to ache viciously. The concentration of his karate lesson had cleared Helgi's mind of his thoughts, his aching as he drove home was the good ache of his body used to its fullest. It was almost nine when he got home, but there were a few slices of cold pizza left in the refrigerator. He took it into his cramped little bedroom, settling down on his bed to eat while he made a more decisive attack on Nietzsche.

"Incipit Tragoedia, when Zarathustra was thirty years old, he left his home and the Lake of Urmi, and went into the mountains and rising one morning with the rosy dawn, he went before the Sun and spoke thus to her. 'You great star! What would be your happiness if you had not those for whom you shine! For ten years you have climbed hither unto my cave, you would have wearied of your light and of the journey, had it not been for me, my eagle, and my snake. But we awaited you every morning, took from you your overflow, and blessed you for it. Lo! I am weary of my wisdom, like the bee that has gathered too much honey, therefore must I descend into the deep, as you do in the evening, when you go behind the sea, and give light also to the netherworld, you most rich star! Like you must I go under. Bless the cup that is about to overflow, that the water may flow golden out of it, and carry everywhere the reflection of your bliss. Thus began Zarathustra's going-under."

The page blurred before Helgi, his sight melting into the images that rang in his mind. Eagle and serpent twining together, around a cup brimming over with golden mead. The grave-snake wriggling in the depths of the mountain, the noblest bird winging on the roads of the air, with the sun-bright drink spilling from his beak in drops like golden seeds. It seemed to him that he could see a bridge of rainbow fire arching to the snow-bright peak of the mountain, that a fair shape stood halfway along it, reaching out. Rapt, he started to move, but a sharp crunching sound broke through his vision, jarring his eyes open. Elric stood with his forepaws on the bed and his hind feet on the floor, his muzzle in Helgi's clean plate. A crust of pizza in his mouth, the elk hound rolled his eyes pleadingly at his master.

"If you get grease on the carpet, I'll have to pay for getting it cleaned, you know," Helgi said automatically, though the words clanged meaninglessly in his ears. He blinked, trying to drive the dizzy vagueness from his head, and patted the bed beside him. "Come on up, boy."

Elric jumped up to the bed and settled down beside him. Helgi hugged the dog close, burying his hands in the elk hound's thick fur. Outside his room's open door grew a forest of darkness, the fluorescent bulb burning in the middle of the ceiling no more than a fire's reflected light cast onto the runes of the German writing before him. I am waiting for the dawn, Helgi thought. He could picture himself sitting before the door of a hut, with a spear in his hand and his dog by his side, staring into the moonless night, though he did not know what he was watching for or what he was guarding. It occurred to him that what he thought of, his ancestors must have lived, and somehow it still lived in him, the light gleaming from the spear tip and the weight of the byrnie on his shoulders.

Siegfried's death did not end the Ring, only brought it back to its beginning, with the Sun glimmering on the waters of the Rhine. The thought seemed to tingle deep within him for a moment, but he had already worn himself out that day, and it sank away as quickly as it had come. He got up and changed into his pajamas, then headed for the bathroom to brush his teeth. Helgi was amazed at how easily Dr. Sachs sight-read his music on a first reading, he played the piano parts as well as Helgi himself could, leaving Helgi free to put his whole strength into singing. When they had gone through the four songs Helgi had brought, the old musician was frowning a little.

"Is something wrong?" Helgi asked.

Dr. Sachs tapped the handwritten sheets of words that rested on the piano beside the music to Helgi's Erl-King song. "Do you believe in what you have written here? Do you know the legend?"

"It came out of a dream I had," Helgi answered slowly.

Beneath the hard gleam of his glasses, Dr. Sachs' eyes had the same far-off look Helgi had seen in them before. Helgi held his breath, afraid the German would not go on.

"Ach," he said finally. "Legends have power, more power than Americans seem to know about. When I was young, my grandmother, she was Alamannisch, from the Black Forest, would tell me about das Wütende Heer, the Furious Host, and Wotan who led it. She would not go out of the house on a stormy winter night, not even to go to church on Christmas Eve."

Helgi clasped his hands behind his back to keep them from shaking. He nodded attentively.

"In Scandinavia you have also such beliefs. It is the oskorei, or aasgaardsreid, Asgard's Ride, in Norway. When I was there in the winter of '42, at a farmhouse near Trondheimach, no matter. Still, I think you must be careful of these songs, because they are true. If you do not know the legends well, I will remind you that Wotan is a very grim god, and it is not so safe to call on him. If you offer yourself up, he is likely to take you.

If you know the stories of the Wild Hunt, you must know that. Even if you are a clever modern person who does not believe in gods and ghosts, perhaps you can trust in Jung or Joseph Campbell or one of these other sensible men who writes about the power of myths and archetypes, and beware of what you are summoning up from your soul. You will forgive me for rambling on at you."

The only answer that came to Helgi's mind was one of the phrases he had read while listening to Die Walküre, Zarathustra's words to the fallen tightrope-walker. He quoted it in German. "'Du hast aus der Gefahr deinen Beruf gemacht, daran ist nichts zu verachten.'" You have made a calling out of danger, there is nothing to be contemptuous of in that. Helgi remembered, but did not speak the following words. Nun gehst du an deinen Beruf zugrunde. Now you go to ground from your calling.

Dr. Sachs raised his heavy eyebrows, but said only, "Now we will work on your phrasing. You are not measuring your breaths as you should. You do not mind if I write with a pencil on this?"

Helgi met Luann for lunch at the cafeteria across the street from the university the next day. By the time he had paid for his cardboard burger and a helping of fluffy green rabbit food, she had already snagged a table for two by the window.

"Mike says you're a pretty good keyboard player, as well as everything else," Luann said half-challengingly, looking sideways up at Helgi with a flick of her ponytail as he set his tray down on the table. "Is it true?"

"True enough for me to be in the band," he answered.

"He also said you managed to scare Widget out of a year's growth. What did you do to him?"

"Just sang."

Too late, Helgi realized how that sounded. He flushed, she giggled. I think this woman is smarter than I am, he thought. I walked right into that.

She peered carefully at him. "You look good with a little color in your cheeks. You're so fair-skinned. How do you stand the summers here?"

"I am a creature of the night," Helgi replied in his best fake Transylvanian accent, taking refuge from his unease in clowning. "I stay in the shadows, stay inside, and only go out by the light of the moon. I must varn you of my unfortunate allergy to garlic, vooden stakes and crosses, also church bells give me migraines. My night life is terrific, though."

"I don't believe in Danish vampires," Luann answered. "Try another one."

"Vampires? Who said vampires? I work for the IRS," Helgi replied, very fast. She snorted laughter, coughed and reached for her napkin. "Has your brother told you everything about me?"

"Brother? Who said brother? I work for the CIA. No, we were just kind of talking, was all. He mentioned that Josh was giving you some hassle about your name."

"If I had tuppence for every time that happened to me," Helgi muttered, "I'd have the Bank of England. Where is your family from?"

"We're mostly a mix, I guess. O'Roarke's probably an Irish name, but there's supposed to be some English in there, and some Indian from way back, and my mother's maiden name was French. Never keep track, never look back, that's us." She broke up a lettuce leaf with her fork, keeping her gaze fixed on his.

"Hmm," Helgi said. There was something in the idea that made him a little uncomfortable, though he could not have pinned it down.

"Coming to the rehearsal tonight?" Luann asked.

"I am."

"Great. I'm looking forward to hearing you. Mike said he was impressed, and he doesn't impress easy."

Helgi grinned. "Is that so? Hey, how come you don't sing with the band?"

"They all told me my voice was too pretty to do rock, or not strong enough, or all that kind of thing. Mainly, I think it's because I'm a girl, or Mike's little sister, or something."

"Hmm." Looking at Luann's sprinkling of freckles and red ponytail, Helgi could easily see her as a younger girl trotting after her brother on short legs, never quite able to catch up, and though he was an only child, his heart squirmed in a moment of sympathy.

"Hey, it's no big deal. Anyway, I'm not sure I'd have time to practice with them."

"What do you want to do with your singing?" Helgi asked. "Are you planning to become a professional?"

"Thinking about it, yes. I guess, hmm, everyone's always told me I have a pretty voice, and I just really wanted to see how far I could take it. And I watched The Sound of Music too many times when I was seven or eight, or something, and I guess it warped me for life. I always feel, well, sort of more real when I'm singing, if that makes any sense. But my voice isn't really strong enough for opera, I had in mind more musicals and such. I did a double major in voice and drama when I was an undergraduate, and I played Aldonza out at the Dinner Playhouse this summer."

Helgi nodded slowly. He did not want to speak, his voice suddenly felt rough as a crow's, but Luann kept talking. "I sang one of Cherubino's arias for my audition, but what I really wanted to do was *Some Enchanted Evening*"."She dabbed at her mouth, then took a deep breath and suddenly began singing it, her high clear voice sounding softly through the noise of the other people in the cafeteria talking. Even Helgi could tell that her voice was not very strong, but her tone was pleasant and her key true, and he was charmed by her ability to sing so naturally and fearlessly.

Luann sang about a verse, a few people clapped when she was done. Looking at Helgi, she let out a brief embarrassed giggle. "I've always wanted to sing that to a man I'd just met. Whoops, it's almost one, I'd better move, I have a class all the way over in Traymore Hall. See you tonight, okay?" She touched his arm lightly, then hurried off, leaving Helgi to wonder how much she had just wanted to sing and how much of the song might have been meant for him? Helgi spent an extra half-hour in the bathroom that evening, mostly messing with his shoulder-length hair.

Normally he just flipped it back and forgot about it, but suddenly his central part looked kind of nerdish to him. He tried the right side, then the left. They were worse. "Short hair?" He asked his reflection. "Nah. A perm? Fuck that, and fuck you, too, hair. No, I don't mean it, please stay with me, don't even think of departing this skull at any point in the foreseeable future. Aah, the hell with it." Helgi pulled the whole reddish-gold mess back and rummaged around for a rubber band. The ponytail made his features look very sharp, high cheekbones standing out like the wings of a stooping eagle. He grimaced at himself, then turned away from the mirror. "What I don't see can't hurt me," he muttered. He wondered what Luann would think of it. Admit it, he thought, you are not standing here messing with your hair because of a sudden attack of vanity. You are doing it because you think this woman is interested in you, and maybe vice versa.

Well, what about Karin?

But Karin was long gone, he had not seen or heard from her for several years. More, she had a military life. She might be posted anywhere in the world. For that matter, she could be married by now. He had hardly known her when he was seventeen he might not even like her now. Was he supposed to spend the rest of his life waiting for the woman of his adolescent dreams to drop into his lap, or pass up a good relationship with someone who felt the way he did about singing in hopes of those dreams coming true someday? Especially when Luann was so much fun to be with, lively and smart, now that Helgi had thought of it, he had never even spoken of Karin as long as fifteen minutes at a time, and even if they met, how could she talk to him about music, or he to her about the Air Force? It seemed to Helgi that his choice now was not between one love and another, but between life and fantasy, and the thought of seeing Luann again warmed him like a hot bowl of soup.

Helgi undid his ponytail and, scowling into the mirror, tried to plait his hair into one thick braid at the back. He didn't know that it looked better, but it didn't look any worse. Whichever, it was time for him to go. Flourescent was already set up in the O'Roarke's garage. Helgi heard their music banging out as he walked around the walk to the back. The garage door was open, a portable fan blowing on the band members, but their faces were already glistening with sweat. Dark crescent were spreading under the armpits of Mike's Grateful Dead T-shirt, the other band members were bare-chested already. Luanne, wearing white shorts and a green halter top, was sitting cross legged on a folding chair in front of the fan, a can of Diet Pepsi in her hand and a thick chemistry text open in her lap. The song fell apart into four different lines that trailed off jaggedly as Helgi approached.

"Yo," called Josh. "Hey, it's Erik the Viking. Pillaged any good towns lately, Erik?"

Helgi merely raised a hand in greeting. "Hi, guys." Mike's keyboard was already set up, with an empty chair behind it. He moved in and sat down. "Hi, Luann. How's it going?"

"Well enough. Can I get you anything to drink? It's Diet Pepsi, water, juice, or beer."

Helgi glanced at the cans of Budweiser beside the other band members. "I'd like a beer, please."

Luann rose gracefully and moved into the house. Mike snickered. "She must like you, Helgi. I can't get her to do that for me. Well, now you're here, let's see what you can do with our music." He handed Helgi a sheaf of papers scribbled with words and intermittent scoring, mostly chord notations with occasional scraps of melody penciled in around them.

"I can deal with it," Helgi said, a little more confidently than he felt. A wave of air-conditioning washed over him as Luann came back through with his beer. "Thanks," he said, taking it from her hand and smiling up at her. His fingers touched hers, lingered a moment. Her hand was cool, damp from the cold-dewed can, her expression, jaw muscles set firmly beneath her soft features and serious gaze of concentration above her smile, reminded him of an novice ice-skater, unsure of whether she was skating or skidding on the slippery ice. He wasn't sure himself, but he popped the top open and took a drink. The Budweiser tasted watery, leaving only an echo of bitter-edged malt on his tongue, but at least it was cold and wet. He set it down beside his foot, turned to Mike as Luann went back to her seat. "Well, I'm ready. What are you waiting for?"

"For you to stop making time with my little sister," Mike answered, his grin curling up beneath the droopy tips of his mustache. Luckily, it was hot enough in the garage that Helgi's face was already flushed. "Okay, dig out 'Dallas Dream', and let's see what we can do with it."

Helgi waited until Rack and Widget had laid him down a good solid
foundation, bass and drums thumping through the concrete floor and up
through the soles of his feet, before he curled his fingers over the keys and
began to weave his own part in through the chords Mike had given him, the
chords Josh was beginning to pound out on his guitar. Helgi hung back a
little through the first two verses, getting the feel of them, but as the third
began he found himself reaching for the levers, switching around the keyboard's voices and letting it scream through Mike's hard-edged tenor voice
and swirling guitar notes.

Luann had closed her chemistry book and sat with her head cocked
towards Helgi, fingers in her ears to mute out a little of the sound booming
around her as she listened The crashing, sudden end of the song took Helgi
by surprise, but he lifted his hands from the keyboard at once with his last
chord still unresolved. He said nothing, it was up to them to accept or reject
him now.

"I think I can live with you," Mike said musingly. "What do you think,
guys?"

Rack said, "Yup."

Josh said, "Sure."

Widget took the longest time to answer, looking from Helgi to Mike. Finally he grunted, "All right."

"You're stupid if you don't take him," Luann said softly, gazing straight at
her brother.

"Ah, what do you know, kid?" Mike asked, grinning.

"Hell of a lot more than you do," Luann shot right back at him. "I know
your A-string's going sharp on you, for one thing. Come on, guys. I'm down
here to hear music, and I want to hear more of it."

It wasn't until closer to the end of the session, when the cicadas were
shrilling through the cooling evening and the big mosquitoes were beginning to fly low and slow to the garage's one light bulb, that Helgi felt sure
enough to say, "Hey, you want to look over a couple of my songs while we're
here?"

He whipped out the copies of his music, he had made one for everyone,
and started passing them around before anyone could say no. Luann laid
her homework down and came to look over Helgi's shoulder while they
played. He had chosen to start with the one that began with the chorus,
"Weird women winging, the white swan's singing," because it was closest to
the music Flourescent was used to playing. Helgi had to stop several times,
playing out the parts as he had them in mind.

Josh didn't read music, and Helgi had never learned to score for percussion, and Widget had a little trouble with the idea of playing triplets in the bass while the singer was working in a duple rhythm. They were rough, they were very rough, but Helgi could feel something coming through, and it heartened him. It worked, he could hear that it would work, just as it had worked in his head while he was composing it. The next song was mostly instrumental, starting slow and simple and weaving into a complex web of music, the lines laid down one on top of the other to build the whole. More Led Zeppelin than Schubert.

The verses were woven in where the instrumentation died down, so that Helgi's voice alone carried the melody over a very soft bass whisper and a rustle of drums, the guitars and keyboards coming in to chord around the last long note of each verse.

"Something sunken, hidden,
sleeps within memory,
down in dark waters' bed,
drowned in waves of years gold
Hidden in halls of stone,
held where only mushrooms
raise their red-capped heads,
rend the soul, too wild dreams
Meetings in the mist-lands,
mounds rise like ancient huts,
Tall grass over gray stone,
growing from fallen bones"

"Pretty damn good," Josh admitted grudgingly when they had made their way through it. "I like it."

"Thanks," Helgi said, trying to hide his surprise. He had guessed Josh for a borderline heavy-metal rocker, never expected he would enjoy a subtle piece like that.

"Hmm," Luann said. "I think I smell a hobbit-pipe around this song somewhere. Maybe the hobbit has been smoking more than tobacco? I thought I heard some definitely psychedelic notes in there."

"The hobbit does not smoke tobacco," Helgi admitted sheepishly. "Other substances constitute classified material and are not discussed in front of witnesses."

Luann grinned. She mimed taking a hit, sucking in with slowly widening eyes, holding it down, and blowing a gout of imaginary smoke into his face.

"Corrupt my sister's morals and die," Mike said.

Luann laughed. "My brother believes a roach clip is something given by the little teeny barber in the Roach Motel. Yeah, and I have some real prime swampland in Louisiana for sale."

While she spoke, Helgi was beginning to feel the uneasy looks of the rest of the band wriggling on the back of his neck already, clammy as the touch of the sweat-soaked T-shirt in the cooling night. He had put his Erl-King song at the bottom of the stack, hoping by the time they got to it they would be too impressed by the rest of his music to refuse to play, but now he himself realized that he himself felt a little tempted to call it a night.

He turned around and looked Widget in the eye, grinning at him. "You aren't afraid to play this one, are you? You sounded kind of nervous about it the other night."

Josh blew a raspberry. "Hell, Widget's a good Baptist, he got his cross on. What's he got to be scared of?"

The flourescent light cast ashes over Widget's caramel skin, glinting gold from the little pendant nestled among his curly black chest hairs, but the bass player showed Helgi his big square teeth, then turned to glare at Josh. "Ain' no law says I got to like every song I hear, is there? Man, I know what I hear, and I know there be somethin' bad in that one. Don' you be making fun of me, I cut you into pieces and eat the pieces."

Remembering how the guitarist had responded to his own challenge, Helgi tensed for a fight, but Josh only laughed. "Not going to let a little honky mojo send you running home to mammy, are ya, Widget?"

Now Helgi did feel uncomfortable. With a start, he realized that he was actually turning his gaze away from Widget, and that made him even more uncomfortable.

"You don' know yo' butt from yo' face," Widget answered. "Hard to tell, at that. Nah, I ain't gonna run out on you. Just you watch outin the night hereafter." He thunked a few hard notes out on his bass. "You got more of these weird two-against-three rhythms in here, Helgi. Why you like them so much, man? You got nothin' better to do than make life complicated?"

"I like them because I like them," Helgi answered. "They fit the music the way I make it. If you don't like it, write your own."

"Never could do that," Widget mumbled. His skin was fair enough for Helgi to see it darken as he looked down, plunking at one of his strings and adjusting the tuning a little.

Helgi wanted to apologies, but couldn't think of how to do it without making things worse. Instead he said, "You got that tuned? Okay. You're starting it, Widget, about so fast....dadada dadada"

Widget plunged into the intro, Mike picked it up, adding a screaming slide to the rising line and wailing down to the long B minor before the others all leapt at the first verse together.

It was halfway through their second rendition, when the ragged lines finally began to pull together, that Helgi first felt the tingle that told him something was happening. He kept singing, listening to the words as if he had not written them, but Dr. Sachs' warning was beginning to ring through his music like the clear notes of an uninvited French horn.

"One-eyed the awful one storming before,
Gallops on ghost-gray, eight-legged horse"

I will remind you that Wotan is a very grim god, and it is not so safe to call on him

"Death as the Erl-King rides on the wind,
Seeking the one who sees him too clear."

If you know the stories of the Wild Hunt, you must know that. The understanding of his song's true meaning did not come to Helgi as a burst of lightning, but rose slowly as the edge of the sun rising into a sky already bright with dawn. Helgi could feel the shivers rippling through his body as he swung into the last verse, from the corner of his eye, he saw Luann hurrying back from the garage into the house.

Helgi heard the door closing, not through his wearied eardrums, but through his bones. For a moment, he could feel his mouth moving and hear the music, but he could not believe the huge deep voice in his ears was his own. The flourescent light bulb seemed to burst in his eyes as though someone had struck it, and in its glowing blue afterimage, he could see the blue-steel helm and shadowed face of the maiden he sang about.

"Sweet in my mouth, the mead of her kiss,
The spear of her song cuts keen as ice,
Battle-bright, she shines through storm,
Rune-wise maid who rides with me"

The afterimage slowly faded back to the bone-white bulb, still unbroken and bright, but the time Helgi had beaten out the last chord, he was chilled to the bone.

The rest of the band members eyed him uncertainly as the distorted echo of their final harmony faded away into the night. Rack shifted uneasily from foot to foot behind his drum set, not meeting Helgi's gaze. Mike stroked his guitar strings, his fingertips muting their sound to nothing even as they rasped over the wire-wrapped cords.

It was Widget who broke their stillness. "You-all still wanna play that song?"

"Give that line up, it's getting old," Josh advised. He laid his guitar carefully in its case and locked it, then knotted his thumb pick into the end of his thin braid. "I'm outta here. See you guys Thursday."

"Me, too," Rack said. "It's past eleven. You-all help me get my set into the car?"

When Rack had packed, and Widget and Josh had driven off, Helgi and Mike dismantled the sound system together. Mike didn't say anything until they had finished. Then he turned to face Helgi squarely. "You sure have yanked Widget's chain. You know, I'm not sure," His eyes seemed very dark, his face whitened by the glare of the light bulb above. "Luann walked out on it too. If that song makes too many people nervous."

"It's because it's powerful," Helgi argued. "You know it's the best of the bunch. The truth, now. Aren't you looking forward to performing it on stage?"

Mike stood looking at Helgi, his rounded face set grimly around the arc of his mustache. "We sounded pretty fine," he admitted at last. "I guess so, but how come?" His voice tailed off.

Helgi wasn't quite sure of the question, but he knew the answer. "Because it's true."

"Uh." Mike straightened his back a little. "I guess Luann probably just went in to crash, anyway."

"Well, tell her I said good night."

"Will do. See you Thursday. Bring any music you've got, we're doing another gig at the Soap around the middle of next month and I'd kind of like to have as much fresh stuff as we can."

"Sure. See you."

CHAPTER XVI

Sigiruna sat on her mother's howe in the gray light of dawn, the dew-damp grass soaking slowly through her gown as she breathed deeply to steady the angry fear that rose and beat against the walls of her heart. Sigigafja had fallen ill a few days after Sigiruna and Bragi came back from God-Home, a sudden fever that had seized her limbs and seethed her brain to sudden storms of madness. At last Ansuwunja had come out of her house, treading among men for the first time in more years than Sigiruna had lived, but even her galdors could do no more than ease Sigigafja's pain and give her a quiet faring. Haganon's frowe had lived long enough to bid her children farewell in the little calm that Ansuwunja's galdor-craft had bought her just before the fever rose to claim her life, but she had never heard even one of the songs of Hailgi Hunding's-Bane that blew like a swift wind across Jutland and Sealand in the moon-turning after Hunding's death.

Then the words Sigiruna had spoken to Hadubroddar had become true, for Haganon had been willing to hear no word of his daughter's marriage for the three years after his wife's death, while the grass grew higher on Sigigafja's mound and the damp peat soaked into the wood of the buried ship that bore the shield-woman's body on her last faring. Often the Skjolding drighten had set his high seat on his wife's howe when the weather was fine, casting his hawk out after rabbits or sitting to deem over quarrels between men, but he had not gone to the mound this year, though the weather was very fine and mild for Ostara-month.

"If Haganon were to come here now, Mother, surely you would give him a better rede than he has gotten!" Sigiruna said aloud. Hadubroddar had sailed to their shores a day after Ostara's feast, with the white shield of peace raised, and his sole aim was to get Sigiruna as his bride. His war band and his fleet were large enough. Though despite the sea-king's boasting, his men seemed no braver or better than any others, but it was his smooth manner and swift tongue that seemed to be winning the day for him.

Hadubroddar often asked his skalds to sing songs of Haganon's young deeds, and often spoke to praise Bragi's promise as a warrior, and because the seventeen winter-old Skjolding had not yet had a chance to bloody his sword, he was all the more easily swayed to Hadubroddar's side. Only Dagar thought little of the sea-king, and he had grown so quiet and brooding that he hardly seemed to be a part of the clan anymore, little chance that he would speak out against the wedding, less that Haganon would heed his voice. Sigiruna had not believed that her father and brother would try to wed her away against her will, but in the past days her doubt had swelled like a mushroom in the damp, and her dreams had all been of battle, of blood spurting from the bodies of her father and brothers and the sleek black ravens glistening in the light of the setting Sun as they hopped about the wolves that tore at the dead.

There would be fighting if she did not wed Hadubroddar, yet she would rather do battle and die than let his heavy arms close about her, there would be men slain before the matter was out, however it went, unless she could find some other path than the ones she saw now. Thus Sigiruna had come out here to seek her mother's help, in hopes that the walkurja would be able to give her daughter some of that wisdom which the dead were said to hold.

"Hadubroddar wishes to wed me, and Hailgi has done nothing," she murmured. But Hunding's-Bane is yet young, Sigiruna thought. He may be still waiting his time, for the balance between the Wolfings and the Hundings is still held steady in Jutland, and for Hailgi to seek wedding-bonds with the Skjoldings now might tip the long frith into open battle again.

Sigiruna shivered hard, the cord of her spine vibrating like a plucked harp string. Though the sky was bright as day, too bright for the dead to come forth beneath its light it seemed to her that she had felt the earth beneath her shifting as though deep roots twisted like adders, as though an underground river were pushing its way up through the howe-mold. The glow of the Sun's white edge dazzled her eyes, and her ears were ringing with the sound of whetstones keening along the edges of swords and spears. Sigiruna closed her eyes, now she could hear the murmuring of men's voices, though she could not make out any of their words.

Then Hailgi's voice sounded clear in her ears, its deep rasp singing against the edges of her nerves. On to Loga Fells! It is a long march yet to the field. Hailgi is going to battle this day, Sigiruna thought, her heart beating more swiftly. He is going to battle, and I must find a place where no one will touch my body while I fare forth to ward him from the dark wights and the idises of his foes who would weave battle-fetters around him. She looked back at the Skjolding hall, at the shingles gleaming like gilded shields in the Sun's new light and the silhouette of the gold-dusted eagle raised at the end of the great roof-beam. The sea-king walked freely there, given full guest-right, and the cold knifed sharply through Sigiruna's guts at the thought of Hadubroddar coming upon her sleeping. I should be safest of all, here on my mother's howe, the Skjolding said to herself.

Here he would not dare to touch me, nor is there anyone in our hall so foolish as to wake one who sleeps upon a mound.

Sigiruna stretched out on her back, closing her hands upon the clear ball of silver-mounted berg-crystal that hung between her breasts. The morning cold was already fading from her limbs as she drew a breath of the soft wind down to the farthest depths of her lungs, she could feel the dark might winding up widdershins from her mother's howe to meet the brightness spiraling deosil from the Sun. Her gray steed was not far from her, as he was never far. It seemed to her that his wolf-shaggy hide was already smoothing beneath the Sun's light, and his neck arched in eagerness as she readied herself to mount. Something was holding her back, something grasped her by the shoulders. Sigiruna struggled a moment, not sure whether she meant to tear herself free of her hide, or settle herself more firmly in it. But then she heard Dagar's voice calling "Sigiruna! Sigiruna" and she had to open her eyes and sit up. Her youngest brother knelt in the damp grass beside her, his pale eyes narrowing as he stared at her.

"What did you mean to do?" He asked.

"What does it matter to you?" Sigiruna countered angrily. "You of all folk should know better than to waken me so, I thought that at least here I would have peace!"

"I thought that you would want to come to the hall and hear what is being spoken," Dagar replied. "Hadubroddar sits in council with our father and our brother, and they are talking less of whether you shall be wedded to him, and more of what the bride-price shall be."

"It is too early" Sigiruna started to say. But she had lost track of time. The Sun was fully up now, and it was no strange thing for her father to hold his councils after breaking his morning fast. "What do they say?"

"Hadubroddar wishes to have you and a share in the Skjolding lands, and our father does not think ill of adding the sea-king's host to our own, nor of the wealth Hadubroddar has spread upon the table. Bragi has spoken of joining his war band for this summer's raiding, and none of the thanes has spoken against it."

Sigiruna glared wild-eyed at her brother for a moment. He sat there so still, his narrow face calm as a mirror's polished surface, when her life was being bartered for such a little thing as Hadubroddar's wealth and friendship! She had drawn back her hand to strike him when sense came to her again, instead she hugged him quickly about the shoulders. "You did well to come to me, Dagar. Now come and stand with me, and we shall see if matters can be changed to the better."

But Dagar drew away from her as they stood, his tall slim body braced as though waiting for a blow. "I shall stand with you until the matter is settled, but if there is nothing to be done, I shall not do battle against my kin, neither with words or with weapons not though you would lift a blade within our very garth. I have little love for Hadubroddar, but it seems to me that the health of the Skjolding clan must be our first thought, and it may be your strength alone that must bear it up."

"There is little to you, if you will not give your word more fully than that," Sigiruna answered angrily. "Let the trolls take you, I do not want such half-hearted help!"

She turned on her heel and strode down the side of the mound, bursting into the hall where the three men sat with chains, brooches, and arm-rings of gold and silver strewn over the table between the platters of bread, sausage, and cheese.

"The land is a gain you will not match else where," Haganon was rumbling. "A sea-king has little hope of winning such a stead, mighty though his band be. This is Skjolding land, my children and their heirs must ever come first upon it, whatever betide."

"Still, it is most fitting that your eldest child should gain the fairest portion, and because a woman cannot lead the host to ward the land, the greatest need in her life is for a worthy warrior to be her husband."

Sigiruna looked about at the thanes. Katilar was nodding, Dice-Agilar smiling, though young Gunthalaukar was frowning, it seemed that he would say nothing, and so with the rest of the men. The words burst from Sigiruna's throat without thought, her spear was not to hand, but she drew her belt knife. "That is not so! And had I such a need, it would be for a better man than one who must marry land to win it."

No sign of his thoughts stirred Hadubroddar's heavy features, he only lifted his hand as if to still Sigiruna, though she had already finished speaking. "It is often said that only he who marries his land truly wins it, for the true leader is like Wodhanar, who took Earth as his woman and fathered Thonarar on her. It may be that you are young to understand such deep lore, but I have learning enough to teach you."

"If you have such learning, you have shown it little. You may know a few of those tales that all folk know, and call upon those that suit your end, anyone may do that. The runes on the rudders of your ships are not well chosen or carved, and for all you may talk of the gods and goddesses, I have seen no signs that your troth is worth your words, I think that you are shameless as a cat's son, and will speak whatever sayings might get you what you wish. I have heard you claim to be true to the gods, but I saw you in the hof at God-Home. You made a great show of baring your chest to Wodhanar's spear when I looked at you, but you did not so much as nod to the others, nor raise your horn when their names were spoken, and you are no holy one whose life is given already, I know this better than any other.

You make offering to Wodhanar because you think men will hold you in awe because of it. This land, though, this land is held by the alf-mounds of the Skjoldings who have ever dwelt here, and the sheaf-god Ingwe-Freyjar whom the Skjoldings hold holy, and though you come of the Swia-folk, ruled by the god-sprung Inglings, you seem to have forgotten the Alfs'-Ruler altogether."

Bragi's face reddened as Sigiruna spoke, he opened his mouth as though to answer her, but closed it again as Haganon rose from his seat and struck his fist hard on the table. The treasures leapt like live things beneath the weight of his blow, jingling on the trembling boards.

"Silence, Sigiruna! You will be still! You have run wild in this hall too long, and in the last year, many men have told me how little hope there is of finding a man who will take you as his bride. The more since you speak so freely of Wodhanar and his offerings, and seldom of Ingwe-Freyjar and his sister, the holy Freyja. Now one has come with open hands, a well-famed warrior who makes his gifts to the god you hail, and you give him words that would win only a raised sword and feud to the death if they were spoken from man to man. You shame our hall and our kin, speaking so to a guest, whatever your thoughts may be. Now hear my deeming. I have sworn that you shall bring a horn of frith to Hadubroddar, and with that horn, if he still wishes to, he shall drink your betrothal ale, and you shall be wed to him at Winter nights."

The Skjolding drighten looked down to Hadubroddar, whose lips had curved into a small, calm smile, then glared heavy-browed at his daughter again. "The terms we spoke of shall stand! If you think you are sold too cheaply, Sigiruna, none but yourself is to blame."

She was too far off to reach Hadubroddar with her belt-knife, and the three at the table were all strong men and good wrestlers, who could easily overpower her together if she attacked one. So Sigiruna sheathed her blade, gathering all the cold hate in her bowels as she glared at her father.

"My bride-price shall be far dearer than you think, if you do not take back your words. Though I have borne the horn to the guest in our hall before, I shall never bear him another, unless it be the bitter horn that men drink beneath the noose in Fetter-Grove. Let Hadubroddar drink his ale without me, he may drink to our betrothal, but those drops shall never fall into Wyrd's Well."

Haganon shook his head. "There were few in all the lands of the North who matched the Skjolding might alone, and now that we have Hadubroddar's sea-band beside us, none are as great as we. The Walsings might have overcome us in the days when Wals lived, but for all Sigimund's might and troll craft, the seas are still rising and the Saxons are scattering. The Wolfings have Hunding's sons at their back. They cannot risk faring from their lands to such a battle, and if they turn against their old foes first, whoever wins must gather his might for several seasons more. The Inglings will be glad enough to see a man of Swia-kin here. You need not look for help from them. You shall be Hadubroddar's bride, and in time you shall see the worth of this. Further, I have given the oath of the clan for this wedding. You cannot break it without shaming us all, and bringing worse shame on the children you might bear after."

Unable to speak, Sigiruna turned and stalked out of the hall, towards the stables where her gray mare waited for her. As she galloped northward, the wind burned against the tears of anger in her eyes, each silent sob tightening her spread-armed grip on the earth. They had all betrayed her. Her father, her brothers, the men she had thought she trusted. I wish they were dead! She thought, but she could not hold her hate, nor bring herself to speak her wish aloud. Sigiruna remembered how Haganon had swung her up in his huge embrace when she was young, how she had sat on his broad shoulders, sure in the knowledge that all the green lands she could see from that height belonged to their kin.

Even now, she knew that her father had not meant to do her ill, it was only that he had no thought and could not guess what was best for her, but he has sworn our kin. He has doomed us all to shame, or me to Hadubroddar! The gray horse was swifter and stronger than old Folwa had been. The Sun was not near her day's height by the time Sigiruna saw Thonarar's holy stone glimmering pale through the oaks' thick trunks. The wind was blowing harder, lashing cold through the trees and casting Sigiruna's hair about her face like foam from winter waves, long tattered tails of white cloud frothed across the sky. A strange trembling dread was rising now in Sigiruna's heart. Legs unsure beneath her, she slipped from her horse's back and bound the reins to an oak's broad limb, then ran along the path, the wind stirring her skirts in a tangle around her legs. Ansuwunja's door was banging open and closed, the branches of the great ash tree above her house whipping about with torn green leaves flying, as though Summer and Winter battled out of season.

"Ansuwunja!" Sigiruna cried. "Ansuwunja, where are you?" A cat yowled from within, then there was only the sound of the wind rushing through the trees, a hundred little whirlwinds tossing the branches about as they swirling Sigiruna's hair into writhing witch-locks. Sigiruna ran into the Frisian's house, but the wind blew harder there. Caught to whirl more fiercely within walls, it cast up a swirling of dust and meal into Sigiruna's eyes, half blinding her so that she must blink and blink to clear her sight with tears of dry hurt. The ale-keg had fallen over, its drink frothing dark to the earthen floor, the stools and table were all overturned, and the high seat's raven-skulls lay broken on the ground. The she-cat crouched wailing in the corner, white fur all bristling with sparks.

The moment Sigiruna's skirt no longer blocked the doorway, the cat flashed out like a weasel down a hole.

"Ansuwunja!"

The lightning shattered through the doorway, thunder deafening the echoes of Sigiruna's cry, the hammering rain followed hard on the stroke.

Suddenly still, Sigiruna lifted her gaze to the high seat where the sheaf-Wodhanar had always stood. He was there no longer. Only a few fallen wheat-heads and a stalk of straw showed where he had been. Though the hard-blowing wind should have cast them away, they lay untouched on the polished seat, where a single drop of blood was slowly soaking in, a dark knot in the wood's pale grain. Ansuwunja's spear was gone as well, and so was her broad-brimmed hat, though everything else lay spilt and spoiled on the floor. A grim thought came to Sigiruna, she turned and walked slowly out into the pounding rain, treading carefully over the slippery grass to stand beneath the ash-tree behind the house.

But the high-arching branches bore no more than fresh leaves. No rope had rasped the wet black bark from the limbs, nor did the Frisian's thin body lie among the tree's twisted roots. Lightning flashed again, stark and white through the blinding rain, and Sigiruna saw the black shape atop the ash-tree. The raven opened its beak, the beating of rain on earth warped its croak, twisting it into words.

"Wodhanar has taken his bride, the Sheaf's queen borne off on the wind. Land's kin shall hold the land. For Sealand the Skjoldings, the Wolfings for Jutland. The Inglings sit in Uppsala now, Skadhe's sons hold Throw-inda-Home. Let the sea-kings roam westward, the wanderers take steads among strangers. New lines shall hallow new lands, and many god-sprung, but ill shall follow, if mound-kin be lost to kin. The tree's branches may reach higher yet, its seeds sprout across great waters, where blood and bone must do for howe and blades be freshly forged. If only the roots stay strong, deep in the home of the dead. The winds from the North blow southward over this land. The folk-tree must hold fast."

The rain was slackening now, the clouds paling already. The raven let out one more croak and took flight, circling heavily upward against the drops pattering on its wings. Sigiruna watched until it was lost against the gray sky, then walked back to her horse. Now she did not spare the spurs. She knew that if she stayed longer she would begin to weep, true sorrow for the loss of her friend bitterly twined with crawling thorns. Ansuwunja's beloved had borne her away, but Hadubroddar must while in the Skjoldings' hall. When she had come home, Sigiruna unsaddled and stabled her mare with the numb thoughtlessness of a drunk moved by habit alone. Half-blinded by the shimmering waves chasing across her eyes, the Skjolding maid did not look before her or think where she was going, but as she came to the top of her mother's howe, her feet caught in the hem of her dress, so that she fell full-length upon the grass.

"If only you were still alive," Sigiruna whispered to her mother. "You knew Ansuwunja as well, and your redes would have saved us all much pain."

Sigigafja had not given herself easily to Haganon, their wedding had been well-blessed with the red mead of wolf and raven, and the eagle had eaten his share of the feast, while Ansuwunja would still ride to joy in the slaughter on the field. Sigiruna knew that the voice whispering these words in her head was not her own. It was her mother's rede she heard, the dead woman's wisdom rising soft from the depths of the howe. The wild beating of her heart began to slow as she breathed more deeply. No one would stir her sleep now, and if they did and she were lost, at least she would not be Hadu-broddar's bride at Winter nights. The gray steed that snuffled at her side now was not the swift-footed mare, but a feller mount, hooves blurred with mist and nostrils flaring at the scent of blood. Now she could hear the far-off sound of byrnies jingling, the blurred mutterings of men's voices. Hailgi's men were already on the field, her hero had need of her, for she could feel the dark wights about him.

She must hurry, before his life was spilled on the earth. Bright-washed afternoon sunlight shifted through swiftly moving bergs of dark cloud, the sprouting fields lit in watery patterns of green. Hailgi's host hastened onward before the wind, hurrying to keep warm beneath its icy lashing. As they crossed along the low tops of Loga Fells, they saw the troops of Hunding's sons drawn up on the field below them. The dog's-head banner flew in several places among the troops. Hailgi guessed that none of Hunding's sons had quite gained rulership over the others. Marching down the winding path to the field, Hailgi saw the light skirts of two maidens by the banner under the arched gray beak-crag of the Eagle Stone. They could not simply run straight onto the field, then. Hailgi glanced about, to Hrothormar and the twelve fur-cloaked men who marched beside him.

"Will you and your men come with me?" Hailgi asked. "I need to go down to Eagle Stone to get Hagalar's daughters off the field, and I need a band they won't set upon lightly if they have treachery in mind."

Hrothormar glanced down at the high stone, his dark eyes glittering from deep within the tangle of fur where beard and hair mixed with bear-hood. He turned his gaze back to Hailgi, opening his mouth in a snarl to show long yellow teeth. Hailgi felt his own hairs tingling in answer, as if a wolf's pelt were prickling out from his skin. He stood his ground, grasping Hrothormar's gaze with his own till the berserk shifted his eyes.

"We'll come, Wolfing," Hrothormar agreed. He waved the other berserks about to surround Hailgi with a living wall of weaponed fur.

"You too, Ansumundar, and you, Swain," Hailgi called. "Come with me."

The berserks moved aside to let the two warriors pass, and they started forward onto the field. Hailgi kept his head high, but he could not help the little pangs of nervousness that tingled through him like sparks flying from fur in the cold. Swain bore Hailgi's raven banner beside him banner in one hand, spear in the other, and the wind lifted the battle-flag so that the raven's wings seemed to beat black against the cloud-white linen. Hailgi could hear the chinking of byrnies and the sound of feet in the mud as the foe men around them shuffled restlessly, moving aside to let them through to the Eagle Stone.

Heming stood beneath the stone's shadow with his helm under his arm. His brown hair had thinned a great deal in three years, though he had gained flesh and color since Hailgi had seen him in Hunding's hall. One of his men held Ingwibjorg, one Gunthahildar. Hailgi marked that their clothing was not torn nor disarranged, and that they stood straight without any signs of pain, but the bruise dark flesh of sleeplessness swelled under both maidens' eyes. He was amazed by how small they seemed now. Ingwibjorg was most of a hand span shorter than he, and her sister still smaller by two fingers' breadth. Ingwibjorg's face was set grimly, jaw muscles tight beneath her plump cheeks, Gunthahildar's fists were clenched on her girdle, as if she were holding her body together by main force.

The berserks opened an aisle so that Hailgi could walk close enough to hail Heming without having to shout. "Hagalar is not here, nor are his men," Hailgi said. "He has kept his word. Let us take the women from the field before we join battle."

Ingwibjorg's grim look melted as her gaze turned towards him, Hailgi saw her pale lips quivering with hope. He remembered what it had been like to walk without weapons among his foes, and knew that the warm glow of anger in his bowels would strengthen his sword-arm. Hailgi hoped that his answering smile would calm her heart, though he thought it might look more like a grimace of fury.

"How can I know that?" Heming replied. "Let me see your troops, call them down to the field."

"I can hardly call them from here, and if I did, you would still have only my word that Hagalar was not hiding behind the hills. But it was shameful of you to take these maidens from their home, and worse for you to threaten them as you do now."

"When the battle is over, if Hagalar and his folk have stayed away, we shall take them home."

"You shall not live that long. How can I trust you not to harm them when the fight turns against you?"

Heming stroked his thick beard, looking from Ingwibjorg to Gunthahildar. Pale as they were, both women met his gaze without flinching, and Gunthahildar showed him her teeth. Hailgi saw that the eating-knives had been taken from their belts, and silently applauded them for having made their disarming needful, he hoped they had at least managed to wound the men who took them.

"Let two of your men go from the field to our ships with these two of mine, and guard them there. Not these bear-sarks, though. They must be plain warriors. Go back, if you will, and send two down to me."

"I have two here," Hailgi replied. He stepped back, taking the banner from Swain's hand. "Swain and Ansumundar, will you guard my foster-sisters from Heming's men?"

Heming's look curdled as the two of them came forward. "You expect me to send my men and my peace-pledges with a troth-breaker? I'd sooner kill the women here and save the trouble."

"Don't speak about what you don't know," Ansumundar rumbled, stepping towards Heming and drawing his sword halfway from the scabbard. "I was true to your father while he lived and after he died, true to my death, till the god chose me for life from the foot of the gallows-tree. Speak like that again, and I'll kill you here and let whatever may fall follow on."

Heming drew his own sword, but did not move forward or speak again, Hailgi guessed that he would not have chosen this fight, but could not back down before his men.

"Are we drightens, or fishwives dickering over a pair of cod?" Hailgi asked Heming sharply. "This won't decide the battle either way, and the day's growing older. Stop fussing. Let them go to your ship."

Heming slid his sword back with a soft grunt of disgust. "All right, then. Go on."

Hailgi and the berserks waited, watching until Ingwibjorg, Gunthahildar, and their four guards had crossed the field and climbed up into one of the ships that lay half-beached by the low tide. Only then did they turn and march back to their own host, which had stopped waiting halfway up the hill.

Freyjawulfar and Raginar had already arranged the formations, they had waited only for Hailgi and the berserks, who would form the point of the swine-wedge. As soon as the sign was given, they would run down from the hill, smashing into the host below with their full strength, and Wodhanar would deem the course of the day after that.

"Are you ready?" Freyjawulfar murmured to Hailgi.

Hailgi swallowed, tightening his hand on the smooth ashen shaft of his spear. There was no more waiting left. The time was on him.

He raised the spear high, turned it to point downwards towards Eagle Stone.

"You all belong to Wodhanar!" Helgi shouted, letting his spear fly in a high arch over the field. He did not see where it struck. He was already running with his sword out and shield up, Hrothormar's berserks surging in a great roaring wave around him as his host swooped down from Loga Fells.

In the shattered fragments of thought between blows, Hailgi knew that his first battle had been easy and clear. Now he hewed and hewed, barely turning strokes that seemed heavier with each swing of the sword, and half the time he could not see whether it was friend or foe before him. Dark shapes seemed to twist in and out of his sight, rain clouding his eyes, it seemed to him that he could hear the hissing of wyrms through his head, and he grasped hilt and shield-grip more tightly against the weakening fear that he might be fey, flinging his blade harder at those who stood against him.

The dark clouds surged and shifted about Sigiruna, she swung her silvery spear, battling her way through to the battle-locked host beneath her. Shafts of sunlight stabbed down to the field through a sudden spatter of rain, and the dark and bright wights writhed and shifted above the host, winged wyrms striking downward with eagle-beaks as the shining shield-women sought to fend them away from the men who strove there. The winds of battle beat against Sigiruna's gray horse, she spurred the steed on, till she could see Hailgi below her. As Sigiruna thrust with her spear, Hailgi's sword cracked through a linden shield and cut through the leather its bearer wore, sticking halfway through his ribs.

Hailgi brought his own shield up to block the wounded man's clumsy stroke, wrenching his blade free to strike again, but Sigiruna saw the bright streak of light that he did not mark flying towards him, the spear's tip thorn-dark within it, and it was her shining shield that knocked the weapon down, snapping the shaft even as the point stuck in Hailgi's own linden. He swept the broken stave around to knock the thrust of another aside and step inside the spear man's range, where the weapon was no more than a staff and his own sword was a torrent of bright blood past the hilt, the clouds darkening its gleaming red until the sun dazzled bright from it again, glittering from the byrnie whose links it pierced as cloud and blood dulled the metal's shine. The twisted battle-wyrms were gathering closer to Hailgi as the ruddy-edged whiteness of his own life-light flared brighter beneath Sigiruna's, their eyes were cold and greedy as the sea.

They should not have him, Sigiruna vowed to herself. She stretched out her hand, and sharp-edged silver hailstones flew icy from her fingertips, hurled fast on the breath of the battle-scream that poured without stopping from her breast. She howled with glee as her missiles struck the dark ones, felling them into empty mist, she clasped her thighs harder on the rough hide of her wolf-steed to drive him forward against Hailgi's foes.

The shapes of battle-women glimmered gray, brightening against the roiling storm as more men fell to the field and the blood reddened the earth in the patches of sunlight between the swiftly moving cloud-shadows. Eight mist-maids ever rode behind Sigiruna, and a host of women strove about her, walkurjas who fared from Wodhanar's hall, or shield-idises riding from elsewhere in the Middle-Garth to ward their own men, the Skjolding did not know which was which. Now Sigiruna's scream rose to a wind that opened the way before Hailgi, sending him onward to the foe she had chosen. For a moment the hound's head blew bright over the field, then the banner-pole splintered beneath Hailgi's sword, the embroidered linen fluttering down to the mud in a rain-swept gust.

The banner-bearer stepped back, swinging the broken pole, Sigiruna pointed, and a spear struck into him, the shaft sprouting bloody from the depths of his chest. He went to his knees, clawing at the weapon as it twisted back down through his body. Suddenly the warped battle-birds arrowed in towards Hailgi's head again, as if drawn by a breath of doom. Sigiruna whirled, striking and heaving her shield desperately as the shouting warrior beneath closed with Hailgi.

The shaft of her spear could not fully block the blow he swung at the Wolfing's helm, only tilt the sword so that its might would glance off instead of caving in the iron. The rain shone white in the sunlight, blowing into Sigiruna's eyes as dazzling tear-stars, blue lightning cracked out through the side of her head as the blow to Hailgi's helm knocked him to his knees in the bloody grass. He lunged low, swinging desperately, and scored through the side of his foe's leg at the knee. The other man went down too, scrabbling for balance as he toppled forward, and Hailgi was already on his feet, stabbing down through the leather band between helmet-rim and byrnie even as his eyes flickered about wildly in search of his next foe.

Sigiruna rode higher, looking over the field. The dark death-wyrms had mostly settled to feed, the idises kneeling beside the living kin who tended to those men who lay dying on the field. A few men were still fighting here and there in the steady drizzle, but others were already taking off their helms. The battlefield shimmered like a rainbow shining over pure gold, hallowed to Wodhanar by the spears that had screamed over it and the blood that had drenched its earth. A new wave of might swept frothing through her as she stretched her own spear down so that its point touched the ground below, drawing up a bright river of the life that had been spilled there.

Sigiruna's horse had lowered his wolfish head, biting sharp-toothed at the bodies that lay there, Wodhanar's harvest, the Awefull One's barley, as the wings of ravens beat around her ears and blackened her sight. Sigiruna called out Hailgi's name through the raven-croaking, called it again, and once more, as she rode upward at the head of her troop of shield-maids. The clouds had grayed the Sun again. Though the clashing of swords still sounded from a couple of small knots of warriors, most already stood bare-headed, sweat-matted hair and beards straggling about their faces, and most of those, far more than Hailgi had feared, were men he knew from his own host. One of Hrothormar's berserks, standing alone in a ring of dead men, swept his blade through the empty air around himself in a last roaring circle. Tottering, he cast back his fur cloak and sank panting to the earth. Freyjawulfar, the left side of his tangled beard matted with dark blood, was kneeling beside one of the fallen, tearing strips from his tunic to bandage his wounds.

Arnugrimar murmured something to another man before his blade moved to the injured man's throat. Thonarabrandar Odd-Eyes was taking a silver ring from a corpse's arm, Bow-Athalwulfar twanging at his damp bowstring in disgust as he shuffled over the field looking for the arrows that he claimed no man but himself could shape rightly. Hailgi suddenly yawned deeply, his limbs beginning to shake under him. His first thought was that he had been wounded without knowing it. A death-wound too deep for his body to admit to before it took him, but no blood stained his byrnie or breeches. He yawned again, rain blowing cold into his mouth. He could not understand what was wrong, but his feet were already bearing him over the dead towards the Eagle Stone. Once he stumbled into something slippery. The man beneath his boots was not quite dead, and screamed miserably as he tried to twist away from the foot in his open guts. Horrified, one boot set firmly on the earth and one skidding in the dying man's bowels, Hailgi stabbed downwards until the scream stopped. He opened his mouth to vomit, but could not.

It was another yawn that stretched his jaws. That blow on the head he thought. But by then he was already sliding down with his back to the Eagle Stone, its cold roughness keeping him from stretching his length on the earth. Sunna's white light cleaved the dark clouds above Loga Fells, one ray shooting down to brighten a streak of pale green on the hill before Hailgi. The little streaks of lightning burst through it like sparks flying from striking swords, and their leaping afterimages gleamed on the high helms of the ones who rode across the heaven-field. Nine weaponed maidens, half-veiled by the shimmering curtain of sun-lit rain. Their byrnies were sprinkled with blood, and bright sparks flew from the tips of their spears. Sigiruna's eyes shone gray on either side of her raven-beaked nose piece, and her fair hair gleamed near-white in the Sun's thin shaft of brilliance. Hailgi pushed himself up and raised his hands and head towards her.

"Will you fare home with me this night?" He cried.

Sigiruna struck her spear against her shield, its thunder resounding about the field as though she had struck the gray sky like an iron gong.

"I think that we have other tasks than to drink beer with the ring-breaker," she called back to him. "My father has promised his maid to the grim son of Granamarar. Yet I have said of Hadubroddar that he is shameless as a cat's son. The folk-leader will come in too few nights, unless you show him to the wal-stead, or else take the maid from the kind ruler. I wish to have no other battle-boar than you, although I see my kin's wrath before me, for I have broken my father's rede."

Hailgi knew the name of Hadubroddar the son of Granamarar, he had won some fame by slaying the Gautish drighten Isung, though he was still a sea-raider with no land and few kin of his own, just the sort of man Berg-ohildar had thought would seek Sigiruna's hand. "Have no awe of Isung's Bane! There must be a din of blades first, or else I will see myself dead! You need not fear Haganon's wrath, nor the ill-mindedness of your clan. Maiden, you shall live with me, and have a good clan, as I see for myself."

"If you would have me, then gather your host and fare to Freki Stone on Sealand's coast. The wedding has been set for the Winter nights feast, but come swiftly, my Wolfing, for I have waited as long as I may."

Sigiruna struck her spear against her shield again, and this time the lightning which burst from it blinded Hailgi. When the cool grayness of the rain-light soothed his eyes to sight again, he was sitting in the mud with his back to the Eagle Stone and a half circle of men standing about looking down at him.

"Are you hurt, Hailgi?" Freyjawulfar asked.

Hailgi shook his head. He tried to push himself up again, but was too worn out to stand. Hrothormar came forward towards him. His fit past, the berserk-drighten was swaying where he stood, his dark eyes vague, but he put out a shaking hand for Hailgi to grasp. His other hand against the stone, Hailgi raised himself with Hrothormar's help, and they stood steadying one another a moment.

"Thank you," Hailgi murmured softly, letting go of the other's grip. He felt firmer on his feet already, steady enough to take a couple of steps as his strength began to drip back into his veins.

Then he glanced towards the empty boats, and his memory slapped sudden life into him. "Hagalar's daughters! Are they" Ansumundar stood nearby, but Swain and the women were nowhere to be seen.

"They're all right," Ansumundar rumbled. "Black Wulfar and his brother Wormar, who were watching them, thought they'd get a vengeance-blow in when Heming went down, but we'd thought they'd try it. Wulfar went for me, but Wormar struck at the girls first. That Swain, he's a good boy he was right there in the way before that nithling could do them any harm, but he's not much of a fighter. Wormar cut the boy a pretty bad one on the shield-arm right away, but Ingwibjorg hit Wormar with an oar before he could finish the job, and then I got him right through the neck, clean as if he'd laid his head on a chopping block."

"How badly hurt is Swain?"

"He won't use that arm again for much," Freyjawulfar answered before Ansumundar could speak. "The blow went halfway through his elbow joint. I'd say he's lucky if he doesn't lose it altogether."

Hailgi didn't know what to say. He looked out over the wal stead, where the rain was coming down harder. At least the rain kept the flies away, he thought, and it seemed to be washing away some of the battlefield stink of shit and blood as well, or else his nose was growing used to the smell.

"They've left us enough boats, anyway," he mused. "Let the wounded go back to Hagalar's hall with Ingwibjorg and Gunthahildar and as many whole men as it takes to row them. The rest of us will go on to Hunding's hall for our feast. Someone find Hunding's sons and load their bodies to come with us. They were athelings and ought to be buried with their kin." Hailgi stopped, thinking of how pale Ingwibjorg and Gunthahildar had been in the hands of their guards, and feeling a sudden surge of sympathy swinging up in him like the echo of Ingwibjorg's full skirt swaying around his legs like Lingwe's touch, which he could never cast from his body again. "Let it be known that if I hear of any man raping or mishandling a woman around Hunding's hall, which is now mine, I will drown him in the bog for Nerthuz myself."

Hailgi went to help load the two boats that would bear the wounded back to Hagalar's hall. Swain was already lying down in one. The rain had soaked the neat bandage on his arm, fading the blood on it to a pale pink splotch that spread even as Hailgi watched.

Swain brought a smile to his lean face as he looked up at Hailgi, leaning up against the rowers' seat behind him. "I might have done better, but then, I might have done worse too. He's dead and the girls are alive, and that's what you wanted, isn't it?"

"You've done very well," Hailgi answered, even as Gunthahildar broke in, talking so fast that her words stuttered over each other.

"He took the blow that was meant for me. He leapt right in the way of the sword. I think I've never seen anyone so brave." Her voice was very high, like a harp-string tightened far above its note. "I bandaged him myself." She raised her skirt to show where she had cut the strips from its hem.

"Well done." Hailgi leaned down to clasp Swain's hand. "I knew I could trust you with my honor."

A flush of pleasure rose to brighten Swain's white face for a moment before ebbing again. "I guess I've proven you were right to take me as your man, after all."

"I knew it all along," Hailgi assured him. He drew his father's ring from his arm, bent the soft gold back and forth until the coils parted.

One half he put back on his other arm, the other he set in Swain's hand. "Take this, and the victory-luck my father gave us be with your healing as well. The sooner you're whole, the gladder I'll be." Hailgi turned to Ingwibjorg. "You too, I hear you were very brave."

"I hit the man with an oar while he was swinging at someone else. How much bravery does that take?" Ingwibjorg pushed her wet hair back from her face. The rain had darkened it into a sodden mass, the rings under her eyes were shockingly dark against her paleness, as though she had been beaten.

"They didn't hurt you, did they?"

"No, they knew we were worth something." She smiled tiredly at Hailgi.

"I was so glad to see you coming for us there. Come back to my father's hall as soon as you can, and I promise I'll greet you with more joy. I'd never seen battle before today, and I'm so..." She sank down on one of the benches, but was on her feet again in a moment as Helmbernu and Arnugrimar came down the beach bearing Athalwulfar the Tall up between them.

His left leg was twisted at an odd angle, but half of his right foot had been sheared cleanly off. Tired as he was, Hailgi got out to help. There were many wounded, and it would be a long time still before he would be able to think on Sigiruna's words or to sleep. Sigiruna lay still on her mother's howe, staring up at the clouds rising against the blue of the western sky, rising from Jutland, as the storm swept on past Hailgi's battlefield. The cold lightless flame of howe-fire flickered all about her, the might of the mound burning through the gold that lay hidden in it.

Her woolen cloak and dress were damp and chill as if they had decked a corpse, but the feeling was thrumming back into her hands and feet as her heart drove the blood harder through her body and her breasts rose higher with her living breaths. She tried to raise herself on one arm, but the muscles shook so badly that she fell back again, lying still for the sun to stroke life into her. Hailgi was safe, sig-blessed as he would ever be while she could fight above him and he kept Wodhanar's favor. And he knew her plight, now war could keep her from Hadubroddar's hands, and perhaps all the Skjoldings' life would not be spilt in the battle. When she was able to sit up again, Sigiruna looked out over the Skjolding lands.

The walkurja-sight was still in her eyes, so that she could see the small broad shapes of the field-wights at their frolic over the frothing seeds, the green and silver heat-waves of the land's might rippling about them. Carefully she stood up, walking along the glistening path to the Skjoldings' hall. Her anger was gone from her, all flung forth in the battle, now she would be able to speak less ill, and perhaps to gain more of what she wished with the weight of calm redes.

As Sigiruna's foot came down within the hall's threshold, ice froze through her limbs. She stood still, shocked and staring. The battle had already come to pass. Her father sat in his high seat with his half-severed head lolling on one shoulder, Bragi's breast gushed blood around a spear-shaft, and the brains ran gray through the deep gash in Hadubroddar's helm, and the wounds gaped dark upon his thanes. The ravens walked between them, free as hens in the hall, and the hounds that nuzzled and snapped at the bloodied corpses were gray gaunt wolves. Yet the men there had not all died in fight, there was a rope around Katilar's neck, as around Hrabanawulfar's and only Dagar's shape showed the brightness of life, and he sat cradling a sling-wrapped sword-arm.Sigiruna's knees dropped beneath her and she toppled forward, barely able to catch herself before her head struck the floor. The men were around her at once, lifting her up and turning her over.

"Back, let her breathe!" Haganon's voice boomed. Sigiruna blinked, and blinked again, as she stared up at him. No sign of blood showed on the fair braids of his gray-stranded beard, and his face was bright as if the Sun shone on it. They were all living folk who crowded around her, Dice-Agilar and Herwobrandar and Hadubroddar, Bragi and Dagar, and her youngest brother's arms both moved freely as he knelt down.

"Nothing is wrong," Sigiruna croaked. Dagar shook his head, pressing her back down. Sigiruna knew that she must be pale and cold, for his touch was as hot as if he had been holding a bowl of steaming broth. Though the walkurja sight was faded, she knew what she had seen. All were doomed to die, her father and Bragi and all the good thanes who had drunk their ale and slept within their hall. It would be a long mourning, that started so early before their death. Only Dagar would live, and she did not know what wound had scathed his sword-arm. The last man of the Skjoldings might be doomed to while his age as a cripple.

Though the tears were warming her eyes, Sigiruna tried to bend her mouth into a smile. Wyrd was set, if she let it lie. She knew that there was nothing to be won from stealing the gladness from her kinsmen's last days, though she herself must weep silent in bed every night. There was no more revenge to take on Haganon for giving her to Granamarar's son, since his oath had already doomed him to death. She could hold her walkurja-craft back, or ward her own kin and let Hailgi's folk die. She knew the runes well, could she not doom Hadubroddar to death, and let Hailgi and her own menfolk live? Battle was not so easily ended with one man's death, when many were met, nor was there any surety that the Skjoldings and Wolfings could make frith over the bodies of their friends. She would have to choose.

To cast her life with the glimmering in the darkness and the whispers of the dead, or trust in the kin she had known, and pay her geld for luring Hailgi to death by dwelling with Hadubroddar. The sea-king was not a lucky man, the gods would not thole him too long. Sigiruna shivered on the bench like a half-drowned hawk, hooding her eyes against the brightness of the men around her. First Hailgi must cross the waters, then, if she knew the ways of her kin and their land, he would be met at the shore by one troop, at Freki Stone by the second. He had not beaten the sons of Hunding easily, and her father spoke the truth. It would be long before he gathered his might, perhaps for too long before he came to Sealand. That thought was a dead relief, cold as clay long from the firing, she did not know if it was better or worse than the shivering wind of mourning and hope that might yet bear Hailgi to her over the corpses of her kin.

CHAPTER XVII

The morning after the battle, Hoilogae was awakened by the cool dripping of rain on his left cheek. He rolled over, away from the leak in the roof, but although his blanket was warm, the fleas were biting and he could not get back to sleep. The smell of cooking porridge crept into his nose, and he could hear the low voices of men muttering nearby. Hoilogae got up, stretched till his fingertips grazed the hall's roof, and breathed deeply. The cool dampness in the air came to him as a welcome relief from the days of dry heat, it seemed to him as he stood there that his own roots were reaching deep into the thirsty earth, drinking his share of the sweet gray rain that fell, nourishing as ale, to the grain-fields. Hoilogae took a wooden bowl and a horn spoon from one of the benches and went to the big clay pot that rested squat among the coals, scooping out a bowlful of porridge. His father, Attalae, and Hedhinaz were sitting near the open doorway and talking as they ate, he went to join them. Most of the other warriors, both their own men and Hrothagaisaz's wounded, were still sleeping, worn out from the fighting and the feast.

"Well, Hoilogae," Herwawardhaz said as Hoilogae sat down beside him, "now that you've won these lands, what do you mean to do with them?" In the soft grey light from the doorway, the older drighten's face looked more restful than Hoilogae could yet remember. His brow smoothed and the tight-drawn bow of his mouth unstrung, the strands of gray blending easily into the streaks of sun-gold through his light brown hair.

Hoilogae gestured towards Hrothagaisaz, who lay on a heap of straw with his cloak over him. He was curled up on his side, eyes shut and a soft snore bubbling out of his mouth. "First we go to Sigisharjaz."

"Not for two or three moons yet, unless you mean to let the faring do what you didn't have the stomach for," Hedhinaz replied. His ash-pale hair had come loose from its ties, he brushed it back impatiently. A huge bruise had swollen to blacken his left cheek in the night, and he sat with his swollen ankle propped up against the bench on the other side of the table, the fighting, Hoilogae thought, must have strained it again. "It may be that you won't have to, such wounds often catch the rot, even with the best care."

"I mean that he shall be given it. We won this hall for the sake of our mother, to whom it should fall by right, and there is no more herb-crafty wife here in Jutland, nor one who knows the charms of healing better." Except, he thought, that Swaebhon might. I wonder where she is I wonder.

Hedhinaz dropped his hand, stroking the hilt of the iron sword at his belt. Attalae seemed to be paying scant attention, scraping the last porridge from the bottom of his bowl as he looked out at the silvery rain-mists drifting slowly across the wind-stirred green fields and the woods beyond, but Hoilogae could feel the old warrior's keen thought stirring through their words like the point of a knife blade.

"Hrothagaisaz is your enemy, you know," Herwawardhaz said softly.

"He was," Hoilogae answered, his voice firm. "He may be again, as it is deemed. For now he is my guest."

"There is a difference," Attalae murmured, "between not seeking to flee your orlog and willingly seeking to bring it upon yourself." He did not look at Hoilogae as he spoke, but still stared out at the shifting shapes of the wind through the rain and over the fields.

"A man is his orlog," Hoilogae replied, "it is his might as well as his doom, and mine was laid before this, why should I not rejoice in it, whatever it be? In any case, I have given my word now, and must hold to it with my full strength, and we shall bring Sigislinthon here to take her place in the land of her kin."

"Who would you have rule in Glazaleunduz?" Herwawardhaz wiped a driblet of porridge out of his beard. His tone was mild, so that Hoilogae could not tell what he thought. "It is a far way from here to there, and our war band is small to hold so large a land as we have won, nor can one drighten be at both ends at once. Do you mean to give up this stead and take that for yourself?"

"Let that be as you think best. But when matters are settled between Hrothagaisaz and myself, I shall go to seek Swaebhon the daughter of Aiwilimae for my wife, and we must wait to see what comes of that."

"I know neither the maiden's name nor that of her father," Herwawardhaz mused. "Attalae?"

"They are not known to me," Attalae rumbled. For a moment Hoilogae thought that he would say more, but he did not. Herwawardhaz seemed about to speak, then his glance slipped down to the sword at Hoilogae's side, and his half-parted lips opened only to take in another spoonful of porridge.

Hedhinaz suddenly leaned over the table towards Attalae. "Did Hrothamaraz have daughters?"

"Two who lived to womanhood." Attalae tapped his bronze spoon twice against the side of his empty bowl with a hollow clunking sound. "One is married to the drighten Gunthawulfaz, who dwells a long way to the south, the other died of a fever last year. You will find no bride fit for you in this household, even if you were old enough to wed."

"I have my own sword, and am blooded in battle, and you have not stilled my voice when we have spoken of the things of men." The hard edge of Hedhinaz's voice flashed like a drawn dagger. "Why, then, should I be thought too young to wed?"

"Because being a warrior is not the same as being the fro of a household, with a wedded frowe beside you," Attalae told him. His gray beard hid the deepening lines around his mouth, but Hoilogae could hear the sadness that blurred his tones like a faint veil of rain. "That asks for more than you have learned yet."

Hoilogae let his mind slip from their talk, staring out at the gray trunks of the beeches rising like shore-cliffs behind the tossing waves of silver-green barley, misted by the swiftly driving rain. It seemed to him that he could feel the grain settling into the earth again, springing and falling, sleeping and sprouting, its slow wheel of planting and harvest rolling on in frith with no shouting of swords or blood to jar it aside, and this stretched as far as he could see, all the way north to the mound where Herwamundaz dwelt. The words rose from Hoilogae's throat without his own thought, like the deep notes rising through the bronze bell of a lur-horn.

"You need have no fear that Glazaleunduz will be unsafe without you this summer. There will be no more warring on any of our lands this year, nor for a little time to come. For now, let Hedhinaz hold the northern part for you, while Mother and you rule here in her udal lands."

Hedhinaz's mouth twisted as though he had bitten into a fruit and found it rotten. Hoilogae realized that in the moment he spoke, his brother's mind had looked forward farther than his, to a day when Hoilogae would rule Sigislinthon's lands alone, and Hedhinaz hold only Glazaleunduz.

"Is Hedhinaz not too young to hold a stead by himself?" Attalae asked before Hedhinaz could speak. "A wedding is only one household, but in Glazaleunduz he must be fro for all."

"Only let me do it, and see!" Hedhinaz flared, turning on Attalae. "If you believe my brother speaks true, what have we to lose?"

Attalae scratched thoughtfully under his beard, regarding Hedhinaz for a very long time. "It would surprise me indeed if, as young as you are, you could learn to rule well. Still, Glazaleunduz is not too far from here for Herwawardhaz to know of your doings. It might perhaps be done."

"It will be done!" Hedhinaz answered. He sat bolt upright, his narrow frame quivering with tension like an arrow just shot into a target. Hoilogae realized Attalae's ploy, while Hedhinaz thought he had to prove himself worthy of Glazaleunduz, he would strive with all his might towards that goal and not turn his thoughts against his brother. Wisely done, Hoilogae applauded silently.

"I shall go with Hoilogae," Attalae went on, more slowly. "It is not in my mind to let him go alone where he is going, for he shall need more guarding than he can give himself along the way."

Herwawardhaz glanced at Hoilogae, then at Hedhinaz, then looked away past them, at an empty space near the left doorpost. "My sons have both become men now," he murmured. "Very well, it shall be so." He turned his gaze to the older warrior. "We shall miss you, Attalae, but I cannot hold you if you choose to go."

Attalae's answer was lost in his gray beard, and it was only the rain-shadowed light from the doorway that cast a gray veil over his wrinkled face. The harvest-tide was almost to its end by the time Sigislinthon ran her palms over the new scar on Hrothagaisaz's leg and stated that it was healed well enough for him to make the long faring to Sigisharjaz's Holm.

Though Hrothamaraz's son had been lucky, his wound closing cleanly without pus or stink, he had healed somewhat slowly. Sigislinthon said that he was at fault, for trying to get up and walk before she said he could, but Hoilogae wondered sometimes if his mother's craft might not have held the wound open longer than it might otherwise have been, trying to hold back the day when her son must go. Counting himself and Attalae, Hoilogae's troop numbered two dozen. Hrothagaisaz took only six warriors with him, for many of his men had died in spite of the care Sigislinthon and their wives had given, and Hoilogae meant to send no more than an equal number back with the news of Sigisharjaz's deeming, while the rest went on with him in search of Swaebhon.

Further, the harvest was not yet done, so the total of men who could be spared was small. Thus they gathered at the door of the hall in the cold gray dawn, beside a small ox-cart loaded with their food and with gifts which Hoilogae meant to give to Sigisharjaz in thanks. Sigislinthon and Herwawardhaz came out of the hall to bid the wayfarers fare well. Hoilogae's mother embraced him, looking up into his face. The clouded sky reflected grayly from her blue eyes as from a still lake, although she smiled, her fine features showed little of joy.

"Fare well, my son, and come home soon," Sigislinthon told him. Without letting go of, she pressed a bag of waxed leather into his hand. "If you should be wounded on the way, make a poultice with the powder in here and bind it on. It will keep the rot out and speed your healing. Tell Hedhinaz that I love him, and hope that he and some of his folk, and you, will be able to come here for the Yule feast. None should be without kin at Yule time."

"I hope so too. But Swaebhon must live far from here, if no one has heard her name or her father's, and the winter storms are coming up. It may be that we will not be able to travel back as swiftly as we would like."

"It may be," Sigislinthon agreed. She leaned her fair head against her son's chest for a moment, then straightened up again. "I love you, Hoilogae. Come home safely."

Hoilogae patted his mother's shoulder awkwardly. "I love you, too," he answered. "I'll be home as soon as I can be. Anyway, I have Attalae to take care of me."

"So you do." Sigislinthon let go of him, turning towards Attalae. She did not embrace him, but stood straight and stark as a young birch in winter, staring at him for a moment. "Now all is as it would have been had you won me for Herwawardhaz when you first asked," she said at last. "May this faring go more smoothly for you and have a swifter end."

"That, at least, it shall certainly have," Attalae answered.

Herwawardhaz hugged his son around the shoulders, the wide brown wing of his cloak engulfing both of them for a moment. "My blessing on your faring and your wooing," the drighten rumbled. "If Swaebhon's bride-price is not beyond imagining, I shall surely make it good for you. There is a sealed bag in the wagon, which you should reach into when you have found her. No man should go wooing empty-handed, least of all one of your clan and deeds."

"I thank you, Father. I hope that I shall be able to adorn our clan with another wedded atheling-frowe, and with more children soon after."

The gleam of teeth breaking through Herwawardhaz's beard showed Hoilogae that he had spoken rightly. "Go on, now," Herwawardhaz said, clapping Hoilogae on the back. "There is little time, if you mean to reach Sigisharjaz before the winter storms rise on the sea. Attalae, my best wishes go with you as well. Remember that you are growing aged. You have the right to make the young men do all the work for you, and claim the best ale at night."

"Perhaps we should play at swords together more often, if you think I am growing aged." Attalae grinned at Herwawardhaz, but Hoilogae, standing a little closer to the old warrior, marked the faint tremble of his lips. It is I who must care for him now, Hoilogae thought, and the thought brought him no joy.

Hrothagaisaz stood a little apart from them, thick blond brows drawn together as he stared back at the hall that had been his father's. His brown eyes narrowed a little, his mouth tightening beneath his sparse golden beard as though he were tallying up a heavy sum in his head, so that his thoughts lent a look of keenness to his blunt features. A sparse scattering of grass, now yellow-brown, had grown up to shadow the scorched place on the earth where the funeral pyre had burned, like pale hair half-hiding a scar. If he could win any blessing from the cindered bone mingled with flint and earth, it was none that Hoilogae could hear. Still, Hrothagaisaz stood straight without a man or a stock to lean on, and walked without a limp.

Herwawardhaz and Sigislinthon walked with the traveler past the fields
that were already reaped, where the short brown rows of stubble whispered
plots against the cold bite of the wind. When all the grain had been gathered, the dry stalks would be seared to the ground, to ready the fields for the
next spring time's planting. Luka's fiery shears cropping Sibjon's fair hair, as
some told it, that he might bring her new tresses of gold for another bright
harvest-tide. Then the fro and frowe went on to join the rest of their folk at
the harvest, and Hoilogae's band began to move northward, walking against
the wind's sharp ice-arrows.

The faring to the hall which was now Hedhinaz's went more swiftly than
the way southward had gone. The cold and the threat of the winter sea-
storms ahead pricked the traveler on. The harvest at Glazaleunduz was already done with, when they got there, the burnt fields sodden black beneath
the lowering gray evening sky. The scent of baking bread rose on the white
plume billowing out from the hall's smoke hole.

Hoilogae went ahead of the troop, scraping the mud from his shoes on
the edge of the stone threshold and knocking once on the hall's door. The
sounds from within stilled for several breaths, while Hoilogae waited for the
door to open. When it finally swung aside, Hedhinaz stood there with his
iron sword drawn in one hand and a foam-topped horn in the other. The
blade shook a little in his hand as he looked at Hoilogae.

"Who are you?" Hedhinaz's voice had deepened in the last months, its
sharp edge tempered a little by the thickening of his throat.

In his moment of bewilderment, Hoilogae marked that his brother's amber luck necklace, or another like it, was around his throat again, and that
Hedhinaz had grown nearly two finger widths taller. Then he remembered
that he had drawn his own dark cloak up against the cold wind in his ears,
and Hedhinaz had no way to expect him. He cast back the fold of wool from
his head. "Do you often greet your guests like this?"

"Only those who knock a single time as the night begins to darken. Or do
you not know that Winter nights has come, and that with it sometimes come
the dead to the lands of the living?" Hedhinaz's eyes flickered over Hoilogae's
shoulder, to the place where Herwamundaz's mound loomed dark against
the twilight. It seemed to Hoilogae that he could remember a train of folk
with torches in their hands, singing as they walked out to the mound with
bread and meat and ale, but snow had been falling then, not rain, perhaps it
had been a different feast.

"We are alive, anyway. Will you bid us come in?"

Hedhinaz swung his arm wide, as if to open the door a second time.
"Come in, my brother, with all your folk, and guest with me for this feast."
He looked over Hoilogae's shoulder. "Welcome, Attalae, and you, Hrothagaisaz. Hurry in, the sky is getting dark and it is nearly time to go to the
hof."

Hoilogae and Attalae entered first, followed by Hoilogae's men. Hedhinaz greeted each of them in turn, Ingwawaldaz and Ingwagairaz, Dagastiz,
Thonarabernu, Hrotharikijaz, the four sons of Hlothowairar, and the rest.

He made a sweeping gesture of welcome to Hrothagaisaz's men, since he could not greet them by name, Hrothagaisaz waited until all the others had gone in before he stepped over the threshold-stone.

"Be welcome in our hall, Hrothagaisaz son of Hrothamaraz," Hedhinaz said. Hoilogae could hear no bitter spoor of mockery in his brother's voice, but Hrothagaisaz, looking down at the younger man, had set his face stiffly as a bronze mask. Hedhinaz lifted the horn to Hrothamaraz's son. It was the gold bound aurochs horn used at the holy sumbel-drinking, which whispered to Hoilogae who else Hedhinaz might have expected to knock on his door at Winter nights' beginning. "I have no frowe to bear you the horn, but I bid you take and drink from it as my guest."

"It seems to me that the sons of Herwawardhaz find it easy to offer hospitality." Hrothagaisaz's words were slow, grinding stonily against the sides of his throat, but he took the horn and drank deeply from it, the ale's foam dripping down from either side of his sparse golden beard like froth from a wolf's jaws. The fire's light seemed to spark against the flecks of green in his eyes as he lowered the horn. "Still, I find it a lighter thing to accept here in Glazaleunduz, and I thank you for it, Hedhinaz."

There was room for all the men who had come with them to sit in Hedhinaz's hall, small as it seemed next to the fresh memory of the hall Hoilogae had won. Hedhinaz had let benches be built, and two narrow tables that stretched the length of the house on either side of the fire-pit in the middle of the floor. It would be cold in winter without cows or sheep inside, but there was hardly room for them. The hens were still nesting in the rafters, though, and Sigislinthon's best rooster strutted about the floor. Many of Herwawardhaz's men had come home rather than take steads in a strange place, and they were here with their wives and children, the younger bairns playing beneath the tables and in the straw along the walls. The planks of the tables and benches were smoothly hewn, but the wood still smelled new and raw, the faint spoor of beech-sap still sharp through the scents of smoke and bread.

Hoilogae dipped his clay mug into one of the tall frothing ale-pots that stood on the table before him, careful not to scoop up any of the wild apples that floated dark in the pale foam. He gathered a handful of hazel nuts and blackberries from the bronze bowl beside it to still his rumbling stomach. The ale did not taste quite so fine as that Sigislinthon had brewed, there was less of the sweetness of honey and fruit in it, and more of some herb's sharp bitterness. Still, Hoilogae could feel its strength in the empty pit of his stomach, and it was welcome after the day's cold walk. He cracked one hazel nut against another in the palm of his hand and picked the broken meat out.

As Hoilogae looked up, Hrothagaisaz was handing the sumbel-horn back to Hedhinaz. The young fro filled it again and went to light a torch from the fire, then walked to the door.

"Rise and gather your torches," Hedhinaz called, sharply as sword scraping along sword. "The night is falling, now we must go to the hof."

Hoilogae and those who had fared with him had no torches, but every man and woman of Glazaleunduz had a pitch-tipped stick to thrust into the fire. At Attalae's gesture, Hoilogae lifted one of the ale-pots instead, bearing its weight easily behind his brother as they walked out into the swiftly-gathering darkness. The torches' wind-battered flames threw their shadows long and wavering over the blackened field, each walker's shade looming into a twisted giant in turn as they passed by Herwamundaz's mound on their way to the pen where the gold horned hof-oxen were kept. Both his hands full, Hoilogae could not hold his cloak down against himself, and the strengthening wind whirled it up to beat about his face, its corners lashing spatters of ale from the pot he bore.

One of the oxen was already standing close to the gate, its gilded horns towering over its dark misted shape, and it was this ox that Attalae led out behind Hedhinaz. Hoilogae set his ale-pot down beside the harrow as Hedhinaz lowered his brand to light the hof's flames. The burning pitch of the torches and the sweetness of the apple wood fire masked the smell of the old blood in the walls and earthen floor of the hof as the folk gathered around the heaped harrow-stones. Hedhinaz looked frail as a single stalk of grain next to the ox, his ash-blond hair gilded ruddy by the firelight.

The shifting shadows on the walls drew Hoilogae's gaze to them as Hedhinaz began to speak, calling Fro Ingwaz and Nerthuz, calling the kin who had fared to the worlds of the dead. Hoilogae could see the shades thickening, moving where the living men and women stood still, and knew that the alfs and idises, the elder fathers and mothers of the clans gathered there, were among them, awaiting the gift Herwamundaz's young kinsman would give for all his folk. It seemed to Hoilogae that the ox's golden horns stretched high as the branches of a great tree, towering into the darkened heavens above, its roots reaching down far below his sight, to where the first seed's orlog had set all the limbs' turning shapes. Red lightning flickered in a swift sword-stroke, and a torrent of dark rain poured down from the tree over the harrow's stones, its warm might sinking swiftly to strengthen the deepest roots.

Hedhinaz swept the bronze sword in his hand around in a great circle, shaking it like a twig towards the eight winds to bless every corner of the hof and all the folk within. Hoilogae felt the hot drops sprinkling over him, sinking into his bones and blood and seed where the ghosts of his elder kin lurked in every smallest shape of his body and soul, and their new-fed life surged up in him like sap at winter's end. Taking the gold-bound horn from Attalae, Hedhinaz raised it and spoke, his words crashing like waves against Hoilogae's ears as he hailed the holy ones gathered around the harrow. Thanks for victory and a good harvest, for winter warding against the darkness and a fair year of frith to come. Thus he called, so that all who were there could hear. Then he drank and passed the horn about, and each spoke in turn.

Many of the men hailed Fro Ingwaz with thanks for his warding in the summertime battle, others spoke to Thonaraz, either calling on him as the Warder or to thank him for sending the spring rains and the summer heat-lightning which ripened the grain, and yet others raised their horn to Tiwaz, giver of wise deemings.

The women hailed Nerthuz, Frijjo, and the Frowe most often, though some of them also called on the manly gods, and both men- and women-folk blessed the land-wights and their kin who dwelt in the howes.When the horn reached Hrothagaisaz, he held it for a long time, then said only, "Hail to thee, Hrothamaraz my father," before drinking and passing it to Hoilogae. The horn felt light in Hoilogae's grasp, light and empty. He dipped it into the ale-pot. Hands wet with beer, he held its smooth curve firmly as he spoke.

"Hail to Wodhanaz, who has given me victory, and to Swaebhon daughter of Aiwilimae, on whom I shall look within the Middle-Garth's ring before Austarjon's next bright dawn."

He had to drink carefully, for he had dipped up one of the crab-apples from the ale-pot in the horn, but he could still hear the gasps. Other men did not dare to speak the name of the Ansuz at sumbel, for the gods drew closest within the drinking-ring, and orlogs laid there could not be unshaped, nor wyrd unraveled when it had turned there.

"Hail to ye, gods and wights all!" Hedhinaz said, taking the horn from his brother and drinking a last time to close the ring. He poured the rest of the drink out over the harrow-stones, beer mingling with blood and spattering to hiss in the fire. The crab-apple bounced from a stone, rolling into the flames where it began to crackle and blacken, its sweet scent rising through the copper-bright smell of the fresh blood.

Hedhinaz bent and cut a large piece of meat from the fallen ox, then went to the door, waiting for the rest to follow him. Hoilogae lifted his lighter beer-burden and went after his brother. The ox was borne by the four sons of Hlothawairar in the firelight, there was no telling one of them from another, their muscle-gnarled bodies beneath black hair and beards alike as four bronze swords from the same clay mold. Hoilogae's brother did not falter on the path to Herwamundaz's mound, but led his folk straight over the rustling grass to its height. He bent to lay the meat carefully on the mound, and Hoilogae poured out the ale beside it. The elder youth thought he could hear his brother whispering, but he could not make out the words. One of the women Wulfahaidhaz, the wife of Laithingaz squatted down, careful of her seven-months' swollen belly, and laid three small loaves by the meat. Then Hedhinaz led them back to the hall.

"You have gotten your luck-necklace again," Hoilogae said to his brother as the ox-meat seethed with spear-leeks and grain in the great bronze cauldron of southern work, one of Herwamundaz's treasures which was only used at the holy feasts.

A flush darkened Hedhinaz's narrow face as he turned his gaze aside. "Mother saw it when the peddler came through here, and bought it back for me," he muttered. "I gave her the little iron knife did you not see that she wore it?"

"I had supposed she had simply bought another like it from him. She spoke of its help in her leech-craft, when she was healing the wounded, and often used it to make fires with. You did well to give it to her."

"That meat will be done by now, I think." Hedhinaz picked up his bowl and walked over to the cauldron, speaking softly with Wulfahaidhiz and her sister Ingwadis who stood stirring the broth.

Hoilogae, Hrothagaisaz, and their men began the sea-faring early the next morning, while most of the other folk were still sleeping off their ale. The sea etin Agjiwaz, too, had been at his brewing. White crests of foam capped the gray waves and lined the edge of the water's path up the strand. The wind blew a gust of spray and light rain into Hoilogae's face, and he drew his cloak more tightly about himself. They took three long boats as well as the smaller boat Hoilogae and Attalae had borrowed from Sigisharjaz. The largest of these would be coming back with Hrothagaisaz, his band, and seven of Hoilogae's men, the other two would fare onwards in the search for Swaebhon.

Hoilogae heard Ingwawaldaz muttering into his brown beard, glancing at the water as he helped to load the boats. The cold had stung Hrothagaisaz's fair skin ruddy, so that no whitening could betray any fear, but he shifted uneasily from foot to foot, staring at the boats.

"We'd best split the in-landers up," Attalae said softly. Hrothagaisaz did not turn to look at them, but even beneath his thick gray cloak, Hoilogae could see the warrior's heavy shoulders stiffening at the rede-giver's words. "Some of them are sure to be sea-sick. I'd wager an arm-ring that no more than one or two of them have ever been on the ocean before, and if the weather's rough, we can't risk having too many men puking instead of working in a single boat. It'll be hard enough for us to keep together as it is."

When the boats were loaded, Hoilogae poured the ale out to Agjiwaz and Ran, its foam mingling with the sea-froth left on the smooth sand as the beer-darkened water drew back to the sea.

"Up into the boat, Attalae," Hoilogae ordered. "It's a heavy push to take us out there, and getting your feet wet in this weather will do you no good."

"Nor will it you, nor anyone else," grunted the old man, but he climbed up into the ship anyway, sitting down heavily by its prow.

Hedhinaz came up to Hoilogae. The young fro was still dressed in his feast finery, ruddy-brown tunic and cream-colored cloak, with a thick cap of white wool on his head and the glittering rings of bronze and gold adorning his arms. "Fare well, my brother. May your wooing go well and the Ansuz whom you called on look kindly upon you."

"Stay well, my brother, and be blessed in frith."

After a moment of awkward silence, Hoilogae stepped forward and embraced his brother. The edges of Hedhinaz's lengthening bones pressed sharply against the thick wool, but Hoilogae could feel the growth of his brother's strength in their embrace. He let go quickly, turning to the boats and tossing his cloak into the bottom of the one where Attalae sat. The wind flayed his tunic's warmth away at once, but it was better than getting his cloak soaked in the icy water. Hoilogae his palms against the ship's stern, the other men did as he had done and gathered around, bending the backs and heaving until the vessels began to slide over the sand and into the ocean. The ships leapt and bucked against the waves, it was not long before several of the men, Hrothagaisaz among them, were leaning over the side of the boat. Thonarabernu chuckled deep in his throat as he pulled his oar.

"So the Awesome One gets his share of the feast after all." Though the big man laughed, his scarred knuckles brushed swiftly over the amber ax-head at his throat on the oar's back swing. Ingwawaldaz glanced nervously at him through a tangle of brown hair, thrusting thumb through fist to turn away any ill-luck his jest might have brought them.

Although the rowing was hard, it warmed Hoilogae and his men from the sea's wet chill about their thighs, and soon those who were not sick began to feel more heartened in spite of the rain spattering sharp into their faces. After a little, Thonarabernu began to sing with the rhythm of the oars, if his deep bass was not sweet or well-tuned, at least it was strong and its beat even. One by one the others began to join him, until even Attalae was beating his hard palms against the bench he sat on and croaking along. Only Hoilogae did not know the song, though the sound of the others' voices stirred him so that he would have liked to sing with them.

The faring to Sigisharjaz's Holm was a hard one. Between the need to row and the need to bail, those men who were not undone by seasickness got little sleep, and their fight against the waves lengthened the way, so that they were two nights on the sea and the day was lowering towards sunset again by the time Attalae took the rudder and gestured that their ship should lead the others in. The mixture of spray, rain, and bilge water had soaked their clothes as thoroughly as if they had been swimming in the sea, and dried fish was little cheer to the stomach, so that none of them showed a very brave appearance as they waded up onto the shore to make their boats fast. Thonarabernu and Theudorikijaz turned the boat Hoilogae had borrowed upside down to dump the bilge water out, then the gifts they had brought for Sigisharjaz were piled in, and Arnuz and Herwamundaz joined the other two in heaving the little ship to their shoulders.

Hrothagaisaz stood apart from the others, with his men behind him. He clearly meant to keep away from Hoilogae's folk from this point, as Hoilogae supposed was his right. Although his face was still greenish-pale from the faring, the grey ash that had dimmed his look while he was Hoilogae's guest no longer veiled him. The bed of coals seemed freshly stirred to fire. The path up to Sigisharjaz's hall was not an easy one to walk side by side, but Hoilogae would not walk behind the other, and Hrothagaisaz would not walk behind him. While they were still a little way from the hall, the doors opened and Hoilogae saw that men with iron weapons stood there.

"I come to give Sigisharjaz's ship back to him, I, Hoilogae, Herwawardhaz's son!" Hoilogae called, his voice ringing off the hills that humped low over the island. "I come in friendship, as I came before, with Arnulita Athalwulfaz's son beside me, and I would ask for Sigisharjaz's rede in deeming a case of were-gild. Tell your drighten that I have come!"

Sigisharjaz's thanes did not answer, but moved aside, their ranks spreading apart from the back as though a spear had been cast slowly through them. Then Sigisharjaz himself was standing in the doorway, a small figure, nearly a head shorter than the thanes who flanked him, with a spear in one hand and a horn in the other.

"Welcome, Hoilogae and Arnulita, and you as well, Hrothagaisaz. I had heard that you might seek my rede, but I had awaited your coming some time earlier."

Hrothagaisaz stepped swiftly forward, putting himself between Sigisharjaz and Hoilogae. "I was wounded, as you may have heard, and could not travel before this, else we would have been here while the summer's weather held."

"I see you have had a hard faring. Come into my hall. I give you all guest right." Sigisharjaz drank from his horn and held it out, first to Hrothagaisaz, then to Attalae, then to Hoilogae.

"Hail to thee, in Wodhanaz's name," Hoilogae said as he lifted the horn to his host. A small grim smile twitched beneath the drighten's iron beard, and it seemed to Hoilogae that he saw the lid over Sigisharjaz's right eye droop a little.

When Hoilogae drank, he almost choked in surprise. It was not the malty ale, but true mead, brewed with honey and perhaps a little fruit. His head was already beginning to spin when he handed the horn back to the drighten. The mead was far stronger than the ale he had grown used to, and he had not eaten well on the faring. Hoilogae saw that its strength had touched Hrothagaisaz's broad cheekbones with color as well, and Attalae caught a last golden drop from his frost-gray mustache with the tip of his tongue. The hall was not nearly so full as when Hoilogae had seen it last, though Sigisharjaz's war band was still at least twice the size of Herwawardhaz's. Hoilogae guessed that many of the men would have gone back to their homes for the winter, when no fighting was expected and the sea cut Sigisharjaz's Holm off from the lands around for much of the time. Gunthahildioz sat in the seat beside her husband's, beneath his eagle-banner.

She turned her head towards the doorway as if trying to hear what was happening, the spindle still twirled slowly down from her hands, its white thread lengthening, until one of the serving maids came to speak to her. Then she set her spinning aside and rose, taking a pitcher from one of the tables. Long brown skirt swishing about her ankles, Sigisharjaz's frowe made her way slowly down the hall. Her amber necklaces shone from her white tunic, glowing softly beneath the ruddy glitter of the twisted golden torc around her throat. Hoilogae marked how carefully Gunthahildioz walked, how her blue eyes squinted through the twilight dimness. He guessed that her sight must have grown much worse in the past months.

When ale had been poured for everyone and all their men except the boat bearers were seated at the benches, Hoilogae, Attalae, Hrothagaisaz, Sigisharjaz, and Gunthahildioz walked to the high seats together. The drighten and his frowe sat down, leaving the others standing before them. Sigisharjaz thumped the butt of his spear three times on the ground, the wind of his movement stirring his pale eagle-banner.

"Now tell me of your case. You first, Hrothagaisaz, then you, Hoilogae." His deep gray eyes, almost black in the evening shadows, met Hoilogae's. "I will settle this matter before there is any talk of gifts between us."

Each of the men told his tale as clearly as he could, knowing that Sigisharjaz had already heard the story several times. The drighten tugged at his short iron-gray beard, though he leaned back in his seat and sipping at his mead as he listened to them. It seemed to Hoilogae that his dark eyes stared beyond their heads, cold as sea-polished stones. A shiver went through Hoilogae. It was the old eagle's gaze he saw glinting black from the drighten's face, and a grim shadow misted Sigisharjaz's look, as though his long sight showed him something ill. His deeming will be death for one of us, Hoilogae thought. One of us may not leave this hall. He did not touch his sword, for he did not wish Sigisharjaz to scent the hint of foe-ship in his thoughts, but his arm tightened with readiness. He would not be brought down easily. Sigisharjaz heaved himself slowly to his feet. He slammed his spear-butt down, his deep voice boomed out through the hall.

"Hoilogae owes no were-gild for a death in battle. The strife was fairly sought, as geld for the old score between Sigislinthon and Hrothamaraz. Sigislinthon and her sons have full right to Swafnijaz's udal lands. However, no word was spoken of those lands south and east, which Hrothamaraz won with his own strength, leaving no kinsman alive to claim by another right. If Hoilogae chooses to fight over those lands with Hrothagaisaz on my fields tomorrow, then shall the matter be decided there, if not, he must yield them up to the son of Hrothamaraz, and that be counted a fair reckoning, and frith hold between the clans of Sigislinthon and Hrothamaraz for no less than three full years. How say you, Hoilogae?"

His heart beating like the wings of a swan freed from a snare, Hoilogae turned his gaze away from Sigisharjaz to look at Hrothagaisaz. The fair man's jaw was set, his chin jutting like a boulder at the base of a cliff, and Hoilogae could hear his hard breathing. Hrothagaisaz had lain still for a long time while his leg healed, though he moved without a limp, he would still be easy game in a single fight now, and both of them knew it. In three years they might have woven a lasting frith between them, and Hoilogae knew that the other would never be more than a fair match for him on the field.

"I did not let Hrothagaisaz live to kill him now. I led the host to win my mother's udal lands, with no wish to take more. I will yield the lands beyond the last mounds of her kin in the east and south, and hold to three years of frith, as you have deemed." Hoilogae heard a few hisses of disappointment. The single combats that often took place on Sigisharjaz's Holm were among the joys of the thanes in the great drighten's war band.

Sigisharjaz looked at Hrothagaisaz. The tautness of the young warrior's face had not eased, his jaws did not move easily as he croaked out, "I will accept the deeming, and keep the three years of frith."

"Then so it is!" Sigisharjaz struck the butt of his spear thrice on the ground again. When he spoke again, his voice was softer. "What have you brought, Hoilogae?"

Hoilogae stepped aside, waving the four thanes who bore Sigisharjaz's boat on their shoulders forward. "You were kind to lend us this ship for our faring across to Wejlunduz's home. I am sorry not to have brought it back before this, but I hope what you will find what I have laden it with a fair enough geld for my lateness." He nodded, and his men put the boat down before Sigisharjaz's seat.

The great drighten stared down at the boatload of gifts, then threw his head back with the barking laugh of an old dog-wolf, sloshing mead over the gilded rim of his horn to darken his rust-brown sleeve like a stain of fresh blood. "A fair geld indeed," he said when he had stopped laughing. "And I have a gift for you in turn." Sigisharjaz reached down, opening the wooden chest by his seat and pulling out a plain iron sword. "For you, Attalae. My thoughts tell me that you shall need it on your way. For you, Hoilogae, I have something else, a spear to point the way to what you seek." He raised his head, bellowing, "Ansuthewaz! To me!"

The tall, slender man who came forth might have been mistaken for a thane at first glance. He strode proudly upright with clean-shaven chin lifted high, and ruddy metal gleamed around his throat. But he wore no weapon, his dark tunic was woven of rough wool, and a closer glance showed that the ring adorning his neck was not a freeman's twisted torc, but the closed collar of a thrall. His light brown hair was cropped very close to his skull. He stopped beside Hoilogae, looking down at Sigisharjaz. "I am here."

"Here is my gift for you. A thrall from Aiwilimae's land. He can guide you there and show you the way to the drighten's hall. Only you must swear not to ask him to go inside or speak with anyone there."

"That I swear willingly," Hoilogae answered. "I could not have asked for a gift that brings me more joy."

The skies were clear the next day, sunlight glinting from the little choppy waves. Hoilogae and those men who would go with him had a long faring up to Gautland and around the coast to the west and north, till they reached the strand of a sound that no man had ever crossed and come back from, the waters that stretched on to the rim of the worlds. Those waters, Ansuthewar said, would be fierce at this time of year, and the land-wights were unkind to seafarers, but Hoilogae had made his vow on the sumbel-horn, and there was no way for him to turn aside from it.

When they went down to the water, Sigisharjaz and Gunthahildioz went with them. The frowe held to her husband's arm as though they were newly wedded, but Hoilogae could see how gently Sigisharjaz guided her feet away from the rough places in the path, and how the age settled on his face when his fierce wariness sank beneath other thoughts. A piece of white linen was draped over her free arm, the drighten held a spear butt-end down in his loose hand, using it as a staff.

As soon as she felt the smooth sand of the waves' wake under her feet, Gunthahildioz let go of her husband's arm, standing firmly on her own. She stretched the cloth she held out to Hoilogae. "This is my own gift to you, to bring you victory in your search for Swaebhon."

As Hoilogae unfolded the banner, the wind caught it, lifting the cloth up to tug against his hands. The black raven stitched into the white linen seemed to flap his wings in the stiff breeze.

"None knows better than the raven how to find his old friend," Sigisharjaz's deep voice rumbled. "Unless some troll-craft turns you about on the way, he shall guide your ship on the fairest paths to your goal." He turned the spear about in his hand. As he handed it butt-first to Hoilogae, the young battle-leader saw the two deep grooves running about the shaft, where the banner's ties might be fastened to the spear. "Wodhanaz blesses your faring with victory."

"I thank you," Hoilogae replied, but, remembering the shape he had seen between the mounds, he did not know whether he spoke to the man or the god.

Sigisharjaz and Gunthahildioz stayed on the beach, watching the three ships go their way. They were there as long as Hoilogae could see, till their holm faded into a dim cloud on the blue horizon.

Attalae coughed, drawing a piece of dried fish out of one of the bags and beginning to gnaw on it. "Sigisharjaz arranged things very well for himself," he mused. "Now there is no drighten in Jutland or Sealand who can be counted as his like, either in lands or in folk, and your clan will always have a threat at its back, which will keep you from spreading farther than you have thus far. True, you could not threaten him now, but in three years you might think of offering battle to some of his holdings in Jutland. And Hrothagaisaz is beholden to him for a fair deeming now. He knows that he could by no means have hoped for better, and that he holds his lands by Sigisharjaz's good will."

"I had thought Sigisharjaz trustier than that."

"Oh, he's trusty, in his own way, like the Ansuz whom he follows. None would doubt that he is openhanded, and that the gifts he gives are worthy of his thanes' troth. But he will seek his own good before all, and you must not forget that in dealing with him."

"Do you wish to put up the banner?" Ansuthewaz asked. His voice was both low and soft, but his words came clearly through the sounds of the sea and the talking of the thanes around him.

Hoilogae tied the banner's fastening-strings around the grooves in the spear shaft, making the battle-flag fast. After a little shuffling through the bags, he found some light rope and lashed the spear upright against one of the ship's ale-casks. The raven fluttered out before them, showing them the path over the sea.

Thinking on the thrall's proud bearing and the keen look in his brown eyes, as well as Sigisharjaz's strange words of the night before, Hoilogae could not help asking, "How did you come here from Aiwilimae's lands? You seem too good a man to be kept as a thrall." It was in his mind that, if they came to Swaebhon's hall as Sigisgairaz had they would, he could reward Ansuthewaz with his freedom, so that the former thane would be able to come among his old friends again.

Ansuthewaz's narrow cheekbones flushed beneath his light tan. "I broke an oath," he replied shortly, and turned away. Hoilogae asked no more.

CHAPTER XVIII

The figures spread out in front of Helgi, deep red as blood-stains against their pale background. He was hardly looking at them, doodling absently as the faculty supervisor who taught Music Theory I two days of the week went on about relative majors and minors. Here was a skeleton-ship with prow and stern both curled up like snakes, centipede-leg oars stretching down from it and a pair of stick-dogs running before it, here a man's long-legged figure raised a huge-bladed ax in an open-fingered hand, and above the ship, another man lifted a spear, Helgi tried to neaten its end, ended up with the weapon's shaft reaching most of the way across the page, much longer than the man who wielded it. Silly stuff, a couple of bare footprints, like the logo on his Hang Ten shirts, an outstretched arm with long skinny fingers, a neat vertical row of little circles, shaded in. An even-armed cross inside a circle, to which he added a head, arms, and long skinny legs, then a couple of extra lines sticking out on either side of the middle.

"The relative minor of a key can always be found by going a step and a half down from the major. Thus the relative minor of C is A minor." Keith brushed a few strands of his waist-length brown hair back out of his face. One nicotine-stained fingertip pointed to the appropriate keys on the diagram of a keyboard that had stretched the length of the chalkboard since the beginning of the year.

By his sun-wheel man, Helgi drew a stick-figure with long hair and arms reaching out, then, to either side, a straight line with branches marked by a series of vees. The ones on the man's tree were point-up, like a row of spears planted one behind the other, the ones on the woman's were point-down, like a line of geese flying down to earth. Helgi looked at it a while, added a couple of spirals here and there, then began to weave a twisting line of runes between the little red figures, just writing what came into his head. THIS PAPER WAS ONCE OF TREE. THIS INK WAS ONCE RED EARTH. A MAN KNOWS LITTLE. I MIGHT HAVE CARVED IN STONE..

Helgi thought the words over, he liked the sound of them, but could go no farther. He turned over the page in front, a blue-lined layer of white lying over the little red shapes that still showed faintly through the unwritten paper. He was glad when the bell rang and he could hurry out to meet Luann in the faculty lounge.

"Hey, should we go off-campus for lunch?"

"Where at?" She blinked her eyes slowly, running a knuckle along the curve of one cheek as she looked up at him. "I warn you, I have gotten my RDA of ptomaine for the week. I am not eating at the cafeteria again."

"We could go over to The French Place for a croissant or something," Helgi offered. "What good is working at a university in the best part of town if you can't eat with the Yuppies once in a while?"

"Why, a university here offers immense opportunities for acts of class-related sabotage, of course." It took Helgi a moment to catch it, he stifled his groan as she went on, "I gather that you're asking me?"

"I gather that I've just been suckered into paying for lunch," Helgi answered ruefully. "Yeah, I guess I am asking you. How about it?"

"Delighted." The corners of Luann's eyes crinkled in an almost Oriental way as she grinned up at him. "It's a date. Meet you outside the Art Building at quarter past."

Helgi moved up against the building's side to keep in its thin sliver of shade while he waited for her, the brick rough and gritty against the backs of his thighs and calves. The moist Dallas heat pressed on him like the weight of a sweaty ox leaning against him, forcing his back into the wall. He glanced at his watch. He was five minutes early. The sunlight polished Luann's hair to bright copper as she made her way across one of the wide squares of lawn towards him. From a little way off, her bare legs and arms looked tanned against the pale yellow of her shorts and green of her blouse, it was only close up that Helgi could see her brownness breaking up into masses of freckles.

"Let's go, I'm starved," she said.

They dashed across the street without waiting for the light, Helgi holding back his stride so that Luann could keep up with him. Their momentum carried them through the swinging doors of The French Place. Helgi drank in the air conditioned coolness like a draught of spring water, leaning his head back to let the stream from one of the overhead vents flow over his flushed face. He ran his hands through his hair, lifting the damp mass and letting it drop, as if he had just taken off a motorcycle helmet.

Beside him, Luann wiped her forehead with the back of her hand. "A hair," she sighed, looking around for a place to sit. As always, The French Place was crowded, mostly with students from Jefferson, though Helgi spotted a few pairs of older businesswomen doing lunch meetings over salads and quiche or croissants.

"I just want a croissant, really," Luann told him. "And an iced tea, with lemon and two sugars."

"You sure? No pastries or anything?"

Luann patted her stomach. "Fat like a pig. Like a serious oinker. Don't even mention French pastries in my presence. A plain croissant, well, yes, you could get me a Caesar salad too, if you insist."

Helgi joined the long line snaking up to the cash register, shifting from one foot to the other as he considered the choices laid out before him. When he returned, tray-laden, to the table, Luann was gone, although she had left her purse and his backpack sitting sentry on their chairs, with his trombone case laid slantwise over their part of the table like the bar of a black 'Do Not' sign. Helgi set it down, replacing it with their food, and took the tray over to the little cart where the used trays were stacked. He wasn't sure whether it would be uncouth to start eating without her or not. Instead he chose to burn his tongue on his coffee. Shit, why do I always do this? He thought. Just once, why don't I wait to drink it until it's cool? But the rich earthy aroma of the French-roast beans came so clearly through the pain in his mouth that he could hardly complain, somehow it never tasted quite as strong and fine when it was cooler.

He sipped the black brew more carefully, blowing out over it and sucking in quickly.

"Didn't mean to run out on you," Luann said, moving her purse off the chair and taking its place. She picked up her knife and fork, beginning to break the lettuce leaves in her salad. "Sorry about that, it looked as though you might be waiting in line forever."

"It's the price we pay for coming here," Helgi answered solemnly. "Great delights always call for great sacrifices." He cut into his croque monseiur, watching the pale strings of molten cheese stretch out over the pink ham as he separated the first bite from the rest of it.

After they had eaten and chatted about their classes a while longer, Helgi asked her, "By the way, how come you walked out on my last song the other night?" The paper napkin he was twisting beneath the table's edge parted soundlessly under his fingers.

Luann sipped at her iced tea, dabbing at her lips with her own napkin and smiling at him. "How long did it take you to notice I was gone?"

If her casual voice hid an edge of irony, Helgi did not hear it, but though her tone warned him of nothing, her words seemed to soften the ground under his feet, so that he felt as though he were walking through a green meadow spread over a bog's hidden betrayals. He opened his mouth, then closed it again. "Uh, I was concentrating pretty hard," he offered lamely. "It's a difficult song."

"Yeah, I could hear that. It's okay, I know you came over to work with the band. If you'd come to see me, it would have been a different story." Luann was still smiling, but it seemed to Helgi that he could hear the softness of shoes sinking into waterlogged peat beneath her voice.

"If I'd come to see you, I wouldn't have been spending my time with those guys," he answered. "No, I was just wondering if you didn't like that one as well as the others."

"Hmm." Luann turned her head, looking out at the street for a moment. The strong light from the window shone through her thin frost of makeup to show the faint splotches of freckles on her nose and cheek. "Not that I didn't like, exactly, well, no, I mean I could tell that it was a better song, but I guess I didn't like it as well. I don't mean, I'm sorry." She met his eyes again, her hand reaching out and then dropping to lie halfway across the table, palm up. Helgi covered it with his own. Luann's hand was cold and damp from her iced-tea glass, smooth beneath his touch, he could not feel her bones in her soft grip.

"That's okay," Helgi said, letting the leaping beat of his heart in his ears drown out the dark tide roaring beneath it. Later he would think about it. "Everyone has a favorite." Then, like a hunter unwilling to leave a wounded stag to heal or die, "Why that one? Any particular reason?" He held her hand carefully, willing his grip not to tighten, using all the control his throat had learned to keep his voice light. "Was it the style, or what?"

"I'd have to hear it again before I could really say," Luann answered softly, looking down at their hands. "I'm sure I'll get another chance next week. I mean, it is a good song, all right? I was just real tired, and it was so intense, and listening to Flourescent practice at full volume for four hours isn't exactly easy on the ears, you know?" Helgi could see the tightening around the edges of her mouth, as though she were reining in more words than she wanted to say.

"I'm sorry," Helgi said. He let go of her hand, then thought that she might think he was pulling away from her, and patted it awkwardly. "Hey, if you don't want a whole pastry, I'll split one with you. I'm still kind of hungry. What do you say?"

"I say a chocolate Napoleon, how about it? My parents are real diet fiends, I never see that kind of thing at home. But at least there's no rent."

"Hmm, I moved out when I started college. I have my own place now. It's not much, but you could come over and see it any time you'd like."

"Might be fun," Luann answered. "Where do you live?"

"Over by I-30, in Oakcliff. I've got to warn you, the roaches rent from the landlord, and I sublet from them."

"I can deal with it."

The echo of Luann's words about his song caught Helgi at odd moments through the day, stinging his mind away from whatever he was trying to concentrate on. That evening, he realized that he had been sitting and staring at the same page of his lesson plans for fifteen minutes.

"Enough of this shit," he muttered, slamming the workbook closed. He stripped off shorts and shirt, changing into his gi trousers and locking the door carefully behind him before picking his way over the toys that littered the stairwell and going out into the back yard where the sprinklers were just sputtering into stillness.

The evening was still warm, the worst of the heat had faded, but mosquitoes were whining in to the light of the porch lanterns. Helgi thought about lighting a citronella candle and decided against it. He would be moving fast. He went through a quick series of stretches, then started to practice his katas, beginning with Kihone, the most basic series of blocks and punches. Focus, he told himself, clean focus. He moved straight into the next one, Heian Sho-dan, trying to imagine enemies moving at him from all sides. Block down, strike, turn, over the top, strike, it's a good song, Dr. Sachs said so, turn, strike, shit, no, the move is age-uke, rising block, like I haven't been doing this kata for almost six years! Angry with himself, Helgi tried to focus his energy into his movements, blocking upwards with the hard punching blow that could break an arm as well as deflecting a downward strike. Upwards again, now he could almost see the shadow of an opponent rising tall before him, striking at him with awesome speed and strength.

Helgi's bare foot skidded on the wet grass as he stepped into the third rising block, and he was barely able to recover his balance. He paused a moment, making sure his stance was good before he looked over his shoulder and whipped around for gi-danborai, a downward block against a strike to the groin. It's a good song, dammit! Punch to the solar plexus, turn into gi-danborai, strike, and his foot slipped on the grass again. Helgi's extended arm flailed a moment as he caught himself and stepped back into position. Breathing hard, he stood in front stance, right arm stretched out. What the hell does her taste in songs matter? He asked himself. She wants to sing in musicals, after all. Anyway, no one likes everything all the time, and she liked the other ones, didn't she?

Helgi slowly drew himself upright, then turned around and went inside, sitting down in front of his synthesizer. Look, he said to himself, the song is just fine. Better than fine, it is powerful. How the hell do you think you can perform in public if one person's criticism upsets you? Don't you believe in yourself? The keyboard seemed to waver in his sight, black keys stretching into dark wave-peaks and white keys frothing forward from their edges. The sparse stubble over Helgi's voice-box was barely heavy enough to feel scratchy under his fingers, rough, grating, and off-key, serious problems with tone and pitch. I remember when your singing used to sound like shit let him sing the psycho songs, man, you do the rest. The words wound one around the other, like the growth rings of a tree, the eldest as fresh with living sap as the last.

I believe in my songs, Helgi thought. I don't think I believe in my singing. But it wasn't my singing she walked out on, it was the song.

He sighed, pressing the synthesizer switch to ON. The instrument came on with a soft hum of unshaped power, a toneless resonance like the roaring of the sea in a shell's depths. Across the room, the digital numbers glowed green from the VCR's monitor. 8.13, changing to 8.14 as he watched. Practice would help his voice, and doing his lesson plans would help him keep his job at the university, his trombone lay waiting inside its dark sheath, but sitting at the synthesizer moping wasn't going to do a damn thing for him. He pulled his book of warm-up exercises out of the music stacked beside the keyboard.

Helgi had just started his first song when he heard the feet on the stairs, the loud laughter and trailing words, "gonna have us a party!"

"Shit," he muttered, snapping his synthesizer off as the heavy bass beat began to thunder through the ceiling. Helgi could have plugged in his headphones and cranked the instrument up loud enough to drown out his neighbors, but he was still restless. He wanted to move, to run all his doubts and worries out of his system.

When he had shut and barred the window, Elric followed him eagerly to the door, turning wet brown eyes up to the collar and leash that hung on a nail in the door frame. Helgi thought about it a moment, then shook his head. He wanted to be alone, without even the sound of his dog's panting to shake his own rhythm.

"You already had one walk this evening," he said sternly. "And I need you here to watch the house."

Elric lowered his muzzle and whined, skulking back to sit by the synthesizer as Helgi unbarred the door and slipped out. As the two locks turned over, Helgi heard the elk hound raising a small mournful howl. The better for people to know that there was a good-sized dog in his apartment, he thought.

Two of the Claymore boys, the six year-old and the eight year-old, were on the stairs picking up their toys, broad butts rising and falling as they jostled each other for favorite trucks. They turned around as Helgi came down, giggling snottily. They were shirtless in the heat, tubby bellies slopping over their shorts, Helgi thought the whole family must have a glandular problem.

"Hey, Karate Kid," the six year-old called. "Beat anyone up today?"

The eight year-old held out a grubby palm, intoning "Take the pebble from my hand, Grasshopper," in a bad Oriental accent. Usually Helgi put up with their ribbing, but he wasn't up for it tonight.

"Move it, you chubby little monsters," he snarled, pushing between them. They fell back, quieted for a second, but as he locked the apartment door behind him, he heard the piping mutter, "Jeez, is he ever on the rag tonight. D'you think."

Helgi started to run, his feet beating smoothly against the pavement. He was dripping sweat within two blocks, but was not breathing hard, he could feel his legs stretching, his muscles and bones sliding back into a good balance, freed of the worry that had cramped through him at the memory of Luann's words. He passed under the freeway, sparing barely a flickered glance for the drunk who lay slumped against a concrete pillar with his tattered dark hat over his face, jogged in place as a couple of cars zoomed past on the access road with stereos booming out their open windows, and ran across.

The neighborhood was nearly all poor black and semi-legal Mexican on this side of the freeway. Helgi knew his white body must look strange to the men who glanced up from their lawn-chairs as he ran past, glimmering like a ghost in the darkness.

"Ain't it kinda hot to be runnin' like that, man?" An old black man with a fluff of gray hair called out from behind his porch screen. Helgi only lifted a hand in greeting and kept going, though the breath was starting to rasp hard in his lungs now.

He did not notice the three young men in the shadows beneath the freeway until he had already crossed the access road and rounded the first concrete pillar. When he saw them standing before him, he was already trapped. The two looking at him were black, thin and hard as coiled steel wire, the taller one was just shoving a package of something into the pocket of his ragged jeans. The other, now swinging around to face Helgi, was an older, chunky built Mexican. All three of them stood where they were, clearly not meaning to let him pass. Helgi's stomach clenched into an icy knot, the rush of adrenalin sweeping away all the tiredness of his run.

"What you doin' out here so late, white boy?" The taller of the black men asked. "Don' you know it past yo' bedtime?" Although he wore a scraggly little goatee and had shaved his head, Helgi was sure the other was no older than seventeen.

"He don' know nothin', he jus' a chickenrunnin' from something over yonder, dat sure," the shorter one answered. The Mexican only smiled, putting his hand in his pocket. A pickup truck roared past under the freeway, but did not stop, or even honk.

"Runnin' somewhere he should not," the taller one affirmed. "Bad things can happen to little white boys in the wrong neighborhood. See it on the evenin' news every day. They can get shot, they can get cut. They can get beaten within an inch of their lives."

The cold chunk of fear in Helgi's stomach had begun to glow now, a hot anger sizzling low in his throat. The pillar was at his back, he could not dodge out into the street, and the concrete rampart on the other side sloped up too sharply for him to run up it.

"Whinin' already?" The one with the shaved head asked. "Whinin' an' shakin', man, you is scared!" He laughed raucously, but it was the Mexican's hand in whom the six-inch blade gleamed dully, flickering like a dim torch-flame in his easy underhanded grip. The heavy man tossed a wave of long black hair out of his face and stepped forward lightly, balancing on the balls of his feet and smiling at Helgi.

All Helgi's strength burst forward in a single move, practiced too long for thought. His right foot whipped around, aimed at the Mexican's elbow rather than his knife, but as the other drew his arm back sharply, Helgi's foot struck his hand. The knife arched glittering past the edge of Helgi's sight, as his foot came down, his momentum snapped his right hand out to back fist the Mexican's temple. The moment the blow had landed, Helgi's whole body twisted to drive the stiffened knuckles of his left hand straight into the other man's throat as a loud joyous shout burst from his own. The Mexican dropped like a sack of grain, head thumping hard against the concrete.

The two blacks had dropped back a few steps, when Helgi looked up at them, his face twisted into a snarl and chin wet with slaver, they turned and ran, their footfalls echoing from the stone roof and slanted walls of the free-way. Helgi had actually leapt over the Mexican's body and run after them, almost to the access road on the other side, when he realized what he was doing and stopped, bending over and panting with shock. He drew his arm across his wet mouth. For a few moments he stared at the glistening trail of spittle on his white skin, then wiped his arm on his gi trousers. The knuckles of his right fist were swelling, the knuckles of his left had begun to thrum with shock. The cars still roared by on the access road, paying no more at-tention to Helgi standing there dazed than they had to the fight beneath the overpass. Helgi could not stop himself. He turned, walking back to where the Mexican lay sprawled across the narrow sidewalk.

The man's head had turned to the side, a little blood drooled black from his mouth. Helgi did not need to touch him to know he was dead. The back fist to the temple alone might have killed him, but his throat was staved in, his neck a strange hollow of flesh. Helgi could not see where the knife had landed.He walked away again. He was not shaking yet, but the sudden raspy croak made him leap and whirl. It was a moment before he realized that the sound came from the drunk on the other side of the far pillar, who cleared his throat and spat into the road as Helgi walked carefully around him.

"Eh, what's all the shouting about?" The drunk muttered. His dark hat had slewed over to the side, one eye gleamed up at Helgi, pale gray in the street-light's fluorescence. "Y'leave some crow-chow over there?" His laugh turned into a harsh run of hacking coughs, flecking his grizzled beard with spittle. He spat up another mouthful of phlegm, then rummaged in his rags and drew out a flat pint bottle. He shook it, staring ruefully at the quarter-inch of dark liquid in the bottom, then unscrewed the cap with a shaking hand and tossed it onto the street, lifting the bottle up to Helgi. "G'wan, you look like you need it. I've had my share already."

Numbly Helgi took it from his hand, wiping the neck off on his trousers before he drank. The rough whiskey chewed its way down his throat like an acrid gasp of gunpowder smoke, but his own hands stopped shaking as its warmth spread out from his belly. "Thank you," he gasped. The drunk answered only with a loud, bubbling snort. After a moment, Helgi realized that the man had fallen asleep again and was snoring. He laid the bottle carefully beside its owner and walked back to his apartment. Helgi's legs were steady until he had gotten in and locked the door, sliding the last deadbolt home, then he began to shake so badly that he could not stand. He dropped down on the chair before his synthesizer and sat for a few moments with his hands trembling on the silent keys.

A burst of laughter floated through the music from upstairs, Elric ambled over to his master, sniffing Helgi's trousers before he stood up on his hind legs and began to lick the sweat from Helgi's chest. Helgi sat there until he had stopped shaking again, then got up to open the window and turn on the fan, its soft breeze stirring through the muggy night-warmth. He toweled off, then knelt down to get some milk from the refrigerator, stunned all the while at how ordinary every movement was as though he had simply run beneath the overpass and home, as he had done on other nights. Then a siren sounded, keening through the sounds of traffic and the upstairs music, and Helgi's aching fingers froze on the milk jug's nubbed plastic handle as if it were a knife-hilt. The police could have found the body already they could have asked the old drunk.

The siren wail rose and rose, and faded into the distance again. Not this time, but later? It seemed to Helgi suddenly that he ought to pray, to say a few words, if not for the soul of the man he had killed, then for himself. But only Macbeth's words came to mind, shuddering cold as corpse-sweat through him as he crouched by the open refrigerator.

"One cried, God bless us! Amen, the other,
As they had seen me with these hangman's hands.
Listening their fear, I could not say, Amen,
When they did say, God bless us."

Why should I? Helgi asked himself then. It was better than a fair fight. He was armed, and I was not. If I had not killed him, it would be me lying dead, there below the freeway. If I owe anything to God, it is only thanks for victory. Helgi closed the refrigerator door and stood up. He was about to speak when other words rose to the surface of his mind, shimmering quiet as ripples on a dark well. Victory-Father bless the victory runes. So the silversmith had written on the card that went with Karin's valknútr, holy to the god Óðinn (Wotan). Another shiver ran through Helgi's body, but this time it was a shiver of awe, lifting his gaze upward to the ghost-patterns glimmering against the cracked yellow ceiling. The thumping of the music from upstairs seemed very far away now, lost beneath the wind that roared in Helgi's ears.

More words streamed into his mind, thundering on the chords that had borne them there. Wer meines Speeres Spitze fürchtet durchschreite das Feuer nie! "Who fears the point of my spear shall never stride through the fire!"

As Helgi breathed in, it seemed to him that he could feel the spear-point pressing sharp against his breastbone. He lifted his throbbing hands as though calling the unseen weapon to strike deeper, softly speaking names remembered from The Norse Myths, newly learned from Wagner.

"Victory-Father, Battle-Father, Father of the Slain," Helgi murmured. "One-Eyed, Grim, Raven-God, Father of Magical Songs ." The last words burned sweet in his throat sweet and cold as the ghost-given drink he had dreamed before his audition. "Thank you, Odin. I give the man I slew to thee, for victory!"

I've had my share already. The drunk's speech came back to Helgi, sharp as the memory of the old man's bright eye gleaming from beneath his tilted hat.Helgi stood still and dumb as a stock of wood, stunned breathless. Even if you are a clever modern person who does not believe in gods and ghosts, perhaps you can trust in Jung or Joseph Campbell or one of these other sensible men who writes about the power of myths and archetypes, and beware of what you are summoning up from your soul.

"Wotan," he whispered. "Winner of the runes" and then again, "Galdor-Smith Shaper of Magical Songs."

The tingling slowly faded from Helgi's body as his breathing eased again. Now he felt charged with energy, as though sparks would fly from his hair if he shook his head. He looked at the clock. It was only quarter past nine. He still had time to get to the Book stop on Mockingbird before they closed. When he came back, he had two books. Teutonic Magic and Teutonic Religion, both by the same author, Kveldulf Gundarsson, the maker of Karin's valknútr. Helgi could not keep his thoughts still long enough to read either of them, instead he skipped through, letting phrases graze like glancing arrow-shots across his eyes.

"The rune ansuz is the rune of Odhinn as the lord of life and death alike. Of wrath, wisdom, and mighty words, of the godly melding of greatness and madness. The Teutonic belief is that humans are sib to the gods, from leader of the dead he became chooser of the dead and Valfather, father of the slain, hence finally the chooser of victory in battle. As the lord of runes and incantation, Odhinn also became the lord of poetry. He is a lord of oaths and of betrayal, of making and unmaking. As a god of war, he makes his heroes invincible till he himself comes to take them in battle."

It was almost two in the morning when Helgi finally closed his eyes to sleep, but when his alarm clock screamed him awake, he found to his surprise that he had slept without dreaming, so far as he could remember. He stopped at the 7-11 on the corner to buy a newspaper on the way to class, but there was nothing in it about a Mexican found slain beneath I-30. That afternoon, Luann's little rust mobile weaved northward through the traffic on Central Expressway after Helgi's, following him closely.

He had given her directions to his apartment, but she insisted that she could never find a place until she'd driven to it. The clouds were rising high in front of them, blocking off the sunlight, Helgi drove with the air conditioner off and windows rolled down, letting the cool, damp wind from the north flow through the car as the heavy bass line beat out from its speakers. Once or twice, the clouds in the distance glimmered with lightning, but the storm was too far away for him to hear the thunder over the radio's noise.

It was like this in Dallas every year when summer and winter shifted places. The cold winds sweeping down over the flat plains from Canada met the heat that rose from Mexico like two giant football players crashing together, kicking up huge thunderclouds into the sky and spinning out into a season of tornadoes and flooding.

"Lo!" Helgi said to Luann as she got out of her car, sweeping his hand grandly towards the apartment. "The castle lyeth before you. Beware of the great water-serpents in the moat, and ward yourself from the packs of rabid wolves roaming wild through our woods." As if on cue, thunder rumbled faintly in the distance. Helgi felt the first splatter of rain on his head, then saw a few sparse drops spreading dark on the pale concrete sidewalk. A gust of cool wind blew another spattering of rain into his face, he hurried to open the door before the downpour could start. Helgi and Luann made it through the door just before the first heavy shower of rain fell on them, hail-sized drops beating down hard enough to spray a fine mist up from the concrete.

As soon as Helgi had unlocked his own door, Elric bounded out, leaping up on Luann. She stumbled backwards under the shock of his weight, trying to fend him off. Helgi grabbed the elk hound by his collar Elric was massively strong, but Helgi had discovered long ago that where the dog's head went, his body must follow, and wrestled him away. "Down, boy! No! Down! Sit! Behave yourself, Elric!"

Elric sat back on his haunches, tongue hanging out, looking up at Helgi as proudly as if he had just brought down a moose for his master.

"Bad dog," Helgi said, as sternly as he could. "No hunting the guests. Food is forthcoming only to those who are patient."

Luann brushed at the red marks Elric's nails had left on her bare thighs, casting a wary glance at the dog. "And there I thought you were kidding about the wolf-packs. Silly me."

"I really am sorry about that, Luann. He didn't hurt you, did he? You don't need to worry about him, he doesn't bite or anything."

"He scratched me a little. I think I'll survive. You don't have any other attack pets, do you?"

"Not a one. I am the most dangerous beast in this house." Helgi showed her his teeth. "Arrrgh." He tried to laugh, but it was as if a shadow of ice had passed through his bones, chilling him with the truth of his words.

Luann, bending to pat Elric on the head, did not see how Helgi's body stiffened. "This reassures me?"

A flash of lightning glimmered through the window as a sudden fusillade of heavy drops shattered on the glass. "Hey," Luann said, "Do you have a TV? We probably ought to check the weather channel to see what's going on tornado season and all that."

Helgi turned his little black-and-white on, twisting the dial until the twenty-four hour weather report came on. TORNADO AND FLASH FLOOD WATCH FOR DALLAS AND TARRANT COUNTIES GOLF-BALL SIZED HAIL REPORTED IN ARLINGTON.

"Well, I guess you'll be here a while," Helgi said. "Pick a seat, any seat. Can I make you coffee or tea?"

"Coffee would be nice. Milk and sugar, please."

As soon as Helgi had poured the coffee and sat down, Elric lay down on his feet like a furry bag of warm stones as the thunder grumbled through another lightning-flash. Though Helgi had not been counting seconds, he could tell that the thunder this time came more swiftly. The storm was moving in fast.

"You certainly are civilized," Luann said approvingly. "Lots of guys don't bother with offering coffee and pointing out the john and all that."

"Uh, my mother kind of pressed it into me. Taking care of guests in her house is real important to her. I think it's an ethnic thing."

Luann rubbed her nose thoughtfully. "I think that's neat. It's funny, though you don't look ethnic."

Without thinking about it, Helgi raised his fist to punch her lightly on the shoulder, as he would have punched Mark. He stopped the movement halfway and let his hand drop, embarrassed. "We're Danes, remember? White folk can be ethnic too, you know."

Luann grinned. "White is beautiful."

"Equal rights for whites."

She raised a fist. "White power."

The two of them both stopped laughing at once, as though the same ugly ghost had tightened one hand on each throat. Luann's gaze drifted towards the window, Helgi looked down at the wavy water-lines of the gray linoleum, gray as the concrete. He'd been in the wrong neighborhood, sure enough.

Helgi coughed. "Then there are those who want to put all the Norsemen on a boat and ship us back to Scandinavia. It worked the first time, too. Leif Erikson and his horde went back to Greenland, and America stayed one hundred percent American until Christopher Columbus landed."

Luann paused a moment, with the smirk that told Helgi she was about to unleash some really devastating witticism, when the hard thrumming of the rain outside changed to the sharper notes of hail. The ice-stones glittered white as a torrent of frozen wheat in the blue-white flash of lightning, the thunder rattled the windowpanes, shaking through Helgi's bones. A moment later the lightning struck another roll of thunder. When Helgi blinked its brightness from his eyes, he knew that something was wrong, but not what.

"It's getting kind of dark in here, isn't it?" Luann said. "You could turn on the lights?"

Helgi heaved Elric from his feet and went over to flip the wall-switch, but no light answered. Now he knew what had caught his eye. The television screen had gone dead black. "I think that last one must have gotten the power lines. I fear that we are now in a state of blackout." Another flash of lightning caught his eye, he looked out the window. "Hey, am I hallucinating, or are those hailstones really as big as golf balls?"

Luann came over to stand beside him at the window. "You're hallucinating. You've got to be. Hail stones don't get that big."

"That's a relief to know." He paused. "Shit, those are big hallucinations."

Soon Helgi had his flashlight propped up on the table behind the synthesizer, casting a wide halo of light upon the ceiling. He turned his chair around and Luann moved hers next to his.

"You know," Luann said thoughtfully, looking up at him, "that flashlight is just so tacky, it's romantic."

Sitting with Luann's bare thigh pressing against his, Helgi found it hard to think of an answer. He coughed, trying to distract himself, and started to play the theme from "Love Boat" one-handed.

"Minor sixth, descending and ascending," Luann said promptly.

Helgi looked at the keyboard, sure enough. "Yes, but can you recognize it with your back turned?"

Luann swung her legs around so that she faced the other way, towards the fire. "Try me and see."

"Ummm. Star Trek." He played the first few notes.

"Minor seventh up, half-step down, I lose it after that. That's a good way to memorize intervals, though. I mean, everyone can remember the way songs start."

"I gladly take credit for any and all strokes of genius," Helgi replied.

"Uh huh. How did you batter up your hands, by the way? Those knuckles look pretty bad."

Helgi tried not to twitch, but he knew she must have felt his leg-muscle tightening against hers. "Oh, practicing karate."

"The board bit back, huh?"

"My school doesn't break boards. Think about it, when was the last time you were walking down the street and got mugged by a rogue piece of wood?" Helgi answered by rote, playing the first bars of the theme from "Karate Kid" a tune he knew well, he heard the Claymore kids whistling it just about every time he practiced in the back yard.

By the time the lights came back on, the storm had faded to a soft dripping of rain through the darkness.

Helgi went over to the TV, flicking channels until they heard "weather report."

The newscaster was a middle-aged man with puffy hair, standing in front of a satellite map. The area around DFW was shaded in various grays, radiating out from a dark center just south of Dallas, Helgi knew that in color TV, that center would have been deep warning red. "The danger area of the worst storm this season has moved out of Dallas County, but Tarrant County is still under tornado and flash flood warnings until eight-thirty tonight. Rescue efforts are continuing for the car swept away in Killian Creek north of Plano this afternoon, but it is now feared that the flash flooding have claimed their second victim of the year. Remember, do not attempt to cross running water on the roadway, no matter how shallow it looks."

"Do you want to call out for a pizza?" Luann asked. "Can I stay here a while to avoid flash floods?"

For a moment Helgi could not answer. With her there, he could not think of Odhinn or the runes hidden in his books, but he also could not think about his killing, and he hardly noticed when sirens screamed past outside. "Sure."

It was almost ten when Helgi walked Luann out to her car. Fuzzy halos glowed around the streetlights, but the dampness in the air was hardly even a light drizzle. Muted light shone behind the curtains in the apartment's upstairs window, a faint silhouette passed through it and was gone.

"Thanks for coming over," Helgi said.

Luann opened the car door. She did not get straight in, but stood with one palm against the wet side of the car, leaning slightly against it with her right hip curving out as she looked up at him. "Thanks for having me over," she answered softly.

Helgi leaned down and kissed her on the lips, he could taste the pizza's spice lingering in her mouth. After a moment, Luann's arms wrapped lightly about his back. Helgi reached around her shoulders, drawing her closer until her breasts pressed warm against the bottom of his ribcage.

A faint flowery scent seemed to hang about her, whether from perfume or her shampoo he did not know. He could feel the hot tide of blood beginning to flood to his groin as a smile curved her lips beneath his, and drew back, a matching warmth rising to heat his cheeks.

"I thought you'd never get the hint," Luann murmured, letting go of him. She patted him lightly on the shoulder. "Take care of yourself, okay? I'll see you tomorrow."

"Yeah, tomorrow." Helgi stepped away, letting her slip into her car. He waited until the last brightness of her taillights had faded around the corner before walking back to the apartment. Instead of going straight in, he stood on the doorstep for a few moments, inhaling through his nose and exhaling through his mouth until his breathing was smooth again.

With Luann gone, the apartment seemed still and strange, a nameless anxiety seemed to press against Helgi as if, instead of being long gone, the storm had yet to strike. After a while he went out again, heading down to the 7-11. For his first steps down the dark street, he had to brace his back hard to keep from jerking about at every sound, or edging far around the two black men who stood waiting by the bus stop in front of the apartment. He had won the fight, Helgi reminded himself. And he knew that if he let fear of another one keep him from walking on the street where he lived at night, he would have lost the battle in the end, and failed the god who had given him the victory.

When he got home, Helgi spread the paper out on the table, going through it until he found the article he had feared to see. A Mexican, his corpse apparently robbed of all documents and money, if he had carried any, but identified by the police as Jesus Gonzales, better known as El Angelito, had been found dead beneath the freeway. Gonzales had been a small-time drug dealer with a couple of convictions on his record, the police suspected his death to be the result of a deal gone bad.

Helgi leaned back with a deep sigh. If the other two had been buying drugs, they were unlikely to tell the cops anything, especially not that a strange white guy had just walked down the street and killed their dealer with his bare hands. "Thank you, Odhinn," he murmured, the strange words tasting more familiar, less blasphemous in his mouth even as he spoke them. He laid the paper aside and picked up Teutonic Magic again.

"The Germanic time-sense is not threefold, but twofold. Time is divided into 'that-which-is', a concept encompassing everything that has ever happened not as a linear progression, but as a unity of interwoven layers, and 'that-which-is-becoming', the active changing of the present as it grows from the patterns set in that-which-is. For the Teutonic mind, all that has been is still immediate and alive, the present only exists as it has been shaped by the great mass of what is, and the future only as the patterns which that which is becoming now should shape in turn. The Teutonic concept of time and being is fully expressed in one of the most ancient images of the Germanic peoples the ever-green tree with the well at its foot."

Since Columbus Day Monday was a holiday for everyone, Flourescent met for practice that morning. Even with the garage door open and the fans going, it was scorchingly hot. Helgi's shorts were soaked with sweat by the time they had gotten through the first song.

"Y'know, this sucks," Josh said suddenly, unslinging his sax and putting it aside. "It's way too fucking hot in here to practice during the daytime." He picked up the can of Dr. Pepper by his feet and drained it, then let out a long bubbling belch, glancing at Luann as though daring her to complain.

"So?" Mike asked. "What do you want to do about it?"

"I've got an idea. I think it's a pretty fucking good idea, and you will too."

"Woo, an idea," Widget chorused. "Woooo." He leaned back, fluttering his fingers and rolling his eyes at Josh in mock awe. "First time, man."

"Shut the fuck up. Now my brother-in-law, Roy, he and his wife are in Lewisville visiting her parents for the holiday, and he said I could use his boat while he was gone as long as I was real careful to clean it up afterwards. I say "Rack drowned him out with a sharp drum roll", "thank you, asshole. I say, why don't we get a few six-packs and some food, and head out to White Rock Lake for the day?"

Mike took off his guitar, shaking his head in admiration. "A good idea. Who'd of thought it? Everyone coming along?"

"Yeah." "Yup." "Bet'cha ass." "Sure am." "Of course," Helgi said, a little after the others, though he wasn't sure. Playing music was one thing, when they were all woven together in a single braid of sound and thought, but he could not even imagine telling the rest of Flourescent anything he had been thinking or doing in the past days. "Sorrow eats your heart, if you cannot speak all your soul to another."

Mike looked at his sister. "You sure you want to come, Luann? Don't you have some work to do or something, ears to train, hair to wash, that sort of thing?"

"I want to come."

"We want her to come," Helgi added, looking Mike straight in the eye. "We all do. Nothing could make us happier." He glared about at the other band members. "Right, guys?"

"Except to come ourselves," cracked Josh. "But I ain't even breathing hard yet."

"Yeah, yeah." Rack beat another swift roll on his drums, tossed the sticks up spinning and caught one in each hand before he stood up. "Well, y'all, I'm ready to go. Y'all got an ice chest for the beer, or do we need to stop by my place?"

Helgi rode in the front of the van with Mike, Luann sitting squeezed between them. With the front windows rolled down all the way and the radio booming out at full blast, there was no way Helgi could talk to Luann, but he put his arm around her shoulders and she leaned up against him like a petted cat. He was hardly willing to let go of her when they got to the 7-11, but she let him lift her down, and kept hold of his hand afterwards. Mike unlocked the back and the rest of Flourescent tumbled out.

"Beer!" Josh shouted in a deep bear-voice. Rack and Widget's higher voices echoed him as the three of them charged towards the doors.

"Lo, the battle-cry of Flourescent was raised, and the heroes charged boldly into the field," declaimed Luann, gesturing with her free hand.

One corner of Mike's mouth twisted up beneath his droopy mustache. "Yeah, but we'll see who ends up paying for most of it."

Helgi shrugged. "It's the price you pay for having a band." He checked his wallet. A ten, a five, and three ones, plus mixed change. "I can help out some."

Mike looked at his sister. "What about you?"

Luann patted her pockets. "Broke as a um, let me see, what breaks?"

"Day breaks. Voices break. It is ofttimes said that limbs break, when one stupidly or deliberately forgets one's wallet and attempts to freeload off one's brother for the millionth time. I am being persecuted. You're persecuting me and you, "he gestured towards Helgi, "are helping her. However, it's too hot to stand out here being persecuted."

Rack, Widget, and Josh were already standing in front of the cold beer, arguing enthusiastically about what kind to get. They ended up splitting the beer buy between Michelob Dark and Dry, with a six-pack of wine coolers for Luann. By the time Flourescent roared out of the 7-11 parking lot, they were breaking the open container law six times over. Helgi glanced around for cops, then raised his beer and drank deeply, sighing as it cooled his throat.

"You could be in a commercial for that stuff," Luann said, sipping at her wine cooler. "I thought you only liked the better beers."

"Beer is beer," Helgi answered, drinking again.

"Ain't that the truth?" Widget whooped from the back.

Helgi noticed that there was a bag in Luann's lap that hadn't been there before, with more in it than suntan lotion. "Did you get something else while we were busy arguing over the beer?" He asked her.

She opened the sack a little to show him a stack of newspapers. "Well, they had a pretty good selection of the rag-papers, with a few fascinatingly disgusting headlines. So if we get bored on the lake, we can always play Tabloid Trash."

Cars of all sorts, draped with tanned and lotion-gleaming bodies, lined the shores of White Rock Lake pickup trucks with their tailgates down, sports cars whose drivers sprawled on the beach towels spread out over their hoods and looked out over the lake through arrogant sunglasses, station wagons with Garfield ice chests in the backs and little kids squatting on the trunks. The chrome fittings of a motorcycle gleamed here and there between the cars, Helgi saw a couple of bikes chained to trees. A shifting kaleidoscope of music from full-volume boom boxes and car stereos beat in through the open windows as Mike's van drove slowly down the speed-bumped road around the lake. Few people swam in White Rock Lake, but two water-skiers skidded over its green surface, their wakes spraying each other as their boats swung dangerously close.

A red sailboat rocked gently in the stillness on the other side of the lake, a few rowboats crawled slowly over the water. The young man who looked after the boathouse where Roy's boat was stored sat hunched on a stool with his long brown hair cloaking his face, staring intensely at a car magazine. He glanced up just long enough to read the numbered tag on the key Josh dangled in front of him, then waved them on in. Roy's boat was a big rowboat, with plenty of room for the six of them plus Josh's boom box and their two family-sized ice chests.

Luann got in at once, sitting in the prow with her feet up on a rower's bench, watching and making the occasional helpful comment as Flourescent dragged the little craft down the muddy path from the boathouse to the water. As they got it to the lake's edge, Mike, Rack, and Widget stepped away, leaving Helgi and Josh at the stern to push the boat into the water. Helgi's feet sank deep into the mud as the two of them shoved, the force sending it out to float free.

The three men on the shore cheered, Luann raised an imaginary microphone to her mouth. "With a single surge of their mighty muscles, the heroes launched the ship into the wild surf," she narrated.

"Thank you, Howard Goat, smell," Mike replied. He sat down on the grass, taking off his sneakers and peeling back his socks before he waded out. "Ow shit! Watch out for broken glass on the bottom, guys." He climbed up into the boat and sat down to look at his foot.

"Is it bad?" Helgi asked.

"Nah, just needs a Band-Aid."

"I think Roy's got some first aid shit in the box," answered Josh. "Lemme see." He flipped off his thongs and waded out to the boat, scuffling more carefully through the mud. Helgi followed him. The little craft tilted under his weight, rising half out of the water, for a second he thought that it was about to flip over, but Mike quickly moved to balance him, and the two of them were able to counterweight Josh.

Once inside the boat, Josh flipped up one of the bench-tops to show a wooden compartment full of fishing tackle and assorted junk. He reached down, stirring through it for a few moments before coming out with a little tin box. "Here you are, and" Grinning like a wild boar, he reached down again and brought out a bottle. "Roy's good buddy, Jack Daniels!" Josh shook the bottle, it gurgled three-quarters full. "Son of a bitch must have forgotten he left this in here. Well, if he forgot it."

"Finders keepers," Widget agreed as he hauled himself up over the side. "We is the finders, and that sure be a keeper!"

On shore, Rack was still struggling with his black cowboy boots. "Hurry up, or we'll leave you behind!" Mike shouted. "How the hell do you wear those boots on a day like this?"

"Fuck you," Rack grunted, pulling the second one off. He rolled his jeans up and made his way out to the boat. "Hey, gimme some of that."

Luann grabbed the bottle from Josh's hand before Rack could get it. "Medicinal purposes come first, guys. Give me your foot, Mike disinfectant."

"Hell of a waste," Josh grunted.

Luann spread Mike's cut open and dripped some of the whiskey onto it. "Shit, that hurts!" He complained.

Luann gave him the bottle. "Think of this as painkiller."

"Well here's to the great future of Flourescent!" Mike took a deep swig and passed the whiskey to Helgi.

Helgi didn't like whiskey much, but he could hardly turn down the toast. He lifted the bottle. "Someday we're going to play Reunion Arena." He took a little sip and handed the bottle on to Josh before putting his arm around Luann again.

When the whiskey reached her, she stared for a moment at the sunlight gleaming on the dark green glass and glimmering from the liquid that sloshed inside. "To Flourescent's new songwriter," she murmured, so softly that Helgi could hardly hear her. She drank, making a face at the taste and opening the ice chest to get out another wine cooler. "Ptoo, how can you guys drink this stuff? I've had better-tasting cold medicine."

"It's hard work," Rack drawled, "but I think I can handle it."

They rowed out farther on the lake, the boat rocking slowly forward like the back of a fat and lazy old mare, until the solid rock of Q102 booming out of their radio was the only music they could hear. Luann got out the suntan lotion and turned around, arching her back towards Helgi. He rubbed the cream into her skin, kneading gently at the delicate strands of muscle under her thin padding of softness. Unlike the girls in his karate class, who were either wiry or solidly built, Luann felt surprisingly fragile to him. Any careless move might rend her sinews from her bones, he felt, he lightened his touch, and she looked back at him.

"That feels good," she said. "Could you do it a little harder, please?"

After he had rubbed her back thoroughly, she rubbed his. The two of them leaned back together in the sunlight, letting the radio's heavy bass beat drown out the sound of the others talking. Although the sun was beating full onto them, it was cooler over the water than on land. Helgi looked over the side, wondering whether he could see any fish, but the lake's depths were murky green. He knew there were fish in there. Mostly slimy-skinned catfish, boneless as sharks, cruising over the mud and trash at the lake's bottom with their long mouth-tendrils quivering, but every so often someone would catch a bass in White Rock Lake. No one seemed to be fishing today, though, any fishermen in the crowd on shore were probably waiting for sunset, when the fish fed. Laguz,the rune meant "water", it spoke of sunken things, the dangers of the deep and the sharp-toothed Lorelei, a beckoning woman above the surface, a dark fish below. It seemed to Helgi that he could feel his thoughts sinking down through the layers of the lake, down to something glimmering in the blackness

"What are you thinking?" Luann asked drowsily.

"Oh, nothing much."

The song ended and the DJ's voice came on. "Now for the news despite a severe battering from heavy storms on the way, the recreated Viking ship Eiriksson, sailing out of Bergen, Norway, landed in Hudson Bay about twenty minutes ago, just as scheduled. We couldn't get out there to interview them, but here we have the Metroplex's very own Viking, Erik Eriksson, to give us his thoughts on this. Over to you, Erik."

A few seconds of unintelligible sing-song followed, Helgi recognized the voice of the Muppet Show's Swedish Chef at once.

"Erik says, just remember that the Norse discovered this country first, and so what we're really celebrating now is Leif Eriksson's Day. So here's a triple-shot of mead for all you Norsemen out there, Yngwie Malmsteen with 'I Am A Viking', followed by Led Zeppelin's 'Immigrant Song' and Todd Rundgren's 'Song of the Viking'. A happy Leif Eriksson's Day from Q102."

As the high notes of Yngwie Malmsteen's guitar screamed out, Helgi realized that everyone in the boat was looking at him. He raised his beer, saying "Happy Leif Eriksson's Day," and poured a little over the side as they returned the greeting. The froth floated on the lake's ripples like sea-foam, slowly settling into the green water as Yngwie Malmsteen sang about steel and slaying. After a while, they dug the bread and sandwich makings out of the ice chests. Rolling up a tube of ham, mustard, and Wonder Bread in one hand, Josh grabbed Luann's bag of tabloids with the other.

"What's this shit? You brought papers along? Hey, the National Enquirer, all right!" He took the tabloid out and spread it out on his lap before starting another sandwich.

"You guys want to play Tabloid Trash?" Luann asked. She started passing out papers.

"Hey, get this," Rack said after a little while. "'Minks in woman's fur coat come alive, claw her to death. Her maid says, "he went into a high falsetto,"'It was horrible! I came in and there she was on the bed, her flesh torn to shreds, as if a hundred little animals had attacked her with teeth and claws. Her mink coat was beside her. I picked it up and I swear, it moved in my hand!'"

"'Woman raped by Bigfoot in Oregon National Park,'" Josh read in a deep pretentious voice that slid up to the same high register as Rack's for the quote. "'Once it was all over, he was very gentle, really.'"

"Okay, here's one for you, Helgi," said Rack. "'Nessie has Swedish cousin! Two American tourists, Mark and Ann Tremont, boating in Trondheim Fjord,'"

"Which is in Norway," Helgi added.

"Were nearly capsized when the Norse Nessie surfaced under their boat. Ann Tremont says, "It was horrible, the neck must have been fifteen feet long! It was dark gray and slimy looking, like a giant slug, with a stringy mane growing all the way down the back of its neck." Luckily for the couple from White Springs, Nevada, "Trondie" didn't want dinner she just wanted to welcome the tourists to Sweden.'"

"You laughin'," said Widget unexpectedly, "but my cousin saw somethin' like that in Lake Waco, coupla years back."

"No shit?" Josh drawled. "Maybe you should write it up for the Enquirer."

"This your cousin in the service?" Asked Rack. "If he's the one who saw it, I might believe it."

"Sure is. Y'all remember meetin' him, he come to our first gig?"

Josh lay back on his rower's bench, dangling his feet over the side. "Was he that big black dude who came in with the fine white babe? Thought sure there were some ol' boys there gonna haul him out and lynch him."

"Thass him. Anyway, him and a couple of homeboys were passin' through Waco, and they thought they'd go to the lake. So they did a little midnight requisitionin' and found them a boat, paddled out to the island out there. And before they could even start drinkin', before one drop of beer or whiskey could pass their lips, what do you think stuck its head up out in front of them?"

Luann laughed. "The Loch Waco Monster."

"Yeah, you laugh, girl. My cousin say its neck about four feet long and big around as my thigh, head like a snake's head, but bent over at a funny angle, he say it was dark brown or black, real shiny and slimy lookin', it just stick its head up, look around a little, and go right back down."

"Water moccasin," said Mike. "They get real big. Lucky those guys weren't swimming out there."

"Nah, he say he thought of that, but he seen them water snakes all his life. He say its head tilted wrong, and there no ripples or anythin' behind it, like a snake swimmin'. Besides, you figure four foot of the snake out of the water, how much be down under? No snakes that big in Texas, 'cept for maybe pythons in the zoo or some such."

"Could of been a snappin' turtle," Rack suggested. "They get real big, too."

"Same thing, man, same 'xact thing. How big you think that fuckin' turtle be? He say no sign of a shell showin' in the water behind it, either that make its neck as long as you is tall. Far as I concerned, snappin' turtle like that be a fuckin' monster."

"What did your cousin think it was?" Helgi asked.

Widget shrugged. "He had no idea, man. None at all."

A few heavy clouds were beginning to drift in by sunset, black against the ruddy light, and a light wind had started to blow, so they rowed back to shore. Luann was the only one still sober enough to drive, she drove them back to her parents' house and made iced tea.

"Don't we gotta pack up and get outta here before your folks get home?" Josh asked, waving drunkenly at the band setup that still occupied most of the garage.

"They're at a dinner with some of the other people from my father's department. They won't be back till late, and if you get caught driving like that, our butts are the ones in trouble."

Josh leaned against the wall, sliding down slowly to the concrete floor and landing with his legs crossed Indian-style. "Well, someone get the fucking boom box out of the van, then. We need some music in here."

After a little while, Luann and Helgi crept into the house. It was smaller than Helgi's house, only one storey. A waist-high counter half-separated the living room from the kitchen, a big sliding-glass door opened out from the living room to the fenced back yard. Helgi saw a dark door-lined passage stretching back from the other side of the living room, and guessed that the bedrooms would be back there.

"We could sit out in the back yard if you like," Luann suggested, her fingers wringing nervously at the edges of her shorts. "Or I could show you my room."

"How well is your yard stocked with mosquitoes?"

She rolled her eyes. "How many mosquitoes do you want? We've got 'em all. Every size, every shape, every color. Come on, my room is this way."

Luann's room was sand-colored with white accents fringed white bedspread, fluffy white lampshade, white desk wedged into the corner by the window. A framed print of blue and yellow watercolor flowers painted in a style that looked streaky and drippy to Helgi hung over the desk, balanced by a Garfield calendar on the other side of the window. Her school books were neatly stacked up on the desk, edges squared off as perfectly as their differing sizes allowed. The top shelf of the cabinet beside the bed held fiction. The Name of the Rose, The Handmaid's Tale, If On A Winter's Night A Traveler. The bottom two shelves held Luann's CDs.

Luann gestured to the bed. "Well, sit down. Can I get you anything else to drink or anything?"

Helgi put his empty glass of iced tea carefully down on the desk and sat down. "No, thanks."

Luann sat down beside him, leaning up against him as she had on the boat and turning her face up towards his. Suddenly certain, Helgi put his arms around her as they kissed. This time he did not pull away when he felt the heat growing in his groin, but rather drew her more closely to him. He could feel the tight knots of her nipples pressing against his bare chest through her thin halter top, his excitement shook him deeply, as though they sat on the deck of a pitching ship. Luann's soft hands stroked down his back, her eyes were half-closed as they kissed. Helgi could not help wondering if she had ever done it before, but he would not have asked.

The knot of her halter top fell free under his hands. Luann's breasts were very white against the rest of her body, sprinkled with a few pale freckles like a light dusting of cinnamon on whipped cream, her little nipples were a deep rose-brown. Luann leaned back her head as Helgi's fingers touched her breasts, Helgi bent his head to kiss her throat, following the soft line down between her collar bones. Her nipples crinkled in turn under his tongue. He felt dizzy, unbelieving, and at the same time he wanted to shout with joy. Luann reached for the elastic waistband of his shorts, pulling them down and stroking him firmly as he unbuttoned and unzipped hers. Her underwear were white cotton with a little froth of lace around the edges.

"Wait," she said, drawing away from him. She pulled her shorts and underwear the rest of the way down, kicking them free with her thong sandals. Luann went over to her closet and stood on tiptoe, reaching up to the top shelf and rustling around for a few moments. Helgi could not look away from her. Her stretch threw the delicate lines of her back into full definition, shoulder bones arching like tiny wings and buttocks curving smoothly out from her slender waist.

When she turned around, Helgi saw a three-pack of Saxon condoms and a tube of spermicidal jelly in her hands. "The O'Roarkes take no chances," she told him, handing the condoms to him. "I hate to sound unromantic, but, on with it, my man."

Helgi tore open one of the foil sections. For a moment he could only stare at the flat rubber thing in his hand. He had seen rubbers discarded in parks, when Mark and he were freshmen, they had spent two hours daring each other to buy a pack, and when they had the things, they had used them for a water balloon fight. He could feel himself beginning to wilt.

"Here, let me do it," Luann said. She took the rubber from his hand and stroked it smoothly onto him. It felt uncomfortably tight to Helgi, but he was afraid to say anything, for all he knew, they were supposed to feel that way.

Luann also looked critically at it. "It's a bit small for you. We'll have to get another brand next time. God forbid it should burst at the moment of truth. However, if God should be so negligent" she held up the spermicidal jelly"we have another weapon in store." She glanced sideways up at him. "Um, you can put it in if you like."

Helgi took the tube from her hand and watched as Luann lay down on the bed, knees up and head propped on the pillow so that she could watch him. Although he had seen plenty of pictures in magazines, he was still astounded by the beauty of the dewy pink petals spreading open between her legs, by the idea that he could touch her with his own hands, his own body. The sight of the jelly tube's white plastic nozzle entering her was as unreal as a clock melting over the back of a chair. He squeezed carefully until he was sure he had enough of the stuff inside her, then tossed the tube aside and lowered himself over Luann on hands and knees. She sighed as he slid slowly into her, wrapping her arms around his neck and drawing his head down so that they could kiss as they made love. Helgi felt as though great waves were surging through him, flinging his whole body into each thrust, Luann was soft and yielding as foaming water beneath him, her arms around his back dragging him deeper into her at each stroke.

He did not remember whether he had made any noise when he came, he only remembered her tightening around him again and again, gripping hard to the very roots of his body until he burst asunder. Helgi and Luann lay together for a little while, Helgi melting within her. Finally Luann glanced up at the clock.

"It's past ten-thirty, and my parents are supposed to be getting home by eleven. I know it's silly for people our age to be worrying about that, but since this is their house, I think."

Helgi kissed her again before he pulled out. The full rubber slipped easily from him. "Um, what do I do with?"

Luann got up and took a few Kleenex from the box on her desk, wrapping the condom up and arcing it neatly into her white wicker wastebasket. "That. You can wash first the bathroom is just across the hall."

Helgi was about to protest, but she laid a finger on his lips. "You won't take nearly as long as I will. Go."

Helgi stuck his head out of the door, looked both ways, saw no one, he could still hear the dim thumping of the bass from the radio in the garage, and streaked across the hall.

When Luann came back from her turn in the bathroom, fully dressed, Helgi suddenly felt terribly awkward again. He wanted to tell her that it was his first time, that it had been wonderful, unbelievable, and he was desperately afraid that she would say something like, "Well, you'll probably get better eventually then." Instead she stood on tiptoes to kiss him again, then grinned wickedly. "That was good. We're going to have to do it lots and lots."

"Um, yeah. I hope so."

Luann put her arms around him, giving him a quick squeeze. "I guess you'd better go now. The parental units ought to be driving in pretty soon. God, and I'd better go tell those drunken idiots to pack their stuff up and get out of the garage. I hope they're in a fit state to drive home, because I don't want to explain them to my parents. I hate living at home, you know that?"

"Ah. Yeah. Um..." The words stuck in his throat a moment, then burst through like hail tumbling suddenly from a cloud. "I love you, Luann."

"I'm so glad you said that, I love you, too." They kissed one more time, then Luann clapped her hands sharply together. "All right, get them li'l doggies moving, mush!"

Dazed by the bright waves of awe and joy breaking through him, Helgi did not know how he made it home. "You won't believe this, Elric," he said softly to the elk hound who lay on the bed beside him.

Elric rolled over for Helgi to scratch his stomach, nosing upside-down at his master's thigh to encourage him. "You don't really care, do you?" Helgi asked as Elric's hind legs kicked happily under his attentions. "I didn't think so. And they say a dog is a man's best friend. Ha." He smiled quietly. "I actually did it, Elric. I actually did. Believe it."

A sharp snare-roll of rain beat against the window, Helgi saw the faint flicker of lightning through the clouds, but heard no thunder. He wondered if anyone was still out on the lake this late. He could imagine, if they'd stayed, being on the water in the small boat as the wind rose, the waves that tossed it about one with the waves of drunkenness in their heads, the shore hidden by the storm-darkness and the driving rain no more hope of making land than if they were in the middle of the ocean.

That brought the ship Eiriksson to his mind storm-tossed, battered by wind and wave, but knowing there was a harbor before them if they held their course. But what about the first time, the first sailing into the unknown waters, over the depths no sounding-line of that time could fathom?

"Here be dragons," Helgi whispered, as the gusts of rain-sharp wind whipped across his window. He tightened his fingers in the warmth of Elric's thick fur. When he closed his eyes, it seemed to him that he could feel the waves tossing about him, see the pale gulls blown like dead leaves on the storm wind against the blackening sky.

Helgi propped a sheet of fresh music paper and a pencil on his synthesizer, flicking the instrument on. He would start in the bass, he thought, a strong beat of swiftly leaping intervals. Horns? No, strings, a vibrato shaking through the song's roots, so that the beat gave no steadiness of land for the listener to rest against. But none of the notes he played sounded right, though he flicked back and forth between instrumental settings, he could not hear the sea in his music, no matter how he tried to shape what he felt into sound. The music paper was blank as a stretch of white sand before him, only its horizontal lines rippling like wave-marks in his tired sight. After a while he turned the synthesizer off, leaving the paper's whiteness untouched, and went to his bedroom.Nudging Elric aside, Helgi lay down on his back with his arms crossed across his chest. He meant only to think for a little while, to see if he could make the sounds any clearer in his mind, but it was not long before he had slipped into soft dazed thoughts of Luann, and from there to sleep.

CHAPTER XIX

Hailgi sat in Hunding's high seat that night, dealing out the treasures taken from the slain. Though he had kept some of the finest pieces with his own gear, he meant to give all of it away, sooner or later. Some would be gifts for other drightens, some he had picked out for Bergohildar as his father had done after every battle, and some he would give to Sigiruna as part of her morning-gift. While they had not come out of the battle unscathed Hailgi guessed that they might have lost as many as one man in five, and many were wounded, so that the true toll would not be known till all fevers had run their courses. They had utterly destroyed the war band of Hunding's sons, and won a great deal. Ingwibjorg and Gunthahildar, helped by the hall's bonds maids, poured out the ale for the victors, although it seemed to Hailgi that Gunthahildar might have spent more time sitting beside Swain, her dark head leaning close to his bright one. Ingwibjorg still looked very pale, as though she had taken a hard-bleeding wound in the battle, and the grimly clenched set of her face showed Hailgi that something was still not well with her. When Ingwibjorg came up to refill his horn, and it was no bull's or aurochs' horn, but one made of fine Frankish glass, with white lines swirling around the blue-green glass to the round bead at its tip, Hailgi had found it in the hall and chosen it for his own. Hailgi caught her hand as she drew the pitcher back. Her skin felt soft as cream under his calloused fingers.

"Ingwibjorg," he whispered to her, "are you really all right? Has any man tried to harm you?"

"No one's touched me." She looked pointedly at his hand on hers. "Except you. You can let go of me any time now, you know."

"Are you angry with me for something?"

"Not yet. I will be if you keep bothering me. I told you, I'm tired."

"Then why don't you go lie down? You and Gunthahildar will have one of the drighten's chambers to yourselves for the night. It won't do your sister any harm to get up from that bench and help the serving maids with the night's ale-pouring. I don't know that your father would think Swain the best match for her."

"And what do you know about it?" Ingwibjorg flared. "You haven't been in much of a hurry to choose a bride for yourself. Anyone would think."

If I crush this glass too tightly, it will shatter, Hailgi thought. He eased his hold and opened his other fist, forcing his body to lean back in the chair and speaking as softly as he could. "What?"

"Oh, never mind. Leave me be." Ingwibjorg walked away, back through the door that led to the room where she would sleep. For a moment, Hailgi thought of going after her, but could not.

The ale that had been brewed in the hall of Hunding's sons was stronger than that served at home, except for high feasts such as Yule and Winter nights, even their small beer was stronger than elsewhere. Little wonder this hall was known as a quarrelsome place, Hailgi said to himself as he sipped cautiously. A loud whoop of laughter went up from the other end of the hall. Skald-Thonarabrandar was standing, his tall frame swaying slightly like a scraggly pine-tree in the wind, and speaking some verse that Hailgi could not quite make out over the noise, though the man made no staves that were not scurrilous and obscene. Hailgi beckoned to Gunthahildar. He had to wave twice before Swain noticed and said something to her. Hagalar's youngest daughter got up and came over to him.

"What do you want?"

"Go see what's wrong with your sister."

Gunthahildar cocked her head to the side like a plump sparrow, putting a finger under her little pointed chin. "I can tell you that without asking." She pointed at Freyjawulfar Long-Ears, who sat by the fire with his boots almost scorching in the coals, then to Theudowinar who roared with laughter at Skald Thonarabrandar's verse, to Hrothormar Bear-Sark, who stood among his berserks with a full horn in his hand, pouring the whole horn full down his throat in a single draught. "Do any of them look like good matches for a maiden Ingwibjorg's age?" Gunthahildar put her hands on her hips, looking down on him. As her mouth tightened, it seemed to Hoilogae that he could see Wulfaruna's young ghost in the shape of her face. "And there you sit, leader of the host, young and reasonably good looking, and haven't given her a single word for the last three years, and now you are fro in your own lands and can wed whoever you choose. You saved her from Hunding's sons, like a proper hero in a good song, but you gave her no more care than a piece of precious gold work. You looked at her to see if she was damaged, and that was all."

"I never swore oaths of love to her, nor said even once that I wished to marry her. This is not my fault. As far as weddings go, what are you doing with Swain? He is no drighten, nor a drighten's son, nor does he come of any atheling-kin. Doesn't your father wish a better match for you?"

"He is the trusted man of the strongest drighten in northern Jutland, the leader of the host, he is an atheling because you have made him one, and he has shown it by his bravery and troth. If Ingwibjorg sees little hope for a pleasing marriage among the drightens of our land, what should I look for? I know you will not do ill by Swain in the years to come, nor may my father look ill upon him, when he was wounded saving my life."

"Do you wish me to speak for him to your father?"

"That would be kind."

"Then I shall."

Gunthahildar leaned forward and kissed Hailgi lightly on the lips. For a moment he remembered the soft warmth of her sister's kiss, and it choked him so that he could not speak. He cleared his throat with a draught of ale as Gunthahildar went back to Swain's side. The bonds maiden who came up to refill his horn was a small woman, young and well-rounded. Her skin was brown from the sun, and sun-streaks reddened her brown braids. As well as Hailgi could tell in the dark hall, she seemed to be the fairest of the serving women. Hailgi took her hand gently in his, her callouses scraping against his own, and looked up into her hazel eyes. She did not pull back, but smiled down at him. Though several of her teeth were broken, none seemed rotted. The warm strength of fresh ale and a clean whiff of rosemary lightened the stale-grain odor underlying her breath. And she was a woman, and seemed willing. Hailgi knew that the ale and the darkness would go far in blurring the differences between her and any other.

"Do you wish to come with me?" He asked her, his voice low.

She leaned against the arm of his seat. "I will, gladly." She giggled, swaying a bit. Hailgi drank from the horn and lifted it up to her. The bonds maid set her pitcher on the table before him and took the glass vessel with both hands, holding it very carefully as she drank.

Hunding's hall had grown oddly since the old drighten's death. None of his sons were willing to leave it to any one of the others or even give over their father's chamber, so they had let more rooms be built behind the one that Hunding had dwelt in, until the hinder part of the hall had become a cluster of little houses, each sharing a wall on either side and a roofed aisle running between them.

Hailgi had not been willing to turn the wives and children of Hunding's sons out so swiftly, but Heming's wife was dead and his bairns fostered by another family, so that chamber and the one that Hunding had owned stood empty now. Hailgi led the woman into the little half-house that had been Heming's, finding a shelf for his horn by touch.

"Shall I light the torches?" She asked. "Or the fire?"

"No. No, leave them be."

Hailgi sent Ingwibjorg and Gunthahildar back the next morning with those wounded who could ride easily. The two women had brought little with them and took little away, though Hailgi offered them their choice of those fine pieces he had kept back the night before as gifts for other drightens.

"You have already done a great deal for us," said Gunthahildar, though it did not stop her from choosing a large cloak-pin of gold and a twisted golden arm-ring with garnet-eyed beast-heads at each end. Ingwibjorg took nothing, only gnawed at her lower lip as her little sister picked over the treasures. The unfair guilt in Hailgi's belly was cold and slimy as a slug's trail, though he had sworn no oaths, he still felt that he had somehow betrayed Ingwibjorg's hopes.

In the cloud-darkened morning light, her eyes were deep green and un-forgiving as the sea beneath a storm-sickened sky, and he could not look into them very long. Still, he could not bring himself to make apologies to her, for if he had wronged her he would have made greater amends, and since he knew he had not, he would not humble himself to her. The other drightens and most of their men went with the women, only a few of those warriors. Men who had come from small steadings and wished to take their plunder in land instead of treasures, claiming a share of earth from those they had slain, stayed behind. Hailgi had spoken to Freyjawulfar about Gunthahildar and Swain, and he had promised to speak to Hagalar in turn. The rain had stopped falling, but the sky was still gray, drops dripping from the new green leaves. Hailgi watched them ride down the muddy path until the last warrior had ridden from his sight among the trees. The next days would not be easy. The sons and wives of the thanes who had fallen in battle, and those carls who had stayed in their fields or come living from the fray, would have to swear troth to him. Hailgi knew that he would have to slay or outlaw those who refused, if one of them did not simply take the chance to knife him where he stood.

It would be best to put Ansumundar over them when that was done, Hail-gi thought. Ansumundar knew better than anyone how to protect himself and which of the folk there could be trusted, but Hailgi himself needed to go home to his own lands and begin gathering his strength for the attack on Sealand. That would be a hard thing, for he would need to leave Ansumun-dar with a good guard, and it was not at all certain that he could rouse the other drightens to do battle for the sake of his chosen bride, simply because he wanted her and her father had promised her to someone else. Still, if he had to go alone against Hadubroddar's host, Hailgi knew that he would do it, even if he were doomed to die in the doing. Hailgi saw the wives and children of Hunding's sons first. They gathered before him in the hall, each mother bringing her bairns forward to swear their oaths of troth on the heavy gold arm-ring that Hailgi held out to them.

The ring that Hunding and his sons had used for their oaths. The eldest child there, a young, plain-faced maiden with long brown braids, could not have had more than ten or eleven winters. It would be a little time before these children were likely to become dangerous, and by then he hoped to have won their loyalty. Nevertheless, Ansumundar loomed beside him with hand on sword-hilt, for a knife flicked suddenly from hiding could make even a weak arm deadly. Most of the other men were in the hall as well, drinking ale or small beer and playing at dice beside the long cooking fire, but they were too far away to ward Hailgi from any stroke. The badly wounded lay bedded down near the fire as well, those who were able joining in the dicing and drinking that drew their minds from their pain. The rest lay quietly, only speaking or groaning every now and then.

None were fevered yet, save for Ansugairar whose belly-wound had stunk of onions last night, he shifted about and moaned, dark hair sweat-dampened and stolid face flushed. His kinsmen had brought him off the field before they knew how deep his wound was, and watched to make sure that no one stole his silver arm ring or his knife but Hailgi had little doubt that they would choose to end his pain soon. Hailgi knew Aiwulfar's wife Wulfadis to be Hagalar's eldest daughter. She was taller and thinner than her sisters, her angular body and face more like her father's than theirs. Though she was only three years older than Hailgi, the years among Hunding's sons had not been kind to her. Her face was worn as a soapstone carving left to the winter weather, her straw like hair was already graying, but no red of tears or sleeplessness ringed her silver-blue eyes. The two small children behind her held back, glancing out from her skirts.

Wulfadis lifted one little hand in each of her own and placed them on the oath ring. The knuckles of her long bony fingers were swollen and reddened beneath the rings of bright copper that she must have put on to ease the pains in her hands.

"Hailgi is no foe of ours. Now you must swear by Ingwe-Freyjar and Nerthuz and the mighty god that you shall not bear weapon against him nor break troth with him. Do you swear it?"

The children were silent, looking up at Hailgi. Their eyes were very blue against their tanned faces. Neatly dressed as they were, in little tunics with no breeches, he could not tell whether they were boys or girls.

"Say, 'I swear it'," Wulfadis prompted. The two bairns echoed her words. "And I swear it for myself, Hailgi. You did well, to keep my sisters safe after Heming had brought them to the battlefield."

"Your father placed his trust in me. I could do nothing else."

"Still, there are men who would not have taken such care for two women in battle's heat."

Such as the sons of Hunding? Hailgi wondered. It would make his work here easier, if that were so.

The smaller of Wulfadis' two children looked up into Hailgi's face. "We've said it. Will you give our papa back now?" The child asked.

Wulfadis whirled as the larger one burst into a sharp volley of sobs, pulling both of them away without a backward glance before Hailgi could say anything. Not knowing what else to do, Hailgi looked towards the group of women and children, beckoning the next family forward.

As Hailgi was taking the last oaths from the families of Hunding's sons, he heard the rumble of thunder growing nearer and the rain pattering more loudly against the roof of the hall. Though the smoke-hole was roofed from the rain by a layer of wood that stood just high enough above it to let smoke out and light in, the wind blew a spattering of drops in to hiss in the fire below.

As the fresh gust of wind brushed his face, Hailgi was suddenly aware of the nearness of the hall. The smells he had numbed himself to, stale smoke and old meat, wounded men's blood, piss in the dirty straw and years of hounds and unwashed bodies, were pressing in to choke him. He felt that the walls were growing narrower and the ceiling lower as he watched.

Hailgi stood, kicking a stinking pile of reeds aside as he started to walk to the door. "I'm going out for a ride," he told Ansumundar. "I'll deal with the next lot when I get back I just need to get out and breathe for a little while. Wulfadis, would you get the bonds maids to sweep and put out fresh straw?"

Wulfadis looked up from her two children, who were both sobbing in her skirts now. Hailgi marked that her own face was still dry, though her children's sadness, or the shadows in the hall, seemed to have grooved the furrows of her skin more deeply. "I'll do that."

Hailgi pulled the hood of his deep scarlet cloak up over his head as he went out, the tightly woven wool shedding some of the rain. Some of the horses of Hunding's men had been turned out into the field so that Hailgi's men could stable their own, the loose steeds would be claimed or sold very soon. The lightning seemed to flicker over his head, but he counted twelve heartbeats before he heard the thunder.

The weather had made the horses restless. They whinnied and stamped, one tall black gelding kicking against the door of his stall as Hailgi walked past. Wigablajar raised his head and nickered a welcome.

"Ah, you're glad to see me, aren't you?" Hailgi stroked the horse's soft nose over the stall-gate for a few moments before coming in to saddle him.

Thonarar's Hammer boomed nearby as Hailgi led Wigablajar out of the stables. The fallow steed shied, but Hailgi stroked him and spoke to him soothingly before mounting up. He could feel the horse calming beneath the pressure of his thighs, his nervousness shifting into an eagerness to be off and running.

The lightning licked overhead, lighting the wood's spring greenness with a sudden gold-white flash. Hailgi's hood blew back, his cloak flowing behind him and the rain pouring into his face like a waterfall rushing down from the high cloud-crags. The galloping eased his mind, as though he were leaving Ingwibjorg and Sigiruna and Wulfadis all behind in the pounding of his horse's hooves through the mud.

A tall figure in a rain-darkened cloak stepped out on the path in front of him. "Hold" the man shouted, lifting his spear. His voice was lighter and clearer than Hailgi's, but with a familiar hemp-rough undertone.

Hailgi reined in his horse before he could dash the man down, trotting the last few steps and stopping before him. "Who are you?" He asked, drawing his sword. This close, he could be amazed at his challenger's size. Though the man seemed more slimly built than Ansumundar, he was taller and his shoulders broader. Hailgi was not sure that even being mounted was such a great advantage, but he would not give way. "What do you want here?"

The man tossed back the hood of his cloak. His pale hair was soaked down, his short golden beard dripping. He had been walking with his face turned up to the rain. It was his fairness that struck Hailgi at once. Chiseled planes slanting down beneath high cheekbones, golden eyebrows peaking on a broad forehead above ice-blue eyes, delicately-cut mouth not hidden by his beard. "Get down off that horse and I'll show you, or stay on it, if you like!" The stranger's speech was that of a Saxon, tones oddly twisted to Hailgi's ears and some words spoken more shortly. "It makes no difference to me." He swung his spear in a hissing arc through the air.

The flash of lightning lit the challenger's face stark white, as though he had been carved from a glacier's heart. Its red afterimage, blinking behind Hailgi's lids was not that of a man, but of a great wolf, its jaws open in a silent laugh.

Bright as the lightning was, its thunder did not sound again till Hailgi had spoken. "We may fight if you wish, but I tell you, Sinfjotli, son of Sigimund and Sigilind the Walsings, it is not seemly for you to raise your weapon against a kinsman of the Wolfing line. Now I have named your name, but you do not yet know mine, or you would not have spoken as you have, after troubling yourself to come this far to this land."

The darkness at the heart of Sinfjotli's winter-light eyes swelled outwards, swallowing the blue around them as he stared upward at his mounted kinsman. All Hailgi's hairs prickled up underneath his gaze. Pack member or prey, he thought. There is nothing else to wolves. It seemed to him that his own gaze narrowed to the other's eyes, sharpening into the point of a spear keen as the one that stood in Fetter-Grove. Then he felt the steely strength of a slim hand gripping his shoulder, and knew that Sigiruna stood behind him to strengthen him. He wanted to look back, but dared not turn his eyes from the Walsing's. At last Sinfjotli blinked the blackness from his eyes, rubbing at them as though he had just stepped from a dark hut into the brightest summer sunlight. The touch on Hailgi's shoulder was gone, as if he had dreamed it. Though he glanced swiftly backwards, he saw nothing but rain-dripping beeches behind him.

"You are Hailgi Hunding's-Bane, there is no one else you might be. I have come in search of you, because I wished to spend the summer in your war band, and to try your strength, because I have heard the songs of you."

"As I have heard the songs of you, Sinfjotli. They say you are a berserk who was raised as an outlaw in the woods of Gautland, a werewolf and the son of a werewolf. How should I trust you in my war band?" Hailgi was careful to rein in his breath so that Sinfjotli could not hear it, but his will could not calm the thudding of his heart. If I do not best him now, with my words, he thought, I will surely never best him, neither I nor any warrior in my band could better his strength with a blade.

The Walsing smiled, showing strong bright teeth. "Because we are kin. How else?"

"Kin-strife has never been far from the Wolfing line." Another prickling rippled up Hailgi's back, he could hear Sinfjotli's breathing. He was treading through the underbrush with the beast close by him, now bravery must be weighed with care. "The songs have told of your father's deeds in Gautland, and your own how he slew his sister's sons, and you killed your half-brothers."

Sinfjotli was no longer smiling. His stance had shifted so that he was poised to fight or flee, head lifted as though he caught the hunter's scent on the wind.

"We had a great geld to pay then, for a great kin-slaughter. It was not the Walsings who first broke troth, then or ever. As for the slayings, they were not freely chosen, but our need forced them upon us. Have you never been driven by the might of need?"

"I have known it" Hailgi admitted"both in a deed of shame and the deed that avenged it. And I know how it can shape. Still, I would have more reason to trust in you before I let a wolf run freely in my hall."

Sinfjotli turned his spear thoughtfully in his hand. "Are you afraid of me?"

"I am not. But there are those who name me wise for my years, and I know that a spear in the back may slay the strongest of heroes. I have another battle to fight soon, where I must trust every man in my band to place his trust in me. You do not seem like a man who can easily bear being second to another. I think you would always be testing me to see which of us might overcome the other, and I have enough trials without seeking out more."

The Walsing regarded Hailgi quietly for a moment, his eyes narrowing as if he were considering the other's words. Hailgi began to think of the ways Sinfjotli might find to attack him, and how he would counter them. Then Sinfjotli twitched convulsively, leaning his head back and stretching his neck out so that Hailgi could see the white gleam of his throat between fair beard and dark cloak.

The gesture lasted only a moment, Hailgi thought the Walsing did not even know that he had made it. Does he have fits, too? Hailgi wondered. Stranger things might be awaited from the son of the Walsing twins, but it would not go far in making Sinfjotli an easy companion within his war band.

Sinfjotli cast his eyes downward to the muddy road. His voice was very low as he said, "I will swear to follow you for the summer, till I go back to the hall of the Walsings for the Winter nights feast, I will swear to stand by you in battle and do as you wish, even as I would for my own father. Whatever you may have heard in the songs of the Walsings, you have surely never heard that we have ever broken our oaths."

"That is so."

Sinfjotli straightened his back, but his gaze still rested near to Wigablajar's hooves. Thus downcast, he looked younger than his size and thick beard had led Hailgi to think, still more boy than man. In actual count of winters, Hailgi remembered then, the two of them were near to an age, but Sinfjotli had grown up in the forest of Gautland and was still young in the world of men.

Hailgi guessed that the Walsing was not often denied what he wished to have, whether because of his father's unbridled love for him, or because there were few his size and fame could not easily cow. The more I say no to him, Hailgi thought, the more set he will become on winning a place in my band, and who knows what he might do to get it? It was not hard for him to see the bodies of the dead in a heap, the bloody corpses become their own mound, and Sinfjotli standing before it demanding to be given the place of the men he had bested. Whatever he did, slaying him would surely bring Sigimund's vengeful wrath down swiftly. I must treat him carefully, Hailgi said to himself. Sinfjotli stood there patiently, his fair brows lowered and all his thoughts in the gaze he cast down before Hailgi. Though the drighten was not sure why the other had changed his mood so swiftly from challenge to supplication, he could not help feeling a oddly warm glow of liking, as though Sinfjotli's gestures had somehow disarmed all his own feelings of mistrust and anxiousness.

Hailgi drew his sword, stretching the point down towards Sinfjotli, who laid his right hand upon it. "Swear, then."

The Walsing swore his oath, and Hailgi answered, "I swear to deal with you fairly, as befits a drighten towards a true thane, for your own sake and that of the bonds of kin which we share." He dried his sword on a part of his tunic that his cloak had shielded from the rain, then shifted back in his saddle, so that Sinfjotli would have room to sit before him. "Will you ride back with me?"

Sinfjotli's gaze flashed up. "Let your horse run as he will, and I will run with him. I know little of horses, but that one does not look so fine that I cannot match his speed, and better it where the road is not smooth."

"A fine boast, if it's true." Hailgi nudged Wigablajar around, kneeing the steed into a gallop. Sinfjotli's first smooth burst of speed brought him up past the mud flying from the horse's rear hooves, then he was pacing Hailgi. The Walsing's dark cloak flowed out behind him, flapping like a battle-flag in the wind of his running. The pathway narrowed ahead of them, curving around a huge oak. To Hailgi's amazement, the Walsing moved ahead of him, running before the galloping horse, the hem of his sodden cloak spattering muddy droplets through the rain.

Wigablajar jibbed suddenly, shying back from the flapping cloak. It took all Hailgi's strength and skill to wrestle him back onto the path, and by that time, Sinfjotli had already rounded the curve. Hailgi touched his horse's sides lightly with his spurs, speeding after the Walsing.

The crack of the branch above him was his only warning as Sinfjotli dropped out of the oak to the horse's back. Hailgi did not waste strength wrestling against him, he hit Sinfjotli low with his shoulder, moving with the path of his kinsman's movement to help Sinfjotli's own weight and momentum carry him over into the mud. The Walsing rolled as he hit the ground, coming up on his feet with his spear in his hand and grinning brightly through the mud on his face as Hailgi reined Wigablajar in. Hailgi's flash of anger was already fading into laughter.

"You've taken a lot of trouble to show me you don't know how to mount a horse," he called down. "Shall I show you how to do it?"

"I think I can manage," Sinfjotli answered. He walked up to Wigablajar, laying a hand on the horse's back. Wigablajar stepped back suspiciously, blowing through his nose.

"Sa, sasteady now," Hailgi murmured to his steed, stroking him. He had heard before that horses had little love for berserks, the animals could smell the bear, or wolf-pelt lurking beneath the human hide.

Steadying himself with one hand, Sinfjotli suddenly leapt up, swinging a leg over Wigablajar's back. The horse stepped backwards suddenly, and Hailgi had to grab onto Sinfjotli to keep him from sliding off again.

Hailgi tugged on Wigablajar's reins as his steed danced about. It seemed to him that he could feel Sinfjotli's unsureness, the tightening of the Walsung's huge muscles. "You really haven't ridden before."

Sinfjotli shook his head, flinging a scattering of muddy drops from the ends of his hair. "The only steed I know is the brine-mare, I can steer the sea-steed well, but my father has had little to do with these others." He paused, his head cocked slightly upward, as though he were listening to something. "I know a stave that may give me some help in this, though."

The Walsing touched the horse's neck, tracing a rune, on Wigablajar's wet hide and murmuring, "Ehwaz horse, the high born's joy. Heroes speak from the war-steed's back, Sleipnir is fleetest of beasts."

Wigablajar stilled at once, standing quiet until Hailgi nudged him into a walk.

"I had not heard that you knew the runes." It did not surprise him, however, often runic wisdom was taught within the berserk-bands, for those two of Wodhanar's gifts had been given together to the ancient tribes of the Erulians, so that even now a mighty runester might name himself in his own inscriptions, 'EK ERILAR I the Erulian'.

Though Hailgi could not read the runes well or write them with cunning, he knew their names and shapes, and could recognize by sight a few of the inscriptions that men often wore on bracteates or carried with them on little sticks of wood for luck, the holy words that filled their bearers with might. 'ALU, LAUKAR, GIBU AUJA'.

"Now that I have come into the world of men, I use them less than we did in our cave. There we were wargs in the wood, with every man's hand against us, now my father is a great drighten and fro over much of the Saxon land, and there is little time to think too deeply on such matters." Sinfjotli turned to look his kinsman in the eye. His blue gaze seared Hailgi's thoughts, not with fire but with ice, cold-strong enough to burn, "I have found that men fear me enough for my strength and fame, without adding rune-might as well. No one makes friends where he is wary. Though no one hates me and many toast me in the hall, there is no one among my father's folk whom I may name friend."

Hailgi heard Freyjawulfar's voice in his mind again, its echo ringing faintly from the back of his skull like a shout finally striking a faraway mountain. You must sleep alone after this. "I think we might name one another friend," he said at last. "I would be glad to learn more of what you know, if you will teach it."

"I can, though I think the frowe who stood behind you earlier could teach you more."

Pressed against Sinfjotli's broad back as he was, Hailgi could not hide his start from the Walsing.

"Have I misspoken?" Sinfjotli asked. "I did not mean to" His voice trailed off, as though he himself was not sure what he meant to say.

"What did you see?" Hailgi asked calmly.

"A maiden who much resembled yourself, so far as I could tell beneath her helm." Sinfjotli's baritone voice fell into a soft chant, its hemp-scratched undertones weaving into a binding rope of fascination that caught Hailgi's breath from him. "She wore a byrnie over a white gown, and a sheathed sword where other women wear their keys, and her hand rested on your shoulder, and her might strengthened your own. Her eyes were gray, but the keenness in her look seemed much like that of Sigilind my mother, as though she were also a daughter of Wodan. I think her to be very wise, she who can ride water and air to your side, for she is a living woman and no wraith who does this."

Hailgi's heart clenched upon itself with joy. "It is Sigiruna the daughter of Haganon whom you saw, she whom I shall wed, and no other. For her sake we shall go to do battle on Sealand before Midsummer's, if her father Haganon does not wish to break her betrothal to Hadubroddar and give her to me."

"Now that is a worthy sake for battle!" Sinfjotli answered, grinning back at Hailgi. "I see I did well to come to your band."

When the two of them walked into the hall together, the sounds of talking stilled suddenly as the folk inside turned from whatever they were doing to look at Sinfjotli. Hailgi marked how his thanes straightened their backs, a few hands hovering close to belt-knives or sword-hilts, Bow-Athalwulfar watched from the corner of his eye as he stood and strung his weapon with an air of false casualness, plucking at its string like a harpist. Some of the women shrank back from Sinfjotli's gaze, but Hailgi saw one fair-haired and slender maiden breathing deeply to raise her breasts as she smiled at him, and Alfarath's widow sat playing with her loosened hair and eying the new thane through its ruddy brown strands.

"Who in Thonarar's name is that, Hailgi?" Ansumundar grunted, eying the Walsing as if he were sizing up a troublesome bull. "Where did you find him? He's not one of Hunding's folk."

"This is my kinsman, Sinfjotli the Walsing," Hailgi announced, raising his voice so that everyone in the hall could hear him clearly. "He has come from the Saxon lands, to fight as a thane in my band for this summer, and I welcome his help."

Hailgi heard a few breaths drawn in sharply as he spoke Sinfjotli's name. The tale of the Walsing's birth was as well-known as his other deeds. Still, it seemed that no one had the mood to challenge. Wulfadis was quietly filling his new glass horn with ale, Hailgi guessed that she had as much right to welcome a guest in the hall as any of the women.

Arnugrimar's scratchy voice broke the silence. "Does this mean that you ween to fight again this summer?"

Hailgi straightened his shoulders. He had not meant for this moment to come so soon. He had not thought about it. "Tomorrow I shall send to Haganon the Skjolding, to ask for his daughter Sigiruna in marriage. If he will not grant me this, then we must go against him, to take her and to add those lands on Sealand and the Skjoldings' wealth to our own."

As Hailgi spoke Wulfadis came up to them with the glass horn in her hands, ready to offer it to Sinfjotli. Hailgi took it from her before she could say anything, raising it high. "This oath I swear. That I shall make Sigiruna my bride at this year's Winter nights' feast, and get a bairn upon her that same night, so that my line shall not end nor our clan-soul be homeless in the years to come. So Wodhanar hear it, so Thonarar hallow it!" He drained the horn in a single draught, his head already beginning to spin.

Helmbernu, eyes bright and face ruddy from a morning of drinking, leapt to his feet, swaying a little as he thrust his spear upward. The point stuck in the roof-beam, the fair-headed thane glanced up in surprise, but recovered quickly. "Hail Hailgi!" He called, and the others took up the shout. Skald-Thonarabrandar ran forward with his new shield in his hand, followed by Ingwiwulfar, Skegga Grimar, and Athalfrithar. Before Hailgi could utter a sound, his men had swung him onto the shield and were heaving it up to their shoulders, about to bear him around the hall. Hailgi did not see quite what happened next, but suddenly the shield rose another two hand spans, so that he had to duck quickly and shift to the side to keep his head from striking the main roof beam.

Sinfjotli must have come up in the middle of the shield-bearers, and lifted their weight from them, now the Walsung was carrying Hailgi about by himself, as easily as he might bear a platter of bread. Most of the men were still shouting, Ansumundar had snatched up a shield and was beating his sword against it, and a few others were starting to follow his lead, but a scowl writhed through Skald-Thonarabrandar's scraggly black beard, and it was not excitement or ale that reddened Ingwiwulfar's plump cheeks. There will be trouble here, Hailgi thought, as he drew his sword and brandished it.

"That's right!" Thonarabrandar Odd-Eyes shouted. "Your sword will be sheathed in Skjolding flesh, one way or another!" He grabbed a leek from one of the plates on the table, casting it at Hailgi like a spear. Hailgi caught it neatly with his left hand, waving the shining herb above his head as his men called more jokes and wedding-night redes to him.

The rain had washed from the sky by the next morning, leaving the air clear and clean as new ice, already bright with the pale morning sunlight. A pair of wood-pigeons sat on the hall's roof, cooing throatily back and forth to one another. Most of Hailgi's men were gathering before the hall with their own steeds and those they had chosen from the booty. Hailgi looked about for Sinfjotli, but did not see him until he looked upward to the men who already sat on horseback. The Walsing had chosen a large gelding with a mottled gray-black hide, and sat on the steed's back as though he had grown up in the saddle.

Sinfjotli raised a hand to Hailgi. "Sleeping late? Getting lazy?"

"Things to do," Hailgi answered.

Ansumundar led Hailgi's own horse up to him. "You sure I can't come with you?"

"I need you here," Hailgi answered. "You know these folk, which none of the rest of us do. If I took you with me, I'd have to leave twice the men behind that I'm leaving now."

The big thane grunted, but Hailgi could see the pleased flush spreading at the roots of his red beard. "How long is this for?"

"You may as well move into Hunding's chambers. Unless you choose to, you won't be moving out any time soon. I'll send Sigga and your sons to you as soon as we get back to my own hall. Oh, and mayhap Swain and Gunthahildar will be coming to take a stead here soon. I'd like to do my best for them."

Ansumundar nodded. "I can take care of it. Swain's a good boy."

Hailgi clapped the thane's oaken shoulder. "Stay well, Ansumundar."

"Fare well, Hailgi."

"Hai, why so downcast?" Sinfjotli asked Hailgi as they rode along, a little ahead of the others. "What could be troubling your mind on such a fine day, with a good battle only a little ahead of you?"

The thoughts of seeing Ingwibjorg again, of whether he could try to explain himself to her, or were better just to leave her be, lifted from Hailgi's mind like the weight of a nightmare fading in Sunna's rising light. "Why do you think something is troubling my mind?" He countered sharply.

"My father often has just such a look, when he sits in his high seat late at night with his horn, and then I know that he is thinking of my mother Sigilind, for he will not gaze straight at Borghild his wife."

As they rounded a bend in the path, they saw a doe standing ahead of them, the sunlight gleaming ruddy from her pelt and her head raised to sniff at the wind. Before either of them could move, she had whirled on graceful hoof-points, leaping over a low stand of bushes and disappearing into the cool green shadows of the forest.

"He had no wish for me to come here," Sinfjotli murmured, so softly that Hailgi could hardly understand him. "And I had little wish to leave him alone, but I could not stay with him too long. I do not know why."

It seemed to Hailgi then that the moving patterns of leaf-shadow and sun shifted over Sinfjotli's face like the passing of years, forward and back, so that he could see the youth avenging his grandfather and the man who rode beside him and the old man that Sinfjotli would become, if it were not Sigimund the Walsing he saw there. Men said that Sigimund and his son were more alike than two brothers. And it seemed to him then that he understood why Sinfjotli sought his own place away from his father's hall, and it seemed to him that there was little hope for him to find it, for Sinfjotli could be nothing other than a Walsing, even as he himself could be no one other than Hailgi.

"I have heard, Hailgi," Sinfjotli went on, "that your father was newly laid in the howe when the sons of Hunding offered battle to you. I did not mean to cause you sorrow."

Hailgi had not thought of Sigismundar, but his memory pricked him with no guilt for it, for he knew that his father's luck still ringed his arm with the gold coils Sigismundar had given him as blessing, and there had been no doubt between them when Hailgi had led the host away, nor did the old drighten rest lonely in his howe while Hailgi was still fro of his lands. "You have not," Hailgi answered, his heart brightening with his voice. "Others have tholed a far worse wyrd than you and I. I think neither of us has cause for sorrow." He untied the skin of ale that hung at his belt, took a drink, and passed it over to the other.

Sinfjotli tilted his head back as he drank, his throat gurgling beneath his fair beard. "I have often heard it said that the Danes brew fine ale. I am willing to swear that this is true, the Danish woman Borghild is the finest brewer in Saxony, and this drink is as good as hers." He handed the ale skin back to Hailgi.

"There was talk once of marrying me to her," Hailgi said thoughtfully after another draught.

Sinfjotli's laugh was startlingly light and clear. "Better well hanged than badly wedded. You should give thanks to Frija that things were not done so, when your own bride waits for you in Sealand. Do you think we'll hunt for our supper this evening?"

"No, we've got plenty of food with us, and we're not so far from Hagalar's hall."

"So that is the hall where your songs began! I asked the gate-warder there where Hunding's garth was, but did not bother to find out who his own drighten was."

Hailgi looked sharply at Sinfjotli, a hot trembling rising up in his guts. "And what do these songs say of that hall?"

"Nothing that is counted to your shame by anyone," the Walsing answered quickly. For a moment, the sunlight dazzled light from his blue eyes as he met Hailgi's gaze, then the shadow of a branch dimmed their brightness. "Only that the woman's garb hid you ill from your foes, for you could not hide your strength or the keenness of your gaze from Blindi Bale-Wise, and there is not one of the songs that does not end with Hunding's death."

Hailgi unlocked his hands from their white-cramping grasp on the reins, drawing breath back into his aching lungs. I had thought all memories of that long past, he cried silently to himself, I thought Hunding's blood had wiped it away forever.

"You need not fear that Sigiruna has heard ill of you," Sinfjotli added.

"That I do not fear," Hailgi answered, his heart suddenly lightened by the thought.

Without asking or being asked, Sinfjotli set up Hailgi's tent that night and then cast his own gear down on one side. Once Sunna had set, the night grew cold quickly, with no more ale than that in the skins they had brought, it was not long before most of the men were creeping into their tents and rolling themselves in their cloaks. Hailgi lay on his stomach, staring through the tent's flap at the fire burning just outside, the little snakes of brightness creeping over and around the thick branches. They wavered in his sight, as though the darkness shimmered like water between him and the writhing golden wyrms. It seemed to Hailgi as if he were looking down into a very deep well, that the shadow of the tent-stakes stretched up into high branches above his head. He had seen the shadows in the water before. It seemed to him that a woman's twisted shape, skirts flowing out to melt into the back of a black wolf, wavered there before him, and that a young man stood facing her with a sword in his hand.

She stretched her hand out towards him, and a silent chill ran over Hailgi as the youth raised his sword. It seemed to him as though the weapon had struck against an unseen bell, whose tolling was too deep for him to hear, but grated up through his bones. Then the water rippled over them, their shadows stretching towards one another like snakes coiling out to twine about each other and melt together. It seemed to him that the dark wyrms in the well's depths were weaving about the tree's gnarled roots as they gnawed, weaving a shape that he did not know, except that layer lay upon layer, coiling ever upwards to where he stood until he could feel the cold snake's coils moving against his right ankle.

Hailgi's eyes burst open to the low flames as he jerked his feet back from the slithering at his feet and leapt up with a yell, flinging his cloak away from his body. Sinfjotli was also on his feet, at first Hailgi saw his eyes open wide in shock, then, as the firelight glittered off the adder slithering out into the open, he began to laugh, pointing at Hailgi.

"Only a snake."

This Hailgi could not bear. Too angry to speak, he lunged after the snake, grabbing it by the tail and swinging it like a whip at Sinfjotli. Still laughing, the Walsing did not even try to dodge. He merely held a palm out, letting the snake's open jaws smack into it.

Hailgi stood breathing hard, he could feel his limbs shaking, but the sight of the trickle of dark blood beginning to run down Sinfjotli's pale wrist sobered him. Men had died of adder-bites before, though it was not common. At the least, Sinfjotli would not grip a blade easily for days. But the Walsing did not show any pain or fright as the snake worked its bale into his hand, though his laughter was quieting at last.

"What did you think was so funny?"

"The look on your face," Sinfjotli answered. "It's only a little snake, why were you frightened?"

"You'll think more of it when your hand swells black," Hailgi answered. "You witling, pluck that thing off yourself and let me see what I can do to leech it."

"There's hardly need for that," Sinfjotli answered, but he pried the snake's jaws apart and tossed it out. "Look. Its bale has not scathed me, and such pin-pricks are little to a Walsing." The bloody tooth-prints showed clearly as drops of black against the white skin, but Sinfjotli's hand was neither swelling nor changing color. "Had you not heard that none of the Walsings can be harmed by poison on our skins, and that my father Sigimund can bear it within as well as without, so that no drink of bale can do him ill?"

"I had heard it," Hailgi said slowly, "but I had given the words little heed. Tales often say strange things. This, I gather, is why you did not think to look about to see whether there might be an adder-hole where you set the tent?"

"The thought did not come to me." Sinfjotli grinned. "But I was glad to see that you were only startled by the wyrm, and not afraid of it or too weak-souled to touch it."

If I had been? Hailgi was about to ask, but it seemed to him that some of the tales he had heard of the Walsings would give him an answer he would rather not hear. "That would not have been fitting for one of my line," Hailgi replied gravely.

Then he thought. I cried out, why has no one come to see what the matter is? Have Helmbernu and Bow-Athalwulfar gone to sleep on watch?

Hailgi shook his cloak out before he wrapped it around himself again and crept out of the tent-flap, walking between the tents and sleeping men. Everything was very quiet, it was a moment before he realized that he could not hear anyone snoring, but the stillness was that of the host holding its breath. A sudden fright came over him, he bent down to touch the nearest shoulder. The hard flesh was warm beneath his hand, and the man turned over so that Hailgi could recognize the huge brush of hoar-streaked beard that gave Skegga-Grimar his name.

"Is all well, Hailgi?" The warrior whispered.

Hailgi did not soften his voice, but rather raised it so that everyone could hear. "All is well. Go back to sleep."

After a little time, he could hear the sound of his men breathing again, and their breaths slowly deepening into snores. Hailgi walked back to his tent, where Sinfjotli sat cross-legged by the flap, staring at the flames as they burned lower and lower, his eyes black in their sinking light. Hailgi sat down beside him.

"I was dreaming when the snake came upon me," Hailgi said softly after a little while, and went on to tell Sinfjotli all he could remember of his dream. The Walsing listened gravely until he was done.

"It seems a true dream to me," Sinfjotli murmured at last, "but I am not sure how to read it. I am less skilled at that than, let us see." He rose suddenly and left the tent, his bare feet whispering over the damp grass. Hailgi watched the Walsing's pale shape move soundlessly into the woods, waited until he came back with his hands full of twigs.

"Carve me a smooth place on each one, so," Sinfjotli told him, drawing his own belt knife and scraping a little patch of bark from one of the twigs. Hailgi did likewise, until each of the sticks had been marked. "Now prick your finger, and when I finish carving each stave, redden it with your blood." Sinfjotli set to graving a rune into each of the twigs and murmuring as he did. " Fehu, Uruz, Thurisaz, Ansuz, Raidho, Kenaz, Gebo, Wunjo." The Walsing's whispering chant of the rune, names seemed to twine through Hailgi's bones as he touched the staves in turn. " Hagalaz, Nauthiz, Isa, Jera, Eihwaz, Perthro, Elhaz, Sowilo."

Although Sinfjotli's voice grew no louder, its echoes rang through and through Hailgi's skull until he could hear nothing else. " Tiwaz, Berkano, Ehwaz, Mannaz, Laguz, Ingwaz, Dagaz, Othala."

By the time he had marked the last rune-stave, Hailgi was as dizzy as if he had drunk a full horn of mead on an empty stomach. He could feel the might tingling in his fingertips as he reached towards them, he could not help his need to grasp them, to take them up and hold the staves in his hands.

"That's right," Sinfjotli murmured. "Now, Wyrd's waters flow through you. Let them fall to show the shaping in your dream."

Unwillingly, Hailgi loosed his grip, letting the twigs fall down before the fire. Only a few landed with their runes facing up, the rest of the staves were dark. Sinfjotli crouched lower, peering at the bloodied twigs. "Here's Perthro, the lot-box," he murmured, pointing at one. "It was Wyrd's well you saw, roots stretching deep into the hidden waters. Gebo and elhaz and dagaz all together. That is sure to be your wedding to Sigiruna, and this is a fair sign, that it is set so strongly in your shaping." Hailgi looked closer at the three staves.

It seemed to his fire-dazed sight that the middle one shimmered into a white shadow like swan-wings rising up to ward, the crossed lines of the first flowing in and out of each other to become the bright glow of the third with the day-star shining from the point in the middle. But Sinfjotli was already going on, pointing to the three staves which lay nearby. "This is called thurisaz, or sometimes thorn. Often it bodes ill. Here by it is Tiwaz, Tiw's rune and the rune of the age-old spear. Together these two must betide a battle, with weapons cast against you, and sig is not sure, for they are very strong staves when blended so. Beside it is Ansuz, Wodan's rune. I say you will do well to pledge him gifts to be given after this battle, lest he should choose his own, for he will not be far from the wal-stead. Now the staves say no more to me."

The Walsing swept the twigs up in his hand and tossed them to smolder and spark in the dying fire. "Has this eased your heart?"

"It has, and I thank you."

When they left Hagalar's hall the next morning, Hailgi's war band was the greater by a third. As if to make up for his lack of aid against Hunding's sons, Hagalar had sent well over half of his own thanes with them. Many of the men went from Hagalar's lands by ship, for they would be sailing to Zealand with a full fleet, but most of those who had come by horse still rode.

Although Hailgi and his men saw the armed men gathered before his hall from a long way off, they did not draw weapons nor ready for a fight, for Hagalar's ships rocked easily in the harbor below them, and Hailgi could see the banners of the other drightens who had ridden to fight against Hunding's sons with him. It was no surprise to Hailgi that Hagalar's men had already ridden out to summon the other war bands.

They were well used to gathering a host in a hurry. Sinfjotli riding beside him like a twin, Hailgi spurred Wigablajar into a gallop, flying down the low hill and through the host gathered before the hall. Sinfjotli kept his place as though the two of them had been roped together, till the moment when they pulled up sharply a few inches from the doors which stood open before them. The two young warriors slid from their horses. Hailgi glanced about for someone to hand his reins to, but Sinfjotli was already taking them from his hands.

"I'll take care of these," the Walsing said in a low voice. "You go on." He gestured towards the inside of the hall where the other drightens sat with their ale-horns, as Bergohildar came out to embrace her son.

Hailgi could feel his mother's bones thin and sharp beneath his arms as he hugged her. It seemed to him that her flesh had wasted since he saw her last, but glimmering tears of joy brightened her blue-green eyes, and his heart warmed with joy as he thought gladly of the treasures he had saved out for her.

"Mother, I've brought you."

Bergohildar raised a finger to his lips to still them, as if he were still a child. "Hush, my dear. Later. You have more to do now than to talk with your mother though I have nothing better to do than wait for you."

Hrothormar Bear-Sark stood as Hailgi walked in, raising the horn to him. "Hail, Hailgi! Know that I and my folk will stand behind you, whatever fainter hearts decide!"

Raginar set his ale-horn down carefully and rested his wide scarred fist on his belly where it swelled out just above his sword-belt. "A berserk who does not wish to die in the straw may make no difference between bravery and recklessness at another's whim." Raginar's shield-hand tugged at the blond braids of his thick beard.

"The rest of us wish more reason to go to battle than a young man's green lusts. Because of the troth we owed your father and because you led us well against Hunding's sons, we have come to hear you out."

Hailgi looked at Freyjawulfar, who sat with his lanky legs up on the bench and horn propped against his knee, then at Theudowinar, who rested the cleft of his clean-shaven chin against his knuckles and stared at Hailgi from between the long dark strands drooping over his eyes. "Are you two of a like mind?"

"I have spoken to you of my mind before," Freyjawulfar answered. "I will give you no help here. For your own sake and your father's, it is best if we can turn you back from this rashness. I bid you think on what befell the Ingling Sigisgairar. He was a true fro to his folk, but Sigilind brought shame to his house and blight to his land. Sigiruna is of the same sort. She will be no better bride than the Walsing was."

The swift wind of Sinfjotli's leap through the door choked Hailgi's breath in his throat. Freyjawulfar's horn flew aside, scattering ale over all of them like blood at a blessing, Sinfjotli had heaved him up off the bench and was shaking the drighten as though he were a straw man left out to the winter winds. It seemed to Hailgi that he could see the gray wolf-hide blurring over the Walsing's face even as Sinfjotli began to growl and snarl. Hrothormar was on his feet at the first sound of Sinfjotli's wolf-voice, but it was not the bear-sark who growled in answer.

Hailgi felt the snarl grating up through his own throat as though something deep within him had voiced it. He and Hrothormar together grasped Sinfjotli's arms, straining to break his hold even as Freyjawulfar brought up a feeble knee. Still Sinfjotli held his victim. Angered by his failure, Hailgi let go of the Walsing and swung back his arm, hitting Sinfjotli in the jaw as hard as he could. Sinfjotli dropped Freyjawulfar and turned towards Hailgi. His eyes were still black with the wolf-wod. A tingle of fear rushed through Hailgi's veins no, it was not fear, but an answering wod rising within. He wanted to fling himself upon Sinfjotli, but something still chained him back. A fetter of words, an oath well-laid.

"Will the Walsing break his oath?" Hailgi asked softly. "Is this how you follow your father's wishes?"

Sinfjotli stood stock-still for a moment, then made his curious twitch again, showing Hailgi his throat. He shuddered as the blackness shrank back to the center of his eyes. "Only let this man unsay the words he spoke of my mother. She was the truest bride ever born, who died in the Ingling's burning hall rather than break her oath even to the man who slew her father and brothers by treachery. I myself saw her walk back into the flames. There is no man here with such bravery."

Freyjawulfar leaned hard on the bench, pushing himself up. "There is not. That also I have heard of her, that no maid in the North-lands was her match for strength of soul and truth of word, I spoke ill and without thought. I say now that it would be a fair thing if Hailgi could win a bride so true, if he could win her without the kin strife or breaking of oaths that brought Sigigairar to his end, and if he could hold the favor of the gods and goddesses, as the Ingling did not." He looked about the hall, his dark eyes vague, until his gaze lighted on his fallen horn and the half-grown hound lapping the ale from it. He stood, limping painfully over to pick it up again.

"Do you still speak against the wedding, then?" Sinfjotli challenged.

Freyjawulfar turned his horn over in his hands, looking unhappily at the new crack running half its length from the deep dent in its gilded lip-binding. "If Haganon will give Sigiruna to Hailgi, I will not gainsay it."

"He will not give her freely!" Hrothormar Bear-Sark broke in. A long-toothed grin split his grizzled brown beard. "Now I would count it a sad thing if such a maid might be won without a rich red geld to be paid, and if Wodhanar's hounds and hawks went hungry at his wish-daughter's wedding feast!"

"What have we to do with Hailgi's wooing?" Theudowinar's deep slow voice replied. "If he wishes the maid, let him win her, but this is no matter to gather all the folk over. What good will we get from it?"

"Haganon is a rich folk-leader. There are many fair lands in Sealand which we may share between us, as well as a goodly store of gold and silver to be won by it," Hailgi answered. "Did I not deal fairly with you after we had beaten the sons of Hunding, did you not come home with a great fee for little blood shed? If you follow me again, I can pledge you and your sons a great plenty of the river's brightness."

Raginar leaned back against the wall, the wyrm-wrought cloak pin of gold that had been part of his booty glittering as he moved. "The river's brightness will do us little good if we bring our men back to the field too soon, when many are but half-healed better to hold less as living men than more in the howe. And you speak truly. We have won much. We will not go hungry for lack of more for some time yet. Let us have a year to rest, then perhaps we may talk of this again."

"That will be too late!" Hailgi cried. "If we do not hasten, Sigiruna will be wedded at Winter nights."

Raginar only laughed. "Widows can be made," he said casually, but Frey-jawulfar was already breaking in.

"How is it that you know this, Hailgi? Your ears must be long indeed for I had heard nothing of it."

In the moment of stillness, Hailgi could clearly hear the sound of dice being thrown outside and Thonaraharjar's cry of, "High cast and mine!" The brown hound lying in the shaft of sunlight slanting in through the door twitched in its sleep, a few flies buzzed up and settled on its flanks again.

Theudowinar tugged on one of the strands of dark hair hanging over his face, pulling it away from his eyes. "How do you know this, Hailgi?"

As silent as the hall was, Hailgi barely heard, and did not know the voice that whispered behind him, "Hailgi, go to your father's howe." Still, once he had heard the rede, he could not withstand it. He swept his arm about as though gathering all the men there within a single chain, as though binding them together to follow the way to Fetter-Grove.

Hailgi walked from the hall without looking back. He barely noticed the warriors giving way before him, their faces changing as though a cloud's shadow passed over them. The wind that blew from the howe did not cast his cloak back nor ruffle his hair, the long grass stood straight and still about him, but the wind blew strongly enough that he could feel himself leaning into it as he walked, clenching his jaw and tightening his fists against its might. So he made his way up to the top of Sigismundar's mound, and when he turned to face those who had walked behind him, the wind whirled about him, flapping the dark wings of his cloak up and whipping through his amber braids.

Hailgi opened his mouth to speak, though he did not know what he would say. Then he heard the voice rising from his throat, and hardly knew it was his own. Huge and deep, harsh with the resonant echo of a raven's croak that rose to the scream of an eagle in his ears as the wod rose and rose in his head.

"Now I have called the host together, I, Hailgi, the Hallowed One. Who of you shall stand against me?" Hailgi cast his arm upwards. Two ravens circled above the mound, black as storm-clouds against the pale blue sky. "Now I speak from my father's howe, I speak with the redes of my eldest kin, who live still within my blood and bone. This I know, as the ravens know it. There must be battle, but we shall be sig-blessed. Wodhanar wrought for this long ago. It is not written but that I must fight for my bride.

Nor shall his favor fall on those who hold back, for this battle shall end with men hanged in Fetter-Grove, and Wodhanar's spear shall be well-drunk on red mead when Sigiruna and I speak our oaths of wedding. But those who help shall win his blessing, and should you think his care is a chancy thing, well you know that his anger is worse, as is the anger of the Wolfing kin!" Hailgi's hands had curved into claws, and the froth was dripping from his mouth as he howled the last words. The other drightens were stumbling back from him, their hair and beards streaming back in the wind that blew from him and their eyes wide with awe.

Only Sinfjotli stood beside the Wolfing, the Walsing's strong hand on Hailgi's shoulder keeping him upright. Freyjawulfar, Raginar, Hrothormar, and Theudowinar stopped a few paces down the mound, standing before their men who had gathered around its base. Their upturned faces were pale beneath the white sunlight, as though Hailgi looked down on a host of the slain. It was Hrothormar Bear-Sark who first shook the fetters of awe from his shoulders, his hoarse voice roaring "Hailgi!" The rest of them took up the cry as though their shouting eased their fear, some crashed spears or swords against their linden shields.

"Wodan favors you," Sinfjotli said beneath the noise. He was more than half holding Hailgi up now, but the Walsing's strength was great enough to hide how much help he was giving his drighten. "Come, you must eat now, to settle yourself in the Middle-Garth again."

Together the Wolfings went down from the top of the mound, leading the host back to the hall. Sinfjotli did not leave Hailgi's side until he had seen the first bites of bread and cheese washed down by a draught of Bergohildar's ale, only then did he rise to fill a wooden plate with food for himself.

"Send to gather your men and ships," Hailgi said to the other drightens when his shaking had stilled. "I do not know whether the battle will be by land or sea, I have heard that Hadubroddar is a sea-king, and he may wish to fight us on the wave. Raginar and Freyjawulfar, I would have you call your kinsmen as well, call Herwolathar and his men from Brandar Isle and Hedhinar's Isle, Freyjabrandar and his host from Stave Ness and High-Garth, and bid them here to my father's haven Arrow-Sound."

"That will take some time," Raginar murmured, twisting his fair beard-braids about one another. "My sister's son Herwolathar is a sea-king, who is like to be out harrying already, if we wait for him, Hadubroddar will surely be ready for us by the time the host is gathered."

"We must bring our fullest might to the field," Hailgi answered, his words sure and steady as a stone-built mound. "This fight will be a harder one than the last, but I know that there is far more to be won, you need not fear that sharing the treasure of those two drightens will leave you with a little part."

"That was not in my mind, you know I have never been close-handed!" Raginar replied hotly, a tide of blood rushing through his cheeks to the pale edge of his beard.

Hailgi laughed. "That is so. So call your kin and let them share in the name and wealth of this faring! It is in my mind that Hadubroddar will know that we are coming, no matter what we do, I do not think Sigiruna has let him linger in dreams of her love."

Hrothormar grasped the spear that leaned against the wall by his seat. "Such a maid should rather call men to battle," he grinned. "I find it fair that she seeks to test your strength." He thumped the shaft's butt against the earthen floor as he began to chant a stave from the tale of Hildar, who had egged her father and lover to slay each other, and brought them to life again each day so that the fight could begin anew.

"'Wound-maid Wodhanar rowned forth,
willed Frodhi's law be spilled there,
bears roar bade of spear-play -
blithe-of-gems wrought strife-runes.'"

It seemed to Hailgi that he could hear the bear growling in Hrothormar's voice, the dark undertone rising to a roar with the berserker's last words. Hrothormar's dark eyes were very wide, staring over Hailgi's shoulder, Hailgi braced his will like an iron collar to keep his neck from turning. "Frey-jawulfar, how do you find this rede?" Hailgi asked, breaking the tale before Hrothormar could chant himself farther into a fit.

"I find it fair enough, and better-thought than I had hoped," the tall drighten answered slowly. A drift of graying hair shadowed his eyes, he slouched down in his cloak like an owl settling to sleep in its feathers. "The wait will do us no harm, a few more men may grow hale enough to fight in the time it takes us to gather the greater host together."

"What of you, Theudowinar?"

Theudowinar pressed the knuckles of his fists together until the gold spirals on the fingers of his right hand furrowed the flesh of the fingers of his left. He spoke very slowly, as though dredging each word from the depths of his chest. "I see that you will not look with friendly eyes upon anyone who will not help you here. If such a battle and such a wedding may turn well, you are surely the man to turn them. It seems to me that I must go with you, though the best planning can hardly make this wise."

"So is it set and sworn?" Hailgi asked, looking at each of them in turn. Only Hrothormar did not turn his gaze away from Hailgi's, but each of the drightens murmured his agreement.

"Well shall this be remembered!" Sinfjotli cried. "Now you have cast your weirds as men ought."

Hrothormar rumbled his liking for the Walsing's words, but Hailgi marked the sideways glances Freyjawulfar and Raginar gave one another, and how Theudowinar's lids hooded his eyes for a moment. I will be loath to lose my friend when the summer is over, Hailgi thought, but he knew now that Sinfjotli could never dwell within his hall for more than a season.

CHAPTER XX

Thunderstorms tossed back and forth over Dallas that week, battling with sunshine hazed by muggy heat. Helgi had given up on trying to dry out his sneakers. They squished like peat moss beneath his tread with every step he took. The morning of Flourescent's Friday gig dawned dark gray, though no thunder startled Helgi from his bed, he could feel its charged weight in the cool air, like rounds heavy in a gun. Luann was waiting for him outside the music building when he got there. She whirled herself towards him, tripped on the last turn, and fell ungracefully into his arms. Helgi caught her, lifting her to her feet.

"I meant to do that," Luann said, grinning ruefully. "Really."

"Of course you did. I believe you."

"That's why I love you, did you know." She pulled his head down for a swift kiss, then looked up at the sky. "Ah, the elements, always perverse, in any other circumstances the rain would be pouring down, lightning flashing and thunder crashing, and then we could re-enact the lovers-in-the-storm scene of your choice."

Helgi glanced up at the seething clouds, greenish-gray as a lake beneath a stormy sky. He could see the choppy swirls in the clouds where the warm and cool winds twisted against each others like struggling adders. "It looks more like Wizard of Oz weather to me. Go on, sing 'Somewhere Over the Rainbow, see if a tornado touches down to sweep away Jefferson's music department."

Luann shook her head, gesturing down the concrete walkway where Dr. Mason was striding briskly towards the building. "The Wicked Witch of the West is on her way, I fear, and we are not in danger of being too early for our classes." She took his hand and they walked inside together.

Although the sky darkened through the day, the rain had not begun to fall by the time Helgi got home. Elric bounded up to meet him, the elk hound's fur bristling up from his body as he barked joyfully and ran to the closet where his leash waited.

"You want a walk before it starts raining, huh?" Helgi checked his watch. Two hours yet.

Lively after three housebound days, Elric dragged Helgi along behind him at a half-run. It was only when the hound stopped, sitting suddenly, that the first shiver rippled over Helgi's skin. No breath of breeze stirred the brown-edged leaves hanging limply from the trees in the yards around them, the heavy air pressed in against Helgi's chest so that he could barely draw breath. Elric raised his nose to the sky, sniffing deeply as though he were drawing in the lightning that waited hidden in the green-gray clouds like fire in flint. The elk hound whimpered, a line from Schubert's *"Geistertanz"* ran through Helgi's mind.

"Was winseln die Hunde beim schlafenden Herrn? Sie wittern die Runden der Geister von fern." Why do the dogs whimper by their sleeping master? They sense the rounds of the ghosts from afar. Then Elric howled like a wolf, the rising and falling cry scraping up and down Helgi's spine. A few blocks over, another howl answered him, and another from farther away.

As Elric lifted his muzzle to howl again, a gust of wind struck Helgi in the face, another whirling a twist of tree-ripped leaves in behind it. The first sparse raindrops splattered the pale sidewalk with dark gray blotches the size of a child's hand print. A white track of lightning glimmered far away, then a second, glowing red as a spearhead fresh-drawn from the forge against the black clouds. Helgi stood staring, the sharp taste of the city-tainted rain in his open mouth as a sheer veil of ice-blue lightning sheeted across the seething sky. If he had not had the leash's loop wrapped around his wrist, Elric's lunge would have torn it from his hand. As it was, the elk hound jerked him off balance into a headlong run. The phone had just started ringing when Helgi and Elric burst dripping in. Helgi grabbed it with one hand, with the other, he shielded his eyes from Elric's shower of spray as the elk hound shook himself.

"You weren't planning to go anywhere tonight, were you?" Helgi's mother asked without any preamble.

"I have to. Flourescent is playing at Bar of Soap tonight. They can't perform without me, more than half of the songs are mine and I sing lead on them."

Helgi could almost see his mother standing in her kitchen, the afternoon shadows deepening the little lines about her eyes and mouth. "I know how important this is to you, Helgi." She paused. "It can't be more important than your safety. I think you should call in and beg off. There was a report just a few minutes ago of a tornado touching down very near Oakcliff. I don't want you on the road tonight. Your father has already decided to stay at his office until the worst of the weather has passed."

Helgi looked at his watch again. "I don't have to go for another hour and a quarter, maybe a little less, if I plan to drive very slowly. You know how fast these storms blow out, Mom, the worst of it will probably be past by then. I'm twenty-two years old and living on my own, I think I can drive without parental assistance, he added silently to himself."

"Where is it? And do you have to go on any back roads?"

"It's across from the main entrance to Fair Park. It's highways nearly all the way there."

"Just be careful not to drive through any moving water, even if you can see the road beneath it. With all the storms we've had, most of the city is in danger of flash flooding."

"Okay."

It was still raining heavily when Helgi drove off. Although he thought it was well before sunset, the sky was so dark that he had to put his lights on to see as far as thirty feet in front of him. The rain glowed lightning-white in the headlight-beams, shining bright around the streetlights above him. Helgi drove slowly, keeping to the middle lane, murky torrents frothed down the gutters on either side of the road, sometimes splashing above the edges of the curbs. Helgi sang along with Jim Morrison as he drove, pitching his voice to cut through the drumming of the rain on his car's roof and tapping on the wheel to the driving beat of *People Are Strange.* He took the turn out onto the freeway very slowly, careful of the dark shapes suddenly hulking up out of the rain around him.

Helgi tightened his hands on the steering wheel as he crossed an overpass, fighting the hard gusts of wind that battered his car back and forth. His windshield burned blue with lighting, blinding him for several heartbeats as the thunder crashed around him. When he could see again, the side of his car was almost scraping the right guard rail. His glance flickering behind him to make sure the way was clear, he twisted the wheel hard, slewing back to the middle lane in a fan of dark water. The steering wheel seemed to pulse under his hands, warm and sweaty as a horse's neck, it was a moment before he realized that it was his own thudding heartbeat he felt in his grip. Grimly he bore down on the gas pedal, plowing through the water on the road, his wake flying up like a white wing on each side of the car.

Helgi could hardly hear the radio over the storm's noise now. The wash of rain over his windshield was so heavy that he no longer needed the windshield wipers. The rippling torrent kept the glass clear. Another searing flash of lightning rocked the car, the brightness one with its bone-shaking thunder. Helgi closed his eyes tightly to drive the burning afterimage away, holding the steering wheel steady and hoping that he could keep the car's path straight. He was moving smoother and faster now, skimming over the road. He knew that he was hydroplaning, the water smooth as ice under the wheels of his car.

Even with his lights switched up to bright, Helgi could see little through the dark rain. He was as blind as if he were flying through a thundercloud, but he thought there were no other car-lights around him. Only the lightning cut through the black storm, a red spear-flash so bright it seemed to burst inside his skull. It seemed to him that he could hear a sound like a thousand far-off screams, the rising clash of wood and metal, he did not know whether it was a real sound or the echo of the thunder still deafening his ears.

My god, I've got to get off the road, he thought, but the wind seemed to be blowing from behind him, bearing his car forward more and more swiftly over the water, silver flashes of lightning glimmered like sunlight glinting on a plane's wings, bright through the black clouds above the red and blue streaks that forked down to earth.

"The Northmen never turn away from storms," Helgi muttered, his voice drowned beneath the booming of the thunder. He was not alone, Mike, Josh, Widget, Rack, they were all counting on him to be there, how could he tell them he had abandoned them because he was too fearful to drive in bad weather?

The echoing noise in his head was growing louder and louder, screaming over the thunder like a freight train. Helgi knew there were no tracks crossing his path, he knew. He glanced into his rear view mirror.

"Oh, shit!"

The long snake-shape stretching down from the clouds to the road was blacker than the sky around it, dark against the lightning that played behind it. It swayed like a bad actress playing a whore, walking behind Helgi as though the smooth black path of the freeway were drawing it along. He stepped on the gas, flying down the road before the tornado's rising scream. The rain battered against his windshield, hard and sharp as a hail of arrows, the shining lightning streaked over his head, white spears flung against the black funnel. I am going to die, Helgi thought. The speed of his driving thrilled through his body, the storm sang in his ears, tornado cry blending into the thunder's ceaseless bass. I am going to die, I am doomed, I am going to die. And he was not afraid, he could feel the wind bearing him up in its howling as the car pitched like a ship on the waves, the storm-gusts swinging it back and forth across the highway.

The whole road was a running torrent, he did not mark the white froth of the waters that poured faster and harder over it until he had already plowed into the flood. The current caught his car like a dance-partner, swinging it halfway around. Helgi felt his lips pulling hard against his teeth, he could not hear whether he was laughing or moaning as he wrestled with the wheel, pulling himself straight against the flood. He rose halfway from his seat, treading down on the gas pedal with his full weight as he set his shoulders to hold the wheel steady. Something roared deeply in Helgi's ears, its note shaking through his chest, his cheeks and chin were wet with froth, as though a spray of water had broken through his windshield. He felt as though he were wrestling to break a giant's grip, as though the flood clutched his car in great arms of foamy water.

The next lightning-flash burst white through his body like a bomb dropping, he did not hear the thunder as his car spun out of control, whirling wildly. Blinded, Helgi could not see what had happened nor where he was going. He did not feel himself move, but when his sight cleared, his car was resting with its rear wheels in the muddy gravel of the road's shoulder and his right foot was jammed down hard on the brake. His ears rang with the thunder's grumbling and the rumble of the rain on the car-roof, he could not hear nor see the dark sky-funnel any longer.

Helgi wiped his mouth dry with his sleeve. He grasped the wheel as tightly as he could, trying to keep his hands from trembling, and slowly steered his car back onto the road. "Odhinn," he muttered, and laughed shakily. "You nearly had me there or did you help me out?" But no answer came, only the rain beating on the car and the resounding blows of thunder about him.

It seemed to Helgi that the rain was softening as he drove, the space between lightning and thunder stretching farther and farther. After a while, he began to see other vehicles creeping through the storm, their headlights on bright like his own. His glance flickered to his watch for a second. He had gone faster than he'd thought, even as slowly as he was driving now, he would be almost half an hour early for setting-up.

As soon as he had gotten into the bar, he called his mother. She answered on the first ring.

"Helgi? Were you near the...."

"It's all right, I made it safely. No problems. I heard the warning on the radio and went another way." White man lies through teeth, Helgi thought to himself.

"Well, thank God for that. What time are you coming home?"

"Eleven or twelvish, I guess."

"All right. Be careful."

As soon as he was off the phone, Helgi ordered a Bass Ale and took it over to the corner by the window, where he could sit and watch the far-off lightning and the rain haloing the streetlights. The pink squiggle of neon above the window brightened the glass in warm flashes, gleaming off Helgi's cold-dewed bottle. By the time he had finished the beer and ordered another, his hands had stopped shaking and his breathing was easy again.

Looking out the window, Helgi didn't see his fellow band members coming from the back room until he heard Mike's sharp voice in his ear. "Boozing before the performance, Helgi? Shame on you. I bet Pavarotti never does that."

"I bet Pavarotti never has to drive to a performance with a fucking tornado after his car," Helgi replied, more hotly than he meant to.

"You saw it? We were wondering thought you lived out that way. We came early 'cause of the storm warnings."

"I was on the road right in front of it."

"What'd you do?"

"Kept driving, what else? I figured if I ignored it, it'd go away, and it did."
Helgi took a long pull of beer.

Rack let his breath out in a long whistle. Widget shook his head. "Shit,
man, you be crazy. You be crazy as a shit house rat."

"And the luckiest motherfucker on the face of the planet," Josh added.
"Can I buy you a beer?"

"After we play, sure. I think two's my limit for now."

Luann only stared at him, her brown eyes almost black against her pale
face. "I can't believe you did that," she said at last. "You idiot. You stupid
idiot. I am so appalled, I don't know what to say."

"Hey, it's okay," Helgi answered her softly. Out of the corner of his eye, he
saw the rest of Flourescent retreating quietly towards the back room, and
thought, oh, shit, I really am in trouble. "I'm here. I made it safely. Not so
much as a scratch on my car." He spread his arms out wide. "See? I'm alive.
I'm okay."

"You could have been killed."

"But I wasn't.", "Or?," the thought came to his mind, an echo of the madness he had felt earlier"maybe I was. It is my ghost that you see here, come
back over the rushing river of death for one last night with you, and one last
performance with Flourescent."

"Not funny, Helgi. Do you know how scared I was?"

"I'm sorry. Really. If I'd known a tornado was going to touch down behind
me, I would've stayed home."

"And then you come in here and make jokes about it."

Helgi reached out and took Luann's hand in his, grateful for the soft
warmth of her skin beneath his icy fingers. She stiffened a little, but did not
pull away. "I really am sorry. I couldn't run out on the band when I knew
they were depending on me. Besides, I didn't want to stand you up."

Luann slid into the chair beside him. "I guess I can't complain about that. I
was just so worried."

Helgi put his arm around her shoulders, then drew her close enough for a
kiss, holding her tight until her lips had warmed his.

"You're half-frozen," she accused. "And your nose is cold like a dog's.
When you finish that beer, I'm going to get you some coffee to warm you
up."

Although they still had an hour until the performance started, Flourescent was already set up. Mike sat cross-legged beneath the single light, reading Zen and the Art of Motorcycle Repair, Josh was doing some last-minute
tuning on his guitar while Rack thumped softly on his drums. Widget stood
in a dark corner, looking upward as if he were talking to someone very tall.
Helgi realized that he was, his companion was wearing a black leather jacket, and his skin was so black that the shadows had hidden him from Helgi's
gaze for a moment.

"Yo, Helgi," Widget called. "This here's my cousin Rof from the Air Force, I was tellin' you about?"

Helgi came over to them, looked up into Rof's face. The Air Force man was almost six inches taller than Helgi himself, his muscles bulging huge against his jacket's scuffed skin, his hair was cropped in a tight cap against his skull. His dark gaze was steady, he did not blink or shift his eyes away from Helgi. I might be able to believe his lake-monster story, was Helgi's first thought.

"Rof, this be Helgi, he writes spooky songs kind yo' woman likes, I think." Widget cackled, his square teeth flashing. "She goin' be here tonight, you better watch out."

"Pleased to meet you, Helgi," Rof rumbled, sticking out his hand. His calloused handshake was gentle, but Helgi could feel the strength lurking behind it. "What you be talkin' about my woman, Widget? What the hell you think you know 'bout women? Only women you know about, be Miss Rosie Palm and her five sisters."

"You is signifyin', Rof," Widget said ominously. "You don' be startin' that shit with meyou got a mouth like molasses, man, I goin' to dance on yo' head."

"You think so? You not goin' to dancegoin' to shit yo' pants."

"You got my shit in yo' head, you chickenshit, man, you dead."

Helgi watched the two of them, appalled, and yet somehow eager, his blood rushing toward the moment when the knife's steel would gleam, its iron edge slicing open a red pathway. He did not know which would draw first, but he was sure Widget would end up dead. The other three band members, though. They were going on with what they were doing, as though nothing were happening.

The big man crouched down to look his smaller cousin in the eye, snapping his fingers as he spoke. "I know you eat that shit, man, you lick it up real good, you'd fuck it if it let you, you'd fuck it if you could."

"Yo' momma fucks that shit, Rof, she fuck it day and night. You no match for me, Rof, go find a dick to bite."

"That dick up yo' butta knife make yo' mouth shut?" Rof threatened.

"You got no knife, you some faggot's wife," Widget replied smartly.

Helgi didn't realize how close he was to them, nor that his hands, half-curled into fists, had raised to a fighting position, until Rof looked at him and laughed. "What's the matter, white boy, you never heard anyone signifyin' before?"

Josh's raucous laughter joined Rof's. "Hey, Rof, don't scare him," the guitarist called. "His family's from uptown, he's probably never seen a real black Neeegro up close in his life before."

Helgi could not laugh. He bit his lips together hard, locking his tongue behind his teeth.

"Shut yo' mouth, white trash," Rof replied amiably. "Don' worry, Helgi, ain't no one gonna be fightin' here. This be," he coughed, suddenly assumed a supercilious English accent two octaves above his natural pitch"one of the quaint ethnic traditions of the American Negro sub-culture. In other words, we be doin' it regular. Wouldn' be a nigger left in Dallas if we cut each other up every time."

Helgi tried to laugh with him, but could only manufacture an uncertain smile. The mocking of the two blacks beneath the freeway was still sharp in his memory keen as the edge of the Mexican's knife.

Rof patted him on the shoulder. "Not used to hearin' that kind of talk, are you? You okay, Helgi. Relax. Where you really from? Widget say yo' family's foreign."

"My mother's family is Danish. I've lived in Plano most of my life I live in Oakcliff now," he added, flashing a swift glare at Josh.

"You into yo' roots." Rof softened his voice, so that Helgi thought no one else could hear him. Black in his dark face, his eyes gleamed like deep water at night, twinned wells drawing Helgi's gaze in deeper. It seemed as though the two of them were alone in a vast hall, shadows stretching out before and behind them far past where the little room's walls had bound them. "Into that time, back when yo' folk knew things, when you was kin to the earth and sky, worshipin' a crazy, one-eyed death-god, no fear of yo' own doom. You got that look in yo' eyes, can't describe it, but I've seen it before. Well? Am I right?"

"You could be," Helgi admitted. His gaze still locked with Rof's, his next words, soft as breath, came without thought, as though his throat had become a brass horn with someone else whispering through it, the words seemed strange to him. "You look deeply. I think that you see things no one else does, things other people say aren't there to see. Am I right?"

"You could be," Rof murmured. They stood staring at each other another moment before the big man turned his eyes away. Helgi thought he caught the words, "not lookin' to trade mojo with," in Rof's next breath, but could not be sure. His own nerves were tingling, he felt as though he had just had a narrow escape from deep water, though he could not say why.

"Hey, Rof, where's that chick you were with last time?" Josh called. "She get tired of you already?"

"My woman be in later," Rof answered. "She had to fill out some paper-work, say she come on when she done you look cat-eyed at her, you be eatin' yo' dick. Be warned."

"Oscar Meyer don't make weenies that big," Josh replied. He flicked his guitar on, ran his finger along the A-string with a rising screech, then cut the note off dead. Helgi looked at his watch again, then wandered out front to find Luann, hoping that talking with her would still his vibrating nerves.

By the time they were ready to start, the bar was full out front, the juke-box going full blast, but only Luann and Rof were sitting in the back room where the band's "stage" was roped off. Helgi was about to ask Mike if this was normal, but the juke box cut off suddenly. Mike thumped the micro-phone, bringing a few howls of protest from out front.

"Ladies, gentlemen, freaks, punks, and everyone else, except Yuppies, we proudly present, for the second time in Bar of Soap, Flourescent!" A couple of people out front applauded, no one else seemed to notice. Mike brought down his hand, and the band swept into "Dallas Dream."

By the time the second song of the set, Helgi's first, "Weird women wing-ing"was halfway done, the back room was crowded, strange faces blurring in a haze of smoke before Helgi's sight as the music curled out from under his fingers, the song howling from his throat. He was singing well, he knew it, he could feel his voice thrumming through his whole body.

"Black storm-clouds brightening, the bone-heap lightening,

The hawk wheels above, its circles tightening,

Stares down at snake, at the storm-beaten lake,

Warriors fallen, where dead men wake."

The applause startled Helgi as if it shook him from a dream, thundering waves of sound rising and falling in his ears. There were not enough people there to make so much noise, he thought, it seemed to him that his head magnified the echoes a hundred times, as though he stood at the bottom of a great amphitheater, its walls rippling like water above him. Although Rof beat his pale palms together, no show of white teeth lightened his dark face. His deep stare was focused just past Helgi, as if he were trying to see through a shadow behind the singer's right shoulder, but Luann was grinning like a jack-o-lantern, her mouth opening and closing in sound-drowned cheers. By the end of the first set, Helgi was dripping with sweat, his hands trembling with exhaustion. He was as adrenaline-burned as if he had just sparred for an hour without a break, he did not know how he would make it through the second set.

"Doing good, man," Josh said, putting a cold bottle of beer into Helgi's hand. "Damn good. You look like you could use a little refreshment."

"That's so. Thanks." He could feel the cool, bubbling draught tingling out through his body as he drank, like rain sinking into a parched field.

Luann came around behind Helgi, kneading at his shoulders. She was rubbing too lightly to do much good, she did not have the strength to loosen his knotted muscles, but he was grateful for the rhythmic pressure that eased his nerves and for the simple feeling of her human touch.

"What do you think?" Helgi asked, leaning his head back to look at her upside-down.

Luann tweaked his nose. "Vanity, vanity. You should have noticed, idiot. If I'd yelled any louder I would have ripped my throat right out."

"Good?"

"Best you've ever done." She bent over to kiss him.

Flourescent had chosen Helgi's Erl-King song as the last piece of the night.

By the time they got to it, Helgi was hollow with exhaustion, as though a strong wind had blown the marrow from his bones. He did not know how he could call up the strength to sing, but suddenly the speakers were humming through stillness and all the eyes around him gleamed like puddles of rain under streetlights. Now it was the song that must breathe life into the singer, Helgi raised his hands, bringing them down in the first run of music, and drew in his breath as Widget began to beat out the triple bass-line that held the song together.

"Wind is howling through black pines."

Then his sight blurred, till the keyboard in front of him was white wings flashing through the night, the notes rushing smoothly as water beneath his unthinking fingers as the wind roared through him, its taste cold as grave-earth in the back of his mouth.

"I give this death as a gift to myself,
As Erl-King's daughter cuts my chains loose.
Gray-shining, grips me, pulling me up,
My bride and my bane, bright the death-maid."

Karin drove slowly through the heavy rain, the slanting lines of water glowing in her jeep's headlights. Although the tornado warning had ended a couple of hours ago, after the touchdowns near Mesquite and Plano, the watch would last until ten that night.

Her head ached from the hours of paperwork, her shoulders cramping as if she had been holding an M-16 at arm's length all afternoon. If she hadn't promised Rof that she would meet him at the Bar of Soap, she would have simply grabbed a quick beer at the officers' mess and then gone back to crash at her quarters.

"Hvorfor er jeg so træt?" Karin muttered. She did not know why she should be so tired, just one training flight that morning, and then only office work. Her body should be aching for some kind of action, a workout or at least a long run.

Perhaps she was coming down with something. She felt like it, cold and a little dizzy, as if she had just stood up too fast after giving blood. The steady swishing of the windshield wipers beneath the sheets of water that poured over the glass was lulling her eyes half-shut. Karin gripped the wheel hard, biting the inside of her lower lip to rouse herself as she thought of the scalding heat and bitter black edge of a cup of strong coffee. That would set her to rights quickly enough, she hoped. She guided the jeep carefully along the curve of the Fair Park exit ramp, down the broad road that led to the gravelly parking lot behind the Bar of Soap.

By the time she had walked through the alleyway and ducked into the bar, Karin's hair and the shoulders of her uniform were soaked. She could hear the wailing sound pouring from the keyboard in the other room, the rhythms of the other instruments pounding along behind it. It seemed to her that she could feel her strength surging up on the thundering beat, she pushed along through the crowd, into the back room where the band was playing. Rof leaned against the wall, his black leather jacket melting into the shadows as he stared at the keyboardist with the dark stern glare that Karin had come to know, that she thought marked his heart coming as close to fear as it could.

She made her way to him, slipping her hand around his thick waist, he glanced down at her and smiled, draping his own arm over her shoulder and drawing her a little closer to him. If anyone from base saw them now, their asses were grass, but if she'd wanted to live forever. The keyboardist looked up and seemed to freeze with his hands on the keys, holding his chord till it slid into a mad discord against the other musicians. His eyes, huge and dark in his white face, locked on Karin's a moment, then he threw back his head and howled, the sound dropping till he hit the song's next notes.

"Sharp is the spear I raise in my hand,
  I too shall ride and I too shall run"

Karin clutched Rof's waist hard, his heavy solidness anchoring her against the deep voice thundering through her ears, the words that seemed to sweep her up through the clouds of blue smoke swirling against the back room's dim lights. She could not shift her gaze from the keyboardist as he sang. His high cheekbones glistened with sweat, pale as if his skull shone bare, and the fury of his music seemed to shake through his broad shoulders as he tossed his head, his long amber braid whipping about. It seemed to her that she had seen his face before, its sharp edges hovering ghostly at the edge of her memory, but it was the rough depth of his voice as his song dropped down to the words that stirred his name forth from her mind. Hel og hægl-bygge, Karin thought, den sanger er Helgi Hadding! She was still breathless with the shock when Rof bent down to shout, "Beer?" Through the music.

Karin held up three fingers, gesturing at Rof, then herself, then at Helgi. He probably wasn't old enough to drink yet, but she was damned if she'd let him go thirsty after his performance. The applause shook through Karin's bones like thunder when the song was over. The lights were already coming up. It must have been the last of the set. A beer bottle in each fist, she elbowed her way through the crowd, stepping easily over the low rope that closed the audience away from the band. As she came closer, Helgi stood up, he staggered, and two of the other band members, the rhythm and lead guitarist, stepped in to pound him on the back. As Helgi, coughing from their blows, leaned against the wall, Karin pressed a beer into his hand. One hand on the wall, Helgi pushed himself up, staring blurry eyed around himself a second before he blinked his eyes clear to stare at her. He was a little taller than Karin now, nicely filled-out, not as heavy as Rof, but lithely muscled, like a martial artist. He had been doing karate, Karin remembered.

"Don't you remember me, Helgi Hadding?" She asked. "Has it been that long?"

"Karin. Of course I, what are you doing here?"

"Rof said his cousin was playing, and I promised I'd come and hear." The skinny rhythm guitarist was actually the band's leader, Karin remembered, she turned to him. "Your singer looks dead, you can't want any more work out of him. Can I steal him for a little while?"

"Go on," the bandleader said to Helgi. "We'll clear up here, but I hope like hell you're planning to take Luann with you."

It was only then that Karin saw the short red-haired girl who had come to stand beside Helgi, the sweat beading on her forehead and lips pressed white together as she stared up at the Air Force officer. Helgi put his arm around her shoulders, gesturing at Karin with the other hand.

"Luann, this is Karin Jensen. She used to live in our neighborhood."

The tight drawstrings seemed to ease at the corners of Luann's eyes and mouth. "Oh. Rof's girlfriend."

Karin grinned down at her. "That's right. Um." Yes, now she remembered, "I saw you when Flourescent was playing first, didn't I? Before they got Helgi?"

"Probably."

"Karin, this is Mike's sister Luann, my girlfriend," Helgi added, a little belatedly.

"Pleased to meet you." Karin looked around for Rof, but could not see him, either he was in the front room looking for a table, or he had gone for a piss. "Come on, let's see if Rof's been kind enough to capture a place for us out front."

Karin and Rof sat facing Helgi and Luann, long legs turned awkwardly under the small table so that no one was treading on anyone else. The jukebox was back on at full volume again, booming out "Beds Are Burning." Helgi was staring straight at her, his eyes unblinking and keen as an adder's. Karin leaned against Rof's shoulder, her blood beating swiftly in her temples.

"What are you doing these days?" She asked.

Helgi leaned closer to her, shouting, "What?"

"I said, what are you doing these days?" Karin had to raise her voice as loudly as she could without actually screaming before Helgi finally heard her question.

"Graduate study in music. Jefferson."

The twist of red neon blinking on the wall behind Karin washed Helgi and Luann in a lurid light, tinting Luann's sweat-blurred makeup a fevered shade of pink, darkening the shadows around Helgi's eyes and beneath his cheekbones. Wisps of hair had frayed loose from his braid, hanging shaggy around his white face. Karin had seen enough recruits run till they fainted from exhaustion to know that he had come very near to the farthest reaches of his strength. Maybe he shouldn't be drinking, but she was not Helgi's mother, and she had no right to tell him what to do.

"I'm stationed at the base down here now. I just got promoted to captain a few weeks ago, and they moved me here." Karin twitched her sleeve to show off the stripes.

"Congratulations."

Then Helgi could think of nothing better to say to Karin. She was before him, as he had always dreamed, the blinking neon light behind her casting flashes of warm bronze light over the silvery whiteness of her helmet-cut hair. Mute as he was, he could not help looking at her white throat to see if his silver chain still glinted around her neck, but she was in uniform now, of course. She might not be allowed to wear jewelry, even if she still had the piece, he didn't know what the rules were in the military. She would not be afraid if she knew he had killed a man, she had not walked out on his Erl-King song, but come in while he sang.

"I should have changed before I left, but I was in a hurry to get here. Just as well, isn't it?" Karin's smile flashed like a snake striking from hiding, and Helgi felt the twinge through his bones. I thought this was over, I thought she was past, he cried silently to himself, but said nothing. Instead he pressed his thigh against Luann's under the table.

They talked of nothing for a while longer, until Helgi's yawns grew wider than his hand could cover. Luann walked out the door at the back of the bar with him, they stood together for a few moments.

"Did she really live near you?"

"Her family still does. She's five years older than I am, I guess?" The words stuck in his throat, but he had never been able to draw them up so far before. "She's always thought of me as a little brother, sort of."

"That's good. Keep it that way." Luann gave him a little shake, then drew him down for a kiss. "I love you, Helgi. Drive carefully, and try to avoid any and all major weather formations in future."

Although Helgi had thought he would be asleep behind the wheel by the time he got home, the cool air rushing through the car had woken him up again, filling him with restless energy. He took Elric for a short walk around the block, then got a Coke and sat down at his synthesizer. The blank sheet of music paper still sat where he had left it a few days ago, but now he knew the feel of the waters storming around him. He shifted a few of the synthesizer's levers, and suddenly it was there in his room. The tornado's roaring, the grip of the water dragging at him, and high above, the scream of the lightning spearing through the sky. His whispered voice was more a chant than a song, a steady beat through the gusting music.

"Now I know you, white-armed maid,
fair-whirling in the foam,
I trust no troll-kind, traitors all,
you'd drag me down to your dark hall,
dread lover, to your home.
Sky and sea do battle still,
wave snatching me from wind,
mast on storm-torn sail rasping,
cloud-rain clasping, sea-spray grasping,
both reaching out to rend."

Helgi hammered down a thunderous bass, letting the light keen oboe-notes spatter faster and faster from his right hand as he sang softly...

"The wyrms writhe up from water's depths,
the dead long-hidden breed, their hordes
are still no more, but stand to words
where grains of gold are kept.
The snake-prowed ship must show the way,
the sea is foe more stark than storm,
when lightning spears the lashing worm
from grim-helmed cloud-wight gray.
The sea's arms clutch as soft as love,
Her gifts, I cannot cast from me,
but through the waters, wending free,
the wind howls wish above."

Suddenly Helgi found himself modulating to a single minor chord in both hands, its keening sound held until he broke into an arpeggio rippling upward, freeing his left to scribble the notes before he lost them.

"Sun spear through clouds, burn rainbow-fire,
swan-white, the brightening brand lifts higher.
Sleeping, now wakened, never forsaken,
Dawn's glow for gloaming but once mistaken.
Sun spears through sky, the rainbow growing
bridge of air-brightness, its flames fair-glowing.
Choosing that trying, harsh raven-crying,
short life more shining for brave dying."

CHAPTER XXI

The sailing along the coast of Gautland was good. The weather held fair, so that Hoilogae and his men camped ashore every night, and could sometimes hunt. After days of dry fish and hard bread, the strong taste of deer-meat cheered and strengthened them, and it seemed that the faring was blessed. Still, Hoilogae did not sleep easily. Every night, he strained through dark drowsiness for a sight of Swaebhon, and his dreams were troubled by the rasping of rocks and the rough deep laughter of the etin-kin. It seemed to him that something stood between himself and his beloved. Had Ansuthewaz not seemed so sure of the path, he would have ordered the ships to sail another way, until he felt the sea-road between them clear again. After a few days, the gently sloping hills and bright-leaved woods gave way to stark cliffs of mottled pink granite rising high from the waves that frothed about their roots.

"Now we should steer a little away from the land," Ansuthewaz told them. "The land-wights here are seldom the kind folk of Jutland or Gautland. It is trolls who dwell in the rocky cliff-caves and seek the lives of men. Even in the daylight hours, I have heard of keels dashed out where no one saw rocks, and ships overturning when no wave struck them. It is best not to make land again until we reach Aiwilimae's harbor."

Even from farther out at sea, they could all see how the cliffs reached higher and higher towards the heavens. Sometimes a bright stream of water tumbled down the dark rocks like a thread of gold in the sunlight, now and again they passed the mouth of a narrow arm of the sea reaching deep into the land. Hoilogae saw the pang of pain on Ansuthewaz's face as they crossed before one of these firths and the thrall looked up to the dark pine-trees that furred the sweeping slopes on either side of the water. He was too kind-hearted to speak to Ansuthewaz about the hidden thoughts whose torment his face mirrored, but he heard the thrall whisper softly, "I must soon be home," and the stab of pain that closed Ansuthewaz's eyes leapt joyously in Hoilogae's heart.

The lightly-clouded sky was already darkening with sunset, so the change in the weather caught them wholly without warning, the brutal might of the wind striking the ships to swing them against the rising waves. Hoilogae opened his mouth to shout to the men in the other ship, but the wind caught him in the face, ripping the sound of his words away, blinding his eyes and stilling his mouth with a slap of ice-grained snow. He barely caught himself against a bench as the ship lurched in a hard sideways roll. We are going over, he thought for a frightful moment before the boat righted itself. Swaebhon, are we to be lost so close?

"Make for land!" Hoilogae shouted, not sure whether anyone could hear him or not. "For land!" Crouching to grasp the benches as he went, he made his way to Attalae's side and took the rudder from the old man's grip. Attalae sat down on a rower's bench, gasping against the snow-weighted wind.

Although the boat rolled from side to side, Hoilogae could not feel it moving. "Row, you slugs!" He shouted. "Row!" The high cliff-walls of the firth would shield them against this cruel northern wind, and they might be able to reach land in safety.

Attalae glanced back swiftly, then braced himself against Hoilogae's shoulder as he stood on his toes to shout in his drighten's ear. "They're rowing!" He cried. "The boat's not moving! There's troll craft at work."

Hoilogae strained his eyes through the spray-salted snow, trying to see the other ship. "Where are they?"

"Don't know! I can't see!" Attalae cried back.

Hoilogae reached down to grasp Ansuthewaz by the neck of his tunic, hauling him up to the rudder. "Help Attalae!" He screamed at the thrall. As soon as Ansuthewaz had a good grip, Hoilogae let go of him and grasped the banner-spear, pulling it free of the ropes that lashed it to the ale-cask. Its point was iron, he could find no better help. Bracing himself against the left side of the boat and one rowers' bench, Hoilogae stabbed outwards into the wind with his spear. It met only air and snow. The ship heeled over onto its side, and Hoilogae could feel himself beginning to fall felt his hand slipping from Swaebhon's grasp. Desperately he stabbed downward, into the water. This thing had stood between them, now he could slay it! His spear struck something hard. It felt as though its iron tip were staving through thick timbers, sinking deeply into something soft beneath them. Then the boat rolled back, and Hoilogae's spear came free with it. Now the ship began to move under the beating of its oars, but the wind howled louder around Hoilogae's ears, the grainy snow clawing at his face, and the waves were tossing the boat about like a leaf flying free on the wind. Hoilogae whipped his spear around, stabbing out again and again, but the iron scathed nothing. Before another gust of snow filled his eyes, Hoilogae saw the high dark shadows of the cliffs looming before him. The wind would drive them onto the rocks if they could not steer free. He took his place at the rudder beside Ansuthewaz and Attalae, lending all his strength to help slant the ship across the wind, away from the cliff-edges.

Suddenly, as though something had broken, they were flying swiftly into the firth with the wind at their backs. By the time they were close enough for Hoilogae to see the high rock that rose before them through the blowing snow, it was too late for them to turn aside. In a blurred flash, he saw a huge clawed hand raised before them, saw ice-white teeth and a twisted gray limb three times the thickness of a man's, and he braced his spear against his shoulder, the iron point jutting out before the ship's prow.

The crash of striking threw Hoilogae backwards, lightnings of pain bursting from his back and flashing through his eyes as he struck the rowers' benches. He slumped into the bilge water between them, his arms too numb from the shock for him to move them. He could hear the sound of men talking around him, but their voices kept fading in and out. Then Attalae was heaving him up as Thonarabernu's body made a strong wall behind the bench for him to lean on. Holtagastaz held a cup of ale to Hoilogae's mouth, steadying his head with one small hand. Hoilogae sipped carefully. The heaving of the boat seemed much less, but his stomach was beginning to twist. He leaned over, spewed a thick mess into the bilge, and sipped at the ale again to clear his mouth of the sour fish taste. Something was strange, but he could not think what.

"I don't see their ship," Thonarastanaz's scratchy voice remarked behind him. "Do you think they had time to get to shore?"

Biting back a groan, Hoilogae pulled himself up. Although the day was swiftly darkening, the air was clear and still, the ship rocking gently on the quiet water between the lengthy clusters of rocks at the bases of the two sheer cliffs stretching inland for the length of the firth. They were alone on the water, alone, except for the shattered bits of Hoilogae's spear bobbing on the low waves between the boat and the rock-berg in the middle of the firth, and the few pieces of broken planking floating on the sea behind them. No one had to speak to answer Thonarastanaz's question.

The first hint of returning feeling was beginning to tingle painfully in Hoilogae's arms. He raised one carefully, let his hand drop to his lap again. "We'll stop here tonight." Weak as his voice was, it sounded clearly through the newly quiet air. "Tomorrow we'll send their funeral gifts to the Awesome One's hall."

Ansuthewaz bent down to speak in Hoilogae's ear. "That is not wise. I know this stead now. It is called Hati's Firth, and ill wights dwell here."

Hoilogae swung his head towards the sheer cliffs that lined the firth. "We can't make land here, and it's getting too dark to go on. Everyone shall be wary tonight, and we shall sleep beneath our shields. That must be enough. We have won through so far, and must win through till dawn."

Attalae was peering into Hoilogae's eyes as he slumped back. "It's hard to tell in this light, but I think your head isn't too badly hurt. Your luck is strong, Hoilogae. Few will be able to say they have seen a braver deed. Now raise your feet up out of the bilge and let us stretch you out on the bench. I'll keep watch for the first part of the night, and wake another at midnight, but you must sleep the night through."

It was dark when Hoilogae opened his eyes, the cliffs looming high and black against the faint starlight. The moon was down. There was no sound except the faint lapping of the water against the sides of the boat and the soft breathing of the sleeping men. Hoilogae ached all over, but the aching drew to two tight knots of pain in his low back and the back of his head. He turned a little on the bench, trying to get more comfortable. Attalae was still on watch. Hoilogae recognized the old man's beak like nose and jutting beard as the shadow at the boat's stem turned its head. Hoilogae had just settled his limbs, ready to go back to sleep, when the voice came whispering over the water. Its tone was like a woman's, an older woman, her throat coarsened from years of breathing the cooking fire's smoke, but deep as a man's, with rocks grating beneath the words.

"Who are the heroes in Hati's Firth? The ship is adorned with shields. You seem brave, I think you fear little. Make known to me your kin-leader's name!"

Attalae's head drooped down towards his chest, then jerked up, as if he had started awake. Unhurriedly he drew his iron sword, laying it over the prow of the boat. "He is called Hoilogae, and you may never win harm for our leader. Iron walls the atheling's ship, and witches may not harm us."

Hoilogae heard the slow scraping of rock dragging over rock. It seemed to him that he could see something moving in the shadow of the cliffs, but he could not make it out.

"How are you called, ill-willed hero?" The voice whispered from the darkness. "How do your kin call you? The folk leader trusts you, to let you dwell in the fair ship's stem."

"I am called Attalae, and I shall be awful to you! I am the most furious towards hags! I have often dwelt in the spray-wet stem, and slain night-riders. How are you called, corpse-greedy ogress? Hag, name your father! You should be nine rosts beneath the earth, and bushes growing on your bosom."

The whispering voice was louder now, scraping down Hoilogae's spine. "I am called Rime-Gardhaz, my father is called Hati. I know him to be the most ill willed etin. He took many brides from their dwellings, before Hoilogae hewed him." The shadows where Rime-Gardhaz stood were beginning to shift as the Moon's edge brightened over the horizon, Hoilogae thought he could see the shape standing tall among the rocks.

"Ogress, you were in front of the warrior's ships, and lay in the firth before us!" Attalae cried. Hoilogae wondered that his shout did not waken the other men, but the thanes lay still, breathing softly as though untroubled. "You would have given the hero's men to Ran, if his spear had not come to your heart-flesh."

"You are deluded, Attalae," the troll-woman's voice rumbled more softly from the cliff, its scratchy dark sound winding around them like an adder's scaly coils. "I say that you are in a dream, you let your eyebrows sink." Attalae's head was nodding forward a little, but Hoilogae saw his hand move to his sword's iron blade, and his head jerk upright again as Rime-Gardhaz's murmurings went on. "My mother lay before the mild one's ships, I drowned the sons of Hlothowairaz in the harbor." The huge twisted shape in the shadows laughed, the sound of high waves breaking on rocks.

As the light of the half full Moon brightened, Hoilogae could see that it cavorted more swiftly, though the cliff-shadow still hid its shape from clear sight. "You would whinny, Attalae, if you were not gelded. Rime-Gardhaz tosses her tail! I think that your heart is in your hinder parts, Attalae, though you have a stallion's voice." Her low laugh seemed to twine cold around Hoilogae's balls, and he swiftly shifted so that his iron sword lay over his groin.

Hoilogae saw Attalae's left hand move into a thumb-through-fist gesture above his crotch as the old warrior shouted back, "You would think me a stallion, if you knew how to try me, and I stepped from water to land! You'd be well-beaten, if I went at it with full thought, and your tail would sink, Rime Gardhaz!"

The shadow-shape's wriggling slowed. Now it seemed to be moving like a lizard to the edge of the rocks. Once Hoilogae saw what might have been the out thrust of a craggy breast, another time, he thought a glimmer of reflected moonlight shone between stony legs, but he could be sure of none of it. "Attalae," the troll called softly. "Attalae, come onto the land, if you trust your might, and I shall meet you in Warin's Bay. Staved-in ribs shall you get, hero, if you come within my claws!"

"I may not go before the warriors waken, who ward the wise one. It would not be unanticipated to me, if the witch suddenly came up under the ship."

The shadows were silent for a little while as the Moon rose, it seemed to Hoilogae that the night's bright drighten was faring faster than he remembered, while the troll-woman's charms still held his men asleep. No she could not touch the Moon, but the stone-slowness of the troll-kin must lie on the harbor, if they could hear her voice and see her move. He heard a faint grating of rock, a rustling of moss, and suddenly knew that the etin-wife was looking at him.

"Awaken, Hoilogae!" Rime-Gardhaz called. Hoilogae rose in a single swift movement with a grunt of pain, drawing his sword and holding the iron before himself. "Deal with Rime-Gardhaz, for you hewed Hati to death! If she could sleep with the battle-boar one night, then she would have bettering for all bales!"

You! Hoilogae thought. It was you above all who wished to tear me from Swaebhon, who wished to keep us apart, you who are my beloved one's true foe. The cold hate burned in him, as he had never felt it. He thought of the dead, and of the troll-maid's dragging claws, and let his fury answer for him.

"You are loathsome to mankind! He is called the Loathly One, who shall have you the thurse who dwells in Tholl Island, a hound-wise etin, worst dweller in the wastes, he is a fitting man for you!"

Hoilogae could see Rime-Gardhaz's huge head raising, swinging about, as she seemed to sniff at something in the still air.

"You would rather have her, who rode above the harbor last night with your men." It seemed to Hoilogae that he could hear an echo of wistfulness in her grating voice, like the crying of gulls echoing from the high cliffs. "The gold-dight maiden seemed to bear might above me, here she stepped from water to land and so made safe your ship. It was she alone who ruled, so that I was not able to be the bane of the leader's men."

Now the sky's brightening came not only from the Moon, but behind the troll woman's cliff, to the east, Hoilogae could see the sky graying as the stars faced. The cliff's shadow, he hoped, would hold the dawn from Rime-Gardhaz's sight until it was too late for her, but he could see her rocky shape beginning to sink down into the water, the sea foaming white around her. Now his cold anger stilled to clear thought, he could see what he must do, if they were to pass safely without the troll-wife lurking each night to attack them, or calling her kin in the sea.

"Hear now, Rime-Gardhaz!" Hoilogae said. "If I better your harms, then tell the war leader truly. Was it one wight who warded the atheling's ship, or fared many together there?"

She was silent for a moment, but sank no further into the water. Hoilogae realized that while he had his iron sword out, she would not believe his offer. Unwillingly he sheathed it. Then Hoilogae thought that the troll-woman was stretching a clawed hand towards him, he could feel something cold and scaly rubbing against his skin, and he shuddered.

"They were three times nine maidens, though one rode before, a white maiden under helm. Their steeds shivered, and from their manes flew dew in deep dales, hail in high woods. From thence comes good harvest to men, what I saw was all loathly to me."

Attalae suddenly sprang up from his place in the bow, slashing his own sword down between Hoilogae and the cliffs. "Look eastward, Rime-Gardhaz! Hoilogae has dazed you with Haljon-songs! By land or by sea, the leader's ship is safe, and the ruler's men as well."

Hoilogae pointed to the east as Sunna's first ray struck over the cliff-edge, brightening through the shadows. For a single moment he saw Rime-Gard-haz clearly, the great rocky woman-shape with the waves frothing up around her knees, her saucer-sized red eyes and fanged maw open in shock as she stared up at the eastern Sun. In her left claw, she held a man's thighbone with a few tatters of flesh still hanging from it, her right was still stretched out to Hoilogae. The troll-woman's scaly gray-green skin was already graying to stone as she froze in the light.

The bone dropped from her claw, her shape melting until she seemed no more than a huge twisted boulder, one which might be thought to look something like a woman from the right angle, in the right light. "Now it is day, Rime-Gardhaz," Hoilogae called, "but Attalae has held you to your life-leaving. Mocked, you shall be a harbor-mark, there where you stand in a stone's likeness!"

Attalae sheathed his sword and sagged down on the bench beside Hoilo-gae, his breath coming hard. A tinge of blue-gray shadowed his lips even beneath the new Sun's golden light, and his face was ashen. Hoilogae sat down beside him, laying his arm around the old man's shoulders as though the warmth of his own body could fill Attalae with new strength. They sat like that in silence for a moment, until Thonarabernu shifted beneath his shield and suddenly let out the loudest, most resonant snore Hoilogae had yet heard. Hoilogae could not help laughing, and Attalae laughed with him, knuckling his red-rimmed eyes.

"We might as well wake them now," the old warrior said. "Myself, I could do with breakfast and a little rest before we go on."

"You stay there, I'll take care of it."

Hoilogae got up from the bench and made his way over to the keg of strong ale. He reached behind himself to rub at his aching back, but his touch only made the pain worse. Sighing, he bent down to draw two mugs of ale, and carried them back to Attalae together with some hard bread and dried fish. The two of them sat together and ate, watching. One by one, Hoilogae's thanes opened their eyes to the rising light.

"Why didn't you wake me for my watch?" Hraidhamannaz asked, sitting up and looking down his long nose at Attalae. Sleep had rucked his gold-en-brown hair up into a crest like an ice-bird's. "You shouldn't have stayed up all night. You don't look well."

"We were talking, and I forgot the time," Attalae answered mildly. "I shall try not to do it again."

Ansuthewaz sat down on Hoilogae's other side, looking out at the rock that loomed above the waves. "Odd that I didn't mark that boulder last night. I had thought that I knew all the harbor-signs in this land."

Hoilogae glanced over at the sun-washed stone. If he looked hard, with his eyes half-closed, he could still see the shape of Rime-Gardhaz's arm beckoning to him, even as her astonished head turned towards the east. "I think there shall be little fear in Hati's Firth for those who come after us. This, too, Swaebhon shall know of when we have reached her father's hall."

Ansuthewaz rasped a thumb thoughtfully over the light stubble on his chin. Although the thrall held his hand steady, Hoilogae could see the faint trembling of his other arm, braced against the side of the boat. "Do you mean to bring her back with you?"

"How else?"

The thrall shrugged, his sea-blue eyes turning back to the tall rock that jutted out from the water's edge.

Worn from his night-battle, Hoilogae slept through most of the next day as his ships sailed north from Hati's Firth. At sunset, Ansuthewaz told them that Aiwilimae's land was no farther than a half-day's faring.

"Then if we keep on through the night," Attalae said, "we should make haven by Aiwilimae's burg at dawn." The old warrior gestured to the cliffs that sheered up from the ocean, there was nowhere that a ship might safely come to shore. "I can sleep as well faring as anchored in the harbor, and I am an old man, who has grown weary of wind and sea. I say that we may as well press on, if we are so close."

Hoilogae looked westward, to the crimson-pink glow of the Sun's last light fading between deep blue sea and deep blue sky. "I find that a good plan. I myself will take the helm in the last part of the night."

Thonarastanaz and Thonarabernu agreed loudly, and no one raised words against it, for the way had been long, but Ansuthewaz stared over the side, into the ocean, as though he sought after a glimmer of the gold burning in Ran's hall. It was in Hoilogae's mind that Sigisharjaz had done the thrall no kindness by sending him on this faring, but there was nothing he could do to better Ansuthewaz's harm, and it seemed to him that they would have had little hope of finding Aiwilimae's lands without him.

Hoilogae went to his place by the prow a little past midnight. The Moon was down, but the stars shone clear through the blue-black sky, the path of Wodhanaz's wain glittering pale as milk against the darkness. He pulled his cloak more tightly around him. Softly as the wind whispered over the sea, he could feel the warmth draining from him like ale draining from a cask. It was blessing enough that the weather had been no worse, this far north and so late in the year, he told himself, it seemed that everyone had said so at least once in the course of the faring. Still, the sons of Hlothawairaz lay in a colder bed than his that night, together with nearly half those men who had come north with him, and if it was not for his sake, he did not know why they had found their deaths.

He had sat thinking thus for some time, his mood sinking lower, when he heard a rustling beside him as another cloak-muffled figure settled to the helmsman's bench. "Couldn't you sleep, Attalae?" He asked softly.

"Not Attalae," Ansuthewaz's low voice answered from the cloak's dark folds. "The cold crept into my bones, and so I awoke, and it seemed to me that lying alone with my thoughts would do me little good."

"Then sit here, and be welcome. Will you share a horn of ale with me? Since we are so close, I think there is little need to hoard it longer?"

Hoilogae did not see Ansuthewaz's head turning, but he heard the whisper of the thrall's movement against the cloak that hid him. "I have a cup of my own," Ansuthewaz answered. "Drink as you will, I shall keep you awake and bring you safe to the stone that marks Aiwilimae's haven."

Hoilogae filled his horn and Ansuthewaz's cup. The ale came slowly from the tap, when he drank, he found the ice-crystals cold and keen as a scattering of iron edges through the draught. Still, the drink's strength warmed him more than he was used to, as though the cold had kindled its might into a need-fire.

After a while, his tongue eased by the ale, Hoilogae said, "Tell me of Swaebhon."

"What is there to tell?" Ansuthewaz answered. "You shall see her soon enough." Hoilogae could hear the bitterness tainting the other man's voice, like an herb's taste coming sharp through ale too young-brewed.

"Still, I would know. Will you tell me?"

"Aiwilimae's man Chaidhamariz sold me to Sigisharjaz, and he gave me to you. I cannot stop you from asking what you will."

Hoilogae said nothing, and after a while Ansuthewaz spoke again, his voice lower, as though he had remembered that men slept behind them. "Men say that she is fair. She is pale as a dead woman, with white-gold hair long enough to twist a bowstring from, and she may be two fingers widths or so less than yourself in height. Her father little weens that she shall wed, for she has dealt ill with all those men who came to ask for her in marriage. I do not know what he will say when you come to him, he is not often known to joy in strangers, and looks with mistrust at those who come with south-forged weapons in their hands. You must be careful not to step onto his land before sunrise, else he is sure to think that you come for battle, and his spears will be cast against you before you can hail him."

"This is well to know," Hoilogae murmured slowly. "Why did you keep it hidden before?"

"Not because I meant to keep it hidden, or lead you into an ambush. But I was little willing to think on the hall where we are going, and so it did not come to my mind."

"Would you be freed from my keeping, when we make shore? I will give you food and weapons, and you may go where you list, if you so choose."

"Where should I go? I would stir the rime-cold sea with my hands, wandering a wretch's paths. Wyrd is full-reded. Winter is coming on. The lands on the way to the north are not like your warm home. You have never seen such mountains, where the snow may lie higher than a man's head and the lakes are blue with ice at summer's peak. The eagle would soon bear my flesh over the high seas, or the hoary wolf share his spoils with the Ansuz. It seems to me that I can ask no better cheer than wan-hope, to live empty-souled, forsaken by all joy, though I am not yet ready to die."

The thrall's words weighed ill against Hoilogae's mood, but he was not sure how to answer them. If I had lived my eighteen years, he wondered, would I know how to speak to such a man? That thought led him to another, so that he answered slowly, "I know little of woe, but I know that shame can be overcome, if you have the mood for it."

"Shame among men can be overcome, but orlog cannot be unsaid, once it is spoken. Look to the turning of your own wyrd, Hoilogae Herwawardhaz's son, and do not trouble yourself with bonds you cannot unloose. You owe me no troth, nor have I any to give to you."

"I do owe you troth," Hoilogae answered hotly. "You have fared with me, and warned us before Hati's Firth, and warned me of another danger now. If you cannot escape your wyrd, there is no need to make it more woeful than it must be, and a strong mood is better than a sorrowful one for any man, on any road. Now it seems to me that, though you have lost your luck and your place, you are still a man of some worth. If you will not take freedom, you have seen that I mean to set you to no worse tasks than are fitting for you, and while you live, you ought to be of a better cheer than you have chosen for yourself now."

"I have hardly earned these words from you," murmured Ansuthewaz. "Still, it seemed to me that the bravery and the high mood I had before were not fitting to a wretched thrall, and I knew no other way than wan-hope, nor did I await other than shame at the hands of those whom my orlog must bring me to serve. I must think on what you have said, but it seems to me that you have spoken well."

Ansuthewaz turned his back on Hoilogae, staring down into the dark waters again. After a while, Hoilogae heard him drinking, then the thrall went back to his place and lay down as if to sleep. Hoilogae sipped at the draught in his horn. His speech with Ansuthewaz had eased his own mind. He could feel his mood rising higher as he looked towards the coast and thought that morning would not be too long in coming. The land was white above the cliffs, a great stretch of pale stone bright in the starlight. Hoilogae wondered how folk could live there, and then he saw how the whiteness lay upon the dark spears of the pine-trees, scattered over the rocks. It was no wonder that he felt so cold. With Winter nights only a little past, the northern lands were already well-shrouded in snow. If winter comes so swiftly here, Hoilogae thought, we are not likely to fare back soon. We have cast our lots for a full season's dwelling, whether Aiwilimae looks well or ill upon us.

He glanced up at the glittering sky, as if Swaebhon might have left some spoor on the Ansuz's Way for him to follow, but no track marred the clear air, nor stirred the keen-pricking stars. His breath came more swiftly as he thought of her, the warmth kindling within his ribs' hearth-ring as he touched the hilt of his sword. It seemed to Hoilogae that the scratchy wool of his tunic and the smooth leather of his leg-wrappings tingled against his skin, the freezing wind on his face opening his eyes to wider wakefulness until the grains of snow and keen rock-edges on the shore were clearer in his silver-lit sight than in the Sun's full brightness. The wind was blowing from the east now, sharp with the clean scent of snow-laden pines over the sea's brine-smell.

Although the day was still far from him, Hoilogae felt his heart lifting towards the morning where Swaebhon waited for him, decked in her bridal linens. It seemed to him that he could see her, fair in the snowy dawn, beckoning him closer, spear raised in her hand. Hoilogae started, jerked his drooping head up from his chest. He had been asleep for a few moments, he thought. The coast seemed farther away, as though a sea-current had caught them while his eyes were closed. He took up his oars, dipping them into the water and beginning to stroke back towards the shore. The work warmed him, so that he was little willing to stop when he had gotten the ship back onto course, instead he kept pulling, hastening the way towards the north as well as he could.

The eastern sky was just beginning to pale when the cliffs suddenly parted, opening into a long crooked firth. Hoilogae would have passed it by, as they had passed many others on the faring, but Ansuthewaz had crept up silently behind him, and whispered, "It is here. Go to the end of the firth."

Hoilogae steered the boat into the firth as well as he could with the currents swinging it about from rock to rock. Ansuthewaz watched silently, but said nothing and did not offer his help, nor did Hoilogae wish to ask.

The land along the firth was snow-whitened, save for one dark patch at the farthest point, and it was for this place that Hoilogae steered as the sky grew lighter. One by one, his men were beginning to stir, before they were halfway to the firth's end, Attalae had come forward to sit by Hoilogae. By the time the sky's blueness had faded into the pale yellow of sand-roses' petals, they were close enough to see the gleam of bronze spear-points, ruddy as flames above the men who had gathered in the snow about the dark spot.

"It seems that we are not anticipated," Attalae said dryly. "Messengers must fare swiftly here, I heard no signal-horn blowing."

"A mounted watcher saw us from the cliff as we came into the firth," Ansuthewaz replied. "There is a well-hidden path through the trees to Aiwilimae's hall."

"Untrusting folk, these Northerners," Thonarastanaz said dryly. His hand had dropped to toy with the hex-shaped amber bead that hung from his sword's hilt on a leather thong, he shifted his weight, moving the sword in its scabbard to be sure it would draw swiftly. "You'd think these rock-walls would ward them well enough. If I had such a burg at home, I'd count myself safe."

"Perhaps there's something well worth having here," Hraidhamannaz suggested brightly. "If we hadn't lost so many at Hati's Firth." Though the youth tried to speak as off-handedly as an older man, his voice trailed off as he looked into the waters. Hoilogae could not remember whether any of the men in the lost boat had been Hraidhamannaz's near kin, or only his friends, his thanes were still half-strangers to him, for all he had tried to ken them better.

As they came closer and the dawn brightened, Hoilogae saw that the dark patch he had marked before was a wide slab of gray stone, ringed about by summer-green grass. It did not seem strange to him that the grass should grow so brightly when the snow covered everything around it. It was so fair to see that he thought it could hardly be otherwise. The stick-shapes hacked into the cloud-pale stone were painted with red ochre, bright as if the fresh wounds in the living rock still bled. There, a man lifted a spear three times his length. That, Hoilogae's soul told him, was the spear of the Ansuz in a living man's hand, with the two four-legged lines that showed wolves running beneath it. Across the stone, Thonaraz lifted his great ax to hallow the wedding of the man and woman who stood between two trees, one with branches lifted, one's limbs sinking towards the earth. The footprints of Nerthuz showed where the holy one had passed, the path humans would follow at the rites. At the stone's base, the prow and stern of a ship curled up proudly, alf-cups, twice dyed with ochre and the blessing-blood, spotted the gray stone like great spatters of red rain.

"Do you see that man there, who stands at the fore of the host in war-helm and a bearskin cloak?" Ansuthewaz asked Hoilogae.

Hoilogae followed the line of the thrall's gaze to the shore. Once he saw the man, he could not have taken him for any but the war band's drighten. The bronze horns of the war-helm twisted high above his head, his golden hair and beard spilled over the brown-black fur he wore, and gold glinted from the hilt of his sword. "That is Aiwilimae, with whom you must deal. Now do not ask me to show my face here, or to speak, hereafter I must be as a dead man." Ansuthewaz wrapped himself in his cloak, lying face-down on the bench.

The war-helmed man cupped his hands to his mouth and shouted, his mighty bass voice carrying over the water. "Who are you, who have come to Aiwilimae's land with swords by your sides and shields hanging your ship? I do not ken your banner, but the spear-point is iron, you must have fared up from the south."

"I am Hoilogae, son of Herwawardhaz!" Hoilogae shouted back. "I have not come to do battle unless I must, I am here to ask for your daughter Swaebhon in marriage, and shall not leave until she is by my side."

"Ill norns have led others to swear such oaths, and those men have won only woe by it. Strangers are little welcome in my lands, and wooers are little welcome to my daughter. Turn your ship and fare southward again, or go north to hunt the white bears. It is one to me what you do, so long as you leave my shores."

Hoilogae drew his sword, the hilt smooth in its hand. The light of the sunrise rippled red down the hallowed blade's wyrm-markings, bright as if its iron were new-come from the forge's fire. "My faring here has been longer than you know, and I have not come this far to turn away now. If there is no other choice, I am willing to fight my way to shore, and battle up to your hall if I must. Though it would be better for you to take the gifts I offer, and give guest-right in turn as befits a drighten, I mean that we shall be kinsmen soon, and strife among kin can bring nothing but woe."

"Brave words for a boy," Aiwilimae answered. "Who are you to tell me what befits a drighten? You shall not land here, my bowmen can shoot you dead where you stand. Nor shall you take part in my land once dead. Your corpses shall gladden the fish and the gulls. Turn around and go away, or else find your death!"

Hoilogae saw the bronze arrow-tips glinting as Aiwilimae's bowmen drew their weapons. He stepped up onto the steersman's bench to give them a clear shot. Living, he could not break his oath, but once he was dead, his men could go home.

They heard the woman's voice before they saw her, its high keen clearness cutting through Aiwilimae's next words. "What are you doing, Father? Let these men come to land. They have fared a long way. Now I swear by the spear and horn I hold that they shall have guest-right in our hall until Austarjon's feast! Would you make an oathbreaker of me?"

Aiwilimae turned his head, looking up at the snow above the gray stone. Hoilogae saw the glitter of the bronze spear-blade first, then the movement of gray-white fur as Swaebhon cast back the hood of her cloak and lifted the silver-bound horn she held to her lips. He was still too far from her to see her face clearly, but her pale brightness shone white as winter sunlight, he could not turn his eyes from her.

The bowmen lowered their weapons before Aiwilimae spoke. "Come to land, then, Hoilogae son of Herwawardhaz. Frith shall not be broken between us now, though I will not speak of what may come later. Come freely. if woe follows for you, then it is for no sake of mine, for my daughter Swaebhon rules in this."

Swaebhon came down over the gray stone as Hoilogae's men took up oars again and rowed into land, her feet finding the path only by long habit. The travel-grime was no more than a thin mist over Hoilogae's fairness in her sight, his amber hair and beard bright above the wyrm-glittering sword in his hand. But it was Hoilogae's gaze that held her, night-gray eyes fearless as a wolf-drighten's at the head of his pack as her own joy brightened on his face. The horn trembled in Swaebhon's hands, a few drops spilling golden trails through the white frost on its rim. Now it was she who must call all her bravery forth to meet him, for it seemed to her that the might of Hoilogae's nearness beat up through the hallowed rock and all about her like great wings that would hammer the flesh from her bones if her strength wavered a moment.

The dawn-light spilled from Swaebhon's gray-blue eyes, glimmering into rainbows in Hoilogae's blurring sight, the ghostly fire burning against the swan-white snow that stretched out behind her. He did not mark his own movement, and hardly felt the icy water freezing his feet and calves as he waded from the boat to shore, there seemed to be nothing in the world out-side of Swaebhon's day-brightening gaze and the white horn he took from her hand. The draught she had given him was sweet as mead, but paler and stronger than any he had tasted, ice-crystals frosted the horn's silver bind-ing, and when Hoilogae, gasping from the strength and cold of the drink, lowered it again, he could taste blood in his mouth where the frozen metal had bitten his lip.

"Hail to you, Hoilogae, and welcome! That is well-done, to come to me with your blade drawn, and to woo a walkurjon with weapons."

Hoilogae saw then that he had not sheathed his sword, he moved to put it back, but Swaebhon caught him by the wrist, her strong cold hand turning his so that the light flowed along the blade's layers of iron, catching and flaming up along the higher edge.

"Wejlunduz wrought well for you. Such a sword has not yet been seen in the Middle-Garth. Still, the sword would be of little use if you had not the hard soul to wield it, and that you have shown better than any. Now bring your men to shore, I think they are more weary from the faring than you are, and we shall greet them in our hall as is fitting."

Swaebhon drew the hood of her wolf-fur cloak up over her head again and strode back over the stone and into the snow without another word, leaving Hoilogae to look after her for a moment before he licked the blood from his lip and turned back to the others.

Aiwilimae stood beside the stone's foot, looking up at him. This close, Hoilogae could see that the drighten's fair hair was blended thickly with silver. Aiwilimae's heavy eyebrows were still drawn close and his wind-pale eyes narrowed, but it seemed to Hoilogae that it was bewilderment, rather than anger, that creased the Northman's wind-ruddied brow into deep folds.

"It seems that you are favored in my hall, whether I will it or not," Aiwili-mae rumbled. "Have you broken your fast this day?"

Hoilogae gestured towards the east, though the sky was nearly as light as full day now, the Sun's edge had not yet risen over the high land. "There has been little time for that."

"Then come with me, there is enough food in my hall. Although I do not often deal so kindly with strangers who come armed to my shores, no one has ever said that my men went hungry. You will want to eat soon before you fall over. Swaebhon's winter-mead is not for drinking on an empty stomach."

Hoilogae's men had drawn the boat up onto the shore, now they came to stand behind him. He could feel them like a warm wall at his back, their company cheering to him. Only Ansuthewaz still lay on his bench as though he were asleep.

One of Aiwilimae's warriors, a thin man wrapped in silvery sealskins with a huge scar shining red through his ash-blond beard, leaned over the side of the boat, poking lightly at Ansuthewaz with the butt of his spear. "What's wrong with this one? Is he ill, or dead?"

"He is wretched, and a thrall," Hoilogae answered sharply. "Leave him be."

The warrior grinned lopsided up at Hoilogae. "Even a wretched thrall might like to come out of the snow into a warm place, and have some food after a long faring. If he's not fit to serve athelings, there are cattle and horses in our hall, and another pair of hands to shovel dung is always welcome. If he is ill, the frowe Swaebhon has herb-lore to cure most fevers, even the worst wounds, so long as the guts are not pierced."

"He is in his place. If he will not come to the hall, you must leave him be."

"I hope you southern folk treat your oxen better than you do your thralls," the scarred man replied. He stepped away from the boat and said no more, but Ansuthewaz stirred, standing with a fold of his cloak wrapped over his face as though the cold pained him and climbing slowly over the side. It seemed to Hoilogae that this boded well that Ansuthewaz must have taken heart from their night's words, and overcome the wan-hope that had made his speech so sorrowful before, and the thought gladdened him.

The smell struck Hoilogae together with the warmth as he stepped into Aiwilimae's hall. A thick must of cows and horses, dogs and old straw and unwashed men. After the days and nights of clean sea-wind, the air inside was almost choking, Hoilogae's head spun after a couple of breaths, although he was not sure his dizziness did not stem from the drink Swaebhon had given him. The hall was built long and low, with the beasts stalled near the door. Only a little light came from the smoke holes above, so that it might have been night as easily as day, but the fires were burning well, and it seemed to Hoilogae that he could feel good cheer within that garth.

Swaebhon sat at the far end of the hall, at the high-table, the whiteness of her wolf skin cloak reddened by the fire behind her. Food was already set out for the men, steaming bowls of porridge and herrings pickled in brine and herbs, women were bringing pots of warmed ale from the hearth-stones to the tables. Aiwilimae led Hoilogae and Attalae up to the high-table and seated them across from Swaebhon and himself before he lifted the war-helm from his head and placed it carefully on one of the rafters, hanging his thick woolen cap on a peg below it. Though his hair was otherwise long and thick, a bald spot the size of Hoilogae's palm gleamed on the crown of his skull, as though the helm had worn it bare through years of warring.

"Now you may tell me more of yourself and your faring," the northern drighten said. He stabbed a piece of pickled herring with his knife, eating it carefully from the keen bronze. "How did you come to hear of Swaebhon, and how did you find your way here?"

Swaebhon sat silently, eating her porridge with a little spoon of gold-worked horn. Now that Hoilogae was here, it seemed to her that she could find no words to say to him. It was enough for her to sit and look at him, wondering that the beloved of her dream-farings should truly walk within the Middle-Garth's ring, and be as fair in the flesh as in her soul-sight. A little blood tinged the high slopes of Hoilogae's cheekbones beneath her gaze, or perhaps it was only the fire's light on his paleness, but he seemed as rapt as she, neither speaking nor moving, still as he had been when he sat on the howe and she rode the winds above.

Yet it seemed to her as though a crumbled leaf of wormwood had been stirred into the sweet porridge. Her father glared at Hoilogae as though all his thoughts ran towards slaying the Jutlander, and Hoilogae seemed corpse-white already, his eyes darkened by lost sleep and the bones standing starkly in his face as though his flesh were starting to sink. Is this the death I was to bring him, that my father be his bane? She wondered. Swaebhon gripped her spoon until it began to bend under her strength, but she struggled to make her gaze show only joy. If ill was to come so soon, all the less should it taint Hoilogae's moment of gladness.

"Sigisharjaz spoke to us, and told us the way to follow," Attalae answered. "I have heard that you have had dealings with him, you must know that his rede is not lightly set aside."

"Not for those who dwell close to him, though his arm does not reach so far that I, or any of the folks within many days' march of me, need care for his wishes. I would guess that you must come out of Jutland or Sealand, we find amber seldom here, but I see that many of your men carry the Frowe's sea-fallen tears as luck-pieces. Sigisharjaz has never fared so far north, nor have any of his men, and my shores are not so easy to find." He turned to Hoilogae. "You, how did you come to be so set upon a woman whom you have never seen, and of whom I doubt you had heard in the usual turnings of things, any more than anyone here in the Northlands had heard of you or your father Herwawardhaz? Now I know that if your man has not lied to me, you are at least hiding something from me."

STEPHAN GRUNDY

Hoilogae clenched his fists beneath the table. Could Aiwilimae have heard of Herwawardhaz's witless son? But such tales traveled no farther than men's names were known, and the shores of Glazaleunduz clearly lay outside the northern drighten's ken.

"Father, there will be time to ask questions over the whole winter," Swaebhon broke in. "You are rough-mannered with your guests, you would do better to ask of their faring, and if they have need of anything."

"You are very like your mother," the Northman said, his voice was rough, but Hoilogae could see the glint of his narrow eyes softening as he looked at his daughter. "She, too, would have had me deal with strangers as if they were friends, and often said that I must speak more mildly to guests in my hall. If I had known that you might be won by the first man who came to you with his sword out for battle, instead of greeting you with gifts and soft words, I should have found you such an eager warrior long ago, and saved myself much trouble."

"You would have had a long search to find the man I wanted," Swaebhon answered. "Hoilogae may not have been known to you, but I knew of him, if you showed a better temper towards strangers, you would learn more of other lands." Though Hoilogae sat there before her, she was little willing to say more, it seemed to her that what lay between them should not be spoken of before others.

"Other lands mean little to me," Aiwilimae said, though he replied to Swaebhon, he was looking straight at Hoilogae. "Nor do I have any way of knowing your worth, you who call yourself Hoilogae. It might be that you are a landless rover, come up north in hopes of winning a bride and fair fields where you may call yourself an atheling and not fear that anyone knows to gainsay you, there are no tales of your worth here."

Hoilogae rose to his feet, his porridge steaming untouched before him. It seemed to him that the earthen floor swayed beneath his feet, as though he were still at sea, and he could hear the wind rushing past his ears. "I need not stay where my worth is spoken of so, nor am I minded to eat food given so grudgingly. Come, Attalae, it seems to me that if we leave now, we may make home again before the worst of the winter storms have blown up. Swaebhon, will you follow me to my father's hall and dwell with me there, to be frowe over a great land when our time has come?"

Swaebhon smiled at him, and reached out her hand across the table as though she would take his, but Attalae had risen as well, laying his hands on Hoilogae's shoulders. Though the old man's touch seemed little weightier than dried leaves, it cooled Hoilogae's anger a little and brought him down to his seat again.

"He speaks fairly, Hoilogae," Attalae said. "He knows nothing of your line or deeds, nor is there anyone he may trust to tell him. It is too much, to ask an old man to give up the only jewel of his line to a seafarer with no more proof than the stranger's words, it seems to me that he will not easily get another child such as Swaebhon. And you have already drunk this hall's mead, scorning its food is unfitting for you."

Aiwilimae's right hand came out from under the table, the blood rushing to darken his scarred knuckles, and Hoilogae knew that the drighten's hand had been tightened on his sword. "You can hardly call me old, for you are far older than I. Still, that is true, Swaebhon's mother died in the birthing, and I have seen no maid to match her since, except my daughter. I am little willing that she should go so far from me, and less willing to send her with a man I know nothing of, to an unknown land."

Attalae sliced a piece of herring in two, swallowing a bit of it whole and clearing his mouth with a sip of ale before he spoke again. "I know that one of your men has been to Sigisharjaz's hall, and not so long ago. Ask him if he heard the names of Herwawardhaz or Hoilogae while he was there. Else wise, send another messenger to Sigisharjaz, he will easily find out if we have told you the truth. We are in no hurry to fare home, and a season together will do these two no harm."

"It seems well to me that Hoilogae's deeds should be told and known among all here," added Swaebhon. "Call together the Thing, if you will, Father, and let those who have cause speak. Or bring your best warriors to him, let your single-harriers meet him in fight upon field or holm, and let him show you his strength on their bodies. I would not find that ill to watch, and you should see then what manner of man has come to wed me."

"It seems to me that you put much trust in this man already, to ask this for him. But I shall call the Thing, and let matters go as they will afterwards."

The porridge had been made with rich cream, and sweetened with honey, it warmed Hoilogae well, and steadied him against the mead's rushing wod.

Aiwilimae belched, wiping his mouth with a fold of his cloak. "Now there are other things we may speak of. Did you bring more amber than your luck-pieces? It is rare here, and gladdens those who get it."

"Let us not speak of trade either," answered Attalae. "As you saw, we came in but one boat, the other was lost in Hati's Firth. If we had brought amber, it would be meant for wooing-gifts, and it would be ill to speak of such before the Thing. Men might say that we had bought your daughter with it. Else wise, if we had none, it might be thought that the lack had harmed our wedding-chances, and only because we traveled lightly and held Hoilogae's fame and strength to be worthier burdens for our little boat than his weight in the Frowe's wave-born tears."

"You're a smooth-tongued old man, aren't you? I see why you were thought worth your weight in the boat. Are you Herwawardhaz, or some kin of his?"

"I am not. But I have given him rede all his life, and thus he and his folk call me Attalae, for I am like a little father to them. If your man whiled more than a night in Sigisharjaz's hall, it is likely that he heard my name spoken, for though I am no drighten nor land-proud fro, I am not without fame of my own."

"That seems not unlikely to me," Aiwilimae admitted grudgingly. Then no one else said anything for a time. Attalae looked at his herring, cutting it as neatly as a woodworker readying beam to be fitted into beam, and Aiwilimae's gaze roamed through the hall, measuring his own men against Hoilogae's little band. Hoilogae was content to sit looking into Swaebhon's eyes. Though she did not speak, knowing that she lived within the Middle-Garth's ring was more than he had set his hope's trust in, and sharing her gaze was joy enough for him. The warmth he felt put him in mind of the green grass around the holy stone, and after a little time he asked, "Is there a tale to that stone which snow does not cover?"

"It has always been so, since folk can remember," Swaebhon answered. "Even in winter's depths, the gods will not suffer snow to hide it from them, but the grass is green there all year. Thus we have always known it to be holy, and held the rites there since our kin came up from the south, for more years than any of us can tell, though it has not been long since I was given sight of the shapes hidden in the rock, and let them be carved and colored where you see them now."

When they had finished eating, Aiwilimae stood and pulled his woolen cap over his head again. "Now, are you minded to come hunting with me? We will need to fill our smokehouse well with meat now, if we are to feed all of you over the winter, and it is often said among us that hunting is the measure of a man."

Hoilogae glanced at Attalae in a heartbeat of hope, surely the old rede-giver would have some way to hide Hoilogae's lack of skill? Then Hoilogae's anger stung him like a chill wind, burning the blood into his face. Was he still a witling, that he must trust in another for his proof? A deeper flush followed the first, like one wave rolling over another. A flush of shame. Neither warmth nor food had brought the color back to Attalae's cheeks, nor reddened the blue ice-tinge of his lips, the darkness was still pooled in the hollows around his eyes, as it had been since his night-speech with the etin-wife, and Hoilogae marked how the rede-giver's hand shook as he laid his spoon into his empty bowl. "I will go, but you must stay here and rest," Hoilogae said swiftly. "I think our long faring has dealt worse with you than with any of us."

Attalae gestured Hoilogae closer to him, spoke softly in his ear. "Are you so skilled in hunting that you think you can go thus without me? I am more hale than I look, I know I have strength enough for this."

Hoilogae closed his teeth on the tip of his tongue before the stinging fury could spill out. Attalae's words were true, and there was nothing ill in lacking a craft he had never been taught. "Your rede is sure to be good," he murmured. "How would you give it to me, if I were as hale as you are now? I count your life as worth more to me than a boar's or deer's."

Aiwilimae chopped his hand through the air. "It seems to me as well that you should rest here, Attalae. I will not have it said that I ran a guest to death , and I would see how matters go with Hoilogae alone."

"Wait here," Swaebhon said to Hoilogae before he could answer. "You are too lightly clad to be out in the snow with us all day, I shall find you some better clothes, and hunting-gear, and skis for your feet as well, for you cannot keep up with us without them." She glided away swiftly, leaving the three men.

"Hoilogae has not gone on skis before, for we have no need for them in Jutland," Attalae said quickly. "You must not think that he can show you his full worth if he must learn a new skill at the same time."

Aiwilimae lifted two long curved pieces of wood from the rafter where they had lain, sitting down and beginning to bind them to his feet with the sinews that pierced them. "There is no trick to going on skis, nor to hunting from them," he grunted, pulling the sinews tight.

Swaebhon came back into the hall, sliding one foot in front of the other, on her feet were pieces of wood like those her father wore. She laid Hoilogae's clothes out before him. A cloak of gray wolf skin, hooded like her own, a tunic of a thick brown and white pelt such as Hoilogae had never seen before, and leg-wrappings of the same fur, as well as another pair of skis. Awkwardly he bent to bind them on.

"No, you have them the wrong way round," Swaebhon said, crouching gracefully before him and untying his knots with one hand as she pushed away the hound that had come up to sniff at her with the other. "There. So, and so. Now stand, and let me clothe you."

Hoilogae felt somewhat foolish, but he did as she told him, letting her slip the tunic over his head. As she wrapped the wolf skin cloak around his shoulders and pinned it shut with a bronze brooch, a strange feeling came over him. It seemed that each wolf-hair thrilled to one of his nerves, ten thousand needle-points tingling over his body, that he could hardly hold himself back from running out of the hall, as though he would run through the snow and the woods in search of something that fled before him, the hot taste of blood and flesh already sweet in his mouth.

Swaebhon's hand passed over Hoilogae's hair, stilling the fierce trembling in his limbs and clearing the red mist from his sight. "The wood-hound's hide is well suited to you, I have no doubt that you are ready for the hunt," she murmured to him. "Have you brought your own bow, or shall we lend you one?"

"I am no bowman," Hoilogae answered. "But give me a spear, and I shall show you how I may hunt best."

Aiwilimae gestured towards the spear that bore the banner Sigisharjaz had give him. "You have brought a spear with you, and an iron-tipped one at that."

"That spear is hallowed to Wodhanaz's game," Hoilogae replied.

The skis were harder to manage than Hoilogae would have thought, watching the ease with which Aiwilimae and Swaebhon glided ahead of him. As well as the two ski-poles, he had his borrowed spear to manage, and it kept throwing him off-balance. Soon his wolf-cloak was as white as Swaebhon's, furred with snow from several tumbles. The gray hounds frisked about him, delighting in his clumsiness, it seemed to him that they had more mind to play with him than to hunt boar or deer. Hoilogae was half-glad that the Northerners were too used to their ski-skills to look back often, but it still seemed to him as if he sat by the fire again with folk walking about him as if he were only a stock or stone. He would not call Swaebhon back to watch him fall, but though he could see her white shape before him, it seemed as though she were farther than she had been since he first saw her in the clouds. Though he wished to, he did not cry out his weeping rage.

He gripped his ski-poles tighter, tearing through the soft snow and crushing it to ice in his wake. His mind all on his skis, Hoilogae did not mark when the two Northerners had passed from his sight, nor when he might have turned from the path until he looked up, and found that he was alone among the dark trees. Only one of the three dogs was still at his side, and the only ski-tracks in the snow were those stretching back from his own feet. Hoilogae had never learned any art of reading wood-paths, and one way looked much the same as another to him. When he looked up through the pine-branches, he saw only the heavy clouds hanging a little above the tree-tops, he could not tell where the Sun rode behind the thick grayness, nor guess which way north might lie, and in any case, he did not know which way he had come from Aiwilimae's hall. The wisest thing, Hoilogae knew, would be to follow his tracks back. He would never catch up with Swaebhon and Aiwilimae, unless they had turned back for him.

But then he would have to admit that he had lost his way, and that he had not sense enough to follow a clear track, that he was, after all, little more than the witling men had thought him for eighteen winters. The wolf-cloak still thrilled through his nerves, filling him with restless strength. He could not turn his thoughts back to the hall, nor was he willing to turn away from the hunt until he had brought down game worth having. The hound sat on his haunches, looking up at Hoilogae with long pink tongue lolling out. So far north, it seemed to the Jutlander that there was little parting the dogs from wolves. This hound's chest might have been thicker than a wolf's, his legs a little shorter and forehead broader, but if he had not known him for tame, he might never have marked those things. He bent down, rubbing his hand over the thick-furred head.

"You'll lead me to them faster than I could find them by myself, I think," he said to the hound. "Go on, I trust you to show me the way." He clapped his hands sharply.

The dog stood, raising his gray muzzle and sniffing the ice-sharp air. After a few moments, he trotted briskly off between the trees, and Hoilogae followed as best he could. The skis felt easier on his feet now, though it felt strange to be gliding over the snow rather than breaking his way through it as he half-remembered doing, sometime before. The hound lowered his head, swinging it from side to side. Now and again he stopped to snuffle up a little snow as though the spoor he sought lay beneath it, leaving a black earth-scar against the whiteness. It was this that first made Hoilogae doubt that he was finding his way back to Aiwilimae and Swaebhon, but now he was moving more swiftly over the snow, the wind of his going rustling through his fur.

He knew that Swaebhon could not be too far from him, knew it as surely as a wolf who hears another howling in answer, and the thought sped up his skis, as though her arm steadied the balance of his spearless hand. The hound's trot broke into a run, and suddenly Hoilogae was skimming over snow that seemed smooth as ice beneath his skis, a frozen spray of rime-dust winging up from their edges. It seemed to him that he could hear his spear's blade cutting through the air before him as he steered straight between the trees, as though the weapon were drawing him in its wake. He knew that if he struck a stone or root now, he could not break his fall, but the snow grew smoother and thicker as the trees thinned, till Hoilogae and the hound broke through into a clearing where two elk, a wide-antlered bull and a bare-headed cow, stood dark in the snow.

The elk raised their long noses, ears twitching back as their velvety nostrils flared. Hoilogae did not hesitate, but flung his spear straight at the bull elk. The wood-drighten reared back as the weapon sank into his flesh, sharp hooves striking out at the air as if to batter the foe who had pierced him. Slowly the slain elk went to his knees in the snow, head still held high and antlers spreading towards the clouds like two great hands reaching up. The cow turned to run, but Hoilogae's hound was already heading her off, driving her back towards him. Shouting hoarsely, Hoilogae flung himself at her without thought. The blow of her hoof whistled a finger's-breadth from his ear.

Before she could strike again, the hound had her hamstring in his jaws, wrestling her off-balance. The elk's coat was rough against Hoilogae's face, her wet smell heavy around him. He stabbed and stabbed again with the knife in his hand, slashing until a sudden waterfall of hot blood soaked his face and pelt. Hoilogae went down with the elk, it was his luck that she toppled away from him, so that he landed across her. For a moment he heard only his own harsh breaths and the sound of the dog worrying at the elk's sinews. Then the dull knocking of wood on wood came through to his ears. He looked up. Swaebhon and Aiwilimae stood at the edge of the clearing, beating their ski-poles together. Grinning brightly at him, Swaebhon called, "Hail, Hoilogae! You have proved the best of hunters today, for we found no game." She skied swiftly over to him, grasping his bloody hands and pulling him to his feet.

The hood of her cloak had fallen back, so that her long hair tumbled free over her shoulders, the cold had kindled a warm flush of crimson over the high sweep of her cheekbones. Hoilogae held onto her hands, drawing her closer. Her cold lips parted beneath his, so that he tasted the heat of her mouth, he could feel the strength of her body through the soft padding of wolf-fur, and his own strength surging to meet hers. When they broke from each other, Swaebhon's white face and cloak were ruddied with smeared patterns of blood. Aiwilimae's cough grumbled up from deep in his chest, mingling with the harsh calling of the ravens that circled overhead.

Hoilogae turned to face him. "You cannot say that I did not earn that kiss," he said mildly.

"You know little of the huntsman's art," the Northman answered. "No hunter would be fool enough to come so close to an elk, nor to try killing it with only a knife and a hound. I saw how you floundered and stabbed at it, that was no clean kill."

"Leave off teasing him, Father," Swaebhon cried. "You know that you have not seen such bravery since you yourself were a youth, and slew an aurochs with your dagger. If you count Hoilogae as a fool for this, he is not the only fool among us."

Aiwilimae's laugh was a deep rumbling roar, that might have passed for a growl of anger if he had not been grinning so widely. "So, he is not. Now I have a better measure of the man, I think. Look to yourself, anyone would think that you had helped him in the kill, with its blood on you like that." He poled over to a sapling, drawing the small hand-ax at his belt and beginning to chop at it near the roots.

Swaebhon bent to scoop up a handful of snow, scrubbing her face with it until her skin glowed pink and clean. Hoilogae was glad to do the same, stripping away the stiffening blood from his face and hair. The two Northerners worked quickly, chopping saplings and lashing them into a rough framework to drag the elk on. Hoilogae could not help them in that, but he drew the spear from the bull's chest and cleaned it carefully, then sliced open his preys' bellies and dragged out the guts so that the dogs might have their share and leave the rest of the meat alone.

Two of the ravens had settled in one of the tree-tops nearby, a bolder pair were already landing in the clearing, croaking resonantly as they waddled towards the elk. Swaebhon and Aiwilimae hardly spared the birds a look, when Hoilogae tried to shoo them away, they merely flapped out of reach of his lunge and landed a little way from him, as though waiting their share of the elks' entrails. Now and again, Hoilogae glanced sideways at Swaebhon, admiring the smooth swiftness of her movements, the strength and ease of her ax-blows and the deftness with which she tied the leather thongs. It seemed to him that he had never seen anything so fair as the short glittering arcs of her ax's bronze blade, nor so pure as her single-minded gaze as she shifted the branches into their pattern, one atop another.

The pink tip of her tongue poked out of her mouth as she worked, Hoilo-gae could hardly hold himself from going to her and kissing her again. Heav-ing the two carcasses up took the full strength of all three hunters. It was slow and clumsy going back to the hall, and none of them made more sound than a grunt as they dragged the elk behind them, but Swaebhon's hand pressed against Hoilogae's again and again. Between the ridges of callus on her palm, the maiden's skin was soft as a bee's velvety back.

Now and again Hoilogae felt a tight throbbing in his groin as she touched him, such as he had never known before, he could not tell what it might mean, but it seemed to him that it was she who roused it in him and only she who could still it. They laid their burden down outside one of the outbuildings around Aiwilimae's hall, and Swaebhon called several of the thanes out to help with the butchering. The meat had to be cut into strips and set in great clay pots of herb-scented brine, later, Swaebhon said, they would hang it to smoke in the bath-house.

"What do you mean by that?"

"It is too cold for us to wash ourselves outdoors in the winter-time, and so we have long since had another way. But you shall find out about it soon. The bath-house will be hot by sunset, and it will do you good to clean your-self."

Two of Aiwilimae's men stayed outside when they had stripped the elk, picking out the best bones for craft work, the rest went back inside. After the hunt, the hall seemed hotter and smellier than it had before, and even when Swaebhon had taken his cloak away, Hoilogae could still smell the elk's blood growing stale in his hair and clothes. Attalae had gone to sleep on a bench near the fire, as had several of Hoilogae's other men, but Thonar-abernu and Ingwawaldaz were gambling with three of Aiwilimae's thanes as cheerfully as if they were back in Herwawardhaz's lands. Though Hoilogae would not have set the thrall to such work, Ansuthewaz was shoveling dung from a bay stallion's stall, swinging the wooden tool with the strength and speed that must have made him a good warrior once.

Hard as he was working, the thrall kept muffled in his cloak, as though he were still traveling through the snow. When Swaebhon came back into the hall, she bore a heaped platter of bread and smoked fish in one hand, a spin-dle dangled from the other, the distaff under her arm. The flax she spun was pure white, glimmering through the dimness like a swan's wings through cloud, and the thread was fine as a sword's edge.

"Now come and sit beside me, Hoilogae," Swaebhon said after they had eaten. She patted the bench beside herself invitingly. "I have much spinning to do, and it will help me if you wind the distaff. I should like to hear the tale of your battle with Hrothamaraz, as I know my father would as well."

"I have much to do," Aiwilimae grunted, heaving himself from the bench. "The two of you may talk as you please, but the Thing shall be held three days from now, and you may count nothing sure between you till then." He gathered his bear-cloak around himself, stumping over to the horse-stalls. "Hai, thrall, saddle that one and lead him out to me."

Hoilogae held his breath, watching as Ansuthewaz laid down his shovel and did as the drighten bid him without speaking. The thrall kept his head lowered all the while, and Aiwilimae spared him no more than a glance, taking the reins and leading the horse from the hall without looking back.

Swaebhon's gaze had followed Hoilogae's, now she said, "You must be a proud man, to bring a serving-thrall for yourself when you might have had another thane in his place."

"He was a gift given to me on the way, and I could not turn him out, he would not take his freedom, though I offered it to him."

"Then wyrd must have fettered him to his state," Swaebhon answered lightly. "Now tell me of the battle."

It seemed to Hoilogae that he stuttered and stumbled as he spoke, and the more so when her hands lay over his to wind the distaff more easily, but after a little while he found himself used to her closeness, as though he had never been without her. Then his words came smoothly as the shining thread spinning from her hands, and he felt that he had never known such happiness. Sunset came earlier than Hoilogae had thought it would, and he knew that the northlands would be cruelly dark and cold by Yule-time.

He, Attalae, Aiwilimae, Swaebhon, five of his thanes, and five of Aiwili-mae's followed the northern drighten to the farthest of the outbuildings, which stood by a little frozen lake. The setting Sun's red light lay in bloody streaks over the snow-field behind it, as though battle had come and gone there.Cold as it was, Aiwilimae, Swaebhon, and their thanes at once began to undress cheerfully, casting their cloaks and tunics aside into the snow. Clad only in her white shift, Swaebhon paused a moment to laugh at Hoilo-gae's confusion.

"Our thralls will take the dirtied clothes, and those who come to bathe next will bring fresh ones, for you as well. You need not fear to leave your sword here, either, the care of it is the honor of our hall. Now come on, it's too cold to stand out here talking." With that, she stripped off her shift and kicked her shoes from her feet. Hoilogae was struck dumb and still by the fairness of her white body, as though battle-fetter lay over him, awed by the wide curves of her breasts and her cold-tightened nipples, by the long lithe muscles of her legs and arms. Swaebhon was not minded to stand in the snow for him to look at, she slipped swiftly through the bath-house's door behind her father.

"Now I see why Aiwilimae wards his lands so carefully," Hraidhamannaz murmured. "There is a treasure any man would wish for, if she would only look kindly upon him."

"Our drighten's daughter has no care for men, if they be not hunting-companions or willing to fight for her joy," a burly brown-bearded Northman answered him.

"It seems to me that I saw her sitting with her head close to our drighten's all day, and her looks were not unkind to him."

"Soon you'll find what other men have found, and that is likely to be to your cost. Now take your clothes off and get in there so the rest of us can come in as well."

Hoilogae was little surprised that Aiwilimae had brought his men along as a guard, but he stripped quickly and cast his clothes aside as Swaebhon had done, shivering naked in through the dark hut's low door.

The heat gripped Hoilogae's body all at once, sinking in to still his shivering. He breathed deeply, tasting the tang of pine-smoke in the hot air. A heap of stones glowed red between a ring of torches in the middle of the hut. Three rows of tables, each higher than the other, lined the walls, and rough linen mats lay over them. Aiwilimae and Swaebhon were already sprawled out on the highest table across from the door, Swaebhon's slim form and her father's bulk bright through the gloom, at the drighten's right hand was a large clay vessel with the handle of a wooden scoop sticking from it, and another sat at his daughter's side.

"Up here, by me," Swaebhon called to him. "Be careful not to touch the walls or the roof, they are sooty."

Hoilogae climbed over the tables to where Swaebhon and her father lay, stretching himself out beside her as the others came in one by one. Watching him, Swaebhon let a little sigh breathe from her lungs. Hoilogae was as fine to look upon as she could have hoped, she thought. His shoulders and chest were broad with a warrior's strength, and she had seen his might that day, but he was lightly boned and lithe for his height. The muscles of his stomach and thighs stood out beneath his white skin as he moved, his manhood was large and well-shaped, a fit wedding-gift to give her on the holy stone when the day came. Though his hair, still dirty with the elk's blood, hung about his face in snarled troll-tangles, that wildness made him no less fair in Swaebhon's sight.

She longed to clasp him, to draw him to her and feel his strong body against hers, but the time for that was yet to come, and her father and the thanes were already watching them closely enough.

"Let your men stay on the lowest rung," Aiwilimae grunted. Hoilogae raised himself on one elbow, glancing swiftly at the northern drighten. Though the heat had already eased him too much for anger, something of his thoughts must have shown, for Aiwilimae shook his head. "No, I do not mean to make them less by this, but the heat is greatest at the roof, and least at the ground. Swaebhon says that your folk do not have this way, and so it is best for them to have the coolest place at first."

Swaebhon turned, stretching like a lynx beneath Hoilogae's gaze. A fine glaze of sweat already sheened her skin, droplets trickling down the slopes of her breasts. For a moment, Hoilogae felt the strange throbbing in his groin again, but the heat soothed the feeling away almost before he was aware of it. He lay back, content to look at her as she was looking at him. Aiwilimae leaned forward, casting several dippers full of water onto the glowing stones.

A great cloud of steam hissed up, and Hoilogae suddenly felt the heat pressing in on him, choking his throat. He breathed deeply and evenly, and the feeling passed away in a little time. The sweat was starting to run freely down his body now, long trails streaking through the shiny droplets that pearled his grimy skin. Swaebhon lifted her mass of wet hair out from behind her back, draping it over the table-edge behind her, Aiwilimae lay without moving, his eyes heavy-lidded against the sweat pouring down his face.

"Bathing here is finest in the early spring, when the birch-leaves are coming out but the water is still iced," Aiwilimae muttered, soft as if he were talking to himself. "Then we beat each other with the twigs, and that is good for cleaning, and strengthens the heart, and their smell is finer than any-thing else." He cast more water onto the stones, sending up a fresh cloud of steam.

"Bend your head down," Swaebhon said to Hoilogae, taking the dipper out of her clay pot. "I mean to wash your hair, for the elk's blood is still in it." Hoilogae propped himself up on his elbows, arching backwards so that his hair was completely under the warm water. Swaebhon's fingers were gentle as she worked his head clean, soaking out the clots of blood and untangling the snarls, he had not thought to comb his hair on the faring, and no one else had thought to remind him.

After Aiwilimae had thrown water onto the stones several times, Hoilo-gae's men began to twitch and mutter about being boiled alive.

"I could stay in here far longer," Aiwilimae said regretfully, "but these southerners will not know what to do until someone shows them. Come, you two." He clambered off the table, and Hoilogae and Swaebhon followed him to the door, Hoilogae's thanes rising eagerly to their feet behind their leader. "Now, do just as I do, the bath is not done until this is over."

Aiwilimae flung the door open and leapt out with a great shout, plunging full-length into the snow and rolling over and over. Theudorikijaz looked out with his mouth open, shaking his head so that droplets of sweat flew from the wet points of his red curls.

"Come on," Hoilogae whispered to him. "You don't want these Northmen to think we're too weak to do as they do. Do you?" He glanced at Swaebhon. She laughed, poising herself with arms above her head and diving smoothly into the snow as though it were water. Hoilogae followed her with a roar. He gasped as the ice bit into his skin gasped with pleasure almost too keen to bear, spreading out his arms and rolling joyfully in the snow. He could feel the hot blood tingling through his whole body, rushing dizzyingly into his head, though he was lying full-length in the snow, he felt as warm as if fur cloaked him.

When he got to his feet, Hoilogae heard the sound of laughter all around him. More of Aiwilimae's thanes and a few women were standing about with torches in their hands and fresh clothes slung over their arms, stamping their feet against the cold as they waited to strip and hurry into the bath-house. They were laughing at the surprised grimaces of Hoilogae's men as the strangers rolled in the snow, but there was no unkindness in their mirth. A stocky blond woman handed Hoilogae a fresh tunic and shoes of soft elk-hide, giving him his sword-belt when he was dressed. He could not keep himself from drawing the blade a little way from the sheath to be sure of it, but it had been kept as safely as Swaebhon had promised.

Those who had just bathed took the torches and the dirty clothes from those who were going in, hurrying back to the hall before the cold could get its grip on them again. Hoilogae glanced behind him to see how Attalae had fared, but the old rede-giver was right at his shoulder, taking three steps for every two of Hoilogae's. "You don't need to worry about me," Attalae panted when he met Hoilogae's gaze. "I thought I was going to die in there at first, but now I feel like a young man again. Ai, and I'm thirsty, I think I must have sweated every drop from my body."

"You will soon grow used to it, and think there are few things more pleasant," Swaebhon told him as they entered the hall again. "Come over here by the fire, Hoilogae. Yes, you look much finer now that you're clean, I'm sure I do as well. You will have to build me a bath-house when you have taken me south."

"I'm sure that will be no hardship," Hoilogae answered. Now that a pale grey shift clouded Swaebhon's body, he could not help thinking more and more of the firm bowls of her breasts, the ringlets of fine gold between her legs, and the stirrings that the bath-house's heat had soothed from him were rising in him again. He could feel his breath coming more quickly as he looked at her, he knew his face was flushed.

There were several other women in the hall now, some talking as they spun by the fire and some carrying food and drink to the bathers. One of these women put a horn of beer into Hoilogae's hand. He raised it to Swaebhon. "Hail to you, and to our wedding soon." He drank deeply, the cool juniper-scented draught sinking into his throat like rain into thirsty earth.

Swaebhon took the horn from Hoilogae's hand as soon as his lips had parted from it, raising it high. "Hail to you, my hero," she answered, and drank in turn. The smooth rim was warm where his mouth had touched it, warm as the kiss they had shared that day. Swaebhon could not forget that Wodhanaz's gifts all bore a price, nor what that geld would be, but the paying was yet to come, thank the gods, it was yet to come, and would not mar their joy together.

CHAPTER XXII

It was still dark when Sinfjotli shook Hailgi awake. A young man stood beside the Walsing, holding a torch whose light shadowed the long hollow planes of his cheeks, but glittered from the sparse golden hairs on his upper lip and chin. Hailgi needed only a moment to recognize Raginar's sister-son Herwolathar, who had come in late with his fleet last night.

"The water is a little rough, but I see no sign of storms yet," the young sea-king said. "If the weather holds, we shall have a smooth faring towards Sealand." Herwolathar touched the amulet that hung around his neck, a seafarer's Hammer, chip-carved with a design of wyrms woven about one another in a charm to bind the water's rage and hold the wearer safe on the wave. The Hammer itself was a heavy one, made of gold, if Agjiwar's wrath or some witch's spell should overcome the magic of Thonarar's sign, the gold would make sure that Herwolathar got warm welcome when he came to Ran's hall.

Bergohildar and her women were already handing out bowls of porridge thickly mixed with chunks of salt pork and cooked greens, together with horns of small beer. Though her voice was too soft to hear and the fire-shadows hid the movement of her lips, it seemed to Hailgi that his mother murmured beneath her breath over each bowl as she stirred it and gave it to one of his men. The stream of smoke rising through the roof-hole clouded the sky, so he could not tell how soon full dawn would come.

Bergohildar came to her son with Sigismundar's drinking-horn in her left hand and a bowl of porridge in her right. "Now hail to you, Hailgi," she said softly. "Freyjar bless you with battle-boar's might, Wodhanar bring death to your foes, and to you the victory, Tiwar deem the day rightly, and Thonarar hallow it, bringing the gods' blessing to all that passes."

Hailgi took the horn from her hand, raising it so that a stream of froth spilled over the rim, dripping down white from the tip to the hard-packed floor like a rivulet falling from a crag. "Hail to them, and to the mothering Earth who gives at need," he answered, drinking deeply from the horn. Warmth spread out from the draught, running swift through the streams of Hailgi's body, this was not the small beer that his men had surely been given as a morning-drink, but Bergohildar's strongest ale, rich with the sweetness of honey and keen with the herbs she had brewed into it.

"Surely you don't mean for me to be drunk so early, Mother?" Hailgi said, laughing in surprise.

Bergohildar smiled back at him, reaching out to tuck a stray strand of hair back into his warrior-braid. "You should not fare from home without the best I can give you. This is the last of a brew which your father often enjoyed, and no better time for you to drink of it."

"Indeed not, and I thank you, Mother." Hailgi took another deep draught of the ale before he sat down. Cradling the horn against his side to keep it from spilling, he began to eat his porridge. Bergohildar had stirred a thick lump of butter into his portion, he could taste its richness through the hot grain and meat, together with a hint of honey. "You've never sent me off better fed."

"You've never had a mightier battle before you," Bergohildar answered. She lifted her hands, even in the shadows Hailgi could see how her finger-joints were swollen, like oak-galls on slender birch-twigs. "Beware of the sea today, Hailgi. Although the stars are clear this morning, I can feel the storm in my joints, this is more than the pain of weaving too long."

"You should not be working this morning, if your hands hurt you," Hailgi answered. "Sit by me and rest."

Bergohildar settled down beside her son, but rose again before Hailgi had finished the last of his porridge. "I must send food out to Herwolathar's men. If they did not come onto shore last night, they will be glad of something hot to wake them, I think."

Hailgi scraped a few more mouthfuls from the bottom of his bowl, washing his mouth clear with a draught of ale. More men were coming into the hall, weapons at their belts and bags of gear slung over their backs.

"Time to roust the last of our sleepers," Herwolathar said to Hailgi. "Come with me?"

Horn still in his hand, drinking carefully as he walked, Hailgi followed the young sea-king out and down to the shore. The sky was beginning to lighten in the east, the war-ships dark against the growing brightness, sails and wyrm-prows down, awnings raised over the sleeping men, they seemed like the shadows of great sea-birds bobbing on the water with wings folded and heads tucked for sleep. Here and there, the white heads of waves rose and fell in the sound. Hailgi and Herwolathar walked quietly to the row of small boats that lay high on the shore, pale arcs of sand flying out of their strap-shoes and more pouring in through the open leather work with each step. Together they dragged two of the boats to the water's edge, struggling through the soft sand that weighted their feet until they reached the firmer ground of the waves' wet wake. Herwolathar gestured Hailgi into his boat first, hauling it out till Hailgi's oars caught the water and it floated free of the shore.

Dragging his own craft into the waves, Raginar's kinsman leapt easily in and caught up the oars in a single swift movement, pulling towards the nearest of the warships. Hailgi's boat seemed to fight him, bucking beneath him like an unbridled steed, he was better used to riding than rowing, and hardly used to these little shore-craft at all. It seemed to him that he could feel the depths dragging at him, and something seemed ill to him in the greed of the waters tugging at his boat. But this is only because I am seldom on the sea, Hailgi thought.

I wish that Sinfjotli were here with me, he spoke of steering the brine-mare. Then it seemed to him that he could see the horse-rune, ehwaz, that Sinfjotli had traced upon Wigiblajar. What harm can it do to try? Hailgi thought. Letting the oars rest beneath his arms a moment, he leaned forward and traced the same rune upon the prow of the boat, murmuring its name beneath his breath. The rocking and plunging of the little craft did not cease, nor did it move more easily through the rough water, but it seemed to Hailgi that now he was moving with it, his oars treading through the waves' tugging and tossing like a horse's sure feet stepping through a tangle of boulders and brush. By the time Herwolathar looked back, Hailgi had already caught up with him, so that the two flanked the stem of the first warship. They each caught one of the ropes that dangled down from the heavy woolen awning, holding tight as they rowed along the ship's sides and peeled back its covering as if stripping the hide from a dead horse.

Sunna was halfway up the sky by the time all the ships were loaded and ready to cast off. Most of the warriors' gear had been tucked tightly away with the awnings and tent-covers lashed down over it to keep the worst of the spray off, they had stowed a good portion of food and drink as well, for it might be a day's full faring to the haven where they meant to land, and there was no knowing what they would find when they got there. A stiff breeze tugged at the sails, whipping the waves up higher so that the boats bucked against their anchors, struggling to cross the border between the pale blue-green waters close to shore and the dark blue-gray a little farther out where the sound's sandy bottom sheered suddenly down, an underwater cliff-edge dropping to the depths. From the bridge of his own flagship where he stood beside Sinfjotli, Hailgi marked how Herwolathar glanced up at the sky, but the wind-bridge was blindingly clear, blue-bright as its own reflection in a silver mirror, and Sunna's light was the gold-white of worn gilt, shattering into thousands of glimmers over the froth-capped waves.

"A fair day for faring," the Walsing said cheerfully. "Are we ready to lift anchor yet?"

Hailgi looked at the ships about him, their bright-checked sails lifting in the wind. Most showed the red war-shields in rows along their sides, many were decked with gold or silver, or had their keels carved with rows of twisting beasts whose silver ring-eyes shone from the darkened wood. Herwolathar's banner had a flint thunder-ax mounted at the top of the pole, above the flag embroidered with a red gull that fluttered beneath, Freyjawulfar's standard was a gold-adorned oaken boar, while Raginar's iron-bound flag was wrought with an eagle, and Hrothormar and his berserks fared beneath the sign of Wodhanar's Raven. Now the time had come for Hailgi to raise his own standard. The pole that leaned against the mast was topped with the wooden image of a snarling wolf's head, the sign of the Wolfing line, but beneath it the banner Hailgi's mother had woven for him was wound around the stave.

Sinfjotli had carved an inscription into the wood for him, 'I SINFJOTLI WALSING RISTED RUNES FOR HAILGI WOLFING', with the thrice-written bindrune 'GA, for GIBU AUJA, "I give luck" .' Hailgi saw that the other drightens were watching him, that men stood with their hands on the anchor-ropes, ready to free their ships as soon as he gave the sign.

He breathed in deeply, the cold salt wind thrumming through his lungs and singing in his skull. It seemed that he could feel the might of all the men surging up behind him, that he stood at the tip of a great spear poised to fly straight and swift across the waters. Hailgi lifted Sigismundar's war-horn to his mouth, and Sinfjotli heaved up the anchor as the Wolfing let the first blast howl deep over the waves.

Their ship leapt ahead of the others, cleaving a frothy furrow through the waves as it skimmed before the driving wind, the crashing of the water against the hull blended with the clashing of shield against shield along the ship's sides as the warriors raised their shout. "Hailgi!"

With the horn's next note, Sinfjotli unfurled Hailgi's banner and lifted it high. The six-rayed star-sign- the holy sign of Hailgi's name, shone white within its red hex on a blue-black field, bright as lightning across the night sky. Hailgi waited for him to fix the standard's stave into its socket at the ship's stem, then blew the third blast as the Walsing raised the war-ship's beast-head, half-wyrm, half-horse, with a rust-red mane of iron spirals curling down its long neck, and heaved it into place, the fierce circles of its red eyes staring out to the open sea. Sinfjotli slid two wooden bolts home, locking the wyrm-prow into its stead.

Hailgi heard the answering horns behind him, and turned to see the other ships, rank by rank, pulling free of the sound's depths and lifting their heads to the wind that bore them along. He did not look long at the shore behind him, the pale rim of sand before the low silver-green hills that darkened to thick beech-woods at the fields' edges and the brown-gold thatch of the farmers' houses. Instead he turned his gaze towards the sea, thinking, I shall not look upon my home-shore again until Sigiruna stands beside me.

"A brave boast," Skald-Thonarabrandar murmured, "but is it wise to speak so before weathering all the storms?"

Hailgi started, he had not known he was speaking. "Do you see storms ahead?"

"I need not be a spae-man to know that we will soon weather the Grim One's hail and the rain of the walkurjas, or that Hildar's storm will soon rattle on the shingles of Walhall's roof, and that it takes both strength and luck for the helm-ash to stand before Wodhanar's winds." Skald-Thonarabrandar laughed. "I have the word-gems, but not the gold to set them in this day, perhaps it is I who am fey for this battle."

"Do not speak so!" Hailgi told him sharply. "As you say, it will be struggle enough without us daring Wyrd to do her worst."

A seagull cried sharply above them, the wind flinging its white-winged shape out before the ships' billowing sails like a little cloud flying before the storm. It was far ahead of them before Hailgi could blink.

"Still, we are not going so slowly ourselves," Sinfjotli said, and Hailgi realized that he had been watching the bird as well. The Walsing sat down on the deck, untying the straps of his shoes and taking them off so that he could brush the caked sand from his feet.

"No." Hailgi looked up to the wind-scoured sky again. The gull was out of sight now, but behind them, where the glittering water already hid the shore, he could see the streaks of pale cloud stretching long swan-necks out over the bright heavens. "Mother warned me that a storm was coming," he murmured absently.

"What?" Sinfjotli knocked his shoes against the deck, shaking a few clumps of wet sand out of the toes. The Walsing brushed the grains over the planking with a wide sweep of his hand, then tied the shoe-straps together and hung them about his neck. "Better to be barefooted on board ship," he commented, straightening up. "It helps you keep your balance...so" Suddenly he leapt up, landing on the hull's narrow edge. Knees flexed, gripping the wood with his toes, Sinfjotli swayed easily with the pitching and rolling of the ship. He grinned down at Hailgi. "Come on, you can do this too, can't you?"

Hailgi swore under his breath, but he would not back down before the Walsing. He took off his own shoes and hung them about his neck, hoping that the gilded spur-spikes fixed in their heels wouldn't cut his throat when he fell. For a moment he balanced himself with one hand against the side, swaying with the boat's rhythm, then sprang up to the narrow ridge of wood within grabbing reach of Sinfjotli. If I fall, Hailgi thought, he's coming down with me. To his surprise, Hailgi found himself balancing easily on the swaying hull-edge, moving with the waves beneath the boat, he felt as though he were dancing, for all his feet were still. There was something dizzying about swaying between water and wind with the tossing wood beneath him, a kind of clear-headed drunkenness that had him laughing as he tipped his head back to stare at the rushing sky, the gray-winged clouds flying over the Sun.

One wave, higher than the rest, broke over the ship's bow, its spray showering cold over Hailgi to shatter his daze. The wood beneath his feet lurched, he was barely able to turn his fall into a leap, landing flat-footed on the deck. Sharp splinters of shock drove up his calves, but now he could hear Herwolathar shouting.

The young sea-king had steered his flagship over near to Hailgi's, and was shouting, "Reef sails and row for shore!"

Sinfjotli had walked along the hull's edge, now he was standing between the prow and Hailgi's standard with a hand braced on each, his hair whipping forward like blond wings beating about his face. If he heard Herwolathar, he gave no sign of it, but Herwolathar gestured back at the purple-gray storm clouds rising behind them like misted cliffs of black stone. He had taken the gold Hammer from his neck, it flashed in his hand like a weapon. "We can't sail in that! Turn back!"

Red lightning flashed jagged across the darkening cloud bank behind the fleet, long tatters of pale mist shrouded the sky above and ahead of them, dimming Sunna's light. Hailgi counted thirteen heartbeats before the low thunder rumbled across the sea, shaking the sails with the strengthening wind. The waves were breaking higher and higher along the ships' sides, their salty spray spattering into Hailgi's mouth like rime-cold blood. He felt the wod rising within him as the deck leapt and plunged like an unbroken stallion beneath his feet, the lightning flashed blue-white through the black avalanche of clouds tumbling down towards them. "I will not!" He shouted, raising his hands towards the sky as if to grasp the fleeting streak of brightness. "We must fare onward!"

With his last words, a wave leapt tall over the bow, spraying cold froth into his face as the ship's nose dug hard into the sea. Now Hailgi knew what he had felt. It was not the storm wind they had to fear, but the sea who wished to drag them down, the daughters of Agwijar and Ran calling living men to their cold water-bed. "Sails higher!" He cried, hoping that his men could hear him over the crashing waves. Skald-Thonarbrandar skidded over the wet deck to help Ingwawulfar haul on the ropes, the thin warrior's face was milk-white beneath the lowering greenish light of the storm, his arm-sinews standing out like knife-edges as he wrestled with the sail. Hailgi could feel the wind pulling them upward as the waves rose to crash over the sides of the boat, tilting the deck back and forth till Hailgi could no longer stand upright, but had to cling to the prow. Blinking the burning salt from his eyes again and again, he looked back to see how his men fared.

Skald-Thonarabrandar and Ingwawulfar held to the mast together like
lovers, the rest clutched to the sides, holding tight for their lives, their faces
corpse-pale. Only Sinfjotli showed no sign of fear, but he was no longer
laughing, he held to the boat's side with one hand, bending to bail with the
other. Skegga-Grimar opened his mouth, body heaving as he spewed an
arc of vomit out over his beard, it stained the deck for a heartbeat before
another wave broke over the side, washing the pale planks clean again. The
lightning flickered more brightly, thunder speaking deep between the crashing of the waves and the screaming of the wind about the mast. Hailgi could
see the waves rising higher, tossing great sprays of white foam about.

The etin-maids shaking their hair. The ship tilted back, stem out of the
water, for a moment Hailgi thought that it would tumble backwards, but the
wind caught it and slammed it down, a mast-high tower of foam springing
up. The lightning flashed white overhead, bone-shaking thunder crashing
in the burst of its afterimage. Blinking the light from his blinded eyes, it
seemed to Hailgi that he saw a woman's shape in the spray, reaching out
towards his sail, and that the wind blew her grasping arm back. Now and
again, Hailgi caught sight of the rest of the fleet through the driving rain as
the waves flung them about, great water-cliffs rising and falling between the
boats. A bolt of lightning lit the spray, the cloud of drops around them burning blue-white for a heartbeat as the thunder shook the ships.

In its brightness, Hailgi saw Raginar's eagle-sign black against its white
field, its wings flaring to blind him as the next bolt shattered the standard's
iron-shod pole. A wave rose between them, higher than the mast, twisting
in the wind to fling a long white cape over Hailgi's ship as it broke far above
his head. The wall of water smashed down on him, its mighty grasp nearly
tearing him away from the prow. His ears rang from the blow, high shrieks of
cruel laughter howling through his head as another great fist of water struck
him, knocking one arm loose from the figurehead. Hailgi scrabbled against
the deck, barely getting his grip again before the next wave could rip him
away from the wood and over the side. Cold fire flickered blue and gold over
the mast, the same corpse-light burned on Hailgi's standard, the wolf's head
shimmering like a marsh ghost beneath the storm-flames that ate no wood.

The wet hairs prickled up on Hailgi's arms, he felt that his hide might
spark like amber-rubbed fur, answering the lightning that leapt about the
ships. Gasping a mouthful of water and wind, Hailgi stared up past the
lightless burning mast and the white shapes of spray that danced higher and
higher between the boats, up at the lightning-torn sky. The bolts followed
without a breath between them, the ceaseless booming of thunder dulled
by the water filling his ears. Dazzled as his salt-burning eyes were, he saw
clearly through the lightning and the seething darkness, saw the hooves of
the gray horses churning the clouds, the sparks flying from the spears of the
nine women riding aloft over the waves, and Hailgi kenned Sigiruna again.
Her cloud-gray helm hid her face, but the fair hair streamed long beneath
its rim, and the lightning glinted from her byrnie like sunlight on silver. Her
spear hissed down, a great wave falling back as its shining length struck into
the water.

The sea roared around Hailgi, its voices all howling together through the thunder, he could make out no words, but their wrath shook through his bones. A huge swell flung his ship upward, it seemed that they flew for a moment, then she crashed down, water rushing over the sides as if they had been stoven in all at once. The boat wallowed downward. Hailgi could feel the sea's strength grabbing at his thighs, and gasped as deeply as he could, knowing he might not taste air again. The wind's slap was hard as a shield-strike, catching the sail again and heeling the ship over to starboard, but when she righted, the water was no deeper than Hailgi's ankles.

Hailgi's body was numb with the cold of water and wind, he could not feel the wooden scales of the beast-prow beneath his hands, nor the grip of his arms about its neck, nor the planks beneath his bare feet. It seemed to him as though he were no longer there, as though he watched the tossing ship from somewhere still between the struggle of sea and sky. Sigiruna's shield was white as a swan's wing, sweeping down between his ship and the towering wave whose watery arms stretched out to embrace him, the track of her spear seared his eyes as she beat the sea-etins back again and again. Beyond her, Hailgi could see the ghost-gray shapes of the other battle-maids in flashes through the rain, but she alone shone bright to his gaze, white-clad and fair as Sunna's light through the storm.

Hailgi did not think of what he did, nor of his life, but he had let go of the wyrm-prow and stood on the plunging deck with head and hands raised towards Sigiruna. It seemed to him that he could feel his might pouring into her, hers into him, their life-tides flowing full as they blended together, that the lightning brightened a rainbow-glimmering bridge through the storm between them. Her spear screamed down to the water again as the deck tilted and he fell, its thunderclap struck hard and wooden against Hailgi's body, knocking the breath from him. Leaning on the side of the boat, Hailgi struggled to his feet. The water filling his mouth at his next breath was sweet, not salt, rain beating down the spray as the swells sank beneath the wind that still blew the ships along their path. Overhead, the clouds were breaking up, shifting veils of late afternoon sunlight slanting low through the thinning rain. Tears washing the seawater from his salt-scoured eyes, Hailgi scanned the sky, but Sigiruna and her maids were gone.

One by one, Hailgi's men let go of their holds and stretched cramped muscles or bent to bail the last of the water out of the ship. Hailgi scanned them swiftly. Skald-Thonarabrandar and Ingwawulfar, Sinfjotli, Helmbernu, Thonarabrandar Odd-Eyes, Skegga-Grimar and Bow-Athalwulfar, they, and the rest of the men who had sailed with him, were all there. Hailgi could see the other ships now, the nearer ones clear and the farther ones gray shadows behind the scatters of drizzling rain. He unslung his father's war-horn from his side and raised it to his mouth, blowing three long blasts and waiting for the answers. There was Raginar's horn, though his standard was shattered, his ship was still whole. There sounded Freyjawulfar's no aurochs horn, but an ancient coil of bronze, whose years no one could tell. Hrothormar Bear-Sark had no horn, the shout of the berserks came from his ship.

One by one, Hailgi tallied the blasts, and let his breath out in a long sigh of relief when the last had sounded. Not one craft had foundered in the storm.

"I never heard of such luck," Skegga-Grimar said quietly. "The idises who favor you must be mightier than any." The skin that showed about the edges of the warrior's huge beard was still porridge-pasty and his legs seemed to buckle with each step, but he made his way across the deck towards Hailgi.

Skegga-Grimar reached out towards his drighten, Hailgi took his thane's water-wrinkled hands in his own, holding them till he could feel the warm blood surging back into them. "I was not out here alone."

"We would not have come through without you," Skegga-Grimar insisted firmly, and Hailgi was wise enough to say no more.

"Hai, that was a ride worth having," Sinfjotli spoke up brightly. "I would have come for this alone."

Hailgi did not miss the way Ingwawulfar's black brows lowered, his little eyes glowering up at the Walsing like an old boar's. "Why did you come?" The thane muttered deep in his throat. "Do you think Hailgi Hund-ing's-Bane needs you by his side? To stand in his father's place, perhaps?"

The two Thonarabrandars and Arnugrimar moved closer to him, as if to brace their shoulders with his in a living shield-wall. Sinfjotli looked down at them, lip curling back to show the white sheen of his teeth.

Before the Walsing could answer, Hailgi broke in, "Though Sinfjotli was not one of this band when we fought Hunding's sons, and will not be one of us for long, he is my kinsman, of whom I have few enough. You must not begrudge me his company for this summer before he fares to his father's hall again, for back without brother is bare, and his friendship is worth more than a little to me." Hailgi held Ingwawulfar's dark gaze with his own until the set of the thane's thick shoulders eased, then turned to Thonarbrandar Odd-Eyes.

"Do you think you could pry out something to eat and drink? I'm starving, myself." He had spoken to loose the man's anger, not because he was hungry, but once the words were out of his mouth he realized how empty he was, hungry enough to feel dizzy and weak, though he did not dare to show it now.

Odd-Eyes grinned. "Could do with some food myself. Funny, when we started out I thought I'd never eat again." He crouched by the heap of gear, prying at the knots of the wet ropes with the point of his belt-knife.

Herwolathar's red gull-flag fluttered out as the sea-king's ship tacked across towards Hailgi's. Hailgi could see Herwolathar gesturing towards the low cloud-bank before them, but not hear his words.

"What?" He shouted.

"Sealand, I said!" Herwolathar called back. "We'll make harbor soon!"

Though Sunna was setting, the sky was still light as day when Herwolathar's ship guided the rest towards the gentle crescent of Una Bay. The border between pale sands and green fields was dark with men, their byrnies and spear-points shining dully in the evening brightness. Behind them rose the silhouettes of crossed tent-posts carved with the heads of beasts, Hailgi guessed it likely that the watchers had been camped there since whenever the Skjoldings had learned that he was gathering his host.

Skegga-Grimar rasped his fingers through the huge tangle of his beard, staring at the men drawn up there. "I guess making land safely tonight was too much to hope for." He looked up at Hailgi. "Is it given to us to fight tonight, or shall we wait in the harbor till morning?"

Hailgi looked up at the sky, breathing deeply. It seemed to him that a great still note rang through the pale blue of the ancient etin's high skull-bowl, stilling the Wolfing's limbs as he gazed west to the pinkish light seeping into the sky like blood into clear seawater. "There shall be no blade-play tonight. Dawn will be early enough tomorrow, when our strength has come back to us."

"I won't speak ill of that," Ingwawulfar agreed.

"Drop anchors!" Hailgi called out to the other ships. "We'll rest here tonight."

"Wisely chosen!" Freyjawulfar shouted back, as the other drightens set their men to dropping anchors.

Hailgi did not have to say anything to his men. Ingwawulfar and Arnugrimar bent down at once, heaving at the heavy iron weight. Sinfjotli, however, though he seldom held back when he might show his strength, only stood gazing thoughtfully at the shore as the others lifted the anchor to the boat's rim and pushed it over to splash into the water.

After a few moments, the Walsing turned towards Hailgi. "There is one there who is clad as a high atheling, with a broad gold ring on the hilt of his sword and a fair gilded dragon-head for the nose-piece of his helm. Little though I know of horses, it seems to me that he is mounted on a fine one, there, you see, beside that little river? I am minded to call to him, to see what manner of man he is and whether his soul may be lessened with strong words or words of nithing, it seems to me that this would make landing easier."

Hailgi thought on this a moment, but before he could speak he saw that the man Sinfjotli had pointed out was riding forward to the water's edge, till each rising wavelet foamed a little higher around his bay's hocks. A proud man, to ride an uncut stallion, Hailgi thought, perhaps too proud for his own good, Sinfjotli might have judged him well.

The atheling's keen tenor voice swept easily over the quiet water. "Who is the land-ruler that steers the host, and has brought this great host to land? I am Gunthamundar the son of Granamarar, I am of good kin."

Sinfjotli swept Hailgi's crimson shield up from its place on the ship's side, lifting it high. The gilded rim and the two golden eagles that flanked the shield-boss gleamed brightly in the evening light. "You will be able to say this evening when you tie up your bitches and give the swine their swill, that it is the Wolfings who have come out of the east, girded for war, to Gnipa Grove. I, Sinfjotli, say that Hadubroddar shall find Hailgi here, a leader too strong to flee, in the fleet's middle. He who has often sated eagles while you kissed bond maids by the quern!"

Though the helm's bright brow-ridges and nose-piece hid Gunthamundar's face above his broad brown mustache, Hailgi could see the warrior's thick shoulders bunching with rage. His stallion danced a step sideways, as though his glittering spurs had nicked its sides. "You remember few old tales, if you speak thus about athelings!" He shouted. "You have eaten wolves' carrion and been the bane of your brothers, you sucked wounds with a cold mouth, and hid in a cave, loathsome to everyone."

The flush rose into Sinfjotli's high cheekbones like sunset's red glowing on snowy mountain peaks, and his free hand gripped the side of the ship so hard that Hailgi heard the wood creak. "You were the most harmful scathe-walkurja, grim and ill-willed, with All-Father. Wodan's champions all had to battle for your sake, false woman. You were a seeress in Warin's Isle, betrayal-wise woman, bringing lies together. You said that you would have no man, no byrnie-clad warrior, except Sinfjotli! We got nine wolves on Saga Ness. I alone was the father."

Gunthamundar thrust his thumb through his clenched fist, shoving it towards Sinfjotli. "You were no father to Fenrir-wolves, though older than all of them. As I remember, you were gelded by thurse-maids on Thonar's Ness, before Gnipa Grove. You were Sigigairar's step-child, and lay beneath rocks where you had your home, used to wolf-songs out in the woods. Ill deeds came aye to your hand, when you ripped the breast of your brother, making yourself known by shameful works. You were a stallion's bride on the bright field, gold-bridled, ready to race. I spurred you downhill on a great course, slender under saddle, cow."

Sinfjotli raised his right hand, shaping a sign in the air. It seemed to Hailgi that he could see a lightless wake of red where the Walsing's fist moved, so that the thurse-rune, burned red in his hidden sight for a moment. "You seemed an uncouth fellow to me when you milked Gullnir's goats, a tattered troll-queen another time, Imdhar's daughter! Will you trade taunts longer?"

Gunthamundar drew his sword, slashing it in a double figure about his head so that the edges caught the fading evening light. "I would first sate the ravens on your corpse-meat at Freki Stone, before I ever tied up bitches or gave swine their swill. May the trolls deal with you. I have heard that the Walsings were ever half troll-kin, how else could a brother get a son on his sister, unless she were shameless as a troll-queen?"

Hailgi saw the shadows gathering around Sinfjotli's head, as though his shape were becoming more and more wolfish, he heard the Walsing's snarl, and swiftly put a hand on Sinfjotli's arm, speaking so that Gunthamundar could hear his voice as well. "Sinfjotli, it would be more fitting for you to fight in battle and to gladden the eagles than to brandish these needless words, though the ring-breakers share in the feud. I await no good from the sons of Granamarar, but it befits drightens' kin to speak the truth.

They battled well at Moinsheimar, and brandished swords with strong souls." He turned towards the shore and shouted to Gunthamundar. "Go now and tell Hadubroddar and Haganon that Hailgi Hunding's-Bane is come, to claim Sigiruna as his bride. If they will not give the maid over to me, then the hosts shall do battle, and those of your kin who are not slain in fight shall be bound for Fetter-Grove gifts to Wodhanar all, serving as his wish-maid's bride-price."

"Sigiruna shall be wedded to none but Hadubroddar," Gunthamundar called back. "Though the hope of marriage gladdens her little, far less does she list to lend her skirts to you, whoever you may have slain. I see now why you have come here. You and she are near enough of a size to trade clothes!"

If Gunthamundar's words went on, or his men laughed, the roaring in Hailgi's ears drowned the sound out. He did not feel the hard planking beneath his feet, the distance between ship and shore seemed to blur till nothing but the gilded dragon-beak above Gunthamundar's moving lips shone in his sight. Now it was Sinfjotli who grasped Hailgi's arm, the Walsing's hard hand dragging the young drighten back from the side of the boat where he would have leapt over.

"Wodan's noose will choke the words from your throat quickly enough," the Walsing called out. "Fetch the rest of the host, or stay to face us yourself if you dare. the day's light shall show you your death!"

The echo of Gunthamundar's laugh seemed to last for a long time. At last Granamarir's son turned his horse and rode back through the line of warriors that guarded the shore.

"I should sorrow little at taking that man to Fetter-Grove, if Wodhanar shapes it so," Thonarbrandar Odd-Eyes said, to which Skald-Thonarbrandar answered,

"Many with their mouths fart,
men with tiny seed-sacks,
that one's leek is lacking
length beyond a flea's thumb.
Short was Freyjar's sight there,
saw those cheeks as fart-mounds,
placed man-tong in tongue-stead,
toolless left bairn-smithy."

The harsh laughter of Hailgi's men rose over the rustlings and muttering from the shore. "That's good!" Arnugrimar shouted. "Say it again, louder, so everyone can hear!"

Skald-Thonarbrandar grinned and raised his voice, speaking the stave again. By the time he had finished the fourth line, Hailgi saw a tall black-bearded warrior raising his spear, the weapon was ripping the air before the fifth was full-spoken.

Lithe as a dancer for all his size, Sinfjotli leapt in front of Skald-Thonarbrandar and caught the spear in flight, flipping it over in his hand and casting it back in a single heartbeat. It flew over the head of the man who had first flung it, sinking deep into one of the warriors behind him, Hailgi heard the grunt of pain as the man went down, hidden behind the others who stood there.

"We know well what is fitting," called Sinfjotli. "We can give a gift for a gift as well as any!" No one answered from the shore, and it seemed to Hailgi that his feat must have taken the mood to taunt from them.

Bow-Athalwulfar had the cover off his weapon and was bending the bowstave to string it, Hailgi shook his head. "This would be an ill time to give them the thought of trading shots. Indeed," he went on, half-musing to himself, "it might be well for us to move back out of arrow range, they are sure to begin shooting as soon as it is light enough tomorrow." He gave the order, waving the other ships as close as they could come so that he could talk with the other drightens without the men on shore hearing every word.

Although Hailgi was leading the host, he knew that he knew little about fighting up from water to land, and saw that the older drightens, too, were looking at the young sea-king Herwolathar as though they would not scorn his rede for his youth.

"No one chooses to fight from the sea against a ready foe, but the Norns shape as they will," Herwolathar said as soon as all the ships' leaders had gathered at the nearest edges of their boats. He was murmuring, almost whispering, no one there, Hailgi thought, would know better than he how easily a voice could float over the water. "The slope to the beach looks short here, but steep. And we have luck in this. It drops off like a cliff just a little beyond where we were anchored, so we can bring our ships in close enough that we can jump from their prows into waist-high water. Best to come in with the ships as fast as we can at first light, and wade in to shore with shields up. I've heard that you shaped the swine-wedge in the fight against the sons of Hundingsomeone among you has learned Wodhanar's battle-wisdom?"

"We've shaped the swine-wedge before, and more often than that one time," Hrothormar Bear-Sark grunted. "My men and I are not strange to its point, though Sigihelmar, who most often came in the front rank, fell in the last battle. Still, it seems to me that Sinfjotli the Walsing could take his place and our strength be none the littler for his help, nor the number of berserks less."

"So. I would say gather into the swine-wedge if you can, and hit them with it at a good pace. If the arrow-fire from shore isn't too heavy, the rest of us may be able to lock into a shield-wall. It's likeliest that they will have already raised their own shield-burg, they'd be fools not to, since they can hold their ground and we must come to them, but your swine-wedge should break it if anything can." The sea-king's blue eyes flickered up to Sinfjotli, who stood quietly at Hailgi's side.

"Sinfjotli and I shall go at its tip," Hailgi said quickly. "That is the most fitting place for us."

"Well enough. What do you ween shall happen when we have reached the land? I do not think we see their full host drawn up there, it is likely that we shall be outnumbered by a few, once the rest have gotten here."

"Then we shall fight as we can, and trust to our idises and Wodhanar's deeming," Hailgi answered. "Does anyone here know how far Haganon's burg stands from the shore?"

"It is some five or six leagues," replied Freyjawulfar. "Somewhat less than half a day's march beyond the beach are several large hills, around the meadow where Freki Stone stands. They are likely to wait till we have gotten onto that field, and come at us from the hills then. Past that is Haganon's burg. It is said to be strongly fenced, though, he is a wary man, who did not ween that his men would always be strong enough to keep a foe from his walls."

Theudowinar nodded. "I have heard this as well. If any of them escape when we win past Freki Stone, or if they have left a last guard there, we are likely to have yet a third battle before we can break through to the hall. Haganon's sons Bragi and Dagar are yet young, so I would be little surprised if Haganon chose to leave the hall in their keeping with a small band rather than bringing them to the field."

"Aye," Freyjawulfar murmured. "I have heard somewhat of Dagar as well. He shows less promise as a warrior than the others of his kin, if more than most youths. But it is said that, young as he is, he kens herblore and healings as well as any wise woman or spae-man, for he learned the skill from his mother, who was said to be the most herb-crafty frowe in men's memory. If he should live through the day, he must be watched carefully, for he could do us either much help or great harm."

Raginar's eyes narrowed as he looked towards the shore, folding one arm across his paunch as his other hand tugged thoughtfully on one of his blond beard-braids. "And I guess there can be no thought of burning the hall, with your prize inside, Hailgi?"

Hailgi nodded firmly. "There cannot."

Freyjawulfar laughed dryly. "It is said, 'do not praise a woman till she is burned'."

"You have little wit if you mock at this," murmured Sinfjotli, but his voice was so quiet that Hailgi thought no one but himself heard it. "No matter what, we shall not see Sigiruna burned while Hailgi or I live. And I am sure there is wealth worth having in Haganon's burg, which shall be worth a little more work."

"Still," Theudowinar mused, his dark eyes fixed calmly on Hailgi, "it seems to me that we are leaving rather more to blessing and luck than is usually the way of wise men."

Overhearing his words, Skegga-Grimar came to the boat's side and leaned over. "Usually, yes. Have we not already seen what blessing and luck follow Hailgi? I would place no greater trust in any drighten in the Middle-Garth, it seems to me that we have already won through a worse battle beneath him this day."

Raginar coughed, Hrothormar Bear-Sark waved a heavy hand. "The same thought is in my mind, but Wodhanar has little care for those who let their wits grow weak under his blessing. Our way is not shaped so as to smooth the path of the attacker, and by that it seems to me that the land-wights will be loath to let us pass as well, for this has long been the home of the Skjolding line. I fear to count this as an easy way, for Wodhanar should not battle Freyjar on his own land."

The tents and the low hills beyond had sunken to shadows in the fading light. Here and there, Hailgi could see the fires springing up, three of them seemed to burn in a triangle around his ship's maned wyrm-prow, silhouetting it black against the far-off flames.

"I have heard that Freyjar does not make maids to weep, nor any man's wife, and that he looses the fetters from all. His might surely will not be raised for this ill marriage. But let us take the prows from our ships and bear them with us. If we have not time to befriend the land-wights, and that seems little likely to me as well, since the Skjoldings have surely been their friends since early days we must strike fear into them. Though that is no fair deed and I am loath to bring harm to the land, the friends of our foes must be our foes for now. If we must pay for it with cattle and swine afterwards, well, cattle and swine must be slain for our feasting in any case, and the Skjoldings will surely have herds large enough that we need not begrudge the hidden folk their meat as geld for the harm we have done them and a gift for friendship afterwards. It is true that I may mean to bring Sigiruna to my home, and never while here, yet I would not be known as Land-Waster, whether the folk be friends or foes."

"That is well-spoken," Freyjawulfar approved. "It seems that you may yet become a worthy fro for your lands, as well as a battle-drighten."

"Though the sea has little love for him," Herwolathar said. He laughed, but his cracked thumb-nail brushed swiftly over the ridges of the gold Hammer at his neck. "I know that Ran's daughters do not take well to being scorned, it is in my mind that a gift to them and to the Awesome One would not go far astray."

"It would not," Hailgi agreed. Though the shore's humped outline was wholly dark now, the last light from the sky still shone blue off the still sea around them, brightening to white in the trail stretching from the half-full Moon, a lightning-line of blue brightness cutting through the shore's black curve where the little river ran. "Dawn shall come early, if no one has better plans than we have made, we may as well sleep."

Hailgi looked around at the faces of the other drightens, shadowy in the darkening twilight. None of them spoke until Raginar turned away, saying, "Sleep well, then."

They did not draw up the awnings that evening, the night was warm, with no wind, and they meant to waken as soon as the light changed. Though Hailgi's limbs dropped easily into his blankets and his body ached from the day's struggle, sleep did not come to him. He knew that most of the men around him would be dead by Sunna's next setting, that this still blue night would be short, and the day very long and dark. Now that no wod bore him up, he had little joy in the thought of wading through Wodhanar's bloody harvest another time. He did not have to think to recall the feeling of living entrails beneath his feet, the sound of Athalwulfar's voice crying, 'It hurts, Hailgi, it hurts!' Or the stink of onions mixed with shit and fever-rot from Ansugairar's belly-wound.

"Yet it will be different when we have begun," he murmured to himself. Though now the memories chilled his heart, he knew that when the Wolfing blood roused in him, nothing would stay his fierceness.

"What will be?" Sinfjotli's voice asked drowsily from the roll of blankets beside Hailgi.

"I'm only mumbling. Go back to sleep."

For the sake of a woman? Hailgi asked himself. So many lives, that I may have my bride? He rolled over uneasily, wriggling until the Moon's light no longer shone straight into his face.

More than that, surely. Wodhanar never wreaks without a reason, and he makes his choices long before sending his walkurjas onto the field. It was his might I felt on the howe-mound, whose wod flowed into my words, there is more wisdom in this than I can rede. For a moment it seemed to him that he might wake Sinfjotli up, but the Walsing was snoring so softly and peaceably that Hailgi had no heart for disturbing him. it seemed to him that Sinfjotli would have few enough chances for quiet rest while he lived. Instead the Wolfing slid from between his blankets, quietly sitting up on his bench. Ar-nugrimar stood hunched over the prow, holding the first night-watch, even through Skegga-Grimar's sonorous snores, Hailgi could hear the watch-man tearing off a piece of dry fish with his teeth and chewing on it noisily. Barefoot, noiseless, Hailgi moved towards the stern where the spears lay. He took his own up. The Moon's light gleamed from the three neat sets of paired silver rings set in the black iron and the silver dots centering each circle, so that the inlaid patterns glowed like three pairs of eyes along the spear-blade.

With this spear, he would hallow Hadubroddar's host to Wodhanar to-morrow and claim the dawn's red for his own. It was a fair weapon, with its silver inlay and glass-smooth shaft of ash wood, light and finely balanced, ready to scream through the air at his cast, as fair as his sword, in its way, but neither of them had any worth without a strong hand to wield them, and a brave soul behind that hand. I must be more than Wodhanar's weapon, Hail-gi thought, more than his will-less work-tool, sent here and there for a sake I do not know. The god surely does not give his wish-daughters to thralls, nor call slaves to sit by him on his benches in Walhall, and if it is said that he is harsh to his kin in the Middle-Garth, it is also said that he loves us well, when we are brave enough to be worthy of him.

I did not have to come here. I might have held what I won from Hunding's sons, and wedded Ingwibjorg, and lived a long time in good fame and joy. But even as he thought that, he knew it was false. He could not have borne the thought that Sigiruna dwelt with another man, whether in sorrow or in joy. In time, his heart told him, that knowing, and knowing he had forsaken her when she called to him, would have fettered his soul till he no longer stirred or spoke, but sat biting the coals by the fire till he sank down dead in the straw.

If she is doomed to be my death?

Then so she shall be, I was not born a coward, and all must pay the geld of life with a dying someday. At the very least, it shall be no shameful death Sigiruna brings me, but one shining with bravery, that men may not easily forget, she shall spur me to a worthy end, as she has spurred me to all I have wrought thus far. Hailgi rasped the ball of his thumb over the spear's edge. It seemed a little dull to him, so he drew the little whetstone from his belt-pouch. Though quiet, the stone's sound against the iron seemed harsh as the crying of a far-off raven in his ears.

CHAPTER XXIII

Helgi lay on the scraggly backyard grass with the morning sunlight warming his back and brightening the pages of the books and scores spread out before him, occasionally scribbling down a few words in his notebook. Elric lay beside him, now and again the elk hound rolled his eyes at the bag of Fritos beside his master's hand or thumped his tail hopefully. Helgi had been drafted to do a major lecture in "Nietzsche and Wagner" in a couple of weeks, now Dr. Mason wanted to see his outline on Monday, and he and Luann had planned to spend the afternoon together and go out to celebrate his birthday that evening. He still didn't know what he was going to write about, he had come outside in hopes that the fresh fall air would blow some thoughts into his head.

A cool gust of breeze rustled through the dry brown leaves of the pecan tree on the other side of the chain-link fence, shaking a couple of nuts loose. One of them thumped into the grass beside Helgi, he reached out, skinned its hull away, and cracked its thin shell in his fist, chewing absently on it. He had given up on reasoning, now his eyes flicked randomly back and forth from Nietzsche's words to Wagner's, searching for a spark to kindle fire in his head.

"To accept the Unreal as a condition of Life. That is to freely, in a dangerous manner, make a stand against the usual feelings of worth, and a philosophy which dares this alone places itself beyond Good and Evil."

"One can hardly hear one's own thoughts, no one will heed the knight. I call that bravery, to keep singing. His heart's in the right place. A true poet-hero!"

Helgi looked thoughtfully up at the shifting fragments of blue sky through the leaves. A mockingbird looked back down at him from the highest branch, opening its beak to give out a brief warble. It flicked its gray tail as though casting off a sprinkling of salt, then flew away.

"The 'unfree will' is mythology. In real life there are only strong and weak wills."

"'Who are you, then, who seeks to restrain me?' 'Fear the guardian of the rock! A fire sea flows around the woman, glowing flames lick around the crag, the fire burns against him who desires the bride. Go back then, rash child!' 'You go back, boaster! There, where the flames burn, to Brünnhild, I must go within!"

After a moment of thought, Helgi turned over a sheet of paper and wrote, "The Hero Wills," at the top of the fresh page, then underlined it carefully. Now that he had a title, the rest of the outline, he thought, should come to him easily. He glanced down at the page in front of him again. "Their thought is in reality much less a discovery than a renewed recognition, renewed remembering, a return and homecoming to a distant ancient common home of the soul, from which every concept was once grown, philosophy is thus far a kind of highest rank of atavism."

Helgi grinned. That he knew already. For a moment the words seemed to shimmer in his sight, beneath the ghostly red angles of a rune., Othala, "inherited land," rune of the mound and the clan, of the wisdom and might drawn from dead kin and past lives. He turned to the front piece of Siegfried, gazing thoughtfully at the nineteenth-century painting. The dark dragon reared up out of the mist before the hero, embers of fire glowing red in the depths of the wyrm's throat and eyes. Siegfried's pale shape shone against him. Long blond hair spilling down over the hero's muscular back to the wolf skin wrapped about his waist, a star of light glinting from the tip of his sword. The background of the Meistersinger fore plate was a flowery meadow. A young man in blue medieval breeches and tunic, with a sword girded to his waist, stood singing before a collection of soberly clad men, in the foreground, a white-bearded old man leaned on his staff beside a flower-crowned maiden. Still. "The human is something that should be overcome. Be the Over-Human the meaning of the earth!"

Beneath his title, he wrote, "I. Wagner's Past and Nietzsche's Future." He was about to go on when Elric's ears suddenly pricked up, the hound swiveling his head back towards the house. After a breath, Helgi heard the faint sound of his telephone ringing. He hurried inside, Elric trailing behind him, and thundered up the stairs quickly enough to catch it before the caller hung up.

"Happy birthday, Helgi."

Helgi's heart clenched like a knot yanked suddenly tight. It was Karin's voice on the other end. "Uh, thanks. And happy Halloween to you."

Karin's glittering laugh showered down the phone-line. "It surely is. How would you like to spend the day in costume?"

"Huh?"

"I was thinking that Rof and I could show you around the base for your birthday, but you'd have to impersonate a member of the Air Force. We could all be in deep shit for breaking regs. What do you say?"

"I'd love to," Helgi answered without a moment's thought.

"Great. We'll be there to pick you up in about an hour and a half. Oh, get your hair tied up safely on top of your head. I think we can probably hide it under a cap if you can pin it down tightly enough."

The phone clicked down before Helgi could say anything else. He stood staring at the dull white shine of the receiver for a few moments, then slowly hung it back on the wall.

"What have I gotten myself into?" He asked Elric. The elk hound looked up sympathetically, but offered no answer. Helgi had only the vaguest idea about military regulations, but he was pretty sure impersonating a member of the Air Force on-base could get him into a lot of trouble if he got caught.

"So I won't get caught." Helgi went out to gather up his books, then stood looking into the mirror, trying to think of what to do with his hair. After a little while, he started plaiting it into several small braids, pinning them to the top of his head with a mass of bobby pins.

Without hair framing them, the lines of his cheekbones and jaw stood out in sharp relief, the edges of his skull pressing hard against the skin as though the flesh had suddenly fallen away from his face. He checked his watch. Forty-five minutes had passed, as long again to go. Helgi picked up Jenseits von Gut und Böse again and opened it, but Nietzsche's sentences twined away from his eyes, verbs slithering from subjects and subjects changing place with objects, he could not concentrate long enough to wrest meaning from the words. Meistersinger, Siegfried, same thing. At last Helgi slipped his shoes off and went out to the yard to stretch and run through a series of katas, hoping that the physical exercise would still the cold trembling in his bones. He felt stiff at first, but as the blood rushed more swiftly through his body, Helgi could feel his strength rising, speeding each strike and kick more surely.

By the time he had reached Bassai-dai, it seemed to Helgi that he could see the shadow-shape of his foe before him, hands and feet flickering out for him to block, his own fists and heels sinking into the dark-mist form as he spun and struck and kicked in the swift battle-dance. Now a block broke a limb, now a killing strike thumped home, but the ghost in Helgi's mind-sight sprang anew from each of his blows, striking at him faster and harder each time. Helgi was breathing hard when he finished the kata, his T-shirt wet at breastbone and back. One of the little braids flopped loose over his face as he made the short bow that completed the kata. Brushing it back, he heard the sound of clapping and looked up. Rof's eyes gleamed dark through the links, Karin was climbing up the fence, a bundle wrapped in a trash bag under her arm.

"You didn't answer the doorbell, so I thought you might be out here," she said as she jumped down, bending her knees to land lightly on the ground.

Rof heaved himself up behind her, the flimsy wire-net shaking under his weight as he pulled himself over. "Happy birthday, Helgi," he rumbled. "Is you ready to get us thrown into the stockade, court-martialed, and shot at sunrise, just 'cause the captain here thought she had a clever idea?"

"I hope not."

Karin handed Helgi her bag. "Well, go see how these fit you." She looked at him more closely. "Be careful when you put the jacket on. It's mine, and if you move your shoulders too hard, you just might split the seams. I guess I'd forgotten how much you'd grown, I remembered you as a skinny little kid."

"That was a few years ago," Helgi answered, trying to smooth the prickles of irritation from his voice. He could not miss the glint of Rof's teeth, nor the glimmering white of his eyes as the big man met Karin's sideways glance.

"So it was. You've gotten good at karate since then, too. What belt are you?"

"First dan, going for second in March."

"Excellent. Go on, now. We have to be back at base by one."

She still thinks she's my big sister, Helgi thought as he hurried up to his room, annoyed. How do I convince her? He slapped himself lightly across the cheeks. "What are you thinking of, moron?" It was silly of him to think of drawing Karin's attention away from Rof, and Helgi had Luann, he had no business planning to break up their relationship.

Luannah, shit. Helgi reached for the phone and dialed Luann's number with one hand as he undressed himself. The phone rang twice, then he heard Mr. O'Roarke's dry voice saying, "You have reached 527-3194. Please leave your number and a message at the tone."

"Uh, Luann, I'm going out for a while. I may be a little late this afternoon, so you might want to call before you come over to make sure I'm home."

Helgi kicked away his jeans and stepped into Karin's gray-green uniform pants. They were almost too tight for him to get over his thighs. He took a deep breath and tugged hard, muttering, "The hero wills." The slacks were tighter at his waist, so that he could barely button them, her boots were both short and narrow for him, and raising his arms to put her cap onto his head strained her jacket almost to splitting.

Helgi straightened the jacket and stood tall, looking at his reflection a moment. What he saw was an Air Force man with the wings of a pilot, braced tightly to attention by a uniform that he had slightly outgrown. Beneath the rim of his cap, Helgi's gray eyes were dark as black-iced pools in the snow, the uniform tinging them with a slight greenish cast. With all his hair hidden, his face looked strange to him, younger, more finely chiseled, the slight bulges of muscle at the narrow corners of his jawline more clearly defined.

Helgi turned and walked stiffly down to the front door, where Karin and Rof stood waiting for him. Karin grinned up at him as he came down the stairs. "You'll do for now, lieutenant. Looks like you need to requisition a new uniform soon, though."

Rof and Karin had come in an Air Force four-seater jeep. They put Helgi in the back, riding up front themselves. The windows were rolled down all the way, so that the cool roar of the wind drowned most of their conversation, but every so often Karin would turn around with more instructions. "Salute everything that moves. Lower ranks will salute you. You salute anyone with more stuff on their sleeve than you have. If anyone of higher rank addresses you. You will answer either, 'Yes, sir!' or 'No, sir!' Got that?"

"'Yassuh, boss massa!'" Helgi answered, saluting Karin at the same time. "The South shall rise again!"

Karin burst out laughing, the delicate lines of her throat tightening as she threw her head back. "Wrong military, wrong side, idiot! The Confederates lost, remember?"

Rof's eyes flicked back at Helgi a moment. "Oh, I dunno about that. Seems to me the military we're in be havin' its moments."

"You stop that talk," Karin warned him teasingly. "Privates are tender little lambs, with fragile morale, and this white boy's not going to find out about some of those moments, either. You love the Air Force, don't you, Helgi?"

"Sir, yes sir!"

"See, Rof? No one's ever going to know that the long golden hair of a musician lurks coiled beneath that gray cap."

"Like a werewolf waitin' for the full moon," Rof agreed. "You sure this is a bright idea? I don't have any particular hankerin' to get busted for it."

"Well, we're doing it now there's no time to turn around and take him home. You don't want to wimp out on us now, do you, Helgi?"

"Hell, no," Helgi answered, as nonchalantly as he could get the words through the cold grip of nervousness in his throat. Karin reached back and whacked him lightly on the shoulder.

"That's, 'Sir, no, sir!' Look in that paper bag under your seat, why don't you? As long as we're breaking regs, we might as well go ahead and shatter them all the way."

"You be crazy, woman," Rof said ominously. "You gonna get yo'self busted or killed someday, stunts you pull. Only reason you ain't been kicked out is that you ain't got caught yet."

"You love me for it and you know it."

"I love you in spite of it, Karin. Not because."

The wet brown paper came apart under Helgi's hands as he pulled three cold-dewed bottles of Elephant beer from under the seat. "Have a beer, Rof?"

"What the hell, you two already got me deeper in shit than I can climb out of without a ladder. Sure, gimme that beer."

Too late, Helgi realized that he had nothing to uncap it with, but Rof popped the top off with his thumb, flicking it out the window.

"Should be a knife in one of those pockets, Helgi," Karin called back to him.

Once they had passed the glaring glass of the tall cluster of buildings that was downtown Dallas, the traffic cleared swiftly, till they rumbled alone through the flat brown fields that stretched out to the dim line of the horizon. A formation of wasp-nosed planes, blotched brown and yellow, roared above through the empty sky, Rof squinted up through the windshield. "Whose be those?"

Karin craned her neck out the window. "I think that's Jeff's flight. Wonder what he's doing up today? I thought his leave started yesterday."

"Nah, he worked a deal with Major Mike for Thanksgiving week. Jeff got a new rug rat, he wants to be home fo' the holiday, and there a gun show on in Fort Worth this weekend Major Mike was all set to go AWOL if he couldn't be wanglin' an early leave for it."

"That figures. I bet he fucks his guns when no one's looking."

"Nah, that might gum up the mechanism. He just stare at them real hard, polish with one hand an'whip his weasel with the other." Rof laughed, pulling off the freeway onto the access road. "If I remember rightly, there be a 7-11 just up here. We got to ditch these bottles and get some mints or some such before we check back in. Don' want to be caught goin' out to the birds with beer on yo' breath, top of everythin' else, do we?" He spun expertly into the 7-11's parking lot, coming to a stop a hairsbreadth from the curb. "I'll take care of that shit you two stay here, figure out yo' story. I got a feelin'yo' gonna need it. There be trouble ahead of you. I can hear it now," suddenly Rof's speech shifted into a nasal East Coast preppie-accent . "Due to the occurrence of certain contingencies which could not have been provided for in the original plan, we have now deemed it expedient and desirable to carry out a strategic backwards advance with a lowered number of personnel" His voice rose to a high squawk. "Run away! Run away!"

Rof collected their bottles and got out, then stuck his head back in through the open window for a moment. "This story better be a good one. I know."

Helgi blinked, remembering how Rof had spoken to him when they first met the depth of the other man's sight, the strange feeling he had gotten when Rof turned away. Karin, too, seemed sobered by her boyfriend's words. She sat considering Helgi for a little while, chewing on her lower lip. "Hmm. Lieutenant Hadding, serial number whatever your Social Security number is. TDY, that's temporary duty. Assigned in from Holloman AFB, New Mexico. It's a good story. With a bit of luck, it'll get you up in the back seat of my F-16D. Think you can remember it?"

"Yes, sir! Lieutenant Hadding, 919-21-7119, just assigned from Holloman, sir!"

"Very good!" Karin patted him on the shoulder.

"What's an AFB?"

Karin sighed. "Air Force Base. No, we do not speak English in the Air Force. We speak acronymese. Just remember not to tell anyone anything you don't have to, and we won't have any trouble. You know how to stand at attention and at ease?"

"We did it in the marching band."

"Okay, it's basically the same. If you see anyone with a lot of sleeve decoration, salute and stand at attention till he, or she, tells you to stand at ease. I
can't think of anything else, but it's okay, the base is usually a little slower on
weekends anyway."

After they had been driving a while longer, Helgi could see a smooth-
topped hill looming up from the flat earth. Its carefully mounded shape
was too even to be natural, and even from this distance, he could see the
bright yellow points of signs posted about its edge. Karin turned around and
shouted, "You'll have to get down under those tarps now. We're almost at the
turn-off for the base."

Helgi wriggled between the two back seats, crawling behind the pile of
tarpaulins in the back and pulling them over him. He began to sweat almost
at once, the dust and the musty smell were stifling. Carefully he moved one,
then another, until he had just a crack of light to suck air through. Now that
he couldn't see out the window, the jeep seemed to be bouncing about twice
as hard, shuddering and grumbling asthmatically, and his stomach began
to feel a little queasy. He felt them turn off the highway, jerking down onto a
road that felt as though it had been hastily cobbled together from rocks and
potholes.

When the jeep jolted to a stop at last, Helgi thought he heard the sound of
Karin and Rof speaking, though the tarpaulins muffled their voices to a dull
wind-roaring. Then the vehicle coughed back into life again, rolling forward.
Eventually the jeep stopped again, Helgi wanted to get out at once, but then
it occurred to him that he had better wait till one of the others said it was all
right. For all he knew, there might be a horde of Air Force people crowding
around them that moment. Helgi lay in his hiding place for what seemed
like a very long time. A warm drop of sweat trickled over his forehead, slow
and maddening as the track of a fly. He wanted to reach up and wipe it off,
but he didn't know who might be watching through the windows.

At last Karin opened the back of the jeep and heaved the tarpaulins off
him. "All clear, Lieutenant. Brush the dust off your uniform and get your ass
in gear. We've got some birds to inspect."

Helgi crawled out of the jeep and brushed himself off, looking around.
They were in a big concrete parking lot framed by low brown buildings.
Each of the parking places was numbered, Helgi could see that they were
divided into groups by type of vehicle. Rof snapped the jeep's doors closed
and locked them behind Helgi. The two of them fell into step behind Karin
as she strode off, her boot-heels clicking against the concrete. This really
is like marching band, Helgi thought, as he felt his years of habit matching
foot and pace to the pattern she and Rof were setting.

"Over there are the barracks," Karin said, waving her hand at one set of desert-brown buildings. "That is where the enlisted personnel neaten the corners of their beds, polish their boots, and all those other thrilling things, when they aren't being set to useful and educational duties. There," she gestured at another, "is the mess hall. Mess it is called, and mess it is, fortunately for the cooks, military personnel do not fall under the jurisdiction of the SPCA. The officers' mess is a vast improvement. Actually, you won't be seeing either of them, for good and sufficient reasons, among them being that I don't want to be barfed on when I take you up, and the fewer people who see you anyway, the better. Over yonder," she pointed straight ahead of them, "are the hangars, where our birds nest. Recon planes to the right, bombers to the left, fighters, where we are going, straight down the middle. That smaller building there by the hangars is where Rof works when he's not actually with my plane."

"What is it you do?" Helgi asked him.

"I be crew chief, do maintenance and repair. Guys like me don' fly no birds. Well, I guess it time to leave you now. I got work to do, if you be goin' up today. See you in the hangar."

A skinny soldier with a rifle slung over his shoulder stood in front of the hangar, rolling a piece of gum from one side of his mouth to the other. His eyes widened and he straightened to attention when he saw Karin approaching, snapping off a salute which she returned at once, Helgi a little belatedly.

"At ease, soldier," Karin said. "Is Dalworth in there? I've got a training flight to carry out."

"Sir, yes, sir! He's in his office, sir!"

"Carry on, private." Karin turned towards the door just as Helgi heard a soft cough behind him. She whirled, stiffening to attention and snapping off a salute at once, Helgi did the same before he got a good look at the person who was standing there. It was an older man, about Helgi's height but more heavily built, with a solid paunch pressing his gray uniform jacket outward. Beneath his cap, his crew cut was so short that his head looked almost shaven, with only a thin dusting of gray pepper-grains over the pink skull. A white pad of bandaging hid his right eye. Some of the spider leg-scars cutting through the eyebrow above it were hoary with age, but a couple of shiny red lines radiated from the bandage's edge as well, and the wiry black hairs of stitch-knots sprouted from one fresh scab. Helgi glanced at the man's sleeve. Three stars. He couldn't quite remember what rank got which, but he was sure that stars were important.

"At ease, Jensen," the officer said. His voice echoed deep in his wide chest, rumbling as though he spoke from the bottom of a tympani. Helgi noticed that he pronounced Karin's last name as she herself did. Yensen. "You too, Lieutenant. Captain, what are you doing here? Damn looie told me you were off-base."

"Sir, I remembered I had some paperwork to do, so I decided to come back for a few hours."

"You don't do paperwork in the hangar, Jensen." He peered closely at Helgi so closely that Helgi could see the edge of his contact lens floating clear against his blue iris. "Who are you, lieutenant?"

"Sir, Lieutenant Hadding, 919-21-7119, transfer from Holloman, sir!" Helgi barked in his best military manner. The sound came straight from his tightened gut, louder and clearer than he had meant it to, its echo hanging in the cool autumn air a moment like the sound of a deep horn.

The officer blinked, drawing back a little. "Are you new on base, Hadding?"

"Yes, sir."

"Is Hadding one of yours, captain?"

"Yes, sir. TDY."

"Is he your cousin or something?"

"Nossir. No relation."

"Huh. Must be my eyesight. I suppose you brought him over today as an excuse to play with a plane and show off what a hot-shit flyer you are while pretending to be an IP. I suppose in about ten minutes I'm going to see one of those Lawn Darts up there wasting fuel and cluttering the airspace, like it existed for no purpose other than your private pleasure. I'd better not see it up there all afternoon, unless you've got a better excuse than the one you're about to give me. Playtime don't last forever, you know." He paused, glaring at Karin to see if she would say anything. "Go on, Jensen."

"Sir, I considered it highly desirable that Hadding have the opportunity to familiarize himself with the F-16s and their workings under the instruction of the most competent officer available, as per his assignment."

"Huh. Hadding, Captain Jensen is an officer and a gentleman, a credit to the service and all that. She might get that urgent paperwork done sometime before next year, but she is possibly the best pilot on this base. Strap yourself in good and watch every move she makes, down to the least twitch of a nosehair. Engrave every word she says about these birds on the surface of your brain, brand them on your butt, if you can't remember them any other way." He grinned tightly, showing a flash of smooth ceramic bridgework. "You haven't flown an F-16 before, have you, Lieutenant?"

"No, sir."

"You're here to do it. Lucky bastard. Well, you may think you're a pilot, you may have your wings and your time on the AT-38, but when Captain Jensen takes you up, don't forget your barf-bag. And consider a diaper to go with it."

"Yes, sir!"

The officer turned back to Karin. "Jensen, my wife's expecting you over for her bridge club and dinner afterwards tomorrow evening. You show up late and your ass is grass, is that clear?"

"As crystal, sir. I hope your operation went well, sir?"

"None of your damn business, Jensen. I can still see well enough to tell whether you've done your paperwork or not. Which means it had damn well better be done. Carry on, Captain."

Karin saluted him, Helgi's arm-snap following hers by half a heartbeat. The officer saluted them back and walked away, his steps firm and steady exaggeratedly so, Helgi thought he seemed to be concentrating on placing each foot in line.

Helgi heaved a silent sigh of relief, trying to keep his knees from sagging as Karin waved him into the hangar behind her. The building seemed very dark after the clear air outside. As Helgi's eyes settled, the sharp snouts of the planes slowly began to rear up out of the shadows above him, pale as moonlit clouds against their deep gray wings and back-fins, he could see the dark shapes of the seats dimly through the clear bubbles covering them.

"The General Dynamics F-16, my Viper," Karin breathed, her murmur rustling through the hangar's stillness like a soft wind. She reached up to stroke the side of the one before her. Her long-fingered hand white against its smooth gray enamel. Now Helgi noticed the shape painted on the nose. A white swan in flight, fine-feathered wings lifted and long neck outstretched like a spear flying into the wind. "Oh, but wait till we're up!" Drawing her hand back, she smiled at him. Helgi had never been able to imagine the clear look of joy on Karin's face. Her unbound smile brushing the grimness from the sharp set of her high cheekbones like a veil of cobwebs, easing the knots at the corners of her jaw and brightening her pale gray eyes to sky-blue. Now her brightness was a rough hand plucking at his heartstrings, but he smiled back at her, hoping that his look of happiness would do in place of the words fettered in his throat. She coughed suddenly, glancing around to make sure no one else was there. "You stay here. I've got to go fill out our mission card. BFM, Basic Flight Maneuvers, I think that's the program for today."

His mouth dry, Helgi watched Karin go between the planes, the smooth sway of her hips, her strong stride, the edge of fair hair gleaming between the rim of her cap and the pale nape of her neck like a gilded helmet-edge. He could feel every muscle in his body straining to burst free of the tight bonds of the uniform he wore, his scalp itched fiercely beneath his knotted hair, and he could not scratch it. He breathed deeply, as though about to release a mighty note from his throat, staring at the keen shapes of the fighter planes ranged before him. You want freedom, your soul thirsts after the stars, your wild hounds want freedom, they bark with desire in their cellar, when your soul sets out to free all captives. When Karin came back, she had a helmet on her head, another dangled by the strap from her hand, together with a neat cloth package. Over her uniform, she wore a thick flight suit, the greenish-gray color of tornado light.

"Hold still, now." She whipped Helgi's cap off and the helm on in the same motion, buckling it tightly under his chin. "Arms up, careful, there! Breathe, but not too deeply." She helped him put his own flight suit on. It was tight around Helgi's stomach and thighs, the vest pressing hard against his upper body. "It's supposed to feel like that, it keeps the blood from draining from your head. You need it, too, the F-16 is stressed up to 9g. Without some extra help, there's a pretty high risk of G-LOC. That's gravity-induced loss of consciousness to you. Not recommended for one flying a fighter plane." Strapping a harness onto his back, she reached around his chest to buckle it. "This clips onto the parachute built into your seat, I'll show you the ripcord. If we should have to punch out not that there's much chance of it, count to one hundred and pull the ripcord hard. It will open your parachute, and you may survive landing." Karin grinned at him. "You're not scared, are you?"

"Of course not," Helgi answered. It was true. His heart was beating harder, his breath coming more swiftly, but not from fear.

She led him around the side of the plane before them. "Ah, here he comes now." A short, broad-shouldered youth about Helgi's age, dressed in khaki with a baseball-type cap hanging lopsided from his cropped skull, was wheeling a ladder between the planes.

"There y'go, ma'am," he said, rolling it up to the plane and stepping back. Karin went up the ladder, Helgi following her. He didn't see exactly what she did, but suddenly she was lifting the clear bubble above the seats. She spoke so softly that he could barely hear her. "You get in front there. He's coming up to strap us in. Get ready for some exciting maneuvers, to celebrate surviving the gaze of the Dread Eye."

"Huh?" Helgi got in, settling himself into the reclining seat as the Air Force man climbed up the ladder behind him. Helgi sat still to be strapped in. He was trying to keep any nervousness from twitching on his face or in his hands, but a light dew of sweat still cooled his forehead.

"Fine, Rogers," Karin said when she, too, had been secured in her seat. "Carry on." The hatch lowered as Rogers climbed back down the ladder.

"What were you about to say?"

"Uh oh, yes, the Dread Eye. Only one of his eyes works. He took a piece of shrapnel over the other, north of the Red River in Nam. Med's been quacking unsuccessfully on it since, and it only seems to get worse and worse. He sits on high and sees everything, not unlike Odin." She turned her head, flashing him a quick grin, "or possibly Sauron, depending on how bad the other eye's hurting him. How he managed to get out of a medical is one of the great wonders of the Air Force, they did manage to promote him into a desk job, but he's likely to be here when we're all gone. As Rof often says ." She assumed a deeper voice, doing a bad imitation of Rof's accent, "'He be one bad mofo, man'. We were lucky to get off that easily. I thought we were both dead when he started asking about you."

"He must like you, though. I mean, inviting you over"

"His wife is relieving my poor delicate sensibilities of the terrible strain of having to associate with these crude male-type people from, er, ah, lower socio-economic classes, all week. She kindly provides me with a few hours of genteel feminine company, sprinkled richly with delicate hints about finding a nice officer, their son, zits and all, graduated from West Point, not actually quite at the bottom of the class, you get the idea. Yeah, the Dread Eye can be quite a decent fellow. Even fatherly, in his own idiosyncratic way. Now, you see all that stuff in front of you? What it does, is" Helgi hardly heard what she was saying, the string of numbers and letters were so much gibberish to him. The ground crew were doing something right below the plane, Helgi saw the top of Rof's dark head vanishing beneath the shadow of a wing.

The hangar door drew up before them, the sunlight spreading towards them from the widening crack like the edge of a golden wave running up a gray beach.

"Permission to taxi?" Karin asked.

A man's voice crackled over the intercom. "Permission given, Captain."

Helgi felt the deep scream through his bones before he heard it through the muffling helmet, the plane was already alive, surging forward into the sunlight before he could draw another breath. He thought the back fin barely cleared the retreating door, but then they were out of the hangar, slowly driving over the wide gray stretch of concrete. They stopped for a few moments, then the intercom spoke again. "Permission for take-off, Captain Jensen."

The plane sped forward along the runway. Helgi could feel the F-16's might gathering beneath him, readying for its great leap then, dizzyingly fast, they were diving upward into the clear cool sky. The air clamped down hard on Helgi's ears, he gulped twice, bursting the pressure back outward. Beneath them, the little shapes of the Air Force trucks blurred into thin greenish trails against the brown earth, a ghost-wisp of white mist brushed past them and was gone, its clear dew streaking tiny tear-tracks back over the clear plastic. This was not like a passenger plane, Helgi realized. Here he was not simply traveling through the sky, but truly in it, with only a thin transparent shell shielding him from the naked wind.

"Prepare to go up, and try not to lean forward," Karin shouted. The F-16's nose tilted sharply upward, then farther up. Helgi realized that he was actually lying head-down as the plane struck straight upward like a lightning bolt flung from earth to sky, the roaring blood crashing against his temples with each heartbeat. He did not know whether he heard the thunder behind them or only felt it, echoing through his skull as they clove the thin air.

Suddenly they were twisting to the side, the violent turn pulling the flesh down from Helgi's face and crushing him tightly against the seat. A shower of lightless sparks shattered in his eyes, their colors flashing blinding auroras against the blue sky. He felt drunkenly light-headed in the grip of the might hurling him forward, weightless as an arrow's screaming flight.

"You all right?" Karin called, her voice a thin flute over the engine's roar.

"Wonderful!" Helgi howled back. "Keep going!"

The plane sheered off from its line, tumbling upward. The two fields, brown and blue, whirled around Helgi, sky and earth changing places in his dizzy sight. A ribbon of white wove before and behind them. They were twisting in and out of their own trail, braiding and knotting their tufted string of cloud. Karin's laughter came muffled through the padding of Helgi's helmet, mingling with the resonance of his own through his skull-bones. Something dark, a hawk? It blurred past beside them, tumbling away in their wake. Without warning, the F-16 turned nose-down and dropped, the brown fields and buildings beneath sharpening at each heartbeat as they plummeted towards the ground.

Helgi's throat clutched, choking off his gasp, then it seemed to him that the wind caught their wings again, lifting them from the dive and bearing them upward in a smooth swift curve like the long arc of a spear's flight. Ahead of them, Helgi saw the chrome and glass towers of downtown Dallas rising from the plain. A cluster of silvery snakes raising their heads together, lashing black tails around and over one another into the twisted tangle of freeways spread out around the city's center.

"Now, this is how it would be if we were really fighting. This is called the 'High Yo-Yo'. The bandit's in a level turn, and we get up and pull across the top of our egg. Climb up high into the clouds, if there were clouds," Karin pulled the plane's nose back hard, till they were lying on their backs as the F-16 screamed straight up again. "Get up over them, so," she whipped them over and across, "and dive out of the sun shooting." They plunged down in another breathless dive, pulling out and looping back in a long upward turn, a powerful undertow of gravity dragging at Helgi's flesh as though to pull it from his bones. "Maybe jinking to avoid ground fire, like so." The Falcon rolled over to the side, twisting here and there like a horse galloping through a field of pike men, then shot straight back up again.

Helgi didn't hear Karin's sigh, but when he glanced back, he saw the rise and fall of her shoulders as they leveled out again, high above the fields. "All brown and tired-looking down there, isn't it?" She said. "If only we were at the base in Colorado then I'd show you something worth seeing! The mountains are bright this time of year, with snow here and there, you can fly straight down the canyons, along the river-gorges. If you've got the guts and the reflexes for it. Of course, pilots crash during training there every so often, but that happens no matter where you are. The cloud patterns are trickier too, you have to rely on the instruments more, and more on your own skill and luck, when the cross-winds catch you at the wrong moment." She flashed a quick glance up at him before turning her attention to her control panel again, turning into a wide soaring circle. "And sometimes you see things in the clouds, or the rocks, sometimes, when you're up there alone, you can feel them watching you."

"What sort of things?" Helgi asked, not sure whether she was teasing him or not. "'Them' who?"

"Trolls. Ghosts. That sort of thing, oh, the sort of thing you were singing about, say, you, of all people, shouldn't be surprised. "This is the 'Low Yo-Yo', another way of cutting off a turning bandit. Hang onto your guts, we're going down."

Helgi's body slammed against the straps holding him in as the Falcon rolled over and dropped nose-first, hurtling down to earth. They seemed only a breath away from impact when the plane's nose began to rise again, swinging up from the ground.

After a few more maneuvers, Karin guided the F-16 into a more stately descent, sweeping back down.

"So soon?" Helgi asked.

"It is not healthy to draw the gaze of the Dread Eye for too long," Karin replied solemnly. "I think I've probably pushed as far as I can for today."

The hangar door scrolled slowly up before them, and the F-16 rolled in. When Helgi reached to undo his buckles, he found that his fingers were so numb and bloodless that he could barely grasp the straps. Now that they were down on the earth again, he could taste the bitter lacing of disappointment through the calm that was slowly sinking into his bones.

"I see why you wouldn't do anything else," he murmured, almost to himself. He thought that Karin had not heard him over the engine, but when its roar had dimmed into silence, she turned around to smile at him.

"Not 'wouldn't'. Couldn't."

The next words walked out of Helgi's mouth before he could stop them, "Do you take Rof up often?"

Karin let her head loll to one shoulder, rolling it backwards to the other as though she had a crick in her neck. "Can't. Regulations. Tech sergeants don't get joyrides, and if I tried to stretch things in his favor, someone might just notice that something was going on between us. This, also, is frowned upon severely and could get us both into serious deep shit."

"Because he's black?" Go on, Helgi, dig your grave with your mouth, that's right, Helgi thought.

"Because I'm an officer and he's an enlisted man," Karin explained patiently. "The Air Force is an equal opportunity organization. It says so in all official literature. Which is not to say that there aren't a few good ol' boys on base who would just love to lynch the two of us on "fraternization" if they had any clue, so we have to be three times as careful as anyone else. This does not always make for an easy relationship, but when it works, it's worth it." She unlatched the cover, standing up and stretching her arms. Below, Rogers was already rolling the ladder up beside the plane again. "Out of there, Lieutenant. I wasn't lying about that paperwork, and now that the Eye has lit upon it, I'd really damn better get it done."

Helgi climbed down the ladder, stretching his cramped muscles as well as he could without breaking the uniform's seams while Karin followed Rogers through the planes again. When she had done whatever it was she had to do, she came back and waved him to follow her through the complex to another low building.

"In here," she said as she led him through a maze of corridors, "is where I contemplate the sins of my life, and sort of generally pay for the privilege of having pretty stripes on my sleeve and being able to order other people around. As mostly an instructor, I get to do more paperwork than I ever wanted to." She unlocked the door, showing him into a small cubicle. The chair behind the desk was a padded swivel chair on wheels, the one in front of it was a wooden slat-chair, painted drab gray. Several sheaves of paper were strewn around the computer on top of the desk, and more were spilling from the end of the single bookshelf above it. "Sit down and make yourself uncomfortable. This will probably take about forty-five minutes, I think. Honest, I wasn't expecting to get caught out on it. I really am sorry. I should have known when Rof warned me, he's good at. Help yourself to the books if you like." Karin sat down, muttering something under her breath as she shuffled through the mess of papers on top of her desk.

Helgi looked at the books. The Last Enemy, Art of War, Poetic Edda, Ideas, Concepts, Doctrine. Basic Thinking in the U.S. Air Force 1963-1988, a couple of plane manuals and several issues of the Air Power Journal, Saga of the Volsungs, Fighter Combat. The Art and Science of Air-to-Air Combat, Folk Songs of Scandinavia. One in particular caught his eye. Our Troth, edited by Kveldúlf Hagan Gundarsson.

"I know that writer!" Helgi said. "Or at least I've read his other books it is the same guy, isn't it?"

Karin's smile glimmered like the ghost-brightness of the Northern lights across the snow. "Oh, yes. Are you actually Asatro?"

"I, I'm not sure." He had seen the word Ásatrú, true to the gods, in Teutonic Religion. "I think so. At least," there was too much in his heart to say. The hoard of words choked in his throat. There would be time later, time to tell Karin everything, time to hear her tales of trolls, "I'm learning the runes. I've called on Odhinn."

Karin sat up sharply, it seemed to Helgi that he could hear a deep chord thrumming between them, as though her nerves were plucked harp strings. Her gaze fixed him tightly, so that he could not move or breathe. Helgi was not sure whether she meant to strike or embrace him. He waited, stones truck, like a troll in daylight, until she let her own breath out in a long slow gust. "We'll talk about that later. I think it will need time in the telling. Would you like to borrow that book? You can have it for a little while, but get your own copy soon. What with all the Bibles in everyone else's office, I like having it here."

"Oh, yes," Helgi breathed. He pulled out Our Troth and set it carefully aside, then got out Folk Songs of Scandinavia as well. Sitting down, he started to read the English words set in italics below the Danish lyrics, trying to hear the notes in his head.

"'Hear me, knight sir Åge,
dearest, my beloved,
may I follow thee into black earth,
into thy grave?'
'So is it in the black earth,
in the grave with me,
as in the blackest Hell-mists,
when sorrow is for thee!
For every time thou weep'st for me,
and thy soul is sad,
then my coffin fills within
with living blood"

Karin rested the point of her chin against her right fist, staring gravely down at her papers and writing with her left hand. The sleeve of her uniform had fallen away from her forearm a little, her fine-boned wrist glimmering white against the storm-green material. The pink tip of her tongue poked out of her mouth as she wrote, bearing down hard with her pen to mark through all the layers of carbon copy.

"Now the white cock crows
I must go to earth.
All corpses sink to the ground,
I must therewith.
Now the red cock crows,
I must go to earth.
All the dead must go to ground,
I must therewith.
Now the black cock crows,
I must to earth.
Now all the gates are closing,
Now must I follow with"

Helgi did not realize that he had been humming aloud until Karin looked up. "'Åge og Else'."

"What?"

"That's the ballad's name. Åge is the dead man, and Else is his lover." She sang softly, her clear soprano filling the little room like the scent of roses. "'Hjem gekk jomfru Else-lille, / hun var så sorgefuld. / måneds-dag derefter / lå hun i sorten muld.' Home went the maiden Else, she was so sorrow-filled. A month's day thereafter, she lay in the black mold. It was always one of my favorite." She laughed ruefully, looking at the wall beyond Helgi's head. "Rof hates it. He thinks it's morbid. It's all his mother's fault, I think."

"His mother?"

"She's some kind of, witch woman." It seemed to Helgi that Karin's pale eyes darkened as she spoke, like the sky rising into storm. "Big scary lady, as tall as he is and twice as dark, but she's very thin, she looks like a skeleton painted black, and her eyes burn. She's all hung about with bead-necklaces of different colors, if the books on Santeria I read had any truth to them, she must be an impressive priestess. I went over there once and she wouldn't talk to me, she, well, I'll tell you all about it later. Rof grew up with this woman, and if you sing about the dead coming back to visit the living, he takes it very seriously."

"You don't? Who was telling me about trolls and ghosts in the mountains?"

Karin stared at him for a moment, as if she was weighing him. "Maybe so. The first time I flew up there, but that's a story for a long night and a few beers, when you can tell me about you and Odhinn. Anyway, I do like 'Åge og Else'. Maybe because I believe, I liked your song, too, what I heard of it."

"Rof didn't?"

"He said he was just about to walk out when I got there." Helgi didn't know what showed in his face, but Karin added hastily, "You should take that as a compliment. It means he felt something in it. There's something about your music that goes right up the spine. I like it."

"My voice?"

"Your voice, at least as much. There's, something about the way it sounds," Karin shook her head. "Now you're fishing for compliments, Helgi. Quit it. Let me finish this shit off and get you home. Olaf and Carol are in town for a few days, and I promised my parents I'd make it over there by late afternoon." She gripped her ballpoint firmly in her fist and began to inscribe her papers, then looked up again.

"If you're bored, you can sing a little more loudly. It won't bother me, I'd like to hear it."

Helgi glanced at his watch. If they left in half an hour, they might be back by six. He hoped Luann had gotten his message.

Val-raven flies in the evening, he cannot fly by day. "He shall have only evil fortune, the good luck he never may, but the raven flies in the evening, Herr Olaf, he rode so wide through the land, To his bridal ale bade he the folk stand, So light goes the dance, so light through the grove."

At last Karin shuffled her paperwork into a neat heap and stood up. "That's that done. Ready to go?"

"Yes. Can I borrow this?"

"Keep it. Happy birthday. Maybe you can use some of it in your own songs. I'd like to hear how that turns out, if you do."

"You know," Helgi said as they drove back towards Dallas, "I really liked that book you gave me for my birthday, what, two years ago?"

"Umm, I remember, The Norse Myths. Yes. Did you ever manage to read what I wrote?"

"I did. After you told me about it, I found a book that had the different runic alphabets in it and deciphered it all."

"Good for you! I rather thought you might. I still have that pendant you gave me, that silver valknútr."

It seemed to Helgi that something closed on his throat, so that he could neither draw nor loose his breath, and a faint pang stabbed through him like the echo of an old wound. He coughed, then croaked, "Um. Yeah, I'm glad."

"I even figured out the maker's inscription, finally. Sigfödhr saelsigruna merki 'Victory-Father bless the sign of victory-runes'. A good sign for a fighter-pilot to have, I think. You chose well." They were running up near the tail of a big sixteen-wheeler, Karin stopped talking for a moment, moving over a lane and stepping on the gas to shoot ahead of the truck before weaving back into the traffic before it. "You've got a girlfriend now, right? That little redhead you were with at the Soap, Rof told me her name, but I forgot it."

"Luann O'Roarke. She's Mike's sister Mike's the bandleader."

"Funny, I thought you were."

"No, I just write the songs. It's Mike who arranges all our gigs and everything."

"Have you made any recordings, demo tapes or anything?"

"No. I just joined Flourescent at the end of August."

"That's right, I heard them once earlier in the summer when you weren't there. They weren't anything special then."

"Flattery, flattery. Flattery will get you everywhere. You really think so?"

Karin reached out one-handed to push the beanie off his head. "You want me to write it out in runes for you? Trust me, du unge helt."

"What?"

She laughed a little embarrassed laugh. "It's hard to remember that you don't speak Danish. Never mind. It's probably safe for you to take your hair down now."

Helgi began to unpin his braids, combing them out with his fingers. "How can I get in touch with you? Have you got a phone number I could reach you at?"

"I do, but you have to be careful calling me during the day. You probably won't be able to reach me then anyway, but just in case you really have to talk to me, I'll give you my office number as well as my home phone. If anyone else answers the office phone, unless it's Rof, hang up. You promise?"

"I promise."

"Okay, look in the glove compartment. I'm pretty sure there's paper and a pen in there."

When the jeep swung up in front of Helgi's apartment, Luann's rust mobile was already parked in the street behind Helgi's Impala, and Luann herself was leaning against the door.

"Sorry I can't come in and say hello to your girlfriend, but I'd better be moving on," Karin said. "I didn't expect to be this late."

"That's okay. Thanks for everything." Helgi met her sky-pale gaze straight on, staring into Karin's eyes until a tinge of pink washed over her high cheekbones. For a moment he almost hoped that she might lean over to kiss him, but she did not. He could feel the warmth in his own cheekbones as he ducked away from her stare and got out of the jeep.

Luann was staring angrily at him. As he came closer, Helgi saw that her brown eyes were red-rimmed, the makeup scrubbed away from her lids and freckled cheeks, and it seemed to him that a faint sea-scent of damp salt rose from her face.

"Didn't you get my message?" He asked. "How long have you been waiting for me?"

Luann glared up at him. "About an hour and a half. I was out most of the day shopping for your birthday present, and then I thought I'd come straight here. Clever, huh? I didn't think you could be gone that long, since your car was here. So I waited and waited" Her voice dropped to a low hiss. "Fucking waited. Where were you, anyway? Why are you wearing that silly costume?"

"Rof and Karin wanted to take me onto the base and show me the planes, since it's my birthday. I had to wear the uniform to get in."

"Rof and Karin, huh?" Luann said, her voice cooler. "I didn't see Rof in that jeep."

"No, he had to stay back to do some work at the base, but Karin is visiting her family this evening. Look," said Helgi before Luann could chase the question any farther, "it's just past six. I'll call the Magic Time Machine right now and see if we can still get a reservation for tonight. My parents took me there for my birthday about five years ago it's a great place to eat on Halloween. You know, the waiters dress up in costume and do their acts all year-round, but on Halloween they really go wild."

"I've heard it's awfully expensive."

"I've got a bit of money saved. I really am sorry about being late, Luann."

"I might forgive you. Maybe. Good food may mellow me. Go call the restaurant."

The Magic Time Machine's phone was busy for fifteen minutes or so, but finally Helgi managed to get through and secure a reservation for eight o'clock. He came back into the living room to find Luann dipping into the little bowl of candy he had left on the table.

"Hey, that's for the Trick-or-Treaters."

"Are you really expecting anyone this year?"

Helgi looked out at the graying light through the window's dirty panes. "No one except the monsters from downstairs. I think we had about three at my parents' house last year, and they all came before dark. I guess people are afraid." He stopped. He could feel the words taking shape in his head, like shadows coming clear from the fog. The night of the dead is claimed by fear again. Where now is the harvest, the sheaves and frothing ale? Gone into dark waters, but the old ghosts remain, "Hey, just a second. I think I feel a poem coming on."

A bright glitter of surprise edged Luann's laugh, as though Helgi had startled her out of her anger. "Go change your clothes first. You look silly in that. Was it one Karin outgrew?"

"It was one of hers, yeah." Helgi was shocked at the raw tone of his own voice. Luann drew back a step, almost as if she were afraid he might hit her.

"Did I say something wrong?"

"I don't think. Never mind. Back in a second." Helgi hurried into his bedroom, tearing off the Air Force uniform and flinging his closet open. He tried to think of what Luann was wearing, but no shapes came to his mind. Only a vague blur of pale green beneath her red hair, and, very clear, the deep brown tear-pools of her eyes. Still, they had been planning to go out anyway, so he didn't think she had jeans on.

After a few moments of dithering, Helgi put on his one good suit. It was a little tight in the shoulders, so that he still could not move his arms easily, but it would do for that night. His hair hung in matted tendrils around his face, when he had brushed it out, the tracks of the day's tight little braids fluffed it up into a semi-Afro around his sharp features.

"My God, you look good," Luann said when he came back down. "You ought to wear a suit more often. Maybe you ought to take me out more often, huh? The hair looks good that way too, it doesn't have that depressed Scandinavian limpness to it."

"Thank you ever so. I'll remember you said that."

"What is it with this Karin person anyway?" Luann asked suddenly. "You had a major crush on her, didn't you?"

"I guess I did," Helgi admitted. "So?"

"Had. Past tense. Over is over. Dead is dead. Gone is gone. This is a good thing. Let's keep it that way."

With the coffin he knocked on the door, For he had no skin, 'Get thou up, my little Else! Let thy betrothed in!'

"We won't talk about her any more. Luann, there's no reason for you to be jealous."

"No, she's just six feet tall, blonde, and gorgeous like a model, with big breasts and long legs, and you were obviously deeply infatuated with her at some point in your young and impressionable adolescence. No reason at all."

"She's five-eleven," Helgi corrected. "Anyway, she's also six or seven years older than I am and attached to someone else at the wrists and ankles. You're not exactly ugly, you know. I mean, the world is full of men who don't even like tall blondes. There are many who prefer short redheads."

"Name three."

Helgi bent down to drop a swift kiss on the top of Luann's head. "No more of that shit. Leave it lie."

Luann stepped away from him. "Oh, before I forget to tell you. You've got to call Mike right away. He wants to talk to you ASAP."

"How come?"

"Just go call him."

Helgi went back into the kitchen, dialing Mike's number. Mike answered on the eighth ring. "Yo?"

"Hello?"

"Hi, Helgi. Good timing, I was right about to walk out the door. I guess Luann gave you the message?"

"All she said was for me to call you."

"Oh. Okay. Look, we've got a really excellent gig in Deep Ellum for Saturday evening, the 21st. Fairly new club, called The Blue Door. You can make it, right?"

"Of course. What does "really excellent" mean?"

"It means, 'they're paying us fifty dollars each'. Which is real good. That leads me to the next thing."

"Yeah?"

"There are a couple of places who might be interested in us, but they say they want to hear a demo tape. Now, we don't have a demo tape."

"No."

"It would be possible for us, say, real soon now, like the Sunday after the gig, to rent a studio for a few hours and generate one, if everyone were willing to throw in some money towards it. Like the money from this upcoming gig."

"Ah Hah. I see where this is leading."

"Everyone else I've asked thinks it's a great idea."

"It is. But why don't I think you've talked to anyone else yet?"

There was a long embarrassed silence on the other end of the phone. Then Mike mumbled, "I figured you'd be the likeliest one to want to put money into it."

"I see. Yes. The answer is yes. Does the place you have in mind have their own synthesizer, or should I bring mine?"

"The only thing they have is recording equipment, so you'll want to bring yours if it's any better than mine. I'll call around and see if I can get everyone else, and we'll plan to rehearse Monday evening like always. I really want to get that new song of yours into shape for the recording, and any others you might come up with in the next couple of weeks. Is that okay by you?"

"Yeah, fine. See you then."

"Sure thing."

Grinning, Helgi came back into the living room. "Did Mike tell you what was going on?"

"He told me. I thought I'd let him surprise you." The tight corners of Luann's mouth eased up into a smile. "So we have something to celebrate beside your birthday Flourescent's first real, genuine, paying gig. Do you want to open your present now, or wait until we get back?"

"I'll wait, I guess. You don't want to give me a hint, do you?"

"Nope. Suspense is good for the soul, and your soul is desperately in need of a retread at the moment."

"Was that a hint? Let me see. New shoes?"

Luann shook her head, carefully curled red hair bouncing softly about her shoulders. "No way, nuh-uh, I'm not even going to hint. You made your choice and you're stuck with it."

"There is something else on your mind," Dr. Sachs said halfway through their lesson, lifting his hands from the piano and turning to face Helgi. "You are not thinking about singing at all, and you are not singing very well as a result."

Helgi looked down at the silvery patterns weaving through the old German's pale green carpet. "I guess that's so," he muttered.

Dr. Sachs stood up, patting Helgi kindly on the shoulder. "Forget about this lesson. You are not learning anything today. Instead you shall come and have a glass or two of wine with me, and enjoy the fine weather in the garden, and perhaps you may eventually feel like telling me what is bothering you badly enough to choke your throat and keep you from hitting two notes on pitch in a row. The old man may have some advice worth hearing, after all. Or failing that, it may ease you simply to tell me, whether you find an answer or not. 'Sorrow eats your heart, if you cannot speak all your soul to another'. It is a good day for such things, I could never have imagined this warm sunlight in the middle of November when I was young. Shall we go into the garden?"

Helgi followed Dr. Sachs through the house into the kitchen. As the old musician opened the refrigerator and bent to take a bottle from the bottom shelf, Tiberius slunk around the corner and stood up on his hind legs, pawing at his master's hands and miaowing loudly.

"Bad cat, Tiberius. Greedy beast! You know you are not to be fed again till evening." Dr. Sachs disengaged the Siamese's claws from the back of his hand, sweeping the cat's length away from himself as he took out the wine with the other hand. "Ach, but you know we are having something nice, and you can't bear to be without your share, isn't it? There. Since cats do not drink wine, I shall pour a nice saucer of milk for you, and you must be happy with that till dinnertime. He is, perhaps," Sachs added to Helgi, "a kobold in disguise, and therefore it is good to be kind to him."

Tiberius crouched down over his milk, rumbling softly as he lapped at it. Dr. Sachs got two glasses from a higher cupboard, and the two of them went out into the garden. "No, leave the door open behind us. Tiberius will no doubt wish to come and join us when he has finished his milk."

The sunlight did not seem warm to Helgi, but pleasantly cool, with a light breeze ruffling the dried leaves from the trees. Just above the creek's bank was a small wooden table with a bench running along either side. A scattering of brown oak-leaves and acorns lay over the polished wood, Dr. Sachs brushed them off, lowering himself onto the bench facing the creek and gesturing Helgi to sit down beside him.

"This wine is what we call Weißherbst, the German rosé. Are you ein Weinkenner, a connoisseur?"

"Not really. I'm more of a beer-drinker."

"Ah. You will not often find the Weißherbst in the stores here, it is not well known outside Germany. This bottle is from the Waltershofener area of Baden, in Tuniberg, near to the Kaiserstuhl. The ground is volcanic there, and its wines draw the fire up through their roots." He poured out a glassful for each of them, the pale November light glowing softly through the sunset-pink wine. "Prosit!"

"Prosit!" Helgi echoed, and they drank. The wine was fruity and a little sweet, with a soft honeyed overtone. For a little while the two of them sat quietly, sipping at their wine and watching the creek rush by. Helgi could see where its flood had sunken a little after the October storms had eased, the tree roots writhing from little water-eaten caves in the naked earth, but the stream was still running fast and muddy near the height of its banks.

Helgi heard a faint rustle behind them and glanced back. Tiberius was creeping slowly down from the house, lifting his seal-gloved paws high above the fallen brown leaves. A gust of wind stirred through the grass. The Siamese crouched down, wriggling his rear a moment and then letting out a soft cry as he sprang forward to pounce on a leaf, or so Helgi thought, until he saw the thrashing beneath the cat's paws.

"Tiberius! What do you have there?" Dr. Sachs half-rose from his seat. Tiberius lifted his head, insolent blue eyes looking straight up at them. The head, and tail-lengths of a garter snake wriggled on either side of his mouth like a great dark mustache. He scampered a few steps, dropped the snake, and leapt onto it again, growling as he lowered his head.

Dr. Sachs sat back down, sighing. "There is no making him anything but a cat. I wish he would leave me the little snakes. They are useful against insects and vermin, but he will not understand this. Does his hunting disturb you? You are not too soft-hearted to bear the sight of it?"

"No." Helgi took another sip of wine, and suddenly the words gushed out of him. "The problem is a woman."

Dr. Sachs laughed softly. "This is little surprise. One who doesn't love you, or one whom you don't love?"

"I don't know. Two women, really and I'm not sure about either of them."

Sachs held up a gnarled hand. "Slowly, slowly. Tell me from the beginning."

So Helgi told him about the Tolkien song he had set with Karin in mind and the gifts they had given each other, about Luann, about Karin and Rof, and the whole history of Flourescent, and finally, about his fight beneath the bridge. The old German sat silent, turning the clear glass stem of his goblet and watching the amber-pink wine swirl in its bowl. Then Helgi saw the pattern shaping from his flowing words, clear as the bark of a crooked stick suddenly resolving into the rough scales and bright black eyes of a rattlesnake. He stopped speaking, drained his goblet, and spoke again.

"I love Karin, and I don't love Luann. I like her a lot, and she's the only woman I've ever slept with. I don't mean to hurt her, but I don't see any way out of it. Luann just can't, she'll never understand. I don't know that Karin loves me."

"Still, you have made a strong impression on her. That is a good beginning. Are you sure that she would be best for you? You have not described her as someone who means to have a long life."

"She is alive," Helgi answered softly, "and I do love her, with all my life."

"Yes, so you do." Dr. Sachs looked down at the rushing waters below them, his blue eyes blurring behind his wire-rimmed glasses. "Für Deutschland zu sterben," he murmured, his voice soft as a whisper rising up through the layers of many years. "I once knew many young men with such great loves, who lie in the black earth now, and are little mourned by the lands that keep their bones. Pure fools, who little knew what they fought for, and were betrayed by their own trust. But it seems to me that some of them fell as heroes, why-ever they fell. I am breathing this air and drinking this good wine because Walther Friedhelm held his post past his hour and died when he might have left it and lived. As with him, so with many another who chose death over life." He reached for the bottle, refilling Helgi's glass and topping up his own. "I have become an old man who rambles. Also, if you have made up your mind, there can be no good for anyone in pretending that it has not been made up. Get on with it, and court this air-woman with all the heart that is in you, and use the gifts she awakens in you to their fullest, as you have already chosen to do."

"Yes. Yes, I have."

Tiberius leapt up onto the table, the gutted snake in his mouth drooling blood onto the polished wood from head and tail-tip. Although it still twitched weakly along its length, Helgi knew the snake was dead already. The Siamese dropped his prey in front of Dr. Sachs, then settled down on his haunches and began to wash the blood from his dark mask with tongue and paw.

After he left Dr. Sachs' house, Helgi stopped at the next gas station to call Luann.

"Hello? Luann?"

"I am. Hello, Helgi."

"Luann, I need to talk to you. Can I come over?"

"Could we go out somewhere? I haven't eaten yet. I've got enough money for a pizza."

"I'd rather talk to you in private. We can go out afterwards, if you still want to."

"This does not sound good. Are you in trouble?"

"Not really. Look, I'll be right over. 'Bye."

Helgi's hands were steady as he hung up the phone and stepped out into the steel-blue light of the lowering evening. The Sun had sunken behind the trees of the White Rock Lake park, leaving their tattered silhouettes dark against the pale sky, and the air was growing cold very swiftly, prickling up a scattering of goosebumps on Helgi's bare arms beneath the sleeve-edges of his black T-shirt.

Luann was waiting by the door when he got there, the light that spilled out around her darkening her shape to a shadow. "Okay, what is it?"

"Let's go inside. It's cold out here."

"If you'd wear a jacket, it wouldn't be. Come in, then."

Helgi followed her through the living room, where Mr. and Mrs. O'Roarke sat in the blue light of the television, watching the news. Mr. O'Roarke was tall and thin, with thinning red hair cropped closely around the edges of a long horsey face and black-edged glasses. His wife was short and plump, the dull light smoothing the age of her rounded face till she could have been Luann's elder sister. They looked up to greet him as he passed, Helgi lifted a hand in answer.

Luann sat down on her bed without turning on the light, Helgi stayed standing, his eyes fixed firmly on hers. He could not think of any way to creep into what he had to say, so he said it straight out, "Luann, I have to break up our relationship."

Luann's eyes widened like pools of dark blood spreading over her white skin. "It's her, isn't it?"

Helgi nodded.

"You shit," she whispered. "You said you loved me." Luann's hands curled into tight fists in her lap.

"I really believed it, too. Luann, I never thought I'd see her again. I had no idea that she could come back like this. I am very sorry. I'll make it up to you any way I can, if you'll tell me how to. You don't want to keep a relationship going where you know you aren't my choice."

"So I was just a way to get laid in the meantime, huh? Or to get into Flourescent?"

"No! Luann, I really believed I loved you. I would never have."

"Never have looked at another woman, if you thought you had a chance to get her. Right. I understand. Well, you don't have to look at me any longer. Get the fuck out of this house, you liar. Out. I am terminating this conversation right now. You are not welcome here. If Flourescent keeps you, they're going to have to find a new place to practice. I never want to see or hear from you again, you understand me?" Luann's voice was cracking into tears as she stood, her fists bunched at her side. "I hope she tells you to fuck off and her boyfriend dribbles your head from here to New Orleans."

Helgi had nothing else to say. He turned around and went out, walking silently through the O'Roarkes' living room and out to his car. Although the dark's coldness sank into his bones as he drove, he did not turn on the heater, nor was he shivering. He was going to have to quit Flourescent, he knew, find another band, or else save up some money and tape his songs by himself, dubbing one part over another till he had all the voices he needed behind him. Luann's words had cut him more deeply than he had thought at first. Now, with their echo still ringing behind the muttering of the old Impala's engine and the shock-paleness of her face reflected in every streetlight's white glow, Helgi could not help wondering about his own truth. I never lied to her, he thought.

I told her what was in my thoughts, what I truly felt then, and I never made any promises to her. If I couldn't tell her about Karin, it was only because I hadn't told myself yet. The thought made Helgi no happier, but it seemed to ease the deep aching sting of shame that had lodged in his guts. He drove carefully, holding back his foot when he wanted to tread on the pedal with his full weight and shoot weaving among the long row of lights trailing the length of Central Expressway.

The phone was ringing when Helgi got in. He leapt through the living room in three large bounds, his shoulder slamming off the kitchen doorframe as he stretched for the receiver.

"Helgi, this is Mike."

"I'm here. I was about to call you."

"Hadding, you asshole, what did you do to my sister?"

"I broke off our relationship."

"Yeah, because you want to trade her in on Widget's cousin's girlfriend. You know how incredibly fucking stupid you are, Helgi?"

"Don't call me stupid, goddamn it!" Helgi roared. "You don't have any idea." He stopped, breathed deeply. "Look, Mike, I told Luann the truth. It was my fault, I am responsible. She saw what was going on before I did. If I hadn't broken us up, she would have eventually. Do you think I should have lied to her and kept the relationship going?"

For a moment Helgi heard nothing but the hiss of the phone line. Then, "I think you should have engaged your brain before running your mouth to her. Damn, Helgi, couldn't you have talked to me first? I could have told you some things."

"Like what?"

"Like, the Jensen woman is a certifiable psycho. You're weird enough by yourself that I was starting to worry about you a little, and hanging around her is only going to make it worse. I mean, we are talking about a woman whose basic purpose in life is to fly a very fast plane with the intention of killing people. This is not normal. On top of that, Widget says she's some kind of witch or Satanist or something."

"Widget's no candidate for a mental health award himself. What does he know? He probably says the same thing about me when I'm not there to hear."

"Plus, Rof will rip off your head and shit down your neck if he even thinks you might be trying to take Karin away from him. I'm serious, Helgi. You may know some karate, but Rof is a bad dude. He will hurt you, man. He may stop before he kills you, but you will wind up in the hospital."

"Maybe so, but he'll be there in the next bed beside me. What are you bitching about, anyway? I thought you were pissed off at me for breaking up with Luann. Why should you care if I get into a fight with Rof?"

"Flourescent can't make it without you! Aw, fuck," Helgi heard Mike's deep gasp, almost like a sob, then the guitarist went on, more calmly. "Look, Helgi, you know and I know that your songs are what made the difference at our last gig. If Rack quits, to hell with him, he's replaceable. Same with Widget or Josh, there's musicians in search of a band all over the place. Getting a songwriter like you is something different, and I don't believe I know anyone else who could sing your songs, there may be better voices out there, but there aren't any like yours. If Rof breaks your head, Flourescent is S.O.L shit outa luck."

"I thought I was going to have to quit the band when I broke up with Luann anyway."

"You can't do that. She'll get over it. She doesn't own our parents' house, anyway, and she doesn't have to watch us while we're practicing, she can't keep you out."

"She thought I'd used her to get into the band."

"She ought to know better than that. If we hadn't needed you, I wouldn't have taken you no matter what she said. Hell, she never paid very much attention to us before you joined, anyway, what would she know?"

"I don't know. But I still feel responsible, and I want to make it up to her somehow."

"Quitting Flourescent won't do it. You want my advice? Just leave her alone for a while and let it blow over. Luann may have a bad temper, but she forgets her grudges pretty quickly. She'll be talking to you again by the end of the month, just wait and see. But promise me that you won't go sniffing around Karin and get yourself hurt, okay?"

"I can't promise that. Do you think I would have done this tonight if I hadn't made up my mind?"

Helgi heard Mike's sigh, like a dry gust of wind through old leaves. "I was hoping that by now you'd be coming down from whatever you were on. I really was. I guess I should have known better. Show for rehearsal Thursday night, same time, same channel, and try at least to live till this weekend, okay?"

"Okay."

Helgi hung up, then went up to his room and picked up the phone.

Karin sat in her apartment's one chair, rubbing her temples and waiting for the aspirin to kick in. It had not been a good day. She had almost gotten into a shouting match with that asshole Captain Shale, over something stupid. Hel tager mig, she thought, I can't even remember what started it, but basically, the problem was that Shale thought she should be making bread and having babies, and she thought he should still be shoveling pig shit on that farm in Texarkana where he was spawned. The Dread Eye had ranked both of them to the dogs and back, as if they were raw recruits, and given them weekend duty together as an object lesson in cooperation. Karin had plans with her family.

Rof had been crabby all day too, glaring sideways at her with that peculiarly dark look he got when he was having problems with his mother. Karin didn't know if he was angry with her and wouldn't say, or if the old witch was giving Rof some sort of trouble about her again, or what. Or perhaps he was still upset by Helgi's music, he had grunted something about the band's next gig and a demo tape, then refused to say anything else. The phone rang. Karin let it sound twice, fully prepared to let it ring until the caller gave up, then she thought that it might be her mother, and she would have to explain about not being free that weekend after all.

"Captain Jensen speaking."

"Hello, Karin." She recognized Helgi's voice at once, though the line lent its tone an odd distant resonance.

"Hello, Helgi. Hey, I heard your group's playing in Deep Ellum Saturday. Congratulations. What's the name of the place?"

"The Blue Door. Mike says it's kind of a new club. Are you going to be there?"

"I can't. The baleful gaze of the Eye fell upon me, and behold, I am stuck with weekend duty." Karin paused for breath, wondering if she should tell Helgi about the whole mess. He didn't deserve it, though, and if he hung around her much longer, he'd get plenty of chances to see her being bad-tempered. "Rof said he'd probably show up for at least part of the evening, though. I also heard that you're about to make a tape. Will you give me a copy?"

"Of course. News sure does get around, doesn't it?"

"Rof's family is pretty close-knit. What one of them knows at noon, all the rest know by two o'clock. Anything else going on?"

"Well, I broke up with Luann tonight."

Karin tried to remember what Helgi's girlfriend looked like, got only a vague idea of shortness and red hair. The two of them had seemed pretty attached, though, Helgi was probably calling for a little sympathy. Maybe dealing it out would take her mind off her own problems. "That's too bad. Was it your idea, or hers?"

"Mine."

"You want to talk about it?"

"Not over the phone."

"Oh. Well, tell you what Rof and I both have the Friday after next, Thanksgiving Friday free. What about all of us going out for pizza or something, if you're not too stuffed with turkey leftovers to move? I know it's kind of a long time to wait, but I'm stuck here immovably till then."

"That'll be fine."

"Look, Helgi," Karin said, her voice softer, "if you need to talk to me, I am here. Don't be shy, okay? Shy men get on my nerves."

"I'll keep that in mind. Thanks, Karin. I'll be all right."

"If you're sure, well, see you when I get free then. Take care."

"You, too."

Luann sat as far away from Helgi as possible in the teachers' lounge the next day, turning her head away ostentatiously whenever he glanced in her direction. Whenever Helgi looked at the tight set of her small shoulders and the red ponytail drooping over the back of her neck, he felt a vague chill of guilt in the pit of his stomach, as if he had swallowed a frozen stone, but it always melted away in a few breaths. He was more engaged in working out the words and notes and hidden runes of a new song. A song that did not come quite so easily this time, one that he would have to perform alone.

CHAPTER XXIV

The day of the Thing was very bright, Sunna's light burning white on the fresh-fallen snow and flashing like lightning from the blade of the great bronze ax that Aiwilimae bore in both hands. The northern drighten nodded as they walked along the firth's edge to the moot-field, looking up at the blue-white sky. "Tiwaz means us to see clearly. However the deeming falls, you may await its going rightly."

"I have no fear of its falling against me," Hoilo-gae answered, touching the hilt of his sword so that the iron would turn away any ill-luck his words might bring.

Two tall lur-players, brothers whose fair hair hung lank about their broad faces, stood inside the coils of their horns with their hands cupped over the mouthpieces to keep the metal warm. Swaebhon sat on a stool between them, her hood down and pale braids spilling over her white pelt. As Aiwilimae stepped within the stakes that marked the Thing-stead, the players raised the instruments to their mouths. The light flashed bright from the lurs' shining bronze bells as they blew out a chord that shivered through Hoilogae's bones.

"Those are new-made," Attalae whispered to Hoilogae, an overtone of awe in his voice. "They have not lost the craft of that casting here, though we have not made such horns in Jutland since my father's time."

Aiwilimae's muscles bunched beneath his bearskin cloak as he lifted the huge ax, swinging it around his head in a lightning-bright arc. "Now Thonaraz hallow this Thing-stead, and drive out all ill wights and witches' charms!" He bellowed. "Here a man has come to seek my daughter's hand, with great boasts of his might. Tiwaz and Waron, oath-fro and frowe, show us the truth of his claims, Frijjo, help us to deem the worth of this wedding!" He plunged the ax-blade into the snow, holding it there as the gathered men, Hoilogae's and his own, stared silently, as the count of heartbeats length-ened into the count of breath. At last he drew it out and turned to Hoilogae. "Now set your sword-hand on this ax, and tell us your name and lineage, your deeds and your hopes for land and rule."

The ax was cold beneath Hoilogae's palm, though not so cold as he had feared, he thought that his skin would not freeze to it. In a strong voice, he recounted all of his kin from Herwamundaz on his father's side and Sigis-brandaz the grandfather of Swafnijaz on his mother's and told where their howe-mounds were, as well as he could remember.

"It was a little before Midsummer's that I wore the war-helm and led the folk-host against Hrothamaraz who had slain my mother's father, and we were blessed with victory. Because of this, which was done at my rede, my father and mother are fro and frowe in her udal lands now. Those lands are four full days march from one side to the other, over flat and fruitful fields, and I expect that they shall be my udal part. My younger brother Hedhinaz holds rule for my father in Glazaleunduz, which is a smaller land, but lies on the northern coast of Jutland, and there much fine amber is gathered, so that it is counted a rich holding. Nor am I unfriendly with Sigisharjaz, the greatest drighten of Jutland, whose fame you have heard even here. It was he who gave me the rede to seek Swaebhon, and his rede as well that sent me to Wejlunduz, who wrought a sword for me the like of which has not been seen before, as you may see it now!"

Sword-hand still on the ax, Hoilogae drew his blade awkwardly with his shield-hand, holding it high so that all could see the wyrm-pattern of the iron. "Before Thonaraz and Tiwaz, and Wodhanaz who has given me victory and who sent his maid to name me, I swear that all I have said is the truth!"

"Now take your hand from the ax, and hold it up so that all may see it," Ai-wilimae said to Hoilogae in a low voice, watching him keenly. Hoilogae lifted his palm easily from the metal, its cold had not scathed him. "The gods have not spoken against your oath, are there any men here who may speak?"

The scar-faced warrior in the sealskin cloak stepped forward. "I, Chaid-hamariz, do not say that this man lies, but I heard a different tale of Her-wawardhaz's eldest son when I came to Sigisharjaz's hall at the last winter's end. Then it was said that the line of his wife Sigislinthon lay in shame, for Swafnijaz was yet unavenged, and that the shame was born in their eldest son. It was said that he would not speak and no name would fasten to him, that he was a coal-biter in the hall, or sat weaponless and witless on a mound, barely able to watch his father's sheep, and it was said that this showed some weakness brought forth from both their lines. I do not mean to do you harm, nor wish to make you my foe," he added softly to Hoilogae, "but it seems to me that you are very unlike the one named as the son of Herwawardhaz, drighten in Glazaleunduz."

"It is true I did not speak for long, and that it was long before my name was given to me," Hoilogae answered. "I have washed the hearth-ashes from my fame and the shame from my parents' lines with the blood of my foes, and that more than once. If you wish to hear of deeds closer to your home, here is one. Though one of our ships was lost in the struggle at evening, we lay a full night without harm in Hati's Firth. There you will find a new haven-mark, a tall stone that was the etin's daughter Rime-Gardhaz, and it will be long before ships find their deaths there again. That you may see for yourself if you fare to that firth."

Aiwilimae hefted the ax thoughtfully in his hands, narrow eyes flickering over its frost-dulled sheen as though he sought to find a flaw in it. "Your words wax higher and higher, and none but yourselves and the gods may know the truth of them. It seems to me that if you are not a hero, you must be mad."

"I can swear to the truth of what he says," Attalae broke in. "Chaidhamariz, if you have not forgotten, you saw me in Sigisharjaz's hall, and that his frowe brought me ale and seated me beside the drighten."

"That I remember," the thin warrior admitted, scratching at the edge of his scar as though he could think of nothing else to do with his hands. "You are one of whom he thought well."

Aiwilimae stepped forward. The great bronze ax hissed through the air between Chaidhamaraz and Attalae. "You are also Hoilogae's man. Now, my men, you have heard what has been said. Does it seem to you that these boasts are trusty enough to win the fairest maid of the northlands, and to take her from her father's hall to a far-off land where we know no one and the ways are strange to us? Which of you would give his own daughter to this outland warrior on these strengths?"

Hoilogae looked around at the fur-muffled men of Aiwilimae's land. He saw friendship on none of their faces, one or two spat into the snow, though a few looked at him with measuring eyes and nodded slowly. Still, none of them spoke, until one whose voice marked him as old spoke from beneath the hoar-silvered fox-tails edging his dark cloak, "There must be another man to speak for him, one known to us as trusty. He may be famed in Jutland, or a friend of Sigisharjaz, but that is little here in the northlands. Until he is known to us, or someone will take his part, we should not give him the last child of our atheling-line."

Hoilogae looked at Attalae and Attalae shook his head. "We may stay here longer than we willed."

"What must I do?" Hoilogae asked. Though he tried to still it, he could hear the shrill note of wan-hope in his voice, he knew now that Aiwilimae would never choose to give his beloved child away.

"Stay here for a time, a year, or two, until you have had time to prove yourself before all."

Swaebhon rose from her seat then, striding forward to set her hand on her father's ax. "That is not needful, for there is one man who is known to all of us and who has had time to learn of Hoilogae's deeds, yes, and who was with him in Hati's Firth. Someone go to fetch the thrall who hides his face in the horse-stalls, pull the fold of his cloak from his head, and bring him here before us."

Hoilogae shifted his blade from shield-hand to sword-hand. "That we must not do. I swore that I would not ask him to go inside or speak. He chose to come in of his own will, but he must not speak for my sake."

"Calm yourself, Hoilogae," the old man in the fox-trimmed cloak said. "You sought to spare him from having to relive his shame, but it is too late, for now we all know the name he bore and the oath-breaking that stripped him of it. Yet he was a trusty man, he merely had the ill-luck to swear an oath, the keeping or breaking of which was not in his power at the last. Though he may no longer swear troth as a free man, there are many here who once thought well of him and might still heed his words."

"It is so," one of the other Northmen said, and a few other voices murmured assent. "A trusty man may still be true, however his luck has turned against him." "Swaebhon's rede is good, let someone fetch him."

Hoilogae closed his eyes, till he felt Swaebhon's hands on his shoulders. "You are not to blame, Hoilogae," she whispered to him, her pale grey eyes cold and still as the winter sky above. "I knew Ansuthewaz when he first came back. He could not hide from me. I gave him his name, 'the Ansuz's thrall'."

"Still, I owed him some troth. I should not have let him come to this."

"The matter is out of your hands now. See, here he comes, and this may not turn so ill for him."

Back straight and head held high, Ansuthewaz walked between the two warriors who had gone to fetch him. He over topped the taller of them by three finger-widths, and the shorter had to hasten his stride to keep up with the thrall. The Sun's white winter-light shone cruelly clear on the greasy mat of Ansuthewaz's hair, on the grime darkening his face and the stains of horse dung crusting his cloak, Hoilogae could not keep his nostrils from tightening as he caught the smell on a gust of wind.

Ansuthewaz stopped just outside the Thing-stakes, gazing straight at Hoilogae. He said nothing, but the betrayed look in his brown eyes was rending as the human gaze of a speared seal.

"Tell us of Hoilogae," Swaebhon called to him.

"Men wondered greatly over him in Sigisharjaz's Holm, for Herwawardhaz's son was known as a witling, yet when he came to that hall, there was no doubt that he was a man of might. He borrowed a little boat to fare on an errand only the drighten knew, and when he brought it back again, it was full of fine goods that he had won when he slew Hrothamariz, and those he gave to Sigisharjaz in thanks for the loan. The storm came up from Hati's Firth and broke his other ship before I could warn him, but he struck into the sea, and the storm sank before him. I do not know what passed in that night, but I know that when the dawn came, a great boulder stood where none had been before, and it looked more than a little like a troll-queen to my eyes. I know that he swore an oath to me, concerning what might come to pass in this land."

"It was not Hoilogae who let you be called here, but I myself," Swaebhon answered. "He spoke against it, but to no good, for you were already known. He did not swear that you should not be asked to speak, only that he should not ask you."

"Then his luck is better than mine." Ansuthewaz looked over the men gathered within the moot-ring. "Has any of you anything else to ask me?"

"You need speak no more," Aiwilimae rumbled.

Ansuthewaz jerked his head in a brief nod, and began to walk again, striding around the edge of the stake-marked stead. Hoilogae thought that he must mean to go along the cliff-path that turned up to the forest, but he did not turn at the path, nor slow his step. Then Hoilogae lunged after him, running with all his strength, but he was far too late, Ansuthewaz had dropped from sight before Hoilogae had taken three steps, the gulls swirling up angrily from the cliff's edge where he had been. No sound came through the waves' crashing and the birds' sharp cries.

Hoilogae whirled, striding towards Swaebhon. Fair as wrought silver, un-clouded by any shock or sorrow, her face did not change as he stood before her. "You knew that this would happen," he said, his voice low enough that no one else could hear. "It was your deeming that brought Ansuthewaz to his death."

"So it was. You and I wrought it together. Did you find his stead fitting to him, or see that he lived well beneath his wyrd?" Swaebhon took his hand. "Come, let us look upon him." She spoke a little louder, so that the men gathered about, still silent from shock, could hear her. "It is my task to ready the death-rites here, and no one may stay me in doing it."

The two of them walked down the narrow path that wound safely be-tween the cliff-crags, down where the sea foamed and swirled between gull-whitened rocks. Ansuthewaz lay half in, half out of a sea-pool at the tide's edge, the waves sweeping over his face and drawing back from him again. His legs drooped in the water that covered him to the waist, his shoul-ders were flung back, lying flat against the rock behind him as though his backbone had become serpent-lithe. The dead man's arms were outspread, his mouth gaped, sea-water brimming over his lips, and his hair lifted like fronds of seaweed with each wave that passed over him. The sky's brightness gleamed blue off his brown eyes as though mirrored in a still bog-pool. If he had bled, the sea had washed it away already.

Hoilogae crouched down, reaching out to touch Ansuthewaz's hand. He was cold as if his ghost had been long gone, cold as Hoilogae's own ice-chilled fingers. A shiver ran through Hoilogae as he looked at the dead man. I too shall die, he thought. And for what?

"His name was Wulfaz, the son of Childiowulfaz," Swaebhon said. "Now it is again."

Hoilogae gazed at the man's pale face, trying to guess at the last sight that had widened his eyes so. It seemed to him that it could not have been so ill, the stark lines were gone from around the dead man's mouth, as though the waves had washed them away with the filth of the horse-stalls. As Hoilogae stared, it seemed to him that Wulfaz had flung his arms wide to embrace the sky, that the Sun's light shone off his eyes like the reflection of a polished shield-boss in his sight, scouring them free from the tarnish of his wan-hope.

"A gift to Wodhanaz." Against the wave-crashing, Hoilogae could not hear whether the voice that spoke was low or high, his own or Swaebhon's, but it was the walkurjon who went on, "He leapt into Walhall."

"That is the stead fitting to him," Hoilogae answered slowly. "You did not choose ill."

"It was he who chose to win his worth again at the last. He might have turned away, and sat biting the coals of another man's fire for his lifetime, and been cast into the bog like a cow dead of sickness at the last."

"Now he shall be burned as a man, with a man's weapons at his side, and neither know his shame longer nor be known for it," Hoilogae murmured, then, to the one who lay there. "Come, Wulfaz. I should have liked to have known you." He lifted Wulfaz's arms, wrapping them about his shoulders from behind, and heaved himself up with the dead man on his back. He might have been lifting a sack of grain, he could feel how the bones were shattered inside the skin, so that the body slithered from side to side as he walked.

Swaebhon let him go up the path before her so that she could steady him if his foot slipped on the narrow way, and so they came back to the cliff-top and passed within the stakes that marked the Thing-place.Hoilogae laid his burden down in the snow before Aiwilimae's feet, turning the dead man's head carefully to hide the porridge-thick mess spilling from the back of his caved-in skull.

"Now he has proved the worth of his word," Hoilogae called out, his voice rough through the still air. "Let no one say that he was not true."

Aiwilimae stared down at the body for a little time, holding his ax over it as though he might let its edge fall at any moment. "I do not give my daughter to you with a glad heart, nor can I wish you blessing save that I wish her all happiness. But if she will go with you, I cannot keep her from you now. Tiwaz and Waron witness that I have said it, and Frijjo bring weal to the wedding."

Though Hoilogae awaited it, no one, not even his own men, struck sword against shield at the Northman's words. Those who were gathered there stood still as if fettered, until Swaebhon's laugh shattered through the icy air. "There is no cause for stillness now! Be joyful. One is freed from bonds, and two have taken them on. I say that Hoilogae and I shall be wed at Austarjon's dawn, and no feast shall be finer. Now bring branches and a burning brand to the holy stone, for there is a bale-fire to be laid for this true thane, and a betrothal fire to be lit for us, that the gods may see our brightness." She whirled into Hoilogae's arms, he clasped her tightly to him, their mouths melting into a kiss that lasted till the sparks spun before Hoilogae's eyes and the roaring in his ears rose above the sound of the thanes' shouting and bronze striking wood. By the time of the Yule feast, the days had waned to mere glimmers of grayness marking night from night, and the wind howled snowflakes about the hall without ceasing.

Now the men and women stayed by the fire, many of them sleeping in Ai-wilimae's hall, and told tales of trolls and ghosts over their ale as the thread spun thicker on the women's distaffs and the thin wood-shavings coiled down from the men's whittling-knives to the icy earth-floor or flared up in the fire. Swaebhon delighted in these stories, tossing her long hair back as she leaned forward to listen more eagerly or waving her horn about as she told tales of her own. As the last daylight of Yule-night had faded from the sky, Hoilogae and Swaebhon kindled a fire together, she holding the lower piece of wood steady while he turned the bow-drill until a little coal began to glow under it. Together they blew it up to a strong flame, feeding it with straw and twigs, then set it to the great pine log that lay across the fire pit in the middle of the hall as the gathered folk watched in silence.

Once the flame faltered, and then no breath could be heard, but at last it got its grip on the bark, eating its way around the tree's bole and flaring into brightness as it tasted the amber-gold resin bleeding from the lopped branches' stubs, and then a great cheer went up. Swaebhon poured a precious draught of her winter-mead for each of the folk in the hall, two women lifted drums from the rafters and began to play, and others to clap their hands and sing with them. After a little while, Aiwilimae and two of his stoutest men left the hall. When they came back, their furry cloaks white with snow, Aiwilimae was gripping a twisted ring in the nose of a huge boar, a yellow-toothed tusker of the half-wild kind that his folk herded in the woods by their settlement. The boar was grunting angrily, squealing now and again as he dug in his hooves and Aiwilimae yanked at the ring, but at last the Northman was able to bring the beast over to the hearth.

"Hail to you, Fro Ingwaz and Frowe Holdon!" He called. "We hallow this swine to you, for battle-boar's bravery and a fair harvest." Aiwilimae looked around the hall, his gaze meeting the eyes of each of the folk in turn. "Who counts himself the bravest here? Who has the high mood of a hero, who will match himself to Fro Ingwaz's battle-might?"

"None but I!" Hoilogae answered, striding boldly forward and drawing his sword. "Now I have done the highest deed of all this year. Many men have led battles, and some few, if the tales told last night held truth, have dealt with the troll-kind and left them stone in the light, but only I have won Swaebhon's oath to be my wife."

A yellow-toothed grin split Aiwilimae's blond beard. "Then show your might!" He gave the ring in the boar's nose a hard twist and let go. Squealing with rage, the swine lunged forward, but Hoilogae had already whirled to the side, bringing his sword down with all the strength of his turning. A fountain of dark blood burst from the boar's neck over the fire, half-quenching the log with a great hiss of coppery steam, his head rolled to the side as the flames sizzled back over the drenched wood. Hoilogae leaned down, stabbing his sword deeply into the pig's head. The blood ran over the hilt and down his arms as he heaved it up two-handed and bore it slowly about the hall for each of the folk to touch in turn.

The boar's flesh took a long time seething, the women often had to take fresh stones from the fire with their tongs and cast them into the clay cauldron to keep its water cooking-hot. There was plenty of bread, and more ale to drink while waiting for it. A rough wrestling contest began in the meantime as well, with the thanes taking turns to see whose strength might prove greatest while those who watched called out rede and wagers, and another round of stories was told at the fire. When the swine's flesh was all eaten, Aiwilimae's folk, both men and women, began putting on their cloaks. Some brought masks out of hiding as well, the rough wooden faces of beasts and birds and grimacing trolls, and tied them on beneath their caps, while those who owned horses set saddles upon them. A few folk slung the straps of small drums over their shoulders, and more were carrying pipes of bone or hollow wood. Hoilogae's men stood together in the middle of the hall, watching in bewilderment.

"What do they mean to do?" Hraidhamannaz asked.

Aiwilimae looked down at him through the eye slits of a snarling bear, whose wooden maw was set with real teeth. The mask warped his speech, as though his words echoed back and forth through it. "The Ansuz rides at the head of the gods and ghosts tonight, and we ride with him. Thus the last sheaf's seeds are scattered, its life freed to hallow the fields for another fruitful harvest. You are strangers here, you may stay inside, if you have no mood for the gods' ride, but none of us may choose to hold back from it."

Swaebhon's mask was the green-gray face of a troll-woman, huge point-ed ears flaring up between long braids of twisted black and gray horsehair and wide mouth opened in a sharp-toothed grin. Hoilogae helped her tie it on, tugging affectionately at the long fair braid of her own hair dangling down her back. The mask she tied on him in turn was that of a wolf with gaping mouth. The fur had been stuck on with pine-resin, its scent sharp in Hoilogae's nostrils with every breath he drew. Three women stood by the fire lighting the brands from a large pile and handing them to the masked folk, Swaebhon took two and gave one to Hoilogae. Though Aiwilimae was fro in the hall, it was the old man who had spoken against Hoilogae at the Thing who stood by the door, blowing a sharp note on his bone flute to call the folk to their places in the long line snaking back through the hall. His mask was a man's face swollen into the blue-black grimace of one long dead, he did not wear his fox-trimmed cap now, but was dressed all in black wool, with a long staff held in his left hand and the flute in his right.

He cocked his head as though he were listening for words in the wind, then flung the door open, shouting, "Out of the way! Let the way be clear!"

Swaebhon caught Hoilogae by his free hand as they ran out into the whirling snow behind the old man. Aiwilimae rode his stallion, his hoof beats pounding beside them, Hoilogae could hear the pipes and drums behind them, weaving in and out of the howling wind that cast the torch-flames back in streaks of fire. Borne up by the speed of his running, he felt the laughter deep in his throat, though he could not hear it. The long wyrm of fire-points wove over the fields, the folk scattering the snow like a great wind as they rode and ran. Hoilogae could feel things bursting beneath his feet, hot might prickling his soles like barley-hairs at each step. Still Swaeb-hon's grip drew him on, faster and faster. Now it seemed to Hoilogae that they were racing between the horses, now they were running alone through the shining snowflakes, now they were hastening among the masked throng again, the twisted faces and beast-faces leaping out of the storm around them as the flute-song pierced through his skull and the drums beat in his bones. Once he was sure he glimpsed Attalae, the old rede-giver's gray hair fluttering like a banner in the wind as he ran a little ahead of Hoilogae, but a flurry of snow veiled him again.

Then Hoilogae felt something heavy slithering and bumping against his back, boneless arms wrapping about his neck. He gasped for air, tucking his chin down to keep its grip from his throat, but it slid off in the next moment. Some of the folk that ran with them had lost their masks, bare faces shone white in the snow, though never long enough for Hoilogae to see any of them clearly. He glanced backward. The torchlight glimmered from the nar-row cheekbones and dark eyes of Ansuthewaz, Wulfaz, and struck a spark from his bronze sword-hilt. Hoilogae blinked and the sight was gone, he did not know who ran beneath the gaping white mask behind him. A horsed shadow loomed up against the whirling flakes before them, raised spear stretching into a long streak of blackness through the storm. No, the torch's smoke streamed back from Aiwilimae's hand till he turned and the wind swept it away.

The torches had burned almost to their nubs by the time the runners came panting to the hall again. Hoilogae and Swaebhon were the first in. As they passed between the door-posts, one of the men who sat by the fire, Hoilogae was not sure who, made a choked cry, and Thonarabernu rose halfway from the bench, lifting the amber ax-head that dangled from his sword-hilt. Then Hoilogae pulled off his mask, and they broke into laughter.

"Hai, Hoilogae, we didn't know you," Attalae called, his sleepy voice a little slurred with ale. "That's what comes of keeping company with troll-queens."

Hoilogae glanced at Swaebhon, who had not taken her mask off yet. "You're fair in every shape, but I like your other face better," he said jestingly to her.

Her sudden unearthly cackle made everyone in the hall start. "What makes you think I have another face?" She cried in a high harsh voice that ran over Hoilogae's nerves like a scraping-tool over a fresh hide. She lifted her arms towards him, shadowy fingers crooked into great claws, the flickering firelight widened the troll-woman's grin and opened her mouth.

Hoilogae caught her hands in his as if to wrestle with her, but drew her in to him instead, thrusting his face against the mask hard enough for the troll-woman's teeth to cut his lips as he pressed his kiss through her mouth to Swaebhon's.

"Out of the way, you two!" Aiwilimae shouted. "Or I'll lead my horse right over you."

Hoilogae and Swaebhon moved aside to let the horses through the doorway, and she turned around so that Hoilogae could untie her mask. Her eyes were heavy-lidded as if she were half-asleep, but she smiled softly at him as she reached out to brush the blood from his mouth. "You're never without a wound, are you, my hero? It's well for you that I know the crafts of healing."

"Well for you, too. What should you do without me?"

Swaebhon crooked her arm around his shoulders. "I should be very sad. But don't think you can run away from me and leave me grieving like other women when their men have left them. I can run as swiftly as you, and ski more swiftly, and I dare say that I'm more used to swimming as well, if you leave me, I shall chase you down where-ever you go." With her free hand, she traced a shape through the melting snow on his fur-wrapped chest. Three triangles overlapping each other. "See. I have bound you with my knot. You cannot get away from me now."

"I think this bond will not be so hard to bear," he answered her, smiling.

The days waxed more swiftly after Yule, though the cold strengthened, but at last the snow began to shrink together with the nights and the birches to bud under the Sun's lengthening light. One morning, not long before daylight began to outstrip darkness, Hoilogae and Swaebhon were walking along the beach in search of clams when they heard a sound over their heads like the barking of a full pack of dogs.

Hoilogae looked up to the cliff-edge, but Swaebhon pointed out over the sea, where a flock of long-necked geese traced their straggling wing-pattern against the cloud-feathered sky.

"See, they've come bringing the storms in their wings," she told him. "We'll have rain for the next days, and likely thunder as well. The Moon was full last night, when he's waned and begun to wax new, the worst of the storms should be past, and we can hold Austarjon's feast, and our wedding."

The night before Austarjon's feast, Hoilogae was not allowed to see Swaebhon. The women and men went to the bath-house separately after sunset, after leaping into the ice-rimmed pond, the men came back to the hall, but Chaidhamariz told Hoilogae that the women had a place of their own.

"They go into the woods, to a holy stone that stands in a birch grove. What they do there, no man knows."

"Did you never try to follow them?" Hraidhamannaz asked from the next bench. The young warrior's eyes were bright over the rim of his horn, the sap of curiosity clearly rising in his veins.

Chaidhamariz shook his head. "No man can see what they see and be a man. Women have wisdom of their own, it may be greater than ours, but I would not pay that price for it."

Hraidhamannaz swiftly moved his clenched fist before his groin, thumb thrust through fingers to ward.

Though the Northmen had bedded him down in soft furs on clean straw and fragrant herbs that night, Hoilogae could not sleep, but turned restlessly, staring at the pink glow of the coals through their gray fur of ash. The hall grumbled like a huge beehive with the sound of men snoring, a sound so familiar to Hoilogae by now that he hardly marked it. Quietly he climbed out from between the furs and bound his shoes to his feet, casting his wolf-cloak around his shoulders. One of the dogs sleeping by the fire raised its head, then got to its feet, following as he eased the hall-door open and stepped out into the night. The Moon's thin white edge was very bright among the stars, silvering the fresh green shoots that furred the field and the new leaves of the birches that stood here and there among the dark pines. Hoilogae followed the path that led along the cliff's edge, the gray hound padding silently after him.

Below, the swirling edges of foam glimmered white against the black water, drawing his gaze down. He could not see the rocks, but the patterns of froth showed him where they broke the waves. For a long time he stood there with the hound beside him, looking over the cliff, until his feet were numb with cold and his eyelids had begun to droop heavy before his sight. The burdens the women bore on their night-faring to the mountain were lighter than those they had carried when the birch-sap rose baskets of flowers for weaving into wreaths, and torches to light the way, but still they went slowly. The pathway was not easy to follow in the darkness and flickering flames. Swaebhon was naked beneath the heavy furs that wrapped her. She must be twice-cleaned that night, as a new bride and as the one who would call the gods and speak the blessings at dawn.

Often she strode ahead of the others, until their long shadows in the torchlight melted into the darkness beneath the trees and only glimmers of the full Moon's light through the branches showed her the edges of the path, it was hard to hold herself back, when she knew that the dawning would bring Hoilogae into her embrace at last. The softness of the wind rustling through the woods hid a cruel edge of ice, but the snow had melted early that year, the sodden leaf-mold was black as coal, and squished beneath Swaebhon's fur-shrouded feet as if she were walking through a bog. Behind her, the other women were singing in a full-throated chorus that would warn wandering beasts away, their song drowned out the owls' hooting and the voices of the other night birds, but now and again Swaebhon heard the long rising howls of a far-off wolf pack.

The wolves would make no threat to such a host of women, and Swaebhon was gladdened to know that they found her wedding-eve fair. Though she knew well enough that there was no beauty in her singing, Swaebhon joined in the next verse, thumping the butt of her spear on the ground with the beat and making up in loudness what she lacked in tone. It was good to be singing with the other women again, it was very good not to feel their cold gazes clinging to her back like little leeches.

"Wed to a good mana woman is merry,
gladsome and gleefulgoes to wedding bed
Fro Ingwaz has forgedthe frolicsome tool,
her husband's own hammershe'll have at her will!"

Thonaragardhaz reached up to thump Swaebhon on the shoulder with her little fist. "Softer, Swaebhon, you'll scare off every land-wight between here and Hoilogae's country," she scolded, but there was no hate in her voice. Swaebhon only smiled down at her, blinking away the smoke from the smaller woman's torch.

"That will be a long faring, but at least we no longer need fear passing Hati's Firth."

Child-hagardhaz was the first to step into the grove, going to the Moon-whitened stone and laying her hands upon it.

"Frijjo, Frowe Holdon, bright and dark goddesses all!" She called. "Hail upon Austarjon's night! Now we ask your blessings, for our folk's fairest maid shall be given at dawn, to a hero like those of elder days. Cleanse her and hallow her, here in this holy stead, that their wedding may bring blessing on all our folk, and new life to the lands." Child-hagardhaz turned to face the other women, a black boulder against the Moon's light. "Come within, Swaebhon," she said, her deep voice sending a raspy shiver up the maiden's spine.

Swaebhon bent to untie the laces holding her leg-wrappings on, stepping barefoot onto the wet earth before she let her fur cloak fall over Thonaragardhaz's outstretched arm. Cold as the wind was on her naked body, Swaebhon's own warmth glowed within her as though she had just come from the bath-house. She strode boldly into the clearing, going to the stone and leaping upon it. Standing so high, she could see the faint glimmer of brightness that ringed the holy grove. Shadows moved outside, the dark troll-women roaming in search of prey on this last night before the year's weight tipped fully over to summer, and within the grove, Swaebhon could see the fairer shadows of the idises, the womanly clan-ghosts who helped and blessed their living kin.

As the might of the holy stone tingled up through her bare feet, Swaebhon's nipples tightened, and she felt a sweet throbbing between her legs. I will have Hoilogae very soon, she told herself, but there was little soothing in that thought, rather, she longed even more to feel his broad chest pressing against her breasts, his strong thighs clasped tightly between her own. The first cleansing was by fire. The torch-bearers wove about the stone in the simple steps of the old dance, Thonaradis beat on her little drum. Each woman swung her torch about Swaebhon, the flames licking too fast to burn her and the pine-smoke rising thick about her.

Thrice Frowe Holdon had been burnt, when she first came to the halls of the gods, thrice she had risen more brightly from the flames like smelted gold, thrice the women danced with their torches. It had happened before that a careless or hateful torch-stroke had set a bride's hair on fire, leaving her scarred or dead, but no torch scathed Swaebhon that night. The second cleansing was by water. Each of the women had a small flask of birch-bark, filled at a running stream between dawn-light and sunrise the morning before. As they danced, the flying water glittered like ice in the Moon's light, splashing coldly over Swaebhon's body to wash away the soot-marks a few of the torches had left upon her thighs and belly. Sagenon, the gray-clad teller of tales, dwelt in the sunken halls, where she and Wodhanaz drank from golden cups as the waves roared above them, there the two of them spoke of what had been, and that memory was ever in the hallowed waters of Wyrd's burn.

Often brides wept when the other women cast the cold waters over them, remembering their sorrows or ill deeds they had done. But Swaebhon had only Wulfaz to remember, and no need to weep. He had made and met his end well. Thonaradis thumped slowly on her drum as the dancers broke from the ring, the women going to the birch trees around the clearing. Swaebhon heard their whispering like leaves in the wind as they asked the holy trees for their gifts before lifting knives and cutting long thin branches free. The third cleansing was by the birch's might, now the dance began again, the switches singing through the air to strike against Swaebhon's body, thighs and buttocks, belly and breasts. The pain was sharp and stinging, lashes keen as knife-edges of beaten bronze, this would stir the life that slept in her womb, so that Hoilogae's seed might kindle her children.

The goddess Gabhjo had lashed on her four sons, mighty oxen fathered by an etin, driving them with her whip between sunrise and sunset, she had ploughed a great piece of land from the coast of the Swihonez and dragged it out into the sound, where it became the island called Sealand. Most brides cried out before the three birch-rounds were done, when a switch cut hard across a tender nipple or thighs already sore from the beating, but Swaebhon bit her lip silently till the blood came, for the harder the other women struck, if she could keep silence, the more surely her womb would fill, the stronger her children would be.

When the third round was done, Child-hagardhaz filled a cow-aurochs' horn with honey-mead, calling the blessings of the goddesses and idises again. She poured a little of it out before the stone, then lifted it up to Swaebhon, who drained the horn in a single draught. Swaebhon's head was spinning, she crouched down carefully on the stone, letting the other women help her to the earth again before they began to rub her body with the soothing salve which would ease the sting of the birching and smooth the welts away by morning. The deep chord of the lur-horns woke Hoilogae a little before dawn, its sound shaking through the hall.

The ringing of a brass gong answered them, a woman's voice shouting through it, "Wake up! Awake, you sleepers! You men, wake up!"

When Hoilogae had rubbed the sleep from his eyes, he saw that a fresh white tunic had been laid out for him, with two thin arm rings of coiled gold lying on it like glittering snakes above his sword belt's dark leather. No food or drink was set upon the tables, the folk would go fasting to the holy stone that morning. A few women had already come into the hall, but Hoilogae could not see Swaebhon.

Attalae came over to help Hoilogae dress more swiftly. The rede-giver's silvered hair was neat and his eyes bright, as though he had been awake for a while. "So far, this has all turned out much better than I had looked for. Enjoy this day's blessing while you can, Hoilogae, the Ansuz has been kind to you after all." He draped the wolf-fur cloak around Hoilogae's shoulders and stepped back to look at the young man, then brought a bone comb from his belt-pouch. "Comb your hair quickly, we must go down to the stone soon."

As Hoilogae gave Attalae's comb back, Aiwilimae came to put his arm around Hoilogae's shoulders, leading him to the doorposts to stand between the two lur-players. "When they begin to walk, you go before them down to the holy stone," the Northman said softly. "Swaebhon will take care of you from there. Take off your shoes, you must go over the stone bare-footed."

It was only a few minutes longer before the lur-horns' bronze bells swung from east to west, the brothers who bore them stepping forward as one. Hoilogae strode out between them into the paling light of dawn, treading carefully over the dew-wet grass. No sign would be worse than for his foot to slip now. Swaebhon stood upon the rock, fair in the growing brightness. Though an edge of ice was still keen in the air, she wore only a skirt of white flax-cords, a broad golden collar about her neck, and a crown of new-bloomed flowers. Her long hair fell unbound down her bare back.

Between her breasts, she held a large dipper of gold with a handle shaped like a horse's head. At her feet, a large clay cauldron steamed gently into the cold dawn air beside a basket filled with the eggs of wild geese and ducks and the green sprays of leeks. Hoilogae came over the stone from its eastern side, following Nerthuz's red footprints to her as the two lur-players took their place on either side of the carven rock and Aiwilimae came to stand before them with his great bronze ax. Swaebhon's brightness seemed to fill the sky behind her with pale-gold light, pink fire burning in feathery streaks before the hidden Sun. She stretched out her free hand to draw the sword from his side, clasping his palm together with the hilt so that they raised it together.

"Hail, Austarjon!" She called. "The winter is done, I hail you, dawn's light at the shining door. Drive your wain over the marches of darkness. Let the seeds spring to life in its wheel-tracks. Hail, shining maid!"

Hoilogae did not know that he would speak till the words sprang from his mouth, clear as the lurs' call through the dawn air. "Hail to you, Wodhanaz! The winter is done, I hail you, eldest Ansuz! Drighten of the dead, bring life from the hidden worlds again, to greet the rising Sun. Hallow our battles with brightness, our workings with wisdom, as we fare up to day's light. I hail you, Spear-God!"

Aiwilimae heaved his ax up over their heads. "Thonaraz, your ax hallow this year-dawn! Hallow the fruitful field, hallow the bearing womb. Nerthuz, mighty one, fair and wise, rise from the depths with weal-full hands. We live by your gifts, we hail you here! Now Ingwaz from east fares, battle-boar bright, the wain rides behind. Now Sunna takes her holy stead, and etins all flee her light."

One hand still on Hoilogae's sword, Swaebhon reached her gold dipper down to the cauldron at her feet, filling it with the steaming drink. "Let Wodhanaz witness. His work waxes towards full. I swear by him, eldest Ansuz, and by Frijjo his frowe, that I will be true to you, my Hoilogae, that my life and love are yours, as long as you will have them." She drank from the shining cup and raised it towards him.

"Wodhanaz and Frijjo hear my oath," Hoilogae answered. The salty water that filled his eyes shone gold in the morning sun, dazzling all the shapes around him, but his voice flowed freely, a deep river of gladness streaming from his heart. "I give my life and love to you freely together, for I hold you dearer than all. Swaebhon, you were my dream and my waking, you are my life and my death, and the holy gift fasting my name and soul to me. I swear that I shall never turn from you, nor shall any other ever content me while the worlds last, until the doom of the gods."

Grain and honey were blended in the golden draught, a faint sea-spoor of bitter salt sharpening its sweetness. Hoilogae drained the cup and clasped her to him. Each of the folk, Hoilogae's men as well as the Northerners, came forward in turn for a drink from Swaebhon's beaker, each bent to take an egg and a leek from the basket at her feet as Aiwilimae swung his ax above them. At last she bore her gifts to the lur-players, then to her father, leaving the dipper and basket in his hand and bearing two goose-eggs and two leeks back for Hoilogae and herself.

They stood in silence as the light brightened in the East, till the Sun's edge first glowed over the land. Then the lur-players blew a great chord of greeting that rang out over the firth, growing louder and louder till it rose into thundering echoes through the sudden silence. They turned back towards the hall, Aiwilimae bore his ax forward between them, leading the folk away and leaving Hoilogae and Swaebhon alone. Hoilogae sheathed his sword, Swaebhon took his cloak from his shoulders and spread it over the stone. Now, at last, as she stepped free of her cord-skirt to stand naked in the Sun's light, Hoilogae understood what had bewildered him before. How his whole being yearned towards her, seeking her own. He cast his tunic aside, clasping Swaebhon close, they sank to the gods' rock together as she reached to guide him in.

Hoilogae did not know how long it lasted, even as he had heard that men forgot the worst of wound-pain after healing, or women the worst of birthing, his joy whelmed him too strongly for his mind to bear its full memory. He only knew that a moment came when his heart burst within him, the great roaring in his ears drowning his cry as lightning seared his sight. When he could breathe and see again, his manhood was drooping down between the dawn-pink streaks on her white thighs, and Swaebhon was stroking his hair and shoulders, kissing him breathlessly. They rested like that a little while, then, with their clothing draped over their arms, each with an egg in one hand and a leek in the other, walked naked back to the hall.

A great cheer went up as they came in, and suddenly the air was full of flowers raining softly down on them. Hoilogae felt men hitting him lightly on the shoulders and back, and a dark-eyed girl reached up to push a bite of honey-dripping bread into his mouth. Two finely carved chairs, garlanded with flowers, stood near the fire where none had before, Hoilogae let himself be pushed into one and pulled his cloak up over himself as Swaebhon, wrapping herself in her own fur again, settled into the other. Fiercely hungry, Hoilogae did as he saw her do, chipping the top from his egg and drinking its contents down, then biting into his leek.

Attalae gave him a loaf of bread, an older woman with silver-spun hair brought a little pot of honey and a larger one of mead to set between the new-wed pair.

"Now do not forget this," Attalae said, lifting the bag that Herwawardhaz had given at their parting. Hoilogae could feel its golden weight, and the still flames of gold and amber within the linen covering.

"Swaebhon, here is a morning-gift for you, from the lands of my father."

Swaebhon unknotted the bag's mouth slowly, spreading it out on her lap. There were the adornments of a high atheling-frowe. A neck-torc of twisted gold, and arm- and finger-rings to match, a chain of smoothed amber, glowing like honey and butter against the dark linen, and two amber shapes, swan and boar.

"These gifts are fair," she answered. "Though I would be content with yourself alone, I shall wear them gladly, as they adorn me brightly, so shall I soon adorn your clan, with myself and the children I bear."

"You will be leaving soon," Aiwilimae said. Alone of the folk there, he was not glad, his thick brows drooped and his voice was heavy, with none of the joy that had uplifted it on the hallowed rock.

"We should fare home before long, yes. I think that I will have much to do."

"I shall give you another ship for the faring. You will have many goods to take with you, for Swaebhon shall not go without the things to which she is accustomed."

Swaebhon reached out to clasp her father's hand. "Be of better cheer, Father. I could have won no greater happiness, and your life is far from at an end. You shall wed again before long, and there shall be children in your hall again, and it may be that my children shall fare north to see you sometimes."

Aiwilimae straightened his back, shaping his mouth into a smile. "Let me not cloud your wedding-day. If I may hope to see your children in my hall, daughter, and know that you are joyful, that is enough for me." He laid his hand on Hoilogae's head. "I did not think to give you my blessing, but now I give it freely. As you love my daughter, may the god you call on always deal as kindly with you as he has this day, and may he bless your wedding with strong children and sig in all things."

Aiwilimae's hand was cold. For all his fair words, his touch seemed to weigh like a barrow-stone on Hoilogae's head, and the raven-rasp of his voice whetted Hoilogae's spine with a low shiver. The Jutlander glanced up at his bride's father. For a moment, it seemed to him that Aiwilimae's right eyelid drooped over darkness, and that his left eye stared beyond the wooden walls, as though he saw something grim standing just beside the hall's door where other gazes could not light on it. But Swaebhon gleamed amber-bright within, her teeth sharp against Hoilogae's lips as he bent over to kiss her. Her bare arms tightened around him, and he knew that he would love her even if she were the worst of trolls.

CHAPTER XXV

The sky was still dark when Hailgi awoke, but the Moon's stead in the sky before them and the chill in the air told him that it would soon be dawn. He pulled on his byrnie, a shiver rippling through his body as the cold metal-weave slithered down over him. Wrapping his cloak back over the metal shirt, Hailgi waited for the heat of his body to warm the icy links as he sat with his new helmet in his lap. It was a helm that Sigismundar had ordered made for his son by the best-known smith in the south a little before the old drighten's last Yule. The messenger had only come from the Rhine with it a few days ago, and Hailgi had felt that he should not show it till the day of the battle, lest a glance of the wrong sort should ill-wish it. It was finely wrought, with the gilded shape of a garnet-eyed raven for the nasal and silver figure-plates around the rim, each shape carefully beaten into the metal by the Rhinelander's skilled hammer, chip-carved and graven to sharpen the detail. The figures' edges stood out keenly in the Moon's light. Here a warrior rode with spear aimed at the wyrm below him, an eagle flying before his head and a raven behind, here a pair of spear-carrying twins in horned helms danced as mirror-images, here a man with sword and wand danced before a wolf-masked figure, who held a spear towards him with its point down.

Then the patterns began again, following each other around the helmet's rim, they seemed a little different each time, though Hailgi could not quite say how, but he was sure that the smith had changed each pattern a bit in the shaping. For a moment he was tempted to wrap it back up and put it away carefully, wearing his old helm in the battle instead. But a drighten must go as a drighten. How else would his foes know where to strike? Hailgi lowered the helm slowly onto his head, its thick leather padding warming quickly. As he bent to shake Sinfjotli awake, he saw the glints struck by the Moon from his helmet mirrored in the Walsing's eyes. Sinfjotli rolled to his feet, stretching his arms up like a tree against the star-bright sky.

"Hai, that's a fine piece of work, and it looks like a fair day for hallowing it." The Walsing leaned a little closer to see the helm, running his finger along the rim. "I've never seen a helmet wrought like that, with figure-plates and all, but there's something about the working that's not so strange." His sharp-arched brows drew together. "My father's sword is plainly wrought, adorned only with an ice-stone in its hilt, but it's the only metalwork I've ever seen done so fairly. Where did you come by this?"

"My father ordered it from the Rhine, from Ragin the Smith, some time ago."

Sinfjotli nodded. "I've heard of Ragin. His work surely lives up to his fame."

By then the others were wakening, those who had byrnies groaning softly at the cold bite of the metal as they put them on. Ingwiwulfar began to pass out pieces of bread, dried fish, and cheese, Thonarbrandar Odd-Eyes went to stand by the cask of small beer, filling cups and horns as they were passed to them. Hailgi felt no will to eat, his blood was beginning to prickle in his veins like ale-wort starting to bubble with yeast, and each breath seemed to fan the coals warming in his body. Sinfjotli did not listen to him when he said he wasn't hungry, but pushed a large slice of bread under a thicker piece of cheese into his hand.

The Walsing ate as he spoke, speaking through great bites of his own food. "You'll need it later. If you don't eat now, you'll burn out all your might on the field and fall asleep halfway through the day. Look over there, how Hrothormar and his men are going at it. They know what they're doing. Bread and cheese are good. Your stomach takes them in quickly, they won't weigh you down too heavily."

Hailgi judged that the light was good enough to go in when the shape of the boar cresting Freyjawulfar's helm was clear in his sight. They did not blow horns this time, but when Hailgi lifted his spear, all the oars dipped into the water together and the fleet stroked in towards the beach. When Herwolathar waved that they were close enough, Sinfjotli heaved the anchor over the ship's stern and ran to the prow. Hailgi leapt into the water with him, gasping at its first cold shock, but his strength was already heating him as, shield held high in one hand against arrows and spear ready to cast in the other, he ran towards Hrothormar's berserks who were already struggling into their swine-wedge. Hailgi heard the first arrows hissing into the water like hail around him, one thunking into his shield, they could not waste too much time gathering into formation. He spared only a quick glance backward, Hrothormar's men knew what they were doing.

Drawing his arm back, Hailgi cast his spear, shouting, "You all belong to Wodhanar!"

The swine-wedge rumbled forward behind Hailgi and Sinfjotli, breaking the waves into a great spray of foam on either side. Drawing his sword, Hailgi heard the horns blowing on the beach as if they were very far away, their echo splashing in his ears with Sinfjotli's howling as the swine-wedge drove through the knee-high water. Then they burst free of the water, shooting forward onto the beach, where a wall of locked linden-shields gleamed to block their way. Hailgi and Sinfjotli hit the shield-wall with the full weight of the berserk-formation behind them, their shields crashing against the foes' linden so hard Hailgi's sight burst into a great flare of lightning and his breath was knocked from him as he stumbled forward over the writhing body of the man who had fallen before his rush.

His shield was shattered, he cast it from him, hewing around himself two-handed, blood springing up in the brightening dawn like foam spraying from a ship's prow. The froth was wet on his face as the Walsing's howl echoed from his own throat, the byrnied men were moving slowly around him, slowly as if they moved through water, while Hailgi's own blade bloodied the wind. Lightning-sparks shot up through the day's reddening light as his sword struck a gilded helmet, sweeping about to cut through the leather throat-piece beneath. The edge stuck in the man's spine, he tugged it loose, bringing it up just in time to sweep aside the blow of a spear-shaft. The wood splintered under Hailgi's strength, the spear-man stumbling, Hailgi stepped forward to run him through.

The light was blurring in his eyes, his body moving more and more swiftly, as though he no longer guided his own limbs, it seemed to him that his flesh had gone clear as glass, lit by the sunrise-flame that burned hotter and hotter within him, yearning ever upward to the bright bridge of light stretching down from the dawn-glowing Sun as his blade whirled and flashed between the streaks of red light flaring along its length. After a time, Hailgi knew that he was moving more and more slowly, and then not at all. He tried to raise his arm again, but it would not rise, unseen fetters bound it fast to his body. "Sigiruna, Sigiruna!" He cried out, but the brightness was already falling from his sight, the roaring in his ears resolving into words like the blurred green of a far-off meadow resolving into single blades of grass to the nearing sight.

"Soft, Hailgi, soft," Sinfjotli was murmuring into his ear. It was the Walsing's strong arms that pinned Hailgi's own to his body, Hailgi saw as his stinging sight cleared, and Sinfjotli's strength that kept him upright. He breathed deeply, struggling to get his feet beneath him again. The sweat was dripping from his nose and chin, his tunic was wringing wet and the cap of down-padded leather under his helmet soaked through. Hailgi lifted the helm from his head, turning his face up to the cool breeze stroking over his wet hair. The battle had lasted a very long time, the Sun was well into the sky now, shining clear as a gem set in the polished blue bowl of the old etin's skull.

"How did we fare?" He asked, his howl-ripped voice harsh and ugly in his own ears.

"Could have been better," Hrothormar answered. "Could have been worse. Raginar's dead, and Freyjawulfar took a bad cut to the thigh. It won't cripple him, but it'll be a while before he marches again. I'd guess that about a third of the men are dead or death-doomed, but when we add the wounded to that, we've lost a full half of our strength. On the other hand, I don't know that we'll be met by so many at Freki Stone, it seemed to me that I marked a good many more men on the beach this morning than there were last night. They hoped to stop us here, where they had the clearest advantage. I've no doubt of that."

"Then why?" Hailgi coughed. He tried to swallow, but his mouth was too dry. "Why not the full host?"

"Ah." Hrothormar raised a bushy eyebrow. "They didn't know where we'd land, and it's too far to march from Haganon's burg by night to fight at dawn. These were the watchers from the coastlines all around. They could have gone to Freki Stone easily and slept this morning while they waited for us, but they didn't. Now, I'd guess that this was easily half of their strength, so we're still fairly matched, except that they'll have rested all day at Freki Stone, and we have a long march after heavy fighting."

Hailgi wanted to speak again, but his throat was too dry to make any sound. Helmet under his arm and sword still unsheathed in his hand, he walked slowly through the dead, dragging his feet through the blood-clotted sand to the little river that cut through the beach, letting himself drop to his knees and plunging his face into the water. It was a bit brackish, but cold, Hailgi drank in great gasps of it, feeling the drink flow through all the tiny sweat-drained riverbeds of his body like a storm after long drought.

He stopped before he felt that he had drunk enough, he knew that he would cast his stomach up if he drank himself full. Hailgi pushed himself upright again, brushing away the clusters of flies that had gathered to drink the sweat and the blood from his body. He was beginning to ache badly now. A huge welt swelled along the length of his shield-arm where he had taken the brunt of the first shock, and his ribs hurt along that side as well, he was not sure that a couple of them were not cracked. Still, whether he was hurt or not, his sword needed cleaning. He bent down to cut a piece of gray wool from the tunic of one of the corpses lying on the field, a big man whose neck had been half cut-through from behind. As Hailgi tugged and sliced, the dead man's head rolled to the side, its weight tearing the wound's red flesh farther open.

It was Skegga-Grimar who lay there, his beard and mouth and eyes filled with clotting black sand. His trust in Hailgi had won him little. Hailgi crouched to brush the bloody muck from Skegga-Grimar's eyeballs, the flies buzzing anxiously up and back with each movement of his hand. The dead man's eyes were clammy under his fingers, he could not clear them very well, but had to leave a ring of black sand around the edge of each. Hailgi cleaned his sword in the river and dried it on the piece of Skegga-Grimar's tunic, polishing it till no fleck of dry blood or drop of water stained the rippling patterns of its metal any longer. His fair new helm had taken a few scratches in the fighting, and one of the plates with the horn-helmed twins had been cut almost through between the two dancers, but he thought that it could be fixed without too much trouble.

He was still too weak from his battle-fit to help those who were carrying the wounded men to small boats and ferrying them out to the ships, but he walked among the dead, looking at their faces to see who had fallen. Thonarabrandar Odd-Eyes' green eye stared sightlessly at the sky, a welter of blood and brains spilled where his brown eye had been. Thurir had been gutted like a fish, a clean stroke that had gone from belly to breastbone. To Hailgi's relief, the quiet thane no longer drew breath and his skin was already cool, his wound must have finished him quickly near the first of the fight.

Hailgi had not forgotten that Thurir would have given him to the bog once, but that was long past no one then could have told that Hagalar's thane would have died for Hailgi's sake. Raginar's men had already borne his body back to his ship. His wife's howe would be opened again when they came back to Jutland and he would be laid beside her, as he had wished. Many of the men he did not know, but more than a few of them were his own thanes or Hagalar's, whose faces were well-known to him.

After a time, Hailgi marked that Sinfjotli sat with his knees drawn up and his arms locked around them, staring at him. "Is something wrong?"

"Why are you walking among the dead like that?"

"I knew these men, and they died for me. I am not downcast, for I know that they died bravely and well, in a fight they chose to follow, but I must not forget their names or their faces, for I shall see them again in Walhall, and they will be eager to know how they are remembered in the Middle-Garth. Many of their kin shall wish to set rune stones to say how and where they fell. This, too, I must be able to remember."

Sinfjotli nodded. After a few moments, he got up and walked by Hailgi. They almost did not recognize Gunthamundar's corpse when they came to it. The Jutlandish drighten had been stripped of his helm, arm-rings, and byrnie, as well as his ring-hilted sword, it was only the broad brown mustache over a clean-shaven chin that jarred Hailgi's memory, and when he looked for them he could see the red marks the helm had pressed into the dead man's forehead and the dusty black ring-traces of his byrnie on his white tunic to either side of the blood-torrent that had spilled from his open neck like a flood of red vomit. Hailgi glanced at Sinfjotli to see if he would say anything, but the Walsing only looked down at the corpse silently for a moment before going on. Hailgi's spear was sunk deep in the guts of an older man, whose face had been trodden into a red ruin beneath his matted mess of silvery hair. After some looking, he found the eagle-shapes that had adorned his shield as well, but the shock of its breaking had twisted them and cracked the gilding away.

When the wounded and the prisoners had been taken to the boats, the host rested on the shore before going on. As the cloud of flies thickened over the dead, many of the men, Hailgi among them, plunged into the sea or the river with their clothes on to wash away the sweat and blood that drew the insects to the living. Sinfjotli had taken his tunic off, but not bothered to wash. He lay on his back in the grass with his arms folded over his chest, he did not seem to notice the flies that lit on his face and body. Hailgi knew that their bites would not scathe him, and no one but Sigimund and Sinfjotli himself could know what the Walsing had grown used to in the caves of Gautland. Still, it made his skin crawl a little to see the flies creeping so peacefully over Sinfjotli's still form, as if Sigimund's son had already fallen dead without a mark on him. After he had eaten a little bread and drunk a cup of small beer, Hailgi lay down beside his friend.

Drugged by the Sun's warmth on his exhausted body, he was swiftly asleep, and did not rouse until the Sun was a little past her midday height.

"Ready to go on?" Hrothormar Bear-Sark asked, his shadow falling over Hailgi's body as the young drighten yawned and rubbed his eyes. "Frey-jawulfar says we ought to start soon if we hope to make Haganon's burg before sunset."

Hailgi stood up and stretched, hiding his wince of pain as the movement pulled against his ribs. Though his muscles had stiffened and he ached worse than before, the tide of his strength had flooded back in as he slept, and he knew that he could do battle again. When Sigiruna awoke, she knew by the warmth and dryness of the air against her face that the Sun was long risen, and knew that this time, her dreams of Hailgi's battle on the shore had been more than dreams. He had won through. Gunthamundar lay dead on the shore, as she had seen him, with nothing to mark him of higher birth than the other corpses, and Hailgi and his men were marching towards Freki Stone. Though she had thought of holding herself back, of weakening his host or letting him fall, Sigiruna's true will had betrayed her at the last, and she had warded him in her sleep. Even as she washed her face and dressed, Sigiruna could hear the sound of the men's voices in the hall.

"The signal fire," Haganon was saying. Sigiruna came closer to the door, listening for a moment. "That should have been done by now, if they are still fighting, there will be none left alive."

The door opened beneath Sigiruna's hand before she had touched it. Dagar stood there, the white sling on his arm glimmering against his plain dark tunic, his hair was not braided as befitted an atheling-youth, but drawn back in a long tail of tarnished gold. Sigiruna felt a glow of anger heating her heart, like iron brightening beneath the bellows' blast. She knew well enough that he would have woken her, had he found her sleeping there. He would have gladly drawn her back from the battle, in hopes that it would mean Hailgi's death. It is no ill thing that he would help his kin, she thought, as she had thought an hundred times since Dagar had first spoken his will-ingness to let her be wed to Hadubroddar. That is the best of troths, without which nothing would stand. Still, that made the sight of him no easier to bear.

Their mother's fine lines were too clear in his calm face, his healer's move-ments, too careful and sure like Sigigafja's for Sigiruna to see any ghost but hers in Dagar's shape, or feel anything but the sharpest betrayal when he spoke against her.

"Why are you dressed as a thrall this day?" Sigiruna asked. "Will you not meet your foes as an atheling?"

"You know well I should be readying myself to fall on the field, if it were easier to swing a sword with a broken arm." Dagar's voice was not loud, but his gaze was keen as the bitter edge of wormwood in herb-brewed ale. "In-stead there will be wounded to tend, and much blood to stain my clothing. I think that you were better dressed in black yourself the more so, since you have ruled that someone you love must die."

"It was not I who wished my betrothal to Hadubroddar," Sigiruna answered. She spoke as coldly as she could, though she could feel her throat closing around the words. "But I fear that you shall live out the day, unless Hailgi chooses to send you to Fetter-Grove as a gift for his victory."

Another man might have made the sign of Thonarar's Hammer to ward off the words, or traced a Sun-wheel over his heart to call the might of the Wans. Dagar only answered, "He may do that, the songs say that he was eager enough to give bound men to Wodhanar before. Perhaps he is a fit match for you."

"What do you know of Wodhanar? I think that you have little right to speak of what Hailgi has given him, but those who are hallowed to the god are his, whether they fall by a foe's sword or by Wodhanar's own spear. You need not blame Hailgi for bringing his captives to Fetter-Grove."

Dagar shrugged. "That may be. But it is late in the day for you to be rising, and I am sure that I know why. From your words, Hailgi must have won past the shore, or you would be weeping now instead of threatening. I shall go and tell our kinsmen, that they may ready themselves to meet him, unless you would rather speak the words yourself, since this fighting is all for your sake and no other's."

Sigiruna bit hard on the inside of her cheek, but she knew that Dagar had the right of it. She could not tell herself that she had not chosen all the warriors within the Skjoldings' hall to die, she could not un-name herself as walkurja, nor as Hailgi's betrothed. So she steadied herself as well as she could, walking proudly into the hall where the men sat in their byrnies, stroking whetstones over sword-edges or squinting down the shafts of arrows to be sure of their straightness. The sound of the thanes' speech rippled down into whispers as Sigiruna strode before her father's high-seat, where he sat with Bragi at his left hand and Hadubroddar in the guest-chair at his right. Though she did not walk quietly, none looked at her.

She felt gray as a ghost, and as she gazed over the men, their half-seen wounds glimmered red through the glassy waters filling her eyes. It seemed to her that she felt her own flesh torn, deep enough for the pain to become numbness. In the old tale, Hildar had brought death to father and lover both, but the songs never said that she had seen the marks of their slaying while they lived, nor that she had felt herself bearing ale in the barrow of the fresh-slain while the men she poured for still breathed and laughed. Sigiruna's sorrow was yet worse, for though she had not seen Hailgi's death, she knew that it must follow their love, sure as seeds fell from every sheaf. Yet he lived. That was her only joy. When Haganon looked up at his daughter, Sigiruna was not sure what she read in the creases of his weathered face. Her own tangled thoughts entwined her so that she was not sure whether she hoped for words of anger or words of love from him, and thus she spoke first.

"The battle on the shore is over. Hailgi fought with the berserk-wod on him, and was sig-blessed, now he marches to this hall, with a great host of hale men still behind him." It was hard for Sigiruna to bite back the next words in her mind, it was as though the slick muscular body of an adder sought to squirm up from her throat. Yet her father sat as a warrior, past his prime, with his silver-gilt hair thin as winter grass and the crevasses of his face running deep into his beard, but the bear-strength still showed in his broad shoulders and massive chest, and the pride of the Skjoldings still straightened his back and glinted from his flint-keen eyes. At best more words would be worthless, but at worst he might heed her, and give over the battle and his oaths for the sake of frith, and Sigiruna knew that such shame must never darken the Skjolding line.

"Then it is time for us to set helm on head and sword to side, and ready ourselves to meet him before Freki Stone!" Haganon answered, his deep voice rumbling through the hall.

Bragi's grin split the new red beard which had only frothed from his face in the last year, and his whetstone sang along the edge of his sword in one last joyous stroke before he sheathed it at his side. "The men of the Skjoldings are glad to do battle!" He answered his father. "I have waited long for this day, blessed be the gods who have given me a chance to swing my sword at last!"

Sigiruna saw some of the older thanes sighing and shaking their heads, but more of the younger ones, and all of Hadubroddar's men, were cheering Bragi on. Oh, my brother Sigiruna thought. From where she stood, she could feel the life seething in him, strong as yeast bubbling and foaming through a pot of rich wort, and yet as easily spilt, the glittering links of the byrnie weighting his young body would soon be split and his hot blood gushing out like new ale from a cloven cask.

"You have done well, Sigiruna, to give me this news," Haganon said, his voice low beneath the shouting of the warriors. He heaved himself up from his seat, resting heavy hands upon Sigiruna's shoulders for a moment. "Now, my daughter, I must ask an oath of troth from you. I will not ask you to aid me with your walkurja-craft as your mother did. You must swear not to work against our own men with spells, nor ride above the battlefield to ward our foes. Even that grim maid Hildar did not choose between her father and beloved in the end, though she had stirred their strife to flame, but worked it so that both hosts fell, and raised both again from the slain."

Sigiruna looked into her father's blue eyes for a moment. No flaws marred their brightness, nor dulled the sharp points of his pupils. Though he might be old, Haganon had set himself for this battle joyfully, and it seemed to Sigiruna that she loved him more now than ever. For a moment her heart almost wavered within her, and then she saw Hadubroddar looking at her, his big hands clasped in his lap with the patience of one who believes he has only to wait a little while to win what he wills.

"I will do no battle this day," Sigiruna answered, "for either side. I have made my choice, now it is you men who must play it out."

Haganon smiled at his daughter, but Sigiruna heard Dagar's deep breath. He would hold her to account for their kinsmen's death that day, nor would he be wrong in doing it. Still, Sigiruna let her father fold her in his hard-ringed embrace, hugging the broad span of his chest in turn, and was glad for this last touch of his living flesh. She had mourned enough already. Hailgi's ribs still hurt with every deep breath, but the marching had worked the worst of the stiffness from his body after they had been going for a while. Though he would not carry it in the fighting, Sinfjotli, still bare-chested, bore Hailgi's standard beside him. The fields were tall and golden, the long barley-hairs and the thicker heads of wheat rippling beneath the light breeze. Had Herwolathar not come before the Moon reached full, Hailgi would have had to choose between breaking his oath and faring to Sealand with only those men who could be spared from the harvest.

As it was, bringing in the grain would be no easy task with so many fallen, it seemed to him that Wodhanar's horse might get a great share of the crop that winter. While Hailgi had been asleep, lots had been cast to see who would have to carry the ships' dragon-prows against the land-wights, and the task had fallen to Theudowinar and one of the men who had fared with Freyjawulfar, a broad-built warrior with a wild shock of curly brown hair. Theudowinar walked slowly, glancing about himself with hooded eyes, as if the ill gaze of the land-wights weighted heavily upon him, but the other man laughed and joked with those around him, making no great weight of what he carried. Soon he began to sing, his strong baritone ringing cheerfully through the clear air, and some of the others joined in.

"'There's a maidenmy heart's seeking,
white her breastsand bright her eyes.
There's a maidenmy heart's seeking,
though her brothersbear me ill'"

By the time the Sun was halfway down the sky, Hailgi could see the hills that ringed the field around Freki Stone and the light glinting here and there from the dark shapes of the men on top of them. He raised his helmet, setting it down on his head. "Lock shields," he said, his voice coming dully through the metal and padding into his own ears. "This time it is they who must break our shield-burg."

Sinfjotli handed Hailgi's standard to Skald-Thonarabrandar who marched behind them. Hailgi and Sinfjotli raised the shields they had taken from dead men on the beach, locking the edges, Herwolathar took his place in the shield-wall on Hailgi's other side. The host moved forward at Hailgi's pace, treading steadily towards the field. Hailgi felt that he rode the head of a great wyrm, its feet beating down to shake the earth beneath him in a steady drum-rhythm, he could feel his breath rising and falling through the body of the host behind him as they made for the gap in the ring of hills.

Through the opening he could see the tall gray stone standing alone on the green meadow. Freki Stone, the Greedy, would be well-fed with the blood of men. As the land began to crest beside him and the bright byrnies to sweep down from above, Hailgi aimed his spear straight for the rock, crying, "Wodhanar have you all!" He saw the brightness leaping from its tip in a great flare of lightning as it struck Freki Stone, and then the hail was whirling white around him as a crack of thunder burst against his shield. He staggered with the shock, but did not go down. There were men before him, hewing high, yet the shield-wall was still locked, Sinfjotli and Herwolathar holding their places beside him.

A silvery hailstone hissed along the side of his face, its touch was cold, but the wetness in his beard seemed warm. The sky had gone black as stormy night, though Hailgi could still see the leather cap and blond beard of the warrior whose spear jabbed at his face too swiftly to block. Hailgi bent his head and sliced upward, shearing the shaft through as the point glanced from his helmet. A swirl of snow blurred his sight for a moment, flakes glowing blue in the lightning's flash. The hilt of his sword seemed very warm in his palm now as he swung it over the edge of the shield-wall again and again, but Sinfjotli's shoulder grazed Hailgi's a moment, and the Walsing's bare flesh was cold and blue as death.

One great blow struck off the bright-helmed head of the man who faced him, but the warrior's last strike rose nevertheless, and only Hailgi's luck let him turn its aim from his neck to his shield-rim. The snow was coming harder and faster now, a great wind blowing it from the black sky into Hailgi's face. He saw the men and swords before him only as shadows against the white storm, helms blurring into the shapes of beast-heads and wild masks. The lightning showed the blood running freely from their bodies, black in its white glow entrails roiling within gaping wounds, hearts beating in open rib cages.

The snow-laden wind was cold with the stink of rotting death, as though they fought within an old mound, Hailgi could feel the wyrm-writhing beneath his feet as he pressed forward over the fallen towards the stone that loomed higher and higher against the lightning-lit sky, slicing at the blistered faces that rose and fell before him. Though he could feel the deep roaring in his throat, the voice that sang in his ears was high as the voice of a flute, a keen silvery wind-sound whose ice numbed his skull even as the soundless depth rumbling through his bones beat faster and faster, sweeping his sword about through shapes that splattered blackly beneath his blows. A flash of lightning showed Hailgi the tree-shape of his own veins deep brown against his white forearm beneath the rust-dark links edging his byrnie's sleeve, showed him, clearly, the distorted blue features of the man who faced him, whose swollen abdomen burst in a great gush of dark muck at the touch of the Wolfing's blade. The gold ring coiled about Hailgi's left arm burned with cold howe-fire against his blackening skin, the tiny lightless flames danced on his helmet's gilded nose-piece.

The shield-wall had broken. Hailgi was fighting alone now, beneath the
pillar of stone that stretched up to the black clouds like a great spear and
the hills closing in on him like walls of gray rock. The next flash of lightning
gleamed from bare white cheekbones with dark flesh hanging from them in
strips, ribs pale over the tattered flaps of skin that drooped beneath them,
as the twisting wyrm-clouds drooped down from the sky's low roof. Hailgi
wanted to cry out, but his mouth was full of icy mold, the snow filling the
pools of his eyes. He shook his head, kept fighting grimly, he could not have
stopped. Now Skegga-Grimar, his bearded skull rolling on his shoulder,
swung his sword up against Hailgi, now Athalwulfar's curly head rose at the
edge of Hailgi's sight, and he saw the white maggots seething in the youth's
guts and the raven-plucked hollows of his eyes.

A man rode beyond them, spear stretched high and blue-black cloak
wrapped tight around him, or was it the dark stain of death spreading over
his naked back? He did not turn his head towards Hailgi, nor seem to mark
the Wolfing as his gray steed galloped past. A red glow was rising through
the black clouds. Hailgi knew it was the glow of the bale-fire, and turned
to fight his way towards it. There, he thought, he would find an end to this
endless battle. His limbs were too heavy and cold, the weight of the earth
was dragging him down, and at last he felt himself sinking to the ground.
Still the bloody glow did not go away, but spread upward through the black
clouds, burning them away where it touched, and it seemed to him that he
heard a man's low voice through the sinking storm wind.

"Sigiruna of Seva-Falls, Hadubroddar shall never sink into your arms
now." The man coughed, bubbles breaking through the deep sound. When
he spoke again, his voice came very slowly. "The gray-furred witch-mounts
tear men's limbs, all Granamarir's sons have lost their lives now."

Hailgi breathed a deep sigh. I must have won. I must have. He stared up
at Freki Stone, deep gray against the red glow of sunset and the pale blue
sky beyond, where the black shapes of ravens circled lower and lower. I am
breathing, I must still live. He braced one arm beneath himself, bit his lip
against the pain and pushed himself up until he was half-sitting. Then it
seemed to him that he could not be seeing truly, that he was still mazed by
the nightmare of his battle, for Sigiruna was walking among the dead, her
long fair hair rippling in the light wind and the hem of her pale gray kirtle
stained with blood.

She turned her gray gaze toward him, Hailgi sat speechless, thinking that
he would have tholed it all again for this sight of her shining above the dark
slaughter-stead. He could see the tears on her white face, their clearness
tinged with red by the sinking Sun, he lifted his right arm, gesturing towards her with his sword to show that he was still alive. A bright smile broke
through her look of sorrow as she ran towards him.

"Hail to you, Hailgi! Now Ingwar's kin shall live in joy, for you have felled the boar too strong to flee, who slew many sea-kings in sword-play. The red rings are seemly for you, as is the ruler-maid. Hale shall you hold Haganon's daughter and Hringstead, sig and land, the strife is closed."

Sigiruna reached down and took Hailgi's hands, helping him up. Though his legs shook under him, it did not seem to him that he was badly wounded. He looked around the field. Sinfjotli stood near Freki Stone, rivulets of sweat streaking white through the blood crusting his broad chest, Hrothormar sat with his back to the rock and his head between his knees, shaking like an aspen leaf in the aftermath of his fit. Other men were moving painfully over the field, Hailgi knew most of them, and knew that he had truly won the day, but far more lay dead on the blood-dark field. Only a few feet from them, Bow-Athalwulfar raised his heavy head with a soft moan. His hand reached out, fingers scrabbling through the slippery grass, then his head drooped back again and he was still.

"Not only good was given to you, Sigiruna," Hailgi answered as he lifted his helmet from his head, the words heavy with the earthen weight that still lay on his own heart. "I say that certain norns ruled in this. Haganon and Bragi must both have fallen on this field, and I brought about their bane. Beneath the hills there, a strong warrior still battled when headless, there on the earth must lie most of your kinsmen. You have won great woe in this war, with the strife stirred between mighty men."

Sigiruna made no sound, but Hailgi saw the sunset-lit pools deepening in her gray eyes. He put his arm about her shoulders, both to comfort her and to keep himself upright. "Take heart, Sigiruna. You have been as Hildar to us. None of the Skjoldings could ever win against what had been shaped for them."

"I would choose life for those who are fallen, if I could still hold you in my embrace," Sigiruna answered. She dashed the tears from her eyes with the back of her hand, and did not know whether they were tears of sorrow or joy, Hailgi's gray gaze drew her own, so that all the dead on the field seemed to fade into a ruddy mist behind his shining shape. It seemed to her that, though she stood on the green earth in her own hide, the keen sight of her walkurja-riding was still with her. For she had seen nothing so fair as the Wolfing's high-boned face before her, nor felt any might like that which thrummed through her body at his touch. "It was not shaped so, nor did I choose ill. For you are here with me, and have come alive through the darkest day, when many others fell. Now I have shed tears enough for the dead, and we must see to the living while we still have light. My brother Dagar is waiting for the wounded at our hall, he will not fight against you, for he broke his arm half a moon ago and is by no means fit for weapon-play yet. Thus his idises saved him from death." She raised her hand, touching Hailgi's jaw gently.

Sigiruna remembered clearly how the tip of Hunding's blade had scored it once, her own might had turned the stroke that would have split Hailgi's head, but could not save him altogether from harm. "This new wound is worse than the first, I can see the groove it cut in your jawbone. That can be seen to later, the bleeding has almost stopped." Sigiruna gestured towards the wain that stood on the edge of the field. "I drove that down from the burg, we shall do best to carry the wounded to it. What do you mean to do with those who fought against you, the men of the Skjoldings and Hadu-broddar's band?"

"The dead shall be burned as is fitting. It is yours to say what shall be done with your father and brother, whether you wish them burned or laid in the howe."

"Ship-burial has long been the way of the Skjoldings, who fare thus over the dark seas to God-Home, as Skjold Sheaf did at the beginning of time, and that shall be done with them. But what of the living whom we take from the field, those folk you promised to Wodhanar at this battle's beginning?"

Hailgi's voice was deep and rough in Sigiruna's ears. The echo of the ravens croaking above the battlefield tingled a shiver down her spine. "I have promised them to Wodhanar, and those words cannot be unspoken. Those who are worst wounded shall be slain now, for there is no good in length-ening their pain only to give them another death, the rest shall be taken to Fetter-Grove at Winter nights, and given to the god when we swear our wedding-oaths before him in that hallowed stead."

Sigiruna nodded. She had known it should be so. The words she had spoken to Dagar that morning had been true as rune-sticks. Lightly cast, but falling into the shapes already cut in Wyrd's well. "That is as it should be." Then Hailgi caught his breath, and it seemed to her that she could feel him staggering slightly. Sigiruna marked now that beneath the drying blood on his face, he was pale as a dead man, only the amber of his hair and beard bright against his fair skin.

She knew that he was not too deeply wounded, but he had borne the berserk-wod raging through him twice that day, and had slept among the slain for a little time. "Are you strong enough to help me with the wound-ed?" Sigiruna asked. "There will be time to count the dead tomorrow, but we must bring the living from the field before night-fall." Though no wolves walked on Sealand, the grim battle-wights had fed well. Even now she could see their shadows, wisps of cloudy mist above the field. They would grow stronger with night. She would leave no living man as their prey.

"I shall help you gladly, as soon as I have cleaned my sword."

Sigiruna looked about the field. One man stood taller than the rest, his golden hair gleaming blood-streaked as the dawn sky. Though his blond mustache and short beard were caked with blood as if he had torn at his foes' flesh with his teeth, she could easily see that he was kin to Hailgi. He had fought without byrnie, and seemed not to mark the flies swarming to the blood drying on his chest and arms. By that, as well as his size and his fairness, she knew that he could be no other than Sinfjotli the son of Sigi-mund. She raised her arm, gesturing to him.

"Hai Walsing!" Sigiruna called. "Come over here, Sinfjotli! I have work for you as well."

Sinfjotli strode swiftly over the dead and the dying, little recking whether the bodies beneath his feet tried to squirm away or not. His eyes were very wide, only the thinnest rim of blue ringing the swollen blackness of his pupils as he stared down at her.

"What would you have me do? I may not turn aside from your bidding."

"Gather the wounded who cannot walk half a league by themselves, and put them in that cart over there."

The cart Sigiruna had driven down from the Skjoldings' hall was no finely carved wain such as the land-fro and frowe might ride about in, it was a broad wagon, with a few scraps of dried grain from harvests past still pricking out between the planks, and it held a good many men. When the wain was full, Hailgi and Sinfjotli climbed up beside Sigiruna. She slapped the reins lightly against the horses' necks, clucking to them. One of the wounded men moaned in pain as the cart jarred into motion behind the two wide-backed geldings, though the way was wide and smooth, it would be no easy faring for some. As they drove over the hills around the battlefield, Hailgi saw the peaked roof of the Skjoldings' hall rising high above the palisade of spear-sharp timbers around it. The wooden beam cresting the thatch had been carved and gilded, its round scalloping gleaming red as war-shields in the Sun's last light. A gold-dusted eagle lifted its wings at one end of the beam, at the other, above the doorway, was carved the shape of a wolf. A young man stood between the doorposts.

Hailgi knew at once that he was Sigiruna's brother Dagar. His tail of hair was a darker gold than hers, but, even in the Sun's reddening light, his skin was as just as pale, and the same high cheekbones and narrow jawline lent his face a look of far-off calm as he watched Sinfjotli leap from the wagon while Hailgi and Sigiruna helped each other to the ground. His right arm hung in a dark sling, as Sigiruna had said. The silver hilt of his sword glittered brightly, but Hailgi thought its brightness was that of metal little handled, rather than that of metal worn shiny by use. Though he did not touch the weapon as they came to the doorway, he did not move aside either, only gazed calmly at Hailgi. His eyes were pale blue, gleaming with an odd brightness, like the clear sky mirrored in an icy pond.

"You have slain my father and brother." Dagar's voice was the high clear voice of a boy. Hailgi realized that, though the youth was a little taller than himself, he could not have been more than fifteen winters.

"If it was by my hand, I do not remember, many things happened in the battle past. But I believe that they are dead, and I shall not deny that it was for my sake and at my will. If you wish to challenge me to fight, I shall go to the holm with you when you have gained the full strength of your arm again."

"That may come to pass as it may. But if you wish to come within here, you must move me from the way yourself. I shall not give you greeting, nor ask you to lay your weapons aside as if you were a guest."

Sigiruna set her palm against her brother's chest and began to step forward. Although it seemed to Hailgi that she was hardly pushing at all, Dagar stumbled backward till the door was clear. "If you want to help, Dagar, there are wounded in the cart. You could bring them in and drive it down to the field for another load. Be sure that you bring only those with a good hope of life. You know that we have not so many medicines or skilled healers that we can waste them on those likely to die, and those who live of our host are doomed to Fetter-Grove in any case."

Dagar turned his face away from his sister as if she, too, reeked of the battlefield's stink. He walked out of the hall without looking at any of them, his head held high.

"Wait here a moment," Sigiruna ordered the two men. "I must welcome you to this hall as is best fitting." She went in and came back to the door in a few moments with a gold-bound horn in each hand, giving them to Hailgi and Sinfjotli where the two warriors stood on the threshold. "Hail to you, Hailgi, who have won this hall and its maid for your own," she said. "And hail, Sinfjotli, our kinsman and guest. May this hall ever be a home open to you."

"Hail to you, Sigiruna, my bride," Hailgi answered. He could find no better words. Her greeting had crushed the last tiny squirming of shame from his days in a woman's garb, hallowing the need and pain that had driven him, the fresh corpses that had bridged the way between them.

The aching in his chest was more than bruised ribs and battle-weariness. It was joy strong and deep enough to hurt, like the spring's first plunge into the icy sea. His restlessness was at an end, the day won. Though both of them were near-bereft of living kin, Hailgi could already feel the strand twining between them, the living and the dead who would be brought forth in his seed and Sigiruna's womb again. He did not let the tears drop, but they warmed his eyes as he gazed on her, and her mouth trembled into a smile. Sigiruna's draught was pure honey-mead, strong with a hint of sweetness, Hailgi could feel it easing his ribs already as Sigiruna took him by the hand and led him into the high-roofed hall. The fires burned along its length in sword-straight pits, running down either side of the hall. Beside the high seat sat two gray Irish hounds, whose heads rose higher than Hailgi's waist.

Hailgi tightened his hand over Sigiruna's, warming her cold fingers with his own as he drew her closer to him. She tilted her head back a little, and their lips met. Hailgi could taste the salt of his own blood and her tears as they kissed, the echo of her mead still sweet in his mouth. After a little, he let her bring him to the high seat and took his place there between the tall pillars as Dagar began to lead the wounded in. Sinfjotli had gone out again while Hailgi's back was turned, now he followed Sigiruna's brother, carrying in a man with a tattered strip of blood-caked tunic tied about the stump of his leg. When Sinfjotli's burden turned his fair head, Hailgi knew him. The maimed man was Fastawulfar, who had fared with Hailgi against Hunding.

"This is your place now. Stay here and rest, Hailgi, I know that you fought a harder battle than any."

"I must see how my folk have fared," he answered. He tried to stand again, but his legs gave way.

"You can ask for yourself, they are coming in now."

As she spoke, Skald-Thonarabrandar limped in. He still held Hailgi's standard, though the pole had been deeply gashed, the cloth ripped in several places and the white star-sign splattered with blood.

"Hai, Hailgi!" He called, coming up to stand before his drighten. Though no blood stained the thane's breeches, he winced every time he put weight on his right foot. "Did I hold your trust well?"

"None better," Hailgi assured him, taking the battered standard from his hands. Tightening his lips against the pain, he tried to slide the gold ring from his shield-arm. The flesh had already swollen black and red around it, he had to bend its coils several times before he could get it off. Finally he was able to wind the ring free, handing it to Skald-Thonarabrandar, who tightened it onto his own arm at once. "How many of our men are still living, and how many of the wounded likely to die?"

"I came from the field before a count was made, but it seemed to me that less than a quarter of our number were still hale enough to walk by themselves, and few of those did not have some wound. It will be long before this battle is forgotten, I have never heard of such a mighty one since living men can remember." The tall thane paused, looking down at the hounds who had risen to sniff at him. "It seems to me that I should make a stave on it, but none of my words seem fitting now. It may be that my drops of Wodhanar's mead were no better than fool-poet's leavings, after all, and fighting in the sunlight has left me mightily thirsty."

There was still mead in Hailgi's horn, he handed it to Skald-Thonarabrandar. "Sigiruna gave me this draught, it may bring better words to you."

The thane raised the horn high, drinking until a few golden drops spilled along the straggles of his black beard and the color rose into his hollow cheeks. "Ah, that feels better. I do not know if?," He muttered something else, too soft for Hailgi to hear it, then, blue eyes brightening, he began to chant.

"Wal-god's wassail-stealings
whelm to flood in helm-land,
one-eyed eagle's crowned high
Ygg's spear-tree with sig-joy.
Shining, Walhall's shingle
shattered 'neath blade's rattle,
There Bale-Eye reaped barley,
bleak troll-steed grew sleeker!"

"A fair stave," Sigiruna said as she came back towards them with a pitcher of Roman glass in her hand. She took the horn from Skald-Thonarabrandar, refilling it and giving it back to Hailgi. "I saw how you limp, you should not stand too long. Come and sit at this bench here before your drighten. There is drink here, and the other women will bring food in soon. We slaughtered swine at mid-day, we knew that one host or the other would want meat in the evening."

Skald-Thonarabrandar sank down gratefully onto the bench, taking up a cup and letting Sigiruna fill it.

"Now, Hailgi, will you let me see to your hurts?"

"They are little enough," Hailgi answered. "It would seem better for both of us to see to those who have been badly wounded." He took a deep draught from his horn, then leaned it against the side of his seat.

Trying to hold himself straight and not breathe too deeply, Hailgi heaved himself to his feet. He thought that he might have taken another blow or two on his cracked ribs in the second battle, the links of his byrnie were broken, though he could see no blood beneath. But he was able to walk to the far end of the hall where the wounded were being laid in fresh straw and blankets, as the hall's women brought warm water and bandages for them. Hailgi knew nothing of herb craft, but he could cut off the head of an arrow that had gone through flesh and pull the shaft out the other side, and he knew how to tie a bandage as well as anyone.

Sigiruna showed him how to stitch the worst wounds closed, working calmly and washing the blood from her hands whenever her fingers became too slippery to hold her needle properly. She had chosen well. of those who they had brought from the battlefield, there were none without hope of healing, if the wounds did not rot in their bodies. Many of the worst hurts she smeared with a thick sticky salve, its honey-scent sweet through the reek of stale blood and sweat. Hailgi could not help but notice the tear-reddened faces of the women bringing bandages, and thought it must be bitter for them, to have to help in healing the men who had slain their husbands or sons or brothers, bitterer still, if they had guessed the doom he had laid upon the men of their own folk who lay wounded there. Surely I would not bear it so well, he thought. Surely I would, but no.

Their hope now lay in being useful to those who had won the day, trying to keep the drighten's good will so that he would not sell them as thralls or cast them to his men, and perhaps being lucky enough to find a warder among the land's new fros. Hailgi knew that, had wyrd fettered him to their place, his only other choice would have been to die on the bale-fire of the slain, as women sometimes did in hopes of faring to Walhall beside their husbands. But though few chose death of their own wills, it was always easy to find, and most would wait to see what came to pass in life before setting their own feet onto the last road.

Hailgi did not mark that Dagar had come back until he heard the youth's clear voice. "There are no more there who will need to ride in the wain. Those left are either death-doomed or hale enough to walk."

"Then you have done well," Sigiruna answered. "Even so, you will need to make up more of this salve no, it were better if I did it, while you tend to these men, I think."

"Do you expect me to grind bale-worts into it?" Dagar challenged.

Sigiruna looked up from the flap of torn flesh she was stitching back over a groaning man's thigh. Hailgi did not know the man under her hands, he might have been one of the Skjoldings' men, or one of those who had come with Herwolathar. "I do not know what you might do. Your thoughts have ever been closed to my sight. But I know the herbs for this one medicine as well as you do, while you are better at sewing wounds and bandaging them so that they do not open again."

Dagar bent down, taking the needle from her hands and pulling the thin sinew taut without another word. He did not look at Hailgi as he worked, but kept his face turned away, his thick skein of gold-streaked hair falling between them so that Hailgi could see nothing of his expression. Sinfjotli bore Hrothormar Bear-Sark in, laying him down gently. The drighten's face was white under his grizzled beard, his eyes closed and his hands pressed tightly to his middle.

"I could not find a wound on him," Sinfjotli explained, "but it seems to me than he has taken more harm than from the berserk-fit alone."

No blood stained Hrothormar's tunic, but he moaned aloud when Hailgi touched his belly.

"He must be hurt inside," Dagar said coldly. "Perhaps he was struck with a shield-rim or the butt of a spear. There is nothing you can do for him. You should have left him on the field for the night to take."

Hrothormar's eyes opened, and he looked up into the dark thatch. "The shields on the roof are very bright," he murmured vaguely. "This hall seems fair, but I would have my weapons by me, there will be many fights yet before I see the wolf and the great bale-fire, or the greedy wyrm."

"I have done little harm," Sinfjotli answered as Hrothormar's eyes closed again and his chest sank with a soft sigh. The Walsing turned to Hailgi. "Herwolathar lives and is mostly unhurt, likewise with Theudowinar. For such a harsh battle, it has not turned too ill for those who fared with you. Come. You have done your share here. They are setting the food on the table, and you look no better than one of the slain."

Hailgi had been bending down too long, he could not hold back the soft sound between his teeth when he straightened again. Sinfjotli took him by the shoulders. "Where are you wounded?"

"It is no great thing. My ribs are sore, and they sting a little. No more."

The Walsing thumped his fist lightly against the broken links on the left side of Hailgi's byrnie. Hailgi was ready for him, and made no sound, but he could feel the blood draining from his head and his knees weakening beneath the pain. "I think it more likely that they are broken. Come, let us have your byrnie off."

Biting his lip, Hailgi unloosed his sword-belt and raised his arms so that Sinfjotli could tug the mail-shirt over his head. The Walsing pulled his friend's tunic up as well, nodding as he looked at Hailgi's chest. The broken bone had not cut through, but Hailgi could clearly see its jagged edge pressing against his skin at the center of a deep red bruise that seemed to be swelling and darkening as he watched. A network of woven ring-welts ran almost the length of his side, where the byrnie's links had been driven into his flesh.

"I thought that a little hurt would not leave you so pale. Now you shall rest for a while, eat and drink the good mead here till your pain is somewhat less, and then I expect that Sigiruna shall see to you herself."

Hailgi buckled his sword-belt back on and let Sinfjotli help him back to the high seat at the end of the hall. He ate and drank without noticing what he was putting into his mouth, as the last of the living came into the hall. The thin blond skop who had come with Herwolathar was singing something, but Hailgi found the man's Alamannish accent hard to understand unless he listened to it closely, it was more pleasant to hear his harp-chords and clear tenor voice without striving to make out the words. Hailgi could not help making his own count as his gaze ran over the grimed and bloody faces of the men who crowded to the tables in search of food and drink. Ingwawulfar still lived, so did Arnugrimar and Thonaraharjar, Gleaugir was among the badly wounded with a shattered collarbone and a deep spear-mark in his thigh, but likely to live.

Athalfrithar was not there, nor Jofugairar nor Sigihadur. Freyjawulfar's man who had carried the dragon-prow against the land-wights sat sideways on the bench with his swollen foot up, waving at Hailgi with a grin as the drighten's glance passed him. Hailgi thought the tally of the fallen might not be so bad as Skald-Thonarabrandar had believed. Even without counting the badly wounded, he guessed that two out of every five men who had marched from Una Bay with him were still living. Harsh as the battle had been, it seemed to Hailgi that his host had fared better than they might have expected. Against their own survivors, only two of the men doomed as Wodhanar's gifts were hale enough that they had to be bound, and by far the greater number of the living wounded were the folk who had come with Hailgi. When the last of the wounded had been seen to, Dagar left and Sigiruna came up to sit beside Hailgi.

"Where has your brother gone?" Hailgi asked her.

"There is a hut near the hall, where all of our healers' supplies are kept. I think that he is likely to sleep there, if I know him at all well enough to guess at what he may do. He blames both of us for what has fallen, which is fair enough. There is a finer bed ready for you, with down cushions and soft sheets, when you have let me wash you clean and tend to your hurts. Sinfjotli tells me that at least one of your ribs is badly broken, and your face will not scar so badly if you will let me stitch it." She leaned forward, brushing her lips so softly over his wounded jaw that he hardly felt her touch. "Now look in those bags by your feet. I believe that you will find many pleasing things there, which your men might be minded to share in."

Someone, Hailgi did not know who, had collected together much of the booty from the slain, the finest of the swords and helms as well as arm rings and cloak-pins. The goods in one bag bore no stain of battle, and included two horns with fine bindings and tips of gilded silver, he guessed that Sigiruna had brought that portion to him. There was no doubt in Hailgi's mind that all of those treasures would go to his men. Those who had lived through the day had earned as rich a reward as he could give them. It was pleasant to hand out the gifts to the thanes who had fought for him, to see how Skald-Thonarabrandar's face lit as he took the horns in payment for the stave he had made earlier that evening, to mark how the fair glitter of a broad silver fibula at Arnugrimar's throat drew the gaze away from the old thane's ugly face, how the bright gold against his bandaged arm seemed to ease the tightening of pain at the corners of Leugar's eyes.

It was more pleasant to sit with Sigiruna beside him, where he could look into her blue-gray eyes and know that she was not a wraith who would be gone with the storm-clouds, but a living woman whose warm hand lay gently over his bruised one, whose joy in him seemed no less than his in her. Still, Hailgi was glad when the last of the gifts had been given, for he was beginning to yawn often and each deep breath stabbed through his side like a fresh wound.

Hailgi had drunk a great deal against the pain in his chest and arm, and in time had to get up to piss, then he had to fend away both Sinfjotli's and Sigiruna's offers of help before he could get three steps from his seat. When Hailgi came back, Sigiruna was standing in the hall's doorway waiting for him. She slipped her arm around his waist as though she would hold him up at need, walking back through the hall with him and thus to the chambers behind the high seat. Torches burned all around the little room, and a fire glowed to one side, with a large bucket of water steaming beside it.

The bed was large enough for two, its finely embroidered crimson blanket turned down to show the white pillows and linen sheets beneath. Sigiruna's Roman pitcher, filled with mead that glowed amber-gold through its clear glass, stood on a little table by the bed, on the other side was a loom, the white linen web on it nearly full-woven. The sweet scent of herbs and clean straw rose from beneath Hailgi's feet. Sigiruna unbuckled his sword-belt, laying the weapon aside, then drew her own knife. Its edge glittered keenly in the firelight.

"What do you mean to do?" Hailgi asked.

"Your tunic will never be clean again, it is the filthiest thing I have ever seen, and the blood is set in it now, since you would sit in it for hours after the fight. I will cut it off, and spare you some pain."

Bewildered, Hailgi stood still to let her slice the cloth cleanly down the back and arms. Breaking the crusted blood from him here and there, Sigiruna unwrapped the wool from his body. That done, she briskly untied the string of his breeches and pulled them down, then crouched to take his shoes off.

"This is likely to hurt," Sigiruna warned him as she dipped a clean cloth into the hot water and began to rub his body. Though she went very gently over his injuries, she had not lied, only Hailgi's pride kept him from asking her to leave him be. She had to stop and wring blood and grime from the cloth several times before she finally began to wash carefully about the edges of the cut on his face. Hailgi bore it well, even when she poured a little mead onto the cloth from her pitcher and dabbed it onto the open flesh. He did not make so much as the least hissing of breath when she drew the wide strips of linen tight around his rib-cage, nor flinch at all when she pierced his skin with her needle and drew the sinew through behind it to sew a neat seam along his jaw. At last she bit the thread off and wiped the blood of the needle-pricks away.

"This is not how I thought our first night together would go," Sigiruna admitted when at last they sat together on the bed's edge, each holding a goblet of mead. She reached out to stroke Hailgi's shoulder, her touch soothing his ridged muscles down. "I do not know quite what I had thought."

"I had not expected that my first hope would be to get healing from you," Hailgi answered. "After faring so well in my first fights, I may have thought that I would take no hurt at all in this battle. I can hardly complain of being scathed, though, I am sure that the worst of it was my own doing, when I broke through the shield-wall on the beach."

"In any case, you will be healed by Winter nights, and ready to keep the vow you made in the hall you won from Hunding's sons." Sigiruna moved closer to him on the bed, leaning her head onto his shoulder so that her long hair rippled down his back. "We shall have much time to talk about it between now and then, so that each of us knows very well what the other wishes for that night. Tomorrow when you rise we must see to burning the dead, and set the men to building the ship-mound for my father and brother."

"You must have rule over that, as you best know how it should be done. Nor will I grudge you time enough to mourn for them, it seems to me that the hurts you have taken this day are far worse than mine."

Hailgi could see the water gleaming in Sigiruna's eyes, but her voice was steady as she answered, "I knew they were death-doomed before they ever trod the field, and mourned them already when they were first chosen to fall. Age was beginning to weight my father's arm, and Bragi's had not come to its full strength, though his warrior's mood was full-waxed. They fell as they ought, and shall fare as they ought, and no Skjoldings have ever asked for better. How many of your men do you think can help with mound-building?"

"That will depend on their choice. Most of those who fared with me shall take their treasures home again in the next days, since harvest is almost upon us. But many will stay. They hope to take steads here."

"Their help with the harvest is much-needed, as well," Sigiruna murmured. "And the Moon is half-waned. It will not be so long till Winter nights, and I have much to ready before our wedding."

She took Hailgi's goblet from his hand and set both empty vessels on the table, then unbound her own belt and slipped her dress over her head as if they had been wedded for years. Hailgi stared at her, awed at her fairness, though he was too tired and sore for more than a glint of desire to spark in his body. Sigiruna drew back the covers and got into bed, gesturing that Hailgi should slide in beside her. Careful of his ribs, he lowered himself between the sheets, she moved over to him till he could feel the warmth of her body along the length of his, the tips of her breasts just brushing his bandages and her breath mingling honey-sweet with his own.

Though he would have liked to stay awake, whispering to Sigiruna and feeling her beside him, the wave of tiredness that had hung over Hailgi all evening was crashing down now. He could no longer keep his eyes open, and his mind was already melting into a soft daze of mead and warmth, away from the aching in his ribs and arm and face. By the time Sigiruna had brought Hailgi back to the battle-field in her own small wain the next day, the dead had already been laid in a great heap, bedded on dry branches and blanketed with pitch. No one had found Hailgi's own spear on the field yet, but Sigiruna had given him one to hallow the pyre with. He could think of no words to say, he cast the weapon one-handed, its glittering edge cutting an arc over the dead before it stabbed into the ground on the other side of the heap. When the spear's shaft no longer thrummed against the earth, Herwolathar brought Hailgi a burning torch. He stood with the fire in his hand a few moments, looking at the pyre.

The shiny blackness hid what the eagles and ravens had done to the corpses, so coated, they looked as strange and nonhuman as the deep brown bog-wights that folk sometimes dug from their homes in the peat. Hailgi was not sure whether he himself wished to be burned or buried in a howe, he knew that some rulers were both burned and buried, so that their ashes should still bring luck to their lands. Anyway, it would not be his choice in the end. He set his torch to a rivulet of pitch dripping down from the higher branches. It flared up at once, hissing and sputtering as a coil of rich pine-scented smoke unfolded into the air like a gray adder arising from sleep. Still, Hailgi's work was not done yet. He had his gift to make to the land-wights, to pay the geld for the fright he had given them and ask their friendship again. That would not be done by Freki Stone, but near the edge of one of the wheat-fields, on a small howe there.

A rowan tree grew at the top of the mound where the Skjoldings made those gifts. Its leaves were still green, but its clusters of berries were already bright red. Dagar already stood under the tree, with one ox to either side of him. He held the slaughter-ax from Haganon's hof in his hand. Though the weapon was heavy, Hailgi marked that Dagar's arm did not tremble under its weight, there was wiry muscle on the youth's light bones.

"We shall give the gift together, slaying one each," Dagar said firmly when Hailgi held out his hand for the ax. "You have offended these wights, but I know them. The alfs here are my kinsmen and the land-trolls have long been friends of the Skjoldings."

"It would be ill of me to drive my wife's brother from her lands, nor was that in my mind to do," Hailgi replied. "I cannot deny your right to take part in this gift, and I say that you shall still hold land here when Sigiruna and I have gone. Here I must hark to the words of Freyjar's son."

Dagar gave the oxen's tethers to Hailgi, shifting his sling so that he could lay his free hand on the left ox's head as he gazed past the Wolfing to the green hills before Freki stone and the golden fields around them. Sigiruna's brother did not speak, but it seemed to Hailgi of a sudden that he was standing on the banks of a great river, whose swift-churning waters shook through the ground around him. Dagar brought the ax down one-handed between the ox's horns with a swift whipping motion, using all the strength in his body. It dropped under the blow, dead weight before it hit the ground.

Hailgi took the bloodied ax from the Skjolding's hands. With his broken rib, he could not be sure of matching Dagar's blow to the ox's skull, but he had enough strength in his shoulders to cleave through his beast's thick neck-muscles and spine. Breathing deeply, Hailgi looked about him as Dagar had done. It seemed to him that the edge of his gaze caught clear shapes stirring like heat-ripples over the grain, over the hills. He tightened his grip on the ax. It was not for himself alone that the land-wights' good will was needed, but if he could not win it back, everyone in these lands would go hungry in the years to come.

"Hear me," he murmured softly, not speaking to the folk who stood at the edge of the field, but to those who moved within the mound. "I bring you a geld, to pay for the harm I did when I brought the dragon-prows into your land. Know that hereafter I shall not harm you again, but ward you from other men's deeds as best I may. I mean to give you worship and gifts as is fitting, I wish there to be friendship and frith between us, and among all the folk, living or hidden, who dwell in these lands about us."

The ox bellowed, raising its head as Hailgi swung the ax with a soft grunt of pain. The blade cut cleanly through the back of its neck, it fell like the other, and Hailgi knew that the land-folk had taken his gift. The harvest-time passed slowly for Hailgi. He could not swing a sickle or bend to bind sheaves while his ribs were healing, so he had to sit in the hall with the other wounded or outside in the late summer sunshine. It was not long before he found that he was trying not to speak to or look at those men he had doomed to Fetter-Grove, stubbornly, he forced himself to talk to them, to learn their names and faces.

This gift to Wodhanar would not be without price for him, Hailgi swore to himself. So he did not turn his face away when Hrabanawulfar's little daughter ran to her father, tugging at his gold-brown braids and beard to get him to lift her up, he watched without blinding himself when Hjalmamarir's dark-eyed wife lifted a cup of ale to the lips of the youth she had wedded only a few days before the battle, or combed his hair where he sat bound before her. Thus he marked at once when Thonarastainar Broad-Nose fell ill with wound-rot, the tall thane tossing uneasily in his straw with sweat matting his dark hair to his forehead.

Hailgi thought little of it that morning, it was more surprising that none of the others had sickened in the quarter-moon since the battle. By afternoon, Thonarastainar Broad-Nose lay still, only breathing harshly, and seven more of the twelve wounded prisoners were already beginning to thrash with fever, while Dice-Agilar had twice made a high cast without remembering to sweep in any of his winnings, staring blankly at the dice as if their marks were blurring in his eyes. Hailgi looked more keenly about the hall. None of his own men showed any sign of illness. Then it seemed to the Wolfing that he knew where he might find an answer for what was happening. He got up and left the hall, walking towards Dagar's healer-hut. The door was closed, but he could hear the voices of Sigiruna and her brother through it quite clearly.

"Dagar, I know you are never without a reason. Now tell me why."

"Men may fall ill at any time," Dagar answered. "See, I am already making a salve which may help stop their wound-rot from spreading."

"Yes if it kills them first. But why do you seek to hasten the doomed towards death?"

"If you must know," Dagar answered, and Hailgi heard something rustling inside, "It was for your sake."

"Mine?"

"Yes, yours!" The youth flared. "Yours and our family's. Do you think it should be told how you gladly cast Wodhanar's spear into the bodies of our father's thanes, men who were friends in our hall and true to our kin? Or how you stood by Hailgi while he cast it, and swore your wedding-oath to him on the bloodied point afterward? If they should chance to die of wound-fever, well, that happens to many men, and there is no shame to our father's memory in it."

"What of Hjalmamarir and Katilar, who are not wounded? What had you planned for them?"

"Men die in many ways. Who can say? Perhaps there was something in their water a sudden flux, that killed in a few hours, perhaps one or the other was stricken by elf-shot, or else the Ansur claimed his own without calling on human hands to aid him."

"Was?"

"Might be. I have done nothing to them, I could not turn my lore."

"These are not easy deaths you would have chosen to deal, for the most part."

"Easier than this long waiting, that makes men into cattle for the Winter nights slaughter. They are already hallowed to Wodhanar. What does it matter whether he takes them sooner or later, here or in his holy grove? I wish to have little to do with that grim god. Freyjar does not deal so, and I will not ask him to heal men only so that Wodhanar may eat them."

Hailgi flung the door open, stepping into the dark hut and taking a deep breath of its herb-musted air. Sigiruna and Dagar stared at him from across the table where Dagar stood grinding something in his stone mortar. Their faces shone white in the dimness, and Hailgi could clearly see the red welt of Sigiruna's hand on her brother's face.

Dagar stepped back from Hailgi, his sling rose, then fell back, as though he had thought to fling his injured arm across his face to fend off a blow.

"Now it would seem to me fitting, if you were doomed to be one of those given to Wodhanar at that feast!" Hailgi cried out wrathfully. "You shall not tend the wounded any longer, for there is no trustworthiness in you, if you fail in the healing you claimed to offer. I asked for no oaths from you, since I did not know whether you would wish to call me to a holm later, as was surely your right. Now I say that you shall come to Fetter-Grove with us, and when Sigiruna and I swear our oaths of wedding on Wodhanar's spear, you shall swear your oath of troth on that same bloodied blade, or else be slain by it where you stand, in place of those you wished to keep from it."

"At least some of them are free of your reach by now," Dagar answered. "Nor will I say that I have wrought ill. Freyjar holds the fetters of health and sick-death, but I would not call him here for this, since there is little use in wasting his might on those sworn as slain. You might slay me now, if you choose to, but you and I will both know why I died. I did not give poison, only kept the strongest healing herbs and the clean bandages for those men who were not doomed to death by your word, for whom there was hope, as there is none for your gift to your god.

It seemed to me no worthy thing, to heal so that you might have more to kill, and their knowing of doom must have weakened them as well, so that their souls had no strength to fend the wound-rot from their bodies."

"Are you able to heal the harm you have allowed?"

"That I cannot do. Perhaps the strongest of the men will live through it, those who see dawn's light tomorrow certainly shall. If not, you must content yourself with Hjalmamarir and Katilar, so that the ravens of Fetter-Grove grow but a little fatter."

"And what shall I do with you? Folk would think it strange if I bound you or locked you away without saying why, when I have let you run free and shown you all the honor a son of the Skjoldings should have."

Sigiruna came around the table to stand beside Hailgi. "My brother has never been an oathbreaker. Let him swear by our father's grave and the honor of the Skjolding line that he will not seek to get in the way of the Winter nights sacrifice, nor use his herb-craft for any ill, and then you may be sure of him."

"Do you swear that, Dagar?"

Sigiruna's brother swallowed, looking angrily down at the herb-bloodied pestle that shook in his hand. "In no way willingly, nor shall I willingly swear on Wodhanar's spear, for now I bear him less love than ever before. I see little other way than speaking these oaths. So be it. I swear by my father's grave and the honor of the Skjolding line that I will not seek to get in the way of the Winter nights sacrifice, nor use my herb-craft for any ill. And may the trolls take you for this."

He turned his mortar upside down, scraping the green-black mess into a small pot, and plunged both mortar and pestle into the bucket of water by the table. The last tremors of anger still shaking through his hands, Hailgi stood staring at the youth until Sigiruna took him by the arm.

"Come, Hailgi," she said. "We may yet be able to save some of them, if the fever has not gone too far and their strength does not fail."

The harvest feast in the hall of the Skjoldings was quiet, though they had been able to bring in more than enough grain to feed those who had survived. Still, there were too many dead for there to be much joy in the mood there. Freyjar's barley-bearded sheaf-shape, throned above the high seat, looked down at benches where the women outnumbered the men by more than half, as though they feasted in the hall of Frija or the Frowe instead of the burg of a great war leader. And there were the death-doomed sitting beside Hailgi and Sigiruna. Hjalmamarir, Katilar, Hrabanawulfar, Aiwiwindar, and Brandar, and Dagar sat there as if he counted himself among their number.

Everyone there knew what should become of them now, and it seemed to Hailgi that the gaze of their eyes grayed the fires' brightness like a fine mist through the hall. He knew that he had not thought of what his oath would mean, had thought that it would be no worse than the time before, and never once set before himself that he would have to keep his chosen men among the others until Winter nights. Though he had unbound them himself for the feast, none of them had tried to strike him or to get away, it seemed to him that he could see their belief in their doom in the sunken hollows around Katilar's dark eyes, in the way Hjalmamarir gently stroked his wife's deep golden hair as she clung red-eyed to him and in the way Brandar clenched his blue-veined hands on the edge of the table, as if to hold tightly to the feeling of the smooth wood while he still lived. Then Herwolathar's bright laughter broke through the quiet murmuring as the ship-drighten tossed a wreath of woven grain to one of his men.

"There's a fair farm for you to hold, now that I have land here to give out!" He called as the other men cheered.

Perhaps it is only me, Hailgi thought. No, Sinfjotli, who sat on his other side, was also quiet, his chin propped on his hand as he stared out into the middle of the hall.

"Why are you so quiet?" He asked the Walsing. "Does the drink not please you?"

"I am only thinking that I must go from here very soon, and back to my father's hall. I should not have stayed so long away, but I wish to see you wedded before I leave."

"Well, we are faring to Fetter-Grove tomorrow." Hailgi paused. "I shall be sorry to see you go."

"As I to leave you." Sinfjotli glanced beyond Hailgi and Sigiruna, to the five men who sat quietly among their wives and children. "Have you ever heard the tale of my mother's first two children, the sons of Sigigairar?"

"I have heard that Sigimund slew them as part of the revenge he took for his father."

"There is more to the tale." Sinfjotli took a deep drink from his horn. "Sigilind sent them to my father, one at a time, so that he might test them to see if they were true Walsings, if they could help in his revenge."

"And?"

"They were not brave enough. So, at Sigilind's bidding, he slew them."

"Why are you telling me of this?"

"Only because it came to my mind. I cannot name that deed ill, for if my brothers had not died then, I should not have been born, and no one could say what might have become of the Walsing-line."

The faring from Sealand to Jutland the next morning was clear, a cold winter wind speeding Hailgi's ships along the waves. Sigiruna had dressed plainly for the faring, meaning to put her wedding-dress on when they got to Fetter Grove. Though she said she had not sailed often before, Hailgi was glad to see that she was not seasick, but balanced easily on the tilting deck beside him, looking up at the white gulls swooping through the sky.

"It is fine to fly alone like that, but finer to sail with you," she said, putting her arm about Hailgi's waist. "This seems to be an easier faring than your last one. Ran's daughters know now that I have claimed you, and they have no hope of drawing you into their halls."

"Ran's daughters are said to be fair," Hailgi answered teasingly.

Sigiruna only laughed. "It's too late. You have made your choice already."

"So I have." He put his own arm around her so that their thick cloaks overlapped like the wings of birds sharing a nest.

When they neared the coast of Sealand, Hailgi sent his other ship southward, to tell Bergohildar to ready the Winter nights feast, and turned his own toward the north, towards Fetter-Grove. The Sun's light had just begun to deepen into the rich red-gold of her setting by the time they cast anchor before the grassy mound by the gray stone.

Hailgi thought to take Sigiruna in to shore in the small landing-boat, but she cast off her cloak and leapt overboard without a thought, standing in the waist-deep water. "I'll carry the mead-cask, if you'll hand it down to me," she offered. "You'll have enough to do with the men there."

Hailgi lifted the cask over the side of the ship, lowering it carefully into her hands as she braced herself for its weight. Though it was not a small cask, it did not seem too heavy for her strength, but she had brewed, filled, and chosen it, after all. Sigiruna balanced the cask easily on one shoulder. "Now give me my cloak and my wedding-dress. I will have my clothes changed by the time you get to shore, I'm sure." Hailgi rolled up the cloak into a bundle for her, then handed down the other bag she had brought with her.

As Sigiruna waded through the low waves to the shore, Hailgi turned back to the men in the boat. He was about to call for help in lifting the prisoners into the small boats when Hrabanawulfar said, "Unbind my feet. I will get in by myself, and set foot on the shore by myself, just as I must walk into Fetter Grove."

Hailgi looked into the warrior's craggy face, meeting his blue gaze straight on. If all five were unbound, but twice twelve had fared there with Hailgi, and that number included Sinfjotli and Sigiruna as well, though not Dagar, who sat on one of the rowers' benches staring coldly at Hailgi.

"You others?"

Katilar jerked his narrow head forward once and flung his neatly plaited braids backward. The dark-haired thane was dressed in a crimson tunic with deep blue embroidery twining about hem and sleeves, as if he meant to rejoice at Sigiruna's wedding feast, a silver ring glittered just below his right elbow. The others, too, were dressed finely. Hrabanawulfar and Hjalmamarir wore their byrnies and good steel helms, and Brandar was wrapped in a cloak of blue-white fox furs from the far North. Aiwiwindar's wife had decked him in a tunic of pure white linen trimmed with southern silk. The thane's belly pressed hard against the shining garment, and Hailgi could see that he would not be able to move his arms easily in it. It must have been Aiwiwindar's own wedding-tunic, ten or fifteen years ago.

"So it shall be, then." Hailgi gestured to Skald-Thonarabrandar, Arnu-grimar, Ingwawulfar, and Sinfjotli. Each of them crouched down to untie the bonds on one captive's feet and retie them loosely enough that the men would be able to walk.

Dagar waded to the shore as his sister had, scowling at her as she came out from behind the grassy mound but saying nothing. Hailgi only stared a moment. He had seen Sigiruna finish the white linen weave, seen her stitching the black and red triangles that wove into a single band of interlocked walknots around the hem and the gold wyrms that twisted around her neck and sleeves, but he had not seen the twisted bridal crown of gold wires and smooth-cut rock crystals that adorned her fair head, nor had he guessed that she might weave fine gold wires to glitter along the length of her unbound hair over her dark blue cloak.

Though there were no flowers in the wood at winter's beginning, Sigiruna had picked three of the white-flecked red mushrooms that spread through the mound's tall grass, bright over the gray stone.

Those she carried in her left hand together with the gold-bound horn she had first greeted Hailgi with, in her right, she held a tunic that matched her bridal dress.

"Put this on quickly, Hailgi," she called so that everyone could hear her. "I have waited long enough for this evening, I am not minded to wait longer."

Hailgi felt the blush coming to his cheeks as he heard his men laughing behind him. He changed tunics as fast as he could, though the Sun had not set, the night-frost was already beginning to bite in the wind. Then he set his helmet upon his head. One of the Skjoldings' thralls was a clever metalsmith, who had repaired it so that the harms could hardly be seen, and Sigiruna had said that she wished him to bear it at their wedding.

Hailgi bound the loose loops of rope onto Sigiruna's slender ankles and wrists, then she did the same for him, tying her knots carefully so that he could neither slip nor be hurt by them. The two of them tied up Sinfjotli together, as if they were playing a game. The Walsing looked down at them with a slight smile on his lips, Hailgi knew that no matter how well they bound him, his strength was great enough to break the rope if he chose. But Sinfjotli would go into Fetter Grove as the rest of them did. That, too, Hailgi knew. Remembering what had been done before, Hailgi had Freyjawinar and Gunthahadur take the captives away one by one, so that they could empty themselves before the procession started into the woods. The beech leaves rustled brown over their heads, the grass beneath their feet, only the red and orange of mushrooms brightened the wood-path in the lowering light.

At first Hailgi thought that the earth had begun to tremble beneath his feet, then it seemed to him that it was a deep growl he heard, the sound shaking in his bones. His first thought was of the wolf that had come upon them in Fetter Grove before, and he glanced back at the others. Sigiruna glided easily behind him, giving no sign that she heard anything. Behind her walked Dagar, fists clenched on the length of rope that linked his wrists, Hrabanawulfar strode steadily as if he were on his way to the battlefield, but Hailgi's own hands were trembling so badly that he could not keep them open, the low growl growing to a wind-roaring in his ears as the edges of his sight blurred into shadows creeping through the trees. I am afraid, he thought wonderingly. Why should I fear?

No ill is likely to come to me this night, but only joy, and how could I find worse here than I have already lived through? He forced his palms flat against his thighs, striding ahead through the fallen leaves and dry grass. The markings on the gray slab of stone that led into Fetter Grove were very dark in the reddening light through the brown leaves, the shadowed blackness within the alf-cups stretching deeper than Hailgi could see. The spear-wielder's silhouette stood out starkly against the gray rock, the huge man raising his weapon as a warning to those who stood bound on the pathway outside the grove. Sigiruna stepped lithely onto the stone, pulling the bung from her keg with her teeth as she twisted the tap.

Red-gold in the Sun's light, the shining mead streamed down into the highest alf-cup and along their line, welling dark over the rim of each and spilling to the next. Something gold and round as a Roman coin glittered in her hand a moment, then spun out to fall before the wooden shape of Wodhanar. Before the trembling in his limbs could overwhelm him, Hailgi stepped onto the stone, following Sigiruna's dark-cloaked shape over it to the holy stead. The rock's might prickled against his soles as if he were walking barefoot through a bin of sharp-haired grain, it seemed to him that he could feel the wind blowing icy over his body, though the brown and golden leaves of the grove hung still in the cold air. Wodhanar's eagle-helm shadowed the crude-carved features of his wooden face, hooding his empty eye socket in darkness.

No sign showed where the bodies of Hailgi's last gift to him had hung, their bones must have dropped to the ground long ago, and been carried off by those who walked freely through the grove where living men must go bound. Hailgi stopped at the rock's edge beside Sigiruna.

"Wodhanar, grant us leave to come here," he murmured softly. "Fettered, we come to Fetter Grove, with gifts won in fight, to bid you share in the wedding-joy you have brought us." He took Sigiruna by the hand and they stepped into the grove together, going to the harrow to lay the things she held upon it.

One by one, the others filed in, captives together with free men. Dagar hung back till last, for a moment, Hailgi thought he would not come in, but at last the youth stepped onto the rock and made his way over it to take his place in the half-circle bent around Wodhanar. Hailgi looked at Sinfjotli, expecting that the Walsing would lift him up so that he could unbind the god's spear, but Sigiruna was already stepping between them. Hailgi and Sinfjotli each cupped their hands together, bending down so that Sigiruna could step into the living stirrups they had made for her.

She knew that her weight would be no burden to them, it seemed to her as though she were already in the air before they touched her, as though their hands were as misty as the wind-steed that swept her over Hailgi's battle-fields. The bindings lashing the spear to the branch fell free as she touched them, she leapt down with the weapon in her hand, bending her knees at the shock of landing but keeping herself upright. Giving the spear to Hailgi, Sigiruna took up the horn and filled it from her keg. She broke off a piece of one of the mushrooms, dropping it into the draught. This was the last kindness she could give to these men.

The bitter-edged death-drink that would daze their minds, drowning out their last fear and letting the swift flight of Wodhanar's weapon wing them free towards Walhall. Slowly she strode toward Hrabanawulfar, bearing the horn in both hands. "Drink the draught I have readied, and let it gladden you towards what has been shaped for you," she told him, her voice steady despite the blurring of her eyes.

"Let Wodhanar know that you were among the first to taste the mead of my wedding feast."

Hrabanawulfar took the horn from her and raised it. As he tilted his head back and back, Sigiruna saw the warrior's voice-box rising and falling beneath the brown grain-plaiting of his beard as though he were singing. Though he still wore his byrnie, it would do him little good against a spear flung hard and straight from so near. Hailgi's strength behind the weapon's blade would break the links asunder like woven linen. When he had finished the drink, Hrabanawulfar stepped up on the rootless tree-stump, standing still as Hailgi looped the rope over a stout branch and made the noose fast about his neck. Sigiruna could hear the thane's breathing coming faster, the darkness was already swelling out from the center of Hrabanawulfar's blue eyes.

As Hailgi tied the knot, Sigiruna could not help seeing the little fingers of Hrabanawulfar's daughter braiding the strands of her father's beard, nor forget how the child's grave look and lowered brown brows had echoed Hrabanawulfar's as she had stood on the beach watching the ships sail out.

Just so, Sigiruna had stood on the shore to watch Haganon sail away, her father's sword glinting in the sunlight as he raised it to wave at her until she could see him no more, just so, she had stood at the door of the mound, looking for the last time at the ship that would bear Haganon and Bragi over the waters to God-Home. Sigiruna took the rope's loose end and stood ready by the stump as Hailgi lifted the spear, aiming it carefully. The left side of Hailgi's ribcage twinged a little as he moved his arm, but his bone had knitted well. His sharp cry rang out as Hrabanawulfar's choked off, the warrior's body turning as it swung free. Sigiruna's shoulders were already beginning to shake from the strain of holding him, as though she were weeping, but her first mighty pull on the rope had broken his neck.

Sinfjotli caught the dead man by the legs, holding his weight up while Sigiruna made the rope fast, Hailgi tugged Wodhanar's spear out from between the broken byrnie-links, careful to keep out of the way of the blood springing forth in the weapon's wake. This close, Hailgi could smell the rich wet scent of the dead man's seed blending with the sharp copper-salt of his blood. Hailgi looked into Sigiruna's eyes as she pulled the knot tight. A rush of warmth flooded into his groin, and his knees began to shake. He reached out to take Sigiruna's hand a moment, she clasped his palm hard, and he could feel the thumps of her heartbeat trembling through her fingers. It would not be long, Hailgi told himself, trying to still his own racing breath, it would not be long now. Brandar turned to shrug his pale fox-cloak from his shoulders into the hands of Freyjawinar, who stood behind him.

"Take this to my son Brandabernu," he murmured. "I shall have no need of it in Walhall, I have heard that Wodhanar has several ways to keep his thanes warm." Brandar laughed softly, raising his bound hands to brush a wave of his loose red-gold hair from his forehead. "Now, Sigiruna, I shall drink your mead, I always said that I should dance at your wedding-feast. I am glad to know that my words are still worthy."

Hailgi could see the horn shaking in Brandar's long hands as he drank it empty and swallowed the piece of mushroom, but the thane did not let his smile ease as Hailgi set the stump on end again beneath a second branch, nor as he put his head through the noose the Wolfing had readied, nor when Sigiruna raised Wodhanar's spear. The Skjolding maid bit her lip hard, its pinkness whitening beneath her teeth, her fierce gaze never left Brandar's eyes as she flung the spear straight into his body. Its impact nearly tore the rope out of Hailgi's hands, he yanked down hard with all his strength, kicking the stool at the same time. Hjalmamarir was the last of the captives to be slain. The young thane grinned as though he would have liked to speak words as brave as Brandar's, but no words seemed to come to him, he drank his death-draught in silence, and stepped onto the tree-stump in silence. Only then did the lock on his throat seem to ease.

He looked Hailgi in the eyes, whispering as though the noose were already choking him, "My frowe may well be carrying a child now I thank you for our last night together. If the child is a son and chosen for life, see that he is given my name, if a daughter, then when she is old enough to understand, tell her to name her first son after me. I wish to live among my kin again."

"That shall be done," Hailgi answered, stepping back and readying himself to cast Wodhanar's spear for the last time.

Hjalmamarir's body was still turning at the rope's end when Sigiruna braced one palm against his ring-shirted chest and pulled the spear from him with the other. Most of his blood missed her, gushing free to drown the round golden pendant that she had cast onto the earth before the tree, but a few spatters showed black on the white linen of her wedding dress when she came back to stand behind the harrow.

The bloody spear in her hand was dark against the reddened sky, the red light shone richly from the gold binding and gilded eagle-tip of the horn as she filled it again and bore it to Hailgi. Hailgi put his hands over hers, the ropes linking their wrists crossed in the horn's shadow. As he touched her, it seemed to him that all his fears and sorrows dropped from his shoulders like a heavy cloak, that no solid earth held his feet's roots, as though he were soaring on unseen wings, the wind bearing him far above the fells.

A deep blue mist, glimmering with lightless sparkles, seemed to swirl up about Sigiruna's sun-bright face, drowning everything around her in Hailgi's sight, the gale in his ears roared at full strength, but he could hear the eagle's sig-scream in his voice as he spoke through the howling wind. "I hail you, Sigiruna, my bride, dear-bought and yet well-bought, with blood of kin and friends! Here, in this holy stead, I swear myself to you. Let us always be bound together by these wedding-oaths, as we are bound here in Fetter-Grove." He glanced back to the great ash-tree at the five dead men dangling behind Wodhanar's wooden shape, at the god's shadowed eye and deep-pooled socket.

A gust of icy wind set the corpses swinging, turning at the ends of their ropes. It seemed to Hailgi that he could feel the cold kindling into warmth under the god's gaze, the fire running up from his groin as if his body had been a stock of dried wood waiting for the torch, and he grasped Sigiruna's hands more tightly, turning his gaze back to her. "Let Wodhanar witness our wedding now, and send us his bairn-apples, so that our line shall wax mighty and our names not be forgotten in the Middle-Garth's ring."

The silver plates of Hailgi's helm, weapon-dancers, wolf-sark, eagle and raven, gleamed brightly in Sigiruna's gray eyes as she looked at him, her own eyes, gazing at him from the reflection in his, were shadowed dark beneath the helm's rim. Though she whispered softly as swan-feathers rustling. Her murmuring meant for Hailgi alone, still her words carried easily through the soundless clearing. "I hail you, Hailgi, my husband, sig-blessed and blessed with love, as Wodhanar has wrought for us. I swear myself to you now by horn and hallowed spear, here within Fetter-Grove. Gladly shall I bear your bairns, and gladly dwell with you. Whether life or death befall us both, our line shall wax mighty, and our names not be forgotten in the Middle-Garth's ring."

Hailgi drank first, then Sigiruna. A third of the hornful was left when they were done, this they poured out on the harrow before Wodhanar together. The rope between Hailgi's wrists was too short for him to embrace his bride as he wished to do, but he grasped her hands and drew her close. Tears brightened Sigiruna's eyes as he kissed her. Hailgi wondered at this a moment, but the warm rush of joy from his heart to his head was already stinging behind his own lids and blurring his sight into a wreath of rainbow fire around Sigiruna's face. Too strong to pour from his mouth in words, Hailgi's gladness had to rush free through his gaze. The tears flowed over the bone rims of his eyes like mead overflowing from a cup, spilling the brightness of the setting Sun over his face. Sigiruna filled the horn again and passed it to Sinfjotli. He drank deeply, wiping a few drops from his beard with the back of his hand when he was done.

As soon as he had passed the horn to Skald-Thonarabrandar who stood beside him, the Walsing caught Sigiruna by the waist, swinging her around and lifting her up to kiss her. After that, each of the men claimed his luck-kiss from the bride in turn, although none of the others tried to lift her from her feet as Sinfjotli had done. When everyone had drunk a good draught of the wedding-mead, Sigiruna beckoned Dagar forward. Sigiruna's nearness and her mead had flooded all other thoughts from Hailgi's mind, so that he would have gone without calling Dagar to give his oaths, but now that the Skjolding stood before him, he could not forget how Dagar had let nine of the twelve wounded prisoners die of fever, and might have killed them all with his herb-craft, had his soul turned only a little harder. Hailgi tilted the spear downward so that Sigiruna's brother could lay his hand on the bloody point. Dagar grasped it hard, so that Hailgi thought he must surely be cutting his fingers, though it was growing too dark to see whether the brightness of new blood ran over the weapon's crusted edges.

"Here on Wodhanar's spear, although I little wished to do this, I swear frith between us, Hailgi." Dagar stopped for a moment, as though tallying the worth of his words as he chose between them. "I shall not seek to bring you harm, by wort or weapon, hand or rede, so long as you turn none of these against me. I swear this by the holy oath of the Skjoldings, by Leiptar's bright waves and Unthio's spray-cold stone, if I break it may the ship of our clan ferry me soon over the waters to our age-old kin-home!" He held up his hand, Hailgi still could not see whether the blood on it was his own or all came from the spear, but the holiness of the oath would hold in any case. "Now you have your oath, is it enough?"

"It is enough," Hailgi answered.

The Moon was up by the time they had cast off, his full brightness showing their path clearly over the waters. Hailgi and Sigiruna sat sharing one cloak, looking out over the prow at the dark shadows of the headlands against the white shore-edges where foam melted into sand. Here and there, Sigiruna could see the amber glow of little fires on the black land.

Folk were feasting well on this hallowed night, for it had been a fair summer. She snuggled closer to Hailgi, leaning into the curve of his shoulder. "Is
your hall far?"

"Not very far," Hailgi answered. "Once we have rounded this point, we will
see another, and the hall's harbor is just beyond that."

"I am eager to be there." There would be a warm hall-fire for them to sit
before, Sigiruna thought, men and women calling wedding-redes with the
friendliness that she would ever have missed in the Skjolding hall. The
Winter nights feast would be ready, with fresh-slain meat and ripe apples,
and perhaps a special dish of leeks for the wedded couple's fruitfulness. Her
mother had told her that the full moon was the best time

"So am I. I am eager to fulfill the second half of my vow."

"What was that?"

Though Hailgi's face shone pale gray in the moonlight, Sigiruna could
feel the heat of the blush rising to his cheeks. "I vowed to wed you at Winter
nights, as I have done, and to get a son with you this same night."

Sigiruna could feel her own laugh running through Hailgi's body as well,
her face warming against him. "That oath, I think, shall also be made true."

CHAPTER XXVI

The Blue Door was bigger than the Bar of Soap, with a small raised stage right by the bar. Even in the dim lighting, Helgi could see the difference in the people who were starting to gather there. The bar's lights gleamed blue from the shiny leather of jackets or pants, no long blue tattoo-sleeves wove downward from the armholes of denim vests, and the polish had not been kicked from boots or worn from chrome snaps. Helgi hefted his synthesizer up onto the edge of the stage, then climbed up after it.

"Ready to play?" Mike asked from behind him.

"Yeah. Hey, Mike, there's something I want to do tonight."

"What?"

"I've got this song I want to do with just keyboard and vocals. I'm not sure where in the set I'll need to put it, but when I give the sign, I want everyone to back off and go away."

Mike pulled hard at one side of his mustache, as though the stinging tug eased something in him even as it tightened his lips into a lopsided twist of disgust. "Jesus, Helgi."

"I've got to do it. Trust me." Helgi stared at Mike until the band leader's brown eyes dropped.

"What is with you this week, Hadding? I'm beginning to think you've gone over the edge and landed on your head, you know that?"

"Mike I really don't want to know what you think. Look, I won't ask for anything like this again. This is strictly a one-time thing, okay?"

"Yeah, one-time." Mike snorted as though he were about to spit on the stage, then his eyes flickered to the bouncer lurking by the front door, and he swallowed. "Okay, fine, as long as you stop being a fucking prima donna and start acting like a human being again. You used to be kind of a likable guy, you know. Shit, you think just because."

"Look, Mike," Helgi started hotly, then lowered his voice. "I'm sorry. I didn't mean to well, whatever, I didn't mean to do it. This is very important to me. It won't fuck up the gig, I promise."

"Probably not. Okay, fine, apology accepted."

"Helgi," Rof's deep voice rumbled. Helgi turned to face him, standing on the edge of the stage, he was looking down at the tight cap of Rof's hair and the broad spread of his scuffed-leather shoulders. The blue lighting cast an odd grayish sheen over the tech sergeant's dark skin, a rim of white glimmered at the edge of his dark eyes as they rolled up to meet Helgi's for a moment. "Karin says hello, and sorry she couldn' make it. Wants to know if you can meet us next Friday evening fo' pizza."

"I already told her I would," Helgi answered boldly.

The bluish gleam of the lights on Rof's cheekbones shifted, tightening inward, but the big man only said mildly, "That so? Must'a wanted to check fo' sure, then. Nothin' goes wrong, pick you up at seven-thirty."

Behind Helgi, Mike's breath sighed softly out again.

"Well, I better move my butt. Promised yo' drum man I'd help carry his set in he none too eager to leave pieces of it unattended in the back lot." Rof turned around and moved slowly off through the thickening crowd. Helgi noticed that he never touched or bumped into anyone. Simply glided through the space that formed around him.

"Death-wish," Mike muttered, shaking his head as he crouched down to hook up their speakers.

By the time they started the second set, a thin blue haze of smoke hung in the air, blurring Helgi's sight whenever he tried to look straight at the lights. It was getting warmer and warmer on-stage. It seemed to him that he could feel a glow of heat kindling inside him, his music heating his body like the rubbing of wood against wood. After the second song, he left his keyboard and walked over to Mike.

"Now," he whispered.

Mike waved the other band-members back as Helgi shifted his synthesizer to the foreground, careful not to yank on or trip over any of the cables weaving across the stage. The faces before him were blurring, pale as fish in the blue light, except for Rof who stood solid and dark by the edge of the stage, unfazed by the smoke's soft glow. As Helgi stepped forward, Rof lifted the bottle of Shiner Bock in his hand slightly, like a fencer saluting an opponent. Helgi did not shift his glance from the other man a moment. He felt his gaze strengthening, the gleam behind his eyeballs stretching out like two wind-swept trails of smoke sweeping together into a single spear. Helgi started very low, a slow minor key whispering in the bass, notes to be felt rather than heard. His mouth opened, the wind began to breathe from it, far down at the bottom of his range.

Even if he were singing clearly, he knew no one there would understand the words "Ravnen mun flyver om aftenen, om dagen han ikke må" Their sounds told little to Helgi himself, but he remembered the English translation. Val-Raven flies in the evening, he cannot fly by day. The deep notes of his voice tingled through his body, rising from the base of his spine through the top of his skull. It seemed to him that he could see the huge muscles of Rof's shoulders lifting beneath the scuffed black leather, as though the other man were bracing himself to wait for a blow, and Helgi began to sing more strongly as he wove the first thread of an upper line, an high wordless human voice, in through the ceaseless rolling of his bass.

"Ravens rise in the evening,
Raw is the gray dawn-light.
High over howe-mound wheeling,
hailing the dead, rune-wailing.
Ravens rise in the evening,
red day is swan-maid's wedding.
High over holy grove fly
hallowing birds, to gallows!"

Keeping the bass line going with his left hand, Helgi shifted levers with his right, adding the clear calling of horns to the middle range, lifting and leaping in battle-notes above his own voice. Rof lifted his hand to something that hung about his neck then jerked it down, as though the little dark bag had stung him.

"Fair she finds wolf's gore-howl
fear-words loath to hearing,
Wraiths kens well the gray maid, weird steed, eight-hooved, rearing.
Witch's son, be watchful!
Will you loose blood-spilling?
Will you woo her Hel-runes, Wodan's keen spear boding?"

Helgi crouched over his keyboard as over a bed of coals in winter's cold, spinning the notes out more and more swiftly into a web over the room, stilling the last murmured voices and catching the eyes that glimmered all around like beast-eyes in the darkness. The cold rushing of the song gripped his hands, bearing down harder and harder on the notes shivering out of the speakers, he could feel the might flowing from him, pressing against Rof, who stood braced hard on the wooden floor, head lowered and jaws clenched as if he were walking into a strong wind.

Helgi could not hear Rof's words, but he saw the other man's blue-black lips moving, and then it seemed to him as if he were standing before a high stone wall, that all his sounds bounced from like spray from the foot of a cliff that the wall was mirrored in his own throat, blocking the sounds from his voice. He could not see into Rof's eyes. The blue gleam of the lights shining off their darkness hid their depths from him. Helgi breathed deeply, calling up his will for the next staves and sharpening his tone into a keen cutting edge as he shifted levers again to the high howl of woodwinds keening over a thundering river of strings and the deep drum-beat of the rocks below.

"Gift Norn-spun forth, weft-geld,
given in blood, long riven,
You will not know that wooing,
worth of death and birth-strife.
Dare not to wield this warring!
Wound by earth and bound down,
Ne'er you'll know her fierceness,
Nor love, in joy and warring."

As Helgi sang the last line, it seemed to him that the wall broke within his throat, letting his notes soar free to pierce clearly through the room. Rof's eyes were wide now, the light no longer glancing from their curves, Helgi felt the brightness of his own gaze pressing into their depths like a spear stabbing into soft peat. Helgi drew a deep breath for the last stave, and Rof stepped backward, crossing his heavy arms across his chest as though to hold sprung ribs in by main force.

"I cast you from cliff's height,
keenest my blade, ween I.
Above, high, hovers leaves ne'er! -
holy love, fair soul-maid.
Rune-carved stock and stone fair,
streams white, from heaven gleaming,
Eagle, raven, Ygg-wolf,
You must now be dooméd!"

As Helgi brought down the last crashing chord, the bottle of beer fell from Rof's hand, spewing a stream of foam out over the floor. The big man turned abruptly, shouldering his way out through the still crowd to the door. As it closed behind him, Helgi clearly heard a man's voice say, "Drunk nigger," in the breath of space before the clapping roared up to deafen him.

Helgi's chest ached as though he had run longer than his strength would carry him, his hands trembled with the echoes of his music still running through them, but the rush of victory sang light through his head. Breathless, his T-shirt soaked and hair dripping with sweat, Helgi stood to drink in the waves of sound till they rolled back and Mike came to the front of the stage again. Helgi was ready to leave by seven o'clock that Friday afternoon. He had stretched out well and chosen his loosest jeans, T-shirt, and denim jacket, clothes which wouldn't bind him in a fight.

When Rof and Karin came to get him, Helgi noticed Rof was wearing his leather jacket and old black jeans rubbed almost white at the knees. Like his own, heavy enough for warmth, loose enough for fighting. Karin wore blue jeans, a denim jacket like Helgi's own over her pale blue blouse. The valknutr's woven triangles gleamed silver at her throat. Sigfödhr sælsigruna merki. Karin and Rof had come in a car this time, an old rickety Buick, the collision-scars all down its sides blackened into shadow-holes by the streetlight above it. Rof opened Karin's door and then walked around to the driver's side while Karin unlocked the rear door behind her seat for Helgi.

"I thought if we came early enough, we might be able to get a table at Campisi's," Karin explained as Rof revved the motor. "Central's not clogged too badly on the southbound side, and I'm tired of eating at Pizza Rut. What do you say?"

"Sounds good," Helgi started.

Rof's voice drowned him out. "Yeah, but we take at least half an hour to get there, mo' like fo'ty-five minutes. Friday night, vacation weekend at that? We be standin' in line for a year."

"Hmm." Karin chewed her lip, looking back at Helgi. "Well, there's a place over by the shopping center at Northwest and Skillman that serves dark beer by the pitcher."

They were able to get a booth to themselves in the pizza restaurant. Helgi and Rof slid in facing each other, Rof right by the wall and Helgi in the middle of his bench so that they both had leg room. Karin stood waiting with the pitcher of beer in her hand until they had arranged themselves, then sat on the outer side of Rof's bench with her legs to the other side of Helgi's, putting the beer down in the middle of the table beside the single candle burning there.

"They make these booths too small," Rof grumbled.

Karin laughed. "Too small for the three of us, that's for sure. Beer, guys?" She poured Helgi's glass full, then Rof's, and lastly her own, raising it as she glanced from Helgi to Rof. "Well, here's to the Air Force!"

"May the Force be with you," Helgi said gravely, a split second before they drank. Karin managed to gulp her mouthful down, though her face went red with the struggle, Rof snorted explosively, spraying a fine mist of beer over the table.

"Good one," Karin said when she got her breath back. "Hey, Helgi, did you bring that tape with you?"

Helgi reached into the pocket of his jacket, bringing it out and passing it over the table to her. She took it and made it disappear into her own jacket's pocket. "Thanks. I've been looking forward to hearing these."

Helgi did not miss the way Rof's heavy brows lowered over his eyes, darkening their sockets to night-caves. "Ain't much good in there for you," he muttered. "You think on that spook-shit too much as it is."

Karin and Helgi both looked at him. If Rof flushed, his dark skin hid it, but his words grew no louder. "We come here to talk. Might as well be, everyone say what they thinkin', no good in hidin' it."

"No," Karin agreed thoughtfully, running a knuckle along the delicate slant of her jaw. She picked up her glass of beer and drank deeply before turning her gaze back to Helgi. "So, how are you surviving your break-up? Do you want to talk about it?"

"I'm surviving it all right. I told you, it was my idea."

"Why?"

"Because of you," Helgi said, looking straight into her light eyes. "Because I love you."

Karin said nothing, but held him in her gaze for a long time.

At last Rof's raw voice broke the silence. "What the hell you be thinkin' of, Helgi? You don' give a shit whether she be another man's woman or not?" He clenched his huge fists on top of the table, leaning over so closely that Helgi could smell the acrid scent of his flesh, his upper lip lifted, showing square teeth very white against his dark face. "Case you hadn' noticed, boy, we have a relationship here, so you can jus' go an' piss into the wind. I hear one word more of this shit outa you, yo' dead meat, you understand?"

"There's a parking lot out back," Helgi answered softly. To his surprise, he felt no fear, only a great calm, laced with sharp twinges of eagerness. "You want to go out there with me? If one of us has to die over this, it might as well happen here and now."

"The winner gets me, is that it?" Karin asked, a flush of red spreading over her high cheekbones and the little muscles at the hinges of her jaw clenching. Her left hand closed tightly on the valknútr's sharp points as she leaned forward, her beer-cool breath gusting the candle's flame into a bright finger flickering towards Helgi. "I say crap on that, guys. I am not the prize in a fucking Crackerjack box. If you two want to fight it out, that's great. I think it'll sure as hell be worth watching, but you better not forget that I'm the one who chooses. Otherwise I'll bury the survivor on the left, so posterity can tell which was which."

Rof turned his head towards Karin, his fierce expression sagging like a tent with its poles cut through. "Seemed to me we had a relationship," he breathed to her. "Seemed to me we put trust in each other, spite of every-thin'. Are you sayin' that's over now?"

"I'm not saying anything," Karin answered. "I'm only saying that neither of you is going to make my choices for me, least of all about this." Her voice softened into the quiet sound of ruffling fur. "Being lovers does not con-stitute a marriage vow, Rof. If you wanted one, you should have asked me earlier."

Rof's heavy head lowered for a moment, then he looked up again, staring at Karin as though Helgi weren't there. Carefully he reached out to draw one dark finger along the line of her cheek. "Will you marry me, Karin? I'll quit the Force if I got to."

Helgi held his breath till the rising bee-hum in his ears nearly drowned Karin's answer. "No. Not now. Not until I've made up my mind."

Rof's hand dropped from her like a hawk shot dead in flight, but he said nothing more. A voice broke through the music on the restaurant's speakers. "Table 9, large pepperoni and mushroom, large ham."

"That's us," Karin said, sliding out of the booth and rising gracefully to her feet. "Don't kill each other while I'm gone, you two. If you've got to fight, I want to see it."

Rof lowered his head like a boar ready to charge, staring unblinkingly at Helgi. The single candle on the booth's table flickered twin candle-flames from his eyes, haloing the two tiny black reflections of Helgi's head, where the tinier glints of the firelight in Helgi's own gaze glittered like sparks from flint. The table-top's polished wood pressed hard and smooth against Helgi's own fists, he could hear Rof's breath hissing softly in and out, waves rolling up and down a pebbly beach. Helgi's own wind seemed locked in his lungs, coiled there like a snake waiting to strike, but his limbs were loose and ready to answer the other's challenge.

Rof's shape was blurring in Helgi's sight, the candlelight on his purple-black skin brushing his heavy features into an broad nonhuman mask as his wide shoulders blended into the booth's shadows, the darkness sweeping up above him and blending into his body below as though his candlelit face were carved upon a great smoke-blackened pillar. Slowly Helgi pushed his breath out, as though he were pushing against a huge rock with all his strength, his thumbs thorn-thrusting through his fists at the same time. For a moment nothing happened, then Rof shifted in his seat and glared down into the depths of his beer before he lifted it and drained half the glass.

Karin was coming back, a wide round platter of pizza held high in either hand. "Frisbee, anyone?" She put one on the table before each of the men, then wriggled back into her place. Her knee brushed against the right side of Helgi's thigh as she settled herself again, sending a streak of heat up his leg, and for a moment Helgi envied the dark skin that hid the tides of Rof's blood.

Helgi stayed up late that night, working on his "Nietzsche and Wagner" lecture until twelve-thirty. He was half-undressed, jeans pooled on the floor about his ankles, T-shirt pulled up over his face, when the little pebbles rattled against his window like a swift shower of hail. He let his T-shirt fall and tugged his jeans back up, holding them with one hand as he drew the curtain aside. Rof stood in the white halo of a streetlight, head tilted back to look up at Helgi's window. He raised a shadow-hand to beckon to Helgi, his leather jacket lifting behind his arm like a black wing. Helgi closed the curtain, zipping his jeans. He did not bother to put jacket or shoes on, but hurried downstairs, unlocking and locking the door as softly as he could. Rof was already coming down their walkway, Helgi balanced on the balls of his feet, his hot readiness battling with the chill of the icy concrete beneath his soles and the icy wind blowing over the skin of his arms and face.

"You can open those fists any time, white boy," Rof said, his voice soft as a scythe slicing through rain. "I ain't gonna fight with you now."

"What happened?"

"Ain't what's happened yet, I don' think. I just want to talk with you, see what's goin' on in yo' head. Seems to me I got that right, we got something in common, after all."

"I guess so. You want to come in?"

Rof shook his head. "Out here good enough. I'll wait fo' you to get a coat. May take a while."

"Nah. I'm okay."

"Come set in the car, then."

Helgi followed him, getting into the passenger side. Something brushed against the top of his head. He reached up to find a flap of cloth dangling from the roof, shedding crumbs of foam beneath his fingers.

Rof rolled down the window on his side of the car, pulled out a packet of cigarettes and tapped one out.

"Want a smoke?"

"No, thank you."

Rof shrugged and flicked the flint on his lighter. The flame flared brightly off his broad nose and cheeks, glistening from the crumpled cellophane that still half-wrapped his pack of Marlboros. He breathed in deeply, letting the lighter's fire die to darkness as the cigarette's coal glowed to life, then blew the gray cloud out for the wind to sweep away. "Thought I'd stopped this fo' good," he apologized. "Can't be smokin' around the fuel or the planes, no good to be hankerin' all the time, so I quit. Sometimes, ain't nothing else will do for it." He tapped the thin rim of ash away on the window's edge, brightening the naked coal a moment. "So. What be Karin to you, Helgi? Why are you doin' all this?"

"Karin to me", Helgi thought. The words came slowly to his mind, like dawn's first blue brightening against the night-stars. My dream and my wakening, my life and my death hard-bought and yet well-bought. He could not bring them forth through his throat not while he spoke. Even as Helgi knew that, his mouth was opening so that he half-sang, half-chanted, the words coming to his lips without embarrassment as he remembered Rof's own shameless rhyming. "Holy love and living dreams, life and death and waking all, words to heal my wounded throat, wind-ways fair beneath my feet. Before your eyes saw her, I loved, and sang till harshness harrowed voice. Without her, I would never live a wooden stock, a silent stone, nameless, wordless, cast from home." Helgi stopped suddenly, breathless in the echo of his own voice. His ears were already burning as though Rof's laughter scorched them, but the big man only moved his hand slowly from mouth to window, knocking the long gray ash from the end of his half-burnt cigarette.

"Don' often hear a white man let his words free like that," Rof murmured. "You different, Helgi. Maybe that why," He was silent for a little while, then went on. "Karin and I, we neither of us members of the club. Woman and a black manthings ain't easy fo' us. Better fo' her some ways, bein' an officer, yeah, some ways, but not all. I got plenty of friends around, got women when I want them, but I bet it be no surprise when I tell you I was the first man to kiss her since she got outa high school. Plenty of women get along fine in the Air Force, get along with the men, get along with the other women, but not her. She was happy flyin', all right, but on the ground she was bone-lonely. 'Spect most of the men around think she be a dyke, and even them who don't be scared of her.

She look at me and you think with all the Vikin' stuff she be talkin', no one would care more about my skin you think she be lookin' to find herself a big blond Nazi, but not her. She come home to my family, even try to talk to my momma," Rof's cigarette had burned down to a nub. He crushed the coal between his fingers and put the butt carefully into the car's ashtray, then lit another. "Well, I ain't blind, least not the way most people be blind. Ain't deaf, neither. I know what you be doin' what I wonder is, do you know it?"

"Know what?" Helgi asked cautiously. He felt as though he were tracing the carven lines of a knot work pattern in the dark, trying to work out its shape from the weave of the round wooden edges under his fingers.

"Yo' songs, yo' power things you be callin' on. Don' know what you sang at me last week, if it wasn' a spell. I wouldn' say this where anyone else could hear. I got no love for seein' thoughts like 'superstitious nigger' behind people's eyes, an' that just what most folk think, but I know you ain't thinkin' that."

He paused, and Helgi could hear the denim rustling of his hands tightening and opening against his thighs, dry as a rattlesnake's scales slipping through the sand. "I think maybe you won already. I don' know how to fight mojo too well, and don' have anyone I can call help from. I ." The ash fell from his new cigarette end, leaving its single fire-eye glowing balefully in the dark. "May as well speak true to you. My momma, she wise in the ways of what, you may not know what the orishas are, but some folk call what she do voodoo, others Santeria. She been a horse for the orishas many a year, she know them all as well as anyone livin'. She say she know the god Karin worships, that old man with his big black hat and one eye missin'. He be very like Baron Samedi, or Papa Gedde if you like, you know those names?"

Helgi shook his head. "He be death an' life, he be the dancer at the crossroads. I seen the altar my momma sets for him, white skulls an' black cocks and an old gray gravestone. Your one-eyed god, he mad, he fierce. Bloody as the war-smith Ogun, tricky as Eshu, an' I don' know where his wild words come from. My momma see his eye shining clear in Karin's gaze, she cast the cowries and talk to Oya, and she was dead set against us from the start, so she ain't gonna lend me her magic against yours, 'cept that you don' hurt me with yo' spells, can't do more'n push me away. So that's done, no good tryin' to struggle agin' two. I got to warn you.

You can pay yo' own prices, but if they bring harm or sorrow to Karin, you be dead, and it'll be my hands that do it. I 'spect you'll hurt me pretty bad, could be they'll wind up buryin' us both, but I promise, you will die."

"Rof. Rof, I love Karin. I don't mean to bring any harm or sorrow to her. Why do you think I would?"

"You gave her that death-knot, didn' you?"

"What are you talking about?" Helgi asked. The words fell weakly from his mouth. He knew the answer well enough by now.

"That silver pendant she wear, with the three locked triangles. Lovin' Karin, I couldn' go long without findin' out about her myths and her folk, she sure cared to know about mine. So I read plenty when I had time, borrowed some of her books, found others other places. And there was that sign, and it was called the Valknut. Book said that meant 'knot of the slain', just like Valhalla be 'hall of the slain', like Valkyries be 'choosers of the slain', all children of that one-eyed god, that same one god whose sign that is, whose name I ain't gonna speak. I warned her about it, but she didn' listen. An' you gave it to her."

"It's also the sign of victory," Helgi answered. "And more than death," His voice trailed off, he could see the silver triangles before him, the light glinting red from the ice-melt metal, twisted around blackness, the tip of a spear cutting the shape through the mist, aimed at his heart.

"Don' know about that. Anyway, I've said my say, got to be movin' on. You really love her, you think. Karin be brave, and crazy, she need someone with his feet on the ground, someone to keep her from burnin' herself up across the sky. I don' think you be that man. You go on now, Helgi, an' we all think on this."

Helgi got out of the car without a word, standing on the curb and watching until the last track of Rof's taillights around the corner had sunken into darkness. His bare feet were numb with cold, he could not feel the rough concrete under them. When he got up to his room, Elric was already asleep on his bed. Helgi eased his feet under the elk hound, letting Elric's warmth soak feeling back. He was no longer sleepy, he could not still his thoughts long enough to see meaning in them. After a while, he put his own copy of the demo tape into his player, fast-forwarding it to the song he had sung at Rof. When he had listened to it, Helgi rewound the tape, closing his eyes to see Karin's gleaming helm of hair and wide gray gaze before him, feeling the swooping brilliance of her flight in the leaping of his own voice. Again and again, Helgi rewound and started the song. Karin would be listening to it, if not now, then sometime soon.

CHAPTER XXVII

Shattered gleams of sunlight sparkled from the dark waves as Hoilogae's ships drove forward into Glazaleunduz's curving bay, the keen wind at their backs. Swaebhon stood at the prow, her long hair whipping forward around her face and bare feet braced against the wood as she swayed with the ship's rocking. Sitting behind her, Hoilogae bent his back to pull hard against the current swinging the boat sideways, but his gaze still rose to the land, to Herwamundaz's howe rising tall and green beyond the bone-pale curve of the beach. They were still too far away for him to see the little flowers, yellow and white, that sprinkled the mound like a scattering of gold and silver through the grass, but Hoilogae's memory cast the sight up to him so that it seemed that he already sat on the hill again, with the Sun's warmth steeping the sweet new scents from grass and flowers into the air about him, with the wind-scoured depth of the sky-bowl above him ringing through his head as the gulls winged dizzily high above.

For a moment Hoilogae, caught in his mind, did not see those who were gathering on the shore. Then the movement drew his eyes. The blurred shadows resolved into the shapes of armed men hastening towards the beach as the deep note of an aurochs horn cleared the wave-lapping from his ears, sun-glints of bronze swords sparkling along the pathway. Hoilogae's shoulders tightened as he glanced swiftly over them, he thought at once of a battle, of his brother slain and home-hall taken by another. Then his gaze lit on Hedhinaz's ash-blond braid and the storm cloud gleam of the iron sword in his brother's hand. Hoilogae's breath eased from him, his shoulder-sinews loosened. He pulled his oars in, rising to his full height beside Swaebhon and calling out, "Hai, Hedhinaz, sheathe your blade! No foe comes to you now, but your brother Hoilogae and his bride!" Hoilogae put his arm around Swaebhon's waist, she let the swaying of the boat nestle her body against his, her head upon his shoulder. Hedhinaz did not answer, but stood still as if fettered, staring at the two of them a moment. Then he shook himself as if to cast the gray cloak from his shoulders and slid his sword into its sheath.

"Come and be welcome!" He called, his voice keen as a gull's cry through the splashing waves. Behind him, the sun-flashes of bronze went out one by one, clouded in cloaks and sheaths as the men pressed nearer to the beach, craning their necks to see who had come back. "How went your faring?"

"The number of dead has not grown less," Swaebhon answered him, "nor will all here be joyful at the tidings we bear. Still, your drighten has won what he sought, and the names of the living and the dead who fared with him shall grow greater when his stories are told."

The keel of the boat grounded with a bump, so that Hoilogae and Swaebhon had to steady each other where they stood. Hoilogae could see the ruddy flush rising into Hedhinaz's winter-pale cheeks, though his brother's eyes did not shift from Swaebhon for a moment.

"Frowe, you are mistaken if you think to name Hoilogae my drighten. He is my brother, but I, Hedhinaz, am fro and drighten here in Glazaleunduz where our father set me over his own udal lands, and it is I who have the right to bid you welcome here, so long as Herwawardhaz and Sigislinthon still dwell in our clan's southerly holdings and keep them safe against the iron-folk from the south."

Hoilogae leapt over the side of the boat, into the waves that swelled cold from thigh to waist and sank again around him. "Come to my arms, Swaebhon. I shall carry you to land, you need not wet your dress."

Swaebhon only laughed. She reached down, steadying herself with a hand on Hoilogae's shoulder. He felt strong-rooted and steady as an old ash-tree beneath her weight. "The faring has been long, and washing will do harm neither to my dress nor myself." She leapt overboard beside him, her splash breaking over him. Her pale skirts belled up in the water around her as she kissed Hoilogae on his wet cheek, then turned, laying her hand upon the boat. She meant to help drag it onto shore, but Hoilogae's old rede-giver reached over the side to lift her hand away from the wood. "The two of you go on," Attalae said. "We'll take care of this ourselves." He looked back at the men behind him.

"Aye, go on," Thonarastanaz said, his grin splitting his broad blond beard as he, too, heaved himself into the water. "If you must help us, frowe, get up there and see if Hedhinaz will give you some ale to greet us with, that's worth more than another hand hauling the ships in."

Swaebhon sighed good-naturedly as Hoilogae took her hands in his. "You would think that I were an old woman already, or that the babe in my womb were near full term," she complained, smiling at him.

Hoilogae stopped dead, staring at her. It seemed to Swaebhon that she could feel the shock of joy bursting through him, its echo warm in her own body. "You didn't tell me?"

Swaebhon reached out to smooth the short-cropped beard along his jawline, then patted him on the cheek. "I thought you should have guessed by now, when in more than a moon and a half. I wondered why you had not asked. You were never told of women's ways and the turning of our wombs with the Moon, were you? Yes, I have borne our child in me since Austarjon's feast. Surely that is not hard for you to believe?"

Hoilogae clasped Swaebhon to him, kissing her as the water rose and fell again around them. His body was very warm through their wet clothes, like a baking-shovel just lifted from the coals, his touch drove the sea's cold from her, though he already held her more gently and did not crush her as tightly to himself as he had before. "This day could not be fairer," he murmured to her as they pushed towards the shore.

When the waves were just lapping around their ankles, Hoilogae stopped again. "At least I shall bear you onto my father's land you and our bairn."

Her eyes flickered up towards the land, towards the high burial mound, still ringed by armed men. Now, for the first time, Swaebhon truly felt herself in a strange stead. Though she knew the howe from her soul-faring, she knew no more of the old one who dwelt in that mound than whatever Hoilogae had inherited, whereas in her father's lands she had known the names and lines of all the dead, and often gone to their howes. If she had any foothold in this new land, it was only through Hoilogae and the child in her womb, whose blood and bones had mingled with this earth through many lives of men. "That I would count fitting."

Swaebhon put one arm around Hoilogae's neck, scattering a great spray of sun-bright droplets out around them as she leapt up into his arms. He bent his knees, bracing himself as her full weight landed in his arms, she was no little thing to catch, though not too much for his strength. Once she was firmly settled, he carried her easily. He felt the life kindling in her womb and his own joy lifting her into the air, lightening his burden. Swaebhon was laughing, a pale flush of pink glowing on her high cheekbones as Hoilogae bore her up the beach without a stumble. He did not mark when he passed Hedhinaz, but by the time the long grass was whipping around Hoilogae's wet ankles, his brother had caught up with them again, pacing them towards Herwamundaz's mound and holding his place by their side as Hoilogae climbed up the flower-spattered slope.

Hedhinaz was not yet as tall as his brother, but had grown swiftly in the last half-year, he was shorter than Swaebhon by no more than two finger widths. The young drighten's skin seemed to stretch tightly over knobby bones and thin taut muscles, the sharp edges of his body pressing hard against the fine white wool of his tunic and cloak, so that Hoilogae thought of how Wejlunduz had beaten his metals out to make them ever longer, thinner, harder, but more brittle, if his heat ever went amiss. When they had reached the top of the mound, Hoilogae eased Swaebhon down. She did not let go her hold on him, but kept her arm about his shoulders as they looked down together on the low rolling swells of green land about Herwamundaz's mound, edged by the deeper green shadows of the beech-wood beyond.

"Here you became Hoilogae," she murmured. "This hallowed stead was not often far from my mind in the times that came after that. It is well that you brought me to earth here, well that the dead should bless the living, for I know that the braid of your clan is well-woven from this knot on. A fair birth, a fair being, and a fair passing away. None may ask for more."

"I bid you welcome here in my father's lands, my bride," Hoilogae answered. He would have said more, but Hedhinaz spoke half an heartbeat later.

"I bid you welcome, frowe, and you, my brother. While I live, you and your children shall always be greeted gladly in these lands that Herwamundaz won may his blessings ever be upon you."

Herwawardhaz's youngest son lifted his narrow head proudly, looking down to the men who were beginning to leave their places about the mound and past them to the sun-brightened sea, but Hoilogae crouched down to lay his palms upon the grass, feeling the might that lay in the earth beneath like the hidden strength in the coils of a sleeping adder. The faces of the men who had drowned in Hati's Firth swirled up before him, pale against the dark waters of his mind. The black hair and beards of Hlothowairaz's sons, their heavy features near as like as those of twins', Dagastiz's red-gold curls above his beak-sharp nose and narrow blue eyes, Ingwawaldaz's glance dark through his tangle of brown hair, his brother Ingwagairaz laughing to spite the seasickness twisting his belly. Hoilogae did not know where they would come to the light again, but it seemed to him that he could feel the stirring within the mound, a soft tremor like the first stirring of a child in the womb, and that he himself was trembling with it.

"If our child is a son, we shall name him Herwamundaz after my fore-father who dwells here," Hoilogae said, his voice dropping within his throat till he could feel its resonance down through his groin. He stood, placing his right palm flat against the layer of wet wool clinging to Swaebhon's smooth belly.

"That is well-done," she answered.

"Do you not fear that it may turn with him as it did the last time a father tried to fasten that name to his bairn?" Asked Hedhinaz sharply. "Eighteen winters or more of sheep-tending is no good birthing-gift to give a firstborn son, I should think." He stood looking up at his brother, legs braced firmly and shoulders set, as though he awaited a blow from Hoilogae, as though he thought Hoilogae would shove him from the mound.

"You need not fear that I seek to take what you hold, my brother," Hoilogae answered mildly. "Between them, our parents' lands are enough for both of us. You shall have and hold Glazaleunduz, and are like in time to have more, if you go on as fiercely as you have begun."

Hoilogae did not know whether the dark tide sweeping over his brother's face rose from shame or anger, not till Hedhinaz turned his gaze towards the grass, staring at the amber-bodied bee which embraced the heart of a white-petaled flower by his foot till it had buzzed unsteadily up and settled on one of the golden milk-blooms nearby.

"As I said," he murmured, "you shall always be a welcome guest here, my brother. I fear the winter ale this year was not so good as that our mother brews, but I kept some of hers back, so you shall have a proper greeting cup. I hope that when you go south, you will ask her from me if she would be willing to brew ale for Glazaleunduz again, should I send her the grain for it."

"That I shall do gladly."

Swaebhon brushed a wave of fair hair from her face with the back of her hand, looking thoughtfully at Hedhinaz. "I know a little of brewing, it is said, at least your brother found my drinks none too ill. Will your frowe be angered if I offer to teach her my craft, or leave my worts working here?"

"I have no frowe yet," Hedhinaz answered, raising his gaze to meet hers. "But I do not doubt that those here will gladly learn what you will teach, and I shall be grateful if you will set worts working in my hall."

Together the three of them walked back down the mound to the beach. Hoilogae's men, and those Aiwilimae had sent with Swaebhon, had already drawn the boats up onto the sand. Three of the Northmen were carrying Swaebhon's chests of clothing towards the hall. The other strangers stayed a little apart, but the men who had fared with Hoilogae were already talking with their friends and kin. A ring of men, Hraidhamannaz and Thonaraber-nu among them, stood around one, when they shifted, Hoilogae saw the bent form of a man whose black hair and beard were thickly streaked with white. He did not cry out, but his clenched fists pressed deep into his thighs as he rocked back and forth. His silent face was so twisted that it took Hoilo-gae a moment to recognize him. Hlothawairaz, who had lost all his sons in the staving of a single boat, and had no comfort save the friendship of the men who stood still watch around his grief. Hoilogae took a step towards him, but Swaebhon laid a hand upon his arm.

"You must speak to him later," she murmured, "and alone. The sight of you will not gladden him now, nor will he hear your words."

Attalae stood leaning against the side of the ship, Hoilogae marked that the brown hem of the rede-giver's tunic was not wet, as the others' were, nor did the sand cake on his shoes' tight-drawn leather. Of a sudden, the old man seemed frail to him as a sheaf of dried straw, but Attalae smiled at them bravely enough.

"Greetings, Hedhinaz," the old man said.

"Greetings to you, Attalae. Shall I hail you as a guest, or as a man who has come back to his home?"

The aged warrior laughed. "That I do not know yet. But a horn of ale would be fitting to either, and a comfort to an old man who has fared a long way."

The long benches and tables in Hedhinaz's hall were no longer so pale as they had been, nor did any spoor of sap cut through the scents of old smoke and the fresh grasses on the floor.

Still, it seemed to Hoilogae that something else had changed, and then he realized that the house had been built up to half again its old length, with a second fire pit dug to keep it warm. The young woman who sat on a little stool by the old hearth, reaching in with her tongs now and again to bring out a red-hot stone and cast it into the clay stew-pot at her feet, wore a thrall's ring about her neck, such as Hoilogae could not remember having seen in Glazaleunduz before, her wide-boned face in its close-cropped frame of red hair was not so much as a shadow in the mists of Hoilogae's memory. Something turned in his guts as he looked at the ring she wore.

It seemed ill for him to speak of his fear, even to himself, but he knew that he would fear asking her what her name was or where she had come from, with the memory of Ansuthewaz still stark in his mind.

"You have not been idle here," Hoilogae said to his brother.

"No, for there was much to be done, and much that still may be. The storms were strong at winter's end this year, stronger than I remember them ever being. Indeed, we could not plant until quite late. The storms brought us more weal than woe, for they cast up a great harvest of amber. We were gathering when we might have been planting, and the last seeds have only now been sown, but the amber harvest has brought us good trade, even so early, better, with our parents up the trade route in place of a foe's clan."

Attalae looked about the hall, stroking his short gray beard. He nodded slowly. "You must be a fro well-fit for these lands. Though the harvest will be the truest proof of that, as it must always be."

Hedhinaz looked at the thrall-woman by the fire. "Hai, go and fetch ale, and tell the other women to get their pitchers out as well, we've got plenty of men who will be wanting drink soon, if you don't mind being given drink by a thrall," he added hastily to the others.

"No, I shall bear the ale myself, at least to you three, if you say that I may, Hedhinaz, and you ween that there is no woman of better birth in this hall," Swaebhon answered.

"Till I am wed myself, no one save my mother shall have better right to pour ale here."

Swaebhon turned to the thrall-woman. "Show me where the ale and the pitchers are kept, then."

The young woman rose to her feet, dusting off her skirts. She was a full head shorter than Swaebhon, though as broad in the hips and shoulders. She did not speak, but smiled up at the other woman, gesturing for Swaebhon to follow her.

"I bought her from a trader only a few days ago," Hedhinaz said. "She is a maiden of the iron-folk, brought up from the lands south of Jutland. It is a little difficult to speak with her, for the southerners' tongue is nothing at all like ours and she has not known ours long, but she is clever with embroidery and a fine cook, and the man who sold her to me said that she is skilled at metalwork as well, though I will not count that true till I have seen her doing it."

Attalae laughed, reaching out to thump Hedhinaz on the shoulder. "And what else is she skilled at?"

Even with the full light of early afternoon slanting golden through the open door and filtering through the two smoke holes, it was too dark to see more than the shadow of Hedhinaz's blush, but his chipped teeth shone clear in the grin that slowly followed it. "She says she is glad to serve a man who is kind to her."

Swaebhon's horn-bearing shadow darkened the long rectangle of light a moment before she stepped between the doorposts. Her wet skirt clung tight against her thighs, swishing heavily between her legs. She carried the gold-bound hof horn in her right hand, holding a large clay pot crooked in her left arm.

"Hail to you, Hedhinaz, and thanks for the guest-right you have given us," Swaebhon said, handing the horn to Hoilogae's brother first.

Hedhinaz took the vessel in both hands, drinking deeply. His eyes closed as he raised the horn higher and higher, the sharp rock of his voice-box rising and falling beneath the sparse hairs of his beard as he poured the ale down his throat. At last he lifted the horn from his mouth again, a long shudder running through his body, and gave it back to her. "Hai, this did not hold as well over the winter as it might have, our mother's ale does not often go not drunk for so long, I suppose. Frowe, your brewing craft will be wholly welcome here."

Swaebhon skillfully tilted the pot she held, spilling a long dark stream from its rim until a second black rivulet trickled over the ring of gold about the horn's lip and down along its curve. "Hail to you, Hoilogae, my beloved husband."

The ale's herb-taste had grown very strong, dark and bitter in the back of Hoilogae's throat. The draught was cold as if it had been drawn up from a very deep well, with an earthy mustiness behind its brine-bitter edge, its strength lay in his stomach like a warm stone. As he drank, he could hear his heart's heavy drum thumping in his ears, it seemed to be beating harder and harder, laboring against the ale's weight. A bitter chill ran from the back of Hoilogae's throat through his body when he lowered the empty horn, though he did not show his shuddering. In a moment it had passed off, leaving him warmed through and a bit light-headed.

"It is not so ill a drink," Hoilogae answered. "Though I found your mead sweeter."

"Shall again, when I have found where the sig-wives build their hives in this land and had a little time to brew." Swaebhon poured the horn full once more. "Hail to you, Attalae, and to your homecoming. You have done well by Hoilogae, and given him rede truly, you do not bring a little score of deeds with you."

Attalae's pale lips curved beneath his pale beard. "That is so." He took the horn from her hand, looking into the darkness within its gold ring for a moment. Swiftly he raised it, casting the ale down his throat without a heartbeat's pause. Hoilogae saw no stirring beneath his hoar-silver beard, Attalae seemed to be drinking the horn dry in a single swallow. Then the re-de-giver's throat clutched convulsively, and the gold-rimmed horn fell from his hand into the straw. Attalae's dark eyes opened wide, he flung his right hand out, clawing emptily at the air as his left hand tightened at his chest. Hoilogae reached out towards him, but the old warrior's knees had already buckled under him, dropping him to the herb-strewn floor.

The last dark drops of ale drooled from Attalae's open mouth, from the rim of the horn beside him, even before Hoilogae had knelt to place his palm above the old man's heart, he knew that Attalae was dead. The taste in Hoilogae's mouth was bitter-edged as the ale's aftertaste, but salt, a warm drop splashed down onto his hand, another darkening Attalae's tunic like a spot of blood. The tears spilled silently from his eyes as he gently wiped the ale from the old man's beard and lifted Attalae's empty body up in his arms. Hedhinaz's mouth was open, a dark doorway between the slanting planes of his face, Swaebhon closed her eyes a moment, laying her long-fingered hands over her belly as though to soothe the child within. At once the hall seemed very full to Hoilogae, sometime while they were drinking, the Northmen and the Jutlanders had come in together, and many of the women with them, and now they were all pressing about to see.

"Back," Hoilogae said, his tear-harsh voice croaking in his own ears. "Wodhanaz has walked here, he chose Attalae's death. Get back from his path."

Hoilogae heard the feet shuffling back through the straw and herbs on the floor. He did not miss the wideness of Hraidhamannaz's blue eyes in his pale face, nor how Thonarabernu clutched to the finger-polished amber axehead at his throat, nor the way Hedhinaz's thrall muttered and wove her fingers about in strange signs. But Thonarastanaz, though he stepped back with the rest, was nodding sagely and pulling at his beard. "Aye," Hoilogae heard him say softly, "we knew Attalae was near the end, didn't we see the blue shadow of the Ansuz's cloak over his face, whenever he'd helped with the rowing? Kind of the Old One, to let him see his homeland again, and have a last horn of ale to cheer him on his way."

"So your welcome feast becomes a funeral arvel. I could have wished a happier homecoming for you." Hedhinaz gestured to the table set crosswise at the end of the hall before his high seat. "Let Attalae rest there for now. If we hurry, we may have branches enough for his burning by sunset."

Swaebhon trod closer to Hoilogae, looking down at the dead man in his arms for a long moment. "Gather the branches and ready the pyre now," she said. "But he must wait the night in the hof, he who had it built, and someone must keep the night-watch beside him."

"That is my right," Hoilogae answered at once.

"I shall watch with you," Hlothawairaz rasped beside him. Surprised, Hoilogae turned to look at the other man. Hlothawairaz's eyes were red and swollen, but the tears had dried from his face, leaving no spoor along the deep crevasses of the old man's skin. "You can tell me more of my sons, and of their deaths."

"As well as I can, I will," Hoilogae promised, though his heart drooped within him at the thought. Carefully as if Attalae were still living, he bore the rede-giver's corpse to the table before the high-seat, easing him down and straightening his limbs and tunic so that the dead man lay with all his dignity. Attalae's eyes were still open, staring dully up at Hoilogae. Now that the first shock of the old warrior's death was fading from Hoilogae's flesh, Hoilogae knew that he was not surprised at it, the wonder was that Attalae had lived long enough to see his homeland again.

"Not so ill to bear as you had feared, is it?" Swaebhon whispered to him. Then, louder, "Come, Hoilogae. I shall help you gather branches, and you shall show me more of these lands while the light lasts. Let Attalae rest here, and his goods should be brought and heaped about him, and a clean and fair tunic put upon him."

Hoilogae glanced at Hedhinaz. His younger brother bit his lip as Swaebhon spoke, as though reining back his words. When she was done, Hedhinaz asked, "Do you ween burning so much better than howe-burial for him? He did not fall in battle, nor was he one of those folk that men fear after their death, but he loved this land and its folk."

Swaebhon put her hand over Attalae's chest, as though feeling for his heartbeat. Her breasts rose and fell as she breathed deeply, her gray eyes staring deeply into the dead man's. Now it seemed to her that she could see the life lingering like the ghostly brightness of a torch-flame against the sudden darkness of its quenching. She knew that light well. The old man had dealt with trolls, and once heard the voice of an older rede-giver than himself, and such folk did not always go easily over the dark waters, for all that he had hailed Thonaraz with his feasting-horn.

But the wind would bear him swiftly to God-Home, and a fine bench-seat awaited him there, sweet mead and the sight of friends and kinsmen who had fared before him. "Better to burn him," she said at last. Then, "What do you have for a bath-house? The faring has been long, and I should like to be clean by tomorrow."

"There is a river where we wash ourselves," Hoilogae answered. "I shall take you there now, if you like, before we go for the wood."

Armed with wood-axes, Hoilogae and Swaebhon walked along the fields. Some of them were already well-grown with green shoots of grain, in others, the sprouts were just pricking through the earth.

Swaebhon cast her gaze over the grain, murmuring deep in her throat. The planting must have been late indeed that year, for though these southern lands looked warm and rich, it was less well-grown than that about Aiwilimae's hall would be by now. "If your summer is not long this year," she said, "the harvest will not be so good. Your brother is not without a share in your boldness to have made the choice he did, nor shall he go untested in the might he's taken for himself."

Hoilogae nodded, and Swaebhon followed his gaze over the low green fields. This seemed a tame and quiet land against her memories of the sheer cliffs and mountains of the North, its grass and grain and beeches pale before the mind-shadows of dark pines, but the threat of hunger lurked beneath its swells as surely as rocks waiting at a cliff's foot.

Hoilogae's thoughts must have been much the same, for he stopped, turning to her again. "How do you find this land?" He asked her. "Does it seem fair in your eyes?"

Swaebhon did not look over to the beech-woods, nor back to Herwamundaz's howe and the sea beyond, but gazed into Hoilogae's sky-gray eyes, reaching out to take his calloused hand in her own. "All that is here seems fair to me, Jutland shall be a fair home for me to bear our bairns into. It may be that I shall miss the mountains and the howling of the wind through the pines, or long now and again to climb high fells, as all folk long for the lands that gave them birth when they are far away.

Still, I shall not miss them too greatly while you are here with me, and shall be joyful at my choice. If, that is," she added, "you build me a proper bath-house soon. I have never gone so long in my life without a good steaming, and shall need it more and more as I grow closer to birthing. Now, where is this river you were telling me of?"

They walked further on, beneath the rustling beech-trees. Hoilogae watched admiringly as Swaebhon stepped lightly over the storm-cast branches, her bare feet hardly leaving any track in the deep leaf-mold. Of course, she must have been taught to wood-walk since she could toddle on her own two legs, but he was sure that her grace could not be matched by any other hunter, woman or man.

"From the tracks," Swaebhon mused, "there must be good hunting here, and like summer all year round, if you have no need to go on skis."

"Not quite like summer," Hoilogae answered, "but the winters must be far less fierce here than in your home, and do not last so long." They had come to a fork in the path. One way led to the holy horse-grove, the other to the river. Hoilogae led her down the second way, till they reached the edge of the rushing water. The river was not very deep here no deeper than Hoilogae's chest in the very middle, but the rocks cutting the water to bubbling tatters were sharp and slippery.

Swaebhon untied her belt and flung her dress from her in a single movement, laying her ax down on the heap of dirty white wool. Standing, she raised one foot to rest it on a water-black rock, looking back at Hoilogae over her shoulder. The leaf-broken sunlight dappled her white skin with shadows and gold, shading one of her blue-gray eyes and brightening the other to a wolf's pale amber. Hoilogae undressed more slowly, unwilling to break his gaze for so much as a moment, then came towards her. She laughed and leapt over the rocks, sinking into the rushing water until her hair floated all around her. Hoilogae followed her in, bending his knees until he had sunken as deeply as she. The river was cold as snow melt, seizing his bones and shaking them.

He pushed off from the rocky bottom, paddling against the current to warm himself. Swaebhon grasped his hands, dragging him upriver towards herself. In spite of the cold, Hoilogae felt his body's heat rising to her touch. He closed his eyes as he kissed her, shaken by the strength of his desire through the icy water, she was already pulling him onto her, into her own warmth. Attalae would cross a broader and colder river in his faring, whose knives were sharper than the rocks pressing hard-edged against Hoilogae's feet. This Hoilogae knew, and held tightly to Swaebhon, moving more swiftly to keep the drill-fire they'd kindled alight, flaming higher in his body.

He did not know whether it was her heat warming his icy flesh now, or whether it was his life that Swaebhon sucked from him as her strong cold arms clutched him tight to her. Still, Hoilogae clung to her, the rushing water bearing them up like a torrent of rain-laden wind. Swaebhon kissed the corners of Hoilogae's eyes when they were done, and her mouth tasted of salt afterwards. They held each other in the rushing water until the river had washed all the warmth from them.

The storms Hedhinaz had spoken of had broken a great many branches, and cast down a good number of trees, so that Hoilogae and Swaebhon soon had as much dry deadwood as they could carry. By the time the Sun's setting reddened the western sky, a pyre stood high-built before Herwamundaz's mound, but Attalae's body lay on a stretcher of branches in the hof, before the harrow. The bier was woven into the shape of a boat, a skeleton-craft for a ghost's faring. In the hof's fire pit, the flames burned low. Their light gleamed from the beaten bronze leaf of Attalae's spear-head, the gold work on his knife, and sword, sheaths, and the gold rings snaking around his arms.

The torches cast a ruddy brightness over the old warrior's silvered hair and beard, softly shading his wrinkles, so that their light showed him as a man in his prime. Hoilogae stood silently at Attalae's head, Hlothawairaz at his feet, as the folk filed by one by one, setting down their gifts of food and goods by the dead man's side, and Hoilogae remembered how carefully Attalae had packed their boat with enough food and water to carry them through any mishap in faring. Hedhinaz was the last to leave the hof. As the door closed behind him, Hlothawairaz sighed, sinking down to the ground and twisting the butt of his torch deep into the earthen floor. A drop of burning pine-sap fell from it, hissing to darkness as Hoilogae, too, lowered himself to sit by Attalae's head. The same light that smoothed Attalae's face carved the lines deeper into the living man's flesh, his face a mask of cre-vassed bark, thick nose and squared chin jutting from it like the stumps of ill-cut branches. Hlothawairaz's broad body was a hunched shadow beside the torch, the man crouching into his own darkness.

"Tell me of my sons," Hlothawairaz said. "Hlothamundaz, Hlothamariz, Hlothagairaz, and Hlothabrandaz. The four hopes of my father's line. Tell me what came to pass with them, and how they met their end."

It seemed to Hoilogae that the man who sat the length of Attalae's body away from him could have been the death-ravaged ghost of any of the four he named. His looks, save for the wearing of age, were so close to his sons'. The blood of shame rose to Hoilogae's cheeks. He had hardly known Hlothawairaz's sons since they had come from the mists into his clear sight, he could say little about them. Hoilogae's speech stumbled as he told what had come to pass in Hati's Firth, till he came to Rime-Gerdhaz's boast, "'My mother lay before the mild one's ships, I drowned the sons of Hlothawairaz in the harbor.'" Then the rest of the tale flowed more easily, till Hlothawairaz had heard how the troll-queen stood in the harbor, a lifeless stone.

"It may not be told," Hlothawairaz said, and a cough stopped his words. Hoilogae heard him clear his throat before he spoke again. "It may not be told, then, whether my sons died of faring with you or of not staying closely enough by you, when all those in your ship came hale through the firth."

"It may not be told," Hoilogae agreed heavily.

Hlothawairaz rose, but did not take his torch up again. "I shall not keep this watch, after all. You hold your place here, as you must, but I do not know what I shall do." He walked to the door and out into the darkness without looking back, leaving Hoilogae where he sat by Attalae's body.

When the torches had burned to earth and gone out, Hoilogae had no way more to mark the night's passing. No breath of air stirred the ash over the fire's coals, he did not know the stars he saw through the smoke hole, for no one had ever showed him how to reckon by the night's beacons. He sat very still in the darkness, waiting for the morning without thought. He did not sleep, nor did his lids begin to droop over his eyes, but nothing stirred with-in or without until the light through the hof's smoke hole had begun to pale.

Then Swaebhon stood in the doorway, white against the storm-gray light of dawn, and lifted her arm towards him, fire curling up from the torch in her hand. Hedhinaz stood behind her, as she stepped aside, he came forward, bending down to take the other end of the gift-laden bier. Together Hoilogae and his brother hefted the branch-boat, raising it to their shoulders and carrying it out into the cold dawn-light. Attalae's head rolled to the side, and Hoilogae saw the dark purple-blue stain of death hooding the skull beneath his thin silver hair, stretching down the nape of his neck. That stain would be spread over his back as well, Wodhanaz had cast his cloak over the corpse. Bracing the bier against his chest, Hoilogae reached out with one hand to straighten the rede-giver's head, so that Attalae's sightless eyes stared at the sky again.

Did I bring him death, or lengthen his life? Hoilogae wondered. No one stayed closer by me than he did, from beginning to end, but that was his choice, and he was a free man. Hoilogae recognized many of the men and women gathered at the foot of Herwamundaz's mound, but Hlothawairaz did not stand among them. Hoilogae and Hedhinaz lowered the death-boat into the middle of the branches, steadying it as it settled creakily into the pyre. His sight blurred, Hoilogae stared down at Attalae's bone-white face. The flesh had already sunken into the hollows of the old warrior's skull, making his dark eyes wider than Hoilogae had ever seen them in life. The rising light brightened the eastern side of Herwamundaz's howe to a bitter pale green. Now Hoilogae's earlier words ached in his throat and he longed to still the might in the mound again, so that he might free his son's naming to bring Attalae's soul into the Middle-Garth again, but that he could not do.

Hoilogae reached down, gripping Attalae's cold shoulders as if the warmth of his own hands could somehow shake the rede-giver to life again, or bring the words sprouting from his throat. Attalae might fare to green God-Home, to the unending battle of Walhall or Frowe Haljon's dark still realm, and be born again in time, but Hoilogae knew that the two of them would not sit talking again while he lived, and that sorrow clutched his throat dumb as it had ever been before Swaebhon gave him his name. Oh, fare well, Hoilogae thought to his old friend, his heart speaking the words his voice could not yet loose. You foe to troll-wives, may Thonaraz ward you from their clutches on this faring, as you always saw the way clearly in life, may your path through death be clear before you, and Wodhanaz not forget the gifts you gave him, nor how you worked well for what he shaped before my birth.

"May Wodhanaz not forget," Swaebhon answered, her call low and clear through the cold dawn air.

No breeze stirred the dew-heavy grasses, but suddenly the sound of a great storm wind rushed through Hoilogae's ears, as the still sky shattered into the furious barking of a pack of hounds in full cry. Hoilogae let go of Attalae's body, opening his hands and stepping backward. He could hinder him no longer. Hedhinaz knew that barking and wind-rushing. He had heard it often at dawn and dusk, every planting, and harvest-time. The geese were rising from the boggy lake where the gifts to the holy ones were often cast, their wings clapping with the echoes of the storm. He saw their long necks stretching against the paling clouds, dark and light together, as the flock wheeled above the howe and Hoilogae's wife lowered her torch to the pitch-blackened branches. As the fire flared up, it seemed to Hedhinaz that Swaebhon's face grew suddenly brighter, rainbow flames glimmering around her swan-white shape, fair against the shadow of the mound, fair as lightning against the flock of storm-birds flying above her.

The sight of her thrilled through his nerves like the cold burning of ice, spearing keenly up through his heart to transfix the breath in his throat as the geese barked and shouted over his head. Swaebhon's sky-gray eyes shone pure as cloud-light mirrored in a still lake, her face lit with awesome joy as the wind of the passing wings stirred the long waterfall of her hair. All the light of her gaze brightened the tears filling Hoilogae's eyes, the two of them clasping hands through the flames that shot adder-swift along the dry wood. The fire burst up from Attalae's hair and woolen tunic, the amber ax-head at his throat burning sweet and bright as pine-sap, and Hedhinaz clutched his fists tight, his teeth crushing the sound in his mouth until the muscles of his jaw cramped.

Swaebhon and Hoilogae stood together until nothing was left by which Attalae might have been known. Only blackened meat, shot through here and there with veins of red-glowing gold like wyrms wound through dark rock, and the sagging shapes of his knife and sword, whose bright bronze heat had burned their scabbards away. The fire was still flaming strongly, but the first drops of rain were hissing into it now, spattering cold against Hoilogae's arms and face. When Hoilogae looked over at his younger brother, Hedhinaz jerked his head away, so that Hoilogae could not see what filled his eyes. The rain was falling a little harder, sheening Swaebhon's white cheeks like the keenest stroke of a whetstone against Wejlunduz's iron and darkening Hedhinaz's braid to the shade of spoiled grain.

"Do you mean to stay long?" Hedhinaz asked his brother.

Hoilogae shook his head. "It would be well if we came to the place where we mean to dwell and settled now, I think. I have had enough of wandering for this year, and there is much to be done to make a home for Swaebhon here. No, we shall leave as soon as we may, if you will trade a cart and horses for our ships."

Hedhinaz's thin lips curled into the half-smile Hoilogae was used to seeing on his face. "I hope your frowe is a better bargainer than you are yourself, my brother. Don't worry, I shall see that you have everything you need for the faring southward. You may leave tomorrow morning, if you wish, though I would have you stay and feast with me tonight."

"We shall stay a little longer than that," Swaebhon answered. "Now, if you will show me where you keep your stores for brewing, and let me speak with whichever of your women is herb-craftiest, I shall be sure that you have a good lot of wort working when I leave, so that at least you shall not be thirsty by Yule-tide."

Hedhinaz gazed over Swaebhon's shoulder as though he did not wish to look at her face, and it seemed to Hoilogae that some troubling thought muddied his brother's sharp features. The rain had soaked its way through their clothes by now, a cold wind was rising, blowing it more sharply into their faces as it whipped the fire to a last fierceness against the falling waters.

"All of that can be done inside," Hedhinaz said. They left the pyre to burn, going down the grassy slope to Hedhinaz's hall.

Bowls of warm milk were waiting on the high table for Hoilogae, Hedhinaz, and Swaebhon when they got in, together with bread and cheese. Hedhinaz sent his thrall-maid out, she came back as they were finishing their breakfast. Behind her was Wulfahaidhaz, wavy fair hair flattened by the rain and water-drops trickling off the pointed tip of her nose. The young woman clutched her wool-muffled babe closer to her breasts as she came nearer to Swaebhon, until the child began to howl.

"She wants feeding, I think," Swaebhon said. "Sit down, I promise you have nothing to fear from me."

Wulfahaidhiz settled herself down on the bench, a little way from Swaebhon, and pulled one breast out of the top of her dress. Hoilogae marked how her eyes closed a little, as if echoing the tight-closed eyes of the babe that sucked hungrily at her nipple.Swaebhon waited until the child had drunk her fill before asking Wulfahaidhiz how matters stood with the brewing-grain, whether it had been malted yet, or begun to sprout.

Hoilogae listened to them talk with half an ear, but he knew nothing of what they were saying, and after a while he grew restless and wandered off, looking at the newly daubed walls of the lengthened hall and the tight bundles of fresh thatch above his head until he longed to be out in the open air again. Hoilogae looked back at the high table. Hedhinaz had gone somewhere else, Swaebhon and Wulfahaidhaz were still talking without a glance towards him. He slipped out into the rain. Attalae's pyre had gone out, though the black branches still cracked in showers of sparks as they gave way under each other's weight. Nothing was left of the old rede-giver but blackened bones beneath a cloak of charred flesh, cooling swiftly under the falling rain, his skull had caved in like the roof of a burnt house, the last coals still glowing in the shelter of its curved walls.

Hoilogae knew that the settlement's potter he could not remember the woman's name, but her thin height and long fall of gold-brown hair, streaked with clay-dust like the gray of age, came easily to his mind was already shaping an earth-hive a little longer than Attalae's thighbones, just long enough for his half-melted sword to be laid crosswise in. It seemed to Hoilogae then that he greatly longed to be able to give words and voice to what howled within him, but he could not even name it, let alone shape it, though he felt as though his heart were rending through his rib-cage in a fury to free itself from the bone that fettered it. He had done with weeping, no more tears came to him, though his mind shadowed flesh over Attalae's burnt bones again, and the echo of the rede-giver's voice still rang in his ears. I await my end, it shall come before yours. Only that I am old. Hoilogae walked on, down the path where he and Swaebhon had trodden the day before. The rain had washed their spoor from the track.

Though he could hear the river down the one pathway, he did not turn towards it, but took the other half of the fork, walking towards the holy grove. The rain grayed the shapes of the horses who stood grazing beneath the dripping oak-leaves. Hoilogae walked towards them in silence, his feet crunching on the hulls of old acorns as the rain fell harder and faster. The holy steeds did not seem to mind him, or mark that he was there, he stood still in the middle of the grove, beneath the cold waterfall streaming from the cloud-cliffs, waiting to see what should come. After a while, he found that he was staring into the eyes of the wind-gray stallion who stood beneath an ash-tree, beside the great slanting slab of gray stone. The horse raised his right fore-hoof, stamping three times on the rock. Slowly Hoilogae walked over to him, looking down at the wet stone.

The rainwater had pooled into three little cup-dents that lay in a straight line along the rock, a little stream running from highest to lowest and spilling over the last rim into the gray-green lichen that clung to the stone below. As Hoilogae stared at the wide slab of stone, it seemed to him that he could see other shadows in the roughness of the rock and the patterns of pale moss against its deep gray. A man lifting Wodhanaz's long spear, the curling prow and stern of a fleet of framework boats, like the boat that had borne Attalae on his last faring. Hoilogae coughed, his rough croak echoing through the clearing. The sound came again, though not from his throat, something rustled above him. Looking up, he saw the black wings spreading near the top of the ash-tree. Two ravens, glossy in the rain, rose heavily from their perch, circling up into the gray sky. Every day after breakfast, when Swaebhon went to the brewing-house, Hoilogae took chisels and mallet and went out to the hallowed grove.

No one followed him, or asked what he was doing, but he chipped at the stone until Sunna's setting reddened the western sky each day, with only the horses and the birds who flew freely through the grove to watch him. The work went more easily and skilfully than he had thought it would, or else his sight half-blinded him to what he wrought. He could see, if he tried, the clumsiness of the lines that shaped the straight bodies and four stick-legs of the two wolves that ran beneath Wodhanaz's feet, but it was far easier for him to see their foam-streaming jaws, frothing with hunger for the dead who fared in the skeleton branch-boats under the god's spear, if they were not hunting dogs, eager to bring down elk and deer for the feast that would come when the ships reached shore. Hoilogae saw each hair in the thick gray pelts of Wodhanaz's hounds, he could feel their hot breath upon his hand when he reached towards their rock-carved shadows, but he could not say how they were meant to be known.

Hoilogae finished the carving of the stone in good time, dyeing each shape bright with red ochre on the day that Swaebhon deemed her hand no longer needful for all the worts she had set to working, the day when the last sod was cut and laid over the mound that covered the clay casket holding Atta-lae's bones. Their wagons were already loaded, two ox-carts and one drawn by horses, to bring Hoilogae, those men and women who wished to go with him, and Swaebhon's Northmen south to the hall where Herwawardhaz and Sigislinthon waited. Hedhinaz had spared nothing in readying their fare-well feast. He had slain both swine and sheep, and sent all the settlement's children out to gather great bowls of the early strawberries.

Still, Hoilogae thought his brother did not look easy in his high seat, that he shifted about as if the sharp ends of his bones pressed painfully against the wood, as if he had not made peace with his place yet.

"When you go south," Hedhinaz said suddenly, turning on his seat to face his brother, "speak to our father about finding a wife for me. It seems to me," He looked down at the shadowed earthen floor, and Hoilogae saw his brother's cheekbones darkening as Hedhinaz tried again. "I have heard that," His voice went up on the last words, he cleared his throat, coughing to knock it back to a man's deepness. "The grain seems to be growing well enough now, but it is a long way till harvest, and if I am fro here, I must not go another year unwed, I have heard that the holy ones take that ill. I have sent here and there, but heard no word of any fitting maid, and it seems to me that our father could help greatly from his new stead, if he did not think I were still too young to take a wife."

He glanced over Hoilogae's shoulder at Swaebhon, who sat half-turned away, talking with the dark-haired Northman Bernu on her other side, the corner of his mouth twisted, as if in disapproval, but he said nothing else.

"I shall speak to him," Hoilogae promised.

"That is well. And for your wife, I have a gift, a blessing for her fruitfulness and joy." Hedhinaz reached into the shadows between the legs of his seat. Hoilogae heard a rustling of cloth, then a soft rattling, and then Hedhinaz was sitting straight again, with a huge necklace of rich clear amber dangling from his hand. The smallest pieces were no smaller than a hazelnut, and the largest was near as large as a small wild apple, the Frowe's sea-tears had been carefully smoothed and polished with flax-seed oil, shining like rubbed gold above the warm glow of fire and thin-rayed glimmers of sun-spangles within their depths. Hedhinaz stood and walked over to Swaebhon, tapping her on the shoulder. She whirled, raising a hand as if she thought to be attacked, then Hoilogae heard her draw in a deep breath, sucking the flesh tight under her cheekbones as Hedhinaz draped the thick string of amber about her neck.

"That is a mighty drighten's gift indeed," Swaebhon murmured, then, Hoilogae could not tell whether she was teasing or not, "but should you not keep such gifts for your own wedding, instead of draping them on your brother's wife?"

"I have another, at least as fair, for the maid who shall wed me," Hedhinaz answered, "and it is in my mind that this is best fit for you. It is a gift from our clan as well, I do not think that Hoilogae has already given you the like."

"He brought me the gift I most desired," Swaebhon answered, reaching across Hoilogae's lap to brush her fingers over the hilt of the sword at his side. "Still, I own that I have never seen a necklace so fair within the Middle-Garth's ring, and the gift shows the giver's might."

Later that evening, when Swaebhon and Hoilogae rested alone together in the house that had been Attalae's, Hoilogae ran his fingers over the smooth warm curves of the amber where it lay between her breasts and said, "I know my brother even less well than I had thought, it had seemed to me that he had little liking for you."

Swaebhon turned herself a bit so that her husband's hands would caress her nipples, though she was well-sated, it was pleasant to have Hoilogae stroking her body. Still, the thought of Hedhinaz was like a thorn-tip pricking through her warm ease, she could not forget his hungry gaze, nor the way his teeth had tightened on his lower lip when she touched the hilt of Hoilogae's sword. "It seems well to me that he should be wed soon," she replied. "I think there is little ill in him, but much strength that might be turned against himself if he sets his foot wrongly, and he has only enough of your wisdom to trouble him. If the sight of his soul is not awakened by another, he will never see more than shadows, nor long for what he does not know." She draped an arm over Hoilogae, stroking his back. "Your work has knotted your shoulders badly, turn over, and let me rub them for you."

"Do you know what I was doing?"

"How should I not? It was well done and didn't you carve Attalae's welcome on God-Home's shore, and help to bring him to that home?"

"I did not know, I was never sure."

"Now you are?"

Hoilogae nodded, the sinews of his neck tugging beneath her hands as she kneaded them. "Now I am," he said firmly, and Swaebhon knew that he spoke the truth.

Hoilogae and Swaebhon rode down the Host-Way in the horse-drawn wagon, the others following behind them. Long before they came within sight of Sigislinthon's hall, a dark-haired boy whom Hoilogae did not know hailed them, "Hai, who are you and what do you wish here in the lands of Sigislinthon and Herwawardhaz?" He raised his shepherd's staff as though he did not see the spears and sheathed swords Hoilogae's party carried, glaring fiercely up at them.

"I am Hoilogae, their son," Hoilogae answered mildly. "I have come back from my long faring, I am sure they will be glad to see me."

The boy's blue eyes widened, he started to say something, but his tongue broke into a spatter of stuttering. At last he calmed, and said, "Are you truly Hoilogae, and alive? No one thought you would come back. Men said that you had gone down to the north, to the lands of the dead, that your wyrd was short, but full-reded."

"My wyrd is not full-reded yet, and I was some little way from the lands of the dead, though there are some who did not come back with me. Run ahead, if your sheep may be trusted to graze by themselves for a while, and tell my mother and father that I and my bride are coming."

The boy turned around, breaking into an easy run along the road before the plodding horses. Soon he had passed behind a swell of green grass, and was lost to sight.

More of the gilt had worn from Sigislinthon's hair, leaving it heavily silvered, Herwawardhaz's body seemed to have thickened, and he moved less easily than Hoilogae remembered, as though his joints were made of swift-rusting iron. Still, both of them came forward quickly enough to greet their son as he and Swaebhon climbed down from the horse-wagon. Her mouth open, Sigislinthon stared up at Hoilogae's bride as her husband embraced Hoilogae and clapped him on the back.

"You are both welcome here, as long as you will stay always, most welcome," Sigislinthon said, her face flushing with the brightness of her smile. She raised the guesting-horn to Hoilogae, who drank deeply of the rich fruity ale and passed it to Swaebhon. "These are your lands, as you know, Hoilogae, both by blood and bones laid in earth and by the strength of your sword, and I am gladdened more than anything to see you alive and well. And you, frowe, are as fair a bride as I might have dreamed for my dear son." She met Swaebhon's gaze a moment, but her eyes flickered swiftly past the younger woman, over the folk who were bringing the ox-carts up beside their leader's wagon.

"Aye, we are gladder to see you than we have been since you left," Herwawardhaz answered. "It is time for you to take part in ruling this land you have won, after all, and I am greatly pleased to see you so well-wed. Where is Attalae, why has he not come with you?"

"Attalae lies by Glazaleunduz, we shall not see him here again, I think," Hoilogae answered. "He lived long enough to see his home-shores and drink a last horn of his homeland's ale. But you know well enough that he was old, and all men must die."

"All men," Herwawardhaz echoed. "You might have brought better news with you, but your homecoming and wedding are gladness enough. Come in, now, you and your folk, and when you have rested and eaten, we shall talk of how best to order these lands. You and your frowe."

"Swaebhon, the daughter of Aiwilimae, who is drighten far along the northern way," Swaebhon answered. "Hoilogae and I must build our hall and rule our part for more than the two of us, for I already have our child in my womb, and am like to give birth at Yule-tide."

Sigislinthon closed her eyes as though she had caught a glimpse of the Sun's brightness, then stepped forward and cast her arms about the other woman. "Hail and welcome again, Swaebhon! May you always find joy here, and your blessings grow as they have begun."

"So long as I am by Hoilogae, I shall always find joy where-ever I am, and Wodhanaz bless the two of us," Swaebhon answered.

There was a great deal to be done that summer, for Swaebhon would have a hall built for her by the nearest lake, no short walk from Sigislinthon's hall, and a bath-house as well, and houses also had to be put up for all those folk who had fared with them. Two of the Northmen, Bernu and Hrothabernu, had married widows of the last summer's fighting before the beginning of harvest, and they had those feasts to hold. They were two days into the harvest when Swaebhon held Hoilogae's hand to her swollen belly so that he could feel the kicking of the child in her womb.

Though no wife had yet been found for Hedhinaz, and news from Glaza-leunduz said his harvest was late in the reaping, as it had been in the sowing, it was also said that there was no fear of starvation among his folk. Just as the harvest had been late, the snow also came late that year, but once it fell, it fell thickly. By Yule Eve it lay as high as Hoilogae's knees on the fields, and rose to the eaves on the north side of his hall where the wind had blown it into a great drift. Swaebhon had been restless the night before, now, with morning graying outside, she stood combing her hair by the half-open door, without a cloak, as if it were summer. Sparks crackled out beneath the hard strokes of her arm, her long hairs swirled as if the wind lifted them, wrapping around her to cling to the great chunks of amber on her necklace. Now and again she paused, her face tightening, then went back to her combing with greater strength.

"Are you well?" Hoilogae asked. "Can I do anything for you?"

Swaebhon let her comb rest halfway through a stroke, laying the other hand across the great swell of her belly. "I am very well. But you must go at once and stoke the bath-house up as quickly as you can, for I am like to give birth today and that is where it is best done. My waters have not yet burst, but I can feel that it will not be long before they do. When you have done that, go to fetch your mother, I think that she well knows how to help in birthing, and I would have her beside me."

Hoilogae clasped Swaebhon carefully, kissing her before he flung his cloak about his shoulders and hurried out into the snow to ready the bath-house.

Although Hoilogae wanted to stay with his wife when the birthing began, Sigislinthon would not let him into the steam-hut with the women.

"Go back to your hall," his mother called through the crack in the door. "Drink a horn of ale, that never hurt any man in your stead. Nothing is happening yet, and you can't help here."

Instead of going back to the hall, Hoilogae walked out to the lake's edge. The snow hid the ice in the middle, but the marsh-grasses stuck up about the sides, grayish-brown skeletons against the whiteness. He did not go out onto the ice, the older men had warned him against it, saying that it might not be thick enough to bear a man's weight safely for a little time yet. Slowly Hoilogae made his way around the edge of the lake, his fur-wrapped legs sinking to the knee at every step.

The air was clear now, every black twig in the wood on the other side sharp against the heavy sky, but the leaden light foretold snow soon to come. He walked until he had come to the top of one of the small mounds that rose in a low uneven ring about the lake. No one knew how old they were, or who lay within, but the holy folk dwelt there, all the same. The snow was very thin on the top of the mound, no more than a white glaze over the spiky shoots of winter-brown crowberry-plants.

Hoilogae arranged part of his cloak beneath him, sinking down onto that and wrapping the rest of the fur garment tightly around himself. Now it was Swaebhon who battled, for her life and their child's, now it was he who must help her, as best he knew how. Hands muffled in the thick wolf-fur, Hoilogae drew his sword from its sheath. The storm-boding light reflected oddly off it, the metal gleaming with the dull gray-black sheen of flint. Hoilogae knew nothing of birthing, he did not know how to begin. But he looked up at the darkening sky and thought of Swaebhon riding above him in the seething clouds of winter's end, as he had first seen her, the walkurjon, Wodhanaz's daughter.

"Wodhanaz, Ansuz," he murmured. "Open the way, bring Swaebhon and my child from the dark house to life and light again."

It seemed to Hoilogae then that his sight split, neatly as two rock-crystals sheering apart beneath a chisel's tap. He was still looking out over the white spread of snow above the water, staring at the first fine swan-feathers drifting down from the heavy sky, but the bath-house was also growing nearer to his eyes, and it seemed to him that a gray shape padded four-legged beside him, though he could not turn his gaze towards it. The door of the bath-house stood open a crack, so that it was easy for Hoilogae to slip in. Swaebhon lay naked in the heat, her legs braced apart and hands pressing against the glistening mound of her belly. She made no sound, but her mouth was fixed open in a wide wolf-toothed snarl, tendrils of sweat-drenched hair writhed about her face as she tossed her head in pain. Sigislinthon wore only a cord-skirt and a strand of amber, as though it were the hottest day in summer.

Hoilogae heard his mother say, "There, I can see the crown. Push!" She put her hands beside Swaebhon's, the two of them straining hard. It seemed to Hoilogae that the shadows thickened around Swaebhon's face, mis-shaping it into a troll-queen's grimace as she struggled to bring their child forth.

The gathering wave sank back, Sigislinthon stood again, wiping her face with the back of her wrist. "It won't be too much longer now."

"Cast more water on the stones," Swaebhon said through her teeth. "The heat will help."

Sigislinthon bent to scoop up a ladleful of water, casting it over the glowing rocks. It hissed up in a cloud of steam, though Hoilogae did not feel the heat, he felt stronger, like a ghost given shape by marsh-mist.

"Ah, there," Sigislinthon murmured. The muscles of Swaebhon's belly had begun to ripple again, a long wyrm-shudder crawling over the mound. This time, Hoilogae bent with her, his sword still held in his left hand, he laid his right over the women's hands, pushing with them. His gaze was fixed on Swaebhon's eyes, clear gray through the shadowy mask of pain twisting about her face, he bore down as hard as he could, for he knew that the birthing would not otherwise end until she was dead.

"Harder, don't stop now, it's coming," Sigislinthon whispered. "Keep going, don't ease up. The crown's out. There!"

Hoilogae could feel the sinking beneath his hands as the babe slid from Swaebhon's body, feel the long shuddering breath that set it free. Sigislinthon lifted the bloody child up, looking at it closely, then slapped it sharply across the bottom. The babe coughed air in, let out a long high howl, a glittering stream arched up from the little pizzle between his legs, splattering against the bath-house's roof.

For a moment the weariness dropped from Sigislinthon's face as she smiled, in the dull red light of the glowing stones, she might have been no older than Swaebhon. Hoilogae wondered why she did not cut the thick strand that bound child and mother, but she laid the babe on Swaebhon's sunken stomach, pressing downward again until something dark and glistening slid from the younger woman's womb. Only then did Sigislinthon tie the two knots to bind the flow of life, only then did she raise her little iron blade to cut.

In the same moment, Hoilogae lifted his sword. The two blades came down at the same time, cutting the ruddy-shining cord. A spray of blood burst forth, its warm droplets sprinkling Hoilogae, and suddenly he could see nothing but the gray sky and white snow, the black trees beyond the lake and the shadows of hall and bath-house a little farther away, misted by the soft-falling snowflakes. Hoilogae's legs were numb beneath him, a thick layer of snow lying over his furry hood. He stood up, hurrying clumsily towards the bath-house with the blood prickling hot and painful into his limbs again.

Hoilogae was almost to the door when Sigislinthon came out, leaving the door ajar behind her. Well-warmed by the heat inside, she still wore only her cord-skirt, but though she had not bothered to put on cloak or shoes, she had wrapped the child she carried in a good woolen blanket.

"How fares Swaebhon?" Hoilogae asked anxiously. "Is she well?"

"She sleeps," Sigislinthon replied. "It was a hard labor, the strongest women do not always have the easiest time in childbirth, but your son is whole and well."

"My son," Hoilogae echoed. He did not take the child from her arms yet, that he could not do till the name-giving. Sigislinthon lifted the babe up so that he could look more closely. The child's eyes were bright, very pale against his crumpled red face.

Sigislinthon laughed. "Yes, newborns always look like that when they've just come from the womb. He's a fine strong boy, who I think is like to favor your father's side of the family."

Hoilogae stood staring silently at his son for a few moments longer, overcome by his still bright joy. The child stared back at him, squinting as if the darkening afternoon's light was too strong for his new-opened eyes, and Hoilogae thought he might have stood there looking down at his babe till his legs fell beneath him. Swaebhon had been the one who bore the child, who had bled and suffered, he must think of her first. "Should Swaebhon be left to sleep on the planks in there? I shall bring her to her bed." He pushed through the door, hurrying into the bath-house.

Swaebhon lay quite still on her back, legs together and hands clasped between her breasts, her sweat-dank hair smoothed straight. Her eyes were closed, her mouth hung open a little. The rich scent of blood hung in the bath-house's warm air, though Sigislinthon had already washed the dark stains away. Hoilogae's heart clutched within him. He could not see any rising or falling of Swaebhon's chest, he did not think she slept. He went to his knees beside the platform where she lay, bending his head close to hers.

"She breathes," Sigislinthon said, "but it is very soft and slow, listen!" It did seem to Hoilogae that a soft breath of air stirred from his wife's mouth, light as a touch of swan down on his cheek. "My foster-father slept so at times, and told us that we must never move him then, for he would not be able to wake after. I do not know what has come over her. She was giving the child that first suckling which brings down the milk, and then she suddenly gave a great yawn, and stretched herself down like that." Sigislinthon looked down at Swaebhon's sleeping body for a moment, her left hand coming up to grasp her necklace and her right going down to pick up the knife. "If she kens the same crafts he did, Frahanamariz," she added in a whisper, her hands tightening on amber and iron "she must have gone forth, she must be wandering in another hide, through this world or another. I do not know why, she has spoken of such things no more than he ever did."

"I shall sit with her till she wakens, then."

"That you may not do, if she does not waken soon. Tonight is Yule, and you must be in the hall to give the feasting-gifts to the gods as the Sun sets. You must lead the folk to set out the food for the holy ones in the mounds, and light the Sun's wheel when she stands at her lowest stead, however things go with your wife.

She is a wise woman, and strong, so that I think you need fear no more for her wandering ghost than you fear when she goes to hunt in the woods. You stay here for now, while I go find Fraujadis. She has enough milk in her breasts for another child, and will surely be glad to give yours suck for a while. If you go out, do not close the door all the way." The child began to squall at once as Sigislinthon set him down on the floor and bent to tie her shoes onto her feet, then flung a light cloak over herself and took the baby up again.

Hoilogae sat still by Swaebhon, watching until his mother came back. "The light is fading fast, now you must go to the hall," Sigislinthon said. "Have no fear. I shall keep a good watch over your bride."

The dark sky and clouds of snow swirling on the wind from the North Sea would bring Yule-night down early, Hedhinaz thought as he stood by the hof and looked out at the frothing gray waves. They would need more wood to keep the fires going all night. On other nights one might wrap in furs and thick wool, sleeping through the bitterest cold, but to forsake the watch or go cold on Yule would be an ill sign to the gods indeed, the more so in a year when, without their help, the harvest would have failed and the folk gone hungry. He could call up some of his men to go into the wood, but it seemed to him that there was no need.

As many stout branches as he could bind into a bundle and carry on his shoulders, added to what was in the hall already, would be enough to make sure the fires burned all night, and that was the drighten's duty first. Hedhinaz put two fingers in his mouth, whistling sharply. It was not long before one of the settlement's gray hounds came running up to him, snow scattering behind its feet. With a good hound beside him, his wood-ax in his hand and his iron sword at his side, Hedhinaz thought that he would have little enough to fear, even should he come upon a wolf-pack, wolves did not often come so near to the settlement, anyway. Hedhinaz and his dog started off towards the wood, carefully skirting Herwamundaz's mound.

The snow did not seem to lie as thickly there as elsewhere, Hedhinaz could see the brown grass showing through here and there about the top of the mound. Swaebhon must be bearing her child soon, Hoilogae's child. What if I went north, as he did? Hedhinaz wondered. What if I, too, followed the northern way down to the dead-lands or the high etin-homes, seeking my bride as my brother did? But he knew that he could not. He had no sureness to call him from the duty he had taken up, no holy maid had spoken to him. Thus weighted, Hedhinaz went under the bare black weave of branches, kicking through the snow to see where he might turn up fallen wood that might be good for burning. The wind had stopped blowing, the broad snowflakes drifting straight down between the laced twigs. Hedhinaz could hear no sound except for his own feet breaking through the crust of the snow, and beside him the panting of the hound that cocked its head and looked bright-eyed up at him.

After a while Hedhinaz came, as he had thought he would, to the long corpse of a tree that had fallen a little after Winter nights. The branches had not yet been stripped from it, and so he set to work, scraping the snow away and swinging his ax as hard as he could at the bare bark. The bronze bit in easily, chips flying about until the branch was thin enough for him to snap free with his hands. A few more chops broke it into pieces that he could carry easily, and then he went on to the next. Before long, Hedhinaz was warm enough to cast his dark cloak aside, and went on cutting wood with the snowflakes melting from his face and arms. When Hedhinaz thought he had enough wood, he bundled it up in his cloak and turned back. The snow had begun to fall more swiftly, blotting out his tracks on the path, and the lowering evening light blurred one tree into another from only a little way off, but he knew he was not far from the settlement, and there was only one path to follow in any case.

Still, the walking did not seem so easy now, Hedhinaz had tired himself cutting wood, and his snow-soaked leg wrappings kept coming untied as he trudged through the knee-deep snow. At last he had to stop to shake the wood from his cloak and wrap the garment around himself again, binding his branches into a heavy bundle with his wood-ax on top. As soon as he had tied the wood to his back and looked about himself, Hedhinaz realized that he must have turned down the wrong fork in the pathway, though he did not know how he had done it. The wood's edge and the houses beyond should have been within sight, but they were not. He recognized nothing but the dark smooth beech-trunks with the snow heaped about their roots. Hedhinaz shivered in the stillness, he wished he could hear some wood-sounds, even the wind through the trees. It seemed to him as if he and his hound were walking through a dead land, where the twisted roots lay beneath the snow like winter-frozen adders, the dark branches above still as thin bones in the howe.

He reached carefully down to pat the dog's head, cold fingers seeking the warmth under the snow-crystals melting in its thick gray fur, then, without thinking, bent lower still. When Hedhinaz straightened, he held a solid knob of gray-black flint in his left hand, the ripple-marks of its breaking smooth and hard against his palm. He did not know why, but it seemed to him that he felt better for holding the stone. Hedhinaz was about to turn and go back up the path when the hound suddenly stiffened, pointing its nose forward and barking sharply three times.

"Sa, easy boy," he murmured, his right hand tightening on the hilt of his sword. His eyes flickered around quickly, but he saw nothing move, and heard nothing. What he could not outfight, he might outrun, but the beech-trunks were too smooth for easy climbing, and Hedhinaz had most often been at weapons-practice or listening to his father, Sigislinthon, and Attalae talk while the other boys were climbing trees.

The hound had begun to shiver. Hedhinaz drew his sword, waiting. He heard it before he saw it. A wind-rustling through the branches, then a low howl crawling cold up the back of his spine, as the dog lifted his nose and whined. Hedhinaz tightened his hand on the flint, the sharp edges pressing painfully into his flesh. At first it seemed to Hedhinaz that a thick whirl of gray snow was blowing down the path towards him. Then he saw the red coal-glow of eyes, and the shapes suddenly leapt into clearness around them. Before him rode a huge gray-clad woman, the top of her head brushing against the high beech-branches, and the wind of her riding blew the snow away behind her.

Her hoar-streaked black braids, coarse as horse-hair, writhed around her misshapen face, coiling over her wide pointed ears and trailing out behind. Her skin was gray-green as moldy bread, she rode on a great wolf, whose red eyes glowed palm-broad and whose mouth dripped thin rivers of white froth. A pair of wyrms twisted over the wolf's neck as her reins, she held their heads in one hand, stretching the other out towards Hedhinaz. Herwawardhaz's son lifted his sword, holding the iron up between them. The troll-woman laughed, her high sharp voice searing through his head like a spike of white-hot bronze.

Her teeth were jagged as rock-tips showing black through the froth that seethed in her mouth-cave.

"Will you have me follow you, Hedhinaz?" She called. "Will you have me follow you?"

"No!" He answered. He raised his flint in the other hand, ready to cast it at her.

She laughed again, but Hedhinaz could see the dark blood-tears spilling from her glowing eyes, scattering to threads of hissing steam in the snow as she tossed her hair back. "You shall pay the geld for that, tonight at the oath-draught!" The troll-woman cried. She pulled sharply on the left wyrm, the wolf reared, beating at the snow-white air with his black claws, and whirled about, his hind legs kicking up a great cloud of flakes that hid the two of them from Hedhinaz's sight.

Something pushed against Hedhinaz's thigh, he nearly cried out, jumping away and striking down with his fist. His knuckles just grazed the hide of the dog, which sat looking up at him in bewilderment.

"Come on," Hedhinaz said, roughening his voice to hide its shaking. "It's getting dark, and we must be back to start the Yule feasting." He sheathed his sword, but still held tight to the piece of flint in his left hand as they walked back along the path.

Hedhinaz did his best to laugh and be merry at the feast, singing with a full voice when he led the train out through the snow to put porridge and meat and ale on Herwamundaz's howe and shucking his cloak to take his turn in the wrestling between the two fire pits, but when he was not thinking hard on gladness, the troll-woman's voice sounded sharp in his skull again. Though he could not hear her words clearly, or remember quite what she had said, and the broad eyes of her wolf glowed without light behind his lids whenever he blinked.

"What ails you, Hedhinaz?" Hrotharikijaz asked him. The young thane he was only a few years older than Hedhinaz, punched his drighten lightly on the shoulder, bloodshot blue eyes peering closely into Hedhinaz's face. "Too much ale already? That's fine strong stuff Hoilogae's wife brewed for us, all right, but I'd thought you'd learned to hold it by now."

"It's not the ale," Hedhinaz answered absently. He glanced down at the horn in his hand, he could still see the firelight shining from the dark draught halfway down its curve.

"Still brooding over the old man?"

"Hlothawairaz?" Hedhinaz had spoken without thought, he thrust thumb through fist, warding off ill-luck.

"Him," Hrotharikijaz agreed, touching the lump of raw amber that hung beneath his scraggly brown beard. His gaze flicked towards the door, but no knock sounded. "It wasn't your fault, you couldn't have known that he meant to slay himself so. Poor old man, I don't think any of us could have helped him."

"No. No, nothing is troubling me."

"Well, if the ale's not at fault, perhaps you need to drink more of it." Hrotharikijaz waved to Keradwinia. "Hai! Over here, the drighten needs drink."

The southern woman finished pouring for Thonarabrandaz and carried her pitcher over to Hedhinaz, leaning against his shoulder like a friendly hound as she poured his horn full again. Hedhinaz put his arm around her, hugging her lightly to him and patting her soft cropped hair, but her warmth did not soothe him now, as it often did in the nights.

Keradwinia smiled up at him, firelight sparkling in her hazel eyes. "You should be merrier," she said, low and teasing. "What has a fine man like you, and fro over a good land and folk, to look so strange about?"

Hedhinaz smiled back at her. "Nothing, I hope."

At midnight, Dagastiz and Harigastiz led in the best boar of the herd, the heavy muscles of their shoulders straining as they held him before the high seat. Wulfahaidhaz bore in the gold-bound hof horn, filled with pure honey-mead from the one pot of that brew Swaebhon had been able to make, she stood on Hedhinaz's other side as each of the folk came up to lay one hand on the boar's head and the other on the horn, speaking an oath and setting the words with a sip of mead.

As fro in the hall, Hedhinaz spoke last, taking the horn from Wulfahaidhaz and raising it high in his right hand, resting the other on the herd-boar's sharp bristles. He paused a moment, looking about the firelit hall, at all the pale faces turned towards him. He could hear the wood crackling beneath the fire's jaws, the soft breathing of the folk around him and the little sounds of Hrabanahildioz's baby daughter suckling at her breast beneath her dark fall of hair. The wind was rising outside, he could hear its low howl about the gables as a sprinkling of snow swirled in through the smoke hole. It seemed to him that the same cold breath blew through his own body, he had to swallow hard to keep the froth from spilling over his lips as he spoke.

"I swear this oath, by the bristles of the boar and the holy draught, that I shall have Swaebhon the daughter of Aiwilimae, the wife of Hoilogae my brother, for my own bride!" Hedhinaz cried, and before he could stop to hear his own words, he had drunken the last swallow of mead from the hallowed horn.

The boar's tether dropped from Dagastiz's limp hand, Harigastiz grasped quickly at the twisted ring in the swine's nose to keep him from breaking free. Hrotharikijaz sat down suddenly on one of the benches, and Hrabana-hildioz's child began to wail. Hedhinaz glanced about the hall. Some of the folk turned their gazes away, but more stared in horror, the firelight casting red gleams over the shadowed darkness of their eyes.Slowly, like bale creeping through his veins, Hedhinaz knew what he had done, and it ate into him swift as fire eating pitch and dry branches. He could not stand there within the ring of folk any longer, he broke and ran, bursting out into the snow-filled night with no thought other than that he must make his way south along the wilderness ways, southward to find Hoilogae.

After the midnight hallowing, when the youngest and the oldest of his folk had gone to sleep, Hoilogae crept out to the bath-house where Sigislinthon still sat by Swaebhon. He had brought his mother her share of the feast earlier, now he carried only a pitcher of ale.

"She still breathes, nothing has changed," his mother murmured to him. She took the pitcher from his hand, filling her little ale-pot and his horn.

"If you'd like to go in, I'll stay here till sunrise," Hoilogae offered.

"I think that would be all right. I'll come back out before first light."

Once or twice during the long night, Hoilogae felt his eyelids drooping, but some far-off sound, either the wind or a wolf-howl he could not tell which called him back to full wakefulness. Swaebhon did not move, and her skin was cold, though Sigislinthon had spread several blankets over her. Only by laying his head against her heart could Hoilogae tell that she was still alive.

Hoilogae's head was beginning to droop down again when something rustled in the darkness, jerking him up sharply. It was still dark, but the sky had cleared, he could see two icy stars through the door-crack.

"Hoilogae?" Swaebhon murmured, her voice very soft and weak. "Hoilo-gae, are you there?"

"I'm here. Are you all right?"

"I'm cold. Come here to me."

Hoilogae stripped off his tunic and crawled under the blankets to her at once, lying full-length beside her so that his warmth could soak into her. He reached down to the pitcher on the floor, shaking it to see if it was empty. There was still some ale left, Hoilogae held the pitcher to Swaebhon's mouth, tilting it carefully.

"My mother says our son is well and strong, though the birthing was hard."

"That's all right, then." Swaebhon yawned. "Will you stay with me while I sleep? I am very tired." She turned onto her side, curling up to nestle against him. Hoilogae held her as her breathing softened and deepened into the breaths of sleep, his heart easing with it. Though it was warm under the blankets now, and he lay comfortable, he knew that it would be no hard thing for him to keep the Yule-watch till dawn.

CHAPTER XXVII

Hair still wet from showering, Helgi had just come in from his Tuesday karate session and settled down to study when the phone rang.

"Ja? Hello?"

"Hello. Dr. Sachs?"

"Ach, Helgi, I am glad you are home at last. I have just had some bad family news my elder brother suffered a severe stroke this afternoon, and my sister Elisabeth and I must fly back to Wiesbaden to see him tomorrow. I am likely to be gone for at least a week, perhaps longer. In any case, I called because Elisabeth and I are holding two tickets for Die Walküre this Friday. I am sorry to miss it, James Morris is singing Wotan, and Gary Lakes is Siegmund. I thought that you could perhaps go in my place, with one of your friends. You have not seen Wagner live before, have you? Also, you shall begin with this. I would advise you to become familiar with the score before you go, though the Dallas Opera now shows English supertitles. I must leave early tomorrow, but I shall put the tickets in an envelope beneath my doormat."

"That's awfully nice of you, Dr. Sachs. I really am sorry about your brother."

"Ach, we all grow old. Those who live past youth. Sooner or later, well, it happens as it must. Pay the closest attention to James Morris. He is everything in a singer that you should wish to become, and Die Walküre is Wotan's opera. Then you shall tell me all about it when I come back."

"I'll do that, Dr. Sachs. Thank you."

Helgi went straight upstairs to call Karin as soon as he had hung up the downstairs phone.

"Captain Jensen speaking."

"Karin, are you free Friday evening?"

"I might be. What for?"

"I have two tickets to Die Walküre. I thought you might like to come with me."

The plastic of the receiver slick beneath Helgi's palm, his breath echoing loudly in his own ears as he waited for her answer.

"I know the story from the saga of the Völsungs, but it's not the same as Wagner's version, is it? I've never seen any of the Ring Cycle. I was off on maneuvers when the Met broadcast their performance, and I was so angry. Of course I'll come. What time does it start?"

"I'm not quite sure. I'll be able to tell you everything tomorrow."

"All right. Anyway, you've got a date."

Karin's jeep pulled up in front of Helgi's apartment at precisely five-thirty that Friday afternoon, its headlights bright through the gathering dusk. When she stepped out, Helgi saw that she was wearing a skirted uniform, three pins gleaming over the storm-blue curve of her left breast. Beneath her dark cap, her hair shone silver in the streetlight's white glow, and his valknútr was bright beneath her throat.

Helgi came out to meet her, touching his suit's breast-pocket to make sure that the tickets were still there. He wasn't sure whether to kiss Karin or clasp her hand, instead he hugged her lightly about the shoulders, as if she were his cousin. "Well, I'm ready to go. Is that your dress uniform?"

"It is. See, you've learned a lot about the Air Force already. I thought since we were going to the opera, I should wear my best, and I don't own any opera-going dresses."

"What constitutes an opera-going dress?" Helgi asked as they got into the jeep.

"Sequins. Lots of sequins, and maybe a few rhinestones and other glitter-things, but mostly sequins on black fabric. Dresses like that, however, are hard to find in my size. And besides, I haven't had a chance to go to the opera since I was a teenager, when, of course, I didn't want to. You don't mind that I'm in uniform, I'm sure." She revved the motor, backed out of the driveway and smoothly shifted to fling the jeep forward.

"Of course not. You look wonderful. I'm proud to be going out with you, Captain Jensen."

Karin glanced sideways at him as she rounded the corner. "You're not bad yourself, Helgi. Though the suit doesn't produce quite the effect I had in mind for you. Put you in a tunic and give you a sword, I'm sure you'd look far more like Siegmund ought to than any operatic tenor does."

"Hmm. Thanks. Though my singing teacher sent me to see Wotan, actually."

They had come to the access ramp for Central. Karin eased her foot's weight on the gas pedal a moment before bringing her leg down hard and sending them shooting out onto the freeway. "I'm not surprised. Wotan, Óðinn is the source of all song, after all. Do you remember reading that?"

"I remember him discovering the runes."

"Stealing the mead of poetry. Flying back to Asgard in the shape of an eagle, bearing the three draughts of mead he'd drunk."

As the memory came back to him, Helgi took up where Karin had left off. "Spewing them out into three vessels in the gods' courtyard, but a few drops fell outside the gates, and those anyone can claim. Those are the fool-poet's leavings."

Karin turned her head to smile at him a moment, grinning with the same night-breaking delight Helgi had seen on her face as she spoke of flying. "You do remember! I think you've gotten a full draught of Óðinn's mead, yourself, the songs on that tape are wonderful. Has your group ever thought about records?"

"No one's given us a chance to yet."

"I bet it won't be long, then. That was very clever of you, to use the Danish lyrics for "Valravnen" as background on that one song. I had to play it three times over before I realized why it sounded so familiar. Though pronouncing Danish is not so easy as you seem to think."

"Will you teach me how?" Helgi asked boldly.

"I'll be glad to."

Their seats were quite near the front, so that Karin and Helgi had to look up at the stage. The first thunderous torrent of strings caught Helgi by surprise. A waterfall of sound rushing suddenly over him, blinding as a spring thunderstorm. As he stared up at the dark stage, a deep green light began to brighten between shadowed tree-trunks. a man's figure ran desperately between them, dodging and turning, his outline twisting. From man to wolf and back again. Lightning flashed with the bright call of the brass, the runner's steps faltered, then quickened again. As the music slowed, the light brightened, till the fleeing man staggered within the doorposts of a hut, collapsing by the fire.

"Wes Herd dies auch sei, hier muß ich rasten!" Whoever's hearth this is, I must rest here! This man was Siegmund, Helgi knew, Wehwalt, the Wolfing, as he would name himself here in Hunding's hall, and the woman now gliding from behind the tree that held the hut's roof up was Sieglinde.

Helgi watched, awed and entranced, ravished by the music. By the end of the second act, he was crouching at the edge of his seat, fists clenched tightly on his crushed program as he stared up at the battle.

Siegmund and Hunding below, Wotan and Brünnhild above. Wotan stretched his spear down, crying, "Zurück vor dem Speer! In Stücken das Schwert!" Back from the spear! In pieces the sword! As Siegmund's sword shattered on its shaft and its point pierced the hero through. Wotan stared down at his son's body, the ancient sorrow, the death of his sons at his hands, his own steed bearing his slain kin over the wind-bridge to Walhall. Weighting his grim face before he turned the bale-glow of his one eye against the surviving warrior. Helgi could feel the god's burden heavy in his own throat as he silently whispered Wotan's slow words to Hunding.

"Geh hin, Knecht knie vor Fricka. Meld ihr, daß Wotan's Speer gerächt, was Spott ihr schufGeh!" Go hence, knave, kneel before Fricka. Tell her that Wotan's spear avenged what caused her shame. Go!

Helgi's gaze turned towards Karin as the lights came up. She sat sprawled against the back of her seat as though flying straight upward in her plane, her eyes wide and stunned. The clear tear-tracks over her white cheeks shone like mother-of-pearl in the auditorium lighting. Helgi gently put his hand over hers on the armrest between them. Karin's skin was very cold to his touch. She shook herself, sitting up straight and wiping the tears from her face with the back of her hand, and it was only then that Helgi realized that his own face was wet. Embarrassed, he took the handkerchief from his suit pocket and blew his nose.

"Wagner changed the story," Karin murmured, her voice husky as if she had been drinking akavit, "but the soul is still there."

Helgi cast about for something to say, but could think of no words that would describe what he had seen. The words and music had already been fully shaped.

"You felt it too, didn't you?" Karin asked. Helgi nodded. She stood up, straightening the skirt of her uniform and adjusting her beret. "Do you want something to drink?"

"I wouldn't mind." Helgi reached back for his wallet, but Karin waved the gesture away.

"No, my treat. You brought me here, after all, I should at least buy the drinks."

The opera house had saved their most spectacular effect for last. As Wotan struck his spear against the rock to summon up Loki, a flickering ring of fire-red light rose up around him, ringing the shapes of the god and the Valkyrie who slept enchanted at his feet. This close, Helgi could just see the clear weave that hung rippling before the stage, where the flames were being projected and brought to life, but knowing how it was done stole nothing from the whole, from the huge dark figure of Wotan, his wide-brimmed hat hanging low over one eye, standing in the ring of fire upon the crag with his spear raised high. As Wotan thundered out his last words, Helgi grasped Karin's hand, holding tightly to her. "Wer meines Speeres Spitze fürchtet, durchschreite das Feuer nie!" Who fears my spear-point shall never stride through the fire!

When they had finally made their escape from the clogged parking lot, Karin said, "Do you want to go straight home, or shall we stop somewhere for food? I'm hungry."

"So am I. What's open at this time of night?"

"Good question. No good answer. I guess Denny's is the least disgusting of the lot, and the one on Northwest serves drinkable coffee."

"What about Rof?" Helgi asked when they were sitting over their third coffee-refill.

"What about him?"

"Well, what's going on with him?"

Karin's eyes narrowed as she looked at Helgi. "I expect he's asleep. He doesn't normally stay up very late if he can help it. You speak German, don't you?"

"Pretty well. Why?"

"Was that really a very inferior translation on the overhead screen, or was it just my imagination? I thought I caught a lot of words that were almost the same as in Danish or Old Norse, but none of them showed up in the supertitles."

"Like what?"

"Some of Wotan's titles. I was sure I heard Brünnhild calling him Sigfödhr and Valfödhr."

"Siegvater, Walvater, Victory-Father, Father of the Slain. No, that wasn't translated."

"It's too bad, really." Karin tossed her head slightly, as though she still had long hair to shake out of her eyes. "Óðinn has so many names, and they all describe him perfectly. How many can you remember?"

Her challenge pricked Helgi's memory, spurring the names up from its depths. "Grímr and YggrHoar-Beard, Bale-Eyed, Blind All-Father, Masked One, Wand-Bearer, Lord of Ghosts. That's all."

"More than many people know. Spear-God, Lord of the Hanged, Song-Smith, Bale-Worker," Karin's voice trailed off. Then she looked straight into Helgi's eyes, her gaze blue-gray as light gleaming from a blade's edge. "You said that you had called on Óðinn."

"Yes. It was after," Slowly the story came forth from his mouth, like a winter-chilled snake edging carefully into the first light of spring. Karin listened, leaning forward slightly as Helgi spoke and nodding every so often.

"Óðinn's blessing indeed," she said gravely when he was done. "I had thought that you would be a good fighter. I am glad to know that I was right."

Helgi felt a sudden surge of bright blood rushing into his heart, swelling it with joy. "That was when I started reading about the runes. It was when, I felt touched by Wotan's spear."

"Yes. Just as you gave me the valknútr." Karin's hand moved to the sharp-edged triangles of her pendant as though she had touched it without thinking many times. "Now you know better what it means, but I knew then, and I wore it still, for I thought that Óðinn had touched you without your knowing it, even then." She looked down at her coffee cup, cradling it carefully in her long fingers, then set it firmly down on the table. "You know, Helgi, this has been a wonderful evening. Thank you very much."

"You're welcome. You really ought to thank my singing teacher's brother. If he hadn't had a stroke, we wouldn't have gotten those tickets."

"Then his ill-luck was good luck for us. But I'm so glad to have come. I wish I could," Karin's voice trailed off. Her eyes closed a moment, as though she looked at a shape shadowing from the darkness behind her lids. She spoke softly, and Helgi knew she was quoting something. "The pilot is of a race of men who since time immemorial have been inarticulate, who, through their daily contact with death, have realized, often enough unconsciously, certain fundamental things. It is only in the air that the pilot can grasp that feeling, that flash of knowledge, of insight, that matures him beyond his years, only in the air that he knows suddenly he is a man in a world of men. 'Coming back to earth' has for him a double significance. He finds it difficult to orient himself in a world that is so worldly, amongst a people whose conversation seems to him brilliant, minds agile, and knowledge complete, yet a people somehow blind. It is very strange," She coughed. "Well, give your teacher my thanks when you see him again, and best wishes for his brother's recovery."

Karin drove slowly back towards base, still dazed by the music ringing through her mind and the sight of the broad-hatted, cloaked shape standing tall and black against the flickering flames of Brünnhilde's rock, his spear lifted high, its shadow stretching out over the whole stage. The words of the Edda came unbidden to her mind. Sigurðr rode up on Hind's Fell and turned southward towards Frankland. He saw a great light on the fell, as if fire burned and lighted up to heaven. How fair it is to see it in Miðgarðr! Karin thought. Even if only on the stage. She was not the only one whose heart had moved, she could still feel the crushing grip of Helgi's calloused hand on her own, and remember how his pale cheeks had glimmered when the lights came up. It seemed to her that there was something in the striving of his music that was akin to what she had heard that night.

Karin tramped down hard on her brake just before she went through the red light, the jeep's tires screaming beneath her as they spun to a stop. And am I so shallow, that I can break up with Rof just because Helgi is such a good musician? A musician who is also Asatro in his heart, if he does not know enough to name himself so yet, who remembers some of the names of Óðinn, with the god's mead singing in his voice as he speaks them? A skald and a warrior, who has slain his man in fight already? Rof also knew a few of Óðinn's names, Karin remembered him saying, "Yo' High One, the Grimyo' Hoar-Beardyo' One-Eye" and now that she thought of it, she could not ever remember Rof speaking the name of Óðinn, or looking straight at the god's picture on her wall.

Still, he loved her. Karin thought of Rof's big hands caressing her body, gentle and thorough with the same care he put into polishing her plane and seeing to each of its parts in turn. She in the air, and he on the earth. For the last six months, she had thought she could not have asked for more. Taking off had felt like Rof swinging her suddenly upwards, her weight so light to his strength that she might have been made of mist, and landing had been like coming into the solid grasp of his arms again. If he had asked her to marry him before Helgi had spoken to her, if he had been willing to leave the Air Force for her, but then there would have been nothing between them but themselves, the first link between them sundered. Karin did not know what she should do, but she was sure that she must make her choice soon. If she drew it out too long, it was sure to shatter one of her men, and neither of them had earned that suffering. It was almost two in the morning when Karin opened the door of her apartment, but she was not yet sleepy. She put Helgi's tape into her little music box and turned it on, plugging in her headphones so that she wouldn't wake up the neighbors, some of those poor bastards might be on duty tomorrow, after all.

Opening the door of the little refrigerator by her bed, she stared at her choices. She almost always ate in the officer's mess, so the only food in there was a slightly moldy piece of cheese, surrounded by bottles of Elephant beer and a lone, half-empty carton of skimmed milk. After a little thought, she pulled out a beer, letting herself sink into Helgi's song as she slowly poured the frothing draught into the drinking horn she had bought at Scarborough Faire that last June. It was his solo, the one that began with the chorus of "Valravnen""Witch's son, be watchful! / Will you loose blood-spilling? / Will you woo her Hel-runes, / Wodan's keen spear boding?"

Helgi is using a skald's alliteration, a true Norse form of poetry, in this song, Karin suddenly realized. Internal rhyme instead of end-rhyme, as close to proper dróttkvætt form as he could get in English. I wonder if he knows, if he did it on purpose? Then she thought a little more closely on the words, and her hand tightened suddenly on the horn's smooth surface. There is troll-craft in his voice, he is singing a spell! And it had to be against Rof, whose mother was a witch-woman, who would surely know what Helgi was saying, if no one else did. That must have taken no little bravery, but Karin had seen it in Helgi's eyes at the pizza place. He had no fear of the bigger man, and she knew that she would never see his gaze shifting away from her when she spoke of Óðinn. It was no little thing, to find a man who both shared her belief that the gods of her kin were real and mighty, and had the bravery to trust in the darkest of them, the Father of the Slain. Enn ec sagðac hanom, at ec strenðac heit þar í mót at giptaz öngom þeim manni, er hroeðaz kynni, but I said to him, that I had sworn an oath in turn never to wed any man, who knew how to be afraid. Sigrdrifa's words.

The Valkyrie had spoken thus to Óðinn, so that he set the fire about her rock, which only Sigurðr, Siegfried might pass.

"Jeg har vælged," Karin said aloud, I have chosen and tilted her horn to drink. She brushed her fingertips over the smooth silver of her valknútr, and a cold shiver tingled through her body. Helgi had bound her with the knot of the slain years ago, long before he seemed to be anything to her but the neighbors' child. Now she was not sure which of them was the chooser, and which the chosen, but there was no doubt in her heart as to how it must end. She looked across at the gray-white gleam of Óðinn's face against the picture's black background, the brightness of his single eye staring at her.

Far worse, never to have found her hero. From the moment she had sworn her oath to the Air Force, she had taken up her own death, and if it came with such joy, Óðinn had truly blessed her. The Jensens' Yule party started early, and the last exam that Helgi had to supervise and collect papers from ended late. It was almost six-thirty by the time he escaped from the classroom and made his way to the parking lot. Although the cool weather had been making it cranky lately, Helgi's Impala started without any trouble. He drove with the window rolled down, letting the wind brush his hair back as if he were riding a motorcycle bare-headed. He was not surprised to see the Jensens' block lined with cars. He had to thread his way twice through the tangle of one-way streets around their house before he could find a parking place.

The Air Force jeep was parked in front of the Jensens' house. Remembering how Karin had leapt out of the bushes at him before, Helgi walked more warily, ready for her attack, but no attack came. When Helgi lifted his hand to knock on the door, it opened before him as though the wind of his gesture had swung it back. Karin stood in the doorway before him with a glass of frothy white eggnog in her right hand, the sound of harp music shimmering out around her. Her left hand was adorned with a sun-spangled piece of amber set in a band of gold knot work. The valknut's silver points gleamed against her creamy skin within the half-round of her white blouse's low neckline, her red skirt fell just past the backs of her knees, leaving her taut calves bare above sandals of woven black leather. A tinge of indigo glimmered on her eyelids, brightening the light gray of her eyes to silver-blue dawn, but she wore no other makeup.

"Hilsen, min helt," she said, handing him the eggnog. "Come and be welcome at our feast."

Helgi took the glass from her hand, drinking as he crossed the threshold. The brandy's strength burned through the cool cream and sweetness, sinking into his empty stomach. He glanced around the room, but Rof's shape loomed nowhere in the candle-light, nor did his broad shoulders spread shadowy above the back of chair or sofa. Except for Olaf, who stood by the mantel twisting the legs of one of the straw goats to make it stand more steadily, Helgi seemed to be the largest person in the room.

Karin leaned forward, brushing her lips swiftly across his. Helgi did not feel the shock he had expected at her touch. Rather, it was as though her kiss opened something far within him, like a well-digger suddenly breaking through the roof of a deep underground river to let the sweet cold water rise slowly into daylight. Helgi stepped forward, but she did not move back, and then his arms were around Karin, binding her to him. Her breasts pressed softly against his chest, he could feel the lithe muscles of her back and shoulders beneath her linen blouse.

Karin looked closely into his eyes as they kissed again, their gazes mingling with their breath.

"Merry Yule," she murmured.

"As merry as I could have hoped," Helgi answered. "I think I've just gotten the year's finest gift."

"Oh, no, there's more to come. Ah, but what have you brought with you? One gift always looks for another, you know."

Helgi let go of her with one hand, slapping himself lightly on the forehead. "I left the presents in the car. I guess I was thinking of something else."

"Really." Karin grinned, and clasped hands with him as they went out the door together. The back of hers felt satiny beneath his fingers, but her palm was as hard as his, ridged with lines of callouses.

As they were carrying the boxes back to the house, Karin stopped by the door of her jeep. "Helgi, why don't we drive down to Highland Park and look at the Christmas lights? I haven't gone to see them this year, and I'd like to."

"So would I. You want to go in and tell them where we're going?"

"They'll never notice we're gone."

Karin drove as fast and easily as she flew, speeding down Central Expressway to Mockingbird.

"Careful how you drive here," Helgi said, looking fondly over at her. "This is not exactly a Highland Park vehicle, and I bet the streets are crawling with cops at this time of year."

"We won't have any trouble. You know, if you reached under the seat there, you just might find something nice."

Helgi reached down till his fingers met a smooth curve of plastic, pulled out a thermos. He unscrewed the cap and sniffed it. Hot chocolate, freely dosed with peppermint schnapps. "You planned this!" He accused her, delighted. "You knew"

"I did," Karin admitted, smiling back at him.

Though he knew the sound of his words might bring the avalanche down on him, Helgi could not keep himself from asking, "Why me?"

"Lots of reasons. You are you. You sing what I would sing if I could write songs, you have the voice and the words to speak my thoughts for me. You're not afraid to speak the name of Óðinn. You don't want to protect me from myself, and mainly," she reached out and squeezed his shoulder, "because I love you, Helgi. And that is something I came to know, which is just because it is."

The two of them drove slowly down the side streets where rainbows of light blinked from each law, outlining the branches of trees and the eaves of houses. Helgi and Karin passed the chocolate back and forth between them, occasionally leaning across to kiss between sips. Some of the light displays were appallingly gaudy. One yard had not only a Santa and sleigh on a lawn full of fake snow, but a giant Christmas tree surrounded by tool-wielding elves, a fake snowman with blinking eyes, and the words 'HAPPY HOLIDAY SEASON' strobing in red and green bulbs on the roof, but some were sheerly beautiful, sprays and swirls of colored lights glowing in trees and along roofs like frozen auroras.

As they got closer to Southern Methodist University, the displays grew smaller, but more tasteful, until Karin stopped in front of a duplex within sight of the university.

"This one is my favorite," she said softly. "They do this every year."

The house had not caught Helgi's eye at first, but now he looked more closely at it. A small pine tree stood in front of a diamond-paned window like the one in Helgi's own living room. The tree was adorned with pure white lights, which glimmered again as a myriad of bright points from each of the little glass panes behind it. Behind the window, bright against deep blue curtains, were an array of clear ornaments. Little crystal boars and goats, ringed with different sorts of crystal snowflakes, hung against the window, and a row of crystal animals sat along the windowsill. At each end of the sill was a large piece, a peaked slab of crystal, carved in inverse relief from behind. The one on the right showed a swan rising from the reeds, a wolf looked from the one on the left. The fine texturing of the swan's feathers, the wolf's eyes and the highlights of its fur, glimmered icy white in the light of the pine's star-points. Helgi unbuckled his shoulder-belt, sliding over to put his arm around Karin. Entranced together, they stared at the lights and the crystal.

"Do you want to go down to Turtle Creek now?" Karin whispered to him. Helgi nodded, moving reluctantly back to his seat and buckling himself in again as Karin started the jeep. They drove along past the creek for a while, until they had come to a place where no cars were passing and trees shielded the road from the streetlights, then Karin parked the jeep and unbuckled her own belt.

"There's more room in the back. Come on," She turned the jeep's internal lights on for a moment, Helgi saw the blankets and pillows spread out in back before the lights went out again. Together they crawled back in the darkness, limbs entangling in their clothes as they began to undress each other. Helgi could feel the strength beneath Karin's velvety skin, the heat of her silk-veiled nipples against his bare chest and her lips on his neck. She unzipped his jeans and tugged them halfway down, shaken by the pleasure of her caresses, Helgi swiftly unbuttoned her skirt, stroking his hands along her silky flanks.

"I love you, Karin," Helgi murmured. "I've always loved you. Oh, Karin," It was his own words that came to him now, as he tasted the mint-chocolate in her mouth, then the light salty flavor of her skin. Sun spear through clouds, burn rainbow-fire, swan-white, the brightening brand lifts higher.

Karin pulled Helgi closer, opening to him in the darkness and drawing him in. The song rang in his skull as he thrust into her, rising high to thrill along every nerve in his body like fire bursting along pitch-streaks through dry wood. Sleeping, now wakened, never forsaken, dawn's glow for gloaming but once mistaken.

"Helgi, Helgi!" Karin cried out, clasping him more tightly with legs and arms. Sun spears through sky, the rainbow growing, bridge of air-brightness, its flames fair-glowing.

"I love you, Karin. Karin, my love!" Choosing that trying, harsh raven-crying, short life more shining for brave dying.

Karin and Helgi did not roll away from each other when they were done, but lay together, stroking each other's bodies as the light dew of sweat chilled on their skins. At last Karin sat up, fumbling through their cast-off clothes for a moment.

"Ah, here it is."

"What?"

"My Yule present to you. Give me your hand."

Helgi stretched out his left hand to her. She took it in both of her own, slipping something onto his fourth finger. He could feel the weight of the gold at once. Drawing his hand back to touch the ring, he felt the intertwining of knot work strands around the smooth warmth of amber.

"This is the mate to yours, isn't it?"

"They belonged to my great-grandparents."

Helgi clasped her left hand in his so that their rings touched. "Karin, I swear that I will hold you in my heart above everything, and give my life and love to you freely. You are my dream and my waking, my death and my life, hard-bought and yet well-bought. My songs are yours with the soul that speaks in them, as long as the world lasts." He reached up to touch the valknútr's warm metal with his other hand. "If this is Wotan's mark, let him hear. I think that I first touched your heart with it, and so I know no fairer sign."

Helgi heard Karin's soft choking breath, the tears warming her voice as she whispered, "Helgi, min helt, I swear that I will be true to you, that my life and love are yours, as long as you will have them. Blessed with victory and blessed with love, whether life or death befall us both." She wrapped her right hand around Helgi's fingers and the valknútr. "Wotan, Óðinn, Sigfather, Valfather. However we call him, let him hear the love we have found, which shall not wane nor pass away."

CHAPTER XXIX

Hailgi straightened his back, shaking his sickle clean of the stalk-shreds that clung to the blade's long curve. Though his ribs had been healed almost a year, they still ached sometimes, and now the storm-warning pain was twisting harder and harder in his side. He pressed his hand against his ribcage, staring up at the sky. The clouds rose high before him, long pale battle-banners stretching out from the north ahead of the towering gray sky-army bearing down over the sea towards the land. It was well that the harvest was almost done, Hailgi thought. He looked over the stretch of sheared brown stubble, the last of his fields. Arnugrimar was still swinging his scythe, his wife Gunthadis binding the sheaves behind him, Hildiwulfar stood in the stubble, his heavy arms crossed on his chest beneath the spread of his gray-blond beard and sweat-sheened face set in the look of a man who has done his share, Dagar wiped his tunic's sleeve over his forehead before he bent again to scoop up an armload of grain-bundles.

Around the field, the other men and women were straightening as Hailgi had done, stretching off the strain of a long day bent swinging the sickle, or going to cast their sheaves onto the high-heaped wagon by the roadside. One gold-brown clump of wheat still stood in the middle of the field, the sharp-headed stalks swaying close together like a last squadron of spearmen raising their weapons amid a slain host. As the cloud-veils shifted, a thin plane of sunlight slanted down through them, brightening a long stripe of brown stubble and gilding the heads of the last standing sheaf against the deep blue clouds in the northern sky. Beside Hailgi, Sigiruna bent to sweep the last stalks up in her arms, binding them together in a swift neat movement and knotting her string tight. Bits of dry grass and grain furred her pale gray dress all over, sticking out along her long braid like thick hair-ends, a few had even gotten stuck in the twisted cords of her belt. Two darker gray spots showed over her nipples. Her breasts had been very full for a first bearing, and, though little Sigismundar fed as heartily as a child of good kin should, they often leaked between feedings.

Sigiruna glanced over at the sky's edge, at the far-off glimmers of lightning flickering where the clouds hung darkest above the sea. "There's good time to cut the last sheaf, and get the wain under cover before the storm reaches us, I think," she said.

Hailgi helped his wife gather her last stack of sheaves, carrying them over to the wagon. The two bay draft horses harnessed to it flicked their ears against the flies, shifting their hooves and widening their nostrils to shift the air. They would have a full burden to pull. The harvest had been very rich that year, so that it seemed to Hailgi that Wodhanar had not been ill-pleased with the share given at last summer's end. The other folk in the field were already gathering into a ring around the last sheaf. Arnugrimar's daughter Guntharun hung back behind the others, pulling her skirts more tightly around her stocky hips and gazing sideways at the clump of standing grain, her thick pale brows drawn close. The other unmarried women stayed back with her. Skegga-Grimar's twins Sigiborg and Thonaragardhar stood with their arms about each other's slender waists like two birch trees growing from one stump, Ingwahildar stood alone, blue eyes turned towards the ground as she pushed a tangle of dark hair back from her narrow face.

If one of them should stumble and brush against the stalks, she would never marry. Hailgi had heard that in the wild North, maidens were sometimes still given to the Last Sheaf in marriage, and sometimes ploughed into the ground when the harvest had been bad. When I see Sinfjotli again, if he can ever spare time from his new bride to come down to Jutland again. I must ask him if that was so in Gautland, Hailgi thought.Hailgi stepped into the ring of folk, laying his left hand upon the last sheaf and drawing in his breath to speak as he raised his scythe. Then he saw the strange man walking through the shorn field towards them. A tall hoar-bearded man clad in rough brown wool, his gray cloak drawn tightly around him against the sharpening wind and his staff thumping on the earth in an even rhythm between his footfalls.

"Is Hailgi Hunding's-Bane among you?" The man called. "The frowe Berg-ohildar said I should find him."

"I am Hailgi Hunding's-Bane," Hailgi shouted back. "Come here, and tell me what you have to say."

Hildiwulfar and Skald-Thonarabrandar moved apart from each other, letting the graybeard into the circle. As the man came closer, Hailgi saw that he was not so old. Though the skin showing between his thick curly tangle of gray hair and gray beard was weathered and pocked, no crows' feet gripped the corners of his dark eyes, and he strode through the stubble with the strength of a young man, raising a hand in greeting.

"Hail, Hailgi. I am called Epli-Karl, I have come from the Saxon lands, from the hall of the Walsings."

"Do you have news of Sinfjotli?" Hailgi broke in. "Do you bring a message from him?"

Epli-Karl's thick brows drew inward, he shook his head. "I have heard that you were his friend, I fear my news will not gladden you. Sinfjotli the son of Sigimund the Walsing is dead. He was poisoned by Sigimund's wife Borghild, in revenge for her brother Hlothawairar whom he slew to win Sigrid of Frisia as his bride." A drift of cloud passed over the Sun, shadowing the stranger for a moment before her light shone full again.

"Poisoned?" Hailgi echoed. No, that could not be. He remembered how Sinfjotli had laughed with the adder dangling from his palm, swinging it like a child's play-whip. "The Walsings."

"I shall tell you how it happened. I was not there, but I have heard it from one who was, the Alamannic skald Paltwini." Epli-Karl waved his arms as he spoke, as though he were shaping his words from the air, his tale moving his whole body. He did not smile, but his eyes were bright and his voice strong. "Sigimund had readied a great funeral arvel for Hlothawairar, and a great were-gild to be paid to Borghild, heaps of gold and amber, fine cloth and furs. When the first of the toasts to the gods was drunk, she bore Sinfjotli's horn to him, but he looked sadly into it and would not drink to Wodhanar or Thonarar. He spoke softly, but men who were standing near thought that he might have said that the ale was bespelled. Sigimund seized it from him," Epli-Karl grasped a great handful of air," and drank it off in one draught, he took no harm from it.

At the second hornful, Sinfjotli spoke more loudly, and was heard to say that the drink was full of deceit, and he thought he should not drink ale brewed with hate. Borghild wept then, and said that he meant to shame her, but Sigimund took the horn and drank it dry, and said that there would be no talk of shame. The last toast was to Hlothawairar, and Borghild dared Sinfjotli to drink, saying that if he would not, he would show that he did not have the brave mood of the Walsings. Still Sinfjotli looked into the horn as if he saw some ill in it, and said that the ale was muddied. Sigimund had drunk a great deal, his son's share as well as his own, and he cried then, so that everyone could hear, "Let your beard filter it, my son!" And Sinfjotli drank then, and he fell down dead before the horn was empty, without a mark on him. Sigimund lifted the body in his arms, and bore it out of the hall. He was gone a long time, and when he came back he was alone, and no mound was ever raised or bale-fire set for his son."

"That was not the death he deserved," Hailgi said slowly. "He was a warrior, the best I have ever known, and never unfriendly with Wodhanar. He ought to have died in battle, it is ill that the last branch of the clan-ash fell to a kinswoman's treachery. How could this have come to pass so?"

"Just as I have said. His wyrd was full-reded, as often, it struck where his might could not ward him."

Hailgi looked down at the sheaf of dry grain bunched together in his grasp, then up at the purple-blue northern sky. The rising clouds had covered the Sun's light now, shadowing the whole field, very faint and far, the thunder rumbled soft over the sea. His ribs were throbbing as though they had broken anew. If Sinfjotli's strength could not save him, there was naught to be trusted but Wyrd, and the life-threads of lightning gilding the blue clouds now seemed thinly spun. Arnugrimar coughed meaningfully, rubbing at the little wart on the side of his nose as he, too, looked over at the flickering lightning rising from the sky's edge. Whatever was in Hailgi's heart, the grain needed to be brought into the storehouse soon, or there would be that much less ale for the springtime feasting.

Hailgi raised his scythe-hand again to fell the last sheaf, then the blood-dark tide swept up through him, casting his head back and crushing the dry stalks beneath his fingers. He could not shape his howl into words, though it tore raven-clawed at the back of his throat, but he raised his grisly song of woe to the gray-swept sky's roof. The dry stubble rustled as the folk stepped away from him, Hailgi saw Skald-Thonarabrandar's eyes wide and black in his pale face, Sigiborg's knuckles pressed white against her mouth. A flush brightened the high bones of Dagar's cheeks as he stumbled back from Hailgi's cry, but he stared at the Wolfing as if daring him to some deed. Sigiruna alone did not move. Her cloud-gray eyes seemed ready to spill tears, but she did not blink the water free, only gazed at Hailgi. He saw her lips moving, murmuring something, but his own voice drowned her words like thunder drowning the whisper of rain.

Hailgi's eyes were still dry when the rough echo of his shout no longer sounded over the field, he did not know when, or how, he should be able to weep. Instead he brought his scythe around in a great sweeping curve, cutting a clean arc between the grain-heads and the earth. From now till planting time, these fields belonged to no living folk. Wodhanar would lead his raging host over them, or Thonarar might hunt thurse-maids through the dead stalks and snow, but no human would tread there in the winter-time. Hailgi stared at the last sheaf raised high in his hand, golden against the dark sky.

The wheat-heads looked like a cluster of plaits to him, long braids trailing off into the swift-fading afterimage of lightning through the clouds. Sigiruna had told him that the Skjoldings shaped the last sheaf into a man, and bore him in from the fields, for Ingwe-Freyjar watched kindly over the holy kings of his kin. But in Jutland, the sheaf was always left outside for Wodhanar's winds to take. The Wolfings' ruler ever knew the gift he must make to his clan-god, though the rough grain might stand in his stead for a time.

"Wodhanar," Hailgi said, letting the old words carry him on, though his voice clanged hollow and harsh in his ears. "Wodhanar, have this fodder for your steed. One year thistle and thorn, the next year better grain." He thrust the sickle into his belt, holding out his hand for the cord that Sigiruna pressed into it, a threefold plait of black, white, and red threads. A lightning-thread of gold glimmered bright along its length. The pale gold of Sigiruna's hair, woven to brighten the strand as the Norns brightened the length of a hero's life.

Hailgi wound the cord slowly about the last sheaf, knotting it tightly again and again. His bonds would have to hold through the winter, lying beneath the storm-dark sky for the ravens to peck and tear at. His first grief-wod had faded already, leaving a still heaviness upon him like a heap of stones and earth. Only when Hailgi had laid the last sheaf on the ground did he see the dark blood staining its dry stalks. He looked at his left hand in dull surprise. The scythe's sharp point had nicked him deeply, slicing down at the base of his left forefinger to leave a little flap of skin hanging free against his palm and the blood pouring down his hand to spatter on the grain and the dark earth below it. He clenched his fist tightly, striding from the field. Behind him, he could hear the swishing of the others moving through the dry stalks like a storm wind, the first drops of rain were spattering down by the time he had reached the wagon. He leapt up to the driver's seat, gathering the reins and slapping them against the horses' necks to urge them forward.

At the door of the last storehouse to be filled, all worked as fast as they could, Epli-Karl along with Hailgi's folk, hurrying to get the grain inside as the sparse raindrops thickened. Arnugrimar and Guntharun leapt up beside Hailgi to cast the bundles of grain down to the others, who cast them through the storehouse door. There would be time to stack them neatly later. Hailgi pressed his wounded hand against the side of his tunic now and again to keep from bleeding on the grain, the dark wool hid the stain of his blood. As Hailgi flung the last bundle to Dagar and straightened up again, a huge spear-shot of lightning flashed overhead, blinding him.

Hailgi blinked the light away, counting three breaths before the thunder rattled the wood beneath his feet, and jumped down to the ground again. Something struck him on the head, and again. Still dazzled, he looked back over the brown fields. The gray veil of rain had suddenly frozen to a white torrent of hail rattling down through the dry grasses, sharp as the hoof beats of a host of tiny riders. Sigiruna grasped Hailgi's hand, pulling him along towards the hall. Her rough touch hurt, but he bore it without complaining, lengthening his stride to keep pace with her. Long-legged as he was, Epli-Karl matched their speed easily, on Hailgi's other side, Dagar turned his face up to the sky as he ran, the little ice-stones catching in his tangled hair.

When they had passed the threshold-pillars, Sigiruna looked at her bloodied palm and shook her head. "It must soon be time for you to do battle again." She glanced up at Hailgi's mother, who stood by the doorway with a pitcher. "Bergohildar, would you like to bear the ale, or would you rather tend to your son?"

Bergohildar's plait-crowned head moved from side to side like a heavy bloom swaying on a slender stalk. "If you let him hurt himself, he's yours to take care of." She smiled up at her wedding-daughter. "Your Siggi has been howling, he's asleep now, but you'll need to feed him soon."

The food was already set out on the long tables. It was not the best feast-fare, that they would not have until Winter nights, when they slaughtered the beasts that were too weak to live through the winter, but it was good enough for hungry harvesters. a thick stew, with smoked fish and leeks, plenty of buttered bread to mop it up with and ale to wash the meal down with.

"Come up and sit beside us," Hailgi said to Epli-Karl. "I would hear more of what you have to tell."

"Ah, there is not so much, really," the young graybeard said, but he came to the head of the table all the same, settling himself between Hailgi and Dagar and beginning to eat with a good will. Sigiruna sat down on Hailgi's other side with a bowl of water and a long strip of linen, taking his hand in both of hers and beginning to wash the blood from it as Hailgi spooned stew into his mouth with the other hand. He could hear the hailstones rattling down the thatched roof, a sharper sound than the pattering of rain. Winter shall be upon us soon, Hailgi thought.

"What of Sigimund?" Sigiruna asked while she worked. "What has he done with Borghild? Was Sinfjotli avenged by any means?"

"I have heard," Epli-Karl said, his mouth half-full, "that Sigimund did her no harm, but sent her straight back," he waved his piece of bread over the table, "to her father's hall. In spite of his age, Sigimund is looking for," he traced a pair of rounded curves in the air with both hands, "who can bear him children and he has sent his men out through all the northern lands in this search. At least, that was what Paltwini told me. He was about to leave for his homeland on that same errand, to see if there were any fit women southward along the Roman marches."

A high wail rose from behind the door as Sigiruna tied Hailgi's bandage tightly and cut the unused length of linen free with her belt-knife. She sighed, standing up. "Don't tell them any more news while I'm gone," she ordered the wanderer, pointing her knife at him before she sheathed it again and went back into the chamber she and Hailgi shared.

Dagar leaned forward over the table. "Do men say anything else of Sinfjot-li, or his death?" The Skjolding youth asked. "Was he greatly mourned?" No edge cut through the smooth tones of his high voice, but it seemed to Hailgi that he could see the iron gleaming in Dagar's blue eyes. The youth was well able to hide his thoughts, but Hailgi knew that Epli-Karl's words had gladdened him, even as news of Hailgi's own death would have. Ingwe-Frey-jar's bright boar is also an eater of the dead, Hailgi thought. It seemed to him for a moment that he could see the mighty-tusked battle-beast snuffling through the earth of a shallow woodland grave, and the chill he felt was damp as thawing earth.

"He is greatly mourned here, however it may have been in Sigimund's hall," Hailgi replied, thinking. Whether you had reason to love him or not! Hailgi would not say that, it had taken Sigiruna's brother this whole year to settle himself, however uneasily, in Jutland. His own forebodings were surely grown from sorrow at Sinfjotli's fall, for all his grim thoughts, Hailgi had no wish to make things worse with his wife's brother. So he only added, "He was my dearest friend. Tell us, if you will, what is thought of his death."

"It is thought ill that a warrior should die of woman-brewed bale," the news-bearer replied. "It is also true that the folk past the Walsings' marches sleep more easily now that Sinfjotli is dead. He terrified many athelings, and all agreed that no one was like to him, no one but Sigimund himself, and Hailgi Hunding's-Bane. There is still wonder over what came to pass with his corpse, but Sigimund will not talk of that."

"Have you been to Sigimund's hall yourself?" Hailgi asked.

Epli-Karl nodded his shaggy head. "Sigimund is fond of well-told tales, and open-handed as well." He mimed a gesture Hailgi knew well. A ring drawn from an arm and flipped across the hall. Then he pushed his tunic's brown sleeve up. A coil of gold wound thrice just above his elbow. "I should have stayed there, if the cheer in that hall had been better. But the last of the Walsings is twice in mourning. Once for Sinfjotli, and once for his sister Sigilind."

Sigiruna had come back so quietly that Hailgi did not hear her, or know she was there until he felt her light touch stroking his shoulder. "Yes, it is hard to outlive folk you love," she murmured. "Matters go more easily for the first to fall, and wyrd has not often been easily shaped for any of that kin."

"And a good death is surely better than an ill life," Dagar answered. He and his sister stared at each other for a moment, Hailgi shifted uncomfort-ably in his seat, remembering the heat and stink of the men who had died in sickbed in the Skjoldings' hall. But Sinfjotli was still clearest in his memory of that time.

The Walsing's easy laugh, his joy in balancing on the ship's edge and the pupils of his eyes swelling to dark pools as he gazed gravely at the runes, and the odd cast to his voice when he had spoken of leaving his father's hall. It seemed to Hailgi that he could see his friend silver-haired, Sinfjotli's broad shoulders beginning to cave beneath a weight of sorrow, the thought brought a prickling of tears to the backs of his eyes, but still he did not weep. It is ill to outlive those you love, he thought, but it seems that wyrd was shaped for me. We were both given to Wodhanar, but he died and I live, with no foes about me, unless the blue-cloaked god takes me by sickness or mischance, I am like to live many years yet.

"What became of Sinfjotli's wife?" Sigiruna asked.

"She went back to Frisia. She would not stay where he had died, I have heard that she truly loved him."

"As well she might," said Sigiruna. "Of all the maids in the Northlands, only I have found a man who could be called the Walsing's match." She leaned over to kiss Hailgi swiftly, her mouth warm with the tastes of fish and leeks and butter.

Sleep did not come easily to Hailgi that night. He lay awake in the darkness, listening to the soft breathing of Sigiruna and little Siggi, the softer whispering of the rain falling onto the thatch and dripping from the eaves. What had Sigimund done, that no bale-fire was laid or howe raised for Sinfjotli? The thought stirred at the roots of Hailgi's sorrow. He did not know how such a thing could have come to pass. I could carve a rune-stone after his memory, Hailgi thought, or at least Sigiruna and I could carve it together.

She kens the runes well, and I could surely wield a hammer and chisel as well as any other man. But that was not enough. How could Sinfjotli be dead, if no one had seen him burned or buried, if no funeral arvel had been drunk about his corpse? A mere draught of poison surely something lay hidden behind that, something more than Epli-Karl's words could tell. After a little while, Hailgi slid out from between the blankets, careful not to wake Sigiruna. The cold night air shivered his naked skin into goosebumps, tightening his man-tools close to his body, the earthen floor seemed mushroom-damp beneath his bare feet.

He padded over to the gashed banner-pole in the corner, running his fingers over the runes Sinfjotli had risted. It seemed to him that their sig, might still be tingle beneath his touch, warm as fire-laced blood. How could that be, if Sinfjotli's blood had grown cold in his bale-stilled veins? Hailgi could feel his own blood beating hot in his fingertips as he gripped the rune-carved staff more tightly, hear his heart drumming through the rushing wind of his breath.

Hailgi stood holding the banner-pole until the cold had soaked all through his body. Then he wriggled back under the covers until he lay full-length against Sigiruna again.

"You're cold," she muttered sleepily, but turned over to lay an arm across Hailgi's shoulders, milk-full breasts pressing against his chest. "Where have you been?"

"Nowhere."

Dark as it was, Hailgi could just make out the pale gleam of Sigiruna's eye-whites as she reached up to stroke his hair and face. "You have not been out, anyway." Hailgi felt the wave of air rising and falling through her body as she sighed. "It should have gone no better with him if he had stayed here with us. That was his wyrd. Though knowing that lightens little for us."

"I still do not believe that he is dead, nor that Sigimund left his dear son to be torn by the ravens and eagles, or to be meat for wolves. I cannot be easy in this matter, nor mourn for Sinfjotli, until I know more."

Sigiruna sat up in the bed, her white body glimmering in the darkness. "Then put on your clothes, and go out to cut a tine for rune-casting. We shall carve them together, and read them together, and see what is shaped in this. The Walsing's life was closely bound with ours."

As she spoke, Siggi began to cry. Sigiruna got up to take the child from the cradle, wrapping the warm blankets around the two of them like a cloak before she put her left breast to his mouth.

Hailgi did not bother to dress or put on shoes. No one would see him so late at night. He flung his cloak about his body, tiptoeing quietly through the hall to pick up the little firewood-ax by the hearth and going out into the rainy darkness. The mud was cold and slimy beneath his bare feet, the wet stalks of dead grass slipping beneath his steps as the wind lashed his face with icy rain. Still, Hailgi moved surely through the darkness. He knew where he was going, he had trodden this path before. The tree he sought stood at the top of a little hill. The old gallows-ash, where ill-doers were sometimes hanged though that had not happened in Hailgi's lifetime, and where the ravens still nested in their season. Hailgi's steps slowed as he came closer to the ash-tree. The fallen twigs crackled and splintered beneath his tread, stabbing into his feet, the tree itself was no more than a thicker darkness in the rain.

He put his hand out to grasp a branch. The wet bark was rough as stone to his touch, the wood as solid, bearing Hailgi's weight easily. As he held to it a moment, it seemed to him that he could feel the sap falling back to the great tree's roots, sunken deep into the mound it stood on, their weave mirroring the weaving of the branches above as though the tree stood half-sunken in still waters. Though Hailgi could not see the ash's leaves, he could hear the wind rustling wetly through them, the rain pattering on them. He knew that winter's age had already yellowed their edges, that they would be dropping soon. A gust of wind shook a scattering of heavier drops from the tree, spattering cold over Hailgi's face and into his mouth, as threads of lightning flickered over the northern sky's dark weft. Swift as a mercy-stroke, Hailgi brought his ax down, shearing the thin branch cleanly through.

He held it in his hand a moment, feeling the life slowly beginning to ebb away from the wood. Still, tree-stuff never wholly died. Once shaped in its growing, it would wait to be filled with life again and again as the sap sprang at each winter's end, as the hallowed house-pillars still rang with the life of the clan within, as Wodhanar's might dwelt in the holy image in Fetter-Grove. This Hailgi knew. Sigiruna had taught him that the tree's life would show the shapes of Wyrd's turning of the runes, even as he stained them with his blood. Silently Hailgi bore the branch down to the hall, never turning his head to look back at the old ash-tree's black shape against the storm. Sigiruna had built up the fire by the time he got back, sitting cross-legged beside it with the blanket still spread over her shoulders. Hailgi sat down beside her, stripping the leafy twigs from his branch and casting them to hiss in the flames.

He cut the wood into twenty-four little tines, scraping a bit of bark away from each so that he could rist the runes into them with the point of his knife. Staining them was easy. Sigiruna had only to untie his bloodied bandage, for the work had opened his cut again. When Hailgi had reddened each of the runes, whispering the name of each to give it life with his breath, he gathered them in his cupped palms. Sigiruna put her hands over his. The air sighed in and out of her lungs, her breath and his rising and falling as one, her might streaming through him and his through her. As one, they turned their hands upward. The runes spattered from their fingers before the flickering flames. Perthro,, lay in the middle of the pattern, the rag-ged-bloodied stave black against the white ash-wood.

"That shows wyrd," Hailgi said slowly. "Whatever comes of this is deeply set. The runes show what shall be." He moved his hand lightly above the fallen tines. "Raidho,, ansur,, lagur,, it seems to me that should show a faring over water. Eihwar, standing beside themI do not know what that should be, but there is dagar, the rune of day. That should be a fair ending to it. There is othala, the udal land, the rune of the kin's inheritance, with gebo,, the gift, beside it."

"Eihwar," Sigiruna whispered, her long forefinger tracing the sign. "The yew-rune, the needle-ash greenest of trees in winter, bale-berried, springing forth even when its stem has rotted. It does not always show joy, even with the day-rune beside it, but it need not be a rune of ill either. Nor is dagar only a fair ending. Most folk die at the doors of dawn."

"It seems to me," Hailgi started slowly, staring down at the shadowed staves before him, "that I must go over the sea to Sigimund's hall, to visit my kinsman there, even as he once sent his son to me. That is the gift for a gift which gebo shows, as I know that it should be."

"That would not be badly done, and the runes may be read so without confusing or spoiling them. And you are Sigimund's nearest kin, after all the nearest that lives, now. Yes, it seems to me that you ought to go as soon as the Winter nights feasting is over."

"I would rather fare before. I cannot call him among the dead now, for my heart does not know him dead, yet I would gladly see you giving him the horn in our hall again, though he were a gray ghost or mouldering from barrow-earth. Now that I know ill has befallen him, I must have an end, or I cannot rest. And it is said that Sigimund and Sinfjotli were nigh the same man. I would see my friend in his full age, as Wyrd should have shaped it."

"Still, you must make the blessings for your folk."

Hailgi nodded slowly. He knew that he could not be sure of crossing the North Sea twice and still being back in time for Winter nights, and he must be at home for the harvest-thanks, whatever might betide. As well as what his own lands had borne, he would soon be getting cows and grain from the lands he had overcome, where his men sat in his stead, all together, the gods and goddesses had dealt kindly with him that year, and it would be ill of him to slight them by being elsewhere at a time of holy feasting.

"If I must wait, I must. How shall I find my way when I go?"

"You might trust in your luck and your shaping to bring you to Sigimund's shore, but it seems to me that you would be surer to ask Epli-Karl for his help. He seems a good man to have with you, and it will not be tiresome to have him guesting in our hall."

Sigiruna fell silent, looking down at the runes again. Her high-boned face was very still and grave beneath the shifting golden veils of the firelight.

"What else do you see written there? It seems to me that you have not told me all you know?"

"I have no wish to speak of what might be, if my words might turn it into being. Wyrd's well is about us when the runes are cast," she touched the perthro-tine lightly, "and reading can be shaping, as risting is."

"Then cast the runes into the fire, so that the reading of the staves is done, and speak to me in riddles or kenning. Let the reading be mine."

Sigiruna stared at the staves a moment longer, but made no move to pick them up. "After all, you are already chosen," she murmured. "This may be, or it may not. The steed for your faring may be the gray horse which can ride over both wave and wind, the eight-legged horse of the ravens' drighten the troll-woman's steed may run over the rainbow's flickering fires. The ash-tree where the old eagle has nested might be felled by the wind of his wings, laid in the earthen kin-home, though I do not know what gift or wedding should take place in that mound. That is still murky to me. Would you know more, or what?"

"Is there more to tell?" Hailgi asked quietly. "What more do you see?"

"Only that the yew springs ever-green above the well's ancient ring, the waters sprinkling down from its leaves each day. But that we know of old, little sight shows me that." Sigiruna drew in a deep breath, gazing across the fire at the smoky darkness of the wall. "Yet I see dagar beside the tree-rune. What these staves mean is clouded in my sight, as though the Norns do not mean that I give warning. I do not know," she went on, her voice soft as the rustling of feathers, "whether these runes rede towards your wyrd, or Sinfjotli's. It seems to me that the Walsing's wyrd is not fully turned, but that more shall come than I can see clearly yet."

"I must go to Sigimund's hall."

"That you shall do, my beloved. It is fair to see that you have no fear in you, and do not grudge giving the gift you promised in earlier times." Sigiruna scooped the runes up in a single swift movement, flinging them into the fire, then turned to draw Hailgi towards her, holding him tight as his arms went around her in turn, as they kissed till a tinge of blood sweetened their mouths, casting their tangle of blankets on the floor to shield their love from the cold earth.

The day after Winter nights was dark and stormy, the winds flinging the seagulls about far above the white-haired waves. Sigiruna, Epli-Karl, and Hailgi stood on the strand, looking from the small boat Hailgi had made ready to the tossing water. Hailgi's words of foreboding had come true. He had slept ill since the news had come, for he could not feel Sinfjotli's death, only the shock of betrayal and the echoing words, Let your beard filter it, my son! Now Hailgi's knees seemed to weaken beneath him, for this faring to find a dead man seemed a little too much like faring to the lands beyond the wider waters, yet it would be better to go down in the doing than to live without answer or rest.

"Bravery is a fine thing," Epli-Karl said, "but you can be too brave, you know."

"I have sailed through a worse storm than this," Hailgi answered.

"So I have heard in the songs. I have also heard that you were in a bigger boat then."

Siguruna shifted little Siggi from her right hip to her left. "I think that drowning is not your wyrd. And if you mean to go, you should go now. Wait, and the weather will keep you back for many days, but if you show the Weather-Maker that you do not fear his storms, he is as like to look well upon you."

If Hailgi had held any doubt about the faring in his heart, Sigiruna's words crushed it from him then. He gazed at her for a few quickening heartbeats, her long hair blowing like a rippling banner in the wind, her eyes mirroring the waves' dark blue-gray and her pale mouth curving into a faint smile as she looked at him. "My fairest treasure," He did not finish his thought, but stepped forward to kiss her, patting his son on the head. "I am sorry to be leaving you as well, Siggi. Be good, my son, and I'll bring you something fair from the Saxon lands to play with."

Siggi blinked up at his father, smiling wetly as Hailgi tickled him through the blankets. "Do you think he'll even know that I'm gone?" Hailgi whispered to Sigiruna.

"I've heard that small children know a great deal more than they seem to. It could be that he shall."

Hailgi and Epli-Karl bent to push their boat towards the water. The first wave-edge had just split about the bow when Sigiruna said, "What do you think you're doing?"

Hailgi looked up in surprise, but she was not speaking to him. Dagar stood between his sister and the boat, a large bag slung over his back. He wore byrnie and sword, and carried a helm under his arm, a leather thong knotted about his forehead bound back his pale hair.

"I mean to go with you," he said to Hailgi. "I have brought enough food and water for myself, as well as my fighting gear and such medicines as we might need on the way, and that boat is heavily laden, and seems to me a little larger than two men can easily deal with, should the winds turn against you. There is reason for you to take me, can you think of any reason for me not to come with you?" The Skjolding did not ease the bag from his back, he stood a little bent under its weight as he stared coolly at Hailgi, waiting for his answer.

"Why should you wish to come with us? Sinfjotli was no friend of yours, nor do I believe that you mourn for his death. If you mean to gloat because he has fallen, there is no place for you here."

"I do not mean to gloat, nor shall I speak any ill words to Sigimund in his grief." Dagar looked away from Hailgi, up at a swirl of white mist slowly melting into the gray cloud-sea behind it.

"Then why should you wish to come?"

Dagar stood silent a long time, staring at the shifting darkness of the sky. Hailgi heard the first shower of rain hissing across the waves, glancing over his shoulder, he saw the wind driving the gray mists closer, more swiftly. At last the Skjolding braced his shoulders and raised his head, the wind blowing his fair hair back from his face like sand blown away from the edge of a hidden rock.

"I was not fostered out of our father's hall, but stayed to learn our mother's herb-craft while she lived. Now I am a man grown, and I should find it fair to see more of the world besides Sealand and Jutland, and to come into a hall which my sister does not rule, to see how things may be done by other folk. I have told you the truth, and I ask nothing that you cannot easily give me. And my oath to you has held true for a year now, it seems to me that you have little cause to fear me."

"Nor do I fear you, whether you have sworn oaths to me or not. Let it be so, then. if you will dare the waves beside us, and fight any foe who comes upon us, you have every right to fare with us." Hailgi was ready to unsay the words as soon as they had leapt from his mouth, but he could not call them back, no more than he could raise from the dead Haganon and Bragi. Dagar would fare with them, whether it gave him joy or not.

Dagar turned to his sister. "Stay well, Sigiruna, and your bairn. If I live through this faring, I shall come back to this hall with Hailgi, and stay here for a little time at least. I do not mean to forsake you or to speak ill of you to others, whatever betide."

"That is good to know," Sigiruna answered. "Fare well, my brother, and keep your frith with Hailgi, I hope that this faring may bring a better friendship between you."

The Skjolding slung his bag into the boat, setting his helmet down beside it and unbuckling his sword-belt so that he could bend over and let his ring-mail slide from his shoulders. Thus lightened, he dug his heels into the sand, helping Hailgi and Epli-Karl shove the boat forward.

With the three of them pushing, the little craft swung free of the land easily. The other two waded out with it, Hailgi hung back, for Sigiruna had waded in to where he stood, the hem of her dress swishing about her calves with the rising and sinking of the rain-pocked waves. "Fare well, my beloved," she said, her murmur near-hidden beneath the sounds of sea and rain. "Fare well and watch Dagar closely, if you do not come back to me, I will fear that his troth shattered on the sea."

"There is little to fear," Hailgi answered. "As you told me before, he has ever been true. Whether frith is in his heart or not, secret slaying does not lurk there. I shall always come back to you." He embraced Sigiruna and his son together as he kissed her. "Stay well, my beloved."

Hailgi waded out to the boat, catching hold of its rim and hauling himself in. Sigiruna was already standing on the beach as the men unfurled the sail, she stood there gazing as long as Hailgi could see her, till they had rounded the curve of the coast.

At first the wind drove them swiftly along, the keel scoring a deep froth-wound through the waves as the rain-soaked sail belled heavily out, splashing its spray cold over the backs of their necks. Hailgi had little work at the helm. The wind was blowing from the north, sending them southward towards the Saxons' land. Behind him, Epli-Karl and Dagar were talking. Fragments of their speech blew past his ears like dry leaves.

"Come to Hailgi's hall?"

"I swore an oath, Fetter-Grove, last Winter nights, Sigiruna and Hailgi," then, louder and clearer,"at Sigiruna's will!"

Epli-Karl's deeper voice came less clearly through the waves and the sound of the wind in the creaking sail, but Hailgi caught the words, "seem a likely young man," a few wind-torn sentences later, he raised his voice. "Hai, Hailgi, there's little need of steering now. We're straight on course, as near as I can tell. You may as well turn about and have some ale with us."

Though the rain had lightened somewhat, Hailgi had little wish to sit with it blowing into his face. He waited for the next swell's peak to pass, then swung across to sit on the bench between Epli-Karl and Dagar, where his back would be to the driving showers. Dagar glanced sideways at him, blue eyes narrowed, but he did not move away from Hailgi, and after he had drunk from the horn in his hand he passed it to the Wolfing. Hailgi took a good draught of the ale. It was Epli-Karl's horn they were drinking from. A long black aurochs-horn with a long shoulder-strap dangling between the two rings of leather riveted along its length. The horn's dark skin was scarred and battered, but it gleamed within as though rubbed with beeswax.

When they had passed the horn a few more times, Dagar asked, "How did you come by your name? It seems a strange one."

The storyteller laughed, shaking a scattering of rain from his curly gray head. "There's little story to it. My kin live where many apple-trees grow. It is a land well-known in its own part of the country, and so when I began my wandering the name fastened to me," he thumped his two fists against his broad chest, "and clung! Your own name is more interesting, 'Day', your parents must have had bright hopes for you."

"It may have been so, though they did not look to see a hero of old songs in me." Dagar looked at Hailgi as he gave him the horn, his fine-boned face drawn into lines tighter than his fifteen winters might have graven. Hailgi did not answer, only drank and passed the ale on.

"There are many more tales left to be told before the doom of the gods, I'm sure," Epli-Karl replied. "You are no older than Hailgi was when he slew Hunding, if the songs tell truly?"

"About that they do, yes," Hailgi growled. He waited to see if the storyteller would ask him any more questions, but Epli-Karl only looked into the gleaming depths of his horn, tilting it until the last dark drops rolled out to be lost in the rain.

"No more there, I'm afraid," he said cheerfully, "and perhaps we ought to save the rest for later. We can't count on a wind like this all the way."

"I wish we could, it would save us some rowing-blisters," Dagar answered. Then he smiled, as Hailgi had not seen him do before. His grin drove the shadows from his face, suddenly the Skjolding did not look at all like his sister to Hailgi's eyes. "Still, it will do us no harm to enjoy the rest while we have it, and this kind wind is also very cold."

"Another horn full would be little loss to us," Hailgi agreed.

"Well-chosen words, I'm sure that's a good rede." Epli-Karl leaned backward, twisting the tap of their cask to fill the horn again. Hailgi marked how easily he did it, moving with the boat as it swayed on the swells. The wayfarer had surely spent much time at sea. "And we need not fear going thirsty once we have gotten to Sigimund's hall. The difficulty is to keep from being drowned in ale and mead, more so for you who will be sitting and talking with him as kin. It takes many horn fulls to reach his head, and no one has yet seen him sleepy or sick from drink, and he often forgets that other men may take bale from Wodhanar's gift as well, as I have found to my cost. But there is never lack of symbel there, no more than in Walhall."

Though the rain had stopped well before sunset, they made landfall early that night, before the light had grayed too dark for them to tell rock from wave. After they had made their boat fast on the shore, Dagar set to kindling and feeding up a fire while Hailgi and Epli-Karl put up their sleeping tent.

"It will be close, with three in the tent," Hailgi told Dagar. "But you chose to come, unless you want to sleep in the open, this will have to do."

Dagar poked another stick into the little pile of half-burnt twigs where his flames were beginning to lick out here and there, turning it over and over so that the bark would char off and leave the wood beneath to catch fire. "I shall take no harm from it."

Epli-Karl squatted down by the fire, stretching his hands out to the fledgling warmth. "Nightfall is a little way off, does anyone want to see if we might be able to find some small game? I would find roast rabbit better than cold smoked fish."

Hailgi looked towards the meadow that spread brown and tangled behind the sand, the winter-gold woods around its edge. "Rabbits should not be hard to find there. But we brought no bows, and a snare will not bring us game by nightfall."

"I am not unskilled with a sling," Epli-Karl admitted.

"Then I would be little help to you. You must go without me. Dagar?"

The Skjolding shook his head. "I can shoot well enough, but I did not bring my bow either, and the sling's art is one I have never learned."

Epli-Karl nodded, rising to his feet. "If I'm not back by nightfall, you can safely take it that the rabbits have killed and eaten me." He strode off into the wet brown meadow, unwrapping a length of cloth from somewhere beneath his cloak. The tall grasses and dried seed-stalks rose to his waist, then he stooped, perhaps to pick up stones, and was gone as if he had ducked beneath a wave.

Hailgi looked at Dagar, who still squatted tending his fire. The sticks were beginning to burn well now as Dagar carefully poked them about, laying larger and larger pieces of wood upon the blaze. Hailgi marked that his long fingers were stained with fading splotches of brown and green, spotted white with old scars from a score of little cuts. The leaping flames glittered off the few little beard-hairs that curled from his jaw.

"Dagar," Hailgi said, "would you care to be fostered somewhere else next year?"

Dagar's mouth opened in surprise as he looked up. He shut it again, pale eyes narrowing into wariness. "I am too old for fostering out. That ought to have been done years ago, if it were to be done at all."

"'Fostering' may have been the wrong word. But you know well that athelings' sons often go to other drightens' war bands, even when they are full-grown, just as Sinfjotli" Hailgi's voice choked in his throat.

"Yes. Where do you think I would go, then? Although I was trained well enough with the other youths of the Skjoldings' hall, my best skills are not at fighting, and I have no wish to go to a stranger's hall, only to be mocked at as an herb-wife." Dagar slowly turned the end of the stick he held about in the fire until it was well-charred, then plunged the burning tip into the wet sand to quench its flame. He reached out for one of the round beach-stones, rubbing the blackened stick against it until the point was sharp enough to be pushed through a rabbit's flesh. "You have not done so ill by me, after all," he muttered softly. Then the muscles bunched at the hinges of his jaw, clamping his mouth closed.

"I know a hall where you would not be mocked at, I think," Hailgi said, his mind rushing only a little ahead of his words. "That is the hall of Hagalar, who was my foster-father, the thanes there have learned long since that it is not well done to speak scornfully of the sons of athelings, for the gray heath-dweller may lie hidden beneath many guises, as once beneath a woman's skirts."

"So it is said."

"Hagalar's elder daughter Ingwibjorg is a fair maiden, with less than a hands-count of winters more than you have, and she is still unwed, so far as I know. There are few men fitting for her, and fewer who are young enough for her to find fair, but a son of the Skjolding line would be no ill match for her."

Dagar rubbed at his forehead, pushing the knotted leather headband back. It had chafed a little in the wetness, leaving a red stripe across his pale brow. "You offer much kindness to the son of your foe."

Hailgi sighed. "To the brother of my wife, who is also one of my kin, as I have said before," he answered patiently. "The battle is long over, and should not have been fought at all if Sigiruna had been given as she wished. Since that day, can you say that I have ever dealt with you as did not befit a kinsman?"

Dagar's voice was muffled as though he spoke through a mouthful of carded wool. "I cannot say that."

"Though Sigiruna was never born to be a frith-weaver, she has nevertheless bound us into one hall. So let there be no more talk of foes and the sons of foes. If you feel so, you should not have fared here with me."

The Skjolding looked up from his fire, staring at Hailgi as though measuring him for a dosage of an herbal remedy. His gaze was not wholly comfortable, but Hailgi stared back until Dagar's eyes dropped.

"I would not have called Sinfjotli's death fitting to him, either," Dagar said softly.

Hailgi did not know how to answer this, he was not sure what Dagar meant by it, or why he was saying this now. To cover his confusion, he coughed, looking over to the meadow where Epli-Karl was striding back towards them in the gathering gloom. A brace of rabbits dangled from the tall man's hand.

"Hai, you've hunted well," Hailgi called out to him.

"Not badly, though the deer in this land seem to be rather on the small side," Epli-Karl answered. He came over to crouch down by the fire with the other two. Hailgi marked that both rabbits had been struck on the head, a little blood dribbling from their broken skulls. Epli-Karl began to skin one, Dagar took the other, slitting it up the belly with his belt-knife and neatly disemboweling it.

Hailgi kept the middle watch that night, sitting as close to the fire as he could without singing his cloak and occasionally tossing another piece of wood onto the flames. The Moon was down, the stars gleaming here and there between the wispy patches of darkness that crept swiftly across the sky. Wavering lines of pale foam rose and fell along the black sea, Hailgi could see that the tide was just starting to go out, and thought that his turn at watch must surely be close to an end. One of the two in the tent was snoring in a deep, regular rhythm, though his ears were keen, Hailgi was just barely able to hear the sudden hitching cry above that sound. At first he was not sure where it came from, or what had made the noise, he got quietly to his feet, settling his helm onto his head and closing his palm about the hilt of his sword. Then the soft cry sounded again, more clearly, and he realized that the noise came from their tent. He walked over, pulling the flap open so that the firelight would shine in. Epli-Karl lay on his back, mouth open, it was he who was snoring. Dagar had thrown off his cloak and was curled up on his right side, his eyes shut tightly. As Hailgi watched, his whole body jerked, as if he had just taken a blow beneath the heart, his mouth opened, but no sound came out, and his right arm convulsed hard, drawing in and then flinging out violently.

Hailgi crouched down, shaking the Skjolding gently by the shoulder with one hand while making the sign of Thonarar's Hammer over him with the other. Dagar's tunic was soaked through with chill sweat, his muscles oak-tight beneath the wet wool. "Wake up, Dagar," Hailgi murmured to him. "Dagar, come back. No troll, or witch-reins may hold you, but Thonarar's Hammer strike the ill wights down. Dagar, wake up."

Dagar's body jerked again, he cried out as his eyes leapt open. For a moment he lay shivering and staring.

"You were dreaming," Hailgi said, as gently as he could. "Unless you were mare-ridden, it was a dream."

"Why did you waken me?"

"You cried out in your sleep, it seemed to be no joyful dream. What was it you saw?"

"I saw" Dagar shook himself, wiping the sweat from his face with a corner of his cloak. "No, I don't remember, but it does not seem to me as though it were an ill dream it does not seem so. I know that I was not mare-ridden, anyway." He pulled his cloak up around himself again, shifting to lie on his back. "Still, it may have been no bad thing that you woke me. How long before my turn to watch?"

"Not very long, I think." Hailgi backed out of the tent, straightening and looking up at the cloud-swept stars till he found a clear pattern to make his guess by. "No, it is not long at all."

Dagar sat up and crawled out, shaking the sand from his cloak. "I may as well start now, in that case. I don't think I'll fall asleep quickly now, and if I am awake, you need not be."

Hailgi lifted the helm from his head, shaking his hair free, and crept back into the tent. He lay down in the warm hollow Dagar's body had left in the sand, tugging his cloak up about his ears to shut out the worst of Epli-Karl's snoring. The Skjolding might have been dreaming of fighting, or of making love, neither sort of dream was strange to Hailgi. It would not be an ill thing at all for Dagar to marry Ingwibjorg, Hailgi thought then, we shall go to visit Hagalar as soon as the planting is done, and see how matters may stand. Their sea-faring was harder in the next days, as they swung around the western coast of Jutland. Though they always kept close to the land, the waves of Agwijar's first winter fury flung the boat about as if they had been in the middle of the open sea, and it often took the full strength of all three of them to keep their small craft afloat and on course. The land grew lower as they sailed southward, till they were passing by settlements built on huge flat-topped mounds, which the sea often made into islands at high tide.

"Now we are not far from Sigimund's lands," Epli-Karl said when he saw these mound-hamlets. "Soon we shall come to the mouth of a great river, that is the Elbe, and Sigimund's hall is not much farther."

Dagar paused in his bailing, standing with his bucket half-emptied to look at the land. "This does not seem to me the best place to have built," he said. "Why should folk have settled here? It looks to me as though those hills were raised by men, as though they chose to dwell in the middle of the sea."

"Your eyes are sharp," Epli-Karl answered. "I have heard that the sea was much lower in old days, but then," he swung his arm to sketch the swell of a great wave in the air, "it began to rise in the time of our grandfathers. No one will choose to leave his lands, and so they built higher and higher. Still, Agwijar is far from beaten, he takes more and more each year, and someday he may yet claim this ground for his own.

The Saxons get along well enough, for they are good sea-men and often fare to the shores of Britain and Gaul in search of gold and other fine things, and what they bring back adorns these mounds very well indeed." He shaded his eyes with his hand, gazing along the coastline to a far-off glimmer of sunlit water against the white sand. "Ah, there, I knew we were getting nearer. Are you two feeling strong? Even with the wind at our backs, it's a hard pull into the river, though a short one."

Cold as the clear winter air was, the sweat was running down Hailgi's face by the time they had lowered sail and tied their boat up in the reeds at the river's edge, the work of rowing had kindled a bright red glow in Dagar's fair cheeks, and dark crescents stained the armpits of Epli-Karl's light brown tunic. Sigimund's hall rose high above them on its mound, on the slope nearest the river, a brown-braided maiden, wrapped in thick dark wool, walked slowly along behind a herd of cows, tapping one every now and again with her stick.

"Hrafanhild!" Epli-Karl shouted as they splashed through the ankle-deep water. "Is Sigimund home?"

"If he hasn't gone out, he is," the maiden answered. Her voice was low and clear as the slow hollow clanging of the cows' bells. "But what brings you back here so soon? I thought you meant to go north to Gautland." Hailgi marked that she, like Sinfjotli, spoke her words more shortly than he was used to, her strong Saxon accent sent a pang of memory through him.

"I did, but," the young graybeard spread his hands wide, "plans change. Instead I have brought Hailgi Hunding's-Bane and Dagar the Skjolding here to visit Sigimund." His speech changed as he spoke, words shortening to echo Hrafanhild's Saxon accent.

Hrafanhild gazed down at them coolly, but Hailgi could see her dark eyes widening a little. "Come up to the hall, it will do our drighten good to see you, I think." Her lips tightened then, as though she were reining back more words, she said nothing more.

Hailgi and Dagar both tarried by the boat long enough to put on their byrnies, though they carried their helms beneath their arms. They would come proudly, but they came in frith, after all. Hrafanhild dropped her stick, muttering something to her cows, and came down to join them. Hailgi could see that she was trying not to stare at him, she glanced away every time he looked at her.

"Has Sigimund been well?"

"He has not been ill," Hrafanhild replied shortly. "No more so than might be guessed."

A large stone propped the hall's door open to let the wind and sunlight in, would be few enough chances to air it as the winter weather grew worse, Hailgi guessed. A few chickens wandered aimlessly about between the benches, scratching or pecking into the rushes on the earthen floor. The only person in the hall was a broad-hipped woman with blond hair cut short around her snub face, who was chasing the straw into piles with vigorous sweeps of her broom.

"Hai, Frithawunjo, where's the drighten?" Hrafanhild asked.

The heavy woman raised her broom, swinging it through the air in a circle. "He went out somewhere. How should I know? It's not me that owns him, is it?" She bent down to gather one of her piles, grunting as she slung it to flare and hiss in the fire pit in the middle of the floor. Hailgi marked that a broad, calf-high mound of earth rose behind the fire, he did not know what it might be or why it was there. "If he's not out hunting, and I don't think he is, at least I didn't see his bow on his back or boar-spear in his hand, you might try asking old Egeberht the Smith, or else Osfrith the Woodcarver."

I do believe he said something about wanting to get a good pile of war-gear ready by the time planting's over, thinks he might have to fight for a new wife, I don't doubt." She laughed, showing teeth like a ragged mouthful of yellow-brown grain. "Good to see you here again, Karl. Sit you down, all of you men, and I'll fetch you some ale, if you've a mind to wait for Sigimund. Hai, wait you two must be some fine athelings, with those byrnies and gold-worked helms. What are you doing here? I'll send someone out to find the drighten at once for you. Who are you?"

"This is Dagar the Skjolding, and I am Hailgi Hunding's-Bane."

Frithawunjo's mouth dropped open, she pressed a freckled hand to her broad bosom. "And here am I nattering, and no atheling-frowe in the hall to give you a fit welcome-draught. Hrafanhild, you'd best give them drink, Sigimund wouldn't like it if we let them stand thirsty in his hall. I'm sure you can breach that cask of Roman wine for these two, and get the glass cups out of the drighten's chamber to serve it in. Ohhh, I'll go see if I can find him, right now."

She bustled out, leaving Hrafanhild to stare after her and shake her head. The young woman muttered something under her breath, then turned back to the men. "Please, sit yourselves by the high seat, and I shall fetch you drink. Are you hungry?"

"Somewhat," Hailgi admitted, following her to the far end of the long tables and taking his place by the empty chair. Sigimund's high seat was made of massive oak, intricately carved all over, with a cushion of white Northern fox-fur in it and a deep scarlet cloak, richly embroidered in gold, slung over the back. Sinfjotli would not have been dwarfed by it, nor Ansumundar, but Hailgi could see that even his own feet would swing a little above the floor if he were to sit in it.

Epli-Karl's gaze followed Dagar's to the mound in the middle of the hall. "That is where the Walsings' apple-tree, the barn stock, once stood, and grew through the roof. Then the hall was burnt, Sigimund had it rebuilt when he won his lands again, but would not plant another tree in the barn stock's stead."

Hrafanhild bore a blue-green cone of glass in each hand when she came back. At first Hailgi thought that the dark drink was ale, but when its scent reached him, he knew that it was not anything he had ever tasted before. Roman wine, Frithawunjo had said, Sigimund must have gotten it in a raid on Britain or Gaul. He wanted to take a little on his tongue to taste it before drinking deeply, but that would not have been fitting for a guest-draught. Instead he raised it, saying, "To the drighten of this hall, and the welcoming maid."

Hrafanhild's round cheeks flushed, but she did not drop her gaze as Hailgi and Dagar drank. The wine tasted strange to Hailgi, musty and just a little sweet, it was as strong as pure honey-mead, glowing nicely in his stomach when he had downed the first swallow. A long shadow fell across the short square of sunlight on the hall-door's threshold. Taking a second sip of wine, Hailgi coughed and choked, spraying the dark drink over the table like blood from a lung-wound. Sinfjotli stood in the doorway, alive and hale, his wide shoulders blocking the ruddy sunlight as his keen blue eyes gazed down the length of the hall to his guests. His hair and beard were longer than Hailgi remembered, plaited into many small braids, sunlight glowed from the hex-cut ice-stone in the hilt of his sword.

Cold as the day was, he was bare-chested and barefooted, wearing only gray breeches and a short blue cloak pinned askew about his shoulders. One hand held a flat piece of interwoven metalwork, perhaps a shield-adornment, in the other, he had a gold-bound drinking horn. It took Hailgi three breaths to see the silver streaking the hair and beard of the man before him, the deep-graven forehead-lines that even the hall's length and dimness could not hide. For all he had known that Sigimund would look much like his son, he had hardly believed that the two of them could be so alike, the same man in youth and strong old age. Dagar, too, stared round-eyed at the Walsing, but Epli-Karl watched his fellow travelers with a small smile curling beneath his gray beard, as though awaiting their shock.

"Hail to you, Hailgi and Dagar," Sigimund called, walking between the tables towards them. His voice seemed deeper than Sinfjotli's had been, roughened by many more years of battle-shouting, but it was still the voice that Hailgi knew well. "Greetings, and welcome in the Walsings' hall. If I had known that you were coming, I should have been readier to greet you, in a manner more fitting to athelings." His gaze turned to their companion. "Welcome back to my hall, Karl, I hope you can stay longer this time."

Hailgi coughed his windpipe free of wine. "Hail, Sigimund." He raised his beaker to his host, downing the rest of the drink as Hrafanhild came back to put a silver cup down in front of Epli-Karl and refill their glass vessels from her pitcher, emptying the last of it into Sigimund's horn as he sat down in his high-seat.

"Ah, you've brought out the wine," Sigimund said to her. "That is well-done. Have a cupful yourself, if you like, Frithawunjo is seeing to some food." He turned his gaze towards his guests. "I am glad to have you here, Hailgi, though I wish you could have come to better joy. Epli-Karl must have told you the tidings."

Hailgi nodded, unable to speak.

"It was a great sorrow to the Wolfing hall as well," Dagar said unexpectedly.

"And to the Skjoldings?" Then Sigimund seemed to catch himself, he shook his hoar-streaked head and looked away from Dagar. "No, forget I spoke. I had forgotten."

Dagar scratched the toe of one shoe through the straw, staring at the wall behind Sigimund. The silence trailed on through the cold air until Hailgi spoke. "We should not have stayed away from this hall so long kin are the joy of kin."

Sigimund's gaze seemed less fierce to Hailgi than Sinfjotli's had been, his eyes were still and bright as the eyes of an adder mirroring the icy winter sky. Neither of them looked away from the other, but Sigimund nodded. "So, it is said. Tell me, has Sigiruna come with you? I would wish to see her again, if I might, she was yet a young maiden, too young for wedding, when I met her before. Still, you have been lucky in your choice, and songs of the two of you are often sung in this hall."

"As are songs of the Walsings in ours." It was said in some of those songs, Hailgi remembered, that a white-clad sig-wife had been seen above Sigimund's head in battle, her shield warding him from harm, some folk thought this woman to be Sigimund's mother, the walkurja Hleod, and others said that she was his sister Sigilind. But that, like the question that had brought him here, could not be spoken of by the light of day, nor while they were sober and still half-strangers to one another.

Frithawunjo came in with a platter of food, fresh white cheese and warm bread and blackberries in a broad wooden bowl, and set it down on the table between them. "Do you want some meat as well?" She asked, looking from Sigimund to his guests. "I guess you do, if you rowed up the river, you're like to have missed your mid-day meal. The smoking from the Winter nights slaughter isn't done yet, but there's some good hors meat sausage, should anyone be hungry for it, or I could heat the last of the slaughtering-stew."

The four of them sat eating, drinking, and talking while the doorway-light lengthened on the floor. Though Hailgi had drunk enough for the tip of his nose to grow numb, he had not drunk too much to feel how the air bit colder and colder as the afternoon stretched on, nor to see how Dagar sat hooded in his cloak like a falcon in its feathers against the icy breeze creeping in from the door. The cloud-shadows were drifting over the sunlight through the doorway now, but Sigimund stood up, casting his short cloak back as though he did not feel either the cold or the wine and mead he had drunk.

"Well, there are still some things I must see to before dark today," he said. "You may come with me if you choose, though it's not likely to be interesting, I have only to talk to our smith, or stay here, or whatever you will." He paced to the door, looked up at the sky. "I don't think there's enough daylight left for much of a hunt, even if the storm doesn't get here before nightfall, though if your luck is with you. You might come across a stag or boar. You may use whatever gear you please, you may be free with anything in this hall."

"I thank you for the offer. We'll try hunting, I think," Hailgi said, thinking that at least being out in the cold air would clear his head. The others were no better off than he, he saw Dagar stagger as the youth pushed himself to his feet, and Epli-Karl did not walk too surely. For a moment Hailgi saw, clear as the carven wooden tables before him and the brindled hound curled by Frithawunjo's feet at the fire, Sinfjotli's hand white and unblackened by bale, the adder swinging from it by its fangs. The memory wrenched at him, but he walked over to the boar-spear by the wall, balancing his steps against the spinning in his head as if he stood swaying with the wave tossing on the edge of a boat.

The wind cut more keenly outside, though the three of them walked swiftly before it, the clouds were rolling up from the sea, great gray riders driving hard over the wind-road. But the walking warmed them up, and the drink still cheered their blood, so that Hailgi and Dagar were soon laughing at Epli-Karl's tales.

"So we were sleeping in one of those sunken earth-houses that you find sometimes in Frisia and Saxony, and I woke up in the middle of the night with something dripping on my head. Roofs leak often enough in the rain, there's nothing strange about that, though this water smelled a little off, but I was tired, and I went back to sleep. Well, when we got up in the morning, we found that our horses had pulled their tether-stakes out, and gone over onto the house-roof to graze, they'd been pissing on us all night!"

It was little surprise that they found no game. Hailgi was sure their noise had warned every beast for miles around. The day grew dark early beneath the heavy clouds, and the air was cold as if it were mid-winter. Hailgi was just about to say that they ought to turn back when the first snowflakes began to swirl down, white glimmers against the few brown leaves still blowing on the wind.

Epli-Karl glanced up at the blackened sky. "Well, we'd best hurry back before it starts coming down too hard for us to find our way. Strange, it usually doesn't snow like this here before Yule-tide."

Sigimund was already back in the hall when the three wayfarers came shivering in with the snow melting from their hair and beards, Hrafanhild stood beside him, pouring his horn full. "Hai, did you find any game?" The Walsing called. "You look wild as trolls from the far North."

"Have you seen trolls often before?" Dagar stuttered through chattering teeth.

Sigimund laughed. "No, though I heard them howling about the mouth of my cave often enough when I dwelt in Gautland. Hrafanhild, bring these cold wood-wights some furs or such to warn them." He leaned his head back, raising his voice. "Frithawunjo! Bring wood, build up the fires." Sigimund grinned at them. "We'll have a proper feast in here tonight, even if it's just for the four of us. Some of the thanes may come in later, but it's the time of year when folk think on staying home with their kin, and more so in this weather."

As the evening wore down, Hailgi marked that the strong mead was making Dagar more and more talkative. Though the Skjolding's voice would always be light, it had begun to sink to a man's depth by the summer's beginning, but now Dagar sounded shrill as when Hailgi had first met him. His clear piercing tone was a boy's as he asked, "How was it for you, those years between your father's death and your vengeance? How did it seem, and how did you bear it?"

Sigimund closed his eyes a moment, as if the sap-scented smoke from the fires stung them. "Strangely, my foe man's words were often a comfort to me. He told me of a Northern saying. That 'a thrall takes his vengeance at once, a coward never'. I knew that I was neither thrall nor coward, and thus, if I waited and watched for the time that seemed to match the rede I had. I was sure to take my revenge and free the ghosts of my father and brothers....still" The Walsing stared silently into the darkness beyond the fire-ring's glow. Just as Hailgi was about to raise his voice, to shift Sigimund's mood into some brighter thing if he could, the hall's drighten went on.

"It seemed to me like a long thorn lodged in my cloak, something that pricked me to waking every morning and sleep every night, and never ceased to pierce the sore in the whole day's course between. And still, it must have been easier to me than to my sister Sigilind, who had to dwell in their slayer's hall, pour him ale and sleep in his bed all those long dark winters while Sinfjotli grew to manhood."

Dagar nodded, his voice was slurred as he said, "I think I can guess at her thoughts."

Hailgi knew that the mead was working as strongly in him as in Dagar, but he cared little. He had not come this long way for any purpose other than to ask Sigimund the question that coiled about his heart.

"What became of Sinfjotli's body? What howe or bale-fire did you find for him?"

Sigimund did not look straight at Hailgi, but the Wolfing could see the dark centers of his eyes swelling to eclipse their keen blue, the hoarfrost seemed to lie more heavily on the Walsing's fair hair and beard as he spoke, and his voice was very slow and deep, like the voice of a dead man.

"I bore his body from the hall. A great pain struck me through the chest and left arm, but I was not too weak to carry him. I did not know where I went, or how long, but in time I came to a sound. There was a man in a little boat, he said that he would bear Sinfjotli across, and get his geld when he came back for me. I laid my son's body in the boat, and the ferryman rowed away, and he did not come back again."

The hairs were crawling upright on the back of Hailgi's neck, like grain-stalks lifting their heads behind a strong wind. A sudden cold had seized his limbs, stilling the thudding of his heartbeat against his eardrums. He stared at Sigimund without speaking. Epli-Karl yawned deeply, his jaws widening too suddenly for him to cover them with his hand. He raised his heavy eyebrows, then opened his mouth as if to say something. The movement stretched into a second yawn. "Oh," he murmured, his voice thick and blurred, "I think I must sleep now." The storyteller yawned yet again, pushing himself up and stumbling to a bench nearer the fire. He wrapped himself tightly in his cloak and lay down, his breath deepening to snoring within a few heartbeats.

Sigimund shrugged. "Some folk have little head for drink." He raised his horn to drain it, a few fire-gilded drops dribbling over the hoary plaits of his beard, then glanced about. "Hrafanhild has been drinking little, surely she cannot be asleep as well."

Hailgi did not see the Saxon maiden anywhere, but Frithawunjo sat slumped against the wall behind them with mouth open and eyes closed, snoring softly.

"Is it really so late?" He began to ask. The words froze in his mouth half-way through. Hailgi sat still as though chains of cold iron lay over all his limbs, staring at the hall-door as it slowly swung open. Hrafanhild went out for a piss, or else a thane is coming in late, he told himself, but that thought did not break the icy fetters that bound the hall in stillness.

The shape that glided out of the gray-white swirls of night snow was tall and pale. it seemed like a woman clad in a white dress, with the cloud-gray hide of a wolf draped over her so that the pelt's face hid her own, two eye-glints gleaming through the wolf's empty eye holes. She bore a pitcher before her in one hand, in the other, she held a piece of weaving with only a few threads straggling free from its edge. A fiery shock pierced through the ice of Hailgi's limbs with the well-known movements of her body. He knew that this was Sigiruna, however she had come here. Now he could move again, he lifted his horn, smiling up at her. But she went first to Sigimund, filling the Walsing's horn from her pitcher before turning to tread the short step to Hailgi himself. He put his hand over hers as she steadied his horn. Her fingers were cold enough to numb his, but she clasped his hand for a moment before turning to walk out as silently as she had come.

Hailgi raised his horn to drink as she departed. The little ice-crystals in the mead melted against the heat of his mouth, their cold piercing the draught's sweetness as Hailgi opened his throat and let the drink pour down until it began to choke him. Sigimund did likewise, his bright gaze fixed on the hall's swinging door.

"Now you have had your wish," Hailgi said hoarsely. "Now you have seen Sigiruna."

The Walsing looked down at him, the ice-edged heat of the mead still burning in his fierce blue eyes. "It seems to me that more has come to pass here. For I would have said that she who brought us that draught was my sister Sigilind, though the wolf-hide hid her face, I would know her from any other frowe."

"Wolf-hide?" Dagar murmured, his voice very queer and small. "I saw no wolf-hide, nor any maiden."

"What did you see?" Hailgi asked.

"I saw only a shadow, as might be cast by a very tall man in a hooded cloak, and it seemed to me that I saw the glimmer of a spear-point for a moment."

It seemed to Hailgi that all the mead he had drunk rushed to his head in a single breath, spinning the hall about him. He gripped the hard wooden edge of the bench as tightly as he could, breathing deeply until the moment of whirling wod had passed. At last he was able to say, "I think that I had best go to sleep now."

Dagar nodded without speaking, staring broad-eyed at Hailgi and Sigimund. More keenly than ever before, Hailgi felt the Skjolding's youth. Though he might have a man's height and years, Dagar's wide blue eyes in his narrow face made him look more child than youth to Hailgi at that moment.

Sigimund stood, and Hailgi and Dagar did likewise. "You can sleep here in the hall, I have more blankets than I can use, or, if you choose, there is a small house just outside the back door which I had readied for you, the fire lit and the beds made up. There you may stay as long as you like."

"I would find that fair," Hailgi said, gathering his strength to stand. The drink-wod that had whelmed him earlier was ebbing from his head, leaving a pounding pain behind in his temples. "Dagar, what of you?"

"I shall do as you do," the Skjolding answered.

The winter in the north of Jutland was bitter cold, but short, though the ground froze hard as a rind of iron, it melted early for the first planting, the plough's wooden boar-tooth breaking the last rim of ice beneath the softening earth. Ostara's feast was bright, bidding well for a warm summer and a good harvest year. It was a little before sunrise on the third day of summer when Hailgi and Sigiruna walked Dagar to the horses' fenced garth. Dagar bore a small chest on his shoulder, Hailgi and Sigiruna each carried one of his bags, and Hailgi also had two horse-saddles over his other arm. Though the path to Hagalar's hall was clear, and there had been little trouble with outlaws during Hailgi's rule, the Wolfing drighten had insisted that Dagar go byrnie-clad and armed.

Despite his thick cloak, the dawning coolness had sunk chill into the iron links, cutting cold through the wool of Dagar's tunic, but he bore it without shivering, though he glanced enviously at Hailgi, who seemed warm enough in his red cloak and tunic of light linen. Even in the mist-grayed dawn, Dagar could see that the long hairs clinging to the shoulder of the cloak like threads of gold were paler than the Wolfing's own amber, Sigiruna must have leaned her head there not long ago. Dagar eased his chest down to the wet earth, crushing the little needle-fine grasses that pricked green through the mud. He put two fingers in his mouth, whistling to the horse Hailgi had given him. The tall bay gelding, Dagar had not given him a name yet, lifted his head, but did not stir his hooves from the ground. Dagar took one of the saddles from Hailgi, walking toward his horse as the Wolfing went to saddle another, a sturdy brown mare with black mane and tail. Sigiruna helped her husband to load Dagar's goods onto the mare. Her long hair, unbound like a maiden's, swung back from her face, her breasts swaying as she heaved the little chest up to the saddle. She steadied it there while Hailgi bound it on, his long fingers brushing over hers as they worked.

Dagar turned his face away from the tenderness that softened Hailgi's sharp features in the misty light as his gray eyes gazed into Sigiruna's across the mare's back, away from his sister's answering smile and the rising brightness glowing on the high curves of her cheekbones. Dagar brushed a little dust from the arch of the bay's glossy neck, pulling the last strap tight and tugging at the saddle. Though it was easier to have a pair of cupped hands to step up into when mounting, more so when he was weighted by a byrnie, Dagar wished no help. He placed his palms flat on the saddle-back, heaving himself up and flinging his leg over. The horse turned his head, regarding him calmly with one large dark eye. Dagar had little trust that he would not bite, and hastened to pull the steed's head straight, nudging him into a walk and guiding him to the mare who stood with reins drooping between her neck and Hailgi's fist.

"The whole length of the path is clear, I am told," Hailgi said, passing the mare's reins up to Dagar, "and there is little risk of missing Hagalar's hall, anyway. If you find the wood-way difficult, you need only make your way to the beach and follow the coast around to the west, and in due time you will come to his lands. You should have nothing to fear, though keep a keen watch on the sea, there is always the risk of raiders from Gautland or one of the southern lands, Saxony or Frisia. Well-horsed as you are, though, even raiders should be little danger to you, so long as you see them in time and have a clear path to run on."

Dagar looked down into Hailgi's face. The pink scar cutting through his close-cropped amber beard along the jawline, narrow nose a little crooked, as though it had been broken in an old fight, he does not look so very like Sigiruna, Dagar thought. Still, the spoor of manhood did not hide the high-boned fairness Hailgi shared with the Skjoldings, and the wide gray eyes staring up at Dagar from beneath sharp dark brows might have been Sigiruna's own, save that there seemed to be more kindness in Hailgi's gaze.

"I shall take care," Dagar said. "I thank you for all your help. Fare well, Hailgi, and you, my sister."

Sigiruna patted him on the shoulder. "Fare well, brother. May you find life with Hagalar to your liking."

Dagar glanced back only once as he rode along the path through the green-sheened fields. Hailgi and Sigiruna stood with their arms about each other's waist and heads together, amber hair mingling with pale as they watched him ride away. They raised their hands to wave when they saw Dagar looking back at them, he waved back once, and then set his head firmly towards the road ahead. Dagar nudged his horses into a trot as they passed beneath the weave of green-leafed branches, moving down the wood-path at a good pace. Once a fox dashed before him, a ruddy streak in the lightening mist, something dangled from its mouth, though he could not see what. Though the white mist still dimmed her light, the Sun was well-risen by the time Dagar came to the overgrown path cutting away from the main road through the woods. Few folk rode this way. It was easier to fare by sea.

Dagar turned his horses down the pathway, riding over the thorny green blackberry vines and trampling the white dog-roses under hoof till he came to a boggy clearing where the high shoots of hwanna and milk-weed brushed against the bellies of the horses. Then he slid from the bay's back, his shoes sinking deep into the mud so that the cold slime oozed over his feet. He tied the mare to an oak by the side of the clearing and unloaded her, taking several long ropes from the chest she had borne. First he squatted down in the mud to fasten a knot about each of the gelding's legs, leaving enough slack that the horse could walk easily, then he did the same for himself with a second rope, and bound his wrists with the third.

The fourth he carried in one hand, tugging at the bay's reins with the other. The path turned upward, onto firmer earth. Walking was not easy here. The blackberry vines and trails of dog-rose coiled thorny about Dagar's ankles, catching at the rope between his legs so that he often had to bend down to unhook the thorns from the rough hemp. Clumps of nettles as high as his waist grew in the way, and these he had to skirt carefully, stamping the tall grasses down around them as the little morning-birds called mockingly over his head. Dew-white spiderwebs spread over the wood-growth before him like patches of frost on the green leaves, though Dagar walked carefully, he could not keep his cloak from brushing them away as he made his way down the path.

At last the Skjolding came to the slab of carven stone, deep gray beneath the morning dampness. The alf-cups brimmed with dew, a darker trail tracing the path from each to the next. Dagar breathed deeply, tightening his hand on the gelding's reins, and lifted his foot to step upon the threshold-stone. The Sun's light came golden through the white mist, the woven leaves of ash and oak breaking her brightness into a thousand gilded spear-shafts through the grove, but the old ash-tree's shadow fell through the fog, graying the wooden shape of Wodhanar beneath. Five rotting rope-ends still dangled from its branches, black in the brightening light. Dagar's mouth was dry, his throat choked with memory as he led his horse forward to stand before the tree. For a long moment, he stared at the god's helm-hidden face, at the crudely curved beak and staring eyes of the eagle-head jutting forward from Wodhanar's helmet. This was not the god he loved, not the god of his clan, but his goal was revenge for the sake of revenge, and he would not ask Freyjar for that nor had he sworn frith on the sheaf of his kin.

"Wodhanar," Dagar whispered. "I swore an oath on your spear, I was little willing to swear. My father and brother lie dead in their howe, by the will of my sister's man, and I have borne my shame as long as I may. Now I would make sacrifice for revenge. Lend me your spear, and give that ill-sworn oath back to me."

Dagar dropped the horse's reins, came forward to move the rootless stump beneath the high branch where Wodhanar's spear-shaft was bound. It was not easy to climb with his hands and feet tied, twice he swayed, nearly losing his balance, but at last he could reach up for the chain fettering the spear to the hanging-tree. The iron links dropped from the branch, clattering on a curve of bone that showed white through the old leaves behind Wodhanar's seat. It seemed to Dagar that he had hardly lifted the spear at all, but it was free in his hand, the heavy dark ashen shaft turning smoothly in his palm. Dagar climbed down from the stump, leaning the spear against the tree's trunk. He did not know how a horse might be hanged, but he took the bay's reins up again, leading the horse beneath the highest branch that he could reach. That blackened rope-end dangling there. Hjalmamarir had swung from that branch, his wife had borne a daughter afterwards, who was of an age with little Siggi. Dagar did not look down to see whether the hard lengths breaking beneath his feet were fallen branches or chewed bones, but tossed one end of his last rope over the branch and knotted it, then tied the other around the neck of his steed.

"Wodhanar, have this gift, for my oath given back, and revenge!" He cast the spear as hard as he could. The bay reared as the weapon sank in. The branch above the horse shook, two last blackened winter-leaves floating down. Then the gelding dropped to his knees, the rope pulling his head up so that he stared up through the branches at the clear sky. His dark eyes rolled back, the whites shining around them.

Dagar came forward, bracing his feet against the earth and working the spear free of the horse's chest. He stepped to the side, knowing how the dark heart-blood would gush forth, the spray spattered his face with salty drop-lets, staining Wodhanar's arm and the side of his cloak deep red. The spear in his hand, Dagar walked from Fetter-Grove. If he lived, he would bring it back afterwards, if not, he knew that Hailgi would bear it to the holy stead, and chain it to the old tree again.

CHAPTER XXIX

The storms passed on after the birth of Hoilogae's son Herwamundaz, dark cloud-packs
howling up towards the North. Three days into
Yule-time, the sky was clear and bright as a mirror
of polished silver, the Sun glittering from the
tiny ice-crystals blanketing the fields and howe-
mounds. Hoilogae and Swaebhon were walking over the lake together, their feet crunching
through the snow shielding its ice. They walked
with cloaks overlapping to keep warm, as close
beneath the shining sky as if they lay under a
single blanket.

"I still remember little of the birthing," Swaebhon said reflectively. "Only
the warmth in the bath-house, and how easy it was to fall asleep afterwards,
I know that it hurt a great deal, but I cannot remember more."

Hoilogae caressed her beneath their cloaks, stroking the rough linen
along the curve of her flank. He wanted to speak, but could say nothing,
she had borne her pain, and Herwamundaz, for his sake. Hoilogae knew
his thoughts must be graven on his face as clearly as pictures into stone, for
Swaebhon laughed, stopping and tilting her head back a little to kiss him.
Their lips were very cold, but Hoilogae could feel the warmth in her mouth
beneath, like a hot spring seething under frozen earth.

"You need not feel so," she said. "My hurts have already healed, and all the
women tell me it will go more easily next time. A woman who lives past her
first child is likely to have many more, unless she die of child bed fever, but
that happens seldom among our folk. And our Herwamundaz is a strong little warrior, isn't he? As fine-looking as his father, and as brave and fierce. Did
you hear how he shouted yesterday, when I came a little late to feed him?"

"I heard," Hoilogae said, smiling. "A full-grown boar could hardly have
matched him. If his arm grows to match his voice, there will not be such
another hero as Herwamundaz between here and your father's hall."

"Before I wed you, I had not thought that I should want children. They
seemed noisy and smelly to me, great trouble and little use for a long time.
Now there is nothing I would trade for our little Werwothough I should like
to have a little daughter next time, I think."

"I'll do my best," Hoilogae answered. They walked on a little further, between the low white mounds on the other side of the lake and into the wood. The leafless beeches gleamed in their casing of ice, the Sun's light flashing bright from the twigs as they clattered and shifted in the light breeze, dropping a powdering of fresh snow over the ice-crusted pathway. Here and there, a brown stalk or withered leaf stuck through the white heaps. The small birds left no track on the hard layer of ice, but the sharp hooves of the deer had punched through it to sink deep into the soft snow beneath, just as Hoilogae and Swaebhon broke through with every step. Mingled with the deer-spoor were wider tracks, large and round.

Swaebhon crouched down in the snow to look more closely. "These tracks are very fresh, if we had come out here a little sooner, we should have had a sight worth seeing. Those wolves are gaining fast on the deer they follow, but they shall have a good fight when they meet him. That is a strong stag, in good health, and the wolves must have been very hungry to risk him instead of looking for easier meat. This is very close to human dwellings for such a chase, the more so in this land, where you have settled so widely and have no mountains nor great rivers to keep you from the beasts." She straightened up, brushing a little melting snow from her hands. "I shall find it fair to go out hunting again, I am sure that I shall be quite strong enough for a good chase in another two or three days."

"Are you tired now?"

"No, not yet. It is good to be out in the clean air, and there is little enough sunlight at this time of the year. We ought not waste it." Swaebhon pulled the pins of coil-wrought bronze from the long twist of winter-pale hair knotted about her skull, running her fingers through it and letting it fall free as she leaned her head back to gaze up at the sky. She pointed upward. "Ah, see there?"

Hoilogae looked up as well, through the branches that spread dark against the blue sky like a net of cracks over a robin's egg. Two black shapes floated above, tilting wide wings against the unseen wind. One called hoarsely to another, its deep resonant quork, quork clear as a lur-horn's voice through the icy woods.

"Someone has made a good kill, there will be more ravens here soon. Shall we follow the tracks?"

When they had tracked the chase for a while, Swaebhon turned to Hoilogae and put a finger to his lips. "Listen," she whispered. "Do you hear them?"

He did. A far-off snapping and growling, coming clearly through the still woods.

"We must go softly and carefully from here. They will not wish to let us close."

The wolf-pack had caught the stag between two great trees, an ash and a broad-trunked oak. The snow was torn up all around, stained reddish-black with gouts of blood. Four wolves, a brindled red-black pair, a deep gray dog-wolf, and a golden-gray bitch, were tearing at the stag's wide-antlered carcase, another gray wolf lay crumpled in the snow, the blood slowly thickening in his fur. The golden-gray bitch-wolf looked up, snarling. The fangs were very white in her gaping mouth, her yellow eyes glowed like hot bronze in their black sockets as she glared up at them. Carefully Hoilogae and Swaebhon backed away until they could see the pack and their kill no longer. By the time they came out of the woods, thin swan-feathers of cloud were already sweeping across the pale sky, dimming the Sun's brightness a little as she dropped towards the tree-tops.

Even from across the lake, Hoilogae could see the wagon in front of the hall, the two horses harnessed before it shifting restlessly in the snow and snorting out little white clouds of cold smoke. Swaebon's fine eyebrows drew together, deepening the straight crease between her sky-gray eyes. "I wonder who has come to our hall," she said slowly. "Those are not our horses, nor do they belong to Herwawardhaz and Sigislinthon, unless they have traded for new ones since we were last there."

One of the horses was gray, one white, but both had black manes and tails. Hoilogae did not know them either, though they looked like fine beasts. "I do not know whose they might be," he answered. "Still, if we have guests, we ought to hasten to meet them."

As Hoilogae and Swaebhon came into the hall, the first thing that Hoilogae marked was the horned bronze helmet on the head of the man who stood braced with his back to them, facing the empty high-seat. He was wrapped in heavy black wool, the long braid down his back was only a little fairer than his cloak, though the light from the door and smoke hole brought the reddish sheen from its darkness. Herwamundaz was howling, his loud high voice going straight through Hoilogae's head, though Fraujodis held the child inside her own garments and was trying to push her plump breast at his mouth, murmuring, "Werwo, Werwo, drink, that's a good baby," he was not sucking.

Hoilogae strode up to the helmed man. A shudder of awe running through his body, he took the helm-bearer by the shoulder, swinging him about. "Who are you, to wear the war-helm into my hall at Yule-tide?"

The man looked up at him, slowly blinking his blue eyes. His face was square, rough-carven as the end of an oaken beam, though he was shaven, his beard was too dark and thick for the keen edge of a bronze, or even iron, razor to scrape away easily, and the stubborn hair-roots darkened his cheeks. "I do not wear it for myself," the helm-bearer replied. "I bring you a bidding to single battle, as is lawful in the days of Yule-tide, whatever oaths are otherwise made."

Hoilogae grasped the ringed hilt of the sword at his side. Swaebhon had come up beside him, she laid her hand upon his shoulder.

"Whose bidding do you bear?" Hoilogae asked, his voice rough as the chisel-rasp of bronze on stone. "Who wishes to meet me in single battle?" Hedhinaz, he thought suddenly, the name darkening his mind like the blood of anger rising into his brother's pale cheeks, but no. Whatever he might think, he was sure that Hedhinaz was true, and had no sake to fight him for.

"I bear the bidding of Hrothagaisaz, son of Hrothamaraz, whom you slew and whose father's iron blade you took from his kin. He calls you to fight him alone at the Thing-place on Sigisharjaz's Holm on Yule's last day, and to give that sword back, if you are not afraid to strike iron on iron."

"I cannot give that sword back. I have already given it to another, my brother Hedhinaz, who earned it well in fight, even if he were here, and not north in Glazaleunduz, I could not take it from him to prove my own strength. In any case, Hrothamaraz bore it against me, and saw then that I had no fear of striking iron on iron. But I will gladly meet Hrothagaisaz at the Thing-place on Sigisharjaz's Holm, and fight him alone in the ring of hallowed linden-stakes on Yule's last day, and there it shall be seen how the gods deem in the sakes that bring us there!" Hoilogae raised his voice louder and louder to be heard over his son's shrieking, until he was roaring with his full throat.

The helm-bearer was a brave man. He had not backed away, though Hoilogae's words and gaze had slowly drained the cold-stung ruddiness from his face like rushing river-water leeching the color from ill-dyed linen. "I shall bear that message back to him," he said, turning to leave.

"Wait. The Sun shall set before too long, we should not send you out hungry into the darkness. However matters may stand with your drighten, I see no need to say that you yourself are at odds with me, at least not till you have taken the war-helm from your head and named your own quarrel for yourself. Though you have come to our hall with words from a foe, I would have you stay this night as a guest, and leave at dawn, with the full day to travel. There are nine nights yet left in Yule, and one will not make much difference in your riding towards Hrothagaisaz's hall, unless the worst of snowstorms should come upon us in the morning."

"You make a fair offer, and I am minded to take it, if you will swear to me that I will be safe here."

"I offer you full guest-right. If that offer were not honorable, my oath would mean no more."

"So be it, then." Hrothagaisaz's messenger lifted the helm from his head, easing it down slowly upon the table as if its weight were far greater than the measure of its bronze. He wore a soft leather cap beneath it, but when he pushed that back, Hoilogae saw the war-helm's red ring on his forehead. Herwomundaz had stopped squalling, in the moment of stillness, Hoilogae could hear the soft sounds of the child's suckling.

At some time while they were talking, Swaebhon had glided away, now she stood beside Hoilogae again. There was a horn in her hand, which she lifted to their guest. "Drink and be welcome, here in our hall."

"I thank you for this guestright," the man answered. "My name is Fritharikijaz, son of Frithguntharaz." He raised the horn, drinking deeply. When he lowered it, Hoilogae felt that the knots of muscle along his jaw had eased, the tight lines of his forehead and mouth loosening. "Your ale deserves its good fame," he said. "Now, where do you keep your beasts? I must unyoke my horses, and bring them within walls before the Sun has fully set. I do not know how such matters go in the Northlands at Yule-tide, but,"

"It is the same," Swaebhon answered firmly.

The Sun went down swiftly at Yule, her light was glowing long and red over the fields of snow to darken the bare woods beyond by the time they had finished seeing to Fritharikijaz's horses. When the three of them walked back into the hall, it was already near-full.

Some of the men and women were feeding up the fires with armloads of new-brought wood, traces of snow hissing away as the damp bark slowly dried and burst into flame, other folk were carrying about the bread the women had baked in the daytime, or reaching into the fire with tongs to lift the glowing stones from the coals and drop them into the large clay stew-pots standing by the hearth. Two of the strongest men in the settlement, Brandahardhaz and his mother's sister's son Harjabaldaz, were carrying in a shoulder-high cask of ale so that the women would not have to go out to the brewing-house when they needed to refill their pitchers. Swaebhon's loom was set up by her seat, she usually wove when she and Hoilogae sat inside by the fire. Now she sat skimming the black-threaded shuttle through the white upright-threads, watching the men as they ate and drank. It seemed to Hoilogae that his beloved was paler than usual, as though she had not healed as well from the birthing as she claimed, and he thought that this quietness was not like her.

Hoilogae leaned over to her, speaking softly into her ear. "Swaebhon, are you tired, or ill? Would you like to go to sleep? I shall spread your blankets for you, and make sure you are left alone."

"I am not tired or ill," Swaebhon answered. "Only thoughtful. I shall go with you to Sigisharjaz's Holm, but I fear we must leave our son behind us. Little Werwo is too young for such a faring at this time of year."

"Ah, but things will be easier when this is done, and it is better so. Else wise we should have awaited a host to march on us the very day the frith Sigisharjaz set between Hrothagaisaz and I came to end. Now there will be only one man dead, or at the worst two, and no harm done to the fields. Alas, I am still sure of my sword, so long as you are with me, my sig-wife, I know that no ill can come for me."

"I have ever worked to make it so," Swaebhon answered. Still, Hoilogae could see the crease between her eyebrows deepening, dark as a short straight scar in the firelight.

"Herwamundaz will be all right," Hoilogae said. "He likes Fraujodis' milk nearly as well as he likes your own, he is a healthy child, and isn't she a fine mother and nurse, with four children out of six still living and well? I know it is hard to leave him behind, but we shall be back soon enough."

Hoilogae and Swaebhon set off for the coast lands the next day, with a band of eight thanes, four Northmen and four Jutlanders. They rode in an ox-drawn wagon, and Hoilogae wore the war-helm again, his high-horned shadow stretching along the road before the cart. No one would stop him, no one would dare not to offer him food and drink, for while he bore the helm, the host's full might was in him and the gods would hold him hallowed. Only one who dared to do battle could hinder his path. The cold bit deeply along the bronze, even through his tufted cap, but it was little worse to bear than the heat of summer had been, and once the Sun had been up a little while, her light began to warm the metal.

The traveling went more slowly than they had thought it would. The ox-cart moved sluggishly through the snow, and twice Hoilogae had to climb down from the wagon to help his men clear a fallen tree from the road, breaking the ice that gripped the limbs with the back of their axes and heaving the trunk aside. Swaebhon had brought her length of new cloth, now full-woven, with her. Though Hoilogae thought it unlike her, she sat stitching in the wagon as the men hauled on the heavy weights, never stirring a step to help them or stilling the movement of her fingers. The sky grayed as they went on, the milky veils of cloud thickening until a dull ruddy glow in the west showed that Sunna was setting. Hoilogae looked about for path-signs. They had just passed Thonaraz's lightning-blasted oak, and were not far from the mounds marking the marches of Sigislinthon's udal lands.

"A little farther, and then we must make camp," he said. "I think there are no houses of living men close enough to reach by darkness, even should we turn back, but I think that those who dwell ahead will greet us kindly on this night, and their homes will shelter us from wind and snow."

Hoilogae gazed keenly at his warriors as he spoke. The four Northmen Bernu, Chaidhamariz, Wiwastanaz, and Ehwastanaz, looked back at him, though their glances flickered to Swaebhon when he met the eyes of each one, but the Jutlanders turned their gazes away altogether. Theudorikijaz grasped the amber boar dangling on a thong from the hilt of his sword, opening his mouth as though he was about to say something, but then shut it again. The lowering ruddy light through the trees darkened the freckles on his left cheek to a single splotch of brown lichen, the right side of his face seemed pale in the shadow.

"These are my kin," Hoilogae said softly. "If they bear me ill-will, there is no hope for what might be, either now or when I am dead. We must not go to them with fear, but rather with friendship, for we have dwelt well in their lands and they have been kind to us in turn."

Theudorikijaz's throat bobbled under his skimpy red beard and he nodded. Hraidhamannaz said nothing, but Hoilogae could see the fair young warrior's shaven jaw tightening. The two older thanes, Eburabrandaz and Katilaz only picked up the leads of the oxen and began to walk again, if any fear lurked beneath the wide spread of Eburabrandaz's brown beard, or the gray cloak wrapped tight around Katilaz's wiry frame, they showed no sign of it. When they had come within sight of the mounds, Hoilogae got down from the wagon again. Swaebhon followed him, bearing a horn of mead and two pieces of fish hard-baked in bread. The two of them stopped between the snowy howes. The silence rang louder and louder in Hoilogae's ears, his skull hummed like a hive of bees with it, thrumming almost painfully between his eyes. It seemed to him that he could see the snow burning coldly over the mounds, blue light flickering against whiteness at the corners of his sight. The howe-dwellers would be awake that night, nor would they be bound to the garths that kept them at other times. It would be little wonder if any surprise guests came to the campfire that night.

"My kinfolk, I have been bidden to battle. Thus I wear the war-helm on my head, and have a sword by my side, but to you I come always in frith and love." Though Hoilogae spoke softly, he could hear his own voice ringing through the earth and snow, the high-heaped rocks beneath the mounds' softer blanketing. "Hail to you, holy folk, hail to you, my kin."

The voice in Hoilogae's head was hoarse and sharp as rotten stone cracking away underfoot, his sight dazed by the shifting blue lights on the snow, it was a moment before he saw the movement on the mound, or knew that the words sounded in his ears as well as his skull. "Hail to you, Hoilogae. I think you must go little further."

Someone's gasp behind him cut off quickly as the shape rose from the snow. Thin beneath the darkening sky, its tattered cloak and long hair streaming out into shadow. It tottered down the mound as though its feet had rotted beneath it. Hoilogae stood his ground, only reaching back to take the horn of mead and one of the fish-rolls from Swaebhon so that he could offer them as was fitting. It was not until the mound-man was nearly upon him that Hoilogae could see the sharp features beneath the matted hair. Though the face was white and blue with cold, the ice-glazed eyes wide and staring as those of a carved god-shape, Hoilogae knew his brother at once, and a great sadness settled chill into his bones.

"Hail to you, Hedhinaz," he said, stretching out the horn towards his brother. "Be welcome among us this Yule night, as my kin shall always be dear to me." He did not know whether Hedhinaz would be able to take the drink or not. He had heard tales in the North last Yule-tide. The tears rose to Hoilogae's own eyes, though the frozen air drew the warmth from them before they could spill over the rims of his cheekbones.

But when Hedhinaz's ice-cold hand touched his on the horn's smooth curve, Hoilogae knew that his kinsman was no ghost or walking lich, but still living. He drew a deep breath of relief, the chill air burning down into his lungs, as Hedhinaz took the horn from his hand and drank. "What tidings do you bring from the north? Drighten, how were you driven out of your land, so that you come alone to find us?"

"I have done a great ill, much harm. I have chosen the high-born one, your bride, at the oath-draught." Hedhinaz's lips hardly moved as he spoke, his words came thickly as though the cold had frozen his whole mouth. "Yet I think it was not wholly I who worked there. On Yule Eve, as the sky was darkening, I met a troll-woman in the wood, who rode on a wolf, she offered to follow me, and I would not have her, and then she said that I would pay for it at the oath-drinking, and I spoke as I would not have wished to then, before the gods and ghosts and all my folk."

Hoilogae stared into his brother's blue-rimmed eyes, dark as seawater against his white face. His own fist had drawn back at Hedhinaz's words, like an adder coiling to strike. Even now, Swaebhon wore the rich strand of amber his brother had given her before Hoilogae's own eyes. It needed little wisdom to know that the words must have been waxing in Hedhinaz's mind since the summer planting, little more for him to see past Swaebhon's mirrored brightness in his brother's eyes, beyond the snowy paleness of the mound behind her to the deep bale-well from which the deepest roots of Hedhinaz's vow had sprung.

Though Hoilogae had not yet touched him, Hedhinaz was already swaying like a tree with rotten roots, set upon by a strong wind. Hoilogae was about to turn his head back to Swaebhon, but then he knew that he did not need to look back for her gaze to strengthen him, he could feel her there by him, as she would be while he lived, while he lived. His brother had battled long against his own will, and had he not already striven beyond his strength for years to stand in Hoilogae's place? There is little to wonder at here, Hoilogae thought. It was carved long since. He opened his hand, slowing its strike until he grasped Hedhinaz gently by the arm to hold up his brother's thin body.

The words came without thought, as though another spoke through his throat, a deep voice, rough as hemp and grim with fore-knowledge. "The troll-woman rode alone on the wolf at darkening-time, offering to follow you. She knew that Sigislinthon's son would have to do battle on Sigishar-jaz's field. You have given no sake for strife! Your ale-speech must soon come true for both of us, Hedhinaz. A drighten has bidden me to the island. On Yule's last day, I shall come there, and I doubt that I shall come back from that. Then may all be done for good, what shall be."

Hoilogae clamped his teeth together hard, but the cold words had already blown through, leaving his throat raw and hot with anger. He would pay Wodhanaz his geld in time, but not be led like a sheep to slaughter. He had chosen open-eyed to wed Swaebhon, and till the shape that called his doom appeared before his eyes, he would not let himself trust in it. He would battle ill words and ill-seemings till the walkurjon claimed his life herself. Hedhinaz flinched back, as though his brother's thoughts had scorched his frozen flesh, and reached for the sword at his side. His clawed blue fingers could not close on the hilt, but he clasped it in his palms, drawing it forth and holding it point-up before Hoilogae. "Hoilogae, you said that Hedhinaz was worthy of good from you, and of great gifts, but it is more seemly for you to redden your sword than to give frith to your foes. Now if you must do battle, do battle with me here, and lay me in a mound in your land afterwards, where you and Swaebhon shall be laid together in time, and then my oath shall be kept, for we shall sleep in one bed and not part from each other afterwards."

"It is too late for that," Hoilogae replied harshly. Then he knew that though he could not rinse the acorn-bitterness from his voice, he might yet clean it from his words, and so he spoke on. "I have taken one challenge already, and till I have met it, there is no one who may stand in my way, nor hinder my going, as this helm tells you full well." He stepped forward, closing his hands around Hedhinaz's and guiding the blade back to its place in the sheath at the youth's side. "I shall neither do battle with you nor take your sword from you. I bear you no ill-will. I must finish making our greetings to our kin, but you shall let Swaebhon tend to you, for I think that you are not well."

At Swaebhon's bidding, the men set up the largest tent around her as she kindled fire by rubbing wood against wood, the mound-dwellers looked unkindly on spark-striking. Though Theudorikijaz was little willing to do it, the offer of a horn of Swaebhon's mead swayed the red-haired thane. He let Hedhinaz huddle against him beneath their cloaks, though Hoilogae could see his blotchy face paling and the shudders running through his body as he let the other youth share in his warmth. When Swaebhon and Hoilogae had fed the fire up to a good blaze, Swaebhon heated water in the little clay pot she had brought.

"Now, Hedhinaz, show me your feet," she told him. Hedhinaz bit his lip as he straightened his legs, and Hoilogae could hear his brother's breath hissing between his teeth. Black blood crusted Hedhinaz's shoes and the foot-wrappings beneath them, in the end Swaebhon had to cut the leather away. Hedhinaz's still face did not change as she pulled the bloody wrappings from his feet, and Hoilogae guessed that he could not feel what she was doing. Without haste, Swaebhon began to wipe his feet with a piece of wool dipped in the hot water, rubbing them firmly.

"Do you feel anything yet?" She asked him.

"No."

The rest of the thanes were setting up their tents so that Hoilogae and Swaebhon were between them and the mounds, Wiwastanaz had scraped a wide circle clean of snow in the middle of the camp-garth and was squatting in it with his own fire-sticks, his furry brown cloak spread out around him. The dark-haired Northerner looked up as Hoilogae came near, his hands never resting as he worked to drill flame from wood.

"Don't need to worry much about your brother," Wiwastanaz said, his light voice even. "Swaebhon's got a good touch with frostbite, it happened often enough in the northlands. If his feet haven't frozen right through, she can bring the blood back to them, and if worst comes to worst, I've seen her chop rotting limbs right off and still keep the life in the man afterwards."

"Do you mean, are you saying he might be crippled?" That might be a fair geld for his ill words at the oath-drinking, Hoilogae thought before he could still his mind.

Hoilogae did not know whether the anger scoring his guts showed on his face, but Wiwastanaz bent his head to blow on the little coal he had brightened in the wood. He did not speak for a few minutes, not till a strong flame was flickering reddish glints from his close-cropped brown beard and sharpening the shadow of the long nose jutting above it.

Then he said, "I saw the way he came down the mound, and how hard it was for him to stand. I won't lie about my thoughts. Hedhinaz may well have lost his feet to the snow, he wouldn't be the first, or the last. But still, you needn't worry, we'll take good care of him for you. He can't be ruling his folk by the strength of those skinny arms alone, so I doubt he'll lose his place in Glazaleunduz. Surely not while he can still get good men to back him up."

"You'll go with Swaebhon, if she must go to Glazaleunduz after this?"

"We will. All of us who came from the north swore to Aiwilimae that we'd keep her safe and see that no one did her ill, or brought her sorrow if it could be helped. We'll go with her, whether she stays or leaves."

"Thank you," Hoilogae said softly. "It eases my mind to know that. And if she goes to Glazaleunduz, you will give your strength to my brother and help him in all things, as you have helped me?"

Wiwastanaz nodded, feeding another stick slowly into his fire. "You need not fear. For your sake as well as hers, we'll do well by him." As Hoilogae began to turn away, the Northerner glanced up sharply. "Hoilogae, you won't go away from the tents this night, will you?"

"I won't."

"Good. It seems to me that here," Wiwastanaz looked up at the darkening shadows behind the great tent, the grayish-whiteness of the two mound-tops against the black trees, and he did not need to finish speaking the thought in his mind.

"I remember that you knew many stories of ghosts and trolls," Hoilogae suddenly found himself saying. "Will you tell me one now?"

"Now?"

"Yes, now. I would hear such a story."

By the time Wiwastanaz's tale was done, the other men had gathered around the fire, holding their stiff hands out to the blaze as they listened. After a few moments of nervous silence, Katilaz rubbed the wart on the side of his stubby nose and said, "Now, that reminds me of something that my mother's half-brother said happened to him once. He was driving a few of those spotted cows he breeds down past the end of the Host-Way, planning to do some trading at the first summer gathering down there, and."

Hoilogae walked back into Swaebhon's tent. His brother was sitting up by himself now, and Theudorikijaz was drinking his reward, the fire warming the color back into his face. Hedhinaz's fists were clenched on two large stones, beads of sweat dribbling down his white forehead as he stared over Swaebhon's bent head. She was still working on the youth's feet, but Hoilogae could see Hedhinaz's mouth tighten each time her thumbs pressed against his soles.

"He won't lose his feet, at least," Swaebhon said. "I may be able to save most of his toes as well, though they're less sure."

Hoilogae squatted down beside his brother, putting his hand on Hedhinaz's shoulder. His brother turned his head painfully, looking into Hoilogae's eyes. This close, Hoilogae could see the little blond hairs beginning to sprout along Hedhinaz's sharp jaw, the fair down thickening on his upper lip. Though the tight skin over the keen bone-edges of his high cheeks was still pale, the blue tint of ice had melted from his face, and his eyes were no longer set in their wide wild death-stare.

"Have you not taken enough hurt already?" Hoilogae asked, as gently as he could. "Why did you come so, without horse or food or folk to help you? It is not like you, to fare so, it does not befit a drighten."

Hedhinaz looked down, the muscles of his jaw tightening as he bit down on something. For a moment Hoilogae feared that his brother was chewing his own tongue, then a bulge moved here and there against Hedhinaz's cheeks, and Hoilogae knew that Swaebhon had given him something to bite against the pain, a strip of leather, perhaps, or a little piece of wood.

"I was ashamed," he muttered through the thing he chewed. "I could not stay in the hall, so I ran out, and then I was lost in the storm. It took me a while to find my way here. I was sleepy. I was just going to sleep on the mound a while, I knew our kin would take care of me."

Swaebhon straightened one of her braid-coils, pushing the bronze pin in more firmly. "You would have slept a long time," she told him, "and I do not doubt that you knew it when you lay down in the snow." She pressed at his foot again. "Do you feel that?"

"Yes. It does not hurt so much now."

"That?"

"Yes."

"That?"

"No. No. Nor that. Hoilogae, who is it that has bidden you to battle?"

"Hrothagaisaz the son of Hrothamaraz." Hoilogae's voice cleared as he spoke, the bitter anger slowly settling from his thoughts like the cloud of mud sinking to the bottom of a cow-stirred pond. "Hedhinaz, think on this. I have no doubt that he would have done this last Yule, had I not been in the Northlands. He has waited his time patiently since his father's death, and I have no mind to disappoint him now."

"You ought to have killed him when you first saw him." Hedhinaz bit down again, then coughed hard. He shifted the thing in his mouth to one side and spat into the fire. Hoilogae did not like the dullness of his eyes, nor the red patches beginning to brighten on his cheeks. "It would have gone better for you if."

Hoilogae slapped his brother across the face. Though it was no hard blow, Hedhinaz's head jerked beneath it, and Hoilogae saw his gaze brightening into the well-known glare before it dimmed again.

"You are not yourself, Hedhinaz, you are not thinking of your words. I know the choice I made better than you do, and I know that I could have made no better choices than those which brought me to Swaebhon and the birth of my son Herwamundaz. If I am to die this Yule-tide, it is well enough. You shall live on in the place you have won, and if you find my death so sorrowful, then you must strive harder to make your life worthy of all I have left you."

"It is far from time to mourn," Swaebhon broke in. She raised her head to stare up at the two of them. Her gray eyes glowed like a wild beast's, the fire-light shining out of their depths. "Neither of you is dead yet, and wyrd may be read both rightly and wrongly. Do you feel that, Hedhinaz?"

Hedhinaz's breath gasped out before he could bite it back, and Hoilogae saw the tears standing in his brother's eyes.

"That?"

Hedhinaz shook his head. "You will walk, and stand to fight, but two toes on your right foot, and one on your left, must be cut off if the life does not come back to them this night, and that we must do tomorrow, before they begin to rot." She scooped a handful of warming-stones out of the clay pot, tossing them back into the fire. "Theudorikijaz, go out and scrub this with snow, and bring it back full of clean snow, and if they are cooking out there, bring us some food."

The red-haired thane nodded, laying his empty horn down on his side and rising to his feet. "Shall I bring the kegs from the wagon as well?"

"Yes, do, if they're left out too long, they're likely to freeze and burst."

Hoilogae and Swaebhon waited a long time for Hedhinaz to go to sleep that night. Though he soon seemed to be breathing with the soft depth of slumber, something about the tight set of his shoulders and the way he was curled made Hoilogae doubt that his brother was really asleep. At last Hedhinaz shifted, and a little string of fire-sheened drool slowly began to pearl from the corner of his mouth to the wadded cloak under his head, and that he would not have done while waking, even to feign sleep.

Only then did Hoilogae wriggle out of his tunic and Swaebhon out of her shift, only then did Hoilogae pull his bride close enough to feel her warmth all along his body. He caressed Swaebhon's milk-filled breasts as softly as he could, careful not to let his calloused palms rasp against her sore nipples, she snuggled closer, kissing the hollow of his throat.

"Hoilogae, you are very fair and brave," Swaebhon murmured. "I am gladder of my choice than ever." Her hands stroked up the insides of his thighs as she kissed him again.

"My beloved, my dear one," Hoilogae whispered back. "My life would have been little without you, and my death hardly worth the name."

For a little time they lay kissing and stroking one another, till the sound of Swaebhon's swift breathing blended with Hoilogae's own and she shifted to pull him onto her. "Have no fear of hurting me," she said softly to him. "I am full-healed, and even if I were not, no pain should keep me from you in these nights."

In the dark, Hoilogae could not know whether any blood mingled with the warmth that eased his way into Swaebhon's body, nor whether any pain edged her soft gasps as she tightened her arms about his back and her thighs about his own. The thought that soon he must part from her was pain enough to spur him on, tightening the sweet noose in his groin as he thrust in again and again.

"Hoilogae, Hoilogae, my hallowed one!" Swaebhon cried in a near-silent whisper, and the tightness within Hoilogae's body broke, his seed spilling out into her as she clutched him hard to her.

Hedhinaz was able to walk by the time Hoilogae's band dragged the boat they had borrowed from Sigisharjaz's man Theudowulfaz up onto the rocky shore of Sigisharjaz's Holm. Though the stumps of his toes still bled a little when he strained himself, he said that he would not lean on anyone, nor would he use an oar for a crutch. Mindful of this, Hoilogae and Swaebhon walked very slowly before the others, making their way up the winding path that led to Sigisharjaz's hall. The going was treacherous, which slowed them even more.

The rocks beneath the sun-brightened snow were slimed with a thin glaze of ice, and some of them were loose underfoot. Hoilogae did not know the two men who stood at the hall-door with spears, though their matching broad faces and masses of straight yellow hair made him think that they must be brothers. Staring at the war-helm on his head, they stood aside without a word as he and Swaebhon passed between the door-posts. Though the Sun stood a little past her day's height, men and women still snored on many of the benches or in the straw by the walls. Sigisharjaz's thralls or bond-folk were carefully cleaning the hall around the sleepers, casting armloads of soiled hay into the fire and strewing fresh about. Sigisharjaz himself sat beneath his eagle-banner with Gunthahildioz beside him, talking softly with his wife. It was a moment before the gray-haired drighten looked up at Hoilogae.

Then he was out of his seat in less than an eye blink, dark eyes glaring like the coals of a bale-fire as he grasped the iron-tipped spear that leaned against the wall behind his high-seat.

"Who wears the war-helm here, in the days of holy feasting and the gods' frith?" Sigisharjaz roared. "Name your names and tell your tidings, or Wodhanaz shall have you here and now!"

Around the hall, eyes slowly opened, men began to roll from their benches to their feet, fumbling for swords and eating knives.

"Wodhanaz shall have me when he chooses. That is already written," Hoilogae called back to him. "I do not bear the helm against you, but Hrothagaisaz has called me to do single battle here on your holm, on Yule's last day, and I have come to answer that calling."

Sigisharjaz set his spear back into its place and walked down between the tables to meet them. "Then hail to you, who have come to fight as a hero on my holm!" He reached out to clasp Hoilogae's forearm in his strong grip, then rose up on his toes to hug him about the shoulders. "It will be good to see you do battle. I have long thought that you must be a warrior of worth, and all I have heard tells me the same. And hail to you, Swaebhon and Hedhinaz and the rest of you. You are all welcome guests this Yule-tide. Come up to sit beside me, and my frowe shall pour you a greeting-draught."

The bonds maids were already hurrying to bring Gunthahildioz a pitcher and cups. She sat still, her silvered head turned a little away from them, but even from halfway down the hall, Hoilogae could see that the milky whiteness had wholly drowned her eyes. Sigisharjaz's wife poured the ale with slow care, measuring from memory so well that not a drop was spilled.

When she was done pouring, Gunthahildioz rose to her feet. Her strands of amber clicked softly against each other as she held out the first cup. "Hail to you, Hoilogae, and be welcome here."

"Hail to you, and to Sigisharjaz, the blessings of all the holy ones be on your hall this Yule-tide," he answered, and drank as Gunthahildioz greeted the others. She had heard the names of Swaebhon and Hedhinaz, but each of the thanes had to speak his name in turn so that she could hail him.

"Attalae, too," the frost-haired frowe murmured at last, lifting her own cup for a moment before she drank. No one said anything, though Hedhinaz shifted nervously. Hoilogae glanced down at his brother's feet. The dark blood was beginning to soak through the thick wrappings over them.

Sigisharjaz settled himself in his seat. "Sit you down by me, then. Hildalinthon, bring us food. I am sure these folk are hungry after their faring." He went on as the wayfarers found places at his table. Hoilogae and Swaebhon beside him, the rest on the other side, with Hedhinaz straight across from the hall's ruler. "Swaebhon, it is fair to see you, and to know that Hoilogae's wish-maiden is worth all his trials. I had heard that you were with child. Did the birthing go well?"

"Very well," Swaebhon answered. "We have a strong son, whom we have named Herwamundaz."

"Ah, that is good. Attalae told me that the name was mighty in Glaza-leunduz. What of you, Hedhinaz? What brings you away from your folk at Yule-tide?"

"I made an oath, and I wish to stand by my brother."

Sigisharjaz nodded his iron-gray head slowly, gazing at him. "I have heard that you are yet unmarried."

"That is so." For all Hedhinaz struggled to meet the old drighten's gaze, Hoilogae could hear the faint tremble in his voice, like the shaking of muscles strained past their strength.

"Hmm. We shall talk more of this later, you and I. Now, Hoilogae, tell us what news there is from Sigislinthon's lands. We have heard little since your home-coming."

It was two nights later, on the evening before Yule's last day, that Hrothagaisaz's ship beached on the shore of Sigisharjaz's Holm. Though Fritharikijaz marched behind his drighten, Hrothagaisaz bore the war-helm himself now, his hazel eyes lighting beneath the shadow of his horns as he looked up to the hall-door where Hoilogae stood.

"Well-met!" Hrothamaraz's son called, his voice merrier than Hoilogae had yet heard it. "Are you ready for battle? Have you brought my sword back to me?"

"I answered your man, I shall answer you in the same way. I shall gladly fight you, but if you want your father's iron, you must ask the man who holds it."

Hrothagaisaz frowned beneath his golden beard, tightening his hand upon the gold-wired hilt of his sword. "Bronze or iron, I shall do battle with you all the same. No fear shall hold me back from it."

"Then I know that Sigisharjaz shall welcome you in his hall, and ween our battle to be a worthy sight."

Though more mead and ale flowed through the nights of Sigisharjaz's Yule-tide feasting than Hoilogae had yet seen, few drank too deeply on the night before the combat. There was no one who wished to sleep through it. Hedhinaz sat silent across from Sigisharjaz, hardly touching the slice of rich boar-meat or the cup of mead before him, but Hoilogae sat with one arm about Swaebhon's shoulders, letting her lift his horn to his lips, and though the war-helm weighted his skull, his heart was light and merry as he tasted the mead's honey and fruit in her mouth. Hrothagaisaz's horns rose on the other side of the hall's fro and frowe, and Hoilogae thought that he often heard his foe man laugh that night, though he could not be sure. Hrothagaisaz had never laughed within the halls of Hoilogae's kin. Hoilogae woke by himself at dawn, when the light was just slipping through the smoke hole in the little house Sigisharjaz had lent to Hoilogae and Swaebhon. Swaebhon lay on her back, her mouth open and hair spread all about her head in a great pale spray. Propping himself up on one elbow, Hoilogae leaned over her, kissing her until her gray eyes opened. She pulled his head back down, holding him to her for a moment before she sat up and reached for the bag she had laid beside the bed the night before.

"This is the tunic you shall wear," she said, unfolding the garment from her sack. It was the black-and-white weave she had been working on, now stitched with sharp lines of madder-red along the hem. Hoilogae stood up, naked in the cold air, and let Swaebhon drape it about him, fastening it over his shoulders with his two finest golden brooches. She wrapped the broad sword-belt she had woven for him around his waist, then bound his leg-wrappings and shoes onto him, afterwards setting his gray wolf-cloak upon his shoulders and pinning it with a golden pin. At last she put Hoilogae's thick-tufted cap onto his head, lowering the war-helm on top of it. He could feel her hands shaking, but her voice was strong as she spoke.

"Let all this ward you well, my beloved. All my might is with you. We shall win, or fail, together."

Swaebhon dressed herself quickly, and the two of them walked together through the snow to the hall. Although the Sun had not yet risen, Hoilogae could see that the sky was clear as water through the dawning's dimness. Cold as it was, it would be a fair day for fighting. Hedhinaz and Hrothagaisaz were already in the hall, sitting in their places at Sigisharjaz's table. Hedhinaz's fair head was bent over his bowl of porridge, but Hrothagaisaz sat straight, slowly chewing each mouthful as though he meant to be sure that no ill chance could choke him before the battle's beginning. A pile of fresh-cut stakes lay heaped beneath the drighten's eagle banner. These were the linden staves that would mark the battling-ring.

"Hail to you, Hoilogae and Swaebhon," Sigisharjaz called cheerfully. "When the Sun is fully up, we shall go to the Thing-stead."

"She shall not go," Hrothagaisaz said. He turned his gaze towards the hall-drighten, blunt jaw set hard beneath his beard's thick gilding. "Hoilogae's wife shall not come, for she is a walkurjon and a witch. If she passes within Tiwaz's garth, there will be no fair battling in that ring."

Hoilogae walked over to stand before his foe. "Who are you, to say who may or may not watch us fight? If you will not have Swaebhon within the hallowed ring, then meet me here and now in this hall!"

Hrothagaisaz rose to his feet. The glints of green in his hazel eyes shone like flecks of verdigris on bronze as he answered, "If Sigisharjaz and Gunthahildioz say that such a battle would be fair, then I can do little. This is Yuletide, when we must meet in Tiwaz's Thing-stead or not at all. But they must say that, and be willing to swear to it on the Ansuz's spear."

Hoilogae looked at the drighten and his frowe. Sigisharjaz rose to lift his spear from its place, but stood silent with the weapon in his hand, staring at Swaebhon. "Gunthahildioz?" Hoilogae asked softly.

Gunthahildioz's teeth worried at her lower lip, her right hand rose to her bosom, thumb rubbing over the plum-sized bead of amber that shone in the middle of her finest strand. The snow-veiling of her eyes seemed to thicken as she turned her head towards Swaebhon. Hoilogae found that he was holding his breath, the air hissed from his lungs in a long slow sigh as she spoke. "Swaebhon may fare as far as the stakes that mark the Thing-stead, but she must stay without. Let the Ansuz choose for himself, what he shall have from the warriors' garth."

Sigisharjaz led the host to the battling-place, a bundle of linden-wood stakes in each arm. Hoilogae and Hrothagaisaz walked behind him, after them came Hedhinaz and Swaebhon, and then all the crowd of warriors and women who would watch the battle. The Thing-stead was marked out by a circle of eight widely-planted oak trees. One growing before each of the eight winds blowing from the rim of the world's ring. In the middle stood a great stone, more than a man's height, which had been raised longer ago than anyone could tell. Some called it the Stone of the Brave, others the Greedy Stone. Hoilogae stopped a few steps before the southern oak, taking Swaebhon in his arms again.

She leaned her head upon his shoulder. "It may be that you are not fey yet," Swaebhon murmured, her voice muffled by the fur of his wolf-cloak. "I know that you are the worthier of Wodhanaz's choosing."

"Have no fear. I shall not shame you, my beloved, come what may." Hoilogae kissed Swaebhon, gazing into her gray eyes until the white skin of her face and the white snow around her melted into a single lightning-brightness, dazzling his sight.

He had no wish to part from her, but at last she lifted her head and said, "Sigisharjaz has set all the linden-stakes but one, it is time for you to go within."

"My beloved" Hoilogae's voice caught on something sharp in his throat, he kissed Swaebhon swiftly one more time, then turned to step within the ring of oaks, walking over the trodden snow to where Sigisharjaz stood with the last stave in his hand.

"Now I shall ask one more time," Hrothagaisaz said, raising his keen voice so that everyone could hear. "Will you give me the iron sword that was my father's, so that we may do battle fairly as befits men?"

"I shall tell you again," Hoilogae answered, the anger slowly glowing up within him like a bow-drill's fire in the cold, "that sword is no longer mine to give."

"But it is."

Hedhinaz had spoken, his voice bleak as stone under snow. Now he untied his belt and drew the iron sword from it, holding it out to Hoilogae hilt-first. "It seems to me that I cannot keep your gift any longer. Take it, and do as you will with it." His dark eyes did not flinch away, nor did Hoilogae see any wavering in the sharp lines of his younger brother's face. Yet if I take it, I must give it, he thought, and there is a little less likelihood that I may live out the day.

Slowly Hoilogae closed his fingers around the hilt. Hedhinaz's hand dropped away, still holding the sheath, and Hrothamaraz's blade was free. "Hrothagaisaz, I won this sword in battle. As you know well, you have no claim on it, nor must I do as you have asked. Yet I shall fight you now as you have whetted me to, iron on iron, if you will swear one thing to me. Should you be the winner here, you shall give my own sword to my brother Hedhinaz, and it shall be his together with my bride Swaebhon, and all the lands that I hold. This was never his fight, nor was it any but I who chose it, and it shall not lessen my brother's holdings."

"That I shall swear, and do swear it, by Thonaraz and Ingwaz," Hrothagaisaz answered. "May the Ansuz hear that oath! Your life alone shall be geld enough for my father. I do not wish to hold what you have held, neither sword nor woman."

Hoilogae gave him the sword. Hrothagaisaz hefted it, its sharpened edges shining bright against the black iron core. His green-flecked gaze lifted, staring past Hoilogae's shoulder. "Now I am ready."

The two helmed warriors turned to face Sigisharjaz together. The drighten lifted his hands towards the bright sky. "Hail, you holy ones. Tiwaz, Wodhanaz, I hail you here! Let the deeming of battle be made, this last Yule day on Sigisharjaz's field. Let these single-harriers meet with none to aid them, but their own might and hallowed luck to shape the day!"

Hoilogae and Hrothagaisaz stepped onto the untrodden snow within the ring of linden-stakes, and Sigisharjaz brought the last stave down into the ground with all the strength of his broad shoulders. Now the thing was done. Neither could pass beyond the ring until one of them had fallen. The Sun's lifting light stretched the shadows of their swords long over the glittering snow, the shadows of their helm-horns twisted against the brightness as Hoilogae and Hrothagaisaz slowly began to circle each other, each trying to move so that the Sun would shine into the eyes of his foe. Hrothagaisaz lunged first, Hoilogae met the blade with his own, and Hrothagaisaz barely managed to block the answering stroke.

Hoilogae followed him, pressing in hard, but Hrothagaisaz leapt to the side, backing a little so that Hoilogae would have to charge in with the light in his eyes. Hoilogae could see Swaebhon's shape pale through the trees, a birch behind the oaks. He whirled his sword in a glittering arc, Hrothagaisaz backed another step, and Hoilogae ran to come in at him from the other side. Their swords caught, the edge of Hoilogae's cutting into Hrothagaisaz's. Wejlunduz's metal had not yet been matched. For a moment they strove together, strength against strength.

Then Hoilogae heaved Hrothagaisaz back, the iron of the other's blade sliding down Hoilogae's with a high scream that went straight through Hoilogae's skull. A bronze sword would have been sheared. The folk along the edges of the ring were shouting now, clashing sword against dagger, but the sound melted to sea-roaring in Hoilogae's ears as he glimpsed Hedhinaz's white face clenched tight above his black cloak, hands twisting on the empty scabbard and the Sun's pale light frosting his gleaming hair. Your ale-speech must soon come true for both of us, Hedhinaz. The two of them closed again, trading blows fast and hard. Hrothagaisaz's helmet had slid askew on his head, his lips were rucked back, and Hoilogae could hear his breath hissing through his clenched teeth as they beat at each other. Hoilogae knew that he was the stronger, that Hrothagaisaz's arm would tire soon.

The edge of the other's blade was jagged against the blue-white sky now, its metal wounded many times by Hoilogae's sword. The forge-fires would have to give it new birth before it could be wielded again, though it might yet serve for this one battle. Hrothagaisaz aimed a cut down at Hoilogae's leg, as he moved to block it, the other shifted his grip, driving the blow up at Hoilogae's head. Hoilogae leapt back, the wind of the sword's point tearing past his cheek, and swung in again. Hrothagaisaz dodged, but not swiftly enough. The tip of Hoilogae's blade ripped through his cloak and tunic, tearing a wide flap of wool loose, a bright line of blood sprang out along the pale skin over his ribs. The troll-woman rode alone, on the wolf at darkening time. It seemed to Hoilogae that he could taste the blood in his mouth again, the keen edges of Swaebhon's troll-teeth cutting into his lips.

Yet it was not Hoilogae, but his foe, who was wounded, it was Hrothagaisaz's limbs that were slowing, not his. The thought strengthened Hoilogae to spring forward, crying out as he drove his sword forward again. The white light of Sun and snow burning in his eyes, it seemed to Hoilogae that his leap lengthened and lengthened, falling forward with no ground beneath his feet. He leapt into Walhall. Then the icy rock skidded away beneath the toe of his back foot as his body slammed into the ground. I slipped on the ice, he thought. After all this. He could not breathe. The earth's blow had knocked all the air from him, numbing the whole front of his body, and his mouth was full of grainy snow. I did not do unfairly by Hrothagaisaz, Hoilogae thought, and he has not slain me yet. If he is willing to deal fairly with me, and not win by mischance, if I can get up. He pushed down with the strength of his arms and chest, pushing himself away from the earth.

Then a black cloud passed over the Sun's light, whelming his head with darkness. Hoilogae blinked his sight clear again. He lay on his back with Hrothagaisaz standing over him, but the other man's sword-arm hung at his side, the blade dangling with its point in the snow. He did not raise the weapon to strike, but neither did he reach to help Hoilogae from the ground. Hoilogae drew a deep breath. Numb though he was, it seemed to him that something moved strangely in his belly, and that the stink of his first battle was rising about him. He lifted his head to look. His own blade lay beside him, its wyrm-marking dyed with blood to the hilt. The wound gaped from the bottom of his ribs on the left side to beneath his hipbones on the right side, the blood did not hide the twisting of his guts, nor the keenness of the stroke that had sheared them through.

A second shadow hid the light from Hoilogae's eyes as his head fell back. He stared wide-eyed into Sigisharjaz's lined face, he could not look away from the old drighten's iron-framed gaze, but whispered, "The battle is over. Bid the bright maid to come to me swiftly, if she wishes to find the ruler still living."

Sigisharjaz nodded. The wind from the hem of his dark cloak blew over Hoilogae's face as the drighten turned, rising to a roaring in his ears as the first wave of pain slammed through his body. Hoilogae thought he might have tried to curl on his wound, but he could not move. He had bitten through the inside of his cheek, the blood flowed sweet and rich over his tongue, the pain in his mouth a little sting through the great gnawing agony in his belly. Then Hoilogae's sight brightened. He thought that he was staring into the Sun's white light, but his eyes cleared a little. The light shone fair on Swaebhon's up-swept cheek, ones as on the wings of a swan in flight, her storm-gray eyes glimmered brightly as she gazed at him, and her cold strong hand stroked his face.

"Hail to you, Swaebhon," Hoilogae murmured. "Be of strong soul. We shall gaze upon each other in a world after this, but the blade has come near to my heart."

Swaebhon's lips parted as if she would speak, but Hoilogae saw her white-furred shoulders beginning to shake as though she held a heavy weight, and the light beginning to spill from her eyes.

"Swaebhon, I bid you not to weep, my bride. If you," The words came harder and harder to him. He could feel his lips moving, the ringing of his voice in his chest, but the pain was rising to drown all the sound in his ears. "If you will hear my speech that you make your bed with Hedhinaz, and let the young battle-boar have your love."

Swaebhon bent to kiss him, Hoilogae did not know whether the salt in his mouth was his blood, or her tears. "I said in the home we loved, when you gave me rings, that I wished to be in your arms alone, and never in those of an unknown battle-boar. Hoilogae, Hoilogae, my love."

"So it must be, " Hoilogae stopped, biting his lip and tightening his numb fists against another wave of pain. When it had stilled a little, he said, "as you love me, see that Hrothagaisaz keeps his oath."

"I will see to it myself," Hedhinaz's voice said, breaking sharp and glittering as amber flaking into shape beneath an iron edge. Hoilogae's sight was too blurred to see his brother's face, but he saw Hedhinaz's thin shape stooping, and the brightness of iron and blood shining on the blade in his hand. "Kiss me, Swaebhon! I will not come back to the lands of our home before I have avenged Herwawardhaz's son, who was the best of heroes beneath the Sun's light, and the last day of Yule, where men may fight alone on this field in spite of all frith-bonds, is not yet to an end."

Swaebhon rose to her feet. The fair shape and the dark blurred together a moment, then her bright face sank into Hoilogae's view again. "Hoilogae, my beloved, my chosen," she murmured. "I have seen these wounds before. You might live for a day."

Hoilogae let his head sink to one side, then heaved it across to the other. "My walkurjon," he whispered. He could say no more. He felt Swaebhon's warm kiss on his mouth, and his heart was glad enough as her cold caress stroked across his throat.

CHAPTER XXXI

The mead tasted cool and sweet, slipping easily from the smooth rim of the ceramic Scarborough Faire goblet down Karin's throat. She gave the half-full cup back to Helgi, who raised it to drink in his turn. The hot sunlight through the leaves of the pecan trees above them dappled his face with a web of gold strands through shadow, gleaming from the sheen of suntan lotion over his white shoulders and chest.

"What's the next show?" She asked.

Helgi unrolled his shed T-shirt to get at the Faire program, glancing quickly down the list of times and names. "Merlin the Magician, well, we saw that this morning. The jousting doesn't start for another hour yet. If we get up now and run, don't walk, over the river and across the other side of the Faire we could catch the end of the Living Chess Match."

Karin laughed. "It's too hot for anyone to run anywhere. I did all the summer running I'll ever need to do in Basic. I nearly ended up with a medical, too, for massive and repeated sunstroke." She put her arm around Helgi's bare shoulders, running her short fingernails over the curve of his bicep. "But the Armed Forces work on a simple and reasonable principle. If a man dies the first time you hang him, keep hanging him till he gets used to it. Actually, speaking of sunstroke, you're looking a little pink in the cheeks you could probably use a little more sunblock. Hold still, now," she dug the tube out of her purse, carefully smearing a few dabs of lotion onto Helgi's cheeks and nose. "There you go."

Helgi glanced down Karin's pale blue halter-top, into the deep crevasse between her breasts. "Hmm, I think you could use a bit of sunblock as well. If you'll just let me put it on"

She slapped his hand away. "Not in public, you don't." Karin tugged the light fabric up to cover a little more of her bosom, then smeared a generous glob over the skin that still showed. "Well, what now?"

The two of them looked out at the colorful tops of the stalls and booths rising above the heads of the people wandering among their rows. Most of the men were shirtless, backs deeply tanned or blistering red in the scorching sunlight of April's last weekend, nearly everyone wore shorts, except for the Renaissance lord in his thick brocade cloak and lady in her velvet skirt who swept through the crowd talking loudly about King Henry's new wife. One of the men who stood in the pecan's shade near Helgi and Karin shook his crew cut head.

"How the hail do they stand wearin' that shit in this weather?" He said loudly as he wiped a trail of sweat from the tanned swell of belly lopping over his cut-off jeans. The two performers didn't even glance in his direction, Karin was sure that they must have heard the question many times before.

"We could just go wandering and see what we find," Helgi suggested.

When Helgi and Karin had gotten two of the big turkey drumsticks that were the Faire's pride and refilled their cup, they started walking about the booths. Arms about each other's waist, they moved from shade to shade as they considered the medievalist crafts on display. Ceramics and pewter goblets, paintings and costumes, jewelry, leather work, and book-binding, At last they made their way to the row of stalls built under the trees by the creek where the air was a little cooler. Most of these booths were open at the back so that the breeze from the water could blow through them. Nearly all of them were two stories high, Karin knew that many of the artists, who traveled from fair to fair, lived and worked there all week, sleeping above the booths where they sold their wares. Helgi tilted his head, staring at one of the wooden signs hanging along the row, Karin followed his gaze. She knew at once which had caught his eye the wooden shield with a sword and spear crossed behind it. The shield was white with a red rim and boss, red runes were painted on the pale background.

Slowly Helgi spelled them out to himself, saying the words aloud when he was sure of them. "'Sigurðsson ok Gundarsson, Niflungar'. Ummwhat are Niflungar?"

Karin put her hands over his eyes. "Don't look at what's in the booth. I'll give you a hint. The German word isn't very different from the Norse, and you should know it. It means 'mist-folk'."

Mist, Nebel"Nibelungen, as in the Ring Cycle? Dwarves? Sigurðsson and Gundarsson are smiths, right?"

"Got it in one." Karin slid her hands down the side of his face, pulling his head close for a kiss.

As they got closer, Helgi saw that the booth was divided into two parts. One half filled with glass-topped cases of jewelry, one half with weapons of various sorts. The outlines of spears were carved into the posts at the four corners of the booth, and its roof was shingled with gilded shields, a few empty stools stood about the floor-planks. Behind one of the cases, a little woman was talking with a young black couple, pointing out different pieces to them. On the other side of the booth, a broad-shouldered man with close-cropped gray hair and beard sat hunched on a wooden bench beneath the sword-hung wall, running a whetstone along the edge of a palm-wide dagger. He was barefooted, wearing an unbleached tunic and deep red breeches beneath a deep blue cape, his belt was tooled in a complex knot work design, and a well-worn, leather-sheathed sax, a one-edged knife with a sharp slope from back to point, of the sort Helgi's books described as best for rune-risting, hung from it. As Karin and Helgi walked towards him, he looked up. "Good morrow, gentles."

"Uh, good morrow," Helgi replied. "Are you Sigurðsson or Gundarsson? Or do the dark elves not come out in the daytime?"

The man raised his dark eyebrows in surprise. His eyes were very blue, Helgi could see the rims of contact lenses floating in them, and the left one slewing off unfocused to the side. "The lord is a wise rune-reader, and not unwitting of lore. I am Grímr Sigurðsson, Kveldúlfr Gundarsson is faring over the whale-roads now, but I see that his work is not unknown to you." He gestured at the valknútr hanging from Karin's neck.

"Neither the silver smithing nor the word smithing," Helgi admitted. "I'm sorry he's gone, if he were still working here, I would have come back next week to ask him to sign my copies of his books."

The smith peered more closely at Helgi. "Wait. I've seen you before. Were you here a few years ago?"

"Texas Renaissance Festival," Helgi admitted. "I bought the valknútr there."

"Yes, I remember you well enough now. A boy going by a fine Norse name, who looked at every one of my weapons I seem to remember that you wanted a sword, I think it was one of the ring-hilts, and the lady who was with you went to some trouble to discourage you before you decided to spend your pennies in Kveldúlfr's half of the shop. Still, I can't complain. It is good to see one of his pieces in such a fair setting."

Karin was laughing now, so that Helgi could feel himself blushing even through the sun-heat still burning in his cheeks. "So my treasure was only your second choice, was it? Lo, how the sins of your past come to light." She looked down at Grímr. "Do you still have that sword?"

"Not that one, but one like it, yes. I have a much better ring-hilted sword, the other one was one of my early efforts, a little clumsy and sold cheap for a wall-hanger, I'm afraid." He set his sharpening aside and stood, looking over the wall. "Yes, here." He lifted the sheathed blade down, holding it out across his wrists for the two of them to look at. Helgi recognized the gilded ring that pierced the top of the pommel, though not the woven serpent-design on the guard, he had remembered a great-sword, a little too heavy for him to swing one-handed, but that had been four years ago.

"Clear!" Grímr said, drawing the sword from its red-brown leather sheath. Even in the booth's shadow, the metal seemed to ripple as the smith swung it up, holding it two-handed before him. "A ring is on the hilt, in the heart is soul"

"'Awe is in the edge, for owning is winner,'" Karin finished. Her face was grave now, a little trickle of sweat running down her pale forehead. "How much is it?"

"I'm afraid this is one of my most expensive pieces, three thousand, but look at the blade. You won't find Damascus steel this cheaply anywhere else."

"How can you sell it so cheaply, then?" Helgi asked.

"I forge for more than making a living, and I'm giving the two of you a special price, at that. I usually charge mundanes a good bit more, twice as much or more for a weapon like this, but if you can read the runes, it doesn't matter to me whether you're Faire folk or not. Here, step out back and swing it, see how it feels in your hand." He turned the sword with a quick flick of his wrist, offering the hilt to Helgi.

Helgi took the sword from him. The hilt fitted snugly into his palm, his fingers curling around it. He walked out the other side of the booth, taking a few steps down the overgrown slope that led down to the creek. The sword swung easily in his hand. Up, across, hissing through the air like an adder, a flock of severed green leaves floating down in its wake.

"Give me a year, and I could make a fine swordsman out of you," Grímr approved. "Which art?"

"Shotokan, second dan." Helgi came back into the booth. Little willing though he was to do it, he turned the blade as Grímr had done, letting the other take the hilt from him.

Karin considered the sword for a moment. "Three thousand's a good price for it, all right, but a bit hard to afford on a captain's pay," then she grinned, her gray eyes brightening. "Grímr, how well do you know the lore? Are you willing to risk the price of the sword on it?"

A slow grin curled under the sword smith's beard like a lizard's tail coiling through dry grass. "What are you offering, m'lady?"

"If you can ask a question either of us can't answer, I'll pay the mundane price for the blade, if either of us can stump you. You give it to us free."

Grímr ran his gaze up and down the sword's bright edge, then over Karin and Helgi. "Pretty high stakes, when neither of us knows the other. You sound very sure of yourself, for someone without much money to spare. I think you should know that I've been at this a while getting the full price for this blade wouldn't hurt me, but I'd rather not see a nice young couple like the two of you walk away broke."

"If we lose, I'll chip in half," Helgi murmured to Karin. With a year and a half of reputation-building behind them, Flourescent was doing well. Helgi had a bit of money in the bank, and there were a few good gigs lined up for the next couple of months.

"We won't lose," she whispered back to him, then, louder, "We're willing to risk it if you are."

"Are you absolutely sure about that?"

Helgi suddenly realized what had been bothering him since first reading the shield, a memory from the book he had learned the runes from, and spoke before he could start doubting himself. "We already seem to know something you don't, or why else would you spell out Viking names in runes from the Elder Futhark, instead of the Viking Age runes?"

The sword smith nodded slowly. "The Elder Futhark is easier to read than the Younger, and more folk know it. Perhaps I wouldn't be cheating you, after all." He turned the sword over and over, considering it as though he meant to buy it himself, then looked brightly up at them. "Hell, why not? It would have made sense to our ancestors. What terms shall we set for the questions?"

Karin thought for a moment. "We can deal with Old Norse lore or Wagner, as you choose," she answered at last. "With just one exception, questions to which only Óðinn knows the answer are strictly out of bounds, unless you promise to tell us the answer when the game is done."

Grímr's grin widened, his teeth showing like the silver rim of a blade drawn a quarter-inch from the sheath, and a prickle ran down Helgi's spine. Questions to which only Óðinn There was no hint of a smile on Karin's face as she met the gaze of the smith's one good eye. "Sharp one, aren't you? I gather there's no hope for using any of Heiðrekr's riddles on you, either." Karin shook her head. "Well, you must promise not to ask me what you have in your pockets or anything of that like. Since you're the challenger, you start."

"I'll start with a simple one, then. Who is it that draws the Sun's wagon across the sky?"

"An easy question to answer, but I think you meant to hide a trick in it. Not nice, Karin. The poems of the Elder Edda say that the Sun's horses are Árvaki and Alsviðr, but Snorri Sturluson says in the Prose Edda that her wagon is drawn by Skinfaxi, 'Shining Mane'. My turn now. Name me the names of Valkyries, all of them that are known."

Not an easy question, for there was no single source that listed all the names. Karin dredged her memory. She knew the ones from 'Grímnismál' best, then there were the thular-lists, "Hrist and MistSkeggjöld and Skögul, Hildr and Thrúðr, Hlökk and Herfjötur, Göll and Geirölul, Randgriðr and Ráðgríðr, and Reginleif, they bear ale to Óðinn's warriors. There are others. SkuldGunnr, Göndul, and Geirskögul, Hrund and Eir, Herja, Geiravör, Hjörthrimul, Svipul and Sveið, Geirdriful and Skalmöld, Thögn and Thrima, and Hjalmthrimul." Those were all the lists Karin knew, now she would have to think. "Brynhildr was also a Valkyrie, and Sváva and Sigrún, some say that Guðrún the wife of Sigurdhr Fáfnir's-Bane might be tallied among their number as well, but I do not know the truth of that, though the Norwegians say that she leads the oskorei, the Wild Hunt, to Ásgarðr."

Karin stopped, but Helgi spoke before Grímr could open his mouth. "There are also Gerhilde and Helmwige, Waltraute and Schwertleite, Ortlinde, Grimgerde, and Rossweisse, Siegrune and Brünnhilde we have named already, and I think that Karin Halfdan's daughter might be counted among them as well."

The smith nodded, taking up his dagger and whetstone again. He dipped his forefinger into the little wooden cup that stood beneath his bench, sprinkling a few drops of oil on the stone before he began to sharpen. "Pull up those stools and sit down, you two, this may not be over too soon. Your turn."

Helgi and Karin sat down facing him. Karin remembered the words that the etin Vafthrúðnir had spoken to Óðinn, when the god came to match wisdom with him. Now you are wise, guest, fare to the etin's bench, and we shall speak in our seats together, we shall wager our heads in the hall, guest, over wisdom-speaking. Though Grímr had not been a rare name in the Viking Age, it was also one of the god's best-known names. The Masked One, the Grim.

Karin turned her head, meeting Helgi's eyes. Helgi felt her gaze spurring him on, though his mouth had gone suddenly dry, he spoke, translating the words from Siegfried in his head. "Which was that kindred, to whom Wotan showed himself baleful and yet who lived most dear to him?"

Grímr sang his answer softly, the ringing strokes of his whetstone keeping the beat, his voice was deep and rough, but kept the tune well enough. "Die Wälsungen sind das Wunschgeschlecht, das Wotan zeugte und zärtlich liebte, zeigt' er auch Ungunst ihn." The Walsings are the wish-kindred that Wotan fathered and loved tenderly, though he showed himself harsh to them as well. "There is more to that question. Not the Walsings alone, but all of Wotan's children and wish-children, answer it. Some were Skjoldings, some Skilfings, some were Wolfings, some Öðlings, and many of the great heroes of the north, Starkaðr and Víkarr, Egill Skalla-Grímsson and his kin, Hadding, Haraldr War-Tooth. Dearest of all to Óðinn was his shining son Baldr, and Loki was not alone in bringing about the holy one's death, but the blind god also had a hand in the deed. Now tell me, if you count yourself wise enough to win this sword. What wyrd shall befall Óðinn in the last battle, at the doom of the gods?"

This Helgi knew, though the question seemed too easy for him to trust, but he answered strongly. "He shall fight against the Wolf Fenrir, and the Wolf shall swallow him, and his son Víðarr shall avenge him by ripping the Wolf's jaws asunder." He paused a moment for breath, and Karin went on, "No more than that is written of Óðinn's wyrd, but the worlds shall be born anew, and Baldr and his slayer shall come alive again from Hel, the val-gods shall rule the wide wind-home, so that Óðinn's work shall not be through, nor his name lost to the living, nor his wyrd full-wrought, when that battle is over." Karin leaned forward, her elbow resting on Helgi's knee as she held up one finger.

"Now, Grímr, I think that you are wise, so tell us this, as you know much. What shall come to pass with Óðinn's wish-sons and daughters, those heroes who fall fighting against the etin-hordes, when the worlds are reborn, when Baldr comes again to the halls of his kin? Is there death beyond death for them, or how shall they pass through the fires, when the Muspilli come to burn the worlds?"

Grímr put down his sharpening-work and leaned back against the booth's wall. The blades clattered against the wooden planking as he gazed at the two of them. "You know that the World-Tree shall not be all burnt, but a shoot of the old stem shall live, and two human folk, Líf and Lífthrasir, shall hide there and come forth again, just as Baldr and the blind warrior come forth from Hel's hold, as Fenrir's maw is sundered, that it not be Óðinn's last grave. What more there is to be known of this, you must find for yourselves. I can tell you no more, nor answer your questions as fully as you have answered mine. Few can seen what lies beyond Óðinn's battle with the Wolf." He held out the sheathed sword to Karin, laying it across his wrists as he had before. "I believe this is yours, wise-understanding one. May the two of you use it well and joy in it, while you live and beyond."

Karin stood, drawing the sword from its sheath. She gazed at the wyrm-pattern metal of the blade for a little while, then brought the hilt up to touch the gilded ring to her valknútr. "My Helgi, min helt, this sword is yours, as I am," she said, her clear high voice ringing from the rippling steel like a hammer-stroke.

Helgi also stood, reaching out to clasp her hands on the sword's hilt. "And yours, as I am, Karin." Together they slid it back into the sheath that Grímr held out for them.

"You two thirsty, by any chance? I've got some home-brewed mead upstairs. It's a lot better than the commercial swill they sell over yonder, I promise."

"Sounds good to me," Helgi said. Karin nodded her head in agreement, and the sword smith heaved himself from the bench, making his way up the rickety wooden stairs. The long horn he brought down was bound with silver at the rim, and dark-carved runes wound about its creamy sides, it was tipped with a silver eagle's head whose eyes glittered like little blood-drops.

"Hail to the singer, and the Valkyrie," Grímr said, raising the horn to Helgi and Karin and drinking so deeply that a few golden drops dripped down on either side of his hoary beard.

"How did you know I was a singer?" Helgi asked as Grímr handed him the horn.

"I know the sound of your voice. I don't spend all my time at forge and Faire, and a man with bad eyesight learns to listen, and your voice is hard to forget. Your songs, as well, are sprung out of need, and answer it well."

"Hail the master of the mead," Helgi said, raising the horn to Grímr with a small nod of his head. He tilted the vessel up carefully, mindful of the warnings he had read about the way a horn-draught could drench an unwary drinker, but the sudden rush of mead from horn had still filled his mouth and throat before he knew it. He swallowed without sputtering, amazed at the rich sweet spice and the strength of the draught.

Óðinn brought the mead up from the mountain's roots, the dark world of death, he shares it with his favored ones, that they gain the gift of song. Now Helgi remembered, as well, reading of how Óðinn had shown himself in disguise to the Danish king Hrólfr kraki and offered him weapons, how the god had given the Völsungs their sword, and a one-eyed tramp beneath the bridge where El Angelito lay, offering Helgi a draught from his bottle.

Tightening his hand on the horn to keep it from shaking, Helgi passed it to Karin. She raised it likewise to their host. "Hail the Galdor-Smith."

They passed the horn around and around. Helgi guessed that it must have held more than a bottle-full of the strong mead. When the horn was empty and Helgi and Karin stood up to leave, Grímr peered closely at each of them for a moment.

"It will not be too long before you drink my mead again, I think. Indeed, I shall be glad to have you guest with me, should you choose to spend the night at the Faire."

Karin glanced westward. The sun was still halfway up the sky. "Not tonight, I think?" her voice trailed off as though she meant to say more, but could not. Despite the afternoon heat, a cold chill shivered beneath Helgi's skin. Surely he had not heard what he might have.

"Not tonight," Grímr agreed gravely. "Farewell, and work swiftly, Helgi. I understand that singing can be a calling of danger, as many well-known musicians have shown with their deaths of late." This time his smile was one-sided, almost cruel, a twitch of the mouth beneath his gray mustache. "If you live long enough to be known at all, and die well enough, you may trust that you will become famous in your falling. it is the blood of the slain that bears the words most widely, as is always the way with Óðinn's children."

"As has often happened before," Helgi agreed. "Though I trust that I still have a few songs left to write."

Grímr nodded. "I think so. If you call mightily enough to the gods you sing of so gladly, be sure that they will hear you, and your life and death may be counted worthwhile."

Helgi was edging down Central towards Mike's parents' house that Monday afternoon, radio and air-conditioner both up full-blast. He was almost past the exit ramp leading to Royal Lane when he heard a dull crump! Beneath his car. The old Impala jerked hard to the left. "Shit!" Helgi yelled, "Shit, shit, shit!" He twisted the wheel, swinging the car one hundred twenty degrees as the little blue Volvo behind him honked plaintively and rolling down the ramp to stop by the side of the access road. Switching his dead-car blinkers on, Helgi got out to look, though he already knew what he was going to see. Sure enough, his left front tire was sagging under the car's weight, deflating like a broken balloon of elephant-hide. Sighing, Helgi went back to haul the spare tire and the jack out of the trunk. The muggy Dallas heat was already trailing long fingers of sweat down his back as he squatted to start changing the tire.

By the time Helgi got back on the road, he was thirty minutes late for the practice, mucky with sweat and auto grease, and generally ill-disposed towards the world, the more so since he was now stuck right in the middle of rush hour. He fumed as he inched along the road in the clog of traffic, staring balefully at the little dashboard clock and tapping his foot on the gas pedal as he practiced light shira-uke chops on the steering wheel. Being late for Flourescent practices always made him feel bad. He just knew Mike was bitching to the others at that very moment about Helgi being a "prima donna ."

"Tough shit," he muttered to the absent bandleader. "You never had a flat tire?"

Even with his windows closed, Helgi could hear the music booming out of the open garage door as he drove up. He recognized the heavy bass beat and screaming guitars of Metallica at once. Rack's drums were set up, with Rack sitting behind them and bashing at apparently random intervals, but none of the other instruments were out of their cases. Mike and Widget were sitting on their folding chairs, drinking beers and grinning like goons, Josh stood by the garage door shaking a Budweiser, his muscular arm pumping up and down as though he were hammering something to death with the beer-can.

They're plotting something, I just know it, Helgi thought. He rolled down his window a crack. "I got a flat on the way over, goddammit!" He snarled. "Josh, if you're thinking of spraying me with that, remember, I know twenty-three ways to break your arm and forty-one ways to smash your nuts back up into your abdominal cavity."

"Go on and try it!" Josh whooped. "We got a recording contract!"

Helgi slammed the ignition off, leaping out of the car and spreading his arms to the frothing white torrent of beer-foam that gushed over his face and chest like a sudden cloudburst. Josh grabbed him roughly around the waist, swinging him up off his feet and around in a circle before dropping him and hammering him on the back till Helgi had to start ducking and fending off the guitarist's enthusiastic blows.

"All right! Who's it with?" Helgi asked when he got his breath back.

"Chrysalis!" Mike answered, a jack-o-lantern grin lighting his round face.

Beer dripping down his cheeks, Helgi stopped dead, staring at him. "You're shitting me."

"S'help me God, Helgi, we have a contract with Chrysalis. I didn't want to tell anyone until, anyway, my dad's lawyer looked it over this afternoon, and he said it was fine. I called your house, but you'd already left. What took you so long getting here?"

"Had a flat, then I got stuck in traffic. Shit! How much are they paying us?"

"Four thousand each as an advance, ten percent thereafter. You keep rights to all printed music and lyrics and all that, if anyone wants to publish it, they have to deal with you separately."

Closing his mouth, Helgi looked around at the other band members.

"Yeah, four thousand," Josh said. "We can all buy imported beer now." He popped the top on another can of Budweiser. Holding it at arm's length above his mouth, he poured a long stream of beer in, the froth splattering over his face and tanned shoulders. Rack drummed out a loud cymbal roll, then threw one of his sticks up. It struck the ceiling, spinning off to clatter along the cement floor by Helgi's feet.

Widget just shook his curly head, smirking the dazed smirk of the stoned. "Did we do it, or what?" He said softly. "Man, I'd never'a thought, I mean, shit."

"Yeah," Helgi agreed. "You got another beer for me?"

Mike reached down into the cooler by his feet and tossed him a can of Michelob Dry. Helgi caught it one-handed. "Have a beer. Have all the beer you want, but don't fry your brain too hard, you have to write another song or three real soon now."

"Say what?" Helgi popped the top and took a long drink. The beer was slightly bitter and he could taste the lingering metal of the can, but its coolness felt good sinking down his throat.

"Two seriously long songs, or three shorter ones. They wanted to ax 'Dallas Dream', 'Water Moccasin', and 'Late Night Fever' and replace them with more of your material."

Helgi looked closely at Mike. A light sheen of sweat lay over the band leader's flushed cheeks, his droopy red mustache blurred the set of his mouth, and Helgi could not tell whether the little lines at the edges of his eyes were drawn taut by excitement or something else. His own lines from years before came floating up into his mind. Scars on soul are cruelest scarred. Coldest cries, who cries alone.

"They probably just wanted a consistent sound for the first album," Helgi said, shrugging. "Once we've gotten better-known, we'll be able to be more diverse again."

"Yeah. Hey, I'm not complaining about it, but you'd better get your butt in gear. We're supposed to go in to make the recording on May twenty-first, which means we don't have much time to learn more music."

"Do you think it should be two long songs, or three short ones?"

Mike tugged thoughtfully at the end of his mustache, but it was Widget who spoke up first. "Make it two long songs, man. That be quicker to learn, and it give us a good finale, showpiece sort of thing."

"I could go for that," Josh agreed. He dragged the back of his arm across his froth-wet face. "Yeah, have one real butt-buster at the end of the whole thing."

"With" Rack rattled a quick snake-warning on his snares,"lots of percussion. Shit, I'm gonna get me a bigger set, have drums you never dreamed of. Jason Bonham'll have nothing on me."

Mike smiled. "Got any ideas yet, Helgi? Were you working on anything?"

"Not at the moment," Helgi admitted. Although he had only drunk half his beer, he felt vague and dizzy, the clutter of music stands and electrical cords in the corner of the garage dissolving before his eyes as the screaming music of Metallica faded in and out of his ears. It's the heat, he thought. He pulled up one of the folding chairs up, sinking down onto the little hard seat and drinking a little more beer. "Ask me again at the end of the week. Hey, are we going to practice today, or are we just going to party?"

Mike kicked the empty can at his feet. It spun away, scattering a shower of pale drops to sink dark into the concrete floor as he got another beer can out of the cooler. "What do you think? Get that song written, then we'll practice our butts off."

Buoyed up by his good mood, Helgi was nearly fifteen minutes early to his singing lesson the next afternoon. His music books under his arm, he walked up between the neatly manicured squares of green lawn. Tiberius was sitting in the window, staring out with his dark ears laid back. As Helgi came closer, the old Siamese let out a plaintive, glass-muted yowl.

"You've decided to be a watch-cat today, huh?" Helgi said to him, ringing the bell. "You won't get rid of me that easily, cat, no matter how loudly you yowl at me."

Tiberius' ears pricked up at the sound of the bell. He slipped down from the window-sill, a few seconds later, Helgi heard him meowing on the other side of the door, and waited for Dr. Sachs to say, "Schlechter Kater! 'Raus mit dir!" But no human voice spoke, and after a little while, the Siamese jumped back up into the window, gazing out with wide blue eyes. Helgi checked his watch. Twelve minutes still until the start of his lesson. Dr. Sachs was probably out somewhere, or in the back garden. He settled himself to the left of the porch, in the shade of one of the broad-branched live oaks that flanked the pillars holding the porch roof up. Now and again he would look at the cat in the window, and Tiberius would stare scornfully back at him, as if to say, I own only one man, and you are not that man. At precisely six o'clock, Helgi got up and rang the doorbell again. He had never known Dr. Sachs to be late for a lesson, he was sure now that the old German must have been out in back. But he waited, and the door did not open. After a couple of minutes, Helgi stepped carefully over the grass, looking past Tiberius into the window. The house was all cool and quiet inside, lit only by the pale blue light through the curtains, the oaken tables were clear, without even the usual books lying upon them, the bookshelves neat as always.

"Well, perhaps he got caught in traffic or something," Helgi said to himself, and settled himself again.

The setting sunlight was shining straight into Helgi's eyes by seven o'clock, his bladder was achingly full and sitting in the heat for more than an hour had made him feel a little out of sorts, as well as worried. At last he got up and stretched himself, shaking the prickling blood back into his right foot. The most likely thing, he thought, was that Dr. Sachs had called while he was out to cancel that afternoon's lesson.

Tiberius had not left the window the whole time, now he yowled again as Helgi turned to leave.

"Don't eat too many snakes, cat," Helgi advised. "I'm sure they're bad for your digestion."

When Helgi got home, he dialed Dr. Sachs' number. After three rings, Helgi heard his teacher's voice. "Dr. Johannes Sachs speaking." Helgi was about to open his mouth when the voice went on. "I am not now at home. Please leave a message and I shall call you back. Ich bin im Moment nicht zum Hause" Helgi waited unhappily while Dr. Sachs repeated the message in German, then said, "Dr. Sachs, this is Helgi Hadding. I came over this afternoon, but you weren't there. Please call me if it's possible to schedule another lesson before next week."

"People do forget things, you know," Helgi said to Elric as he hung up. "It's been known to happen before this, anyway." Elric looked up at him moistly, unconvinced, then turned his plaintive gaze towards the leash hanging by the door.

After he had walked Elric, Helgi tried calling Dr. Sachs again, but got the answering machine again. Annoyed and frustrated, he went to his room, turning on his computer and staring at the screen. He wanted to think about starting his new song, or at least to turn on his synthesizer and practice singing, but he had a whole stack of papers to grade by Wednesday. Helgi was walking towards the door of the Music building, bracing himself to step out into the heat, when he felt a light, but sharp prod in his shoulder. He turned around to see Ms. Devereaux looking up at him. "Helgi, do you have a class now?" Her voice was lower and softer than he had ever heard it in his lessons with her, tightly as her dark bun pulled the flesh of her face back, he could see the slight puffiness about her neatly outlined eyes.

"Uh, no Why?" Helgi asked, the sick dread already creeping through him like a snake's cold smooth fang sliding into his vein. Only half-aware of what he was doing, he began to twist Karin's ring on his finger, rubbing his thumb rhythmically over the warm smooth amber.

Ms. Devereaux opened the nearest door. The empty classroom was very like all the others in the Music building, rows of desk-topped chairs ranged before a chalk-frosted blackboard and a battered upright piano near the windows. "Helgi," it seemed to him that Ms. Devereaux's voice nearly caught in her throat, but he saw her breath lifting from her diaphragm, carrying her words on, "Johannes, Dr. Sachs is dead."

The blood dropped from Helgi's face as though his throat had been cut. "When did it happen?" He asked in a small breathless whisper, thinking, *My god, he might have been in there dying, all that hour, if I had only done something, gone up through the garden or something to see if he was all right.*

"Early yesterday morning. He must have been expecting he was able to call the hospital, but by the time the ambulance got there, he was already gone."

Helgi stared dumbly at her. "He never told me about Norway," Helgi heard himself saying. "I thought he was going to a couple of times, but he never did."

"What?"

"In ever mind. Is there, when is his funeral going to be?" Helgi breathed as Dr. Sachs had taught him, deep and slow, gathering the strength in his belly to support his voice. He could not let himself fail now.

"His body is being sent back to Germany. His family," Ms. Devereaux tugged the waistband of her black skirt straight, tucking a loose fold of grey blouse into it. "He will be buried with the rest of his family, as he wished. We are holding a memorial service for him in the chapel here Thursday afternoon." She coughed softly into her hand. "Helgi, do you have any songs prepared that might be appropriate? I think he was awfully proud of you. He used to say, 'See, you have sent me a problem, and I found that he was a genius after all.' I think of all his students," She coughed into her hand again. "Could you?"

"If I have an accompanist, the song I have isn't so well known. 'Hell dig, Liv', it's a Swedish song, with music by a Finnish composer, Oskar Merikanto."

Ms. Devereaux shook her head. "I don't know him, but if we can find the music in the library, and if you have a couple of hours to work with me this evening, I can accompany you."

They walked slowly to the Music library together. "I don't remember the name of the book Dr. Sachs copied it out of," Helgi whispered, "but it was some sort of collection, let me see." He dug his wallet out of his pocket, scuffled in it until he could find the folded scrap of paper where he had written the name. "'Hell dig, Liv', in Suomalaisia Yksinlauluja (Finnish Solo Songs). Recording, Matti Salminen, 'Myrskylintu'."

The Jefferson chapel was full for Dr. Sachs' memorial service, and some were standing at the back of the church. Masses of white lilies hid the altar, heaped before the plain Lutheran cross, a basket of pale flowers bloomed at the end of every pew. Dr. Mason sat in the front row, together with Dr. Richie and the other instructors, some of whom Helgi knew by name, some only by face. Although Luann wasn't there, Mike was, sitting near the back with a crowd of other students or ex-students whom Helgi didn't know. A table had been set up near the altar, covered with lilies in place of the body that was not there.

Helgi himself sat at the aisle end of the right front pew, Ms. Devereaux was already in place at the piano. As the minister, Dr. Meyer, the head of the Divinity department, spoke, Helgi tried to close his ears, staring at the cracked blond wood where he rested his elbow and breathing as deeply and carefully as he could. He would not let any tears block his throat, he thought. He must prove himself worthy of his teacher. Still, he could not keep himself from hearing the minister's words. "As a young man, Johannes Sachs studied music in Berlin, supporting himself through his training by playing the piano and singing in nightclubs. He completed his doctorate in nineteen forty-eight, emigrating to the United States four years later and taking a post as a singing instructor at Oberlin, nd I shall never know now what he did in Norway, or what he saw there," Helgi thought. It may be that only he knows, knew.

Carefully Helgi eased the knot from his throat by shaping the words of the song over soundless breath and imagining the sound of his own singing, as he wanted it to sound, air flowing free and rich as the sunset-rose Baden wine, taste warmed with the fires of the volcanic earth. Full tone, Dr. Sachs had said, this is a song of triumph, you must let your joy sing through you. But it was hard, when he could hear someone's muffled sniffle along the row beside him, he could not keep from seeing his teacher lying pale and dead where the lilies rested, or his stocky body sinking to the green and blue Oriental rug beside the telephone, strong shoulders crumpling in over his chest and metal-rimmed glasses askew on his nose, as the gray light of dawn slowly rose through the water-green filter of his curtains.

"Dr. Sachs served as head of the Music Department here at Jefferson for twenty-three years, during which he built his department into one of the best in the country, especially for vocal studies. He was beloved by students and instructors alike, as a fine teacher and a fine man who never failed to care about each of his students, both as musicians and as people. Although his age and failing health finally forced him to retire seven years ago, he continued to take a keen interest in the department's activities, and taught Jefferson students privately until the end of his life."

Dr. Meyer gathered the folds of his black robe about his spare figure, stepping down from the pulpit, and Helgi glanced at Ms. Devereaux, who made a tiny gesture of beckoning. He swallowed hard, standing and walking slowly up to stand beside the piano. His father's tuxedo was a little short at his ankles, tight about his shoulders, but it did not hamper his breathing or his throat in any way, and that was all that mattered.

The title of the song and name of the singer were in the program, along with the Swedish words that Dr. Sachs had carefully coached Helgi in and an English translation. Helgi did not say anything, only drew his draught of breath, staring above the heads of the dark-clad students in the back road and listening for the two deep solid A minor chords which announced his entrance.

"Hell dig liv, i din skönhet och prakt! Hail thee, life, in your beauty and light,

  Du föder och döder, stolt i din storhet,in birthing, in slaying, proud in your greatness, och härliga makt,"and ruling might.

Helgi would not look at the mound of flowers where no body lay, he swallowed hard to clear his throat in the two and a half measures of grace the piano chords gave him.

"Du evigt unga, i vår som i höst,
Thou ever young one, in spring as in fall,
dina sånger segrande stiga
your songs, victorious, rise up
genom vindarnas dån
through the wind's din,
och den döendes röst.
and the dying one's call.

The piano broke into a series of glittering waterfalls down from the treble, but Helgi could hear Dr. Sachs speaking through them. Here, most of all, you must use the full resonance in your chest. You can make a fine dark tone, Helgi, see that you do it, without losing any of your projection, the sound must still ring in your head. It struck him that there must be few here who had not heard the old German's dry tones speaking so, in classes if not one to one, but his deep sobbing gasp came from the bottom of his diaphragm, as Dr. Sachs had taught him, and he did not miss his next entrance.

"Hell dig, mörke, fruktade död,
Hail to you, dark, frightening death,
livets lydige slav,
life's obedient slave,
stumma föryngrings gåta,
dumb riddle of renewal,
slocknada, spirande liv i grav!
withering, sprouting life in the grave!
Andra och ständigt skiftande släkten
Another, and endlessly shifting kin
stiga på nytt ur de gamlas spår.
rises up new where the old has grown,
Aftonrodnan är morgonväkten.
Evening's reddening is morning's waking,
Livet skördar, vad döden sår."
Life shall harvest what death has sown.

The piano-notes ran swiftly upward, rising to a great peak, Helgi let his voice flow full from his depths, full volume, to fill the hall of mourners and drown out the battering of tears behind the gates of his eyes.

"Hell dig, liv, i din skönhet och prakt!
Hail thee, life, in your beauty and light.
Du dödar och föder, stolt i din storhet
in slaying, in birthing, proud in your greatness,
och härliga makt!"
and ruling might!

Ms. Devereaux beat the rapid chords to their final crashing end, then lifted her hands from the piano, letting the last note die away with Helgi's voice. For a moment there was silence, Helgi saw a few of the students glancing sideways at their neighbors. Then the front row began clapping, the sound rising back from them in a great wave that beat against Helgi's ears. The hot tears were filling his eyes now, but he bowed, gesturing to Ms. Devereaux in acknowledgment as Dr. Sachs had taught him to do. My god, Helgi thought, I did that well. I really did. He could not have spoken, even if he had wanted to, the three twined strands of sorrow, awe, and joy bound his throat tight. He only bowed his head until the clapping had died down, then walked slowly back to his place as Dr. Richie came up to the microphone to speak his eulogy.

Here, his back to everyone but the front row, and his head turned towards the aisle, away from them, Helgi could loose the heat knotted against his throat in a slow trickle of blood-salty tears. Even now, Dr. Sach's corpse might be faring home over the water, if he had not already gone to ground among his kin in Germany. Helgi glanced through blurred eyes at the flowers by the altar. At once a half-angry pang wrenched through his heart. It seemed to him evilly unfair that Dr. Sachs had been taken away, instead of being let to lie in state where he might have heard Helgi's song and the kind words his colleagues were speaking of him, it seemed a betrayal, to have no more than the blooming mound to mourn over. He clenched his fists tight against his thighs as a tear traced down his cheek like a hot fingertip.

After the service was over, Helgi moved through the crowd in a daze, muttering something appropriate in answer to all the compliments till at last Ms. Devereaux laid her hand upon his arm, looking up at him.

"That was well-sung," she said softly. "Dr. Sachs would have been proud to hear it."

Helgi nodded, clearing his throat twice so that he could get words out. "Thank you. I wish," I wish he could have, he thought, but couldn't say it. "Do you know what's happened to Tiberius?"

"Poor cat, I'm taking care of him right now, but he's not doing very well. He prowls around the house and meows the way Siamese cats do. He's obviously waiting for," Ms. Devereaux tugged a tissue out of her purse, pressing it against her face and blowing her nose hard. When she looked up again, the neat dark lines around her eyes were smudged, her eyelashes spiky with moisture. "Of course he's disoriented by the move, the poor old thing. Cats are like that."

Helgi was just fumbling in his pocket for the key to the apartment when he heard the rumble of Karin's jeep behind him. He turned, walking back down the walkway to meet her. She was in civvies, a light green blouse and a darker green skirt that fell to just below her knees, her heels raised her to his height.

Karin stopped with one hand on the jeep's door, staring at him. "Hel og haglbyge, Helgi, where on earth are we going for you to wear a tuxedo? If you'd warned me, I would have come in my full dress blues."

Helgi blinked, looking for words. Of course she didn't know, he hadn't told her he hadn't wanted to talk to anyone last night.

"It's not where we're going, it's where I just was. My, my singing teacher, Dr. Sachs, he died Tuesday. I was at his memorial service. I sang for him, I mean, for the service."

Karin hurried to hug him, clasping him tightly against her strong warm body. "Helgi, my Helgi, min helt. No wonder you are so pale, if you have been dealing with the dead. Come, let us go in where it is cool, and you shall sit and recover yourself before we talk about what to do this evening, if you want to go out."

"I do," Helgi answered strongly, swallowing back the rising heat in his throat. "It is, I wish I had told him about the recording contract. I wish I had called him on Monday."

"Ah, but he must have known it would happen soon." Karin tilted her head and leaned up against Helgi, kissing him softly on the eyes. "It is always hardest for the ones who are left behind, I think that grief lasts longer than the pain of leaving. I hope with all my heart that I do not outlive you, my Helgi."

Helgi found that he had turned the amber of his ring inward, clutching his fist about it. When he opened his hand, he saw that the gold setting had left white dents in his palm. "I don't think I could outlive you by long, either," he answered huskily, tightening his arms around Karin's shoulders.

She kissed his lips, stroking his hair smooth. "My dear Helgi, but you have enough mourning for the dead without worrying about the living, this must be a wake as well as a celebration tonight. Will you also sing this song for me? I should like to hear it."

Helgi and Karin stopped by Helgi's parents' house after dinner so that Helgi could return his father's tuxedo. Roger Hadding answered the door.

"Hello, you two. How did your performance go, Helgi?"

"Fine."

Helgi's mother looked up from the dining room table, pushing the newspaper's crossword puzzle away and laying down her pencil. "Well, sit down and join us if you'd like. Coffee or tea, Karin?"

"Coffee, please," Karin said, pulling a chair out and sitting down. Helgi settled down beside her, more carefully, he had drunken well at dinner, enough to make him cautious about how he moved while his parents were watching.

"I was quite impressed with that sword you got for Helgi at Scarborough Faire, Karin," Roger Hadding said. His grin lightened his long face, its creases overwriting the small wrinkles about his eyes and mouth.

"It's a fine one, isn't it?" She agreed. "You're interested in weaponry?"

"I was pretty interested in that sort of thing when I was your age. I went to the occasional Society for Creative Anachronism event, even fought in a couple of their tournaments. I was never committed enough to invest in a live-steel sword of my own, though."

Helgi looked at his father in disbelief, trying to picture a chain-mail shirt draped over his bony frame in place of his white open-collared sports shirt, his knotty fingers wrapped around a blade's hilt instead of the coffee mug's handle. The image came more easily than he had thought. To his surprise, he could see Roger Hadding as a lean and grizzled warrior, the long slanting of his cheeks darkened by white-flecked stubble and his dark eyes gazing grimly from beneath his shaggy brows.

Helgi's father was still speaking. "Whereas I expect to see the two of you going out to raid monasteries any time now. I guess you're still interested in Norse mythology, huh?"

"Always," Karin answered, smiling back at him. "But you know something about it yourself, don't you?"

"I used to, once upon a time. It's been a while, and I'm mostly a Tolkien fan anyway, but when I hear Helgi quoting the Prose Edda, it takes me right back to my undergraduate days."

Karin's gray glance flickered over to Helgi. "Only the Prose Edda?" She asked teasingly. "Not the Poetic? Shame on you, Helgi."

Helgi spread his hands. "Hey, it's not my fault. I ordered it from the Jefferson bookstore a couple of months back, but they said the publisher was out of stock."

Helgi's father raised his graying eyebrows. "You should have told me you were looking for it. I've still got my old Poetic Edda around here, I think I'm not quite sure where, but I'm sure I haven't gotten rid of it. Kirsten, what did you do with that load of surplus books when we rearranged our room?"

"They should be in a box in the attic. It's labeled 'Roger's Books', just for those who weren't sure."

Karin had to leave fairly early, since she was flying the next morning, but after Helgi had walked her out to her jeep and kissed her goodbye, he got a flashlight and went up the little wooden staircase that led from the corner of the study to the attic. The door squeaked alarmingly when he pulled it open, a warm wave of musty air, edged with a hint of mothballs, spilled over him. He flicked the flashlight on, shining it into the darkness. Two fat chairs, covered in shiny black plastic, squatted on either side of the doorway like great toads, behind the chairs, towers of dust-brown cardboard boxes rose nearly to the ceiling's low beams, the black crevasses between them stretching farther into shadow than Helgi could see.

He sneezed, setting a cloud of dust-motes to dancing in the flashlight's beam, and stepped cautiously onto the creaky wooden floor, running his light up and down the box-heaps to read the inscriptions left by his mother's neat hand. 'PICTURES AND PAPERS, MISMATCHED CROCKERY DO NOT DROP!, HELGI'S OLD STUFF, PARTS AND PIECES, KIRSTEN'S EASTER HAT, TREE ORNAMENTS, TREE LIGHTS, ROGER'S BOOKS'. The box of books was in the middle of a stack, Helgi had to prop the flashlight against the bottom box of the next heap, its slanted brightness casting his shadow high and hulking against the ceiling as he carefully dismantled his chosen tower until he had 'ROGER'S BOOKS' free.

Helgi slit the tape holding the lid closed with his thumbnail, then lifted aside book after book until he came to a large red-gold paperback with The Poetic Edda written black on its cover, which he set down by the flashlight. Although he repacked the books, he did not bother heaping up the stack again, there was still enough room in the attic for many more piles of boxes. When Helgi came into his own room, he stood still a moment, looking at his sword. He had driven three long nails slantwise into the wall to hold the weapon above his bed, and it was fine to see it resting there. Elric was already waiting for him on the bed, Helgi nudged the elk hound aside, settling himself into the spot the dog had warmed and opening the book.

He had already seen enough quotes from it in his other books, enough so that many of the verses and names were familiar, and the broken lines of alliteration no longer seemed strange to his eye.

"Easily knownto Ygg's chosen
are the heavenly halls.
the rafters, spear shafts,the roofs, shield-shingled,
and the benches strewn with byrnies."

Helgi flipped through the book, glancing here and there until the title of one poem caught his eye. "The Lay of Helgi Hjörvardhr's-Son."

"A ring is on the hilt, in the heart is soul,
awe is in the edge for owning's winner.
A blood-dyed wyrm on the blade turns,
upon the guard an adder winds tail."

Helgi reached up to lift his sword from its resting place, stroking the gilded ring and running his fingers along the twisting snake-design on the guard. Now I know what Karin and Grímr were quoting from, he thought. He turned back to the beginning of the poem, reading more and more slowly as the words sank into his mind, after a few moments, Elric pricked up his ears, gazing darkly at his master, and Helgi realized that he was actually chanting the poem aloud.

"'What gift do you give with Helgi's name,
and, bright-lightening bride, what you offer?
Think wisely of all well must you speak,
I'll have none of it have I not thee!'
'Swords are lying in Sigar's Holm
one of those, of all is best.
A ring is in the hilt'"

Helgi did not read the interspersed sections of prose aloud, only moved his lips soundlessly. One time Hedhinn fared home by himself through the wood on Yule evening, and found a troll woman, who rode a warg and had wyrms for reins, and offered to follow him. Helgi thought himself fey, and thought that Hedhinn had seen his fetch when he saw the woman riding on the wolf. Helgi put the book down, clenching his sword's hilt tightly to stop his hands from trembling. He felt as though he had tried to dig a small stone free of the earth, only to find that it was the tip of a great pillar running down to its roots in the living bedrock, a stone fountain springing up from an underground lake. The last echoes of the dinner's wine were still ringing in his head, dazing him from clear thought, and after a moment he opened the book again, going on to read of the doom of Helgi Hjörvardhr's-Son.

"The Second Lay of Helgi Hunding's-Bane," Helgi turned the pages back, yes, there was a First Lay as well. He chanted more swiftly as he read through them, the rough dark sound of the alliterative lines stirring something deep within him.

"Then shone light from Loga Fells,
and from that light the lightning flashed,
the mighty hero saw maidens riding.
their byrnies were bloody-sprinkled
and from their spears the sparks flew forth."

Helgi got Sigrún in marriage, and they had sons. Helgi did not grow old. Dagr, Högni's son, made sacrifice to Óðinn for revenging his father. Óðinn lent Dagr his spear

By the time Helgi had read all three of the poems, he was no longer trembling, the shaking in his limbs had risen to a pure high ringing like a strong wind blowing through harp strings. He drew his sword, staring at the wyrm-pattern metal. The light ran up and down the blade, its reflection glimmering off his mussed bedclothes and shelves of books, glancing from the crumpled clothes on the floor as Helgi turned the weapon in his hand.

He could feel the awe-might thrilling in it, its echo tingling through Karin's ring on his other hand, the long snake-ripples of dark metal wove among the bright, drawing his eye in through the shining reflections. It seemed to Helgi that it was not his own half-mirrored face he saw, but that Karin's gray eyes looked out from the gray metal, the wind-waves of the sword's patterning rippling over her fair-helmed head.

He reached out to touch the glittering point, brushing his hand against it as lightly as if he were stroking Karin's velvety cheek. The sword's bright edge slit his hand like a razor, the sting piercing him a few heartbeats later. It was not a deep cut, but the blood began to drip at once, running deep red along the length of the blade. Thoughtfully Helgi put the sword down and went to get a box of tissues from the bathroom. Pressing one wad against his hand to stop the bleeding, he cleaned the blade carefully with another, watching out for the edges. He knew that nothing would rust iron as fast as blood or sweat. Elric sniffed at him as he worked, licking a few drops of blood from Helgi's arm and trying to push his nose under the makeshift bandage. Helgi elbowed him gently away, polishing the sword clean and tossing the streaked tissues into the wastebasket on the other side of the room.

"The sword still bites," he murmured to himself. If Helgi were to lift the blade and bring it down, it would shear through Elric's thick fur and flesh, or his own gray slacks and the muscles of his leg, as surely as the edge of a bulldozer's shovel shearing through earth. The blood would be bright in his light bulb's flourescent glow. The sword was no imitation of fantasy, but as real as the wad of blood-soaked Kleenex Helgi pressed against his wounded hand. Now it seemed to him as though he stood before an underground river breaking forth from the earth, storming along its long-dry bed in a huge torrent of white froth, the rushing might seemed to bear him up, so that he could not sit still, but sprang to his feet, swinging the sword up. Its tip narrowly missed the paper lamp-shade hanging from the center of the ceiling, the bright reflection of the light bulb underneath trailing from the sword's point in a long arc of blue.

The words of the Helgi-poems were still ringing in his mind as he laid the sword down across the top of his synthesizer, rummaging along the mess of papers on his shelves for a clean sheet of music paper and a pen. Helgi Hjörvardhr's-Son, Helgi Hunding's-Bane. They had taken their doom up without fear. Helgi did not know what his might be, but he was sure that it was real and deadly as the sword-edge glittering over his levers and keys, that he must choose it and weave it and bring it forth in his song. He propped the Poetic Edda open beside the sword, then lowered his hand to the lever that opened the synthesizer to its flow of electricity. The small dark circle beside the switch brightened to glowing red, the faint hum of power rose from the speakers like a rising swarm of bees, and Helgi began to write.

CHAPTER XXXI

Hailgi and Sigiruna watched Dagar go till his mounted shape was no more than a gray shadow far off in the white morning mists. Sigiruna shook herself. "I hope that he will be well-treated in Hagalar's hall."

"There is little doubt of it. Hagalar is kind, though he knows well how to deal with difficult youths, my fostering there was mostly a joyful time. Things must be easier there now, as well, since he no longer stands between two great foe men."

"Yes, you have told me how you could not freely pass in and out of his garth, and how not a day went by that the watch was not kept for a war band bent on battle. You have ever done well, my Hailgi."

"I hope that this will turn out as well. Dagar, seems he is not so unlike myself at his age, I think."

Sigiruna's pale straight brows drew together in puzzlement. "I do not see how. Were you not already first in the host, a well-known hero, did you not seek death before frith-making, and battle before all things?"

"Yes, but," Hailgi's throat betrayed him, he could not voice the words he wanted, nor could he grasp them clearly, but his thoughts melted away like a stirring of fog against fog. "I think," he said slowly at last, "that Dagar will not be content to be anything but what he himself is, nor to let anything but his own will shape him. It may be better for him in a strange place, where no one thinks they know what he ought to be."

"By that you mean me, I suppose," Sigiruna said. Her laugh washed the sting from her words like dock-leaves washing away a nettle's bite. "Ah, well, I cannot say that you are wrong. And it may be that I know my own brother least of all. Whatever I may see of other thoughts, his have always been closed to me, his heart a garth where I might never tread, and thus I have ever let you rule over what should become of him." She glanced swiftly eastward, where the mist shone golden as harvest over the fields. "Well, that is done, and the day's work will be starting soon. There is plenty of grain left from the planting, more than in most years. I had thought to brew a large batch of ale, for that will keep longer than grain or meal, without danger of rot or mice creeping into it, and I have never heard anyone complain that there was too much drink poured in a hall. And that means I shall be at the malting the whole day, for your mother brews in another way than I, and I cannot teach these Jutish women the way I wish to do it."

Hailgi looked up at the brightening sky. Though the mist still veiled the ground, no clouds flared in the Sun's light, the day would be fair. "I think it would not be an ill day for me to go hunting," he said. "It will be bright later, and Wigablajar has rested too long in his garth, it will do him no harm to stretch his legs."

"Neither him nor you," Sigiruna replied. She prodded his stomach, just above the belt-buckle. "Though you have gotten no fatter over the winter's resting, in spite of the good harvest and the full-fatted beasts we had for feasting, I can tell you are restless, you had best go out hunting, before you begin to start fights within the hall, and kill your good thanes before you have a chance to lead them into battle."

"I have seldom started fights," Hailgi began hotly, then stopped, laughing. "It may be that you are right. Anyway, it is a fine day for hunting, and fresh meat will be good to have as well. Short as the winter was, I think that the deer will not be too thin to eat by now, and if I am lucky I may find a boar as well."

"So long as you are careful of the tusks, I know full well where a boar usually strikes," answered Sigiruna. Her hand brushed swiftly over the front of his breeches. "I know that I am not through with you yet, my Hailgi, I think it is written that we shall have more than one son."

The woods' first green was just unfolding from the bud, the beech-branches sheened green in the mist-filtered sunlight as Hailgi rode with his strung bow and an arrow in his hand. It was no easy skill, to shoot from horseback, but there was still plenty of sausage left from the slaughtering at summer's end, so that it would be little matter whether he rode home with game or not. Soon the seas would be still enough to fare a good way over, and then Hailgi meant to take his band raiding. Maybe south along the coast, to the lands of Lingwe's kin, it would not be ill to meet him in battle, or perhaps westward to the shores of Britain, where they might find fine Roman glass and craft-work as well as gold. It would be good to bring back Roman wine as well, to show honor to high atheling-guests with as Sigimund did, though Hailgi had to admit to himself that the southern drink was little to his own liking.

Even from horseback, Hailgi could see the prints clear across the pathway. A fine large deer had passed that way, its weight driving its hoof prints deep through the layers of damp leaves, into the rotting mold. Hailgi turned Wigablajar, gripping hard with his knees and pulling back on the reins as he touched his steed's side lightly with the gilded spurs riveted into his shoes. The horse leapt over the stand of bushes where the deer had leapt before, turning in among the trees to follow the sharp hoof-tracks. Hailgi followed the deer's spoor for a good way, twisting here and there between the trees without heed for the thick clumps of nettles sprouting high and green through the budding tangle of brown-wooded vines. He was too high-mounted to tell the freshness of the cloven tracks very closely, but their edges were still sharp, the deer must have been there that day.

At last the hoof prints led down to a rocky stream-bed. Although Hailgi rode up one side of the froth-edged brook and down the other, he could not find where the track led on from there, but he knew the stream, and he knew that he would come to a good path a little way up it. Wigablajar's hooves splashed through the clear brown water, clattering against the rounded stones as Hailgi turned his head towards the north. The horse's muscles gathered, he sprang up the stream's bank, crashing through the greening spikes of the low crow-berry bushes and onto the road again. Wisps of mist still hung about the ground, faint ghosts edging the pathway and fading before Hailgi as he rode, but the Sun shone brightly behind him, her tree-broken light casting his mounted shadow long and dark along the trodden way ahead. The Wolfing could see where Dagar's horses had passed, the bowed crescents of their shoe-prints dark through the tender green shoots.

Though Sigiruna's brother had spoken little of his hopes for Hagalar's hall, Hailgi could see that he had ridden as one who was eager, never stopping or turning aside to pluck a fresh store of the herbs that sprang up by the edges of the road. He nocked an arrow as he rode, turning his point here and there at half-draw as if each of the pale swirls of mist might hide a deer's high-horned shape. Still, he did not pull his bow fully back or let his shaft fly, even in jest, he might easily spare the loss of an iron point, but there was no telling who might be scathed if he shot unknowing. Caught up in his game, it was some time before Hailgi looked down at the road again to see if a real stag might have chanced to pass that way. No cloven marks marred the smooth ripples of grass-grown mold, the little green blades stood unscathed as the first shoots of grain sprouting in a well-kept field.

Hailgi glanced back along the path. Only Wigablajar's hoof-prints had scored the way behind him, and the little pile of horse-apples in the middle of the road still steamed freshly in the cool morning air. Hailgi tugged Wigablajar to a stop. The pale horse tossed his head and nickered, stamping his left fore hoof hard against the path as Hailgi sat in thought. Dagar could hardly have gotten lost, more likely, he had turned down towards the north and ridden along the coast, or gone between the trees to pick herbs for his leech-craft. There was no need to follow him. Now that farewells were said, Hailgi thought that Dagar could hardly want anything less than to have Sigiruna's husband dogging his tracks to his new home. If the pale ripple of a weasel's long back disappearing between the green shoots of bramble-vines had not caught his eye, Hailgi would not have looked to the northern side of the track, and he would not have seen the hoofmark beneath the leaves.

There it was. As large a deer-track as those he had been following earlier, if not better. The deer must have stood by the roadside a moment, then turned back between the beeches' gray trunks. Hailgi gladly followed its track, urging Wigablajar on with little nudges of his knees. When the hoof prints finally disappeared into a thick hedge of brambles and nettles, Hailgi was not truly lost. He knew that if he kept going northward, he would come to the sea, and the road was somewhere to the south of him, but he was not sure how far he had come towards the west, or how often he had turned back eastward. It would still be a while till noon, but the Sun was edging closer towards her height, so that Hailgi thought it was not likely that he would come upon much game. Still, it was a fair day for a ride, with the last morning dampness still cooling the bright air, it was good to stretch his muscles on horseback again after the winter's stillness and the long work of planting. He would simply ride, and see where his path led him.

Something rustled heavily behind Hailgi. He turned half-around on Wigablajar's back, drawing his bow to full, then eased the string as he saw the wide black wings flapping up through the green-misted beech-branches, the raven rising to join its mate who circled through the pale blue sky above. It seemed to Hailgi that there would be little good in shooting a raven, and he had heard woodsmen say that the black birds might lead wolves or men to game knowing that they would have a share of the kill in their time. He pulled Wigablajar's head around, gazing upward through the fine-leafed tree-weave. The two dark birds tilted their wings against the air, flying about a wide wind-ring before they flapped slowly towards the north-east. Bow still half-drawn, Hailgi followed, knee-touching Wigablajar into a trot through the low crow-berry bushes and white-petaled dog-roses. His glance flickered from the sky to the woods around him and back, sharp flashes of gray bark and pale blooms, keen-edged unfolding leaves and ravens' spread wing-feathers all blending into the day's brightness.

Hailgi did not know where he was until the pale gray beeches suddenly darkened to thick gnarled oaks with ash-trees standing slender among them, and the Sun's light shifted brightly through the thinning branches before him. He wheeled Wigablajar sharply around before his gaze could fall upon the wooden shape that he knew waited not far before him, he had already come more deeply than he should have. The bowstring slackening between his fingers, Hailgi tilted his head back to see where the ravens had gone. They had flown from his sight, he could not tell which wind-road had led them from Fetter-Grove.

"Hailgi!" Dagar's voice called, high and sharp as an arrow's iron keening. "Hailgi, look at me!"

Taken by surprise, Hailgi swung Wigablajar's head slowly towards the west. Dagar was mounted on the brown mare, the Skjolding's deep gold hair streamed over his byrnied shoulders like rivulets of muddy foam over gray rocks. Though the Sun's light glowed in his pale blue eyes, he did not squint or blink against her brightness. He might have been blinded already, for all the harm the mighty sky-shield shining behind Hailgi did him.

Dagar sat still on his horse, and raised in his hand was a bloody spear, the great spear from Fetter-Grove, which he must have taken from Wodhanar's hand. Hailgi began to bend his bow, but his arms moved too slowly, as though the grave-cold were already stilling them. Then Wodhanar's spear was in the air, its shrieking song binding Hailgi's limbs for the long moment of its flight. A great clap of thunder burst around Hailgi, the afterimage of the lightning burned pale blue in his eyes, its glow drowning everything around him. Then he saw the two little black shapes circling through the brightness, the jagged edges of their wings sharpening as they grew in his sight. He was lying on the ground, the mud cold against his back, he could not draw breath or turn his head, only stared up into the sky as the ravens' wings spread and spread above him to cover its brightness with feathers dark as earth.

Suddenly riderless, Hailgi's fallow horse rolled white-rimmed eyes at Dagar a moment before it bolted, crashing through a thick stand of nettles and the bushes beyond. Dagar rode closer, looking down. Hailgi lay on his back, arms out flung, bloody froth dribbled from his gaping mouth into his beard. The shaft of Wodhanar's spear jutted high above him like a slim ash-sapling springing from his broken chest.

The Wolfing's fallen bow had caught on a low crow-berry bush a few paces from his right hand, his arrow lay in the mud a little farther on. Two black flies were buzzing just above his face, but he did not move or blink, even when one of them settled on his open eye like a second pupil against the gray iris. Dagar's limbs were all shaking now, his heart racing as though he had eaten thimble-flowers or the purple blooms of storm-hat. He could not believe that Hailgi had fallen so easily, but there he lay with the wide spray of bright blood sinking into the earth all around him, the muddy peat-water seeping into his amber-fair hair and the spreading stain of wetness darkening his pale blue breeches. Now I have avenged my father, Dagar thought, but his heart was numbed as by the first shock of a bone breaking, and he felt none of the wonder or gladness which he had awaited upon the lifting of his shame.

The second thought followed hard on the first, like thunder after lightning. Hailgi was ever kind to me. The other fly had landed on the edge of Hailgi's upper lip, treading lightly down over the red foam rimming his mouth. Dagar slid from his own horse's back, bracing his foot hard against the slippery grass as he grasped the spear-shaft in both hands again. Hailgi's body lurched as Dagar tugged at the weapon, both flies flying up as the Wolfing's head rolled to one side. A second gout of blood poured out behind the spearhead, soaking rapidly through Hailgi's red tunic like a dark spill of ale. More flies buzzed around the body now, anxiously gathering to hide the blood and stains beneath their black cloud. Dagar swung the spear's haft over Hailgi to drive them away, he might have been swinging it through a patch of mist.

Unbinding his roll of blankets from the mare's back, Dagar bent to heave at the Wolfing's body. As he turned Hailgi over, more blood flowed from the dead man's lips, and Dagar heard his soft sigh. He started violently, letting go of Hailgi's shoulder. The body flopped back into the mud, Hailgi's face turned to the other side, away from Dagar, as though he did not wish to look at the oath-breaker any longer.

"You knew full well that I did not make that vow willingly, and you too paid the geld of shame by breaking the frith others had meant to keep. You have no cause to turn your face from me," Dagar said to Hailgi, but the Wolfing made no reply. "Now come with me, I shall bear you back to your kin-home. I shall deal no worse with you than you dealt with my father and brother, but see that you are laid in a fair howe, with horse and hounds you shall fare no less well-weaponed to the holy halls than you meant for me to fare to your foster-father." Carefully Dagar lifted a corner of his blanket, wiping the slimy mud away from Hailgi's cheek and out of his beard and hair as best he could.

He grasped the Wolfing's tunic, pushing with all the strength in his shoulders, and this time Hailgi's body rolled easily onto the wide square of wool. When he had bound Hailgi safely into the blanket, Dagar fettered his own hands and feet again. He had little wish to leave the Wolfing's body alone, even for a short time, but it was full daylight. "Wolves seldom roam before sunset," he whispered to himself, but the rustling of his voice did not comfort him. Still, Wodhanar must have his spear back, and without much tarrying. It was not well for the god's weapon to stay outside the hallowed garth too long. White bone already ringed the dark sockets of the bay gelding's empty eyes, Dagar did not wish to gaze too closely at the signs of the ravens' feasting on his face, but hurried towards the rootless stump as swiftly as he dared to with the fetter-rope binding his ankles.

When the Skjolding had mounted up, bracing himself against the spear's shaft for balance, he looked down to the god's shape, and his heart stopped in his breast, a whirlwind of dizziness buzzing through his head. The blood-blackened fold of the wooden cloak over Wodhanar's spear arm was moving slowly, lifting upward a little before it lowered again. He did not know how long he stood staring, fettered by the cold dread in his limbs, before he realized that what he saw was the thick black swarm of flies crawling over the blood-soaked wood, rising and settling as they fought for their places on Wodhanar's cloak. Dagar did not need to speak. The ravens were already rising from the old ash-tree's crown, and through the trees beyond it, he could just see the warm brown of his mare's hide. He lifted the spear, sliding its butt back down through Wodhanar's hand, and looped the bright chain about shaft and branch as it had been before.

The way back to the settlement seemed long and slow. Dagar had tied Hailgi's blanketed body tightly to the mare's back, but walked himself, leading her by the reins. She was heavily laden, with all Dagar's possessions as well as Hailgi's corpse, Hailgi's bow dangled by her side, tied to her saddle. The brown mare walked with her head dangling low, now and again trying to turn aside for a mouthful of grass or milkweed, and Dagar had to pull hard on the reins to keep her following him. A dull ache was beginning to throb out from his right shoulder, as though the spear-cast had strained him beyond his strength. I have killed Hailgi Hunding's-Bane, he thought, the hero men thought to be best under the sun. Dagar did not look to left or right as he led the mare along the road through the fields, though a couple of men looked up from their work to shout greeting to him. One of Sigiruna's maidservants, the young Gautish woman Hildagardhar who had taken over little Sigismundar's nursing a few moons earlier, sat on a stool before the hall door. Her slim fingers moved swiftly on her small tablet-loom, weaving out a long pattern-band in blue and gold that would do as a woman's thin belt, or for edging a feasting tunic's hem.

"Where is Sigiruna?" Dagar asked. His voice no longer sounded clear to him, but darkened by the hoarse echo of awe and dread. Hildagardhar looked up, blue eyes wide. Though the Sun had already burned a tinge of summer-red across her broad-boned cheeks, Dagar could see the blood draining from her face.

"She...she's gone to the brewing-house," Hildagardhar stammered. "Wait, wait here, I'll get her." The Gautish woman dropped her weaving and fled, mud spattering from her shoes as she ran.

Dagar cut the ropes that bound Hailgi's corpse to the mare, easing him down to the threshold of the door. It was not long before he saw Sigiruna striding over the muddy stretch of earth from the brewing-house. Her hair was tied back in a long tail, a few strands sticking to the sheen of sweat on her heat-pinked face, dark droplet-stains spattered the creamy wool of her dress. Sigiruna's step faltered as she drew near, looking down bloody bundle at the hall's door. Her shoulders heaved with her deep breath, her mouth dropping open as though her heart, too, were struck still within her.

Dagar spoke as if to himself, his whisper hardly passing beyond his own ears. "I am loath, sister, to tell you sad tidings because my need has made me bring my kinswoman to weeping. That hero who was best in the world and ever stood first among warriors, he fell this morning at Fetter-Grove. Here I have brought him home, as you may see for yourself."

He bent to unwrap the blanket. The traces of mud showed very dark against Hailgi's white skin in the Sun's light, the Wolfing's eyes stared black from his pale face, head drooping to the side like a hanged man's. Sigiruna's shrill eagle-scream rang through Dagar's head, her voice sounding high and keen through the echoes of her cry inside his skull as the white shaft of her arm lifted to point at him.

"All the oaths shall bite you which you swore to Hailgi, by Leiptar's bright waves and Unthio's spray-cold stone! That ship should not glide which bears you, though a good wind fills the sails, that horse should not run which runs under you, though you would flee from your foes, that sword should not bite which you brandish, unless it sings about your own head. Then would Hailgi's death be revenged upon you, if you were a warg in the woods outside, wealth and all joy forsaken, having no meat but cold corpses."

It seemed to Dagar that he could already see the bale-fire burning in Sigiruna's eyes as she cried out against him, the lines of her whitening face drawn into a sword-sharp troll's mask. He had felt her fist on his face often enough, now he waited for her hand to grasp her own belt-knife, or lunge for the sword at his side, but she did not move, only stood with her hand pointing towards him as though arrows of ice might fly from her fingertips, or the lightning of her rage spring forth to eat his heart.

"You are mad, sister, and out of your wits, to bid such an ill-shaping for your brother," Dagar said gently. "Wodhanar alone ruled all bale, from our father's death to this, for he bore runes of battle-sake between kinsmen." He stepped forward slowly, taking her hand in both of his. "Now your brother offers you red rings, the holy waters' stead and Battle-Dale. Ring-adorned bride, you shall have half our homeland, to pay for your harms, you and your children, or else I shall go from here to Sealand and dwell in the hall of the Skjoldings, and leave all the lands here to you and whoever you shall choose. You often whetted me to battle and to brave deeds. You know that it was not a man's part to leave our father and brother unavenged, though you wed their slayer and bore his son. Now I have done what I had to. The soul of our kin is cleansed."

Sigiruna looked down at Hailgi's face again, and the tears began to drip from her eyes, as though all her strength had spilled from her body with the flowing of Hailgi's blood. "I shall never sit joyful at Sefa Fells," she said, her voice small and choked, "nor enjoy life early, nor at night, unless the light shine upon the ruler again and Wigablajar, that gold-bitted steed, runs hither under the hero. Then I might greet him gladly." She crouched down, the mud soaking into her hem as she stroked Hailgi's matted hair back, brushing the earth from his face as her tears fell upon him. "Hailgi caused such terror among all his foes and their kinsmen, they were as goats running mad on the fells before a wolf, filled with dread. So was he among heroes like the nobly shaped ash-tree among bushes, or the dew-dripping stag above all other animals, horns glowing up to the heavens. Hailgi, my Hailgi." Sigiruna bent to embrace the Wolfing's body, her long hair-tail falling forward to stream over his shoulder as she lifted Hailgi from where he lay, heaving him up with her arms locked about his chest. The bloodied blanket fell away as she bore him into the hall, and Dagar heard a higher cry from within.

"Hailgi! My son, my son!"

Now I am ruler here, Dagar thought, till someone chooses to avenge Hailgi in turn. His legs were steady as stone beneath him as he strode into the hall, walking around the table where Sigiruna and Bergohildar were straightening Hailgi's clothes and pulling his bloodied cloak over the great rent in his chest while two of the thrall-maids stood whispering to each other. Dagar sat down in the high seat, looking over the hall.

"You," he called to the bonds women, "go out and call all the folk here to the hall. What has happened here may not be hidden, but if any will vengeance, it must be taken now or not at all."

The two women stared at him, Dagar half-rose from the seat, his hand on the hilt of the sword. "Go!" He shouted, and they ran from the hall. He stood again, walking down to Bergohildar and Sigiruna and touching the older woman on the shoulder. The tears brightened all the crevasses running down Bergohildar's face as she looked up at him. Dagar could not tell her not to weep, but he said, "Bergohildar, you need not fear for what shall happen to you. You shall live here in honor for all of your days, and have rule over whatever you will, I give you your own choice, in deeming the were-gild for your son."

"I have no wish for were-gild," Bergohildar answered, her voice cracking under all the weight of her years. "I ought to have died with Sigismundar, as I wished to, I shall not long outlive his son. You shall live knowing that you murdered a man who wished you only weal, and broke oaths to murder a kinsman."

"It was no murder. If you look well, you will see that the spear went in from the front. Hailgi saw me, and had his bow half-nocked in his hand already when I hailed him, so that he might have shot me before I could cast the weapon."

"He must have awaited no ill from you, even though he saw the spear in your hand, both fear and troth-breaking were ever far from his thoughts. But that is over, and you have slain him. Now the only were-gild I will take shall be the goods of my wedding, and those you shall put with me when you lay me in the howe where Sigismundar is sleeping, for I have little wish to live longer in this hall. You, Sigiruna, shall have it for your own, and reap what you sowed when your troll-craft whetted Hailgi to slay the heroes of the Skjolding clan."

The old frowe brushed a muddied strand of bright hair from her son's face and bent to lay a single kiss on his pale brow, then straightened herself and walked from the hall, treading with a slow care, as if she were trying to hide the staggering of drunkenness. Dagar went back to the high seat, settling himself as the first thanes rushed in. Rage twisted Arnugrimar's ugly face as he raised his sap-stained ax, behind him came Hildawulfar and Skald-Thonarabrandar, their bare swords bright in their hands.

"Hold!" Dagar called. "There will be time for vengeance, once you have heard what has happened. Then you may choose for yourselves, whether to call me to battle or let were-gild be paid for the Wolfing leader. Sigiruna, take Hailgi's tunic from him, let the wound be seen, so that all may know how I came upon him."

Sigiruna drew her belt-knife, cutting through the blood-stiffened linen. She tugged it away from Hailgi's bare skin as if he could still feel the pain of the cloth coming unstuck from his wound, slicing down each of the sleeves and easing the spoiled fabric from beneath his body. The splinters of Hailgi's breastbone shone white against the glistening dark red of the wound, all might see that the spear had struck from the front. When most of the settlement's men had gathered, Dagar rose to his feet. "Now hear. I have avenged Haganon and Bragi, as was my due, and I avenged them fairly, as you may see for yourselves if you look at the wound on Hailgi's body. Wodhanar's blessing was upon the deed, for the slaying was done at Fetter-Grove, and I struck with Wodhanar's spear."

Skald-Thonarabrandar walked forward to stand before the table where Hailgi lay. "How may we know that you tell the truth?" The lanky thane asked. "There are many spears in the world, and Wodhanar seldom speaks his will to men."

"Go to Fetter-Grove, if you doubt me. You may see the spoor of the slaying upon the ground without, and the gift I made to Wodhanar within, and the drighten's blood still standing upon the spear-point of the god, which pierced him through."

Skald-Thonarabrandar tightened his fist on his sword's hilt. "You are no coward, to come again into this hall," he said slowly, "for no one here did not love Hailgi Hunding's-Bane, and few do not have the gold rings he gave in their keeping. Had he fallen in battle with his friends around him, none of us should have come again from that field, and his slayer least of all, if we had not fallen first. But come to Fetter-Grove with us, and we shall see if matters are as you have said, for few are brave enough to stand against what Wodhanar has deemed. It was not the part of a coward to come at Hailgi from the front, nor to raise a spear's point against him where he might meet it. Though you went byrnied while he was bare, I cannot say that you have not done as a man should. Yet I do say now that, whatever has passed there, you shall not rule in Hailgi's hall while I live, and I do not doubt that any of the folk here would say the same."

"I have already said that Hailgi's hall and lands shall be Sigiruna's portion for her husband's death, if she will take them, and she may rule here as she likes, and choose who she will to sit beside her. Half our homestead I have sworn to her as well, but I shall dwell in the hall where my father dwelt, by the high mounds of the Skjoldings. I have no more wish to stay here than you have for me to stay. Now follow me, and I shall show you where Hailgi fell."

Sigiruna watched the men go from the hall. She wanted to cry out, or to run after them, but her limbs seemed fettered, and the earth weighted her body down as if all her might had already fared with Hailgi. She knew that she would not ride over air and water again, nor tread the cloud-roads with lightning sparking from her spear, while she lived, she could not follow her beloved to the high halls of the gods.

"Frowe," said Hildagardhar timidly, "can I do anything?"

Sigiruna looked down at the fair little Gaut-maid, who stood wringing the long woven strips dangling down from the knot of her belt. "Go and get water and cloths, so that I may clean the drighten's body. After that, set the bond-men to digging so that a howe may be raised, and send others into the woods to find his horse, he must ride as is fitting."

She cut Hailgi's breeches away as well. They were bloody and soiled, and no one else would ever wear them. Sigiruna cast all the rent cloth into a single heap on the floor, she would tell the bond maidens to burn it all. When Hildagardhar came back with the pot of water, Sigiruna began to sponge the blood from Hailgi's cooling body, wiping her cloth over the little knot where his ribs had not quite healed straight. He had ever been a bad patient, never lying still to heal or telling her when he hurt. Her tears had all flowed, leaving dry sobs to shake her shoulders as she cleaned the mud from his face and hair. She had ever known that they would have to pay their geld to Wodhanar someday. For that she had chosen Hailgi, but she had not thought the day would come so soon, or that his fall would leave her alive and alone.

Once more Sigiruna bent to clasp her arms about Hailgi's bare white chest, raising him up. She was used to the heaviness of dead men, but Hailgi's bloodless body was lighter than she had weened him to be. His head resting against her shoulder, she bore him easily into their chamber and laid him down on their bed. Sigiruna still remembered how to deal with the battle-slain, that knowledge had not left her. Leeks grew all about the back of the hall, now she went out and pulled up three, their white stems shining in the sunlight as she brought them out of the earth. These she cut and pressed into the wound. Though the day was warming swiftly, they would help to keep Hailgi's body from rotting before he was laid in the howe. After that she packed the bloody spear-hole before and behind with bandages of coarse linen to soak up the last of the blood so that it would not soil his burial clothes, and bound another wrapping of leeks about his chest with a broad strip of finer linen.

676

Hailgi's limbs were not yet stiff, so that Sigiruna could easily guide his arms into the sleeves of his wedding-tunic, and pull his byrnie on over that before she girded his sword to his waist. She could not yet bear to set his helmet upon his head, but she set it beside him, its polished silver plates casting a broken veil of light over the keen lines of his face. Sitting down on the bed by Hailgi, Sigiruna took her fine-toothed comb from the table beside them. She lifted his head to her lap and began to comb the last flecks of earth from his beard and hair, as she had often combed him while he lived. She could not forget how he had smiled up at her then, laughing when she said that she had found a louse or flea on him or when she chided him for the great matted tangles his helmet had often rucked his hair into. Though Sigiruna could weep no more, it seemed to her that there would never be an end to the freshening of her sorrows.

There was nothing in the hall which Hailgi had not touched, she would never pour ale again without feeling his fingers over hers on the horn, nor taste the sweet mead without thinking of his kisses. If it were not for little Sigismundar, who lay happily chewing on the blanket in his cradle, Sigiruna thought she would have put on her wedding-dress then, and gone to dig up the roots of storm-hat or dwale, and let Dagar lay them both in the mound together. But she had her son to think of, and she knew that it was not given to her to put an end to her own life before Wodhanar chose her again. The earth-door of Sigismundar's howe was still dark by the time Hailgi's had been full-built. The old drighten's mound had been broken on the day of Hailgi's death, so that Bergohildar's body could be borne in and laid beside her husband.

Now the heaped mold of Hailgi's howe rose brown against the grass-sheened fields and the green woods beyond. Down to the east, past the pale strand, Dagar's ship floated with furled sails on the turning tide, ready to fare back to the Skjoldings' hall. A strong wind was blowing from the north, flinging Sigiruna's hair and her dark cloak back and stirring the mane of the fallow horse whose gold-adorned reins she held. The howe's wide gate stood open, the reddening evening light showing the white linen of the fine bed Sigiruna had made there, the bowl of dried apples, the bread and the keg of strong mead she had set within for her husband. Dagar stood beside her, holding the leashes of two great hunting hounds. The two Skjoldings watched silently as Skald-Thonarabrandar, Arnugrimar, Ingwawinar, and Hildawulfar bore Hailgi's bier up from the hall, the long train of his folk following behind his body.

Gold glittered on Hailgi's arms beneath his byrnie-sleeves, and the silver adorning his helm gleamed like ruddy gold in the light of the lowering Sun. Sigiruna led Wigablajar aside so that her husband could be carried to the door of the howe. Though two bright rounds of Roman-minted silver weighted his eyelids and the helmet's raven-shaped nose piece spread over his face, it seemed to Sigiruna that she could see Hailgi's still features as well as if no metal hid them, that he was still gazing at her, and saw all the little worms of sorrow gnawing within her. She did not wish to weep, but though she made no sound, she could not still her burning tears as she looked down at him. They splashed onto the breast of his byrnie, soaking into the white linen beneath.

"My Hailgi," Sigiruna whispered. Even here, at the gates of the howe, he was her beloved, she would not have chosen otherwise, not even had she known from the beginning the very day of his fall. "Let no one hinder your passing, but ride swiftly up to God-World, along the rainbow's shining fire. Haimdalar, warder of the holy garth, awaits you at the head of the shivering bridge, Wodhanar shall greet you in that hall where the shingles are all shields, where the posts are the shafts of spears. Fare well, my holy one. The gates of Walhall are open for you!"

At her gesture, Hildagardhar carried little Sigismundar forward, lowering the child so that he could lay his chubby little hand on his father's byrnied breast. Sigiruna did not know whether her son would remember this moment, but she knew that it would lie beneath the layers of his life like a leek's seed deep within the herb's shining root, and shape him with the strength Hailgi had left him. Breathing deeply to keep her hands from shaking, Sigiruna lifted her knife to Wigablajar's throat where the great vein pulsed beneath his gleaming yellow-brown hide. This, too, was well-known to her. She had often slain horses at Winter nights, and her blade was so keen that the fallow steed did not flinch away from its edge, if he felt it cutting in at all. Sigiruna helped Skald-Thonarabrandar and Ingwawinar to drag the horse's heavy body in, arranging him by the side of the mound with his legs tucked neatly beneath him.

Arnugrimar and Hildawulfar bore Hailgi's bier in through the door, and the three of them lifted him carefully from the wooden framework onto the bed's soft linen. The worst of the stiffness had passed from his limbs already, so that Sigiruna had little trouble straightening him and wrapping his hands about the fine horn of Frankish glass he had brought from Hunding's hall. As the men carried the bodies of the hounds in to lay at Hailgi's feet, Sigiruna kissed her husband one last time. His lips were cold as if he had been outside in the rain, the faint taste of rot in his mouth no stronger than the staleness of morning's first wakening.

Sigiruna stood watching as the bondsmen heaped up the earth again to fill the mound's broad opening. Only once did she turn to look down at the darkening sea. The sail of Dagar's ship was pale against the water, its square shape waning beneath the wind's strong blast as she gazed at it. The day after Hailgi's burial was gray and gloomy, the new green shoots bending flat before the showers of rain that blew across the fields. Sigiruna wandered silently about the hall, or stared out the door at the shifting clouds, while little Siggi played in the straw and crawled about with the dogs licking his face.

Now and again she would pick her son up, letting him nuzzle his face against her breasts, but when he began to cry, she had to call Hildagardhar to come give him suck. When Sigiruna could no longer bear to stay inside, she walked out, following the low ridge that led up to the mounds of the Wolfing clan. The fresh earth of Hailgi's howe was black beneath the rain, rivulets of muddy water snaking down its sides. If the weather had held good, they might have turfed it over that morning, but leaving it another day or two would do little harm. Her shoes slipping in the mud, Sigiruna climbed up to the top of the mound. All her soul's keen sight could not pierce through the black mold, but she remembered Hailgi as her craft had once shown him to her.

The young hero standing in the boat's prow, small and slim before the grown thanes watching from the strand, his amber-fair hair streaming about his shoulders and his sword shining brightly as he dared them to follow him to battle, his jaw bleeding from the tip of Hunding's blade and the shadow of the byrnie he had borne still marking his tunic as he stared up at the sky in wonderment, his gray eyes bright with awe and love. Hailgi's cheek dripping blood beneath his helmet, the might in his arms as he clasped her hands in his and rose to his feet, smiling at her even as the pain of the broken ribs drained the color from his face and his strong body glimmering pale against hers in the darkness, the warmth of his arms about her and his soft kisses on her mouth and breasts and thighs. Sigiruna wept and wept, she could not still her tears, and here there was no one to see how her shoulders shook, or how she clasped her knees, rocking back and forth on the howe till her strength was all spilt.

She had heard that Wodhanar's wish-daughters were not meant to weep, she had not cried when she had smoothed the death-snarl from her father's grim face, nor when she had combed the pale hair of her brother Bragi over his forehead to hide the great gash in his skull. Men died, it was ever so, but she had chosen Hailgi for her own, and ought to have been allowed to bear him to Walhall herself, and share his bed there. By the time she could weep no more, the rain was falling in a cold thick torrent, the wind driving its waves hard over the earth, and the sky was beginning to darken. The storm had washed the salt tracks from Sigiruna's face and the heat from her eyes by the time she got back to the hall. Hildagardhar was sitting in a pile of fresh straw near the fire with Sigismundar before her, the two of them laughing as they patted palms together. Sigiruna stood silently in the doorway watching them for a little while, until a cold gust of wind swept through the door behind her, spattering heavy drops all around her faint shadow on the earthen floor.

Hildagardhar glanced up guiltily, her laughter stilling swift as the smacking of palm against cheek. Sigismundar gurgled happily on, his little hand reaching out for her wrist. Sigiruna glided over, picking the child up and hugging him to her wet breasts.

"Mama's back, my sweet," she murmured to him. Sigismundar little liked being taken from his warm place, and answered her with a loud wail. She bounced him gently up and down in the crook of one arm, petting his soft fair hair with the other until he stopped crying. "Has Guntharuna cooked anything for dinner?"

"Guntharuna's gone to bed already. She said she thought she had a little fever truly, she didn't look very hale, and this is the time of year for sickness."

"Well, that's all right. I'm not very hungry, I'll get some bread from the bake-house later, or maybe some cheese. Have you eaten?"

"I had some sausage, frowe, and I've fed Siggi already."

"Good." Sigiruna sat down in the high seat with her son in her arms. It seemed to her that she could already see the clean lines of Hailgi's features showing beneath his plumpness, his dark gray eyes were very wide and bright in his little face, and his warm weight in her lap felt solid and comforting.

"My treasure, my sweet," she murmured to him. "You shall grow into a strong hero someday, you shall take up a sword, and wave it like this, and like this." Sigiruna guided her son's little arm gently through the motions of striking and parrying, Sigismundar laughed as he looked up at his mother.

Hildagardhar poked at the fire, arranging another few sticks on it, then settled herself on the nearest bench to weave at her tablet-loom. After a while she stood, carrying her work up to the high seat. "Frowe, is there any more of this yellow thread in the hall? I thought I had enough to finish off this belt, but it looks as though I'm an ell short."

Although the light was fading, Sigiruna still knew the color at once. It was one of Haitharikijar's new dyeing-batches, which Hildagardhar had been weaving into everything she made lately, the dyer had mixed a little red in with the yellow, giving it a fine rich amber-tone. She had meant to get some from him to embroider around the hem of Hailgi's red tunic. It was so nearly the color of his hair, but then they had been busy with the planting, and,

"No, there's not. You can go over to Haitharikijar's house and see if he's got any left, if you like. We'll be all right here. What does he want for it?"

"I gave him half a cheese last time."

"Well, go ahead and take a whole one out of the storehouse for him. There's twelve rolls of fine flax-thread that I want dyed deep blue, and another three to dye red. And take a torch with you, I don't doubt it will be full dark before you get back."

Sigismundar was squirming in her lap, making 'I-want-down' noises. Sigiruna set him on the floor, letting him crawl over to pull the tail of one of the dogs sleeping by the fire. The hound raised its head to growl softly, Sigiruna carried her son to another part of the hall where he could prowl without risking bites. Even within the hall, Sigiruna could hear the barking of the geese passing overhead and the flapping of their wings through the ceaseless whisper of the rain on the thatch. Last year, she and Hailgi had ridden through the marshes together. It was just before she got too big with Sigismundar to risk getting on horseback, and shot their arrows up at the hound-noisy flocks.

There had been goose enough for the whole settlement to feast that night, with plenty of strong ale still left from Ostara's night. Sigiruna dashed the tears away from her eyes with the back of her hand. I must stop weeping, she thought, there is enough water about us already, without me adding a river to it! The hall seemed very lonely and cold, with only herself and the sleepy dogs and Sigismundar tossing the straw about himself, and no more than the single fire burning to light it. Suddenly the door banged open. Hildagardhar ran in, sodden braid flinging a spray of water from its end and the flying hem of her cloak scattering mud behind her. Her eyes were wide and wild, her hands empty.

"Sigiruna! Sigiruna, I saw him! I saw"

"What did you see?" Sigiruna leaned forward in the high seat. Her fists clenched painfully. "Who?"

"The drighten, I saw him riding through the clouds, on his fallow horse, bloodied as he fell, with a train of slain warriors behind him, I heard the barking of his hounds. I thought that I was dreaming, or deluded, or else that the doom of the gods had come, but he was spurring his steed onward, and I thought that he was faring homeward again. It seemed to me that I heard him speaking, I know that I could take no other man's voice for his, but I thought that I heard him say that you should go out from the hall, if you listed to find the folk-leader, that the howe is open and Hailgi has come. He was drenched in blood, and he bade that you should come and still the wound-flow."

681

Sigiruna grabbed a burning brand from the fire, running out into the rain. Her dress was soaked through in seconds as if she were standing under a waterfall, her feet slipping in the mud as she hastened breathlessly along the dark path towards the mounds. The torch's sputtering flames showed her the blackness gaping on the side of Hailgi's howe, casting a few bright sparks from the metal within. The heavy weight of earth was cold through his body, his bones weighting his limbs like stone. Hailgi remembered the swift rushing of the wind around him, riding down through the sunset-glowing clouds, but Walhall had already faded to a shining blur in his mind, a dream too fair for him to hold after wakening. Slowly he turned his head, the cold rounds of metal fell from his eyes, clanging against the side of his helmet.

He could see the blue howe-fire burning over the rings on his arms, icy flames dancing over the squares of gold that adorned his pale steed's bridle and the gilded collars of the hunting hounds at his feet. His glass horn lay in his hands, smeared by the blood that had oozed through his byrnie, he remembered its rippled smoothness beneath his fingers, but could not feel it now. The only thing he felt was the burning pain in his breast where the hot sorrow-drops had fallen on him, glowing against his icy body like a coal laid on frost-numbed flesh.

Then the ruddy light flickered warmly over him, he saw the brightness of the living fire coming nearer, and heard the light steps splashing through the mud. His body did not move easily beneath his will, but he was able to pull one curled hand away from his drinking horn and push himself up onto his side. Sigiruna stuck the butt of her burning brand into the earth beneath the edge of the howe-roof and ran to him. The golden tears of joy spilled from her eyes again as she embraced him, her living breath warm on his lips. "

I am so glad to see you" she murmured"glad as Wodhanar's hungry hawks learning of the slain and warm corpses, or seeing the dew-sprinkled day." She set his glass horn aside and lay down by Hailgi, running her hands over his mailed back and clasping him hard to her as though her warmth could kindle life from his coldness again. "Living or not, I would kiss you, and you shall cast your bloodied byrnie from you. My poor Hailgi, your hair is all hoary with frost, and you are drenched in death-dew, the hands of Haganon's kinsman are spray-cold, ruler, how shall I heal your hurts?"

It was hard for Hailgi to draw breath into his broken lungs, harder still for him to press it out. The words came slowly from deep in his throat, harsh and dragging in a single low tone. "You alone, Sigiruna, have caused Hailgi to be drenched in harm-dew. Gold-adorned one, sun-bright maid, you weep bitter tears before you go to sleep. Each falls bloody on the battle-leader's breast, burning spray-cold into me, pressing with sorrow. Thus I have come hither from Walhall's benches, your weeping has weighed me down, bearing me to earth again."

"Hailgi, my Hailgi," Sigiruna whispered. She lifted the helmet from his head, smoothing his hair back from his face. "If I had known that my weeping would cause you harm, I should never have dropped a single tear, though my heart burst beneath their weight. But let me pour the mead that I set in the mound for you, and we shall drink it together, as we drank on our bridal night."

She helped him to sit up, leaning his back against the curve of the earthen wall. The pain in Hailgi's breast was already easing as he watched Sigiruna, white against the ruddy brightness of her torch and the blue howe-flames, fill his horn with mead, its golden light shining green through the blue glass. Slowly he raised one arm to take the vessel from her warm hand. He held it gently in the curve of his palm, he knew that the least of his strength would shatter the fragile glass, but he moved his hand very carefully, and was able to tilt the horn against his lips at last. It was easier for him to let the mead flow down than to try to swallow, but he could feel the strength she had brewed into it glowing within him, as if he were gulping a fire-warmed drink after a long faring through the snow, and his voice sounded a little more like a living man's when he spoke again.

"Well shall we drink this dear draught, though I have lost my lands and hopes. No one shall sing songs of sadness, though the wound bleeds in my breast. Now my bride has come into the howe, beloved atheling-maid, beside the dead." He lifted the half-empty horn towards Sigiruna, she uncurled his hand from it and raised it to her own lips, draining the draught.

"My Wolfing, I have made a bed for us here, free from sorrow. I would sleep in your arms, folk-leader, as with my dear one in life."

Though Hailgi could not feel his cold face shifting with his thoughts, a faint spoor of his wonder brightened his slow voice as he answered her. "I say that nothing will be unawaited sooner or later at Sefa Fells, if you lie in the dead warrior's arms, white in the howe, while still alive, Haganon's daughter, atheling-born!" He reached out to draw Sigiruna to him, holding her living body as carefully as he had held the glass horn.

"Now my sorrows are at an end," she whispered into his ear. "Now I shall weep no more, since we are together this night, and I know that you have not forsaken me, though you ride over the high wind-roads while I must wait within the Middle-Garth's ring."

"Be of strong soul, my walkurja. Now I know that a seat shall soon be readied for you in Walhall, a fair home for both of us to dwell in for a while, and we shall never be apart too long."

Sigiruna let out her breath in a warm soft sigh, and Hailgi could feel the curve of her smile against his cheek. "That gladdens my heart, more than I may tell. My Hailgi, I would give you a full share of my strength, so that we might stay together and fare together, and not be away from each other a moment."

"That may not be, but I know that we shall see Ostara's next dawning together, my beloved."

Sigiruna bent to fill the horn, then leaned up against Hailgi again. He lowered his arm about his shoulders, she held the mead to his lips, and they sat drinking and whispering softly together for a time. It seemed to Hailgi that he could feel her life soaking slowly into him like rain seeping down through the earth, and after a while he was able to raise his arms above his head so that she could draw the chill links of his byrnie from his body.

"I should have brought hot water to wash you with, and fresh bandages for your wound," Sigiruna said, shaking her head as she laid her hand above the thick patch of chill blood that had soaked through his tunic. "If I had stopped for a moment to think."

"You came as swiftly as you could, and I would not have been without you for that time," Hailgi replied. "My pain is eased, my breast no longer bleeds, and I can ask for no more. Though those who come to Walhall are the pale dead, drenched in blood, with broken byrnies and shattered shields, there is always healing within its door-posts, sure as there is always fighting on Sig-Father's fields each day."

"It is well enough, then, to know that you are hale and glad there." Sigiruna kissed him again. She did not close her eyes, but gazed deep into his own. Hailgi did not know what she might see there, for the burning branch at the howe-door had guttered out a little while ago, but her arms tightened around his shoulders as she pressed her mouth harder against his. Though she did not shiver, the cold blue flames dancing over his arm-rings showed him how the hairs stood up on her arms, her white skin stippled with the cold.

"I wish that I could warm you better," Hailgi murmured. "But I cannot, you must wrap yourself in the blankets you have laid here."

Sigiruna stood up, untying her belt and stripping her wet dress from her shoulders before she climbed back into the bed. "Now lie down beside me, my Hailgi, and these blankets shall cover us both."

It was less hard for Hailgi to ease himself down than it had been for him to sit up, and soon he lay in Sigiruna's warm embrace beneath the bed covers. He did not know what more might be, until he felt the heat of her touch between his thighs, and then it seemed to him that his life was not wholly spilled, but one deed might yet be done.

Hailgi felt the dawning as a slow thrill through his cold limbs, like the deep note of a far-off battle-horn shaking through the air. He tried to raise his head, but it had grown heavier, though he could still feel Sigiruna's warmth beside him, her borrowed life was already fading from his limbs.

"Sigiruna," he said. He could hear his voice growing deeper and slower as he spoke, sinking to the depths of his broken breast. "Put my byrnie on me again, gird me with my sword, and put my helmet on my head. It is time for me to ride the reddening ways, and let the fallow horse tread the flight-paths. I must go westward, over the wind-helm's bridge, before Salgofnir wakes the sig-folk."

"I am little willing for you to go," Sigiruna answered, but no tears dimmed the brightness of her face against the dark howe-shadows. She lifted his arms into the sleeves of his byrnie, tugging the ring-weave over his head and girding his sword on him.

The warmth of Sigiruna's kiss had faded from Hailgi's lips before she lifted her mouth from his. She shimmered fairer and fairer as his sight brightened, but Wigablajar stood saddled, and Hailgi could wait in his howe no longer.

CHAPTER XXXIII

Helgi stood at the fore of the darkened stage, his sword gripped in both hands and pointing downward. His pale face shone very bright against the black background, reddish-gold hair glowing over the shoulders of his black T-shirt, the light reflecting from his blade picked out the shadows of his black jean laden legs. Mike, Widget, and Josh were ranged behind him, single lights brightening their faces from the darkness around them and gleaming smoothly from the curves of the guitars slung against their bodies. Rack sat off to the side, his spotlight glittering off the chrome fittings of the drums that rose around him like the steel-braced walls of a fortress. Above their heads, the words 'FLOURESCENT HEROIC MADNESS' glowed in bright letters, the pure white shapes edged with a lightning-shiver of blue light.

Helgi turned the CD over in his hands, looking at the list of titles on the back. 1. Erl-King (Hadding) 3' 48", 2. Through the Sunrise (Hadding) 2' 56"all his titles, his words and music gathered inside the little flat plastic box like a tree's might lurking in the seed. There were Mistlands, Weird Women, Night-Driving. Ending with Call to the Gods and, finally, the song that crowned them all, 16. Karin's Song (Hadding) 5.23.

"It's awesome," Helgi said. Though the garage trapped the August heat, amplifying it like a microphone shriek bouncing back and forth between the concrete walls, a shiver ran up to meet the drop of sweat trickling down his bare spine as he turned the CD back over to look at the cover picture again. "I can't believe, I mean, we did it."

"Betcha ass," Mike agreed. He took another one from the stack piled up on the chair beside his music stand, flipping it up in the air and catching it. "That sword was just the thing, gives us that truly crazed quality that catches the eye. Have you heard us on the radio yet? They were playing 'Night-Driving' on Q102 about an hour ago. I just about shat when I heard it. I think, hell, I think we've made it. Any day now, we'll be getting money for nothing and chicks for free."

Helgi pried the plastic cover up, slipping the little booklet out of its place. Yes. There were his lyrics, his words, printed out for everyone to see, black and stark against the white page, beneath the line of italicized print that said In memory of Dr. Johannes Sachs. True musician, true teacher, and true friend. As he blinked, it seemed to him that the shapes of the letters shone red behind his eyelids, a sudden stream of electricity running live as blood through their neon.

Helgi tugged the shimmering disc from its place. He could see his face mirrored behind the letters embossed into its silvery surface, pale and slightly blurred as though he stood in a mist, two brilliant rainbow-beams glowed out from the clear hole in the middle, their bands of colored fire cutting slantwise up through the foggy reflection of his forehead and down over the point of his chin. "Have you heard it?"

"Excreteth Ursa Major on the Milky Way?" Mike's eyes flickered to the pale streak on his freckled wrist before he reached down to pick up the crumpled digital watch at his feet. "We could probably put it on now, might as well, if you can't stand to wait any longer. It'll be a couple of hours before anyone else makes it over. Unlike some people, they have to work during the day."

"Unlike you, the unemployed."

Mike's slightly soured look split into a wide grin. "Hey, boy, I ain't unemployed no more! Neither are you, come to think of it. We are musicians, opium-producing parasites on the body of the American proletariat, it is true, but nevertheless we have ceased to be totally functionless drones."

"This is so," Helgi agreed, grinning back at him. "How many copies did you say they printed?"

"Thirty thousand. Fucking good, for a first recording." Mike leaned down, pressing a button on the side of his portable CD player. The disk-slot slid open, he laid the glimmering circle into it, pushing it home and punching it to life.

Helgi sat silently, listening as the first runs of his keyboard glittered out above the deep thrumming of Widget's bass. By habit, he began drawing breath three beats before his entrance, but then let the air flow from his lungs in a long soft sigh as the first words rang out like a gust of snow-cold wind blasting through the muggy-hot garage. "'Wind is howling through dark pines'"

Though Helgi was used to the sound Dr. Sachs' old tape recorder had played back from his lessons, the dark glow of his voice on CD was new to him. It seemed to him that the bright round had cleared the spoor of harshness from his throat without stealing the aching edge of his strength, the storm-clean tones of his hopes singing through the speakers' black grids.

"Is that really what I sound like?" Helgi asked. His eyes warmed with unshed rain as he spoke, he could not help it, with the echo of all the old wounding-words still ringing in the back of his throat.

"Yeah, it is. You surprised? It's never quite the same when you hear a recording of yourself. You've gotten real good since we made that first demo tape. You want to hear the difference?"

"Uh." My, your voice has certainly improved, Helgi, I remember when your singing used to sound like shit. But the pain in his throat had eased already, the memories hurting no worse than the rain-woken ache of a bone broken long ago, the healing was in the voice that sang from the speakers now, his inheritance from Dr. Sachs. Helgi picked up the red can of Coke by his feet, pressing its ice-cold edge between the low swells of his pecs. "Yeah. Why not?"

"Just a sec, I'll be back."

The house-door fanned a blast of cool air over Helgi as Mike closed it behind him. With no one there to hear, Helgi sang as softly as he had years ago, when he feared being heard, "'The hunt hares above as I sink to the ground, The willow-gray maiden wheels in the sky, Blood raining black from the host of the slain, the hemp of the hang-noose harsh brushing my face. I give this death as a gift to myself," Helgi got up to turn the CD player off when Mike came back in, slipping the disc into its sleeve beneath the ranged gazes of the band.

"Okay, let's run this up so you can hear the same song."

The first thing Helgi noticed was how ragged Widget's bass sounded against his keyboard runs, how Josh's guitar and Rack's drums shifted just a little out of phase with the rhythm. Then Helgi was singing. He could not mistake his voice for anyone else's, but it was far from the sound on Flourescent's CD. Harsh, dragging a little, as though he had to force it up through his throat. Still, he could hear the strength lurking in it. It seemed to be the sunken darkness of sleep that flattened the tones, that only an hour or two of wakening could bring the sound up to the brighter pitch and speed of full life.

Helgi felt his throat opening out as he listened, as though he could shape the voice of the singer on the tape into his own clear depth. Seeing how expectantly Mike was looking at him, Helgi nodded. "Okay, you've convinced me."

'Erl-King' had been the last song on the demo tape, when it was over, Mike flicked it back out and put another of their CDs in, pushing the machine's buttons until the low guitar scream that started, "Through the Sunrise' was rising and rising to ring through the swift chromatic flickering of Helgi's keyboard notes against the garage's walls. "Are we fine, or what?"

"We are fine," Helgi agreed. "I bet Dr. Sachs is, would have been proud of us. You know, I was scared to show him my music at first. I didn't think he'd think it was well, real music, but he worked on everything with me. He was really enthusiastic."

"Yeah. I guess if he used to support himself by performing at nightclubs, he wouldn't have any reason to object to rock. It's hard to imagine, isn't it? You could have knocked me over with a feather when Dr. Meyer told us that at the service. I would have thought he was, well, just too dignified to do that sort of thing, even when he was our age. I know this is horrible, I felt like a shit at the time, but for the rest of the service, I couldn't keep from trying to imagine him as the host in Cabaret. It was an awfully strange image."

"Umm." It seemed to Helgi that the damp weight of the heat was pressing down harder on him, dimming the brightness of the sunlit concrete outside and dulling the edge of the music ringing out of the speakers.

"Hey, I'm sorry, Helgi," Mike said softly. "You still miss him, don't you?"

"Yeah."

Mike's low brow furrowed as he rolled the end of his mustache thoughtfully between his thumb and index finger. "Hmm. Uh. Hey, if I tell you something, will you promise not to breathe a hint or a whisper?"

"I promise," Helgi said at once. Beneath the brightening lure-flame of his curiosity, he could feel a network of darker thoughts. Did Dr. Sachs tell him what he never told me, was he more of a favorite student than I was? Does he know? "Not a hint or a whisper, I swear it."

"Okay." Although they were alone in the garage, Mike leaned closer to Helgi, so close that Helgi could feel the moist warmth of his breath and smell the slight musky scent of his aftershave and sweat, see the tiny golden threads radiating out from his pupils through his brown irises. His skin was thicker-pored than Luann's, the red hair-roots just pricking through along his jaw and chin. "No one knows this but me," he murmured, "and it's not certain, so I really don't want you talking. It would be a bad thing if it got out."

"Didn't I just promise not to tell?" Helgi asked, but his slight irritation nettled his curiosity more hotly, like the prickle of adrenalin glittering hungry through a wolf's blood at the first sight of his quarry. He found that he was leaning closer to Mike, ear towards mouth, close and quiet as if they were waiting in a little hunters' blind together. "Go on, say it."

"It is possible. It is just possible, " Mike whispered. "Well, Jimmy Page is going to be playing Reunion Arena in the middle of October, and it is just possible that Flourescent may be chosen as his opening band."

Helgi gripped Mike by the shoulders, clutching hard enough that the bandleader winced and shifted away, his sweat-slicked muscles slipping under Helgi's grasp. "You mean it? Us? Jimmy Page? Reunion Arena?

"Hey, I told you it's not certain. You could stop mauling me before you break something, Helgi. Really."

"Sorry." Helgi let go of him. The marks of his hands flanked Mike's freckle-blotched shoulders in white for a moment, then flushed red as the blood rushed back into the skin. "That is, that is just amazing. When did you hear it?"

"Just a couple of days ago. They want a hot new local band, is the rumor, and lo, here we be, well- known enough to draw attention but fresh enough for people not to be tired of us, brilliant and exciting, and visibly integrated, with a low profanity and sexism content in our lyrics. I don't know that this will have anything to do with the final choice, but I suspect it won't hurt us."

"When will we know?"

"Should be by early next month. Or that's what I'm told, anyway. But you see why I don't want the other guys to know. I don't want to get their hopes up if it doesn't work out."

"Yeah. No, I won't tell anyone. Except, well...."

"Yeah, you want to tell Karin. You just can't restrain yourself from letting her know this news. If you tell anyone else, or she tells anyone, and this gets out before it's settled, your ass is grass, Hadding."

"Gotcha." Helgi reached over to fast-forward the CD.

"What're you doing?"

Helgi paused, his finger resting on the button's smooth curve. "I want to hear the last one."

"Like, you can't wait forty-five minutes and listen to the rest of it? You have an urgent appointment?"

"No, come on, I want to hear it."

The song started with sound effects, a low snake-hiss sharpening into the pattering of raindrops and rising to a waterfall's full torrent, then a spark-bright note from Mike's guitar zinged through, just before the deep roll of Rack's bass drum. At first the harsh croaking sound blended into the music, weaving through the undertones of Helgi's dark voice as he began to sing. Then the strange noise rose to a loud and raucous squawking, breaking Helgi's concentration away from the music. Mike got up, walking to the end of the garage door's shadow and looking out.

"What's going on?"

"It's just a couple of big old crows. We get them hanging around our garbage cans a lot. They're really hyper-excited about something this time, though."

Helgi rose to join him. Behind the driveway leading to the O'Roarkes' garage was a thick hedge of dark-leaved bushes, higher than Helgi's head. The two crows were flying in a tight circle over it, croaking and squawking wildly. One of them turned in the air, pecking at the other, and they dropped flapping for a few feet together before breaking apart again. A black feather drifted slowly down into the bushes beneath them.

"They must have found a dead dog in there," Helgi said. Raven croaked to raven, on high gallows-tree, awaiting meat. Y'leave some crow-chow over there? "Or something," he added slowly.

Mike sniffed at the air. "Could be. How delicious. I think I'll be generous and leave it for them."

The big dark birds winged a little higher over the bushes, then suddenly shot straight out of their air-circle like stones from a sling. Helgi heard their muffled croaking over the house for a moment, then the sound of the song swept it away.

"Strange things happen all the time," Mike said, raising his voice so that Helgi could hear him over the sound of his own singing and the high keen notes shimmering above it. "I guess maybe they weren't as hungry as they thought they were."

"Maybe not," Helgi said absently, his mind already wrapped in his music again.

The autumn storms whirled back and forth over Dallas between sullen afternoons of heavy sunshine, their lightnings playing about the sphere that topped Reunion Tower's slim pillar and casting the jagged edges of the city's skyline black against the huge spread of the sky over the broad flat horizon. Helgi often woke up in the middle of the night, creeping softly downstairs and out of the apartment.

The thrilling that ran through his bones like electricity humming through a speaker kept him from sleeping, drove him out in his car to ride over the black roads with the windows rolled down and the warm wind or cold rain streaming over his face as a heavy bass beat boomed out from the Impala's radio. The week leading up to The Concert was a hard one for Helgi. He had two mid-term exams to grade, one in "Schubert and his Contemporaries" and one in Composition Theory 101. Helgi finally had to turn off the radio while he worked. The strain of listening in hopes that they would play one of Flourescent's songs was almost as distracting as the manic delight that still rushed through him whenever he heard his own voice singing from the speakers, whenever he heard a DJ saying "Flourescent, from their first CD, Heroic Madness" or "Flourescent, opening for Jimmy Page this Friday."

Thursday's storm raged all night, great claps of thunder shaking Helgi from his uneasy sleep. He had not set his alarm clock. He was sure his excitement would wake him early, but when he finally opened his eyes and glanced blearily over at the digital clock's green glow, he saw that it was already 10.13.

Helgi rolled out of bed, nearly tripping over Elric as he landed. The elk hound gave him a reproachful woof. Helgi reached down and patted him. "Sorry about that. Just give me a second to get dressed, okay?"

After the thunderstorm, the morning was glistening-clear, the autumn's first edge of ice slicing along the wind. Here and there, the trees in people's gardens had begun to turn, brown and gold edging the oaks and a few clusters of rich bright red leaves crowning slender maple saplings. The pavement's stony cold had numbed Helgi's bare feet against its roughness by the time they had gone a block. Though he wore only shorts and a light T-shirt, and goosebumps stippled his bare arms and legs, he was not cold.

The air's sharpness only brightened his body's own warmth. Elric was no longer quite as eager to run as he had been when he was a puppy, but when Helgi began to jog along the sidewalk, the elk hound tore out in front of him as though he would drag his master along in his track, running faster and faster to keep ahead until he was going full speed with Helgi pacing him closely enough that the leash never tightened on Elric's neck. It was only eleven-thirty when they got back. His head light from the run, Helgi was not hungry, but he knew the performance would take his full strength, so he made himself sit down and eat a bowl of cornflakes. He was just rinsing the bowl out in the sink when the doorbell rang.

"Just a minute," he shouted. He wiped his hands dry on his T-shirt as he hurried downstairs to open the apartment door. "Karin! What are you doing here this early?"

"I'm not AWOL," Karin answered. The deep blue skirt of her dress uniform rustled about her long legs as she stepped over the threshold and hurried upstairs with him. "Not quite. Really. How could I stay away from you, today of all days, my Helgi?" In spite of her uniform, she wore the silver valknútr at her throat, the amber ring that matched his glowed on her finger, and a light shadow-tinge of shimmering dawn-blue brightened her gray eyes.

Helgi embraced Karin, kissing her deeply as she tightened her arms about his back. "I'm glad you're here. The waiting was starting to get to me."

"You'll have to get used to it," she answered without letting go of him. "I've heard that musicians on tour spend most of their time just sitting and waiting in hotel rooms."

"There's a price for everything, I suppose." He kissed her again. "Is it really all right for you to be here?"

"I won't get into any trouble for it. I'm flying tomorrow, combat practice, at that, so I'm supposed to be in bed early tonight and not drink any alcohol." She laughed. "We'll see about that, but I'm planning to be moderately good, anyway, so I thought I should come and see you now." Karin tilted her head, shaking her dark cap off to fall on the table by the door. Her fine blond hair was a little mussed, Helgi ran his fingers through it to straighten it.

"Is anyone else home?" She asked.

"Not a one. Would you like something to drink?"

"It's not too early for beer, is it? No, it's almost noon. Your shoulders are awfully tense, too, it feels as though you could use a little mellowing. You stay there, I'll get it."

Karin came back a few moments later with a froth-topped glass stein of dark beer in each hand. "I bring you beer, apple of the byrnie-Thing," she said, handing one to Helgi. She lifted her own glass. "Hail and good luck to you, my beloved singer, min helt."

"My Valkyrie," Helgi answered, smiling at her.

"Still a mess," Karin said, shaking her head as she kicked a couple of dirty socks aside. "You'd never get away with this in the military, you know."

"A good reason not to be in the military," Helgi answered, swatting her lightly on the rear.

"Don't do that, you'll tempt me to spill my drink, and I warn you, my man. Your one percent is vulnerable." With her free hand, Karin faked a grab at his groin.

"Oh, do that again. Only do it slower this time."

They settled down on the bed, leaning against the wall together. "Are your parents coming to the concert?" Karin asked.

"Of course they are. My father likes Jimmy Page. They may even," Helgi added, glancing sideways at her, "want to hear the opening band."

"Ow. Got me. There just seems to be something strange and unnatural about the Older Generation listening to rock of their own free wills."

"They aren't even quite fifty yet, you know. They were young and crazy in the late sixties."

"I guess someday our kids are going to be saying something similar about us, huh?" Karin snuggled a little more closely to him, resting the sharp point of her chin on his shoulder. "When you're well-known as a Wagnerian singer and I'm a general in the Air Force, they'll never believe we were young and crazy people who drank beer and screwed in the middle of the day, like we're just about to be doing." She drank off the last of her draught, putting the empty stein down at the side of the bed by her purse, and Helgi did the same. "Come here, min helt."

Helgi and Karin lay together in each other's warmth for a long time before they got up to wash and dress again. This time, Helgi pulled on the snug black jeans and black T-shirt he planned to wear for the performance. He struck a pose and flexed his muscles. "How do I look?"

"Yum," Karin said. She moved close to him, running her palms slowly down over his buttocks. "I'm not sure it's safe to let you go out there. Lust-maddened women will storm the stage before you ever get the chance to sing. Your hair's all messy, though, wonder how that happened?"

"Couldn't imagine."

Karin sat down on the bed, digging a green plastic comb out of her purse. "Sit down here, and I'll do something with it."

Helgi settled himself at her feet, leaning his head back into her lap.

"You have such nice hair," Karin said as she worked the comb gently through his tangles. "Such a lovely amber-gold color. It's funny. When I was little my hair was down to my waist and I hated it I was a little troll, I hated combing, hated washing, when my mother couldn't catch me to clean and braid it I went around in this sort of grubby cloud, and I couldn't wait till I was old enough to tell my mother I wanted it cut off. Now I wish I could grow it long again, but alas." She sighed. "I suppose it wouldn't be practical, anyway, even if I braided it, there'd always be the risk of it getting loose and getting into my eyes at the wrong moment."

"Your hair's beautiful the way it is," Helgi replied, gazing upside-down at her as she bent over him. It was strange to look at Karin like this. The sides of her face slanting down like steep cliff-sides from the little peak of her chin and the dark wings of her eyebrows underscoring her sky-light eyes, her blond hair like a bowl of pale bone, holding her face in its cupped shape. "Though I'm sure it would be beautiful long."

"Flatterer. Shameless flatterer. I love you so. Shall I braid your hair, or let it flow free?"

"Let it flow, I think the idea is for us to look the way we do on the CD cover."

"Oh, good. Are you going to wear your sword? Of course you are."

"I hadn't"

"You need it for your last song," Karin said firmly. "I won't have you going on-stage without it. You will wear it, and draw it, and hopefully not decapitate any of the other band members while you still need them."

It was a little past two when Helgi and Karin finally dismantled the shiny black nest of cords entwining his synthesizer's keyboard, control panel, computer connection, and speakers, boxing each part of the instrument individually and carrying them out to Karin's jeep. Helgi could already feel the slight trembling in his hands, like the marching of a far-off host shaking faintly through the earth, the weight of his sword laying along his thigh kept him from chasing the thoughts out of his mind for a single moment. A fine veil of mist, rippled by thin lines of darker cloud, lay across the sky, dimming the sunlight to a pearl-pale glow.

"Doesn't look as though it's going to rain tonight," Helgi said hopefully, getting into the jeep himself and pulling his shoulder-belt tightly across his body.

"Are you nervous?" Karin asked as the jeep coughed to life.

"No," Helgi answered, running his left hand down the sword's smooth scabbard. The dividing line was a sharp edge. Not nervous, but nerved, all the thin cords threading through his body drawn tight as steel strings, ringing with the sympathetic echo of the night's music rehearsing itself again and again in the back of his mind. "I can't wait." He tossed back his hair, letting his deep breaths still the eager shivering in his belly as his voice burst free from his throat.

"Spute dich, Kronos! Fort den rasselnden Trott! Bergab gleitet der Weg" Stir yourself, Time! Forth at a rattling trot! From the mountain glides the wayKarin listened quietly, a small smile curving her lips as she drove faster and faster.

"Trunknen von letzten Strahl, Reiß mich ein Feuermeer, mir ins schäu-
menden Aug, mich geblendeten Taumelden in der Hölle nächtliches Tor."
Sweep me, drunk from the last ray, a sea of fire in my foaming eye, blinded
and swaying through Hella's night-door. Karin shifted gears, lunging out
onto the freeway just before a red BMW, whose angry honking followed
them along the road. "Töne, Schwager, ins Horn! Rassle den schallenden
TrabDaß der Orkus vernehme. wir kommen! Daß gleich an der Tür der Wirt
uns freundlich empfange." Sound the horn, coachman! Rattle at a ringing
trot. That the underworld shall know, we come! That the friendly host may
welcome us at the gate.

Early in the day as it was, all the real security-people who weren't watching the outside of the arena were off guarding Jimmy Page's hotel room or
something, or so Helgi figured, once he and Karin had gotten his equipment
taken care of and headed back towards the room that had been assigned to
Flourescent, they were only challenged once. The security guard who sat on
a stool before the backstage entrance was about Helgi's age, a very skinny
young man whose immense mass of wavy brown hair draped over the copy
of programming and meta programming he was reading and hid all but the
letters 'lstrom' on his name tag. He had a walkie-talkie and a nightclub on
his belt, but no gun. There was something vaguely familiar about his wide-
mouthed, bony face, Helgi was sure he had seen him before, but didn't know
where.

"Hi, Helgi," the guard said, putting his book down. His hair shifted, showing his name to be E. Gullstrom. "Congratulations."

"Thanks."

"Everyone else is in there already. They said for me to tell you you're late."

"Late? Not possible, it can't be three yet."

"Probably not." Gullstrom looked up at Karin. "I've seen you over at the
Bar of Soap, haven't I?"

"It is not unlikely," she admitted.

"Not to sound fascist or militarist or anything non-politically correct like
that," Karin raised her eyebrows, gesturing down at her uniform. The security guard shrugged. "Anyway, I've got to see your backstage pass before I let
you come in."

"What would you do if I just walked in anyway?" Karin asked. "There's
two of us, and we're both bigger than you are, not to mention that Helgi's
armed."

"I'm not stupid. I would peacefully stand aside and let you by," Gullstrom
grinned like a golliwog"and club you on the back of the head the moment
you had passed."

"Good man." Karin got her pass out of her purse for him to inspect.

Flourescent's dressing room was comfortably furnished, with overstuffed chairs and a refrigerator in the corner. A large bowl of potato chips and a smaller bowl of dip sat on the low table between the ring of chairs, Rack was dipping and eating one-handed without looking at the bowls, apparently deeply absorbed in the Batman comic book he held in front of his face. Mike was pacing about the room with a Pepsi in one hand and a cigarette in the other, Josh and his current girlfriend, a tall bosomy Mexican girl named Juanita, sat on one of the sofas passing a little stone pipe back and forth. A bluish haze of smoke already hung about the bare white light bulb in the middle of the ceiling, harsh tobacco and sweet marijuana blending uneasily. Widget was winding a new string onto his bass, cursing in a low steady mutter. As Helgi and Karin came in, he glanced up and nodded without meeting their eyes, then turned his gaze back to his work.

"Took you long enough to get here," Mike said, his cigarette showering a few ashes onto the stained gray carpet as he passed them. "Now you can sit and twitch with the rest of us. There's food and drink in the fridge, if you want any. Before you start getting your hopes up, I have been told that we are extremely unlikely to see Jimmy Page or Jason Bonham or any of the rest of them until the party afterwards, when they will be mobbed with press people and special guests and all of that, but at least we will be able to say we shared their air."

Rack suddenly laid his comic aside, pressing his palms together and bowing himself double. "We're unworthy! We're unworthy! We're scum!"

No one laughed, though one corner of Karin's mouth curved up. Mike stopped pacing for a second to glare at the drummer. "If you even think of doing that Wayne's World shit near Jimmy Page, I swear I will pay Helgi to karate-kick your ass from here to San Antonio, okay?"

"Hey, be mellow, Mike," Josh advised. "Four hours is too long to sit and watch you freak out." He took the pipe from Juanita, toking deeply on its lipstick-stained mouthpiece. "Share the smoke, have a beer, drop a Valium, anything. We've still got plenty of time before we have to go on, and watching you prowl around like that is making my eyeballs twitch."

"I very much doubt that that's what's making your eyeballs twitch. You just better have come down by the time we go on, is all." Still, Mike swung around one of the chairs, dropping heavily into its padded seat as Helgi and Karin settled themselves across from him. "What about you, Helgi? Are you ready to go on? No sore throat or anything?"

"I'm all ready."

"Great. I've talked with the lighting people. No special effects for us yet, but I've arranged a few minor things so that we're not, you know, just standing there like lumps on a log for forty-five minutes. Actually," Mike stood again. "Come on. We need to practice our entrance. We need to practice it because we won't be able to see when we come on, and we have to be able to get into place without nose-diving off the stage or knocking over microphones or anything like that."

Reunion Arena and the cloudy night sky above were dead black, only the bluish ghost-glow of the city lights showing above the amphitheater's high curving walls and the tiny red eyes of cigarettes glowing here and there among the great rustling sea of people beneath. Helgi breathed deeply, counting his paces as he walked from the wings into the darkness. He did not dare to put his weight fully down with each new step, twice cables moved beneath his searching foot, but at last his count of paces was full and his hand closed on the cold metal stem of his microphone. He knew Karin was there in the darkness before him. The security guards would have escorted her to her place in the front row by now. Now that he stood between earth and sky, his feet on the stage's cable-wound platform with the hidden flashes of electricity running all around him and the thousands of eyes staring up into the darkness where he waited, the last trembling was fading from Helgi's body. He could feel his limbs strong and supple as an ash-tree's branches, the current of his hair stirred in the light wind blowing over the stage, the flame that laced his veins brightened with each breath he took, ready to flare to a mighty bonfire around him.

Mike's voice rang out, high and sharp, the speakers' hum warping it against the back of the arena's walls. "Now, for the first time at Reunion Arena. Flourescent!" The applause started slowly, but rose faster and faster, until Mike's words cut through its beating again. "Rack McKinley!"

The first spotlight's halo cast Helgi's shadow dimly before him, but he knew that he himself was still dark.

"Widget Jackson! Josh Levine! Mike O'Roarke, and Helgi Hadding!"

As Mike spoke his name, Helgi drew his sword, holding it point-down before himself. The white brilliance bursting around him in the huge thunder of hand-clapping blinded him a moment, but Widget's bass was already thumping out its sure beat, the triple rhythms pounding up through Helgi's soles like the rushing of an underground river beating up through stone. Helgi saluted the throng of darkness before him, sheathing his sword and raising his hands to the keyboard as he awaited the chord change that would call forth the first runs of 'Erl-King'.

The second to last piece, Helgi's other new song 'Call to the Gods', was different than anything Flourescent had done before. Helgi did not sing, but chanted over the rumbling of Rack's drums and the wailing of Mike's guitar. He started slow, the speakers booming his whisper out over the hushed arena.

"The ravens flew back at sun set, the battlefield lay bloody, and the cross rose high above the slain. The first flames sprang from the dead on the pyre, lighting the sky red, and men said that Ásgarðr burned. That the Heathen gods had fallen with their heroes on the field. From the wood, an old man watched, and the bale-fire lit his single eye. His eight-legged horse had carried many slain through the smoke of their burning, and borne them back to earth again. He was the lord of ghosts, who knew that death was not the end. The Heathen temple crashed in fire and the Christians spoke Mass where it had stood, in twilight rested the gods. A woman spun within the hall, chanting tales to her daughter, a singer whispered the words of ancient lays, and a woodcarver cut the Dragon-Slayer's story deep into the doors of a church, candle-flames glimmering in the night, the true, half-awake, keeping the long watch as the Yule log burned every year and the folk set their gifts on the burial mounds of their kin, or hung them on hallowed trees.

"The Sun of the North wheeled hidden through the darkness, through life-age on life-age, the great waters ran hidden beneath the stone, like blood dark in the veins, while the riverbed above seemed dry and rocky. But evening's reddening lights morning's wakening. Twilight leads to dawn, and new life springs forth from the bones in the mound. Now the water of Wyrd's Well bursts forth in Sunna's morning brightness, shining holy and fair. Now we hail the gods, wakening and rising among us!"

Helgi stretched his hands up towards the sky, gazing high into the mist of light that hung over the amphitheater. He could see the huge pillars of darkness standing all about, the hof's high-timbered cloud-roof, glittering with the lights that burst before his eyes.

"Hail to Wodan, Walhall's drighten, hail the rister of runes! All-Father, Yggr, eagle-high, wyrm-deep. Hail for singing spear, hail for mead of might! Hail to Frija, Fensalir's ruler, weaver of wisdom-threads. Bright queen of household, holy wyrd-kenner, seeress, spindle-turner, hail for care and kin!"

As Helgi cried out the call to each god, it seemed to him that the pillars slowly reshaped themselves, carven masks standing forth from the black wood and coming to life with his breath, till the ghost-shapes of the holy ones rose high all about him, strengthened by the breath of all the folk below, by the power thrumming through speakers and booming out of Helgi's throat.

"Hail Fro Ing, for frith and joy, greetings to life-stead's god. Giver of harvest, helmed as boar-warder. Hail thee, mound-god hidden, hail thee, holy of gods! Hail the Frowe, falcon-winging, Brísingamen's bright maid. Fiery as gold, fair-lighting in sea, singer of clear seith-songs, hail thee, Lady of love!"

Now Helgi could no longer hear drum and guitar, though he knew they were playing behind him. Now there was only the wind in his ears, as though he stood on a mountain's peak and called out alone to the great ones who ringed him round.

"Hail to Tiw, true and high god, worthy leavings of Wolf. One-Handed, awesome, oath-god mighty, bright Irminsul's upholder, hail thee, holy law-god! Hail to Thonar, thurses' slayer, holder of holy steads aye. Wyrm's lone bane, Bilskírnir's king, holding the high-seat posts. Hail the Hammer-God! Hail thee, Loki, aloft bright-faring, Wodan's friend, rich in wit. Thonar's wise wain-friend, wily gift-bringer, have thy oath-given horn, not lies, but laughter I hail! Hail ye all, my elder kin, stock and strength of my clan. In mound deep-rooted, rowning your wisdom, spring forth, live in my soul, as I stand true in your troth!"

The applause was so loud that Helgi could hardly hear it. It seemed like the crashing of waves against his ears, its weight swaying him where he stood. Though the sweat was pouring down his face, the wind blowing over him cooling it to grave-dew, he was not tired. His nerves were thrilling through him as though his whole body were coming to life after frostbite, his heart beating hot beneath his sweat-chilled ribs. Now the time had come, as he had dreamed it. Karin sat bright in the darkness below him, her face turned up and gray eyes gazing at him from beneath the pale-gilded helm of her hair. Now he had the song that he had always wanted to sing to her, the voice and words to bring it forth into Reunion Arena's great ring, beneath the eyes of the gods and goddesses that gazed down upon him. The crown of all his striving, the magical galdor-song that might bring his death, as Wyrd had once shaped the deaths of the two Helgis before him, but was Wotan's fair payment for song and victory and love, 'Karin's Song'.

It was Helgi's hands that shaped the first storm, bringing forth the rising torrent of rain from his synthesizer until its waterfall poured foaming and howling through the whole dark-peopled amphitheater, a single hollow note shrieking high above it, piercing his skull like an arrow of ice. A bright strobe-light burst behind his back with each keen stroke of Mike's guitar, the sound ripping the air into trembling waves. The booming of the drums was so loud that Helgi felt rather than heard it, its dark might beating against him like a fall of stones. His own breath seemed cold in his throat, cold as a gust of snow-glittering wind, but his voice was all unfettered now. Borne up by the keen tightening in his guts, rising free from his aching chest, as his hands on the keyboard wove the echoes from the ring-walls together into a single crest of sound.

"Eagles scream out from highest fells,
  hallowed water falls blood shining from the sky
  wounded by your flight,
  clouds scored with lines of light,
  weave-threads of destiny.
You shimmer over ravens' height,
  rainbow-white your heat rain shining in the sun
  all bright on gallows-grove
  where heroes hanged shall prove
  gone under, not undone."

Now Helgi strode away from the synthesizer, leaving its last notes to ring and ring and grow as Rack battered against the cage of his drums, fighting to break them both free of the black chord Josh and Mike's guitars wrapped around them in the synthesizer's echo. Helgi drew his sword, gazing up to the low dark curve of the sky above. It seemed to him that the bone-shaking sound booming from the speakers enclosed Reunion Arena like a mound of black earth, the great shapes of the holy ones around lightless as foxfire in the darkness. Then two great pillars of white light speared high up from either side of the stage, spreading into broad pale shields where they struck the heavy cloud-roof. Standing between the two shafts of brightness, Helgi raised his blade, flinging his voice forth into the night.

"Runes all rock-carved, ring and sword,
  reddened by battle for my bride
  deaths you deemed, dark by my side,
  the day's first light showed doom.
  You hailed me holy, and hero called
  Helgi upon the mound below,
  woke once to life and once in howe,
  now brightest dawn has come."

Two great wings of damp cloud rolled forth from the sides of the stage, the dry-ice mist roiling and turning in the sharp white beams that flanked Helgi. The seething fog billowed up around him, rolling slowly out into the audience. It seemed to Helgi that the posts of pale light above him were spreading over the clouds above, swan wings unfolding to glow blue-white against the darkness as the dizzying wind rushed through his ears, but he could still see Karin shining fair through the mist below him, and feel the might pouring into him from her gaze like mead into a cup.

Helgi laid his sword on top of his synthesizer and beat down upon the keys again, riding the song's high bridge over the whirling, razor-edged river of the guitars' music rushing beneath him until he had crossed and his voice sounded alone over the hoof-beating of the drums that carried him onward.

"Chooser of the Slain! Your fetters bind and loose,
  call forth the ravens black
  with spear raised in your hand,
  pull tight the threefold noose.
  Chooser of the Slain! Your glance is awe and death,
  you bear life's ale-cup sweet,
  with healing in your hands,
  to bring the dead new breath.
  Chooser of the Slain! Your steed a wood-mad wolf,
  the Masked One's cloak is dark,
  but fearless we ride on
  to bridge death's roaring gulf."

The guitars swept in, their fierce torrent bearing Helgi to his feet so swiftly that bright mushrooms burst behind his dazzled eyelids, the light-pillars' brightness shining from his sword as he brandished it against the cloud of still dark shapes before him, beneath the silvery swan who shimmered above.

"White of dawn and day's blood-red,
dark must be the knot's third strand,
I ween no fear, though wise man warned
the wild one's spear should point to tomb.
Weave in and out, wind death to life,
we shuttle back and forth through cloud,
make bed of love from burial shroud,
burned thrice, rise bright through doom.
Away from here, from earth's folk-ring,
all hurts are healed, Grim's hall is fair,
Wolf-riding witch-wife, wend through air!
Wish-maid, we fare to Wotan's home!"

As Helgi sang his last words, he swung his sword high over his head. The bright tip seemed to score through the white wings above him, a ray of red laser-light flashed off it, bursting Helgi's sight into a blinding fireball as Mike's guitar screamed out behind him and Widget's bass dropped down and down into the black depths and all the lights went out. For a moment, the deep roar of silence was louder in Helgi's ears than the music, his eyes blinded by the brightness of the sword's afterimage flashing blue against the darkness. Then the stage lights flicked on again, the shrieking and clapping and stamping rose and rose until it seemed to Helgi that he stood in the middle of a battlefield thundering with guns and the shrieks of the dying. He raised his head weakly, lifting his sword once more to answer the applause before he could stagger off-stage.

His eyes still dazzled, Helgi nearly tripped over the little man standing at the stage's left wing before he noticed there was someone in his way.

"Hey, watch what you're doing with the bloody sword," the man said, his English voice light and friendly. "That was an extremely good performance, by the way. You really got out there and sang your bollocks off, though the rest of the band isn't up to your standard, I'm afraid."

Helgi blinked, staring down at the thin face, the cloud of curly dark hair above the brightly tie-dyed silken shirt. *My god, I almost stabbed Jimmy Page!* He thought, belatedly sliding his sword back into the sheath. "Uh, thanks," he croaked.

"Are you the songwriter, too?"

"I am."

"'Strive ever to more! 'If you are truly mine, and do not doubt it, and if you are ever joyful, then death comes as the crown.' Crowley, as if you couldn't have guessed. Well, I'll see you at the party afterwards." The fans outside had begun to stamp and chant in rhythm, JIM-MY! JIM-MY!, Jimmy Page sauntered slowly away from the stage, heading back for his own dressing room.

Helgi glanced back out. The roadies had started to clear away Rack's drums and his own synthesizer, getting the stage ready for the main act, the other members of Flourescent were just walking off. In the dim lighting of the wings, they all looked pale and drained, drenched with sweat as if they had been standing in a storm, but they were still grinning.

Josh punched Helgi hard on the shoulder. "Man, that was the best ever. You and your sword, awesome."

Though deep shadows bruised the skin beneath them, Mike's eyes glittered with maniac glee. "Yeah, awesome. Christ, just wait, we'll be the main act next time, just you see. Did you hear the way they were screaming for us? I've been to concerts where really big groups didn't get that kind of applause, I tell you."

Rack laughed, beating a swift tattoo against the wall with his sticks. Only Widget shook his head. The warm coffee-color of his skin had faded to an unhealthy gray under the muted lighting. "'Fraid that music's just a little too thick for my blood," he muttered, so softly that Helgi could barely hear it through the ringing echo in his ears. None of the others even seemed to notice that the bassist was speaking. "Don't know if?"

"You okay, Helgi?" Josh suddenly asked, leaning close enough that Helgi could smell the stale smoke on his breath. "You don't look so hot."

"Just tired. It took a lot out of me." His voice was hoarse now, as though his throat had splintered under the weight it had borne that night.

Mike unslung his guitar, pulling his sweat-soaked shirt away from his chest and shaking a few droplets from his face. "Well, you can't die now. I think we've just got enough time to put on dry clothes and get back here for the start of Jimmy Page's set, if we really move our butts with major fastness. Probably can't shower, but fuck, who's going to smell us anyway?"

Helgi was just pulling up his jeans when he heard Karin's exasperated voice outside the dressing room door, "Well, if I see anything I don't recognize, I'll throw a rock at it, all right?" Then the lower mutter of the security guard who had replaced Gullstrom.

Glancing around to make sure no-one else's genitals were actually hanging out, he went to the door and opened it. "It's okay, we're all decent."

Karin flung her arms tightly around Helgi, kissing him hard enough to leave a tinge of blood in his mouth. "Helgi, min helt, det var så vidunderligthat was so wonderful. Oh, my Helgi," the brightness glowed out from her eyes, too pure and strong to find more shape in words than his song had given it, but he could feel the uplift of joy surging through her, and tightened his own arms about her shoulders.

"All for you," Helgi murmured, the keen joy in his own heart piercing through his body as though it would lay his inmost caverns open to Karin's touch.

Mike coughed loudly. "Hey, if you don't mind, some of us want to get out of this room before the concert's over."

Helgi and Karin moved aside from the door, letting the others hurry out. "Do you want to go back for the rest of it?" Helgi asked her.

"I want to be with you. My Helgi, this is your night, I want to do what you want to do." Karin tilted her head to the side, looking up at him. She was as disheveled as if she had been on-stage with the band, her short blond hair spiky with drying sweat and her pale eyes wide and bright against the faint shadows of smeared mascara beneath them, her breaths were still coming swift and deep as though she had been fighting.

"When do you have to be back on base?"

"When I go back. Look, let's rent a hotel room. Let's have a night all to ourself, where no one can find us. What do you say?"

The faint roaring of the audience suddenly rose as though a great volume-control had been turned up. There would be the concert, and the party afterwards, and Jimmy Page. Helgi's parents had been invited, and might even come to the party for a little while, but surely wouldn't expect him to go home with them, he could go off with Karin afterwards. Then it would be hours before he was alone with her again, and now she was here in his arms, with the echo of his last song still ringing through their bones, and he wanted nothing else in the world.

It felt to Helgi as though the sudden rush of blood into his groin had pulled a noose tight about his throat, he was hardly able to croak out, "Let's go."

The parking lot was dark and still, the only person there was the security guard who sat reading a gun magazine in his glass box at the exit. He glanced at Helgi's lot pass and nodded, pressing the button that lowered the barrier before them.

After stopping at the first liquor store they came to for two bottles of chilled champagne, Karin and Helgi drove on to the Holiday Inn on Mockingbird. The plump frill-haired woman behind the counter looked suspiciously at them when they checked in, her apricot lips pursing as she tapped chipped red nails over the computer keys, but at last she admitted that the hotel did have a room with a double bed and shower, which she supposed they could rent for the night. As she spoke, her chins pouched over the little gold cross pinned to her collar, Helgi had no doubt that she wanted to add something about youthful fornications. The two of them were barely able to hold in their laughter until the elevator's door slid shut behind them. Then they collapsed in each other's arms as the little chamber rose upward. "We should have checked in as Mr. and Mrs. John Smith," Karin said. "I swear, I thought she'd tell us to go away and screw elsewhere."

Their room was painted pale blue and trimmed in sterile white, the white Formica and chrome of the bathroom gleaming disinfected and the bed's white linen showing no stain of human touch. Karin peeled the glistening cellophane envelopes off the two plastic cups by the sink, Helgi untwisted the champagne bottle's wires, pressing with his thumbs until the cork sprang out to bounce sharply off the big mirror facing the foot of the bed. The golden wine frothed up, spilling over the bottle's rim, Karin lunged over to him, getting her cup under the foam before it poured out onto the bedspread.

When the two cups were filled, Helgi and Karin settled themselves cross-legged on the bed. "Here's to us," Karin murmured. "I am so glad we chose each other." She lifted her champagne towards him. The little bubbles were still rising bright through the straw-pale wine, the cold had already dewed the clear plastic with a mist of frost. Her fingers brushed against Helgi's as they clicked cups dully together, her bright gaze did not leave his as they drank deeply. He drained his cup in one draught, the chill bubbling drink flowing smoothly down to soothe the song-torn edges of his throat as its warmth soaked slowly out through his body.

Karin drank her cup off as well, then refilled both of them. "Ah, I can see that doing you good already." She stroked a fingertip lightly over his cheek. "Your color is starting to come back now. My poor Helgi, I wasn't sure you'd live until I could get you here."

"Now I expect that you have a way of healing me in mind," Helgi answered, looking at her over the rim of transparent plastic as he sipped more slowly at his second cupful.

Karin reached out to brush the sweat-crusted hair back from his forehead. "I might."

When they had drained the first bottle of champagne, Helgi and Karin undressed each other slowly, kissing as they stroked the garments from each other's body. He cupped one of her breasts in each hand, bending to run his tongue along the musky-salt crevice between them, she threw her head back, her long white throat bare to the line of kisses Helgi laid gently along it. Their mirror-reflections glimmered in the corner of Helgi's eye, a single pale shape blurred by the slow ripples of their movements as the soft fair curls of Karin's groin tickled at the root of Helgi's manhood. He wanted to push her down on the bed then, but her muscles tightened against him. "Let's shower together first," she whispered. "Come on."

The shower nozzle was high enough for Helgi and Karin to stand together under it. Karin twisted it on, a torrent of clear water flowed warm over their bodies as Helgi pulled her closer to him. The flood's brightness shone from Karin's face, the shower stall gleaming white as a sunlit cloud around them. The full strength of the water beat hard on their heads, spraying about their shoulders to half-choke their deep gasping breaths of pleasure as Karin raised on her toes and guided Helgi into her. Her warm sheath tightening on him.

His strength held her up, moving slowly beneath the rushing fall of water, the touch of her body thrilled all through him, her wide gray gaze and the soft wolf-moans breathing from her parted lips kindling his need-fire more brightly against the shining torrent that poured down over them. Helgi clasped Karin to him as hard as he could, murmuring her name over and over as the glowing threads tightened through his body and 'Karin's Song' pounded in the back of his skull like raven-wings beating through the bowl of the sky, till he spilled the last of his life out into her. Helgi and Karin lay awake in their bed most of the night, making love and talking softly between times as they sipped at the warming champagne. Helgi did not know when their whispering slipped into sleep, but the ringing of the telephone jolted him sharply awake.

Karin reached over his body to answer it. "Hello?" She said blearily. "Oh. Yes, thanks." She dropped the receiver back into place. "Wake-up call. If I don't get straight back to base now, I really will be in deep shit." Helgi tightened his eyelids hard as she dialed the lights up to full, blinking against the sudden brightness.

The heating had gone off during the night, if it had ever been on, the chill of early morning lay gray in the air, and rain was spattering lightly against the window. Karin looked pale and unreal as a ghost as she sat up among the night-tossed blankets, her hair sticking up in wild peaks and tiny light-ning-cracks of red scarring the whites of her eyes.

"I can take a taxi home," Helgi offered. "I've still got some money on me, and that'll save you at least forty-five minutes."

Karin leaned forward to kiss him, brushing her lips across his so lightly that Helgi could barely taste the morning staleness on her breath. "That'll help. I do love you, Helgi." She got out of bed, walking naked to the cur-tained window. Pulling one corner aside, she looked out at the graying dawn.

"'Time for me to ride the reddening ways,'" Helgi murmured, "'and let the fallow horse tread the flight-paths.'"

Karin let the curtain fall, turning to gaze at him as she completed the quote. "'I must go westward, over the wind-helm's bridge, before Salgofnir wakes the sig-folk.'"

Helgi and his host rode away, but the women fared home to their dwell-ing. When they had dressed, Helgi went out to the parking lot with Karin to kiss her goodbye. The soft rain soaking through his hair and T-shirt, he watched as the little clouds of smoke coughed out of the tailpipe of her jeep, as it rolled away from him, heaving out into the blurry gray sea of rainy mist over the road. When he could see her no more, he went back into the hotel to call for his taxi.

Helgi had just gotten out of the shower and was ready to go to bed when the phone rang

"Hello?"

"Lo," said his father, "it's the famous rock star."

"Uh, yeah."

"That was really a very impressive performance, Helgi. We're sorry we missed the party, but we were both too exhausted afterwards to even think of doing anything else. I'd forgotten how a really good concert takes it out of you. Did you have a good time?"

"Excellent."

"How did you get home? Did Karin bring you?"

"Karin had to leave pretty quickly, so I decided to take a taxi."

"Did you get to talk to Jimmy Page?" Roger asked.

Helgi grinned into the receiver. "He said he liked my music."

"All right! You've been approved by the best. Not that there was ever any doubt, of course."

Helgi made appropriate noises at appropriate intervals as his father talked about the concert, then put his mother on to do the same. At last Kirsten said, "Do you have any plans for today?"

"I thought I'd just rest and recover. I'm still pretty tired."

"I'm not surprised. Well, at least you're getting the chance to party with rock stars while you're still young and strong enough to appreciate it. As opposed to us old folk who conk out at ten-thirty or eleven with our ears bleeding and heads ringing. If someone had told me, twenty years ago. Well, never mind that. Go to bed, you've earned a good rest."

Helgi slept until late in the afternoon. When he woke up, he felt, not very lively, his bones still weighting heavy in his flesh, but warm and comfortable enough, as though the tide of restless strength that had been flowing up through him for weeks had ebbed away all at once, leaving him drained and at peace. He lay in bed for a little while, resting in his own warmth as if he were soaking up the day's last sunlight and quietly sorting through the last night's events in his head. Content and happy, he finally pushed Elric's sleepy weight from his feet, got up and changed into clean clothes.

"Come on, I'll take you for a walk. How about it? Walk?"

Elric had the leash in his mouth before Helgi had gotten out the door of his room. Wrapping his faded denim jacket around himself, Helgi collared his hound and started out. The sidewalks were still wet, the sky rippled gray and the air chill and damp on his face, but the rain had stopped for the moment. Though Elric lowered his head and tugged at the leash, Helgi walked slowly behind him. Suddenly the elk hound sat back on his haunches, pointing his nose straight up and barking. For a strange moment, the sky seemed to magnify his barks an hundredfold, as if a great pack of ghostly hounds were running through the clouds. Then Helgi saw the flock of wild geese flying low overhead, their long necks and wide-spread wings black as the shadows of swans against the rain-gray light.

Their barking and rushing wing-noise stirred Helgi like a voice calling from far away, he thought of the winding of a hunter's horn, and the wind rustling over the marshes. It seemed to him that their melancholy cries told him something, but he could not think what, it was like listening to Karin talk Danish with her family, being able to understand words and sometimes even phrases, but not quite able to bring the whole together in his mind. By the time Helgi got back to the house, the cold wind had cleared his head, sweeping away the warm peace of his first moments awake. Now he felt alive and prickly, as though he were waiting for something more, as though he was still waiting to perform, or awaiting Karin's knock at the door. He drank a Coke, prowled around his room, and reviewed about half a page of his first lecture for Monday. His throat was still tired from the concert, so he didn't want to sing. Finally he took his trombone out of its case, beginning a slow series of warm-up scales.

The music calmed him while he played, but when he stopped, his mouth tired and swollen beneath the smooth rim of the trombone's mouthpiece, he was no stiller than before.

Helgi got to the phone before its third ring. "Hello?"

"Hadding." The deep voice was rough and strange, unfamiliar to Helgi. He could hear music in the background, another voice talking with the low mindless drone of television or the radio behind it. "Hadding, this is Rof. You remember me?"

Helgi's hand tightened on the receiver, an edge of cold fear slicing through his guts. "Is something wrong with Karin? Is she in trouble?"

"I tell you when I see you. You just get yo' butt over here."

"Where?"

"Bar of Soap."

The streetlights were on already, shining from the black streets, the dark road was slick beneath Helgi's wheels as though it had been wet with blood. He drove as fast as he could, speeding down the freeway towards the high-clustered buildings of downtown Dallas, the colored neon lines and squiggles that glowed through the low-hanging mist, as Robert Plant's mellow voice sang from the Impala's radio *"No Quarter,"* calling on the cold winds of Thor.

A circle of light spread and shrank over the sphere on top of Reunion Tower, then its lights began flashing on and off like a strobe. Helgi swung hard around the long circular exit ramp leading down to Fair Park, finally turning into the gravel parking lot behind Bar of Soap. He did not run down the alley and into the bar, but strode as swiftly as he could. There were already a few people inside, but Helgi couldn't see Rof anywhere. A thread of confusion snaking through his taut worry, he made his way to the bar and ordered a Bass Ale. His cold beer in his hand, he was just turning away when he saw the huge dark figure shouldering his way through from the little hallway where the toilets were. Rof wore his black leather jacket, but still had his fatigues on underneath it.

As he came closer, Helgi could smell the whiskey on his breath, though his dark skin and the dim lighting hid the worst ravages on his face, Helgi could see that his bloodshot eyes were swollen and wet.

Rof and Helgi sat down facing each other in the last empty booth. "Now tell me," Helgi said, gripping the cold neck of his bottle. "What's happened?"

"Karin's dead. Just two or three hours ago."

Rof's mouth kept moving, but Helgi didn't hear anything he was saying. For a moment he simply sat, staring blindly at the other man as the thoughts came slowly through the cold cloud in his skull. I was wrong. I was wrong. I thought I was writing my own doom. I was supposed to die first.

"Again. Tell me again. What happened?" Helgi took a long drink of his beer, the taste of hops bitter as the numbing glow of absinthe through the pale grain.

"She went up, she was scheduled to fly today. ACM, that be combat practice, to you, and Karin jus' come out of the clouds, divin' fast and pullin' up and then her plane blew up, all at once, jus' a fireball in the sky. Nothin' left, few pieces of hot shrapnel came down, nothin' of her. They sayin' it might be mechanical failure, some flaw in the makin', but hell, I done checked that damn plane a hundred times over, went over it again myself jus' yesterday with a fine-tooth comb. While she was off with you, 'steada doin' what she suppose to." Rof swallowed hard, clenching his big fists on top of the table. "I stake my soul, man, there was nothin' wrong with that plane. Nothin' wrong with her flyin', either, even when she half-dead from gettin' no sleep and doin' what-all the whole night, never was a pilot like Karin. So you tell me, Helgi Hadding. You tell me what happened."

Helgi said nothing. Slowly he got to his feet, steadying himself against the low back of the booth, and walked over to the jukebox beside the bar, running the searching finger of his gaze along the list of bands and titles beneath its smeared plastic top. He dug out his wallet, dropped in fifty cents, and punched the buttons for his choice. By the time he had gotten back to his seat, his own voice was already sounding over the bar's speakers. "Eagles scream out from highest fells." Helgi fumbled for his place, sat down blindly. For a moment, he could see nothing but the ghostly swan-wings bursting into a fireball at the tip of his high-swung sword, the glimmering silver wings flaming into a bright streak across the clouds. He had lifted his blade too high and cut down the swan.

He had called down the lightning-strike of Wotan's spear. It will not be too long before you drink my mead again.

Rof nodded slowly. "Yeah. Oh, I warned her 'bout that song, I got a bad feelin' first time I heard it, strongest I'd ever had, but she only be laughin' at me, say the only bad feelin' I had was jealousy."

"I," Helgi could not say anything more. He had no tears. It seemed as though they had all flowed and dried long before, and though the words of Karin's death burned achingly through his body, he could not weep beneath the sound of his own song.

"'Chooser of the Slain! Your steed a wood-mad wolf, The Grim One's cloak is dark, but fearless we ride on, to bridge the roaring gulf.'" Helgi drained the rest of his Bass Ale, remembering how Karin had brought beer to him, and thinking of the words of Helgi Hunding's-Bane. Well shall we drink this dear draught, though I have lost my lands and hopes. Something brighter was already glowing beneath the harsh friction of sorrow through his flesh, a coal from dead wood. My doom. Our doom, which we both knew from the first. He felt no fear, the unshed tears pooled in the back of his eyes were sinking away already, leaving his sight and his voice rinsed clear behind them.

"'Away from here, from earth's folk-ring, all hurts are healed, Grim's hall is fair.'"

"Come on," Helgi said. "I think we can discuss this better out back."

Helgi and Rof went out into the cold night together, walking between the cars in the parking lot and around the dumpster. Beyond the paved lot was a wider plot of raw earth, where cars could be left when something big was going on in Fair Park, but there was no one parked there now, and no lights brightening the long shadowy stretch. The rain had muddied the rocky ground, Helgi could feel it slippery beneath his sneakers, and marked how carefully Rof was setting his feet. Watch well, Karin, he thought. Though no wolves feast on the fallen afterwards, our last fight must still be worthy. My name and my words shall live. The gods be called forth to earth whenever my music is played, and Wotan be well-paid for his gifts.

When they were far enough into the darkness that Helgi thought no casual passer-by from the road or the parking lot would see them, he stopped, turning to face Rof. Helgi could not see his face, except for the white rims of his eyes, though he could hear Rof's respiration, the quickening breaths coming fast and deep as sobs.

"Say it," Rof said. "I want to hear you say it."

The mist was falling more heavily, slicking the big man's leather jacket and cooling the heat of Helgi's face. Above, the city's lights brightened the foggy rain to a ghostly bluish haze.

"It was for my sake Karin died, my spell-song that named her doom, my sword that struck down the swan," Helgi said slowly. "She chose me, and I her, for she was always Wotan's wish-daughter, who loved me above all, and you would have given her neither the death nor the life she wished."

Rof's fists snapped out as he leapt for Helgi. Helgi caught the first blow on his forearm, twisted out of the way of the second and struck back, kicking hard at the same time. His fists struck against hard flesh and bone, shoulder and arm, his foot met the other's thigh. Rof backed up a step, then lunged forward again. Helgi felt his knuckles striking in below the ribs, but Rof hardly seemed to notice, swinging with the full weight of his body behind the blows. It seemed to Helgi now that he fought a shadow in the blackness, the tireless opponent of his katas who could never be hurt nor killed, no matter how often Helgi's blows beat against his death-dark shape. Only once, when Helgi's strongest side-kick sank deep into Rof's side.

A killing blow, deep enough to burst organs and rupture bowels, did the big man groan and stagger, but the force of his turn had made Helgi slip as well, and he was barely able to recover his balance before the other's raven-shadow loomed over him again, his fists flying down like stones pounding against Helgi's aching arms. Helgi's anger strengthened him, for he had never beaten this shadow, who had always been a half-step ahead of him, daring him to move faster and more strongly, mocking each slip of his foot or missed note in his voice and pricking him to go beyond his body's bounds , and now the masked shape was goading him on to his death, but his heart would burst and fling him beyond the dark man who blocked the way, if he did not fail and sink before him.

After a time, the gasping breaths seemed to rip hot out of Helgi's throat, he was no better than half-blocking, turning away the worst force of each blow, but bright sparks shot from his swelling right eye through his head, and he could feel something grating in his ribcage with each breath.

Though the other was slowing, Helgi knew that his strength could not last against Rof's. As the big man closed in, flinging himself into another blow, Helgi half-stepped to the side, turning so that Rof's fist skimmed through the air before his face, but the slimy mud under his feet betrayed him as he swung his strength into his own punch. His left leg skidded forward, the strike that should have hammered Rof's temple in skating off his chest instead, and Rof's own blow caught him across the face, bursting a fireball through the bowl of his skull. Helgi flung a hand up to fend off the second strike and straightened his forward leg at the same time, wrenching his whole body forward against Rof's. The other man went down hard, but grabbed Helgi's own leg as he fell. Helgi's supporting foot slipped in the mud, bringing him down on top of Rof. He struck for the throat, but Rof was already grasping his arms, and had brought his knees up to block Helgi's own knee-strike at his groin.

Helgi twisted his arms free as Rof heaved beneath him, lurching to throw Helgi's lighter body off to the side. Then Rof's dark shadow blotted out the faint glow of the clouds above, Helgi felt the warm drops of blood streaming onto his face, heard them choking thicker in Rof's breath, the other man's death-gasps loud as thunder in his ears. A great flare of pain lit his body, his broken ribs giving way beneath the weight crushing his chest, but the pain was already fading beneath the high howling song of the wind in Helgi's ears as the starbursts beating against his face brightened into a single rainbow glow, weaving up into a high fiery bridge over the rushing blackness, and Karin's hand gripped his to pull him up behind her.

Helgi oc Sváva er sagt at væri
"It is said of Helgi and Sváva that they ndrborin. Were born again."
-Helgaqviða Hjörvarðzsonar- Song of Helgi Hjörvarðr's-Son
Þat var trúa í fornescio, at menn væri
"That was the belief in early times, that
endrbornir, enn þat er nú kölluðmen
were born again, but now that is
kerlingavilla. Helgi oc Sigrún er
called an old wives' tale. Of Helgi and
kallat at væri endrborin. Hét hann þáSigrun
it is said that they were born
Helgi Haddingiascaði, en hon Kára,
again. He was then called Helgi
Hálfdanar dóttir, svá sem qveðit íHaddings'
prince, and she Kára
Káralióðom, oc var hon valkyria.
Hálfdan's daughter, as it is said in
'Song of Kára',
  and she was a valkyrie."
  -Helgaqviða Hundingsbana önnor Second Song of Helgi Hunding's-Bane

BIOGRAPHY

From his humble beginnings, Gundarsson would make his mark on the world by writing on the most rare and obscure myths breathing new life into them, for a new generation of readers. His fictional works written under Stephan Grundy focused on mythology and history and were met with international success. Along with his fictional works, Gundarsson made a name for himself writing books on Germanic Paganism (also known as heathenry) and Germanic Culture. He is an Elder in the organization The Troth where he has dedicated a majority of his life influencing major changes in the organization, including the development of anti-racist and anti-sexist ideals.He has fought for equality in transgendered communities, as well as fighting for the acceptance of Loki. Gundarsson has shaped heathenry through his numerous academic and fictional works as well as his extensive articles, thesis papers and his creation and sustainment of the lore program within The Troth. His hobbies included wood-working, jewelry making and gardening as well as historical re-enactment. He is currently attending medical school in Ireland supported by his loving wife Melodi where they maintain a local hof called The Tribe of Thor.

The Three Little Sisters LLC

Our staff appreciate the dedication it takes to write, and we know how frustrating it is finding a quality publishing house that cares about its books, its authors and staff. Three Little Sisters LLC is a house built by people who love to read, and all of them want to see your work out there. We specialize in small market books. This means our titles are not ones you would find elsewhere or ones that just don't fit at the big houses. Our books are written by authors who capture the imagination, foster pure spirituality, delve into worlds of fantasy or inspire us with poems. We are all from different backgrounds but all joined in a common mission to keep books alive for future generations.

Visit Us At: www.3littlesisters.com

Made in the USA
Columbia, SC
14 October 2021